# THE
# FIONAVAR
# TAPESTRY

# GUY GAVRIEL KAY

# THE
# FIONAVAR
# TAPESTRY

## THE
## SUMMER TREE

## THE
## WANDERING FIRE

## THE
## DARKEST ROAD

HARPER PERENNIAL

*The Summer Tree* was first published by McClelland & Stewart Limited in 1984.
The first paperback edition was published by Collins Publishers in 1986.
The first HarperCollins Publishers Ltd edition was published in 1992.

*The Wandering Fire* was first published by Collins Publishers in 1986.
The first paperback edition was published in 1987. The first
HarperCollins Publishers Ltd edition was published in 1989.

*The Darkest Road* was first published by Collins Publishers in 1986.
The first paperback edition was published in 1987. The first
HarperCollins Publishers Ltd edition was published in 1992.

These three books were first published together in this
omnibus edition in 1995.

---

Canadian Cataloguing in Publication Data

Kay, Guy Gavriel
The fionavar tapestry

Contents: The summer tree — The wandering fire — The darkest road.
ISBN 0-00-647950-2

I. Title.   II. Title: The summer tree.   III. Title: The wandering fire.
IV. Title: The darkest road.

PS8571.A935F5 1995    C813'.54    C95-930651-X
PR9199.3.K38F5 1995

---

17 18 HC 30

Printed and bound in the United States

# ACKNOWLEDGEMENTS

At the beginning of the first edition of *The Summer Tree*, in 1984, I acknowledged my parents, my brothers and my wife, with love. Some things do not change. My thanks also to Martin Springett and Sue Reynolds, and to my agents and editors in many countries, over two decades.

# THE FIONAVAR
# TAPESTRY

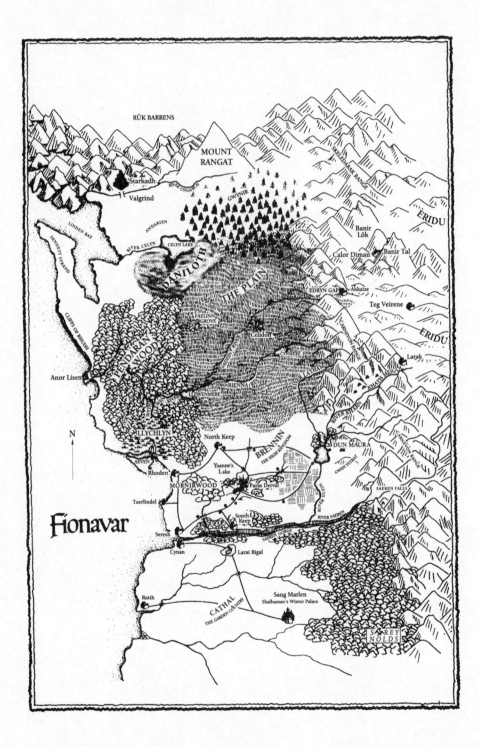

# BOOK 1

# THE SUMMER TREE

The Summer Tree *is dedicated to the memory
of my grandmother,*
*TANIA POLLOCK BIRSTEIN*

*whose gravestone reads, "Beautiful, Loving, Loved,"
and who was all of these things.*

# CONTENTS

# THE CHARACTERS

## The Five:

KIMBERLY FORD
KEVIN LAINE
JENNIFER LOWELL
DAVE MARTYNIUK
PAUL SCHAFER

## In Brennin:

AILELL, High King of Brennin
THE EXILED PRINCE, his older son
DIARMUID, younger son and heir to Ailell; also Warden of the
    South Marches

GORLAES, the Chancellor

METRAN, First Mage of Brennin
DENBARRA, his source
LOREN SILVERCLOAK, a mage
MATT SÖREN, his source, once King of the Dwarves
TEYRNON, a mage
BARAK, his source

JAELLE, High Priestess of the Goddess

YSANNE, Seer of Brennin ("the Dreamer")
TYRTH, her servant

COLL, lieutenant to Diarmuid
CARDE
ERRON
TEGID
DRANCE } the men of South Keep, members of
ROTHE     Diarmuid's band
AVERREN

MABON, Duke of Rhoden
NIAVIN, Duke of Seresh
CEREDUR, Warden of the North Marches

RHEVA ⎫
LAESHA ⎭ ladies of the court of Ailell

LEILA ⎫
FINN ⎭ children in Paras Derval

NA-BRENDEL, a lord of the lios alfar, from Daniloth

# In Cathal:

SHALHASSAN, Supreme Lord of Cathal
SHARRA, his daughter and heir ("the Dark Rose")

DEVORSH ⎫
BASHRAI ⎭ Captains of the Guard

# On the Plain:

IVOR, Chieftain of the third tribe of the Dalrei
LEITH, his wife
LEVON
CORDELIANE ("LIANE") ⎫ his children
TABOR

GEREINT, shaman of the third tribe

TORC, a Rider of the third tribe ("the Outcast")

# The Powers:

THE WEAVER at the Loom

MÖRNIR of the Thunder
DANA, the Mother
CERNAN of the Beasts
CEINWEN of the Bow, the HUNTRESS
MACHA ⎫
NEMAIN ⎭ godesses of war

RAKOTH MAUGRIM the UNRAVELLER, also named SATHAIN,
the HOODED ONE

GALADAN, Wolflord of the andain, his lieutenant

EILATHEN, a water spirit
FLIDAIS, a wood spirit

# From the Past:

IORWETH FOUNDER, first High King of Brennin

CONARY, High King during the Bael Rangat
COLAN, his son, High King after him ("the Beloved")
AMAIRGEN WHITEBRANCH, first of the mages
LISEN of the Wood, a deiena, source and wife to Amairgen
REVOR, ancestral hero of the Dalrei, first Lord of the Plain

VAILERTH, High King of Brennin in a time of civil war
NILSOM, First Mage to Vailerth
AIDEEN, source to Nilsom

GARMISCH, High King before Ailell
RAEDERTH, First Mage to Garmisch; beloved of Ysanne the Seer

# OVERTURE

*After the war was over, they bound him under the Mountain. And so that there might be warning if he moved to escape, they crafted then, with magic and with art, the five wardstones, last creation and the finest of Ginserat. One went south across Saeren to Cathal, one over the mountains to Eridu, another remained with Revor and the Dalrei on the Plain. The fourth wardstone Colan carried home, Conary's son, now High King in Paras Derval.*

*The last stone was accepted, though in bitterness of heart, by the broken remnant of the lios alfar. Scarcely a quarter of those who had come to war with Ra-Termaine went back to the Shadowland from the parley at the foot of the Mountain. They carried the stone, and the body of their King—most hated by the Dark, for their name was Light.*

*From that day on, few men could ever claim to have seen the lios, except perhaps as moving shadows at the edge of a wood, when twilight found a farmer or a carter walking home. For a time it was rumoured among the common folk that every seven-year a messenger would come by unseen ways to hold converse with the High King in Paras Derval, but as the years swept past, such tales dwindled, as they tend to, into the mist of half-remembered history.*

*Ages went by in a storm of years. Except in houses of learning, even Conary was just a name, and Ra-Termaine, and forgotten, too, was Revor's Ride through Daniloth on the night of the red sunset. It had become a song for drunken tavern nights, no more true or less than any other such songs, no more bright.*

*For there were newer deeds to extol, younger heroes to parade through city streets and palace corridors, to be toasted in their turn by village tavern fires. Alliances shifted, fresh wars were fought to salve old wounds, glittering triumphs assuaged past defeats, High King succeeded High King, some by descent and others by brandished sword. And through it all, through the petty wars and the great ones, the strong leaders and weak, the long green years of peace when the roads were safe and the harvest rich, through it all the Mountain slumbered—for the rituals of the wardstones, though all else changed, were preserved. The stones were watched, the naal fires tended, and there never came the terrible warning of Ginserat's stones turning from blue to red.*

*And under the great mountain, Rangat Cloud-Shouldered, in the wind-blasted north, a figure writhed in chains, eaten by hate to the edge of madness, but knowing full well that the wardstones would give warning if he stretched his powers to break free.*

*Still, he could wait, being outside of time, outside of death. He could brood on his revenge and his memories—for he remembered everything. He could turn the names of his enemies over and over in his mind, as once he had played with the blood-clotted necklace of Ra-Termaine in a taloned hand. But above all he could wait: wait as the cycles of men turned like the wheel of stars, as the very stars shifted pattern under the press of years. There would come a time when the watch slackened, when one of the five guardians would falter. Then could he, in darkest secrecy, exert his strength to summon aid, and there would come a day when Rakoth Maugrim would be free in Fionavar.*

*And a thousand years passed under the sun and stars of the first of all the worlds. . . .*

# PART I

# SILVERCLOAK

# CHAPTER 1

In the spaces of calm almost lost in what followed, the question of *why* tended to surface. Why them? There was an easy answer that had to do with Ysanne beside her lake, but that didn't really address the deepest question. Kimberly, white-haired, would say when asked that she could sense a glimmered pattern when she looked back, but one need not be a Seer to use hindsight on the warp and weft of the Tapestry, and Kim, in any event, was a special case.

With only the professional faculties still in session, the quadrangles and shaded paths of the University of Toronto campus would normally have been deserted by the beginning of May, particularly on a Friday evening. That the largest of the open spaces was not, served to vindicate the judgement of the organizers of the Second International Celtic Conference. In adapting their timing to suit certain prominent speakers, the conference administrators had run the risk that a good portion of their potential audience would have left for the summer by the time they got under way.

At the brightly lit entrance to Convocation Hall, the besieged security guards might have wished this to be the case. An astonishing crowd of students and academics, bustling like a rock audience with pre-concert excitement, had gathered to hear the man for whom, principally, the late starting date had been arranged. Lorenzo Marcus was speaking and chairing a panel that night in the first public appearance ever for the reclusive genius, and it was going to be standing room only in the august precincts of the domed auditorium.

The guards searched out forbidden tape recorders and waved ticket-holders through with expressions benevolent or inimical, as their natures dictated. Bathed in the bright spill of light and pressed by the milling crowd, they did not see the dark figure that crouched in the shadows of the porch, just beyond the farthest circle of the lights.

For a moment the hidden creature observed the crowd, then it turned, swiftly and quite silently, and slipped around the side of the building. There, where the darkness was almost complete, it looked once over its shoulder and then, with unnatural agility, began to climb hand over hand up the outer wall of Convocation Hall. In a very little while the creature, which had neither ticket nor tape recorder, had come to rest beside a window set high in the dome above the hall. Looking down past the glittering chandeliers, it could see the audience and the stage, brightly lit and far below. Even at this height, and through the heavy glass, the electric murmur of sound in the hall could be heard. The creature, clinging to the arched window, allowed a smile of lean pleasure to flit across its features. Had any of the people in the highest gallery turned just then to admire the windows of the dome, they might have seen it, a dark shape against the night. But no one had any reason to look up, and no one did. On the outside of the dome the creature moved closer against the window pane and composed itself to wait. There was a good chance it would kill later that night. The prospect greatly facilitated patience and brought a certain anticipatory satisfaction, for it had been bred for such a purpose, and most creatures are pleased to do what their nature dictates.

Dave Martyniuk stood like a tall tree in the midst of the crowd that was swirling like leaves through the lobby. He was looking for his brother, and he was increasingly uncomfortable. It didn't make him feel any better when he saw the stylish figure of Kevin Laine coming through the door with Paul Schafer and two women. Dave was in the process of turning away—he didn't feel like being patronized just then—when he realized that Laine had seen him.

"Martyniuk! What are you doing here?"

"Hello, Laine. My brother's on the panel."

"Vince Martyniuk. Of course," Kevin said. "He's a bright man."

"One in every family," Dave cracked, somewhat sourly. He saw Paul Schafer give a crooked grin.

Kevin Laine laughed. "At least. But I'm being rude. You know Paul. This is Jennifer Lowell, and Kim Ford, my favourite doctor."

"Hi," Dave said, forced to shift his program to shake hands.

"This is Dave Martyniuk, people. He's the centre on our basketball team. Dave's in third-year law here."

"In that order?" Kim Ford teased, brushing a lock of brown hair back from her eyes. Dave was trying to think of a response when there was a movement in the crowd around them.

"*Dave!* Sorry I'm late." It was, finally, Vincent. "I have to get backstage fast. I may not be able to talk to you till tomorrow. Pleased to meet you"—to Kim, though he hadn't been introduced. Vince bustled off, briefcase in front of him like the prow of a ship cleaving through the crowd.

"Your brother?" Kim Ford asked, somewhat unnecessarily.

"Yeah." Dave was feeling sour again. Kevin Laine, he saw, had been accosted by some other friends and was evidently being witty.

If he headed back to the law school, Dave thought, he could still do a good three hours on Evidence before the library closed.

"Are you alone here?" Kim Ford asked.

"Yeah, but I—"

"Why don't you sit with us, then?"

Dave, a little surprised at himself, followed Kim into the hall.

"Her," the Dwarf said. And pointed directly across the auditorium to where Kimberly Ford was entering with a tall, broad-shouldered man. "She's the one."

The grey-bearded man beside him nodded slowly. They were standing, half hidden, in the wings of the stage, watching the audience pour in. "I think so," he said worriedly. "I need five, though, Matt."

"But only one for the circle. She came with three, and there is a fourth with them now. You have your five."

"I have five," the other man said. "*Mine*, I don't know. If this were just for Metran's jubilee stupidity it wouldn't matter, but—"

"Loren, I know." The Dwarf's voice was surprisingly gentle. "But she is the one we were told of. My friend, if I could help you with your dreams. . . ."

"You think me foolish?"

"I know better than that."

The tall man turned away. His sharp gaze went across the room to where the five people his companion had indicated were sitting. One by one he focused on them, then his eyes locked on Paul Schafer's face.

Sitting between Jennifer and Dave, Paul was glancing around the hall, only half listening to the chairman's fulsome introduction of the evening's keynote speaker, when he was hit by the probe.

The light and sound in the room faded completely. He felt a great darkness. There was a forest, a corridor of whispering trees, shrouded in mist. Starlight in the space above the trees. Somehow he knew that the moon was about to rise, and when it rose . . .

He was in it. The hall was gone. There was no wind in the darkness, but still the trees were whispering, and it was more than just a sound. The immersion was complete, and within some hidden recess Paul confronted the terrible, haunted eyes of a dog or a wolf. Then the vision fragmented, images whipping past, chaotic, myriad, too fast to hold, except for one: a tall man standing in darkness, and upon his head the great, curved antlers of a stag.

Then it broke: sharp, wildly disorienting. His eyes, scarcely able to focus, swept across the room until they found a tall, grey-bearded man on the side of the stage. A man who spoke briefly to someone next to him, and then walked smiling to the lectern amid thunderous applause.

"Set it up, Matt," the grey-bearded man had said. "We will take them if we can."

"He was good, Kim. You were right," Jennifer Lowell said. They were standing by their seats, waiting for the exiting crowd to thin. Kim Ford was flushed with excitement.

"Wasn't he?" she asked them all, rhetorically. "What a *terrific* speaker!"

"Your brother was quite good, I thought," Paul Schafer said to Dave quietly.

Surprised, Dave grunted noncommittally, then remembered something. "You feeling okay?"

Paul looked blank a moment, then grimaced. "You, too? I'm fine. I just needed a day's rest. I'm more or less over the mono." Dave, looking at him, wasn't so sure. None of his business, though, if Schafer wanted to kill himself playing basketball. He'd played a football game with broken ribs once. You survived.

Kim was talking again. "I'd love to meet him, you know." She looked wistfully at the knot of autograph-seekers surrounding Marcus.

"So would I, actually," said Paul softly. Kevin shot him a questioning look.

"Dave," Kim went on, "your brother couldn't get us into that reception, could he?"

Dave was beginning the obvious reply when a deep voice rode in over him.

"Excuse me, please, for intruding." A figure little more than four feet tall, with a patch over one eye, had come up beside them. "My name," he said, in an accent Dave couldn't place, "is Matt Sören. I am Dr. Marcus's secretary. I could not help but overhear the young lady's remark. May I tell you a secret?" He paused. "Dr. Marcus has no desire at all to attend the planned reception. With all respect," he said, turning to Dave, "to your very learned brother."

Jennifer saw Kevin Laine begin to turn himself on. Performance time, she thought, and smiled to herself.

Laughing, Kevin took charge. "You want us to spirit him away?"

The Dwarf blinked, then a basso chuckle reverberated in his chest. "You are quick, my friend. Yes, indeed, I think he would enjoy that very much."

Kevin looked at Paul Schafer.

"A plot," Jennifer whispered. "Hatch us a plot, gentlemen!"

"Easy enough," Kevin said, after some quick reflection. "As of this moment, Kim's his niece. He wants to see her. Family before functions." He waited for Paul's approval.

"Good," Matt Sören said. "And very simple. Will you come with me then to fetch your . . . ah . . . uncle?"

"Of course I will!" Kim laughed. "Haven't seen him in *ages*." She walked off with the Dwarf towards the tangle of people around Lorenzo Marcus at the front of the hall.

"Well," Dave said, "I think I'll be moving along."

"Oh, Martyniuk," Kevin exploded, "don't be such a legal drip! This guy's world-famous. He's a legend. You can study for Evidence tomorrow. Look, come to my office in the afternoon and I'll dig up my old exam notes for you."

Dave froze. Kevin Laine, he knew all too well, had won the award in Evidence two years before, along with an armful of other prizes.

Jennifer, watching him hesitate, felt an impulse of sympathy. There was a lot eating this guy, she thought, and Kevin's manner didn't help. It was so hard for some people to get past the flashiness to see what was underneath. And against her will, for Jennifer had her own defences, she found herself remembering what love-making used to do to him.

"Hey, people! I want you to meet someone." Kim's voice knifed into her thoughts. She had her arm looped possessively through that of the tall lecturer, who beamed benignly down upon her. "This is my Uncle Lorenzo. Uncle, my room-mate Jennifer, Kevin and Paul, and this is Dave."

Marcus's dark eyes flashed. "I am," he said, "more pleased to meet you than you could know. You have rescued me from an exceptionally dreary evening. Will you join us for a drink at our hotel? We're at the Park Plaza, Matt and I."

"With pleasure, sir," Kevin said. He waited for a beat. "And we'll try hard not to be dreary." Marcus lifted an eyebrow.

A cluster of academics watched with intense frustration in their eyes as the seven of them swept out of the hall together and into the cool, cloudless night.

And another pair of eyes watched as well, from the deep shadows under the porch pillars of Convocation Hall. Eyes that reflected the light, and did not blink.

It was a short walk, and a pleasant one. Across the wide central green of the campus, then along the dark winding path known as Philosophers' Walk that twisted, with gentle slopes on either side, behind the law school, the Faculty of Music, and the massive edifice of the Royal Ontario Museum, where the dinosaur bones preserved their long silence. It was a route that Paul Schafer had been carefully avoiding for the better part of the past year.

He slowed a little, to detach himself from the others. Up ahead, in the shadows, Kevin, Kim, and Lorenzo Marcus were weaving a baroque fantasy of improbable entanglements between the clans Ford and Marcus, with a few of Kevin's remoter Russian ancestors thrown into the mix by marriage. Jennifer, on Marcus's left arm, was urging them on with her laughter, while Dave Martyniuk loped silently along on the grass beside the walkway, looking a little out of place. Matt Sören, quietly companionable, had slowed his pace to fall into stride with Paul. Schafer, however, withdrawing, could feel the conversation and laughter sliding into the background. The sensation was a familiar one of late, and after a while it was as if he were walking alone.

Which may have been why, partway along the path, he became aware of something to which the others were oblivious. It pulled him sharply out of reverie, and he walked a short distance in a different sort of silence before turning to the Dwarf beside him.

"Is there any reason," he asked, very softly, "why the two of you would be followed?"

Matt Sören broke stride only momentarily. He took a deep breath. "Where?" he asked, in a voice equally low.

"Behind us, to the left. Slope of the hill. Is there a reason?"

"There may be. Would you keep walking, please? And say nothing for now—it may be nothing." When Paul hesitated, the Dwarf gripped his arm. "Please?" he repeated. Schafer, after a moment, nodded and quickened his pace to catch up to the group now several yards ahead. The mood by then was hilarious and very loud. Only Paul, listening for it, heard the sharp, abruptly truncated cry from the darkness behind them. He blinked, but no expression crossed his face.

Matt Sören rejoined them just as they reached the end of the shadowed walkway and came out to the noise and bright lights of Bloor Street. Ahead lay the huge stone pile of the old Park Plaza hotel. Before they crossed the road he placed a hand again on Schafer's arm.

"Thank you," said the Dwarf.

"Well," said Lorenzo Marcus, as they settled into chairs in his sixteenth-floor suite, "why don't you all tell me about yourselves? Yourselves," he repeated, raising an admonitory finger at grinning Kevin.

"Why don't you start?" Marcus went on, turning to Kim. "What are you studying?"

Kim acquiesced with some grace. "Well, I'm just finishing my interning year at—"

"Hold it, Kim."

It was Paul. Ignoring a fierce look from the Dwarf, he levelled his eyes on their host. "Sorry, Dr. Marcus. I've got some questions of my own and I need answers now, or we're all going home."

"Paul, what the—"

"No, Kev. Listen a minute." They were all staring at Schafer's pale, intense features. "Something very strange is happening here. I want to know," he said to Marcus, "why you were so anxious to cut us out of that crowd. Why you sent your friend to set it up. I want to know what you did to me in the auditorium. And I really want to know why we were followed on the way over here."

"*Followed?*" The shock registering on Lorenzo Marcus's face was manifestly unfeigned.

"That's right," Paul said, "and I want to know what it was too."

"Matt?" Marcus asked, in a whisper.

The Dwarf fixed Paul Schafer with a long stare.

Paul met the glance. "Our priorities," he said, "can't be the same in this." After a moment, Matt Sören nodded and turned to Marcus.

"Friends from home," he said. "It seems there are those who want to know exactly what you are doing when you . . . travel."

"Friends?" Lorenzo Marcus asked.

"I speak loosely. Very loosely."

There was a silence. Marcus leaned back in his armchair, stroking the grey beard. He closed his eyes.

"This isn't how I would have chosen to begin," he said at length, "but it may be for the best after all." He turned to Paul. "I owe you an apology. Earlier this evening I subjected you to something we call a searching. It doesn't always work. Some have defences against it and with others, such as yourself, it seems, strange things can happen. What took place between us unsettled me as well."

Paul's eyes, more blue than grey in the lamplight, were astonishingly unsurprised. "I'll need to talk about what we saw," he said to Lorenzo Marcus, "but the thing is, why did you do it in the first place?"

And so they were there. Kevin, leaning forward, every sense sharpened, saw Lorenzo Marcus draw a deep breath, and he had a flash image in that instant of his own life poised on the edge of an abyss.

22

"Because," Lorenzo Marcus said, "you were quite right, Paul Schafer—I didn't just want to escape a boring reception tonight. I need you. The five of you."

"We're not five." Dave's heavy voice crashed in. "I've got nothing to do with these people."

"You are too quick to renounce friendship, Dave Martyniuk," Marcus snapped back. "But," he went on, more gently, after a frozen instant, "it doesn't matter here—and to make you see why, I must try to explain. Which is harder than it would have been once." He hesitated, hand at his beard again.

"You aren't Lorenzo Marcus, are you?" Paul said, very quietly.

In the stillness, the tall man turned to him again. "Why do you say that?"

Paul shrugged. "Am I right?"

"That searching truly was a mistake. Yes," said their host, "you are right." Dave was looking from Paul to the speaker with hostile incredulity. "Although I am Marcus, in a way—as much as anyone is. There is no one else. But Marcus is not who I am."

"And who are you?" It was Kim who asked. And was answered in a voice suddenly deep as a spell.

"My name is Loren. Men call me Silvercloak. I am a mage. My friend is Matt Sören, who was once King of the Dwarves. We come from Paras Derval, where Ailell reigns, in a world that is not your own."

In the stone silence that followed this, Kevin Laine, who had chased an elusive image down all the nights of his life, felt an astonishing turbulence rising in his heart. There was a power woven into the old man's voice, and that, as much as the words, reached through to him.

"Almighty God," he whispered. "Paul, how did you know?"

"Wait a second! You *believe* this?" It was Dave Martyniuk, all bristling belligerence. "I've never heard anything so crackbrained in my life!" He put his drink down and was halfway to the door in two long strides.

"Dave, please!"

It stopped him. Dave turned slowly in the middle of the room to face Jennifer Lowell. "Don't go," she pleaded. "He said he needed us."

Her eyes, he noticed for the first time, were green. He shook his head. "Why do you care?"

"Didn't you hear it?" she replied. "Didn't you feel anything?"

He wasn't about to tell these people what he had or hadn't heard in the old man's voice, but before he could make that clear, Kevin Laine spoke.

"Dave, we can afford to hear him out. If there's danger or it's really wild, we can run away after."

He heard the goad in the words, and the implication. He didn't rise to it, though. Never turning from Jennifer, he walked over and sat beside her on the couch. Didn't even look at Kevin Laine.

There was a silence, and she was the one who broke it. "Now, Dr. Marcus, or whatever you prefer to be called, we'll listen. But please explain. Because I'm frightened now."

It is not known whether Loren Silvercloak had a vision then of what the future held for Jennifer, but he bestowed upon her a look as tender as he could give, from a nature storm-tossed, but still more giving, perhaps, than anything else. And then he began the tale.

"There are many worlds," he said, "caught in the loops and whorls of time. Seldom do they intersect, and so for the most part they are unknown to each other. Only in Fionavar, the prime creation, which all the others imperfectly reflect, is the lore gathered and preserved that tells of how to bridge the worlds—and even there the years have not dealt kindly with ancient wisdom. We have made the crossing before, Matt and I, but always with difficulty, for much is lost, even in Fionavar."

"How? How do you cross?" It was Kevin.

"It is easiest to call it magic, though there is more involved than spells."

"Your magic?" Kevin continued.

"I am a mage, yes," Loren said. "The crossing was mine. And so, too, if you come, will be the return."

"This is ridiculous!" Martyniuk exploded again. This time he would not look at Jennifer. "Magic. Crossings. Show me something! Talk is cheap, and I don't believe a word of this."

Loren stared coldly at Dave. Kim, seeing it, caught her breath. But then the severe face creased in a sudden smile. The eyes, improbably, danced. "You're right," he said. "It is much the simplest way. Look, then."

There was silence in the room for almost ten seconds. Kevin saw, out of the corner of his eye, that the Dwarf, too, had gone very still. What'll it be, he thought.

They saw a castle.

Where Dave Martyniuk had stood moments before, there appeared battlements and towers, a garden, a central courtyard, an open square before the walls, and on the very highest rampart a banner somehow blowing in a non-existent breeze: and on the banner Kevin saw a crescent moon above a spreading tree.

"Paras Derval," Loren said softly, gazing at his own artifice with an expression almost wistful, "in Brennin, High Kingdom of Fionavar. Mark the flags in the great square before the palace. They are there for the coming celebration, because the eighth day past the full of the moon this month will end the fifth decade of Ailell's reign."

"And us?" Kimberly's voice was parchment-thin. "Where do we fit in?"

A wry smile softened the lines of Loren's face. "Not heroically, I'm afraid, though there is pleasure in this for you, I hope. A great deal is being done to celebrate the anniversary. There has been a long spring drought in Brennin, and it has been deemed politic to give the people something to cheer about. And I daresay there is reason for it. At any rate, Metran, First Mage to Ailell, has decided that the gift to him and to the people from the Council of the Mages will be to bring five people from another world—one for each decade of the reign—to join us for the festival fortnight."

Kevin Laine laughed aloud. "Red Indians to the Court of King James?"

With a gesture almost casual, Loren dissolved the apparition in the middle of the room. "I'm afraid there's some truth to that. Metran's ideas . . . he is First of my Council, but I daresay I need not always agree with him."

"You're here," Paul said.

"I wanted to try another crossing in any case," Loren replied quickly. "It has been a long time since last I was in your world as Lorenzo Marcus."

"Have I got this straight?" Kim asked. "You want us to cross with you somehow to your world, and then you'll bring us back?"

"Basically, yes. You will be with us for two weeks, perhaps, but when we return I will have you back in this room within a few hours of when we departed."

"Well," said Kevin, with a sly grin, "that should get you, Martyniuk, for sure. Just think, Dave, two extra weeks to study for Evidence!"

Dave flushed bright red, as the room broke up in a release of tension.

"I'm in, Loren Silvercloak," said Kevin Laine, as they quieted. And so became the first. He managed a grin. "I've always wanted to wear war-paint to court. When's take-off?"

Loren looked at him steadily. "Tomorrow. Early evening, if we are to time it properly. I will not ask you to decide now. Think for the rest of tonight, and tomorrow. If you will come with me, be here by late afternoon."

"What about you? What if we don't come?" Kim's forehead was creased with the vertical line that always showed when she was under stress.

Loren seemed disconcerted by the question. "If that happens, I fail. It has happened before. Don't worry about me . . . niece." It was remarkable what a smile did to his face. "Shall we leave it at that?" he went on, as Kim's eyes still registered an unresolved concern. "If you decide to come, be here tomorrow. I will be waiting."

"One thing." It was Paul again. "I'm sorry to keep asking the unpleasant questions, but we still don't know what that thing was on Philosophers' Walk."

Dave had forgotten. Jennifer hadn't. They both looked at Loren. At length he answered, speaking directly to Paul. "There is magic in Fionavar. I have shown you something of it, even here. There are also creatures, of good and evil, who co-exist with humankind. Your own world, too, was once like this, though it has been drifting from the pattern for a long time now. The legends of which I spoke in the auditorium tonight are echoes, scarcely understood, of mornings when man did not walk alone, and other beings, both friend and foe, moved in the forests and the hills." He paused. "What followed us was one of the svart alfar, I think. Am I right, Matt?"

The Dwarf nodded, without speaking.

"The svarts," Loren went on, "are a malicious race, and have done great evil in their time. There are few of them left. This one, braver than most, it would seem, somehow followed Matt and me through on our crossing. They are ugly creatures, and sometimes dangerous, though usually only in numbers. This one, I suspect, is dead." He looked to Matt again.

Once more the Dwarf nodded from where he stood by the door.

"I wish you hadn't told me that," Jennifer said.

The mage's eyes, deep-set, were again curiously tender as he looked at her. "I'm sorry you have been frightened this evening. Will you accept my assurance that, unsettling as they may sound, the svarts need not be of concern to you?" He paused, his gaze holding hers. "I would not have you do anything that goes against your nature. I have extended to you an invitation, no more. You may find it easier to decide after leaving us." He rose to his feet.

Another kind of power. A man accustomed to command, Kevin thought a few moments later, as the five of them found themselves outside the door of the room. They made their way down the hall to the elevator.

Matt Sören closed the door behind them.

"How bad is it?" Loren asked sharply. The Dwarf grimaced. "Not very. I was careless."

"A knife?" The mage was quickly helping his friend to remove the scaled-down jacket he wore.

"I wish. Teeth, actually." Loren cursed in sudden anger when the jacket finally slipped off to reveal the dark, heavily clotted blood staining the shirt on the Dwarf's left shoulder. He began gently tearing the cloth away from around the wound, swearing under his breath the whole time.

"It isn't so bad, Loren. Be easy. And you must admit I was clever to take the jacket off before going after him."

"Very clever, yes. Which is just as well, because my own stupidity of late is terrifying me! How in the name of Conall Cernach could I let a svart alfar come through with us?" He left the room with swift strides and returned a moment later with towels soaked in hot water.

The Dwarf endured the cleansing of his wound in silence. When the dried blood was washed away, the teeth marks could be seen, purple and very deep.

Loren examined it closely. "This is bad, my friend. Are you strong enough to help me heal it? We could have Metran or Teyrnon do it tomorrow, but I'd rather not wait."

"Go ahead." Matt closed his eyes.

The mage paused a moment, then carefully placed a hand above the wound. He spoke a word softly, then another. And beneath his long fingers the swelling on the Dwarf's shoulder began slowly to recede. When he finished, though, the face of Matt Sören was bathed in a sheen of perspiration. With his good arm Matt reached for a towel and wiped his forehead.

"All right?" Loren asked.

"Just fine."

"Just fine!" the mage mimicked angrily. "It would help, you know, if you didn't always play the silent hero! How am I supposed to know when you're really hurting if you always give me the same answer?"

The Dwarf fixed Loren with his one dark eye, and there was a trace of amusement in his face. "You aren't," he said. "You aren't supposed to know."

Loren made a gesture of ultimate exasperation, and left the roc. with a shirt of his own, which he began cutting into strips.

"Loren, don't blame yourself for letting the svart come through. You cou. done anything."

"Don't be a fool! I should have been aware of its presence as soon as it tried . come within the circle."

"I'm very seldom foolish, my friend." The Dwarf's tone was mild. "You couldn't have known, because it was wearing this when I killed it." Sören reached into his right trouser pocket and pulled out an object that he held up in his palm. It was a bracelet, of delicate silver workmanship, and set within it was a gem, green like an emerald.

"A vellin stone!" Loren Silvercloak whispered in dismay. "So it would have been shielded from me. Matt, someone gave a vellin to a svart alfar."

"So it would seem," the Dwarf agreed.

The mage was silent; he attended to the bandaging of Matt's shoulder with quick, skilled hands. When that was finished he walked, still wordless, to the window. He opened it, and a late-night breeze fluttered the white curtains. Loren gazed down at the few cars moving along the street far below.

"These five people," he said at last, still looking down. "What am I taking them back to? Do I have any right?"

The Dwarf didn't answer.

After a moment, Loren spoke again, almost to himself. "I left so much out."

"You did."

"Did I do wrong?"

"Perhaps. But you are seldom wrong in these things. Nor is Ysanne. If you feel they are needed—"

"But I don't know what for! I don't know *how*. It is only her dreams, my premonitions. . . ."

"Then trust yourself. Trust your premonitions. The girl *is* a hook, and the other one, Paul—"

"He is another thing. I don't know what."

"But something. You've been troubled for a long time, my friend. And I don't think needlessly."

The mage turned from the window to look at the other man. "I'm afraid you may be right. Matt, who would have us followed here?"

"Someone who wants you to fail in this. Which should tell us something."

Loren nodded abstractedly. "But who," he went on, looking at the green-stoned bracelet that the Dwarf still held, "who would ever give such a treasure into the hands of a svart alfar?"

The Dwarf looked down at the stone for a very long time as well before answering.

"Someone who wants you dead," Matt Sören said.

# CHAPTER 2

The girls shared a silent taxi west to the duplex they rented beside High Park. Jennifer, partly because she knew her room-mate very well, decided that she wouldn't be the first to bring up what had happened that night, what they both seemed to have heard under the surface of the old man's words.

But she was dealing with complex emotions of her own, as they turned down Parkside Drive and she watched the dark shadows of the park slide past on their right. When they got out of the cab the late-night breeze seemed unseasonably chilly. She looked across the road for a moment, at the softly rustling trees.

Inside they had a conversation about choices, about doing or not doing things, that either one of them could have predicted.

⟡══◉═══⟡

Dave Martyniuk refused Kim's offer to share a cab and walked the mile west to his flat on Palmerston. He walked quickly, the athlete's stride overlaid by anger and tension. *You are too quick to renounce friendship*, the old man had said. Dave scowled, moving faster. What did *he* know about it?

The telephone began ringing as he unlocked the door of his basement apartment.

"Yeah?" He caught it on the sixth ring.

"You are pleased with yourself, I am sure?"

"Jesus, Dad. What is it this time?"

"Don't swear at me. It would *kill* you, wouldn't it, to do something that would bring us pleasure."

"I don't know what the hell you're talking about."

"Such language. Such respect."

"Dad, I don't have time for this any more."

"Yes, hide from me. You went tonight as Vincent's guest to this lecture. And then you went off after with the man he most wanted to speak with. And you couldn't even *think* of asking your brother?"

Dave took a careful breath. His reflexive anger giving way to the old sorrow. "Dad, please believe me—it didn't happen that way. Marcus went with these people I know because he didn't feel like talking to the academics like Vince. I just tagged along."

"You just tagged along," his father mimicked in his heavy Ukrainian accent. "You are a liar. Your jealousy is so much that you—"

Dave hung up. And unplugged the telephone. With a fierce and bitter pain he stared at it, watching how, over and over again, it didn't ring.

⊷⇒◠⇐⊶

They said good-night to the girls and watched Martyniuk stalk off into the darkness.

"Coffee time, amigo," Kevin Laine said brightly. "Much to talk about we have, yes?"

Paul hesitated, and in the moment of that hesitation Kevin's mood shattered like glass.

"Not tonight, I think. I've got some things to do, Kev."

The hurt in Kevin Laine moved to the surface, threatened to break through. "Okay," was all he said, though. "Good night. Maybe I'll see you tomorrow." And he turned abruptly and jogged across Bloor against the light to where he'd parked his car. He drove home, a little too fast, through the quiet streets.

It was after one o'clock when he pulled into the driveway, so he entered the house as silently as he could, sliding the bolt gently home.

"I am awake, Kevin. It is all right."

"What are you doing up? It's very late, Abba." He used the Hebrew word for father, as he always did.

Sol Laine, in pyjamas and robe at the kitchen table, raised a quizzical eyebrow as Kevin walked in. "I need permission from my son to stay up late?"

"Who else's?" Kevin dropped into one of the other chairs.

"A good answer," his father approved. "Would you like some tea?"

"Sounds good."

"How was this talk?" Sol asked as he attended to the boiling kettle.

"Fine. Very good, actually. We had a drink with the speaker afterwards." Kevin briefly considered telling his father about what had happened, but only briefly. Father and son had a long habit of protecting each other, and Kevin knew that this was something Sol would be unable to handle. He wished it were otherwise; it would have been good, he thought, a little bitterly, to have *someone* to talk to.

"Jennifer is well? And her friend?"

Kevin's bitterness broke in a wave of love for the old man who'd raised him alone. Sol had never been able to reconcile his orthodoxy with his son's relationship with Catholic Jennifer—and had resented himself for not being able to. So through their short time together, and after, Kevin's father had treated Jen like a jewel of great worth.

"She's fine. Says hello. Kim's fine, too."

"But Paul isn't?"

Kevin blinked. "Oh, Abba, you're too sharp for me. Why do you say that?"

"Because if he was, you would have gone out with him afterwards. The way you always used to. You would still be out. I would be drinking my tea alone, all alone." The twinkle in his eyes belied the lugubrious sentiments.

Kevin laughed aloud, then stopped when he heard the bitter note creeping in.

"No, he's not all right. But I seem to be the only one who questions it. I think I'm becoming a pain in the ass to him. I hate it."

"Sometimes," his father said, filling the glass cups in their Russian-style metal holders, "a friend has to be that."

"No one else seems to think there's anything wrong, though. They just talk about how it takes time."

"It does take time, Kevin."

Kevin made an impatient gesture. "I *know* it does. I'm not that stupid. But I know him, too, I know him very well, and he's . . . There's something else there, and I don't know what it is."

His father didn't speak for a moment. "How long is it now?" he asked, finally.

"Ten months," Kevin replied flatly. "Last summer."

"Ach!" Sol shook his heavy, still-handsome head. "Such a terrible thing."

Kevin leaned forward. "Abba, he's been closing himself off. To everyone. I don't . . . I'm afraid for what might happen. And I can't seem to get through."

"Are you trying too hard?" Sol Laine asked gently.

His son slumped back in his chair. "Maybe," he said, and the old man could see the effort the answer took. "But it hurts, Abba, he's all twisted up."

Sol Laine, who had married late, had lost his wife to cancer when Kevin, their only child, was five years old. He looked now at his handsome, fair son with a twisting in his own heart. "Kevin," he said, "you will have to learn—and for you it will be hard—that sometimes you can't do anything. Sometimes you simply can't."

Kevin finished his tea. He kissed his father on the forehead and went up to bed in the grip of a sadness that was new to him, and a sense of yearning that was not.

He woke once in the night, a few hours before Kimberly would. Reaching for a note pad he kept by the bed, he scribbled a line and fell back into sleep. *We are the total of our longings,* he had written. But Kevin was a song-writer, not a poet, and he never did use it.

⟡

Paul Schafer walked home as well that night, north up Avenue Road and two blocks over at Bernard. His pace was slower than Dave's, though, and you could not have told his thoughts or mood from his movements. His hands were in his pockets, and two or three times, where the streetlights thinned, he looked up at the ragged pattern of cloud that now hid and now revealed the moon.

Only at his doorway did his face show an expression—and, this was only a transitory irresolution, as of someone weighing sleep against a walk around the block, perhaps.

Schafer went in, though, and unlocked his ground-floor apartment. Turning on a lamp in the living room, he poured himself a drink and carried the glass to a deep armchair. Again the pale face under the dark shock of hair was expressionless. And again, when his mouth and eyes did move, a long time later, it was to register only a kind of indecision, wiped away quickly this time by the tightening jaw.

He leaned sideways then to the stereo and tape deck, turned them on, and inserted a cassette. In part because it was very late, but only in part, he adjusted the machine and put on the headphones. Then he turned out the only light in the room.

It was a private tape, one he had made himself a year ago. On it, as he sat there motionless in the dark, sounds from the summer before took shape: a graduation recital in the Faculty of Music's Edward Johnson Building, by a girl named Rachel Kincaid. A girl with dark hair like his own and dark eyes like no one else in this world.

And Paul Schafer, who believed one should be able to endure anything, and who believed this of himself most of all, listened as long as he could, and failed again. When the second movement began, he shuddered through an indrawn breath and stabbed the machine to silence.

It seemed that there were still things one could not do. So one did everything else as well as one possibly could and found new things to try, to will oneself to master, and always one realized, at the kernel and heart of things, that the ends of the earth would not be far enough away.

Which was why, despite knowing very well that there were things they had not been told, Paul Schafer was glad, bleakly glad, to be going farther than the ends of the earth on the morrow. And the moon, moving then to shine unobstructed through the window, lit the room enough to reveal the serenity of his face.

⊶═◉═⊷

And in the place beyond the ends of earth, in Fionavar, which lay waiting for them like a lover, like a dream, another moon, larger than our own, rose to light the changing of the wardstone guard in the palace of Paras Derval. The priestess appointed came with the new guards, tended and banked the naal flame set before the stone, and withdrew, yawning, to her narrow bed.

And the stone, Ginserat's stone, set in its high obsidian pillar carved with a relief of Conary before the Mountain, shone still, as it had a thousand years, radiantly blue.

# CHAPTER 3

Towards dawn a bank of clouds settled low over the city. Kimberly Ford stirred, surfaced almost to wakefulness, then slipped back down into a light sleep, and a dream unlike any she'd known before.

There was a place of massive jumbled stones. A wind was blowing over wide grasslands. It was dusk. She almost knew the place, was so close to naming it that her inability tasted bitter in her mouth. The wind made a chill, keening sound as it blew between the stones. She had come to find one who was needed, but she knew he was not there. A ring was on her finger, with a stone that gleamed a dull red in the twilight, and this was her power and her burden both. The gathered stones demanded an invocation from her; the wind threatened to tear it from her mouth. She knew what she was here to say, and was broken-hearted, beyond all grief she'd ever known, at the price her speaking would exact from the man she'd come to summon. In the dream, she opened her mouth to say the words.

She woke then, and was very still a long time. When she rose, it was to move to the window, where she drew the curtain back.

The clouds were breaking up. Venus, rising in the east before the sun, shone silver-white and dazzling, like hope. The ring on her finger in the dream had shone as well: deep red and masterful, like Mars.

The Dwarf dropped into a crouch, hands loosely clasped in front of him. They were all there; Kevin with his guitar, Dave Martyniuk defiantly clutching the promised Evidence notes. Loren remained out of sight in the bedroom. "Preparing," the Dwarf had said. And now, without preamble, Matt Sören said more.

"Ailell reigns in Brennin, the High Kingdom. Fifty years now, as you have heard. He is very old, much reduced. Metran heads the Council of the Mages, and Gorlaes, the Chancellor, is first of all advisers. You will meet them both. Ailell had two sons only, very late in life. The name of the elder," Matt hesitated, "—is not to be spoken. The younger is Diarmuid, now heir to the throne."

Too many mysteries, Kevin Laine thought. He was nervous, and angry with himself for that. Beside him, Kim was concentrating fiercely, a single vertical line furrowing her forehead.

"South of us," the Dwarf continued, "the Saeren flows through its ravine, and beyond the river is Cathal, the Garden Country. There has been war with Shalhassan's people in my lifetime. The river is patrolled on both sides. North of Brennin is the Plain where the Dalrei dwell, the Riders. The tribes follow the eltor herds as the seasons change. You are unlikely to see any of the Dalrei. They dislike walls and cities."

Kim's frown, Kevin saw, had deepened.

"Over the mountains, eastward, the land grows wilder and very beautiful. That country is called Eridu now, though it had another name long ago. It breeds a people once brutal, though quiet of late. Little is known of doings in Eridu, for the mountains are a stern barrier." Matt Sören's voice roughened. "Among the Eriduns dwell the Dwarves, unseen for the most part, in their chambers and halls under the mountains of Banir Lök and Banir Tal, beside Calor Diman, the Crystal Lake. A place more fair than any in all the worlds."

Kevin had questions again, but withheld them. He could see there was an old pain at work here.

"North and west of Brennin is Pendaran Wood. It runs for miles to the north, between the Plain and the Sea. Beyond the forest is Daniloth, the Shadowland." The Dwarf stopped, as abruptly as he'd begun, and turned to adjust his pack and gear. There was a silence.

"Matt?" It was Kimberly. The Dwarf turned. "What about the mountain north of the Plain?"

Matt made a swift, convulsive gesture with one hand, and stared at the slight, brown-haired girl.

"So you were right, my friend, from the very first."

Kevin wheeled. In the doorway leading from the bedroom stood the tall figure of Loren, in a long robe of shifting silver hues.

"What have you seen?" the mage asked Kim, very gently.

She, too, had twisted to face him. The grey eyes were strange—inward and troubled. She shook her head, as if to clear it. "Nothing, really. Just . . . that I do see a mountain."

"And?" Loren pressed.

"And . . . " she closed her eyes. "A hunger. *Inside*, somehow. . . I can't explain it."

"It is written," said Loren after a moment, "in our books of wisdom, that in each of the worlds there are those who have dreams or visions—one sage called them memories—of Fionavar, which is the First. Matt, who has gifts of his own, named you as one such yesterday." He paused; Kim didn't move. "It is known," Loren went on, "that to bring people back in a crossing, such a person must be found to stand at the heart of the circle."

"So that's why you wanted us? Because of Kim?" It was Paul Schafer; the first words he'd spoken since arriving.

"Yes," said the mage, simply.

"Damn!" cried Kevin softly. "And I thought it was my charm."

No one laughed. Kim stared at Loren, as if seeking answers in the lines of his face, or the shifting patterns of his robe.

Finally she asked, "And the mountain?"

Loren's voice was almost matter-of-fact. "One thousand years ago someone was imprisoned there. At the deepest root of Rangat, which is the mountain you have seen."

Kim nodded, hesitated. "Someone . . . evil?" The word came awkwardly to her tongue.

They might have been alone in the room. "Yes," said the mage.

"One thousand years ago?"

He nodded again. In this moment of misdirection, of deceit, when everything stood in danger of falling apart, his eyes were more calm and compassionate than they had ever been.

With one hand Kim tugged at a strand of brown hair. She drew a breath. "All right," she said. "All right, then. How do I help you cross?"

Dave was struggling to absorb all this when things began to move too quickly. He found himself part of a circle around Kim and the mage. He linked hands with Jennifer and Matt on either side. The Dwarf seemed to be concentrating very hard; his legs were wide apart, braced. Then Loren began to speak words in a tongue Dave didn't know, his voice growing in power and resonance.

And was interrupted, by Paul Schafer.

"Loren—is the person under that mountain dead?"

The mage gazed at the slim figure who'd asked the question he feared. "You, too?" he whispered. Then, "No," he answered, telling the truth. "No, he isn't." And resumed speaking in his strange language.

Dave wrestled with the refusal to seem afraid that had, in large part, brought him here, and with the genuine panic that was building within him. Paul had nodded once at Loren's answer, but that was all. The mage's words had become a complex rising chant. An aura of power began to shimmer visibly in the room. A low-pitched humming sound began.

*"Hey!"* Dave burst out. "I need a promise I'll be back!" There was no reply. Matt Sören's eyes were closed now. His grip on Dave's wrist was firm.

The shimmer in the air increased, and then the humming began to rise in volume.

"No!" Dave shouted again. "No! I need a promise!" And on the words he violently pulled his hands free from those of Jennifer and the Dwarf.

Kimberly Ford screamed.

And in that moment the room began to dissolve on them. Kevin, frozen, disbelieving, saw Kim reach out then, wildly, to clutch Dave's arm and take Jen's free hand even as he heard the cry torn from her throat.

Then the cold of the crossing and the darkness of the space between worlds came down and Kevin saw nothing more. In his mind, though, whether for an instant or an age, he thought he heard the sound of mocking laughter. There was a taste in his mouth, like ashes of grief. *Dave*, he thought, *oh, Martyniuk, what have you done?*

# PART II

# RACHEL'S SONG

# CHAPTER 4

It was night when they came through, in a small, dimly lit room somewhere high up. There were two chairs, benches, and an unlit fire. An intricately patterned carpet on the stone floor. Along one wall stretched a tapestry, but the room was too darkly shadowed, despite flickering wall torches, for them to make it out. The windows were open.

"So, Silvercloak, you've come back," a reedy voice from the doorway said, without warmth. Kevin looked over quickly to see a bearded man leaning casually on a spear.

Loren ignored him. "Matt?" he said sharply. "Are you all right?" The Dwarf, visibly shaken by the crossing, managed a terse nod. He had slumped into one of the heavy chairs and there were beads of perspiration on his forehead. Kevin turned to check the others. All seemed to be fine, a little dazed, but fine, except—

*Except that Dave Martyniuk wasn't there.*

"Oh, God!" he began, "Loren—"

And was stopped in mid-sentence by a beseeching look from the mage. Paul Schafer, standing beside Kevin, caught it as well, and Kevin saw him walk quietly over to the two women. Schafer spoke softly to them, and then nodded, once, to Loren.

At which point the mage finally turned to the guard, who was still leaning indolently on his weapon. "Is it the evening before?" Loren asked.

"Why, yes," the man replied. "But shouldn't a great mage know that without the asking?"

Kevin saw Loren's eyes flicker in the torchlight. "Go," he said. "Go tell the King I have returned."

"It's late. He'll be sleeping."

"He will want to know this. Go now."

The guard moved with deliberate, insolent slowness. As he turned, though, there was a sudden *thunk,* and a thrown knife quivered in the panelling of the doorway, inches from his head.

"I know you, Vart," a deep voice said, as the man whipped around, pale even by torchlight. "I have marked you. You will do what you have been told, and quickly,

and you will speak to rank with deference—or my next dagger will not rest in wood."
Matt Sören was on his feet again, and danger bristled through him like a presence.

There was a tense silence. Then:

"I am sorry, my lord mage. The lateness of the hour . . . my fatigue. Welcome home,
my lord, I go to do your will." The guard raised his spear in a formal salute, then spun
again, sharply this time, and left the room. Matt walked forward to retrieve his dagger.
He remained in the doorway, watching.

"Now," said Kevin Laine. "Where is he?"

Loren had dropped into the chair the Dwarf had vacated. "I am not sure," he said.
"Forgive me, but I truly don't know."

"But you have to know!" Jennifer exclaimed.

"He pulled away just as I was closing the circle. I was too far under the power—I
couldn't come out to see his path. I do not even know if he came with us."

"I do," said Kim Ford simply. "He came. I had him all the way. I was holding
him."

Loren rose abruptly. "You did? Brightly woven! This means he has crossed—he is
in Fionavar, somewhere. And if that is so, he will be found. Our friends will begin to
search immediately."

"Your friends?" Kevin asked. "Not that creep in the doorway, I hope?"

Loren shook his head. "Not him, no. He is Gorlaes's tool—and here I must ask of
you another thing." He hesitated. "There are factions in this court, and a struggle taking place, for Ailell is old now. Gorlaes would like me gone, for many reasons, and
failing that, would take joy in discrediting me before the King."

"So if Dave is missing . . . ?" Kevin murmured.

"Exactly. I think only Metran knows I went for five—and I never promised him so
many, in any case. Dave will be found, I promise you that. Can I ask you to keep his
presence a secret for this time?"

Jennifer Lowell had moved to the open window while the others talked. A hot
night, and very dry. Below and to her left, she could make out the lights of a town, lying almost directly adjacent to the walled enclosure of what she assumed to be Paras
Derval. There were fields in front of her, and beyond them rose the thick, close trees
of a forest. There was no breeze. She looked upward, apprehensive, and was desperately relieved to find she knew the stars. For though the slender hand on the window
ledge was steady, and the cool green eyes gave little away, she had been badly thrown
by Dave's disappearance and the sudden dagger.

In a life shaped of careful decisions, the only impulsive act of significance had
been the beginning of her relationship with Kevin Laine one night two years ago.
Now, improbably, she found herself in a place where only the fact that she could see
the Summer Triangle overhead gave her any kind of security. She shook her head
and, not lacking in a sense of irony, smiled very slightly to herself.

Paul Schafer was speaking, answering the mage. "It seems," he said softly—they
were all speaking quietly—"that if you brought us here, then we're already a part of
your group, or we'll be seen that way anyhow. I'll keep my mouth shut."

Kevin was nodding, and then Kim. Jennifer turned from the window. "I won't say anything," she said. "But please find Dave soon, because I really am going to be very frightened if you don't."

"Company!" Matt growled from the doorway.

"Ailell? Already? It can't be," said Loren.

Matt listened for a moment longer. "No . . . not the King. I think . . ." and his dark, bearded face twisted into its version of a smile. "Listen for yourself," the Dwarf said.

A second later Kevin heard it, too: the unsteady carolling of someone coming down the hallway towards them, someone far gone in drink:

> *Those who rode that night with Revor*
> *Did a deed to last forever . . .*
> *The Weaver cut from brighter cloth*
> *Those who rode through Daniloth!*

"You fat buffoon!" another voice snarled, rather more controlled. "Shut up or you'll have him disinherited for bringing you in here." The sardonic laughter of a third person could be heard, as the footsteps made their tenuous way up the corridor.

"Song," the aggrieved troubadour said, "is a gift to men from the immortal gods."

"Not the way you sing," his critic snapped. Loren was suppressing a smile, Kim saw. Kevin snorted with laughter.

"Shipyard lout," the one called Tegid retorted, not quietly. "You betray your ignorance. Those who were there will never forget my singing that night in the Great Hall at Seresh. I had them weeping. I had—"

"I *was* there, you clown! I was sitting beside you. And I've still got stains on my green doublet from when they started throwing fruit at you."

"Poltroons! What can you expect in Seresh? But the battle after, the brave fight in that same hall! Even though wounded, I rallied our—"

"Wounded?" Hilarity and exasperation vied for mastery in the other speaker's voice. "A tomato in the eye is hardly—"

"Hold it, Coll." The third man spoke for the first time. And in the room Loren and Matt exchanged a glance. "There's a guard just ahead," the light, controlling voice went on. "I'll deal with him. Wait for a minute after I go in, then take Tegid to the last room on the left. And keep him quiet, or by the river blood of Lisen, I *will* be disinherited."

Matt stepped quickly into the hallway. "Good even, Prince." He raised his dagger in salute. A vein of blue glittered in the light. "There is no guard here now. He has gone to bring your father—Silvercloak has just returned with four people who have crossed. You had best move Tegid to a safe place very fast."

"Sören? Welcome home," said the Prince, walking forward. "Coll, take him quickly."

"Quickly?" Tegid expostulated. "Great Tegid moves at his own pace. He deigns not to hide from minions and vassals. He confronts them with naked steel of Rhoden and the prodigious armour of his wrath. He—"

"Tegid," the Prince said with extreme softness, "move now, and sharply, or I will have you stuffed through a window and dropped to the courtyard. Prodigiously."

There was a silence. "Yes, my lord," the reply came, surprisingly meek. As they moved past the doorway Kim caught a glimpse of an enormously fat man, and another, muscled but seeming small beside him, before a third figure appeared in the entranceway, haloed by the wall torch in the corridor. *Diarmuid*, she had time to remember. They call him Diarmuid. The younger son.

And then she found herself staring.

All his life Diarmuid dan Ailell had been doing that to people. Supporting himself with a beringed hand upon the wall, he leaned lazily in the doorway and accepted Loren's bow, surveying them all. Kim, after a moment, was able to isolate some of the qualities: the lean, graceful build, high cheekbones in an over-refined face, a wide, expressive mouth, registering languid amusement just then, the jewelled hands, and the eyes . . . the cynical, mocking expression in the very blue eyes of the King's Heir in the High Kingdom. It was hard to judge his age; close to her own, she guessed.

"Thank you, Silvercloak," he said. "A timely return and a timely warning."

"It is folly to defy your father for Tegid," Loren began. "It is a matter far too trivial—"

Diarmuid laughed. "Advising me again? Already? A crossing hasn't changed you, Loren. There are reasons, there are reasons . . ." he murmured vaguely.

"I doubt it," the mage replied. "Other than perversity and South Keep wine."

"Good reasons, both," Diarmuid agreed, flashing a smile. "Who," he said, in a very different tone, "have you brought for Metran to parade tomorrow?"

Loren, seemingly used to this, made the introductions gravely. Kevin, named first, bowed formally. Paul followed suit, keeping his eyes on those of the Prince. Kim merely nodded. And Jennifer—

"A peach!" exclaimed Diarmuid dan Ailell. "Silvercloak, you have brought me a peach to nibble." He moved forward then, the jewellery at wrist and throat catching the torchlight, and, taking Jennifer's hand, bowed very low and kissed it.

Jennifer Lowell, not predisposed by character or environment to suffer this sort of thing gladly, let him have it as he straightened.

"Are you always this rude?" she asked. And there was no warmth in the voice at all, or in the green eyes.

It stopped him for an instant only. "Almost always," he answered affably. "I do have some redeeming qualities, though I can never remember what they're supposed to be. I'll wager," he went on, in a swift change of mood, "that Loren is shaking his head behind my back right now in tragic disapproval." Which happened to be true. "Ah well, then," he continued, turning to look at the frowning mage, "I suppose I'm expected to apologize now?"

He grinned at Loren's sober agreement, then turned once more to Jennifer. "I am sorry, sweetling. Drink and a long ride this afternoon. You are quite extravagantly beautiful, and have probably dealt with worse intrusions before. Indulge me." It was prettily done. Jennifer, somewhat bemused, found she could only manage a nod. Which succeeded in provoking yet another sublimely mocking smile. She flushed, angry again.

Loren cut in sharply. "You are behaving badly, Diarmuid, and you know it."

"Enough!" the Prince snapped. "Don't push me, Loren." The two men exchanged a tense look.

When Diarmuid spoke again, though, it was in a milder tone. "I did apologize, Loren, do me some justice." After a moment, the mage nodded.

"Fair enough," he said. "We don't have time to quarrel, in any case. I need your help. Two things. A svart attacked us in the world from which I brought these people. It followed Matt and me, and it was wearing a vellin stone."

"And the other thing?" Diarmuid was instantly attentive, drunk as he was.

"There was a fifth person who crossed with us. We lost him. He is in Fionavar—but I don't know where. I need him found, and I would much prefer that Gorlaes not know of him."

"Obviously. How do you know he is here?"

"Kimberly was our hook. She says she had him."

Diarmuid turned to fix Kim with an appraising stare. Tossing her hair back she met the look, and the expression in her own eyes was more than a little hostile. Turning without reaction, the Prince walked to the window and looked out in silence. The waning moon had risen—overly large, but Jennifer, also gazing out, did not notice that.

"It hasn't rained while you were gone, by the way," said Diarmuid. "We have other things to talk about. Matt," he continued crisply, "Coll is in the last room on the left. Make sure Tegid is asleep, then brief him. A description of the fifth person. Tell Coll I'll speak with him later." Wordlessly, Matt slipped from the room.

"No rain at all?" Loren asked softly.

"None."

"And the crops?"

Diarmuid raised an eyebrow without bothering to answer. Loren's face seemed moulded of fatigue and concern. "And the King?" he asked, almost reluctantly.

Diarmuid paused this time before answering. "Not well. He wanders sometimes. He was apparently talking to my mother last night during dinner in the Great Hall. Impressive, wouldn't you say, five years past her death?"

Loren shook his head. "He has been doing that for some time, though not in public before. Is there . . . is there word of your brother?"

"None." The answer this time was very swift. A strained silence followed. *His name is not to be spoken*, Kevin remembered and, looking at the Prince, wondered.

"There was a Gathering," Diarmuid said. "Seven nights past at the full of the moon. A secret one. They invoked the Goddess as Dana, and there was blood."

*"No!"* The mage made a violent gesture. "That is going too far. Who summoned it?"

Diarmuid's wide mouth crooked slightly.

"Herself, of course," he said.

"Jaelle?"

"Jaelle."

Loren began pacing the room. "She will cause trouble, I know it!"

"Of course she will. She means to. And my father is too old to deal with it. Can you see Ailell on the Summer Tree now?" And there was a new thing in the light voice—a deep, coruscating bitterness.

"I never could, Diarmuid." The mage's tone had suddenly gone soft. He stopped his pacing beside the Prince. "Whatever power lies in the Tree is outside my province. And Jaelle's, too, though she would deny it. You have heard my views on this. Blood magic, I fear, takes more than it gives back."

"So we sit," Diarmuid snarled, stiff anger cracking through, "we sit while the wheat burns up in fields all over Brennin! Fine doings for a would-be royal house!"

"My lord Prince"—the use of the title was careful, admonitory—"this is no ordinary season, and you do not need me to tell you that. Something unknown is at work, and not even Jaelle's midnight invocations will redress the balance, until we touch what lies beneath."

Diarmuid sank into one of the chairs, gazing blankly at the dim tapestry opposite the window. The wall torches had almost burnt out, leaving the room webbed with lighter and darker shadows. Leaning against the window ledge, Jennifer thought that she could almost see the threads of tension snaking through the darkened spaces. *What am I doing here*, she thought. Not for the last time. A movement on the other side of the chamber caught her eye, and she turned to see Paul Schafer looking at her. He gave a small, unexpectedly reassuring smile. *And I don't understand him, either,* she thought, somewhat despairingly.

Diarmuid was on his feet again by then, seemingly unable to be still for any length of time. "Loren," he said, "you know the King won't come tonight. Did you—"

"He must! I won't let Gorlaes have—"

"Someone's here," Paul said sharply. He had quietly ended up in Matt's post by the door. "Five men, three with swords."

*"Diarmuid—"*

"I know. You haven't seen me. I won't be far," and the heir to the throne of Brennin leaped in a rustle of cloth and a moonlit flash of yellow hair through the window, reaching out, almost lazily, for a handhold on the wall outside. For God's sake, Kevin thought.

Which was all he had time for. Vart, the surly guard, appeared in the doorway. When he saw that Matt was nowhere to be seen, a thin smile flicked across his face.

"My lord the Chancellor," Vart announced.

Kevin wasn't sure what he'd expected, but it wasn't what he saw. Gorlaes, the Chancellor, was a big, broad-shouldered, brown-bearded man of middle years. He smiled generously, showing good teeth as he came sweeping in. "Welcome back, Silvercloak! And brightly woven, indeed. You have come in the very teeth of time—as ever." And he laughed. Loren, Kevin saw, did not.

The other man who came in, an armed aide close beside him, was stooped and very old. The King? Kevin wondered, for a brief, disoriented moment. But it was not.

"Good evening, Metran," Loren said deferentially to this white-haired new arrival. "Are you well?"

"Well, very well, very, very," Metran wheezed. He coughed. "There is not enough light in here. I want to see," he said querulously. A trembling arm was raised, and suddenly the six wall torches blazed, illuminating the chamber. *Why*, Kim thought, *couldn't Loren have done that?*

"Better, much better," Metran went on, shuffling forward to sink into one of the chairs. His attendant hovered close by. The other soldier, Kim saw, had placed himself by the door with Vart. Paul had withdrawn towards Jennifer by the window.

"Where," Loren asked, "is the King? I sent Vart to advise him I was here."

"And he has been so advised," Gorlaes answered smoothly. Vart, in the doorway, snickered. "Ailell has instructed me to convey his greetings to you, and to your—" he paused to look around, "—four companions."

"Four? Only four?" Metran cut in, barely audible over a coughing fit.

Gorlaes spared him only the briefest of glances and went on. "To your four companions. I have been asked to take them under my care as Chancellor for the night. The King had a trying day and would prefer to receive them formally in the morning. It is very late. I'm sure you understand." The smile was pleasant, even modest. "Now if you would be good enough to introduce me to our visitors I can have my men show them to their rooms . . . and you, my friend, can go to your richly deserved rest."

"Thank you, Gorlaes." Loren smiled, but a thin edge like that of a drawn blade had come into his voice. "However, under the circumstances I count myself responsible for the well-being of those who crossed with me. I will make arrangements for them, until the King has received us."

"Silvercloak, are you implying that their well-being can be better attended to than by the Chancellor of the realm?" There, too, Kevin thought, his muscles involuntarily tensing: the same edge. Though neither man had moved, it seemed to him as if there were two swords drawn in the torchlit room.

"Not at all, Gorlaes," said the mage. "It is simply a matter of my own honour."

"You are tired, my friend. Leave this tedious business to me."

"There is no tedium in caring for friends."

" Loren, I must insist—"

*"No."*

There was a cold silence.

"You realize," said Gorlaes, his voice dropping almost to a whisper, "that you offer me little choice?" The voice came up suddenly. "I must obey the commands of my King. Vart, Lagoth . . ." The two soldiers in the doorway moved forward.

And pitched, half-drawn swords clattering, full-length to the floor.

Behind their prone bodies stood a very calm Matt Sören, and the big, capable man named Coll. Seeing them there, Kevin Laine, whose childhood fantasies had been shaped of images like this, knew a moment of sheer delight.

At which point a lithe, feral figure, shimmering with jewellery, swung easily through the window into the room. He landed lightly beside Jennifer, and she felt a wandering hand stroke her hair before he spoke.

"Who makes this noise at such an hour? Can a soldier not sleep at night in his father's palace without—why, Gorlaes! And Metran! And here is Loren! You have returned, Silvercloak—and with our visitors, I see. In the very teeth of time." The insolence of his voice filled the room. "Gorlaes, send quickly, my father will want to welcome them immediately."

"The King," the Chancellor replied stiffly, "is indisposed, my lord Prince. He sent me—"

"He can't come? Then I must do the family honours myself. Silvercloak, would you . . . ?"

And so Loren carefully introduced them again. And "*A peach!*" said Diarmuid dan Ailell, bending, slowly, to kiss Jennifer's hand. Against her will, she laughed. He didn't hurry the kiss.

When he straightened, though, his words were formal, and both of his arms were raised in a wide gesture of ritual. "I welcome you now," he began, and Kevin, turning instinctively, saw the benign countenance of Gorlaes contort, for a blurred instant, with fury. "I welcome you now," Diarmuid said, in a voice stripped of mockery, "as guest-friends of my father and myself. The home of Ailell is your home, your honour is ours. An injury done you is an injury to ourselves. And treason to the Oak Crown of the High King. Be welcome to Paras Derval. I will personally attend to your comfort for tonight." Only on the last phrase did the voice change a little, as the quick eyes, malicious and amused, flashed to Jennifer's.

She flushed again, but he had already turned. "Gorlaes," he said softly, "your retainers appear to have collapsed. I have been told, in the few hours since I've been back from South Keep, of entirely too much drinking among them. I know it is a festival, but really . . . ?" And the tone was so mild, so very reproachful. Kevin fought to keep a straight face. "Coll," Diarmuid went on, "have four rooms made ready on the north side, please, and quickly."

"No." It was Jennifer. "Kim and I will share. Just three." She resolutely avoided looking at the Prince. Kimberly, watching him, decided that his eyebrows went higher than they had any right to go.

"We will, too," said Paul Schafer quietly. And Kevin felt his pulse leap. Oh, Abba, he thought, maybe this will do it for him. Maybe it will.

"I'm too hot. Why is it so hot everywhere?" Metran, First of the Mages, asked, of no one in particular.

⋄⊷══◯◯══⊷⋄

The north side of the palace, opposite the town, overlooked a walled garden. When they were finally alone in their room Kevin opened the glass doors and stepped out onto a wide stone balcony. The moon, waning, was high overhead, bright enough to illuminate the shrubs and the few flowers below their room.

"Not much of a garden," he commented, as Paul came out to join him.

"There's been no rain, Diarmuid said."

"That's true." There was silence. A light breeze had finally come up to cool the evening.

"Have you noticed the moon?" Paul asked, leaning on the parapet.

Kevin nodded. "Larger, you mean? Yes, I did. Wonder what effect that has?"

"Higher tides, most likely."

"I guess. And more werewolves."

Schafer gave him a wry look. "I wouldn't be surprised. Tell me, what did you think about that business back there?"

"Well, Loren and Diarmuid seem to be on the same side."

"It looks that way. Matt's not very sure of him."

"Somehow that doesn't surprise me."

"Really. What about Gorlaes? He was pretty quick to call in the marines. Was he just following orders, or—"

"Not a chance, Paul. I saw his face when Diarmuid made us guest-friends. Not happy, my friend."

"Really?" Schafer said. "Well, that simplifies things at least. I'd like to know more about this Jaelle, though. And Diarmuid's brother, too."

"The nameless one?" Kevin intoned lugubriously. "He of no name?"

Schafer snorted. "Funny man. Yes, him."

"We'll figure it out. We've figured things out before."

"I know," said Paul Schafer, and after a moment gave a rare smile.

"Oh, Romeo, Romeo, wherefore art thou, Romeo?" came a plaintive cry from off to their left. They looked over. Kim Ford, languishing for all she was worth, swayed towards them from the next balcony. The leap was about ten feet.

"I'm coming!" Kevin responded instantly. He rushed to the edge of their own balcony.

"Oh, fly to me!" Kimberly trilled. Jennifer, behind her, began almost reluctantly to laugh.

"I'm coming!" Kevin repeated, ostentatiously limbering up. "You two all right there?" he asked, in mid-flex. "Been ravished yet?"

"Not a chance," Kim lamented. "Can't find anyone who's man enough to jump to our balcony."

Kevin laughed. "I'd have to do it pretty fast," he said, "to get there before the Prince."

"I don't know," Jennifer Lowell said, "if *anyone* can move faster than that guy."

Paul Schafer, hearing the banter begin, and the laughter of the two women, moved to the far end of the balcony. He knew, very well, that the frivolity was only a release from tension, but it wasn't something to which he had access any more. Resting his own ringless, fine-boned hands on the railing, he gazed out and down at the denuded garden below. He stood there, looking about him, but not really seeing: the inner landscape demanded its due.

Even had Schafer been carefully scanning the shadows, though, it is unlikely that he would have discerned the dark creature that crouched behind a clump of stunted shrubs, watching him. The desire to kill was strong upon it, and Paul had moved to within easy range of the poison darts it carried. He might have died then.

But fear mastered bloodlust in the figure below. It had been ordered to observe, and to report, but not to kill.

So Paul lived, observed, oblivious, and after a time he drew a long breath and lifted his eyes from sightless fixation on the shadows below.

*To see a thing none of the others saw.*

High on the stone outer wall enclosing the garden stood an enormous grey dog, or a wolf, and it was looking at him across the moonlit space between, with eyes that were not those of a wolf or a dog, and in which lay a sadness deeper and older than anything Paul had ever seen or known. From the top of the wall the creature stared at him the way animals are not supposed to be able to do. And it called him. The pull was unmistakable, imperative, terrifying. Looming in night shadow it reached out for him, the eyes, unnaturally distinct, boring into his own. Paul touched and then twisted his mind away from a well of sorrow so deep he feared it could drown him. Whatever stood on the wall had endured and was still enduring a loss that spanned the worlds. It dwarfed him, appalled him.

And it was calling him. Sweat cold on his skin in the summer night, Paul Schafer knew that this was one of the things caught up in the chaotic vision Loren's searching had given him.

With an effort brutally physical, he broke away. When he turned his head, he felt the motion like a twist in his heart.

"Kev," he managed to gasp, the voice eerie in his own head.

"What is it?" His friend's response was instant.

"Over there. On the wall. Do you see anything?" Paul pointed, but did not look back.

"What? There's nothing. What did you see?"

"Not sure." He was breathing hard. "Something. Maybe a dog."

"And?"

"And it wants me," Paul Schafer said.

Kevin, stunned, was silent. They stood a moment like that, looking at each other, not sharing, then Schafer turned and went inside. Kevin stayed a while longer, to re-assure the others, then went in himself. Paul had taken the smaller of the two beds that had been hastily provided, and was lying on his back, hands behind his head.

Wordlessly, Kevin undressed and went to bed. The moon slanted a thin beam of light into the far comer of the room, illuminating neither of them.

# CHAPTER 5

All the night they had been gathering. Stern men from Ailell's own birthplace in Rhoden, cheerful ones from high-walled Seresh by Saeren, mariners from Taerlindel, and soldiers from the fastness of North Keep, though not many of these because of the one who was exiled. From villages and dust-dry farms all over the High Kingdom they came as well. For days they had been trickling into Paras Derval, crowding the inns and hostels, spilling out into makeshift campgrounds beyond the last streets of the town below the palace. Some had come walking west from the once rich lands by the River Glein; leaning on the carved staffs of the southeast they had cut across the burnt-out desolation of the grain lands to join the dusty traffic on the Leinan Road. From the grazing lands and the dairy lands in the northeast others had come riding on the horses that were the legacy of their winter trading with the Dalrei by the banks of the Latham; and though their horses might be painfully gaunt, each mount yet bore the sumptuous woven saddle-cloth that every Brennin horseman crafted before he took a horse: a weaving for the Weaver's gift of speed. From beyond Leinan they came as well, dour, dark farmers from Gwen Ystrat in their wide, six-wheeled carts. None of their women, though, not from so near Dun Maura in the province of the Mother.

But from everywhere else the women and children had come in noisy, festive number. Even in the midst of drought and deprivation, the people of Brennin were gathering to pay homage to their King, and perhaps to briefly forget their troubles in doing so.

Morning found them densely clustered in the square before the palace walls. Looking up they could see the great balustrade hung with banners and gaily coloured streamers, and most wonderful of all, the great tapestry of Iorweth in the Wood, brought forth for this one day that all the folk of Brennin might see their High King stand beneath the symbols of Mörnir and the Weaver both, in Paras Derval.

But all was not consigned to high and sacred things. Around the fringes of the crowd moved jugglers and clowns, and performers doing glittering things with knives and swords and bright scarves. The cyngael chanted their ribald verses to pockets of laughing auditors, extemporizing satires for a fee upon whomever their benefactor designated; not a few revenges were thus effected in the clear, cutting words of the cyngael—immune since Colan's day from any law save that of their own council. Amid the babble, pedlars carried their colourful goods about or erected hasty booths from which to display their craft in the sunlight. And then the noise, never less than a roar, became a thundering, for figures had appeared on the balustrade.

The sound hit Kevin like a blow. He regarded the absence of sunglasses as a source of profound and comprehensive grief. Hung-over to incapacity, pale to the edge of green, he glanced over at Diarmuid and silently cursed the elegance of his figure. Turning to Kim—and the movement hurt like hell—he received a wry smile of commiseration, which salved his spirit even as it wounded his pride.

It was already hot. The sunlight was painfully brilliant in a cloudless sky, and so, too, were the colours worn by the lords and ladies of Ailell's court. The High King himself, to whom they'd not yet been presented, was further down the balcony, hidden behind the intervening courtiers. Kevin closed his eyes, wishing it were possible to retreat into the shade, instead of standing up front to be seen . . . red Indians, indeed. Red-eyed Indians, anyhow. It was easier with his eyes closed. The fulsome voice of Gorlaes, orating the glittering achievements of Ailell's reign, slid progressively into background. What the hell kind of wine did they make in this world, Kevin thought, too drained to be properly outraged.

The knock had come an hour after they'd gone to bed. Neither of them had been asleep.

"Careful," said Paul, rising on one elbow. Kevin had swung upright and was pulling on his cords before moving to the door.

"Yes?" he said, without touching the lock. "Who is it?"

"Convivial night persons," came an already familiar voice. "Open up. I've got to get Tegid out of the hallway."

Laughing, Kevin looked over his shoulder. Paul was up and half dressed already. Kevin opened the door and Diarmuid entered quickly, flourishing two flasks of wine, one of them already unstopped. Into the room behind him, also carrying wine, came Coll and the preposterous Tegid, followed by two other men bearing an assortment of clothing.

"For tomorrow," the Prince said in response to Kevin's quizzical look at the last pair. "I promised I'd take care of you." He tossed over one of the wine flasks, and smiled.

"Very kind of you," Kevin replied, catching it. He raised the flask in the way he'd learned in Spain, years before, to shoot a dark jet of wine down his throat. He flipped the leather flask over to Paul who drank, wordlessly.

"Ah!" exclaimed Tegid, as he eased himself onto a long bench. "I'm dry as Jaelle's heart. To the King!" he cried, raising his own flask, "and to his glorious heir, Prince Diarmuid, and to our noble and distinguished guests, and to . . ." The rest of the peroration was lost in the sound of wine voluminously pouring into his mouth. At length the flow ceased. Tegid surfaced, belched, and looked around. "I've a mighty thirst in me tonight," he explained unnecessarily.

Paul addressed the Prince casually. "If you're in a party mood, aren't you in the wrong bedroom?"

Diarmuid's smile was rueful. "Don't assume you were a first choice," he murmured. "Your charming companions accepted their dresses for tomorrow, but nothing more, I'm afraid. The small one, Kim"—he shook his head—"has a tongue in her."

"My condolences," said Kevin, delighted. "I've been on the receiving end a few times."

"Then," said Diarmuid dan Ailell, "let us drink in joint commiseration." The Prince set the tone by commencing to relate what he characterized as essential information: a wittily obscene description of the various court ladies they were likely to meet. A description that reflected an extreme awareness of their private as well as public natures.

Tegid and Coll stayed; the other two men left after a time, to be replaced by a different pair with fresh wine flasks. Eventually these two departed as well. The two men who succeeded them, however, were not smiling as they entered.

"What is it, Carde?" Coll asked the fair-haired one.

The man addressed cleared his throat. Diarmuid, sprawled in a deep chair by the window, turned at the sound.

Carde's voice was very soft. "Something strange. My lord, I thought you should know right away. There's a dead svart alfar in the garden below this window."

Through the wine-induced haze descending upon him, Kevin saw Diarmuid swing to his feet.

"Brightly woven," the Prince said. "Which of you killed it?"

Carde's voice dropped to a whisper. "That's just it, my lord. Erron found it dead. Its throat was . . . ripped apart, my lord. Erron thinks . . . he thinks it was done by a wolf, though . . . with respect, my lord, I don't ever want to meet what killed that creature."

In the silence that followed this, Kevin looked over at Paul Schafer. Sitting up on his bed, Schafer seemed thinner and more frail than ever. His expression was unreadable.

Diarmuid broke the stillness. "You said it was below this window?"

Carde nodded, but the Prince had turned already and, throwing open the doors, was on the balcony and then dropping over the edge. And right behind him was Paul Schafer. Which meant that Kevin had to go, too. With Coll beside him and Carde just behind, he moved to the edge of the balcony, swung over the balustrade, hung by his hands a dizzy instant, and dropped the ten feet to the garden. The other two followed. Only Tegid remained in the room, his mountainous bulk precluding the descent.

Diarmuid and Paul had moved to where three men were standing by a stunted clump of shrubbery. They parted to let the Prince in among them. Kevin, breathing deeply to clear his head, moved up beside Paul and looked down.

When his eyes adjusted to the dark, he wished they hadn't. The svart alfar had been almost decapitated; its head had been clawed to shreds. One arm had been torn through, the shoulder remaining attached to the body only by an exposed strip of cartilage, and there were deep claw marks scoring the naked torso of the dark green, hairless creature. Even in the shadows, Kevin could see the thick blood clotting the dried-out soil. Breathing very carefully, shocked almost sober, he resisted an impulse to be sick. No one spoke for a long time: the fury that was reflected in the mangled creature on the ground imposed its own silence.

Eventually Diarmuid straightened and moved back a few steps. "Carde," he said crisply, "I want the watch doubled on our guests as of now. Tomorrow I want a report on why that thing wasn't seen by any of you. And why you didn't see what killed it, either. If I post guards, I expect them to be useful."

"My lord." Carde, badly shaken, moved off with the other guards.

Coll was still crouching beside the dead svart. Now he looked over his shoulder. "Diar," he said, "it was no ordinary wolf that did this."

"I know," said the Prince. "If it was a wolf."

Kevin, turning, looked at Paul Schafer again. Schafer had his back to them. He was gazing at the outer wall of the garden.

At length the four of them walked back to the balcony. With the aid of crevices in the palace wall, and a hand over the balustrade from Tegid, they were all soon in the room once more. Diarmuid, Tegid, and Coll departed shortly after. The Prince left them two flasks of wine and an offer; they accepted both.

Kevin ended up drinking almost all of the wine himself, primarily because Paul, for a change, wasn't in a mood to talk.

"We're on!" Kim hissed, prodding him with an elbow. They were, it seemed. The four of them stepped forward in response to Gorlaes's sweeping gesture and, as instructed, waved to the loudly cheering crowd.

Kimberly, waving with one hand and supporting Kevin with the other, realized suddenly that this was the scene that Loren had conjured up for them in the Park Plaza two nights before. Instinctively she looked up over her shoulder. And saw the banner flapping lazily overhead: the crescent moon and the oak.

Kevin, grateful for her arm, did manage a few waves and a fixed smile, while reflecting that the tumultuous gathering below was taking a lot on faith. At this height they could have been any four members of the court. He supposed, impressed with himself for thinking so clearly, that the public relations thing would probably focus on the nobility anyhow. The people around them knew they were from another world—and someone seemed to be awfully unhappy about it.

His head was killing him, and some indeterminate fungus seemed to have taken up residence in his mouth. *Better shape up fast*, he thought, *you're about to meet a king*. And there was a long ride waiting tomorrow, with God knows what at the end.

For Diarmuid's last offer had been an unexpected one. "We're going south tomorrow morning," he'd said as the dawn was breaking. "Across the river. A raid of sorts, though a quiet one. No one to know. If you think you can manage, you may find it interesting. Not altogether safe, but I think we can take care of you." It was the smile on the last phrase that got both of them—which, Kevin realized, was probably what the manipulative bastard had intended.

The great hall at Paras Derval had been designed by Tomaz Lal, whose disciple Ginserat had been, he who later made the wardstones and much else of power and beauty in the older days.

Twelve great pillars supported the high ceiling. Set far up in the walls were the windows of Delevan—stained-glass images of the founding of the High Kingdom by Iorweth, and the first wars with Eridu and Cathal. The last window on the western wall, above the canopied throne of Brennin, showed Conary himself, Colan young beside him, their fair hair blowing back as they rode north through the Plain to the last battle against Rakoth Maugrim. When the sun was setting, that window would blaze with light in such a fashion that the faces of the King and his golden son were illuminated as from within with majesty, though the window had been crafted almost a thousand years before. Such was the art of Delevan, the craft of Tomaz Lal.

Walking between the huge pillars over mosaic-inlaid tiles, Kimberly was conscious for the first time of feeling awe in this place. The pillars, windows, ever-present tapestries, the jewelled floor, the gem-encrusted clothing of the lords and ladies, even the silken splendour of the lavender-coloured gown she wore . . . She drew a deep, careful breath and kept her gaze as straight as she could.

And doing so, she saw, as Loren led the four of them to the western end of the hall, under the last great window, a raised dais of marble and obsidian and upon it a throne carved of heavy oak, and sitting upon the throne was the man she'd only glimpsed through the crowd on the balcony earlier in the day.

The tragedy of Ailell dan Art lay in what he had fallen from. The haggard man with the wispy, snow-white beard and blurred, cataract-occluded gaze showed little of the giant warrior, with eyes like a noonday sky, who had taken the Oak Throne fifty years before. Gaunt and emaciated, Ailell seemed to have been stretched thin by his years, and the expression with which he peered forward to follow their approach was not welcoming.

To one side of the King stood Gorlaes. The broad-shouldered Chancellor was dressed in brown, with his seal of office hung about his neck and no other ornament. On the other side of the throne, in burgundy and white, stood Diarmuid, the King's Heir of Brennin. Who winked when her gaze lingered. Kim turned away abruptly to see Metran, the First Mage, making his slow wheezing way, attendant solicitously at hand, to stand with Loren just in front of them.

Seeing Paul Schafer gazing intently at the King, she turned back to the throne herself, and after a pause she heard her name being spoken in introduction. She stepped forward and bowed, having decided earlier that under no circumstances was she going to try anything so hazardous as a curtsy. The others followed suit. Jennifer did curtsy, sinking down in a rustle of green silk, and rising gracefully as an appreciative murmur ran through the hall.

"Be welcome to Brennin," the High King said, leaning back in his throne. "Bright be the thread of your days among us." The words were gracious, but there was little pleasure in the low desiccated tones in which they were spoken. "Thank you, Metran, Loren," the King said, in the same voice. "Thank you, Teyrnon," he added, nodding to a third man half hidden beyond Loren.

Metran bowed too low in response and almost toppled over. His aide helped him straighten. Someone snickered in the background.

Loren was speaking. "We thank you for your kindness, my lord. Our friends have met your son and the Chancellor already. The Prince was good enough to make them guest-friends of your house last night." His voice on the last phrase was pitched to carry.

The King's eyes rested for a long moment on those of Loren, and Kim, watching, changed her mind. Ailell might be old, but he certainly wasn't senile—the amusement registering in his face was far too cynical.

"Yes," said the King, "I know he did. And herewith I endorse his doing so. Tell me, Loren," he went on in a different tone, "do you know if any of your friends play ta'bael?"

Loren shook his head apologetically. "Truly, my lord," he said, "I never thought to ask. They have the same game in their world, they call it chess, but—"

"I play," said Paul.

There was a short silence. Paul and the King looked at each other. When Ailell spoke, his voice was very soft. "I hope," he said, "that you will play with me while you are with us."

Schafer nodded by way of response. The King leaned back, and Loren, seeing this, turned to lead them from the hall.

*"Hold, Silvercloak!"*

The voice was icily imperious. It knifed into them. Kim quickly turned left to where she'd noticed a small grouping of women in grey robes. Now that cluster parted and a woman walked forward towards the throne.

All in white she was, very tall, with red hair held back by a circlet of silver on her brow. Her eyes were green and very cold. In her bearing as she strode towards them was a deep, scarcely suppressed rage, and as she drew near, Kimberly saw that she was beautiful. But despite the hair, which gleamed like a fire at night under stars, this was not a beauty that warmed one. It cut, like a weapon. There was no nuance of gentleness in her, no shading of care, but fair she was, as is the flight of an arrow before it kills.

Loren, checked in the act of withdrawing, turned as she approached—and there was no warmth in his face, either.

"Have you not forgotten something?" the woman in white said, her voice feather-soft and sinuous with danger.

"An introduction? I would have done so in due course," Loren replied lightly. "If you are impatient, I can—"

"Due course? Impatient? By Macha and Nemain you should be cursed for insolence!" The red-haired woman was rigid with fury. Her eyes burned into those of the mage.

Who endured the look without expression. Until another voice interceded in rich, plummy tones. "I'm afraid you are right, Priestess," said Gorlaes. "Our voyager here does at times forget the patterns of precedence. Our guests should have been presented to you today. I fear—"

"Fool!" the Priestess snapped. "You are a fool, Gorlaes. Today? I should have been spoken to *before* he went on this journey. How *dare* you, Metran? How dare you send for a crossing without leave of the Mother? The balancing of worlds is in her hands and so it is in mine. You touch the earthroot in peril of your soul if you do not seek her leave!"

Metran retreated from the enraged figure. Fear and confusion chased each other across his features. Loren, however, raised a hand and pointed one long, steady finger at the woman confronting him. "Nowhere," he said, and thick anger spilled from his own voice now, "nowhere is such a thing written! And this, by all the gods, you know. You overreach yourself, Jaelle—and be warned, it shall not be permitted. The balance lies not with you—and your moonlit meddling may shatter it yet."

The Priestess's eyes flickered at that—and Kim suddenly remembered Diarmuid's reference the night before to a secret gathering.

And it was Diarmuid's lazy voice that slid next into the charged silence. "Jaelle," he said, from by his father's throne, "whatever the worth of what you say, surely this is not the time to say it. Lovely as you are, you are marring a festival with your wrangling. And we seem to have another guest waiting to be greeted." Stepping lightly from the dais, he walked past all of them, down to the end of the hall, where, Kim saw as she turned to watch, there stood another woman, this one white-haired with age and leaning on a gnarled staff before the great doors of Ailell's hall.

"Be welcome, Ysanne," said the Prince, a deep courtesy in his tone. "It is long since you have graced our court." But Kim, hearing the name spoken, seeing the frail figure standing there, felt something touch her then, like a finger on the heart.

A current of sound had begun to ripple through the gathered courtiers, and those lining the spaces between the pillars were crowding backwards in fear. But the murmur was only faint background for Kim now, because all her senses were locked onto the seamed, wizened figure walking carefully towards the throne on the arm of the young Prince.

"Ysanne, you should not be here." Ailell, surprisingly, had risen to speak, and it could be seen that, even stooped with years, he was the tallest man in the room.

"True enough," the old woman agreed placidly, coming to a halt before him. Her voice was gentle as Jaelle's had been harsh. The red-haired Priestess was gazing at her with a bitter contempt.

"Then why?" Ailell asked softly.

"Fifty years on this throne merits a journey to pay homage," Ysanne replied. "Is there anyone else here besides Metran and perhaps Loren who well recalls the day you were crowned? I came to wish you bright weaving, Ailell. And for two other things."

"Which are?" It was Loren who asked.

"First, to see your travellers," Ysanne replied, and turned to face Paul Schafer.

His responding gesture was brutally abrupt. Throwing a hand in front of his eyes, Schafer cried out, "No! No searching!"

Ysanne raised her eyebrows. She glanced at Loren, then turned back to Paul. "I see," she said. "Fear not, then, I never use the searching—I don't need it." The whispering in the hall rose again, for the words had carried.

Paul's arm came down slowly. He met the old woman's gaze steadily then, his own head held high—and strangely, it was Ysanne who broke the stare.

And then it was, then it was, that she turned, past Jennifer and Kevin, ignoring the rigid figure of Jaelle, and for the first time saw Kimberly. Grey eyes met grey before the carven throne under the high windows of Delevan. "Ah!" cried the old woman then on a sharply taken breath. And in the softest thread of a whisper added, after a moment, "I have awaited you for so long now, my dear."

And only Kim herself had seen the spasm of fear that had crossed Ysanne's face before she spoke those quiet words like a benediction.

"How?" Kim managed to stammer. "What do you mean?"

Ysanne smiled. "I am a Seer. The dreamer of the dream." And somehow, Kim knew what that meant, and there were sudden, bright tears in her eyes.

"Come to me," the Seer whispered. "Loren will tell you how." She turned then, and curtsied low before the tall King of Brennin. "Fare kindly, Ailell," she said to him. "The other thing I have come to do is say goodbye. I shall not return, and we shall not meet again, you and I, on this side of the Night." She paused. "I have loved you. Carry that."

"Ysanne—" the King cried.

But she had turned. And leaning on her staff, she walked, alone this time, the length of the stunned, brilliant hall and out the double doors into the sunlight.

⋄⇒◉⇐⋄

That night, very late, Paul Schafer was summoned to play ta'bael with the High King of Brennin.

The escort was a guard he didn't know and, walking behind him down shadowy corridors, Paul was inwardly grateful for the silent presence of Coll, who he knew was following them.

It was a long walk but they saw few people still awake. A woman combing her hair in a doorway smiled at him, and a party of guards went by, sheathed swords clinking at their sides. Passing some bedrooms Paul heard murmurs of late-night talk, and once, a woman cried out softly on a taken breath—a sound very like a cry that he remembered.

The two men with their hidden follower came at length to a pair of heavy doors. Schafer's face was expressionless as they were opened to his escort's tapping and he was ushered into a large, richly furnished room, at the centre of which were two deep armchairs and a table set for ta'bael.

"Welcome!" It was Gorlaes, the Chancellor, who came forward to grip Paul's arm in greeting. "It is kind of you to come."

"It *is* kind," came the thinner voice of the King. He moved out from a shadowed corner of the room as he spoke. "I am grateful to you for indulging an old man's sleeplessness. The day has worn heavily upon me. Gorlaes, good night."

"My lord," the Chancellor said quickly, "I will be happy to stay and—"

"No need. Go to sleep. Tarn will serve us." The King nodded to the young page who had opened the door for Paul. Gorlaes looked as if he would protest again, but refrained.

"Good night then, my lord. And once more, my deepest well-wishes on this brightly woven day." He walked forward, and on one knee kissed the hand Ailell extended. Then the Chancellor left the room, leaving Paul alone with the King and his page.

"Wine by the table, Tarn. Then we will serve ourselves. Go to bed—I will wake you when I want to retire. Now come, my young stranger," Ailell said, lowering himself carefully into a chair.

In silence, Paul walked forward and took the other chair. Tarn deftly filled the two glasses set beside the inlaid board, then withdrew through an inner doorway into the King's bedroom. The windows of the room were open and the heavy curtains drawn back to admit whatever breath of air might slide in. In a tree somewhere outside a bird was singing. It sounded like a nightingale.

The beautifully carved pieces glinted in the light of the candles, but the face of the tall King of Brennin was hidden as he leaned back in his chair. He spoke softly. "The game we play is the same, Loren tells me, though we name the pieces differently. I always play the black. Take you the white and begin."

Paul Schafer liked to attack in chess, especially with white and the first move. Gambits and sacrifices followed each other in his game, designed to generate a whirlwind assault on the opposition king. The fact that the opposition this night *was* a king had no effect on him, for Schafer's code, though complex, was unwavering. He set out to demolish the black pieces of Ailell just as he would have those of anyone else. And that night, heartsick and vulnerable, there was even more fire in his game than usual, for he sought to hide from torment in the cold clarity of the black-and-white board. So he marshalled himself ruthlessly, and the white pieces spun into a vortex of attack.

To be met by a defence of intricate, resilient subtlety. Whatever Ailell had dwindled from, however his mind and authority might seem to waver, Paul knew, ten moves into the game, that he was dealing with a man of formidable resources. Slowly and patiently the King ordered his defences, cautiously he shored up his bulwarks, and so it was that Schafer's freewheeling attack began to exhaust itself and was turned inexorably back. After almost two hours' play, Paul tipped over the white king in resignation.

The two men leaned back in their chairs and exchanged their first look since the game had begun. And they smiled, neither knowing, since there was no way they could know, how rare it was for the other to do so. Sharing that moment, however, as Paul raised his silver goblet to salute the King, they moved closer, across the twin gulfs of worlds and years, to the kind of bonding that might have allowed them to understand each other.

It was not to happen, but something else was born that night, and the fruit of that silent game would change the balance and the pattern of all the worlds there were.

Ailell spoke first, his voice husky. "No one," he said, "no one has ever given me a game like that. I do not lose in ta'bael. I almost did tonight."

Paul smiled for the second time. "You almost did. You may next game—but I'm not very certain of it. You play beautifully, my lord."

Ailell shook his head. "No, I play carefully. All the beauty was on your side, but sometimes plodding caution will wear down brilliance. When you sacrificed the second rider . . ." Ailell gestured wordlessly. "I suppose that it is only the young who can do a thing like that. It has been so long for me, I seem to have forgotten." He raised his own cup and drank.

Paul refilled both goblets before replying. He felt drained, simplified. The bird outside, he realized, had stopped singing a long time ago. "I think," he said, "that it is more a question of style than of youth or age. I'm not very patient, so I play the way I do."

"In ta'bael, you mean?"

"Other things, too," Paul answered, after a hesitation.

Ailell, surprisingly, nodded. "I was like that once, though it may be hard for you to credit." His expression was self-deprecating. "I took this throne by force in a time of chaos, and held it with my sword in the early years. If we are to be a dynasty, it begins with me and follows with . . . with Diarmuid, I suppose." Paul remained silent, and after a moment the King went on. "It is power that teaches patience; holding power, I mean. And you learn the price it exacts—which is something I never knew when I was your age and thought a sword and quick wits could deal with anything. I never knew the price you pay for power."

Ailell leaned over the board and picked up one of the pieces. "Take the queen in ta'bael," he said. "The most powerful piece on the board, yet she must be protected when threatened by guard or rider, for the game will be lost if that exchange is made. And the king," said Ailell dan Art, "in ta'bael you cannot sacrifice a king."

Paul couldn't read the expression in the sunken, still-handsome face, but there was a new timbre in the voice, something shifting far under the words.

Ailell seemed to notice his discomfort. He smiled again, faintly. "I am heavy company at night," he said. "Especially tonight. Too much comes back. I have too many memories."

"I have too many of my own," Paul said impulsively, and hated himself the instant the words were spoken.

Ailell's expression, though, was mild, even compassionate. "I thought you might," he said. "I'm not sure why, but I thought you might."

Paul lowered his face to the deep wine goblet and took a long drink. "My lord," he said, to break the ensuing stillness with a new subject, any new subject, "why did the Priestess say that Loren should have asked her before bringing us? What does—"

"She was wrong about that, and I will send to tell her so. Not that Jaelle is likely to listen." Ailell's expression was rueful. "She loves to make trouble, to stir up tensions she might find ways to exploit. Jaelle is ambitious beyond belief, and she seeks a return to the old ways of the Goddess ruling through her High Priestess, which is how it was before Iorweth came from oversea. There is a good deal of ambition in my court, there often is around the throne of an aging king, but hers runs deeper than any."

Paul nodded. "Your son said something like that last night."

"What? Diarmuid did?" Ailell gave a laugh that was actually evocative of the Prince. "I'm surprised he sobered up long enough to think so clearly."

Paul's mouth twitched. "Actually, he wasn't sober, but he seems to think pretty clearly anyhow."

The King gestured dismissively. "He is charming sometimes." After a pause he tugged at his beard and asked, "I'm sorry, what were we speaking of?"

"Jaelle," Paul said. "What she said this morning."

"Yes, yes, of course. Once her words would have been true, but not for a long time now. In the days when the wild magic could only be reached underground, and usually only with blood, the power needed for a crossing would be drained from the very heart of the earth, and that has always been the province of the Mother. So in those days it was true that such an expenditure of earthroot, of avarlith, could only be made through intercession of the High Priestess with the Goddess. Now, though, for long years now, since Amairgen learned the skylore and founded the Council of the Mages, the power drain in their magic runs only through the mage's source, and the avarlith is not touched."

"I don't understand. What power drain?"

"I go too quickly. It is hard to remember that you are from another world. Listen, then. If a mage were to use his magic to start a fire in that hearth, it would require power to do it. Once all our magic belonged to the Goddess and that power was tapped straight from the earthroot; and being both drained and expended in Fionavar, the power would find its way back to the earth—it would never diminish. But in a crossing the power is used in another world—"

"So you lose it!"

"Exactly. Or so it was once. But since Amairgen freed the mages from the Mother, the power will be drained from the source only, and he rebuilds it in himself over time."

"He?"

"Or she, of course."

"But . . . you mean each mage has . . . ?"

"Yes, of course. Each is bonded to a source, as Loren is to Matt, or Metran to Denbarra. That is the anchoring law of the skylore. The mage can do no more than his source can sustain, and this bond is for life. Whatever a mage does, someone else pays the price."

And so much came clear then. Paul remembered Matt Sören trembling as they came through the crossing. He remembered Loren's sharp concern for the Dwarf, and then, seeing more clearly still, the dim torches on the walls of that first room, the torches frail Metran had so easily gestured to brightness, while Loren had refrained to let his source recover. Paul felt his mind stretch away from self-absorption, stiffly, as if muscles had been too long unused.

"How?" he asked. "How are they bound to each other?"

"Mage and source? There are a great many laws, and long training to be endured. In the end, if there is still willingness, they may bind with the ritual, though it is not a thing to be done lightly. There are only three left in Fionavar. Denbarra is sister-son to Metran, Teyrnon's source is Barak, his closest friend as a child. Some pairings have been strange ones: Lisen of the Wood was source to Amairgen Whitebranch, first of the mages."

"Why was it strange?"

"Ah," the High King smiled, a little wistfully, "it is a long tale, that one. Perhaps you may hear a part of it sung in the Great Hall."

"All right. But what about Loren and Matt? How did they . . . ?"

"That, too, is strange," Ailell said. "At the end of his training, Loren sought leave of the Council and of me to travel for a time. He was gone three years. When he returned he had his cloak, and he was bonded to the King of the Dwarves, a thing that had never happened before. No Dwarf—"

The King broke off sharply. And in the abrupt silence they both heard it again: a barely audible tapping on the wall of the room across from the open window. As Paul looked at the King in wonder, it came again.

Ailell's face had gone queerly soft. "Oh, Mörnir," he breathed. "They *have* sent." He looked at Paul, hesitating, then seemed to make a decision. "Stay with me, young Paul, Pwyll, stay and be silent, for you are about to see a thing few men have been allowed."

And walking over to the wall, the King pressed his palm carefully against it in a place where the stone had darkened slightly. "*Levar shanna*," he murmured, and stood back, as the thin outline of a door began to take shape in the seamless structure of the wall. A moment later the demarcation was clear, and then the door slid soundlessly open and a slight figure moved lightly into the room. It was cloaked and hooded, and remained so a moment, registering Paul's presence and Ailell's nod of endorsement, then it discarded the concealing garment in one smooth motion and bowed low before the King.

"Greetings I bear, High King, and a gift to remember your crowning day. And I have tidings needful for you to hear from Daniloth. I am Brendel of the Kestrel Mark."

And in this fashion did Paul Schafer first see one of the lios alfar. And before the ethereal, flame-like quality of the silver-haired figure that stood before him, he felt himself to have grown heavy and awkward, as a different dimension of grace was made manifest.

"Be welcome, Na-Brendel of the Kestrel," Ailell murmured. "This is Paul Schafer, whom I think we would name Pwyll in Fionavar. He is one of the four who came with Silvercloak from another of the worlds to join the fabric of our celebration."

"This I know," said Brendel. "I have been in Paras Derval two days now, waiting to find you alone. This one I have seen, and the others, including the golden one. She alone made the waiting tolerable, High King. Else I might have been long hence from your walls, with the gift I bear undelivered." A flame of laughter danced in his eyes, which were green-gold in the candlelight.

"I thank you then for waiting," said Ailell. "And tell me now, how does Ra-Lathen?"

Brendel's face went suddenly still, the laughter extinguished. "Ah!" he exclaimed softly. "You bring me quickly to my tidings, High King. Lathen Mistweaver heard his song in the fall of the year. He has gone oversea and away, and with him also went Laien Spearchild, last of those who survived the Bael Rangat. None now are left, though few enough were ever left." The eyes of the lios alfar had darkened: they were violet now in the shadows. He stopped a moment, then continued. "Tenniel reigns in Daniloth. It is his greeting I bring to you."

"Lathen gone now, too?" the King said, very low. "And Laien? Heavy tidings you bear, Na-Brendel."

"And there are heavier yet to tell," the lios replied. "In the winter, rumour came to Daniloth of svart alfar moving in the north. Ra-Tenniel posted watch, and last month we learned that the word was not false. A party of them moved south past us, to the edgings of Pendaran, and there were wolves with them. We fought them there, High King. For the first time since the Bael Rangat, the lios alfar went to war. We drove them back, and most of them were slain—for we are still something of what we were—but six of my brothers and sisters fell. Six we loved will never now hear their song. Death has come again to us."

Ailell had collapsed into his chair as the lios alfar spoke. "Svarts outside Pendaran," he moaned now, almost to himself. "Oh, Mörnir, what wrong of mine was so great that this need come upon me in my age?" And aged he did seem then, shaking his head quiveringly back and forth. His hands on the carved arms of the chair trembled. Paul exchanged a glance with the bright figure of the lios. But though his own heart was twisted with pity for the old King, he saw no trace of the same in the eyes, now grey, of their visitor.

"I have a gifting for you, High King," Brendel said at length. "Ra-Tenniel would have you know that he is other than was the Mistweaver. My tidings of battle should tell you that. He will not hide in Daniloth, and henceforth you will see us more often than at the sevenyear. In token of which, and as earnest of alliance and our interwoven threads of destiny, the Lord of the lios alfar sends you this."

Never in his life had Paul seen a thing so beautiful as the object Brendel handed to Ailell. In the thin sceptre of crystal that passed from the lios to the man, every nuance of light in the room seemed to be caught and then transmuted. The orange of the wall torches, the red flickers of the candles, even the blue-white diamonds of starlight seen through the window, all seemed to be weaving in ceaseless, intricate motion as if shuttling on a loom within the sceptre.

"A summonglass," the King murmured as he looked down upon the gift. "This is a treasure indeed. It has been four hundred years since one of these lay within our halls."

"And whose fault was that?" Brendel said coldly.

"Unfair, my friend," Ailell replied, a little sharply, in his turn. The words of the lios seemed to kindle a spark of pride in him. "Vailerth, High King, broke the summonglass as a small part of a great madness—and Brennin paid a blood price for that madness in civil war." The King's voice was firm again. "Tell Ra-Tenniel that I accept his gift. Should he use it to summon us, the summons shall be answered. Say that to your Lord. Tomorrow I will speak with my Council as to the other tidings you have brought. Pendaran will be watched, I promise you."

"It is in my heart that more than watching may be needed, High King," Brendel replied, softly now. "There is a power stirring in Fionavar."

Ailell nodded slowly. "So Loren said to me some time ago."

He hesitated, then went on, almost reluctantly. "Tell me, Na-Brendel, how does the Daniloth wardstone?"

"The same as it has been since the day Ginserat made it!" Brendel said fiercely. "The lios alfar do not forget. Look to your own, High King!"

"No offence was meant, my friend," said Ailell, "but you know that all the guardians must burn the naal fire. And know you this as well: the people of Conary and Colan, and of Ginserat himself, do not forget the Bael Rangat, either. Our stone is blue as it ever was, and as, if the gods are kind, it ever will be." There was a silence; Brendel's eyes burned now with a luminous intensity. "Come!" said Ailell suddenly, rising to stand tall above them. "Come, and I will show you!"

Turning on his heel he stalked to his bedroom, opened the door, and passed through. Following quickly behind, Paul caught a glimpse of the great four-postered, canopied bed of the King, and he saw the figure of Tarn, the page, asleep on his cot in a corner of the room. Ailell did not break stride, though, and Paul and the lios alfar hastened to keep up as the King opened another door on the opposite wall of the bed-chamber and passed through that as well into a short corridor, at the end of which was another heavy door. There he stopped, breathing hard.

"We are above the Room of the Stone," Ailell said, speaking with some difficulty. He pressed a catch in the middle of the door and slid back a small rectangle of wood, which allowed them to see down into the room on the other side.

"Colan himself had this made," the King said to them, "when he returned with the stone from Rangat. It is told that for the rest of his days, he would often rise in the night and walk this corridor to gaze upon Ginserat's stone and ease his heart with the knowledge that it was as it had been. Of late I have found myself doing the same. Look you, Na-Brendel of the Kestrel; look upon the wardstone of the High Kingdom."

Wordlessly the lios stepped forward and placed his eye to the opening in the door. He stayed there for a long time, and was still silent when at length he drew back.

"And you, young Pwyll, look you as well and mark whether the blue of the binding still shines in the stone." Ailell gestured and Paul moved past Brendel to put his eye to the aperture.

It was a small chamber, with no decorations on the walls or floor and no furnishings of any kind. In the precise centre of the room there stood a plinth or pillar, rising past the height of a man, and before it was set a low altar, upon which burned a pure white fire. Upon the sides of the pillar were carven images of kingly men, and resting in a hollowed-out space at the top of the column lay a stone, about the size of a crystal ball; and Paul saw that that stone shone with its own light, and the light with which it shone was blue.

Back in the room they had left, Paul found a third goblet on a table by the window and poured wine for the three of them. Brendel accepted his cup, but immediately began a restless pacing of the room. Ailell had seated himself again in his chair by the gameboard. Watching from the window, Paul saw the lios alfar stop his coiled movement and stand before the King.

"We believe the wardstones, High King, because we must," he began softly, almost gently. "But you know there are other powers that serve the Dark, and some of them are great. Their Lord may yet be bound beneath Rangat, but moving over the land now is an evil we cannot ignore. Have you not seen it in your drought, High King? How can you not see? It rains in Cathal and on the Plain. Only in Brennin will the harvest fail. Only—"

*"Silence!"* Ailell's voice cracked high and sharp. "You know not of what you speak. Seek not to meddle in our affairs!" The King leaned forward in his chair, glaring at the slim figure of the lios alfar. Two bright spots of red flushed his face above the wispy beard.

Na-Brendel stopped. He was not tall, but in that moment he seemed to grow in stature as he gazed at the High King.

When he finally spoke, it was without pride or bitterness. "I did not mean to anger you," he said. "On this day, least of all. It is in my heart, though, that little in the days to come can be the affair of one people alone. Such is the meaning of Ra-Tenniel's gift. I am glad you have accepted it. I will give your message to my Lord." He bowed very low, turned, and walked back through the doorway in the wall, donning his cloak and hood as he moved. The door slid silently closed behind him, and then there was nothing in the room to mark his ever having been there, save the shimmering sceptre of glass Ailell was twisting around and around in the trembling hands of an old man.

From where he stood by the window, Paul could hear a different bird now lifting its voice in song. He supposed it must be getting close to dawn, but they were on the west side of the palace and the sky was still dark. He wondered if the King had completely forgotten his presence. At length, however, Ailell drew a tired breath and, laying the sceptre down by the gameboard, moved slowly to stand by Paul, gazing out the window. From where they stood, Paul could see the land fall away westward, and far in the distance rose the trees of a forest, a greater darkness against the dark of the night.

"Leave me, friend Pwyll," Ailell said at length, not unkindly. "I am weary now, and will be best by myself. Weary," he repeated, "and old. If there truly is some power of Darkness walking the land I can do nothing about it tonight unless I die. And truly, I do not want to die, on the Tree or otherwise. If this is my failing, then so it must be." His eyes were distant and sad as he gazed out the window towards the woods far off.

Paul cleared his throat awkwardly. "I don't think that wanting to live can be a failing." The words rasped from too long a silence; a difficult emotion was waking within him.

Ailell smiled at that, but with his mouth only, and he continued to look out at the darkness. "For a king it may be, Pwyll. The price, remember?" He went on in a different voice, "Some blessings I have had. You heard Ysanne in the hall this morning.

She said she had loved me. I never knew that. I don't think," the King mused softly, turning at last to look at Paul, "that I will tell that part to Marrien, the Queen."

Paul let himself out of the room, after bowing with all the respect he had. There was a queer constriction in his throat. *Marrien, the Queen.* He shook his head, and took an uncertain step along the corridor. A long shadow detached itself from the wall nearby.

"Do you know the way?" Coll asked.

"Not really, no," Paul said. "I guess I don't."

They passed through the hallways of the palace, their footsteps echoing. Beyond the walls, dawn was just breaking in the east over Gwen Ystrat. It was dark still in the palace, though.

Outside his doorway Paul turned to Diarmuid's man. "Coll," he asked, "what's the Tree?"

The burly soldier froze. After a moment a hand went up to rub the broad hook of his broken nose. They had stopped walking; Paras Derval lay wrapped in silence. For a moment Paul thought his question would not be answered, but then Coll did speak, his voice pitched low.

"The Summer Tree?" he said. "It's in the wood west of the town. Sacred it is, to Mörnir of the Thunder."

"Why is it important?"

"Because," said Coll, lower yet, "that's where the God would summon the High King in the old days, when the land had need."

"Summon him for what?"

"To hang on the Summer Tree and die," said Coll succinctly. "I've said too much already. Your friend is with the Lady Rheva tonight, I believe. I'll be back to wake you in a little while; we've got a long ride today." And he spun on his heel to walk off.

"Coll!"

The big man turned, slowly.

"Is it always the King who hangs?"

Coll's broad, sunburnt face was etched with apprehension. The answer, when it came, seemed almost to be against his will. "Princes of the blood have been known to do it instead."

"Which explains Diarmuid last night. Coll, I really don't want to get you in trouble—but if I were to make a guess at what happened here, I'd guess that Ailell was called because of this drought, or maybe there's a drought because he hasn't gone, and I'd guess he is terrified of the whole thing, and Loren backs him because he doesn't trust whatever happens on the Summer Tree." After a moment Coll nodded stiffly, and Schafer continued.

"Then I'd go on to guess, and this is really a guess, that Diarmuid's brother wanted to do it for the King, and Ailell forbade him—which is why he's gone and Diarmuid is heir. Would that be a good guess?"

Coll had come very close as Schafer was speaking. He searched Paul's eyes with his own honest brown ones. Then he shook his head, a kind of awe written into his features.

"This is deeper than I can go. It would be," he said, "a very good guess. The High King must consent to his surrogate, and when he refused, the Prince cursed him, which is treason, and was exiled. It is now death to speak his name."

In the silence that followed it seemed to Paul as if the whole weight of the night was pressing down upon the two of them.

"There is no power in me," Coll said then, in his deep voice, "but if there was, I would have him cursed in the name of all the gods and goddesses there are."

"Who?" Paul whispered.

"Why, the Prince, of course," said Coll. "The exiled Prince. Diarmuid's brother, Aileron."

# CHAPTER 6

Beyond the palace gates and the walls of the town, the depredations of drought came home. The impact of a rainless summer could be measured in the heavy dust of the road, in the thin grass peeling like brown paint on hills and tummocks, in stunted trees and dried-up village wells. In the fiftieth year of Ailell's reign, the High Kingdom was suffering as no living man could remember.

For Kevin and Paul, riding south with Diarmuid and seven of his men in the morning, the way of things registered most brutally in the pinched, bitter features of the farmers they passed on the road. Already the heat of the sun was casting a shimmer of mirage on the landscape. There were no clouds in the sky.

Diarmuid was setting a hard pace, though, and Kevin, who was no horseman and who'd had a sleepless night, was exceedingly happy when they pulled up outside a tavern in the fourth village they came to.

They took a hasty meal of cold, sharply spiced meat, bread, and cheese, with pints of black ale to wash away the throat-clogging dust of the road. Kevin, eating voraciously, saw Diarmuid speak briefly to Carde, who quietly sought the innkeeper and withdrew into another room with him. Noticing Kevin's glance, the Prince walked over to the long wooden table where he and Paul were sitting with the lean, dark man named Erron.

"We're checking for your friend," Diarmuid told them. "It's one of the reasons we're doing this. Loren went north to do the same, and I've sent word to the coast."

"Who's with the women?" Paul Schafer asked quickly.

Diarmuid smiled. "Trust me," he said. "I do know what I'm doing. There are guards, and Matt stayed in the palace, too."

"Loren went without him?" Paul queried sharply. "How . . . ?"

Diarmuid's expression was even more amused. "Even without magic our friend can handle himself. He has a sword, and knows how to use it. You worry a good deal, don't you?"

"Does it surprise you?" Kevin cut in. "We don't know where we are, we don't know the rules here, Dave's gone missing, God knows where—and we don't even know where we're going with you now."

"That last," said Diarmuid, "is easy enough. We're crossing the river into Cathal, if we can. By night, and quietly, because there's a very good chance we'll be killed if found."

"I see," said Kevin, swallowing. "And are we allowed to know why we are subjecting ourselves to that unpleasant possibility?"

For the first time that morning Diarmuid's smile flashed full-force. "Of course you are," he said kindly. "You're going to help me seduce a lady. Tell me, Carde," he murmured, turning, "any news?"

There was none. The Prince drained his pint and was striding out the door. The others scrambled to their feet and followed. A number of the villagers came out of the inn to watch them ride off.

"Mörnir guard you, young Prince!" one farmer cried impulsively. "And in the name of the Summer Tree, may he take the old man and let you be our King!"

Diarmuid had raised a gracious hand at the first words, but the speaker's last phrase brought him to wheel his horse hard. There was a brutal silence. The Prince's face had gone cold. No one moved. Overhead Kevin heard a noisy flap of wings as a dense cluster of crows wheeled aloft, darkening the sun for an instant.

Diarmuid's voice, when it came, was formal and imperious. "The words you have spoken are treason," Ailell's son said, and with a sideways nod spoke one word more: *"Coll."*

The farmer may never have seen the arrow that killed him. Diarmuid did not. He was already pounding up the road without a backwards glance as Coll replaced his bow. By the time the shock had passed and the screaming had begun, all ten of them were around the bend that would carry them south.

Kevin's hands were shaking with shock and fury as he galloped, the image of the dead man engulfing him, the screams still echoing in his mind. Coll, beside him, seemed impassive and unperturbed. Save that he carefully refused to meet the glance of Paul Schafer, who was staring fixedly at him as they rode, and to whom he had spoken a treasonous word of his own the night before.

⇥⬡⬡⇤

In the early spring of 1949 Dr. John Ford of Toronto had taken a fortnight's leave from his residency at London's St. Thomas Hospital. Hiking alone in the Lake District, north of Keswick, he came, at the end of a long day afoot, down the side of a hill and walked wearily up to a farmyard tucked into the shadow of the slope.

There was a girl in the yard, drawing water from a well. The westering sun slanted upon her dark hair. When she turned at the sound of his footstep, he saw that her eyes were grey. She smiled shyly when, hat in hand, he asked for a drink, and before she had finished drawing it for him, John Ford had fallen in love, simply and irrevocably, which was his nature in all things.

Deirdre Cowan, who was eighteen that spring, had been told long ago by her grandmother that she would love and marry a man from over the sea. Because her gran was known to have the Sight, Deirdre never doubted what she had been told. And this man, handsome and diffident, had eyes that called to her.

Ford spent that night in her father's house, and in the quietest dark before dawn Deirdre rose from her bed. She was not surprised to see her gran in the hallway by her own bedroom door, nor to see the old woman make a gesture of blessing that went back a very long way. She went to Ford's room, the grey eyes beguiling, her body sweet with trust.

They were married in the fall, and John Ford took his wife home just as the first snows of the winter came. And it was their daughter who walked, a Dwarf beside her, twenty-five springs after her parents had been brought together, towards the shores of a lake in another world, to meet her own destiny.

The path to the lake where Ysanne lived twisted north and west through a shallow valley flanked by gentle hills, a landscape that would have been lovely in any proper season. But Kim and Matt were walking through a country scorched and barren—and the thirst of the land seemed to knife into Kim, twisting like anguish inside her. Her face hurt, the bones seeming taut and difficult within her. Movement was becoming painful, and everywhere she looked, her eyes flinched away.

"It's dying," she said.

Matt looked at her with his one eye. "You feel it?"

She nodded stiffly. "I don't understand."

The Dwarf's expression was grim. "The gift is not without its darkness. I do not envy you."

"Envy me *what*, Matt?" Kim's brow furrowed. "What do I have?"

Matt Sören's voice was soft. "Power. Memory. Truly, I am not sure. If the hurt of the land reaches so deeply. . . ."

"It's easier in the palace. I'm blocked there from all this."

"We can go back."

For one moment, sharp and almost bitter, Kim did want to turn back—all the way back. Not just to Paras Derval, but home. Where the ruin of the grass and the dead stalks of flowers by the path did not burn her so. But then she remembered the eyes of the Seer as they had looked into hers, and she heard again the voice, drumming in her veins: *I have awaited you.*

"No," she said. "How much farther?"

"Around the curve. We'll see the lake soon. But hold, let me give you something—I should have thought of it sooner." And the Dwarf held out towards her a bracelet of silver workmanship, in which was set a green stone.

"What is it?"

"A vellin stone. It is very precious; there are few left, and the secret of fashioning them died with Ginserat. The stone is a shield from magic. Put it on."

With wonder in her eyes, Kimberly placed it upon her wrist, and as she did, the pain was gone, the hurt, the ache, the burning, all were gone. She was aware of them, but distantly, for the vellin was her shield and she felt it guarding her. She cried out in wonder.

But the relief in her face was not mirrored in that of the Dwarf. "Ah," said Matt Sören, grimly, "so I was right. There are dark threads shuttling on the Loom. The Weaver grant that Loren comes back soon."

"Why?" Kim asked. "What does this mean?"

"If the vellin guards you from the land's pain, then that pain is not natural. And if there is a power strong enough to do this to the whole of the High Kingdom, then there is a fear in me. I begin to wonder about the old tales of Mörnir's Tree, and the pact the Founder made with the God. And if not that, then I dare not think what. Come," said the Dwarf, "it is time I took you to Ysanne."

And walking more swiftly, he led her around an out-thrust spur of hill slope, and as they cleared the spur she saw the lake: a gem of blue in a necklace of low hills. And somehow there was still green by the lake, and the profuse, scattered colours of wildflowers.

Kim stopped dead in her tracks. "Oh, Matt!"

The Dwarf was silent while she gazed down, enraptured, on the water. "It *is* fair," he said finally. "But had you ever seen Calor Diman between the mountains, you would spare your heart's praise somewhat, to have some left for the Queen of Waters."

Kim, hearing the change in his voice, looked at him for a moment; then, drawing a deliberate breath, she closed her eyes and was wordless a long time. When she spoke, it was in a cadence not her own.

"Between the mountains," she said. "Very high up, it is. The melting snow in summer falls into the lake. The air is thin and clear. There are eagles circling. The sunlight turns the lake into a golden fire. To drink of that water is to taste of whatever light is falling down upon it, whether of sun or moon or stars. And under the full moon, Calor Diman is deadly, for the vision never fades and never stops pulling. A tide in the heart. Only the true King of Dwarves may endure that night vigil without going mad, and he must do so for the Diamond Crown. He must wed the Queen of Waters, lying all night by her shores at full of the moon. He will be bound then, to the end of his days, as the King must be, to Calor Diman."

And Kimberly opened her eyes to look full upon the former King of Dwarves. "*Why*, Matt?" she asked, in her own voice. "Why did you leave?"

He made no answer, but met her look unflinchingly. At length he turned, still silent, and led her down the winding path to Ysanne's lake. She was waiting there for them, dreamer of the dream, knowledge in her eyes, and pity, and another nameless thing.

⟡

Kevin Laine had never been able to hide his emotions well, and that summary execution, so casually effected, had disturbed him very deeply. He had not spoken a word through a day's hard riding, and the twilight found him still pale with undischarged anger. In the gathering dark the company passed through more heavily wooded country, slanting gradually downhill towards the south. The road went past a thick copse of trees and revealed, half a mile beyond, the towers of a small fortress.

Diarmuid pulled to a halt. He seemed fresh still, unaffected by the day on horseback, and Kevin, whose bones and muscles ached ferociously, fixed the Prince with a cold stare.

He was, however, ignored. "Rothe," said Diarmuid to a compact, brown-bearded rider, "you go in. Speak to Averren and no one else. I am not here. Coll is leading a number of you on a reconnaissance. No details. He won't ask anyway. Find out, discreetly, if a stranger has been seen in the area, then join us by the Dael Slope." Rothe spun his horse and galloped towards the tower.

"That's South Keep," Carde murmured to Kevin and Paul. "Our watchtower down here. Not too big—but there's little danger of anything crossing the river, so we don't need much. The big garrison's down river, west by the sea. Cathal's invaded twice that way, so there's a castle at Seresh to keep watch."

"Why can't they cross the river?" Paul asked. Kevin maintained his self-imposed silence.

Carde's smile in the gathering dark was mirthless. "That you'll see, soon enough, when we go down to try."

Diarmuid, throwing a cloak over his shoulders, waited until the keep gates had swung open for Rothe; then he led them west off the road along a narrow path that began to curve south through the woods.

They rode for perhaps an hour, quietly now, though no order had been given. These, Kevin realized, were highly trained men, for all the roughness of their garb and speech when compared to the dandies they'd met in the palace.

The moon, a thinning crescent, swung into sight behind them as they wound out of the trees. Diarmuid halted at the edge of the sloping plain, a hand up for silence. And after a moment Kevin heard it, too: the deep sound of water, swift-flowing.

Under the waning moon and the emerging stars he dismounted with the others. Gazing south he could see the land fall sheer away in a cliff only a few hundred yards from where they stood. But he could not see anything at all on the far side; it was as if the world ended just in front of them.

"There's a land fault here," a light voice said close to his ear. Kevin stiffened, but Diarmuid went on casually. "Cathal lies about a hundred feet lower than us; you'll see when we go forward. And," said the Prince, his voice still light, "it is a mistake to make judgements too soon. That man had to die—had he not, word would be in the palace by now that I was encouraging treasonous talk. And there are those who would like to spread that word. His life was forfeit from the time he spoke, and the arrow was a kinder death than Gorlaes would have granted him. We'll wait for Rothe here. I've told Carde to rub you both down; you'll not make it across with muscles that won't move." He walked away and sat on the ground, leaning against the trunk of a tree. After a moment, Kevin Laine, who was neither a petty man nor a stupid one, smiled to himself.

Carde's hands were strong, and the liniment he used was extraordinary. By the time Rothe rejoined them, Kevin felt functional again. It was quite dark now, and Diarmuid threw back his cloak as he suddenly rose. They gathered around him at the edge of the wood and a ripple of soundless tension went through the company. Kevin, feeling it, looked for Paul, and saw that Schafer was already gazing at him. They exchanged a tight smile, then listened intently as Diarmuid began to speak, softly and concisely. The words spun into the almost windless night, were received and registered, and then there was silence; and they were moving, nine of them, with one man left to the horses, over the slope that led to the river they had to cross into a country where they would be killed if seen.

Running lightly beside Coll, Kevin felt his heart suddenly expand with a fierce exhilaration. Which lasted, growing brighter, until they dropped to a crouch, then a crawl, and, reaching the edge of the cliff, looked down.

Saeren was the mightiest river west of the mountains. Tumbling spectacularly out of the high peaks of Eridu, it roared down into the lowlands of the west. There it would have slowed and begun to meander, had not a cataclysm torn the land millennia ago in the youngness of the world, an earthquake that had ripped a gash like a wound in the firmament: the Saeren Gorge. Through that deep ravine the river thundered, dividing Brennin, which had been raised up in the earth's fury, from Cathal, lying low and fertile to the south. And great Saeren did not slow or wander in its course, nor could a dry summer in the north slake its force. The river foamed and boiled two hundred feet below them, glinting in the moonlight, awesome and appalling. And between them and the water lay a descent in darkness down a cliff too sheer for belief.

"If you fall," Diarmuid had said, unsmiling, "try not to scream. You may give the others away."

And now Kevin could see the far side of the gorge, and along the southern cliff, well below their elevation, were the bonfires and garrisons of Cathal, the outposts guarding their royalty and their gardens from the north.

Kevin swore shakily. "I do not believe this. What are they afraid of? No one can cross this thing."

"It's a long dive," Coll agreed from his right side. "But he says it was crossed hundreds of years ago, just once, and that's why we're trying now."

"Just for the hell of it, eh?" Kevin breathed, still incredulous. "What's the matter? Are you bored with backgammon?"

"With what?"

"Never mind."

And indeed, there was little chance to talk after that, for Diarmuid, farther along to their right, spoke softly, and Erron, lean and supple, moved quickly over to a large twisted tree Kevin hadn't noticed and knotted a rope carefully about the trunk. That done, he dropped the line over the edge, paying it out between his hands. When the last coil spun down into darkness, he wet each of his palms deliberately and cocked an eye at Diarmuid. The Prince nodded once. Erron gripped the rope tightly, stepped forward, and disappeared over the edge of the cliff.

Hypnotically, they all watched the taut line of the rope. Coll went over to the tree to check the knot. Kevin became aware, as the long moments passed, that his hands were wet with perspiration. He wiped them surreptitiously on his breeches. Then, on the far side of the rope, he saw Paul Schafer looking at him. It was dark, and he couldn't see Paul's face clearly, but something in the expression, a remoteness, a strangeness, triggered a sudden cold apprehension in Kevin's chest, and brought flooding remorselessly back the memory he could never quite escape of the night Rachel Kincaid had died.

He remembered Rachel himself, remembered her with a kind of love of his own, for it had been hard not to love the dark-haired girl with the shy, Pre-Raphaelite grace, for whom two things in the world meant fire: the sounds of a cello under her bow, and the presence of Paul Schafer. Kevin had seen, and caught his breath to see, the look in her dark eyes when Paul would enter a room, and he had watched, too, the hesitant unfolding of trust and need in his proud friend. Until it all went smash, and he had stood, helpless tears in his own eyes, in the emergency ward of St. Michael's Hospital with Paul when the death word came. When Paul Schafer, his face a dry mask, had spoken the only words he would ever speak on Rachel's death: "It should have been me," he had said, and walked alone out of a too-bright room.

But now, in the darkness of another world, a different voice was speaking to him. "He's down. You next, friend Kevin," said Diarmuid. And there was indeed the dancing of the rope that meant Erron was signalling from the bottom.

Moving before he could think, Kevin went up to the rope, wet his hands as Erron had done, gripped carefully, and slid over and down alone.

Using his booted feet for leverage and control, he descended hand over hand into the growing thunder of noise that was the Saeren Gorge. The cliff was rough, and there was a danger that the line might fray on one of the rock edges—but there was little to be done about that, or about the burning in his hands as the rope slid abrasively through his grip. He looked down only once and was dizzied by the speed of the water far below. Turning his face to the cliff, Kevin breathed deeply for a moment, willing himself to be calm; then he continued, hand and foot, rope and toehold, down to where the river waited. It became a process almost mechanical, reaching for crevices with his foot, pushing off as the rope slid through his palms. He blocked out pain and fatigue, the returning ache of abused muscles, he forgot, even, where he was. The world was a rope and a face of rock. It seemed to have always been.

So oblivious was he that when Erron touched his ankle, Kevin's heart leaped in a spasm of terror. Erron helped him step down onto the thin strip of earth, barely ten feet from where the water roared past, drenching them with spray. The noise was overwhelming; it made conversation almost impossible.

Erron jerked three times on the slack line, and after a moment it began to sway and bob beside them with the weight of a body above. Paul, Kevin thought wearily, that'll be Paul. And then another thought invaded him and registered hard over exhaustion: *he doesn't care if he falls.* The realization hit with the force of apprehended truth. Kevin looked upwards and began frantically scanning the cliff face, but the moon was lighting the southern side only, and Schafer's descent was invisible. Only the lazy, almost mocking n ovement of the rope end beside them testified that someone was above.

And only now, absurdly too late, did Kevin think of Paul's weakened condition. He remembered rushing him to hospital only two weeks before, after the basketball game Schafer shouldn't have played, and at the memory, his heart angled in his breast. Unable to bear the strain of looking upwards, he turned instead to the bobbing rope beside him. So long as that slow dance continued, Paul was all right. The movement of the rope meant life, a continuation. Fiercely Kevin concentrated on the line swaying slowly in front of the dark rock face. He didn't pray, but he thought of his father, which was almost the same thing.

He was still gazing fixedly at the rope when Erron finally touched his arm and pointed. And looking upwards then, Kevin drew free breath again to see the slight, familiar figure moving down to join them. Paul Schafer alighted moments later, neatly, though breathing hard. His eyes met Kevin's for an instant, then flicked away. He tugged the rope three times himself, before moving down the strand to slump against the rock face, eyes closed.

A time later there were nine of them standing spray-drenched by the river bank. Diarmuid's eyes gleamed in the light reflected off the water; he seemed feral and fey, a spirit of night unleashed. And he signalled Coll to begin the next stage of the journey.

The big man had descended with another coil of rope in the pack on his broad back. Now he unslung his bow and, drawing an arrow from its quiver, fitted an end of the rope to an iron ring set in the shaft. Then he moved forward to the edge of the water and began scanning the opposite shore. Kevin couldn't see what he was looking to find. On their own side a few shrubs and one or two thick, short trees had dug into the thin soil, but the Cathal shore was sandier, and there seemed to be nothing growing by the river. Coll, however, had raised his great bow with the arrow notched to the string. He drew one steady breath and pulled the bowstring all the way back past his ear, the gesture smooth, though the corded muscles of his arm had gone ridged and taut. Coll released, and the arrow sang into arching flight, the thin rope hurtling with it high over Saeren—*to sink deep into the stone cliff on the far side.*

Carde, who'd been holding the free end of the rope, quickly pulled it tight. Then Coll measured and cut it, and, tying the free end to another arrow, proceeded to fire the shaft point-blank into the rock behind them. The arrow buried itself in stone.

Kevin, utterly incredulous, turned to Diarmuid, questions exploding in his eyes. The Prince walked over and shouted in his ear, over the thunder of the water, "Loren's arrows. It helps to have a mage for a friend––though if he finds out how I've used his gift, he'll consign me to the wolves!" And the Prince laughed aloud to see the silvered highway of cord that spanned Saeren in the moonlight. Watching him, Kevin felt it then, the intoxicating lure of this man who was leading them. He laughed himself in that moment, feeling constraint and apprehension slip away. A sense of freedom came upon him, of being tuned to the night and their journey, as he watched Erron leap up, grab the rope, and begin to swing hand over hand, out over the water.

The wave that hit the dark-haired man was a fluke, kicked up from an angled rock by the shore. It slammed into Erron as he was changing grips and threw him violently sideways. Desperately Erron curved his body to hang on with one hand, but the wave that followed the first buffeted him mercilessly, and he was torn from the rope and flung into the mill-race of Saeren.

Kevin Laine was running before the second wave hit. Pelting flat out downstream along the strand, he leaped, without pausing to calculate or look back, for the over-hanging branch of one of the knotted trees that dug into the earth by the river. Fully extended in flight, his arms outstretched, he barely reached it. There was no time to think. With a racking, contorted movement he twisted his body, looped his knees over the branch, and hung face down over the torrent.

Only then did he look, almost blinded by spray, to see Erron, a cork in the flood, hurtling towards him. Again, no time. Kevin reached down, tasting his death in that moment. Erron threw up a convulsive hand, and each clasped the other's wrist.

The pull was brutal. It would have ripped Kevin from the tree like a leaf—had not someone else been there. Someone who was holding his legs on the branch with a grip like an iron band. A grip that was not going to break.

"I've got you!" screamed Paul Schafer. "Lift him if you can."

And hearing the voice, locked in Schafer's vise-like hold, Kevin felt a surge of strength run through him; both hands gripping Erron's wrist, he pulled him from the river.

There were other hands by then, reaching for Erron, taking him swiftly to shore. Kevin let go and allowed Paul to haul him up to the branch. Straddling it, they faced each other, gasping hard for breath.

"You idiot!" Paul shouted, his chest heaving. "You scared the hell out of me!"

Kevin blinked, then the too, too *much* boiled over. "You shut up! I scared *you*? What do you think you've been doing to me since Rachel died?"

Paul, utterly unprepared, was shocked silent. Trembling with emotion and adrenalin afterburn, Kevin spoke again, his voice raw. "I mean it, Paul. When I was waiting at the bottom . . . I didn't think you were going to make it down. And Paul, I wasn't sure if you cared."

Their heads were close together, for the words to be heard. Schafer's pupils were enormous. In the reflected moonlight his face was so white as to be almost inhuman.

"That isn't quite true," he replied finally.

"But it isn't far wrong. Not far enough. Oh, Paul, you have to bend a little. If you can't talk, can't you cry at least? She deserves your tears. Can't you cry for her?"

At that, Paul Schafer laughed. The sound chilled Kevin to the core, there was such wildness in it. "I can't," Paul said. "That's the whole problem, Kev. I really, really can't."

"Then you're going to break," Kevin rasped.

"I might," Schafer replied, scarcely audible. "I'm trying hard not to, believe me. Kev, I know you care. It matters to me, very much. If . . . if I do decide to go, I'll . . . say goodbye. I promise you'll know."

"Oh, for God's sake! Is that supposed to make me—"

"*Come on!*" Coll bellowed from the shore, and Kevin, startled, realized that he'd been calling for some time. "That branch could crack any second!"

So they moved back to the strand, to be disconcertingly enveloped by bear-hugs from Diarmuid's men. Coll himself nearly broke Kevin's back with his massive embrace.

The Prince walked over, his expression utterly sober. "You saved a man I value," he said. "I owe you both. I was being frivolous when I invited you to come, and unfair. I am grateful now that I did."

"Good," said Kevin succinctly. "I don't much enjoy feeling like excess baggage. And now," he went on, raising his voice so they could all hear, while he buried again that which he had no answer for and no right to answer, "let's cross this stream. I want to see those gardens." And walking past the Prince, his shoulders straight, head high as he could carry it, he led them back to the rope across the river, grief in his heart like a stone.

One by one then, hand over hand, they did cross. And on the other shore, where sand met cliff in Cathal, Diarmuid found them what he had promised: the worn handholds carved into the rock five hundred years ago by Alorre, Prince of Brennin, who had been the first and the last to cross Saeren into the Garden Country.

Screened by darkness and the sound of the river, they climbed up to where the grass was green and the scent of moss and cyclamen greeted them. The guards were few and careless, easily avoided. They came to a wood a mile from the river and took shelter there as a light rain began to fall.

⊷⇒◯⇐⊶

Beneath her feet Kimberly could feel the rich texture of the soil, and the sweetness of wildflowers surrounded her. They were in the strand of wood lining the north shore of the lake. The leaves of the tall trees, somehow untouched by the drought, filtered the sunlight, leaving a verdant coolness through which they walked, looking for a flower.

Matt had gone back to the palace.

"She will stay with me tonight," the Seer had said. "No harm will touch her by the lake. You have given her the vellin, which was wiser perhaps than even you knew, Matt Sören. I have my powers, too, and Tyrth is here with us."

"Tyrth?" the Dwarf asked.

"My servant," Ysanne replied. "He will take her back when the time comes. Trust me, and go easily. You have done well to bring her here. We have much to talk of, she and I."

So the Dwarf had gone. But there had been little of the promised talk since his departure. To Kim's first stumbled questions the white-haired Seer had offered only a gentle smile and an admonition. "Patience, child. There are things that come before the telling time. First there is a flower we need. Come with me, and see if we can find a bannion for tonight."

And so Kim found herself walking through shade and light under the trees, questions tumbling over each other in her mind. Blue-green, Ysanne had said it was, with red like a drop of blood at the heart.

Ahead of her the Seer moved, light and sure-footed over root and fallen branch. She seemed younger in the wood than in Ailell's hall, and here she carried no staff to lean upon. Which triggered another question, and this one broke through.

"Do you feel the drought the way I do?"

Ysanne stopped at that and regarded Kim a moment, her eyes bright in the seamed, wizened face. She turned again, though, and continued walking, scanning the ground on either side of the twisting path. When her answer came Kim was unprepared.

"Not the same way. It tires me, and there is a sense of oppression. But not actual pain, as with you. I can—*there!*" And darting quickly to one side she knelt on the earth.

The red at the centre did look like blood against the sea-coloured petals of the bannion.

"I knew we would find one today," said Ysanne, and her voice had roughened. "It has been years, so many, many years." With care she uprooted the flower and rose to her feet. "Come, child, we will take this home. And I will try to tell you what you need to know."

"Why did you say you'd been waiting for me?" They were in the front room of Ysanne's cottage, in chairs beside the fireplace. Late afternoon. Through the window Kim could see the figure of the servant, Tyrth, mending the fence in back of the cottage. A few chickens scrabbled and pecked in the yard, and there was a goat tied to a post in a corner. Around the walls of the room were shelves upon which, in labelled jars, stood plants and herbs of astonishing variety, many with names Kim could not recognize. There was little furniture: the two chairs, a large table, a small, neat bed in an alcove off the back of the room.

Ysanne sipped at her drink before replying. They were drinking something that tasted like camomile.

"I dreamt you," the Seer said. "Many times. That is how I see such things as I do see. Which have grown fewer and more clouded of late. You were clear, though, hair and eyes. I saw your face."

"*Why,* though? What am I, that you should dream of me?"

"You already know the answer to that. From the crossing. From the land's pain, which is yours, child. You are a Seer as I am, and more, I think, than I have ever been." Cold suddenly in the hot, dry summer, Kim turned her head away.

"But," she said in a small voice, "I don't *know* anything."

"Which is why I am to teach you what I know. That is why you are here."

There was a complex silence in the room. The two women, one old, the other younger than her years, looked at each other through identical grey eyes under white hair and brown, and a breeze like a finger blew in upon them from the lake.

"My lady."

The voice abraded the stillness. Kim turned to see Tyrth in the window. Thick black hair and a full beard framed eyes so dark they were almost black. He was not a big man, but his arms on the window sill were corded with muscle and tanned a deep brown by labour in the sun.

Ysanne, unstartled, turned to him. "Tyrth, yes, I meant to call you. Can you make up another bed for me? We have a guest tonight. This is Kimberly, who crossed with Loren two nights past."

Tyrth met her eyes for an instant only, then an awkward hand brushed at the thick hair tumbling over his forehead. "I'll do a proper bed then. But in the meanwhile, I've seen something you should know of. . . ."

"The wolves?" Ysanne asked tranquilly. Tyrth, after a bemused moment, nodded. "I saw them the other night," the Seer went on. "While I slept. There isn't much we can do. I left word in the palace with Loren yesterday."

"I don't like it," Tyrth muttered. "There haven't been wolves this far south in my lifetime. Big ones, too. They shouldn't be so big." And turning his head, he spat in the dust of the yard before touching his forehead again and walking from the window. As he moved away Kim saw that he limped, favouring his left foot.

Ysanne followed her glance. "A broken bone," she said. "Badly set years ago. He'll walk like that all his life. I'm lucky to have him, though—no one else would serve a witch." She smiled. "Your lessons begin tonight, I think."

"How?"

Ysanne nodded towards the bannion resting on the table top. "It begins with the flower," she said. "It did for me, a long time ago."

The waning moon rose late, and it was full dark when the two women made their way beneath it to stand by the edge of the lake. The breeze was delicate and cool, and the water lapped the shore gently, like a lover. Over their heads the summer stars were strung like filigree.

Ysanne's face had gone austere and remote. Looking at her, Kim felt a premonitory tension. The axis of her life was swinging and she knew not how or where, only that somehow, she had lived in order to come to this shore.

Ysanne drew her small figure erect and stepped onto a flat surface of rock jutting out over the lake. With a motion almost abrupt, she gestured for Kim to sit beside her on the stone. The only sounds were the stir of the wind in the trees behind them, and the quiet slap of water against the rocks. Then Ysanne raised both arms in a gesture of power and invocation and spoke in a voice that rang over the night lake like a bell.

"Hear me, Eilathen!" she cried. "Hear and be summoned, for I have need of you, and this is the last time and the deepest. *Eilathen damae! Sien rabanna, den viroth bannion damae!*" And as she spoke the words, the flower in her hand burst into flame, blue-green and red like its colours, and she threw it, spiralling, into the lake.

Kim felt the wind die. Beside her, Ysanne seemed carved out of marble, so still was she. The very night seemed gathered into that stillness. There was no sound, no motion, and Kim could feel the furious pounding of her heart. Under the moon the surface of the lake was glassy calm, but not with the calm of tranquillity. It was coiled, waiting. Kim sensed, as if within the pulse of her blood, a vibration as of a tuning fork pitched just too high for human ears.

And then something exploded into motion in the middle of the lake. A spinning form, whirling too fast for the eye to follow, rose over the surface of the water, and Kim saw that it shone blue-green under the moon.

Unbelieving, she watched it come towards them, and as it did so the spinning began to slow, so that when it finally halted, suspended in air above the water before Ysanne, Kim saw that it had the tall form of a man.

Long sea-green hair lay coiled about his shoulders, and his eyes were cold and clear as chips of winter ice. His naked body was lithe and lean, and it shimmered as if with scales, the moonlight glinting where it fell upon him. And on his hand, burning in the dark like a wound, was a ring, red as the heart of the flower that had summoned him.

*"Who calls me from the deep against my desire?"* The voice was cold, cold as night waters in early spring, and there was danger in it.

"Eilathen, it is the Dreamer. I have need. Forgo your wrath and hear me. It is long since we stood here, you and I."

"Long for you, Ysanne. You have grown old. Soon the worms will gather you." The reedy pleasure in the voice could be heard. "But I do not age in my green halls, and time turns not for me, save when the bannion fire troubles the deep." And Eilathen held out the hand upon which the red ring burned.

"I would not send down the fire without a cause, and tonight marks your release from guardianship. Do this last thing for me and you are free of my call." A slight stir of wind; the trees were sighing again.

"On your oath?" Eilathen moved closer to the shore. He seemed to grow, towering above the Seer, water rippling down his shoulders and thighs, the long wet hair pulled back from his face.

"On my oath," Ysanne replied. "I bound you against my own desire. The wild magic is meant to be free. Only because my need was great were you given to the flowerfire. On my oath, you are free tonight."

"And the task?" Eilathen's voice was colder than ever, more alien. He shimmered before them with a green dark power.

"This," said Ysanne, and pointed to Kimberly.

The stab of Eilathen's eyes was like ice cutting into her. Kim saw, sensed, somehow knew the fathomless halls whence Ysanne had summoned him—the shaped corridors of seastone and twined seaweed, the perfect silence of his deep home. She held the gaze as best she could, held it until it was Eilathen who turned away.

"Now I know," he said to the Seer. "Now I understand." And a thread that might have been respect had woven its way into his voice.

"But she does not," said Ysanne. "So spin for her, Eilathen. Spin the Tapestry, that she may learn what she is, and what has been, and release you of the burden that you bear."

Eilathen glittered high above them both. His voice was a splintering of ice. "And this is the last?"

"This is the last," Ysanne replied.

He did not hear the note of loss in her voice. Sadness was alien to him, not of his world or his being. He smiled at her words and tossed his hair back, the taste, the glide, the long green dive of freedom already running through him.

*"Look then!"* he cried. "Look you to know—and know your last of Eilathen!"

And crossing his arms upon his breast, so that the ring on his finger burned like a heart afire, he began to spin again. But somehow, as Kim watched, his eyes were locked on hers all the time, even as he whirled, so fast that the lake water began to foam beneath him, and his cold, cold eyes and the bright pain of the red ring he wore were all she knew in the world.

And then he was inside her, deeper than any lover had ever gone, more completely, and Kimberly was given the Tapestry.

She saw the shaping of the worlds, Fionavar at first, then all the others—her own in a fleeting glimpse—following it into time. The gods she saw, and knew their names, and she touched but could not hold, for no mortal can, the purpose and the pattern of the Weaver at the Loom.

And as she was whirled away from that bright vision, she came abruptly face to face with the oldest Dark in his stronghold of Starkadh. In his eyes she felt herself shrivel, felt the thread fray on the Loom; she knew evil for what it was. The live coals of his eyes scorched into her, and the talons of his hands seemed to score her flesh, and within her heart she was forced to sound the uttermost depths of his hate, and she knew him for Rakoth the Unraveller, Rakoth Maugrim, whom the gods themselves feared, he who would rend the Tapestry and lay his own malignant shadow on all of time to come. And flinching away from the vastness of his power, she endured an endless passage of despair.

Ysanne, ashen and helpless, heard her cry out then, a cry torn from the ruin of innocence, and the Seer wept by the shore of her lake. But through it all Eilathen spun, faster than hope or despair, colder than night, the stone over his heart blazing as he whirled like an unleashed wind towards the freedom he had lost.

Kimberly, though, was oblivious to time and place, to lake, rock, Seer, spirit, stone, locked like a spell into the images Eilathen's eyes imposed. She saw Iorweth Founder come from oversea, saw him greet the lios alfar by Sennett Strand, and her heart caught at the beauty of the lios in that vision, and of the tall men the God had called to found the High Kingdom. And then she learned why the Kings of Brennin, all the High Kings from Iorweth to Ailell, were named the Children of Mörnir, for Eilathen showed her the Summer Tree in the Godwood under stars.

The Dalrei she saw next, in a whirling away to the north and west; on the Plain she watched them in pursuit of the glorious eltor, their long hair tied back. The Dwarves delving under Banir Lök and Banir Tal she was shown, and the distant men of wild Eridu beyond their mountains.

Eilathen's eyes carried her south then, across Saeren, and she saw the gardens of Cathal, and the unrivalled splendour of the Lords across the river. The heart of Pendaran she touched, and in a bright vision, bittersweet, she saw Lisen of the Wood meet Amairgen Whitebranch in the grove and bind herself to him, first source to the first mage; and she saw her die by the sea tower, fairest child of all the turning worlds.

Grieving still for that loss, she was taken by Eilathen to see the war—the Great War against Rakoth. Conary she saw, and knew, and Colan his son, the Beloved. She saw the bright, fierce array of the lios, and the shining figure of Ra-Termaine, greatest of the Lords of the lios alfar—and she saw that brilliant company torn apart by wolves and svart alfar, and most terribly of all by the flying creatures older than nightmare unleashed by Maugrim. Then she watched as, coming too late, Conary and Colan were cut off and trapped in their turn by Sennett, and as a red sun went down on a night, Conary would die, she saw, and her heart exploded within her to see, the curved ranks of the Dalrei ride singing out of Daniloth, out of the mist behind Revor into the sunset. She did not know, though Ysanne did, that she was weeping as the Riders and the warriors of Brennin and Cathal, terrible in their fury and their grief, drove the armies of the Dark back north and east through Andarien to Starkadh, where the Lion of Eridu came to join them, and where the blood and smoke cleared at last to show Rakoth beaten to his knees in surrender.

Then she was shown the binding, and knew the Mountain again for the prison it had become, and she watched Ginserat make the stones. Faster then, the images began to fly, and to Ysanne's eyes the speed of Eilathen's turning became as a maelstrom of power, and she knew that she was losing him. The joy of his release she tasted, even amid her own deep ache of loss.

Faster he spun, and faster, the water white beneath his feet, and the Seer watched as the one beside her who was no longer a girl learned what it was to dream true. To be a dreamer of the dream.

And there came a time when Eilathen slowed and stopped.

Kimberly lay sprawled on the rock, drained of all colour, utterly unconscious. The water spirit and the Seer gazed at each other a long time, unspeaking.

At length, Eilathen's voice was heard, high and cold in the moonlight. "I have done. She knows what she is able to know. A great power is in her, but I do not know if she can bear the burden. She is young."

"Not anymore," Ysanne whispered. She found it hard to speak.

"Perhaps not. But it is no care of mine. I have spun for you, Dreamer. Release me from the fire." He was very close, the ice-crystal eyes gleaming with an inhuman light.

The Seer nodded. "I did promise. It was past time. You know why I needed you?" There was an appeal in her voice.

"I do not forgive."

"But you know why?"

Another long silence. Then, "Yes," said Eilathen, and one listening for it might have imagined gentleness in his tone. "I know why you bound me."

Ysanne was crying again, the tears glinting on her lined face. Her back was straight, though, her head high, and the command, when it came, rang clear. "Then go free of me, free of guardianship. Be free of flowerfire, now and evermore. *Laith derendel, sed bannnion. Echorth!*"

And on the last word a sound burst from Eilathen, a high, keening sound beyond joy or release, almost beyond hearing, and the red-stoned ring slid from his finger and fell on the rock at the Seer's feet.

She knelt to gather it and, when she rose, saw through still-falling tears that he had already spun back out over the lake.

"Eilathen!" she cried. "Forgive me if you can. Farewell!"

For reply, his motion only grew faster, wilder somehow than before, untamed, chaotic, and then Eilathen reached the middle of the lake and dived.

But one listening for it—wanting, praying even, to catch it—might have heard, or imagined she heard, just before he disappeared, the sound of her name called out in farewell in a voice cold and free forever.

She sank to her knees cradling Kim, and rocked her upon her lap as one rocks a child.

Holding the girl, gazing out through almost blinded eyes at the empty lake, she did not see the dark-haired, dark-bearded figure that rose from the cover of a sheltering rock behind them. The figure watched long enough to see her take the ring Eilathen had guarded and slip it carefully upon Kimberly's right hand, where it fit her ring finger as perfectly as the Seer had dreamt it would.

After seeing this, the watching figure turned, still unseen, and walked away from them, and there was no trace of a limp in his stride.

---

She was seventeen that spring, not yet accustomed to men calling her beautiful. A pretty child she had been, but adolescence had found her long-limbed and coltish, prone to skinned knees and bruises from rough play in the gardens at Larai Rigal— activities ultimately deemed unfitting for a Princess of the realm. The more so when Marlen died hunting and she became heir to the Ivory Throne in a ceremony she scarcely remembered, so dazed was she by the speed of it and the death of her brother. Her knee was hurting, from a fall the day before, and her father's face had frightened her. There were no falls after that, for the play in the gardens and on the lake of the summer palace came to an end. She learned to school herself in the ways of a decadent court and, in time, to deal not unkindly with the suitors who began to come in such numbers, and she did grow beautiful, the Dark Rose of Cathal, and her name was Sharra, daughter of Shalhassan.

Proud she remained, as were all of her blood, and strong-willed, a quality rare in dissolute Cathal, though not unexpected in her father's daughter. Within her, too, there flickered yet a secret flame of rebelliousness against the demands of position and ritual that trammelled her days and nights.

Even now the flame burned, within beloved Larai Rigal, where the scent of calath and myrrh, of elphinel and alder enveloped her with memories. Memories that fired her with brighter longing than had any of the men who had knelt before her father's throne seeking her hand, with the ritual phrase: "The sun rises in your daughter's eyes." She was young yet, for all her pride.

And it would have been for all of these reasons, the last perhaps more than any of the others, that when the letters had begun to appear in her room—how, she knew not—she kept them secret unto herself; deeply secret, too, she kept the suspicion, burning like a liena in the gardens at night, of who had sent them.

Of desire they spoke, and called her fair in words more strung with fire than any she had ever heard. A longing was in the lines that sang to her, and it awoke within her breast, prisoner that she was in the place she would one day rule, longings of her own: most often she yearned for the simplicity of mornings that were gone, leaving this strangeness in their place, but sometimes, when she was alone at night, for other things. For the letters grew more bold as time went by, and descriptions of desire became promises of what hands and lips might do.

Still, they were unsigned. Finely phrased, elegantly penned, they bespoke nobility, but there never was a name signed at the close. Until the last one came, as spring was spilling calath and anemone all over Larai Rigal. And the name she read at last gave shape and certainty to what she had long guessed and held in her heart as a talisman. *I know something you don't know* was the refrain that had carried her lightly, even kindly, through mornings in the reception chamber, then closely escorted afternoon walks with one suitor or another along the curving pathways and arched bridges of the gardens. Only at night, her ladies at last dismissed, her black hair brushed and falling free, could she take from its hiding place that last letter and read again by candlelight:

> *Bright One,*
>
> *Too long. Even the stars now speak to me of you, and the night wind knows your name. I must come. Death is a dark I seek not to find, but if I must walk within its provinces to touch the flower of your body, then I must. Promise only that should the soldiers of Cathal end my life it will be your hands that close my eyes, and perhaps—too much to ask, I know—your lips that touch my cold ones in farewell.*
>
> *There is a lyren tree near the northern wall of Larai Rigal. Ten nights past the full of the moon there should still be light enough at moonrise for us to find each other.*
> *I will be there. You hold my life as a small thing between the fingers of your hands.*
>
> *Diarmuid dan Ailell*

It was very late. Earlier in the evening it had rained, releasing the scent of elphinel from below her window, but now the clouds had drifted and the waning moon shone into her room. Gently its light touched her face and glinted in the heavy fall of her hair.

It had been full nine nights before.

Which meant that he had somehow crossed Saeren and was hiding somewhere in the dark of the land, and tomorrow . . .

Sharra, daughter of Shalhassan, drew a long breath in the bed where she lay alone, and returned the letter to its secret place. That evening she did not dream of childhood or of childhood games when at length sleep found her, twisting from side to side all night, her hair loose and spread upon the pillows.

***

Venassar of Gath was so young and shy, he made her feel protective. Walking the next moming on the Circle Path, she did most of the talking. In yellow doublet and hose, long-faced and clearly apprehensive, he listened with desperate attentiveness, tilted alarmingly towards her as she named the flowers and trees past which they walked, and told the story of T'Varen and the creation of Larai Rigal. Her voice, pitched low to exclude their retinue, which walked a careful ten paces ahead and behind, gave no hint of how many interminable times she had done this before.

They walked slowly past the cedar from which she had fallen the day her brother died, the day before she had been named heir to the throne. And then, following the curve of the path over the seventh bridge past one of the waterfalls, she saw the giant lyren near the northern wall.

Venassar of Gath, gangling and discomfited, essayed a series of coughs, snorts, and comments in a hapless attempt thereafter to revive a dead conversation. The Princess at his side had withdrawn into a stillness so profound that her beauty seemed to have folded upon itself like a flower, dazzling still, but closed to him. His father, he thought despairingly, was going to flay him.

Taking pity at last, Sharra carefully placed her hand on his arm as they crossed the ninth bridge, completing the Circle, and walked up towards the pavilion where Shalhassan reclined, surrounded by the scented finery of his court. The gesture launched Venassar into a state of petrified automatism, despite the predatory look it elicited from Bragon, his father, who was sitting beside Shalhassan under the waving fans of the servants.

Sharra shivered as Bragon's glance lingered on her and the smile deepened under his dark moustache. It was not the smile of a potential father-in-law. Beneath the silk of her gown, her body recoiled from the hunger in his eyes.

Her father did not smile. He never did.

She made obeisance to him and moved into the shade, where they brought her a glass of m'rae, deeply chilled, and a dish of flavoured ices. When Bragon took his leave, she made sure he saw the coldness in her eyes, and then smiled at Venassar, extending a hand he almost forgot to touch to his forehead. Let the father know, she thought, with no possibility of mistake, why they would not be returning to Larai Rigal. And the anger in her almost showed.

What she wanted, Sharra thought bitterly, even as she smiled, was to climb the cedar again, past the branch that had broken under her, and, reaching the very topmost point, to turn into a falcon that could fly over the shining of the lake and the glory of the gardens all alone.

"A brute, and the son is a callow fool," Shalhassan said, leaning towards her so only the slaves, who didn't matter, could hear.

"They all are," said his daughter, "the one or the other."

The moon, thinning down, had risen late. From her window she could see it surfacing from the eastern arm of the lake. Still, she lingered within her room. It would not do to arrive on time; this man would have to learn that a Princess of Cathal did not scurry to a tryst like a servant girl from Rhoden or some such northern place.

Nonetheless, the pulse under the fine skin of her wrist was beating far too fast. *A small thing between the fingers of your hands,* he had written. Which was true. She could have him taken and garrotted for his effrontery. It might even start a war.

Which, she told herself, was irresponsible. Shalhassan's daughter would greet this man with the courtesy due his rank and the secrecy the passion in him deserved of her. He had come a long way through very great peril to see her. He would have gracious words to carry back north from the gardens of Cathal. But no more. Presumption such as his had a price, and this, Diarmuid of Brennin would learn. And, she thought, it would be well if he told her how he had crossed Saeren. It was a thing of no small importance to the land she would one day rule.

Her breathing seemed to be under control; the race of her pulse had slowed. The image of the solitary falcon in her mind fell away as on a down drift of wind. It was the heiress of Cathal, well schooled in duty and obligation, who descended, careful of her skirt, down the easy branches of the tree outside her balcony.

The lienae glowed, flying through the dark. About her were woven the deep, disturbing night scents of the flowers. She walked under starlight and the crescent illumination of the moon, sure of her way, for the walled gardens, for all their miles, were her oldest home and she knew every step of all the paths. A night walk such as this, though, was a vanished pleasure, and she would be severely chastised if discovered. And her servants would be flogged.

No matter. She would not be discovered. The palace guard patrolled the outer perimeter of the walls with their lanterns. The gardens were another world. Where she walked, the only lights were those of moon and stars, and the hovering, elusive lienae. She heard the soft chirring of insects and the plashing of the sculpted waterfalls. There was a breath of wind in the leaves, and somewhere, too, in these gardens there was now a man who had written to her of what lips and hands might do.

She slowed a little on the thought, crossing the fourth bridge, the Ravelle, hearing the gentle sound of tamed water over coloured stone. No one, she realized, knew where she was. And she knew nothing beyond rumour, which did not reassure, of the man who was waiting in the dark.

But courage was not lacking in her heart, though it might be foolhardy and unwise. Sharra, dressed in azure and gold, one lapis lazuli pendant hanging between her breasts, came over the bridge and past the curving of the path and saw the lyren tree.

There was no one there.

She had never doubted he would be waiting—which, given the hazards that had lain in his path, was absurd. A besotted romantic might somehow bribe a servant of hers to plant letters, might promise an impossible tryst, but a Prince of Brennin, the heir even, since his brother's exile, would not dice his life away on a folly such as this, for a woman he'd never seen.

Saddened, and angry with herself for feeling so, she walked the last few steps and stood under the golden branches of the lyren. Her long fingers, smooth finally, after years of abuse, reached out to caress the bark of the trunk.

"If you weren't in a skirt, you might join me up here, but I don't imagine a Princess can climb trees anyhow. Shall I come down?" The voice came from directly above her. She checked a sudden motion and refused to look up.

"I've climbed every climbable tree in these gardens," she said evenly, over the acceleration of her heart, "including this one. And often in skirts. I do not care to do so now. If you are Diarmuid of Brennin, then come down."

"And if I'm not?" The tone, for a supposedly infatuated lover, was far too mocking, she thought, and she didn't answer. Nor did he wait. There was a rustle in the leaves above, then a thump beside her on the ground.

And then two hands took one of hers quite comprehensively, and brought it not to his forehead but to his lips. Which was all right, though he should have knelt. What was not all right was that he should turn the hand over to kiss her palm and wrist.

She snatched her hand away, horribly aware of the pounding of her heart. She still hadn't even seen him clearly.

As if reading the thought, he moved out of shadow, to where the moonlight could find his bright, tousled hair. And he did drop to a knee then—letting the light fall like benediction on his face.

And so she did see, finally. The eyes, wide-set and deep, were very blue under long, almost feminine lashes. The mouth was wide as well, too much so, and there was no softness in it, or in the lines of the beardless chin.

He smiled, though, and not mockingly. And she realized that from where he knelt she, too, was in the light to be seen.

"Well—" she began.

"Fools," said Diarmuid dan Ailell. "They all told me you were beautiful. Said it sixteen different ways."

"And?" She stiffened, anger ready as a lash.

"And, by Lisen's eyes, you are. But no one ever told me there was cleverness in you. I should have known. Shalhassan's heir would have to have subtlety."

She was completely unprepared. No one had ever said this. Off balance, she fleetingly remembered all her Venassars, so effortlessly handled.

"Forgive me," this man said, rising to stand beside her, very close. "I didn't know. I was expecting to deal with a very young woman—which you are not, not in the ways that matter. Shall we walk? Will you show me your gardens?"

And so she found herself in stride with him on the northern perimeter of the Circle Path, and it seemed foolish and young to protest when he took her arm. A question, however, insinuated itself as they moved in the scented darkness, haloed by the lienae flying all about them.

"If you thought me so simple, how could you write me as you did?" she asked, and felt her heartbeat slow again, as a measure of control came back to her in his silence. Not so easily, my friend, she thought.

"I am," said Diarmuid quite calmly, "somewhat helpless before beauty. Word of yours reached me some time ago. You are more than I was told you were."

A neat enough answer, for a northerner. Even honey-tongued Galienth might have approved. But it was well within her ability to compass. So although he was handsome and disturbing in the shadows beside her, and his fingers on her arm kept shifting very slightly, and once brushed the edge of her breast, Sharra now felt secure. If there was a twist of regret, another downward arc of the mind's falcon, she paid it no attention.

"T'Varen laid out Larai Rigal in the time of my great-grandfather, Thallason, whom you have cause to remember in the north. The gardens cover many miles, and are walled in their entirety, including the lake, which . . ." And so she went on, as she had for all the Venassars, and though it was night now, and the man beside her had a hand on her arm, it really wasn't so very different after all. I might kiss him, she thought. On the cheek, as goodbye.

They had taken the Crossing Path at the Faille Bridge, and began curving back north. The moon was well clear of the trees now, riding high in a sky laced with windblown clouds. The breeze off the lake was pleasant and not too chilly. She continued to talk, easily still, but increasingly aware of his silence. Of that, and of the hand on her arm, which had tightened and had grazed her breast again as they passed one of the waterfalls.

"There is a bridge for each of the nine provinces," she said, "and the flowers in each part of—"

"Enough!" said Diarmuid harshly. She froze in midsentence. He stopped walking and turned to face her on the path. There was a calath bush behind her. She had hidden there, playing, as a child.

He had released her arm when he spoke. Now, after a long, cold glance at her, he turned and began walking again. She moved quickly to keep up.

When he addressed her, it was while staring straight ahead, his voice low and intense. "You are speaking like someone scarcely a person. If you want to play gracious Princess with the petty lordlings who mince about, courting you, it is none of my affair, but—"

"The lords of Cathal are not petty, sir! They—"

"Do not, please, insult us both! That emasculated whipping-boy this afternoon? His father? I would take great pleasure in killing Bragon. They are worse than petty, all of them. And if you speak to me as you do to them, you cheapen both of us unbearably."

They had reached the lyren again. Somewhere within her a bird was stirring. She moved ruthlessly to curb it, as she had to.

"My lord Prince, I must say I am surprised. You can hardly expect less formal conversation, in this, our first—"

"But I *do* expect it! I expect to see and hear the woman. Who was a girl who climbed all the trees in this garden. The Princess in her role bores me, hurts me. Demeans tonight."

"And what is tonight?" she asked, and bit her lip as soon as she spoke.

"Ours," he said.

And his arms were around her waist in the shadows of the lyren, and his mouth, descending, was upon her own. His head blocked the moon, but her eyes had closed by then anyway. And then the wide mouth on hers was moving, and his tongue—

"*No!*" She broke away violently, and almost fell. They faced each other a few feet apart. Her heart was a mad, beating, winged thing she had to control. Had to. She was Sharra, daughter of—

"Dark Rose," he said, his voice unsteady. He took a step towards her.

"No!" Her hands were up to ward him.

Diarmuid stopped. Looked at her trembling figure. "What do you fear in me?" he asked.

Breathing was difficult. She was conscious of her breasts, of the wind about her, the nearness of him, and of a dark warmth at her centre, where—

"How did you cross the river?" she blurted out.

She expected mockery again. It would have helped. His gaze was steady, though, and he stayed absolutely motionless.

"I used a mage's arrow and a rope," he said. "I crossed hand over hand above the water and climbed a ladder cut into the cliff several hundred years ago. I give you this as between you and me. You will not tell?"

She was Princess of Cathal. "I make no such promise, for I cannot. I will not betray you now in any way, but secrets endangering my people—"

"And what do you think I did in telling you? Am I not heir to a throne, just as you are?"

She shook her head. Some voice within was wildly telling her to run, but instead she spoke, as carefully as she could. "You must not think, my lord Prince, to win a daughter of Shalhassan, merely by coming here and—"

"Sharra!" he cried, speaking her name for the first time, so that it rang in the night air like a bell tolling pain. "Listen to yourself! It is not just—"

And they both heard it then.

The jangling clink of armour as the palace guard moved up on the other side of the wall.

"What was that?" a gravelly voice exclaimed, and she knew it for Devorsh, Captain of the Guard. There was a murmured reply. Then, "No, I heard voices. Two of you go have a look inside. Take the dogs!"

The sound of armoured men walking off jarred the night.

Somehow they were together under the tree. She laid a hand on his arm.

"If they find you, they will kill you, so you had better go."

Incredibly, his gaze on hers, close and above, was undisturbed. "If they find me, they kill me," said Diarmuid. "If they can. Perhaps you will close my eyes, as I once asked." The expression changed then, the voice roughened. "But I will not leave you now willingly, though all of Cathal come calling for my blood."

And gods, gods, all the gods, his mouth on hers was so very sweet, the touch of his hands blindingly sure. His fingers were busy at the fastenings of her bodice, and dear Goddess, her own hands were behind his head, pulling him down to her, her tongue sought his in hunger long denied. Her breasts, suddenly released, strained towards his touch, and there was an ache in her, a burning, something wild being set free as he laid her down on the deep grass and his fingers touched her here, and here, and her clothes were gone from about her, and his from him as well. And then his body along hers was all the night and garden, all the worlds, and in her mind she saw the shadow of a falcon, wings beating wide, fly across the face of the high moon.

*"Sharra!"*

From where they were, outside the walls, they heard the name cried out within the gardens. "What was that?" one of them exclaimed. "I heard voices. Two of you go have a look inside. Take the dogs!"

Two men moved quickly to obey the sharp command, jogging urgently in the direction of the western gate.

But only for a few jangling strides. After that, Kevin and Coll stopped running and looped silently back to the concealing hollow where the others lay. Erron, whose disguised voice had barked the order, was already there. The soldiers of Cathal were, at that moment, flanked ten minutes' walk away on either side. The timing and the plan were Diarmuid's, worked out as they lay watching and listening to the patrol in the early evening.

Now they had nothing more to do but wait for him. They settled quietly into the dark hollow. A few slept, using the time to advantage, for they would be running back north as soon as the Prince rejoined them. There was no talk. Too wound up to rest properly, Kevin lay on his back and watched the slow transit of the moon. Several times they heard the guards cross and cross again in their circuit of the walls. They waited. The moon reached its zenith and began to slide west against the backdrop of summer stars.

Carde saw him first, a black-clad, bright-haired figure on the top of the wall. Quickly Carde checked right and left for the patrol, but the timing, again, was flawless, and rising briefly to be seen, he gave a thumbs-up sign.

Seeing it, Diarmuid leaped, rolled once, and was up running lightly and low to the ground. When he dropped into the hollow beside them, Kevin saw that he was carrying a flower. Hair dishevelled, doublet loose and half unbuttoned, the Prince's eyes flashed with an intoxicated hilarity.

"Done!" he said, raising the flower in salute to all of them. "I've plucked the fairest rose in Shalhassan's garden."

# CHAPTER 7

"He will be found, I promise it." So he had said. A rash promise, and uncharacteristic, but it had been made.

So at about the time Paul and Kevin began their ride south with Diarmuid, Loren Silvercloak was galloping north and east alone in search of Dave Martyniuk.

It was rare for the mage to be solitary—alone, he was stripped of his powers—but he'd needed Matt to stay in the palace, the more so since word had come of the dead svart in the garden. It was a bad time to be away, but his choices were limited, and so, too, were the people he could trust.

So north he rode, gradually curving eastward through the grain land amid the dry crackle of the ruinous summer. All that day and the next he travelled, and not slowly, for a sense of urgency was strong within him. He paused only to ask discreet questions in the farmyards and half-empty towns through which he passed, and to note again, and despairingly, the impact of famine on those to whom he spoke.

There was no word, though. No one had seen the tall dark-haired stranger or heard tell of him. So on the third morning Loren mounted early from where he'd passed the night in a copse of trees to the west of Lake Leinan. Looking eastward he could see the sun rising from the line of hills past the lake and he knew Dun Maura lay beyond. Even by daylight, with a blue sky above, there was for the mage a darkness about that place.

There was no love lost between the Mormae of Gwen Ystrat and the mages who had followed Amairgen's lead out from the dominion of the Mother. Blood magic, thought Loren, shaking his head, picturing Dun Maura and the rites of Liadon enacted every year before Conary came and forbade them. He thought of the flowers strewn by the maidens chanting his death and return as the spring: *Rahod hedai Liadon*. In every world, the mage knew, but his very soul rebelled against the darkness of this power. Grimly he turned his horse away from the country of the Priestesses and continued north, following the Latham on the long ride to the Plain.

He would ask aid of the Dalrei, as he had so often done before. If Dave Martyniuk was somewhere among the great spaces of the Plain, only the Riders could find him.

So north he rode, a tall, grey, bearded figure no longer young, alone on a horse in the wide sweep of the level lands, and the baked earth resonated beneath him like a drum.

He was hoping, even though it was summer, to find a tribe of the Riders in the south Plain, for if he could speak to even one tribe then word would be sent to Celidon, and once his message was lodged at the mid-Plain, then soon all the Dalrei would know, and the Dalrei he trusted.

It was a long ride, though, and there were no villages now among the broad grazing lands in which he could take food or rest. And so he was still galloping alone as that third day drew towards sundown and then dark. His shadow lay long on the earth beside him, and the river had become a glimmering, muted presence to the east, when the urgency that had lain within him since he had left Paras Derval exploded into terror.

Grappling at the reins, he brought his mount to a rearing halt, then held it rigidly still. One moment he remained so, his face drawn suddenly tight with fear, then Loren Silvercloak cried aloud in the onrushing night and wheeled his horse hard to ride in the dark, back, back towards Paras Derval, where something overwhelming was about to happen.

Drumming furiously home under the stars, he gathered his mind and hurled a desperate warning southward over all the empty leagues that lay between. He was too far away, though, much too far away, and without his power. He urged his horse faster, driving like wind in the darkness, but he knew, even as he did so, that he was going to be too late.

⤙≡◯⊜⤚

Jennifer was not happy. Not only was Dave missing, not only had Kevin and Paul ridden off that morning on some crazy expedition with Diarmuid, but now Kim had left as well, with Matt guiding her to the home of the old woman whom people in the Great Hall the day before had called a witch.

Which left her in a large room on the cooler west side of the palace, sitting in a low window seat, surrounded by a gaggle of court ladies whose principal yearning in life seemed to be to elicit all they could from her about Kevin Laine and Paul Schafer, with special and explicit focus on their sexual predilections.

Parrying the questions as best she could, she barely managed to conceal a growing irritation. On the far side of the room, a man was playing a stringed instrument under a tapestry depicting a scene of battle. There was a dragon flying over the conflict. She hoped profoundly that it was a mythical confrontation.

The ladies had all been briefly presented to her, but only two names had registered. Laesha was the very young, brown-eyed lady-in-waiting who seemed to have been assigned to her. She was quiet, which was a blessing. The other was the Lady Rheva, a striking, dark-haired woman who clearly enjoyed a higher status than the others, and to whom Jennifer had taken an effortless dislike.

Nor was this in any degree lessened when it became clear, because Rheva made it clear, that she'd spent the night before with Kevin. It was evidently a triumph in a continuing game of one-upmanship, and Rheva was exploiting it for all it was worth. It was aggravating in the extreme, and Jennifer, abandoned, was in no mood to be aggravated.

So when another of the women gave a sulky toss of her hair and inquired whether Jennifer had any idea why Paul Schafer had been so indifferent to her—"Does he, perhaps, prefer to spend his nights with boys?" she asked, with a barb of malice—Jennifer's brief laugh was entirely humourless.

"There are more obvious possibilities, I should think," she replied, aware that she was making an enemy. "Paul is somewhat discriminating, that's all."

There was a brief silence. Someone tittered. Then:

"Are you suggesting, by any chance, that Kevin is not?" It was Rheva, and her voice had gone very soft.

Jennifer could handle this. What she could not handle was having it continue. She rose abruptly from the window seat and, looking down on the other woman, smiled.

"No," she said, judiciously. "Knowing Kevin, I wouldn't say that at all. The trick, though, is to get him twice." And she moved past them all and out the door.

Walking swiftly down the corridor, she made a very firm mental note to inform Kevin Laine that if he took a certain court lady to bed once more, she would never speak to him again as long as she lived.

At the doorway to her room, she heard her name being called. Her long skirt trailing the stone floor, Laesha came hurrying up. Jennifer eyed her inimically, but the other woman was laughing breathlessly.

"Oh, my," she gasped, laying a hand on Jennifer's arm, "that was wonderful! The cats in that room are spitting with anger! Rheva hasn't been handled like that for years."

Jennifer shook her head ruefully. "I don't imagine they'll be very friendly the rest of the time I'm here."

"They wouldn't have been anyway. You are much too beautiful. On top of your being new, it's guaranteed to make them hate you for existing. And when Diarmuid put out word yesterday that you were reserved for him, they—"

"He *what?*" Jennifer exploded.

Laesha eyed her carefully. "Well, he is the Prince, and so—"

"I don't care who he is! I have no intention of letting him touch me. Who do they think we are?"

Laesha's expression had altered a little. "You mean that?" she asked hesitantly. "You don't want him?"

"Not at all," said Jennifer. "Should I?"

"I do," said Laesha simply, and flushed to the roots of her brown hair.

There was an awkward silence. Speaking carefully, Jennifer broke it. "I am only here two weeks," she said. "I will not take him from you or anyone else. I need a friend right now, more than anything else."

Laesha's eyes were wide. She took a short breath.

"Why do you think I followed you?"

This time they shared the smile.

"Tell me," Jennifer asked after a moment. "Is there any reason we have to stay in here? I haven't been outside at all. Can we see the town?"

"Of course," said Laesha. "Of course we can. We haven't been at war for years."

***

Despite the heat, it was better outside the palace. Dressed in an outfit much like Laesha's, Jennifer realized that no one knew she was a stranger. Feeling freed by that, she found herself strolling at ease beside her new friend. After a short while, though, she became aware that a man was following them through the dusty, twisting streets of the town. Laesha noticed it, too.

"He's one of Diarmuid's," she whispered.

Which was a nuisance, but before he had left in the morning, Kevin had told her about the dead svart alfar in the garden, and Jennifer had decided that for once she wasn't about to object to having someone watch over her. Her father, she thought wryly, would find it amusing.

The two women walked along a street where a blacksmith's iron rang upon anvils. Overhead, balconies of second-floor houses leaned out over the narrow roadway, blocking the sunlight at intervals. Turning left at a crossing of lanes, Laesha led her past an open area where the noise and the smell of food announced a market. Slowing to look, Jennifer saw that even in a time of festival there didn't seem to be much produce on display. Following her glance, Laesha shook her head slightly and continued up a narrow alleyway, pausing at length outside a shop door through which could be seen bales and bolts of cloth. Laesha, it seemed, wanted a new pair of gloves.

While her friend went inside, Jennifer moved on a few steps, drawn by the sound of children's laughter. Reaching the end of the cobbled lane, she saw that it ran into a wide square with a grassy area, more brown than green, in the centre. And upon the grass, fifteen or twenty children were playing some sort of counting game. Smiling faintly, Jennifer stopped to watch.

The children were gathered in a loose circle about the slim figure of a girl. Most of them were laughing, but the girl in the centre was not. She gestured suddenly, and a boy came forward from the ring with a strip of cloth and, with a gravity that matched her own, began to bind it over her eyes. That done, he rejoined the ring. At his nod the children linked hands and began to revolve, in a silence eerie after the laughter, around the motionless figure blindfolded in the centre. They moved gravely and with dignity. A few other people had stopped to watch.

Then, without warning, the blindfolded girl raised an arm and pointed it towards the moving ring. Her high clear voice rang out over the green:

*When the wandering fire*
*Strikes the heart of stone*
*Will you follow?*

And on the last word the circling stopped.

The girl's finger was levelled directly at a stocky boy, who, without any hesitation, released the hands on either side of him and walked into the ring. The circle closed itself and began moving again, still in silence.

"I never tire of watching this," a cool voice said from just behind Jennifer.

She turned quickly. To confront a pair of icy green eyes and the long red hair of the High Priestess, Jaelle. Behind the Priestess she could see a group of her grey-clad attendants, and out of the corner of her eye, she noticed Diarmuid's man edging nervously closer to them.

Jennifer nodded a greeting, then turned back to watch the children. Jaelle stepped forward to stand beside her, her white robe brushing the cobblestones of the street.

"The ta'kiena is as old as any ritual we have," she murmured in Jennifer's ear. "Look at the people watching."

And indeed, although the faces of the children seemed almost unnaturally serene, the adults who had gathered at the edge of the square or in shop archways wore expressions of wonder and apprehension. And there were more people gathering. Again the girl in the ring raised her arm.

> *When the wandering fire*
> *Strikes the heart of stone*
> *Will you follow?*
> *Will you leave your home?*

And again the circling stopped on the last word. This time the extended finger pointed to another of the boys, older and lankier than the first. With only a brief, almost ironic pause, he, too, released the hands he was holding and walked forward to stand by the other chosen one. A murmur rose from the watchers, but the children, seemingly oblivious, were circling again.

Unsettled, Jennifer turned to the impassive profile of the Priestess. "What is it?" she asked. "What are they doing?"

Jaelle smiled thinly. "It is a dance of prophecy. Their fate lies in when they are called."

"But what—"

"Watch!"

The blindfolded girl, standing straight and tall, was chanting again:

> *When the wandering fire*
> *Strikes the heart of stone*
> *Will you follow?*
> *Will you leave your home?*
> *Will you leave your life?*

This time, when the voice and the dancing stopped together, a deep sound of protest ran through the watching crowd. For the one chosen now was one of the youngest girls. With a toss of her honey-coloured hair and a cheerful smile, she stepped into the ring beside the two boys. The taller one placed an arm around her shoulders.

Jennifer turned to Jaelle. "What does it mean?" she asked. "What kind of prophecy . . . ?" The question trailed off.

Beside her the Priestess was silent. There was no gentleness in the lines of her face, nor compassion in her eyes as she watched the children begin to move again. "You ask what it means," she said at length. "Not much in these soft times, when the ta'kiena is only another game. That last one they now say means only that she will leave the life her family has led." Her expression was unreadable, but an irony in the tone reached Jennifer.

"What was it before?" she asked.

This time Jaelle did turn to look at her. "The dance has been done by children for longer than anyone can remember. In harsher days that call meant death, of course. Which would be a pity. She's an attractive child, isn't she?"

There was a malicious amusement in the voice. "Watch closely," Jaelle continued. "This last one they truly fear, even now." And indeed, the people around and behind them had grown suddenly quiet with strained anticipation. In the stillness Jennifer could hear the sounds of laughter from the market, several streets over. It seemed farther than that.

In the circle on the green, the blindfolded girl raised her arm and began the chant for the final time:

> When the wandering fire
> Strikes the heart of stone
> Will you follow?
> Will you leave your home?
> Will you leave your life?
> Will you take . . . the Longest Road?

The dancing stopped.

Her heart pounding inexplicably, Jennifer saw that the slim finger was pointing unerringly at the boy who had carried the blindfold. Raising his head, as if hearing some far-off music, the boy stepped forward. The girl removed her blindfold. They regarded each other a long moment, then the boy turned, laid a hand, as if in benediction, on the other chosen ones, and walked alone from the green.

Jaelle, watching him go, wore a troubled expression for the first time. Glancing at her unguarded features, Jennifer realized with a start how young the woman beside her was. About to speak, she was checked by the sound of crying, and, turning her head, she saw a woman standing in the doorway of a shop behind them in the lane; there were tears pouring down her face.

Jaelle followed Jennifer's glance. "His mother," the Priestess said softly.

Feeling utterly helpless, Jennifer had an instinctive longing to offer comfort to the woman. Their eyes met, and on the face of the other woman Jennifer saw, with an aching twist of new understanding, a distillation of all a mother's sleepless nights. A message, a recognition, seemed to pass for an instant between the two of them, then the mother of the boy chosen for the Longest Road turned her head away and went into her shop.

Jennifer, struggling with something unexpected, finally asked Jaelle, "Why is she hurting so much?"

The Priestess, too, was a little subdued. "It is difficult," she said, "and not a thing I understand yet, but they have done the dance twice before this summer, I am told, and both times Finn was chosen for the Road. This is the third, and in Gwen Ystrat we are taught that three times touches destiny."

Jennifer's expression drew a smile from the Priestess. "Come," she said. "We can talk at the Temple." Her tone was, if not exactly friendly, at least milder than hitherto.

On the verge of accepting, Jennifer was stopped by a cough behind her.

She turned. Diarmuid's man had moved up to them, sharp concern creasing his face. "My lady," he said, acutely embarrassed, "forgive me, but might I speak with you in private for a moment."

"You fear me, Drance?" Jaelle's voice was like a knife again. She laughed. "Or should I say your master does? Your absent master."

The stocky soldier flushed, but held his ground. "I have been ordered to watch over her," he said tersely.

Jennifer looked from one to the other. There was suddenly an electric hostility shimmering in the air. She felt disoriented, understanding none of it.

"Well," she said to Drance, trying to pick her way, "I don't want to get you in trouble—why don't you just come with us?"

Jaelle threw her head back and laughed again, to see the man's terrified recoil. "Yes, Drance," she said, her tone coruscating, "why *don't* you come to the Temple of the Mother with us?"

"My lady," Drance stammered, appealing to Jennifer. "Please, I dare not do that . . . but I must guard you. You must not go there."

"Ah!" said Jaelle, her eyebrows arched maliciously. "It seems that the men here are already saying what you can or cannot do. Forgive me my invitation. I thought I was dealing with a free visitor."

Jennifer was not oblivious to the manipulation, and she remembered Kevin's words that morning as well: "There's some danger here," he'd said soberly. "Trust Diarmuid's men, and Matt, of course. Paul says be careful of the Priestess. Don't go anywhere on your own."

In the dawn shadows of the palace, it had made a good deal of sense, but now, in bright afternoon sunlight, the whole thing was rankling just a little. Who was Kevin, making his way through the court ladies, then galloping off with the Prince, to tell her to sit tight like a dutiful little girl? And now this man of Diarmuid's . . .

About to speak, she remembered something else. She turned to Jaelle. "There seems to be some real concern for our safety here. I would like to place myself under

93

your protection while I visit your Temple. Will you name me a guest-friend before I go?"

A frown flicked across Jaelle's face, but it was chased away by a slow smile, and there was triumph in her eyes.

"Of course," she said sweetly. "Of course I will." She raised her voice so that her words rang out over the street, and people turned to look. Lifting her arms wide, fingers spread, she intoned, "In the name of Gwen Ystrat and the Mormae of the Mother, I name you guest of the Goddess. You are welcome in our sanctuaries, and your well-being shall be my own concern."

Jennifer looked to Drance, questioningly. His expression was not reassuring; if possible, he appeared even more consternated than before. Jennifer had no idea if she'd done right or wrong, or even of exactly what she'd done, but she was tired of standing in the middle of the street with everyone watching her.

"Thank you," she said to Jaelle. "In that case, I will come with you. If you like," she added, turning to Drance, and to Laesha, who had just scurried up, her new gloves in hand and an apprehensive look in her eye, "you can both wait outside for me."

"Come, then," said Jaelle, and smiled.

It was a low-set building, and even the central dome seemed too close to the ground, until Jennifer realized, as she passed through the arched entrance, that most of it was underground.

The Temple of the Mother Goddess lay east of the town on the palace hill. A narrow pathway wound its way further up the hill, leading to a gate in the walls surrounding the palace gardens. There were trees lining the path. They seemed to be dying.

Once they were inside the sanctuary, the grey-robed attendants melted away into shadow as Jaelle led Jennifer forward through another arch. It brought them into the room under the dome. At the far side of the sunken chamber Jennifer saw a great black altar stone. Behind it, resting in a carved block of wood, stood a double axe, each face ground into the shape of a crescent moon, one waxing, one waning.

There was nothing else.

Inexplicably, Jennifer felt her mouth go dry. Looking at the axe with its wickedly sharpened blades, she fought to repress a shudder.

"Do not fight it," Jaelle said, her voice echoing in the empty chamber. "It is your power. Ours. So it was once, and will be again. In our time, if she should find us worthy."

Jennifer stared at her. The flame-haired High Priestess in her sanctuary seemed more keenly beautiful than ever. Her eyes gleamed with an intensity that was the more disturbing because of how cold it was. Power and pride, it spoke; nothing of tenderness, and no more of her youth. Glancing at Jaelle's long fingers, Jennifer wondered if they had ever gripped that axe, had ever brought it sweeping down upon the altar, down upon—

And then she realized that she was in a place of sacrifice.

Jaelle turned without haste. "I wanted you to see this," she said. "Now come. My chambers are cool, we can drink and talk." She adjusted the collar of her robe with a graceful hand and led the way from the room. As they left, a breeze seemed to slide through the chamber, and Jennifer thought she saw the axe sway gently in its rest.

"And so," the Priestess said, as they reclined on cushions on the floor in her room, "your so-called companions have abandoned you for their own pleasures." It was not a question.

Jennifer blinked. "Hardly fair," she began, wondering how the other woman knew. "You might say I've left them to come here." She tried a smile.

"You might," Jaelle agreed pleasantly, "but it would be untrue. The two men left at dawn with the princeling, and your friend has run off to the hag by the lake." Midway through the sentence, her voice had dipped itself into acid, leading Jennifer to realize abruptly that she was under attack in this room.

She parried, to get her balance. "Kim's with the Seer, yes. Why do you call her a hag?"

Jaelle was no longer so pleasant. "I am not used to explaining myself," she said.

"Neither am I," replied Jennifer quickly. "Which may limit this conversation somewhat." She leaned back on the cushions and regarded the other woman.

Jaelle's reply, when it came, was harsh with emotion. "She is a traitor."

"Well, that's not the same as a hag, you know," Jennifer said, aware that she was arguing like Kevin. "A traitor to the King, you mean? I wouldn't have thought you'd care, and yesterday—"

Jaelle's bitter laugh stopped her. "No, not to the old fool!" She took a breath. "The woman you call Ysanne was the youngest person ever to be named to the Mormae of the Goddess in Gwen Ystrat. She left. She broke an oath when she left. She betrayed her power."

"She betrayed you personally, you mean," Jennifer said, staying on the offensive.

"Don't be a fool! I wasn't even alive."

"No? You seem pretty upset about it, though. Why did she leave?"

"For no reason that could suffice. *Nothing* could suffice."

The clues were all there. "She left for a man, then, I take it," Jennifer said.

The ensuing silence was her answer. At length Jaelle spoke again, her voice bitter, cold. "She sold herself for a body at night. May the hag die soon and lie lost forever."

Jennifer swallowed. A point-scoring exchange had suddenly been turned into something else. "Not very forgiving, are you?" she managed.

"Not at all," Jaelle replied swiftly. "You would do well to remember it. Why did Loren leave for the north this morning?"

"I don't know," Jennifer stammered, shocked by the naked threat.

"You don't? A strange thing to do, is it not? To bring guests to the palace, then ride off alone. Leaving Matt behind, which is *very* strange. I wonder," said Jaelle. "I wonder who he was looking for? How many of you really did cross?"

It was too sudden, too shrewd. Jennifer, heart pounding, was aware that she had flushed.

"You look warm," Jaelle said, all solicitude. "Do have some wine." She poured from a long-necked silver decanter. "Really," she continued, "it is most uncharacteristic of Loren to abandon guests so suddenly."

"I wouldn't know," Jennifer said. "There are four of us. None of us knows him very well. The wine is excellent."

"It is from Morvran. I am glad you like it. I could swear Metran asked him to bring five of you."

So Loren had been wrong. Someone did know. Someone knew a great deal indeed.

"Who is Metran?" Jennifer asked disingenuously. "Was he the old man you frightened so much yesterday?"

Balked, Jaelle leaned back on her own cushions. In the silence Jennifer sipped her wine, pleased to see that her hand was steady.

"You trust him, don't you?" the Priestess said bitterly. "He has warned you against me. They all have. Silvercloak angles for power here as much as anyone, but you have aligned yourself with the men, it seems. Tell me, which of them is your lover, or has Diarmuid found your bed yet?"

Which was quite sufficient, thank you.

Jennifer shot to her feet. Her wine glass spilled; she ignored it. "Is this how you treat a guest?" she burst out. "I came here in good faith—what right have you to say such things to me? I'm not aligned with *anyone* in your stupid power games. I'm only here for a few days—do you think I care who wins your little battles? I'll tell you one thing, though," she went on, breathing hard, "I'm not happy about male control in my world, either, but I've never in my life met anyone as screwed up on the subject as you are. If Ysanne fell in love—well, I doubt you can even *guess* what that feels like!"

White and rigid, Jaelle looked up at her, then rose in her turn. "You may be right," she said softly, "but something tells me that you have no idea what it feels like, either. Which gives us a thing in common, doesn't it?"

Back in her room a short while later, Jennifer closed the door on Laesha and Drance and cried about that for a long time.

The day crawled forward webbed in heat. A dry, unsettling wind rose in the north and slid through the High Kingdom, stirring the dust in the streets of Paras Derval like an uneasy ghost. The sun, westering at the end of day, shone red. Only at twilight was there any relief, as the wind shifted to the west, and the first stars came out in the sky over Brennin.

Very late that night, north and west of the capital, the breeze stirred the waters of a lake to muted murmuring. On a wide rock by the shore, under the lacework of the stars, an old woman knelt, cradling the slight form of a younger one, on whose finger a red ring shone with a muted glimmering.

After a long time, Ysanne rose and called for Tyrth. Limping, he came from the cottage and, picking up the unconscious girl, walked back and laid her down in the bed he'd made that afternoon.

She remained unconscious for the rest of the night and all the next day. Ysanne did not sleep, but watched her through the hours of darkness, and then in the searing brightness of the following day, and on the face of the old Seer was an expression only one man, long dead, would have recognized.

Kimberly woke at sunset. Away to the south in that moment, Kevin and Paul were taking up their positions with Diarmuid's men outside the walls of Larai Rigal.

For a moment, Kim was completely disoriented, then the Seer watched as a brutal surge of knowledge came flooding into the grey eyes. Lifting her head, Kim gazed at the old woman. Outside, Tyrth could be heard shutting up the animals for the night. The cat lay on the window sill in the last of the evening light.

"Welcome back," said Ysanne.

Kim smiled; it took an effort. "I went so far." She shook her head wonderingly, then her mouth tightened at another recollection. "Eilathen has gone?"

"Yes."

"I saw him dive. I saw where he went, into the green far down. It is very beautiful there."

"I know," said the Seer.

Again, Kim drew breath before speaking. "Was it hard for you to watch?"

At that, Ysanne looked away for the first time. Then, "Yes," she said. "Yes, it was hard. Remembering."

Kim's hand slipped from the coverlet and covered that of the old woman. When Ysanne spoke again, it was very low. "Raederth was First of the Mages before Ailell was King. He came one day to Morvran, on the shores of Lake Leinan. . . . You know what lies in Gwen Ystrat?"

"I know," said Kimberly. "I saw Dun Maura."

"He came to the Temple by the lake, and stayed there a night, which was brave, for there is no love in that place for any of the mages since Amairgen's day. Raederth was a brave man, though."

"He saw me there," Ysanne continued. "I was seventeen and newly chosen to be of the Mormae—the inner circle—and no one so young had ever been chosen before. But Raederth saw me that night, and he marked me for something else."

"As you did me?"

"As I did you. He knew me for a Seer, and he took me away from the Mother and changed my fate, or found it for me."

"And you loved him?"

"Yes," Ysanne said simply. "From the first, and I miss him still, though all the years have run away from us. He brought me here at midsummer, more than fifty years ago, and summoned Eilathen with the flowerfire, and the spirit spun for me as he did for you last night."

"And Raederth?" Kim asked, after a moment.

"He died three years after of an arrow ordered by Garmisch, the High King," Ysanne said flatly. "When Raederth was slain, Duke Ailell rose in Rhoden and began the war that broke the rule of Garmisch and the Garantae and took him to the throne."

Kimberly nodded again. "I saw that, too. I saw him kill the King before the palace gate. He was brave and tall, Ailell."

"And wise. A wise King, all his days. He wedded Marrien of the Garantae, and named Metran, her cousin, First Mage to follow Raederth, which angered me then and I told him so. But Ailell was trying to knit a sundered kingdom, and he did. He deserved more love than he has had."

"He had yours."

"Late," Ysanne said, "and grudgingly. And only as King. I tried to help him, though, with his burden, and in return he found ways to ensure that I would be left alone here."

"A long time alone," Kim said softly.

"We all have our tasks," the Seer said. There was a silence. In the barn out back, a cow lowed plaintively. Kim heard the click of a gate being shut, then Tyrth's uneven steps crossing the yard. She met Ysanne's gaze, a half-smile tugging at her mouth.

"You told me one lie yesterday," she said.

Ysanne nodded. "I did. One. It was not my truth to tell."

"I know," said Kim. "You have carried a great deal alone. I am here now, though; do you want me to share your burden?" Her mouth crooked. "I seem to be a chalice. What power can you fill me with?"

There was a tear in the old woman's eye. She wiped it away, shaking her head. "Such things as I can teach have little to do with power. It is in your dreams now that you must walk, as all the Seers must. And for you as well there is the stone."

Kim glanced down. The ring on her right hand was no longer shining as it had when Eilathen wore it. It glowered, deep and dark, the colour of old blood.

"I did dream this," she said. "A terrible dream, the night before we crossed. What is it, Ysanne?"

"The Baelrath it was named, long ago, the Warstone. It is of the wild magic," the Seer said, "a thing not made by man, and it cannot be controlled like the shapings of Ginserat or Amairgen, or even of the Priestesses. It has been lost for a very long time, which has happened before. It is never found without reason, or so the old tales say."

It had grown dark outside as they talked. "Why have you given it to me?" Kim asked in a small voice.

"Because I dreamt it on your finger, too."

Which, somehow, she had known would be the answer. The ring pulsed balefully, inimically, and she feared it.

"What was I doing?" she asked.

"Raising the dead," Ysanne replied, and stood to light the candles in the room.

Kim closed her eyes. The images were waiting for her: the jumbled stones, the wide grasslands rolling away in the dark, the ring on her hand burning like a fire in the dream, and the wind rising over the grass, whistling between the stones—

"Oh, God!" she cried aloud. "What *is* it, Ysanne?"

The Seer returned to her seat beside the bed and gravely regarded the girl who lay there wrestling with what lay upon her.

"I am not sure of this," she said, "so I must be careful, but there is a pattern shaping here. You see, he died in your world the first time."

"Who died?" Kim whispered.

"The Warrior. Who always dies, and is not allowed to rest. It is his doom."

Kim's hands were clenched. "Why?"

"There was a great wrong done at the very beginning of his days, and for that he may not have rest. It is told and sung and written in every world where he has fought."

"Fought?" Her heart was pounding.

"Of course," Ysanne replied, though gently still. "He is the Warrior. Who may be called only at darkest need, and only by magic and only when summoned by name." Her voice was like wind in the room.

"And his name?"

"The secret one, no man knows, or even where it is to be sought, but there is another, by which he is always spoken."

"And that is?" Though now she knew. And a star was in the window.

Ysanne spoke the name.

He was probably wrong to be lingering, but the commands had not been explicit, and he was not overly prone to let it disturb him. It intoxicated them all to be abroad in the open spaces, using forgotten arts of concealment to observe the festival traffic on the roads to and from Paras Derval, and though by day the charred land dismayed them, at night they sang the oldest songs under the unclouded glitter of the stars.

He himself had a further reason for waiting, though he knew the delay could not be prolonged indefinitely. One more day he had promised himself, and felt extravagantly gratified when the two women and the man crested the ridge above the thicket.

Matt was quietly reassuring. Kim was in good hands, and though he didn't know where Diarmuid's band had gone—and preferred it that way, he added with a grimace—they were expected back that night. Loren, he confirmed, had indeed gone in search of Dave. For the first time since her encounter with the High Priestess two days before, Jennifer relaxed a little.

More unsettled by the strangeness of everything than she liked to admit, she had spent yesterday quietly with Laesha. In Jennifer's room the two new friends had traded accounts of their lives. It was somehow easier, Jennifer had reflected, to approach Fionavar in this way than to step out into the heat and confront things such as the children's chanting on the green, the axe swaying in the Temple, or Jaelle's cold hostility.

There had been dancing after the banquet that night. She had expected some difficulty in dealing with the men, but against her will she'd ended up being amused at the careful, almost apprehensive propriety of those who danced with her. Women claimed by Prince Diarmuid were very clearly off-limits to anyone else. She'd excused herself early and had gone to bed.

To be awakened by Matt Sören knocking at her door. The Dwarf devoted the morning to her, an attentive guide through the vastness of the palace. Roughly garbed, with an axe swinging at his side, he was a harshly anomalous figure in the hallways and chambers of the castle. He showed her rooms with paintings on the walls, and inlaid patterns on the floor. Everywhere there were tapestries. She was beginning to see that they had a deeper significance here. They climbed to the highest tower, where the guards greeted Matt with unexpected deference, and, looking out, she saw the High Kingdom baking in the rigour of its summer. Then he led her back to the Great Hall, empty now, where she could gaze undisturbed at the windows of Delevan.

As they circled the room, she told him about her meeting with Jaelle two days ago. The Dwarf blinked when she explained how she was made guest-friend, and again when she described Jaelle's questions about Loren. But once more he reassured her.

"She is all malice, Jaelle, all bright, bitter malice. But she is not evil, only ambitious."

"She hates Ysanne. She hates Diarmuid."

"Ysanne, she would hate. Diarmuid . . . arouses strong feelings in most people." The Dwarf's mouth twisted in his difficult smile. "She seeks to know every secret there is. Jaelle may suspect we had a fifth person, but even if she were certain, she would never tell Gorlaes—who *is* someone to be wary of."

"We've hardly seen him."

"He is with Ailell, almost all the time. Which is why he is to be feared. It was a dark day for Brennin," Matt Sören said, "when the elder Prince was sent away."

"The King turned to Gorlaes?" Jennifer guessed.

The Dwarf's glance at her was keen. "You are clever," he said. "That is exactly what happened."

"What about Diarmuid?"

"What *about* Diarmuid?" Matt repeated, in a tone so unexpectedly exasperated, she laughed aloud. After a moment, the Dwarf chuckled, too, low in his chest.

Jennifer smiled. There was a solid strength to Matt Sören, a feeling of deeply rooted common sense. Jennifer Lowell had come into adulthood trusting few people entirely, especially men, but, she realized in that moment, the Dwarf was now one of them. In a curious way, it made her feel better about herself.

"Matt," she said, as a thought struck her, "Loren left without you. Did you stay here for us?"

"Just to keep an eye on things." With a gesture at the patch over his right eye, he turned it into a kind of joke.

She smiled, but then looked at him a long moment, her green eyes sober. "How did you get that?"

"The last war with Cathal," he said simply. "Thirty years ago."

"You've been here that long?"

"Longer. Loren has been a mage for over forty years now."

"So?" She didn't get the connection.

He told her. There was an easiness to the mood they shared that morning, and Jennifer's beauty had been known to make taciturn men talkative before.

She listened, taking in, as Paul had three nights before, the story of Amairgen's discovery of the skylore, and the secret forging that would bind mage and source for life in a union more complete than any in all the worlds.

When Matt finished, Jennifer rose and walked a few steps, trying to absorb the impact of what she had been told. This was more than marriage, this went to the very essence of being. The mage, from what Matt had just said, was nothing without his source, only a repository of knowledge, utterly powerless. And the source . . .

"You've surrendered all of your independence!" she said, turning back to the Dwarf, hurling it almost as a challenge.

"Not all," he said mildly. "You give some up any time you share your life with someone. The bonding just goes deeper, and there are compensations."

"You were a king, though. You gave up—"

"That was before," Matt interrupted. "Before I met Loren. I . . . prefer not to talk about it."

She was abashed. "I'm sorry," she whispered. "I was prying."

The Dwarf grimaced, but by now she knew it for his smile. "Not really," he said. "And no matter. It is a very old wound."

"It's just so strange," she explained. "I can't even grasp what it must mean."

"I know. Even here they do not understand the six of us. Or the Law that governs the Council of the Mages. We are feared, respected, very seldom loved."

"What Law?" she asked.

At that he hesitated, then rose. "Let us walk," Matt said. "I will tell you a story, though I warn you, you would do better with one of the cyngael, for I am a poor tale-spinner."

"I'll take my chances," Jennifer said with a smile.

As they started to walk the outer edges of the hall, he began "Four hundred years ago, the High King went mad. Vailerth was his name, the only son of Lernath, who was the last King of Brennin to die on the Summer Tree."

She had questions about that, too, but held her peace. "Vailerth was brilliant as a child," Matt continued, "or so the records from that time say, but it seems something bent in him after his father died and he came to the throne. A dark flower blossomed in his brain, the Dwarves say when such a thing occurs.

"First Mage to Vailerth was a man called Nilsom, whose source was a woman. Aideen was her name, and she had loved Nilsom all her life, or so the records tell."

Matt walked a few strides in silence. Jennifer had the feeling he was sorry to have begun the story, but after a moment he resumed. "It was rare for a mage to have a woman for source in part because in Gwen Ystrat, where the Priestesses of Dana are, they would curse any woman who did so. It was always rare; it is rarer still since Aideen."

She looked over at him, but the Dwarf's features were quite impassive.

"Many dark things fell out because of Vailerth's madness. At length there came talk of civil war in the land, because he began taking children, boys and girls both, from their homes and bringing them into the palace by night. They would never be seen again, and the rumours of what the High King did to them were very bad. And in these deeds, in all of these deeds of darkness, Nilsom was with the King, and some say it was he who goaded Vailerth into them. Theirs was a dark weaving, and Nilsom, with Aideen by his side, had power so great none dared openly gainsay them. It is my own thought," the Dwarf added, turning his head for the first time, "that he, too, was mad, but in a cooler, more dangerous fashion. It was a long time ago, however, and the records are incomplete, because many of our most precious books were destroyed in the war. There was war at the last, for one day Vailerth and Nilsom went too far: they proposed to go into the Godwood and cut down the Summer Tree.

"The whole of Brennin rose up then, save for the army Vailerth had raised. But that army was loyal and strong, and Nilsom was very strong, more so than the five other mages in Brennin all together. And then on the eve of war there was only one other mage, for four of them were found dead, and their sources, too.

"There was civil war in the High Kingdom then. Only Gwen Ystrat stayed aloof. But the Dukes of Rhoden and Seresh, the Wardens of the North March and the South, the farmers and the townsmen and the mariners from Taerlindel, all came to war against Vailerth and Nilsom.

"They were not enough. Nilsom's power then, sourced in Aideen's strength and her love, was greater, they say, than that of any mage since Amairgen. He wrought death and ruination among all who opposed them, and blood soaked the fields as brother slew brother, while Vailerth laughed in Paras Derval."

Once more Matt paused, and when he resumed, there was a flatness in his voice. "The last battle was fought in the hilly land just west of us, between here and the Godwood. Vailerth, they say, climbed to the topmost towers of this palace to watch Nilsom lead his army to the final victory, after which nothing but the dead would stand between them and the Tree.

"But when the sun rose that morning, Aideen went before her mage, whom she loved, and she told him she would no longer drain herself for him in this cause. And saying so, she drew forth a knife and drained the life's blood from her veins instead and so died."

"Oh, no," Jennifer said. "Oh, Matt!"

He seemed not to have heard. "There is little after that," he said, still very flat. "With Nilsom powerless, the army of Vailerth was overrun. They threw down their swords and spears and sued for peace. Nilsom would not do so, and in the end he was killed by the last mage in Brennin. Vailerth leaped from his tower and died. Aideen was buried with honour in a grave close by the Mörnirwood, and Duke Lagos of Seresh was crowned in this hall."

They had come full circle, back to the benches under the last window, close to the throne. Overhead, Colan's yellow hair was brilliant in the sunlight that poured through the windows.

"It remains only to tell you," Matt Sören said, gazing directly at her now, "that when the Council of Mages gathers at midwinter, Nilsom's is a name whose memory we curse by ritual."

"I should think," said Jennifer, with some spirit.

"So, too," said the Dwarf softly, "is the name of Aideen."

*"What?"*

Matt's gaze was unwavering. "She betrayed her mage," he said. "In the laws of our Order, there is no crime so deep. None. No matter what the cause. Every year Loren and I curse her memory at midwinter and we do so truly. And every year," he added, very low, very gently, "when the snows melt in the spring, we lay the first of the wildflowers on her grave."

From that composed glance, Jennifer turned her head away. She felt close to tears. She was too far from home, and it was all so difficult and so strange. Why should such a woman be cursed? It was too hard. What she needed, she realized, was exercise, fifty hard laps in a pool to clear her head, or else, and better still . . .

"Oh, Matt," she said. "I need to move, to *do* something. Are there horses for us to ride?"

And of all things, *that* cracked the solid composure of the Dwarf. Astonishingly, he flushed. "There are horses, of course," he said awkwardly, "but I fear I will not join you—Dwarves do not ride for pleasure. Why don't you go with Laesha and Drance, though?"

"Okay," she said, but then lingered, unwilling, suddenly, to leave him.

"I'm sorry if I have troubled you," Matt said. "It is a difficult story."

Jennifer shook her head. "More for you, surely, than for me. Thank you for sharing it. Thanks for a lot." And, bending swiftly, she kissed him on the cheek and ran from the hall to find Laesha, leaving a normally phlegmatic Dwarf in a remarkably unsettled state.

And so did it come to pass, three hours later, that the two women had galloped with Diarmuid's man to the crest of a ridge east of the town, where they stilled their tired horses in disbelief, as a small party of ethereal figures ascended the slope towards them, their tread so light the grass seemed not to bend beneath their feet.

"Welcome!" said their leader as he stopped before them. He bowed, his long silver hair glinting in the light. "This hour is brightly woven." His voice was like music in a high place. He spoke directly to Jennifer. She was aware that Drance beside her, the prosaic soldier, had tears shining on his transfigured face.

"Will you come down among the trees and feast with us this evening?" the silver-haired figure asked. "You are most welcome. My name is Brendel of the Kestrel Mark, from Daniloth. We are the lios alfar."

⤞═◉═⤝

The return to Brennin was almost effortless, as if they were being propelled homeward by a following wind. Erron, fluid and agile, went first again on the climb back up the cliff, and he hammered iron spikes into the rock face for the rest of them.

They came again to the horses, mounted, and began galloping north once more on the dusty roads of the High Kingdom. The mood was exhilarated and chaotic. Joining in the bawdy chorus of a song Coll was leading, Kevin couldn't remember feeling happier; after the incident on the river, he and Paul seemed to have been completely accepted by the band, and because he respected these men, that acceptance mattered.

Erron was becoming a friend, and so, too, was Carde, singing away on Kevin's left side. Paul, on the other side, wasn't singing, but he didn't seem unhappy, and he had a lousy voice anyway.

Just past midday they came to the same inn where they had stopped before. Diarmuid called a halt for lunch and a quick beer, which became, given the prevailing mood, several slow beers. Coll, Kevin noticed, had disappeared.

The extended break meant that they were going to miss the banquet in the Great Hall that night. Diarmuid didn't seem to care.

"It's the Black Boar tonight, my friends," he announced, glittering and exhilarated at the head of the table. "I'm in no mood for court manners. Tonight I celebrate with you and let the manners look after themselves. Tonight we take our pleasure. Will you drink with me to the Dark Rose of Cathal?"

Kevin cheered with the others, drank with the others.

⟶⟩═◉⟨═⟵

Kimberly had dreamt again. The same one at first: the stones, the ring, the wind—and the same grief in her heart. And again she woke just as the words of power reached her lips.

This time, though, she had fallen asleep again, to find another dream waiting, as if at the bottom of a pool.

She was in the room of Ailell the King. She saw him tossing restlessly on his bed, saw the young page asleep on his pallet. Even as she watched, Ailell woke in the dark of his chamber. A long time he lay still, breathing raggedly, then she saw him rise painfully, as if against his own desire. He lit a candle and carried it to an inner doorway in the room, through which he passed. Invisible, insubstantial, she followed the King down a corridor lit only by the weaving candle he bore, and she paused with him before another door, into which was set a sliding view-hole.

When Ailell put his eyes to the aperture, somehow she was looking with him, seeing what he saw, and Kimberly saw with the High King the white naal fire and the deep blue shining of Ginserat's stone, set into the top of its pillar.

Only after a long time did Ailell withdraw, and in the dream Kim saw herself move to look again, standing on tiptoe to gaze with her own eyes into the room of the stone.

*And looking in, she saw no stone at all, and the room was dark.*

Wheeling in terror, she saw the High King walking back towards his chamber, and waiting there for him in the doorway was a shadowed figure that she knew.

His face rigid as if it were stone, Paul Schafer stood before Ailell, and he was holding a chess piece in his outstretched hand, and coming nearer to them. Kim saw that it was the white king, and it was broken. There was a music all about them that she couldn't recognize, although she knew she should. Ailell spoke words she could not hear because the music was too loud, and then Paul spoke, and she needed desperately to hear, but the music . . . And then the King held high his candle and began to speak again, and she could not, could not, could not.

Then everything was blasted to nothingness by the howling of a dog, so loud it filled the universe.

And she awoke to the morning sunlight and the smell of food frying over the cooking fire.

"Good morning," said Ysanne. "Come and eat, before Malka steals it all. Then I have something to show you."

✦═◎═✦

Coll rejoined them on the road north of the town. Paul Schafer eased his horse over to the roan stallion the big man rode.

"Being discreet?" he asked.

Above his broken nose Coll's eyes were guarded. "Not exactly. But he wanted to do something."

"Which means?"

"The man had to die, but his wife and children can be helped."

"So you've paid them. Is that why he delayed just now in the tavern? To give you time? It wasn't just because he felt like drinking, was it?"

Coll nodded. "He often feels like drinking," he said wryly, "but he very rarely acts without reason. Tell me," he went on, as Schafer remained silent, "do you think he did wrong?"

Paul's expression was unreadable.

"Gorlaes would have hanged him," Coll pressed, "and had the body torn apart. His family would have been dispossessed of their land. Now his eldest son is going to South Keep to be trained as one of us. Do you really think he did wrong?"

"No," said Schafer slowly, "I'm just thinking that with everyone else starving, that farmer's treason was probably the best way he could find to take care of his family. Do you have a family, Coll?"

To which Diarmuid's lieutenant, who didn't, and who was still trying to like this strange visitor, had no reply at all. They rode north through the heat of the afternoon, the dry fields baking on either side, the far hills shimmering like mirages, or the hope of rain.

✦═◎═✦

The trap door under the table had been invisible until Ysanne, kneeling, had laid her hand on the floor and spoken a word of power. There were ten stairs leading down; on either side the rough stone walls were damp to the touch. There were brackets set into the walls, but no torches, because from the bottom of the stairs came a pale glow of light. Wondering, Kim followed the Seer and Malka, the cat, as they went down.

The chamber was small, more a cave than a room. Another bed, a desk, a chair, a woven carpet on the stone floor. Some parchments and books, very old by the look of them, on the desk. Only one thing more: against the far wall was set a cabinet with glass doors, and within the cabinet, like a captured star, lay the source of light.

There was awe in the Seer's voice when she broke the silence. "Every time I see this . . ." Ysanne murmured. "It is the Circlet of Lisen," she said, walking forward. "It was made for her by the lios alfar in the days when Pendaran Wood was not yet a place of dread. She bound it on her brow after they built the Anor for her, and she stood in that tower by the sea, a light like a star on her brow, to show Amairgen the way home from Cader Sedat."

"And he never came." Kim's voice, though she whispered, felt harsh to her own ears. "Eilathen showed me. I saw her die." The Circlet, she saw, was purest gold, but the light set within it was gentler than moonfall.

"She died, and Pendaran does not forgive. It is one of the deep sorrows of the world. So much changed . . . even the light. It was brighter once, the colour of hope, they said when it was made. Then Lisen died, and the Wood changed, and the world changed, and now it seems to shine with loss. It is the most fair thing I know in all the world. It is the Light against the Dark."

Kim looked at the white-haired figure beside her. "Why is it here?" she asked. "Why hidden underground?"

"Raederth brought it to me the year before he died. Where he went to find it, I know not—for it was lost when Lisen fell. Lost long years, and he never told me the tale of where he went to bring it back. It aged him, though. Something happened on the journey of which he could never speak. He asked me to guard it here, with the two other things of power, until their place should be dreamt. 'Who shall wear this next,' he said, 'after Lisen, shall have the darkest road to walk of any child of earth or stars.' And he said nothing more. It waits here, for the dreaming."

Kimberly shivered, for something new within her, a singing in the blood, told her that the words of the dead mage were true prophecy. She felt weighted, burdened. This was getting to be too much. She tore her eyes away from the Circlet. "What are the other two things?" she asked.

"The Baelrath, of course. The stone on your finger."

Kim looked down. The Warstone had grown brighter as they spoke, the dull, blood-dark lustre giving way to a pulsating sheen.

"I think the Circlet speaks to it," Ysanne went on. "It always shone so in this room. I kept it here beside the other, until the night I dreamt you wearing it. From that time I knew its hour was coming, and I feared the wakening power would call forces I could not ward. So I summoned Eilathen again, and bound him to guard the stone by the red at the heart of the bannion."

"When was this?"

"Twenty-five years ago, now. A little more."

"But—I wasn't even born!"

"I know, child. I dreamt your parents first, the day they met. Then you with the Baelrath on your hand. Our gift as Seers is to walk the twists that lie in the weave of time and bring their secrets back. It is no easy power, and you know already that it cannot always be controlled."

Kim pushed her brown hair back with both hands. Her forehead was creased with anxiety, the grey eyes were those of someone being pursued. "I do know that," she said. "I'm trying to handle it. What I can't . . . I don't understand why you are show-ing me Lisen's Light."

"Not true," the Seer replied. "If you stop to think, you will understand. You are being shown the Circlet because it may fall to you to dream who is to wear it next."

There was a silence. Then, "Ysanne, I don't live here."

"There is a bridge between our worlds. Child, I am telling you that which you know already."

"But that's just it! I'm beginning to understand what I am. I saw what Eilathen spun. But I'm *not* of this world, it isn't in my blood, I don't know its roots the way you do, the way all the Seers must have known. How should . . . how could I *ever* presume to say who is to bear the Circlet of Lisen? I'm a stranger, Ysanne!"

She was breathing hard. The old woman looked at her a long time, then she smiled. "Now you are. You have just come. You are right about being incomplete, but be easy. It is only time." Her voice, like her eyes, was gentle as she told her second lie, and shielded it.

"Time!" Kimberly burst out. "Don't you understand? I'm only *here* two weeks. As soon as they find Dave, we're going home."

"Perhaps. There is still a bridge, and I did dream the Baelrath on your hand. It is in my heart as well—an old woman's heart, not a Seer's vision—that there may be need of a Dreamer in your world, too, before what is to come is full-woven on the Loom."

Kimberly opened her mouth, and closed it again, speechless. Because now it *was* too much: too many things, too quickly and too hard.

"I'm sorry," she managed to gasp, and then, whirling, ran up the stone stairs and out the doorway of the cottage to where there was sunlight and a blue sky. Trees, too, and a path down which she could run to the edge of a lake. Alone, because no one was pursuing her, she could stand there throwing pebbles into the water, knowing that they were pebbles, only pebbles, and that no green spirit, water dripping from his hair, would rise in answer from the lake to change her life again.

In the chamber from which she had fled, the light continued to shine. Power and hope and loss were in the radiance that bathed Ysanne as she sat at the desk, stroking the cat in her lap, her eyes unfocused and blind.

"Ah, Malka," she murmured at last, "I wish I were wiser. What is the use of living so long if one hasn't grown wise?"

The cat pricked up her ears, but preferred to continue licking a paw rather than address herself to so thorny a question.

At length the Seer rose, lowering the affronted Malka to the floor, and she walked slowly to the cabinet wherein the Circlet shone. Opening the glass door, she reached in and took out an object half-hidden on a lower shelf, then she stood there a long time, gazing at what lay in her hand.

The third thing of power: the one that Kimberly, throwing pebbles by the lake, had not seen.

"Ah, Malka," the Seer said again, and drew the dagger from its sheath. A sound like a plucked harpstring ran through the room.

A thousand years before, in the days after the Bael Rangat, when all the free peoples of Fionavar had gathered before the Mountain to see Ginserat's stones, the

Dwarves of Banir Lök had shaped a crafting of their own as a gift for the new High King of Brennin.

With thieren had they wrought, rarest of metals, found only at the roots of their twin mountains, most precious gift of earth to them, blue-veined silver of Eridu.

And for Colan the Beloved they had taken thought and fashioned a blade, with runes upon the sheath to bind it, and an old, dark magic spun in their caverns to make a knife unlike any other in all the worlds, and they named it Lökdal.

Very low bowed Conary's son when they handed it to him, and silently he listened, wiser than his years, as Seithr the Dwarf-King told him what had been laid upon the blade. Then he bowed again, lower yet, when Seithr, too, fell silent.

"I thank you," Colan said, and his eyes flashed as he spoke. "Double-edged the knife, and double-edged the gift. Mörnir grant us the sight to use it truly." And he placed Lökdal in his belt and bore it south away.

To the mages he had entrusted it, the blade and the magic locked within it like a blessing or a curse, and twice only in a thousand years had Colan's dagger killed. From First Mage to First Mage it had passed, until the night Raederth died. In the middle of that night, the woman who loved him had had a dream that shook her to the hidden places of her soul. Rising in the darkness, she came to the place where Raederth guarded the blade, and she took it away and hid it from those who succeeded him. Not even Loren Silvercloak, whom she trusted with everything else, knew that Ysanne had Lökdal.

"Who strikes with this blade without love in his heart shall surely die," had said Seithr of the Dwarves. "That is one thing."

And then softly, so that only Colan heard, he had said the other thing.

In her hidden chamber, Ysanne the Seer, dreamer of the dream, turned the bright rippling blade over and over in her hands, so the light glinted from it like blue fire.

On the shore of the lake a young woman stood, power within her, power beneath her, throwing pebbles one by one.

⊷⇒◉⇐⊷

It was cooler in the wood where the lios alfar led them. The food they were offered was delicate and wonderful: strange fruits, rich bread, and a wine that lifted the spirit and sharpened the colours of the sunset. Throughout, there was music: one of the lios played at a high-toned wind instrument while others sang, their voices twining in the deepening shadows of the trees, as the torches of evening were lit at the edge of the glade.

Laesha and Drance, for whom this was childhood fantasy made true, seemed even more enchanted than Jennifer was, and so when Brendel invited them to stay the night in the wood and watch the lios dance under the stars, it was with wonder and joy that they accepted.

Brendel dispatched someone to ride swiftly to Paras Derval and give private word to the King of their whereabouts. Wrapped in a delicate languor, they watched the messenger, his hair glowing in the light of the setting sun, ride over the hill, and they turned back to the wine and the singing in the glade.

As the shadows lengthened, a grace note of long sorrow seemed to weave its way into the songs of the lios alfar. A myriad of fireflies moved like shining eyes just beyond the torches: lienae they were named, Brendel said. Jennifer sipped the wine he poured for her, and let herself be carried into a rich sweet sadness by the music.

Cresting the hill west of them, the messenger, Tandem of the Kestrel, set his horse into an easy canter towards the walled town and the palace a league away.

He was not quite halfway there when he died.

Soundlessly he fell from his horse, four darts in his throat and back. After a moment the svarts rose from the hollow beside the path and watched in unblinking silence as the wolves padded up from beside them to the body of the lios. When it was clear that he was dead, they, too, went forward and surrounded the fallen rider. Even in death, there was a nimbus of glory clinging to him, but when they were done, when the wet, tearing sounds had ceased and only the quiet stars looked down, there was nothing left that anyone would care to see of Tandem of the lios alfar.

Most hated by the Dark, for their name was Light.

※═◎═※

And it was in that moment, away to the north and east, that another solitary rider checked his own mount suddenly. A moment he was motionless, then with a terrible oath, and fear like a fist in his heart, Loren Silvercloak turned his horse and began desperately to thunder home.

※═◎═※

In Paras Derval, the King did not attend the banquet, nor did any of the four visitors, which caused more than a little talk. Ailell kept to his chambers and played ta'bael with Gorlaes, the Chancellor. He won easily, as was customary, and with little pleasure, which was also customary. They played very late, and Tarn, the page, was asleep when the interruption came.

※═◎═※

As they went through the open doorway of the Black Boar, the noise and smoke were like a wall into which they smashed.

One voice, however, made itself heard in a prodigious bellow that resounded over the pandemonium.

"Diarmuid!" roared Tegid, surging to his feet. Kevin winced at the decibel level engendered. "By the oak and the moon, it's himself!" Tegid howled, as the tavern sounds briefly resolved themselves into shouted greetings.

Diarmuid, in fawn-coloured breeches and a blue doublet, stood grinning sardonically in the doorway as the others fanned out into the dense haze of the room. Tegid wove his way unsteadily forward to stand swaying before his Prince.

And hurled the contents of a mug of ale full in Diarmuid's face.

"Wretched Prince!" he screamed. "I shall tear your heart out! I shall send your liver to Gwen Ystrat! How *dare* you slip off and leave great Tegid behind with the women and the mewling babes?"

Kevin, beside the Prince, had a brief, hysterical vision of Tegid trying to go hand over hand across Saeren, before Diarmuid, dripping wet, reached to the nearest table, grabbed a silver tankard, and threw it violently at Tegid.

Someone screamed as the Prince followed up the throw, which bounced off the big man's shoulder, with a short rush, at the end of which his lowered head intersected effectively with Tegid's massive target of a girth.

Tegid staggered back, his face momentarily achieving a shade of green. He recovered quickly, though, seized the nearest table top, and with one mighty exertion lifted it whole from the trestles, spilling mugs and cutlery, and sending their erstwhile users scattering as raucous curses exploded around him. Wheeling for leverage, he swung the board in a wide, lethal sweep that bade fair to render Ailell heirless had it landed.

Diarmuid ducked, very neatly. So, too, less smoothly, did Kevin. Sprawling on the floor, he saw the board whistle over their heads and, at the spent end of its sweep, clip a red-doubleted man on the shoulder, catapulting him into the patron beside him. A remarkable human demonstration of the domino effect ensued. The noise level was horrific.

Someone elected to deposit his bowl of soup on the red-doubleted gentleman's balding pate. Someone else regarded this as more than sufficient excuse to deck the soup-pourer from behind with a hoisted bench. The innkeeper prudently began removing bottles from the bar top. A barmaid, her skirts aswirl, slipped under a table. Kevin saw Carde dive to join her there.

In the meantime, Diarmuid, springing from his crouch, butted Tegid again before the mountainous one could ready a return scything of the table top. The first reaping had comprehensively cleared a wide space about the two of them.

This time Tegid held his ground; with a joyous bellow he dropped the board on someone's head and enveloped Diarmuid in a bear-hug.

"Now I have you!" Tegid boomed, his face flushed with rapture. Diarmuid's features were also shading towards scarlet as his captor tightened a bone-crushing grip. Watching, Kevin saw the Prince free his arms for a counter-blow.

He had no doubt Diarmuid could manage to free himself, but Tegid was squeezing in earnest, and Kevin saw that the Prince was going to have to use a crippling retort to break the other man's hold. He saw Diarmuid shift his knee for leverage, and knew what would have to follow. With a futile shout, he rushed forward to intercede.

And stopped dead as a terrifying cry of outrage exploded from Tegid's throat. Still screaming, he dropped the Prince like a discarded toy on the sandy floor.

There came a smell of burning flesh.

Leaping spectacularly, Tegid upended another table, rescued a brimming pitcher of ale, and proceeded to pour its contents over his posterior.

The movement revealed, somewhat like the drawing of a curtain, Paul Schafer behind him, holding, rather apologetically, a poker from the cooking fire.

There was a brief silence, an awe-stricken homage to the operatic force of Tegid's scream, then Diarmuid, still on the floor, began to laugh in high, short, hysterical gasps, signalling a resumption of universal pandemonium. Crying with laughter, barely able to stand, Kevin made his way, with Erron staggering beside him, to embrace the crookedly grinning Schafer.

It was some time before order was restored, largely because no one was particularly intent on restoring it. The red-doubleted man appeared to have a number of friends, and so, too, it seemed, did the soup-pourer. Kevin, who knew neither, threw a token bench into the fray, then withdrew towards the bar with Erron. Two serving women joined them there, and the press of events greatly facilitated a rapid acquaintance.

Going upstairs, hand in hand with Marna, the taller of the two, Kevin's last glimpse of the tavern floor was of a surging mass of men disappearing in and out of the smoky haze. Diarmuid was standing atop the bar, lobbing whatever came to hand upon the heads of the combatants. He didn't seem to be choosing sides. Kevin looked for Paul, didn't see him; and then a door was opened and closed behind him, and in the rush of dark a woman was in his arms, her mouth turned up to his, and his soul began again its familiar spiral downward into longing.

Much later, when he had not yet completed the journey back, he heard Marna ask in a timid whisper, "Is it always so?"

And a good few minutes yet from being capable of speech, he stroked her hair once with an effort and closed his eyes again. Because it *was* always so. The act of love a blind, convulsive reaching back into a falling dark. Every time. It took away his very name, the shape and movement of his bones; and between times he wondered if there would be a night when he would go so far that there was no returning.

Not this night, though. Soon he was able to smile at her, and then to give thanks and gentle words, and not without sincerity, for her sweetness ran deep, and he had needed badly to drink of such a thing. Slipping inside his arm, Marna laid her head on his shoulder beside his own bright hair, and, breathing deeply of her scent, Kevin let the exhaustion of two waking nights carry him to sleep.

He only had an hour, though, and so was vulnerable and unfocused when the presence of a third person in the room woke him. It was another girl, not Erron's, and she was crying, her hair disordered about her shoulders.

"What is it, Tiene?" Marna asked sleepily.

"He sent me to you," brown-haired Tiene sniffled, looking at Kevin.

"Who?" Kevin grunted, groping towards consciousness. "Diarmuid?"

"Oh, no. It was the other stranger, Pwyll."

It took a moment.

"*Paul!* What did—what's happened?"

His tone was evidently too sharp for already tender nerves. Tiene, casting a wide-eyed glance of reproach at him, sat down on the bed and started crying again. He shook her arm. "Tell me! What happened?"

"He left," Tiene whispered, barely audible. "He came upstairs with me, but he left."

Shaking his head, Kevin tried desperately to focus. "What? Did he . . . was he able to . . . ?"

Tiene sniffed, wiping at the tears on her cheeks. "You mean to be with me? Yes, of course he was, but he took no pleasure at all, I could tell. It was all for me . . . and I am not, I gave him nothing, and . . . and . . ."

"And what, for God's sake?"

"And so I cried," Tiene said, as if it should have been obvious. "And when I cried, he walked out. And he sent me to find you. My lord."

She had moved farther onto the bed, in part because Marna had made room. Tiene's dark eyes were wide like a fawn's; her robe had fallen open, and Kevin could see the start of her breasts' deep curve. Then he felt the light stirring of Marna's hand along his thigh under the sheet. There was suddenly a pulsing in his head. He drew a deep breath.

And swung quickly out of bed. Cursing an erection, he kicked into his breeches and slipped on the loose-sleeved doublet Diarmuid had given him. Without bothering to button it, he left the room.

It was dark on the landing. Moving to the railing, he looked down on the ruin of the ground level of the Black Boar. The guttering torches cast flickering shadows over bodies sprawled in sleep on overturned tables and benches, or against the walls. A few men were talking in muted tones in one corner, and he heard a woman giggle suddenly from the near wall and then subside.

Then he heard something else. The plucked strings of a guitar.

His guitar.

Following the sound, he turned his head to see Diarmuid, with Coll and Carde, sitting by the window, the Prince cradling the guitar in the window seat, the others on the floor.

As he walked downstairs to join them, his eyes adjusted to the shadows, and he saw other members of the band sprawled nearby with some of the women beside them.

"Hello, friend Kevin," Diarmuid said softly, his eyes bright like an animal's in the dark. "Will you show me how you play this: I sent Coll to bring it. I trust you don't mind." His voice was lazy with late-night indolence. Behind him, Kevin could see a sprinkling of stars.

"Aye, lad," a bulky shadow rumbled. "Do a song for us." He'd taken Tegid for a broken table.

Without speaking, Kevin picked his way forward over the bodies on the floor. He took the guitar from Diarmuid, who slipped down from the window seat, leaving it for him. The window had been thrown open; he felt a light breeze stir the hairs at the back of his neck, as he tuned the guitar.

It was late, and dark, and quiet. He was a long way from home, and tired, and hurting in a difficult way. Paul had gone; even tonight, he had taken no joy, had turned from tears again. Even tonight, even here. So many reasons he could give. And so:

"This is called 'Rachel's Song,'" he said, fighting a thickness in his throat, and began to play. It was a music no one there could know, but the pull of grief was immediate. Then after a long time he lifted his voice, deep when he sang, in words he'd decided long ago should never be sung:

*Love, do you remember*
*My name? I was lost*
*In summer turned winter*
*Made bitter by frost.*
*And when June comes December*
*The heart pays the cost.*

*The breaking of waves on a long shore,*
*In the grey morning the slow fall of rain,*
*And stone lies over.*

*You'll bury your sorrow*
*Deep in the sea,*
*But sea tides aren't tamed*
*That easily—*
*There will come a tomorrow*
*When you weep for me.*

*The breaking of waves on a long shore,*
*In the grey morning the slow fall of rain,*
*Oh love remember, remember me.*

Then the music came alone again, transposed, worked on harder than anything he'd written in his life, especially what was coming now, with his own stupid tears. The part where the melody hurt, it was so beautiful, so laden with memory: the adapted second movement of the Brahms F Major Cello Sonata.

The notes were clean, unblurred, though the candles were blurred in his sight, as Kevin played Rachel Kincaid's graduation piece and gave sound to the sorrow that was his and not his.

Into the shadowed room it went, Rachel's song; over the sleeping bodies that stirred as sadness touched their dreams; among the ones who did not sleep and who felt the pull as they listened, remembering losses of their own; up the stairway it went to where two women stood at the railing, both crying now; faintly it reached the bedrooms, where bodies lay tangled in the shapes of love; and out the open window it went as well, into the late night street and the wide dark between the stars.

And on the unlit cobblestones a figure paused by the doorway of the tavern and did not enter. The street was empty, the night was dark, there was no one to see. Very silently he listened, and when the song came to an end, very silently he left, having heard the music before.

So Paul Schafer, who had fled from a woman's tears, and had cursed himself for a fool and turned back, now made his final turning, and did not turn again.

There was darkness for a time, a twisting web of streets, a gate where he was recognized by torchlight, and then darkness again in corridors silent save for the footfalls that he made. And through it he carried that music, or the music carried him, or the memory of music. It hardly mattered which.

He walked a matrix of crossing hallways he had walked before, and some were lit and others dark, and in some rooms he passed there were sounds again, but no one else walked in Paras Derval that night.

And in time he came, carrying music, carrying loss, carried by both of them, and stood for a second time before a door beyond which a slant of light yet showed.

It was the brown-bearded one called Gorlaes who opened to his summons, and for a moment he remembered that he did not trust this man, but it seemed a concern infinitely removed from where he was, and one that didn't matter now, not anymore.

Then his eyes found those of the King, and he saw that Ailell knew, somehow knew, and was not strong enough to refuse what he would ask, and so he asked.

"I will go to the Summer Tree for you tonight. Will you grant me leave and do what must be done?" It seemed to have been written a very long time ago. There was music.

Ailell was weeping as he spoke, but he said what was needful to be said. Because it was one thing to die, and another to die uselessly, he listened to the words and let them join the music in carrying him with Gorlaes and two other men out of the palace by a hidden gate.

There were stars above them and a forest far away. There was music in his head that was not going to end, it seemed. And it seemed he wasn't saying goodbye to Kevin after all, which was a grief, but it was a lost, small, twisting thing in the place where he had come.

Then the forest was no longer far away, and at some point the waning moon had risen as he walked, for it brushed the nearest trees with silver. The music still was with him, and the last words of Ailell: *Now I give you to Mörnir. For three nights and forever,* the King had said. And cried.

And now with the words and the music in his head, there had come again, as he had known it would, the face for which he could not cry. Dark eyes. Like no one else. In this world.

And he went into the Godwood, and it was dark. And all the trees were sighing in the wind of the wood, the breath of the God. There was fear on the faces of the other three men as the sound rose and fell about them like the sea.

He walked with them amid the surging and the swaying of the trees, and in time he saw that the path they were following had ceased to wander. The trees on either side now formed a double row leading him on, and so he stepped past Gorlaes, music carrying him, and he came into the place wherein stood the Summer Tree.

Very great it was, dark almost to black, its trunk knotted and gnarled, wide as a house. It stood alone in the clearing, in the place of sacrifice, and clutched the earth with roots old as the world, a challenge to the stars that shone down, and there was power in that place beyond the telling. Standing there, he felt it calling for his blood, for his life, and knowing he could not live three nights on that tree, he stepped forward, so as not to turn again, and the music stopped.

They stripped him of his garments then and bound him naked to the Summer Tree at the waning of the moon. When they had gone, it was silent in the glade save for the ceaseless sighing of the leaves. Alone upon the Tree, he felt within his flesh the incalculable vastness of its power, and had there been anything left to fear, he would have been afraid.

And this was the first night of Pwyll the Stranger on the Summer Tree.

# CHAPTER 8

In another wood east of Paras Derval, the lios alfar were still singing as Jennifer drifted towards sleep. Under the stars and the crescent of the risen moon, their voices wove about her a melody of sorrow so old and deep it was almost a luxury.

She roused herself and turned on the pallet they had made for her.

"Brendel?"

He came over to her and knelt. His eyes were blue now. They had been green like her own the last time she looked, and gold on the hillside that afternoon.

"Are you immortal?" she asked, sleepily.

He smiled. "No, Lady. Only the gods are so, and there are those who say that even they will die at the end. We live very long, and age will not kill us, but we do die, Lady, by sword or fire, or grief of heart. And weariness will lead us to sail to our song, though that is a different thing."

"Sail?"

"Westward lies a place not found on any map. A world shaped by the Weaver for the lios alfar alone, and there we go when we leave Fionavar, unless Fionavar has killed us first."

"How old are you, Brendel?"

"I was born four hundred years after the Bael Rangat. A little more than six hundred years ago."

She absorbed it in silence. There was nothing, really, to say. On the other side Laesha and Drance were asleep. The singing was very beautiful. She let it carry her into simplicity, and then sleep.

He watched her a long time, the eyes still blue, calm, and deeply appreciative of beauty in all its incarnations. And in this one there was something more. She looked like someone. He knew this or he sensed it to be so, but although he was quite right, he had absolutely no way of knowing whom, and so could not warn anyone.

At length he rose and rejoined the others for the last song, which was, as it always was, Ra-Termaine's lament for the lost. They sang for those who had just died by

Pendaran, and for all the others long ago, who would never now hear this song or their own. As the lios sang, the stars seemed to grow brighter above the trees, but that may have been just the deepening of night. When the song ended, the fire was banked and they slept.

They were ancient and wise and beautiful, their spirit in their eyes as a many-coloured flame, their art a homage to the Weaver whose most shining children they were. A celebration of life was woven into their very essence, and they were named in the oldest tongue after the Light that stands against the Dark.

But they were not immortal.

The two guards died of poison arrows, and four others had their throats ripped apart by the black onrush of the wolves before they were fully awake. One cried out and killed his wolf with a dagger as he died.

They fought bravely then, even brilliantly, with bright swords and arrows, for their grace could be most deadly when they had need.

Brendel and Drance with two others formed a wall about the two women, and against the charge of the giant wolves they held firm once, and again, and yet again, their swords rising and falling in desperate silence. It was dark, though, and the wolves were black, and the svarts moved like twisted wraiths about the glade.

Even so, the shining courage of the lios alfar, with Drance of Brennin fighting in their midst as a man possessed, might have prevailed, had it not been for the one thing more: the cold, controlling will that guided the assault. There was a power in the glade that night that no one could have foretold, and doom was written on the wind that rose before the dawn.

For Jennifer it was a hallucination of terror in the dark. She heard snarls and cries, saw things in blurred, distorted flashes—blood-dark swords, the shadow of a wolf, an arrow flying past. Violence exploding all around her, she who had spent her days avoiding such a thing.

But this was night. Too terrified to even scream, Jennifer saw Drance fall at last, a wolf dying beneath him, another rising wet-mouthed from his corpse to leap past her to where Laesha stood. Then before she could react, even as she heard Laesha cry out, she felt herself seized brutally as the hideous svarts surged forward into the gap and she was dragged away by them over the body of Diarmuid's man.

Looking desperately back, she saw Brendel grappling with three foes at once, blood dark on his face in the thin moonlight, then she was among the trees, surrounded by wolves and svart alfar, and there was no light to see by or to hope for anywhere.

They moved through the forest for what seemed an endless time, travelling north and east, away from Paras Derval and everyone she knew in this world. Twice she stumbled and fell in the dark, and each time she was dragged, sobbing, to her feet and the terrible progress continued.

They were still in the woods when the sky began to shade towards grey, and in the growing light she gradually became aware that amid the shifting movements of her captors, one figure never left her side: and among the horrors of that headlong night, this was the worst.

Coal-black, with a splash of silver-grey on his brow, he was the largest wolf by far. It wasn't the size, though, or the wet blood on his dark mouth; it was the malevolence of the power that hovered about the wolf like an aura. His eyes were on her face, and they were red; in them, for the moment she could sustain the glance, she saw a degree of intelligence that should not have been there, and was more alien than anything else she had come upon in Fionavar. There was no hatred in the look, only a cold, merciless will. Hate, she could have understood; what she saw was worse.

It was morning when they reached their destination. Jennifer saw a small woodcutter's cabin set in a cleared-out space by the forest's edge. A moment later she saw what was left of the woodcutter as well.

They threw her inside. She fell, from the force of it, and then crawled on her knees to a corner where she was violently, rackingly sick. Afterwards, shivering uncontrollably, she made her way to the cot at the back of the room and lay down.

We salvage what we can, what truly matters to us, even at the gates of despair. And so Jennifer Lowell, whose father had taught her, even as a child, to confront the world with pride, eventually rose up, cleaned herself as best she could, and began to wait in the brightening cottage. Daylight was coming outside, but it was not only that: courage casts its own light.

The sun was high in a blank sky when she heard the voices. One was low, with a note of amusement she could discern even through the door. Then the other man spoke, and Jennifer froze in disbelief, for this voice she had heard before.

"Not hard," the first man said, and laughed. "Against the lios it is easy to keep them to it."

"I hope you were not followed. I absolutely must not be seen, Galadan."

"You won't be. Almost all of them were dead, and I left behind ten wolves against the stragglers. They won't follow in any case. Enough of them have died; they wouldn't risk more for a human. She is ours, more easily than we might have hoped. It is rare indeed that we receive aid from Daniloth." And he laughed again, maliciously amused.

"Where is she?"

"Inside."

The door was flung open, letting in a dazzling shaft of sunlight. Momentarily blinded, Jennifer was dragged into the clearing.

"A prize, wouldn't you say?" Galadan murmured.

"Perhaps," the other one said. "Depending on what she tells us about why they are here."

Jennifer turned towards the voice, her eyes adjusting, and as they did, she found herself face to face with Metran, First Mage to the High King of Brennin.

No longer was he the shuffling old man she'd seen that first night or watched as he cowered from Jaelle in the Great Hall. Metran stood straight and tall, his eyes bright with malice.

"You traitor!" Jennifer burst out.

He gestured, and she screamed as her nipples were squeezed viciously. No one had touched her; he had done it himself without moving.

"Carefully, my dear lady," Metran said, all solicitude, as she writhed in pain. "You must be careful of what you say to me. I have the power to do whatever I want with you." He nodded towards his source, Denbarra, who stood close by.

"Not quite," the other voice demurred. "Let her go." The tone was very quiet, but the pain stopped instantly. Jennifer turned, wiping tears from her face.

Galadan was not tall, but there was a sinuous strength to him, a sheathed intimation of very great power. Cold eyes fixed her from a scarred, aristocratic face under the thatch of silver hair—like Brendel's, she thought, with another sort of pain.

He bowed to her, courtly and graceful, and with a veiled amusement. Then that was gone as he turned to Metran.

"She goes north for questioning," he said. "Unharmed."

"Are you telling me what to do?" Metran said on a rising note, and Jennifer saw Denbarra stiffen.

"Actually, yes, if you put it that way." There was mockery in his voice. "Are you going to fight me over it, mageling?"

"I could kill you, Galadan," Metran hissed.

The one named Galadan smiled again, but not with his eyes. "Then try. But I tell you now, you will fail. I am outside your taught magic, mageling. You have some power, I know, and have been given more, and may indeed have greater yet to come, but I will still be outside you, Metran. I always will be. And if you test it, I shall have your heart out for my friends."

In the silence that followed this, Jennifer became conscious of the ring of wolves surrounding them. There were svart alfar as well, but the giant red-eyed wolf was gone.

Metran was breathing hard. "You are not above me, Galadan. I was promised this."

At that, Galadan threw back his fierce, scarred head, and a burst of genuine laughter rang through the clearing.

"Promised, were you? Ah well, then, I must apologize!" His laughter stopped. "She is still to go north. If it were not so, I might take her for myself. But look!"

Jennifer, turning skyward to where Galadan was pointing, saw a creature so beautiful it lifted her heart in reflexive hope.

A black swan came swooping down from the high reaches of the sky, glorious against the sun, the great wings widespread, feathered with jet plumage, the long neck gracefully extended.

Then it landed, and Jennifer realized that the true horror had only begun, for the swan had unnatural razored teeth, and claws, and about it, for all the stunning beauty, there clung an odour of putrescent corruption.

Then the swan spoke, in a voice like slithering darkness in a pit. "I have come," she said. "Give her to me."

Far away yet, terribly far away, Loren Silvercloak was driving his horse back south, cursing his own folly in all the tongues he knew.

"She is yours, Avaia," said Galadan, unsmiling. "Is she not, Metran?"

"Of course," said the mage. He had moved upwind of the swan. "I will naturally be anxious to know what she has to say. It is vital for me in my place of watch."

"No longer," the black swan said, ruffling her feathers. "I have tidings for you. The Cauldron is ours, I am to say. You go now to the place of spiralling, for the time is upon us."

Across the face of Metran there spread then a smile of such cruel triumph that Jennifer turned away from it. "It has come then," the mage exulted. "The day of my revenge. Oh, Garmisch, my dead King, I shall break the usurper into pieces on his throne, and make drinking cups of the bones of the House of Ailell!"

The swan showed her unnatural teeth. "I will take pleasure in the sight," she hissed.

"No doubt," said Galadan wryly. "Is there word for me?"

"North," the swan replied. "You are asked to go north with your friends. Make haste. There is little time."

"It is well," said Galadan. "I have one task left here, then I follow."

"Make haste," Avaia said again. "And now I go."

"*No!*" Jennifer screamed, as cold svart hands grabbed for her. Her cries cut the air of the clearing and fell into nothingness. She was bound across the back of the giant swan and the dense, putrefying smell of it overwhelmed her. She could not breathe; when she opened her mouth, the thick black feathers choked her, and as they left the earth for the blazing sky, Jennifer fainted for the first time in her life, and so could not have known the glorious curving arc she and the swan made, cutting across the sky.

The figures in the clearing watched Avaia bear the girl away until they were lost in the shimmering of the white sky.

Metran turned to the others, exultation still in his eyes. "You heard? The Cauldron is mine!"

"So it seems," Galadan agreed. "You are away across the water, then?"

"Immediately. It will not be long before you see what I do with it."

Galadan nodded, then a thought seemed to strike him. "I wonder, does Denbarra understand what all this means?" He turned to the source. "Tell me, my friend, do you know what this Cauldron is all about?"

Denbarra shifted uneasily under the weight of that gaze. "I understand what is needful for me to know," he said sturdily. "I understand that with its aid, the House of Garantae will rule again in Brennin."

Galadan regarded him a moment longer, then his glance flicked away dismissively. "He is worthy of his destiny," he said to Metran. "A thick-witted source is an advantage for you, I suppose. I should get dreadfully bored, myself."

Denbarra flushed, but Metran was unmoved by the gibe this time. "My sister-son is loyal. It is a virtue," he said, unconscious of the irony. "What about you? You mentioned a task to be done. Should I know?"

"You should, but evidently you don't. Give thanks that I am less careless. There is a death to be consummated."

Metran's mouth twitched at the insult, but he did not respond. "Then go your way," he said. "We may not meet for some time."

"Alas!" said Galadan.

The mage raised a hand. "You mock me," he said with intensity. "You mock us all, andain. But I tell you this: with the Cauldron of Khath Meigol in my hands, I will wield a power even you dare not scorn. And with it I shall wreak such a vengeance here in Brennin that the memory of it will never die."

Galadan lifted his scarred head and regarded the mage. "Perhaps," he said finally, and very, very softly. "Unless the memory of it dies because everything has died. Which, as you know, is the wish of my heart."

On the last words, he made a subtle gesture over his breast, and a moment later a coal-black wolf with a splash of silver on its head ran swiftly westward from the clearing.

Had he entered the forest farther south, a great deal of what ensued might have been very different.

At the southern edge of the woodcutter's clearing a figure lay, hidden among the trees, bleeding from a dozen wounds. Behind him on the trail through the forest the last two lios alfar lay dead. And ten wolves.

And in the heart of Na-Brendel of the Kestrel Mark lay a grief and a rage that, more than anything else, had kept him alive so far. In the sunlight his eyes were black as night.

He watched Metran and his source mount horses and swing away northwest, and he saw the svarts and wolves leave together for the north. Only when the clearing stood utterly silent did he rise, with difficulty, and begin his own journey back to Paras Derval. He limped badly, from a wound in the thigh, and he was weak unto death from loss of blood; but he was not going to let himself fall or fail, for he was of the lios alfar, and the last of his company, and with his own eyes he had seen a gathering of the Dark that day.

It was a long way, though, and he was badly, badly hurt, so he was still a league from Paras Derval when twilight fell.

⋄⊱⟹◯⟸⊰⋄

During the day there were rumblings of thunder in the west. A number of the merchants in the city came to their doorways to look at the heavens, more out of habit than out of hope. The killing sun burned in a bare sky.

On the green at the end of Anvil Lane, Leila had gathered the children again for the ta'kiena. One or two had refused out of boredom, but she was insistent, and the others acceded to her wishes, which, with Leila, was always the best thing to do.

So she was blindfolded again, and she made them do it double so she truly could not see. Then she began the calling, and went through the first three almost indifferently because they didn't matter, they were only a game. When she came to the last one, though, to the Road, she felt the now familiar stillness come over her again, and she closed her eyes behind the two blindfolds. Then her mouth went dry and the difficult twisting flowered inside her. Only when the rushing sound began, like waves, did she start the chant, and as she sang the last word everything stopped.

She removed the blindfolds and, blinking in the brightness, saw with no surprise at all that it was Finn again. As if from far away she heard the voices of the adults watching them, and further still she heard a roll of thunder, but she looked only at Finn. He seemed more alone every time. She would have been sad, but it seemed so destined that sadness didn't fit, nor any sense of surprise. She didn't know what the Longest Road was, or where it led, but she knew it was Finn's, and that she was calling him to it.

Later that afternoon, though, something did surprise her. Ordinary people never went to the sanctuary of the Mother, certainly not at the direct request of the High Priestess herself. She combed her hair and wore her only gown; her mother made her.

⋄⊰⇒◉⇐⊱⋄

When Sharra dreamed now of the falcon, it was no longer alone in the sky over Larai Rigal. Memory burned in her like a fire under stars.

She was her father's daughter, though, heir to the Ivory Throne, and so there was a matter to be looked into, regardless of fires in her heart or falcons overhead.

Devorsh, Captain of the Guard, knocked in response to her summons, and the mutes admitted him. Her ladies murmured behind fluttering fans as the tall Captain made obeisance and gave homage in his unmistakable voice. She dismissed the women, enjoying their chagrin, and bade him sit in a low chair by the window.

"Captain," she began, without preamble, "certain documents have come to my attention raising a matter I think we must address."

"Highness?" He was handsome, she conceded, but not a candle, not a candle. He would not understand why she was smiling; not that it mattered.

"It seems that the archival records make mention of stone handholds cut many years ago in the cliff above Saeren due north of us."

"Above the river, Highness? In the cliff?" Polite incredulity infused the gravelly voice.

"I think I said that, yes." He flushed at the rebuke; she paused to let it register. "If those handholds exist, they are a danger and we should know about them. I want you to take two men you trust and see if this is true. For obvious reasons"—though she knew of none—"this is to be kept very quiet."

"Yes, Highness. When shall I—"

"Now, of course." She rose, and so, of necessity, did he.

"My lady's will." He made obeisance and turned to go.

And because of the falcons, the moon-touched memory, she called him back. "Devorsh, one thing more. I heard footsteps in the garden the night before last. Did you notice anything by the walls?"

His face showed real concern. "Highness, I went off duty at sundown. Bashrai took command from me. I will speak to him of this without delay."

"Off duty?"

"Yes, Highness. We take turns, Bashrai and myself, in leading the night watch. He is most competent, I suggest, but if—"

"How many men patrol the walls at night?" She leaned on the back of a chair for support; there was a pressure behind her eyes.

"Twelve, Highness, in peacetime."

"And the dogs?"

He coughed. "Ah, no, my lady. Not of late. It was felt unnecessary. They have been used on the hunt this spring and summer. Your father knows about this, of course." His face was animated by unconcealed curiosity. "If my lady feels they should—"

"No!" It was intolerable that he be in the room another moment, that he continue to look at her like this, his eyes widening in appraisal. "I will discuss this with Bashrai. Go now and do as I have told you. And quickly, Devorsh, very quickly."

"I go, my lady," he said in the distinctive voice, and went. After, she bit her tongue, tasting blood, so as not to scream.


Shalhassan of Cathal was reclining on a couch, watching two slaves wrestling, when word was brought to him. His court, hedonistic and overbred, was enjoying the sight of the oiled bodies writhing naked on the floor in the presence chamber, but the King watched the fight, as he heard the news, expressionlessly.

Raziel appeared just then in the archway behind the throne with the cup in his hand. It was mid-afternoon then and, taking the drink, Shalhassan saw that the jewelled goblet was blue. Which meant that the northerner's stone still shone as it should. He nodded to Raziel, who withdrew, their private ritual observed, as every day it was. It would never, ever do for the court to find out that Shalhassan was troubled by dreams of red wardstones.

Turning his thoughts to his daughter, Shalhassan drank. He approved her headstrong nature, indeed he had nurtured it, for no weakling dared sit on the Ivory Throne. Tantrums, though, were irresponsible, and this latest . . . Tearing apart her chambers and whipping her women were one thing; rooms could be restored and servants were servants. Devorsh was a different matter; he was a good soldier in a country with remarkably few, and Shalhassan was not pleased to hear that his Captain of the Guard had just been garrotted by his daughter's mutes. Whatever the insult she might say he had given her, it was a rash and precipitate response.

He drained the blue cup and came to a decision.

She was growing too undisciplined; it was time to have her married. However strong a woman might be, she still needed a man by her side and in her bed. And the kingdom needed heirs. It was past time.

The wrestling had grown tedious. He gestured and the eidolath stopped the fight. The two slaves had been brave, though, he decided, and he freed them both. There was a polite murmur from the courtiers, an approving rustle of silk.

Turning away, he noticed that one of the wrestlers was a little tardy in his obeisance. The man may have been exhausted, or hurt, but the throne could not be compromised.

At any time, in any way. He gestured again.

There *were* appropriate uses for the mutes and their garrottes. Sharra would just have to learn to discriminate.

⟡

The knowledge of approaching death can come in many shapes, descending as a blessing or rearing up as an apparition of terror. It may sever like the sweep of a blade, or call as a perfect lover calls.

For Paul Schafer, who had chosen to be where he was for reasons deeper than loss and more oblique than empathy for an aged King, the growing awareness that his body could not survive the Summer Tree came as a kind of relief: in this failure, at least, there could be no shame. There was no unworthiness in yielding to a god.

He was honest enough to realize that the exposure and the brutal heat, the thirst and immobility were themselves enough to kill him, and this he had known from the moment they bound him.

But the Summer Tree of Mörnirwood was more than all of these. Naked upon it in the blaze of day, Paul felt the ancient bark all along the planes of his body, and in that contact he apprehended power that made what strength he had its own. The tree would not break him; instead he felt it reaching out, pulling him into itself, taking everything. Claiming him. He knew as well, somehow, that this was only the beginning, not even the second night. It was scarcely awake.

The God was coming, though. Paul could feel that slow approach along his flesh, in the running of his blood, and now there was thunder, too. Low yet, and muted, but there were two whole nights to come and all about him the Godwood vibrated soundlessly as it had not for years upon years, waiting, waiting for the God to come and claim his own, in darkness and forever, as was his due.

⟡

The genial proprietor of the Black Boar was in a mood that bade fair to shatter his public image entirely. Under the circumstances, however, it was not entirely surprising that his countenance should display a distinctly forbidding mien as he surveyed his demesne in the morning light.

It was a festival. People drank during festivals. There were visitors in town, visitors with dry throats from the drought and a little money saved for this time. Money that might—money that *should*—be his, by all the gods, if he hadn't been forced to close the Boar for the day to redress the damage of the night before.

He worked them hard all day, even the ones with broken bones and bashed pates from the brawl, and he certainly wasted no sympathy on employees bemoaning hangovers or lack of sleep. There was money being lost every moment he stayed closed, every moment! And to add to the choler of his mood there was a vile, vile rumour running through the capital that bloody Gorlaes, the Chancellor, intended to slap a rationing law down on all liquids as soon as the fortnight's festival ended. Bloody drought. He attacked a pile of debris in a corner as if it were the offending Chancellor himself. Rationing, indeed! He'd like to see Gorlaes try to ration Tegid's wine and ale, he'd like to see him try! Why, the fat one had likely poured a week's worth of beer over his posterior the night before.

At the recollection, the owner of the Black Boar succumbed to his first smile of the day, almost with relief. It was hard work being furious. Eyeing the room, hands on hips, he decided that they'd be able to open within an hour or so of sun down; the day wouldn't be a total loss.

So it was that as full dark cloaked the twisting lanes of the old town, and torches and candles gleamed through curtained windows, a bulky shadow moved ponderously towards the recently reopened doors of his favourite tavern.

It was dark, though, in the alleys, and he was impeded a trifle by the effects of his wars the night before, and so Tegid almost fell as he stumbled into a slight figure in the lane.

"By the horns of Cernan!" the great one spluttered "Mind your path. Few obstruct Tegid without peril!"

"Your pardon," the wretched obstacle murmured, so low he was scarcely audible. "I fear I am in some difficulty, and I . . ."

The figure wavered, and Tegid put out an instinctive hand of support. Then his bloodshot eyes finally adjusted to the shadows, and with a transcendent shock of awe, he saw the other speaker.

"Oh, Mörnir," Tegid whispered in disbelief, and then, for once, was speechless.

The slim figure before him nodded, with an effort. "Yes," he managed. "I am of the lios alfar. I—," he gasped with pain, then resumed, "—I have tidings that must . . . must reach the palace, and I am sorely hurt."

At which point, Tegid became aware that the hand he had laid upon the other's shoulder was sticky with fresh blood.

"Easy now," he said with clumsy tenderness. "Can you walk?"

"I have, so far, all day. But . . ." Brendel slipped to one knee, even as he spoke. "But as you see, I am . . ."

There were tears in Tegid's eyes. "Come, then," he murmured, like a lover. And lifting the mangled body effortlessly, Tegid of Rhoden, named Breakwind, called the Boaster, cradled the lios alfar in his massive arms and bore him towards the brilliant glitter of the castle.

⊹⟫═◖═⟨⊹

"I dreamt again," Kim said. "A swan." It was dark outside the cottage. She had been silent all day, had walked alone by the lake. Throwing pebbles.

"What colour?" Ysanne asked, from the rocking chair by the hearth.

"Black."

"I dreamt her as well. It is a bad thing."

"What is it? Eilathen never showed me this."

There were two candles in the room. They flickered and dwindled as Ysanne told her about Avaia and Lauriel the White. At intervals they heard thunder, far off.

⊹⟫═◖═⟨⊹

It was still a festival, and though the King looked haggard and desiccated in his seat at the high table, the Great Hall gleamed richly by torchlight, festooned as it was with hangings of red and gold silk. Despite their morose King and his unwontedly bemused Chancellor, the court of Ailell was determined to enjoy itself. The players in the musicians' gallery overhead were in merry form, and even though dinner had not yet begun, the pages were being kept busy running back and forth with wine.

Kevin Laine, eschewing both his seat at the high table as a guest of honour and the not-very-subtle invitation of the Lady Rheva, had decided to ignore protocol by opting for a masculine enclave partway down one of the two tables that ran along the hall. Seated between Matt Sören and Diarmuid's big, broken-nosed lieutenant, Coll, he attempted to preserve a cheerful appearance, but the fact that no one had seen Paul Schafer since last night was building into a real source of anxiety. Jennifer, too: where the hell was she?

On the other hand, there were still many people filing into the room, and Jen, he had cause to remember, was seldom on time for anything, let alone early. Kevin drained his wine goblet for the third time and decided that he was becoming altogether too much of a worrier.

At which point Matt Sören asked, "Have you seen Jennifer?" and Kevin abruptly changed his mind.

"No," he said. "I was at the Boar last night, and then seeing the barracks and the armoury with Carde and Erron today. Why? Do you—?"

"She went riding with one of the ladies-in-waiting yesterday. Drance was with them."

"He's a good man," Coll said reassuringly, from the other side.

"Well, has anyone seen them? Was she in her room last night?" Kevin asked.

Coll grinned. "That wouldn't prove much, would it? A lot of us weren't in our beds last night." He laughed and clapped Kevin on the shoulder. "Cheer up!"

Kevin shook his head. Dave. Paul. Now Jen.

"Riding, you said?" He turned to Matt. "Has anyone checked the stables? Are the horses back?"

Sören looked at him. "No," he said softly. "We haven't—but I think I want to now. Come on!" He was already pushing his chair back.

They rose together and so were on their feet when the sudden babble of sound came from the east doorway, and the courtiers and ladies gathered there moved aside for the torches to reveal the enormous figure with a bloodstained body in his arms.

Everything stopped. In the silence Tegid moved slowly forward between the long tables to stand before Ailell.

"Look!" he cried, grief raw in his voice. "My lord King, here is one of the lios alfar, and see what they have done to him!"

The King was ashen. Trembling, he rose. "Na-Brendel?" he croaked. "Oh, Mörnir. Is he . . . ?"

"No," a faint, clear voice replied. "I am not dead, though I might yet wish to be. Let me stand to give my tidings."

Gently, Tegid lowered the lios to stand on the mosaic-inlaid floor, and then, kneeling awkwardly, he offered his shoulder for support.

Brendel closed his eyes and drew a breath. And when he spoke again his voice, by some act of pure will, rang out strong and clear beneath the windows of Delevan.

"Treachery, High King. Treachery and death I bring you, and tidings of the Dark. We spoke, you and I, four nights past, of svart alfar outside Pendaran Wood. High King, there have been svarts outside your walls this day, and wolves with them. We were attacked before dawn and all my people are slain!"

He stopped. A sound like the moaning of wind before a storm ran through the hall.

Ailell had sunk back into his chair, his eyes bleak and hollow. Brendel lifted his head and looked at him. "There is an empty seat at your table, High King. I must tell you that it stands empty for a traitor. Look to your own hearth, Ailell! Metran, your First Mage, is allied with the Dark. He has deceived you all!" There were cries at that, of anger and dismay.

"Hold!" It was Diarmuid, on his feet and facing the lios. His eyes flashed, but his voice was under tight control. "You said the Dark. Who?"

Once more the silence stretched. Then Brendel spoke. "I would not have ever wanted to bear this tale to the world. I spoke of svart alfar and wolves attacking us. We would not have died had it been only them. There was something else. A giant wolf, with silver on his head like a brand against the black. Then I saw him after with Metran and I knew him, for he had taken back his true form. I must tell you that the Wolflord of the andain has come among us again: Galadan has returned."

"Accursed be his name!" someone cried, and Kevin saw that it was Matt. "How can this be? He died at Andarien a thousand years ago."

"So thought we all," said Brendel, turning to the Dwarf. "But I saw him today, and this wound is his." He touched his torn shoulder. Then, "There is more. Something else came today and spoke with both of them."

Once more Brendel hesitated. And this time his eyes, dark-hued, went to Kevin's face.

"It was the black swan," he said, and a stillness fell upon stillness. "Avaia. She carried away Jennifer, your friend, the golden one. They had come for her, why I know not, but we were too few, too few against the Wolflord, and so my brethren are all dead, and she is gone. And the Dark is abroad in the world again."

Kevin, white with dread, looked at the maimed figure of the lios. "Where?" he gasped, in a voice that shocked him.

Brendel shook his head wearily. "I could not hear their words. Black Avaia took her north. Could I have stayed her flight, I would have died to do so. Oh, believe me," the lios alfar's voice faltered. "Your grief is mine, and mine may tear the fabric of my soul apart. Twenty of my people have died, and it is in my heart that they are not the last. We are the Children of Light, and the Dark is rising. I must return to Daniloth. But," and now his voice grew strong again, "an oath I will swear before you now. She was in my care. I shall find her, or avenge her, or die in the attempt." And Brendel cried then, so that the Great Hall echoed to the sound: "We shall fight them as we did before! As we always have!"

The words rang among them like a stern bell of defiance, and in Kevin Laine they lit a fire he did not know lay within him.

"Not alone!" he cried, his own voice pitched to carry. "If you share my grief, I will share yours. And others here will, too, I think."

"Aye!" boomed Matt Sören beside him.

"All of us!" cried Diarmuid, Prince of Brennin. "When the lios are slain in Brennin, the High Kingdom goes to war!"

A mighty roar exploded at those words. Building and building in a wave of fury it climbed to the highest windows of Delevan and resounded through the hall.

It drowned, quite completely, the despairing words of the High King.

"Oh, Mörnir," whispered Ailell, clutching his hands together in his lap. "What have I done? Where is Loren? What have I done?"

◆━◐◖━◆

There had been light, now there was not. One measured time in such ways. There were stars in the space above the trees; no moon yet, and only a thin one later, for tomorrow would be the night of the new moon.

His last night, if he lived through this one.

The Tree was a part of him now, another name, a summoning. He almost heard a meaning in the breathing of the forest all around him, but his mind was stretched and flattened, he could not reach to it, he could only endure, and hold the wall of memory as best he might.

One more night. After which there would be no music to be laid open by, no highways to forget, no rain, no sirens, none, no Rachel. One more night at most, for he wasn't sure he could survive another day like the last.

Though truly he would try: for the old King, and the slain farmer, and the faces he'd seen on the roads. Better to die for a reason, and with what one could retain of pride. Better, surely, though he could not say why.

*Now I give you to Mörnir,* Ailell had said. Which meant he was a gift, an offering, and it was all waste if he died too soon. So he had to hold to life, hold the wall, hold for the God, for he was the God's to claim, and there was thunder now. It seemed at times to come from within the Tree, which meant, in the way of things, from within himself. If only there could be rain before he died, he might find some kind of peace at the end. It had rained, though, when *she* died, it had rained all night.

His eyes were hurting now. He closed them, but that was no good, either, because she was waiting there, with music. Once, earlier, he had wanted to call her name in the wood, as he had not beside the open grave, to feel it on his lips again as he had not since; to burn his dry soul with her. Burn, since he could not cry.

Silence, of course. One did not do any such thing. One opened one's eyes instead on the Summer Tree, in the deep of Mörnirwood, and one saw a man come forward from among the trees.

It was very dark, he could not see who it was, but the faint starlight reflected from silver hair and so he thought . . .

"Loren?" he tried, but scarcely any sound escaped his cracked lips. He tried to wet them, but he had no moisture, he was dry. Then the figure came nearer, to stand in the starlight below where he was bound, and Paul saw that he had been wrong. The eyes that met his own were not those of the mage, and, looking into them, he did know fear then, for it should not end so, truly it should not. But the man below stood as if cloaked in power, even in that place, even in the glade of the Summer Tree, and in the dark eyes Paul saw his death.

Then the figure spoke. "I cannot allow it," he said, with finality. "You have courage, and something else, I think. Almost you are one of us, and it might have been that we could have shared something, you and I. Not now, though. This I cannot allow. You are calling a force too strong for the knowing, and it must not be wakened. Not when I am so near. Will you believe," the voice said, low and assured, "that I am sorry to have to kill you?"

Paul moved his lips. "Who?" he asked, the sound a scrape in his throat.

The other smiled at that. "Names matter to you? They should. It is Galadan who has come, and I fear it is the end."

Bound and utterly helpless, Paul saw the elegant figure draw a knife from his belt. "It will be clean, I promise you," he said. "Did you not come here for release? I will give it to you." Their eyes locked once more. It was a dream, it was so like a dream, so dark, blurred, shadowed. He closed his eyes; one closed one's eyes to dream. She was there, of course, but it was ending, so all right then, fine, let it end on her.

A moment passed. No blade, no severing. Then Galadan spoke again, but not to him, and in a different voice.

*"You?"* he said. "Here? Now I understand."

For reply there came only a deep, rumbling growl. His heart leaping, Paul opened his eyes. In the clearing facing Galadan was the grey dog he had seen on the palace wall.

Gazing at the dog, Galadan spoke again. "It was written in wind and fire long ago that we should meet," he said. "And here is as fit a place as any in all the worlds. Would you guard the sacrifice? Then your blood is the gateway to my desire. Come, and I shall drink it now!"

He placed a hand over his heart and made a twisting gesture, and after a brief blurring of space, there stood a moment later, where he had been, a wolf so large it dwarfed the grey figure of the dog. And the wolf had a splash of silver between its ears.

One endless moment the animals faced each other, and Paul realized that the Godwood had gone deathly still. Then Galadan howled so as to chill the heart, and leaped to attack.

There took place then a battle foretold in the first depths of time by the twin goddesses of war, who are named in all the worlds as Macha and Nemain. A portent it was to be, a presaging of the greatest war of all, this coming together in darkness of the wolf, who was a man whose spirit was annihilation, and the grey dog, who had been called by many names but was always the Companion.

The battle the two goddesses foreknew—for war was their demesne—but not the resolution. A portent then, a presaging, a beginning.

And so it came to pass that wolf and dog met at last in Fionavar, first of all the worlds, and below the Summer Tree they ripped and tore at one another with such fury that soon dark blood soaked the glade under the stars.

Again and again they hurled themselves upon each other, black on grey, and Paul, straining to see, felt his heart go out to the dog, with all the force of his being. He remembered the loss he had seen in its eyes, and he saw now, even in the shadows, as the animals rolled over and over, biting and grappling, engaging and recoiling in desperate frenzy, that the wolf was too large.

They were both black now, for the light grey fur of the dog was matted and dark with its own blood. Still it fought, eluding and attacking, summoning a courage, embodying a gallantry of defiance that hurt to see, it was so noble and so doomed.

The wolf was bleeding, too, and its flesh was ripped and torn, but it was so much larger; and more, more than that, Galadan carried within himself a power that went far deeper than tooth and gashing claw.

Paul became aware that his bound hands were torn and bleeding. Unconsciously he had been struggling to free himself, to go to the aid of the dog who was dying in his defence The bonds held, though, and so, too, did the prophecy, for this was to be wolf and dog alone, and so it was.

Through the night it continued. Weary and scored with wounds, the grey dog fought on; but its attacks were parried more easily now, its defences were more agonizing, more narrowly averting the final closing of jaw on jugular. It could only be a question of time, Paul realized, grieving and forced to bear witness. It hurt so much, so much. . . .

"*Fight!*" he screamed suddenly, his throat raw with effort. "Go on! I'll hold if you can—I'll make it through tomorrow night. In the name of the God, I swear it. Give me till tomorrow and I'll bring you rain."

For a moment the animals were checked by the force of his cry. Then, limp and drained, Paul saw with agony that it was the wolf who lifted a head to look at him, a terrible smile distorting its face. Then it turned back, back for the last attack, a force of fury, of annihilation. Galadan who had returned. It was a charge of uncoiled power, not to be denied or withstood.

And yet it was.

The dog, too, had heard Paul's cry; without the strength to raise its head in reply, it found yet in the words, in the desperate, scarcely articulate vow, a pure white power of its own; and reaching back, far back into its own long history of battle and loss, the grey dog met the wolf for the last time with a spirit of utmost denial, and the earth shook beneath them as they crashed together.

Over and over on the sodden ground they rolled, indistinguishable, one contorted shape that embodied all the endless conflict of Light and Dark in all the turning worlds.

Then the world turned enough, finally, for the moon to rise above the trees.

Only a crescent she was, the last thin, pale sliver before the dark of tomorrow. But she was still there, still glorious, a light. And Paul, looking up, understood then, from a deep place in his soul, that just as the Tree belonged to Mörnir, so did the moon to the Mother; and when the crescent moon shone above the Summer Tree, then was the banner of Brennin made real in that wood.

In silence, in awe, in deepest humility, he watched at length as one dark, blood-spattered animal disengaged from the other. It limped, tail down, to the edge of the glade, and when it turned to look back, Paul saw a splash of silver between its ears. With a snarl of rage, Galadan fled the wood.

The dog could barely stand. It breathed with a sucking heave of flank and sides that Paul ached to see. It was so terribly hurt, it was scarcely alive; the blood so thick upon it, he could not see an untorn patch of fur.

But it *was* alive, and it came haltingly over to gaze up at him, lifting its torn head under the light and succour of the moon it had waited for. In that moment, Paul Schafer felt his own cracked, dry soul open up again to love as he looked down upon the dog.

For the second time their eyes met, and this time Paul did not back away. He took in the loss he saw, all of it, the pain endured for him and endured long before him, and with the first power of the Tree, he made it his own.

"Oh, brave," he said, finding that he could speak. "There can never have been a thing so brave. Go now, for it is my turn, and I will keep faith. I'll hold now, until tomorrow night, for you as much as anything."

The dog looked at him, the eyes clouded with pain, but still deep with intelligence, and Paul knew he was understood.

"Goodbye," he whispered, a kind of caress in the words.

And in response the grey dog threw back its proud head and howled: a cry of triumph and farewell, so loud and clear it filled all the Godwood and then echoed far beyond it, beyond the bounds of the worlds, even, hurtling into time and space, that the goddesses might hear it, and know.

In the taverns of Paras Derval, the rumour of war spread like a fire in dry grass. Svarts had been seen, and giant wolves, and lios alfar had walked in the city and been slain in the land. Diarmuid, the Prince, had sworn vengeance. All over the capital, swords and spears were rescued from places where they had rusted long years. Anvil Lane would resound in the morning to the clanging sound of fevered preparation.

For Karsh, the tanner, though, there was other news that eclipsed even the rumours, and on the crest of it he was engaged in drinking himself happily to incapacity, and buying, with profoundly uncharacteristic largess, drinks for every man in earshot.

He had cause, they all agreed. It wasn't every day that saw a man's daughter initiated as an acolyte in the Temple of the Mother. The more so, when Jaelle, the High Priestess herself, had summoned her.

It was an honour, they all chorused, toasting Karsh amid the bustle of war talk. It was more, the tanner said, toasting back: for a man with four daughters, it was a blessing from the gods. From the Goddess, he corrected himself owlishly, and bought everyone another round with money marked until that day for her dowry.

In the sanctuary the newest acolyte drifted towards the sleep of the utterly exhausted. In her fourteen years she had never known a day like the one just past. Tears and pride, unexpected fear, and then laughter had all been part of it.

The ceremony she had barely understood, for they had given her a drink that made the domed room spin softly, though not unpleasantly. The axe she remembered, the chanting of the grey-clad priestesses of whose number she would soon be one, and then the voice, cold and powerful, of the High Priestess in her white robe.

She didn't remember when she had been cut, but the wound on her wrist throbbed under the cloth bandage. It was necessary, they had explained: blood to bind.

Leila hadn't bothered telling them that she had always known that.

Long past midnight Jaelle woke in the stillness of the Temple. High Priestess of Brennin, and one of the Mormae of Gwen Ystrat, she could not fail to hear, though no one else in Paras Derval would, the supernatural howling of a dog, as the moon shone down upon the Summer Tree.

She could hear it, but she did not understand, and lying in her bed she chafed and raged at her inability. There was something happening. Forces were abroad. She could feel power gathering like a storm.

She needed a Seer, by all the names of the Mother, she needed one. But there was only the hag, and she had sold herself. In the darkness of her room, the High Priestess clenched her long fingers in deep, unending bitterness. She had *need*, and was being denied. She was blind.

*Lost and forever,* she cursed again, and lay awake all the rest of the night, feeling it gathering, gathering.

⊷═◉═⊷

Kimberly thought she was dreaming. The same dream as two nights before, when the howling had shattered her vision of Paul and Ailell. She heard the dog, but this time she did not wake. Had she done so, she would have seen the Baelrath glowering ominously on her hand.

In the barn, among the close, familiar smells of the animals, Tyrth the servant did awaken. One moment he lay motionless, disbelieving, as the inner echoes of that great cry faded, then an expression crossed his face that was composed of many elements, but had more of longing than anything else. He swung out of bed, dressed quickly, and left the barn.

He limped across the yard and through the gate, closing it behind him. Only when he was in the strand of trees, and so hidden from the cottage, did the limp disappear. At which point he began to run, very swiftly, in the direction of the thunder.

Alone of those who heard the dog, Ysanne the Seer, awake in her bed as well, knew what that cry of pain and pride truly meant.

She heard Tyrth cross the yard, limping west, and she knew what that meant, too. There were so many unexpected griefs, she thought, so many different things to pity.

Not least, what she had now, at last, to do. For the storm was upon them; that cry in the wood was the harbinger, and so it was full time, and this night would see her do what she had seen long ago.

Not for herself did she grieve; there had been true fear at her first foreknowledge, and an echo of it when she had seen the girl in the Great Hall, but it had passed. The thing was very dark, but no longer terrifying; long ago she had known what would come.

It would be hard, though, for the girl. It would be hard in every way, but against what had begun tonight with the dog and the wolf . . . It was going to be hard for all of them. She could not help that; one thing only, she could do.

There was a stranger dying on the Tree. She shook her head; that, that was the deepest thing of all, and he was the one she had not been able to read, not that it mattered now. As to that, only the sporadic thunder mattered, thunder in a clear, starry sky. Mörnir would walk tomorrow, if the stranger held, and no one, not one of them could tell what that might mean. The God was outside of them.

But the girl. The girl was something else, and her Ysanne could see, had seen many times. She rose quietly and walked to stand over Kim. She saw the vellin stone on the slim wrist, and the Baelrath glowing on one finger, and she thought of Macha and Red Nemain and their prophecy.

She thought of Raederth then, for the first time that night. An old, old sorrow. Fifty years, but still. Lost once, fifty years ago on the far side of Night, and now . . . But the dog had howled in the wood, it was full, fullest time, and she had known for very long what was to come. There was no terror any more, only loss, and there had always been loss.

Kimberly stirred on her pillow. So young, the Seer thought. It was all so sad, but she knew, truly, of no other way, for she had lied the day before: it was not merely a matter of time before the girl could know the woven patterns of Fionavar as she needed to. It could not be. Oh, how could it ever be?

The girl was needed. She was a Seer, and more. The crossing bore witness, the pain of the land, the testimony in Eilathen's eyes. She was needed, but not ready, not complete, and the old woman knew one way, and only one, to do the last thing necessary.

The cat was awake, watching her with knowing eyes from the window sill. It was very dark; tomorrow there would be no moon. It was time, past time.

She laid a hand then, and it was very steady, upon Kimberly's forehead, where the single vertical line showed when she was distressed. Ysanne's fingers, still beautiful, traced a sign lightly and irrevocably on the unfurrowed brow. Kimberly slept. A gentle smile lit the Seer's face as she withdrew.

"Sleep, child," she murmured. "You have need, for the way is dark and there will be fire ere the end, and a breaking of the heart. Grieve not in the morning for my soul; my dream is done, my dreaming. May the Weaver name you his, and shield you from the Dark all your days."

Then there was silence in the room. The cat watched from the window. "*It is done*," Ysanne said, to the room, the night, the summer stars, to all her ghosts, and to the one loved man, now to be lost forever among the dead.

With care she opened the secret entrance to the chamber below, and went slowly down the stone stairs to where Colan's dagger lay, bright still in its sheath of a thousand years.

There was a very great deal of pain now. The moon had passed from overhead. His last moon, he realized, though thought was difficult. Consciousness was going to become a transient condition, a very hard thing, and already, with a long way yet to go, he was beginning to hallucinate. Colours, sounds. The trunk of the Tree seemed to have grown fingers, rough like bark, that wrapped themselves around him. He was touching the Tree everywhere now. Once, for a long spell, he thought he was inside it, looking out, not bound upon it. He thought he *was* the Summer Tree.

He was truly not afraid of dying, only of dying too soon. He had sworn an oath. But it was so hard to hold onto his mind, to hold his will to living another night. So much easier to let go, to leave the pain behind. Already the dog and wolf seemed to have been half dreamt, though he knew the battle had ended only hours before. There was dried blood on his wrists from when he had tried to free himself.

When the second man appeared before him, he was sure it was a vision. He was so far gone. *Popular attraction,* a faint, fading capacity of his mind mocked. *Come see the hanging man!*

This man had a beard, and deep-set dark eyes, and didn't seem about to change into an animal. He just stood there, looking up. A very boring vision. The trees were loud in the wind; there was thunder, he could feel it.

Paul made an effort, moving his head back and forth to clear it. His eyes hurt, for some reason, but he could see. And what he saw on the face of the figure below was an expression of such appalling, balked desire that the hair rose up on his neck. He should know who this was, he should. If his mind were working, he would know, but it was too hard, it was hopelessly beyond him.

"You have stolen my death," the figure said.

Paul closed his eyes. He was too far away from this. Too far down the road. He was incapable of explaining, unable to do more than try to endure.

An oath. He had sworn an oath. What did an oath mean? A whole day more, it meant. And a third night.

Some time later his eyes seemed to be open again and he saw, with uttermost relief, that he was alone. There was grey in the eastern sky; one more, one last.

And this was the second night of Pwyll the Stranger on the Summer Tree.

# CHAPTER 9

In the morning came something unheard of: a hot, dry wind, bitter and unsettling, swept down into Paras Derval from the north.

No one could remember a hot north wind before. It carried with it the dust of bone-bare farms, so the air darkened that day, even at noon, and the high sun shone balefully orange through the obscuring haze.

The thunder continued, almost a mockery. There were no clouds.

"With all respect, and such-like sentiments," Diarmuid said from by the window, his tone insolent and angry, "we are wasting time." He looked dishevelled and dangerous; he was also, Kevin realized with dismay, a little drunk.

From his seat at the head of the council table, Ailell ignored his heir. Kevin, still not sure why he'd been invited here, saw two bright spots of red on the cheeks of the old King. Ailell looked terrible; he seemed to have shrivelled overnight.

Two more men entered the room: a tall, clever-looking man, and beside him, a portly, affable fellow. The other mage, Kevin guessed: Teyrnon, with Barak, his source. Gorlaes, the Chancellor, made the introductions and it turned out he was right, except the innocuous-seeming fat man was the mage, and not the other way around.

Loren was still away, but Matt was in the room, and so, too, were a number of other dignitaries. Kevin recognized Mabon, the Duke of Rhoden, Ailell's cousin, and beyond him was Niavin of Seresh. The ruddy man with the salt-and-pepper beard was Ceredur, who had been made North Warden after Diarmuid's brother was exiled. He'd seen them at last night's banquet. Their expressions were very different now.

It was Jaelle they were waiting for, and as the moments passed, Kevin, too, began to grow impatient with apprehension. "My lord," he said abruptly to the King, "while we wait—who is Galadan? I feel completely ignorant."

It was Gorlaes who answered. Ailell was sunken in silence, and Diarmuid was still sulking by the window. "He is a force of Darkness from long ago. A very great power, though he did not always serve the Dark," the Chancellor said. "He is one of the andain—child of a mortal woman and a god. In older days there were not a few such unions. The andain are a difficult race, moving easily in no world at all. Galadan became their Lord, by far the most powerful of them all, and said to be the most subtle mind in Fionavar. Then something changed him."

"An understatement, that," murmured Teyrnon.

"I suppose," said Gorlaes. "What happened is that he fell in love with Lisen of the Wood. And when she rejected him and bound herself instead to a mortal, Amairgen Whitebranch, first of the mages, Galadan vowed the most complete vengeance ever sworn." The Chancellor's voice took on a note of awe. "Galadan swore that the world that witnessed his humiliation would cease to exist."

There was a silence. Kevin could think of nothing to say. Nothing at all.

Teyrnon took up the tale. "In the time of the Bael Rangat, he was first lieutenant to Rakoth and most terrible of his servants. He had the power to take on the shape of a wolf, and so he commanded them all. His purposes, though, were at odds with his master's, for though the Unraveller sought rule for lust of power and domination, Galadan would have conquered to utterly destroy."

"They fought?" Kevin hazarded. Teyrnon shook his head. "One did not pitch oneself against Rakoth. Galadan has very great powers, and if he has joined the svart alfar to his wolves in war upon us, then we are in danger indeed; but Rakoth, whom the stones bind, is outside the Tapestry. There is no thread with his name upon it. He cannot die, and none could ever set his will against him."

"Amairgen did," said Diarmuid from the window.

"And died," Teyrnon replied, not ungently.

"There are worse things," the Prince snapped.

At that, Ailell stirred. Before he could speak, though, the door opened and Jaelle swept into the room. She nodded briefly to the King, acknowledged no one else, and slipped into the chair left for her at one end of the long table.

"Thank you for hurrying," Diarmuid murmured, coming to take his chair at Ailell's right hand. Jaelle merely smiled. It was not a pleasant smile.

"Well, now," said the King, clearing his throat, "it seems to me that the best way to proceed is to spend this morning in a careful review—"

"In the name of the Weaver and the Loom, Father!" Diarmuid's fist crashed on the table. "We all know what has happened! What is there to review? I swore an oath last night we would aid the lios, and—"

"A premature oath, Prince Diarmuid," Gorlaes interrupted. "And not one within your power to swear."

"No?" said the Prince softly. "Then let me remind you—let us indeed carefully review," he amended delicately, "what has happened. One of my men is dead. One of the ladies of this court is dead. A svart alfar was within the palace grounds six nights ago." He was ticking them off on his fingers. "Lios alfar have died in Brennin. Galadan has returned. Avaia has returned. Our First Mage is a proven traitor. A guest-friend of this House has been torn away from us—a guest-friend, I pause to point out, of our radiant High Priestess as well. Which should mean something, unless she takes such things to be meaningless."

"I do not," Jaelle snapped through clenched teeth.

"No?" the Prince said, his eyebrows raised. "What a surprise. I thought you might regard it as of the same importance as arriving to a War Council on time."

"It isn't yet a Council of War," Duke Ceredur said bluntly. "Though to be truthful, I am with the Prince—I think we should have the country on war footing immediately."

There was a grunt of agreement from Matt Sören. Teyrnon, though, shook his round honest head. "There is too much fear in the city," he demurred, "and it is going to spread within days throughout the country." Niavin, Duke of Seresh, was nodding agreement. "Unless we know exactly what we are doing and what we face, I think we must take care not to panic them," the chubby mage concluded.

"We *do* know what we face!" Diarmuid shot back. "Galadan was seen. He was *seen*! I say we summon the Dalrei, make league with the lios, and seek the Wolflord wherever he goes and crush him now!"

"Amazing," Jaelle murmured drily in the pause that ensued, "how impetuous younger sons tend to be, especially when they have been drinking."

"Go gently, sweetling," the Prince said softly. "I will not brook that from anyone. You, least of all, my midnight moonchild."

Kevin exploded. "Will you two listen to yourselves? Don't you understand: Jennifer is gone! We've got to do something besides bicker, for God's sake!"

"I quite agree," Teyrnon said sternly. "May I suggest that we invite our friend from Daniloth to join us if he is able. We should seek the views of the lios on this."

"You may seek their views," said Ailell dan Art, suddenly rising to tower above them all, "and I would have his thoughts reported to me later, Teyrnon. But I have decided to adjourn this Council until this same time tomorrow. You all have leave to go."

"Father—" Diarmuid began, stammering with consternation.

"No words!" Ailell said harshly, and his eyes gleamed in his bony face. "I am still High King in Brennin, let all of you remember it!"

*"We do, my dearest lord,"* said a familiar voice from the door. "We all do," Loren Silvercloak went on, "but Galadan is far too great a power for us to delay without cause."

Dusty and travel-stained, his eyes hollow with exhaustion, the mage ignored the fierce reaction to his arrival and gazed only at the King. There was, Kevin realized, a sudden surge of relief in the room; he felt it within himself. Loren was back. It made a very great difference.

Matt Sören had risen to stand beside the mage, eyeing his friend with a grimly worried expression. Loren's weariness was palpable, but he seemed to gather his resources, and turned among all that company to look at Kevin.

"I am sorry," he said simply. "I am deeply sorry."

Kevin nodded jerkily. "I know," he whispered. That was all; they both turned to the King.

"Since when need the High King explain himself?" Ailell said, but his brief assertion of control seemed to have drained him; his tone was querulous, not commanding.

"He need not, my lord. But if he does, his subjects and advisers may sometimes be of greater aid." The mage had come several steps into the room.

"Sometimes," the King replied. "But at other times there are things they do not and should not know." Kevin saw Gorlaes shift in his seat. He took a chance.

"But the Chancellor knows, my lord. Should not your other counsellors? Forgive my presumption, but a woman I love is gone, High King."

Ailell regarded him for a long time without speaking. Then he gave a small nod. "Well spoken," he said. "Indeed, the only person here who truly has a right to be told is you, but I will do as you ask."

"My lord!" Gorlaes began urgently.

Ailell raised a hand, quelling him.

In the ensuing silence there came a distant roll of thunder.

"Can you not hear it?" the High King whispered on a rising note. "Listen! The God is coming. If the offering holds, he comes tonight. This will be the third night. How can we act before we know?"

They were all on their feet.

"Someone is on the Tree," Loren said flatly.

The King nodded.

"My brother?" asked Diarmuid, his face ashen.

"No," said Ailell, and turned to Kevin.

It took a moment, then everything fell into place. "Oh, God," Kevin cried. "It's Paul!" And he lowered his face into his hands.

⊹⟞⟝⊙⟝⟞⊹

Kimberly woke knowing.

*Who kills without love shall surely die,* Seithr the Dwarf-King had said to Colan the Beloved long ago. And then, lowering his voice, he had added for only the son of Conary to hear, "Who dies with love may make of his soul a gift to the one marked with the pattern on the dagger's haft."

"A rich gift," had murmured Colan.

"Richer than you know. Once given, the soul is gone. It is lost to time. There can be no passage beyond the walls of Night to find light at the Weaver's side."

Conary's son had bowed very low. "I thank you," he said. "Double-edged the knife, and double-edged the gift. Mörnir grant us the sight to use it truly."

Even before she looked, Kim knew that her hair was white. Lying in bed that first morning she cried, though silently and not for long. There was much to be done. Even with the vellin on her wrist, she felt the day like a fever. She would be unworthy of the gift if she were undone by mourning.

So she rose up, Seer of Brennin, newest dreamer of the dream, to begin what Ysanne had died to allow her to do.

More than died.

There are kinds of action, for good or ill, that lie so far outside the boundaries of normal behaviour that they force us, in acknowledging that they have occurred, to restructure our own understanding of reality. We have to make room for them.

This, Kim thought, is what Ysanne had done. With an act of love so great—and not just for her—it could scarcely be assimilated, she had stripped her soul of any place it held in time. She was gone, utterly. Not just from life, but more, much more, as Kim now knew—from death as well from what lay after in the patterns of the Weaver for his children.

Instead, the Seer had given all she could to Kim, had given all. No longer could Kim say she was not of Fionavar, for within her now pulsed an intuitive understanding of this world more deep even than the knowledge of her own. Looking now at a bannion, she would know what it was; she understood the vellin on her wrist, something of the wild Baelrath on her finger; and one day she would know who was to bear the Circlet of Lisen and tread the darkest path of all. Raederth's words; Raederth whom Ysanne had lost again, that Kim might have this.

Which was so unfair. What right, what possible right had the Seer had to make such a sacrifice? To impose with this impossible gift, such a burden? How had she presumed to decide for Kim?

The answer, though, was easy enough after a while: she hadn't. Kim could go, leave, deny. She could cross home as planned and dye her hair, or leave it as it was and go New Wave if she preferred. Nothing had changed. Except, of course, that everything had. *How can you tell the dancer from the dance?* she had read somewhere. Or the dreamer from the dream, she amended, feeling a little lost. Because the answer to that was easiest of all.

You can't.

Some time later she laid her hand, in the way she now knew, upon the slab below the table, and saw the door appear.

Down the worn stone stairs she went, in her turn. Lisen's Light showed her the way. The dagger would be there, she knew, with red blood on the silver-blue thieren of the blade. There would be no body, though, for Ysanne the Seer, having died with love and by that blade, had taken herself beyond the walls of time, where she could not be followed. Lost and forever. It was final, absolute. It was ended.

And she was left here in the first world of them all, bearing the burden of that.

She cleaned Lökdal and sheathed it to a sound like a harpstring. She put it back in the cabinet. Then she went up the stairs again towards the world that needed her, all the worlds that needed what it seemed she was.

⊷⟾◉⟾⊷

"Oh, God," Kevin said. "It's Paul!"

A stunned silence descended, overwhelming in its import. This was something for which none of them could have prepared. I should have known, Kevin was thinking, though. I should have figured it out when he first told me about the Tree. A bitterness scaling towards rage pulled his head up. . . .

"That must have been some chess game," he said savagely to the King.

139

"It was," Ailell said simply. Then, "He came to me and offered. I would never have asked, or even thought to ask. Will you believe this?"

And of course he did. It fit too well. The attack was unfair, because Paul would have done what he wanted to, exactly what he wanted to, and this was a better way to die than falling from a rope down a cliff. As such things were measured, and he supposed they could be measured. It hurt, though, it really hurt, and—

"No!" said Loren decisively. "It must be stopped. This we cannot do. He is not even one of us, my lord. We cannot lay our griefs upon him in this way. He must be taken down. This is a guest of your House, Ailell. Of our world. What were you thinking of?"

"Of our world. Of my House. Of my people. He came to me, Silvercloak."

"And should have been refused!"

"Loren, it was a true offering." The speaker was Gorlaes, his voice unwontedly diffident.

"You were there?" the mage bristled.

"I bound him. He walked past us to the Tree. It was as if he were alone. I know not how, and I am afraid here speaking of it, as I was in the Godwood, but I swear it is a proper offering."

"No," Loren said again, his face sharp with emotion. "He cannot possibly understand what he is doing. My lord, he must be taken down before he dies."

"It is his own death, Loren. His chosen gift. Would you presume to strip it from him?" Ailell's eyes were so old, so weary.

"I would," the mage replied. "He was not brought here to die for us."

It was time to speak.

"Maybe not," Kevin said, forcing the words out, stumbling and in pain. "But I think that is why he came." He was losing them both. Jennifer. Now Paul, too. His heart was sore. "If he went, he went knowing, and because he wanted to. Let him die for you, if he can't live for himself. Leave him, Loren. Let him go."

He didn't bother trying to hide the tears, not even from Jaelle, whose eyes on his face were so cold.

"Kevin," said the mage gently, "it is a very bad death. No one lasts the three—it will be waste and to no point. Let me take him down."

"It is not for you to choose, Silvercloak," Jaelle spoke then. "Nor for this one, either."

Loren turned, his eyes hard as flint. "If I decide to bring him down," he said driving the words into her, "then it will be necessary for you to kill me to prevent it."

"Careful, mage," Gorlaes cautioned, though mildly. "That is close to treason. The High King has acted here. Would you undo what he has done?"

None of them seemed to be getting the point. "No one has acted but Paul," Kevin said. He felt drained now, but completely unsurprised. He really should have known this was coming. "Loren, if anyone understood this, it was him. If he lasts three nights, will there be rain?"

"There might be." It was the King. "This is wild magic, we cannot know."

"Blood magic," Loren amended bitterly.

Teyrnon shook his head. "The God is wild, though there may be blood."

"He can't last, though," Diarmuid said, his voice sober. He looked at Kevin. "You said yourself, he's been ill."

A cracked, high laugh escaped Kevin at that.

"Never stopped him," he said fiercely, feeling it so hard. "The stubborn, brave, son of a bitch!"

The love in the harsh words reached through to all of them, it could not help but do so; and it had to be acknowledged. Even by Jaelle and, in a very different way, by Loren Silvercloak.

"Very well," said the mage at last. He sank into a chair. "Oh, Kevin. They will sing of him here as long as Brennin lasts, regardless of the end."

"Songs," said Kevin. "Songs only mess you up." It was too much effort not to ache; he let it sweep over him. Sometimes, his father had said, you can't do anything. *Oh, Abba,* he thought, far away and alone inside the hurt.

"Tomorrow," Ailell the High King said, rising again, gaunt and tall. "I will meet you here at sunrise tomorrow. We will see what the night brings."

It was a dismissal. They withdrew, leaving the King sitting at the last alone in his council chamber with his years, his self-contempt, and the image of the stranger on the Tree in his name, in the name of the God, in his name.

They went outside into the central courtyard, Diarmuid, Loren, Matt, and Kevin Laine. In silence they walked together, the same face in their minds, and Kevin was grateful for the presence of friends.

The heat was brutal, and the sour wind abraded them under the sickly, filtered sun. A prickly tension seemed woven into the texture of the day. And then, suddenly, there was more.

*"Hold!"* cried Matt the Dwarf, whose people were of the caverns of the earth, the roots of mountains, the ancient rocks. "Hold! Something comes!"

And in the same instant, north and west of them, Kim Ford rose, a blinding pulse in her head, an apprehension of enormity, and moved, as if compelled, out back of the cottage where Tyrth was labouring. "Oh, God," she whispered. "Oh, my God!" Seeing with distorted vision the vellin bracelet writhing on her wrist, knowing it could not ward what was coming, what had been coming for so long, so terribly, what none of them had seen, none, what was *here, now, right now!* She screamed, in overwhelming agony.

And the roof of the world blew up.

Far, far in the north among the ice, Rangat Cloud-Shouldered rose up ten miles into the heavens, towering above the whole of Fionavar, master of the world, prison of a god for a thousand years.

But no more. A vast geyser of blood-red fire catapulted skyward with a detonation heard even in Cathal. Rangat exploded with a column of fire so high the curving world could not hide it. And at the apex of its ascent the flame was seen to form itself into the five fingers of a hand, taloned, oh, taloned, and curving southward on the wind to bring them all within its grasp, to tear them all to shreds.

A gauntlet hurled, it was a wild proclamation of release to all the cowering ones who would be his slaves forever after now. For if they had feared the svart alfar, trembled before a renegade mage and the power of Galadan, what would they do now to see the fingers of this fire raking heaven?

To know Rakoth Maugrim was unchained and free, and could bend the very Mountain to his vengeance?

And on the north wind there came then the triumphant laughter of the first and fallen god, who was coming down on them like a hammer bringing fire, bringing war.

The explosion hit the King like a fist in the heart. He tottered from the window of the council chamber and fell into a chair, his face grey, his hands opening and closing spasmodically as he gasped for breath.

"My lord?" Tarn the page rushed into the room and knelt, terror in his eyes. *"My lord?"*

But Ailell was beyond speech. He heard only the laughter on the wind, saw only the fingers curving to clutch them, enormous and blood-coloured, a death cloud in the sky, bringing not rain but ruin.

He seemed to be alone. Tarn must have run for aid. With a great effort Ailell rose, breathing in high short gasps, and made his way down the short hallway to his rooms. There he stumbled to the inner door and opened it.

Down the familiar corridor he went. At the end of the passageway, the King stopped before the viewing slot. His vision was troubled: there seemed to be a girl beside him. She had white hair, which was unnatural. Her eyes were kind, though, as Marrien's had been at the end. He had managed to win love there after all. It was patience that power taught. He had told that to the stranger, he remembered. After ta'bael. Where was the stranger? He had something else to say to him, something important.

Then he remembered. Opening the slot, Ailell the King looked into the Room of the Stone and saw that it was dark. The fire was dead, the sacred naal fire; the pillar carved with images of Conary bore nothing upon its crown, and on the floor, shattered forever into fragments like his heart, lay the stone of Ginserat.

He felt himself falling. It seemed to take a very long time. The girl was there; her eyes were so sorrowful. He almost wanted to comfort her. Aileron, he thought. Diarmuid. Oh, Aileron. Very far off, he heard thunder. A god was coming. Yes, of course, but what fools they all were—it was the wrong god. It was so funny, so funny, it was.

And on that thought he died.

So passed, on the eve of war, Ailell dan Art, High King of Brennin, and the rule passed to his son in a time of darkness, when fear moved across the face of all the lands. A good King and wise, Ysanne the Seer had called him once.

What he had fallen from.

⁘ ⇒◉⇐ ⁘

Jennifer was flying straight at the Mountain when it went up.

A harsh cry of triumph burst from the throat of the black swan as the blast of fire rose far above to separate high in the air and form the taloned hand, bending south like smoke on the wind, but not dissolving, hanging there, reaching.

There was laughter in the sky all around her. *Is the person under the mountain dead?* Paul Schafer had asked before they crossed. He wasn't dead, nor was he under the Mountain anymore. And though she didn't understand, Jennifer knew that he wasn't a person, either. You had to be something more to shape a hand of fire and send mad laughter down the wind.

The swan increased her speed. For a day and a night Avaia had borne her north, the giant wings beating with exquisite grace, the odour of corruption surrounding her, even in the high, thin reaches of the sky. All through this second day they flew, but late that night they set down on the shores of a lake north of the wide grasslands that had unrolled beneath their flight.

There were svart alfar waiting for them, a large band this time, and with them were other creatures, huge and savage, with fangs and carrying swords. She was pulled roughly from the swan and thrown on the ground. They didn't bother tying her—she couldn't move in any case, her limbs were brutally stiff with cramp after so long bound and motionless.

After a time they brought her food: the half-cooked carcass of some prairie rodent. When she shook her head in mute refusal, they laughed.

Later they did tie her, tearing her blouse in the process. A few of them began pinching and playing with her body, but some leader made them stop. She hardly registered it. A far corner of her mind, it seemed to be as remote as her life, said that she was in shock, and that it was probably a blessing.

When morning came, they would bind her to the swan again and Avaia would fly all that third day, angling northwest now so the still-smouldering mountain gradually slid around towards the east. Then, towards sunset, in a region of great cold, Jennifer would see Starkadh, like a giant ziggurat of hell among the ice, and she would begin to understand.

⤙═◎═⤚

For the second time, Kimberly came to in her bed in the cottage. This time, though, there was no Ysanne to watch over her. Instead, the eyes gazing at her were the dark ones, deep-set, of the servant, Tyrth.

As awareness returned she became conscious of a pain on her wrist. Looking, she saw a scoring of black where the vellin bracelet had twisted into her skin. That she remembered. She shook her head.

"I think I would have died without this." She made a small movement of her hand to show him.

He didn't reply, but a great tension seemed to dissolve from his compact, muscled frame as he heard her speak. She looked around; by the shadows it was late afternoon.

"That's twice now you've had to carry me here," she said

"You must not let that bother you, my lady," he said in his rough, shy voice.

"Well, I'm not in the habit of fainting."

"I would never think that." He cast his eyes down.

"What happened with the Mountain?" she asked, almost unwilling to know.

"It is over," he replied. "Just before you woke." She nodded. That made sense.

"Have you been watching me all day?"

He looked apologetic. "Not always, my lady. I am sorry, but the animals were frightened and . . ."

At that she smiled inwardly. He was pushing it a bit.

"There is boiling water," Tyrth said after a short silence. "Could I make you a drink?"

"Please."

She watched as he limped to the fire. With neat, economical motions he prepared a pot of some herbal infusion and carried it back to the table by the bed.

It was, she decided, time.

"You don't have to fake the limp anymore," she said.

He was very cool, you had to give him credit. Only the briefest flicker of uncertainty had touched the dark eyes, and his hands pouring her drink were absolutely steady. Only when he finished did he sit down for the first time and regard her for a long time in silence.

"Did she tell you?" he asked finally, and she heard his true voice for the first time.

"No. She lied, actually. Said it wasn't her secret to tell." She hesitated. "I learned from Eilathen by the lake."

"I watched that. I wondered."

Kim could feel her forehead creasing with its incongruous vertical line.

"Ysanne is gone, you know." She said it as calmly as she could.

He nodded. "That much I know, but I don't understand what has happened. Your hair . . ."

"She had Lökdal down below," Kim said bluntly. Almost, she wanted to hurt him with it. "She used it on herself."

He did react, and she was sorry for the thought behind her words. A hand came up to cover his mouth, a curious gesture in such a man. "No," he breathed. "Oh, Ysanne, no!" She could hear the loss.

"You understand what she has done?" she asked. There was a catch in her voice; she controlled it. There was so much pain.

"I know what the dagger does, yes. I didn't know she had it here. She must have come to love you very much."

"Not just me. All of us." She hesitated. "She dreamt me twenty-five years ago. Before I was born." Did that make it easier? Did anything?

His eyes widened. "That I never knew."

"How could you?" He seemed to regard gaps in his awareness as deeply felt affronts. But there was something else that had to be said. "There is more," Kim said. *His name is not to be spoken*, she thought, then: "Your father died this afternoon, Aileron."

There was a silence. "Old news," the elder Prince of Brennin said. "Listen."

And after a moment she heard them: all the bells in Paras Derval tolling. The death bells for the passing of a King.

"I'm sorry," she said.

His mouth twitched, then he looked out the window. *You cold bastard*, she thought. *Old news*. He deserved more than that, surely; surely he did. She was about to say as much when Aileron turned back to her, and she saw the river of tears pouring and pouring down his face.

*Dear God*, she thought shakily, enduring a paroxysm of self-condemnation. He may be hard to read, but how can you be *that* far off? It would have been funny, a Kim Ford classic, except that people were going to be relying on her now for so much. It was no good, no good at all. She was an impulsive, undisciplined, halfway-decent intern from Toronto. What the *hell* was she going to do?

Nothing, at any rate, for the moment. She held herself very still on the bed, and after a minute Aileron lifted his tanned, bearded face and spoke.

"After my mother died, he was never the same. He . . . dwindled. Will you believe that he was once a very great man?"

This she could help him with. "I saw by the lake. I know he was, Aileron."

"I watched him until I could hardly bear it," he said, under control now. "Then factions formed in the palace that wanted him to step aside for me. I killed two men who spoke of it in my presence, but my father grew suspicious and frightened. I could not talk to him anymore."

"And Diarmuid?"

The question seemed to genuinely surprise him. "My brother? He was drunk most of the time, and taking ladies to South Keep the rest. Playing March Warden down there."

"There seems to be more to him than that," Kim said mildly.

"To a woman, perhaps."

She blinked. "That," she said, "is insulting."

He considered it. "I suppose it is," he said. "I'm sorry." Then he surprised her again. "I'm not good," Aileron said, his eyes averted, "at making myself liked. Men will usually end up respecting me, if against their will, because at some things they value I have . . . a little skill. But I have no skill with women." The eyes, almost black, swung back to hers. "I am also hard to shake from desires I have, and I am not patient with interference."

He was not finished. "I tell you these things, not because I expect to change, but so you will know I am aware of them. There will be people I must trust, and if you are a Seer, then you must be one of them, and I'm afraid you will have to deal with me as I am."

A silence followed this, not surprisingly. For the first time she noticed Malka and called her softly. The black cat leaped to the bed and curled up on her lap.

"I'll think about it," she said finally. "No promises; I'm fairly stubborn myself. May I point out, on the original issue, that Loren seems to value your brother quite a bit, and unless I've missed something, Silvercloak isn't a woman." *Too much asperity,* she thought. *You must go carefully here.*

Aileron's eyes were unreadable. "He was our teacher as boys," he said. "He has hopes still of salvaging something in Diarmuid. And in fairness, my brother does elicit love from his followers, which must mean something."

"Something," she echoed gravely. "You don't see anything to salvage?" It was ironic, actually: she hadn't liked Diarmuid at all, and here she was . . .

Aileron, for reply, merely shrugged expressively.

"Leave it, then," she said. "Will you finish your story?"

"There is little left to tell. When the rains receded last year, and stopped absolutely this spring, I suspected it was not chance. I wanted to die for him, so I would not have to watch him fading. Or see the expression in his eyes. I couldn't live with him mistrusting me. So I asked to be allowed to go to the Summer Tree, and he refused. Again I asked, again he refused. Then word came to Paras Derval of children dying on the farms, and I asked again before all the court and once more he refused to grant me leave. And so . . ."

"And so you told him exactly what you thought." She could picture the scene.

"I did. And he exiled me."

"Not very effectively," she said wryly.

"Would you have me leave my land, Seer?" he snapped, the voice suddenly commanding. It pleased her; he had some caring, then. More than some, if she were being fair. So she said, "Aileron, he did right. You must know that. How could the High King let another die for him?"

And knew immediately that there was something wrong.

"You don't know, then." It was not a question. The sudden gentleness in his voice unsettled her more than anything.

"What? Please. You had better tell me."

"My father did let another go," Aileron said. "Listen to the thunder. Your friend is on the Tree. Pwyll. He has lasted two nights. This is the last, if he is still alive."

Pwyll. Paul.

It fit. It fit too perfectly. She was brushing tears away, but others kept falling. "I saw him," she whispered. "I saw him with your father in my dream, but I couldn't hear what they said, because there was this music, and—"

Then that, too, fell into place.

"Oh, Paul," she breathed. "It was the Brahms, wasn't it? Rachel's Brahms piece. How could I not have remembered?"

"Would you have changed anything?" Aileron asked. "Would you have been right to?"

Too hard, that one, just then. She concentrated on the cat. "Do you hate him?" she asked in a small voice, surprising herself with the question.

It drove him to his feet with a startled, exposed gesture. He strode to the window and looked out over the lake. There were bells. And then thunder. A day so charged with power. And it wasn't over. Night to come, the third night . . .

"I will try not to," he said at last, so softly Kim could scarcely hear it.

"Please," she said, feeling that somehow it mattered. If only to her, to ease her own gathering harvest of griefs. She rose from the bed, holding the cat in both arms.

He turned to face her. The light was strange behind him.

Then, "It is to be my war," said Aileron dan Ailell.

She nodded.

"You have seen this?" he pushed.

Again she nodded. The wind had died outside; it was very quiet. "You would have thrown it away on the Tree."

"Not thrown away. But yes, it was a foolishness. In me, not in your friend," he added after a moment. "I went to see him there last night. I could not help myself. In him it is something else."

"Grief. Pride. A dark kind."

"It is a dark place."

"Can he last?"

Slowly, Aileron shook his head. "I don't think so. He was almost gone last night."

Paul. When, she thought, had she last heard him laugh?

"He's been sick," she said. It sounded almost irrelevant. Her own voice was funny, too.

Aileron touched her shoulder awkwardly. "I will not hate him, Kim." He used her name for the first time. "I cannot. It is so bravely done."

"He has that," she said. She was not going to cry again. "He has that," she repeated, lifting her head. "And we have a war to fight."

"We?" Aileron asked, and in his eyes she could see the entreaty he would not speak.

"You're going to need a Seer," she said matter-of-factly. "I seem to be the best you've got. And I have the Baelrath, too."

He came a step towards her. "I am . . ." He took a breath. "I am . . . pleased," he managed.

A laugh escaped her, she couldn't help it. "God," she said on a rising note. "God, Aileron, I've never met anyone who had so much trouble saying thank-you. What do you do when someone passes you the salt?"

His mouth opened and closed. He looked very young.

"Anyhow," she said briskly, "you're welcome. And now we'd better get going. You should be in Paras Derval tonight, don't you think?"

It seemed that he had already saddled the horse in the barn, and had only been waiting for her. While Aileron went out back to bring the stallion around, she set about closing up the cottage. The dagger and the Circlet would be safest in the chamber down below. She knew that sort of thing now, it was instinctive.

She thought of Raederth then, and wondered if it was folly to feel sorrow for a man so long dead. But it wasn't, she knew, she now knew; for the dead are still in time, they are travelling, they are not lost. Ysanne was lost. She still needed a long time alone, Kim realized, but she didn't have it, so there was no point even thinking. The Mountain had taken that kind of luxury away from all of them.

From all of them. She did pause, at that. She was numbering herself among them, she realized, even in her thoughts. *Are you aware,* she asked herself, with a kind of awe, *that you are now the Seer of the High Kingdom of Brennin in Fionavar?*

She was. *Holy cow*, she thought, *talk about over-achievers!* But then her mind swung back to Aileron, and the flared levity faded. Aileron, whom she was going to help become King if she could, even though his brother was the heir. She would do it because her blood sang to her that this was right, and that, she knew by now, was part of what being a Seer meant.

She was quiet and ready when he came round the side on the horse. He had a sword now, and a bow slung in the saddle, and he rode the black charger with an easy grace. She was, she had to admit, impressed.

There was a slight issue at the outset over her refusal to leave Malka behind, but when she threatened to walk, Aileron, a stony expression on his face, reached a hand down and swung her up behind him. With the cat. He was very strong, she realized.

He also had a scratched shoulder a minute later. Malka, it seemed, didn't like riding horseback. Aileron, it also seemed, could be remarkably articulate when swearing. She told him as much, sweetly, and was rewarded with a quite communicative silence.

With the dying of the wind, the haze of the day seemed to be lifting. It was still light, and the sun, setting almost directly behind them, cast its long rays along the path.

Which was one reason the ambush failed.

They were attacked at the bend where she and Matt had first seen the lake. Before the first of the svarts had leaped to the road, Aileron, some sixth sense triggered, had already kicked the stallion into a gallop.

There were no darts this time. They had been ordered to take the white-haired woman alive, and she had only one servant as a guard. It should have been easy. There were fifteen of them.

Twelve, after the first rush of the horse, as Aileron's blade scythed on both sides. She was hampering him, though. With a concise movement he leaped from the saddle, killing another svart as he landed. "Go on!" he shouted. Of its own accord, the horse sped into a trot and then a gallop down the path. *No way*, Kim thought, and, holding the terrified cat as best she could, grappled for the reins and pulled the stallion to a halt. Turning, she watched the battle, her heart leaping into her throat, though not with fear.

By the light of the setting sun, Kimberly bore witness to the first battle of Aileron dan Ailell in his war, and a stunning, a nearly debilitating grace was displayed for her then upon that lonely path. To see him with a sword in his hand was almost heart-breaking. It was a dance. It was more. Some men, it seemed, were born to do a thing; it was true.

Because awesomely, stupefyingly, she saw that it had been a mismatch from the first. Fifteen of them, with weapons and sharp teeth for close fighting, against the one man with the long blade flashing in his hand, and she understood that he was going to win. Effortlessly, he was going to win.

It didn't last very long. Not one of the fifteen svart alfar survived. Breathing only a little quickly, he cleaned his sword and sheathed it, before walking towards her up the path, the sun low behind him. It was very quiet now. His dark eyes, she saw, were sombre.

"I told you to go," he said.

"I know. I don't always do what I'm told. I thought I warned you."

He was silent, looking up at her.

"A 'little' skill," she mimicked quite precisely.

His face, she saw with delight, had suddenly gone shy.

"Why," Kim Ford asked, "did that take you so long?"

For the first time she heard him laugh.

They reached Paras Derval at twilight, with Aileron hooded for concealment. Once inside the town they made their way quickly and quietly to Loren's quarters. The mage was there, with Matt and Kevin Laine.

Kim and Aileron told their stories as succinctly as they could; there was little time. They spoke of Paul, in whispers, hearing the thunder gathering in the west.

And then, when it became clear that there was something important neither she nor the Prince knew, they were told about Jennifer.

At which point it was made evident that notwithstanding a frightened cat, or a kingdom that needed her, the new Seer of Brennin could still fall apart with the best of them.

⊹⇒◦⇐⊹

Twice during the day he thought it was the end. There was very great pain. He was badly sunburned now, and so dry. Dry as the land, which, he had thought earlier—how much earlier?—was probably the point. The nexus. It all seemed so simple at times, it came down to such basic correspondences. But then his mind would start to spin, to slide, and with the slide, all the clarity went, too.

He may have been the only person in Fionavar who didn't see the Mountain send up its fire. The sun was fire enough for him. He heard the laughter, but was so far gone he placed it elsewhere, in his own hell. It hurt there, too; he was not spared.

That time it was the bells that brought him back. He was lucid then for an interval, and knew where they were ringing, though not why. His eyes hurt; they were puffy with sunburn, and he was desperately dehydrated. The sun seemed to be a different colour today. Seemed. What did he know? He was so skewed, nothing could be taken for what it was.

Though the bells were ringing in Paras Derval, he was sure of that. Except . . . except that after a while, listening, he seemed to hear a harp sounding, too, and that was very bad, as bad as it could be, because it was a thing from his own place, from behind the bolted door. It wasn't out there. The bells were, yes, but they were fading. He was going again, there was nothing to grab hold of, no branch, no hand. He was bound and dry, and sliding, going under. He saw the bolts shatter, and the door opening, and the room. *Oh, lady, lady, lady,* he thought. Then no bolts anymore, nothing to bar the door. Under. Undersea down . . .

They were in bed. The night before his trip. Of course. It would be that memory. Because of the harp, it would be.

His room. Spring night; almost summer weather. Window open, curtains blowing, her hair around them both, the covers back so he could see her by candlelight. Her candle, a gift. The very light was hers.

"Do you know," Rachel said, "that you are a musician, after all."

"I wish," he heard himself say. "You know I can't even sing."

"But no," she said pursuing a conceit, playing with the hairs on his chest. "You are. You're a harper, Paul. You have harper's hands."

"Where's my harp, then?" Straight man.

And Rachel said, "Me, of course. My heart's your harp string."

What could he do but smile? The very light.

"You know," she said, "when I play next month, the Brahms, it'll be for you."

"No. For yourself. Keep that for yourself."

She smiled. He couldn't see it, but he knew by now when Rachel smiled.

"Stubborn man." She touched him lightly with her mouth. "Share it, then. Can I play the second movement for you? Will you take that? Let me play that part because I love you. To tell."

"Oh, lady," he had said.

Hand of the harper. Heart of the harpstring.

Lady, lady, lady.

What had brought him back this time, he didn't know. The sun was gone, though. Dark coming down. Fireflies. Third night then. Last. *For three nights, and forever,* the King had said.

The King was dead.

How did he know that? And after a moment it seemed that very far down, below the burnt, strung-out place of pain he had become, a part of him remained that could fear.

How did he know Ailell was dead? The Tree had told him. It knew the passing of High Kings, it always did. It had been rooted here to summon them far back in the soil of time. From Iorweth to Ailell they were the Children of Mörnir, and the Tree knew when they died. And now he knew as well. He understood. *Now I give you to Mörnir*; the other part of the consecration. He was given. He was becoming root, branch. He was naked there, skin to bark; naked in all the ways there were, it seemed, because the dark was coming down inside again, the door unbolting. He was so open the wind could pass through him, light shine, shadow fall.

Like a child again. Light and shade. Simplicity.

When had all the twisting started?

He could remember (a different door, this) playing baseball on the street as darkness fell. Playing even after the streetlights kicked on, so that the ball would come flashing like a comet out of brightness and into dark, elusive but attainable. The smell of cut grass and porch flowers, the leather of a new fielder's glove. Summer twilight, summer dark. All the continuities. When had it turned? Why did it have to turn? The process changing to disjunctions, abortings, endings, all of them raining down like arrows, unlit and inescapable.

And then love, love, the deepest discontinuity.

Because it seemed that this door had turned into the other one after all, the one he couldn't face. Not even childhood was safe any more, not tonight. Nowhere would be safe tonight. Not here at the end, naked on the Tree.

And he understood then, finally: understood that it had to be naked, truly so, that one went to the God. It was the Tree that was stripping him, layer by layer, down to what he was hiding from. To what—hadn't there once been a thing called irony?—he had come here hiding from. Music. Her name. Tears. Rain. The highway.

He was skewed again, going down: the fireflies among the trees had become headlights of approaching cars, which was so absurd. But then it wasn't, after all, because now he was in the car, driving her eastward on Lakeshore Boulevard in the rain.

It had rained the night she died.

*I don't, I don't want to go here,* he thought, clinging to nothing, his mind's last despairing effort to pull away. *Please, just let me die, let me be rain for them.*

But no. He was the Arrow now. The Arrow on the Tree, of Mörnir, and he was to be given naked or not at all.

Or not at all. There was that, he realized. He could die. That was still his choice, he could let go. It was there for him.

And so on the third night Paul Schafer came to the last test, the one that was always failed, the opening. Where the Kings of Brennin, or those coming in their name, discovered that the courage to be there, the strength to endure, even love of their land were none of them enough. On the Tree one could no longer hide from the living or the dead, from one's own soul. Naked or not at all, one went to Mörnir. And oh, that was too much for them, too hard, too unfair after all that had been endured, to be forced to go into the darkest places then, so weak, so impossibly vulnerable.

And so they would let go, brave Kings of the sword, wise ones, gallant Princes, all would turn away from so much nakedness and die too soon.

But not that night. Because of pride, of pure stubbornness, and because, most surely, of the dog, Paul Schafer found the courage not to turn. Down he went. Arrow of the God. So open, the wind could pass, light shine through him.

Last door.

"The Dvořák," he heard. His own voice, laughing. "The Dvořák with the Symphony. Kincaid, are you a star!"

She laughed nervously. "It's only at Ontario Place. Outdoors, with a baseball game in the background at the stadium. No one will hear a thing."

"Wally will hear. Wally loves you already."

"Since when have you and Walter Langside been so close?"

"Since the recital, lady. Since his review. He's my main man now, Wally." She had won everything, won them all. She had dazzled. All three papers had been there, because of advance rumour of what she was. It was unheard-of for a graduate recital. The second movement, Langside of the *Globe* had written, could not be played more beautifully.

She had won everything. Had eclipsed every cellist ever to come out of Edward Johnson Hall. And today the Toronto Symphony had called. The Dvořák Cello Concerto. August 5, at Ontario Place. Unheard-of. So they had gone to Winston's for dinner, to blow a hundred dollars of his bursary money from the history department.

"It'll probably rain," she said. The wipers slapped their steady tattoo on the windshield. It was really coming down.

"The bandstand's covered," he replied airily, "and the first ten rows. Besides, if it rains, you don't have to fight the Blue Jays. Can't lose, kid."

"Well, you're pretty high tonight."

"I am, indeed," he heard the person he had been say, "pretty high tonight. I am very high."

He passed a labouring Chevy.

"Oh, shit," Rachel said.

*Please*, a lost, small voice within the Godwood pleaded. His. *Oh, please*. But he was inside it now, had taken himself there, all the way. There was no pity on the Summer Tree. How could there be? So open, he was, the rain could fall through him.

"Oh, shit," she said.

"What?" he heard himself say, startled. Saw it start right then, right there. The moment. Wipers at the top of their sweep. Lakeshore East. Just past a blue Chevrolet.

She was silent. Glancing, he could see her hands clasped tightly together. Her head was down. *What was this?*

"I've got something to tell you."

"Evidently." Oh, God, his defences.

She looked over at that. Dark eyes. Like no one else. "I promised," she said. "I promised I'd talk to you tonight."

*Promised?* He tried, watched himself try. "Rachel, what is it?"

Eyes front again. Her hands.

"You were away for a month, Paul."

"I was away for a month, yes. You know why." He'd gone four weeks before her recital. Had convinced them both it made sense—the time was too huge for her, it meant too much. She was playing eight hours a day; he wanted to let her focus. He flew to Calgary with Kev and drove his brother's car through the Rockies and then south down the California coast. Had phoned her twice a week.

"You know why," he heard himself say again. It had begun.

"Well, I did some thinking."

"One should always do some thinking."

"Paul, don't be like—"

"What do you want from me?" he snapped. "What *is* this, Rach?"

So, so, so. "Mark asked me to marry him."

Mark? Mark Rogers was her accompanist. Last-year piano student, good-looking, mild, a little effeminate. It didn't fit. He couldn't make it fit.

"All right," he said. "That happens. It happens when you've got a common goal for a while. Theatre romance. He fell in love. Rachel, you're easy to fall in love with. But why are you telling me this way?"

"Because I'm going to say yes."

No warning at all. Point-blank. Nothing had ever prepared him for this kick. Summer night, but God, he was so cold. So cold, suddenly.

"Just like that?" Reflex.

"No! Not just like that. Don't be so cold, Paul."

He heard himself make a sound. A gasp, a laugh: halfway. He was actually shivering. *Don't be so cold, Paul.*

"That's just the sort of thing," she said, twisting her hands together. "You're always so controlled, thinking, figuring out. Like figuring out I needed to be alone a month, or why Mark fell in love with me. So much logic: Mark's not so strong. He *needs* me. I can see the ways he needs me. He cries, Paul."

*Cries?* Nothing held together anymore. What did crying have to do with it?

"I didn't know you liked a Niobe number." It was important to stop shivering.

"I *don't.* Please don't be nasty, I can't handle it. . . . Paul, it's that you never truly let go, you never made me feel I was indispensable. I guess I'm not. But Mark . . . puts his head on my chest sometimes, after."

"Oh, Jesus, Rachel, don't!"

"It's true!" It was raining harder. Trouble breathing now.

"So he plays harp, too? Versatile, I must say." God, such a kick; he was so cold.

She was crying. "I didn't want it to be . . ."

She didn't want it to be like this. How had she wanted it to be? Oh, lady, lady, lady.

"It's okay," he found himself saying, incredibly. Where had that come from? Trouble breathing still. Rain on the roof, on the windshield. "It'll be all right."

"No," Rachel said, weeping still, rain drumming. "Sometimes it can't be all right."

Smart, smart girl. Once he would have reached to touch her. Once? Ten minutes ago. Only that, before the cold.

Love, love, the deepest discontinuity.

Or not quite the deepest.

Because this, precisely, was when the Mazda in front blew a tire. The road was wet. It skidded sideways and hit the Ford in the next lane, then rebounded and three-sixtied as the Ford caromed off the guard rail.

There was no room to brake. He was going to plough them both. Except there was a foot, twelve inches' clearance if he went by on the left. He knew there'd been a foot, had seen the movie in slow motion in his head so many times. Twelve inches. Not impossible; very bad in rain, but.

He went for it, sliced the whirling Mazda, banged the rail, spun, and rolled across the road and into the sliding Ford.

He was belted; she wasn't.

That was all there was to it, except for the truth.

The truth was that there had indeed been twelve inches, perhaps ten, as likely, fourteen. Enough. Enough if he had gone for it as soon as he saw the hole. But he hadn't, had he? By the time he'd moved, there were three inches clear, four, not enough at night, in rain, at forty miles an hour. Not nearly.

Question: how did one measure time there, at the end? Answer: by how much room there was. Over and over he'd watched the film in his mind; over and over he'd seen them roll. Off the rail, into the Ford. Over.

Because he hadn't moved fast enough.

And why—*Do pay attention, Mr. Schafer*—why hadn't he moved fast enough?

Well, class, modern techniques now allow us to examine the thought patterns of that driver in the scintilla—lovely word, that—of time between the seeing and the moving. Between the desire and the spasm, as Mr. Eliot so happily put it once.

And where, on close examination, was the desire?

Not that we can be sure, class, this is *most* hazardous terrain (it was raining, after all), but careful scrutiny of the data does seem to elicit a curious lacuna in the driver's responses.

He moved, oh, yes indeed, he did. And in fairness—do let's be fair—faster than most drivers would have done. But was it—and there's the rub—was it as fast as he could move?

Is it possible, just a hypothesis now, but is it possible that he delayed that scintilla of time—only that, no more; but still—because he wasn't entirely sure he *wanted* to move? The desire and the spasm. *Mr. Schafer, your thoughts?* Was there perhaps a slight, shall we say, lag in the desire?

Dead on. St. Michael's Emergency Ward.

The deepest discontinuity.

"It should have been me," he'd said to Kevin. You had to pay the price, one way or another. You certainly weren't allowed to weep. Too much hypocrisy, that would be. Part of the price, then: no tears, no release. *What had crying to do with it?* he had asked her. Or no, he had thought that. Niobe, he had said. A Niobe number. Witty, witty, defences up so fast. Seatbelt buckled. So cold, though, he'd been, so very cold. Crying, it seemed, had a lot to do with it, after all.

But there was more. One played the tape. Over and over, like the inner film, like the rolling car: over and over, the tape of her recital. And one listened, always, in the second movement, for the lie. His, she had said. That part because she loved him. So it had to be a lie. One should be able to hear that, despite Walter Langside and everyone else. Surely one could hear the lie?

Not so. Her love for him in that sound, that perfect sound. Incandescent. And this was beyond him; how it could be done. And so each time there came a point where he couldn't listen anymore and not cry. And he wasn't permitted to cry, so.

So she had left him and he had killed her, and you weren't allowed to weep when you have done that. You pay the price, so.

So he had come to Fionavar.

To the Summer Tree.

Class dismissed. Time to die.

This time it was the silence. Complete and utter stillness in the wood. The thunder had stopped. He was cinder, husk: what is left, at the end.

At the end one came back because, it seemed, this much was granted: that one would go in one's own self, from this place, knowing. It was an unexpected dispensation. Drained, a shell, he could still feel gratitude for dignity allowed.

It was unnaturally silent in the darkness. Even the pulsing of the Tree itself had stopped. There was no wind, no sound. The fireflies had gone. Nothing moved. It was as if the earth itself had stopped moving.

Then it came. He saw that, inexplicably, a mist was rising from the floor of the forest. But no, not inexplicably: a mist was rising because it was meant to rise. What could be explained in this place?

With difficulty he turned his head, first one way, then the other. There were two birds on the branches, ravens, both of them. I know these, he thought, no longer capable of surprise. They are named Thought and Memory. I learned this long ago.

It was true. They were named so in all the worlds, and this was their nesting place. They were the God's.

Even the birds were still, though, each bright yellow eye steady, motionless. Waiting, as the trees were waiting. Only the mist was moving; it was higher now. There was no sound. The whole of the Godwood seemed to have gathered itself, as if time were somehow opening, making a place—and only then, finally, did Paul realize that it was not the God they were waiting for, it was something else, not truly part of the ritual, something outside . . . and he remembered an image then (thought, memory) of something far back, another life it seemed, another person almost who had had a dream . . . no, a vision, a searching, yes, that was it . . . of mist, yes, and a wood, and waiting, yes, waiting for the moon to rise, when something, something . . .

But the moon could not rise. It was the dark of moon, new moon night. The last crescent had saved the dog the night before. Had saved him for this. They were waiting, the Godwood, the whole night was waiting, coiled like a spring, but there could be no moonrise that night.

And then there was.

Above the eastern trees of the glade of the Summer Tree, there came the rising of the Light. And on the night of the new moon there shone down on Fionavar the light of a full moon. As the trees of the forest began to murmur and sway in the sudden wind, Paul saw that the moon was red, like fire or blood, and power shaped that moment to its name: Dana, the Mother, come to intercede.

Goddess of all the living in all the worlds; mother, sister, daughter, bride of the God. And Paul saw then, in a blaze of insight, that it didn't matter which, all were true: that at this level of power, this absoluteness of degree, hierarchies ceased to signify. Only the might did, the awe, the presence made manifest. Red moon in the sky on new moon night, so that the glade of the Godwood could shine and the Summer Tree be wrapped below in mist, above in light.

Paul looked up, beyond surprise, beyond disbelief; the sacrifice, the shell. Rain to be. And in that moment it seemed to him as if he heard a voice, in the sky, in the wood, in the running of his own moon-coloured blood, and the voice spoke so that all the trees vibrated like living wands to the sound:

*It was not so, will not have been so.*

And when the reverberations ceased, Paul was on the highway again, Rachel with him in the rain. And once more he saw the Mazda blow and skid into the Ford. He saw the spinning, impossible obstruction.

He saw twelve inches' clearance on the left.

But Dana was with him now, the Goddess, taking him there to truth. And in a crescendo, a heart-searing blaze of final dispensation, he saw that he had missed the gap, and only just, oh, only just, not because of any hesitation shaped by lack of desire, by death or murder wish, but because, in the end, he was human. Oh, lady, he was. Only, only human, and he missed because of hurt, grief, shock, and rain. Because of these, which could be forgiven.

And were, he understood. Truly, truly were.

*Deny not your own mortality.* The voice was within him like a wind, one of her voices, only one, he knew, and in the sound was love, he was loved. *You failed because humans fail. It is a gift as much as anything else.*

And then, deep within him like the low sound of a harp, which no longer hurt, this last: *Go easy, and in peace. It is well.*

His throat ached. His heart was a bound, constrained thing too large for him, for what was left of his body. Dimly, through the risen mist, he saw a figure at the edge of the glade: in the form of a man, but bearing the proud antlers of a stag, and through the mist he saw the figure bow to him and then disappear.

Time was.

The pain was gone. His being was shaped of light, he knew his eyes were shining. He had not killed her, then: it was all right. It was loss, but loss was allowed, it was demanded. So much light, there seemed to be, even in that moment when the mist rose to his feet.

And at last it came, at last, sweet, sweet release of mourning. He thought of Kevin's song then, remembered it with love: *There will come a tomorrow when you weep for me.*

Tomorrow. And so. So. It seemed that this was tomorrow, and here at the end, at the last, he was weeping for Rachel Kincaid who had died.

So Paul cried on the Summer Tree.

And there came then a roll of thunder like the tread of doom, of worlds cracking asunder, and the God was there in the glade, he had come. And he spoke again, in his place, in the one unchanging voice that was his, and forged by the power of that thundering, the mist began to flow together then, faster and faster, to the one place, to the Summer Tree.

Upwards it boiled, the mist of the Godwood, up through the sacrifice, the great trunk of the Tree, hurled into the night sky by the God like a spear.

And in the heavens above Brennin, as the thunder crashed and rolled, suddenly there were clouds piling higher and higher upon each other, spreading from the Mörnirwood to cover all the land.

Paul felt it going. Through him. His. His and the God's. Whose he was. He felt the tears on his face. He felt himself claimed, going, mist boiling through him, ravens rising to fly, the God in the Tree, in him, the moon above the clouds riding in and out, never lost, Rachel, the Summer Tree, the wood, the world, and oh, the God, the God. And then one last thing more before the dark.

Rain, rain, rain, rain, rain.

⤝═◉═⤜

In Paras Derval that night the people went down into the streets. In villages all over Brennin they did so, and farmers bore their children out of doors, only half awake, that they might see the miraculous moon that was answer of the Mother to the fire of Maugrim, and that they might feel upon their faces and remember, though it might seem to them a dream, the return of rain, which was the blessing of the God upon the Children of Mörnir.

In the street, with Loren and Matt, with Kim and the exiled Prince, Kevin Laine wept in his turn, for he knew what this must mean, and Paul was the closest thing to a brother he'd ever had.

"He did it," whispered Loren Silvercloak, in a voice choked and roughened with awe. Kevin saw, with some surprise, that the mage, too, was crying. "Oh, bright," Loren said. "Oh, most brave."

Oh, Paul.

But there was more. "Look," Matt Sören said. And turning to where the Dwarf was pointing, Kevin saw that when the red moon that should never have been shone through the scudding clouds, the stone in the ring Kim wore leaped into responding light. It burned on Kim's finger like a carried fire, the colour of the moon.

"What is this?" Aileron asked.

Kim, instinctively raising her hand high so that light could speak to light, realized that she both knew and didn't know. The Baelrath was wild, untamed; so was that moon.

"The stone is being charged," she said quietly. "That is the war moon overhead. This is the Warstone." The others were silent, hearing her. And suddenly her own voice intoning, her role, seemed so heavy; Kim reached back, almost desperately, for some trace of the lightness that had once defined her.

"I think," she tried, hoping that Kevin, at least, would catch it, would play along, help her, please, to remember what she was, "I think we'd better have a new flag made."

Kevin, wrestling with things of his own, missed it completely. All he heard was Kim saying "we" to this new Prince of Brennin.

Looking at her, he thought he was seeing a stranger.

In the courtyard behind the sanctuary, Jaelle, the High Priestess, lifted her face to the sky and gave praise. And with the teachings of Gwen Ystrat in her heart, she looked at the moon, understanding far better than anyone else west of Lake Leinan what it meant. She gave careful thought for a time, then called six of her women to her, and led them secretly out of Paras Derval, westward in the rain.

In Cathal, too, they had seen the Mountain's fire in the morning, and trembled to hear the laughter on the wind. Now the red moon shone above Larai Rigal as well. Power on power. A gauntlet hurled into the sky, and answered in the sky. This, Shalhassan could understand. He summoned a Council in the dead of night and ordered an embassy to leave for Cynan and then Brennin immediately. No, not in the morning, he snapped in response to a rash question. Immediately. One did not sleep when war began, or one slept forever when it ended.

A good phrase, he thought, dismissing them. He made a mental note to dictate it to Raziel when time allowed. Then he went to bed.

Over Eridu the red moon rose, and the Plain, and down upon Daniloth it cast its light. And the lios alfar, alone of all the guardian peoples, had lore stretching back sufficiently far to say with certainty that no such moon had ever shone before.

It was a reply to Rakoth, their elders agreed, gathered before Ra-Tenniel on the mound at Atronel, to the one the younger gods had named Sathain, the Hooded One, long, long ago. It was an intercession as well, the wisest of them added, though for what, or as to what, they could not say.

Nor could they say what the third power of the moon was, though all the lios knew there was a third.

The Goddess worked by threes.

There was another glade in another wood. A glade where one man alone had dared to walk in ten centuries since Amairgen had died.

The glade was small, the trees of the grove about were very old, extremely tall. The moon was almost overhead before she could shine down upon Pendaran's sacred grove.

When she did, it began. A play of light first, a shimmering, and then a sound following, unearthly like a flute among the leaves. The air itself seemed to quiver to that tune, to dance, to form and reform, coalesce, to shape finally a creature of light and sound, of Pendaran and the moon.

When it was ended, there was silence, and something stood in the glade where nothing had stood before. With the wide eyes of the newly born, dewed so that her coat glistened in the birthing light, she rose on unsteady legs, and stood a moment, as one more sound like a single string plucked ran through Pendaran Wood.

Slowly then, delicately as all her kind, she moved from the glade, from the sacred grove. Eastward she went, for though but newly birthed, she knew already that to the west lay the sea.

Lightly, lightly did she tread the grass, and the powers of Pendaran, all the creatures gathered there, grew still as she passed, more beautiful, more terrible than any one of them.

The Goddess worked by threes; this was the third.

To the highest battlement he had climbed, so that all of black Starkadh lay below him. Starkadh rebuilt, his fortress and his fastness, for the blasting of Rangat had not signified his freedom—though let the fools think so yet awhile—he had been free a long time now. The Mountain had been exploded because he was ready at last for war, with the place of his power rising anew to tower over the northland, over Daniloth, a blur to the south, where his heart's hate would forever lie.

But he did not look down upon it.

Instead his eyes were riveted on the impossible response the night sky held up to him, and in that moment he tasted doubt. With his one good hand, he reached upwards as if his talons might rake the moon from heaven, and it was a long time before his rage passed.

But he had changed in a thousand years under Rangat. Hate had driven him to move too fast the last time. This time it would not.

Let the moon shine tonight. He would have it down before the end. He would smash Brennin like a toy and uproot the Summer Tree. The Riders would be scattered, Larai Rigal burned to waste, Calor Diman defiled in Eridu.

And Gwen Ystrat he would level. Let the moon shine, then. Let Dana try to show forth empty signs in heavens choked with his smoke. Her, too, he would have kneeling before him. He had had a thousand years to consider all of this.

He smiled then, for the last was best. When all else was done, when Fionavar lay crushed beneath his fist, only then would he turn to Daniloth. One by one he would have them brought to him, the lios alfar, the Children of Light. One by one by one to Starkadh. He would know what to do with them.

The thunder was almost spent, the rain a thin drizzle. The wind was wind, no more. A taste of salt on it from the sea, far away. The clouds were breaking up. The red moon stood directly over the Tree.

"Lady," said the God, muting the thunder of his voice, "Lady, this you have never done before."

"It was needful," she replied, a chiming on wind. "He is very strong this time."

"He is very strong," the thunder echoed. "Why did you speak to my sacrifice?" A slight reproach.

The Lady's voice grew deeper, woven of hearth smoke and caves. "Do you mind?" she murmured.

There came a sound that might have been a god amused. "Not if you beg forgiveness, no. It has been long, Lady." A deeper sound, and meaningful.

"Do you know what I have done in Pendaran?" she asked, eluding, voice gossamer like dawn.

"I do. Though for good or ill I do not know. It may burn the hand that lays hold of it."

"All my gifts are double-edged," the Goddess said, and he was aware of ancient blood in that tone. There was a silence, then she was finest lace again, cajoling: "I have interceded, Lord, will you not do so?"

"For them?"

"And to please me," said the moon.

"Might we please each other?"

"We might so."

A roll of thunder then. Laughter.

"I have interceded," Mörnir said.

"Not the rain," she protested, sea-sound. "The rain was bought."

"Not the rain," the God replied. "I have done what I have done."

"Let us go, then," said Dana.

The moon passed away behind the trees to the west.

Shortly thereafter the thunder ceased, and the clouds began to break up overhead.

And so at the last, at the end of night, in the sky above the Summer Tree, there were only the stars to look down upon the sacrifice, upon the stranger hanging naked on the Tree, only the stars, only them.

Before dawn it rained again, though the glade was empty by then, and silent, save for the sound of water falling and dripping from the leaves.

And this was the last night of Pwyll the Stranger on the Summer Tree.

# PART III

# THE CHILDREN OF IVOR

# CHAPTER 10

He landed badly, but the reflexes of an athlete took him rolling through the fall, and at the end of it he was on his feet, unhurt. Very angry, though.

He had opted out, damn it! What the hell right did Kim Ford have to grab his arm and haul him to another world? What the . . .

He stopped; the fury draining as realization came down hard. She had, she really *had* taken him to another world.

A moment ago he had been in a room in the Park Plaza Hotel, now he found himself outdoors in darkness with a cool wind blowing, and a forest nearby; looking the other way, he saw wide rolling grasslands stretching away as far as he could see in the moonlight.

He looked around for the others, and then as the fact of isolation slowly came home, Dave Martyniuk's anger gave way to fear. They weren't friends of his, that was for sure, but this was no time or place to have ended up alone.

They couldn't be far, he thought, managing to keep control. Kim Ford had had his arm; surely that meant she couldn't be far away, her and the others, and that Lorenzo Marcus guy who'd got him into this in the first place. And was going to get him out, or deal with severe bodily pain, Martyniuk vowed. Notwithstanding the provisions of the Criminal Code.

Which reminded him: looking down, he saw that he was still clutching Kevin Laine's Evidence notes.

The absurdity, the utter incongruousness in this night place of wind and grass acted, somehow, to loosen him. He took a deep breath, like before the opening jump in a game. It was time to get his bearings. Boy Scout time.

*Paras Derval where Ailell reigns,* the old man had said. Any cities on the horizon? As the moon slipped from behind a drift of cloud, Dave turned north into the wind and saw Rangat clear.

He was not, as it happened, anywhere near the others. All Kim had been able to do with her desperate grab for his arm was keep him in the same plane as them, the same world. He was in Fionavar, but a long way north, and the Mountain loomed forty-five thousand feet up into the moonlight, white and dazzling.

"Holy Mother!" Dave exclaimed involuntarily.

It saved his life.

Of the nine tribes of the Dalrei, all but one had moved east and south that season, though the best grazing for the eltor was still in the northwest, as it always was in summer. The messages the auberei brought back from Celidon were clear, though: svart alfar and wolves in the edgings of Pendaran were enough for most Chieftains to take their people away. There had been rumours of urgach among the svarts as well. It was enough. South of Adein and Rienna they went, to the leaner, smaller herds, and the safety of the country around Cynmere and the Latham.

Ivor dan Banor, Chieftain of the third tribe, was, as often, the exception. Not that he did not care for the safety of his tribe, his children. No man who knew him could think that. It was just that there were other things to consider, Ivor thought, awake late at night in the Chieftain's house.

For one, the Plain and the eltor herds belonged to the Dalrei, and not just symbolically. Colan had given them to Revor after the Bael Rangat, to hold, he and his people, for so long as the High Kingdom stood.

It had been earned, by the mad ride in terror through Pendaran and the Shadowland and a loop in the thread of time to explode singing into battle on a sunset field that else had been lost. Ivor stirred, just thinking on it: for the Horsemen, the Children of Peace, to have done this thing . . . There had been giants in the old days.

Giants who had earned the Plain. To have and to hold, Ivor thought. Not to scurry to sheltered pockets of land at the merest rumour of danger. It stuck in Ivor's craw to run from svart alfar.

So the third tribe stayed. Not on the edge of Pendaran—that would have been foolhardy and unnecessary. There was a good camp five leagues from the forest, and they had the dense herds of the eltor to themselves. It was, the hunters agreed, a luxury. He noticed that they still made the sign against evil, though, when the chase took them within sight of the Great Wood. There were some, Ivor knew, who would rather have been elsewhere.

He had other reasons, though, for staying. It was bad in the south, the auberei reported from Celidon; Brennin was locked in a drought, and cryptic word had come from his friend Tulger of the eighth tribe that there was trouble in the High Kingdom. What, Ivor thought, did they need to go into that for? After a harsh winter, what the tribe needed was a mild, sweet summer in the north. They needed the cool breeze and the fat herds for feasting and warm coats against the coming of fall.

There was another reason, too. More than the usual number of boys would be coming up to their fasts this year. Spring and summer were the time for the totem fasts among the Dalrei, and the third tribe had always been luckiest in a certain copse of trees here in the northwest. It was a tradition. Here Ivor had seen his own hawk gazing with bright eyes back at him from the top of an elm on his second night. It was a good place, Faelinn Grove, and the young ones deserved to lie there if they could. Tabor, too. His younger son was fourteen. Past time. It might be this summer. Ivor had been twelve when he found his hawk; Levon, his older son—his heir, Chieftain after him had seen his totem at thirteen.

It was whispered, among the girls who were always competing for him, that Levon had seen a King Horse on his fast. This, Ivor knew, was not true, but there *was* something of the stallion about Levon, in the brown eyes, the unbridled carriage, the open, guileless nature, even his long, thick yellow hair, which he wore unbound.

Tabor, though, Tabor was different. Although that was unfair, Ivor told himself— his intense younger son was only a boy yet, he hadn't had his fasting. This summer, perhaps, and he wanted Tabor to have the lucky wood.

And above and beyond all of these, Ivor had another reason still. A vague presence at the back of his mind, as yet undefined. He left it there. Such things, he knew from experience, would be made clear to him in their time. He was a patient man.

So they stayed.

Even now there were two boys in Faelinn Grove. Gereint had spoken their names two days ago, and the shaman's word began the passage from boy to man among the Dalrei.

There were two in the wood then, fasting; but though Faelinn was lucky, it was also close to Pendaran, and Ivor, father to all his tribe, had taken quiet steps to guard them. They would be shamed, and their fathers, if they knew, so it had been only with a look in his eye that he had alerted Torc to ride out with them unseen.

Torc was often away from the camps at night. It was his way. The younger ones joked that his animal had been a wolf. They laughed too hard at that, a little afraid. Torc: he did look like a wolf, with his lean body, his long, straight, black hair, and the dark, unrevealing eyes. He never wore a shirt, or moccasins; only his eltor skin leggings, dyed black to be unseen at night.

The Outcast. No fault of his own, Ivor knew, and resolved for the hundredth time to do something about that name. It hadn't been any fault of Torc's father, Sorcha, either. Just sheerest bad luck. But Sorcha had slain an eltor doe that was carrying young. An accident, the hunters agreed at the gathering: the buck he'd slashed had fallen freakishly into the path of the doe beside it. The doe had stumbled over him and broken her neck. When the hunters came up, they had seen that she was bearing.

An accident, which let Ivor make it exile and not death. He could not do more. No Chieftain could rise above the Laws and hold his people. Exile, then, for Sorcha; a lonely, dark fate, to be driven from the Plain. The next morning they had found Meisse, his wife, dead by her own hand. Torc, at eleven, only child, had been left doubly scarred by tragedy.

He had been named by Gereint that summer, the same summer as Levon. Barely twelve, he had found his animal and had remained ever after a loner on the fringes of the tribe. As good a hunter as any of Ivor's people, as good even, honesty made Ivor concede, as Levon. Or perhaps not quite, not *quite* as good.

The Chieftain smiled to himself in the dark. That, he thought, was self-indulgent.

Torc was his son as well, the whole tribe were his children. He liked the dark man, too, though Torc could be difficult; he also trusted him. Torc was discreet and competent with tasks like the one tonight.

Awake beside Leith, his people all about him in the camp, the horses shut in for the night, Ivor felt better knowing Torc was out there in the dark with the boys. He turned on his side to try to sleep.

After a moment, the Chieftain recognized a muffled sound, and realized that someone else was awake in the house. He could hear Tabor's stifled sobbing from the room he shared with Levon. It was hard for the boy, he knew; fourteen was late not to be named, especially for the Chieftain's son, for Levon's brother.

He would have comforted his younger son, but knew it was wiser to leave the boy alone. It was not a bad thing to learn what hurt meant, and mastering it alone helped engender self–respect. Tabor would be all right.

In a little while the crying stopped. Eventually Ivor, too, fell asleep, though first he did something he'd not done for a long time.

He left the warmth of his bed, of Leith sound asleep beside him, and went to look in on his children. First the boys; fair, uncomplicated Levon, nut-brown, wiry Tabor; and then he walked into Liane's room.

Cordeliane, his daughter. With a bemused pride he gazed at her dark brown hair, at the long lashes of her closed eyes, the upturned nose, laughing mouth . . . even in sleep she smiled.

How had he, stocky, square, plain Ivor, come to have such handsome sons, a daughter so fair?

All of the third tribe were his children, but these, these.

Torc had been having a bad night. First the two idiots who had come to fast had managed to end up, totally oblivious, within twenty feet of each other on precisely opposite sides of a clump of bushes in the wood. It was ridiculous. What sort of babies were they sending out these days?

He had managed, with a series of snuffling grunts that really were rather unnerving, to scare one of them into moving a quarter of a mile away. It was an interference with the ritual, he supposed, but the fast had barely begun, and in any case, the babies needed all the help they could get: the man smell in those bushes had been so strong they'd have likely ended up finding only each other for totem animals.

That, he thought, was funny. Torc didn't find many things funny, but the image of two fasting thirteen-year-olds becoming each other's sacred beasts made him smile in the dark.

He stopped smiling when his sweep of the grove turned up a spoor he didn't recognize. After a moment, though, he realized that it had to be an urgach, which was worse than bad. Svart alfar would not have disturbed him unless there were a great many. He had seen small numbers of them on his solitary forays westward towards Pendaran. He'd also found the trail of a very large band, with wolves among them. It had been a week before, and they were moving south fairly quickly. It had not been a pleasant thing to find, and he'd reported it to Ivor, and to Levon as leader of the hunt, but it was, for the time being, no direct concern of theirs.

This was. He'd never seen one of the urgach, no one in the tribe had, but there were legends enough and night stories to make him very cautious indeed. He remembered the tales very well, from before the bad time, when he'd been only a child in the third tribe, a child like all the others, shivering with pleasurable fear by the fire, dreading his mother's summons to bed, while the old ones told their stories.

Kneeling over the spoor, Torc's lean face was grim. This was not Pendaran Wood, where creatures of Darkness were known to walk. An urgach, or more than one in Faelinn Grove, the lucky wood of the third tribe, was serious. It was more than serious: there were two babies fasting tonight.

Moving silently, Torc followed the heavy, almost overpowering spoor and, dismayed, he saw that it led eastward out of the grove. Urgach on the Plain! Dark things were abroad. For the first time, he wondered about the Chieftain's decision to stay in the northwest this summer. They were alone. Far from Celidon, far from any other tribe that might have joined numbers with them against what evils might be moving here. The Children of Peace, the Dalrei were named, but sometimes peace had been hard won.

Torc had no problems with being alone, he had been so all his adult life. Outcast, the young ones called him, in mockery. The Wolf. Stupid babies: wolves ran in packs. When had he ever? The solitude had made for some bitterness, for he was young yet, and the memory of other times was fresh enough to be a wound. It had also given him a certain dour reflectiveness born of long nights in the dark, and an outsider's view of what humans did. Another kind of animal. If he lacked tolerance, it was not a surprising flaw.

He had very quick reflexes.

The knife was in his hand, and he was low to the gully and crawling from the trees as soon as he glimpsed the bulky shadow in a brief unsheathing of moonlight. There were clouds, or else he would have seen it earlier. It was very big.

He was downwind, which was good. Moving with honed speed and silence, Torc traversed the open ground towards the figure he'd seen. His bow and sword were on his horse; a stupidity. Can you kill an urgach with a knife, a part of him wondered.

The rest of him was concentrating. He had moved to within ten feet. The creature hadn't noticed him, but it was obviously angry and it was very large—almost a foot taller than he was, bulking hugely in the shadows of the night.

He decided to wait for moonlight and throw for the head. One didn't stop to talk with creatures from one's nightmares. The size of it made his heart race—tearing fangs on a creature that big?

The moon slanted out; he was ready. He drew back his arm to throw: the dark head was clearly outlined against the silvered plain, looking the other way, north.

"Holy Mother!" the urgach said.

Torc's arm had already begun its descent. With a brutal effort he retained control of the dagger, cutting himself in the process.

Creatures of evil did not invoke the Goddess, not in that voice. Looking again in the bright moonlight, Torc saw that the creature before him was a man; strangely garbed, and very big, but he seemed to be unarmed.

Drawing breath, Torc called out in a voice as courteous as the circumstances seemed to permit, "Move slowly and declare yourself."

At the snarled command, Dave's heart hit his throat and jackknifed back into his ribcage. *Who the hell?* Rather than pursue this inquiry, however, he elected to move slowly and declare himself.

Turning towards the voice with his hands outspread and bearing only Evidence notes, he said, as levelly as he could, "My name is Martyniuk. Dave Martyniuk. I don't know where I am, and I'm looking for someone named Loren. He brought me here."

A moment passed. He felt the wind from the north ruffling his hair. He was, he realized, very frightened.

Then a shadow rose from a hollow he hadn't even seen, and moved towards him.

"Silvercloak?" the shadow asked, materializing in the moonlight as a young man, shirtless despite the wind, barefoot, and clad in leggings of black. He carried a long, quite lethal-looking blade in his hand.

*Oh, God,* Dave thought. *What have they done to me?* Carefully, his eyes on the knife, he replied, "Yes, Loren Silvercloak. That's his name." He took a breath, trying to calm down. "Please don't misunderstand anything. I'm here in peace. I don't even want to be here. I got separated . . . we're supposed to be in a place called Paras Derval. Do you know it?"

The other man seemed to relax a little. "I know it. How is it that you don't?"

"Because I'm not from here," Dave exclaimed, frustration hitting his voice. "We crossed from my world. Earth?" he said hopefully, then realized how stupid that was.

"Where is Silvercloak, then?"

"Aren't you listening?" Martyniuk exploded. "I told you, I got separated. I need him to go home. All I want to do is get home as fast as I can. Can't you understand that?"

There was another silence.

"Why," the other man asked, "shouldn't I just kill you?"

Dave's breath escaped in a hiss. He hadn't handled this too well, it seemed. God, he wasn't a diplomat. Why hadn't Kevin Laine been separated from the others? Dave considered jumping the other man, but something told him this lean person knew how to use that blade extremely well.

He had a sudden inspiration. "Because," he gambled, "Loren wouldn't like it. I'm his friend; he'll be looking for me." *You are too quick to renounce friendship,* the mage had said, the night before. Not always, Dave thought, not tonight, boy.

It seemed to work, too. Martyniuk lowered his hands slowly. "I'm unarmed," he said. "I'm lost. Will you help me, please?"

The other man sheathed his blade at last. "I'll take you to Ivor," he said, "and Gereint. They both know Silvercloak. We'll go to the camp in the morning."

"Why not now?"

"Because," the other said, "I have a job to do, and I suppose you'll have to do it with me now."

"How? What?"

"There are two babies in that wood fasting for their animals. We've got to watch over them, make sure they don't cut themselves or something." He held up a bleeding hand. "Like I did, not killing you. You are among the Dalrei. Ivor's tribe, the third. And lucky for you he is a stubborn man, or the only thing you would find here would be eltor and svart alfar, and the one would flee you and the other kill. My name," he said, "is Torc. Now come."

The babies, as Torc insisted on calling the two thirteen-year-olds, seemed to be all right. If they were lucky, Torc explained, they would each see an animal before dawn. If not, the fast would continue, and he would have to watch another night. They were sitting with their backs against a tree in a small clearing midway between the two boys. Torc's horse, a small dark grey stallion, grazed nearby.

"What are we watching for?" Dave asked, a little nervously. Night forests were not his usual habitat.

"I told you: there are svart alfar around here. Word of them has driven all the other tribes south."

"There was a svart alfar in our world," Dave volunteered. "It followed Loren. Matt Sören killed it. Loren said they weren't dangerous, and there weren't many of them."

Torc raised his eyebrows. "There are more than there used to be," he said, "and though they may not be dangerous to a mage, they were bred to kill and they do it very well."

Dave had an uncomfortable, prickly feeling suddenly. Torc spoke of killing with disquieting frequency.

"The svarts would be enough to worry about," Torc went on, "but just before I saw you, I found the spoor of an urgach—I took you for it, back there. I was going to kill first and investigate after. Such creatures have not been seen for hundreds of years. It is very bad that they are back; I don't know what it means."

"What are they?"

Torc made a strange gesture and shook his head. "Not at night," he said. "We shouldn't be talking of them out here." He repeated the gesture.

Dave settled back against the tree. It was late, he supposed he should try to sleep, but he was far too keyed up. Torc no longer seemed to be in a talking mood; that was okay by him.

On the whole, it looked all right. Could have been a lot worse. He appeared to have landed among people who knew the mage. The others couldn't be too far away; it would probably work out, if he didn't get eaten by something in these woods. On the other hand, Torc obviously knew what he was doing. Roll with it, he thought.

After about three-quarters of an hour, Torc rose to check on his babies. He looped east, and came back ten minutes later, nodding his head.

"Barth is all right, and well hidden now, too. Not as stupid as most of them." He continued west to look in on the other one. A few minutes later, he reappeared again.

"Well—" Torc began, approaching the tree.

Only an athlete could have done it. With purest reflex, Dave launched himself at the apparition that had emerged from the trees beside Torc. He hit the hairy, ape-like creature with the hardest cross-body block he could throw, and the sword swinging to decapitate Torc was deflected away.

Sprawled flat with the breath knocked out of him, Dave saw the huge creature's other hand coming down. He managed to parry with his left forearm, and felt a numbing sensation from the contact. God, he thought, staring into the enraged red eyes of what had to be the urgach, this sucker is strong! He didn't even have time to be afraid: rolling clumsily away from the urgach's short-range sword thrust, he saw a body hurtle past him.

Torc, knife in hand, had hurled himself straight at the creature's head. The urgach dropped its awkward sword, and with a terrifying snarl, easily blocked Torc's arm. Shifting its grip, it threw the Rider bodily away, to smash into a tree, senseless for a moment.

One on one, Dave thought. Torc's dive had given him time to get to his feet, but everything was moving so fast. Whirling, he fled to where Torc's tethered horse was neighing in terror, and he grabbed the sword resting by the saddle-cloth. A sword he thought. *What the hell do I do with a sword?*

Parry, like crazy. The urgach, weapon reclaimed, was right on top of him, and it levelled a great two-handed sweep of its own giant blade. Dave was a strong man, but the jarring impact of blocking that blow made his right arm go almost as numb as his left; he staggered backwards.

"Torc!" he cried desperately. "I can't—"

He stopped, because there was suddenly no need to say anything more. The urgach was swaying like a toppling rock, and a moment later it fell forward with a crash, Torc's dagger embedded to the hilt in the back of its skull.

The two men gazed at each other across the dead body of the monstrous creature.

"Well," said Torc finally, still breathing hard, "now I know why I didn't kill you."

What Dave felt then was so rare and unexpected, it took him a moment to recognize it.

⟡━◉◉━⟡

Ivor, up with the sun and watching by the southwest gate, saw Barth and Navon come walking back together. He could tell—it was not hard—from the way they moved that they had both found something in the wood. Found, or been found by, as Gereint said. They had gone out as boys and were coming back to him, his children still, but Riders now, Riders of the Dalrei. So he lifted his voice in greeting, that they should be welcomed by their Chieftain back from the dreamworld to the tribe.

"Hola!" cried Ivor, that all should hear. "See who comes! Let there be rejoicing, for see the Weaver sends two new Riders to us!"

They all rushed out then, having waited with suppressed excitement, so that the Chieftain should be first to announce the return. It was a tradition of the third tribe since the days of Lahor, his grandfather.

Barth and Navon were welcomed home with honour and jubilation. Their eyes were wide yet with wonder, not yet fully returned from the other world, from the visions that fasting and night and Gereint's secret drink had given them. They seemed untouched, fresh, which was as it should be.

Ivor led them, one on either side, letting them walk beside him now, as was fit for men, to the quarters set apart for Gereint. He went inside with them and watched as they knelt before the shaman, that he might confirm and consecrate their animals. Never had one of Ivor's children tried to dissemble about his fast, to claim a totem when there had been none, or pretend in his mind that an eltor had been an eagle or a boar. It was still the task of the shaman to find in them the truth of their vigil, so that in the tribe Gereint knew the totems of every Rider. It was thus in all the tribes. So it was written at Celidon. So was the Law.

At length Gereint lifted his head from where he sat cross-legged on his mat. He turned unerringly to where Ivor stood, the light from outside silhouetting him.

"Their hour knows their name," the shaman said.

It was done. The words that defined a Rider had been spoken: the hour that none could avoid, and the sanctity of their secret name. Ivor was assailed suddenly by a sense of the sweep, the vastness of time. For twelve hundred years the Dalrei had ridden on the Plain. For twelve hundred years each new Rider had been so proclaimed.

"Should we feast?" he asked Gereint formally.

"Indeed we should," came the placid reply. "We should have the Feast of the New Hunters."

"It shall be so," Ivor said. So many times he and Gereint had done this, summer after summer. Was he getting old?

He took the two newest Riders and led them into the sunlight, to where all the tribe was gathered before the door of the shaman's house.

"Their hour knows," he said, and smiled to hear the roar that went up.

He gave Navon and Barth back to their families at last. "Sleep," he urged them both, knowing what the morrow would be like, knowing he would not be heeded. Who slept on this day?

Levon had, he remembered; but he had been three nights in the grove and had come out, at the last, hollowed and other-worldly. A difficult, far-voyaging fast it had been, as was fitting for one who would one day lead the tribe.

Thinking so, he watched his people stream away, then ducked back into the darkness of Gereint's house. There was never any light in that house, no matter which camp they occupied.

The shaman had not moved.

"It is well," Ivor said, hunkering down beside the old one.

Gereint nodded. "It is well, I think. They should both do, and Barth may be something more." It was the closest he ever came to giving the Chieftain a hint of what he had seen in the new ones. Always Ivor marvelled at the shaman's gift, at his power.

He still remembered the night they had blinded Gereint. A child, Ivor had been, four summers from his hawk, but as Banor's only son, he had been taken out with the men to see it done. Power for him all his life would be symbolized by deep-voiced chanting and torches weaving on the night plain under the stars of midsummer.

For some moments the two men sat quietly, each wrapped in his own thoughts, then Ivor rose. "I should speak to Levon about tomorrow's hunt," he said. "Sixteen, I think."

"At least," the shaman said in an aggrieved tone. "I could eat a whole one myself. We haven't feasted in a long time, Ivor."

Ivor snorted. "A very long time, you greedy old man. Twelve whole days since Walen was named. Why aren't you fat?"

"Because," the wisest one explained patiently, "you never have enough food at the feasts."

"Seventeen, then!" Ivor laughed. "I'll see you in the morning before they go. It's up to Levon, but I'm going to suggest east."

"East," Gereint agreed gravely. "But you'll see me later today."

This, too, Ivor had grown accustomed to.

*The Sight comes when the light goes,* the Dalrei said. It was not Law, but had the same force, it seemed to Ivor at times. They found their totems in the dark, and all their shamans came to their power in blindness with that ceremony on midsummer night, the bright torches and the stars suddenly going black.

He found Levon with the horses, of course, tending to a mare with a bad fetlock. Levon rose at his father's footstep and came over, pushing the yellow hair back from his eyes. It was long, and he never tied it back. Seeing Levon lifted Ivor's heart; it always did.

He remembered, probably because he'd been thinking of it earlier, the morning Levon had returned from his three-day fast. All day he had slept, bone-weary, the fair skin almost translucent with exhaustion. Late at night he had arisen and sought his father.

Ivor and his thirteen-year-old son had walked out alone into the sleeping camp.

"I saw a cerne, father," Levon had said suddenly. A gift to him, the deepest, rarest gift. His animal, his secret name. A cerne was very good, Ivor thought with pride. Strong and brave, proudly horned like the god for which it was named, legendary for how it would defend its young. A cerne was as good as could be.

He nodded. There had been a difficulty in his throat. Leith was always teasing him about how quick he was to cry. He wanted to put an arm about the boy, but Levon was a Rider now, a man, and had given him a man's gift.

"Mine was a hawk," Ivor had said, and had stood beside his son, their shoulders touching as they looked together at the summer sky above their sleeping people.

"Eastward, right?" Levon said now, coming up. There was laughter in his brown eyes.

"I think," Ivor replied. "Let's not be foolhardy. It's up to you, though," he added quickly.

"I know. East is fine. I'll have the two new ones, anyhow. It's easier country to hunt. How many?"

"I thought sixteen, but Gereint wants an eltor to himself."

Levon threw back his head and laughed. "And he complained about not enough feasting, didn't he?"

"Always," his father chuckled. "How many hunters, then, for seventeen?"

"Twenty," Levon said immediately.

It was five fewer than he would have taken. It put great pressure on the hunters, especially with the two new ones in the band, but Ivor held his peace. The hunting was Levon's now, and his son knew the horses and hunters, and the eltor like no one else did. He believed in putting pressure on them, too, Ivor knew. It kept them sharp. Revor was said to have done the same thing.

So "Good" was all he said. "Choose well. I'll see you at home later." Levon raised a hand; he was already turning back to the mare.

Ivor hadn't eaten yet, or talked to Leith, and the sun was already high. He went home. They were waiting for him in the front room. Because of Gereint's parting words, he wasn't totally surprised.

"This," said Torc, without ceremony, "is Davor. He crossed from another world with Loren Silvercloak last night, but was separated from him. We killed an urgach together in Faelinn last night."

*Yes,* Ivor thought, *I knew there was something more.* He looked at the two young men. The stranger, a very big man, bristled with a certain aggressiveness, but was not truly so, Ivor judged. Torc's terse words had both frightened and pleased the Chieftain. An urgach was unheard-of news, but the Outcast's saying "we" made Ivor smile inwardly. The two of them had shared something in that killing, he thought.

"Welcome," he said to the stranger. And then, formally, "Your coming is a bright thread in what is woven for us. You will have to tell me as much as you care to of your story. Killing an urgach—that was bravely done. We shall eat first, though," he added hastily, knowing Leith's rules with guests. "Liane?" he called.

His daughter materialized instantaneously. She had, of course, been listening behind the door. Ivor suppressed a smile. "We have guests for the morning meal," he said. "Will you find Tabor and have him request Gereint to come? Levon, too."

"Gereint won't want to," she said impertinently. "It's too far, he'll say." Ivor observed that she was keeping her back to Torc. It was shameful that a child of his should treat a tribesman so. He would have to speak to her of it. This business of the Outcast must be ended.

For the moment he said merely, "Have Tabor say that he was right this morning."

"About what?" Liane demanded.

"Go, child," Ivor said. There were limits.

With a predictable toss of her hair, Liane spun and left the room. The stranger, Ivor saw, had an amused look on his face, and no longer clutched the sheaf of papers he carried quite so defensively. It was well, for the moment.

Loren Silvercloak, though, and an urgach in Faelinn Grove? Not for five hundred years had such a creature been reported to Celidon. *I knew,* Ivor thought, *there was another reason why we stayed.*

This, it seemed, was it.

# CHAPTER 11

They had found a horse for him, not an easy task. The Dalrei tended to be smallish people, quick and wiry, and their mounts were much the same. In winter, though, they traded with the men of Brennin in the lands where the High Kingdom ran into the Plain near the Latham, and there were always one or two larger mounts in every tribe, used usually for carrying goods from camp to camp. Riding the placid-tempered grey they had given him, and with Ivor's younger son, Tabor, as a guide, Dave had come out at dawn with Levon and the hunters to watch an eltor chase.

His arms were in pretty rough shape, but Torc had to be just as bad, or worse, and he was hunting; so Dave figured he could manage to ride a horse and watch.

Tabor, skinny and tanned dark brown, rode a chestnut pony beside him. He wore his hair tied back like Torc and most of the Riders, but it wasn't really long enough for that, and the tied part stuck up on the back of his head like a tree stump. Dave remembered himself at fourteen and found an uncharacteristic empathy for the kid beside him. Tabor talked a lot—in fact, he hadn't shut up since they'd ridden out—but Dave was interested and didn't mind, for once.

"We used to carry our houses with us when we moved," Tabor was saying as they jogged along. Up front, Levon was setting an easy pace eastward into the rising sun. Torc was beside him and there seemed to be about twenty other riders. It was a glorious, mild summer morning.

"They weren't houses like we have now, of course," Tabor went on. "We made them of eltor skin and poles, so they were easy to carry."

"We have things like that in my world, too," Dave said. "Why did you change?"

"Revor did it," Tabor explained.

"Who's he?"

The boy looked pained, as if appalled to discover that the fame of this Revor hadn't reached Toronto yet. Fourteen was a funny age, Dave thought, suppressing a grin. He was surprised at how cheerful he felt.

"Revor is our brightest hero," Tabor explained reverently. "He saved the High

King in battle during the Bael Rangat, by riding through Daniloth, and was rewarded with the land of the Plain for the Dalrei forever. After that," Tabor went on, earnestly, "Revor called a great gathering of all the Dalrei at Celidon, the mid-Plain, and said that if this was now our land, we should have some mark of ourselves upon it. So the camps were built in those days, that our tribes might have true homes to come to as they followed the eltor about the Plain."

"How far back?" Dave asked.

"Oh, forever and ever," Tabor replied, waving a hand.

"Forever and Revor?" said Dave, surprising himself. Tabor looked blank for a second, then giggled. He was a good kid, Dave decided. The ponytail was hilarious, though.

"The camps have been rebuilt many times since then," Tabor resumed his lecture. He was taking his guide duties seriously. "We always cut wood when we are near a forest—except Pendaran, of course—and we carry it to the next camp when we move. Sometimes the camps have been completely destroyed. There are fires when the Plain is dry."

Dave nodded; it made sense. "And I guess you have to clear out the damage the weather and animals do in between times, anyway."

"Weather, yes," Tabor said. "But never the animals. The shamans were given a spell as a gift from Gwen Ystrat. Nothing wild ever enters the camps."

That, Dave still had problems with. He remembered the old, blind shaman, Gereint, being led into the Chieftain's house the morning before. Gereint had trained his sightless eye sockets right on him. Dave had met the look as best he could—a staring duel with a blind man—but when Gereint had turned away, expressionless, he'd felt like crying out, *"What did you see, damn you?"*

The whole thing unnerved him. It had been the only bad moment, though. Ivor, the Chieftain, a small, leathery guy with crinkly eyes and a considered way of speaking, had been all right.

"If Silvercloak was going to Paras Derval," he'd said, "then that is where he'll be. I will send word of you with the auberei to Celidon, and a party of us will guide you south to Brennin. It will be a good thing for some of our younger men to make that journey, and I have tidings for Ailell, the High King."

"The urgach?" a voice had said then from by the door, and Dave had turned to see Liane again, Ivor's brown-haired daughter.

Levon had laughed. "Father," he'd said, "we may as well make her part of the tribal council. She's going to listen anyhow."

Ivor had looked displeased and proud, both. It was at that point that Dave had decided he liked the Chieftain.

"Liane," Ivor had said, "doesn't your mother need you?"

"She said I was in her way."

"How can you be in her way? We have guests, there must be things for you to do," Ivor had said bemusedly.

"I break dishes," Liane had explained. "Is it the urgach?"

Dave had laughed aloud, then flushed at the look she'd given him.

"Yes," Ivor had said. But then he added, looking levelly at Liane, "My daughter, you are being indulged because I dislike chastising my children before guests, but you go too far. It ill becomes you to listen at doors. It is the action of a spoiled child, not a woman."

Liane's flippant manner had disappeared completely. She paled, and her lip trembled. "I'm sorry," she had gasped, and spinning on her heel, had fled the home.

"She hates missing things," Levon had said, stating the obvious.

"There they are."

Tabor was pointing southeast, and Dave, squinting into the sun, saw the eltor moving northward across their path. He had been expecting buffalo, he now realized, for what he saw made him catch his breath, in sudden understanding of why the Dalrei spoke not of a herd, but of a swift of eltor.

They were like antelope: graceful, many-horned, sleek, and very, very fast. Most were coloured in shadings of brown, but one or two were purest white. The speed of their sweep across the plain was dazzling. There had to be five hundred of them, moving like wind over the grass, their heads carried high, arrogant and beautiful, the hair of their manes lifting back in the wind of their running.

"A small swift," Tabor said. The kid was trying to be cool, but Dave could hear the excitement in his voice, even as he felt his own heartbeat accelerate. God, they were beautiful. The Riders around him, in response to Levon's concise command, picked up speed and changed approach slightly to intersect the swift at an angle.

"Come!" Tabor said, as their slower mounts fell behind. "I know where he will have them do it." He cut away sharply northward, and Dave followed. In a moment they crested a small knoll in the otherwise level sweep of the prairie; turning back, Dave saw the eltor swift and the hunters converge, and he watched the Dalrei hunt, as Tabor told him of the Law.

An eltor could be killed by knife blade only. Nothing else. Any other killing meant death or exile to the man who did so. Such, for twelve hundred years, had been the Law inscribed on the parchments at Celidon.

More: one eltor to one man, and one chance only for the hunter. A doe could be killed, but at risk, for a bearing doe's death meant execution or exile again.

This, Dave learned, was what had happened to Torc's father. Ivor had exiled him, having no other mercy to grant, for in the preservation of the great eltor swifts lay the preservation of the Dalrei themselves. Dave nodded to hear it; somehow, out here on the Plain under that high sky, harsh, clear laws seemed to fit. It was not a world shaped for nuance or subtlety.

Then Tabor grew silent, for one by one, in response to Levon's gesture, the hunters of the third tribe set out after their prey. Dave saw the first of them, low and melded to his flying horse, intersect the edge of the racing swift. The man picked his target, slid into place beside it; then Dave, his jaw dropping, saw the hunter leap from horse to eltor, dagger flashing, and, with a succinct slash, sever the beast's jugular. The eltor fell, the weight of the Dalrei pulling it away from the body of the swift. The hunter disengaged from the falling beast, hit the ground himself at frightening speed, rolled, and was up, his dagger raised in red triumph.

Levon raised his own blade in response, but most of the other men were already flying alongside the swift. Dave saw the next man kill with a short, deadly throw. His eltor fell, almost in its tracks. Another hunter, riding with unbelievable skill, held to his mount with his legs only, leaning far out over the back of a madly racing eltor, to stab from horseback and bring down his beast.

"Uh-oh," Tabor said sharply. "Navon's trying to be fancy." Shifting his glance, Dave saw that one of the boys he'd guarded the night before was showing off on his first hunt. Riding his horse while standing up, Navon smoothly cut in close to one of the eltor. Taking careful aim, he threw from his standing position—and missed. The flung blade whipped just over the neck of the prey and fell harmlessly.

"Idiot!" Tabor exclaimed, as Navon slumped down on his mount. Even at a distance Dave could see the young Rider's dejection.

"It was a good try," he offered.

"No," Tabor snapped, his eyes never leaving the hunters. "He shouldn't be doing that on his first hunt, especially when Levon has trusted him by taking only twenty for seventeen. Now if anyone else is unlucky . . ."

Turning back to the hunt, Dave picked out the other new Rider. Barth, on a brown stallion, went in with cool efficiency, picked out his eltor and, wasting no time, pulled alongside, leaped from his horse, and stabbing, as the first hunter had done, brought his beast down.

"Good," Tabor muttered, a little grudgingly. "He did well. See, he even pulled it down to the outside, away from the others. The leap is the surest way, though you can get hurt doing it."

And sure enough, though Barth rose holding a dagger aloft, it was in his left hand, and his right hung down at his side. Levon saluted him back. Dave turned to Tabor to ask a question, but was stopped cold by the stricken expression on his companion's face.

"Please," Tabor whispered, almost a prayer. "Let it be soon. Oh, Davor, if Gereint doesn't name me this summer, I will die of shame!"

Dave couldn't think of a single thing to say. So, after a moment, he just asked his question. "Does Levon go in, too, or will he just watch?"

Tabor collected himself. "He only kills if the others have failed, then he must make up the numbers himself. It is a shameful thing, though, if the leader must kill, which is why most tribes take many more hunters than they need." There was pride in Tabor's voice again. "It is a thing of great honour to take only a few extra Riders, or none, though no one does that. The third tribe is known now over all the Plain for how bold we are on the hunt. I wish, though, that Levon had been more careful with two new ones today. My father would have—oh, no!"

Dave saw it, too. The eltor picked out by the fifteenth Rider stumbled, just as the hunter threw, and the blade hit an antler only and glanced away. The eltor recovered and raced off, head high, its mane blown gracefully back.

Tabor was suddenly very still, and after a quick calculation Dave realized why: no one else could miss. Levon had cut it very fine.

The sixteenth hunter, an older man, had already peeled off from the small group remaining. Dave saw that the Riders who had already killed were racing along on the far side of the swift. They had turned the eltor so the beasts were now running back south along the other side of the knoll. All the kills, he realized, would be close together. It was an efficient process, well judged. If no one else missed.

The sixteenth hunter played no games. In fast, his blade high, he picked a slower animal, leaped, and stabbed, pulling it clear. He rose, dagger lifted.

"A fat one," Tabor said, trying to mask his tension. "Gereint'll want that one tonight."

The seventeenth man killed, too, throwing from almost directly over top of his eltor. He made it look easy.

"Torc won't miss," Dave heard Tabor say, and saw the now familiar shirtless figure whip past their knoll. Torc singled out an eltor, raced south with it for several strides, then threw with arrogant assurance. The eltor dropped, almost at their feet. Torc saluted briefly, then sped off to join the other Riders on the far side of the swift. Seeing that throw, Dave remembered the urgach falling two nights before. He felt like cheering for Torc, but there was one more to go, and he could feel Tabor's anxiety.

"Cechtar's very good," the boy breathed. Dave saw a big man on a chestnut horse leave Levon's side—the leader was alone now, just below them. Cechtar galloped confidently towards the racing swift that the others were steering past the knoll. His knife was drawn already, and the man's carriage on his horse was solid and reassuring.

Then the horse hit a tummock of grass and stumbled. Cechtar kept his seat, but the damage was done—the knife, prematurely upraised, had flown from his hand to fall harmlessly short of the nearest animal.

Hardly breathing, Dave turned to see what Levon would do. Beside him, Tabor was moaning in an agony of distress. "Oh no, oh no," he repeated. "We are shamed. It's a disgrace for all three Riders, and Levon especially for misjudging. There's nothing he can do. I feel sick!"

"He has to kill now?"

"Yes, and he will. But it doesn't make any difference, there's nothing he can—oh!"

Tabor stopped, for Levon, moving his horse forward very deliberately, had shouted a command to Torc and the others. Watching, Dave saw the hunters race to turn the eltor yet again, so that after a wide arc had been described, the swift, a quarter of a mile away now, were flying back north, five hundred strong on the east side of the knoll.

"What's he doing?" Dave asked softly.

"I don't know, I don't understand. Unless . . ." Levon began to ride slowly eastward, but after a few strides he turned his horse to stand motionless, square in the path of the swift.

"What the hell?" Dave breathed.

"*Oh, Levon, no!*" Tabor screamed suddenly. The boy clutched Dave's arm, his face white with terrified understanding. "He's trying Revor's Kill. He's going to kill himself!"

Dave felt his own rush of fear hit, as he grasped what Levon was trying to do. It was impossible, though; it was insanity. Was the hunt leader committing suicide out of shame?

In frozen silence they watched from the knoll as the massed swift, slightly wedge-shaped behind a huge lead animal, raced over the grass towards the still figure of Tabor's yellow-haired brother. The other hunters, too, Dave was dimly aware, had stopped riding. The only sound was the rapidly growing thunder of the onrushing eltor.

Unable to take his eyes away from the hunt leader, Dave saw Levon, moving without haste, dismount to stand in front of his horse. The eltor were very close now, flying; the sound of their drumming hooves filled the air.

The horse was utterly still. That, too, Dave registered, then he saw Levon unhurriedly draw his blade.

The lead eltor was fifty yards away.

Then twenty.

Levon raised his arm and, without pausing, the whole thing one seamless motion, threw.

The blade hit the giant animal directly between the eyes; it broke stride, staggered, then fell at Levon's feet. Right at Levon's feet.

His fists clenched tightly with raw emotion, Dave saw the other animals instantly scythe out away from the fallen leader and form two smaller swifts, one angling east, one west, dividing in a cloud of dust precisely at the point where the fallen eltor lay.

Where Levon, his yellow hair blowing free, stood quietly stroking his horse's muzzle, having stolen in that moment, with an act of incandescent gallantry, great honour for his people from the teeth of shame. As a leader should.

Dave became aware that he was shouting wildly, that Tabor, tears in his eyes, was hugging him fiercely and pounding his sore shoulders, and that he had an arm around the boy and was hugging him back. It was not, it never had been the sort of thing he did, but it was all right now, it was more than all right.

Ivor was astonished at the fury he felt. A rage such as this he could not remember. Levon had almost died, he told himself, that was why. A foolhardy piece of bravado, it had been. Ivor should have insisted on twenty-five Riders. He, Ivor, was still Chieftain of the third tribe.

And that vehement thought gave him pause. Was it only fear for Levon that sparked his anger? After all, it was over now; Levon was fine, he was better than fine. The whole tribe was afire with what he had done. Revor's Kill. Levon's reputation was made; his deed would dominate the midwinter gathering of the nine tribes at Celidon. His name would soon be ringing the length of the Plain.

*I feel old,* Ivor realized. *I'm jealous. I've got a son who can do Revor's Kill.* What did that make him? Was he just Levon's father now, the last part of his name?

Which led to another thought: did all fathers feel this way when their sons became men? Men of achievement, of names that eclipsed the father's? Was there always the sting of envy to temper the burst of pride? Had Banor felt that way when twenty-year-old Ivor had made his first speech at Celidon and earned the praise of all the elders for the wisdom of his words?

Probably, he thought, remembering his father with love. Probably he had, and, Ivor realized, it didn't matter. It really didn't. It was part of the way of things, part of the procession all men made towards the knowing hour.

If he had a virtue, Ivor reflected, something of his nature he wanted his sons to have, it was tolerance. He smiled wryly. It would be ironic if that tolerance could not be extended to himself.

Which reminded him. His sons; and his daughter. He had to have a talk with Liane. Feelingly decidedly better, Ivor went looking for his middle child.

Revor's Kill. Oh, by Ceinwen's bow, he was proud!

The Feast of the New Hunters started formally at sundown, the tribe gathering in the huge central area of the camp, from where the smell of slowly roasting game had been wafting all afternoon. Truly, this would be a celebration: two new Riders and Levon's deed that morning. A feat that had obliterated the failures before. No one, not even Gereint, could remember the last time it had been done. "Not since Revor himself!" one of the hunters had shouted, a little drunkenly.

All the hunters from the morning were a little drunk; they had started early, Dave among them, on the clear, harsh liquor the Dalrei brewed. The mood of mingled relief and euphoria on the ride home had been completely infectious and Dave had let himself go with it. There didn't seem to be any reason to hold back.

Through it all, drinking round for round with them, Levon seemed almost unaffected by what he had done. Looking for it, Dave could find no arrogance, no hidden sense of superiority in Ivor's older son. It had to be there, he thought, suspicious, as he always was. But looking one more time at Levon as he walked between him and Ivor to the feast—he was guest of honour, it seemed—Dave found himself reluctantly changing his mind. Is a horse arrogant or superior? He didn't think so. Proud, yes; there was great pride in the bay stallion that had stood so still with Levon that morning, but it wasn't a pride that diminished anything or anyone else. It was simply part of what the stallion was.

Levon was like that, Dave decided.

It was one of his last really coherent thoughts, for with the sunset the feast began. The eltor meat was superlative; broiled slowly over open fires, seasoned with spices he didn't recognize, it was better than anything he'd ever tasted in his life. When the sizzling slices of meat started to go around, the drinking among the tribesmen got quite serious as well.

Dave was seldom drunk; he didn't like surrendering the edge of control, but he was in a strange space that evening, a whole other country. A whole other world, even. He didn't hold back.

Sitting by Ivor's side, he suddenly realized that he hadn't seen Torc since the hunt.

Looking around the firelit pandemonium, he finally spotted the dark man standing by himself, off on the edge of the circle of light cast by the fires.

Dave rose, not too steadily. Ivor raised an inquiring eyebrow. "It's Torc," Dave mumbled. "Why's he on his own? Shouldn't be. He should be here. Hell, we . . . we killed an urgach together, me and him." Ivor nodded, as if the stumbling discourse had been lucid explanation.

"Truly," the Chieftain said quietly. Turning to his daughter, who was serving him just then, he added, "Liane, will you go and bring Torc to sit by me?"

"Can't," Liane said. "Sorry. Have to go get ready for the dancing." And she was gone, quick, mercurial, into the confused shadows. Ivor, Dave saw, did not look happy.

He strode off to fetch Torc himself. Stupid girl, he thought, with some anger, she's avoiding him because his father was exiled and she's chief's daughter.

He came up to Torc in the half-dark, just beyond the cast glow of the many fires. The other man, chewing on an eltor haunch, merely grunted a hello. That was okay. Didn't need to talk; talkers bugged Dave anyhow.

They stood awhile in silence. It was cooler beyond the fires; the wind felt easy, refreshing. It sobered him a little.

"How do you feel?" he asked finally.

"Better," Torc said. And after a moment, "Your shoulder?"

"Better," Dave replied. When you didn't say a lot, he thought, you said the important things. In the shadows with Torc, he felt no real desire to go back to the centre of the clearing. It was better here, feeling the wind. You could see the stars, too. You couldn't in the firelight; or in Toronto, either, he thought.

On impulse he turned around. There it was. Torc turned to look with him. Together they gazed at the white magnificence of Rangat.

"There's someone under there?" Dave asked softly.

"Yes," said Torc briefly. "Bound."

"Loren told us."

"He cannot die."

Which was not comforting. "Who is he?" Dave asked with some diffidence.

For a moment Torc was silent, then: "We do not name him by his name. In Brennin they do, I am told, and in Cathal, but it is the Dalrei who dwell under the shadow of Rangat. When we speak of him, it is as Maugrim, the Unraveller."

Dave shivered, though it wasn't cold. The Mountain was shining in the moonlight, its peak so high he had to tilt his head back to take it in. He wrestled then with a difficult thought.

"It's so great," he said. "So tremendous. Why'd they put him under something so beautiful? Now every time you look at it, you have to think about . . ." He trailed off. Words were too tough, sometimes. Most of the time.

Torc was looking at him with sharp understanding, though. "That," he said softly, "is why they did it." And he turned back to the lights.

Turning with him, Dave saw that some of the fires were being put out, leaving a ring of flame, around which the Dalrei were gathering. He looked at Torc.

"Dancing," his companion said. "The women and boys."

And a moment later Dave saw a number of young girls enter the ring of fire and begin an intricate, weaving dance to a tune laid down by two old men with curiously shaped stringed instruments. It was pretty, he supposed, but dancing wasn't really his thing. His eyes wandered away, and he spotted the old shaman, Gereint. Gereint was holding a piece of meat in each hand, one light, one dark. He was taking turns biting from each. Dave snorted and nudged Torc to look.

Torc laughed, too, softly. "He should be fat," he said. "I don't know why he isn't." Dave grinned. Just then Navon, still looking sheepish about his failure that morning, came by with a flask. Dave and Torc each drank, then watched the new Rider walk off. Still a boy, Dave thought, but he's a hunter now.

"He'll be all right," Torc murmured. "I think he learned his lesson this morning."

"He wouldn't be around to have learned it if you didn't use a knife as well as you do. That," Dave said for the first time, "was some throw the other night."

"I wouldn't have been around to throw it if you hadn't saved my life," Torc said. Then after a moment he grinned, his teeth white in the darkness. "We did all right back there."

"Damn right," said Dave, grinning back.

The young girls had gone, to cheerful applause. A larger operation began now, with the older boys joining a number of the women. Dave saw Tabor move to the centre of the circle, and after a moment he realized that they were dancing the morning's hunt. The music was louder now, more compelling. Another man had joined the two musicians.

They danced it all, with stylized, ritual gestures. The women, their hair loose and flowing, were the eltor, and the boys mimed the Riders they would one day be. It was beautifully done, even to the individual quirks and traits of the hunters. Dave recognized the characteristic head tilt of the second Rider in the boy who imitated him. There was enthusiastic applause for that, then there was laughter as another boy danced Navon's flashy failure. It was indulgent laughter, though, and even the other two misses were greeted with only brief regret, because everyone knew what was coming.

Tabor had untied his hair for this. He looked older, more assured—or was it just the role, Dave wondered, as he saw Ivor's younger son dance, with palpable pride and a surprisingly graceful restraint, his older brother's kill.

Seeing it again in the dance, Dave cheered as loudly as everyone else when the young woman dancing the lead eltor fell at Tabor's feet, and all the other women streamed around him, turning at the edge of the circle defined by the fires to form a whirling kaleidoscope of movement about the still figure of Tabor dan Ivor. It was well done, Dave thought, really well done. A head taller than everyone there, he could see it all. When Tabor glanced at him across the massed people in between, Dave gave him a high, clenched-fist gesture of approval. He saw Tabor, despite his role, flush with pleasure. Good kid. Solid.

When it ended, the crowd grew restive again; the dancing seemed to be over. Dave looked at Torc and mimed a drinking motion. Torc shook his head and pointed.

Looking back, Dave saw that Liane had entered the circle of fire.

She was dressed in red and had done something to her face; her colour was high and striking. She wore golden jewellery on each arm and about her throat; it glinted and flashed in the firelight as she moved, and it seemed to Dave as if she had suddenly become a creature of flame herself.

The crowd grew quiet as she waited. Then Liane, instead of dancing, spoke. "We have cause to celebrate," she sang out. "The kill of Levon dan Ivor will be told at Celidon this winter, and for many winters after." There was a roar of approval; Liane let it die down. "That kill," she said, "may not be the brightest deed we have reason to honour tonight." The crowd hushed in perplexity. "There was another act of courage done," Liane continued, "a darker one, in the night wood, and it should be known and celebrated by all of the third tribe."

*What?* Dave thought. *Uh-oh.*

It was all he had time for. "Bring forth Torc dan Sorcha," cried Liane, "and with him Davor, our guest, that we may honour them!"

"Here they are!" a high voice cried from behind Dave, and suddenly goddamn Tabor was pushing him forward, and Levon, smiling broadly, had Torc by the arm, and the two sons of Ivor led them through the parting crowd to stand beside the Chieftain.

With excruciating self-consciousness, Dave stood exposed in the light of the fires, and heard Liane continue in the rapt silence.

"You do not know," she cried to the tribe, "of what I speak, so I will dance it for you." *Oh, God,* Dave thought. He was, he knew, beet-red. "Let us do them honour," Liane said, more softly, "and let Torc dan Sorcha no more be named Outcast in this tribe, for know you that these two killed an urgach in Faelinn Grove two nights ago."

They hadn't known, Dave realized, wishing he could find a place to disappear, knowing Torc felt the same. From the electric response of the tribe, it was clear that they hadn't had a clue.

Then the music began, and gradually his colour receded, for no one was looking at him anymore: Liane was dancing between the fires.

She was doing it all, he marvelled, spellbound, doing it all herself. The two sleeping boys in the wood, Torc, himself, the very texture, the mood of Faelinn Grove at night—and then somehow, unbelievably, whether it was alcohol or firelight or some alchemy of art, he saw the urgach again, huge, terrifying, swinging its giant sword.

But there was only a girl in the ring of fire, only a girl and her shadow, dancing, miming, becoming the scene she shaped, offering it to all of them. He saw his own instinctive leap, then Torc's, the urgach's brutal blow that had sent Torc smashing into a tree. . . .

She had it dead-on, he realized, astonished. Then he smiled, even through his wonder and stirring pride: of course, she'd listened in while they told Ivor. He felt like laughing suddenly, like crying, like some kind, *any* kind of articulation of emotion as he watched Liane dance his own desperate parry of the urgach's sword, and then, finally, Torc's hurled dagger—she was Torc, she was the blade, and then the toppling, like a mighty tree, of the beast. She was all of it, entire, and she wasn't a stupid girl after all.

Ivor saw the urgach sway and fall, and then the dancer was herself again, Liane, and she was whirling between the fires, her bare feet flying, jewellery flashing on her arms, moving so fast her hair, short as it was, lifted behind her as she exploded in a wild celebration of dance, of the deed in the night wood, of this night, and the next, and the days, all of them, of everything there was before the hour came that knew your name.

With a lump in his throat he saw her slow, the motion winding down until she stopped, her hands across her breasts, her head lowered, motionless, the still point between the fires; between the stars, it seemed to him.

A moment the third tribe was still with her, then there came an explosion of cheering that must have rocketed beyond the camp, Ivor thought, beyond the lights of men, far out into the wide dark of the night plain.

He looked for Leith in that moment, and saw her standing among the women on the other side of the fires. No tears for her; she was not that sort of woman. But he knew her well enough after so many years to read the expression on her face. Let the tribe think the Chieftain's wife cool, efficient, unruffled; he knew better. He grinned at her, and laughed when she flushed and looked away, as if unmasked.

The tribe was still buzzing with the catharsis of the dance and the killing that had led to it. Even in this, Liane had been wilful, for he was not at all sure this was how he would have chosen to tell them of the urgach, and it was his place to decide. It couldn't be kept hidden, for the auberei would have to take word on their ride to Celidon tomorrow, but once more, it seemed, his middle child had gone her own way.

How could he be angry, though, after this? It was always so hard, Ivor found, to stay angry with Liane. Leith was better at it. Mothers and daughters; there was less indulgence there.

She had judged it rightly, though, he thought, watching her walk over to Torc and the stranger and kiss them both. Seeing Torc redden, Ivor decided that not the least cause for joy this night might be the reclaiming of the outcast by his tribe.

And then Gereint rose.

It was remarkable how tuned the tribe was to him. As soon as the blind shaman moved forward into the space between the fires, some collective thread of instinct alerted even the most intoxicated hunter. Gereint never had to gesture or wait for silence.

He'd looked silly before, Ivor reflected, watching the shaman move unassisted between the flames. Not anymore. However he might look with eltor juice dripping from his chin, when Gereint rose in the night to address the tribe, his voice was the voice of power. He spoke for Ceinwen and Cernan, for the night wind and the dawn wind, all the unseen world. The hollowed sockets of his eyes gave testimony. He had paid the price.

"Cernan came to me with the greyness of dawn," Gereint said quietly. *Cernan*, thought Ivor, god of the wild things, of wood and plain, Lord of the eltor, brother and twin to Ceinwen of the Bow.

"I saw him clear," Gereint went on. "The horns upon his head, seven-tined for a King, the dark flash of his eyes, the majesty of him." A sound like wind in tall grass swept through the tribe.

"He spoke a name to me," Gereint said. "A thing that has never happened in all my days. Cernan named to me this morning Tabor dan Ivor, and called him to his fast."

*Tabor.* And not just named by the shaman after a dream. Summoned by the god himself. A thrill of awe touched Ivor like a ghostly finger in the dark. For a moment he felt as if he were alone on the Plain. There was a shadow with him, only a shadow, but it was the god. Cernan knew his name; Tabor dan Ivor, he had called.

The Chieftain was brought unceremoniously back to the reality of the camp by the high scream of a woman. Liane, of course. He knew without looking. Flying across the ring, almost knocking over the shaman in her haste, she sped to Tabor's side, no longer a red spirit of dance and flame, only a quicksilver, coltish girl fiercely hugging her brother. Levon was there, too, Ivor saw; more quietly, but as fast, his open face flashing a broad smile of delight. The three of them together. Fair and brown and brown. His.

So Tabor was in Faelinn tomorrow. At that thought, he looked over and saw Torc gazing at him. He received a smile and a reassuring nod from the dark man, and then, with surprise and pleasure, another from giant Davor, who had been so lucky for them. Tabor would be guarded in the wood.

He looked for Leith again across the ring of fire. And with a twist in his heart, Ivor saw how beautiful she was, how very beautiful still, and then he saw the tears in her eyes. Youngest child, he thought, a mother and her youngest. He had a sudden overwhelming sense of the wonder, the strangeness, the deep, deep richness of things. It filled him, it expanded within his breast. He couldn't hold it in, it was so much, so very much.

Moving within the ring to a music of his own, Ivor, the Chieftain, not so old after all, not so very, danced his joy for his children, all of them.

# CHAPTER 12

Tabor, at least, was no baby. Ivor's son, Levon's brother, he knew where to lie in the wood at night. He was sheltered and hidden and could move easily at need. Torc approved.

He and Davor were in Faelinn Grove again. Their guest had, surprisingly, elected to delay his journey south in order to watch over the boy with him. Tabor, Torc thought, had made a strong impression. It wasn't unusual: he liked the boy himself. Characteristically, Torc gave no thought to the possibility that he himself might be another reason for Dave's reluctance to leave.

Torc had other things to think about. In fact, he had been of two minds about being accompanied that night. He had been looking forward to solitude and dark since the festival. Too much had happened there, and too quickly. Too many people had come over to embrace him after Liane's dance. And in the night, long after the fires had burned down, Kerrin dal Ragin had slipped into the room Levon had insisted he take in the camp. Levon had been smiling when they talked, and when Kerrin appeared in the doorway, Torc had belatedly understood why. Kerrin was very pretty, and much talked about among the hunters; her giggling, scented arrival was not the sort of thing an outcast grew accustomed to.

It had been very nice, more than that, in fact. But what had followed her arrival in his bed did not admit of leisure or tranquillity to let him reflect on all that had occurred.

He'd needed to be alone, but Davor's company was the next best thing. The big man was inclined to silence himself, and Torc could sense that the stranger had things of his own to think about. In any case, they were there to guard Tabor, and he'd not have wanted to meet another urgach alone. The Chieftain had given Davor an axe—the best weapon for one of his size, without training in the sword.

So, weapons to hand this time, the two of them had settled down against a pair of trees close to where Tabor lay. It was a mild, easy night. Torc, outcast no longer, it seemed, let his mind go back, past Kerrin's fair, silken hair, past the naming of Tabor by the god, the tumult of the tribe's response to what he and Davor had done, to the still point, the heart of everything, the moment for which he needed the dark and solitude.

Liane had kissed him when her dance was done.


Fingering the haft of his axe, enjoying the balanced, solid feel of it, Dave realized that he even liked the name they had given him.

Davor. It sounded far more formidable than Dave. Davor of the Axe. Axewielder. Davor dan Ivor—

Which stopped him. From that thought he could feel himself backing away; it was too exposed to even let it surface inside.

Beside him, Torc sat quietly, his dark eyes hidden; he seemed lost in reverie. Well, Dave thought, I guess he won't be an outcast anymore, not after last night.

Which took him back. His, too, had been a tiring night. Three girls, no less, had made their way through Ivor's doorway to the room where Dave slept. Or didn't, after all, sleep.

God, he remembered thinking at one point, I'll bet there's a lot of kids born nine months after one of these feasts. A good life, he decided, being a Rider of the Dalrei, of the third tribe, of the children of Ivor—

He sat up abruptly. Torc glanced at him, but made no comment. *You have a father,* Dave told himself sternly. *And a mother and brother. You're a law student in Toronto, and a basketball player, for God's sake.*

"In that order?" he remembered Kim Ford teasing, the first time they'd met; or had Kevin Laine put it the other way around? He couldn't remember. Already the time before the crossing seemed astonishingly remote. The Dalrei were real, Martyniuk thought. This axe, the wood, Torc—his kind of person. And there was more.

His mind looped back again to the night before, and this time it zeroed in on the thing that mattered much more than it should, more, he knew, than he could allow it to. Still, it did.

He leaned back against the tree again, going with the memory.

Liane had kissed him when her dance was done.


They heard it at the same time: something crashing loudly through the trees. Torc, child of night and woods, knew immediately—only someone who wanted to be heard would make so much noise. He didn't bother moving.

Dave, however, felt his heart lurch with apprehension. "What the hell is that?" he whispered fiercely, grabbing for his axe.

"Her brother, I think," Torc said, inadvisedly, and felt himself go crimson in the dark.

Even Dave, far from a perceptive man, could hardly miss that one. When Levon finally emerged through the trees, he found the two of them sitting in an awkward silence.

"I couldn't sleep," he offered apologetically. "I thought I might watch with you. Not that you need me, but . . ."

There was truly no guile, no hauteur in Levon. The man who had just done Revor's Kill, who would one day lead the tribe, was sheepishly requesting their indulgence.

"Sure," Dave said. "He's your brother. Come sit down."

Torc managed a short nod. His heartbeat was slowing, though, and after a time he decided he didn't really mind if Davor knew. *I've never had a friend*, he thought suddenly. *This is the sort of thing you talk to friends about.*

It was all right that Levon had come; Levon was unlike anyone else. And he had done something the morning before that Torc was not sure he would have dared to try. The realization was a hard one for a proud man, and a different person might have hated Levon for it. Torc, however, measured out his respect in terms of such things. *Two friends*, he thought, *I have two friends here.*

Though he could only speak of her to one of them.

That one was having problems. Torc's slip had registered, and Dave felt a need to walk the implications out. He rose. "I'm going to check on him," he said. "Right back."

He didn't do much thinking, though. This wasn't the sort of situation Dave Martyniuk could handle, so he ducked it. He carried the axe, careful not to make a noise with it; he tried to move as quietly as Torc did in the wood. *It's not even a situation,* he told himself abruptly. *I'm leaving tomorrow.*

He had spoken aloud. A night bird whirred suddenly from a branch overhead, startling him.

He came to the place where Tabor was hidden—and well hidden, too. It had taken Torc almost an hour to find him. Even looking straight at the spot, Dave could barely make out the shape of the boy in the hollow he'd chosen. Tabor would be asleep, Torc had explained earlier. The shaman had made a drink that would ensure this, and open the mind to receive what might come to wake him.

*Good kid*, Dave thought. He'd never had a younger brother, wondered how he would have behaved towards one. A lot better than Vince did, the bitter thought came. A hell of a lot better than Vincent.

A moment longer he watched Tabor's hollow, then, assured there was no danger to be seen, he turned away. Not quite ready to rejoin the other two, Dave took an angled route back through the grove.

He hadn't seen the glade before. He almost stumbled into it, checked himself barely in time. Then he crouched down, as silently as he could.

There was a small pool, glittering silver in the moonlight. The grass, too, was tinted silver, it seemed dewy and fragrant, new somehow. And there was a stag, a full-grown buck, drinking from the pool.

Dave found he was holding his breath, keeping his body utterly still. The moonlit scene was so beautiful, so serene, it seemed to be a gift, a bestowing. He was leaving tomorrow, riding south to Paras Derval, the first stage of the road home. He would never be here again, see anything like this.

*Should I not weep?* he thought, aware that even such a question was a world away from the normal workings of his mind. But he was, he was a world away.

And then, as the hairs rose up on the back of his neck, Dave became aware that there was someone else beside the glade.

He knew before he even looked, which is what caused the awe: her presence had been made manifest in ways he scarcely comprehended. The very air, the moonlight, now reflected it.

Turning, in silence and dread, Dave saw a woman with a bow, standing partway around the glade from where he crouched in darkness. She was clad in green, all in green, and her hair was the same silver as the moonlight. Very tall she was, queenly, and he could not have said if she was young or old, or the colour of her eyes, because there was a light in her face that made him avert his face, abashed and afraid.

It happened very quickly. A second bird flew suddenly, flapping its wings loudly, from a tree. The stag raised its head in momentary alarm, a magnificent creature, a king of the wood. Out of the corner of his eye—for he dared not look directly—Dave saw the woman string an arrow to her bow. A moment, a bare pulsation of time, slipped past as the frieze held: the stag with its head high, poised to flee, the moonlight on the glade, on the water, the huntress with her bow.

Then the arrow was loosed and it found the long, exposed throat of the stag.

Dave hurt for the beast, for blood on that silvered grass, for the crumpled fall of a thing so noble.

What happened next tore a gasp of wonder from the core of his being. Where the dead stag lay, a shimmer appeared in the glade, a sheen of moonlight, it seemed at first; then it darkened, took shape and then substance, and finally Dave saw another stag, identical, stand unafraid, unwounded, majestic, beside the body of the slain one. A moment it stood thus, then the great horns were lowered in homage to the huntress, and it was gone from the glade.

It was a thing of too much moonlit power, too much transcendency; there was an ache within him, an appalled awareness of his own—

"Stand! For I would see you before you die."

Of his own mortality.

With trembling limbs, Dave Martyniuk rose to stand before the goddess with her bow. He saw, without surprise, the arrow levelled on his heart, knew with certainty that he would not rise to bow to her once that shaft was in his breast.

"Come forward."

A curious, other-worldly calm descended upon Dave as he moved into the moonlight. He dropped the axe before his feet; it glittered on the grass.

"Look at me."

Drawing a deep breath, Dave raised his eyes and looked, as best he could, upon the shining of her face. She was beautiful, he saw, more beautiful than hope.

"No man of Fionavar," the goddess said, "may see Ceinwen hunt."

It gave him an out, but it was cheap, shallow, demeaning. He didn't want it.

"Goddess," he heard himself say, wondering at his own calm, "it was not intentional, but if there is a price to be paid, I will pay it."

A wind stirred the grass. "There is another answer you could have made, Dave Martyniuk," Ceinwen said.

Dave was silent.

An owl suddenly burst from the tree behind him, cutting like a shadow across the crescent of the moon and away. The third one, a corner of his mind said.

Then he heard the bowstring sing. *I am dead*, he had time, amazingly, to think, before the arrow thudded into the tree inches above his head.

His heart was sore. There was so much. He could feel the quivering of the long shaft; the feathers touched his hair.

"Not all need die," Green Ceinwen said. "Courage will be needed. You have sworn to pay a price to me, though, and one day I will claim it. Remember."

Dave sank to his knees; his legs would not bear him up before her any longer. There was such a glory in her face, in the shining of her hair.

"One thing more," he heard her say. He dared not look up. *"She is not for you."*

So his very heart lay open, and how should it be otherwise? But this, this he had decided for himself; he wanted her to know. He reached for the power of speech, a long way.

"No," he said. "I know. She's Torc's."

And the goddess laughed. "Has she no other choice?" Ceinwen said mockingly, and disappeared.

Dave, on his knees, lowered his head into his hands. His whole body began to shake violently. He was still like that when Torc and Levon came looking for him.

When Tabor woke, he was ready. There was no disorientation. He was in Faelinn, and fasting, and he was awake because it was time. He looked about, opening himself, prepared to receive what had come, his secret name, the ambit of his soul.

At which point, disorientation did set in. He was still in Faelinn, still in his hollow, even, but the wood had changed. Surely there had been no cleared space before him; he would never have chosen such a place. There *was* no such place near this hollow.

Then he saw that the night sky had a strange colour to it, and with a tremor of fear he understood that he was still asleep, he was dreaming, and would find his animal in the strange country of this dream. It was not usual, he knew; usually you woke to see your totem. Mastering fear as best he could, Tabor waited.

It came from the sky.

Not a bird. No hawk or eagle—he had hoped, they all did—nor even an owl. No, his heart working strangely, Tabor realized then that the clearing was needed for the creature to land.

She did, so lightly the grass seemed scarcely to be supporting her. Lying very still, Tabor confronted his animal. With an effort, then, a very great effort, he stretched himself out, mind and soul, to the impossible creature that had come for him. It did not exist, this exquisite thing that stood gazing calmly back at him in the strangely hued night. It did not exist, but it would, he knew, as he felt her enter him, become a part of him as he of her, and he learned her name even as he learned what it was the god had summoned him to find and be found by.

For a last moment, the very last, the youngest child of Ivor heard, as if someone else were speaking, a part of himself whisper, "An eagle would have been enough."

It was true. It would have been more than enough, but it was not so. Standing very still before him, the creature appeared to understand his thought. He felt her then, gently, in his mind. *Do not reject me*, he heard as from within, while her great, astonishing eyes never left his own. *We will have only each other at the last.*

He understood. It was in his mind, and then in his heart also. It was very deep; he hadn't known he went so deep. In response he stretched forth a hand. The creature lowered her head, and Tabor touched the offered horn.

"Imraith-Nimphais," he said, remembered saying, before the universe went dark.

"Hola!" cried Ivor joyously. "See who comes! Let there be rejoicing, for see, the Weaver sends a new Rider to us."

But as Tabor drew nearer, Ivor could see that it had been a difficult fast. He had found his animal—such was written in every movement he made—but he had clearly gone a long way. It was not unusual, it was good, even. A sign of a deeper merger with the totem.

It was only when Tabor walked up close to him that Ivor felt the first touch of apprehension.

No boy came back from a true fast looking quite the same; they were boys no longer, it had to show in their faces. But what he saw in his son's eyes chilled Ivor to the core, even in the morning sunshine of the camp.

No one else seemed to notice; the tumult of welcome resounded as it always did, louder even, for the son of the Chieftain who had been called by the god.

Called to what? Ivor was thinking, as he walked beside his youngest child towards Gereint's house. Called to what?

He smiled, though, to mask his concern, and saw that Tabor did so as well; with his mouth only, not the eyes, and Ivor could feel a muscle jumping spasmodically where he gripped his son's arm.

Arriving at Gereint's door he knocked, and the two of them entered. It was dark inside, as always, and the noise from without faded to a distant murmur of anticipation.

Steadily, but with some care, Tabor walked forward and knelt before the shaman. Gereint touched him affectionately on the shoulder. Then Tabor lifted his head.

Even in the darkness Ivor saw Gereint's harshly checked motion of shock. He and Tabor faced each other, for what seemed a very long time.

At length Gereint spoke, but not the words of ritual. "This does not exist," the shaman said. Ivor clenched his fists.

Tabor said, "Not yet."

"It is a true finding," Gereint went on, as if he hadn't heard. "But there is no such animal. You have encompassed it?"

"I think so," Tabor said, and in his voice now was utter weariness. "I tried. I think I did."

"I think so, too," Gereint said, and there was wonder in his voice. "It is a very great thing, Tabor dan Ivor."

Tabor made a gesture of deprecation; it seemed to drain what reserves of endurance he had left. "It just came," he said, and toppled sideways to his father's feet.

As he knelt to cradle his unconscious son, Ivor heard the shaman say in his voice of ritual, "His hour knows his name." And then, differently, "May all the powers of the Plain defend him."

"From what?" Ivor asked, knowing he should not.

Gereint swung to face him. "This one I would tell you if I could, old friend, but truly I do not know. He went so far the sky was changed."

Ivor swallowed. "Is it good?" he asked the shaman, who was supposed to know such things. "Is it good, Gereint?"

After too long a silence Gereint only repeated, "It is a very great thing," which was not what he needed to hear. Ivor looked down at Tabor, almost weightless in his arms. He saw the tanned skin, straight nose, unlined brow of youth, the unruly shock of brown hair, not long enough to tie properly, too long to wear loose—it always seemed to be that way with Tabor, he thought.

"Oh, my son," Ivor murmured, and then again, rocking him back and forth as he always used to, not so many years ago.

# CHAPTER 13

Towards sundown they pulled the horses to a halt in a small gully, only a depression, really, defined by a series of low tummocks on the plain.

Dave was a little unnerved by all the openness. Only the dark stretch of Pendaran brooding to the west broke the long monotony of the prairie, and Pendaran wasn't a reassuring sight.

The Dalrei were undisturbed, though; for them, clearly, this exposed spot on the darkening earth was home. The Plain was their home, all of it. For twelve hundred years, Dave remembered.

Levon would allow no fires; supper was cold eltor meat and hard cheese, with river water in flasks to wash it down. It was good, though, partly because Dave was ravenous after the day's ride. He was brutally tired as well, he realized, unfolding his sleeping roll beside Torc's.

Overtired, he soon amended, for once inside the blanket he found that sleep eluded him. Instead he lay awake under the wide sky, his mind circling restlessly back over the day.

Tabor had still been unconscious when they left in the morning. "He went far," was all the Chieftain would say, but his eyes could not mask concern, even in the dark of Gereint's house.

But then the question of Tabor was put aside for a moment, as Dave told his own story of the night glade and the Huntress, except for the very last, which was his alone. There was a silence when he was done.

Cross-legged on his mat, Gereint asked, "'Courage will be needed'—she said exactly that?"

Dave nodded, then remembered it was the shaman, and grunted a yes. Gereint rocked back and forth after that, humming tunelessly to himself for a long time. So long that it startled Dave when he finally spoke.

"You must go south quickly, then, and quietly, I think. Something grows, and if Silvercloak brought you, then you should be with him."

"It was only for the King's festival," Dave said. Nervousness made it sound sharper than he meant.

"Perhaps," Gereint said, "but there are other threads appearing now."

Which wasn't all that wonderful.


Turning on his side, Dave could see the raised silhouette of Levon against the night sky. It was deeply comforting to have that calm figure standing guard. Levon hadn't wanted to come at first, he remembered. Concern for his brother had left him visibly torn.

It was the Chieftain, asserting himself with absolute firmness, who had settled the issue. Levon would be useless at home. Tabor was being cared for. It was not, in any case, unusual for a faster to sleep a long time on his return. Levon, Ivor reminded his older son, had done the same. Cechtar could lead the hunt for ten days or two weeks—it would be good for him in any case, after the loss of face caused by his failure two days ago.

No, Ivor had said decisively, given Gereint's injunction as to speed and secrecy, it was important to get Dave—Davor, he said, as they all did—south to Paras Derval safely. Levon would lead, with Torc beside him in a band of twenty. It was decided.

Logical and controlling, Dave had thought, and coolly efficient. But then he remembered his own last conversation with Ivor.

The horses had been readied. He had bidden formal, slightly stiff farewells to Leith and then Liane—he was very bad at goodbyes. He'd been embarrassed, too, by the knot of girls standing nearby. Ivor's daughter had been elusive and remote.

After, he'd looked in on Tabor. The boy was feverish, and restless with it. Dave wasn't good with this, either. He'd made a confused gesture to Leith, who'd come in with him. He hoped she'd understand, not that he could have said exactly what he'd wanted to convey.

It was after this that Ivor had taken him for that last stroll around the perimeter of the camp.

"The axe is yours," the Chieftain had begun. "From what you have described, I doubt you will have great use for it in your own world, but perhaps it will serve to remind you of the Dalrei." Ivor had frowned then. "A warlike remembrance, alas, of the Children of Peace. Is there anything else you would . . . ?"

"No," Dave had said, flustered. "No, it's fine. It's great. I'll, ah, treasure it." Words. They had walked a few paces in silence, before Dave thought of a thing he did want to say.

"Say goodbye to Tabor for me, eh? I think . . . he's a good kid. He'll be all right, won't he?"

"I don't know," Ivor had replied with disturbing frankness. They had turned at the edge of the camp to walk north, facing the Mountain. By daylight Rangat was just as dazzling, the white slopes reflecting the sunlight so brightly it hurt the eye to see.

"I'm sure he'll be fine," Dave had said lamely, aware of how asinine that sounded. To cover it, he pushed on. "You've been, you know, really good to me here. I've . . . learned a lot." As he said it, he realized it was true.

For the first time Ivor smiled. "That pleases me," he said. "I like to believe we have things to teach."

"Oh, yeah, for sure," Dave said earnestly. "Of course you do. If I could stay longer . . ."

"If you could stay," Ivor had said, stopping and looking directly at Dave, "I think you would make a Rider."

Dave swallowed hard, and flushed with intense, self-conscious pleasure. He was speechless; Ivor had noticed. "If," the Chieftain had added, with a grin, "we could ever find a proper horse for you!"

Sharing the laugh, they resumed their walk. *God*, Dave was thinking, *I really, really like this man*. It would have been nice to be able to say it.

But then Ivor had thrown him the curve. "I don't know what your encounter last night means," he had said softly, "but it means a good deal, I think. I am sending Levon south with you, Davor. It is the right thing, though I hate to see him go. He is young yet, and I love him very much. Will you take care of him for me?"

Mean, unbalancing curve ball. "What?" Dave had exclaimed, bridling reflexively at the implications. "What are you talking about? *He's* the one who knows where he's going! You want me to guard him? Shouldn't it be the other way around?"

Ivor's expression was sad. "Ah, my son," he had said gently, "you have far to go in some ways. You, too, are young. Of course I told him to guard you as well, and with everything he has. I tell you both. Don't you see, Davor?"

He did see. Too late, of course. And clearly, he'd been an idiot, again. Again. And with no time to make it up, for they had looped full circle by then, and Levon, Torc, and seventeen other Riders were already mounted, with what seemed to be the whole third tribe turning out to see them off.

So there had been no last private word. He'd hugged Ivor hard, though, hoping the Chieftain would somehow know that it meant a lot for him to do that. Hoping, but not knowing if.

Then he had left, south for Brennin and the way home, the axe at his saddle side, sleeping roll behind, a few other things behind as well, too far behind for anything to be done.

On the starlit dark of the Plain, Dave opened his eyes again. Levon was still there, watching over them, over him. Kevin Laine would have known how to handle that last talk, he thought, surprisingly, and slept.

On the second day they started just before sunrise. Levon set a brisk but not a killing pace; the horses would have to last, and the Dalrei knew how to judge these things. They rode in a tight cluster, with three men, rotating every second hour, sent ahead a half-mile. Quickly and quietly, Gereint had advised, and they all knew Torc had seen svart alfar heading south two weeks before. Levon might take calculated risks on the hunt, but he was not a rash man; Ivor's son could hardly be so. He kept them moving in a state of watchful speed, and the trees at the outreaches of Pendaran rolled steadily by on their right as the sun climbed in the sky.

Gazing at the woods, less than a mile away, Dave was bothered by something. Kicking his horse forward, he caught up with Levon at the head of the main party.

"Why," he asked, without preamble, "are we riding so close to the forest?"

Levon smiled. "You are the seventh man to ask me that," he said cheerfully. "It isn't very complex. I'm taking the fastest route. If we swing farther east we'll have to ford two rivers and deal with hilly land between them. This line takes us to Adein west of the fork where Rienna joins it. Only one river, and as you see, the riding is easy."

"But the forest? It's supposed to be . . ."

"Pendaran is deadly to those who enter it. No one does. But the Wood is angry, not evil, and unless we trespass, the powers within it will not be stirred by our riding here. There are superstitions otherwise, but I have been taught by Gereint that this is so."

"What about an ambush, like from those svart alfar?"

Levon was no longer smiling. "A svart would sooner die than enter Pendaran," he said. "The Wood forgives none of us."

"For what?" Dave asked.

"Lisen," Levon said. "Shall I tell the story?"

"I'm not going anywhere," said Dave.

"I have to explain magic to you first, I think. You were brought here by Silvercloak. You would have seen Matt Sören?"

"The Dwarf? Sure."

"Do you know how they are bound to each other?"

"Haven't a clue. Are they?"

"Assuredly," said Levon, and as they rode south over the prairie, Dave learned, as Paul Schafer had four nights before, about the binding of mage and source, and how magic was made of that union.

Then as Levon began his tale, Torc came up quietly on his other side. The three of them rode together, bound by the rhythm and cadence of Lisen's tragedy.

"It is a long story," Levon began, "and much of import comes into it, and has grown out of it. I do not know nearly the whole, but it begins in the days before the Bael Rangat.

"In those days, the days before magic was as I have told you it now is, Amairgen, a counsellor to Conary, the High King in Paras Derval, rode forth alone from Brennin.

"Magic in that time was governed by the earthroot, the avarlith, and so it was within the domain of the Priestesses of the Mother in Gwen Ystrat, and jealously they guarded their control. Amairgen was a proud and brilliant man, and he chafed at this. So he went forth one morning in the spring of the year, to see if it need always be so.

"In time he came, after many adventures that are all part of the full tale—though most of them I do not know—to the sacred grove in Pendaran. The Wood was not angry then, but it was a place of power, and never one that welcomed the presence of men, especially in the grove. Amairgen was brave, though, and he had been journeying long without answer to his quest, so he dared greatly, and passed a night alone in that place.

"There are songs about that night: about the three visitations he had, and his mind battle with the earth demon that came up through the grass; it was a long and terrible night, and it is sung that no man else would have lived or been whole of mind to see the dawn.

"Be that as it may, just before morning there came a fourth visitation to Amairgen, and this one was from the God, from Mörnir, and it was beneficent, for it taught to Amairgen the runes of the skylore that freed the mages ever after from the Mother.

"There was war among the gods after that, it is told, for the Goddess was wrathful at what Mörnir had done, and it was long before she would let herself be placated. Some say, though I would not know if it is true, that it was the discord and the chaos of this conflict that gave Maugrim, the Unraveller, the chance to slip from the watch of the younger gods. He came from the places where they have their home and took root in the north lands of Fionavar. So some songs and stories have it. Others say he was always here, or that he slipped into Fionavar when the Weaver's eye was dimmed with love at the first emergence of the lios alfar—the Children of the Light. Still others tell that it was as the Weaver wept, when first man slew his brother. I know not; there are many stories. He is here and he cannot be killed. The gods grant he be always bound.

"Be all of that as it may, in the morning when Amairgen rose up, the runes in his heart and great power waiting there, he was in mortal danger yet; for the Wood, having its own guardians, was greatly angered at his having dared the grove at night, and Lisen was sent forth to break his heart and kill him.

"Of that meeting there is one song only. It was made not long after, by Ra-Termaine, greatest of all singers, Lord then of the lios alfar, and he crafted it in homage and remembrance of Amairgen. It is the most beautiful lay ever fashioned, and no poet since has ever touched the theme.

"There were very mighty peoples on the earth in those days, and among them all, Lisen of the Wood was as a Queen. A wood spirit she was, a deiena, of which there are many, but Lisen was more. It is said that on the night she was born in Pendaran, the evening star shone as brightly as the moon, and all the goddesses from Ceinwen to Nemain gave grant of their beauty to that child in the grove, and the flowers bloomed at night in the shining that arose when they all came together in that place. No one has ever been or will be more fair than was Lisen, and though the deiena live very long, Dana and Mörnir that night, as their joint gift, made her immortal that this beauty might never be lost.

"These gifts she was given at her birth, but not even the gods may shape exactly what they will, and some say that this truth is at the heart of the whole long tale. Be that so, or not, in the morning after his battles she came to Amairgen to break him with her beauty and slay him for his presumption of the night. But, as Ra-Termaine's song tells, Amairgen was as one exalted that morning, clothed in power and lore, and the presence of Mörnir was in his eyes. So did the design of the God act to undo the design of the

God, for coming to him then, wrapped in her own beauty like a star, Lisen fell in love and he with her, and so their doom was woven that morning in the grove.

"She became his source. Before the sun had set that day, he had taught her the runes. They were made mage and source by the ritual, and the first sky magic was wrought in the grove that day. That night they lay down together, and as the one song tells, Amairgen slept at length a second night in the sacred grove, but this time within the mantle of her hair. They went forth together in the morning from that place, bound as no living creatures to that day had been. Yet because Amairgen's place was at the right hand of Conary, and there were other men to whom he had to teach the skylore, he returned to Paras Derval and founded the Council of the Mages, and Lisen went with him and so left the shelter of the Wood."

Levon was silent. They rode thus for a long time. Then, "The tale is truly very complex now, and it picks up many other tales from the Great Years. It was in those days that the one we call the Unraveller raised his fortress of Starkadh in the Ice and came down on all the lands with war. There are so many deeds to tell of from that time. The one the Dalrei sing is of Revor's Ride, and it is very far from the least of the great things that were done. But Amairgen Whitebranch, as he came to be called, for the staff Lisen found for him in Pendaran, was ever at the centre of the war, and Lisen was at his side, source of his power and his soul.

"There are so many tales, Davor, but at length it came to pass that Amairgen learned by his art that Maugrim had taken for his own a place of great power, hidden far out at sea, and was drawing upon it mightily for his strength.

"He determined then that this island must be found and wrested away from the Dark. So Amairgen gathered to him a company of one hundred lios alfar and men, with three mages among them, and they set sail west from Taerlindel to find Cader Sedat, and Lisen was left behind."

"*What?* Why?" Dave rasped, stunned.

"It was Torc who answered. "She was a deiena," he said, his own voice sounding difficult. "A deiena dies at sea. Her immortality was subject to the nature of her kind."

"It is so," Levon resumed quietly. "They built in that time for her the Anor Lisen at the westernmost part of Pendaran. Even in the midst of war, men and lios alfar and the powers of the Wood came together to do this for her out of love. Then she placed upon her brow the Circlet of Lisen, Amairgen's parting gift. The Light against the Dark, it was called, for it shone of its own self, and with that light upon her brow—so great a beauty never else having been in any world—Lisen turned her back on the war and the Wood and, climbing to the summit of the tower, she set her face westward to the sea, that the Light she bore might show Amairgen the way home.

"No man knows what happened to him or those who sailed in that ship. Only that one night Lisen saw, and those who stood guard beside the Anor saw as well, a dark ship sailing slowly along the coast in the moonlight. And it is told that the moon setting west in that hour shone through its tattered sails with a ghostly light, and it could be seen that the ship was Amairgen's, and it was empty. Then, when the moon sank into the sea, that ship disappeared forever.

"Lisen took the Circlet from her brow and laid it down; then she unbound her hair that it might be as it was when first they had come together in the grove. Having done these things, she leaped into the darkness of the sea and so died."

The sun was high in the sky, Dave noticed. It seemed wrong, somehow, that this should be so, that the day should be so bright. "I think," Levon whispered, "that I will go ride up front for a time." He kicked his horse to a gallop. Dave and Torc looked at each other. Neither spoke a word. The Plain was east, the Wood west, the Sun was high in the sky.

Levon took a double shift up front. Late in the day Dave went forward himself to relieve him. Towards sunset they saw a black swan flying north almost directly overhead, very high. The sight filled them all with a vague, inexplicable sense of disquiet. Without a word being spoken, they picked up speed.

As they continued south, Pendaran gradually began to fall away westward. Dave knew it was there, but by the time darkness fell, the Wood could no longer be seen. When they stopped for the night, there was only grassland stretching away in every direction under the profligate dazzle of the summer stars, scarcely dimmed by the last thin crescent of the moon.

Later that night a dog and a wolf would battle in Mörnirwood, and Colan's dagger, later still, would be unsheathed with a sound like a harpstring, in a stone chamber underground beside Eilathen's lake.

At dawn the sun rose red, and a dry, prickly heat came with it. From first mounting, the company was going faster than before. Levon increased the point men to four and pulled them back a little closer, so both parties could see each other all the time.

Late in the morning the Mountain exploded behind them.

With the deepest terror of his life, Dave turned with the Dalrei to see the tongue of flame rising to master the sky. They saw it divide to shape the taloned hand, and then they heard the laughter of Maugrim.

"The gods grant he be always bound," Levon had said, only yesterday.

No dice, it seemed.

There was nothing within Dave that could surmount the brutal sound of that laughter on the wind. They were small, exposed, they were open to him and he was free. In a kind of trance, Dave saw the point men galloping frantically back to join them.

"Levon! Levon! We must go home!" one of them was shouting as he came nearer. Dave turned to Ivor's son and, looking at him, his heart slowed towards normality, and he marvelled again. There was no expression on Levon's face, his profile seemed chiselled from stone as he gazed at the towering fire above Rangat. But in that very calm, that impassive acceptance, Dave found a steadfastness of his own. Without moving a muscle, Levon seemed to be growing, to be willing himself to grow large enough to match, to overmatch the terror in the sky and on the wind. And somehow in that moment Dave had a flashing image of Ivor doing the selfsame thing, two days' ride back north, under the very shadow of that grasping hand. He looked for

Torc and found the dark man gazing back at him, and in Torc's eyes Dave saw not the stern resistance of Levon, but a fierce, bright, passionate defiance, a bitter hatred of what that hand meant, but not fear.

*Your hour knows your name*, Dave Martyniuk thought, and then, in that moment of apocalypse, had another thought: *I love these people*. The realization hit him, for Dave was what he was, almost as hard as the Mountain had. Struggling to regain his inner balance, he realized that Levon was speaking, quelling the babble of voices around him.

"We do not go back. My father will be caring for the tribe. They will go to Celidon, all the tribes will. And so will we, after Davor is with Silvercloak. Two days ago Gereint said that something was coming. This is it. We go south as fast as we can to Brennin, and there," said Levon, "I will take counsel with the High King."

Even as he spoke, Ailell dan Art was dying in Paras Derval. When Levon finished, not another word was said. The Dalrei regrouped and began riding, very fast now and all together. They rode henceforth with a hard, unyielding intensity, turning their backs on their tribe without a demurrer to follow Levon, though every one of them knew, even as they galloped, that if there was war with Maugrim, it would be fought on the Plain.

It was that alert tension that gave them warning, though in the end it would not be enough to save them.

Torc it was who, late in the afternoon, sped a distance ahead; bending sideways in his saddle, he rode low to the ground for a time before wheeling back to Levon's side. The Wood was close again, on their right. "We are coming to trouble," Torc said shortly. "There is a party of svart alfar not far ahead of us."

"How many?" Levon asked calmly, signalling a halt.

"Forty. Sixty."

Levon nodded. "We can beat them, but there will be losses. They know we are here, of course."

"If they have eyes," Torc agreed. "We are very exposed."

"Very well. We are close to Adein, but I do not want a fight now. It will waste us some time, but we are going to flank around them and cross both rivers farther east."

"I don't think we can, Levon," Torc murmured.

"Why?" Levon had gone very still.

"Look."

Dave turned east with Levon to where Torc was pointing, and after a moment he, too, saw the dark mass moving over the grass, low, about a mile away, and coming nearer.

"What are they?" he asked, his voice tight.

"Wolves," Levon snapped. "Very many." He drew his sword. "We can't go around—they will slow us by the rivers for the svarts. We must fight through south before they reach us." He raised his voice. "We fight on the gallop, my friends. Kill and ride, no lingering. When you reach Adein, you cross. We can outrun them on the other side." He paused, then: "I said before there would be war. It seems that we are to fight the first battle of our people. Let the servants of Maugrim now learn to fear the Dalrei again, as they did when Revor rode!"

With an answering shout, the Riders, Dave among them, loosed their weapons and sprang into gallop. His heart thudding, Dave followed Levon over a low tummock. On the other side he could see the river glistening less than a mile away. But in their path stood the svart alfar, and as soon as the Dalrei crested the rise a shower of arrows was launched towards them. A moment later, Dave saw a Rider fall beside him, blood flowering from his breast.

A rage came over Dave then. Kicking his horse to greater speed, he crashed, with Torc and Levon on either side, into the line of svarts. Leaning in the saddle, he whistled the great axe down to cleave one of the ugly, dark green creatures where it stood. Light-headed with fury, he pulled the axe clear and turned to swing it again.

"No!" Torc screamed. "Kill and ride! Come on!" The wolves, Dave saw in a flying glance, were less than half a mile away. Wheeling hard, he thundered with the others towards the Adein. They were through, it seemed. One man dead, two others nursing wounds, but the river was close now and once across they would be safe.

They would have been. They should have been. It was only sheerest, bitterest bad luck that the band of svarts that had ambushed Brendel and the lios alfar were there waiting.

They were, though, and there were almost a hundred of them left to rise from the shallows of Adein and block the path of the Dalrei. So with the wolves on their flank, and svarts before and behind, Levon was forced into a standing fight.

Under that red sun, the Children of Peace fought their first battle in a thousand years. With courage fuelled by rage, they fought on their land, launching arrows of their own, angling their horses in jagged lethal movements, scything with swords soon red with blood.

"Revor!" Dave heard Levon scream, and the very name seemed to cow the massed forces of the Dark. Only for a moment, though, and there were so many. In the chaos of the mêlée, Dave saw face after face of the nightmare svarts appear before him with lifted swords and razor teeth bared, and in a frenzy of battle fury he raised and lowered the axe again and again. All he could do was fight, and so he did. He scarcely knew how many svarts had died under his iron, but then, pulling the axe free from a mashed skull, Dave saw that the wolves had come, and he suddenly understood that death was here, by the Adein River on the Plain. Death, at the hands of these loathsome creatures, death for Levon, for Torc. . . .

"No!" Dave Martyniuk cried then, his voice a mighty bellow over the battle sounds, as inspiration blasted him. "To the Wood! Come on!"

And punching Levon's shoulder, he reined his own horse so that it reared high above the encircling enemy. On the way down he swung the axe once on either side of the descending hooves, and on each side he killed. For a moment the svarts hesitated, and using the moment, Dave kicked his horse again and pounded into them, the axe sweeping red, once, and again, and again; then suddenly he was clear, as their ranks broke before him, and he cut sharply away west. West, where Pendaran lay, brooding and unforgiving, where none of them, man or svart alfar or even the giant, twisted wolves of Galadan, dared go.

Three of them did dare, though. Looking back, Dave saw Levon and Torc knife through the gap his rush had carved and follow him in a flat-out race west, with the wolves at their heels and arrows falling about them in the growing dark.

Three only, no more, though not for lack of courage. The rest were dead. Nor had there been a scanting of gallant bravery in any one of the Dalrei who died that day, seventeen of them, by Adein where it runs into Llewenmere by Pendaran Wood.

They were devoured by the svart alfar as the sun went down. The dead always were. It was not the same as if it were the lios they had killed, of course, but blood was blood, and the red joy of killing was thick within them all that night. After, the two groups of them, so happily come together, made a pile of all the bones, clean-picked and otherwise, and started in, letting the wolves join them now, on their own dead.

Blood was blood.

There was a lake on their left, dark waters glimpsed through a lattice of trees as they whipped by. Dave had a fleeting image of hurtful beauty, but the wolves were close behind and they could not linger. At full tilt they hurtled into the outreaches of the forest, leaping a fallen branch, dodging sudden trees, not slacking pace at all, until at last Dave became aware that the wolves were no longer chasing them.

The twisting half-trail they followed became rougher, forcing them to slow, and then it was merely an illusion, not really a path. The three of them stopped, breathing with harsh effort amid the lengthening shadows of trees.

No one spoke. Levon's face, Dave saw, was like stone again, but not as before. This he recognized: not the steadfastness of resolution, but a rigid control locking the muscles, the heart, against the pain inside. You held it in, Dave thought, had always thought. It didn't belong to anyone else. He couldn't look at Levon's face very long, though; it twisted him somehow, on top of everything else.

Turning to Torc, he saw something different. "You're bleeding," he said, looking at the blood welling from the dark man's thigh. "Get down, let's have a look."

He, of course, hadn't a clue what to do. It was Levon, glad of the need for action, who tore his sleeping roll into strips and made a tourniquet for the wound, which was messy but, after cleaning, could be seen to be shallow.

By the time Levon finished, it was dark, and they had all been deeply conscious for some moments of something pulsing in the woods around them. Nor was there anything remotely vague about it: what they sensed was anger, and it could be heard in the sound of the leaves, felt in the vibrations of the earth beneath their feet. They were in Pendaran, and men, and the Wood did not forgive.

"We can't stay here!" Torc said abruptly. It sounded loud in the dark; for the first time, Dave heard strain in his voice.

"Can you walk?" Levon asked.

"I will," said Torc grimly. "I would rather be on my feet and moving when we meet whatever is sent for us." The leaves were louder now, and there seemed—or was that imagination?—to be a rhythm to their sound.

"We will leave the horses, then," Levon said. "They will be all right. I agree with you—I don't think we can lie down tonight. We will walk south, until we meet what—"

"Until we're out!" Dave said strongly. "Come on, both of you. Levon, you said before, this place isn't evil."

"It doesn't have to be, to kill us," said Torc. "Listen." It was not imagination; there *was* a pattern to the sound of the leaves.

"Would you prefer," Dave snapped, "to go back and try to make nice to the wolves?"

"He's right, Torc," Levon said. In the dark, only his long yellow hair could be seen. Torc, in black, was almost invisible. "And Davor," Levon went on, in a different voice, "you wove something very bright back there. I don't think any man in the tribe could have forced that opening. Whatever happens after, you saved our lives then."

"I just swung the thing," Dave muttered.

At which Torc, astonishingly, laughed aloud. For a moment the listening trees were stilled. No mortal had laughed in Pendaran for a millennium. "You are," said Torc dan Sorcha, "as bad as me, as bad as him. Not one of us can deal with praise. Is your face red right now, my friend?"

Of course it was, for God's sake. "What do you think?" he mumbled. Then, feeling the ridiculousness of it, hearing Levon's snort of amusement, Dave felt something let go inside, tension, fear, grief, all of them, and he laughed with his friends in the Wood where no man went.

It lasted for some time; they were all young, had fought their first battle, seen comrades slaughtered beside them. There was a cutting edge of hysteria to the moment.

Levon took them past it. "Torc is right," he said finally. "We are alike. In this, and in other ways. Before we leave this place, there is a thing I want to do. Friends of mine have died today. It would be good to have two new brothers. Will you mingle blood with me?"

"I have no brothers," Torc said softly. "It would be good."

Dave's heart was racing. "For sure," he said.

And so the ritual was enacted in the Wood. Torc made the incisions with his blade and they touched their wrists, each to each, in the dark. No one spoke. After, Levon made bandages, then they freed the horses, took their gear and weapons, and set forth together south through the forest, Torc leading, Levon last, Dave between his brothers.

As it happened, they had done more than they knew. They had been watched, and Pendaran understood these things, bindings wrought of blood. It did not assuage the anger or the hate, for she was forever lost who should never have died; but though these three had still to be slain, they could be spared madness before the end. So it was decided as they walked, oblivious to the meaning of the whispering around them, wrapped in it, though, as in a net of sound.

***

For Torc, nothing had ever been so difficult or shaken him so deeply as that progression. Over and above the horrors of the slaughter by Adein, the deep terror of being in Pendaran, there was another thing for him: he was a night mover, a woods person, this was his milieu, and all he had to do was lead his companions south.

Yet he could not.

Roots appeared, inexplicably, for him to stumble over, fallen branches blocked paths, other trails simply ended without apparent cause. Once, he almost fell.

*South, that's all!* he snarled to himself, oblivious in his concentration to the aching of his leg. It was no good, though—every trail that seemed to hold promise soon turned, against all sense or reason, to the west. Are the trees moving? he asked himself once, and pulled sharply away from the implications of that. Or am I just being incredibly stupid?

For whichever cause, supernatural or psychological, after a little while it was clear to him that hard as he might try—cutting right through a thicket once—to keep them on the eastern edges of the Great Wood, they were being drawn, slowly, very patiently, but quite inescapably, westward into the heart of the forest.

It was not, of course, his fault at all. None of what happened was. Pendaran had had a thousand years to shape the paths and patterns of its response to intrusions such as theirs.

*It is well,* the trees whispered to the spirits of the Wood.

*Very well,* the deiena replied.

Leaves, leaves, Torc heard. Leaves and wind.

For Dave that night walk was very different. He was not of Fionavar, knew no legends of the Wood to appal, beyond the story Levon had told the day before, and that was more sorrowful than frightening. With Torc before and Levon behind, he felt quite certain that they were going as they should. He was blissfully unaware of Torc's desperate manoeuvrings ahead of him, and after a time he grew accustomed to, even sedated by, the murmurings all around them.

So sedated, that he had been walking alone, due west, for about ten minutes before he realized it. *"Torc!"* he cried, as sudden fear swept over him. *"Levon!"* There was, of course, no reply. He was utterly alone in Pendaran Wood at night.

# CHAPTER 14

Had it been any other night, they would have died.

Not badly, for the forest would do this much honour to their exchange of blood, but their deaths had been quite certain from the moment they had ridden past haunted Llewenmere into the trees. One man alone had walked in Pendaran and come out alive since Maugrim, whom the powers called Sathain, had been bound. All others had died, badly, screaming before the end. Pity was not a thing the Wood could feel.

Any other night. But away south of them in another wood, this was Paul Schafer's third night on the Summer Tree.

Even as the three intruders were being delicately separated from each other, the focus of Pendaran was torn utterly away from them by something impossible and humbling, even for the ancient, nameless powers of the Wood.

A red moon rose in the sky.

In the forest it was as if a fire had started. Every power and spirit of the wild magic, of tree and flower or beast, even the dark, oldest ones that seldom woke and that all the others feared, the powers of night and the dancing ones of dawn, those of music and those who moved in deadly silence, all of them began a mad rush away, away, to the sacred grove, for they had to be there before that moon was high enough to shed her light upon the glade.

Dave heard the whispering of the leaves stop. It frightened him, everything did now. But then there came a swift sense of release, as if he were no longer being watched. In the next instant he felt a great sweep, as of wind but not wind, as something rushed over him, through him, hurtling away to the north.

Understanding nothing, only that the Wood seemed to be simply a wood now, the trees merely trees, Dave turned to the east, and he saw the full moon resting, red and stupefying, atop the highest trees.

Such was the nature of the Mother's power that even Dave Martyniuk, alone and lost, unspeakably far from home and a world he somewhat comprehended, could look upon that moon and take heart from it. Even Dave could see it for an answer to the challenge of the Mountain.

Not release, only an answer, for that red moon meant war as much as anything ever could. It meant blood and war, but not a hopeless conflict now, not with Dana's intercession overhead, higher than even Rangat's fires could be made to climb.

All this was inchoate, confused, struggling for some inner articulation in Dave that never quite came together; the sense was there, though, the intuitive awareness that the Lord of the Dark might be free, but he would not be unopposed. It was thus with most of those across Fionavar who saw that symbol in the heavens: the Mother works, has always worked, along the tracings of the blood so that we know things of her we do not realize we know. In very great awe, hope stirring in his heart, Dave looked into the eastern sky, and the thought that came to him with absolute incongruity was that his father would have liked to see this thing.

⤞══◯═══⤝

For three days Tabor had not opened his eyes. When the Mountain unleashed its terror, he only stirred on his bed and murmured words that his mother, watching, could not understand. She adjusted the cloth on his forehead and the blankets over him, unable to do more.

She had to leave him for a while after that, for Ivor had given orders, swift and controlled, to quell the panic caused by the laughter riding on the wind. They were starting east for Celidon at first light tomorrow. They were too alone here, too exposed, under the very palm, it seemed, of the hand that hung above Rangat.

Even through the loud tumult of preparation, with the camp a barely contained whirlwind of chaos, Tabor slept.

Nor did the rising of a red full moon on new moon night cause him to wake, though all the tribe stopped what they were doing, wonder shining in their eyes, to see it swing up above the Plain.

"This gives us time," Gereint said, when Ivor snatched a minute to talk with him. The work continued at night, by the strange moonlight. "He will not move quickly now, I think."

"Nor will we," Ivor said. "It is going to take us time to get there. I want us out by dawn."

"I'll be ready," the old shaman said. "Just put me on a horse and point it the right way."

Ivor felt a surge of affection for Gereint. The shaman had been white-haired and wrinkled for so long he seemed to be timeless. He wasn't, though, and the rapid journey of the coming days would be a hardship for him.

As so often, Gereint seemed to read his mind. "I never thought," he said, very low, "I would live so long. Those who died before this day may be the fortunate ones."

"Maybe so," Ivor said soberly. "There will be war."

"And have we any Revors or Colans, any Ra-Termaines or Seithrs among us? Have we Amairgen or Lisen?" Gereint asked painfully.

"We shall have to find them," Ivor said simply. He laid a hand on the shaman's shoulder. "I must go. Tomorrow."

"Tomorrow. But see to Tabor."

Ivor had planned to supervise the last stages of the wagon loading, but instead he detailed Cechtar to that and went to sit quietly by his son.

Two hours later Tabor woke, though not truly. He rose up from his bed, but Ivor checked his cry of joy, for he saw that his son was wrapped in a waking trance, and it was known to be dangerous to disturb such a thing.

Tabor dressed, quickly and in silence, and left the house. Outside the camp was finally still, asleep in troubled anticipation of grey dawn. The moon was very high, almost overhead.

It was, in fact, now high enough. West of them a dance of light was beginning in the clearing of the sacred grove, while the gathered powers of Pendaran watched.

Walking very quickly, Tabor went around to the stockade, found his horse, and mounted. Lifting the gate, he rode out and began to gallop west.

Ivor, running to his own horse, leaped astride, bareback, and followed. Alone on the Plain, father and son rode towards the Great Wood, and Ivor, watching the straight back and easy riding of his youngest child, felt his heart grow sore.

Tabor had gone far indeed. It seemed he had farther yet to go. *The Weaver shelter him*, Ivor prayed, looking north to the now quiescent glory of Rangat.

More than an hour they rode, ghosts on the night plain, before the massive presence of Pendaran loomed ahead of them, and then Ivor prayed again: *Let him not go into it. Let it not be there, for I love him.*

Does that count for anything? he wondered, striving to master the deep fear the Wood always aroused in him.

It seemed that it might, for Tabor stopped his horse fifty yards from the trees and sat quietly, watching the dark forest. Ivor halted some distance behind. He felt a longing to call his son's name, to call him back from wherever he had gone, was going.

He did not. Instead, when Tabor, murmuring something his father could not hear, slipped from his mount and walked into the forest, Ivor did the bravest deed of all his days, and followed. No call of any god could make Ivor dan Banor let his son walk tranced into Pendaran Wood alone.

And thus did it come to pass that father and both sons entered into the Great Wood that night.

Tabor did not go far. The trees were thin yet at the edge of the forest, and the red moon lit their path with a strangely befitting light. None of this, Ivor thought, belonged to the daylight world. It was very quiet. Too quiet, he realized, for there was a breeze, he could feel it on his skin, and yet it made no sound among the leaves. The hair rose up on the back of Ivor's neck. Fighting for calm in the enchanted silence, he saw Tabor suddenly stop ten paces ahead, holding himself very still. And a moment later Ivor saw a glory step from the trees to stand before his son.

Westward was the sea, she had known that, though but newly born. So east she had walked from the birthing place she shared with Lisen—though that she did not know—and as she passed among the gathered powers, seen and unseen, a murmur like the forest's answer to the sea had risen up and fallen like a wave in the Wood.

Very lightly she went, knowing no other way to tread the earth, and on either side the creatures of the forest did her homage, for she was Dana's, and a gift in time of war, and so was much more than beautiful.

And as she travelled, there came a face into the eye of her mind—how, she knew not, nor would ever—but from the time that was before she was, a face appeared to her, nut-brown, very young, with dark unruly hair, and eyes she needed to look into. Besides, and more than anything, this one knew her name. So here and there her path turned as she sought, all unknowing, delicate and cloaked in majesty, a certain place within the trees.

Then she was there and he was there before her, waiting, a welcome in those eyes, and a final acceptance of what she was, all of her, both edges of the gift.

She felt his mind in hers like a caress, and nudged him back as if with her horn. *Only each other, at the last,* she thought, her first such thought. Whence had it come?

*I know,* his mind answered her. *There will be war.*

*For this was I birthed,* she replied, aware all of a sudden of what lay sheathed within the light, light grace of her form. It frightened her.

He saw this and came nearer. She was the colour of the risen moon, but the horn that brushed the grass when she lowered her head for his touch was silver.

*My name?* she asked.

*Imraith-Nimphais,* he told her, and she felt power burst within her like a star.

Joyously she asked, *Would you fly?*

She felt him hesitate.

*I would not let you fall,* she told him, a little hurt.

She felt his laughter then. *Oh, I know, bright one,* he said, *but if we fly you may be seen and our time is not yet come.*

She tossed her head impatiently, her mane rippling. The trees were thinner here, she could see the stars, the moon. She wanted them. *There is no one to see but one man,* she told him. The sky was calling her.

*My father,* he said. *I love him.*

*Then so will I,* she answered, *but now I would fly. Come!*

And within her then he said, *I will,* and moved to mount astride her back. He was no weight at all; she was very strong and would be stronger yet. She bore him past the other, older man, and because Tabor loved him, she lowered her horn to him as they went by.

Then they were clear of the trees, and there was open grass and oh, the sky, all the sky above. For the first time she released her wings and they rose in a rush of joy to greet the stars and the moon whose child she was. She could feel his mind within hers, the exulting of his heart, for they were bound forever, and she knew that they were glorious, wheeling across the wide night sky, Imraith-Nimphais and the Rider who knew her name.

***

When the chestnut unicorn his son rode lowered her head to him as they passed, Ivor could not keep the tears from his eyes. He always cried too easily, Leith used to scold, but this, surely this transcendency . . . ?

And then, turning to follow them, he saw it become even more, for the unicorn took flight. Ivor lost all track of time then, seeing Tabor and the creature of his fast go soaring across the night. He could almost share the joy they felt in the discovery of flight, and he felt blessed in his heart. He had walked into Pendaran and come out alive to see this creature of the Goddess bear his son like a comet above the Plain.

He was too much a Chieftain and too wise to forget that there was a darkness coming. Even this creature, this gift, could not be an easy thing, not coloured as she was like the moon, like blood. Nor would Tabor ever be the same, he knew. But these sorrows were for the daylight—tonight he could let his heart fly with the two of them, the two young ones at play in the wind between him and the stars. Ivor laughed, as he had not in years, like a child.

After an unknown time they came down gently, not far from where he stood. He saw his son lay his head against that of the unicorn, beside the silver shining of its horn. Then Tabor stepped back, and the creature turned, moving with terrible grace, and went back into the darkness of the Wood.

When Tabor turned to him, his eyes were his own again. Wordlessly, for there were no words, Ivor held out his arms and his youngest child ran into them.

"You saw?" Tabor asked finally, his head against his father's chest.

"I did. You were glorious."

Tabor straightened, his eyes reclaiming their dance, their youth. "She bowed to you! I didn't ask. I just said you were my father and I loved you, so she said she would love you, too, and she bowed."

Ivor's heart was full of light. "Come," he said gruffly, "it is time to go home. Your mother will be weeping with anxiety."

"Mother?" Tabor asked in a tone so comical Ivor had to laugh. They mounted and rode back, slowly now, and together, over their Plain. On this eve of war a curious peace seemed to descend upon Ivor. Here was his land, the land of his people for so long that the years lost meaning. From Andarien to Brennin, from the mountains to Pendaran, all the grass was theirs. The Plain *was* the Dalrei, and they, it. He let that knowledge flow through him like a chord of music, sustaining and enduring.

It would have to endure in the days to come, he knew, the full power of the Dark coming down. And he also knew that it might not. Tomorrow, Ivor thought, I will worry tomorrow and riding in peace over the prairie beside his son, he came back to the camp and saw Leith waiting for them by the western gate.

Seeing her, Tabor slipped from his horse and ran into her arms. Ivor willed his eyes to stay dry as he watched. Sentimental fool, he castigated himself; she was right. When Leith, still holding the boy, looked a question up at him he nodded as briskly as he could.

"To bed, young man," she said firmly. "We're riding in a few hours. You need sleep."

"Oh, Mother," Tabor complained, "I've done nothing *but* sleep for the—"

"Bed!" Leith said, in a voice all her children knew.

"Yes, Mother," Tabor replied, with such pure happiness that even Leith smiled watching him go into the camp. Fourteen, Ivor thought, regardless of everything. Absolutely regardless.

He looked down at his wife. She met the look in silence. It was, he realized, their first moment alone since the Mountain.

"It was all right?" she asked.

"It was. It is something very bright."

"I don't think I want to know, just yet."

He nodded, seeing once more, discovering it anew, how beautiful she was.

"Why did you marry me?" he asked impulsively.

She shrugged. "You asked."

Laughing, he dismounted, and with each of them leading a horse, his and Tabor's, they went back into the camp. They put the animals in the stockade and turned home.

At the doorway Ivor looked up for the last time at that moon, low now in the west, over where Pendaran was.

"I lied," Leith said quietly. "I married you because no other man I know or can imagine could have made my heart leap so when he asked."

He turned from the moon to her. "The sun rises in your eyes," he said. The formal proposal. "It always, always has, my love."

He kissed her. She was sweet and fragrant in his arms, and she could kindle his desire so. . . .

"The sun rises in three hours," she said, disengaging. "Come to bed."

"Indeed," said Ivor.

"To sleep," she said, warningly.

"I am not," Ivor said, "fourteen years old. Nor am I tired."

She looked at him sternly a moment, then the smile lit her face as from within.

"Good," said Leith, his wife. "Neither am I." She took his hand and drew him inside.

◆⊷═◉═⊶◆

Dave had no idea where he was, nor, beyond a vague notion of heading south, where to go. There weren't likely to be signposts in Pendaran Wood indicating the mileage to Paras Derval.

On the other hand, he was absolutely certain that if Torc and Levon were alive, they'd be looking for him, so the best course seemed to be to stay put and call out at intervals. This raised the possibility of other things answering, but there wasn't a lot he could do about that.

Remembering Torc's comments on the "babies" in Faelinn Grove, he sat down against a tree on the upwind side of a clearing, where he could see anything coming across, with a chance of hearing or smelling something approaching from behind. He then proceeded to negate this bit of concealment by shouting Levon's name several times at the top of his voice.

He looked around afterwards, but there was nothing stirring. Indeed, as the echoes of his cry faded, Dave became deeply aware of the silence of the forest. That wild rush, as of wind, seemed to have carried everything with it. He appeared to be very much alone.

But not quite. "You make it," a deep voice sounded, from almost directly beneath him, "very hard for honest folk to sleep."

Leaping violently to his feet, Dave raised his axe and watched apprehensively as a large fallen tree trunk was rolled aside to reveal a series of steps leading down, and a figure emerging to look up at him.

A long way up. The creature he'd awakened resembled a portly gnome more than anything else. A very long white beard offset a bald crown and rested comfortably on a formidable paunch. The figure wore some sort of loose, hooded robe, and the whole ensemble stood not much more than four feet high.

"Could you trouble yourself," the bass voice continued, "to summon this Levon person from some other locality?"

Checking a bizarre impulse to apologize, and another to swing first and query later, Dave raised the axe to shoulder height and growled, "Who are you?"

Disconcertingly, the little man laughed. "Names already? Six days with the Dalrei should have taught you to go slower with a question like that. Call me Flidais, if you like, and put that down."

The axe, a live thing suddenly, leaped from Dave's hands and fell on the grass. Flidais hadn't even moved. His mouth open, Dave stared at the little man. "I am testy when awakened," Flidais said mildly. "And you should know better than to bring an axe in here. I'd leave it there if I were you."

Dave found his voice. "Not unless you take it from me," he rasped. "It was a gift from Ivor dan Banor of the Dalrei and I want it."

"Ah," said Flidais. "Ivor." As if that explained a good deal. Dave had a sense, one that always irritated him, that he was being mocked. On the other hand, he didn't seem in a position to do much about it.

Controlling his temper, he said, "If you know Ivor, you know Levon. He's in here somewhere, too. We were ambushed by svart alfar and escaped into the forest. Can you help me?"

"I am pied for protection, dappled for deception," Flidais replied with sublime inconsequentiality. "How do you know I'm not in league with those svarts?"

Once more Dave forced himself to be calm. "I don't," he said, "but I need help, and you're the only thing around, whoever you are."

"Now that, at least, is true," Flidais nodded sagely. "All the others have gone north to the grove, or," he amended judiciously, "south to the grove if they were north of it to start with."

*Cuckoo,* Dave thought. I have found a certifiable loon. Wonderful, just wonderful.

"I have been the blade of a sword," Flidais confided, confirming the hypothesis. "I have been a star at night, an eagle, a stag in another wood than this. I have been in your world and died, twice; I have been a harp and a harper both."

In spite of himself Dave was drawn into it. In the red-tinted shadows of the forest, there was an eerie power to the chant.

"I know," Flidais intoned, "how many worlds there are, and I know the skylore that Amairgen learned. I have seen the moon from undersea, and I heard the great dog howl last night. I know the answer to all the riddles there are, save one, and a dead man guards that gateway in your world, Davor of the Axe, Dave Martyniuk."

Against his will, Dave asked, "What riddle is that?" He hated this sort of thing. God, did he hate it.

"Ah," said Flidais, tilting his head. "Would you come to salmon knowledge so easily? Be careful or you will burn your tongue. I have told you a thing already, forget it not, though the white-haired one will know. Beware the boar, beware the swan, the salt sea bore her body on."

Adrift in a sea of his own, Dave grabbed for a floating spar. "Lisen's body?" he asked.

Flidais stopped and regarded him. There was a slight sound in the trees. "Good," Flidais said at last. "Very good. For that you may keep the axe. Come down and I will give you food and drink."

At the mention of food, Dave became overwhelmingly aware that he was ravenous. With a sense of having accomplished something, though by luck as much as anything else, he followed Flidais down the crumbling earthen stairs.

At the bottom there opened out a catacomb of chambers, shaped of earth and threaded through twisting tree roots. Twice he banged his head before following his small host into a comfortable room with a rough table and stools around it. There was a cheery light, though from no discernible source.

"I have been a tree," Flidais said, almost as if answering a question. "I know the earthroot's deepest name."

"Avarlith?" Dave hazarded, greatly daring.

"Not that," Flidais replied, "but good, good." He seemed to be in a genial mood now as he puttered about domestically.

Feeling curiously heartened, Dave pushed a little. "I came here with Loren Silvercloak and four others. I got separated from them. Levon and Torc were taking me to Paras Derval, then there was that explosion and we got ambushed."

Flidais looked aggrieved. "I *know* all that," he said, a little petulantly. "There shall be a shaking of the Mountain."

"Well, there was," Dave said, taking a pull at the drink Flidais offered. Having done which, he pitched forward on the table, quite unconscious.

Flidais regarded him a long time, a speculative look in his eye. He no longer seemed quite so genial, and certainly not mad. After a while, the air registered the presence he'd been awaiting.

"Gently," he said. "This is one of my homes, and tonight you owe me."

"Very well." She muted a little the shining from within her. "Is it born?"

"Even now," he replied. "They will return soon."

"It is well," she said, satisfied. "I am here now and was here at Lisen's birth.

Where were you?" Her smile was capricious, unsettling.

"Elsewhere," he admitted, as if she had scored a point. "I was Taliesen. I have been a salmon."

"I know," she said. Her presence filled the room as if a star were underground. Despite his request, it was still hard to look upon her face. "The one riddle," she said. "Would you know the answer?"

He was very old and extremely wise, and he was half a god himself, but this was the deepest longing of his soul. "Goddess," he said, a helpless streaming of hope within him, "I would."

"So would I," she said cruelly. "If you find the summoning name, do not fail to tell me. And," said Ceinwen, letting a blinding light well up from within her so that he closed his eyes in pain and dread, "speak not ever to me again of what I owe. I owe nothing, ever, but what has been promised, and if I promise, it is not a debt, but a gift. Never forget."

He was on his knees. The brightness was overpowering. "I have known," Flidais said, a trembling in his deep voice, "the shining of the Huntress in the Wood."

It was an apology; she took it for such. "It is well," she said for the second time, muting her presence once more, so that he might look upon her countenance. "I go now," she said. "This one I will take. You did well to summon me, for I have laid claim to him."

"Why, goddess?" Flidais asked softly, looking at the sprawled form of Dave Martyniuk.

Her smile was secret and immortal. "It pleases me," she said. But just before she vanished with the man, Ceinwen spoke again, so low it was almost not a sound. "Hear me, forest one: if I learn what name calls the Warrior, I will tell it thee. A promise."

Stricken silent, he knelt again on his earthen floor. It was, had always been, his heart's desire. When he looked up he was alone.

They woke, all three of them, on soft grass in the morning light. The horses grazed nearby. They were on the very fringes of the forest; southward a road ran from east to west, and beyond it lay low hills. One farmhouse could be seen past the road, and overhead birds sang as if it were the newest morning of the world. Which it was.

In more ways than the obvious, after the cataclysms that the night had known. Such powers had moved across the face of Fionavar as had not been gathered since the worlds were spun and the Weaver named the gods. Iorweth Founder had not endured that blast of Rangat, seen that hand in the sky, nor had Conary known such thunder in Mörnirwood, or the white power of the mist that exploded up from the Summer Tree, through the body of the sacrifice. Neither Revor nor Amairgen had ever seen a moon like the one that had sailed that night, nor had the Baelrath blazed so in answer on any other hand in the long telling of its tale. And no man but Ivor dan Banor had ever seen Imraith-Nimphais bear her Rider across the glitter of the stars.

Given such a gathering, a concatenation of powers such that the worlds might never be the same, how small a miracle might it be said to be that Dave awoke with his friends in the freshness of that morning on the southern edge of Pendaran, with the high road from North Keep to Rhoden running past, and a horn lying by his side.

A small miracle, in the light of all that had shaken the day and night before, but that which grants life where death was seen as certain can never be inconsequential, or even less than wondrous, to those who are the objects of its intercession.

So the three of them rose up, in awe and great joy, and told their stories to each other while morning's bird-song spun and warbled overhead.

For Torc, there had been a blinding flash, with a shape behind it, apprehended but not seen, then darkness until this place. Levon had heard music all around him, strong and summoning, a wild cry of invocation as of a hunt passing overhead, then it had changed, so gradually he could not tell how or when, but there came a moment when it was so very sad and restful he had to sleep—to wake with his new brothers on the grass, Brennin spread before them in a mild sunlight.

"Hey, you two!" cried Dave exuberantly. "Will you look at this?" He held up the carved horn, ivory-coloured, with workmanship in gold and silver, and runes engraved along the curve of it. In a spirit of euphoria and delight, he set the horn to his lips and blew.

It was a rash, precipitate act, but one that could cause no harm, for Ceinwen had intended him to have this and to learn the thing they all learned as that shining note burst into the morning.

She had presumed, for this treasure was not truly hers to bestow. They were to blow the horn and learn the first property of it, then ride forth from the place where it had lain so long. That was how she had intended it to be, but it is a part of the design of the Tapestry that not even a goddess may shape exactly what she wills, and Ceinwen had reckoned without Levon dan Ivor.

The sound was Light. They knew it, all three of them, as soon as Dave blew the horn. It was bright and clean and carrying, and Dave understood, even as he took it from his lips to gaze in wonder at what he held, that no agent of the Dark could ever hear that sound. In his heart this came to him, and it was a true knowing, for such was the first property of that horn.

"Come on," said Torc, as the golden echoes died away. "We're still in the Wood. Let's move." Obediently Dave turned to mount his horse, still dazzled by the sound he had made.

"Hold!" said Levon.

There were perhaps five men in Fionavar who might have known the second power of that gift, and none in any other world. But one of the five was Gereint, the shaman of the third tribe of the Dalrei, who had knowledge of many lost things, and who had been the teacher of Levon dan Ivor.

She had not known or intended this, but not even a goddess can know all things. She had intended a small gift. What happened was otherwise, and not small. For a moment the Weaver's hands were still at his Loom, then Levon said:

"There should be a forked tree here."

And a thread came back with his words into the Tapestry of all the worlds, one that had been lost a very long time.

It was Torc who found it. An enormous ash had been split by lightning—they could have no glimmering how long ago—and its trunk lay forked now, at about the height of a man.

In silence, Levon walked over, Dave beside him, to where Torc was standing. Dave could see a muscle jumping in his face. Then Levon spoke again:

"And now the rock."

Standing together the three of them looked through the wishbone fork of the ash. Dave had the angle. "There," he said, pointing.

Levon looked, and a great wonder was in his eyes. There was indeed a rock set flush into a low mound at the edge of the Wood. "Do you know," he said in a hushed whisper, "that we have found the Cave of the Sleepers?"

"I don't understand," said Torc.

"The Wild Hunt," Levon replied. Dave felt a prickling at the back of his neck. "The wildest magic that ever was lies in that place asleep." The strain in Levon's usually unruffled voice was so great it cracked. "Owein's Horn is what you just blew, Davor. If we could ever find the flame, they would ride again. Oh, by all the gods!"

"Tell me," Dave pleaded; he, too, was whispering.

For a moment Levon was silent; then, as they stared at the rock through the gap in the ash, he began to chant:

> *The flame will wake from sleep*
> *The Kings the horn will call,*
> *But though they answer from the deep*
> *You may never hold in thrall*
> *Those who ride from Owein's Keep*
> *With a child before them all.*

"The Wild Hunt," Levon repeated as the sound of his chanting died away. "I have not words to tell how far beyond the three of us this is." And he would say no more.

They rode then from that place, from the great stone and the torn tree with the horn slung at Dave's side. They crossed the road, and by tacit agreement rode in such a way as to seen by no men until they should come to Silvercloak and the High King.

All morning they rode, through hilly farmland, and at intervals a fine rain fell. It was badly needed, they could see, for the land was dry.

It was shortly after midday that they crested a series of ascending ridges running to the southeast, and saw, gleaming below them, a lake set like a jewel within the encircling hills. It was very beautiful, and they stopped a moment to take it in. There was a small farmhouse by the water, more a cottage really, with a yard and a barn behind it.

Riding slowly down, they would have passed by, as they had all the other farms, except that as they descended, an old, white-haired woman came out in back of the cottage to gaze at them.

Looking at her as they approached, Dave saw that she was not, in fact, so old after all. She made a gesture of her hand to her mouth that he seemed, inexplicably, to know.

Then she was running towards them over the grass, and with an explosion of joy in his heart, Dave leaped, shouting, from his horse, and ran and ran and ran until Kimberly was in his arms.

# PART IV

# THE UNRAVELLER

# CHAPTER 15

Diarmuid, the Prince, as Warden of South Keep, had a house allocated to him in the capital, a small barracks, really, for those of his men who might, for any reason, be quartered there. It was here that he preferred to spend his own nights when in Paras Derval, and it was here that Kevin Laine sought him out in the morning after the cataclysms, having wrestled with his conscience a good part of the night.

And it was still giving him trouble as he walked from the palace in the rain. He couldn't think very clearly, either, for grief was a wound in him that dawn. The only thing keeping him going, forcing resolution, was the terrible image of Jennifer bound to the black swan and flying north into the grasp of that hand the Mountain had sent up.

The problem, though, was *where* to go, where loyalty took him. Both Loren and Kim, unnervingly transformed, were clearly supporting this grim, prepossessing older Prince who had suddenly returned.

"It is my war," Aileron had told Loren, and the mage had nodded quietly. Which, on one level, left Kevin with no issue at all to wrestle with.

On the other hand, Diarmuid was the heir to the throne and Kevin was, if he was anything at all here, one of Diarmuid's band. After Saeren and Cathal, after, especially, the look he and the Prince had exchanged when he'd finished his song in the Black Boar.

He needed Paul to talk it over with, God, he needed him. But Paul was dead, and his closest friends here were Erron and Carde and Coll. And their Prince.

So he entered the barracks and asked, as briskly as he could, "Where's Diarmuid?" Then he stopped dead in his tracks.

They were all there: Tegid, the company from the journey south, and others he didn't know. They were sitting soberly around the tables in the large front room, but they rose when he entered. Every one of them was dressed in black, with a red band on his left arm.

Diarmuid, too. "Come in," he said. "I see you have news. Let it wait, Kevin." There was quiet emotion in the usually acerbic voice. "The grief, I know, is yours most of all, but the men of the South Marches have always worn a red armband when one of their own dies, and we have lost two now. Drance and Pwyll. He was one of us—we all feel it here. Will you let us mourn for Paul with you?"

There was no briskness left in Kevin, only a compounding of sorrows. He nodded, almost afraid to speak. He collected himself, though, and said, swallowing hard, "Of course, and thank you. But there is business first. I have information, and you should know it now."

"Tell me, then," the Prince said, "though I may know it already."

"I don't think so. Your brother came back last night."

Sardonic amusement registered in Diarmuid's face. But it had indeed been news, and the mocking reaction had been preceded by another expression.

"Ah," said the Prince, in his most acid tones. "I should have guessed from the greyness of the sky. And of course," he went on, ignoring the rising murmur from his men, "there is now a throne up for the taking. He would return. Aileron likes thrones."

"It is *not* up for the taking!" The speaker, red-faced and vehement, was Coll. "Diar, you are the heir! I will cut him apart before I see him take it from you."

"No one," said Diarmuid, playing delicately with a knife on the table, "is going to take anything from me at all. Certainly not Aileron. Is there more, Kevin?"

There was, of course. He told them about Ysanne's death, and Kim's transformation, and then, reluctantly, about Loren's tacit endorsement of the older Prince. Diarmuid's eyes never left his own, nor did the hint of laughter sheathed in their depths ever quite disappear. He continued to toy with the dagger.

When Kevin had finished, there was a silence in the room, broken only by Coll's furious pacing back and forth.

"I owe you again," said Diarmuid at length. "I knew none of this."

Kevin nodded. Even as he did, there came a knocking at the door. Carde opened it.

In the entranceway, rain dripping from his hat and cloak, stood the broad, square figure of Gorlaes, the Chancellor. Before Kevin could assimilate his presence there, Gorlaes had stepped into the room.

"Prince Diarmuid," he said, without preamble, "my sources tell me your brother has returned from exile. For the Crown, I think. You, my lord, are the heir to the throne I swore to serve. I have come to offer you my services."

And at that Diarmuid's laughter exploded, unchecked and abrasive in a room full of mourners. "Of course you have!" he cried. "Come in! Do come in, Gorlaes. I have great need of you—we're short a cook at South Keep!"

Even as the Prince's sarcastic hilarity filled the room, Kevin's mind cut back to the pulse beat of time that had followed his first announcement of Aileron's return. There had been sharp irony in Diarmuid then, too, but only after the first instant. In the first instant, Kevin thought he had seen something very different flash across the Prince's face, and he was almost certain he knew what it was.

⋄⋅≡◉⊂⋅⋄

Loren and Matt had gone with Teyrnon and Barak to bring the body home from the Tree. The Godwood was not a place where soldiers would willingly go, and in any case, on the eve of war the last two mages in Paras Derval saw it as fit that they walk together with their sources, apart from other men, and share their thoughts on what would lie in the days ahead.

They were agreed on the kingship, though in some ways it was a pity. For all Aileron's harsh abrasiveness, there was in his driven nature the stuff of a war king of old. Diarmuid's mercurial glitter made him simply too unreliable. They had been wrong about things before, but not often in concert. Barak concurred. Matt kept his own counsel, but the other three were used to that.

Besides, they were in the wood by then and, being men acquainted with power, and deeply tuned to what had happened in the night, they walked in silence to the Summer Tree.

And then, in a different kind of silence, walked back away, under leaves dripping with the morning rain. It was taught, and they all knew the teachings, that Mörnir, if he came for the sacrifice, laid claim only to the soul. The body was husk, dross, not for the God, and it was left behind.

Except it hadn't been.


A mystery, but it was solved when Loren and Matt returned to Paras Derval and saw the girl, in the dun robes of an acolyte of the sanctuary, waiting outside their quarters in the town.

"My lord," she said, as they walked up, "the High Priestess bade me tell you to come to her in the Temple so soon as you might."

"Tell him?" Matt growled.

The child was remarkably composed. "She did say that. The matter is important."

"Ah," said Loren. "She brought back the body."

The girl nodded.

"Because of the moon," he went on, thinking aloud. "It fits."

Surprisingly, the acolyte nodded again. "Of course it does," she said coolly. "Will you come now?"

Exchanging a raised-eyebrows look, the two of them followed Jaelle's messenger through the streets to the eastern gate.

Once beyond the town, she stopped. "There is something I would warn you about," she said.

Loren Silvercloak looked down from his great height upon the child. "Did the Priestess tell you to do so?"

"Of course not." Her tone was impatient.

"Then you should not speak other than what you were charged to say. How long have you been an acolyte?"

"I am Leila," she replied, gazing up at him with tranquil eyes. Too tranquil; he wondered at the answer. Was her mind touched? Sometimes the Temple took such children.

"That isn't what I asked," he said kindly.

"I know what you asked," she said with some asperity. "I am Leila. I called Finn dan Shahar to the Longest Road four times this summer in the ta'kiena."

221

His eyes narrowed; he had heard about this. "And Jaelle has made you an acolyte?"

"Two days ago. She is very wise."

An arrogant child. It was time to assert control. "Not," he said sternly, "if her acolytes presume to judge her, and her messengers offer messages of their own."

It didn't faze her. With a shrug of acceptance, Leila turned and continued up the slope to the sanctuary.

He wrestled with it for several strides, then admitted a rare defeat. "Hold," Loren said, and heard Matt's snort of laughter beside him. "What is your news?" The Dwarf, he was aware, was finding this whole exchange richly amusing. It was, he supposed.

"He is alive," Leila said, and suddenly there was nothing amusing about anything at all.

⋄⊷⊜⊜⊶⋄

There had been darkness. A sense of movement, of being moved. The stars very close, then impossibly far away, and receding. Everything receding.

The next time there was an impression, blurred as through rain on glass, of candles wavering, with grey shapes moving ambiguously beyond their arc. He was still now, but soon he felt himself slipping back again, as a tide withdraws to the dark sea wherein there lie no discontinuities.

Except the fact of his presence.

Of his being alive.

Paul opened his eyes, having come a long way. And it seemed, after all the journeying, that he was lying on a bed in a room where there were, indeed, candles burning. He was very weak. There was astonishingly little physical pain, though, and the other kind of pain was so newly allowed it was almost a luxury. He took one slow breath that meant life, and then another to welcome back sorrow.

"Oh, Rachel," he breathed, scarcely a sound. Forbidden once, the most forbidden name. But then intercession had come, before he died, and absolution allowing grief.

Except that he hadn't died. A thought like a blade pierced him at that: was he alive because he'd failed? Was that it? With an effort he turned his head. The movement revealed a tall figure standing by the bed gazing down at him from between the candles.

"You are in the Temple of the Mother," Jaelle said. "It is raining outside."

Rain. There was a bitter challenge in her eyes, but it couldn't touch him in that moment. He was beyond her. He turned his head away. It was raining; he was alive. Sent back. Arrow of the God.

He felt the presence of Mörnir then, within himself, latent, tacit. There was a burden in that, and soon it would have to be addressed, but not yet, not yet. Now was for lying still, tasting the sense of being himself again for the first time in so very long. Ten months. And three nights that had been forever. Oh, he could go with joy a little ways, it was allowed. Eyes closed, he sank deep into the pillow. He was desperately weak, but weakness was all right now. There was rain.

"Dana spoke to you."

He could hear the vivid rage in her voice. Too much of it; he ignored her. *Kevin*, he thought. *I want to see Kev. Soon*, he told himself, *after I sleep*.

She slapped him hard across the face. He felt a raking nail draw blood.

"You are in the sanctuary. Answer!"

Paul Schafer opened his eyes. With cold scorn of his own, he confronted her fury. This time, Jaelle looked away.

After a moment she spoke, gazing at one of the long candles. "All my life I have dreamed of hearing the Goddess speak, of seeing her face." Bitterness had drained her voice. "Not me, though. Not anything at all. Yet you, a man, and one who turned from her entirely for the God in his wood, have been allowed grant of her grace. Do you wonder why I hate you?"

The utter flatness of her tone made the words more chilling than any explosion of anger would have been. Paul was silent a moment, then he said, "I am her child, too. Do not begrudge the gift she offered me."

"Your life, you mean?" She was looking at him again, tall and slender between the candles.

He shook his head; it was still an effort. "Not that. In the beginning, perhaps, but not now. It was the God who gave me this."

"Not so. You are a greater fool than I thought if you know not Dana when she comes."

"Actually," he said, but gently, for it was a matter too high for wrangling, "I do know. In this case, better than you, Priestess. The Goddess was there, yes, and she did intercede, though not for my life. For something else before the end. But it was Mörnir who saved me. It was his to choose. The Summer Tree is the God's, Jaelle."

For the first time he read a flicker of doubt in the wide-set eyes. "She was there, though? She did speak? Tell me what she said."

"No," said Paul, with finality.

"You must." But it was not a command now. He had a vague sense that there was something he should, something he wanted to say to her, but he was so weary, so utterly drained. Which triggered a completely different realization.

"You know," he said, with feeling, "that I haven't had food or drink for three days. Is there . . . ?"

She stood still a moment, but when she moved, it was to a tray on a low table by the far wall. She brought a bowl of cool soup to the bed. Unfortunately it seemed that his hands didn't work very well yet. He thought she would send for one of the grey-clad priestesses, but in the end she sat stiffly on the bed beside him and fed him herself.

He ate in silence, leaning back against the pillows when he was done. She made as if to get up, but then, with an expression of distaste, used the sleeve of her white gown to wipe the blood from his cheek.

She did rise then, to stand tall and queenly by his bed, her hair the colour of the candlelight. Looking up at her, he felt at a disadvantage suddenly.

"Why," he asked, "am I here?"

"I read the signs."

"You didn't expect to find me alive?"

She shook her head. "No, but it was the third night, and then the moon rose. . . ."

He nodded. "But why?" he asked. "Why bother?"

Her eyes flashed. "Don't be such a child. There is a war now. You will be needed."

He felt his heart skip. "What do you mean? What war?"

"You don't know?"

"I've been somewhat out of touch," he said sharply. "What has happened?"

It may have taken an effort, but her voice was controlled. "Rangat exploded yesterday. A hand of fire in the sky. The wardstone is shattered. Rakoth is free."

He was very still.

"The King is dead," she said.

"That I know," he said. "I heard the bells."

But for the first time now, her expression was strained; something difficult moved in her eyes. "There is more," said Jaelle. "A party of lios alfar were ambushed here by svarts and wolves. Your friend was with them. Jennifer. I am sorry, but she was captured and taken north. A black swan bore her away."

So. He closed his eyes again, feeling the burdens coming down. It seemed they could not be deferred after all. Arrow of the God. Spear of the God. Three nights and forever, the King had said. The King was dead. And Jen.

He looked up again. "Now I know why he sent me back."

As if against her will, Jaelle nodded. "Twiceborn," she murmured.

Wordlessly, he asked with his eyes.

"There is a saying," she whispered, "a very old one: *No man shall be Lord of the Summer Tree who has not twice been born.*"

And so by candlelight in the sanctuary, he heard the words for the first time.

"I didn't ask for this," Paul Schafer said.

She was very beautiful, very stern, a flame, as the candles were. "Are you asking me for pity?"

His mouth crooked wryly at that. "Hardly, at this point." He smiled a little. "Why is it so much easier for you to strike a defenceless man than to wipe the blood from his face?"

Her reply was formal, reflexive, but he had seen her eyes flinch away. "There is mercy in the Goddess sometimes," she said, "but not gentleness."

"Is that how you know her?" he asked. "What if I tell you that I had from her last night a compassion so tender, there are no words to compass it?"

She was silent.

"Aren't we two human beings first?" he went on. "With very great burdens, and support to share. You are Jaelle, surely, as well as her Priestess."

"There you are wrong," she said. "I am only her Priestess. There is no one else."

"That seems to me very sad."

"You are only a man," Jaelle replied, and Paul was abashed by what blazed in her eyes before she turned and left the room.

◆◇══◑◒══◇◆

Kim had lain awake for most of the night, alone in her room in the palace, achingly aware of the other, empty bed. Even inside, the Baelrath was responding to the moon, glowing brightly enough to cast shadows on the wall: a branch outside the window swaying in the rain wind, the outline of her own white hair, the shape of a candle by the bed, but no Jen, no shadow of her. Kim tried. Utterly unaware of what her power was, of how to use the stone, she closed her eyes and reached out in the wild night, north as far as she might, as clearly as she might, and found only the darkness of her own apprehensions.

When the stone grew dim again, only a red ring on her finger, she knew the moon had set. It was very late then, little left of the night. Kim lay back in weariness and dreamt of a desire she hadn't known she had.

*It is in your dreams that you must walk*, Ysanne had said, was saying still, as she dropped far down into the dream again.

And this time she knew the place. She knew where lay those jumbled mighty arches of broken stone, and who was buried there for her to wake.

Not him, not the one she sought. Too easy, were it so. That path was darker even than it was now, and it led through the dead in the dreaming place. This she now knew. It was very sad, though she understood that the gods would not think it so. The sins of the sons, she thought in her dream, knowing the place, feeling the wind rising, and, her hair, oh, her white hair, blown back.

The way to the Warrior led through the grave and the risen bones of the father who had never seen him alive. What was she that she should know this?

But then she was somewhere else, with no space to wonder. She was in the room under the cottage where the Circlet of Lisen still shone, Colan's dagger beside it, where Ysanne had died, and more than died. The Seer was with her, though, was within her, for she knew the book, the parchment page within the book where the invocation could be found to raise the father whole from his grave, and make him name the name of his son to the one who knew the place of summoning. There was no peace, no serenity anywhere. She carried none, had none to grant, she wore the Warstone on her hand. She would drag the dead from their rest, and the undead to their doom.

What was she that this should be so?

At the morning's first light she made them take her back in the rain. An armed guard of thirty men went with her; troops from North Keep who had been Aileron's before he was exiled. With cool efficiency they compassed her about on the ride to the lake. At the last curve the bodies of Aileron's victims still lay on the path.

"Did he do that alone?" the leader of the guard asked when they were past. His voice was reverent.

"Yes," she said.

"He will be our King?"

"Yes," she said.

They waited by the lake while she went inside, and then down the now familiar stairs into the glow cast by Lisen's Light. She left it where it lay, though; and, walking to the table, she opened one of the books. Oh, it was a glory and a terror that she knew where to look, but she did, and sitting there alone, she slowly read the words that she would have to speak.

But only when she knew the place that no one knew. The tumbled stones were only the starting point. There was a long way yet to walk along this path; a long way, but she was on it now. Preoccupied, tangled among interstices of time and place, the Seer of Brennin went back up the stairs. Aileron's men awaited her, in disciplined alertness by the lake.

It was time to go. There was a very great deal to be done. She lingered, though, in the cottage, seeing the fire, the hearth, the worn table, the herbs in jars along the wall. She read the labels, unstoppered one container to smell its contents. There was so much to be done, the Seer of Brennin knew, but still she lingered, tasting the aloneness.

It was bittersweet, and when she moved at last, Kimberly went out the back door, still alone, into the yard, away from where the soldiers were, and she saw three men picking their way on horseback down the slope north of her, and one of them she knew, oh, she knew. And it seemed that amid all the burdens and sorrows, joy could still flower like a bannion in the wood.

⊹⊱⊰⊹

They buried Ailell dan Art in a time of rain. It fell upon the windows of Delevan high above the Great Hall where the King lay in state, robed in white and gold, his sword upon his breast, his great, gnarled hands closed upon the hilt; it fell softly upon the gorgeous woven covering of the bier when the nobility of Brennin, who had gathered for celebration and stayed for mourning and war, bore him out of the palace and to the doors of the Temple where the women took him; it fell, too, upon the dome of that sanctuary while Jaelle, the High Priestess, performed the rites of the Mother, to send back home to her one of the Kings.

No man was in that place. Loren had taken Paul away. She'd had hopes of seeing Silvercloak shaken, but had been disappointed, for the mage had shown no surprise at all, and she had been forced to cloak her own discomfiture at that, and at his bowing to the Twiceborn.

No man was in that place, save for the dead King, when they lifted the great axe from its rest, and no man saw what they did then. Dana was not mocked nor denied when she took her child home, whom she had sent forth so long ago on the circling path that led ever back to her.

It was the place of the High Priestess to bury the High King, and so Jaelle led them forth when the rites were done. Into the rain she went, clad in white among all the black, and they bore Ailell shoulder-high behind her to the crypt wherein the Kings of Brennin were laid to rest.

East of the palace it lay, north of the Temple. Before the body went Jaelle with the key to the gates in her hands. Behind the bier, fair and solitary, walked Diarmuid, the King's Heir, and after him came all the lesser nobility of Brennin. Among them there walked, though with aid, a Prince of the lios alfar, and there were come as well two men of the Dalrei, from the Plain; and with these walked two men from another world, one very tall and dark, another fair, and between them was a woman with white hair. The common folk lined the path, six deep in the rain, and they bowed their heads to see Ailell go by.

Then they came to the great gates of the burying place, and Jaelle saw that they were open already and that a man clad in black stood waiting there for them, and she saw who it was.

"Come," said Aileron, "let us lay my father by my mother, whom he loved."

And while she was trying to mask her shock, another voice spoke. "Welcome home, exile," Diarmuid said, his tone mild, unsurprised, and he moved lightly past her to kiss Aileron on the cheek. "Shall we lead him back to her?"

It was greatly wrong, for she had right of precedence here, but in spite of herself the High Priestess felt a strange emotion to see the two of them, the dark son and the bright, pass through the gates of the dead, side by side, while all the people of Brennin murmured behind them in the falling rain.

On a spur of hill high above that place, three men watched. One would be First Mage of Brennin before the sun had set, one had been made King of Dwarves by a sunrise long ago, and the third had caused the rain and been sent back by the God.

✦⟹⟸✦

"We are gathered," Gorlaes began, standing beside the throne but two careful steps below it, "in a time of sorrow and need."

They were in the Great Hall, Tomaz Lal's masterpiece, and there were gathered that afternoon all the mighty of Brennin, save one. The two Dalrei, and Dave as well, so fortuitously arrived, had been greeted with honour and shown to their chambers, and even Brendel of Daniloth was absent from this assemblage, for what Brennin had now to do was matter for Brennin alone.

"In any normal time our loss would demand space for mourning. But this is no such time. It is needful for us now," the Chancellor continued, seeing that Jaelle had not contested his right to speak first, "to take swift counsel amongst one another and go forth from this hall united, with a new King to lead us into—"

"Hold, Gorlaes. We will wait for Silvercloak." It was Teyrnon, the mage, and he had risen to stand, with Barak, his source, and Matt Sören. Trouble already, and they had not even begun.

"Surely," Jaelle murmured, "it is rather his duty to be here when others are. We have waited long enough."

"We will wait longer," the Dwarf growled. "As we waited for you, yesterday." There was something in his tone that made Gorlaes glad it was Jaelle who'd raised objection, and not himself.

"Where is he?" Niavin of Seresh asked.

"He is coming. He had to go slowly."

"Why?" It was Diarmuid. He had stopped his feline pacing at the edges of the hall and come forward.

"Wait," was all the Dwarf replied.

Gorlaes was about to remonstrate, but someone else came in first.

"No," said Aileron. "For all the love I bear him, I will not wait on this. There is, in truth, little to discuss."

Kim Ford, in that room as the newest, the only, Seer of Brennin, watched him stride to stand by Gorlaes.

And a step above him, directly before the throne. *He will always be like this,* she thought. *There is only the force of him.*

And with force, cold, unyielding force, Aileron looked over them all and spoke again. "In time of council Loren's wisdom will be sorely needed, but this is not a time of council, whatever you may have thought."

Diarmuid was no longer pacing. He had moved, at Aileron's first words, to stand directly in front of his brother, an unruffled contrast to Aileron's coiled intensity.

"I came here," said Aileron dan Ailell flatly, "for the Crown, and to lead us into war. The Throne is mine"—he was looking directly at his brother—"and I will kill for it, or die for it before we leave this hall."

The rigid silence that followed this was broken a moment later by the jarring sound of one man clapping.

"Elegantly put, my dear," said Diarmuid as he continued to applaud. "So utterly succinct." Then he lowered his hands. The sons of Ailell faced each other as if alone in the vast hall.

"Mockery," said Aileron softly, "is easy. It was ever your retreat. Understand me, though, brother. This, for once, is no idle sport. I want your fealty this hour, in this place, or there are six archers in the musicians' gallery who will kill you if I raise my hand."

"No!" Kim exclaimed, shocked out of silence.

"This is preposterous!" Teyrnon shouted at the same time, striding forward. "I forbid—"

"You cannot forbid me!" Aileron rode over him. "Rakoth is free. What lies ahead is too large for me to trifle with."

Diarmuid had cocked his head quizzically to one side, as if considering an abstract proposition. Then he spoke, his voice so soft they had to strain to hear. "You would truly do this thing?"

"I would," Aileron replied. With no hesitation at all.

"Truly?" Diarmuid asked a second time.

"All I have to do is raise my arm," Aileron said. "And I will if I must. Believe it."

Diarmuid shook his head slowly back and forth; he sighed heavily. Then:

"Coll," he said, and pitched it to carry.

"My lord Prince." The big man's voice boomed instantly from overhead. From the musicians' gallery.

Diarmuid lifted his head, his expression tranquil, almost indifferent. "Report."

"He did do it, my lord." Coll's voice was thick with anger. He moved forward to the railing. "He really did. There were seven men up here. Say the word and I will slay him now."

Diarmuid smiled. "That," he said, "is reassuring." Then he turned back to Aileron and his eyes were no longer so aloof. The older brother had changed, too; he seemed to have uncoiled himself into readiness. And he broke the silence.

"I sent six," Aileron said. "Who is the seventh?"

They were all scrambling to grasp the import of this when the seventh leaped from the gallery overhead.

It was a long jump, but the dark figure was lithe and, landing, rolled instantly and was up. Five feet from Diarmuid with a dagger back to throw.

Only Aileron moved in time. With the unleashed reflexes of a pure fighter, he grabbed for the first thing that came to hand. As the assassin's dagger went back, Aileron flung the heavy object hard across the space between. It hit the intruder square in the back; the flung blade was sent awry, just awry. Enough so as not to pierce the heart it was intended for.

Diarmuid had not even moved. He stood, swaying a little, with a peculiar half-smile on his face and a jewelled dagger deep in his left shoulder. He had time, Kim saw, to murmur something very low, indistinguishable, as if to himself, before all the swords were out and the assassin was ringed by steel. Ceredur of North Keep drew back his blade to kill.

"Hold swords!" Diarmuid ordered sharply. "Hold!" Ceredur slowly lowered his weapon. The only sound in the whole great room was made by the object Aileron had flung, rolling in diminishing circles on the mosaic-inlaid floor.

It happened to be the Oak Crown of Brennin.

Diarmuid, with a frightening glint of hilarity in his face, bent to pick it up. He bore it, his footsteps echoing, to the long table in the centre of the room. Setting it down, he unstoppered a decanter, using one hand only. They all watched as he poured himself a drink, quite deliberately. Then he carried his glass slowly back towards them all.

"It is my pleasure," said Diarmuid dan Ailell, Prince of Brennin, "to propose a toast." The wide mouth smiled. There was blood dripping from his arm. "Will you all drink with me," he said, raising high the glass, "to the Dark Rose of Cathal?"

And walking forward, he lifted his other arm, with obvious pain, and removed the cap and pins she wore, so that Sharra's dark hair tumbled free.

⋄⇒◎⇐⋄

Having Devorsh killed had been a mistake, for two reasons. First, it gave her father far too much leverage in his campaign to foist one of the lords on her. The lordlings. Leverage he had already begun to use.

Secondly, he was the wrong man.

By the time Rangat sent up its fiery hand—visible even in Cathal, though the Mountain itself was not—her own explosion of rage had metamorphosed into something else. Something quite as deadly, or even more so, since it was sheathed within exquisitely simulated repentance.

She had agreed that she would walk the next morning with Evien of Lagos in the gardens, and then receive two other men in the afternoon; she had been agreeing to everything.

But when the red moon rose that night, she bound up her hair, knowing her father very, very well, and in the strangely hued darkness and the haste of departure, she joined the embassy to Paras Derval.

It was easy. Too easy, a part of her thought as they rode to Cynan; discipline was shockingly lax among the troops of the Garden Country. Still, it served her purpose now, as had the Mountain and the moon.

For whatever the larger cataclysms might mean, whatever chaos lay before them all, Sharra had her own matter to deal with first, and the falcon is a hunting bird.

At Cynan there was pandemonium. When they finally tracked down the harbour-master, he flashed a code of lights across the delta to Seresh and was quickly answered. He took them across himself, horses and all, on a wide river barge. From the familiarity of the greetings exchanged on the other side of Saeren, it was clear that rumours of quite improper intercourse between the river fortresses were true. It was increasingly evident how certain letters had gotten into Cathal.

There had been rumblings of thunder in the north as they rode to Cynan, but as they came ashore in Seresh in the dark hours before dawn, all was still and the red moon hung low over the sea, sailing in and out of scudding clouds. All about her flowed the apprehensive murmurings of war, mingled with a desperate relief among the men of Brennin at the rain that was softly falling. There had been a drought, she gathered.

Shalhassan's emissaries accepted, with some relief, an invitation from the garrison commander at Seresh to stay for what remained of the night. The Duke, they learned, was in Paras Derval already, and something else they learned: Ailell was dead. This morning. Word had come at sundown. There would be a funeral and then a coronation on the morrow.

Who? Why, Prince Diarmuid, of course. The heir, you know. A little wild, the commander conceded, but a gallant Prince. There were none in Cathal to match him, he'd wager. Only a daughter for Shalhassan. What a shame, that.

She slipped from the party as it rode towards Seresh castle and, circling the town to the northeast, set out alone on the road to Paras Derval.

She reached it late in the morning. It was easy there, too, amid the hysteria of an interrupted, overcrowded festival, a dead King, and the terror of Rakoth unchained. She should, a part of her mind said, be feeling that terror, too, for as Shalhassan's heir she had an idea of what was to come, and she had seen her father's face as he looked upon the shattered wardstone. Shalhassan's frightened face, which never, ever showed his thought. Oh, there was terror enough to be found, but not yet.

She was on a hunt.

The doors of the palace were wide open. The funeral had so many people coming and going back and forth that Sharra was able to slip inside without trouble. She thought, briefly, of going to the tombs, but there would be too many people there, too great a press.

Fighting the first numbings of fatigue, she forced herself to clarity. They were having a coronation after the burial. They would have to; in time of war there was no space to linger. Where? Even in Cathal the Great Hall of Tomaz Lal was a byword. It would have to be there.

She had spent all her life in palaces. No other assassin could have navigated with such instinctive ease the maze of corridors and stairwells. Indeed, it was the very certainty of her bearing that precluded any challenge.

All so very easy. She found the musicians' gallery, and it was even unlocked. She could have picked the lock in any case; her brother had taught her how, years and years ago. Entering, she sat down in a dark corner and composed herself to wait. From the high shadows she could see servants below making ready glasses and decanters, trays of food, deep chairs for nobility.

It was a fine hall, she conceded, and the windows were indeed something rare and special. Larai Rigal was better, though. Nothing matched the gardens she knew so well.

The gardens she might never see again. For the first time, now that she was, unbelievably, here, and had only to wait, a tendril of fear snaked insidiously through her mind. She banished it. Leaning forward, she gauged the leap. It was long, longer than from high branches of familiar trees, but it could be done. It would be done. And he would see her face before he died, and die knowing. Else there was no point.

A noise startled her. Pressing quickly back into her corner, she caught her breath as six archers slipped through the unlocked door and ranged themselves along the gallery. It was wide and deep; she was not seen, though one of them was very close to her. In silence she crouched in the corner, and so learned, from their low talk, that there was more than a simple coronation to take place that day, and that there were others in that hall with designs on the life she had claimed as her own.

She had a moment to think on the nature of this returned Prince, Aileron, who could send men hither with orders to kill his only brother on command. Briefly she remembered Marlen, her own brother, whom she had loved and who was dead. Only briefly, though, because such thoughts were too soft for what she had still to do, despite this new difficulty. It had been easy to this point, she had no right to have expected no hindrance at all.

In the next moments, though, difficulty became something more, for ten men burst through the two doors of the high gallery; in pairs they came, with knives and swords drawn, and in cold, efficient silence they disarmed the archers and found her.

She had the presence of mind to keep her head down as they threw her together with the six archers. The gallery had been designed to be shadowed and torchlit, with only the flames visible from below, so that music emanating therefrom would seem disembodied, born of fire. It was this that saved her from being exposed in the moments before the nobles of Brennin began to file in over the mosaic-inlaid floor below them.

Every man in that gallery, and the one woman, watched, absorbed, as the foreshortened figures moved to the end of the hall where stood a carved wooden throne. It was oak, she knew, and so was the crown resting on the table beside it.

Then he came forward into view from the perimeter of the room and it was clear that he had to die, because she was still, in spite of all, having trouble breathing at the sight of him. The golden hair was bright above the black of his mourning. He wore a red armband; so, she abruptly realized, did the ten men encircling her and the archers.

An understanding came then and, though she fought it very hard, a sharp pleasure at his mastery. Oh, it was clear, it was clear he had to die.

The broad-shouldered man with the Chancellor's seal about his neck was speaking now. Then he was interrupted once, and, more intensely, a second time. It was hard to hear, but when a dark-bearded man strode to stand in front of the throne she knew it was Aileron, the exile returned. He didn't look like Diarmuid.

"Kevin, by all the gods, I want his blood for this!" the leader of her captors hissed fiercely.

"Easy," a fair-haired man replied. "Listen."

They all did. Diarmuid, she saw, was no longer pacing; he had come to stand, his posture indolent, before his brother.

"The Throne is mine," the dark Prince announced. "I will kill for it or die for it before we leave this hall." Even in the high gallery, the intensity of it reached them. There was a silence.

Raucously broken by Diarmuid's lazy applause. "God," the one called Kevin murmured. *I could have told you*, she thought, and then checked it brutally.

He was speaking now, something too soft to be caught, which was maddening, but Aileron's reply they all heard, and stiffened: "There are six archers in the musicians' gallery," he said, "who will kill you if I raise my hand."

Time seemed to slow impossibly. It was upon her, she knew. Words were spoken very softly down below, then more words, then: *"Coll,"* Diarmuid said clearly, and the big man moved forward to be seen and speak, and say, as she had known he would:

"There were seven men up here."

It all seemed to be quite peculiarly slow; she had a great deal of time to think, to know what was about to happen, long, long it seemed, before Aileron said, "I sent six. Who is the seventh?"—and she jumped, catching them utterly by surprise, drawing her dagger even as she fell, so slowly, with so much clarity, to land and roll and rise to face her lover.

She had intended to give him an instant to recognize her; she prayed she had that much time before they killed her.

He didn't need it. His eyes were wide on hers, knowing right away, knowing probably even as she fell, and, oh, curse him forever, quite unafraid. So she threw. She had to throw, before he smiled.

It would have killed him, for she knew how to use a dagger, if something had not struck her from behind as she released.

She staggered, but kept her feet. So did he, her dagger in his left arm to the hilt, just above the red armband. And then, in a longed-for, terrifying access to what lay underneath the command and the glitter, she heard him murmur, so low no one else could possibly hear, "Both of you?"

And in that moment he was undisguised.

Only for the moment, so brief, she almost doubted it had taken place, because immediately he was smiling again, elusive, controlling. With vivid laughter in his eyes, he took the crown his brother had thrown to save his life, and set it down. Then he poured his wine and came back to salute her extravagantly, and set free her hair so that she was revealed, and though her dagger was in his arm, it seemed that it was he who held her as a small thing in the palm of his hand, and not the other way around at all.

"Both of them!" Coll exclaimed. "They both wanted him dead, and now he has them both. Oh, by the gods, he will do it now!"

"I don't think so," said Kevin soberly. "I don't think he will."

"What?" demanded Coll, taken aback.

"Watch."

"We will treat this lady," Diarmuid was saying, "with all dignity due to her. If I am not mistaken, she comes as the vanguard of an embassy from Shalhassan of Cathal. We are honoured that he sends his daughter and heir to consult with us."

It was so smoothly done that he took them all with him for a moment, standing the reality on its head.

"But," spluttered Ceredur, red-faced with indignation, "she tried to kill you!"

"She had cause," Diarmuid replied calmly.

"Will you explain, Prince Diarmuid?" It was Mabon of Rhoden. Speaking with deference, Kevin noted.

"Now," said Coll, grinning again.

*Now,* thought Sharra. *Whatever happens, I will not live with this shame.*

Diarmuid said, "I stole a flower from Larai Rigal four nights ago in such a way that the Princess would know. It was an irresponsible thing, for those gardens, as we all know, are sacred to them. It seems that Sharra of Cathal valued the honour of her country above her own life—for which we in turn must honour her."

Sharra's world spun for a dizzy instant, then righted itself. She felt herself flushing; tried to control it. He was giving her an out, setting her free. But, she asked herself, even then, with a racing heart, of what worth was freedom if it came only as his gift?

She had no time to pursue it, for Aileron's voice cut abrasively through his brother's spell, just as Diarmuid's applause had destroyed his own, moments before "You are lying," the older Prince said tersely. "Even you would not go through Seresh and Cynan as King's Heir, risking so much exposure for a flower. Do not toy with us!"

Diarmuid, eyebrows raised, turned to his brother. "Should I," he said in a voice like velvet, "kill you instead?"

*Score one,* Kevin thought, seeing, even high as he was, how Aileron paled at that. *And a neat diversion, too.*

"As it happens," Diarmuid went on, "I didn't go near the river fortresses."

"You flew, I suppose?" Jaelle interjected acidly.

Diarmuid bestowed his most benign smile upon her. "No. We crossed Saeren below the Dael Slope, and climbed up the handholds carved in the rock on the other side."

"This is disgraceful!" Aileron snapped, recovering. "How can you lie at such a time?" There was a murmur among the gathering.

"As it happens," Kevin Laine called down, moving forward to be seen, "he's telling the truth." They all looked up. "The absolute truth," Kevin went on, pushing it. "There were nine of us."

"Do you remember," Diarmuid asked his brother, "the book of Nygath that we read as boys?"

Reluctantly, Aileron nodded.

"I broke the code," Diarmuid said cheerfully. "The one we could never solve. It told of steps carved into the cliff in Cathal five hundred years ago by Alorre, before he was King. We crossed the river and climbed them. It isn't quite as foolish as it sounds—it was a useful training expedition. And something more."

She kept her head high, her eyes fixed on the windows. But every timbre of his voice registered within her. *Something more.* Is a falcon not a falcon if it does not fly alone?

"How did you cross the river?" Duke Niavin of Seresh asked, with no little interest. He had them all now, Kevin saw; the first great lie now covered with successive layers of truth.

"With Loren's arrows, actually, and a taut rope across. But don't tell him," Diarmuid grinned easily, despite a dagger in his arm, "or I'll never, ever hear the end of it."

*"Too late!"* someone said from behind them, halfway down the hall.

They all turned. Loren was there, clad for the first time since the crossing in his cloak of power, shot through with many colours that shaded into silver. And beside him was the one who had spoken.

"Behold," said Loren Silvercloak, "I bring you the Twiceborn of the prophecy. Here is Pwyll the Stranger who has come back to us, Lord of the Summer Tree."

He had time to finish, barely, before there came an utterly undecorous scream from the Seer of Brennin, and a second figure hurtled over the balcony of the overhead gallery, shouting with relief and joy as he fell.

Kim got there first, to envelop Paul in a fierce, strangling embrace that was returned, as hard, by him. There were tears of happiness in her eyes as she stepped aside to let Kevin and Paul stand face to face. She was grinning, she knew, like a fool.

"Amigo," said Paul, and smiled.

"Welcome back," said Kevin simply, and then all the nobility of Brennin watched in respectful silence as the two of them embraced.

Kevin stepped back, his eyes bright. "You did it," he said flatly. "You're clear now, aren't you?" And Paul smiled again.

"I am," he said.

Sharra, watching, not understanding anything beyond the intensity, saw Diarmuid walk forward then to the two of them, and she marked the pleasure in his eyes, which was unfeigned and absolute.

"Paul," he said, "this is a bright thread unlooked-for. We were mourning you."

Schafer nodded. "I'm sorry about your father."

"It was time, I think," said Diarmuid. They, too, embraced, and as they did so, the stillness of the hall was shattered by a great noise over their heads as Diarmuid's men roared and clattered their swords. Paul raised a hand to salute them back.

234

Then the mood changed, the interlude was over, for Aileron had come forward, too, to stand in front of Paul as Diarmuid stepped aside.

For what seemed like forever, the two men gazed at each other, their expressions equally unreadable. No one there could know what had passed between them in the Godwood two nights before, but what lay in the room was palpable, and a thing very deep.

"Mörnir be praised," Aileron said, and dropped to his knees before Paul.

A moment later, everyone in the room but Kevin Laine and the three women had done the same. His heart tight with emotion, Kevin suddenly understood a truth about Aileron. This, this was how he led, by pure force of example and conviction. Even Diarmuid, he saw, had followed his brother's lead.

His eyes met Kim's across the heads of the kneeling brothers. Not clearly knowing what it was he was acquiescing to, he nodded, and was moved to see the relief that showed in her face. She wasn't, it seemed, such a stranger after all, white hair notwithstanding.

Aileron rose again, and so did all the others. Paul had not moved or spoken. He seemed to be conserving his strength. Quietly the Prince said, "We are grateful beyond measure for what you have woven."

Schafer's mouth moved in what was only half a smile. "I didn't take your death after all," he said.

Aileron stiffened; without responding, he spun and walked back to the throne. Ascending the steps, he turned again to face them all, his eyes compelling. "Rakoth is free," he said. "The stones are broken and we are at war with the Dark. I say to all of you, to you, my brother"—a sudden rawness in the voice—"I tell you that this conflict is what I was born for. I have sensed it all my life without knowing. Now I know. It is my destiny. It is," cried Aileron, passion blazing in his face, "my war!"

The power of it was overwhelming, a cry of conviction torn whole from the heart. Even Jaelle's bitter eyes held a kind of acceptance, and there was no mockery at all in Diarmuid's face.

"You arrogant bastard," Paul Schafer said.

It was like a kick in the teeth. Even Kevin felt it. He saw Aileron's head snap back, his eyes go wide with shock.

"How presumptuous can you get?" Paul went on, stepping forward to stand before Aileron. "Your death. Your crown. Your destiny. Your war. *Your* war?" His voice skirled upwards. He put a hand on the table for support.

"Pwyll," said Loren. "Paul, wait."

"No!" Schafer snapped. "I hate this, and I hate giving in to it." He turned back to Aileron. "What about the lios alfar?" he demanded. "Loren tells me twenty of them have died already. What about Cathal? Isn't it their war, too?" He pointed to Sharra. "And Eridu? And the Dwarves? Isn't this Matt Sören's war? And what about the Dalrei? There are two of them here now, and seventeen of them have died. Seventeen of the Dalrei are dead. Dead! Isn't it their war, Prince Aileron? And look at us. Look at Kim—*look* at her, at what she's taken on for you. And"—his voice roughened—"think about Jen, if you will, just for a second, before you lay sole claim to this."

There was a difficult silence. Aileron's eyes had never left Paul's while he spoke, nor did they now. When he began to speak, his tone was very different, a plea almost. "I understand," he said stiffly. "I understand all of what you are saying, but I cannot change what else I know. Pwyll, I was born into the world to fight this war."

With a strange light-headedness, Kim Ford spoke then for the first time in public as Seer of Brennin. "Paul," she said, "everyone, I have to tell you that I've seen this. So did Ysanne. That's why she sheltered him. Paul, what he's saying is true."

Schafer looked at her, and the crusading anger she remembered from what he had been before Rachel died faded in the face of her own certitude. *Oh, Ysanne*, she thought, seeing it happen, *how did you stand up under so much weight?*

"If you tell me, I will believe it," Paul said, obviously drained. "But you know it remains his war even if he is not High King of Brennin. He's still going to fight it. It seems a wrong way to choose a King."

"Do you have a suggestion?" Loren asked, surprising them all.

"Yes, I do," Paul said. He let them wait, then, "I suggest you let the Goddess decide. She who sent the moon. Let her Priestess speak her will," said the Arrow of the God, looking at Jaelle.

They all turned with him. It seemed, in the end, to have a kind of inevitability to it: the Goddess taking back one King and sending forth another in his stead.

She had been waiting, amid the tense dialogue back and forth, for the moment to stop them all and say this thing. Now he had done it for her.

She gazed at him a moment before she rose, tall and beautiful, to let them know the will of Dana and Gwen Ystrat, as had been done long ago in the naming of the Kings. In a room dense with power, hers was not the least, and it was the oldest, by far.

"It is a matter for sorrow," she began, blistering them with a glance, "that it should take a stranger to Fionavar to remind you of the true order of things. But howsoever that may be, know ye the will of the Goddess—"

"No," said Diarmuid. And it appeared that there was nothing inevitable after all. "Sorry, sweetling. With all deference to the dazzle of your smile, I don't want to know ye the will of the Goddess."

"Fool!" she exclaimed. "Do you want to be cursed?"

"I have been cursed," Diarmuid said with some feeling. "Rather a good deal lately. I have had quite a lot happen to me today and I need a pint of ale very badly. It has only just occurred to me that as High King I couldn't very easily drop in to the Boar at night, which is what I propose to do as soon as we've crowned my brother and I get this dagger out of my arm."

Even Paul Schafer was humbled by the relief that flashed in that moment across the bearded face of Aileron dan Ailell, whose mother was Marrien of the Garantae, and who would be crowned later that day by Jaelle, the Priestess, as High King of Brennin to lead that realm and its allies into war against Rakoth Maugrim and all the legions of the Dark.

⋅✦⋅☰◉☰⋅✦⋅

There was no banquet or celebration; it was a time of mourning and of war. And so at sundown Loren gathered the four of them, with the two young Dalrei Dave refused to be parted from, in the mages' quarters in the town. One of the Dalrei had a leg wound. That, at least, his magic had been able to deal with. A small consolation, given how much seemed to be beyond him of late.

Looking at his guests, Loren counted it off inwardly. Eight days; only eight days since he had brought them here, yet so much had overtaken them. He could read changes in Dave Martyniuk's face, and in the tacit bonds that united him to the two Riders. Then, when the big man told his story, Loren began to understand, and he marvelled. Ceinwen. Flidais in Pendaran. And Owein's Horn hanging at Dave's side.

Whatever power had been flowing through him when he chose to bring these five had been a true one, and deep.

There had been five, though, not four; there were only four in the room, however, and absence resonated among them like a chord.

And then was given voice. "Time to start thinking about how to get her back," Kevin Laine said soberly. It was interesting, Loren noted, that it was still Kevin who could speak, instinctively, for all of them.

It was a hard thing, but it had to be said. "We will do everything we can," Loren stated flatly. "But you must be told that if the black swan bore her north, she has been taken by Rakoth himself."

There was a pain in the mage's heart. Despite his premonitions, he had deceived her into coming, given her over to the svart alfar, bound her beauty as if with his own hands to the putrescence of Avaia, and consigned her to Maugrim. If there was a judgement waiting for him in the Weaver's Halls, Jennifer would be someone he had to answer for.

"Did you say a swan?" the fair-haired Rider asked. Levon. Ivor's son, whom he remembered from fully ten years ago as a boy on the eve of his fast. A man now, though young, and bearing the always difficult weight of the first men killed under his command. They were all so young, he realized suddenly, even Aileron. *We are going to war against a god*, he thought, and tasted a terrible doubt.

He masked it. "Yes," he said, "a swan. Avaia the Black she was named, long ago. Why do you ask?"

"We saw her," Levon said. "The evening before the Mountain's fire." For no good reason, that seemed to make it hurt even more.

Kimberly stirred a little, and they turned to her. The white hair above the young eyes was still disturbing. "I dreamt her," she said. "So did Ysanne."

And with that, there was another lost woman in the room for Loren, another ghost. *You and I will not meet again on this side of the Night,* Ysanne had told Ailell.

On this side, or on the other now, it seemed. She had gone so far it could not be compassed. He thought about Lokdal. Colan's dagger, Seithr's gift. Oh, the Dwarves did dark things with power under their mountains.

Kevin, straining a little, punctured the grimness of the silence. "Ye gods and little fishes!" he exclaimed. "This is some reunion. We've got to do better than this!"

A good try, Dave Martyniuk thought, surprising himself with how well he understood what Kevin was trying to do. It wasn't going to get more than a smile, though. It wasn't—

Access to inspiration came then with blinding suddenness.

"Uh-uh," he said slowly, choosing his words. "Can't do it, Kevin. We've got another problem here." He paused, enjoying a new sensation, as their concerned eyes swung to him.

Then, reaching into the pocket of his saddle-bag on the floor beside him, he withdrew something he'd carried a long way. "I think you've misinterpreted the judgement in the *McKay* case," he told Kevin, and tossed the travel-stained Evidence notes down on the table.

Hell, Dave thought, watching them all, even Levon, even Torc, give way to hilarity and relief. There's nothing to this! A wide grin, he knew, was splashed across his face.

"Funny, funny man," Kevin Laine said, with unstinted approval. He was still laughing. "I need a drink," Kevin exclaimed. "We all do. And you," he pointed to Dave, "haven't met Diarmuid yet. I think you'll like him even more than you like me."

Which was a funny kind of dig, Dave thought, as they rose to go, and one he'd have to think about. He had a feeling, though, that this, at least, would turn out to be all right.

The five young men departed for the Black Boar. Kim, however, following an instinct that had been building since the coronation, begged off and returned to the palace. Once there, she knocked at a door down the corridor from her own. She made a suggestion, which was accepted. A short while later, in her own room, it emerged that her intuitions on this sort of thing had not been affected at all by anything in Fionavar.

Matt Sören closed the door behind them. He and Loren looked at each other, alone for the first time that day.

"Owein's Horn now," the mage said finally, as if concluding a lengthy exchange.

The Dwarf shook his head. "That is deep," he said. "Will you try to wake them?"

Loren rose and crossed to the window. It was raining again. He put out his hand to feel it like a gift on his palm.

"I won't," he said at last. "But they might."

The Dwarf said softly, "You have been holding yourself back, haven't you?"

Loren turned. His eyes, deep-set under the thick grey eyebrows, were tranquil, but there was power in them still. "I have," he said. "There is a force flowing through all of them, I think, the strangers and our own. We have to give them room."

"They are very young," Matt Sören said.

"I know they are."

"You are sure of this? You are going to let them carry it?"

"I am sure of nothing," the mage said. "But yes, I am going to let them carry it."

"We will be there?"

Silvercloak smiled then. "Oh, my friend," he said, "we will have our battle, never fear. We must let the young ones carry it, but before the end, you and I may have to fight the greatest battle of them all."

"You and I," the Dwarf growled in his deep tones. By which the mage understood a number of things, not least of which was love.

*** 

In the end, the Prince had had a great many pints of ale. There were an infinity of reasons, all good.

He had been named Aileron's heir in the ceremony that afternoon. "This," he'd said, "is getting to be a habit." The obvious line. They were quoting it all over the Black Boar, though. He drained another pint. Oh, an infinity of reasons, he had.

Eventually it seemed that he was alone, and in his own chambers in the palace, the chambers of Prince Diarmuid dan Ailell, the King's Heir in Brennin. Indeed.

It was far too late to bother going to sleep. Using the outer walls, though with difficulty because of his arm, he made his way to Sharra's balcony.

Her room was empty.

On a hunch, he looped two rooms along to where Kim Ford was sleeping. It was hard work, with the wound. When he finally climbed up over the balustrade, having to use the tree for awkward leverage, he was greeted by two pitchers of icy water in the face. No one deflected them, either, or the laughter of Shalhassan's daughter and the Seer of Brennin, who were a long way down the road to an unexpected friendship.

Mourning his fate somewhat, the heir to the throne finally slipped back into the palace and made his way, dripping, to the room of the Lady Rheva.

One took comfort where one could, at times like this.

He did, in fact, eventually fall asleep. Looking complacently down on him, Rheva heard him murmur as in a dream, "Both of them." She didn't really understand, but he had praised her breasts earlier, and she was not displeased.

Kevin Laine, who might have been able to explain it to her, was awake as well, hearing a very long, very private story from Paul. Who could talk again, it seemed, and who wanted to. When Schafer was done, Kevin spoke himself, also for a long time.

At the end of it, they looked at each other. Dawn was breaking. Eventually, they had to smile, despite Rachel, despite Jen, despite everything.

# CHAPTER 16

He came for her in the morning.

She thought she had sounded the depths of despair the night before, when the swan had set down before the iron gates of Starkadh. From the air she had seen it a long way off, a brutally superimposed black upon the white plateaus of the glaciers. Then as they flew nearer, she had felt herself almost physically battered by the nature of it: the huge, piled slabs of windowless stone, lightless, unyielding. Fortress of a god.

In the darkness and the cold his servants had unbound her from the swan. With grasping hands she had been dragged—for her legs were numb—into the bowels of Starkadh, where the odour was of decay and corrupting flesh, even among the cold, and the only lights gleamed a baneful green. They had thrown her into a room alone, and filthy, exhausted, she had fallen onto the one stained pallet on the icy floor. It smelt of svart alfar.

She lay awake, though, shivering with the bitter cold for a long time. When she did sleep, it was fitfully, and the swan flew through her dreams crying in cold triumph.

When she woke, it was to the certitude that the terrors she had endured were but a shelf on the long way down, and the bottom was invisible yet in the darkness, but waiting. She was going there.

It wasn't dark in the room now, though. There was a bright fire blazing on the opposite wall, and in the middle of the room she saw a wide bed standing, and with a constriction of the heart she recognized her parents' bed. A foreboding came upon her, complete and very clear: she was here to be broken, and there was no mercy in this place. There was a god.

And in that moment he was there, he had come, and she felt her mind shockingly peeled open like a fruit. For an instant she fought it, and then was enveloped, stricken by the ease with which she was exposed. She was in his fortress. She was his, it was made known to her. She would be smashed on the anvil of his hate.

It ended, as suddenly as it had begun. Her sight returned, slowly, blurred; her whole body trembled violently, she had no control over it. She turned her head and saw Rakoth.

She had vowed not to cry out, but all vows in this place were as nothing before what he was.

From out of time he had come, from beyond the Weaver's Halls, and into the pattern of the Tapestry. A presence in all the worlds he was, but incarnate here in Fionavar, which was the First, the one that mattered.

Here he had set his feet upon the Ice, and so made the northland the place of his power, and here he had raised up jagged Starkadh. And when it was full-wrought, a claw, a cancer in the north, he had risen to the topmost tower and screamed his name that the wind might bear it to the tamed gods whom he feared not, being stronger by far than any one of them.

Rakoth Maugrim, the Unraveller.

It was Cernan, the stag-horned forest god, who set the trees whispering in mockery of that claim, and in mockery they named him otherwise: Sathain, the Hooded One, and Mörnir of the Thunder sent lightning down to drive him from the tower.

And all the while the lios alfar, newly wakened, sang in Daniloth of Light, and Light was in their eyes, their name, and he hated them with an undying hate.

Too soon had he attacked, though the years may have seemed long to mortal men. And indeed there were men in Fionavar then, for Iorweth had come from oversea, in answer to a dream sent by Mörnir with sanction of the Mother, to found Paras Derval in Brennin by the Summer Tree, and his son had ruled, and his son's son, and then Conary had ascended to the throne.

And in that time had Rakoth come down in fury from the Ice.

And after bitter war been beaten back. Not by the gods—for in the waiting time, the Weaver had spoken, the first and only time he had done so. He said that the worlds had not been woven to be a battleground for powers outside of time, and that if Maugrim were to be mastered, it would be by the Children, with only mildest intercession of the gods. And it had been so. They had bound him under the Mountain, though he could not die, and they had shaped the wardstones to burn red if he but assayed the smallest trial of his powers.

This time it would be otherwise. Now his patience would bear ripe fruit for the crushing, for this time he had been patient. Even when the circle of the guardians had been broken, he had lain still under Rangat, enduring the torment of the chain, savouring it then to sweeten the taste of vengeance to come. Not until Starkadh had been raised high again from the rubble of its fall had he come out from under the Mountain, and with red exploding triumph, let them know he was free.

Oh, this time he would go slowly. He would break them all, one by one. He would crush them with his hand. His one hand, for the other lay, black and festering, under Rangat, with Ginserat's unbroken chain around it still, and for that as much as anything would they pay full, fullest measure before they were allowed to die.

Starting with this one, who knew nothing, he saw, and so was trash, a toy, first flesh for his hunger, and fair like the lios, a presaging of his oldest desire. He reached into her, it was so easy in Starkadh, he knew her whole, and began.

She had been right. The bottom was so far down, the truest depths of night lay beyond where she could ever have apprehended them to be. Facing hate in that moment, a blank, obliterating power, Jennifer saw that he was huge, towering over her, with one hand taloned, grey like disease, and the other gone, leaving only a stump that forever dripped black blood. His robe was black, darker even, somehow, a swallowing of light, and within the hood he wore there was—most terrible—no face. Only eyes that burned her like dry ice, so cold they were, though red like hellfire. Oh, what sin, what sin would they say had been hers that she be given over to this?

Pride? For she was proud, she knew, had been raised to be so. But if that was it, then be it so still, here at the end, at the fall of Dark upon her. A sweet child she had been, strong, a kindness in her nature, if hidden behind caution, not opening easily to other souls, because she trusted only her own. A pride in that, which Kevin Laine, first of all men, had seen for what it was, and laid open for her to understand before he stepped back to let her grow in that understanding. A gift, and not without pain for himself. A long way off, he was, and what, oh, what did any of it matter in this place? What did it matter why? It didn't, clearly, except that at the end we only have ourselves anyway, wherever it comes down. So Jennifer rose from the mattress on the floor, her hair tangled, filthy, the odour of Avaia on her torn clothes, her face stained, body bruised and cut, and she mastered the tremor in her voice and said to him, "You will have nothing of me that you do not take."

And in that foul place, a beauty blazed like Light unleashed, white with courage and fierce clarity.

But this was the stronghold of the Dark, the deepest place of his power, and he said, "But I will take everything," and changed his shape before her eyes to become her father.

And after that it was very bad.

You send your mind away, she remembered reading once; when you're tortured, when you're raped, you send your mind after a while into another place, far from where pain is. You send it as far as you can. To love, the memory of it, a spar for clinging to.

But she couldn't, because everywhere she went he was there. There was no escape to love, not even in childhood, because it was her father naked on the bed with her— her mother's bed—and there was nothing clean in any place. "You wanted to be Princess One," James Lowell whispered tenderly. "Oh, you are now, you are. Let me do this to you, and this, you have no choice, you always wanted this."

Everything. He was taking everything. And through it all he had one hand only, and the other, the rotting stump, dripped his black blood on her body and it burned wherever it fell.

Then he started the changes, again and again, tracking her through all the corridors of her soul. Nowhere, nowhere to even try to hide. For Father Laughlin was above her then, tearing her, excoriating her, penetrating, whose gentleness had been an island all her life. And after him, she should have been prepared, but—oh, Mary Mother, what was her sin, what had she done that evil could have power over her like this? For now it was Kevin, brutal, ravaging, burning her with the blood of his missing hand. Nowhere for her to go, where else was there in all the worlds? She was so far, so far, and he was so vast, he was all places, everywhere, and the only thing he could not do was reclaim his hand, and what good would that do her, oh, what good?

It went on so long that time unhinged among the pain, the voices, the probing of her deepest places as with a trowel, effortlessly. Once he was a man she did not know, very tall, dark, a square-jawed face, distorted now with hatred, brown eyes distended—but she did not know him, she knew she did not know. And then he was, most shockingly, himself at the end, giant upon her, the hood terribly thrown back and nothing there, only the eyes, endlessly, only them, raking her into shreds, first sweet fruit of his long revenge.

It had been over for a long time before she became aware. She kept her eyes closed. She breathed, she was still alive. And no, she told herself, her soul on a spar in a darkest place, the only light her own and so dim. But no, she said again within her being; and, opening her eyes, she looked full upon him and spoke for the second time. "You can take them," Jennifer said, her voice a scrape of pain, "but I will not give them to you, and every one of them has two hands."

And he laughed, for resistance here was a joy, an intensifying of pleasure unimagined. "You shall," he said, "give all of yourself for that. I shall make of your will my gift."

She didn't understand, but a time later there was someone else in the room, and for a hallucinatory instant she thought it was Matt Sören.

"When I leave this room," said Rakoth, "you are Blöd's, for he brought me a thing I coveted." The Dwarf, who was not Matt after all, smiled. There was a hunger in his expression. She was naked, she knew. Open.

"You will give him everything he asks," the Unraveller said. "He need take nothing, you will give and give again until you die." He turned to the Dwarf. "She pleases you?"

Blöd could only nod; his eyes were terrifying.

Rakoth laughed again, it was the laughter on the wind. "She will do anything you ask. At morning's end you are to kill her, though. Any way you like, but she must die. There is a reason." And moving forward as he spoke, Sathain, the Hooded One, touched her once, with his one hand, between the eyes.

And oh, it was not over after all. For the spar was gone, the clinging place for what she was, for Jennifer.

He left the room. He left her with the Dwarf. What was left of her.

Blöd wet his lips. "Get up," he said, and she rose. She could not do otherwise. There was no spar, there was no light.

"Beg me," he said, and oh, what sin had it been? Even as the pleading spilled helplessly from her, as his filthy abuse rained down, and then real pain, which excited him—even through it all she found something. Not a spar of light, for there was no light anymore, it was drowned; but here, at the last, the very last thing was pride. She would not scream, she would not go mad, unless he said for her to do so, and if he did that, it was still being taken, after all, she was not giving it.

But at length he tired and, mindful of his instructions, turned his mind to killing her.

He was inventive, and it appeared after a time that pain did impose impossibilities. Pride can only carry one so far, and golden girls can die, so when the Dwarf began to truly hurt her, she started to scream after all. No spar, no light, no name, nothing left but the Dark.

⊷⊶⊙⊷⊶

When the embassy from Cathal entered the Great Hall of Paras Derval in the morning, it was with a degree of stupefaction quite spectacular that they discovered their Princess waiting to greet them.

Kim Ford was fighting a shameful case of the giggles. Sharra's description of the probable reactions on the part of the embassy dovetailed so wonderfully with the reality that she knew with certainty that if she but glanced at the Princess, she would disgrace herself. She kept her eyes carefully lowered.

Until Diarmuid strolled up. The business with the water pitchers the night before had generated the sort of hilarity between the two women that cements a developing friendship. They had laughed for a long time. It was only afterwards that Kim had remembered that he was a wounded man, and perhaps in more ways than one. He had also acted in the afternoon to save both Sharra's life and her pride, and he had told them to crown his brother. She should have remembered all of that, she supposed, but then she couldn't, she simply *could not* be serious and sensitive all the time.

In any case, the Prince showed no traces of affliction at the moment. Using the drone of Gorlaes's voice as cover—Aileron had, a little surprisingly, re-appointed the Chancellor—he approached the two of them. His eyes were clear, very blue, and his manner gave no hint of extreme intoxication a few hours before, unless it lay in the slightly edged quality of his gaze.

"I hope," he murmured to Sharra, "that yesterday discharged all your impulses to throw things at me."

"I wouldn't count on it," Sharra said defiantly.

He was very good at this, Kim realized. He paused to flick her with a brief, sardonic glance, as to an erring child, before turning back to the Princess. "That," he said simply, "would be a pity. Adults do have better things to do." And he moved off, elegant and assured, to stand beside his brother, as the heir to the throne should.

Kim felt obscurely chastened; the water had been awfully childish. On the other hand, she abruptly recalled, he had been climbing into their rooms! He deserved whatever he got, and more.

Which, though manifestly true, didn't seem to count for much. She still felt like a kid at the moment. *God, he's cool*, she thought, and felt a stirring of sympathy for her newest friend. Sympathy and, because she was honest with herself, the slightest flicker of envy.

In the meantime, she was beginning to understand why Gorlaes was still Chancellor. No one else would have put such a flourish into the necessary rituals that accompanied procedures of this sort. Or even remembered them, for that matter. He was still going, and Aileron was waiting with surprising patience, when a second man, in his own way as handsome as the first, came up to her.

"What," asked Levon, without preamble or greeting, direct as wind, "is the ring you have?"

This was different. It was the Seer of Brennin who looked up at him appraisingly. "The Baelrath," she answered quietly. "The Warstone, it is called. It is of the wild magic."

He reacted to that. "Forgive me, but why are you wearing it?"

"Because the last Seer gave it to me. She dreamt it on my hand."

He nodded, his eyes widening. "Gereint told me of such things. Do you know what it is?"

"Not entirely. Do you?"

Levon shook his head. "No. How should I? It is far from my world, Lady. I know the eltor and the Plain. But I have one thought. May we talk after?"

He really was extraordinarily attractive, a restless stallion in the confines of the hall. "Sure," she said.

As it happened, they never got the chance.

Kevin, standing with Paul beside one of the pillars opposite the women, was quietly pleased at how clear-headed he felt. They'd done a lot of ale the night before. Paying close attention, he saw Gorlaes and then Galienth, the Cathalian emissary, conclude their formal speeches.

Aileron rose. "I thank you," he said levelly, "for coming here, and for your gracious words about my father. We are grateful to Shalhassan that he saw fit to send his daughter and heir to take counsel with us. It is a trust we honour, and it is an emblem of the trust we all must share in the days to come."

The emissary, who, Kevin knew, was utterly clueless as to how Sharra had got there, nodded sage agreement. The King, still standing, spoke again.

"In this counsel-taking, all shall be granted speech, for it cannot be otherwise. It comes to me, though, that first right of address here belongs not to myself, but rather to the eldest of us and the one whose people best know the fury of Rakoth. Na-Brendel of Daniloth, will you speak for the lios alfar?" For a moment after he had ended, Aileron's glance met that of Paul Schafer in an enigmatic exchange.

Then all eyes were on the lios. Still limping from his wounds, Brendel advanced, and with him for support came the one who had seldom left his side in three days. Tegid took Brendel carefully forward, and then withdrew, unwontedly diffident, and the lios alfar stood alone in the midst of them all, his eyes the colour of the sea under rain.

"I thank you, High King," he said. "You do me and my people honour in this hall." He paused. "The lios have never been known for brevity of discourse, since time runs more slowly for us than for you, but there is urgency upon us now, and I will not be overlong. Two thoughts I have." He looked around.

"There were five guardian peoples named, one thousand years ago before the Mountain. Four are here today: Brennin and Cathal, the Dalrei and the lios alfar. None of our wardstones turned red, yet Rakoth is free. We had no warning at all. The circle was broken, my friends, and so—," he hesitated, then spoke aloud the thought they all shared, "—and so we must beware of Eridu."

Eridu, Kim thought, remembering it from Eilathen's whirling vision. Wild, beautiful land where lived a race of dark, fierce, violent men.

And the Dwarves. She turned, to see Matt Sören gazing at Brendel with an impassive face.

"That is my first counsel," the lios continued. "The other is more to the point. If Rakoth is but newly free, then even with his power, black Starkadh cannot be raised again for some time. He has announced himself too soon. We must attack before that fortress anchors his might in the Ice again. I say to all of you that we should go forth from this Council and carry war to the Unraveller ourselves. We bound him once, and we will do so again!"

He was a flame; he fired them all with the burning in him. Even Jaelle, Kevin saw, had a blaze of colour in her face.

"No one," said Aileron, rising again, "could have spoken more clearly my own thought. What say the Dalrei?"

In the now charged ambience, Levon walked forward, uncomfortable but not abashed, and Dave felt a surge of pride to hear his new brother say, "Never in our long history have the Riders failed the High Kingdom in time of need. I can say to you all that the sons of Revor will follow the sons of Conary and Colan into the Rük Barrens and beyond against Maugrim. Aileron, High King, I pledge my life to you, and my sword; do with them what you will. The Dalrei shall not fail you."

Quietly Torc stepped forward. "And I," he said. "My life, my sword."

Stern and erect, Aileron nodded to them, accepting it. He looked a king, Kevin thought. In that moment he came into it.

"And Cathal?" Aileron asked, turning to Galienth. But it was another voice that answered him.

"A thousand years ago," said Sharra, daughter of Shalhassan, heir of Shalhassan, "the men of the Garden Country fought and died in the Bael Rangat. They fought at Celidon and among the tall trees of Gwynir. They were at Sennett Strand when the last battle began and at Starkadh when it ended. They will do as much again." Her bearing was proud before them all, her beauty dazzling. "They will fight and die. But before I accede to this counsel of attack, there is another voice I would hear. Throughout Cathal the wisdom of the lios alfar is a byword, but so, too, and often it has been said with a woven curse, is the knowledge of the followers of Amairgen. What say the mages of Brennin? I would hear the words of Loren Silvercloak."

And with a jolt of dismay, Kevin realized that she was right. The mage hadn't said a thing. He had barely made his presence known. And only Sharra had noticed.

Aileron, he saw, seemed to have followed the same line of thought. He wore a sudden expression of concern.

And even now, Loren was hesitating. Paul gripped Kevin's arm. "He doesn't want to speak," Schafer whispered. "I think I'm going to—"

But whatever intervention he had planned was forestalled, for there came then a loud hammering on the great doors at the end of the hall, and as they turned, startled, the doors were opened, and a figure walked with two of the palace guard between the high pillars towards them all. He walked with the flat, halting steps of absolute exhaustion, and as he drew nearer, Kevin saw that it was a Dwarf.

In the loud silence, it was Matt Sören who stepped forward. "Brock?" he whispered.

The other Dwarf did not speak. He just kept walking and walking, as if by willpower alone, until he had come the length of the Great Hall to where Matt stood. And there he dropped to his knees at last, and in a voice of rawest grief, cried aloud, "Oh, my King!"

In that moment the one eye of Matt Sören truly became a window to his soul. And in it they all saw a hunger unassuageable, the deepest, bitterest, most forsaken longing of the heart.

*"Why, Matt?"* Kim remembered asking after her tranced vision of Calor Diman on that first walk to Ysanne's lake. "Why did you leave?"

And now, it seemed, they were to learn. A chair had been set for Brock before the throne, and he had collapsed into it. It was Matt who spoke, though, as they gathered around the two Dwarves.

"Brock has a tale to tell," Matt Sören said in his deep tones, "but I fear it will mean little to you unless I first tell you mine. It seems the time for privacy is past. Listen, then.

"In the time of the passing of March, King of the Dwarves, in his one-hundred-and-forty-seventh year, only one man could be found who would assay the test of full moon night by Calor Diman, the Crystal Lake, which is how we choose our King, or have the powers choose him for us.

"Know you that he who would rule under the twin mountains must first lie at full moon night beside the lake. If he lives to see the dawn and is not mad, he is crowned under Banir Lök. It is a dark ordeal, though, and many of our greatest warriors and artisans have been broken shards when the sun rose on their vigil."

Kim began to feel the first pulsings of a migraine behind her eyes. Blocking it as best she could, she focused hard on what Matt was saying.

"When March, to whom I was sister-son, died, I gathered what courage I had—a youthful courage it was, I confess—and according to the ritual, I shaped a crystal of my own devising and dropped it as a token of intention in Crystal Lake on new moon night.

"Two weeks later the door from Banir Tal, which is the one entrance to the meadow by Calor Diman, was opened for me and then bolted behind my back."

Matt's voice had dropped almost to a whisper. "I saw the full moon rise above that lake," he said. "I saw many things besides. I . . . did not go mad. In the end I offered and was bound to the waters. They crowned me King two days after."

It was building up to a grandfather of a headache, Kim realized. She sat down on the steps before the throne and put her head in her hands, listening, straining to concentrate.

"I did not fail by the lake," Matt said, and they could all hear the bitterness, "but in every other way I did fail, for the Dwarves were not what once we had been."

"Not your fault," Brock murmured, looking up. "Oh, my lord, truly not your fault."

Matt was silent a moment, then shook his head in rejection. "I was King," he said shortly. Just like that, Kevin thought. He looked at Aileron.

But Matt was continuing. "Two things the Dwarves have always had," he said. "A knowledge of secret things in the earth, and a lust to know more.

"In the last days of King March, a faction formed within our halls around two brothers, foremost of our artisans. Their desire, which became a passion and then, in the first weeks of my reign, a crusade, was to find and unlock the secrets of a dark thing: the Cauldron of Khath Meigol."

A murmur rose in the hall at that. Kim had her eyes closed; there was a lot of pain, and the light was hurting now, lancing against her eyeballs. She bent all her will to Matt. What he was saying was too important to lose because of a headache.

"I ordered them to stop," the Dwarf said. "They did, or so I thought. But then I found Kaen, the older, combing the oldest books again, and his brother had gone away without my leave. I grew wrathful then, and in my folly and pride I called a gathering of all Dwarves in the Moot Hall and demanded they choose between Kaen's desires and my own, which were to let the black thing lie where it was lost, while we moved from spells and powers of the old ways and sought the Light I had been shown by the lake.

"Kaen spoke after me. He said many things. I do not care to repeat them before—"

"He lied!" Brock exclaimed fiercely. "He lied and he lied again!"

Matt shrugged. "He did it well, though. In the end the Dwarfmoot chose that he be allowed to go on with his search, and they voted as well that all our energies should be bent to his aid. I threw down my sceptre," Matt Sören said. "I left the Moot Hall, and the twin mountains, and I vowed I would not come back. They might search for the key to this dark thing, but not while I was King under Banir Lök."

God, it was hurting. Her skin felt too tight. Her mouth was dry. She pressed her hands to her eyes and held her head as motionless as she could.

"Wandering in the mountains and the wooded slopes that summer," Matt continued, "I met Loren, who was not yet Silvercloak, nor yet a mage, though his training was done. What passed between us is still matter for we two alone, but in the end I told the one lie of my life to him, because it involved a pain I had resolved to bear alone.

"I told Loren that I was free to become his source, that I wanted nothing more. And indeed, there was already something woven into our coming together. A night by Calor Diman had taught me to see that. But it had given me something else—something I lied about. Loren could not have known it. Indeed, until I met Kimberly, I thought no one who was not a Dwarf could know this thing."

Kim lifted her head, feeling the movement like a knife. They would be looking at her, though, so she opened her eyes for a moment, trying to mask the nausea flooding over her. When she thought no one was watching, she closed her eyes again. It was very bad, and getting worse.

"When the King is bound to Crystal Lake," Matt was explaining softly, "he is forever bound. There is no breaking it. He may leave but he is not free. The lake is in him like another heartbeat and it never stops calling. I lie down at night fighting this and rise up in the morning fighting it, and it is with me through the day and the evening and will be until I die. This is my burden, and it is mine alone, and I would have you know, else I would not have spoken before you, that it was freely chosen and is not regretted."

The Great Hall was silent as Matt Sören fixed each of them in challenge with his one dark eye. All but Kim, who couldn't even look up now. She was seriously wondering if she was going to pass out.

"Brock," said Matt at length, "you have tidings for us. Are you able to tell them now?"

The other Dwarf looked at him, and, noting the regained composure in his eyes, Kevin realized that there had been a second reason why Matt had spoken first and at length.

Within himself, he still felt the deep hurting of Sören's tale, and it was as an echo of his own thought that he heard Brock murmur, "My King, will you not come back to us? It has been forty years."

But Matt was ready for it this time; once only would he expose his soul. "I am," he said, "source to Loren Silvercloak, First Mage to the High King of Brennin. Kaen is King of the Dwarves. Tell us your news, Brock."

Brock looked at him. Then said, "I would not add to your burdens, but I must tell you that what you say is untrue. Kaen reigns in Banir Lök, but he is not King."

Matt raised a hand. "Do you tell me he has not slept by Calor Diman?"

"I do. We have a ruler, but not a King, unless it be you, my lord."

"Oh, by Seithr's memory!" Matt Sören cried. "How far have we fallen from what we were?"

"Very far," Brock said in a harsh whisper. "They found the Cauldron at the last. They found it and restored it."

There was something in his voice; something terrible.

"Yes?" Matt said.

"There was a price," Brock whispered. "Kaen needed help in the end."

"Yes?" Matt said again.

"A man came. Metran was his name, a mage from Brennin, and together he and Kaen unlocked the power of the Cauldron. Kaen's soul, I think, had been twisted utterly by then. There was a price and he paid it."

"What price?" asked Matt Sören.

Kim knew. Pain was splintering her mind.

"He broke the wardstone of Eridu," said Brock, "and delivered the Cauldron to Rakoth Maugrim. We did it, my King. The Dwarves have freed the Unraveller!" And casting his cloak over his face, Brock wept as if his heart would break.

In the uproar that followed, the terror and the fury, Matt Sören turned slowly, very slowly, as if the world were a calm, still place, and looked at Loren Silvercloak, who was looking back at him.

*We will have our battle,* Loren had said the night before. *Never fear.* And now, most terribly, it was clear what that battle would be.

Her head was being torn apart. There were white detonations within her brain. She was going to scream.

"What is it?" a voice whispered urgently at her side.

A woman, but not Sharra. It was Jaelle who knelt beside her. She was too ago-nized to feel surprise. Leaning on the other woman, she whispered on a thin-stretched note, "Don't know. My head. As if—something's crashing in—I don't—"

"Open your eyes," Jaelle commanded. "Look at the Baelrath!"

She did. The pain was almost blinding. But she could see the stone on her hand throbbing with red fire, pulsing to the rhythm of the explosions behind her eyes, and looking into it, her hand held close to her face, Kim saw something else then, a face, a name written in fire, a room, a crescendo of dark, of Dark, and—

*"Jennifer!"* she screamed. *"Oh, Jen, no!"*

She was on her feet. The ring was a wild, burning, uncontrollable thing. She stag-gered, but Jaelle supported her. Hardly knowing what she was doing, she screamed again, "Loren! I need you!"

Kevin was there. "Kim? What?"

She shook her head, tore away from his touch. She was blind with agony; she could scarcely speak. "Dave," she scraped. "Paul. Come on . . . the circle. *Now!*" There was so much urgency. They seemed to move so slowly, and Jen, Jen, oh, Jen. *"Come on!"* she screamed again.

Then they were around her, the three of them, and Loren and Matt, unquestioning, were beside them. And she held up the ring again, instinctively, and opening herself, her mind, cutting through the claws of pain she found Loren and linked to him and then—oh, a gift—Jaelle was there as well, tapping into the avarlith for her, and with the two of them as ballast, as bedrock, she cast her mind, her soul, to its farthest, most impossible compassing. Oh, far, and there was so much Dark between, so much hate, and oh, so very great a power in Starkadh to stay her.

But there was also a spar of light. A dying spar, so nearly gone, but it was there, and Kim reached with everything she had, with all she was, to the lost island of that light and she found Jennifer.

"Oh, love," she said, inside and aloud, "Oh, love, I'm here. Come!"

The Baelrath was unleashed, it was so bright they had to close their eyes against the blazing of that wildest magic as Kimberly pulled them out, and out, all the way out, with Jennifer held to the circle only by her mind, the spar, pride, last dying light, and love.

Then as the shimmering grew in the Great Hall, and the humming before the crossing time, as they started to go, and the cold of the space between worlds entered the five of them, Kim drew one breath again and cried the last desperate warning, not knowing, oh not, if she was heard:

*"Aileron, don't attack! He's waiting in Starkadh!"*

And then it was cold, cold, and completely dark, as she took them through alone.

⊷⟝◉⊂⟞⊹

*Here ends* THE SUMMER TREE, *the first book of* THE FIONAVAR TAPESTRY

⊷⟝◉⊂⟞⊹

# BOOK 2

# THE WANDERING FIRE

# ACKNOWLEDGEMENTS

This second book of the Tapestry was written on the farm of our friends, Marge and Antonios Katsipis, near the town of Whakatane, New Zealand. The shaping of my own world was immeasurably aided by the warmth with which the two of them, and their son, Iakomi, welcomed us to theirs.

The Wandering Fire *is dedicated to my wife,*

*LAURA*

*who came with me to find it.*

# CONTENTS

# THE CHARACTERS

## The Five:

KIMBERLY FORD, Seer of Brennin
KEVIN LAINE
JENNIFER LOWELL
DAVE MARTYNIUK, "Davor"
PAUL SCHAFER, Lord of the Summer Tree ("Pwyll Twiceborn")

## In Brennin:

AILERON, High King of Brennin
DIARMUID, his brother

LOREN SILVERCLOAK, First Mage of Brennin
MATT SÖREN, his source, once King of the Dwarves
TEYRNON, a mage
BARAK, his source

JAELLE, High Priestess of the Goddess
AUDIART, her second in command, in the province of Gwen Ystrat
LEILA, a young priestess

COLL, lieutenant to Diarmuid
CARDE
ERRON
TEGID ⎬ the men of South Keep, members of
ROTHE  Diarmuid's band
AVERREN

GORLAES, the Chancellor of Brennin
MABON, Duke of Rhoden
NIAVIN, Duke of Seresh
CEREDUR, Warden of the North Marches

VAE, a woman in Paras Derval
FINN, her son
SHAHAR, her husband
BRENDEL, a lord of the lios alfar, from Daniloth
BROCK, a Dwarf, from Banir Tal

## In Cathal:

SHALHASSAN, Supreme Lord of Cathal
SHARRA, his daughter and heir ("the Dark Rose")
BASHRAI, Captain of the Honor Guard (eidolath)

## On the Plain:

IVOR, Chieftain of the third tribe of the Dalrei
LEITH, his wife
LEVON
CORDELIANE ("LIANE") } his children
TABOR

TORC, a Rider of the third tribe

GEREINT, shaman of the third tribe

## In Daniloth:

RA-TENNIEL, King of the lios alfar
GALEN
LYDAN
LEYSE } lords and ladies of the lios alfar
HEILYN
ENROTH

## The Powers:

THE WEAVER at the Loom

MÖRNIR of the Thunder
DANA, the Mother
CERNAN of the Beasts
CEINWEN of the Bow, the HUNTRESS
MACHA }
NEMAIN } godesses of war

OWEIN, Leader of the Wild Hunt

# The Dark:

RAKOTH MAUGRIM the UNRAVELLER

GALADAN, Wolflord of the andain, his lieutenant
METRAN, once First Mage of Brennin, now allied with the Dark
AVAIA, the Black Swan
BLÖD, a Dwarf, servant to Rakoth
KAEN, brother to Blöd, ruling the Dwarves in Banir Lök

# From the Past:

IORWETH FOUNDER, first High King of Brennin

CONARY, High King during the Bael Rangat
COLAN, his son, High King after him ("the Beloved")
AMAIRGEN WHITEBRANCH, first of the mages
LISEN of the Wood, a deiena, source and wife to Amairgen

REVOR, ancestral hero of the Dalrei, first Lord (Aven) of the Plain

# PART I

# THE WARRIOR

# CHAPTER 1

Winter was coming. Last night's snow hadn't melted and the bare trees were laced with it. Toronto woke that morning to see itself cloaked and made over in white, and it was only November.

Cutting across Nathan Phillips Square in front of the twin curves of the City Hall, Dave Martyniuk walked as carefully as he could and wished he'd worn boots. As he maneuvered towards the restaurant entrance on the far side, he saw with some surprise that the other three were already waiting.

"Dave," said sharp-eyed Kevin Laine. "A new suit! When did this happen?"

"Hi, everyone," Dave said. "I got it last week. Can't wear the same corduroy jackets all year, can I?"

"A deep truth," said Kevin, grinning. He was wearing jeans and a sheepskin jacket. And boots. Having finished the obligatory apprenticeship with a law firm that Dave had just begun, Kevin was now immersed in the equally tedious if less formal six-month Bar Admission course. "If that is a three-piece suit," he added, "my image of you is going to be irrevocably shattered."

Wordlessly, Dave unbuttoned his overcoat to reveal the shattering navy vest beneath.

"Angels and ministers of grace defend us!" Kevin exclaimed, crossing himself with the wrong hand while making the sign against evil with the other. Paul Schafer laughed. "Actually," Kevin said, "it looks very nice. Why didn't you buy it in your size?"

"Oh, Kev, give him a break!" Kim Ford said. "It *is* nice, Dave, and it fits perfectly. Kevin's feeling scruffy and jealous."

"I am not," Kevin protested. "I am simply giving my buddy a hard time. If I can't tease Dave, who can I tease?"

"It's okay," said Dave. "I'm tough, I can take it." But what he was remembering in that moment was the face of Kevin Laine the spring before, in a room in the Park Plaza Hotel. The face, and the flat, harshly mastered voice in which he'd spoken, looking down at the wreckage of a woman on the floor:

*"To this I will make reply although he be a god and it mean my death."*

You gave some latitude, Dave was thinking, to someone who'd sworn an oath like that, even if his style was more than occasionally jarring. You gave latitude because what Kevin had done that evening was give voice, and not for the only time, to the mute rage in one's own heart.

"All right," said Kim Ford softly, and Dave knew that she was responding to his thought and not his flippant words. Which would have been unsettling, were she not who she was, with her white hair, the green bracelet on her wrist, and the red ring on her finger that had blazed to bring them home. "Let's go in," Kim said. "We've things to talk about."

Paul Schafer, the Twiceborn, had already turned to lead them through the door.

How many shadings, Kevin was thinking, are there to helplessness? He remembered the feeling from the year before, watching Paul twist inward on himself in the months after Rachel Kincaid had died. A bad time, that was. But Paul had come out of it, had gone so far in three nights on the Summer Tree in Fionavar that he was beyond understanding in the most important ways. He was healed, though, and Kevin held to that as a gift from Fionavar, some recompense for what had been done to Jennifer by the god named Rakoth Maugrim, the Unraveller. Though recompense was hardly the word; there was no true compensation to be found in this or any other world, only the hope of retribution, a flame so faint, despite what he had sworn, it scarcely burned. What were any of them against a god? Even Kim, with her Sight, even Paul, even Dave, who had changed among the Dalrei on the Plain and had found a horn in Pendaran Wood.

And who was he, Kevin Laine, to swear an oath of revenge? It all seemed so pathetic, so ridiculous, especially here, eating fillet of sole in the Mackenzie King Dining Room, amid the clink of cutlery and the lunchtime talk of lawyers and civil servants.

"Well?" said Paul, in a tone that made their setting instantly irrelevant. He was looking at Kim. "Have you seen anything?"

"Stop that," she said. "Stop pushing. If anything happens I'll tell you. Do you want it in writing?"

"Easy, Kim," Kevin said. "You have to understand how ignorant we feel. You're our only link."

"Well, I'm not linked to anything now, and that's all there is to it. There's a place I have to find and I can't control my dreaming. It's in this world, that's all I know, and I can't go anywhere or do anything until I find it. Do you think I'm enjoying this any more than you three are?"

"Can't you send us back?" Dave asked, unwisely.

"I am not a goddamned subway system!" Kim snapped. "I got us out because the Baelrath was somehow unleashed. I can't do it on command."

"Which means we're stuck here," Kevin said.

"Unless Loren comes for us," Dave amended.

Paul was shaking his head. "He won't."

"Why?" Dave asked.

"Loren's playing hands-off, I think. He set things in motion, but he's leaving it up to us now, and some of the others."

Kim was nodding. "He put a thread in the loom," she murmured, "but he won't weave this tapestry." She and Paul exchanged a glance.

"But why?" Dave persisted. Kevin could hear the big man's frustration. "He needs us—or at least Kim and Paul. Why won't he come for us?"

"Because of Jennifer," said Paul quietly. After a moment he went on. "He thinks we've suffered enough. He won't impose any more."

Kevin cleared his throat. "As I understand it, though, whatever happens in Fionavar is going to be reflected here and in the other worlds, too, wherever they are. Isn't that true?"

"It is," said Kim calmly. "It is true. Not immediately, perhaps, but if Rakoth takes dominion in Fionavar he takes dominion everywhere. There is only one Tapestry."

"Even so," said Paul, "we have to do it on our own. Loren won't demand it. If the four of us want to go back, we'll have to find a way ourselves."

"The four of us?" Kevin said. So much helplessness. He looked at Kim.

There were tears in her eyes. "I don't know," she whispered. "I just don't know. She won't see the three of you. She never goes out of the house. She talks to me about work and the weather, and the news, and she's, she—"

"She's going ahead with it," Paul Schafer said.

Kimberly nodded.

Golden, she had been, Kevin remembered, from inside the sorrow.

"All right," said Paul. "It's my turn now."

Arrow of the God.

⊷⊨⊙⊫⊶

She'd had a peephole placed in the door so she could see who was knocking. She was home most of the day, except for afternoon walks in the park nearby. There were often people at the door: deliveries, the gas man, registered mail. For a while at the beginning there had been, fatuously, flowers. She'd thought Kevin was smarter than that. She didn't care whether or not that was a fair judgment. She'd had a fight with Kim about it, when her roommate had come home one evening to find roses in the garbage can.

"Don't you have any idea how he's feeling? Don't you care?" Kimberly had shouted.

Answer: no, and no.

How could she come to such a human thing as caring, any more? Numberless, the unbridged chasms between where she now was, and the four of them, and everyone else. To everything there yet clung the odour of the swan. She saw the world through the filtered unlight of Starkadh. What voice, what eyes seen through that green distortion, could efface the power of Rakoth, who had shoveled through her mind and body as if she, who had once been loved and whole, were so much slag?

She knew she was sane, did not know why.

One thing only pulled her forward into some future tense. Not a good thing, nor could it have been, but it was real, and random, and hers. She would not be gainsaid.

And so, when Kim had first told the other three, and they had come in July to argue with her, she had stood up and left the room. Nor had she seen Kevin or Dave or Paul since that day.

She would bear this child, the child of Rakoth Maugrim. She intended to die giving birth.

She would not have let him in, except that she saw that he was alone, and this was sufficiently unexpected to cause her to open the door.

Paul Schafer said, "I have a story to tell. Will you listen?"

It was cold on the porch. After a moment she stepped aside and he entered. She closed the door and walked into the living room. He hung up his coat in the hall closet and followed her.

She had taken the rocking chair. He sat down on the couch and looked at her, tall and fair, still graceful though no longer slim, seven months heavy with the child. Her head was high, her wide-set green eyes uncompromising.

"I walked away from you last time, and I will again, Paul. I will not be moved on this."

"I said, a story," he murmured.

"Then tell it."

So he told her for the first time about the grey dog on the wall of Paras Derval and the fathomless sorrow in its eyes; he told her about his second night on the Summer Tree, when Galadan, whom she also knew, had come for him, and how the dog had appeared again, and of the battle fought here in the Mörnirwood. He told her about being bound on the Tree of the God, and seeing the red moon rise and the grey dog drive the wolf from the wood.

He told her of Dana. And Mörnir. The powers shown forth that night in answer to the Darkness in the north. His voice was deeper than she remembered; there were echoes in it.

He said, "We are not in this alone. He may break us into fragments in the end, but he will not be unresisted, and whatever you may have seen or endured in that place you must understand that he cannot shape the pattern exactly to his desire. Or else you would not be here."

She listened, almost against her will. His words brought back words of her own, spoken in Starkadh itself: *You will have nothing of me that you do not take*, she had said. But that was before. Before he had set about taking everything—until Kim had pulled her out.

She lifted her head a little. "Yes," Paul said, his eyes never leaving her face. "Do you understand? He is stronger than any of us, stronger even than the God who sent me back. He is stronger than you, Jennifer; it is not worth saying except for this: he cannot take away what you are."

"I know this," said Jennifer Lowell. "It is why I will bear his child."

He sat back. "Then you become his servant."

"No. You listen to me now, Paul, because you don't know everything, either. When he left me . . . after, he gave me to a Dwarf. Blöd was his name. I was a reward, a toy, but he said something to the Dwarf: he said I was to be killed, *and that there was a reason.*" There was cold resolution in her voice. "I will bear this child because I am alive when he wished me dead—the child is random, it is outside his purposes."

He was silent a long time. Then, "But so are you, in and of yourself."

Her laugh was a brutal sound. "And how am I, in and of myself, to answer him? I am going to have a son, Paul, and he will be my answer."

He shook his head. "There is too much evil in this, and only to prove a point already proven."

"Nonetheless," said Jennifer.

After a moment his mouth crooked sideways. "I won't press you on it, then. I came for you, not him. Kim's already dreamt his name, anyhow."

Her eyes flashed. "Paul, understand me. I would do what I am doing whatever Kim said. Whatever she happened to dream. And I will name him as I choose!"

He was smiling, improbably. "Stick around and do that then. Stay with us, Jen. We need you back." Only when he spoke did she realize what she'd said. He'd tricked her, she decided, had goaded her quite deliberately into something unintended. But she couldn't, for some reason, feel angry. Had this first tenuous spar he'd thrown across to her been a little firmer she might, in fact, have smiled.

Paul stood up. "There is an exhibition of Japanese prints at the Art Gallery. Would you like to see it with me?"

For a long time she rocked in the chair, looking up at him. He was dark-haired, slight, still frail-seeming, though not so much as last spring.

"What was the dog's name?" she asked.

"I don't know. I wish I did."

After another moment she rose, put on her coat, and took her first careful step on the first bridge.

Dark seed of a dark god, Paul was thinking, as he tried to simulate an interest in nineteenth-century prints from Kyoto and Osaka. Cranes, twisted trees, elegant ladies with long pins in their hair.

The lady beside him wasn't talking a great deal, but she was there in the gallery, and it was not a small grace. He remembered the crumpled figure she had been seven months before, when Kim had brought them desperately from Fionavar with the wild, blazing power of the Baelrath.

This was Kim's power, he knew: the Warstone and the dreams in which she walked at night, white-haired as Ysanne had been, two souls within her, and knowledge of two worlds. It had to be a difficult thing. *The price of power*, he remembered Ailell the High King telling him, the night they played their game of ta'bael. The night that had been overture to the three nights that became his own hard, hardest thing. The gateway to whatever he now was, Lord of the Summer Tree.

Whatever he now was. They had moved into the twentieth century now: more cranes, long, narrow mountain scenes, low boats riding on wide rivers.

"The themes don't change much," Jennifer said.

"Not much."

He had been sent back, he was Mörnir's response, but he had no ring with which to burn, no dreams down which to track the secrets of the Tapestry, not even a horn such as Dave had found, no skylore like Loren, or crown like Aileron; not even—though he felt a chill at the thought—a child within him like the woman at his side.

And yet. There had been ravens at his shoulder in the branches of the Tree: Thought and Memory were their names. There had been a figure in the clearing, hard to see, but he had seen horns on its head and seen it bow to him. There had been the white mist rising up through him to the sky in which a red moon sailed on new moon night. There had been rain. And then the God.

And there was still the God. At night, sometimes, he could feel the tacit presence, immense, in the rush and slide of his blood, the muffled thunder of his human heart.

Was he a symbol only? A manifestation of what he had been telling Jennifer: the presence of opposition to the workings of the Unraveller? There were worse roles, he supposed. It gave him a part to play in what was to come, but something within—and there was a god within him—said that there was more. *No man shall be Lord of the Summer Tree who has not twice been born,* Jaelle had said to him in the sanctuary.

He was more than symbol. The waiting to learn what, and how, seemed to be part of the price.

Almost at the end now. They stopped in front of a large print of a river scene: boats being poled along, others unloading at a crowded dock; there were woods on the far side of the stream, snow-capped mountains beyond. It was badly hung, though; he could see people behind them reflected in the glass, two students, the sleepy guard. And then Paul saw the blurred reflection in the doorway of a wolf.

Turning quickly on a taken breath he met the eyes of Galadan.

The Wolflord was in his true shape, and hearing Jennifer gasp Paul knew that she, too, remembered that scarred, elegant force of power with the silver in his dark hair.

Grabbing Jennifer's hand, Paul wheeled and began to move quickly back through the exhibition. He looked over his shoulder: Galadan was following, a sardonic smile on his face. He wasn't hurrying.

They rounded a corner. Mumbling a swift prayer, Paul pushed on the bar of a door marked EMERGENCY EXIT ONLY. He heard a guard shout behind him, but no alarm sounded. They found themselves in a service corridor. Without saying a word, they clattered down the hallway. Behind them Paul heard the guard shout again as the door opened a second time.

The corridor forked. Paul pushed open another door and hurried Jennifer through. She stumbled and he had to hold her up.

"I can't run, Paul!"

He cursed inwardly. They were as far from the exit as they could be. The door had taken them out into the largest room in the gallery, Henry Moore's permanent sculpture exhibit. It was the pride of the Art Gallery of Ontario, the room that placed it on the artistic map of the world.

And it was the room in which, it seemed, they were going to die.

He helped Jermifer move farther away from the door. They passed several huge pieces, a madonna and child, a nude, an abstract shape.

"Wait here," he said, and sat her down on the broad base of one of the sculptures. There was no one else in the room—not on a weekday morning in November.

It figures, he thought. And turned. The Wolflord walked through the same door they had used. For the second time he and Galadan faced each other in a place where time seemed to hang suspended.

Jennifer whispered his name. Without taking his eyes from Galadan he heard her say, in a voice shockingly cold, "It is too soon, Paul. Whatever you are, you must find it now. If not, I will curse you as I die."

And still reeling from that, he saw Galadan raise a long slender finger to a red weal on his temple. "This one," said the Lord of the andain, "I lay at the root of your Tree."

"You are lucky," Paul said, "to be alive to lay it anywhere."

"Perhaps," the other said, and smiled again, "but no more fortunate than you have been until now. Both of you." There was, though Paul had not seen it come, a knife in his hand. He remembered that knife. Galadan moved a few steps closer. No one, Paul knew, was going to enter the room.

And then he knew something more. There was a deep stirring, as of the sea, within him, and he moved forward himself, away from Jennifer, and said, "Would you battle the Twiceborn of Mörnir?"

And the Wolflord replied, "For nothing else am I here, though I will kill the girl when you are dead. Remember who I am: the children of gods have knelt to wash my feet. You are nothing yet, Pwyll Twiceborn, and will be twice dead before I let you come into your force."

Paul shook his head. There was a tide running in his blood. He heard himself say, as if from far off, "Your father bowed to me, Galadan. Will you not do so, *son of Cernan?*" And he felt a rush of power to see the other hesitate.

But only for a moment. Then the Wolflord, who had been a force of might and a Lord of the mighty for past a thousand years, laughed loud and, raising his hand again, plunged the room into utter darkness.

"What son have you ever known to follow his father's path?" he said. "There is no dog to guard you now, *and I can see in the dark!*"

The surging of power stopped within Paul.

In its place came something else, a quiet, a space as of a pool within a wood, and he knew this, instinctively, to be the true access to what he now was and would be. From within this calm he moved back to Jennifer and said to her, "Be easy, but hold fast to me." As he felt her grip his hand and rise to stand beside him, he spoke once more to the Wolflord, and his voice had changed.

"Slave of Maugrim," he said, "I cannot defeat you yet, nor can I see you in the dark. We will meet again, and the third time pays for all, as well you know. But I will not tarry for you in this place."

269

And on the words he felt himself dropping into the still, deep place, the pool within, which uttermost need had found. Down and down he went, and, holding tight to Jennifer, he took them both away through the remembered cold, the interstices of time, the space between the Weaver's worlds, back to Fionavar.

# CHAPTER 2

Vae heard the knocking at the door. Since Shahar had been sent north she often heard sounds in the house at night, and she had taught herself to ignore them, mostly.

But the hammering on the shop entrance below was not to be ignored as being born of winter solitude or wartime fears. It was real, and urgent, and she didn't want to know who it was.

Her son was in the hallway outside her room, though, he had already pulled on trousers and the warm vest she had made him when the snows began. He looked sleepy and young, but he always looked young to her.

"Shall I go see?" he said bravely.

"Wait," Vae said. She rose, herself, and pulled on a woolen robe over her night attire. It was cold in the house, and long past the middle of the night. Her man was away, and she was alone in the chill of winter with a fourteen-year-old child and a rapping, more and more insistent, at her door.

Vae lit a candle and followed Finn down the stairs.

"Wait," she said again in the shop, and lit two more candles, despite the waste. One did not open the door on a winter night without some light by which to see who came. When the candles had caught, she saw that Finn had taken the iron rod from the upstairs fire. She nodded, and he opened the door.

In the drifted snow outside stood two strangers, a man and a tall woman he supported with an arm about her shoulders. Finn lowered his weapon; they were unarmed. Coming nearer, and holding her candle high, Vae saw two things: that the woman wasn't a stranger after all, and that she was far gone with child.

"From the ta'kiena?" said Vae. "The third time."

The woman nodded. Her eyes turned to Finn and then back to his mother. "He is still here," she said. "I am glad."

Finn said nothing; he was so young it could break Vae's heart. The man in the doorway stirred. "We need help," he said. "We are fleeing the Wolflord from our world. I am Pwyll, this is Jennifer. We crossed here last spring with Loren."

Vae nodded, wishing Shahar were there instead of in the windy cold of North Keep with his grandfather's spear. He was a craftsman, not a soldier; what did her husband know of war?

"Come in," she said, and stepped back. Finn closed and bolted the door behind them. "I am Vae. My man is away. What help can I offer you?"

"The crossing brought me early to my time," the woman called Jennifer said, and Vae saw from her face that it was true.

"Make a fire," she said to Finn. "In my room upstairs." She turned to the man. "You help him. Boil water on the fire. Finn will show you where the clean linen is. Quickly, both of you."

They left, taking the stairs two at a time.

Alone in the candlelit shop, among the unspun wool and the finished craftings, she and the other woman gazed at each other.

"Why me?" said Vae.

The other's eyes were clouded with pain. "Because," she said, "I need a mother who knows how to love her child."

Vae had been fast asleep only moments before; the woman in the room with her was so fair she might have been a creature from the dreamworld, save for her eyes.

"I don't understand," said Vae.

"I will have to leave him," the woman said. "Could you give your heart to another son when Finn takes the Longest Road?"

In daylight she might have struck or cursed anyone who said so flatly the thing that twisted through her like a blade. But this was night and half a dream, and the other woman was crying.

Vae was a simple woman, a worker in wool and cloth with her man. She had a son who for no reason she could understand had been called three times to the Road when the children played the prophecy game, the ta'kiena, and then a fourth time before the Mountain went up to signal war. And now there was this.

"Yes," said Vae, simply. "I could love another child. It is a son?"

Jennifer wiped away her tears. "It is," she said. "But there is more. He will be of andain, and I don't know what that will mean."

Vae felt her hands trembling. Child of a god and a mortal. It meant many things, most of them forgotten. She took a deep breath. "Very well," she said.

"One thing more," the golden woman said.

Vae closed her eyes. "Tell me, then."

She kept them closed for a long time after the father's name was spoken. Then, with more courage than she would have ever guessed she had, Vae opened her eyes and said, "He will need to be loved a great deal. I will try." Watching the other woman weep after that, she felt pity break over her in waves.

At length Jennifer collected herself, only to be racked by a visible spasm of pain.

"We had best go up," said Vae. "This will not be an easy thing. Can you manage the stairs?"

Jennifer nodded her head. Vae put an arm around her, and they moved together to the stairway. Jennifer stopped.

"If you had had a second son," she whispered, "what name would he have had?"

The dreamworld, it was. "Darien," she said. "For my father."

It was not an easy thing, but neither was it a long one. He was small, of course, more than two months early, but not as small as she had expected. He was placed on her breast for a moment, afterward. Looking down for the first time upon her son, Jennifer wept, in love and in sorrow for all the worlds, all the battlegrounds, for he was beautiful.

Blinded, she closed her eyes. Then, once only, and formally, that it should be done and known to be done, she said, "His name is Darien. He has been named by his mother." Saying so, she laid her head back upon the pillows and gave her son to Vae.

Taking him, Vae was astonished how easily love came to her again. There were tears in her own eyes as she cradled him. She blamed their blurring and the shifting candlelight for the moment—no more than that—when his very blue eyes seemed red.

It was still dark when Paul went out into the streets, and snow was falling. Drifts were piling up in the lanes of Paras Derval and against the shops and houses. He passed the remembered signboard on the Black Boar. The inn was dark and shuttered, the sign creaked in the pre-dawn wind. No one else was abroad in the white streets.

He continued, east to the edge of the town and then—though the going became harder—north up the slope of the palace hill. There were lights on in the castle, beacons of warmth amid the wind and blowing snow.

Paul Schafer felt a deep desire to go to those beacons, to sit down with friends—Loren, Matt, Diarmuid, Coll, even Aileron, the stern, bearded High King—and learn their tidings even as he shared the burden of what he had just witnessed.

He resisted the lure. The child was Jennifer's thread in this weaving, and she was owed this much: he would not take that thread away by spreading word throughout the land of a son born that day to Rakoth Maugrim.

Darien, she had named him. Paul thought of Kim saying, *I know his name.* He shook his head. This child was something so unpredictable, so truly random, it numbed the mind: what would be the powers of this newest of the andain, and where, oh, where, would his allegiance fall? Had Jennifer brought forth this day not merely a lieutenant but an heir to the Dark?

Both women had cried, the one who had given birth and the one who would raise him. Both women, but not the child, not this fair blue-eyed child of two worlds.

Did the andain cry? Paul reached down toward the still place, the source of the power that had brought them here, for an answer but was not surprised to find nothing there.

Pushing through the last swirling mound of snow he reached his destination, drew a breath to steady himself, and pulled on the chain outside the arched doorway.

He heard a bell ring deep within the domed Temple of the Mother; then there was silence again. He stood in the darkness a long time before the great doors swung open and the glow of candlelight spun out a little way into the snowbound night. He moved sideways and forward to see and be seen.

"No farther!" a woman said. "I have a blade."

He kept his composure. "I'm sure you do," he said. "But you also have eyes, I hope, and should know who I am, for I have been here before."

There were two of them, a young girl with the candle and an older woman beside her. Others, with more light, were coming forward as well.

The girl moved nearer, raising her light so that his face was fully lit by the flame.

"By Dana of the Moon!" the older woman breathed.

"Yes," said Paul. "Now quickly, please, summon your Priestess. I have little time and must speak with her." He made to enter the vestibule.

"Hold!" the woman said again. "There is a price of blood all men must pay to enter here."

But for this he had no tolerance.

Stepping quickly forward, he grabbed her wrist and twisted. A knife clattered on the marble floor. Still holding the grey-robed woman in front of him Paul snapped, "Bring the Priestess, now!" None of them moved; behind him the wind whistled through the open door.

"Let her go," the young girl said calmly. He turned to her; she looked to be no more than thirteen. "She means no harm," the girl went on. "She doesn't know that you bled the last time you were here, Twiceborn."

He had forgotten: Jaelle's fingers along his cheek as he lay helplessly. His glance narrowed on this preternaturally self-possessed child. He released the other priestess.

"Shiel," the girl said to her, still tranquilly, "we should summon the High Priestess."

"No need," a colder voice said, and walking between the torches, clad as ever in white, Jaelle came to stand facing him. She was barefoot on the cold floor, he saw, and her long red hair was twisted down her back in untended spirals.

"Sorry to wake you," he said.

"Speak," she replied. "And carefully. You have assaulted one of my priestesses."

He could not afford to lose his temper. This was going to be difficult enough as it was.

"I am sorry," he lied. "And I am here to speak. We should be alone, Jaelle."

A moment longer she regarded him, then turned. "Bring him to my chambers," she said.

"Priestess! The blood, he must—"

"Shiel, be silent for once!" Jaelle snapped in a wholly unusual revealing of strain.

"I told her," the young one said mildly. "He bled the last time he was here."

Jaelle hadn't wanted to be reminded. She went the long way around, so he would have to pass the dome and see the axe.


The bed he remembered. He had awakened here on a morning of rain. It was neatly made. Proprieties, he thought wryly—and some well-trained servants.

"Very well," she said.

"News first, please. Is there war?" he asked.

She walked over to the table, turned, and faced him, resting her hands behind her on the polished surface. "No. The winter came early and hard. Not even svart alfar march well in snow. The wolves have been a problem, and we are short of food, but there have been no battles yet."

"So you heard Kim's warning?" *Don't attack, he's waiting in Starkadh!* Kimberly had screamed, as they passed into the crossing.

Jaelle hesitated. "I heard it. Yes."

"No one else?"

"I was tapping the avarlith for her."

"I remember. It was unexpected." She made an impatient movement. "They listened to you then?"

"Eventually." This time she gave nothing away. He could guess, though, what had happened, knowing the deep mistrust the men in the Great Hall that morning would have had for the High Priestess.

"What now?" was all he said.

"We wait for spring. Aileron takes council with everyone who will talk to him, but everyone waits for spring. Where is the Seer?" Some urgency there.

"Waiting also. For a dream."

"Why are you here?" she asked.

Smile fading, then, with no levity at all, he told her: Arrow of Mörnir to Priestess of the Mother. Everything. Softly he gave her the name of the child and, more softly yet, who the father was.

She didn't move during the telling of it or after; no indication anywhere in her of the impact. He had to admire her self-control. Then she asked again, but in a different voice, "Why are you here?"

And he said, "Because you made Jennifer a guest-friend last spring." She hadn't been ready for that—this time it showed in her face. A triumph for him of sorts, but the moment was too high by far for petty score-keeping in the power game. He went on, to take away the sting, "Loren would mistrust the wildness of this too much, but I thought you could deal with it. We need you."

"You trust me with this?"

His turn to gesture impatiently. "Oh, Jaelle, don't exaggerate your own malevolence. You aren't happy with the power balance here, any fool can see that. But only a very great fool would confuse that with where you stand in this war. You serve the Goddess who sent up that moon, Jaelle. I am least likely of all men to forget it."

She seemed very young in that moment. There was a woman beneath the white robe, a person, not merely an icon; he'd made the mistake of trying to tell her that once, in this very room, with the rain falling outside.

"What do you need?" she said.

His tone was crisp. "A watch on the child. Complete secrecy, of course, which is another reason I came to you."

"I will have to tell the Mormae in Gwen Ystrat."

"I thought as much." He rose, began pacing as he spoke. "It is all the same, I gather, within the Mormae?"

She nodded. "It is all the same, within any level of the Priestesshood, but it will be kept to the inner circle."

"All right," he said, and stopped his pacing very close to her. "But you have a problem then."

"What?"

"This!" And reaching past her, he pulled open an inner door and grabbed the listener beyond, pulling her into the room so that she sprawled on the carpeted floor.

"Leila!" Jaelle exclaimed.

The girl adjusted her grey robe and rose to her feet. There was a hint of apprehension in her eyes, but only a hint, Paul saw, and she held her head very high, facing the two of them.

"You may owe a death for this." Jaelle's tone was glacial.

Leila said hardily, "Are we to discuss it with a man here?"

Jaelle hesitated, but only for a second. "We are," she replied, and Paul was startled by a sudden change in her tone. "Leila," the High Priestess said gently, "you must not lecture me, I am not Shiel or Marline. You have worn grey for ten days only, and you must understand your place."

It was too soft for Paul's liking. "The hell with that! What was she doing there? What did she hear?"

"I heard it all," Leila said.

Jaelle was astonishingly calm. "I believe it," she said. "Now tell me why."

"Because of Finn," said Leila. "Because I could tell he came from Finn."

"Ah," said Jaelle slowly. She walked towards the child then and, after a moment, stroked a long finger down her cheek in an unsettling caress. "Of course."

"I'm lost," said Paul.

They both turned to him.

"You shouldn't be," Jaelle said, in complete control again. "Did Jennifer not tell you about the ta'kiena?"

"Yes, but—"

"And why she wanted to bear her child in Vae's house? Finn's mother's house?"

"Oh." It clicked. He looked at slim, fair-haired Leila. "This one?" he asked.

The girl answered him herself. "I called Finn to the Road. Three times, and then another. I am tuned to him until he goes."

There was a silence. "All right, Leila," Jaelle said. "Leave us now. You have done what you had to do. Never breathe a word."

"I don't think I could," said Leila, in a small voice. "For Finn. There is an ocean inside me sometimes. I think it would overrun me if I tried." She turned and left the room, closing the door softly behind her.

Looking at the Priestess in the light of the tall candles, Paul realized that he had never seen pity in her eyes before.

"You will do nothing?" he murmured.

Jaelle nodded her head, still looking at the door through which the girl had gone. "Anyone else I would have killed, believe me."

"But not this one?"

"Not this one."

"Why?"

She turned to him. "Leave me this secret," she said softly. "There are some mysteries best not known, Pwyll. Even for you." It was the first time she had spoken his name. Their eyes met, and this time it was Paul who looked away. Her scorn he could master, but this look in her eyes evoked access to a power older and deeper, even, than the one he had touched on the Tree.

He cleared his throat. "We should be gone by morning."

"I know," said Jaelle. "I will send in a moment to have her brought here."

"If I could do it myself," he said, "I would not ask this of you. I know it will drain the earthroot, the avarlith."

She shook her head; the candlelight made highlights in her hair. "You did a deep thing to bring her here by yourself. The Weaver alone knows how."

"Well, I certainly don't," he said. An admission.

They were silent. It was very still in the sanctuary, in her room.

"Darien," she said.

He drew a breath. "I know. Are you afraid?"

"Yes," she said. "And you?"

"Very much."

They looked at each other across the carpeted space that lay between, a distance impossibly far.

"We had better get moving," he said finally.

She raised her arm and pulled a cord nearby. Somewhere a bell rang. When they came in response she gave swift, careful orders, and it seemed very soon when the priestesses returned, bearing Jennifer.

After that it took little time. They went into the dome and the man was blindfolded. She took the blood from herself, which surprised some of them; then she reached east to Gwen Ystrat, found Audiart first, then the others. They were made aware, manifested acceptance, then traveled down together, touched Dun Maura, and felt the earthroot flow through them all.

"Goodbye," she heard him say, as it changed for her, in the way it always had— the way that had marked her even as a child—into a streaming as of moonlight through her body. She channeled it, gave thanks, and then spun the avarlith forth to send them home.

After, she was too weary to do anything but sleep.

⋅→═◉◺═→⋅

In the house by the green where the ta'kiena had been chanted, Vae held her new child in her arms by the fire. The grey-robed priestesses had brought milk and swaddling clothes and promised other things. Finn had already put together a makeshift crib for Darien.

She had let him hold his brother for a moment, her heart swelling to see the brightness in his eyes. It might even keep him here, she thought; perhaps this awesome thing was so powerful it might overmaster the call that Finn had heard. It might.

And another thought she had: whatever the father might be, and she laid a curse upon his name, a child learned love from being loved, and they would give him all the love he needed, she and Finn—and Shahar when he came home. How could one not love a child so calm and fair, with eyes so blue—blue as Ginserat's wardstones, she thought, then remembered they were broken.

# CHAPTER 3

Paul, on lookout up the road, whistled the all-clear. Dave grabbed the post for support and hurdled the fence, cursing softly as he sank ankle deep in spring mud.

"Okay," he said. "The girls."

Kevin helped Jen first and then Kim to balance themselves on the stiff wire for Dave to swing them up and over. They had been worried that the fence might be electrically charged, but Kevin's checking earlier had established that it wasn't.

"Car coming!" Paul cried sharply.

They flattened themselves on the cold, mucky ground till the headlights went by. Then Kevin rose and he too vaulted over the fence. This part was easy, but the ground was pressure-sensitive farther in, they knew, and an alarm would sound in the guard's underground room when they walked that far.

Paul jogged up and neatly cleared the fence. He and Kevin exchanged a glance. Despite the immensity of what they were about to do, Kevin felt a surge of exhilaration. It was a joy to be *doing* something again.

"All right," he said, low and in control. "Jen, you're with me. Prepare to be as sexy as hell. Dave and Paul—you know what to do?" They nodded. He turned to Kim. "All set, sweetheart. Do your thing. And—"

He stopped. Kim had removed her gloves. The Baelrath on her right hand was very bright; it seemed like a thing alive. Kim raised it overhead.

"May all the powers of the dead forgive me for this," she said and let the light carry her forward past the crumbling Heelstone to Stonehenge.

On a night at the beginning of spring she had taken the second step at last. It had been so long in coming she had begun to despair, but how did one command a dream to show itself? Ysanne had never taught her. Nor had the Seer's gift of so much else offered this one thing to her. Dreamer of the dream, she now was, but there was much waiting involved and never, ever, had Kimberly been called a patient person.

Over and over through the summer of their return and the long winter that followed—and was not over yet, though April had come—she had seen the same image tumble through her nights, but she knew it now. She had known this first step on the road to the Warrior since a night in Paras Derval. The jumbled stones and the wind over the grass were as familiar as anything had ever been to her, and she knew where they were.

It was the time that had confused her, or it would have been easy despite the blurring of the vision in those first dreams when she was young in power: she had seen it not as it now was, but as it had been three thousand years ago.

Stonehenge. Where a King lay buried, a giant in his day, but small, small, beside the one whose secret name he held sacrosanct beyond the walls of death.

Sacrosanct except now, at last, from her. As ever, the nature of this power overwhelmed her with sorrow: not even the dead might have rest from her, it seemed, from Kimberly Ford with the Baelrath on her hand.

Stonehenge, she knew. The starting point. The hidden Book of Gortyn she had found under the cottage by the lake, and in it she had found—easily, because Ysanne was within her—the wards that would raise the guardian dead from his long resting place.

But she had needed one thing more, for the dead man had been mighty and would not give up this secret easily: she had needed to know the other place, the next one, the last. The place of summoning.

And then, on a night in April, she did.

It would have misled her again, this long-sought image, had not she been prepared for the trick that time might play. The Seers walked in their dreams along loops spun invisibly in the Weaver's threading through the Loom, and they had to be prepared to see the inexplicable.

But this she was ready for, this image of an island, small and green, in a lake calm as glass under a just-risen crescent moon. A scene of such surpassing peacefulness that she would have wept a year ago to know the havoc she would wreak when she came.

Not even a year ago, not so much even. But she had changed, and though there was sorrow within her—deep as a stone and as permanent—there was too much need, and the delay had been too long to allow her the luxury of tears.

She rose from her bed. The Warstone flickered with a muted, presaging light. It was going to blaze soon, she knew. She would carry fire on her hand. She saw by the kitchen clock that it was four in the morning. She also saw Jennifer sitting at the table, and the kettle was coming to a boil.

"You cried out," her roommate said. "I thought something was happening."

Kim took one of the other chairs. She tightened her robe about her. It was chilly in the house, and this traveling always left her cold. "It did," she said, wearily.

"You know what you have to do?"

She nodded.

"Is it all right?"

She shrugged. Too hard to explain. She had an understanding, of late, as to why

Ysanne had withdrawn in solitude to her lake. There were two lights in the room: one on the ceiling and the other on her hand. "We'd better call the guys," she said.

"I already have. They'll be here soon."

Kim glanced sharply at her. "What did I say in my sleep?"

Jennifer's eyes were kind again; they had been since Darien was born. "You cried out for forgiveness," she said. *She would drag the dead from their rest and the undead to their doom.*

"Fat chance," said Kimberly.

The doorbell rang. In a moment they were standing all around her, anxious, disheveled, half asleep. She looked up. They were waiting, but the waiting was over; she had seen an island and a lake like glass. "Who's coming with me to England?" she asked, with brittle, false brightness in her voice.

⋅⊱══◑ ◐══⊰⋅

All of them went. Even Dave, who'd had to virtually quit his articling job to get away on twenty-four hours' notice. A year ago he'd carried a packet of Evidence notes into Fionavar with him, so determined was he to succeed in the law. He'd changed so much; they all had. After seeing Rangat throw up that unholy hand, how could anything else seem other than insubstantial?

Yet what could be more insubstantial than a dream? And it was a dream that had the five of them hurtling overseas on a 747 to London and, in a Renault rented at Heathrow and driven erratically and at speed by Kevin Laine, to Amesbury beside Stonehenge.

Kevin was in a fired-up mood. Released at last from the waiting, from months of pretending to take an interest in the tax, real estate, and civil-procedure courses that preceded his call to the Bar, he gunned the car through a roundabout, ignored Dave's spluttering, and skidded to a stop in front of an ancient hotel and tavern called, of course, the New Inn.

He and Dave handled the baggage—none of them had more than carry-ons—while Paul registered. On the way in they passed the entrance to the bar—crowded at lunchtime—and he caught a glimpse of a cute, freckled barmaid.

"Do you know," he told Dave, as they waited for Paul to arrange for the rooms, "I can't remember the last time I was laid?"

Dave, who couldn't either, with greater justification, grunted. "Get your mind out of your pants for once."

It *was* frivolous, Kevin supposed. But he wasn't a monk and couldn't ever pretend to be. Diarmuid would understand, he thought, though he wondered if even that dissolute Prince would comprehend just how far the act of love carried Kevin, or what he truly sought in its pursuit. Unlikely in the extreme, Kevin reflected, since he himself didn't really know.

Paul had the keys to two adjacent rooms. Leaving Kimberly, at her own insistence, alone in one of the rooms, the four others drove the mile west to join the tour buses and pocket cameras by the monument. Once there, even with the daytime tackiness, Kevin sobered. There was work to be done, to prepare for what would happen that night.

Dave had asked on the plane. It had been very late, the movie over, lights dimmed. Jennifer and Paul had been asleep when the big man had come over to where Kevin and Kim were sitting, awake but not speaking. Kim hadn't spoken the whole time, lost in some troubled country born of dream.

"What are we going to do there?" Dave had asked her diffidently, as if fearing to intrude.

And the white-haired girl beside him had roused herself to say, "You four will have to do whatever it takes, to give me enough time."

"For what?" Dave had said.

Kevin, too, had turned his head to look at Kim as she replied, far too matter-of-factly, "To raise a King from the dead and make him surrender a name. After that I'll be on my own."

Kevin had looked past her then, out the window, and seen stars beyond the wing; they were flying very high over deep waters.

⟡⟺◎⟺⟡

"What time is it?" Dave asked for the fifth time, fighting a case of nerves.

"After eleven," said Paul, continuing to fidget with a spoon. They were in the saloon bar of the hotel; he, Dave, and Jen at the table, Kevin, unbelievably, chatting up the waitress over by the bar. Or not, actually, unbelievably; he'd known Kevin Laine a long time.

"When the hell is she coming down?" Dave had an edge in his voice, a real one, and Paul could feel anxiety building in himself as well. It was going to be a very different place at night, he knew, with the crowds of the afternoon gone. Under stars, Stonehenge would move back in time a long way. There was a power here still, he could feel it, and he knew it would be made manifest at night.

"Does everyone know what they have to do?" he repeated.

"Yes, Paul," said Jennifer, surprisingly calm. They'd worked out their plans over dinner after returning from the monument. Kim hadn't left her room, not since they'd arrived.

Kevin strolled back to the table, with a full pint of beer.

"Are you drinking?" Dave said sharply.

"Don't be an idiot. While you two have been sitting here doing nothing, I've gotten the names of two of the guards out there. Len is the big bearded one, and there's another named Dougal, Kate says."

Dave and Paul were silent.

"Nicely done," said Jennifer. She smiled slightly.

"Okay," said Kim, *"let's go."* She was standing by the table in a bomber jacket and scarf. Her eyes were a little wild below the locks of white hair and her face was deathly pale. A single vertical line creased her forehead. She held up her hands; she was wearing gloves.

"It started to glow five minutes ago," she said.

And so she had come to the place and it was time indeed, here, now, to manifest herself, to show forth the Baelrath in a crimson blaze of power. It was the Warstone, found, not made, and very wild, but there was a war now, and the ring was coming into its force, carrying her with it past the high shrouded stones, the fallen one, and the tilting one, to the highest lintel stone. Beside which she stopped.

There was shouting behind her. Very far behind her. It was time. Raising her hand before her face Kimberly cried out in a cold voice, far from what she sounded like when allowed to be only herself, only Kim, and said into stillness, the waiting calm of that place, words of power upon power to summon its dead from beyond the walls of Night.

*"Damae Pendragon! Sed Baelrath riden log verenth. Pendragon rabenna, nisei damae!"*

There was no moon yet. Between the ancient stones, the Baelrath glowed brighter than any star. It lit the giant teeth of rock luridly. There was nothing subtle or mild, nothing beautiful about this force. She had come to coerce, by the power she bore and the secret she knew. She had come to summon.

And then, by the rising of a wind where none had been before, she knew she had.

Leaning forward into it, holding the Baelrath before her, she saw, in the very centre of the monument, a figure standing on the altar stone. He was tall and shadowed, wrapped in mist as in a shroud, only half incarnated in the half-light of star and stone. She fought the weight of him, the drag; he had been so long dead and she had made him rise.

No space for sorrow here, and weakness shown might break the summoning. She said:

"Uther Pendragon, attend me, for I command your will!"

"Command me not, I am a King!" His voice was high, stretched taut on a wire of centuries, but imperious still.

No space for mercy. None at all. She hardened her heart. "You are dead," she said coldly, in the cold wind. "And given over to the stone I bear."

"Why should this be so?"

The wind was rising. "For Ygraine deceived, and a son falsely engendered." The old, old telling.

Uther drew himself to his fullest height, and he was very tall above his tomb. "Has he not proven great beyond all measure?"

And thus: "Even so," said Kimberly, and there was a soreness in her now that no hardening could stay. "And I would call him by the name you guard."

The dead King spread his hands to the watching stars. "Has he not suffered enough?" the father cried in a voice that overrode the wind.

To this there was no decent reply, and so she said, "I have no time, Uther, and he is needed. By the burning of my stone I compel you—*what is the name?*"

She could see the sternness of his face, and steeled her own that he might read no irresolution there. He was fighting her; she could feel the earth pulling him away, and down.

"Do you know the place?" Uther Pendragon asked.

"I know."

And in his eyes, as if through mist or smoke, she saw that he knew this was so, and with the Baelrath would master him. Her very soul was turning over with the pain of it. So much steel she could not be, it seemed.

He said, "He was young when it happened, the incest, and the rest of it. He was afraid, because of the prophecy. Can they not have pity? Is there none?"

What was she that the proud Kings of the dead should beseech her so? "The name!" said Kimberly into the keening of the wind, and she raised the ring above her head to master him.

And, mastered, he told her, and it seemed as if stars were falling everywhere, and she had brought them tumbling down from heaven with what she was.

She was sheer red, she was wild, the night could not hold her. She could rise, even now, to come down as red moonlight might fall, but not here. In another place.

It was high. High enough to have once been an island in a lake like glass. Then the waters had receded all over Somerset, leaving a plain where waters had been, and a seven-ridged hill high above that plain. But when a place has been an island the memory of water lingers, and of water magic, no matter how far away the sea may be, or how long ago it fell away.

And so it was with Glastonbury Tor, which had been called Avalon in its day and had seen three queens row a dying king to its shore.

So much of the filtered legends had been close to true, but the rest was so far off it carried its own grief with it. Kim looked around the summit of the Tor and saw the thin moon rise in the east above the long plain. The Baelrath was beginning to fade even as she watched, and with it the power that had carried her here.

There was a thing to do while it yet burned, and raising the ring she turned, a beacon in the night, back to face Stonehenge, so many miles away. She reached out as she had done once before, though it was easier now, she was very strong tonight, and she found the four of them, gathered them together, Kevin and Paul, Jennifer and Dave, and before the Warstone faded, she sent them to Fionavar with the last red wildness Stonehenge had engendered.

Then the light she bore became only a ring on her finger, and it was dark on the windy summit of the Tor.

There was enough moonlight for her to make out the chapel that had been erected there some seven hundred years ago. She was shivering, now, and not only with cold. The burning ring had lifted her, given her resolution beyond her ordinary reach. Now she was Kimberly Ford only, or it seemed that way, and she felt daunted here on this ancient mound that yet gave scent of sea wind here in the midst of Somerset.

She was about to do something terrible, to set once more in motion the workings of a curse so old it made the wind seem young.

There had been a mountain, though, in the northland of Fionavar, and once it had held a god prisoner. Then there had been a detonation so vast it could only mean one thing, and Rakoth the Unraveller had been no longer bound. There was so much power coming down on them, and if Fionavar was lost then all the worlds would fall to Maugrim, and the Tapestry be torn and twisted on the Worldloom past redress.

She thought of Jennifer in Starkadh.

She thought of Ysanne.

With the ring quiescent on her hand, no power in her but the name she knew, terrible and merciless, she drew upon her need for strength in that high dark place and spoke in her own voice the one word that the Warrior needs must answer to:

*"Childslayer!"*

Then she closed her eyes, for the Tor, the whole Somerset Plain, seemed to be shaking with an agonized convulsion. There was a sound: wind, sorrow, lost music. He had been young and afraid, the dead father had said—and the dead spoke truth or lay silent—Merlin's prophecy had tolled a knell for the shining of the dream, and so he had ordered the children slain. Oh, how could one not weep? All the children, so that his incestuous, marring, foretold seed might not live to break the bright dream. Little more than a child himself he had been, but a thread had been entrusted to his name, and thus a world, and when the babies died . . .

When the babies died the Weaver had marked him down for a long unwinding doom. A cycle of war and expiation under many names, and in many worlds, that redress be made for the children and for love.

Kim opened her eyes and saw the low, thin moon. She saw the stars of spring hang brightly overhead, and she was not wrong in thinking they were brighter than they had been before.

Then she turned and, in the celestial light, saw that she was not alone in that high enchanted place.

He was no longer young. How could he have been young after so many wars? His beard was dark, though flecked with grey, and his eyes not yet fixed in time. She thought she saw stars in them. He leaned upon a sword, his hands wrapped around the hilt as if it were the only certain thing in the wide night, and then he said in a voice so gentle and so weary it found her heart, "I was Arthur here, my lady, was I not?"

"Yes," she whispered.

"I have carried other names elsewhere."

"I know." She swallowed. "This is your true name, though, your first."

"Not the other?"

*Oh, what was she?* "Not that. I will never tell it, or speak it again. I give you an oath."

Slowly he straightened. "Others will, though, as others have before."

"I cannot do anything to alter that. I only summoned because of our need."

He nodded. "There is war here?"

"In Fionavar."

At that he drew himself up: not so tall as his father had been, yet majesty lay about him like a cloak, and he lifted his head into the rising wind as if hearing a distant horn.

"Is this the last battle, then?"

"If we lose, it will be."

On the words, he seemed to coalesce, as if acceptance ended his passage from wherever he had been. There were no longer stars in the depths of his eyes; they were brown, and kind, and of the broad, tilled earth.

"Very well," said Arthur.

And that mild affirmation was what, finally, broke Kimberly. She dropped to her knees and lowered her face to weep.

A moment later she felt herself lifted, effortlessly, and wrapped in an embrace so encompassing she felt, on that lonely elevation, as if she had come home after long voyaging. She laid her head on his broad chest, felt the strong beating of his heart, and took comfort even as she grieved.

After a time he stepped back. She wiped away her tears and saw, without surprise, that the Baelrath was aglow again. She was aware, for the first time, of how weary she felt, with so much power channeling itself through her. She shook her head: no time, none at all, to be weak. She looked at him.

"Have I your forgiveness?"

"You never needed it," Arthur said. "Not half as much as I need all of yours."

"You were young."

"They were babies," he said quietly. And then, after a pause, "Are they there yet, the two of them?"

And the hurting in his voice laid bare for her, for the first time, the true nature of how he had been cursed. She should have known, it had been there to see. *For the children and for love.*

"I don't know," she said, with difficulty.

"They always are," he said, "because I had the babies killed."

There was no answer to make, and she didn't trust her voice in any case. Instead she took him by the hand, and holding high the Baelrath once again with the last strength she had, she crossed with Arthur Pendragon, the Warrior Condemned, to Fionavar and war.

# PART II

# OWEIN

# CHAPTER 4

Ruana essayed the thin chant, having only Iraima to aid him. He had scant hope it would carry as far as it had to go, but there was nothing else he could think of to do. So he lay in the dark, listening to the others dying around him, and he chanted the warnsong and the savesong over and over again. Iraima helped when she could, but she was very weak.

In the morning their captors found that Taieri had died, and he was taken out and devoured. After, the ones outside burned his bones for warmth against the bitter cold. Ruana choked on the smoke that drifted from the pyre. It had been placed in front of the cave, to make breathing harder for them. He heard Iraima coughing. They would not be killed directly, he knew, for fear of the bloodcurse, but they had been without food in the caves a long time now, and breathing the smoke of their brothers and sisters. Ruana wondered, abstractly, what it would be like to feel hate or rage. Closing his eyes, he chanted the kanior once for Taieri, knowing it was not being done in proper accordance with the rites, and asking forgiveness for this. Then he began the other two again in cycle, the warnsong and the savesong, over and over. Iraima joined in with him awhile, and Ikatere as well, but mostly Ruana sang alone.

⟡

They climbed up to Atronel over the green grass, and the high ones of all three Marks were there before Ra-Tenniel. Only Brendel was away south, in Paras Derval, so Heilyn represented the Kestrel. Galen and Lydan, the twins, stood forth for the Brein Mark, and fairest Leyse for the Swan, and she was clad in white as the Swan Mark always were, for memory of Lauriel. Enroth, who was eldest since Laien Spearchild had gone to his song, was there as well—Markless and of all Marks, as were the Eldest and the King alone.

Ra-Tenniel made the throne glow brightly blue, and fierce Galen smiled, though it could be seen that her brother frowned.

Leyse offered a flower to the King. "From by Celyn," she murmured. "There is a fair grove there, of silver and red sylvain."

"I would go with you to see them," Ra-Tenniel replied.

Leyse smiled, elusive. "Are we to open the sky tonight, Brightest Lord?"

He accepted the deflection. This time Lydan smiled.

"We are," said Ra-Tenniel. "Na-Enroth?"

"It is woven," the Eldest affirmed. "We will try to draw him forth from Starkadh."

"And if we do?" Lydan asked.

"Then we go to war," Ra-Tenniel replied. "But if we wait, or if the Dark One waits as he seems purposed to do, then our allies may be dead of this winter before Maugrim comes after us."

Heilyn spoke for the first time. "He has made the winter then? This is known?"

"It is known," Enroth replied. "And another thing is known. The Baelrath blazed two nights ago. Not in Fionavar, but it was on fire."

They stirred at that. "The Seer?" Lyse ventured. "In her world?"

"So it would seem," Enroth said. "Something new is threading across the Loom."

"Or something very old," Ra-Tenniel amended, and the Eldest bowed his head.

"Then why do we wait?" Galen cried. Her rich singer's voice carried to the others on the slopes of Atronel. A murmur like a note of music came to the six of them by the throne.

"We do not, once we are agreed," Ra-Tenniel replied. "Is it not bitterest irony that we who are named for Light should have been forced to cloak our land in shadow for this thousand years? Why should Daniloth be named the Shadowland? Would you not see the stars bright over Atronel, and send forth our own light in answer back to them?"

The music of agreement and desire was all about them on the mound. It carried even careful Lydan, and he, too, let his eyes reach crystal as Ra-Tenniel made the throne shine full bright, and, speaking the words necessary, he undid the spell Lathen Mistweaver had woven after the Bael Rangat. And the lios alfar, the Children of Light, sang then with one voice of praise to see the stars undimmed overhead, and to know that all over the northland of Fionavar the shining of Daniloth would illuminate the night for the first time in a thousand years.

It exposed them, of course, which was the gallant purpose of what they did. They made themselves a lure, the most tantalizing lure there could ever be, to draw Rakoth Maugrim down from Starkadh.

All night they stayed awake. No one would sleep, not with the stars to see, and then the waxing moon. And not with their borders open to the north, where they knew the Unraveller would be upon his towers among the Ice, seeing their taunting, iridescent glow. They sang in praise of the light, that their clear voices might reach him, too, and clearest of them all sang Ra-Tenniel, Lord of the lios alfar.

In the morning they put back the Mistweaver's shadowing. Those sent to keep watch by the borders returned to Atronel to report that a mighty storm was howling southward over the bleak, empty Plain.

⟶⊂⊃⟵

Light is swifter than wind. In the country south of Rienna the Dalrei saw the glow above Daniloth as soon as it went up. The newest storm would take some time to reach them.

Which is not to say it wasn't cold enough on watch by the gates where Navon of the third tribe took his turn on guard. Being a Rider among the Dalrei was still a glorious thing for one who had seen his animal so recently, but there were less pleasant aspects to it for a fourteen-year-old, staring out into the white night for wolves while the wind tore at his eltor cloak, seeking the thin bones underneath.

While word of the light far in the northwest ran wild through the clustered camps, Navon concentrated on his watch. He had slipped up on his first hunt as a Rider; his attempt at a flashy kill had been one of the failures that led Levon dan Ivor to risk his life trying Revor's Kill. Trying and succeeding. And though the hunt leader of the third tribe had never said a word to him, Navon had striven ever since to erase the memory of his folly.

The more so, because every member of the third tribe felt an added pride and responsibility after what had happened at Celidon when the snows began and the wolves had begun to kill the eltor. Navon remembered his first sickening sight of slaughtered grace in the land between the Adein and Celidon itself, mockingly near to the mid-Plain stones. For whereas the Dalrei might kill fifteen or twenty of the flying beasts on one hunt and only by adherance to their stern Law, that day the joined Riders of the third and eighth tribes had ridden over a swell of rising land, to see two hundred eltor lying in the snow, their blood shockingly red on the white drifts of the Plain.

It was the snow that had undone them. For the eltor, so fast over the grass that men spoke of a swift of eltor, not a herd, had hooves ill-adapted to the deep piled snow. They foundered in it, their fluid grace turning to ungainly, awkward motion—and they had become easy prey for the wolves.

Always in autumn the eltor went south to leave the snow behind, always the Dalrei followed them to this milder country on the fringes of the grazing lands of Brennin. But this year the snow had come early, and savagely, trapping the animals in the north. And then the wolves had come.

The Dalrei cursed, turning faces of grief and rage to the north. But curses had done no good, nor had they stayed the next bad thing, for the winds had carried the killing snow all the way south to Brennin. Which meant there was no safe place for the eltor anywhere on the Plain.

And so Dhira of the first tribe had issued a Grand Summoning to Celidon of all nine chieftains and their shamans and advisers. And venerable Dhira had risen up—everyone knew the story by now—and asked, "Why does Cernan of the Beasts allow this slaughter?"

And only one man of that company had stood to make reply.

"Because," Ivor of the third tribe had said, "he cannot stop it. Maugrim is stronger than he, and I will name him now by his name, and say Rakoth."

His voice had grown stronger to quell the murmuring that came at the never-spoken name.

"We must name him and know him for what he is, for no longer is he a presence of nightmare or memory. He is real, he is here now, and we must go to war against him for our people and our land, ourselves and with our allies, or there will be no generations after us to ride with the eltor on the wide Plain. We will be slaves to Starkadh, toys for svart alfar. Each man in this Gathering must swear by the stones of Celidon, by this heart of our Plain, that he will not live to see that sunless day. There is no Revor here with us, but we are the sons of Revor, and the heirs to his pride and to the High King's gift of the Plain. Men of the Dalrei, shall we prove worthy of that gift and that pride?"

Navon shivered in the dark as the remembered words ran through his mind. Everyone knew of the roar that had followed Ivor's speech, exploding outward from Celidon as if it might run all the white leagues north, through Gwynir and Andarien, to shake the very walls of Starkadh.

And everyone knew what had followed when mild, wise Tulger of the eighth tribe had risen in his turn to say, simply, "Not since Revor have the nine tribes had one Lord, one Father. Should we have an Aven now?"

"Yes!" the Gathering had cried. (Everyone knew.)

"Who shall that be?"

And in this fashion had Ivor dan Banor of the third tribe become the first Aven of all the Plain in a thousand years, his name exploding in its turn from the holy place.

They all showed it, Navon thought, pulling his cloak more tightly about him against the keening wind. All of the third tribe partook of both the glory and the responsibility, and Ivor had made sure they had no special status in the distribution of labours.

Celidon would be safe, he'd decided. No wolves would enter there as yet, risking the deep, ancient power that bound the circle of the standing stones or the House that stood inside them.

The eltor were the first priority for now. The animals had finally made their way south to the country by the River Latham, and thither the tribes would follow them; the hunters would circle the gathered swifts—though the name was a mockery in snow—and the camps would be on constant alert against attack.

And so it had come to be. Twice had the wolves ventured to attack one of the protected swifts, and twice had the racing auberei gotten word to the nearest camp in time to beat back the marauders.

Even now, Navon thought, pacing from north to south along the wooden outer wall, even now Levon, the Aven's son, was out there in the bitter cold on night duty around the large swift near the camp of the third tribe. And with him was the one who had become Navon's own hero—though he would have blushed and denied it had the thought been attributed to him by anyone. Still, no man in any tribe, not even Levon himself, had killed as many wolves or ridden so many nights of guard as had Torc dan Sorcha. He had been called "the Outcast" once, Navon remembered, shaking his head in what he thought was an adult disbelief. Not any longer. The silent deadliness of Torc was a byword now among the tribes.

His tribe had more than its share of heroes these days, and Navon was determined not to let them down. He peered keenly into the dark south, a fourteen-year-old sentinel, and not the youngest either.

But youngest or not, he was first to see and hear the lone auberei come galloping up, and it was Navon who raised the alarm, while the auberei went on to the next camp without pausing to rest his horse.

It was, evidently, a major attack.

A very major attack, Torc realized, as he saw the dark, fluid shapes of the wolves bear down on the huge swift that the third and seventh tribes were guarding together. Or trying to guard, he amended inwardly, racing to Levon's side for the hunt leader's orders. This was going to be bad; the wolves were in force this time. In the growing chaos he rose up in his saddle and scanned the swift: the four lead eltor were still roped and held, an ugly thing but necessary, for if this enormous, mingled swift were to take flight then chaos would become hopelessness. As long as the leaders stayed, the swift would hold together, and the eltor were horned and could fight.

And they *were* fighting, he saw, as the lead edge of the wolf attack reached them. It was an unholy scene: wolf snarls, the high-pitched cries of the eltor, the lurid, weaving torches the Riders bore in the darkness, and then eltor blood on the snow again.

Rage threatened to choke Torc's breathing. Forcing himself to stay calm, he saw that the right front edge of the swift was undermanned, and the wolves were racing around for it.

Levon saw it too. "Doraid!" he shouted to the hunt leader of the seventh. "Take half your men for the near flank!"

Doraid hesitated. "No," he said, "I have another idea. Why don't we—"

At which point he found himself pulled from his horse and hurtling into the snow. Torc didn't stop to see where he fell. "Riders of the seventh," he screamed over the noise of the battle, *"follow me!"*

Tabor dan Ivor, bearing a torch for his brother, saw that the hunters of the seventh did indeed follow. His heart swelled, even amid the carnage, to see how the reputation of Torc dan Sorcha enforced obedience. No man on the Plain had a more defiant hatred of the Dark than the black-clad Rider of the third tribe, whose only concession to the winter winds was an eltor vest over his bare chest. His aura was such now that the hunters of another tribe would follow him without a question asked.

Torc beat the wolves to the flank, barely. He and the Riders of the seventh smashed, swords scything, into the wolf pack. They cut it in two and wheeled swiftly to knife back the other way.

"Cechtar," Levon said, cool as ever. "Take twenty men around the other way. Guard the lead eltor on that side."

"Done!" Cechtar cried, flamboyant as always, and raced off over the powdered snow with a group of Riders at his heels.

Rising as high as he could in the saddle, Tabor almost fell, but he balanced himself and, turning to Levon, said, "The auberei got through. I see torches coming from the camp!"

"Good," said Levon grimly, looking the other way. "We are going to need them all."

Wheeling his horse to follow his brother's glance, Tabor saw them too, and his heart clenched like a fist.

There were urgach coming up from the south.

The savage creatures were mounted on beasts such as Tabor had never seen—huge six-legged steeds, as monstrous as their riders, with a viciously curved horn protruding from their heads.

"We seem to have a fight here," said Levon, almost to himself. And then, turning to Tabor with a smile, he said, "Come, my brother, it is our turn."

And the two sons of Ivor, the one tall and fair, the other young yet, nut-brown and wiry, hurled their horses forward towards the advancing line of the urgach.

Try as he could, Tabor couldn't keep up, and Levon soon outdistanced him. He did not ride alone though, for angling to intercept his path, low on his flying horse, came a Rider in black leggings and an eltor vest.

Together Levon and Torc raced directly towards the wide line of the urgach. There are too many, Tabor thought, trying furiously to catch up. He was closer than anyone else, and so saw what happened best of all. Thirty paces from the advancing urgach, Levon and Torc, without a word spoken, suddenly wheeled their horses at right angles, and racing across the line of the huge, six-legged steeds, fired three arrows each at dazzling speed.

Six of the urgach fell.

Tabor, however, was in no position to cheer. Churning fiercely forward in Torc and Levon's wake he suddenly found himself galloping with only a torch in his hand right at the line of monsters.

He heard Levon scream his name, not very helpfully. Swallowing a fifteen-year-old's yelp of apprehension, Tabor angled his horse for a gap in the onrushing line. An urgach, hairy and huge, changed course to intercept him.

"Cernan!" Tabor cried and hurled the torch even as he swung himself under the belly of his horse. He heard the whistle of a sword where his head had been, a guttural roar of pain as the flung torch struck hair and flesh, and then he was through the line and riding away from the fight over the wide sweeping beauty of the white Plain under a waxing moon and all the stars.

Not for long. He checked his horse and turned it, reaching for the small sword slung from his saddle. There was no need—none of the urgach had come after him. Instead they smashed viciously into the terrified eltor and then, hewing and carving the screaming animals like so much meat, they swung, en masse, and hit the left side contingent of Dalrei with a brutal force. There were reinforcements coming—Tabor could see the torches streaming towards them from the camps in the distance but they were not going to be enough, he thought despairingly, not against the urgach.

Levon and Torc were speeding to attack again, he saw, but the urgach were deep within the mass of Riders, their gigantic swords wreaking havoc among the hunters while the wolves, unimpeded, ran wild through the eltor.

He heard hoofbeats behind him. Sword raised, he spun his horse frantically. And a glad cry escaped his throat.

*"Come on, little brother!"* someone shouted, and then Dave Martyniuk thundered by, an axe of Brennin held high, a golden Prince racing beside him and thirty men behind.

Thus did the warriors of Brennin come to the aid of the Dalrei, led by Prince Diarmuid and by the one called Davor, huge and fell, wrapped in battle fury like a red halo under the waxing moon.

Tabor saw them crash in their turn, these trained soldiers of Diarmuid's band, into the nearest wolf pack, and he saw their swords descend in silver sweeps and rise again, dark with blood. Then they hit the massed phalanx of the urgach with Torc and Levon, and brave Cechtar beside, and over the squeals of the dying eltor, the snarl of wolves, Tabor heard, rising above the torchlit carnage, the voice of Davor cry, "Revor!" once and again, and he was young in the tidal wave of his relief and pride.

Then, suddenly, he was young no more, nor was he only a fifteen-year-old newly called Rider of the Dalrei.

From his vantage point behind the battle scene and on a slope above it Tabor saw, off to the east, a dark mass approaching very fast, and he realized that the Dalrei were not the only ones to be receiving reinforcements. And if he could see the urgach at such a distance, then there were very many, there were too many, and so.

And so it was time.

*Beloved.* He formed the thought in his mind.

*I am here,* he heard instantly. *I am always here. Would you ride?*

*I think we must,* Tabor sent reply. *It is time for us, bright one.*

*We have ridden before.*

He remembered, would always remember. *But not to battle. We will have to kill.*

A new note in the mind voice: *I was made for war. And to fly. Summon me.*

Made for war. It was true, and a grief, but the urgach were nearer now, and so.

And so in his mind Tabor spoke her name. *Imraith-Nimphais,* he called, on a cresting of love, and he dismounted from his horse, for on the words she was in the sky above him, more glorious than anything on earth, the creature of his dreaming.

She landed. Her horn was luminous, a silver such as the silver of the moon, though her coat was deep red as had been the moon that gave her life. And where she walked, the snow showed no imprint of her hooves, so lightly did she move.

It had been a long time. His heart full as with light, he raised a hand and she lowered her head, the single horn grazing him like a caress, that he might in turn caress her head.

*Only each other,* he heard, and he sent back affirmation and acceptance. Then: *Shall we fly?* she asked.

He could feel the straining desire run through her, and then through himself, and he said aloud, *"Let us fly, and kill, my darling."*

And Tabor dan Ivor mounted himself upon the flying creature of his vigil, the double-edged gift of Dana that was to bear him, young as they both were, into the sky and away from the world of men. And Imraith-Nimphais did so. She left the ground for the cold wide heavens, carrying the Rider who alone of all creatures had dreamt her name, and to the men below they were as an unleashed comet between the stars and the Plain.

Then Tabor said within, *You see?*

And: *I do,* she replied.

He turned her to where the urgach were riding to the battlefield, and they came down upon them like a killing light. She changed as they sped down, and with her shining horn she killed once, and once more, and many, many times again under the guidance of his hand. And the urgach fled before them and they pursued, slaying, and the wolves broke and fled also, southward away, and the Dalrei and the men of Brennin cheered, amazed and exultant to see the shining thing from heaven come to their aid.

She heard them not, nor did he. They pursued, killing until her horn was sticky and clotted with blood and there were no more of the loathsome creatures of the Dark to slay.

And finally, trembling with weariness and the shock of aftermath, they came down in a white place far from blood and Tabor cleaned her horn with snow. After, they stood close together in the wide silence of the night.

*Only each other,* she sent.

*Only each other at the last,* he replied. Then she flew off, glittering, and as dawn broke over the mountains he began the long walk back to the camps of men.

# CHAPTER 5

"The first battle is always the worst," Carde said, moving his horse towards Kevin so no one else would hear.

The words were meant to be reassuring, and Kevin managed a gesture of acknowledgment, but he was not prone to be dishonest with himself and he knew that the shock of battle, though real, was not his deepest problem.

Nor was it envy of Dave Martyniuk, though honesty compelled admission that this was also a part of his mood now, just after it had all ended, with the electrifying appearance of the winged, shining creature in the sky. Dave had been extraordinary, almost terrifying. Wielding the huge axe Matt Sören had found for him in the Paras Derval armory, he had roared into battle, outpacing even Diarmuid and wreaking violent havoc among the wolves while screaming at the top of his lungs. The big man had even gone one-on-one with one of the enormous, fanged brutes they called urgach. And he had killed it too; blocking a vicious sword thrust, he had launched a backhanded sweep of the axe that had half severed the creature's head and sent it tumbling from the back of its giant steed. Then Dave had killed the six-legged horned beast as well.

And Kevin? Quick, sharp Kevin Laine had been his torchbearer at the time. Oh, they'd given him a sword to fight with, but what did he know about fighting wolves with a sword on horseback? Staying on the plunging horse was challenge enough in the screaming inferno of that fight. And when he had gained enough space to realize how utterly useless he was, Kevin had swallowed his pride, sheathed the sword, and grabbed a burning torch to give Dave light enough by which to kill. He hadn't been too good at that, either, and twice had been nearly felled himself by Dave's whirling axe.

They had won, though, this first real battle of the war, and something magnificent had been revealed in the sky. Kevin clung to the splendour of that image of the winged unicorn and tried to lift himself enough to share the triumph of the moment.

Yet it seemed that someone else wasn't happy; there was a confrontation taking place. He and Carde edged their horses closer to the knot of men surrounding a husky brown-haired Rider and Torc, Dave's friend, whom Kevin remembered from their last days in Paras Derval.

"And if you ever do so again," the brown-haired man was saying loudly, "I will cripple you and stake you out in the Plain with honey on your eyes to draw the aigen!"

Torc, impassive on his dark grey horse, made no reply, and the other man's blustered threat fell fatuously into the silence. Dave was grinning. He was sitting his horse between Torc and Levon, the other Rider Kevin remembered from their last time.

It was Levon who spoke, quietly but with immense authority. "Doraid, be done. And hear me: you were given a direct command in battle, and you chose that moment to discuss strategies. If Torc had not done what I asked you to do, the wolves would have turned the flank of the swift. Do you wish to explain your action here or before the Aven and the leader of your tribe?"

Doraid turned to him furiously. "Since when does the third tribe command the seventh?"

"It does not," Levon replied with equanimity. "But I command this guard, and you were there when that command was given me."

"Ah, yes!" Doraid sneered. "The precious son of the Aven. He is to be obeyed, and—"

"One moment!" a familiarly inflected voice snapped, and Doraid stopped in mid-word. "Do I understand what happened here?" Diarmuid continued, moving into the ring of Riders. "Did this man refuse a direct order? And is he complaining about it now?" The tone was acid.

"He did," Torc spoke for the first time. "And he is. You do understand correctly, my lord Prince."

Kevin had a blinding attack of déjà vu: an innyard to the south, a farmer crying, "Mörnir guard you, young Prince!" And then something else.

"Coll," Diarmuid said.

"No!" Kevin screamed and launched himself in a flat dive from his horse. He hit his friend, Diarmuid's big lieutenant, with a tackle that sent them both flying to land with a double crunch in the snow among the stamping horses of the Dalrei.

He was about a half second too late. There was another man lying in the snow, not far away: Doraid, with Coll's arrow buried deep in his chest.

"Oh, hell," Kevin said, sick at heart. "Oh, bloody hell."

Nor was he eased to hear a chuckle beside him. "Nicely done," Coll said softly, not at all discomfited. "You almost broke my nose again."

"God. Coll, I'm sorry."

"No matter." He chuckled again. "I was half expecting you, in fact. I remember you don't like his justice."

No one was even looking at them. His wild leap seemed to have been utterly pointless. From where he lay on the ground, he saw two men face each other in the ring of torches.

"There were enough Dalrei dead tonight without adding another," Levon said evenly.

Diarmuid's voice was cool. "There will be enough dead in this war without our risking more by allowing what this man did."

"It was a matter then for us, for the Aven, to decide."

"Not so," Diarmuid replied. For the first time he raised his voice. "Let me remind you all, and better now than later, of how things are. When Revor was given the Plain for himself and his heirs, he swore an oath of loyalty to Colan. Let it not be forgotten. Ivor dan Banor, Aven of the Dalrei, holds that title in the same way that Revor himself did: under the High King of Brennin, who is Aileron dan Ailell, and to whom you swore an oath of your own, Levon!"

Levon's colour was high, but his eyes never wavered. "I do not forget it," he said. "Justice is still not served by arrows at night on a battlefield."

"Not so," Diarmuid said a second time. "There is seldom time in war to serve it any other way. What," he asked softly, "does the Law of the Dalrei invoke for what Doraid did this night?"

It was Torc who answered. "Death," he said clearly. "He is right, Levon."

Still on the ground with Coll, Kevin realized that Diarmuid, pupil, once, of Loren Silvercloak, had known exactly that. And after a moment he saw Levon nod his head.

"I know he is," he said. "I am my father's son, though, and I cannot order a death so easily. Will you forgive me, my lord Prince?"

For reply, Diarmuid swung down from his horse and walked over to Levon's. With a formal gesture he served as footman to help the other dismount, and then the two of them, both young, both fair, embraced, as the Dalrei and the men of Brennin shouted their approval.

"I feel like an idiot!" Kevin said to Coll. He helped the other man to his feet.

"We all feel that way sometimes," said the big man sympathetically. "Especially around Diar. Let's go get drunk, friend. The Riders make a lethal drink!"

They did. And there was a great deal of it. It didn't really lift his mood, though, nor did Diarmuid's indulgent response to his precipitate action earlier.

"I didn't know you liked Coll so much!" the Prince had said, triggering a round of laughter in the huge wooden house in which most of them had gathered.

Kevin faked a laugh; he couldn't think of a reply. He had never felt superfluous before, but more and more it was beginning to look as if he was. He noticed Dave—Davor they called him here—huddled with Levon, Torc, and a number of other Dalrei, including a teenage kid, all arms and legs and disordered hair who, he'd been given to understand, had ridden the unicorn that flew. He saw Diarmuid rise up and make his way through a giggling cluster of women to join the group. He thought about doing the same, knowing they would welcome him, but it seemed pointless somehow. He had nothing to contribute.

"More sachen?" a soft voice said in his ear. He tilted his head to see a pretty brown-haired girl holding a stone beaker. Coll winked surreptitiously and shifted a little bit away on the bench, making room.

Oh, well. "Okay," Kevin said. He smiled. "Are you joining me?"

Neatly she slipped in beside him. "For a little while," she said. "I'm supposed to be serving. I'll have to get up if my mother comes. My name is Liane dal Ivor."

He wasn't really in the mood, but she was bright and sharp and carried the ball herself much of the time. With an effort, wanting at least to be polite, Kevin did a little half-hearted flirting.

Later, her mother did appear, surveying the scene with a hostess's eye, and Liane scrambled off with a surprising oath to serve some more beakers of sachen. A little later the conclave at the far end broke up and Dave came over.

"We're leaving early in the morning," he said tersely "Levon wants to see Kim in Paras Derval."

"She wasn't there yet," Kevin protested.

"Gereint says she will be," the other replied, and without amplification strode off into the night, buttoning his coat against the cold.

Kevin glanced at Coll. They shrugged. At least the sachen was good; saved the evening from being a total write-off.

Much later, something else did as well. He hadn't been in his bed very long, was just feeling the heavy covers warming up, when the door opened and a slim figure bearing a candle slipped inslde.

"If you ask me for a beaker of sachen," Liane said, "I'll break it over your head. I hope you're warm in there." She placed the flame on the low table beside the bed and undressed. He saw her for a moment in the light; then she was under the blankets beside him.

"I like candles," she said.

It was the last thing either of them said for a long time. And again, despite everything, the curving act of love took him away with it, so far that the colours of the light seemed to change. Before the flame burnt out he saw her bend back above him like a bow, in her own transcending arc, and he would have spoken then if he could.

Later it was dark and she said, "Fear not. We went so deep because we are near to Gwen Ystrat. The old stories are true after all."

He shook his head. He had to travel a long way back to do that much, and farther still to speak. "Everywhere," he said. "This deep."

She stiffened. He hadn't meant it to wound. How to explain? But Liane stroked his forehead and in a different voice whispered, "So you carry Dun Maura within yourself?" Then she called him, as he thought, drifting, by another name. He wanted to ask. There were questions, but the tide was going out and he was far along with it, much too far.

In the morning when Erron woke him with a shake and a grin, she was, naturally, gone. Ncr did he see her before they rode off, the thirty men of Diarmuid's band, he and Dave, with Levon and Torc alongside.

⟨⇒◎⇐⟩

For Dave the journey northeast to the upper reaches of the Latham had promised reunion and in the end had offered both that and revenge. From the moment he'd understood that the man Diarmuid was to bring back was Gereint of the third tribe, his heart had begun racing with anticipation. There was no way they could have kept him from joining that party of the Prince's men. Loren wanted Gereint for some reason having to do with figuring out the winter, he gathered. That didn't matter so much to him; what mattered was that soon he would be among the Dalrei again.

The roads had been cleared east as far as Lake Leinan, but the going became harder as they turned north the next morning. Diarmuid had hoped to make the camps before sundown, but it was slow going among the drifts and into the teeth of the bitter wind that blew unobstructed down from the Plain. They had given Dave and Kevin wonderfully warm woven coats in Paras Derval. Lightweight, too—they knew how to work with wool and cloth here, that much was obvious. Without the coats they would have frozen. Even with them, when the sun went down, the going became very bad, and Dave had no idea how far away they were from the camps.

Then all thoughts of cold had disappeared, for they had seen torches moving in the night, heard the screams of dying animals and the shouts of men in battle.

Dave hadn't waited for anyone else. He'd kicked his big stallion forward and charged up over a mound of snow, to see a battlefield spread out before him, and, astride a horse between him and the melee, a fifteen-year-old boy he remembered.

Diarmuid, the elegant Prince, had caught up with him as they galloped past Tabor down the slope, but Dave was scarcely aware of anyone else as he plunged into the closest pack of wolves, hewing on either side, aiming straight for the closest urgach, with a memory of deaths by Llewenmere to drive him on.

He remembered little else, as battle fury overtook him. Kevin Laine had been beside him with a torch for light at one point and they told him afterwards that he had slain an urgach and its mount by himself. The six-legged horned beasts were called slaug, they told him. But that was after.

After Tabor, astonishingly, had appeared in the sky overhead, riding a lethal winged creature with a horn of its own that shone and killed.

After the moment when the wolves had fled and the slaug had borne the urgach away in flight, and he had dismounted to stand facing his brothers again. A great deal had been made whole then as he felt Torc's hard grip on his arm and then Levon's embrace.

There had been an interlude of some tension when Diarmuid had had a Dalrei slain for insubordination and then faced Levon down in a confrontation, but that, too, had ended all right. Kevin Laine, for no reason Dave could grasp, had tried to interfere, but no one else seemed to have taken much notice of it.

Then they had ridden back to the camp and to Ivor, who had a new title now but was still the same stocky, greying man he remembered, with the same deep-set eyes in a weather-beaten face. Ivor said, to lift Dave even higher, "Welcome home, Davor. A bright thread in darkness spins you back."

There had been sachen after, and good food by the fires, and many remembered faces. Including Liane's.

"How many times am I going to have to dance an urgach kill of yours?" she asked, bright-eyed, pert, her mouth soft on his cheek where she'd kissed him on tiptoe before moving off.

Tabor had come in quite a while later, and he'd wanted to embrace the boy but something in Tabor's face stopped him. It stopped all of them, even his father. It was then that Ivor had gestured Dave over to join a meeting around a smaller fire off to the side of the room.

With Dave, there were seven people there, and Diarmuid, carrying his own beaker, made a slightly disheveled eighth a moment later. Dave wasn't sure what he thought of this Prince; he'd been rather more impressed with Aileron, the older brother who was now High King. Diarmuid seemed altogether too suave for Dave's taste; on the other hand, there had been nothing soft about the pace he'd set on the ride, or the control he'd asserted in the matter of the Dalrei he'd ordered killed. Ivor, Dave noticed, hadn't brought the issue up either.

And Diarmuid, despite the drinking, seemed very much in command as he concisely outlined the wish of the High King and his First Mage that Gereint the shaman ride back with him to Paras Derval. There to join with the mages in seeking the source of the winter that was slowly grinding them all down under its malevolent heel.

"For it *is* malevolent," the Prince added quietly from where he'd crouched in front of blind Gereint. "The lios have confirmed what we've all guessed. We would like to leave tomorrow—if it suits the shaman, and all of you."

Ivor nodded an acknowledgment of the courteous proviso. No one spoke, though; they waited for Gereint.

Dave had still not gotten over the uneasiness he felt in the presence of this wrinkled ancient whose hollowed eye sockets seemed, nonetheless, to see into the souls of men and down the dark avenues of time. Cernan, god of the wild things, had spoken to Gereint, Dave remembered—and had called Tabor to his fast, to the animal they had seen in the sky. That thought led him to Ceinwen, and the stag in Faelin Grove. And this was his own dark avenue.

He turned from it to hear Gereint say, "We are going to need the Seer as well."

"She hasn't come yet," Diarmuid said.

Everyone looked at Dave. "She was bringing someone," he said. "She sent us ahead."

"Who was she bringing?" the man called Tulger asked from beside Ivor.

But a rare discretion led Dave to murmur, "I think that's for her to say, not me." Ivor, he saw, nodded his agreement.

Gereint smiled thinly. "True," the shaman said. "Although I know, and they have arrived by now. They were in Paras Derval before you left." This was exactly what drove Dave crazy about Gereint.

Diarmuid didn't seem bothered. "With Loren, probably," he murmured, smiling as if at a jest. Dave didn't get the joke. "Will you come then?" the Prince continued, addressing the shaman.

"Not to Paras Derval," Gereint replied placidly. "It is too far for my old bones."

"Well, surely—" Diarmuid began.

"I will meet you," Gereint went on, ignoring him, "in Gwen Ystrat. I will leave tomorrow for the Temple in Morvran. You will all be coming there."

This time even Diarmuid looked discomfited. "Why?" he asked.

"Which way did the wolves fly?" the shaman asked, turning unnervingly to where Torc sat.

"South," the dark man said, and they were silent. There was a burst of laughter from the largest fire. Dave glanced over involuntarily and saw, with a sudden chill, that Liane was sitting next to Kevin, and the two of them were whispering in each other's ears. His vision blurred. Goddamn that flashy skirt-chaser! Why did the slick, carefree Kevin Laines always have to be around to spoil things? Inwardly seething, Dave forced himself to turn back to the conclave.

"You will all be there," Gereint was repeating. "And Gwen Ystrat is the best place for what we will have to do."

Diarmuid stared at the blind shaman for a long moment. Then: "All right," he said. "I will tell my brother. Is there anything else?"

"One thing." It was Levon. "Dave, you have your horn."

The horn from Pendaran. With the note that was the sound of Light itself. "I do," Dave said. It was looped across his body.

"Good," said Levon. "Then if the Seer is in Paras Derval I would like to ride back with you. There is something I'd like to try before we go to Gwen Ystrat."

Ivor stirred at that, and turned to his elder son. "It is rash," he said slowly. "You know it is."

"I don't know," Levon replied. "I know we have been given Owein's Horn. Why else if not to use?" This was reasonable enough on its own terms to silence his father. It happened, however, to be quite wrong.

"What exactly are we talking about?" the Prince asked.

"Owein," Levon said tensely. There was a brightness in his face. "I want to wake the Sleepers and set free the Wild Hunt!"

It held them, if only for a moment.

"What fun!" said Diarmuid, but Dave could see a gleam in his eye, answering Levon's.

Only Gereint laughed, a low, unsettling sound. "What fun," the shaman repeated, chuckling to himself as he rocked back and forth.

It was just afterwards that they noticed that Tabor had fainted.

He'd revived by morning and come out, pale but cheerful, to bid them goodbye. Dave would have stayed with the Dalrei if he could, but they needed him for the horn, it seemed, and Levon and Torc were coming with them, so it was all right. And they'd be meeting again soon in Gwen Ystrat. Morvran was the place Gereint had named.

He was thinking about Gereint's laughter as they set off south again to meet the road to Paras Derval where it began to the west of Lake Leinan. In any normal weather, Levon said, they would have cut across the grazing lands of north Brennin, but not with the ice and snow of this unnatural season.

Kevin was riding, uncharacteristically subdued, with a couple of Diarmuid's men, including the one he'd so asininely jumped the night before. That was fine by Dave;

he wanted nothing to do with the other man. If people wanted to call it jealousy, let them. He didn't care enough to explain. He wasn't about to confide in anyone that he'd renounced the girl himself—to Green Ceinwen in the wood. Nor was he about to recount what the goddess had replied.

*She's Torc's,* he'd said.

*Has she no other choice?* Ceinwen had answered, and laughed before she disappeared.

That part was Dave's own business.

For now, though, he had catching up to do with the men he called his brothers, ever since a ritual in Pendaran Wood. Eventually the catching up took them to the moment in the muddy fields around Stonehenge where Kevin had been explaining to the guards in French and mangled English what he and Jennifer were doing necking in forbidden territory. It had been a remarkably effective performance, and it had lasted precisely until the moment when the four of them had felt the sudden shock of power gathering them together and hurling them into the cold, dark crossing between worlds.

# CHAPTER 6

It was, Jennifer realized, as the now-familiar cold of the crossing receded, the same room as the first time. Not the same as her second crossing, though, when she and Paul had come through so hard they had both fallen to their knees in the snow-drifted streets of the town.

It had been there, while Paul, still dazed, had struggled to his feet under the swinging sign of the Black Boar, that she had felt the first pangs of premature labour. And with these, as she grasped where he had somehow taken them, she had had a sudden memory of a woman crying in the shop doorway by the green, and her way had seemed very clear.

So they had come to Vae's house and Darien had been born, after which a great deal seemed to change within her. Since Starkadh she had become a creature of jarring angles and dislocated responses. The world, her own world, was tinted balefully, and the possibility of ever one day crossing back to ordinary human interaction seemed a laughable, hopeless abstraction. She had been carved open by Maugrim; what healing was there anywhere for that?

Then Paul had come and said what he had said, had opened with his tone, as much as anything, the glimmering of a path. However much Rakoth might be, he was not all, not everything; he had not been able to stop Kim from coming for her.

And he could not stop her child from being born.

Or so she thought until, with a lurch of terror, she had seen Galadan in their own world. And she had heard him say that she would die, which meant the child.

So she had said to Paul that she would curse him if he failed. How had she said such a thing? From where had that come?

It seemed another person, another woman entirely, and perhaps it was. For since the child had been born and named and sent out into the worlds of the Weaver to be her own response to what had been done to her, her one random weft of thread laid across the warp—since then, Jennifer had been astonished at how mild everything was.

No angles or jarrings any more. Nothing seemed to hurt; it was all too far away. She had found herself capable of dealing with others, of surprising acts of gentleness. There were no storm winds any more; no sunshine either. She moved in slow motion, it sometimes seemed, through a landscape of grey, with grey clouds overhead; at times, but only at times, the memory of colour, of vibrancy, would come to her like the low surge of a distant sea.

And all this was fine. It was not health; she was wise enough to understand that much, but it was infinitely better than what had been before. If she could not be happy and whole, at least she could be . . . mild.

The gentleness was an unexpected gift, a compensation of sorts for love, which had been mangled in Starkadh, and for desire, which had died.

Being touched was a difficult thing—not a sharp, hurting problem, but difficult, and when it happened she could feel herself twisting inwardly, a small fragile person who had once been Jennifer Lowell and golden. Even the dissembling at Stonehenge earlier that night, where she and Kevin had deceived the guards into believing that they were Gallic lovers seeking the pagan blessing of the stones—even then it had been difficult to feel his mouth on hers before the guards came. And impossible not to let him sense this, for it was hard to hide things from Kevin. But how, from this mild grey country in which she moved, did one tell a former lover, and the kindest of them all, that he had lain with her in Starkadh, obscene and distorted, black blood dripping from his severed hand to burn her flesh? How to explain that there was no going back past that, or forward from that place?

She had let him hold her, had simulated embarrassed dismay when the guards had come up to them, and had smiled and pouted mutely, as instructed, while Kevin launched into his frantic, incoherent explanation.

Then she had felt the gathering and the cold, as Kim took hold of them, and now they were in this room, their first room in Paras Derval, and it was night again.

The tapestry was the same and the torches were blazing this time, so they could make it out properly: the dazzlingly crafted depiction of Iorweth the Founder in the Godwood, before the Summer Tree. Jennifer, Kevin, and Dave glanced at it, then all three of them looked, instinctively, at Paul.

Scarcely pausing to acknowledge the tapestry, he moved quickly to the unguarded doorway. There had been a guard the last time, Jennifer remembered, and Matt Sören had thrown a knife.

This time, Paul stepped into the corridor and called softly. There was a noisy clatter of weaponry, and a moment later a terrified boy, in gear a size too large for him, came forward down the corridor with a bow drawn none too steadily.

"I know you," said Paul, ignoring the bow. "You're Tarn. You were the King's page. Do you remember me?"

The bow was lowered. "I do, my lord. From the ta'bael game. You are . . ." There was awe in the boy's face.

"I am Pwyll, yes," Schafer said simply. "Are you a guard now, Tarn?"

"Yes, my lord. I am too old to be a page."

"So I see. Is the High King in the palace tonight?"

"Yes, my lord. Shall I—"

"Why don't you lead us to him," Paul said. It was Kevin who heard, and remembered hearing before, the crisp tone in Schafer's voice. There had been an undeniable tension between Paul and Aileron when last they had met. Apparently it still existed.

They followed the boy through a web of corridors and down one drafty flight of stone stairs before they came at length to a pair of doors that only Paul remembered.

Tarn knocked and withdrew; after a startled glance, a tall guard admitted them.

The room had changed, Paul saw. The gorgeous wall hangings had been taken down, and in their place had been hung a sequence of maps and charts. Gone, too, were the deep armchairs he remembered; in their place were a number of hard wooden seats and a long bench.

The chessboard with its exquisitely carved pieces was nowhere to be seen. Instead, a huge table stood in the middle of the room and on it lay an enormous map of Fionavar. Bent over the map, his back to the door, stood a man of average height, simply dressed in brown, with a fur vest over his shirt against the cold.

"Who is it, Shain?" the man said, not pausing in his scrutiny of the map.

"If you turn around you can see for yourself," Paul Schafer said before the guard could make reply

And, very fast, Aileron did turn, almost before Paul's voice died away. His eyes above the beard blazed with an intensity three of them remembered.

"Mörnir be praised!" the High King exclaimed, taking a few quick steps towards them. Then he stopped and his face changed. He looked from one to another. "Where is she?" cried Aileron dan Ailell. *"Where is my Seer?"*

"She's coming," Kevin said, moving forward. "She's bringing someone with her."

"Who?" Aileron snapped.

Kevin looked at Paul, who shook his head. "She'll tell you herself, if she succeeds. I think it is hers to tell, Aileron."

The King glared at Paul as if minded to pursue it further, but then his face softened. "Very well," he said "So long as she is coming. I have . . . very great need of her." After a moment a wry tone came into his voice. "I am bad at this, am I not? You deserve a fairer greeting, all of you. And is this Jennifer?"

He came to stand before her. She remembered his brother and their first meeting. This one, austere and self-contained, did not call her a peach, nor did he bend to kiss her hand. Instead, he said awkwardly, "You have suffered in our cause, and I am sorry for it. Are you well now?"

"Well enough," she said. "I'm here."

His eyes searched hers. "Why?" Aileron asked.

A good question and one nobody had asked her, not even Kim. There was an answer, but she wasn't about to give it now to this abrasive young King of Brennin. "I've come this far," she said levelly, meeting his look with her own light green eyes. "I'll stay the course."

Men better versed in dealing with women had broken off a stare when faced with

Jennifer's gaze. Aileron turned away. "Good," he said, walking back to the map on the table. "You can help. You will have to tell us everything you remember of Starkadh."

"Hey!" Dave Martyniuk said. "That's not fair. She was badly hurt there. She's trying to forget!"

"We need to know," Aileron said. Men, he could outface.

"And you don't care how you find out?" Kevin asked, a dangerous quality in his voice.

"Not really," the King replied. "Not in this war."

The silence was broken by Jennifer. "It's all right," she said. "I'll tell what I can remember. But not to you"—she indicated the King—"or any of the rest of you either, I'm afraid. I'll talk about it to Loren and Matt. No one else."

The mage had grown older since last they had seen him. There was more white among the grey of his beard and hair, deeper lines in his face. His eyes were the same as ever, though: commanding and compassionate at the same time. And Matt Sören hadn't changed at all, not even the Dwarf's twisted grimace that passed for a smile.

They all recognized it for what it was, though, and after the brittleness of Aileron the greeting they received from mage and source marked, for all of them, their true return to Fionavar. When Matt took her hand between his own two calloused ones, Jennifer cried.

"We never knew," Loren Silvercloak said, a roughness in his voice. "We didn't know if she pulled you out. And only Jaelle heard the last warning about Starkadh. It saved many lives. We would have attacked."

"And then the winter came," Aileron said. "And there was no hope of attack or anything. We've been unable to do anything at all."

"We can offer wine to our guests," the Dwarf said tartly.

"Shain, find some cups and serve anyone who wants it," Aileron said absently. "We need Kim badly," he went on. "We have to find out how Maugrim is controlling the winter—it was not a thing he could ever do before. The lios have confirmed that."

"He's making it worse?" Paul asked soberly.

There was a silence. Loren broke it. "You don't understand," he said softly. "He is making it. He has twisted the seasons utterly. These snows have been here for nine months, Pwyll. In six nights it will be Midsummer's Eve."

They looked out the window. There was ice on the glass. It was snowing again, and a bitter wind was howling about the walls. Even with two fires blazing in the room and torches everywhere, it was very cold.

"Oh, God!" said Dave abruptly. "What's happening to the Dalrei?"

"They are gathered near the Latham," Loren said. "The tribes and the eltor."

"Just in that corner?" Dave exclaimed. "The whole Plain is theirs!"

"Not now," Aileron said, and there was helpless anger in his voice. "Not while this winter lasts."

"Can we stop it?" Kevin asked.

"Not until we know how he is doing it," Loren replied.

"And so you want Kim?" Paul said. He had walked away from the others to stand by the window.

"And someone else. I want to bring Gereint here, Ivor's shaman. To see if all of us together can break through the screen of ice and snow to find their source. If we do not," the mage said, "we may lose this war before it begins. And we must not lose this war."

Aileron said nothing. It was all in his eyes.

"All right," said Jennifer carefully. "Kim's on her way, I think. I hope. In the meantime, I guess I have some things to tell Loren and Matt."

"Now?" Kevin asked.

"Why not?" She smiled, though not an easy smile. "I'll just take some of that wine, Shain. If nobody minds."

She and the mage and his source withdrew into an inner chamber. The others looked at each other.

"Where's Diarmuid?" Kevin said suddenly.

"Where do you think?" Aileron replied.

⋯⇒◉⇐⋯

About half an hour earlier, shortly after Matt and Loren had left for the palace, Zervan of Seresh had lain in his bed in the mages' quarters, not sleeping.

He had no real duties left: he had built up the front-room fire to a level that should last the night, and he knew that if Brock returned before the other two, he'd build it up again for them.

It was never a hard life being servant to the mages. He had been with them now for twenty years, ever since they had told him he was not cut from mage cloth himself. It hadn't been a surprise; he'd sensed it very early. But he had liked all three of them—even, though it was a bitter memory, Metran, who had been clever before he had been old, before he turned out to be a traitor. He had liked Paras Derval, too, the energy of the town, the nearness of the palace. It was nice being at the centre of things.

When Teyrnon had asked him, Zervan had been pleased to stay on and serve the mages.

Over twenty years the original liking had grown to something akin to love. The four of them who were left, Loren and Teyrnon, Matt and Barak, were the nearest to family that Zervan had, and he worried over them all with a fussy, compulsive eye for detail.

He had been briefly ruffled when Brock of Banir Tal had come to live with them a year before. But although the new Dwarf was obviously of high rank among his people, he was unobtrusive and undemanding, and Zervan quite approved of his manifest devotion to Matt Sören. Zervan had always thought Matt drove himself too hard, and it was good to have Brock around in support, sharing the same view.

It was from Brock that Zervan had come to understand the source of Matt's occasional descents into deep moodiness and a silence that was marked even in one of taciturn nature. It was clear now to Zervan: Matt Sören, who had been King under Banir Lök, was silent and grim when he was fighting off the ceaseless pull of Calor Diman, the Crystal Lake. All Dwarf Kings, Brock had explained, spent a full moon night beside that lake between the twin mountains. If they survived what they saw, and were still sane, they could claim the Diamond Crown. And never, Brock said, never would they be free of the tidal pull of Calor Diman. It was this tide, Zervan understood, that so often pulled Loren's source awake at night, around the time of the full moon, to pace his room with a measured tread, back and forth, unsleeping until dawn.

But tonight it was Zervan himself who could not sleep. Matt was in the palace with Loren. Brock, tactfully, had excused himself to go off to the Black Boar. He often did something like that, to leave mage and source alone. Zervan, alone in the house, was awake because, twice now, he had heard a sound from outside his window.

The third time Zervan swung out of bed, dressed himself, and went to take a look. Passing through the front room, he threw a few more pieces of wood on each of the fires and then took a stout stick to carry with him. Opening the door, he went out into the street.

It was bitterly cold. His breath frosted, and even through gloves he could feel his fingertips chilling. Only the wind greeted him, and the unnatural snow. He walked around the side of the house towards the back where the bedrooms were and from where he thought he'd heard a sound.

A cat, he thought, crunching through the snow between the house and the one next door. I probably heard a cat. There were no footprints in the snow ahead of him. Somewhat reassured, he rounded the corner at the back of the house.

He had time to see what it was, to feel his mind grapple with the impossibility, and to know why there were no footsteps in the snow.

He had no time to shout or scream or give any kind of warning at all.

A long finger reached out. It touched him and he died.

⤖═◐══⤙

After the numbing wind and icy, treacherous streets, the heat of the Black Boar struck Kevin like an inferno. The tavern was packed with shouting, perspiring people. There were at least four huge fires blazing and a myriad of torches set high in the walls.

It was almost exactly as he remembered it: the dense, enveloping smoke, the smell of meat broiling over the cooking fires, and the steady, punishing level of noise. As the three of them pushed their way through the door, Kevin realized that the Boar seemed even more crowded than it was because most of the patrons were squeezed together in a wide circle around a cleared area in the middle of the tavern. The tables had been lifted from their trestles and overturned and benches had been stacked away to open a space.

With Dave serving as a massive battering ram, Kevin and Paul pushed through behind him towards the front of the crowd near the door. When they got there, amid jostling elbows and spilling beer, Kevin saw that there was a burly redheaded man in a ring formed by the crowd. The man was carrying a smaller figure seated on his shoulders.

Facing them, roaring belligerent defiance that somehow could be heard over the din, was that vast human mountain Tegid of Rhoden, and on his shoulders, laughing, was Diarmuid, Prince of Brennin.

Beginning to laugh himself, Kevin could see wagers flying all through the crowd as the two pairs warily circled each other. Even in wartime! he thought, looking at the Prince. People were standing on tables for a better view; others had gone upstairs to look down on the battle. Kevin spotted Carde and Erron, each with a fistful of wagers, standing on the bar. Beside them, after a second, he recognized Brock, the Dwarf who had brought them word of treachery in Eridu. He was older than Matt, with a lighter-coloured beard, and he was laughing aloud, which Matt Sören very seldom did. All eyes were on the combatants; not a soul had yet recognized the three of them.

"Yield, North Keep intruders!" Tegid roared. Abruptly, Kevin realized something.

"They're Aileron's men!" he shouted to Dave and Paul as Tegid launched himself in a stumbling, lurching run towards the other two.

The big man opposing him sidestepped neatly and Diarmuid, whooping with laughter, barely managed to dodge the grasp of the other rider, who was trying to pull him to the ground. Tegid terminated his run by crashing into a table on the far side of the ring, wreaking ruin among the spectators and almost unseating his rider.

Slowly he turned, breathing stertorously. Diarmuid lowered his head and spoke a series of instructions into the ear of his unstable mount. This time they advanced more cautiously, Tegid waddling wide-footed for balance on the rush-strewn floor.

"You drunken whale!" the opposing rider taunted him.

Tegid stopped his careful advance and eyed him with redfaced ire. Then, sucking air into the bellows of his lungs, he screamed, "Beer!" at a deafening volume. Immediately a girl dashed forward with two foaming pints and Diarmuid and Tegid each drained one in a long pull.

"Twelve!" Carde and Erron shouted together from the bar top. The match had obviously been going on for some time. Diarmuid tossed his tankard back to the serving girl while Tegid hurled his over his shoulder; a patron ducked quickly and tipped over the table on which he and four other men were standing. Had been standing.

It was too much for Kevin Laine.

A moment later the North Keep duo were quite inexcusably thrown to the ground by an attack from behind. It hadn't been subtle; they'd been simply run over. As the howls and screams rose to unprecedented levels, Kevin, mounted firmly on Dave's broad shoulders, turned to the pair from the Boar.

"Have at you!" he cried.

But Tegid had other ideas. With a howl of joy, he rushed, open-armed, towards Dave, grabbed him in a titanic bear hug, and, quite unable to do anything so complex as stop, toppled the four of them to the floor in a tangled, sodden heap.

Once down, he commenced buffeting both of them with fierce blows intended to signify affection and pleasure, Kevin doubted not, but formidable enough to make the room spin for him. He was laughing breathlessly and trying to ward off Tegid's exuberance when he heard Diarmuid whisper in his ear.

"Neatly done, friend Kevin." The Prince was not even slightly impaired. "I would have hated to lose. But down here on the floor we have a problem."

"What?" The tone had affected Kevin.

"I was keeping an eye on someone by the door for the last hour, perched up on Tegid. A stranger, I'm afraid. It wasn't concerning me much because I rather hoped he'd report we were ill prepared for war."

"What kind of stranger?"

"I was hoping to find out later. But if you're here, it changes things. I don't want him reporting that Kim and Paul are back."

"Kim isn't. Paul's here."

"Where?" said the Prince sharply.

"By the door."

There were a lot of people surrounding them by then: Carde and Erron, Coll, quite a few women. By the time they fought through to the doorway it was too late to do anything.

Paul watched the fight with a certain bemusement. It seemed that nothing, really, could induce in Diarmuid a sense of responsibility. And yet the Prince was more than a wastrel; he had proved it too many times in the short while they'd been here in the spring for the issue to still be in doubt.

In the spring. Spring a year ago, actually, if midsummer was approaching; it was on that, and on the meaning of this savage, inflicted winter, that Paul was reflecting. In particular, on something he had noticed on the icy walk from palace to tavern.

So he was preoccupied with implications and abstractions even amid the pandemonium. With only half an eye he saw Kevin mount up on Dave's shoulders and the two of them charge forward to down the North Keep pair from behind.

The roar that followed got his attention and he grinned, taking in the scene. Funny, manic Kevin Laine, in his own way quite as irrepressible as Diarmuid was, and as full of life.

His grin became a laugh as he saw Tegid rumble forward to gather Dave in a vast embrace, and then he winced as all four of them came crashing down.

Thus occupied, thus preoccupied, he didn't even see the figure, cloaked and hooded—even in the broiling heat of the Boar—that was picking its way to his side.

Someone else did, though. Someone who had seen Kevin and Dave and had guessed Paul might be there. And just as the cloaked figure came abreast of him, someone interposed herself.

"Hold it, sister! This one is mine first," said brown-haired Tiene. "You can have the others for your bed, wherever it is, but he is mine, upstairs, tonight."

Paul turned to see the slight, pretty girl whose tears had driven him from lovemaking into the night a year ago and, from that starry night, after he'd heard a song he hadn't been meant to hear, to the Summer Tree.

And it was because he'd been on the Tree and had survived, because the God had sent him back, that the one in the cloak—who was indeed a woman, though not sister to any mortal—had been coming to kill him where he stood.

Until the foolish, interfering girl had stepped between. A hand came out from within the cloak and touched Tiene with one long finger. No more than that, but the girl gasped as an icy, numbing pain shot into her arm where she'd been touched. She felt herself falling, and as she fell, she reached out with her other arm, where the cold had not yet penetrated, and pulled the hood from the other's face.

It was a human face, but only just. Skin so white it was almost blue; one sensed it would be freezing to the touch. She had no hair at all and her eyes were the colour of moon on ice, glacial ice, and cold enough to bring winter into the heart of those who looked at them.

But not Paul. He met her glance and saw her retreat momentarily before a thing she read in his own depths. Around them, unbelievably, no one seemed to have noticed anything, not even Tiene's fall. People were falling all over the tavern that night.

But only one man heard a raven speak, and it was Paul. *Thought, Memory.* Those were the names, he knew, and they had been there, both of them, in the Tree at the end when the Goddess came and then the God.

And in the moment when the apparition before him recovered herself and moved to strike at him as she had Tiene, Paul heard the ravens and he chanted the words given to him, and they were these:

> *White the mist that rose through me,*
> *Whiter than land of your dwelling.*
> *It is your name that will bind thee,*
> *Your name is mine for the telling.*

He stopped. Around the two of them, powers of the first world and so of all worlds, the careening pandemonium continued. No one paid them the slightest mind. Paul's voice had been pitched low, but he saw each word cut into her. Then, as low as before, but driving every syllable, for this was as old and as deep a magic as any there was, he said, "I am Lord of the Summer Tree, there is no secret to my name, no binding there." She had time, she could have moved to touch him and her touch could freeze the heart, but his words held her. Her ice eyes locked on his, and she heard him say, "You are far from the Barrens and from your power. Curse him who sent you here and be gone, Ice Queen, *for I name thee now by thy name, and call thee Fordaetha of Rük!*"

There came a scream that was not a scream, from a throat human and yet not. It rose like a wounded thing, took monstrous flight of its own, and stopped all other sounds in the Black Boar quite utterly.

By the time the last wailing vibration had died away into the terrified stillness, there was only an empty cloak on the floor in front of Paul. His face was pale with strain and weariness, and his eyes gave testimony to having seen a great evil.

Kevin and Diarmuid, with Dave and the others close behind, came rushing up as the tavern exploded into frightened, questioning life. None of them spoke; they looked at Paul.

Who was crouched beside a girl on the floor. She was blue already from her head to her feet, in the grip of an icy death that had been meant for him.

At length he rose. The Prince's men had cleared a space for them. Now, at a nod from Diarmuid, two of them lifted the dead girl and bore her out into the night, which was cold but not so cold as she.

Paul said, "Fruits of winter, my lord Prince. Have you heard tell of the Queen of Rük?"

Diarmuid's face showed no trace of anything but concentration. "Fordaetha, yes. The legends have her the oldest force in Fionavar."

"One of them." They all turned to look at the grim face of the Dwarf, Brock. "One of the oldest powers," the Dwarf continued. "Pwyll, how came Fordaetha down from the Barrens?"

"With the ice that came down," Paul replied and said again, bitterly, "Fruits of winter."

"You killed her, Paul?" It was Kevin and there was a difficult emotion vivid in his face.

*Power*, Paul was thinking, remembering the old King whose place he'd taken on the Tree. He said only, "Not killed. I named her with an invocation, and it drove her back. She will not take any shape for a long time now, nor leave the Barrens for longer yet, but she is not dead and she serves Maugrim. Had we been farther north, I couldn't have dealt with her. I wouldn't have had a chance." He was very weary.

"Why do they serve him?" he heard Dave Martyniuk say, a longing to comprehend incarnate in his voice.

He knew the answer to this question, too; he had seen it in her eyes. "He promised her Ice. Ice this far south—so much of a winter world for her to rule."

"Under him," Brock said softly. "To rule under him."

"Oh, yes," Paul agreed. He thought of Kaen and Blöd, the brothers who had led the Dwarves to serve Maugrim as well. He could see the same thought in Brock's face. "It will all be under him, and for always. We cannot lose this war."

Only Kevin, who knew him best, heard the desperation in Paul's voice. He watched, they all did, as Schafer turned and walked to the doorway. He paused there, long enough to remove his coat and drop it on the floor. He had only an open-necked shirt on underneath.

"There's another thing," Paul said. "I don't need a jacket. The winter doesn't touch me. For what that's worth."

"Why?" It was Kevin who asked, for all of them.

Schafer stepped into the snow before turning to reply through the open door, "Because I tasted it on the Tree, along with all the other shapes of death."

The door swung shut behind him, cutting off the wind and the blowing snow. They stood there in the bright, noisy tavern, and there was warmth all around them, and good companionship. Nor were there many things more dear in any world.

At about the time Paul was leaving the tavern, Loren Silvercloak and his source were making their way home to the mages' quarters in the town. Neither of them was immune to the cold, and though the snow had stopped, the wind had not and in places there were drifts piled as high as the Dwarf's chest. Overhead the summer stars shone brightly down on a winter world, but neither of them looked up, nor did they speak.

They had heard the same story, so they shared the same emotions: rage at what had been done to the woman they had just left in the palace; pity for the hurt they could not heal; and love, in both of them, for beauty that had proven itself defiant in the darkest place. There was something beyond all these in Matt Sören as well, for it had been a Dwarf, Blöd, who had marred her when Maugrim was done.

They did not know of Darien.

At length they reached their quarters. Teyrnon and Barak were elsewhere and Brock was out, with Diarmuid, probably, so they had the large space to themselves. As a matter of deliberate policy they were sleeping in town each night, to reassure the people of Paras Derval that the high ones of the realm were not hiding behind palace walls. Zervan had built the fires up before he went to bed, so it was blessedly warm, and the mage walked over to stand before the largest hearth in the front room, as the Dwarf poured two glasses of an amber-coloured liquor.

"'Usheen to warm the heart,'" Matt quoted as he gave Loren his drink.

"Mine is cold tonight," the tall mage said. He took a sip and made a wry face. "Bitter warmth."

"It will do you good." The Dwarf dropped into a low chair and began pulling off his boots.

"Should we reach for Teyrnon?"

"To say what?" Matt raised his head.

"The one thing we learned."

They looked at each other in silence.

"The Black Swan told Metran that the cauldron was theirs and he was to go to the place of spiraling," Jennifer had said, white and rigidly controlled as she went back in words to the woodcutter's clearing where Avaia had come for her. This was the one thing.

"What will he do there with the dead?" Matt Sören asked now. Hatred deep as a cavern lay in the query.

The mage's face was bleak. "I don't know," he said. "I don't know anything, it seems. Except that we cannot go after him until we break the winter, and we cannot break the winter."

"We will," said the Dwarf. "We will break it because we must. You will do this, there is no doubt in me."

The mage smiled then, softening the harsh lines of his face. "Aren't you tired," he asked, "after forty years of supporting me like this?"

"No," said Matt Sören simply. And after a moment, he smiled as well, the crooked twist of his mouth.

Loren drained the usheen, making a face again. "Very well," he said. "I want to reach for Teyrnon before we sleep. He should know that Metran has the Cauldron of Khath Meigol and has gone with it . . . to Cader Sedat."

He said it as prosaically as he could, but even in the speaking of the island's name they both felt a chill, nor could any of their order not do so. Amairgen Whitebranch, first of the mages, had died in that place a thousand years ago.

Matt braced and Loren closed. They found Teyrnon through Barak, a day's ride off with the soldiers in North Keep. They conveyed what had happened and shared among the four of them doubts that would not go outside the Council of the Mages.

Then they broke the link. "All right?" Silvercloak asked his source after a moment.

"Easy," Matt replied. "It will help me sleep."

At which point there came a heavy knocking at the door. It wouldn't be Brock; he had the key. One glance, only, they exchanged, premonitory, for they were what they were, and had been so for a long time. Then they went, together, to open the front door.

In the night outside, with stars bright behind him and a half-moon, stood a bearded man, broad-shouldered, not tall, time spun far into his eyes, and a woman unconscious in his arms.

It was very still. Loren had a sense that the stars, too, were motionless, and the late-risen moon. Then the man said, in a voice rich and low, "She is only weary, I think. She named this house to me before she fainted away. Are you Loren Silvercloak? Matt Sören?"

They were proud men, the mage and his source, and numbered among the great of Fionavar. But it was with a humbled, grateful awe that they knelt then in their open doorway, both of them, before Arthur Pendragon and the one who had summoned him, and they were kneeling to the woman no less than to the man.

⊹⟞⟝⊙⟝⟞⊹

Another knock on another door. In her room in the palace, Jennifer was alone and not asleep. She turned from contemplating the fire; the long robe they had given her brushed the deep carpets of the floor. She had bathed and washed her hair, then combed it out before the mirror, staring at her own strange face, at the green eyes that had seen what they had seen. She had been standing before the fire a long time, how long she knew not, when the tapping came.

And with it, a voice: "Never fear me," she heard through the door. "You have no greater friend."

A voice like a chiming of bells, sound at the edge of song. She opened the door to see Brendel of the lios alfar. From a long way off she was moved to see his bright, slender grace.

"Come in," she said. "But it is past time for tears."

She closed the door behind him, marvelling at how the flames of the fire, the candle by her bed, seemed to flicker and dance the more vividly with his presence in the room. The Children of Light, the lios were; their very name meant light, and it spoke to them and was answered in their being.

And the Darkest One hated them with a hate so absolute it made all else seem

316

small beside. It was a measure of evil, she thought, who of all mortals needed no such measure, that it could so profoundly hate the creature that stood before her, eyes dry, now, and shading to amber even as she watched.

"There are graces in this King," Brendel said. "Though one would not have thought so. He sent word to my chambers that you were here."

She had been told, by Kevin, of what Brendel had done: how he had followed Galadan and his wolves, and sworn an oath in the Great Hall. She said, "You have no cause to reproach yourself for me. You did, I have heard, more than anyone could have done."

"It was not enough. What can I say to you?"

She shook her head. "You gave me joy as well. My last memory of true delight is of falling asleep hearing the lios sing."

"Can we not give you that once more, now that you are with us again?"

"I do not know if I can receive it, Brendel. I am not . . . whole." It was easier, somehow, for her than for him. There was a long silence in which she suffered his eyes to hold hers. He did not probe within, although she knew he could, just as Loren had not used a Searching on her. None of them would intrude, and so she could hide Darien, and would.

"Will you unsay that?" he asked, the music in him deep and offering pain.

"Shall I lie to you?"

He turned and went to the window. Even the clothing he wore seemed woven of many colours that shifted as he moved. The starlight from outside lit his silvery hair and glinted within it. How could she so deny one who could have stars caught in his hair?

And how could she not? *I will take all*, Rakoth had said, and had come too near to doing so.

Brendel turned. His eyes were golden; it seemed his truest colour. He said, "I have waited here a long time, by Ra-Tenniel's desire and my own. His, that I might give our counsel to this young King and learn what the men of Brennin purpose; mine, to see you here and alive, that I might offer you and ask one thing."

"Which is?" She was very tall, fairer even than she had been, marked by sorrow and shadow and given something thereby.

"That you come with me to Daniloth to be made whole again. If it can be done, it will be there."

She looked at him as if from a great height or a great depth—it was distance either way. She said, "No," and saw pain flare like fire in his eyes. She said, "I am better as I am. Paul brought me this far, he and another thing. Leave it rest. I am here, and not unhappy, and I am afraid to try for more light lest it mean more dark."

There was no answer he could make; she had meant that to be so. He touched her cheek before he left, and she endured the touch, grieving that such a thing should not bring joy, but it did not, and what could she do or say?

The lios alfar spoke from the doorway, the music almost gone from his voice. "There is vengeance then," said Brendel of the Kestrel Mark. "There is only that and always that." He closed the door softly behind him.

Oaths, she thought, turning slowly to the fire again. Kevin, Brendel, she wondered who else would swear revenge for her. She wondered if it would ever mean anything to her.

Even as she stood thus, in the grey country of muting and shadow, Loren and Matt were opening their door to see two figures in the snow with the stars and moon behind.

⋯⊷⫘◗ ⫘⊶⋯

One last doorway, late of a bitter night. Few people left abroad in the icy streets. The Boar had long since closed, Kevin and Dave making their way to the South Keep barracks with Diarmuid and his men. In that pre-dawn hour when the north seemed closer and the wind wilder yet, the guards held close to their stations, bent over the small fires they were allowed. Nothing would attack, nothing could; it was clear to all of them that this wind and snow, this winter of malign intent, was attack enough. It was cold enough to kill, and it had; and it was growing colder yet.

Only one man felt it not. In shirt sleeves and blue jeans, Paul Schafer walked alone through the lanes and alleyways of the town. The wind moved his hair but did not trouble him, and his head was high when he faced the north.

He was walking almost aimlessly, more to be in the night than anything else, to confirm this strange immunity and to deal with the distance it imposed between him and everyone else. The very great distance.

How could it be otherwise for one who had tasted of death on the Summer Tree? Had he expected to be another one of the band? An equal friend to Carde and Coll, to Kevin even? He was the Twiceborn, he had seen the ravens, heard them speak, heard Dana in the wood, and felt Mörnir within him. He was the Arrow of the God, the Spear. He was Lord of the Summer Tree.

And he was achingly unaware of how to tap into whatever any of that meant. He had been forced to flee from Galadan, did not even understand *how* he had crossed with Jennifer. Had needed to beg Jaelle to send them back, and knew she would hold that over him in their scarcely begun colloquy of Goddess and God. Even tonight he had been blind to Fordaetha's approach; Tiene's death had been the only thing that gave him time to hear the ravens speak. And even that—he had not summoned them, knew not whence they came or how to bring them back.

He felt like a child. A defiant child walking in winter without his coat. And there was too much at stake, there was absolutely everything.

A child, he thought again, and gradually became aware that his steps had not been aimless after all. He was in the street leading to the green. He was standing before a door he remembered. The shop was on the ground level; the dwelling place above. He looked up. There were no lights, of course; it was very late. They would be asleep, Vae and Finn, and Darien.

He turned to go, then froze, cold for the first time that night, as moonlight showed him something.

Moving forward, he pushed on the open door of the shop. It swung wide, creaking on loose hinges. Inside, there were still the shelves of cloth and wool, and crafted fabrics across the way. But there was snow in the aisle and piled against the counters. There was ice on the stairs as he went up in the dark. The furniture was all in place, all as he remembered, but the house was deserted.

He heard a sound and wheeled, terror gripping him. He saw what had made the noise. In the wind that blew through a broken window, an empty cradle rocked slowly back and forth.

# CHAPTER 7

Early the next morning, the army of Cathal crossed the River Saeren, into the High Kingdom. Their leader allowed himself a certain amount of satisfaction. It had been well planned, exquisitely timed, in fact. They had arrived at Cynan by night, quietly, and then sent word across the river in the morning only half an hour before the specially built barges had carried them across to Seresh.

He had counted on the main road to Paras Derval being kept clear of snow, and it was. In the biting cold and under a brilliant blue sky, they set off over a white landscape for the capital. The messenger to the new High King could only be a couple of hours ahead of them; Aileron was going to have no time to organize anything at all.

And this, of course, was the point. There had been word back and forth across Saeren, barges between Seresh and Cynan, coded lights across the river farther east—the court of Brennin knew that soldiers from Cathal were coming, but not how many or when.

They were going to look shabby and badly prepared when this glittering force, twenty-five hundred strong, galloped up from the southwest. And not just the horsemen, either. What would the northmen say when they saw two hundred of the legendary war chariots of Cathal sweep up to the gates of Paras Derval. And in the first of them, pulled by four magnificent stallions from Faille, would be not a war leader or mere captain of the eidolath, the honour guard, but Shalhassan himself, Supreme Lord of Sang Marlen, of Larai Rigal, of the nine provinces of the Garden Country.

Let young Aileron deal with that, if he could.

Nor was this trivial display. Shalhassan had ruled a country shaped by intrigue far too long to indulge in mere flamboyance. There was a cold will guiding every step of this maneuver, a controlling purpose to the speed he demanded from his charioteer, and a reason for the splendour of his own appearance, from the pleated, scented beard to the fur cloak he wore, artfully slit to allow access to his curved, bejewelled sword.

One thousand years ago Angirad had led men from the south to war against the Unraveller, and they had marched and ridden under the moon and oak banner of

Brennin, under Conary and then Colan. But there had been no real Cathal then, no flag of flower and sword, just the nine fractious provinces. It was only on his return, covered with the glory of having been at Andarien and Gwynir, at the last desperate battle before the Valgrind Bridge, and then at the binding under Rangat, that Angirad was able to show forth the wardstone they had given him and make a realm, to build a fortress in the south and then the summer palace by the lake at Larai Rigal.

But he had done these things. No longer was the south a nest of feuding principalities. It was Cathal, the Garden Country, and it was no subservient realm to Brennin, however Iorweth's heirs might style themselves. Four wars in as many hundred years had made that clear. If Brennin had its Tree, the boast went in the south, Larai Rigal had its ten thousand.

And it also had a real ruler, a man who had sat the Ivory Throne for twenty-five years now, subtle, inscrutable, imperious, no stranger to battle, for he had fought in the last war with Brennin thirty years ago—when this boy-king Aileron was not yet alive. To Ailell he might possibly have deferred, but not to the son, scarce one year out of exile to wear the Oak Crown.

Battles are won en route Shalhassan of Cathal thought. A worthy thought: he raised his hand in a certain way, and a moment later Raziel galloped up, uneasy on a horse at speed, and the Supreme Lord of Cathal made him write it down. Ahead, the five members of the honour guard that had been thrown hastily together by the shocked Duke of Seresh whipped their horses to stay ahead of the chariots. He thought about passing them but decided otherwise. It would be more satisfying, to the certain degree he allowed such things to satisfy him, to arrive in Paras Derval nipping at the heels of their honour guard as if putting them to flight.

It was, he decided, well. In Sang Marlen, Galienth would monitor the decisions of his daughter. It was appropriate for her to begin to practice the statecraft she had been learning since her brother died. He was not going to have another heir. Escapades such as the one of the previous spring, when she had outraced his envoys to Paras Derval, could no longer be countenanced. He had never, in fact, received a wholly or even moderately satisfactory account of that affair. Not that he really expected one, given with whom he was dealing. Her mother had been exactly the same. He shook his head. It was time for Sharra to be wed, but every time he raised the point she evaded him. Until the last encounter, when she had smiled her falsely deferential smile (he knew it; it had been her mother's once) and murmured into her dish of chilled m'rae that if he but raised the question one more time she would wed indeed . . . and choose Venassar of Gath for her mate.

Only decades of skill had kept him from rising from his couch to let the entire court and the eidolath view his discomfiture. Worse, even, than the prospect of that semi-sentient, gangling excuse for a man beside Sharra on the throne was the thought of vulpine Bragon of Gath, his father, standing behind them.

He had turned the subject to how she should deal with the taxes while he was away. The unprecedented winter, freezing even the lake at Larai Rigal and laying waste T'Varen's gardens, had wreaked its toll everywhere, he explained, and she would have to walk a fine line of judgement between compassion and indulgence. She listened, all outward show of attentiveness, but he saw her smile behind downcast eyes. He never smiled; it gave too much away. On the other hand he had never been beautiful, and Sharra was, exceedingly. With her it was a tool, a weapon even, he knew, as he fought again to keep royal composure.

He had to work at it even now, racing to Paras Derval, remembering his impossible child's superior smile. There was a thought here, he told himself, and in a moment he had made it abstract enough. He raised his half-closed palm again, and moment later Raziel bounced up alongside, gratifyingly unhappy, to record it. After which Shalhassan put his mind from his daughter, looked at the angle of the afternoon sun, and decided they were getting close. He drew himself up straight, shook loose his heavy cloak, combed out his forked beard, and prepared to sweep the horsemen and the war chariots of Cathal, dazzling and crisp of line, into the chaotic capital of his unprepared allies. Then they would see what they would see.

About a league from Paras Derval, everything started to go completely wrong.

First of all, the road was blocked. As the advance guard slowed and his charioteer gradually did the same, Shalhassan peered ahead, his eyes squinting in the glare of sun on snow. By the time they all stopped, the horses stamping and snorting in the cold, he was cursing inwardly with an intensity not even hinted at by his outer equanimity.

There were a score of soldiers mounted before them, clad neatly in brown and gold, weapons presented towards him with high ceremoniousness. A horn blew, sweet and clear, from behind their ranks, and the soldiers turned sharply to line the sides of the wide road, making way for six children, dressed alike in red, brilliant against the snow. Two of them approached past the Seresh honour guard and, unruffled by the movements of his horses, brought to Shalhassan of Cathal flowers of Brennin for welcome.

His face grave, he accepted them. *How did they have flowers in this winter?* Then he turned to see a tapestry being held high on poles by the other four children, and in front of him was raised high a work of sheerest art in a gesture befitting royalty: on this open road, exposed to the elements, they held up for him a woven scene from the Bael Rangat. In evanescent shades, a pinnacle of the weaver's art, Shalhassen saw the battle of Valgrind Bridge. And not just any part of the battle, but the one moment, sung and celebrated in Cathal ever since, when Angirad, first of all men in that glittering host, had set foot on the bridge over Ungarch to lead the way across to Starkadh.

It was a double honour they were doing him. As he lowered his gaze, moved despite all his striving, Shalhassan saw a figure walk beneath the tapestry to stand in the road before him, and he knew that the honour was triple and that he had miscalculated badly.

In a cloak of purest white, falling in thickly furred splendour from shoulder to white boots, stood Diarmuid, the King's brother and heir. *The wastrel*, Shalhassan thought, struggling to fight the immediate overwhelming impression of effortless elegance. Diarmuid wore white gloves as well, and a white fur hat on his golden hair, and the only colour on this brilliant Prince of Snow was a red djena feather in his hat—and the red was exactly the shade the children wore.

It was a tableau of such studied magnificence that no man alive could miss the import, and no man present, of either country, would fail to tell of it.

The Prince moved a finger, no more, and there rang out over the wide snow-covered vista the exquisitely played, heart-stirring sounds of the renabael—the battle summons of the lios alfar, crafted so long ago by Ra-Termaine, greatest of their lords, greatest of their music weavers.

And then the white Prince gestured again, and again it was no more than a finger's movement, and as the music stopped, its echoes falling away in the cold, still air, the player of that music came forward, more graceful even than the Prince, and for the first time in his days Shalhassan of Cathal, quite unbelieving, saw one of the lios alfar.

The Prince bowed. The lios bowed. Over their heads Angirad stood in blood up to his knees and claimed the Valgrind Bridge in the name of Light.

Shalhassan of Cathal stepped down into the road from his carriage and bowed in his turn.

The five guards from Seresh had gone on ahead, doubtless relieved to be thus superseded. For the last league of the approach to Paras Derval, the army of Cathal was led by an honour guard of the men of Prince Diarmuid, precise and formidable; on one side of Shalhassan's chariot walked the Prince himself, and on the other was Na-Brendel, Highest of the Kestrel Mark from Daniloth.

Nor did they go faster than a walking pace, for as they drew nearer the capital, a huge crowd of cheering people lined the roadway, even among the drifted snow, and Shalhassan was forced to nod and wave in measured, dignified response.

Then, at the outskirts of the town itself, the soldiers were waiting. For the entire twisting, ascending route to the square before the palace, the foot soldiers, archers and horsemen of Paras Derval, each one turned smartly out in uniform, stood at equal intervals.

As they came into the square itself, densely packed around its outer edges with still more cheering people, the procession halted again and Prince Diarmuid presented to him, with flawless formality, the First Mage of Brennin and his source, with another Dwarf beside him whom the Prince named as Brock of Banir Tal; the High Priestess of Dana—and she, too, was dazzling in white and crowned in red as well, the thick red fall of her hair; and finally to one of whom he had heard tell, a young man, dark of hair, slim and not tall, whom the Prince named soberly as Pwyll Twice-born, Lord of the Summer Tree.

And Shalhassan could hear the crowd's response even as he met the blue-grey eyes of this young man from another world who was the chosen of the God.

Without another word spoken, these five joined the Prince and the lios alfar. Dismounting because there was no room to sweep up in a chariot, Shalhassan walked forward to the gates of the palace to meet Aileron the High King. Who had done this, all of this, on perhaps two hours' warning.

***

He had been briefed by Sharra in Sang Marlen, given an idea of what to expect. But it was only an idea and not enough, for as Aileron stepped forward to meet him partway, Shalhassan, who had been shown what Brennin could do if it chose, saw what Brennin chose.

Under the unkempt dark hair, the eyes of the High King were fierce and appraising. His stern, bearded face—not so boyish as he'd thought it would be—was fully as impassive as Shalhassan's own, and as unsmiling. He was clad in shades of brown and dun, and carelessly: his boots stained, his trousers well-worn. He wore a simple shirt and over it a short warm vest, quite unadorned. And at his side was no blade of ceremony but a long-hilted fighting sword.

Bareheaded he came forward, and the two Kings faced each other. Shalhassan could hear the roaring of the crowd and in it he heard something never offered him in twenty-five years on his own throne, and he understood then what the people of Brennin understood: the man standing before him was a warrior King, no more and certainly not less.

He had been manipulated, he knew, but he also knew how much control underlay such a thing. The dazzle of the younger brother was balanced here, and more, by the willed austerity of the older one who was King. And Shalhassan of Cathal realized in that moment, standing between the fair brother and the dark, that he was not going to lead this war after all.

Aileron had not spoken a word.

Kings did not bow to each other, but Shalhassan was not a small-minded man. There was a common enemy and an awesome one. What he had been shown had been meant not just to put him in his place but to reassure, and this, too, he grasped, and was reassured.

Abandoning on the instant every stratagem he'd envisaged for this day, Shalhassan said, "High King of Brennin, the army and chariots of Cathal are here, and yours. And so, too, is such counsel as you should seek of me. We are honoured by the welcome you have offered us and stirred by your reminder of the deeds of our ancestors, both of Brennin and Cathal."

He had not even the mild pleasure of reading relief or surprise in the other's dark eyes. Only the most uninflected acceptance, as if there had been no doubt, ever, of what he would say.

What Aileron replied was, "I thank you. Eighteen of your chariots have unbalanced wheels, and we will need another thousand men, at least."

He had seen the numbers at Seresh and here in Paras Derval, knew of the garrisons at Rhoden and North Keep. Without missing a beat, Shalhassan said, "There will be two thousand more before the moon is new." Just under three weeks; it could be done, but Sharra would have to move. And the chariot master was going to be whipped.

Aileron smiled. "It is well." He stepped forward, then, the younger King to the older, as was proper, and embraced Shalhassan with a soldier's grip as the two armies and the populace thundered approval.

Aileron stepped back, his eyes now bright. He raised his arms for silence and, when he had it, lifted his clear dry voice into the frosty air. "People of Paras Derval! As you can see, Shalhassan of Cathal has come himself to us with twenty-five hundred men and has promised us two thousand more. Shall we make them welcome among us? Shall we house them and feed them?"

The shouted agreement that followed did not mask the real problem and, obscurely moved, Shalhassan decided it was time for a gesture of his own, that the northerners not mistake the true grandeur of Cathal. He raised one hand, his thumb ring glinting in the brilliant sunshine, and when he, too, had silence, said, "We thank you in our turn, High King. Shelter we will need, so far from our gardens, but the people of Cathal will feed the soldiers of Cathal and as many of the folk of Brennin as our winter granaries allow."

Let the northern King find words to engender an ovation that equalled *that*, Shalhassan thought triumphantly from behind his expressionless face. He turned to Aileron. "My daughter will arrange for the provisions and the new soldiers, both."

Aileron nodded; the roaring of the crowd had not yet stopped. Cutting through it, Shalhassan heard a lightly mocking voice.

"A wager?" said Diarmuid.

Shalhassan caught an unguarded flash of anger in the narrowed eyes of the young King before turning to face the Prince.

"Of what sort?" he asked repressively.

Diarmuid smiled. "I have no doubt at all that both provisions and soldiers will soon be among us, but I have no doubt either that it will be the formidable Galienth, or perhaps Bragon of Gath, who arranges for them. It will certainly not be your daughter."

"And why," Shalhassan said softly, concealing an inward wince at the mention of Bragon, "are you of this view?"

"Because Sharra's with your army," the Prince replied with easy certitude.

It was going to be a pleasure, and one he would allow himself, to tame this over-confident Prince. And he could; if only because his own apprehensions of such a thing had led him to have the army checked twice on the way from Seresh to Paras Derval for a wayward Princess in disguise. He knew his daughter well enough to have watched for it. She was not in the army.

"What have you to wager?" the Supreme Lord of Sang Marlen asked, very softly so as not to frighten his prey.

"My cloak for yours," the other replied promptly. His blue eyes were dancing with mischief. The white was the better cloak and they both knew it. Shalhassan said so. "Perhaps," Diarmuid replied, "but I don't expect to lose."

A very great pleasure to tame him. "A wager," said Shalhassan as the nobility about them murmured. "Bashrai," he said and his new Captain of the Guard stepped sharply forward. He missed the old one, remembering how Devorsh had died. Well, Sharra, back, in Sang Marlen, would make some recompense for that now. "Order the men to step forward in groups of fifty," he commanded.

"And to remove their headgear," Diarmuid added.

"Yes, and that," Shalhassan confirmed. Bashrai turned crisply again to execute orders.

"This is utter frivolity," Aileron snapped, his eyes cold on his brother.

"We can use some," a musical voice interposed. Brendel of the lios alfar smiled infectiously. His eyes were golden Shalhassan noted with a thrill and, just in time, caught the corners of his mouth curving upward.

Word of the wager had spread through the crowd by now and a laughing, anticipatory sound filled the square. They could see scribbled wagers passing from hand to hand. Only the red-haired Priestess and the grim High King seemed impervious to the lifting mood.

It didn't take long. Bashrai was pleasingly efficient, and in a short while the entire army of Cathal had stepped bare-headed past the palace gates where the two Kings stood. Diarmuid's men were checking them, and carefully, but Shalhassan had checked as carefully himself.

Sharra was not in the ranks.

Shalhassan turned slowly to the white-clad Prince. Diarmuid had managed to maintain his smile. "The horses, I wonder?" he tried. Shalhassan merely raised his eyebrows in a movement his court knew very well, and Diarmuid, with a gracious gesture and a laugh, slipped out of his rich cloak in the cold. He was in red underneath to match his feather and the children.

"The hat, too?" he offered, holding them both out to be claimed.

Shalhassan gestured to Bashrai, but as the Captain, smiling on behalf of his King, stepped forward, Shalhassan heard an all-too-familiar voice cry out, "Take it not, Bashrai! The people of Cathal claim only wagers they have fairly won!"

Rather too late it came clear to him. There had been an honour guard of five, hastily assembled at dawn in Seresh. One of them now walked forward from where they had gathered on the near side of the square. Walked forward and pulling off a close-fitting cap, let tumble free to her waist the shining black hair for which she was renowned.

"Sorry, Father," said Sharra, the Dark Rose of Cathal.

The crowd erupted in shouting and laughter at this unexpected twist. Even some of the Cathalian soldiers were cheering idiotically. Their King bestowed a wintry glance upon his sole remaining child. How, he thought, could she thus lightly bring him so much shame in a foreign land?

When she spoke again, though, it was not to him. "I thought I'd do it myself this time," she said to Diarmuid, not with any degree of warmth. The Prince's expression was hard to read. Without pausing, however, Sharra turned to his brother and said, "My lord King, I am sorry to have to report a certain laxity among your troops, both of Seresh and here. I should not have been able to join this guard, however chaotic the morning was. And I should certainly have been discovered as we came into Paras Derval. It is not my place to advise you, but I must report the facts." Her voice was guileless and very clear; it reached every corner of the square.

In the stony heart of Shalhassan a bonfire burst into warming flame. Splendid woman! A Queen to be, and worthy of her realm! She had turned a moment of acute embarrassment for him into a worse one for Brennin and a triumph for herself and for Cathal.

He moved to consolidate the gain. "Alas!" cried Shalassan. "My daughter, it seems has the advantage over us all. If a wager has been won today, it has been won by her." And with Bashrai quick to aid, he doffed his own cloak, ignoring the bite of wind, and walked over to lay it at his daughter's feet.

Precisely in step beside him, neither before nor behind, was Diarmuid of Brennin. Together they knelt, and when they rose the two great cloaks, the dark one and the white, lay in the snow before her and the thronged square echoed to her name.

Shalhassan made his eyes as kind as he could, that she might know he was, for the moment, pleased. She was not looking at him.

"I thought I had saved you a cloak," she said to Diarmuid.

"You did. How should I better use it than as a gift?" There was something very strange in his eyes.

"Is gallantry adequate compensation for incompetence?" Sharra queried sweetly. "You are responsible for the south, are you not?"

"As my brother's expression should tell you," he agreed gravely.

"Has he not cause to be displeased?" Sharra asked, pressing her advantage.

"Perhaps," the Prince replied, almost absently. There was a silence: *something very strange.* And then just before he spoke again it flashed maliciously in his blue eyes and, a pit yawning before them, father and daughter both saw a hilarity he could no longer hold in check.

"Averren," said Diarmuid. All eyes turned to where another figure detached itself from the four remaining riders from Seresh. This one, too, removed a cap, revealing short copper-coloured hair. "Report," said Diarmuid, his voice carefully neutral.

"Yes, my lord. When word came that the army of Cathal was moving west, I sent word to you from South Keep, as instructed. Also as instructed, I went west myself to Seresh and crossed yesterday evening to Cynan. I waited there until the army arrived and then, in Cathalian colours, I sought out the Princess. I saw her bribe a bargeman to take her across that night and I did the same."

"Wasting my money," said the Prince. There was utter silence in the square. "Go on."

Averren cleared his throat. "I wanted to find out the going rate, my lord. Er . . . in Seresh I picked up her trail without difficulty. I almost lost her this morning, but ah . . . followed your surmise, my lord Prince, and found her in the colours of Seresh waiting with the guards. I spoke with Duke Niavin and later with the other three guards, and we simply rode with her in front of the army all day, my lord. As instructed."

After silence, sound. Sound of a name cried on rising note after rising note to reach a crescendo so high it bade fair to break through the vaults of sky above and earth below, that Mörnir and Dana both might hear how Brennin loved its brilliant laughing Prince.

Shalhassan, calculating furiously, salvaged one meager crumb of nurture from the ashes of the afternoon: they had known all along, but if that was bad it was a comprehensible thing and better that it had been done this way than in two hours, utterly without warning. That was—would have been—simply too formidable.

Then he chanced to see Aileron's face, and even as he mentally added another score to Diarmuid's tally for the day, he felt his one crumb turn to ash as well. It was abundantly clear from the High King's expression—*Aileron hadn't known any of this.*

Diarmuid was looking at Sharra, his own expression benign. "I told you the cloak was a gift, not a wager lost."

Her colour high, she asked, "Why did you do it that way? Why pretend not to know?"

And laughing suddenly, Diarmuid replied, "Utter frivolity," in a passable imitation of his brother. Then, laughing still, he turned to face the black expression, very close to a killing look, in the High King's eyes. It was perhaps more than he had expected. Slowly the laughter faded from his eyes. At least it was gone, Shalhassan thought wryly, though he himself had not wiped it away. The cheering was still going on.

Aileron said, "You knew all along." It was not a question.

"Yes," said Diarmuid simply. "We do things differently. You had your charts and plans."

"You didn't tell me, though."

Diarmuid's eyes were wide and there was a questing in them and, if one knew what to look for, a long desire. Of all the people in that square, only Kevin Laine, watching from among the crowd, had seen that look before, and he was too far away this time. The Prince's voice was even, if very low, as he said, "How else would you have ever known? How else would you have been able to put your planning to the test? I expected you to succeed, brother. We had it both ways."

A long silence. Too long, as Aileron's heavy-lidded gaze remained bleakly on his brother's face. The cheering had run itself down. A moment passed. Another. A stir of cold, cold wind.

"Brightly woven, Diar," Aileron said. And then dazzled them all with the warmth of his smile.

They began to move inside. *Both ways,* Shalhassan was thinking bemusedly. They knew all along *and* they had prepared in two hours. What sort of men were these two sons of Ailell?

"Be grateful," came a voice at his side. "They are ours." He turned and received a golden wink from a lios alfar and a grin from Brock, the Dwarf next to him. Before he knew what he was doing, Shalhassan smiled.

⊹⊱═◉═⊰⊹

Paul had wanted to waylay the Priestess immediately, but she was ahead of him in the procession and turned to the left as soon as she passed through the great doors of the palace, and he lost sight of her in the crowded entranceway. Then, as he fought to get free and follow, Kevin came up and he had to stop.

"He was brilliant, wasn't he?" Kevin grinned.

"Diarmuid? Yes, very." Paul rose on tiptoe to try to see over the people milling about them. There was a banquet being readied; servants and courtiers jostled each other as they crisscrossed the vestibule. He saw Gorlaes, the handsome Chancellor, taking charge of the party from Cathal, which now included, unexpectedly, a Princess.

"You're not listening," Kevin said.

"Oh. What?" Paul drew a breath. "Sorry. Try me again." He managed a smile.

Kevin gave him a searching glance. "You okay? After last night?"

"I'm fine. I walked a lot. What were you saying?"

Again Kevin hesitated, though with a different, more vulnerable expression. "Just that Diarmuid's riding off within the hour to fetch this shaman from the Dalrei. Dave's going and I am too. Do you want to come?"

And how did one explain how dearly one wanted to come? To come and savour, even amid war, the richness of companionship and the laughter that the Prince and Kevin both knew how to engender. How explain, even if he had the time?

"Can't, Kev. I've too much to do here."

"Umm. Right. Can I help?"

"Not yet. Maybe later."

"Fine," Kevin said, feigning a casualness. "We'll be back in three or four days."

Paul saw red hair through an archway. "Good," he said to his closest friend. "Take care." There should have been more, he thought, but he couldn't be everything; he wasn't even sure what, exactly, he could be.

He squeezed Kevin on the shoulder and moved off quickly to intercept Jaelle, cutting through the eddying crowd. He didn't look back; Kevin's expression, he knew, would have forced him to stop and explain, and he didn't feel up to explaining how deeply fear lay upon him.

Halfway across the floor he saw, with a shock, that Jennifer was with the Priestess. Schooling his features, he came up to them.

"I need you both," he said.

Jaelle fixed him with her cool regard. "It will have to wait."

Something in the voice. "No, it won't," Paul said. And gripping her right arm very hard and Jennifer's more gently, he propelled them both, smiling fatuously for the crowd, across the entrance foyer, down a branching hallway, and then, almost without breaking stride, into the first room they came to.

It was, thankfully, empty of people. There were a number of musical instruments laid out on the two tables and on the window seat. A spinet stood in the middle of the room and, beside it, what appeared to be a harp laid on its side, mounted into brackets and with free-standing legs.

He closed the door.

Both women regarded him. At any other time he might have paused to appreciate the order of beauty in the room with him, but neither pair of green eyes was less than cold at the moment, and the darker ones flashed with anger. He had bruised Jaelle, he knew, but she wasn't about to let him see that. Instead, she snapped, "You had best explain yourself."

It was a bit much.

*"Where is he?"* said Paul, hurling the question like a blade.

And found himself nonplused and weaponless when, after a blank instant, both women smiled and exchanged an indulgent glance.

"You were frightened," Jaelle said flatly.

He didn't deny it. "Where?" he repeated.

It was Jennifer who answered. "He's all right, Paul. Jaelle was just telling me. When did you find out?"

"Last night. I went to the house." *The cradle rocking in the icy wind . . . in the empty house.*

"I would rather you checked with me or with Jaelle before doing that sort of thing," Jennifer said mildly.

He felt the explosion coming, moved ruthlessly to curb it, and succeeded, barely. Neither woman appeared quite so smug as they looked at him. He said, paying out the words carefully, "There seems to be a misconception here. I don't know if either of you are capable of grasping this trenchant point, but we are not talking about some cuddly infant with spittle on his chin; we are dealing with the son of Rakoth Maugrim *and I must know where he is!"* He felt his voice crack with the strain of keeping it from rising to a shout.

Jaelle had paled, but again it was Jennifer who answered, hardily. "There is no misconception, Paul. I am unlikely to forget who his father is."

It was like cold water in the face; he felt his anger being sluiced away, leaving behind a residue of sorrow and deep pain.

"I know that," he said after a difficult moment. "I'm sorry. I was frightened last night. The house was the second thing."

"What was the first?" Jaelle asked, not harshly this time.

"Fordaetha of Rük."

With some distant satisfaction he saw her hands begin to tremble. "Here?" she whispered. "So far south?" She put her hands in the pockets of her gown.

"She was," he said quietly. "I drove her back. But not before she killed. I spoke to Loren this morning. Their servant is dead: Zervan. And so is a girl from the tavern." He turned to Jennifer. "An ancient power of winter was in Paras Derval. She tried to kill me as well and . . . failed. But there is a great deal of evil about. I must know where Darien is, Jennifer." She was shaking her head. He pushed on. "Listen to me, please! He cannot be only yours now, Jen. He can't. There is too much at stake, and we don't even know what he is!"

"He is to be random," she replied calmly, standing very tall, golden among the instruments of music. "He is not to be used, Paul."

So much dark in this, and where were his ravens now? It was a hard, a savage thing, but it had to be said, and so:

"That isn't really the issue. The issue is whether or not he has to be stopped."

In the silence that followed they could hear the tread of feet outside in the corridor and the continuing buzz of the crowd not far away. There was a window open. So as not to have to look anymore at what his words had done to Jennifer, Paul walked over to it. Even on the main level of the palace they were quite high up. Below, to the south and east, a party of thirty men or so were just leaving Paras Derval. Diarmuid's band. With Kevin, who might in fact have understood, if Paul had known clearly what he wanted to explain.

Behind him Jaelle cleared her throat and spoke with unwonted diffidence. "There is no sign yet of that last, Pwyll," she said. "Both Vae and her son say so and we have been watching. I am not so foolish as you take me for."

He turned. "I don't take you for foolish at all," he said. He held the look, longer perhaps than necessary, before turning reluctantly to the other woman.

Jennifer had been looking pale a long time, it was almost a year since she'd had a healthy tan, but never had he seen her as white as now she was. For a disoriented instant he thought of Fordaetha. But this was a mortal woman, and one to whom unimaginable damage had been done. Against the white of her skin, the high cheekbones stood out unnaturally. He wondered if she was going to faint. She closed her eyes; opened them. "He told the Dwarf I was to die. Told him there was a reason." Her voice was an aching rasp.

"I know," Paul said, as gently as he could. "You explained to me."

"What reason could there be for killing me if . . . if not because of a child?" How did one comfort a soul to whom this had been done? "What reason, Paul? Could there be another?"

"I don't know," he whispered. "You're probably right, Jen. Please stop."

She tried; wiped at her tears with both hands. Jaelle walked forward with a square of silk and gave it to her awkwardly. Jennifer looked up again. "But if I'm right . . . if he was afraid of a child, then . . . shouldn't Darien be *good?*"

So much yearning in the question, so much of her soul. Kevin would lie, Paul thought. Everyone he knew would lie.

Paul Schafer said, very low, "Good, or a rival, Jen. We can't know which, and so I must know where he is."

Somewhere on the road Diarmuid and his men were galloping. They would wield swords and axes in this war, shoot arrows, throw spears. They would be brave or cowardly, kill or die, bonded to each other and to all other men.

He would do otherwise. He would walk alone in darkness to find his own last battle. He who had come back would say the cold truths and the bitter, and make a wounded woman cry as though whatever was left of her heart was breaking even now.

Two women. There were bright, disregarded tears on Jaelle's cheeks as well. She said, "They have gone to the lake. Ysanne's lake. The cottage was empty, so we sent them there."

"Why?"

"He is of the andain, Pwyll. I was telling Jennifer before you came: they do not age as we do. He is only seven months old, but he looks like a five-year-old child. And is growing faster now."

Jennifer's sobs were easing. He walked over to the bench where she was and sat down beside her. With a real hesitation, he took her hand and raised it to his lips.

He said, "There is no one I have known so fine as you. Any wound I deal to you is more deeply bestowed upon myself; you must believe this to be true. I did not choose to be what I have become. I am not even sure what that is."

He could sense her listening.

He said, "You are weeping for fear you have done wrong, or set loose an evil. I will say only that we cannot know. It is just as possible that Darien will be our last, our deepest hope of light. And let us remember"—he looked up and saw that Jaelle had come nearer—"let all three of us remember that Kim dreamt his name and so he has a place. He is in the Tapestry."

She had stopped crying. Her hand remained in his, and he did not let it go. She looked up after a moment. "Tell me," she said to Jaelle, "how are you watching him?"

The Priestess looked uncomfortable. "Leila," she said.

"The young one?" Paul asked, not comprehending. "The one who spied on us?"

Jaelle nodded. She walked over to the horizontally mounted harp and plucked two strings before answering. "She is tuned to the brother," she whispered. "Exactly how, I don't understand, but she *sees* Finn and he is almost always with Darien. We take them food once a week as well."

His throat was dry again with fear. "What about an attack? Can't they just take him?"

"Why should they be attacked," Jaelle replied, lightly touching the instrument, "a mother and two children? Who knows they are even there?"

He drew a breath. It felt like such naked, undefended folly. "Wolves?" he pursued. "Galadan's wolves?"

Jaelle shook her head. "They never go there," she said. "They never have. There is a power by that lake warding them."

"What power?" he asked.

"I don't know. I truly don't. No one in Gwen Ystrat knows."

"Kim does, I'll bet," said Jennifer.

They were silent for a long time, listening to the Priestess at the harp. The notes followed one another at random, the way a child might play.

Eventually there came a knocking.

"Yes?" said Paul.

The door opened, and Brendel stepped inside. "I heard the music," he said. "I was looking for you." His gaze was on Jennifer. "Someone is here. I think you should come." He said nothing more. His eyes were dark.

They all rose. Jennifer wiped her face; she pushed back her hair and straightened her shoulders. Very like a queen, she looked, to Paul. Side by side, he and Jaelle followed her from the room. The lios alfar came after and closed the door.

⤛≡◯⟩⟨≡⤜

Kim was edgy and afraid. They had been planning to bring Arthur to Aileron in the morning, but then Brock had discovered Zervan's frozen body in the snow. And before they could even react, let alone properly grieve, tidings had come of Shalhassan's imminent arrival from Seresh, and palace and town both had exploded into frenzied activity.

Frenzied, but controlled. Loren and Matt and Brock, grim-faced, all three of them, hurried off, and so Kim and Arthur, alone in the mages' quarters, went upstairs and watched the preparations from a second-floor window. It was clear, both to her untrained glance and to his profoundly expert one, that there was a guiding purpose to the chaos below. She saw people she recognized rushing or riding past: Gorlaes, Coll, Brock again; Kevin, racing around the corner with a banner in his hand; even the unmistakable figure of Brendel, the lios alfar. She pointed them out to the man beside her, keeping her tone as level and uninflected as she could manage.

It was hard, though. Hard because she had next to no idea what to expect when the Cathalians had been greeted and it came time to bring Arthur Pendragon to Aileron, the High King of Brennin. Through three seasons she had waited—fall, winter, and the winterlike spring—for the dream that would allow her to summon this man who stood, contained and observant, by her side. She had known in the deepest way she now knew things that it was a necessary summoning, or she would not have had the courage or the coldness to walk the path she'd trod the night before, through a darkness lit only by the flame she bore.

Ysanne had dreamt it, too, she remembered, which was reassuring, but she remembered another thing that was not. *It is to be my war,* Aileron had said. At the very beginning, their first conversation, before he was King even, before she was his Seer. He had limped to the fire as Tyrth, the crippled servant, and walked back as a Prince who would kill to claim a crown. And what, she wondered anxiously, what would this young, proud, intolerant King do or say when faced with the Warrior she had brought? A Warrior who had been a King himself, who had fought in so many battles against so many different shapes of Darkness, who had come back from his island, from his stars, with his sword and his destiny, to fight in this war Aileron claimed as his own.

It was not going to be an easy thing. Past the summoning, she had not yet seen, nor could she do so now. Rakoth unchained in Fionavar demanded response; for this reason if for no other, she knew, had she been given fire to carry on her hand. It was the Warstone she bore, and the Warrior she had brought. For what, and to what end, she knew not. All she knew was that she had tapped a power from beyond the walls of Night, and that there was a grief at the heart of it.

"There is a woman in the first group," he said in the resonant voice. She looked. The Cathalians had arrived. Diarmuid's men, dressed formally for the first time she had ever seen, had replaced the guard from Seresh. Then she looked again. The first group was that guard from Seresh, and one of them, incredibly, she knew.

"Sharra!" she breathed. "Again! Oh, my God." She turned from staring at the disguised Princess she had befriended a year ago to glancing with astonishment at the man beside her, who had noticed a disguise in one of so many riders in such a tumultuous throng.

He looked over at her, the wide-set dark eyes gentle. "It is my responsibility," said Arthur Pendragon, "to see such things."

Midafternoon, it was. The breath of men and horses showed as puffs of smoke in the cold. The sun, high in a clear blue sky, glittered on the snow. Midafternoon, and at the window Kimberly thought again, looking in his eyes, of stars.

She recognized the tall guard who opened the door: he had escorted her to Ysanne's lake the last time she went. She saw, from his eyes, that he knew her as well. Then his face changed as he took in the man who stood quietly beside her.

"Hello, Shain," she said, before he could speak. "Is Loren here?"

"Yes, and the lios alfar, my lady."

"Good. Are you going to let me in?"

He jumped backwards with an alacrity that would have been amusing were she in any state to be amused. They feared her, as once they had feared Ysanne. It wasn't funny now, though, not even ironic; this was no place or time for such shadings.

Drawing a deep breath, Kim pushed back her hood and shook out her white hair, and they walked in. She saw Loren first and received a quick nod of encouragement—one that did not mask his own tension. She saw Brendel, the silver-haired lios alfar, and Matt, with Brock, the other Dwarf, and Gorlaes the Chancellor.

Then she turned to Aileron.

He hadn't changed, unless it were simply to become more, in a year's time, of what he had already been. He stood in front of a large table that was spread with a huge map of Fionavar. His hands were clasped behind his back, his feet balanced wide apart, and his deep-set, remembered eyes bored into her. She knew him, though: she was his Seer, his only one.

Now she read relief in his face.

"Hello," she said calmly. "I'm told you got my last warning."

"We did. Welcome back," Aileron said. And then, after a pause, "They have been walking on tiptoe around me this past half hour, Loren and Matt. Will you tell me why this is and whom you have brought with you?"

Brendel knew already; she could see the wonder silver in his eyes. She said, raising her voice to make it clear and decisive, as a Seer's should be, "I have used the Baelrath as Ysanne dreamt long ago. Aileron, High King, beside me stands Arthur Pendragon, the Warrior of the old tales, come to make one with our cause."

The lofty words rose and then fell into silence, like waves breaking around the King's rock-still face. Any of the others in this room would have done it better, she thought, painfully aware that the man beside her had not bowed. Nor could he be expected to, not to any living man, but Aileron was young and newly King, and—

"My grandfather," said Aileron dan Ailell dan Art, "was named for you, and have I a son one day he, too, will be." As the men in the room and the one woman gasped with astonishment, the High King's face broke into a joyful smile. "No visitation, not even of Colan or Conary, could be more bright, my lord Arthur. Oh, brightly woven, Kimberly!" He squeezed her shoulder hard as he strode past and embraced fiercely, as a brother, the man she had brought.

Arthur returned the gesture, and when Aileron stepped back, the Warrior's own eyes showed, for the first time, a glint of amusement. "They led me to understand," he said, "that you might not entirely welcome my presence."

"I am served," said Aileron, with a heavy emphasis, "by advisers of limited capacities. It is a sad truth that—"

"Hold it!" Kim exclaimed. "That's not fair, Aileron. That's . . . not fair." She stopped because she couldn't think of what else to say, and because he was laughing at her.

"I know," Aileron said. "I know it isn't." He controlled himself, then said in a very different voice, "I don't even want to know what it is you had to go through to bring us this man, though I was taught as a boy by Loren and I think I can hazard a guess. You are both full welcome here. You could not be otherwise."

"Truly spoken," said Loren Silvercloak. "My lord Arthur, you have never fought in Fionavar before?"

"No," the deep voice replied. "Nor against Rakoth himself, though I have seen the shadows of his shadow many times."

"And defeated them," Aileron said.

"I never know," Arthur replied quietly.

"What do you mean?" Kim asked in a whisper.

"I die before the end." He said it quite matter-of-factly. "I think it best you understand that now. I will not be here for the ending—it is a part of what has been laid upon me."

There was silence, then Aileron spoke again. "All I have been taught tells me that if Fionavar falls then all other worlds fall as well, and not long after—to the shadows of the shadow, as you say." Kim understood: he was moving away from emotion to something more abstract.

Arthur nodded gravely. "So it is told in Avalon," he said, "and among the summer stars."

"And so say the lios alfar," Loren added. They turned to look at Brendel and noticed for the first time that he had gone. Something stirred in Kimberly, the faintest, barely discernible anticipation, far too late, of the one thing she could not have known.

Na-Brendel of the Kestrel Mark had the same sense of belated awareness, but more strongly, because the lios alfar had traditions and memories that went deeper and farther back then did those of the Seers. Ysanne once, and Kimberly now, might walk into the future, or dream some threads of it, but the lios lived long enough to know the past and were often wise enough to understand it. Nor was Brendel, Highest of the Kestrel, least among them in age or understanding.

And once, a year ago in a wood east of Paras Derval, a sense of a chord half heard had come to him, as it came now again, more strongly. With sorrow and wonder both, he followed the sound of a harp to another door and, opening it, bade all three of them come back with him, one for the God, one for the Goddess, and one in the name of the children, and for bitterest love.

Nor was he wrong, nor Kimberly. And as he entered the King's room with Pwyll and the women, Brendel saw from the mage's suddenly rigid face that he, too, understood. Loren and his source and Brock of Banir Tal were standing with Kim by the window. Aileron and Arthur, with Gorlaes, stood over the spread-out map.

The King and the Chancellor turned as they came in. Arthur did not. But Brendel saw him lift his head quickly as if scenting or hearing a thing to which the rest were oblivious, and he saw that Arthur's hands, resting on the tabletop, had gone suddenly white.

"We have been granted aid beyond measure," he said to the three he had brought. "This is Arthur Pendragon, whom Kimberly has summoned for us. My lord Arthur, I would present to you—"

He got no further. Brendel had lived long and seen a very great deal in his days and had shared more through the memories of the Elders of Daniloth. But nothing, ever, could touch the thing he saw in the Warrior's eyes as Arthur turned. Before that glance he felt his voice fail; there were no words one could say, no pity deep enough to touch, to even nearly touch.

Kim saw them, too, the eyes of the one she'd summoned from a vanished island, from the summer stars. To war, she'd thought, because there was need. But understanding in that instant the fullness of the curse that had been laid on him, Kim felt her heart turn over and over as if tumbling down a chasm. A chasm of grief, of deepest love, deeply returned, most deeply betrayed, saddest story of all the long tales told. She turned to the second one. Oh, Jen, she thought. Oh, Jennifer.

*"Oh, Guinevere,"* said Arthur. *"Oh, my very dear."*

All unexpecting had she walked the long corridors and up the stone stairwell. The stone of the walls in its muted shadings matched the serenity of grey she had built inside. It would be all right or, if not, it was not meant to be. There was a hope that Darien might be what she'd so deeply wanted him to be, back in the days when things reached deeply into her. There was a chance; there were people aware of it. She had done what she could, and it was as much as she could.

She entered the room and smiled to see Kim and to see that she seemed to have brought the one she'd waited for. Then Brendel spoke his name and Arthur slowly turned and she saw his eyes and heard him name her by the other name, and there was fire, light, memory, so much love, and desire: an explosion in her breast.

*Then another memory, another explosion.* Rangat's fire climbing to block out her sight of heaven, and the hand, the severed hand, the blood black, as his fortress was, green light, and red his eyes had been, Rakoth's, in Starkadh.

And here as well. They were. And, oh, too brutally between. She had only to cross to the table where Arthur stood. By whom she was loved, even still, and would be sheltered. But the Unraveller lay between.

She could not come, not ever, to such perfect love, nor had she, the first time, or in any of the after times. Not for this reason, though. It had never been Fionavar before. Shadows of the shadow there had been, and the other sword of Light, the other one, brightest, bitterest love. But never Rakoth before. She could not pass, not through that flame, not past the burning of that blood on her body, not over; oh, she could not rise over the Dark and what it had done to her.

Not even to the shore that Arthur was.

She needed grey. No fire or blood, no colours of desire, access to love. She said, and her voice was very clear, "I cannot cross. It is better so. I have been maimed but will not, at least, betray. He is not here. There is no third. The gods speed your blade in battle, and grant you final rest."

There were so many falling stars in his eyes, so many fallen. She wondered if any were left in the sky.

"And you," he said after a long time. "Grant you rest."

So many fallen stars, so many falling still.

She turned and left the room.

# CHAPTER 8

She had no one to blame but herself, of course; Shalhassan had made that very clear. If the heir to the throne of Cathal chose to come to a place of war, she would have to conduct herself in a manner befitting royalty. There was also the matter of saving face as best one could after the disaster of yesterday.

So all morning and into the afternoon Sharra found herself sitting around a table in the High King's antechamber as the tedious business of planning the disposition and provisioning of troops was conducted. Her father was there, and Aileron, cool and efficient. Bashrai and Shain, the Captains of the Guard, stood by to register orders and relay them through runners stationed just outside the room.

The other man, the one she watched most closely, was a figure from the shadowy realm of childhood stories. She remembered Marlen her brother pretending to be the Warrior when he was ten years old, pretending to pull the King Spear from the mountainside. And now Marlen was five years dead and beside her stood Arthur Pendragon, giving counsel in a deep, clear voice, favouring her with a glance and a gentle smile now and again. But his eyes didn't smile; she had never seen eyes like his, not even those of Brendel, the lios alfar.

It continued through the afternoon. They ate over the map and the innumerable charts Aileron had prepared. It was necessary, she understood, but it seemed pointless, somehow, at the same time. There was not going to be a true war while the winter lasted. Rakoth was making this winter-in-summer, but they didn't know how and so they couldn't do anything to stop it. The Unraveller didn't need to risk battle, he wasn't going to. He was going to freeze them to death, or starve them, when the stored food ran out. Already it had begun: the elderly and the children, first victims always, were starting to die in Cathal and Brennin and on the Plain.

Against that brutal reality, what good were abstract plans to use chariots as barricades if Paras Derval were attacked?

She didn't say it, though. She was quiet and listened and, about midafternoon, had been silent so long they forgot about her, and she made her escape and went in search of Kim.

It was Gorlaes, the omniscient Chancellor, who directed her. She went to get a cloak from her chambers and noticed that the white one had already been trimmed to her size. Expressionlessly she put it on and, climbing all the stairs, came out on a turret, high above everything else. Kim was standing there, in furred cloak and gloves but unhooded, her startling white hair whipping into her eyes. To the north, a long line of clouds lay along the horizon and a north wind was blowing.

"Storm coming," Sharra said, leaning on the parapet beside the other woman.

"Among other things." Kim managed a smile but her eyes were red.

"Tell me," Sharra said. And listened as it came out like a pent-up flood. The dream. The dead King and the undead son. The children slain and Jennifer shattered in Starkadh. The one thing unforeseen: Guinevere. Love betrayed. Grief at the heart of it, the heart of everything.

Cold in the high wind they stood when the story ended. Cold and silent, facing the bitter north. Neither wept; it was wind that laid freezing tears on their cheeks. The sun slid low in the west. Ahead of them the clouds were thick on the horizon.

"Is he here?" Sharra asked. "The other one? The third?"

"I don't know. She said he wasn't."

"Where is she now?"

"In the Temple, with Jaelle."

Silence again, save for the wind. As it happened, though for very different reasons, the thoughts of both of them were away to the east and north where a fair-haired Prince was riding at the head of thirty men.

A short while later the sun was lost in trees behind Mörnirwood and the cold became too great. They went inside.

Three hours later they were back on that tower with the King and half the court, it seemed. It was full dark and savagely cold, but no one noticed, now.

Away to the north, very, very far, a luminous pearly light was being cast into the sky.

"What is it?" someone asked.

"Daniloth," Loren Silvercloak replied softly. Brendel was standing beside him, his eyes the colour of the light.

"They are trying it," the lios breathed. "Not for a thousand years has Daniloth been unsheathed. There are no shadows on the Land of Light tonight. They will be looking at the stars later when they fade the shining. There will be starlight above Atronel."

It was almost a song, so beautiful was his voice, so laden with yearning. Every one of them looked at that cast glow and, wondering, understood that it had been like that every night before Maugrim had come, and the Bael Rangat, before Lathen had woven the mist to change Daniloth into the Shadowland.

"Why?" Sharra asked. "Why are they doing it?"

Again it was Loren who replied. "For us. They are trying to draw him down from Starkadh to divert his power from the winter's shaping. The lios alfar are offering themselves so that we might have an end to the cold."

"An ending to it for them as well, surely?" Gorlaes protested.

Never taking his eyes from the light in the north, Na-Brendel answered him. "There is no snow in Daniloth. The sylvain are blooming now as they do each midsummer, and there is green grass on Atronel."

They watched, picturing it, heartened despite the knife of wind by that lifted glow that meant courage and gallantry, a play of light in heaven at the very door of the Dark.

Watching it, Kim was distracted by a sound, very thin, almost a drift of static in her mind. More that than music, and coming, so far as she could tell, from the east. She lifted her hand; the Baelrath was quiescent, which was a blessing. She was coming to fear its fire. She pushed the whisper of sound away from her—it was not hard—and turned her whole being to the light of Daniloth, trying to draw strength and some easing of guilt and sorrow. It was less than forty-eight hours since she had stood at Stonehenge and she was weary, through and through, with so much yet to be done.

Beginning, it seemed, immediately.

When they returned to the Great Hall, a woman in grey was there waiting for them. Grey, as in the grey robes of the priestesses, and it was Jaelle, striding past the Kings, who spoke to her.

"Aline, what is it?"

The woman in grey sank to the floor in a deep curtsy before Jaelle; then she offered a perfunctory version to Aileron. Turning back to the High Priestess, she spoke carefully, as from memory.

"I am to convey to you the obeisance on the Mormae and Audiart's apologies. She sent this in person because it was thought the men here would greater appreciate urgency if we did not use the link."

Jaelle remained very still. There was a forbidding chill in her face. "What urgency?" she asked, velvet danger sheathed in her voice.

Aline flushed. I wouldn't be in her shoes for anything, Kim thought suddenly.

"Again, Audiart's apologies, High One," Aline murmured. "It is as Warden of Gwen Ystrat, not as Second of the Mormae, that she sent me. I was told to say this to you."

Imperceptibly, almost, Jaelle relaxed. "Very well—" she began but was interrupted before she could finish.

"If you are sent by my Warden, you should be speaking to me," Aileron said, and his own voice was fully as cold as Jaelle's had been. The High Priestess stood immobile and impassive. No help there, Kim thought. She felt briefly sorry for Aline, a pawn in a complex game. Only briefly, though; in some ways pawns had it easy.

Aline decided; she sank down into a proper curtsy before the King. Rising, she said, "We have need of you, High King. Audiart requests you to remember how seldom we ask aid and that you therefore consider our plight with compassion."

"To the point!" the High King growled. Shalhassan, just behind him, was taking it all in avidly. It was no time for anything but control.

Again Aline glanced at Jaelle and again found no assistance. She licked her lips. Then, "Wolves," she said. "Larger than any of us have ever seen. There are thousands of them, High King, in the wood north of Lake Leinan, and they are raiding at night among the farms. The farms of your people, my lord King."

"Morvran?" said Jaelle sharply. "What about us?"

Aline shook her head. "They have been seen near the town but not yet in the Temple grounds, High One. If they had been, I am to say, then—"

"Then the Mormae would have linked to tell me. Audiart," Jaelle murmured, "is cleverness itself." She tossed her head, and the red hair rippled down her back like a river.

Aileron's eyes were bright in the torchlight. "She wants me to come and clean them out for her? What says the High Priestess?"

Jaelle didn't even look at him. "This," she said, "is your Warden, not my Second, Aileron."

There was a silence, and then a polite cough and Paul Schafer walked forward towards Audiart's messenger.

"One moment," he said. "Aileron, you spoke of cleaning out the wolves. It may be more than that." He paused "Aline, is Galadan in Leinanwood?"

The priestess had fear in her eyes. "We never thought of that. I do not know."

And so it was time. That was a cue for her, if anything was. Kim schooled her face and, as she did, Aileron's glance swung over to find her.

Would she ever be used to this? Had Ysanne ever grown accustomed to this shuttling back and forth on the timeloom? Only last night, restless and heartsick for Jennifer, she had fallen into half sleep and a blurred, insubstantial dream of a hunt in a wood, in some wood, somewhere, and a rushing thunder over the ground.

She met the King's glance. "Something is there," she said, keeping her voice crisp. "Or someone. I have seen a hunt."

Aileron smiled. He turned to Shalhassan and to Arthur beside him. "Shall we three hunt wolves of the Dark in Gwen Ystrat?"

The dour King of Cathal nodded.

"It will be good to have an enemy to kill just now," Arthur said.

He meant more, Kim knew, than Aileron heard, but she had no space for sorrow because something else from her dream had slotted into place with the High King's words.

"It will be more than a hunt," she murmured. It was never necessary for a Seer to speak loudly. "I'll be coming, and Loren, and Jaelle, if she will."

"Why?" It was Paul, challenging, bearing his own burdens.

"I dreamt the blind one," she explained. "Gereint of the Dalrei will be going to Morvran tomorrow."

There was a murmur at that. It was, she supposed, unsettling for people to hear such things. Not much she could do, or cared at the moment to do, about it. She was very weary, and it wasn't about to get easier.

"We'll leave tomorrow then, as well," Aileron said decisively.

Loren was looking at her.

She shook her head, then pushed her hair back from her face. "No," she said, too tired to be diplomatic. "Wait for Diarmuid."

It wasn't going to get any easier at all, not for a long time, maybe not ever.

⋯⋟══◉══⟨⋯

It was passing away from him. He had seen it coming long ago, in some ways he had willed it to come, but it was still a hard thing for Loren Silvercloak to see his burdens passing to others. The harder because he could read in them the toll exacted by their new responsibilities. It was manifest in Kim, just as her power was manifest: a Seer with the Baelrath and the gift of another's soul, she must be staggering under the weight of it.

Today was a day of preparations. Five hundred men, half from Cathal and half from Brennin, were to ride for Gwen Ystrat as soon as Diarmuid returned. They were waiting because Kim had said to wait. Once it might have been the mages who offered such decisive counsel, but it was passing from them. He had set the thing in motion when he brought the five of them, and he was wise enough, for all Matt's reproachful glances, to let it move without his interference, insofar as that was possible. And he was compassionate enough to pity them: Kim, and Paul who bore the weight of the name Twiceborn, with all such a thing implied, but who had not been able to tap into his power yet. It was there, any fool could see, it might be greater than any of them could fathom, but as of now it was latent only. Enough to set him painfully apart, not enough to give him compensation or direction.

And then there was Jennifer, and for her he could weep. No compensation, or even dream of it, for her, no chance to act, only the pain, so many shadings of it. He had seen it from the first—so long ago, it seemed—before they crossed, when he had read a message in her beauty and a dark future in her eyes. He had taken her anyhow, had told himself he had no choice; nor was that merely sophistry—such, at least, Rangat's exploding had made clear.

Which did not take away the sorrow. He understood her beauty now, they all did, and they knew her oldest name. *Oh, Guinevere,* Arthur had said, and was any fate more harsh in any world than that of the two of them? And the third.

He passed the day alone in untranquil thought. Matt and Brock were at the armories, giving the benefit of their expertise in weapons to the two Captains of the Guard. Teyrnon, whose pragmatic good sense would have been of some help, was in North Keep. They would reach for him that night; he and Barak, too, would have their place in Gwen Ystrat.

If ever any mage, any worker in the skylore, could be said to have a place so near Dun Maura. The tall mage shook his head and threw another log on the fire. He was cold, and not just from the winter. How had it come to be that there were only two mages left in Brennin? There could never be more than seven; so Amairgen had decreed when first he formed the Council. But two, only two, and at such a time? It was passing from them, it seemed, in more ways than one.

Two mages only in Brennin to go to war against Maugrim; but there were three mages in Fionavar, and the third had put himself in league with the Dark. He was on Cader Sedat, that enchanted island, long since made unholy. He was there, and he had the Cauldron of Khath Meigol and so could bring the newly dead back to life.

Whatever else might pass from them, that one was his. His and Matt's. *We will have our battle in the end,* he had said to the Dwarf.

If the winter ever ended. Metran.

⊷⟹⟸⊶

Night came, and with it another storm worse than any yet. Wind howled and whistled down the Plain into the High Kingdom, carrying a wall of snow. It buried farms and farmhouses. It blanketed the woods. It hid the moon, and in the inhuman darkness figures of dread seemed to be moving within the storm and the howling of wind was the sound of their laughter.

Darien lay in bed listening to it. He'd thought at first it was another nightmare but then knew he was awake. Frightened, though. He pulled the covers up over his head to try and muffle the voices he heard in the wind.

They were calling. Calling him to come and play outside in the wild dark dancing of the storm. To join them in this battering of wind and snow. But he was only a little boy, and afraid, and he would die if he went outside. Even though the storm wasn't so bad where they were.

Finn had explained about that. How even though Darien's real mother couldn't be there with them she was protecting him all the time, and she made the winter easier around his bed because she loved him. They all loved him; Vae his mother and even Shahar his father, who had been home from war only once before they had come to the lake. He had lifted Darien up in the air and made him laugh. Then he had said Dari would soon be bigger than Finn and laughed, himself, though not the funny laugh.

Finn was his brother and he loved Dari most of all and he was the most wonderful person in the world and knew everything besides.

It was Finn who had explained what Father had meant when Dari came crying to him after, because there was something wrong about him being bigger than Finn. Soon, Father had said.

Finn had dressed him in his coat and boots and carried him out for a walk. Dari liked it more than anything when they did that. Finn would throw Dari in the snow, but only where it was new and soft, and then fall in himself so they both got all white, rolling about, and Dari would laugh so hard he got the hiccups. This time, though, Finn had been serious. Sometimes he was serious and made Dari listen to him. He said that Dari was different from other little boys. That he was special because his real mother was special, and so he was going to be bigger and stronger and smarter than all the other boys. Even Finn, Finn said. And what that meant, Finn said, was that Dari had to be better, too, he had to be kinder and gentler and braver, so he would deserve what his real mother had given him.

He had to try to love everything, Finn said, except the Dark.

The Dark was what was causing the storm outside, Dari knew. And most of the time he hated it like Finn said. He tried to do it all the time, to be just like Finn was, but sometimes he heard the voices, and though mostly they frightened him, sometimes they didn't. Sometimes he thought it might be nice to go with them.

Except that would mean leaving Finn, and he would never do that. He got out of bed and put on his knitted slippers. He pulled back the curtain and paddled over, past where his mother slept, to the far wall where Finn's bed was.

Finn was awake. "What took you so long?" he whispered "Come in, little brother, we'll keep each other warm." With a sigh of pleasure, Dari kicked off the slippers and crawled in beside Finn, who moved over, leaving Dari the warm part where he'd lain.

"There are voices," he said to Finn.

His brother didn't say anything. Just put an arm around Dari and held him close. The voices weren't as loud here when he was beside Finn. As he drifted to sleep, Dari heard Finn murmur into his ear, "I love you, little one. "

Dari loved him back. When he fell asleep he dreamed again, and in his dream he was trying to tell that to the ghostly figures calling from the wind.

# CHAPTER 9

In the afternoon after the storm—a day so clear and bright it was almost a mockery—
came Diarmuid, Prince of Brennin, back to Paras Derval. With certain others he was
brought to the High King's antechamber, where a number of people waited for him,
and in that place he was presented by Aileron, his brother, to Arthur Pendragon.

And nothing happened.

Paul Schafer, standing next to Kim, had seen her pale when Diarmuid came into
the room. Now, as the Prince bowed formally to Arthur and the Warrior accepted it
with an unruffled mien, he heard her draw a shaky breath and murmur, from the
heart, "Oh, thank God."

A look passed between her and Loren, who was on the far side of the room, and in
the mage's countenance Paul read the same relief. It took him a moment, but he put it
together.

"You thought he was the third one?" he said. "Third angle of the triangle?"

She nodded, still pale. "I was afraid. Don't know why now. Don't know why I was
so sure."

"Is that why you wanted us to wait?"

She looked at him, grey eyes under white hair. "I thought it was. I knew we had to
wait before going to the hunt. Now I don't know why."

"Because," came a voice, "you are a true and loyal friend and didn't want me to
miss the fun."

"Oh, Kev!" She wheeled and gave him a very un-Seerlike hug. "I missed you!"

"Good," said Kevin brightly.

"Me, too," Paul added.

"Also good," Kevin murmured, less flippantly.

Kim stepped back. "You feeling unappreciated, sailor?"

He gave her a half smile. "A bit superfluous. And now Dave's fighting an urge to
bisect me with his axe."

"Nothing new there," Paul said dryly.

"What now?" Kim asked.

"I slept with the wrong girl."

Paul laughed. "Not the first time."

"It isn't funny," Kevin said. "I had no idea he liked her, and anyhow, she came to me. The Dalrei women are like that. They call the shots with anyone they like until they decide to marry."

"Have you explained to Dave?" Kim asked. She would have made a joke but Kevin did look unhappy. There was more to this, she decided.

"He's a hard man to explain things to. Hard for me, anyway. I've asked Levon. It was his sister." Kevin indicated someone with a sideways nod of his head.

*And that, of course, was it.*

Kim turned to the handsome, fair-haired Rider standing just behind them. There had been a reason for waiting for this party, and it wasn't Diarmuid or Kevin. It was this man.

"I have explained," Levon said. "And will do so again, as often as necessary." He smiled; then his expression grew sober and he said to Kim, "Seer, I asked if we might talk, a long time ago."

She remembered. The last morning, before the Baelrath had blazed and her head had exploded with Jennifer's screams and she had taken them away.

She looked at her hand. The ring was pulsing; only a very little, but it was alive again.

"All right," she said, almost curtly. "You, too, Paul. Kev, will you bring Loren and Matt?"

"And Davor," Levon said. "Diarmuid, too. He knows."

"My room. Let's go." She walked out, leaving them to follow her. Her and the Baelrath.

> *The flame will wake from sleep,*
> *The Kings the horn will call,*
> *But though they answer from the deep,*
> *You may never hold in thrall*
> *Those who ride from Owein's Keep*
> *With a child before them all.*

Levon's voice faded away. In the silence Kim became aware, annoyingly, of the same faint static she'd heard two nights ago; again it was from the east. Gwen Ystrat, she decided. She was getting herself tuned in to whatever sendings the priestesses were throwing back and forth out there. It was a nuisance and she pushed it from her mind. She had enough to worry about, starting with all these men in her bedroom. A frustrated woman's dream, she thought, unable to find it amusing.

They were waiting for her. She kept silent and let them wait. After a moment it was Levon who resumed—it was his idea, after all. He said, "I learned that verse from Gereint as a boy. I remembered it last spring when Davor found the horn. Then we located the tree and the rock. And so we know where Owein and the Sleepers are." He couldn't keep the excitement from his voice. "We have the horn that calls them and . . . and it is my guess that the Baelrath roused is the flame that wakes them."

"It would fit," said Diarmuid. He had kicked off his boots and was lying on her bed. "The Warstone is wild, too. Loren?"

The mage, by exercise of seniority, had claimed the armchair by the window. He lit his pipe methodically and drew deeply upon it before answering.

"It fits," he said at length. "I will be honest and say I do not know what it forms."

The quiet admission sobered them. "Kim?" Diarmuid asked, taking charge from where he lay sprawled across her bed.

She was minded to give them a hard time, still, but was too proud to be petty. "I haven't seen it," she murmured. "Nothing of this at all."

"Are you sure?" Paul Schafer asked from by the door, where he stood with Matt Sören. "You were waiting for Levon, weren't you?"

He was awfully clever, that one. He was her friend, though, and he hadn't given away her first apprehension about Diarmuid. Kim nodded, and half smiled. "I sensed he was coming. And I guessed, from before, what he wanted to ask. I don't think we can conclude much from that."

"Not much," Diarmuid concurred. "We still have a decision to make."

"We?" It was Kevin Laine. "Kim's ring, Dave's horn. Their choice, wouldn't you say?"

Levon said, "They aren't really theirs. Only—"

"Anyone planning to take them away and use them?" Kevin asked laconically. "Anyone going to force them?" he continued, driving the point home. There was a silence. Another friend, Kim thought.

There was an awkward cough. "Well," said Dave, "I'm not about to go against what gets decided here, but I'd like to know a little more about what we're dealing with. If I've got the horn that calls these . . . ah, Sleepers, I'd prefer to know who they are."

He was looking self-consciously at Loren. They all turned to the mage. The sun was behind him, making it hard to see his face. When he spoke, it was almost as a disembodied voice.

"It would be altogether better," he said, from between the setting sun and the smoke, "if I could give a fair answer to Dave's question. I cannot. Owein and the Wild Hunt were laid to rest an infinitely long time ago. Hundreds and hundreds of years before Iorweth came from oversea, or the Dalrei crossed the mountains from the east, or even men pushed into green Cathal from the far lands in the southeast.

"Even the lios alfar were scarcely known in the land when the Hunt became the Sleepers. Brendel has told me, and Laien Spearchild before him, that the lios have only shadowy legends of what the Wild Hunt was before it slept."

"Was there anyone here?" Kevin murmured.

"Indeed," Loren replied. "For someone put them under that stone. Tell me, Levon, was it a very great rock?"

Levon nodded without a word.

Loren waited.

"The Paraiko!" Diarmuid said, who had been student to the mage when he was young. His voice was soft; there was wonder in it.

"The Paraiko," Loren repeated. "The Giants. They were here, and the Wild Hunt rode the night sky. It was a very different world, or so the legends of the lios tell. Shadowy kings on shadowy horses that could ride between the stars and between the Weaver's worlds."

"And the child?" Kim asked this time. It was the question that was gnawing at her. *A child before them all.*

"I wish I knew," Loren said. "No one does, I'm afraid."

"What else *do* we know?" Diarmuid asked mildly.

"It is told," came a deep voice from the door, "that they moved the moon."

"What?" Levon exclaimed.

"So it is said," Matt repeated, "Under Banir Lök and Banir Tal. It is our only legend of the Hunt. They wanted greater light by which to ride, and so they moved the moon."

There was a silence.

"It *is* closer here," Kevin said wonderingly. "We noticed it was larger."

"It is," Loren agreed soberly. "The tales may be true. Most of the Dwarf tales are."

"How were they ever put under the stone?" Paul asked.

"That is the deepest question of all," Loren murmured. "The lios say it was Connla, Lord of the Paraiko, and it is not impossible for one who made the Cauldron of Khath Meigol and so half mastered death to have done so."

"It would have been a mighty clash," Levon said softly.

"It would have been," Loren agreed, "but the lios alfar say another thing in their legends." He paused. His face was quite lost in the glare of the sun. "They say there was no clash. That Owein and the Hunt asked Connla to bind them, but they do not know why."

Kim heard a sound, or thought she did, as of quick wings flying. She looked to the door.

And heard Paul Schafer say, in a voice that sounded scraped up from his heart, "I know." His expression had gone distant and estranged but when he continued, his voice was clear. "They lost the child. The ninth one. They were eight kings and a child. Then they made a mistake and lost the child, and in grief and as penance they asked the Paraiko to bind them under the stone with whatsoever bonds they chose and whatsoever method of release."

He stopped abruptly and passed a hand before his eyes. Then he leaned back for support against the wall.

"How do you know this?" Levon asked in amazement.

Paul fixed the Dalrei with those fathomless, almost inhuman eyes, "I know a fair bit about half-death," he said.

No one dared break the silence. They waited for Paul. At length he said, in a tone more nearly his own, "I'm sorry. It . . . catches me unawares, and I'm thrown by it. Levon, I—"

The Dalrei shook his head. "No matter. Truly not. It is a wonder, and not a gift, I know, but earned. I am grateful beyond words that you are here, but I do not envy you."

Which, Kim thought, was about it. She said, "Is there more, Paul? Do we wake them?"

He looked at her, more himself with each passing second. It was as if an earthquake had shaken the room and passed. Or a roll of very great thunder.

"There is no more," he said, "if you mean do I know anything more. But, for what it's worth, I did see something just before we left the other room."

Too clever by half, she thought. But he had paused and was leaving it for her. "You don't miss much, do you?" she murmured. He made no reply. She drew a breath and said, "It's true. The Baelrath glowed for a moment when Levon came up to me. In the moment when I understood what he had come for. I can tell you that, for what, as Paul says, it's worth."

"Something, surely," Levon said earnestly. "It is as I have been saying: why else have we been given the horn, shown the cave? Why, if not to wake them? And now the stone is telling us!" .

"Wild to wild," Loren murmured. "They may be calling each other, Levon, but not for any purpose of ours. This is the wildest magic. And it is in the verse: we will never hold them. Owein and the Hunt were powerful enough to move the moon and capricious enough to do it for their pleasure. Let us not think they will tamely serve our needs and as tamely go away."

Another silence. Something was nagging at the back of Kim's mind, something she knew she should be remembering, but this had become a chronic condition of late, and the thought could not be forced.

It was, surprisingly, Dave Martyniuk who broke the stillness. Awkward as ever in such a situation, the big man said, "This may be very dumb, I don't know . . . but it occurred to me that if Kim's ring is being called, then maybe Owein is ready to be released and we've been given the means to do it. Do we have the right to deny them, regardless of whether we know what they'll do? I mean, doesn't that make us jailers, or something?"

Loren Silvercloak rose as if pulled upward. Away from the angled light, they could see his eyes fixed on Dave. "That," said the mage, "is not even remotely a foolish thing to say. It is the deepest truth yet spoken here." Dave flushed bright red as the mage went on. "It is in the truest nature of things, at the very heart of the Tapestry: the wild magic is meant to be free, whether or not it serves any purpose of ours."

"So we do it?" Kevin asked. And turned to Kim again.

In the end, as in the beginning, it came back to her because she wore the ring. Something nagging still, but they were waiting and what Dave had said was true. She knew that much.

"All right," she said, and on the words the Baelrath blazed like a beacon with red desire.

"When?" Paul asked. In the tinted light they were all on their feet.

"Now, of course," said Diarmuid. "Tonight. We'd best get moving, it's a white ride."

They had lost Matt and Loren and picked up the other Dalrei, Torc, and Diarmuid's lieutenant, Coll.

The mage had volunteered to stay behind and inform the two Kings of what was happening. Torc, Kevin was given to understand, had been there when the horn and the cave were found; he had a place in this weaving. Kevin wasn't about to question it, seeing as he himself had no real place at all. Coll was with Diarmuid because he always was.

Kevin rode beside Paul for the early going, as Diarmuid led them northeast through a gentle valley. It was curious, but the cold seemed milder here, the wind less chill. And when they came around a ridge of hills he saw a lake, small, like a jewel in a setting of white-clad slopes—and the water of the lake wasn't frozen.

"A wind shelter, you think?" he said to Paul.

"More than that. That's Ysanne's lake. Where the water spirit is. The one Kim saw."

"Think that's doing it"

"Maybe." But by then Paul wasn't really with him any more. He had slowed his mount and was looking down at a small cottage by the lake. They were skirting it, passing by on a high ridge, but Kevin could see two boys come out to gaze at the party of riders passing by. Impulsively, Kevin waved and the older one waved back. He seemed to bend, speaking to his brother, and after a moment the little fellow raised a hand to them.

Kevin grinned and turned to say something to Paul, but what he saw in Schafer's rigid features erased the easy smile from his own. They resumed riding a moment later, moving quickly to catch the others. Paul was silent, his face clenched and rigid. He didn't offer anything, and this time Kevin didn't ask. He wasn't sure if he could deal with another rejection.

He caught up to Coll and rode the rest of the way beside him. It was colder when they came to the north end of the valley, and dark by the time they crossed the High Road from Rhoden to North Keep. He was carrying a torch by then, something which seemed, of late, to be his lot. The main illumination, though, more even than the low moon shining through clouds on their right, was the increasing brilliance of the red light cast by the ring Kim wore. *Wild to wild,* Kevin remembered.

And so, led by the Baelrath, they came at length to Pendaran Wood. There were powers there, aware of them, drawn by their presence and by the power of the ring. There were powers beyond these as well: the goddess whose gift had come to more than she had meant, and her brother, god of beasts and the wood. Above these also, Mörnir waited, and Dana, too, knew why the Warstone burned. Very far to the north, in his seat amid the Ice, the Unraveller was still a moment and wondered, though not clearly knowing what, or why.

And far, far above all of this, outside of time, the shuttle of the Worldloom slowed and then was still, and the Weaver, too, watched to see what would come back into the Tapestry.

Kimberly went forward, then, to the edging of Pendaran Wood, led by the flame on her hand. The company waited behind her, silent and afraid. She went without guidance, as if it had all been done before, to the place where a giant tree had been split by lightning so long ago not even the lios alfar had known the night of that storm. And she stood in the fork of that tree, wild magic on her hand, and wilder magic asleep behind the great rock Connla of the Paraiko had put there, and now, at the time of doing it, there was no fear in her heart, not even any wonder. She was tuned to it, to the wildness, to the ancient power, and it was very great. She waited for the moon to clear a drift of cloud. There were stars overhead, summer stars above the snow. The Baelrath was brighter than any of them, brighter than the moon the Hunt had moved so long ago. She drew a breath of gathering, felt the heart of things come over into her. She raised her hand, that the wandering fire might shine through the broken tree. She said:

"Owein, wake! It is a night to ride. Will you not wake to hunt among the stars?"

They had to close their eyes, all of them, at the pulse of red the words unleashed. They heard a sound like a hillside falling, and then there was stillness.

"It's all right," Kim said. "Come, Dave. Your turn now." And they opened their eyes to see a gaping cave where Connla's rock had been, and moonlight shining on the grass before the cave. The Baelrath was muted; it gleamed softly, a red against the snow, but not a flame.

It was by moonlight, silver and known, that they saw Dave stride, with long slow steps, more graceful than he knew in that moment, to stand by Kim and then, as she stepped back, to stand alone in the fork of the tree.

"The fire wakes them," they heard her say. "The horn calls, Dave. You must set them free."

Without a word the big man tilted back his head. He spread his legs wide for balance in the snow. Then, lifting Owein's Horn so that it glinted under the moon, he set it to his lips and with all the power of his lungs he sent forth the sound of Light.

No man there, nor the woman, ever forgot that sound for the length of their days. It was night, and so the sound they heard was that of moonlight and starlight falling on new snow by a deep wood. On and on it went, as Dave hurled the notes aloft to claim the earth and sky and be his own challenge to the Dark. On and on he blew, until it seemed his lungs must crack, his braced legs buckle, his heart break for the beauty vouchsafed him, and the great fragility of it.

When the sound stopped, the world was a different place, all of the worlds were, and the Weaver's hands moved to reclaim a long-still weft of thread for the web of the Tapestry.

In the space before the cave were seven shadowy figures, and each of them bore a crown and rode a shadowy horse, and the outline of each was blurred as through smoke.

And then there was an eighth as the seven kings made way, and from the Cave of the Sleepers came Owein at last after so long a sleep. And where the hue of the kings and of their shadowy horses was a dark grey hue, that of Owein was light grey shading to silver, and the colour of his shadowy horse was black, and he was taller than any of them and his crown gleamed more brightly. And set in it were stones red like the red of the Baelrath, and a red stone was set as well in the hilt of his drawn sword.

He came forward, past the seven kings, and his horse did not touch the ground as it moved, nor did the grey horses of the kings. And Owein raised his sword in salute to Dave and again to Kim, who wore the fire. Then he lifted his head to look beyond those two, and he scanned the company behind them. A moment he did so, and they saw his brow grow dark, and then the great black horse reared high on its legs, and Owein cried in a voice that was the voice of the storm winds, *"Where is the child?"*

And the grey horses of the kings reared high as well, and the kings lifted their own voices and cried, *"The child! The child!"* in a chorus like moaning winds; and the company was afraid.

It was Kimberly who spoke while in her heart she was naming herself a fool: for this, this was the thing she had been trying to think of all afternoon and through the ride to this place of power.

"Owein," she said, "we came here to free you. We did not know what more you needed done."

He whipped his horse, and with a cry it rose into the air above her, its teeth bared, its hooves striking towards her head. She fell to the ground. He loomed above her, wrathful and wild, and she heard him cry a second time, *"Where is the child?"*

And then the world shifted again. It shifted in a way none of them, not one, neither mortal nor forest power nor watching god, had foreknown.

From the fringe of trees not far from her a figure walked calmly forward.

"Do not frighten her. I am here," said Finn.

And so he came to the Longest Road.

⊷⟫◉⟪⊶

From first waking in the morning after the storm he had been uneasy. His heart would begin to race inexplicably, and there would be a dampness on his palms. He wondered if he was ill.

Restless, he dressed Dari in his boots and coat and the hat their mother had made in a blue that came near to the blue of Dari's eyes. Then he took his little brother for a walk in the wood around the lake.

Snow was everywhere, soft and clear, weighing the branches of the bare trees, piling in the paths. Dari loved it. Finn lifted him high, and the little one shook down a white powder from the branches he could reach. He laughed aloud and Finn lifted him up to do it again. Usually Dari's laughter picked up his own mood, but not today. He was too unsettled. Perhaps it was the memory of the night before: Dari seemed to have forgotten the voices calling him, but Finn could not. It was happening more often of late. He had told their mother, the first time. She had trembled and turned pale and then had wept all night. He had not told her of any of the other times Dari had come into his bed to whisper, "There are voices."

With his long strides he carried Dari farther into the grove, farther than they usually went—close to the place where their copse of trees thickened and then merged with the dark of Mörnirwood. It began to feel colder, and he knew they were leaving the valley. He wondered if Dari's voices would be louder and more alluring away from the lake.

They turned back. He began to play with his brother, tossing Dari into snowbanks and piling in after him. Dari was not as light or as easy to throw around as he used to be. But his whoops of delight were still those of a child and infectious, and Finn began to enjoy himself after all. They had tumbled and rolled a good distance from the path when they came to one of the strange places. Amid the piled snow that lay deep on the forest floor, Finn spotted a flash of colour; so he took Dari by the hand and clumped over through the snow.

In a tiny patch of improbably green grass there were a score of flowers growing. Looking up, Finn saw a clear space overhead where the sun could shine through the trees. And looking back at the flowers he saw they were all known to him—narcissus and corandiel except for one. They had seen these green places before, he and Dari, and had gathered flowers to bring home to Vae, though never all of them. Now Dari went to pluck a few, knowing how much his mother liked receiving gifts. "Not that one," Finn said. "Leave that one." He wasn't sure why, but something told him it should be left, and Dari, as always, obeyed. They took a handful of corandiel, with a yellow narcissus for colour, and went back home. Vae put the flowers in water on the table and then tucked Dari into bed for his nap.

They left behind them in the wood, growing in the strange place, that one blue-green flower with red at its centre like blood.

He was still restless, very much on edge. In the afternoon he went walking again, this time towards the lake. The grey waters chopped frigidly against the flat stone where he always stood. They were cold, the waters of the lake, but not frozen. All the other lakes, he knew, were frozen. This was a protected place. He liked to think the story he told Dari was true: that Dari's mother was guarding them. She had been, he remembered, like a queen, even with her pain. And after Dari was born and they came to carry her away, she had made them put her down beside Finn. He would never forget. She had stroked Finn's hair with her long fingers; then, pulling his head close, had whispered, so no one else would hear, "Take care of him for me. As long as you can." As long as you can. And on the thought, as if she had been waiting, annoyingly, for her cue, Leila was in his mind.

*What do you want?* he sent, letting her see he was irritated. In the beginning, after the last ta'kiena, when they discovered that she could do this, it had been a secret pleasure to communicate in silence and across the distances. But lately, Leila had changed. It had to do, Finn knew, with her passage from girl to woman; but knowing this didn't make him any more comfortable with the images she sent him from the Temple. They kept him awake at night; it was almost as if Leila enjoyed doing so. She was younger than he by more than a year, but never, ever, had he felt older than Leila.

All he could do was let her know when he was displeased, and not answer back when she began to send thoughts of greater intimacy than he could deal with. After a while, if he did this, she would always go away. He'd feel sorry, then.

He was in a bad mood today, though, and so, when he became aware of her, the question he sent was sharp and unaccommodating.

*Do you feel it?* Leila asked, and his heart skipped a beat, because for the first time ever he sensed a fear in her.

Fear in others made him strong, so as to reassure. He sent, *I'm uneasy, a little. What is it?*

And then his life began to end. For Leila sent, *Oh, Finn, Finn, Finn*, and with it an image.

Of the ta'kiena on the green, when she had chosen him.

So that was it. For a moment he quailed and could not hide it from her, but the moment passed. Looking out at the lake, he drew a deep breath and realized that his uneasiness had gone. He was deeply calm. He had had a long time to accept this thing and had been a long time waiting.

*It's all right*, he sent to Leila, a little surprised to realize that she was crying. *We knew this was going to come.*

*I'm not ready*, Leila said in his mind.

That was a bit funny: she wasn't being asked to do anything. But she went on, *I'm not ready to say goodbye, Finn. I'm going to be all alone when you go.*

*You'll have everyone in the sanctuary.*

She sent nothing back. He supposed he'd missed something, or not understood. No help for it now. And there was someone else who was going to miss him more.

*Leila*, he sent. *Take care of Darien.*

*How?* she whispered in his mind.

*I don't know. But he's going to be frightened when I go, and . . . he hears voices in the storms, Leila.*

She was silent, in a different way. The sun slipped behind a cloud and he felt the wind. It was time to move. He didn't know how he knew that, or even where he was to go, but it was the day, and coming on towards the hour.

*Goodbye*, he sent.

*The Weaver grant you Light*, he heard her say in his mind.

And she was gone. Walking back to the cottage, he already had enough of a sense of where he was about to go to know that her last wish was unlikely to be granted.

Long ago he had decided he would not tell his mother when the time came. It would smash her as a hammer smashes a lock, and there was no need for any of them to live through that. He went back in and kissed her lightly on the cheek where she sat weaving by the fire.

She smiled up at him. "Another vest for you, my growing son. And brown to match your hair this time."

"Thank you," he said. There was a catch in his throat. She was small and would be alone, with his father away at war. What could he do, though; what was in him to deny what had been laid down? These were dark times, maybe the very darkest times of all. He had been marked. His legs would walk even if his heart and courage stayed behind. It was better, he knew, to have the heart and soul go, too, to make the offering run deeper and be true. He was beginning to know a number of unexpected things. He was already travelling.

"Where's Dari?" he asked. A silly question. "Can I wake him?"

Vae smiled indulgently. "You want to play? All right, he's slept enough, I suppose."

"I'm not asleep," Dari said drowsily, from behind his curtain. "I heard you come in."

This, Finn knew, was going to be the hardest thing. He could not weep. He had to leave Dari an image of strength, clean and unblurred. It was the last guarding he could do.

He drew the curtains, saw his little brother's sleepy eyes. "Come," he said. "Let's dress you quick and go weave a pattern in the snow."

"A flower?" Dari said. "Like the one we saw?"

"Like the one we saw."

They hadn't been outside for very long. A part of him cried inwardly that it wasn't enough, he needed more time. Dari needed more. But the horsemen were there, eight of them, and the part of him that was travelling knew that this was the beginning, and even that the number was right.

Even as he looked, Dari holding him tightly by the hand, one of the riders lifted an arm and waved to him. Slowly Finn raised his free hand and signalled an acceptance. Dari was looking up at him, an uncertainty in his face. Finn knelt down beside him.

"Wave, little one. Those are men of the High King, and they're saying hello to us."

Still shy, Dari lifted a small mittened hand in a tentative wave. Finn had to look away for a moment.

Then, to the brother who was all his joy, he said calmly, "I want to run and catch up with them a moment, little one. I have a thing to ask. You wait and see if you can start the flower by yourself."

He rose then and began to walk away so his brother wouldn't see his face because the tears were falling now. He couldn't even say "I love you" at the end, because Dari was old enough to sense something wrong. He had said it so often, though, had meant it so much. Surely it had been enough in the little time he'd had. Surely it would be enough?

When Vae looked out a while later she saw that her older son was gone. Dari had done a thing of wonder, though: he had traced a perfect flower in the snow, all alone.

She had her own courage, and she knew what had come. She tried to do all her weeping first before going out in the yard to tell her little one how beautiful his newest flower was, and that it was time to come in and eat.

What broke her in the end was to see that Dari, moving quietly in the snow, was tracing his flower neatly with a thin branch in the growing dark while tears were pouring down his face without surcease.

In the twilight he followed them, and then by moonlight and their torches. He even got a little ahead, at first, cutting through the valley, while they took the higher ridges. Even when they passed him, torches, and a red flame on his right, they did not hurry; he was not far behind. Somehow he knew he could have kept up, even if they had been making speed. He was travelling. It was the day, the night, and nearly, now, the hour.

And then it was all three. There was no fear in him; as he'd moved farther and farther from the cottage his sorrow, too, had faded. He was passing from the circles of men into another place. It was only with an effort, as they neared the Wood, that he remembered to ask the Weaver to hold fast on the Loom to the thread of the woman, Vae, and the child, Darien. An effort, but he did it, and then, with that as the last thing, he felt himself cut loose as the fire blazed to let the horn sound and he saw and knew the kings.

He heard Owein cry out for him, *"Where is the child?"* He saw the woman of the flame fall down before Cargail's hooves. He remembered Owein's voice, and knew his tone to be fear and unease. They had been so long asleep in their cave. Who would lead them back into the starlit sky?

Who, indeed?

"Do not frighten her," he said. "I am here." And walking forward from the trees he came past Owein, into the circle of the seven mounted kings. He heard them cry out for joy and then begin to chant Connla's verse that had become the ta'kiena, the children's game, so long afterward. He felt his body changing, his eyes. He knew he looked like smoke. Turning to the cave, he spoke in a voice he knew would sound like wind. "Iselen," he said, and saw his white, white horse come forth. He mounted and, without a backward glance, he led Owein and the Hunt back into the sky.

⋌⇒⇐⋋

It came together, Paul thought, still twisting inside with the dazzle and the hurt. The two verses had come to the same place: the children's game and the one about Owein. He looked around and saw, by the moonlight, that Kim was still on her knees in the snow, so he went and, kneeling, gathered her to his chest.

"He was only a boy," she wept. "Why do I cause so much sorrow?"

"Not you," he murmured, stroking her white hair. "He was called long ago. We couldn't know."

"I *should* have known. There had to be a child. It was in the verse."

He never stopped stroking her hair. "Oh, Kim, we can reproach ourselves fairly for so many things. Be easy on the ones that are not fair. I don't think we were meant to know."

What long premeditating will, Paul thought, down all the years, had been farseeing enough to shape this night? Softly he spoke, to frame it:

> *When the wandering fire*
> *Strikes the heart of stone*
> *Will you follow?*
> *Will you leave your home?*
> *Will you leave your life?*
> *Will you take the Longest Road?*

The ta'kiena had become skewed over the long years. It wasn't four different children to four different fates. The wandering fire was the ring Kim wore. The stone was the rock it had smashed. And all questions led to the Road that Finn had taken now.

Kim lifted her head and regarded him with grey eyes, so like his own. "And you?" she asked. "Are you all right?"

To anyone else he might have dissembled, but she was kindred in some way, set apart as he was, though not for the same thing.

"No," said Paul. "I'm too frightened to even weep."

She read it in him. He saw her face change, to mirror his own. "Oh," she said. "Darien."

Even Diarmuid was silent on the long ride home. The sky had cleared and the moon, nearing full, was very bright, and high. They didn't need the torches. Kevin rode next to Kim, with Paul on her other side.

Glancing at her, and then at Paul, Kevin felt his own sense of grievance slipping away. It was true that he had less to offer here, demonstrably less than his marked, troubled friends, but neither did he have to carry what, so manifestly, they did. Kim's ring was no light, transfiguring gift. It could be no easy thing to have set in motion what had happened to that boy. How could a human child have become, even as they watched, a thing of mist, diffused enough to take to the night sky and disappear among the stars? The verses, he understood, something to do with both verses coming together. He wasn't sure, for once, if he wanted to know more.

Paul, though, Paul didn't have a choice. He did know more, and he couldn't hide the fact, nor the strain of wrestling with it. No, Kevin decided, he wouldn't begrudge them their roles this once, or regret his own insignificance in what had happened.

The wind was behind them, which made things easier, and then, when they dipped down towards the valley around the lake again, he felt it grow milder and less chill.

They were skirting the farmhouse again, retracing their path. Looking down, he saw there was a light, still, in the window, though it was very late, and then he heard Paul call his name.

The two of them stopped on the trail. Ahead, the others kept moving and then disappeared around a bend in the hill slope.

They looked at each other a moment, then Paul said, "I should have told you before. Jennifer's child is down there. He's the young one we saw earlier. It was his older brother . . . so to speak . . . whom we just watched go with the Hunt."

Kevin kept his voice level. "What do we know about the child?"

"Very little. He's growing very fast. Obviously. All the andain do, Jaelle says. No sign yet of any . . . tendencies." Paul drew a breath and let it out. "Finn, the older one, was watching over him, and so were the priestesses, through a girl who was mind-linked to Finn. Now he's gone and there is only the mother, and it'll be a bad night down there."

Kevin nodded. "You're going down?"

"I think I'd better. I need you to lie, though. Say I've gone to Mörnirwood, back to the Tree, for reasons of my own. You can tell Jaelle and Jennifer the truth—in fact, you'd better, because they'll know from the girl that Finn's gone."

"You're not coming east, then? To the hunt?"

Paul shook his head. "I'd better stay. I don't know what I can do, but I'd better stay."

Kevin was silent. Then, "I'd say be careful, but that doesn't mean much here, I'm afraid."

"Not much," Paul agreed. "But I'll try."

They looked at each other. "I'll take care of what you wanted," Kevin said. He hesitated. "Thanks for telling me."

Paul smiled thinly. He said, "Who else?" After a moment, leaning sideways on their horses, the two men embraced.

"Adios, amigo," said Kevin and, turning, kicked his mount to a trot that carried him around the bend.

Paul watched him go. He remained motionless for a long time after, his eyes fixed on the curve in the trail past which Kevin had disappeared. The road was not only bending now, it was forking, and very sharply. He wondered when he'd see his friend again. Gwen Ystrat was a long way. Among many other things, it might be that Galadan was there. Galadan, who he'd sworn would be his when they met for the third time. If they did.

But he had another task now, less filled with menace but as dark, notwithstanding that. He turned his thoughts from bright Kevin and from the Lord of the andain to one who was also of the andain and might yet prove greater than their Lord, for good or ill.

Picking his way carefully down the slope, he circled the farmyard by the light of the moon and the glow of the lamp in the window. There was a path leading up to the gate.

And there was something blocking the path.

Anyone else might have been paralyzed with fear, but Paul felt a different thing, though not any the less intense. *How many twists for the heart*, he thought, *are gathered in this one night?* And thinking so, he dismounted and stood on the path facing the grey dog.

A year and more had passed, but the moon was bright and he could see the scars. Scars earned under the Summer Tree while Paul lay bound and helpless before Galadan, who had come to claim his life. And had been denied by the dog who stood now in the path that led to Darien.

There was a difficulty in Paul's throat. He took a step forward. "Bright the hour," he said and sank to his knees in the snow.

For a moment he wasn't sure, but then the great dog came forward and suffered him to place his arms about its neck. Low in its throat it growled, and Paul heard an acceptance, as of like to like.

He leaned back to look. The eyes were the same as they had been when first he'd seen them on the wall, but he was equal to them now; he was deep enough to absorb their sorrow, and then he saw something more.

"You have been guarding him," he said. "I might have known you would."

Again the dog rumbled, deep in its chest, but it was in the bright eyes that Paul read a meaning. He nodded. "You must go," he said, "Your place is with the hunt. It was more than happenstance that drew me here. I will stay tonight and deal with tomorrow when it comes."

A moment longer the grey dog stayed facing him; then, with another low growl, it moved past, leaving the path to the cottage open. As the dog went by, Paul saw the number of its scars again, more clearly, and his heart was sore.

He turned. The dog had done the same. He remembered their last farewell, and the howl that had gone forth from the heart of the Godwood.

He said, "What can I say to you? I have sworn to kill the wolf when next we meet." The dog lifted its head.

Paul whispered, "It may have been a rash promise, but if I am dead, who can tax me with it? You drove him back. He is mine to kill, if I can."

The grey dog came back towards him to where he still crouched, on the path. The dog, who was the Companion in every world, licked him gently on his face before it turned again to go.

Paul was crying, whose dry eyes had sent him to the Summer Tree. "Farewell," he said, but softly. "And go lightly. There is some brightness allowed. Even for you. The morning will offer light."

He watched the dog go up the slope down which he had come and then disappear past the curve around which Kevin, too, had gone.

At length he rose and, taking the reins of the horse, unlatched the gate and walked over to the barn. He put his horse in an empty stall.

Closing the barn and then the gate, he walked through the yard to the back door of the cottage and stepped up on the porch. Before knocking he looked up: stars and moon overhead, a few fast-moving wisps of cloud scudding southward with the wind. Nothing else to be seen. They were up there, he knew, nine horsemen in the sky. Eight of them were kings, but the one on the white horse was a child.

He knocked and, so as not to frighten her, called softly, "It is a friend. You will know me."

She opened it quickly this time, surprising him. Her eyes were hollowed. She clutched a robe about herself. She said, "I thought someone might come. I left a light."

"Thank you," said Paul.

"Come in. He is asleep, finally. Please be quiet."

Paul stepped inside. She moved to take his coat and saw he wasn't wearing one. Her eyes widened.

"I have some power," he said. "If you will let me, I thought I'd stay the night."

She said, "He is gone, then?" A voice far past tears. It was worse, somehow.

Paul nodded. "What can I say? Do you want to know?"

She had courage; she did want to know. He told her softly, so as not to wake the child. After he had done, she said only, "It is a cold fate for one with so warm a heart."

Paul tried. "He will ride now through all the worlds of the Tapestry. He may never die."

She was a young woman still, but not her eyes that night. "A cold fate," she repeated, rocking in the chair before the fire.

In the silence he heard the child turn in its bed behind the drawn curtain. He looked over.

"He was up very late," Vae murmured. "Waiting. He did a thing this afternoon—he traced a flower in the snow. They used to do it together, as children will, but this one Dari did alone, after Finn left. And . . . he coloured it."

"What do you mean?"

"Just that. I don't know how, but he tinted the snow to colour his flower. You'll see in the morning."

"I probably marred it just now, crossing the yard."

"Probably," she said. "There is little left of the night, but I think I will try to sleep. You look very tired, too."

He shrugged.

"There is only Finn's bed," she said. "I'm sorry."

He rose. "That will suit me very well."

A short while later, in the dark, he heard two things. The first was the sound of a mother crying for her child, and the second was the wind outside growing in strength in the hours before dawn.


The calling came. It woke Dari, as it always did. At first it felt like a dream again but he rubbed his eyes and knew he was awake, though very tired. He listened, and it seemed to him that there was something new this time. They were crying for him to come out with them, as they always did, but the voices in the wind were naming him by another name.

He was cold, though, and if he was cold in his bed, he would die outside in the wind. Little boys couldn't go out into that wind. He was very cold. Rubbing his eyes drowsily, he slid into his slippers and voyaged across the floor to crawl into bed with Finn.

But it wasn't Finn who was there. A dark figure rose up in Finn's own bed and said to him, "Yes, Darien, what can I do?"

Dari was frightened but he didn't want to wake his mother so he didn't cry. He padded back to his own bed, which was even colder now, and lay wide awake, wanting Finn, not understanding how Finn, who was supposed to love him, could have left him all alone. After a while he felt his eyes change colour; he could always feel it inside. They had changed when he did the flower, and now they did so again, and he lay there hearing the wind voices more clearly than he ever had before.

# PART III

# DUN MAURA

# CHAPTER 10

In the morning a shining company left Paras Derval by the eastern gate, led by two Kings. And with them were the children of Kings, Diarmuid dan Ailell, Levon dan Ivor, and Sharra dal Shalhassan; and there were also Matt Sören, who had been a King, and Arthur Pendragon, the Warrior, cursed to be a King forever without rest; and there were many great and high ones beside, and five hundred men of Brennin and Cathal.

Grey was the morning under grey clouds from the north, but bright was the mood of Aileron the High King, freed at last from powerless planning within his walls. And his exhilaration at being released to act ran through the mingled armies like a thread of gold.

He wanted to set a swift pace, for there were things to be done in Morvran that night, but scarcely had the company cleared the outskirts of the town when he was forced to raise his hand and bring them to a stop.

On the snow-clad slope north of the cleared road a dog barked, sharp and carrying in the cold air. And then as the High King, moved by some instinct, signalled the halt, they heard the dog bark three times more, and every man in that company who knew dogs heard frantic joy in the sound.

Even as they stopped, they saw the grey shape of a hunting dog begin to tumble and dash down through the snow towards them, barking all the while, somersaulting head over tail in its haste.

It was Aileron who saw the light blaze in Arthur's face. The Warrior leaped from his horse down into the road and, at the top of his great voice, cried, *"Cavall!"*

Bracing his legs, he opened wide his arms and was knocked flying, nonetheless, by the wild leap of the dog. Over and over they rolled, the dog yelping in intoxicated delight, the Warrior mock growling in his chest.

All through the company, smiles and then laughter began to blossom like flowers in a stony place.

Heedless of his clothing or his dignity, Arthur played in the road with the dog he had named Cavall, and it was a long time before he stood to face the company. Arthur was breathing hard, but there was a brightness to his eyes in which Kim Ford found some belated dispensation for what she had done on Glastonbury Tor.

"This is," asked Aileron with gentle irony, "your dog?"

With a smile, Arthur acknowledged the tone. But his answer moved them to another place. "He is," he said, "insofar as he is anyone's. He was mine once, a very long time ago, but Cavall fights his own wars now." He looked down at the animal beside him. "And it seems that he has been hurt in those wars."

When the dog stood still, they could see the network of scars and unevenly regenerated fur that covered its body. They were terrible to look at.

"I can tell you whence those came." Loren Silvercloak moved his mount to stand beside those of the Kings. "He battled Galadan, the Wolflord, in Mörnirwood to save the life of the one who became the Twiceborn."

Arthur lifted his head. "The battle foretold? Macha and Nemain's?"

"Yes," Kim said, moving forward in her turn.

Arthur's eyes swung to her. "The Wolflord is the one who seeks the annihilation of this world?"

"He is," she replied. "Because of Lisen of the Wood, who rejected him for Amairgen."

"I care not for the reason," Arthur said, a coldness in his voice. "These are his wolves we go to hunt?"

"They are," she said.

He turned to Aileron. "My lord King, I had a reason to hunt before this: to forget a grief. There is a second reason now. Is there room in your hunting pack for another dog?"

"There is pride of place," Aileron replied. "Will you lead us now?"

"Cavall will," said Arthur, mounting as he spoke. Without a backward glance, the grey dog broke into a run.

⸺⊙⊙⸺

Ruana chanted the kanior for Ciroa, but not properly. It had not been proper for Taieri, either, but to the chant he again added the coda asking forgiveness for this. He was very weak and knew he had not the strength to rise and perform the bloodless rites that were at the heart of the true kanior. Iraima was chanting with him, for which he gave thanks, but Ikatere had fallen silent in the night and lay breathing heavily in his alcove. Ruana knew he was near his end, and grieved, for Ikatere had been golden in friendship.

They were burning Ciroa at the mouth of the cave, and the smoke came in, and the smell of charred flesh. Ruana coughed and broke the rhythm of the kanior. Iraima kept it, though, or else he would have had to start again: there was a coda for failing the bloodless rites, but not for breaking the chant.

After, he rested a little time and then, alone, began the thin chants again: the warnsong and the savesong, one after another. His voice was far from what it had been in the days when those of other caves would ask him to come and lead kanior for their dead. He continued, though, regardless: silence would be the last surrendering. Only when he chanted could he hold his mind from wandering. He wasn't even sure how many of

364

them were left in the cave, and he had no idea of what was happening in the other caves. No one had kept a count for many years, and they had been set upon in the dark.

Iraima's sweet voice came back in with him on the third cycle of the warnsong, and then his heart went redgold with grief and love to hear Ikatere chanting deep again with them for a little time. They spoke not, for words were strength, but Ruana shaded his voice to twine about Ikatere's; he knew his friend would understand.

And then, on the sixth cycle through, as the twilight was descending outside where their captors were camped on the slope, Ruana touched another mind with the savesong. He was singing alone again. Gathering what little was left in him, he focused the chant to a clear point, though it cost him dearly, and sent it out as a beam towards the mind he had found.

Then the mind seized hold of the beam he threw and sent back, effortlessly, the sound of laughter, and Ruana plummeted past black, for he knew whom he had found.

*Fool!* he heard, and lancets cut within him. *Did you think I would not blanket you? Where do you think your feeble sounds have gone?*

He was glad he had been chanting alone, that the others need not endure this. He reached inside, wishing again that he had access to hate or rage, though he would have to atone for such a wish. He sent, along the beam the chant had made, *You are Rakoth Maugrim. I name you.*

And was battered in his mind by laughter. *I named myself a long time ago. What power would you find in naming me, fool of a race of fools? Unworthy to be slaves.*

*Cannot be slaves*, Ruana sent. And then: *Sathain.* The mocking name.

Fire bloomed in his mind. Red-black. He wondered if he could have the other kill him. Then he could—

There was laughter again. *You shall have no bloodcurse to send. You shall be lost. Every one of you. And no one will chant kanior for the last. Had you done what I asked, you would have been mighty in Fionavar again. Now I will rip your thread from the Tapestry and wear it about my throat.*

*Not slaves*, Ruana sent, but faintly.

There was laughter. Then the chantbeam snapped.

For a long time Ruana lay in the dark, choking on the smoke of Ciroa's burning, assailed by the smell of flesh and the sounds the unclean ones made as they feasted.

Then, because he had nothing else to offer, no access to more, and because he would not end in silence, Ruana began the chants again, and Iraima was with him, and much-loved Ikatere. Then his heart came from past black towards gold again to hear Tamure's voice. With four they essayed the wide chant. Not in hope it would go as far as it had to go, for they were blanketed by the Unraveller and were very weak. Not to get through to anyone, but so as not to die in silence, not servants, never slaves, though their thread be torn from the Loom and lost forever in the Dark.

◄•═◑◑═•►

Hers, Jennifer understood, was a different fate from Arthur's, though interwoven endlessly. She remembered now. From first sight of his face she had remembered all of it, nor were the stars in his eyes new for her—she had seen them before.

No curse so dark as his had been given her, for no destiny so high, no thread of the Tapestry, had ever been consigned to her name. She was, instead, the agent of his fate, the working out of his bitter grief. She had died; in the abbey at Amesbury she had died—she wondered, now, how she had failed to recognize it by Stonehenge. She had had her rest, her gift of death, and she knew not how many times she had come back to tear him apart, for the children and for love.

She had no idea, remembering only that first life of all, when she had been Guinevere, daughter of Leodegrance, and had ridden to wed in Camelot, now lost and thought to be a dream.

A dream it had been, but more than that, as well. She had come to Camelot from her father's halls, and there she had done what she had done, and loved as she had loved, and broken a dream and died.

She had only fallen in love twice in her life, with the two shining men of her world. Nor was the second less golden than the first. He was not, whatever might have been said afterwards. And the two men had loved each other, too, making all the angles equal, shaped most perfectly for grief.

Saddest story of all the long tales told.

But, she told herself, it would not unfold again this time, not in Fionavar. *He is not here*, she had said, and known, for in this if nowhere else she had knowledge. There was no third one walking here, with the easy, envied stride, the hands she had loved. *I have been maimed but will not, at least, betray*, she had said, while a shower of starlight fell.

And she would not. It was all changed here, profoundly changed. Rakoth Maugrim had set his shadow between the two of them, across the Weaver's casting on the Loom, and everything was marred. No less a grief, more, even, for her, who had seen the unlight of Starkadh, but if she could not cross to love, she would not shatter him as she had before.

She would stay where she was. Surrounded by the grey-robed priestesses in the grey tone-on-tone of where her soul had come, she would walk among the women in the sanctuary while Arthur went to war against the Dark for love of her, for loss of her, and for the children, too.

Which led her back, as she paced the quiet curving halls of the Temple, to thoughts of Darien. And to these, too, she seemed to have become reconciled. Paul's doing. Paul, whom she had never understood, but trusted now. She had done what she had done, and they would see where the path led.

Last night, Jaelle had told her about Finn, and they had sat together. She had grieved a little for that boy among the strewn cold stars. Then Kevin had come knocking, very late, had offered blood as all men were bound to do, and then had come to them to say that Paul was with Darien and so it was all right, insofar as it could ever be all right.

Jaelle had left them, after that. Jennifer had said goodbye to Kevin, who was riding east in the morning. There was nothing she could offer in response to the troubled intensity of his gaze, but her new gentleness could speak to the sadness she had always seen in him.

Then, in the morning, Jaelle, too, had gone, leaving her to walk in the quiet Temple, more serene than she could have ever dreamed herself becoming, until from a recessed alcove near the dome she heard the sound of someone crying desperately.

There was no door to the alcove and so, passing by, she looked and then stopped, seeing that it was Leila. She was going to move on, for the grief was naked and she knew the girl was proud, but Leila looked up from the bench where she sat.

"I'm sorry," said Jennifer. "Can I do anything, or shall I go?"

The girl she remembered from the ta'kiena looked at her with tears brimming in her eyes. "No one can do anything," she said. "I've lost the only man I'll ever love!"

For all her sympathy and mild serenity, Jennifer had to work hard not to smile. Leila's voice was so laden with the weighty despair of adolescence it took her back to the traumas of her own teenage years.

On the other hand, she'd never lost anyone the way this girl had just lost Finn, or been tuned to anyone the way Leila and Finn had been. The impulse to smile passed. "I'm sorry," she said again. "You have a reason to weep. Will it help to hear that time does make it easier?"

As if she had scarcely heard, the girl murmured, "At midwinter full of moon, half a year from now, they will ask me if I wish to be consecrated to these robes. I will accept. I will never love another man."

She was only a child, but in the voice Jennifer heard a profound resolution.

It moved her. "You are very young," she said. "Do not let grief turn you so quickly away from love."

The girl looked up at that. *"And who are you to talk?"* Leila said.

"That is unfair," said Jennifer after a shocked silence.

The tears were glistening on Leila's cheeks. "Maybe," she said. "But how often have you loved, yourself? Have you not waited all your days for him? And now that Arthur is here you are afraid."

She had been Guinevere and was capable of dealing with this. There was too much colour in anger, so she said gently, "Is this how it seems to you?"

Leila hadn't expected that tone. "Yes," she said, but not defiantly.

"You are a wise child," said Jennifer, "and perhaps not only a child. You are not wholly wrong, but you must not presume to judge me, Leila. There are greater griefs and lesser, and I am trying to find the lesser."

"Lesser grief," Leila repeated. "Where is joy?"

"Not here," said Jennifer.

"But why?" It was a hurt child asking.

She surprised herself by answering, "Because I broke him once, long ago. And because I was broken here last spring. He is condemned to joylessness and war, and I cannot cross, Leila. Even if I did, I would smash him in the end. I always do."

"Must it be repeated?"

"Over and over," she said. The long tale. "Until he is granted release."

"Then grant it," said Leila simply. "How shall he be redeemed if not in pain? What else will ever do it? Grant him release."

And with that, all the old sorrow seemed to have come back after all. She could not stay it. There was brightly coloured pain in all the hues of guilt and grief, and coloured, also, was the memory of love, love and desire, and—

"It is not mine to grant!" she cried. *"I loved them both!"*

It echoed. They were near to the dome and the sound reverberated. Leila's eyes opened very wide. "I'm sorry," she said. "I'm sorry!" And she ran forward to bury her head against Jennifer's breast, having voyaged into deeper seas than she knew.

Reflexively stroking the fair hair, Jennifer saw that her hands were trembling. It was the girl who cried, though, and she who gave comfort. Once, in the other time, she had been in the convent garden at Amesbury when a messenger had come, towards sunset. After, as the first stars came out, she had comforted the other women as they came to her in the garden, weeping at the word of Arthur dead.

⋅✦⋅═◉═⋅✦⋅

It was very cold. The lake was frozen. As they passed north of it under the shadow of the wood, Loren wondered if he would have to remind the King of the tradition. Once more, though, Aileron surprised him. As they came up to the bridge over the Latham, the mage saw him signal a halt. Without a backward glance, the King held in his mount until Jaelle moved past him on a pale grey horse. Arthur called his dog to heel. Then the High Priestess went forward to lead them over the bridge and into Gwen Ystrat.

The river was frozen, too. The wood sheltered them somewhat from the wind, but under the piled grey clouds of late afternoon the land lay grim and mournful. There was a corresponding bleakness in the heart of Loren Silvercloak as, for the first time in his days, he passed over into the province of the Mother.

They crossed the second bridge, over the Kharn, where it, too, flowed into Lake Leinan. The road curved south, away from the wood where the wolves were. The hunters were gazing backwards over their shoulders at the winter trees. Loren's own thoughts were elsewhere, though. Against his will he turned and looked to the east. In the distance lay the mountains of the Carnevon Range, icy and impassible save through Khath Meigol, where the ghosts of the Paraiko were. They were beautiful, the mountains, but he tore his gaze from them and focused closer in, to a place not two hours' ride away, just over the nearest ridge of hills.

It was hard to tell against the dark grey of the sky, but he thought he saw a drift of smoke rising from Dun Maura.

"Loren," Matt said suddenly, "I think we forgot something. Because of the snow." Loren turned to his source. The Dwarf was never happy on a horse, but there was a grimness in his face that went beyond that. It was in Brock's eyes, too, on the far side of Matt.

"What is it?"

"Maidaladan," said the Dwarf. "Midsummer's Eve falls tomorrow night."

An oath escaped from the mage. And a moment after, inwardly, he sent forth a heartfelt prayer to the Weaver at the Loom, a prayer that Gereint of the Dalrei, who had wanted to meet them here, knew what he was doing.

Matt's one eye was focused beyond him now, and Loren swung back as well to look east again. Smoke, or shadings in the clouds? He couldn't tell.

Then, in that moment, he felt the first stirrings of desire.

He was braced by his training to resist, but after a few seconds he knew that not even the skylore followers of Amairgen would be able to deny the power of Dana in Gwen Ystrat, not on the night before Maidaladan.

The company followed the High Priestess through Morvran amid the blowing snow. There were people in the streets. They bowed but did not cheer. It was not a day for cheering. Beyond the town they came to the precincts of the Temple, and Loren saw the Mormae waiting there, in red, all nine of them. Behind and to one side stood Ivor of the Dalrei, and the old blind shaman, Gereint; farther yet to the side, with relief in their faces, were Teyrnon and Barak. Seeing the two of them, he felt some easing of his own disquiet.

In front of everyone stood a woman well over six feet tall, broad-shouldered and grey-haired, with her back straight and her head imperiously high. She, too, was clad in red, and Loren knew that this had to be Audiart.

"Bright the hour of your return, First of the Mother," she said with cool formality. Her voice was deep for a woman. Jaelle was in front of them and Loren couldn't see her eyes. Even in the overcast afternoon her red hair gleamed. She wore a silver circlet about her head. Audiart did not.

He had time to see these things, for Jaelle made no reply to the other woman. A bird flew suddenly from the Temple wall behind the nine Mormae, its wings loud in the stillness.

Then Jaelle delicately withdrew a booted foot from the stirrups of her saddle and extended it towards Audiart.

Even at a distance, Loren could see the other pale, and there came a low murmuring from the Mormae. For an instant Audiart was motionless, her eyes on Jaelle's face; then she stepped forward with two long strides and, cupping her hands beside the horse of the High Priestess, helped her dismount.

"Continue," Jaelle murmured and, turning her back walked through the gates of the Temple to the red-clad Mormae. One by one, Loren saw, they knelt for her blessing. Not one of them, he judged, was less than twice her age. Power on power, he thought, knowing there was more to come.

Audiart was speaking again. "Be welcome, Warrior," she said. There was some diffidence in her tone, but she did not kneel. "There is a welcome in Gwen Ystrat for one who was rowed by three Queens to Avalon."

Gravely, and in silence, Arthur nodded.

Audiart hesitated a moment, as if hoping for more. Then she turned, without hurrying, to Aileron, whose bearded features had remained impassive as he waited. "You are here and it is well," she said. "Long years have passed since last a King of Brennin came to Gwen Ystrat for Midsummer's Eve."

She had pitched her voice to carry, and Loren heard sudden whisperings among the horsemen. He also saw that Aileron hadn't realized what day it was either. It was time to act.

The mage moved up beside the High King. He said, and loudly, "I have no doubt the rites of the Goddess will proceed as they always do. We are not concerned with them. You requested aid of the High King, and he has come to give that aid. There will be a wolf hunt in Leinanwood tomorrow." He paused, staring her down, feeling the old anger rise in him. "We are here for a second reason as well, with the countenance and support of the High Priestess. I want it understood that the rituals of Maidaladan are not to interfere with either of the two things we have come to do."

"Is a mage to give commands in Gwen Ystrat?" she asked, in a voice meant to chill.

"The High King does." With time to recover, Aileron was bluntly compelling. "And as Warden of my province of Gwen Ystrat, you are charged by me now to ensure that things come to pass as my First Mage has commanded you."

She would, Loren knew, want revenge for that.

Before Audiart could speak, though, the sound of high thin laughter came drifting to them. Loren looked over to see Gereint swaying back and forth in the snow as he cackled with merriment.

"Oh, young one," the shaman cried, "are you still so fierce in your passions? Come! It has been a long time since I felt your face."

It was a moment before Loren realized that Gereint was speaking to him. With a ruefulness that took him back more than forty years, he dismounted from his horse.

The instant he touched the ground he felt another, deeper, surge of physical desire. He couldn't entirely mask it, and he saw Audiart's mouth go thin with satisfaction. He mastered an impulse to say something very crude to her. Instead, he strode over to where the Dalrei stood and embraced Ivor as an old friend.

"Brightly met, Aven," he said. "Revor would be proud."

Stocky Ivor smiled. "Not so proud as Amairgen of you, First Mage."

Loren shook his head. "Not yet," he said soberly. "Not until the last First Mage is dead and I have cursed his bones."

"So fierce!" Gereint said again, as he'd half expected.

"Have done, old man," Loren replied, but low, so no one but Ivor could hear. "Unless you can say you would not join my curse."

This time Gereint did not laugh. The sightless sockets of his eyes turned to Loren, and he ran gnarled fingers over the mage's face. He had to step close to do so, so what he said was whispered.

"If my heart's hate could kill, Metran would be dead past the Cauldron's reviving. I taught him, too, do not forget."

"I remember," the mage murmured, feeling the other's hands gliding over his face. "Why are we here, Gereint? Before Maidaladan?"

The shaman lowered his hands. To the rear, Loren heard orders being shouted as the hunters were dispersed to the lodgings assigned them in the village. Teyrnon had come up, with his round, soft face and sharp intelligence.

"I felt lazy," Gereint said tormentingly. "It was cold and Paras Derval was far away." Neither mage spoke nor laughed, nor did Ivor. After a moment the shaman said, in a deeper voice, "You named two things, young one: the wolves and our own quest. But you know as well as I, and should not have had to ask, that the Goddess works by threes."

Neither Loren nor Teyrnon said a word. Neither of them looked to the east.

The ring was quiet, which was a blessing. She was still deeply drained by the work of the night before. She wasn't sure if she could have dealt with fire again so soon, and she had been expecting it from the moment they crossed the first bridge. There was power all around her here, she could feel it, even through the green shield of the vellin on her wrist which guarded her from magic.

Then, when prepossessing Audiart spoke of Midsummer, the part of Kim that was Ysanne, and shared her knowledge, understood where the power was coming from.

Nothing to be done, though. Not by her, in this place. Dun Maura had nothing to do with a Seer's power, nor with the Baelrath either. When the company began to break up—she saw Kevin ride back into Morvran with Brock and two of Diarmuid's men—Kim followed Jaelle and the mages to the Temple.

Just inside the arched entranceway, a priestess stood with a curved, glinting dagger, and an acolyte in brown, trembling a little, held a bowl for her.

Kim saw Loren hesitate, even as Gereint extended his arm for the blade to cut. She knew how hard this would be for the mage. For any follower of the skylore, this blood offering would be tainted with darkest overtones. But Ysanne had told her a thing once, in the cottage by the lake, and Kim laid a hand on the mage's shoulder. "Raederth spent a night here, I think you know," she said.

There was, even now, a sorrow in saying this. Raederth, as First Mage, had been the one who'd seen the young Ysanne among the Mormae in this place. He had known her for a Seer and taken her away, and they had loved each other until he died—slain by a treacherous King.

The lines of Loren's features softened. "It is true," he said. "And so I should be able to, I suppose. Do you think I could stroll about and find an acolyte to share my bed tonight?"

She looked at him more closely and saw the strain she had missed. "Maidaladan," she murmured. "Is it taking you hard?"

"Hard enough," he said shortly, before stepping forward after Gereint to offer his mageblood to Dana, like any other man.

Deep in thought, Kim walked past the priestess with the blade and came to one of the entrances to the sunken dome. There was an axe, double-edged, mounted in a block of wood behind the altar. She stayed in the entrance looking at it until one of the women came to show her to her chamber.

Old friends, thought Ivor. If there was a single bright thread in the weaving of war it was this: that sometimes paths crossed again, as of warp and weft, that had not done so for years and would not have done, save in darkness. It was good, even in times like these, to sit with Loren Silvercloak, to hear Teyrnon's reflective voice, Barak's laughter, Matt Sören's carefully weighed thoughts. Good, too, to see men and women of whom he'd long heard but never met: Shalhassan of Cathal and his daughter, fair as the rumours had her; Jaelle the High Priestess, as beautiful as Sharra, and as proud; Aileron, the new High King, who had been a boy when Loren had brought him to spend a fortnight among the tribe of Dalrei. A silent child, Ivor remembered him as being, and very good at everything. He was a taciturn King now, it seemed, and said to still be very good at everything.

There was a new element, too, another fruit of war: among these high ones, he, Ivor of the Dalrei, now moved as an equal. Not merely one of the nine chieftains on the Plain, but a Lord, first Aven since Revor himself. It was a very hard thing to compass. Leith had taken to calling him Aven around the home, and only half in teasing, Ivor knew. He could see her pride, though the Plain would wash to sea before his wife would speak of such a thing.

Thinking of Leith led his mind to another thought. Riding south into Gwen Ystrat, feeling the sudden hammer of desire in his loins, he had begun to understand what Maidaladan meant and to be grateful to Gereint, yet again, for telling him to bring his wife. It would be wild in Morvran tomorrow night, and he was not entirely pleased that Liane had come south with them. Still, in these matters the unwed women of the Dalrei took directions from no man. And Liane, Ivor thought ruefully, took direction in precious few other matters as well. Leith said it was his fault. It probably was.

His wife would be waiting in the chambers given them here in the Temple. That was for afterwards. For now there was a task to be done under the dome, amid the smell of incense burning.

In that place were gathered the last two mages in Brennin, with their sources; the oldest shaman of the Plain, and by far the most powerful; the white-haired Seer of the High Kingdom; and the High Priestess of Dana in Fionavar—these seven were now to move through the shadows of space and time to try to unlock a door: the door behind which lay the source of winter winds and ice on Midsummer's Eve.

Seven to voyage and four to bear witness: the Kings of Brennin and Cathal, the Aven of the Dalrei, and the last one in the room was Arthur Pendragon, the Warrior, who alone of all men in that place had not been made to offer blood.

"Hold!" Jaelle had said to the priestess by the doorway, and Ivor shivered a little, remembering her voice. "Not that one. He has walked with Dana in Avalon." And the grey-robed woman had lowered her knife to let Arthur pass.

Eventually to come, as had Ivor and the others, to this sunken chamber under the dome. It was Gereint's doing, the Aven thought, torn between pride and apprehension. Because of the shaman they were in this place, and it was the shaman who spoke first among that company. Though not as Ivor had expected.

"Seer of Brennin," Gereint said, "we are gathered to do your bidding."

So it came back to her. Even in this place it came back, as had so much else of late. Once, and not a long time ago, she would have doubted it, wondered why. Asked within, if not aloud, who she was that these gathered powers should defer to her.

What was she, the inner voice would have cried, that this should be so?

Not anymore. With only a faint, far corner of her mind to mourn the loss of innocence, Kim accepted Gereint's deference as being properly due to the only true Seer in the room. She would have taken control if he had not offered it. They were in Gwen Ystrat, which was the Goddess's, and so Jaelle's, but the journey they were now to take fell within Kimberly's province, not any of the others', and if there was danger it was hers to face for them.

Deeply conscious of Ysanne and of her own white hair, she said, "Once before, I had Loren and Jaelle with me—when I pulled Jennifer out from Starkadh." It seemed to her the candles on the altar shifted at the naming of that place. "We will do the same thing again, with Teyrnon and Gereint besides. I am going to lock on an image of the winter and try to go behind it, into the mind of the Unraveller, with the vellin stone to shield me, I hope. I will need your support when I do."

"What about the Baelrath?"

It was Jaelle, intense and focused, no bitterness to her now. Not for this. Kim said, "This is a Seer's art and purely so. I do not think the stone will flame."

Jaelle nodded. Teyrnon said, "If you do get behind the image, what then?"

"Can you stay with me?" she asked the two mages.

Loren nodded. "I think so. To shape an artifice, you mean?"

"Yes. Like the castle you showed us before we first came." She turned to the Kings. There were three of them, and a fourth who had been and would always be, but it was to Aileron she spoke. "My lord High King, it will be hard for you to see, but we may all be sightless under the power. If there is anything shaped by the mages, you must mark what it is."

"I will," he said in his steady, uninflected voice. She looked to the shaman.

"Is there more, Gereint?"

"There is always more," he replied. "But I do not know what it is. We may need the ring, though, after all."

"We may," she said curtly. "I cannot compel it." The very memory of its burning gave her pain.

"Of course not," the blind shaman replied. "Lead us. I will not be far behind."

She composed herself. Looked at the others ringed about her. Matt and Barak had their legs braced wide apart, Jaelle had closed her eyes, and now she saw Teyrnon do the same. Her glance met that of Loren Silvercloak.

"We are lost if this fails," he said. "Take us through, Seer."

"Come, then!" she cried and, closing her eyes, began to drop down, and down, through the layers of consciousness. One by one she felt them come into her: Jaelle, tapping the avarlith; the two mages, Loren fierce and passionate, Teyrnon clear and bright; then Gereint, and with him he brought his totem animal, the night-flying keia of the Plain, and this was a gift to her, to all of them—a gift of his secret name.

*Thank you*, she sent; then, encompassing them all, she went forward, as if in a long flat dive, into the waking dream.

It was very dark and cold. Kim fought back fear. She might be lost down here; it could happen. But they were all lost if she failed. Loren had spoken true. In her heart a brilliant anger burned then, a hatred of the Dark so bright she used it to shape an image in the deep, still place to which they had come, the bottom of the pool.

She had not prepared it beforehand, choosing to let the dream render its own truest shape. And so it did. She felt the others registering it, in all their shadings of grief, anger, and hurting love for the thing marred, seeing that clear image of Daniloth defiantly alight, open and undefended amid an alien landscape of ice and snow.

She went into it. Not to the light, though she yearned for it, with all her heart, but straight into the bleak winter that surrounded it. Driving with all her power she reached back for the strength of the others and made of herself an arrow flung from a bow of light hurtling into the shape of winter.

And broke through.

Very black. The image gone. She was spinning. No controlled flight now. She was going into it and very fast and there was nothing to hand, nothing to grab onto, no—

*I'm here.* And Loren was.

*And I.* Jaelle.

*Always.* Brave Teyrnon.

Still dark, though, and going into it so far. No sense of space, of walls, nowhere to reach, not even with the others there. They were not enough. Not for where she had come so far into the workings of Maugrim. There was so much Dark. She had seen it once before, in and out for Jennifer—but now there was only *in* and so far yet to go. Then the fifth one was there and spoke.

*The ring.* She heard Gereint as if he were the voice of the keia itself, creature of the night, guardian of the way to the world of the dead.

*I can't!* she flung back, but even as she formed the thought, Kim felt the terrible fire and there was a red illumination in her mind.

And pain. She did not know that she cried aloud in the Temple. Nor did she know how wildly the light was blazing under the dome.

She was burning. Too near, she was. Too far into the web of Dark, too near the heart of power. The flame was all around, and fire does more than illuminate. It burns, and she was inside. She was—

A balm. A cooling breath as of the night breeze through autumn grasses on the Plain. Gereint. Another now: moonlight falling on Calor Diman, the Crystal Lake. And that was Loren, through Matt.

And then a goad: *Come!* Jaelle cried. *We are near to it.*

And Teyrnon's strength, cool in its very essence: *Farther yet, I think, but I am here.*

So on again she went. Forward and down, now, very nearly lost with how far she had to go. There was fire, but they were guarding her; she could endure it, she would; it was wild but not the Dark, which was an end to everything.

No longer an arrow, she made herself a stone and went down. Driven by need, by a passionate longing for Light, she went into the Dark, a red stone falling into the secret heart, the worm-infested caverns of Maugrim's designs. Into this unplace she fell, having cast loose from all moorings save the one along which she could send back, before she died and was lost, a single clear icon for the mages to shape in the domed room so infinitely far.

Too far. It was too deep and she was going so fast. Her being was a blur, a shadow; they could not hold her. One by one she left the others behind. With a despairing cry, Loren, who was the last, felt her slip away.

So there was fire and Rakoth, with no one to stay either one of them. She was alone and lost.

Or she should have been. But even as she plummeted, burning, a new mind came to hers so far down into the Dark she could scarcely believe it was there.

The burning ebbed again. She could exist, she could move through the pain, and she heard then, as if in a memory of a clean mild place, a deep voice singing.

There was darkness between, like a black-winged creature, screening the other from her. She was almost gone. Almost, but not yet. She had been a red arrow, then a stone. Now she made herself into a sword, red as it had to be. She turned. In this directionless world she somehow turned and, with the last blazing of her heart, she slashed through the curtain, found the other where he lay, and grasped an image to send back. She had to do it alone, for the mages were gone. With her very last power, using fire like love, she threw the vision back, unimaginably far, towards the sanctuary in Gwen Ystrat. Then it was dark.

She was a broken vessel, a reed on which a wind could play if there could be a wind. She was a twinned soul without form. The ring had faded utterly. She had done what she could.

There was someone with her, though, chanting still.

*Who?* she sent, as everything began to leave her.

*Ruana,* he replied. *Save us,* he sent. *Save us.*

And then she understood. And, understanding, knew she could not let go. There was no release for her yet. No directions existed in this place, but from where her body lay his chanting would be north and east.

In Khath Meigol, where the Paraiko had once been.

*We are,* he sent. *We still are. Save us.*

There was no fire left in the ring. With only the slow chanting to guide her in the black, she began the long ascent to what there was of light.

When the Baelrath blazed Ivor closed his eyes, as much against the pain in the Seer's cry as against the surging of red. They had been asked to bear witness, though, and a moment later he forced himself to look again.

It was hard to see in the punishing glow of the Warstone. He could just make them out, the young Seer and the others around her, and he marked the clenched strain on the faces of Matt and Barak. He had a sense of massive striving, of almost shattering effort. Jaelle was trembling now. Gereint looked like some Eridun death mask. Ivor's heart ached for them, journeying so far in such a silent battling.

Even as he thought this, the chamber exploded with echoing voices as, almost simultaneously, Jaelle and Gereint and tall Barak cried aloud in despair and pain. For a moment longer Matt Sören was silent, perspiration pouring down his craggy face; then Loren's source, too, cried out, a deep tearing sound, and fell to the floor.

As he rushed forward with Arthur and Shalhassan to succour them, Ivor heard Loren Silvercloak murmur with numbed tonelessness, "Too far. She went too far. It is over."

Ivor took the weeping Barak in his arms and led him to a bench set into the curving wall. He went back and did the same for Gereint. The shaman was shaking like the last leaf on a tree in an autumn wind. Ivor feared for him.

Aileron the High King had not moved. Nor had he taken his gaze from Kim. The light was still blazing and she was still on her feet. Ivor glanced at her face and then quickly away: her mouth was wide open in a soundless, endless screaming. She looked as if she were being burned alive.

He went back to Gereint, who was breathing in desperate gasps, his wizened face grey, even in the red light. And then, as Ivor knelt beside his shaman, that light exploded anew, so wildly it made the glow from before seem dim. Power pulsed like an unleashed presence all around them. It seemed to Ivor that the Temple shook.

He heard Aileron cry, *"There is an image! Look!"*

Ivor tried. He turned in time to see the Seer fall, in time to see a blurred shaping in the air beside her, but the light was too red, too bright. He was blinded by it, burned. He could not see.

And then it was dark.

Or it seemed that way. There were still torches on the walls, candles burning on the altar stone, but after the crazed illumination of the Baelrath, still raging in his mind's eye, Ivor felt surrounded by darkness. A sense of failure overwhelmed him. Something had happened; somehow, even without the mages, Kim had sent an image back and now she was lying on the floor with the High King standing over her, and Ivor had no idea what she had sent to them with what looked to have been the last effort of her soul. He couldn't see if she was breathing. There was very little he could see.

A shadow moved. Matt Sören rising to his feet.

Someone spoke. "It was too bright," said Shalhassan. "I could not see." There was pain in his voice.

"Nor I," Ivor murmured. Far too late his sight was returning.

"I saw," Aileron said. "But I do not understand."

"It was a Cauldron." Arthur Pendragon's deep voice was quietly sure. "I marked it as well."

"A Cauldron, yes," Loren said. "At Cader Sedat. We know that already."

"But there is no connection," Jaelle protested weakly. She looked close to collapse. "It quickens the newly dead. What does the Cauldron of Khath Meigol have to do with winter?"

What indeed? Ivor thought, and then he heard Gereint. "Young one," the shaman rasped, almost inaudibly, "this is the mages' hour. You have lived to come to this. First Mage of Brennin, *what is he doing with the Cauldron?*"

The mages' hour, Ivor thought. In the Temple of Dana in Gwen Ystrat. The Weaving of the Tapestry was truly past all comprehending.

Oblivious to their beseeching looks, Loren turned slowly to his source. Mage and Dwarf looked at each other as if no one else was in the room, in the world. Even Teyrnon and Barak were watching the other two and waiting. He was holding his breath, Ivor realized, and his palms were damp.

"Do you remember," Loren said suddenly, and in his voice Ivor heard the timbre of power that lay in Gereint's when he spoke for the god, "do you remember the book of Nilsom?"

"Accursed be his name," Matt Sören replied. "I never read it, Loren."

"Nor I," said Teyrnon softly. "Accursed be his name."

"I did," said Loren. "And so did Metran." He paused. *"I know what he is doing and how he is doing it."*

With a gasp, Ivor expelled air from his lungs and drew breath again. All around him he heard others doing the same. In Matt Sören's one eye he saw a gleam of the same pride with which Leith sometimes looked at him. Quietly, the Dwarf said, "I knew you would. We have a battle then?"

"I promised you one a long time ago," the mage replied. He seemed to Ivor to have grown, even as they watched.

"Weaver be praised!" Aileron suddenly exclaimed.

Quickly they all looked over. The High King had crouched and was cradling Kim's head in his arms, and Ivor could see that she was breathing normally again, and there was colour in her face.

In a rapt silence they waited. Ivor, close to tears, saw how young her face was under the white hair. He was too easily moved to tears, he knew. Leith had derided it often enough. But surely it was all right now? He saw tears on the face of the High King and even a suspicious brightness in the eyes of dour Shalhassan of Cathal. In such company, he thought, may not a Dalrei weep?

In a little while she opened her eyes. There was pain in their greyness, and a great weariness, but her voice was clear when she spoke.

"I found something," she said. "I tried to send it back. Did I? Was it enough?"

"You did, and it was enough," Aileron replied gruffly.

She smiled with the simplicity of a child. "Good," she said. "Then I will sleep now. I could sleep for days." And she closed her eyes.

# CHAPTER 11

"Now you know," said Carde with a wink, "why the men of Gwen Ystrat always look so tired!"

Kevin smiled and drained his glass. The tavern was surprisingly uncrowded, given the prevailing energies of the night. It appeared that both Aileron and Shalhassan had given orders. Diarmuid's band, though, as always, seemed to enjoy an immunity from such disciplinary commands.

"That," said Erron to Carde, "is half a truth at best." He raised a hand to summon another flask of Gwen Ystrat wine, then turned to Kevin. "He's teasing you a bit. There's some of this feeling all year long, I'm told, but only some. Tonight's different—or tomorrow is, actually, and it's spilling over into tonight. What we're feeling now comes only at Maidaladan."

The innkeeper brought over their wine. Upstairs they heard a door open, and a moment later Coll leaned over the railing. "Who's next?" he said with a grin.

"Go ahead," Carde said. "I'll keep the wine cool for you."

Kevin shook his head. "I'll pass," he said as Coll came clumping down the stairs.

Carde raised an eyebrow. "No second offers," he said. "I'm not being that generous tonight, not with so few women about."

Kevin laughed. "Enjoy," he said, raising the glass Erron had filled for him.

Coll slipped into Carde's seat. He poured himself a glass, drained it in a gulp, then fixed Kevin with a surprisingly acute glance. "Are you nervous about tomorrow?" he asked softly, so it wouldn't go beyond their table.

"A little," Kevin said. It was the easiest thing to say, and after a moment he realized that it gave him an out. "Actually," he murmured, "more than a little. I don't think I'm in a party mood tonight." He stood up. "I think I'll turn in, as a matter of fact."

Erron's voice was sympathetic. "It's not a bad idea, Kevin. Tomorrow night's the real thing, anyhow. What we're feeling now is going to be ten times stronger. With a wolf hunt under your belt, you'll be ready to bed a priestess or three."

"They come out?" Kevin asked, arrested for a moment.

"Only night of the year," Erron said. "Part of the rites of Liadon." He smiled wryly. "The only good part."

Kevin returned the smile. "I'll wait for tomorrow, then. See you in the morning." He clapped Coll on the shoulder, pulled on his coat and gloves, and walked out the door into the bitter chill of the night.

It is bad, he was thinking, when you have to lie to friends. But the reality was too difficult, too alienating, and it was private, too. Let them think he was apprehensive about the hunt; that was better than the truth.

The truth was that nothing of the desire that every other man in the company was feeling had even touched him. None of it. Only from the talk all around had he even grasped that something unusual was happening. Whatever supercharged eroticism was associated with Midsummer's Eve in this place—so much of it that even the priestesses of the Goddess came out from the Temple to make love—whatever was happening wasn't bothering to include him.

The wind was unholy. Worse even than a December holiday he'd spent once on the prairies. It scythed like a blade under his coat. He wasn't going to be able to stay out long. Nothing could. How, Kevin thought, did you fight an enemy who could do this? He had sworn revenge for Jennifer, he remembered, and his mouth twisted with bitter irony. Such bravado that had been. First of all, there wasn't even a war in which to fight—Rakoth Maugrim was breaking them with a hammer of wind and ice. Second, and this truth had been coiling within him since they had arrived from Stonehenge, he wouldn't be much good for anything even if, somehow, they ended the winter and there was a war. The memory of his useless flailing about during the battle on the Plain three nights ago was still raw.

He had moved past jealousy—hadn't lingered long there anyhow—it wasn't really a part of his nature. He was used to being able to *do* something, though. He no longer envied Paul or Kim their dark, burdensome powers—Kim's grief by Pendaran Wood the night before and Paul's loneliness had wiped that away, leaving a kind of pity.

He didn't want their roles or Dave's axe-wielding strength, and no sane person would want any part of what fate Jennifer had found. All he wanted was to *matter*, to have some way, however slight, of effectuating the heartfelt vow he had sworn.

Two, actually. He had done it twice. Once in the Great Hall when Brendel had brought word of the lios alfar dead and Jennifer taken away. Then a second time, when Kim had brought them home and he looked down at what had been done to a woman he loved and then forced himself not to look away, that the scalding image might always be there if courage ever flagged in him.

It was still there, that image, and—he searched himself for this—he was not lacking in courage. He had no fear of tomorrow's hunt, whatever the others might think, only a bitterly honest awareness that he was just along for the ride.

And this, for Kevin Laine, was the hardest thing in any world to handle. What he seemed to be, here in Fionavar, was utterly impotent. Again his mouth crooked bitterly in the cold, for this description was especially accurate now. Every man in Gwen

Ystrat was feeling the pull of the Goddess. Every man but him, for whom, all his adult days, the workings of desire had been a deep, enduring constant, known only to the women who had shared a night with him.

If love and desire belonged to the Goddess, it seemed that even she was leaving him. What did that leave?

He shook his head—too much self-pity there. What was left was still Kevin Laine, who was known to be bright and accomplished, a star in law school and one in the making, everyone said, when he got to the courts. He had respect and friendship and he had been loved, more than once. His, a woman had told him years ago, was a face made for good fortune. A curious phrase; he had remembered it.

There was, he told himself, no room for maudlin self-pity in a curriculum vitae like that.

On the other hand, all the glitter of his accomplishments lay squarely within his own world. How could he glory in mock trial triumphs anymore? How set his sights on legal excellence after what he had seen here? What could possibly have meaning at home once he had watched Rangat hurl a burning hand into the sky and heard the Unraveller's laughter on the north wind?

Very little, next to nothing. In fact, one thing only, but he did have that one thing, and with the pang of his heart that always came when he hadn't done so for a while, Kevin thought of his father.

*"Fur gezunter heit, und cum gezunter heit,"* Sol Laine had said in Yiddish, when Kevin had told him he had to fly to London on ten hours' notice. *Go safely, and come safely.* Nothing more. In this lay a boundless trust. If Kevin had wanted to tell, Kevin would have explained the trip. If Kevin did not explain, he had a reason and a right.

"Oh, Abba," he murmured aloud in the cruel night. And in the country of the Mother his word for father became a talisman of sorts that carried him in from the slash of wind to the house Diarmuid had been given in Morvran.

There were prerogatives of royalty. Only Coll and Kevin and Brock were sharing the place with the Prince. Coll was in the tavern, and the Dwarf was asleep, and Diarmuid was God knows where.

With a mild amusement registering at the thoughts of Diarmuid tomorrow night, and the deeper easing that thoughts of his father always gave to him, Kevin went to bed. He had a dream but it was elusive and he had forgotten it by morning.

⊷⊷⊷⊷⊷

The hunt started with the sunrise. The sky was a bright blue overhead, and the early rays of sunlight glittered on the snow. It was milder, too, Dave thought, as if somehow the fact of midsummer was registering. Among the hunters there was an electric energy one could almost see. The erotic surges that had begun when they had first entered Gwen Ystrat were even deeper now. Dave had never felt anything like it in his life, and they said the priestesses would come out to them tonight. It made him weak just to think of it.

He forced his mind back to the morning's work. He had wanted to hunt with the small contingent of the Dalrei, but horses weren't going to be much use in the wood and Aileron had asked the Riders to join the bowmen, who were to ring the forest and cut down any wolves that tried to flee. Dave saw Diarmuid's big lieutenant, Coll, unsling an enormous bow and ride over the bridge to the northwest with Torc and Levon.

It left an opening for him, he supposed, and somewhat reluctantly he walked over with his axe to where Kevin Laine stood joking with two other members of the Prince's band. There was a rumour going about that they had gotten an early start on the midsummer festival last night, defying the orders of the two Kings. Dave couldn't say he was impressed. It was one thing to carouse in town, another to be partying on the eve of battle.

On the other hand, none of them seemed the worse for it this morning, and he didn't really know anyone else to join up with so he awkwardly planted himself by the Prince and waited to be noticed. Diarmuid was rapidly scanning his brother's written instructions. When he finished, he looked up, noting Dave's presence with his disconcertingly blue gaze.

"Room for one more?" Dave asked.

He was prepared for a jibe but the Prince said only, "Of course. I've seen you fight, remember?" He raised his voice very slightly, and the fifty or so men around him quieted. "Gather round, children, and I'll tell you a story. My brother has outdone himself in preparing this. Here is what we are to do."

Despite the frivolous tone, his words were crisp. Behind the Prince, Dave could see the eidolath, the honour guard of Cathal, riding quickly off to the northeast behind Shalhassan. Nearby, Aileron himself was addressing another cluster of men, and, past him, Arthur was doing the same. It was going to be a pincer movement, he gathered, with the two hosts moving together from southwest and northeast.

The archers, about two hundred of them, were to ring the wood. The Cathalians were already along the line of the Kharn River, on the eastern edge, and across the northern boundary as far as the Latham. The bowmen of Brennin were posted from the Latham as well, in the north and then, at intervals, around to the south and west. The thinner copses east of the Kharn had already been checked and found empty, Diarmuid explained. The wolves were within the circle of Leinanwood itself and, if all went according to design, would soon be within the circle of the armies. The dogs were to be set loose to drive the wolves towards the forest centre.

"Unless the perfidious wolves have the temerity to disobey the High King's plans, we should meet Shalhassan's forces by the Latham in mid-wood with the wolves between us. If they aren't," Diarmuid concluded, "we blame anyone and everything except the plan. Any questions?"

"Where are the mages?" asked Kevin Laine. He always had questions, Dave thought. One of those. Couldn't just get on with it.

But Diarmuid answered seriously. "We were going to have them. But something happened last night in the Temple. The sources are completely drained. Swords and arrows are all we can use this morning."

And axes, Dave thought grimly. Didn't need anything more. It was cleaner this way with the magic kept out of it. There were no more questions, and no time for more; Aileron had begun moving his company forward. Diarmuid, neat-footed and quick, led them across the Latham bridge to the left flank, and Dave saw Arthur's company take the right.

They were on the southwestern edge of the wood, on the strip of land between forest and frozen lake. Around to the west and north Dave could see the archers, bows drawn, sitting on their horses where the wood thinned out.

Then Aileron signalled Arthur, and Dave saw the Warrior speak to his dog. With a howl, the grey dog exploded forward into Leinanwood and the hunting pack sprang after him. Dave heard faint answering sounds from the northern side as the other half of the pack was released. A moment the men waited; then the High King stepped forward, and they entered the wood.

It grew darker very suddenly, for even without leaves the trees were thick enough to screen the sun. They were moving northwest, before beginning their wide sweep back to the east, so Diarmuid's flank, their own, was in the lead. Abruptly Dave became aware of the smell of wolf, sharp and unmistakable. All around them the dogs were barking, but not urgently. His axe carried at the ready, with its thong looped around his wrist, Dave strode with Kevin Laine on his left and the Dwarf named Brock, bearing an axe of his own, on his right, behind the figure of Diarmuid.

Then, off to their right, Cavall gave tongue again, so loudly that even someone who had never hunted before knew what the sound meant.

"Turn!" Aileron cried from behind them. "Spread out and turn, towards the river!"

Dave's sense of direction was hopelessly gone by then, but he pointed his nose where Diarmuid went and, with quickening heart, set off to find the wolves.

They were found first.

Before they reached the river or the men of Cathal, the black and grey and brindle shapes were upon them. Scorning to be hunted, the giant wolves surged to the attack, and even as he swung the axe in a killing stroke, Dave heard the sounds of battle to the east as well. The men of Cathal had their own fight.

He had no more time to think. Swerving down and to his right, he dodged the fanged leap of a black beast. He felt claws shred his coat. No time to look back; there was another coming. He killed it with a chopping backhand slash, then had to duck, almost to his knees, as another leaped for his face. It was the last clear moment he remembered.

The battle became a chaotic mêlée as they twisted through the trees, pursuing and pursued. Within his breast Dave felt a surge of the obliterating fury that seemed to be his in battle, and he waded forward through snow red with blood, his axe rising and falling. In front of him all the time he saw the Prince, elegantly lethal with a sword, and heard Diarmuid singing as he killed.

He had no conception of time, could not have said how long it was before they broke through, he and the Prince, with Brock just behind. In front of him he could see the figures of the Cathalians across the frozen river. There were wolves to the right, though, engaging the centre of the Brennin ranks and Arthur's flank, as well. Dave turned to go to their aid.

"*Wait!*" Diarmuid laid a hand on his arm. "Watch."

Kevin Laine came up beside them, bleeding from a gash on his arm. Dave turned to watch the last of the battle on their side of the Latham.

Not far off, Arthur Pendragon, with grey Cavall by his side, was wreaking controlled destruction among the wolves. Dave had a sudden unexpected sense of how many times the Warrior had swung that blade he carried, and in how many wars.

But it wasn't Arthur whom Diarmuid was watching. Following the Prince's gaze, Dave saw, and Kevin beside him, the same thing Kimberly had seen a year before on a twilit path west of Paras Derval.

Aileron dan Ailell with a sword.

Dave had seen Levon fight, and Torc; he had watched Diarmuid's insouciant deadliness and, just now, Arthur's flawless swordplay with never a motion wasted; he even knew how he battled in his own right, fuelled by a rising tide of rage. But Aileron fought the way an eagle flew, or an eltor ran on the summer Plain.

It had ended on the other side. Shalhassan, bloody but triumphant, led his men down to the frozen waters of the Latham, and so they saw as well.

Seven wolves remained. Without a word spoken, they were left for the High King. Six were black, Dave saw, and one was grey, and they attacked in a rush from three sides. He saw how the grey one died and two of the black, but he never knew what motion of the sword killed the other four.

It was very nearly silent in the wood after that. Dave heard scattered coughing on both sides of the river; a dog barked once, nervously; a man not far away swore softly at the pain of a wound he'd taken. Dave never took his eyes from the High King. Kneeling in the trampled snow, Aileron carefully wiped his blade clean before rising to sheath it. He glanced fleetingly at his brother, then turned, with an expression almost shy, to Arthur Pendragon.

Who said, in a voice of wonder, "Only one man I ever saw could do what you just did."

Aileron's voice was low but steady. "I am not him," he said. "I am not part of it."

"No," said Arthur. "You are not part of it."

After another moment, Aileron turned to the river. "Brightly woven, men of Cathal. A small blow only have we given the Dark this morning, but better that we have given it than otherwise. There are people who will sleep easier tonight for our work in this wood."

Shalhassan of Cathal was splotched in blood from shoulder to boot and there were bloody smears in the forked plaits of his beard, but, kingly still, he nodded grave agreement. "Shall we sound the maron to end the hunt?" Aileron asked formally.

"Do so," Shalhassan said. "All five notes, for there are six of us dead on this side of the river."

"As many here," said Arthur. "If it please you, High King, Cavall can give tongue for both triumph and loss."

Aileron nodded. Arthur spoke to the dog.

Grey Cavall walked to an open space by the riverbank where the snow was neither trampled down nor red with wolf or dog or human blood. In a white place among the bare trees he lifted his head.

But the growl he gave was no sound of triumph nor yet of loss.

Dave would never be sure which caused him to turn, the dog's snarled warning or the trembling of the earth. Faster than thought he spun.

There was an instant—less than that, a scintilla of time in the space between seconds—and in it he had a flash of memory. Another wood: Pendaran. Flidais, the gnomelike creature with his eerie chants. And one of them: *Beware the boar, beware the swan, the salt sea bore her body on.*

Beware the boar.

He had never seen a creature like the one that rumbled now from the trees. It had to be eight hundred pounds, at least, with savage curving tusks and enraged eyes, and it was an albino, white as the snow all around them.

Kevin Laine, directly in its path, with only a sword and a wounded shoulder, wasn't going to be able to dodge it, and he hadn't a hope in hell of stopping the rush of that thing.

He had turned to face it. Bravely, but too late, and armed with too little. Even as the bizarre memory of Flidais exploded and he heard Diarmuid's cry of warning, Dave took two quick steps, let go of his axe, and launched himself in a lunatic, weaponless dive.

He had the angle, sort of. He hit the boar with a flying tackle on the near side shoulder, and he put every ounce of his weight and strength into it.

He was bounced like a Ping-Pong ball from a wall. He felt himself flying, had time to realize it, before he crashed, pinwheeling, into the trees.

"Kevin!" he screamed and tried, unwisely, to stand. The world rocked. He put a hand to his forehead and it came away covered with blood. There was blood in his eyes; he couldn't see. There was screaming, though, and a snarling dog, and something had happened to his head. There was someone on the ground and people running everywhere, then a person was with him, then another. He tried to rise again. They pushed him back. They were talking to him. He didn't understand.

"Kevin?" he tried to ask. He couldn't form the name. Blood got in his mouth. He turned to cough and fainted dead away from the pain.

It hadn't actually been bravery, or foolish bravado either—there had been no time for such complex things. He'd been at the back and heard a grunt and a trampling sound, so he'd been turning, even before the dog barked and the earth began to shake under the charge of the white boar.

In the half second he'd had, Kevin had thought it was going for Diarmuid and so he yelped to get its attention. Unnecessary, that, for the boar was coming for him all the way.

Strange how much time there seemed to be when there was no time at all. *At least somebody wants me,* was the first hilarious thought that cut in and out of his mind. But he was quick, he'd always been quick, even if he didn't know how to use a sword. He had no place to run and no way on earth of killing this monster. So, as the boar thundered up, grunting insanely and already beginning to raise its tusks to disembowel him, Kevin, timing it with coolest precision, jumped up in a forward somersault, to put his hands on the stinking white fur of the boar's huge back and flip over it like a Minoan bull dancer, to land in the soft snow.

In theory, anyway.

Theory and reality began their radical bifurcation around the axis formed by the flying figure of Dave Martyniuk at precisely the point where his shoulder crashed into that of the boar.

He moved it maybe two inches, all told. Which was just enough to cause Kevin's injured right arm to slip as he reached for the hold that would let him flip. He never got it. He was lying sprawled on top of the boar, with every molecule of usable air cannonballed out of his lungs, when some last primitive mechanism of his mind screamed *roll*, and his body obeyed.

Enough so that the tusk of the animal in its vicious, ripping thrust tore through the outer flesh of his groin and not up and through it to kill. He did his somersault in the end and came down, unlike Dave, in snow.

There was a lot of pain, though, in a very bad place and there were droplets of his blood all over the snow like red flowers.

It was Brock who turned the boar away from him and Diarmuid who planted the first sword. Eventually there were a number of swords; he saw it all, but it was impossible to tell who struck the killing blow.

They were very gentle when it came time to move him and it would have been rude, almost, to scream, so he gripped the branches of his makeshift stretcher until he thought his hands had torn through the wood, and he didn't scream.

Tried one joke as Diarmuid's face, unnaturally white, loomed up. "If it's a choice between me and the baby," he mumbled, "save the baby." Diar didn't laugh. Kevin wondered if he'd gotten the joke, wondered where Paul was, who would have. Didn't scream.

Didn't pass out until one of the stretcher bearers stumbled over a branch as they left the forest.

✧⊷═◉═⊶✧

When Kevin came to, he saw that Martyniuk was in the next bed, watching him. Had a huge blood-stained bandage around his head. Didn't look too well, himself.

"You're okay," Dave said. "Everything intact."

He wanted to be funny but the relief was too deep for that. He closed his eyes and took a breath. There was surprisingly little pain. When he opened his eyes he saw that there were a number of others in the room: Diar and Coll and Levon. Torc, too, and Erron. Friends. He and Dave were in the front room of the Prince's quarters, in beds moved close to the fire.

"I am okay," he confirmed. Turned to Dave. "You?"

"Fine. Don't know why, though."

"The mages were here," Diarmuid said. "Both of them. They each healed one of you. It took awhile."

Kevin remembered something. "Wait a minute. How? I thought—"

"—that the sources were drained," Diarmuid finished. His eyes were sober. "They were, but we had little choice. They're resting now in the Temple, both Matt and Barak. They'll be all right, Loren says." The Prince smiled slowly. "They won't be around for Maidaladan, though. You'll have to make it up to them. Somehow."

Everyone laughed. Kevin saw Dave looking at him. "Tell me," the big man said slowly, "did I save your life or almost get you killed?"

"We'll go with the first," Kevin said. "But it's a good thing you don't like me much, because if you did, you would have hit that pig with a real tackle instead of faking it. In which case—"

"Hey!" Dave exclaimed. "Hey! That's not . . . that isn't . . ." He stopped because everyone was laughing. He would remember the line, though, for later. Kevin had a way of doing that to him.

"Speaking of pigs," Levon said, helping Dave out, "We're roasting that boar for dinner tonight. You should be able to smell it."

After a moment and some trial sniffs, Kevin could. "That," he said from the heart, "was one big pig."

Diarmuid was grinning. "If you can make it to dinner," he said, "we've already arranged to save the best part for you."

"No!" Kevin moaned, knowing what was coming.

"Yes indeed, I thought you might like from the boar what it almost had from you."

There was a great deal of encouragement and loud laughter, fuelled as much, Kevin realized belatedly, by inner excitement as by anything else. It was Maidaladan, Midsummer's Eve, and it showed in every other man in the room. He got up, aware that there was a certain kind of miracle in his doing so. He was bandaged, but he could move and so, it seemed, could Dave. In the big man Kevin read the same scarcely controlled excitement that flared in all the others. Everyone but him. But now there was something nagging at him from somewhere very deep, and it seemed to be important. Not a memory, something else. . .

There was a lot of laughter and a rough, boisterous humour all around. He went with it, enjoying the camaraderie. When they entered the Morvran meeting house—a dining hall for the night—spontaneous applause burst forth from the companies of Brennin and Cathal, and he realized they were cheering for him and Dave.

They sat with Diarmuid's men and the two young Dalrei. Before dinner formally began, Diarmuid, true to his word, rose from his seat at the high table, bearing a platter ceremoniously before him, and came to Kevin's side.

Amid the gathering hilarity and to the rhythm of five hundred hungry men banging their fists on the long wooden tables, Kevin reminded himself that such things were said to be a delicacy. With a full glass of wine to hand, he stood up, bowed to Diarmuid, and ate the testicles of the boar that had almost killed him.

Not bad, actually, all things considered.

"Any more?" he asked loudly and got his laugh for the night. Even from Dave Martyniuk, which took some doing.

Aileron made a short speech and so did Shalhassan, both of them too wise to try to say much, given the mood in the hall. Besides, Kevin thought, the Kings must be feeling it too. The serving girls—daughters of the villagers, he gathered—were giggling and dodging already. They didn't seem to mind, though. He wondered what Maidaladan did to the women: to Jaelle and Sharra, even to that battleship Audiart, up at the high table. It was going to be wild later, when the priestesses came out.

There were windows high on all four sides. Amid the pandemonium, Kevin watched it growing dark outside. There was too much noise, too much febrile excitement, for anyone to mark his unwonted quiet.

He was the only one in the hall to see the moon when it first shone through the eastern windows. It was full and this was Midsummer's Eve, and the thing at the edge of his mind was pushing harder now, straining towards a shape. Quietly he rose and went out, not the first to leave. Even in the cold, there were couples clinched heedlessly close outside the banquet hall.

He moved past them, his wound aching a little now, and stood in the middle of the icy street looking up and east at the moon. And in that moment awareness stirred within him, at last, and took a shape. Not desire, but whatever the thing was that lay behind desire.

"It isn't a night to be alone," a voice from just behind him said. He turned to look at Liane. There was a shyness in her eyes.

"Hello," he said. "I didn't see you at the banquet."

"I didn't come. I was sitting with Gereint."

"How is he?" He began to walk, and she fell in stride beside him on the wide street. Other couples, laughing, running to warmth, passed them on all sides. It was very bright, with the moonlight on the snow.

"Well enough. He isn't happy, though, not the way the others are."

He glanced over at her and then, because it seemed right, took her hand. She wasn't wearing gloves either, and her fingers were cold.

"Why isn't he happy?" A random burst of laughter came from a window nearby, and a candle went out.

"He doesn't think we can do it."

"Do what?"

"Stop the winter. It seems they found out that Metran is making it—I didn't understand how—from the spiralling place, Cader Sedat, out at sea."

A quiet stretch of road. Inside himself Kevin felt a deeper quiet gathering, and suddenly he was afraid. "They can't go there," he said softly.

Her dark eyes were somber. "Not in winter. They can't sail. They can't end the winter while the winter lasts."

It seemed to Kevin, then, that he had a vision of his past of chasing an elusive dream, waking or asleep, down all the nights of his life. The pieces were falling into place. There was a stillness in his soul. He said, "You told me, the time we were together, that I carried Dun Maura within me."

She stopped abruptly in the road and turned to him.

"I remember," she said.

"Well," he said, "there's something strange happening. I'm not feeling anything of what's hitting everyone else tonight. I'm feeling something else."

Her eyes were very wide in the moonlight. "The boar," she whispered. "You were marked by the boar."

That too. Slowly he nodded. It was coming together. The boar. The moon. Midsummer. The winter they could not end. It had, in fact, come together. From within the quiet, Kevin finally understood.

"You had better leave me," he said, as gently as he could.

It took a moment before he realized that she was crying. He hadn't expected that.

"Liadon?" she asked. Which was the name.

"Yes," he said. "It looks as if. You had better leave me."

She was very young, and he thought she might refuse. He underestimated her, though. With the back of her hand she wiped away her tears. Then, rising on tiptoe, she kissed him on the lips and walked away in the direction from which they had come, towards the lights.

He watched her go. Then he turned and went to the place where the stables were. He found his horse. As he was saddling it, he heard bells ring from the Temple and his movements slowed for a moment. The priestesses of Dana would be coming out.

He finished with the saddle and mounted up. He walked the horse quietly up the lane and stopped in the shadows where it joined the road from Morvran to the Temple. Looking north, he could see them coming, and a moment later he watched the priestesses go by. Some were running and some walked. They all wore long grey cloaks against the cold and they all had their hair unbound and loose down their backs, and all the women seemed to shine a little in the full moonlight. They went past and, turning his head to the left, he saw the men coming out to meet them from the town, and the moon was very bright and it shone on the snow and ice, and on all the men and women in the road as they came together.

In a very little while the street was empty again and then the bells were silent. There were cries and laughter not very far away, but he carried his own deep quiet now, and he set his horse towards the east and began to ride.

⊷⇒◯⇐⊷

Kim woke late in the afternoon. She was in the room they had given her, and Jaelle was sitting quietly beside the bed.

Kim sat up a little and stretched her arms. "Did I sleep all day?" she asked.

Jaelle smiled, which was unexpected. "You were entitled."

"How long have you been watching me?"

"Not long. We've been checking on all of you periodically."

"All of us? Who else?"

"Gereint. The two sources."

Kim pushed herself into a sitting position. "Are you all right?"

Jaelle nodded. "None of us went so far as you. The sources were recovering, until they were drained again."

Kim asked with her eyes, and the red-haired Priestess told her about the hunt and then the boar. "No lasting damage to any of them," she finished, "though Kevin came very close."

Kim shook her head. "I'm glad I didn't see it." She drew a long breath. "Aileron told me that I did send something back. What was it, Jaelle?"

"The Cauldron," the other woman replied, and then, as Kim waited: "The mage says Metran is making the winter with it from Cader Sedat, out at sea."

There was a silence as Kim absorbed this. When it sunk in, all she felt was despair. "Then I did no good at all! We can't do anything about it. We can't get there in winter!"

"Nicely planned, wasn't it?" Jaelle murmured with a dryness that did not mask her own fear.

"What do we do?"

Jaelle stirred. "Not much, tonight. Don't you feel it?"

And with the question, Kim realized she did. "I thought it was just an aftermath," she murmured.

The Priestess shook her head. "Maidaladan. It reaches us later than the men, and more as restlessness than desire, I think, but it is almost sundown, and Midsummer's Eve."

Kim looked at her. "Will you go out?"

Jaelle rose abruptly and took a few paces towards the far wall. Kim thought she'd given offence, but after a moment the tall Priestess turned back to her. "Sorry," she said, surprising Kim for the second time. "An old response. I will go to the banquet but come back afterwards. The grey-robed ones must go into the streets tonight, to any man who wants them. The red Mormae never go, though that is custom and not law." She hesitated. "The High Priestess wears white and is not allowed to be part of Maidaladan or to have a man at any other time."

"Is there a reason?" Kim asked.

"You should know it," Jaelle said flatly.

And reaching within, to the place of her second soul, Kim did. "I see," she said quietly. "Is it difficult?"

For a moment Jaelle did not answer. Then she said, "I went from the brown of acolyte straight to the red and then the white."

"Never grey." Kim remembered something. "Neither was Ysanne." And then, as the other stiffened, she asked, "Do you hate her so much? Because she went with Raederth?"

She didn't expect an answer, but it was a strange afternoon, and Jaelle said, "I did once. It is harder now. Perhaps all the hate in me has gone north."

There was a long silence. Jaelle broke it awkwardly.

"I wanted to say . . . you did a very great thing last night, whatever comes of it."

For only the briefest moment Kim hesitated; then she said, "I had help. I'm only going to tell you and Loren, and Aileron, I think, because I'm not sure what will come of it and I want to go carefully."

"What help?" Jaelle said.

"The Paraiko," Kim replied. "The Giants are still alive and under siege in Khath Meigol."

Jaelle sat down quite suddenly. "Dana, Mother of us all!" she breathed. "What do we do?"

Kim shook her head. "I'm not sure. We talk. But not tonight, I guess. As you said, I don't think anything important will happen tonight."

Jaelle's mouth twitched. "Tell that to the ones in grey who have been waiting a year for this."

Kim smiled. "I suppose. You know what I mean. We'll have to talk about Darien, too."

Jaelle said, "Pwyll is with him now."

"I know. I guess he had to go, but I wish he were here."

Jaelle rose again. "I'm going to have to leave. It will be starting soon. I am glad to see you better."

"Thank you," Kim said. "For everything. I may look in on Gereint and the sources. Just to say hello. Where are they?"

Again Jaelle coloured. "We put them in beds in the chambers I use. We thought it would be quiet there—not all the priestesses go out if there are men in the Temple."

In spite of everything, Kim had to giggle. "Jaelle," she said, "you've got the only three harmless men in Gwen Ystrat sleeping in your rooms tonight!"

After a second she heard the High Priestess laugh, for the first time she could remember.

When she was alone, for all her good intentions, she fell asleep again. No dreams, no workings of power, just the deep sleep of one who had overtaxed her soul and knew there was more to come.

The bells woke her. She heard the rustle of long robes in the hallway, the quick steps of a great many women, whispers and breathless laughter. After a while it was quiet again.

She lay in bed, wide awake now, thinking of many things. Eventually, because it was Maidaladan, her thoughts went back to an incident from the day before, and, after weighing it and lying still a while longer, she rose, washed her face, and put on her own long robe with nothing underneath.

She went along the curving hallway and listened at a door where a dim light yet showed. It was Midsummer's Eve, in Gwen Ystrat. She knocked, and when he opened it, she stepped inside.

"It is not a night to be alone," she said, looking up at him.

"Are you sure?" he asked, showing the strain.

"I am," she said. Her mouth crooked. "Unless you'd prefer to go in search of that acolyte?"

He made no reply. Only came forward. She lifted her head for his kiss. Then she felt him unclasp her gown and as it fell she was lifted in Loren Silvercloak's strong arms and carried to his bed on Midsummer's Eve.

＊＝◎⇐＝＊

She was finally beginning to get a sense of what he might do, Sharra thought, of the forms his quest for diversion took. She had been a diversion herself a year ago, but that one had cost him a knife wound and very nearly his life. From her seat at the high table of the banquet hall she watched, a half smile on her lips, as Diarmuid rose and carried the steaming testicles of the boar to the one who had been gored. Miming a servant's gestures, he presented the platter to Kevin.

She remembered that one: he had taken the same leap as she the year before, from the musicians' gallery in Paras Derval, though for a very different reason. He, too, was handsome, fair as Diarmuid was, though his eyes were brown. There was a sadness in them, too, Sharra thought. Nor was she the first woman to see this.

Sadness or no, Kevin made some remark that convulsed those around him. Diarmuid was laughing as he returned to his seat between her father and the High Priestess, on the far side of Aileron. Briefly, he glanced at her as he sat down, and expressionlessly she looked away. They had not spoken since the sunlit afternoon he had so effortlessly mastered all of them. Tonight, though, was Maidaladan, and she was sure enough of him to expect an overture.

As the banquet proceeded—boar meat from the morning and eltor brought down from the Plain by the Dalrei contingent—the tone of the evening grew wilder. She was curious, certainly not afraid, and there was an unsettling disquiet within her as well. When the bells rang, she understood, the priestesses would be coming out. She herself, her father had made clear, would be in the Temple well before that. Already, Arthur Pendragon and Ivor, the Aven of the Dalrei, who had talked entertainingly on either side of her all evening, had gone back to the Temple. Or she assumed that was where they had gone.

There were, therefore, empty seats beside her in the increasingly unruly hall. She could see Shalhassan begin to stir restively. This was not a mood for the Supreme Lord of Cathal. She wondered, fleetingly, if her father was feeling the same upwelling of desire that was becoming more and more obvious in all the other men in the room. He must be, she supposed and suppressed a smile—it was a difficult thing to envisage Shalhassan at the mercy of his passions.

And in that instant, surprising her despite everything, Diarmuid was next to her. He did not sit. There would be a great many glances turned to them. Leaning on the back of the chair Arthur had been sitting in, he said, in a tone of mildest pleasantry, something that completely disconcerted her. A moment later, with a polite nod of his head, he moved away and, passing down the long room with a laugh or a jibe every few strides, out into the night.

She was her father's daughter, and not even Shalhassan, looking over with an appraising glance, was able to read even a hint of her inner turmoil.

She had expected him to come to her tonight, expected the proposition he would make. For him to murmur as he had just done, "Later," and no more was very much what she had thought he'd do. It fit his style, the indolent insouciance.

What didn't fit, what had unnerved her so much, was that he had made it a question, a quiet request, and had looked for a reply from her. She had no idea what her eyes had told him, or what—and this was worse—she had wanted them to tell.

A few moments later her father rose and, halfway down the room, so did Bashrai. An honour guard, creditably disciplined, escorted the Supreme Lord and Princess of Cathal back to the Temple. At the doorway, Shalhassan, with a gracious gesture if not an actual smile, dismissed them for the night.

She had no servants of her own here; Jaelle had assigned one of the priestesses to look after her. As she entered her room, Sharra saw the woman turning down her bed by the light of the moon that slanted through the curtained window. The priestess was robed and hooded already for the winter outside. Sharra could guess why.

"Will they ring the bells soon?" she asked.

"Very soon, my lady," the woman whispered, and Sharra heard a straining note in her low voice. This, too, unsettled her.

She sat down in the one chair, playing with the single gem she wore about her neck. With quick, almost impatient movements, the priestess finished with the bed.

"Is there more, my lady? Because, if not . . . I'm sorry, but—but it is only tonight . . ." Her voice trembled.

"No," Sharra said kindly. "I will be fine. Just . . . open the window for me before you go."

"The window?" The priestess registered dismay. "Oh, my lady, no! Not for you, surely. You must understand, it will be very wild tonight, and the men of the village have been known to . . ."

She fixed the woman with her most repressive stare. It was hard, though, to quell a hooded priestess of Dana in Gwen Ystrat. "I do not think any men of the village will venture here," she said, "and I am used to sleeping with a window open, even in winter." Very deliberately, she turned her back and began removing her jewellery. Her hands were steady, but she could feel her heart racing at the implication of what she had done.

If he laughed when he entered, or mocked her, she would scream, she decided. And let him deal with the consequences. She heard the catch of the window spring open and a cold breeze blew into the room.

Then she heard the bells, and the priestess behind her drew a ragged breath.

"Thank you," said Sharra, laying her necklace on the table. "I suppose that is your sign."

"The window was, actually," said Diarmuid.

Her dagger was drawn before she finished turning.

He had tossed back the hood and stood regarding her tranquilly. "Remind me to tell you some day about the other time I did this sort of thing. It's a good story. Have you noticed," he added, making conversation, "how tall some of these priestesses are? It was a lucky—"

"Are you trying to earn my hate?" She hurled it at him as if the words were her blade.

He stopped. "Never that," he said, though easily still. "There is no approach to this room from outside for one man by himself, and I chose not to confide in anyone. I had no other way of coming here alone."

"What made you assume you could? How much presumption—"

"Sharra. Have done with that tone. I didn't assume. If you hadn't had the window opened I would have walked out when the bells rang."

"I—" She stopped. There was nothing to say.

"Will you do something for me?" He stepped forward. Instinctively she raised her blade, and at that, for the first time, he smiled. "Yes," he said, "you can cut me. For obvious reasons I offered no blood when I came in. I don't like being in here on Maidaladan without observing the rites. If Dana can affect me the way she is tonight, she deserves propitiation. There's a bowl beside you."

And rolling up the sleeves of his robe and the blue shirt he wore beneath, he extended his wrist to her.

"I am no priestess," she said.

"Tonight, I think, all women are. Do this for me, Sharra."

So, for the second time, her dagger cut into him as she took hold of his wrist and drew a line across the underside. The bright blood welled, and she caught it in the bowl. He had a square of Seresh lace in his pocket, and wordlessly he passed it to her. She laid down the bowl and knife and bound the cut she had made.

"Twice now," he murmured, echoing her own thought. "Will there be a third?"

"You invite it."

He stepped away at that, towards the window. They were on the east side and there was moonlight. There was also, she realized, a long drop below as the ground fell sharply away from the smooth Temple walls. He had clasped his hands loosely on the window ledge and stood looking out. She sat down on the one chair by her bed. When he spoke it was quietly, still, but no longer lightly. "I must be taken for what I am, Sharra. I will never move to the measured gait." He looked at her. "Otherwise I would be High King of Brennin now, and Aileron would be dead. You were there."

She had been. It had been his choice; no one in the Hall that day was likely to forget. She remained silent, her hands in her lap. He said, "When you leaped from the gallery I thought I saw a bird of prey descending for a kill. Later, when you doused me with water as I climbed the walls, I thought I saw a woman with a sense of how to play. I saw both things again in Paras Derval five days ago. Sharra, I did not come here to bed you."

A disbelieving laugh escaped her.

He had turned to look at her. There was moonlight on his face. "It is true. I realized yesterday that I don't like the passion of Maidaladan. I prefer my own. And yours. I did not come to bed you, but to say what I have said."

Her hands were gripping each other very tightly. She mocked him, though, and her voice was cool. "Indeed," she said. "And I gather you came to Larai Rigal last spring just to see the gardens?"

He hadn't moved, but his voice seemed to have come very near, somehow, and it was rougher. "One flower only," said Diarmuid. "I found more than I went to find."

She should be saying something, dealing back to him one of his own deflating, sardonic jibes, but her mouth had gone dry and she could not speak.

And now he did move forward, a half step only, but it took him out of the light. Straining to see in the shadows, Sharra heard him say, carefully and masking now—at last—a tension of his own, "Princess, these are evil times, for war imposes its own constraints and this war may mean an ending to all that we have known. Notwithstanding this, if you will allow, I would court you as formally as ever a Princess of Cathal has been courted, and I will say to your father tomorrow what I say to you tonight."

He paused. There seemed to be moonlight all through the room suddenly, and she was trembling in every limb.

"Sharra," he said, *"the sun rises in your eyes."*

So many men had proposed to her with these, the formal words of love. So many men, but none had ever made her weep. She wanted to rise but did not trust her legs. He was still a distance away. Formally, he had said. Would speak to her father in the morning. And she had heard the rawness in his voice.

It was still there. He said, "If I have startled you, I am sorry for it. This is one thing I am not versed in doing. I will leave you now. I will not speak to Shalhassan unless and until you give me leave."

He moved to the doorway. And then it came to her—he could not see her face where she sat in the shadows, and because she had not spoken. . . .

She did rise then and, uttering the words through and over a cresting wave in her heart, said shyly, but not without a thread of laughter, "Could we not pretend it was not Maidaladan? To see where our own inadequate desire carried us?"

A sound escaped him as he spun.

She moved sideways into the light so he could see her face. She said, "Whom else should I ever love?"

Then he was beside her, and above, and his mouth was on her tears, her eyes, her own mouth, and the full moon of midsummer was upon them as a shower of white light, for all the dark around and all the dark to come.

⋅⊱══◯══⊰⋅

It was cold in the open but not so very bad tonight, and there was a shining light on the snow and the hills. Overhead the brighter stars gleamed frostily down, but the dimmer ones were lost in the moonlight, for the full moon was high.

Kevin rode at a steady pace towards the east, and gradually the horse began to climb. There was no real path, not among the snow, but the ascent was easy enough and the drifts weren't deep.

The hills ran north and south, and it wasn't long before he crested a high ridge and paused to look down. In the distance the mountains glittered in the silvery light, remote and enchanting. He wasn't going so far.

A shadow moved among the snow and ice to his right and Kevin swung over quickly to look, aware that he was weaponless and alone in a wide night.

It wasn't a wolf.

The grey dog moved slowly, gravely, to stand in front of the horse. It was a beautiful animal for all the brutal scars, and Kevin's heart went out to it. A moment they were thus, a tableau on the hilltop among the snow and the low sweeping sigh of the wind.

Kevin said, "Will you lead me there?"

A moment longer Cavall looked up, as if questioning or needing reassurance from the lone rider on the lone horse.

Kevin understood. "I *am* afraid," he said. "I will not lie to you. There is a strong feeling in me, though, the more so now, since you are here. I would go to Dun Maura. Will you show me the way?"

A swirl of wind moved the snow on the hilltop. When it passed Cavall had turned and was trotting down the slope to the east. For a moment Kevin looked back. There were lights behind him in Morvran and in the Temple, and dimly, if he listened, he could hear shouts and laughter. He twitched the reins and the horse moved forward after the dog, and on the downhill side the lights and noise were lost.

It wouldn't be very far, he knew. For perhaps an hour Cavall led him down out of the hills, winding east and a little north. Horse and man and dog were the only moving things among a winter landscape of evergreens piled with snow, and the moulded, silvered forms of the tummocks and gullies. His breath frosted in the night air, and the only sounds were the movements of his horse and the sighing of the wind, softer now since they had come down from the high places.

Then the dog stopped and turned to look back at him again. He had to search for several moments before he saw the cave. They were directly in front of it. There were bushes and overhanging vines over the entrance, and the opening was smaller than he'd thought it would be—more a fissure, really. A slantwise path led from it down into what seemed to be the last of the low hills. If the moonlight had not been so bright he wouldn't have seen it at all.

His hands weren't entirely steady. He took a number of slow, deep breaths and felt his heart's hard beating ease. He swung down off the horse and stood beside Cavall in the snow. He looked at the cave. He was very much afraid.

Drawing another breath, he turned back to the horse. He stroked its nose, his head close, feeling the warmth. Then he took the reins and turned the horse around to face the hills and the town beyond. "Go now," he said, and slapped it on the rump.

A little surprised at how easy it was, he watched the stallion canter off, following its own clear track. He could see it a long way in the clear light before the path they had taken curved south around a slope. For a few seconds more he stood gazing west at the place where it had disappeared.

"Well," he said, turning away, "here goes." The dog was sitting in the snow, watching him with its liquid eyes. So much sadness there. He had an impulse to embrace it, but the dog wasn't his, they had shared nothing, and he would not presume. He made a gesture with his hand, a silly one really, and, saying nothing more, walked into Dun Maura.

This time he didn't look back. There would be only Cavall to see, and the dog would be watching him, motionless in the moonlit snow. Kevin parted the ferns and stepped through the bushes into the cave.

Immediately it was dark. He hadn't brought any sort of light, so he had to wait for his eyes to adjust. As he waited, he became aware of how warm it suddenly was. He removed his coat and dropped it by the entrance, though a little out of the way. After a moment's hesitation he did the same with the beautifully woven vest Diarmuid had given him. His heart jumped at a quick flapping sound outside, but it was only a bird. Once it called, then twice, a long, thin, quavering note. Then, a moment later, it called a third time, a halftone deeper, and not so long. With a hand on the right side wall, Kevin began moving forward.

It was a smooth path, and the downward slope was gentle. With his hands outstretched, he could feel the walls on either side. He had a sense that the roof of the cave was high, but it was truly dark and he couldn't see.

His heart seemed to have slowed and his palms were dry, though there was a dampness to the rough walls. The blackness was the hard thing, but he knew, as much as he had ever known anything, that he had not come so far only to trip and break his neck on a dark path.

He went on for a long time, how long he didn't know. Twice the walls came very close together, forcing him to turn sideways to pass through. Once something flying in the dark passed very near him, and he ducked belatedly with a primitive fear. This passed, though, it all passed. Eventually the corridor bent sharply right, and down, and in the distance Kevin saw a glow of light.

It was warm. He undid another button of his shirt and then, on impulse, took it off. He looked up. Even with the new light, the roof of the cave was so high it was lost in the shadows. The path widened now, and there were steps. He counted, for no good reason. The twenty-seventh was the last; it took him out of the path to the edge of a huge round chamber that glowed with an orange light from no source he could see.

He stopped on the threshold, instinctively, and as he did so the hair rose up on the back of his neck and he felt the first pulse—not a surge yet, though he knew it would come—of power in that most holy place, and in him the form the power took was, at last, desire.

*"Bright your hair and bright your blood,"* he heard. He spun to his right.

He hadn't seen her, and wouldn't have had she not spoken. Barely three feet away from him there was a crude stone seat carved roughly into the rock face. On it, bent almost double with age, sat a withered, decrepit old crone. Her long stringy hair hung in unkempt yellow-grey whorls down her back and on either side of her narrow face. With knobbed hands, as deformed as her spine, she worked ceaselessly away at a shapeless knitting. When she saw him startle she laughed, opening wide her toothless mouth with a high, wheezing sound. Her eyes, he guessed, had once been blue, but they were milky and rheumy now, dimmed by cataracts.

Her gown would long ago have been white, but now it was stained and soiled an indeterminate shade and torn in many places. Through one tear he saw the slack fall of a shrunken breast.

Slowly, with uttermost deference, Kevin bowed to her, guardian of the threshold in this place. She was laughing still when he rose. Spittle rolled down her chin.

"It is Maidaladan tonight," he said.

Gradually she quieted, looking up at him from the low stone seat, her back so bent she had to twist her neck sideways to do so. "It is," she said. "The Night of the Beloved Son. It is seven hundred years now since last a man came calling on Midsummer's Eve." She pointed with one of her needles, and Kevin looked on the ground beside her to see crumbled bones and a skull.

"I did not let him pass," the crone whispered, and laughed.

He swallowed and fought back fear. "How long," he stammered, "how long have you been here?"

*"Fool!"* she cried, so loudly he jumped. *Foolfoolfoolfool* reverberated in the chamber, and high above he heard the bats. *"Do you think I am alive?"*

*Alivealivealivealive*, he heard, and then heard only his own breathing. He watched the crone lay her knitting down beside the bones at her feet. When she looked up at him again she held only one needle, long and sharp and dark, and it was trained on his heart. She chanted, clearly but soft, so there was no echo:

> *Bright your hair and bright your blood,*
> *Yellow and red for the Mother.*
> *Give me your name, Beloved,*
> *Your true name, and no other.*

In the moment before he answered, Kevin Laine had time to remember a great many things, some with sorrow and some with love. He drew himself up before her; there was a power in him, an upsurge of desire; he, too, could make the echoes ring in Dun Maura.

*"Liadon!"* he cried, and in the resounding of it, the burgeoning strength within himself, he felt a breath, a touch, as of wind across his face.

Slowly the crone lowered the needle.

"It is so," she whispered. "Pass."

He did not move. His heart was beating rapidly now, though not with fear any more. "There is a wishing in me," he said.

"There always is," the crone replied.

Kevin said, "Bright my hair and bright my blood. I offered blood once, in Paras Derval, but that was far from here, and not tonight."

He waited and for the first time saw a change in her eyes. They seemed to clear, to move back towards their lost blue; it may have been a trick of the orange light on the stone seat, but he thought he saw her straighten where she sat.

With the same needle she pointed, inwards, to the chamber. Not far away, almost on the threshold still, Kevin saw the elements of offering. No brightly polished dagger here, no exquisitely crafted bowl to catch the falling gift. This was the oldest place, the hearth. There was a rock rising up, a little past the height of his chest, from the cave floor, and it came to no level, rounded peak, but to a long jagged crest. Beside the rock was a stone bowl, little more than a cup. It had had two handles once, but one had broken off. There was no design on it, no potter's glaze; it was rough, barely functional, and Kevin could not even hazard a guess how old it was.

"Pass," the crone repeated.

He went to the rock and picked up the bowl, carefully. It was very heavy to his hand. Again he paused, and again a great many things came back to him from far away, like lights on a distant shore, or lights of a town seen at night from a winter hill.

He was very sure. With a smooth, unhurried motion, he bent over the rock and laid his cheek open on the jagged crest. Even as he felt the pain and caught the welling blood, he heard an ululating wail from behind him, a wild sound of joy and grief in one rising and falling cry as he came into his power.

He turned. The crone had risen. Her eyes were very blue, her gown was white, her hair was white as snow, her fingers long and slender. Her teeth were white, her lips were red, and a red flush was in her cheeks, as well, and he knew it for desire.

He said, "There is a wish in my heart."

She laughed. A gentle laugh, indulgent, tender, a mother's laugh over the cradle of her child.

"Beloved," she said. "Oh, be welcome again, Liadon. Beloved Son. . . Maidaladan. She will love you, she will." And the Guardian of the Threshold, old still but no longer a crone, laid a finger on his still flowing wound, and he felt the skin close to her touch and the bleeding stop.

She rose up on her toes and kissed him full on the lips. Desire broke over him like a wave in a high wind. She said, "Twelve hundred years have passed since I claimed my due from a sacrifice come freely."

There were tears in her eyes.

"Go now," she said. "Midnight is upon us, Liadon. You know where to go; you remember. Pour the bowl and the wish of your heart, Beloved. She will be there. For you she will come as swiftly as she did when the first boar marked the first of all her lovers." With her long fingers she was disrobing him even as she spoke.

Desire, power, crest of the wave. He was the force behind the wave and the foam where it broke. Wordlessly, he turned, remembering the way, and crossing the wide chamber, bearing his blood in a stone bowl, he came to its farthest point. To the very brink of the chasm.

Naked as he had been in the womb, he stood over it. And now he did not let his mind go back to the lost things from before; instead, he turned his whole being to the one wish of his heart, the one gift he sought of her in return, and he poured out the brimming cup of his blood into the dark chasm, to summon Dana from the earth on Midsummer's Eve.

In the chamber behind him the glow died utterly. In the absolute black he waited and there was so much power in him, so much longing. The longing of all his days brought to a point, to this point, this crevasse. Dun Maura. Maidaladan. His heart's desire. The boar. The blood. The dog in the snow outside. Full moon. All the nights, all the travelling through all the nights of love. And now.

And now she had come, and it was more than anything could be, more than all. She was, and she was there for him in the dark, suspended in the air above the chasm.

"Liadon," she whispered, and the throaty desire in the sound set him on fire. Then to crown it, and shape it, for she loved him and would love him, she whispered again, and she said, "Kevin," and then, *"Oh, come!"*

And he leaped.

She was there and her arms were around him in the dark as she claimed him for her own. It seemed to him as if they floated for a moment, and then the long falling began. Her legs twined about his, he reached and found her breasts. He caressed her hips, her thighs, felt her open like a flower to his touch, felt himself wild, rampant, entered her. They fell. There was no light, there were no walls. Her mouth made sounds as she kissed him. He thrust and heard her moan, he heard his own harsh breathing, felt the storm gathering, the power, knew this was the destination of his days, heard Dana say his name, all his names in all the worlds, felt himself explode deep into her, with the fire of his seed. With her own transfiguring ecstasy she flared alight; she was incandescent with what he had done to her, and by the light of her desire he saw the earth coming up to gather him, and he knew he had come home, to the end of journeying. End of longing, with the ground rushing now to meet, the walls streaming by; no regret, much love, power, a certain hope, spent desire, and only the one sorrow for which to grieve in the last half second, as the final earth came up to meet him.

*Abba*, he thought, incongruously. And met.

⟼⟾⟸⟻

In the Temple, Jaelle woke. She sat bolt upright in bed and waited. A moment later the sound came again, and this time she was awake and there could be no mistake. Not for this, and not tonight. She was High Priestess, she wore white and was untouched, because there had to be one so tuned to the Mother that if the cry went up it would be heard. Again it came to her, the sound she had never thought to hear, a cry not uttered for longer than anyone living knew. Oh, the ritual had been done, had been enacted every morning after Maidaladan since the first Temple was raised in Gwen Ystrat. But the lamenting of the priestesses at sunrise was one thing, it was a symbol, a remembering.

The voice in her mind was infinitely otherwise. Its mourning was for no symbolic loss, but for the Beloved Son. Jaelle rose, aware that she was trembling, still not quite believing what she heard. But the sound was high and compelling, laden with timeless grief, and she was High Priestess and understood what had come to pass.

There were three men sleeping in the front room of her chambers. None of them stirred as she passed through. She did not go into the corridor. Instead she came to another, smaller doorway and, barefoot in the cold, walked quickly down a dark narrow hallway and opened another door at the end of it.

She came out under the dome, behind the altar and the axe. There she paused. The voice was loud within her, though, urgent and exultant, even in its grief, and it carried her with it.

She was High Priestess. It was the night of Maidaladan, and, impossibly, the sacrifice had come to pass. She laid both hands on the axe that only the High Priestess could lift. She took it from its rest, and swinging around, she brought it crashing down on the altar. Hugely, the sound reverberated. Only when it ended did she lift her own voice in the words that echoed within her being.

*"Rahod hedai Liadon!"* Jaelle cried. "Liadon has died again!" She wept. She grieved with all her heart. And she knew every priestess in Fionavar had heard her. She was High Priestess.

They were awakening now, all those in the Temple. They were coming from their sleep. They saw her there, her robe torn, blood on her face, the axe lifted from its rest.

*"Rahod hedai Liadon!"* Jaelle cried again, feeling it rise within her, demanding utterance. The Mormae were all there now; she saw them begin to tear their own robes, to rend their faces in a wildness of grief and she heard them lift their voices to lament as she had done.

There was an acolyte beside her, weeping. She carried Jaelle's cloak and boots. In haste, the High Priestess put them on. She moved to lead them away, all of them, east, to where it had come to pass. There were men in the room now, the two mages, the Kings; there was fear in their eyes. They stepped aside to let her pass. There was a woman who did not.

"Jaelle," said Kim. "Who is it?"

She hardly broke her stride. "I do not know. Come!" She went outside. There were lights being lit all over Morvran and down the long street leading from the town she saw the priestesses running towards her. Her horse had been brought. She mounted up and, without waiting for anyone, she set off for Dun Maura.

They all followed. Two on a horse, in many cases, as the soldiers bore with them the priestesses who had leaped, crying, from their beds. It was midsummer and the dawn would come early. There was already a grey light when they came up to the cave and saw the dog.

Arthur dismounted and walked over to Cavall. For a moment he gazed into the eyes of his dog, then he straightened and looked at the cave. At the entrance Jaelle knelt among the red flowers now blooming amid the snow, and there were tears streaming down her face.

The sun came up.

"Who?" asked Loren Silvercloak. "Who was it?"

There were a great many people there by then. They looked around at each other in the first of the morning light.

Kim Ford closed her eyes.

All around them the priestesses of Dana began, raggedly at first, but then in harmony, to sing their lament for the dead Liadon.

"Look!" said Shalhassan of Cathal. "The snow is melting!"

Everyone looked but Kim. Everyone saw.

*Oh, my darling man*, thought Kimberly. There was a murmur surging towards a roar. Awe and disbelief. The beginnings of a desperate joy. The priestesses were wailing in their grief and ecstasy. The sun was shining on the melting snow.

"Where's Kevin?" said Diarmuid sharply.

*Where, oh, where? Oh, my darling.*

# PART IV

# CADER SEDAT

# CHAPTER 12

Oldest of three brothers, Paul Schafer had a general sense of how to deal with children. But a general sense wasn't going to be much good here, not with this child. Dari was his problem for the morning, because Vae had her own griefs to deal with: a child's loss to mourn and an almost impossible letter to write to North Keep.

He'd promised to see that the letter got there, and then he had taken Dari outside to play. Or, actually, just to walk in the snow because the boy—he looked to be seven or eight now, Paul judged—wasn't in a mood to play and didn't really trust Paul anyhow.

Reaching back fifteen years to a memory of his brothers, Paul talked. He didn't push Dari to say or do anything, didn't offer to toss him or carry him; he just talked, and not as one talks to a child.

He told Dari about his own world and about Loren Silvercloak, the mage who could go back and forth between the worlds. He talked about the war, about why Shahar, Dari's father, had to be away, and about how many mothers and children had had their men go away to war because of the Dark.

"Finn wasn't a man, though," said Dari. His first words that morning.

They were in the woods, following a winding trail. Off to the left Paul could see glimpses of the lake, the only unfrozen lake, he guessed, in Fionavar. He looked down at the child, weighing his words.

"Some boys," he said, "become like men sooner than others. Finn was like that."

Dari, in a blue coat and scarf, and mittens and boots, looked gravely up at him. His eyes were very blue. After a long moment he seemed to come to a decision. He said, "I can make a flower in the snow."

"I know," said Paul, smiling. "With a stick. Your mother told me you made one yesterday."

"I don't need a stick," Darien said. Turning away, he gestured towards the untrodden snow on the path ahead of them. The gesture of his hand in the air was duplicated in the snow. Paul saw the outline of a flower take shape.

He also saw something else.

"That's . . . very good," he said, as evenly as he could, while bells of alarm were going off in his head. Darien didn't turn. With another movement, not a tracing this time, simply a spreading of his fingers, he coloured the flower he'd made. It was blue-green where the petals were, and red at the centre.

Red, like Darien's eyes, when he made it.

"That's very good," Paul managed to say again. He cleared his throat: "Shall we go home for lunch?"

They had walked a long way and, going back, Dari got tired and asked to be carried. Paul swung him up on his shoulders and jogged and bounced him part of the way. Dari laughed for the first time. It was a nice laugh, a child's.

After Vae had given him lunch, Dari napped for most of the afternoon. He was quiet in the evening, too. At dinnertime, Vae, without asking, set three places. She, too, said very little; her eyes were red-rimmed, but Paul didn't see her weep. After, when the sun set, she lit the candles and built up the fire. Paul put the child to bed and made him laugh again with shadow figures on the wall before he pulled the curtains around the bed.

Then he told Vae what he had decided to do, and after a while she began to talk, softly, about Finn. He listened, saying nothing. Eventually he understood something—it took too long, he was still slow with this one thing—and he moved closer and took her in his arms. She stopped talking, then, and lowered her head simply to weep.

He spent a second night in Finn's bed. Dari didn't come to him this time. Paul lay awake, listening to the north wind whistle down the valley.

In the morning, after breakfast, he took Dari down to the lake. They stood on the shore, and he taught the child how to skip flat stones across the water. It was a delaying action, but he was still apprehensive and uncertain about his decision of the night before. When he'd finally fallen asleep, he'd dreamt about Darien's flower, and the red at its centre had become an eye in the dream, and Paul had been afraid and unable to look at it.

The child's eyes were blue now, by the water, and he seemed quietly intent on learning how to skip a stone. It was almost possible to convince oneself that he was just a boy and would remain so. Almost possible. Paul bent low. "Like this," he said, and made a stone skip five times across the lake. Straightening, he watched the child run to look for more stones to throw. Then, lifting his glance, he saw a silver-haired figure ride around the bend in the road from Paras Derval.

"Hello," said Brendel as he came up. And, then, dismounting, "Hello, little one. There's a stone just beside you and a good one, I think."

The lios alfar stood, facing Paul, and his eyes were sober and knowing.

"Kevin told you?" Paul asked.

Brendel nodded. "He said you would be angry, but not very. "

Paul's mouth twitched. "He knows me too well."

Brendel smiled, but his tell-tale eyes were violet. "He said something else. He said there seemed to be a choice of Light or Dark involved and that, perhaps, the lios alfar should be here."

For a moment, Paul was silent. Then he said, "He's the cleverest of all of us, you know. I never thought of that."

To the east, in Gwen Ystrat, the men of Brennin and Cathal were entering Leinan-wood and a white boar was rousing itself from a very long sleep.

Behind Brendel, Dari tried, not very successfully, to skip a stone. Glancing at him, the lios said softly, "What did you want to do?"

"Take him to the Summer Tree," Paul replied.

Brendel went very still. "Power before the choice?" he asked.

Dari skipped a stone three times and laughed. "Very good," Paul told him auto-matically, and then, to Brendel, "He cannot choose as a child, and I'm afraid he has power already." He told Brendel about the flower. Dari had run a few steps along the shore, looking for another stone.

The lios alfar was as a quiescent silver flame amid the snow. His face was grave; it was ageless and beautiful. When Paul was done, he said, "Can we gamble so, with the Worldloom at risk?"

And Paul replied, "For whatever reason, Rakoth did not want him to live. Jennifer says Darien is random."

Brendel shook his head. "What does that mean? I am afraid, Pwyll, very greatly afraid."

They could hear Dari laughing as he hunted for skipping stones. Paul said, "No one who has ever lived, surely, can ever have been so poised between Light and Dark." And then, as Brendel made no reply, he said again, hearing the doubt and the hope, both, in his own voice, "Rakoth did not want him to live."

"For whatever reason," Brendel repeated.

It was mild by the lake. The waters were ruffled but not choppy. Dari skipped a stone five times and turned, smiling, to see if Paul had been watching him. They both had.

"Weaver lend us light," Brendel said.

"Well done, little one," said Paul. "Shall we show Brendel our path through the woods?"

"Finn's path," said Dari and set off, leading them.

From within the cottage Vae watched them go. Paul, she saw, was dark, and the lios alfar's hair gleamed silver in the light, but Darien was golden as he went into the trees.

Paul had always been planning to come back alone with a question to ask, but it seemed to have worked out otherwise.

As they came to the place where the trees of the lake copse began to merge with the darker ones of the forest, Dari slowed, uncertainly. Gracefully, Brendel swept for-ward and swung him lightly up to his shoulders. In silence, then, Paul walked past both of them as once he had walked past three men at night, and near to this place. Carrying his head very high, feeling the throb of power already, he came into the Godwood for the second time.

It was daylight, and winter, but it was dark in Mörnirwood among the ancient trees, and Paul found himself vibrating inwardly like a tuning fork. There were memories. He heard Brendel behind him, talking to the child, but they seemed very distant. What was close were the images: Ailell, the old High King, playing chess by candlelight; Kevin singing "Rachel's Song"; this wood at night; music; Galadan and the dog; then a red full moon on new moon night, the mist, the God, and rain.

He came to the place where the trees formed a double row, and this, too, he remembered. There was no snow on the path, nor would there be, he knew; not so near the Tree. There was no music this time, and for all the shadows it was not night, but the power was there, it was always there, and he was part of it. Behind him, Brendel and the boy were silent now, and in silence Paul led them around a curve in the twin line of trees and into the glade of the Summer Tree. Which was as it had been, the night they bound him upon it.

There was dappled light. The sun was high and it shone down on the glade. He remembered how it had burned him a year ago, merciless in a blank, cloudless sky.

He put away his memories.

He said, "Cernan, I would speak with you," and heard Brendel draw a shocked breath. He did not turn. Long moments passed. Then from behind a screen of trees surrounding the glade a god came forward.

He was very tall, long of limb and tanned a chestnut brown. He wore no clothing at all. His eyes were brown like those of a stag, and lightly he moved, like a stag, and the horns on his head, seven-tined, were those of a stag as well. There was a wildness to him, and an infinite majesty, and when he spoke there was that in his voice which evoked all the dark forests, untamed.

"I am not to be summoned so," he said, and it seemed as though the light in the glade had gone dim.

"By me you are," said Paul calmly. "In this place."

Even as he spoke there came a muted roll of thunder. Brendel was just behind him. He was aware of the child, alert and unafraid, walking now about the perimeter of the glade.

"You were to have died," Cernan said. Stern and even cruel he looked. "I bowed to honour the manner of your death."

"Even so," said Paul. There was thunder again. The air seemed tangibly charged with power. It crackled. The sun shone, but far off, as if through a haze. "Even so," Paul repeated. "But I am alive and returned hither to this place."

Thunder again, and then an ominous silence.

"What would you, then?" Cernan said.

Paul said in his own voice, "You know who the child is?"

"I know he is of the andain," said Cernan of the Beasts. "And so he belongs to Galadan, to my son."

"Galadan," Paul said harshly, "belongs to me. When next we meet, which will be the third time."

Again a silence. The horned god took a step forward. "My son is very strong," he said. "Stronger than us, for we may not intervene." He paused. And then, with a new note in his voice, said, "He was not always as he is."

So much pain, Paul thought. Even in this. Then he heard, bitter and implacable,

406

the voice of Brendel: "He killed Ra-Termaine at Andarien. Would you have us pity him?"

"He is my son," said Cernan.

Paul stirred. So much darkness around him with no raven voices to guide. He said, still doubting, still afraid, "We need you, Woodlord. Your counsel and your power. The child has come into his strength, and it is red. There is a choice of Light we all must make, but his is gravest of all, I fear, and he is but a child." After a pause, he said it: "He is Rakoth's child, Cernan."

There was a silence. "Why?" the god whispered in dismay. "Why was he allowed to live?"

Paul became aware of murmuring among the trees. He remembered it. He said, "To make the choice. The most important choice in all the worlds. But not as a child; his power has come too soon." He heard Brendel breathing beside him.

"It is only as a child," Cernan said, "that he can be controlled."

Paul shook his head. "There is no controlling him, nor could there ever be. Woodlord, he is a battlefield and must be old enough to know it!" Saying the words, he felt them ring true. There was no thunder, but a strange, anticipatory pulsing ran within him. He said, "Cernan, can you take him through to his maturity?"

Cernan of the Beasts lifted his mighty head, and for the first time something in him daunted Paul. The god opened his mouth to speak—

They never heard what he meant to say.

From the far side of the glade there came a flash of light, blinding almost, in the charged dimness of that place.

"Weaver at the Loom!" Brendel cried.

*"Not quite,"* said Darien.

He came out from behind the Summer Tree, and he was no longer a child. Naked as Cernan, he stood, but fair-haired as he had been from birth, and not so tall as was the god. He was about the height, Paul realized, with a numbing apprehension, that Finn had been, and looked to be the same age as well.

"Dari. . ." he began, but the nickname didn't fit any more, it didn't apply to this golden presence in the glade. He tried again. "Darien, this is what I brought you for, but how did you do it alone?"

He was answered with a laugh that turned apprehension to terror. "You forgot something," said Darien. "You all did. Such a simple thing as winter led you to forget. We are in an oak grove and Midsummer's Eve is coming on! With such power to draw upon, why should I need the horned god to come into my power?"

"Not your power," Paul replied as steadily as he could, watching Darien's eyes, which were still blue. "Your maturity. You are old enough now to know why. You have a choice to make."

*"Shall I go ask my father,"* Darien cried, *"what to do?"* And with a gesture he torched the trees around the glade into a circle of fire, red like the red flash of his eyes.

Paul staggered back, feeling the rush of heat as he had not felt the cold. He heard Cernan cry out, but before the god could act, Brendel stepped forward.

"No," he said. "Put out the fire and hear me before you go." There was a music in his voice, bells in a high place of light. "Only once," Brendel said quietly, and Darien moved a hand.

The fire died. The trees were untouched. Illusion, Paul realized. It had been an illusion. He still felt the fading heat on his skin, though, and in the place of his own power he felt a helplessness.

Ethereal, almost luminous, Brendel faced the child of Rakoth. "You heard us name your father," he said, "but you do not know your mother's name, and you have her hair and her hands. More than that: your father's eyes are red, your mother's green. Your eyes are blue, Darien. You are not bound to any destiny. No one born, ever, has had so pure a choice of Light or Dark."

"It is so," came Cernan's deep voice from the trees.

Paul couldn't see Brendel's eyes, but Darien's were blue again and he was beautiful. No longer a child but young, still, with a beardless open face, and so very great a power.

"If the choice is pure," said Darien, "should I not hear my father as well as you? If only to be fair?" He laughed then, at something he saw in Brendel's face.

"Darien," said Paul quietly, "you have been loved. What did Finn tell you about the choice?"

It was a gamble. Another one, for he didn't know if Finn would have said anything at all.

A gamble, and he seemed to have lost. "He left," said Darien, a spasm of pain raking across his face. *"He left!"* the boy cried again. He gestured with a hand—a hand like Jennifer's—and disappeared.

There was silence, then a sound of something rushing from the glade.

"Why," said Cernan of the Beasts again—the god who had mocked Maugrim long ago and named him Sathain—"why was he allowed to live?"

Paul looked at him, then at the suddenly frail-seeming lios alfar. He clenched his fists. "To choose!" he cried with a certain desperation. Reaching within, to the throb of power, he sought confirmation and found none.

Together, Paul and Brendel left the glade and then the Godwood. It had been a long walk there; it seemed even longer going back. The sun was westering behind them when they came again to the cottage. Three had gone out in the morning, but Vae saw only two return.

She let them in, and the lios alfar bowed to her and then kissed her cheek, which was unexpected. She had never seen one of them before. Once, it would have thrilled her beyond measure. Once. They sat down wearily in the two chairs by the fire, and she made an herbal tea while they told her what had come to pass.

"It was for nothing then," she said when the tale was done. "It was worse than nothing, all we did, if he has gone over to his father. I thought love might count for more."

Neither of them answered her, which was answer enough. Paul threw more wood on the fire. He felt bruised by the day's events. "There is no need for you to stay here now," he said. "Shall we take you back to the city in the morning?"

Slowly, she nodded. And then, as the loneliness hit home, said tremulously, "It will be an empty house. Cannot Shahar come home to serve in Paras Derval?"

"He can," said Paul quietly. "Oh, Vae, I am so sorry. I will see that he comes home."

She did weep, then, for a little while. She hadn't wanted to. But Finn had gone impossibly far, and Dari now as well, and Shahar had been away for so long.

They stayed the night. By the light of candles and the fire, they helped her gather the few belongings she had brought to the cottage. When it grew late they let the fire die, and the lios slept in Dari's bed and Paul in Finn's again. They were to leave at first light.

They woke before that, though. It was Brendel who stirred and the other two, in shallow sleep, heard him rise. It was still night, perhaps two hours before dawn.

"What is it?" Paul asked.

"I am not sure," the lios replied. "Something."

They dressed, all three of them, and walked out towards the lake. The full moon was low now but very bright. The wind had shifted to the south, blowing towards them from over the water. The stars overhead and west were dimmed by the moon. They shone brighter, Paul saw, in the east.

Then, still looking east, he lowered his glance. Unable to speak, he touched Brendel and Vae and then pointed.

All along the hills, clearly visible in the light of the moon, the snow was starting to melt.

He hadn't gone far, nor been invisible for long—it wasn't a thing he could sustain. He heard the god go off in the guise of a stag and then the other two, walking slowly, in silence. He had an impulse to follow but he remained where he was among the trees. Later, when everyone had gone, Darien rose and left as well.

There was something, like a fist or a stone, buried in his chest. It hurt. He wasn't used to this body, the one he had accelerated himself into. He wasn't used to knowing who his father was either. He knew the first discomfort would pass, suspected the second would. Wasn't sure how he felt about that, or about anything. He was naked, but he wasn't cold. He was deeply angry at everyone. He was beginning to guess how strong he was.

There was a place—Finn had found it—north of the cottage and high up on the highest of the hills. In summer it would have been an easy climb, Finn had said. Darien had never known a summer. When Finn took him, the drifts had been up to Dari's chest and Finn had carried him much of the way.

He wasn't Dari anymore. That name was another thing lost, another fragment gone away. He stood in front of the small cave on the hill slope. It sheltered him from the wind, though he didn't need shelter. From here you could see the towers of the palace of Paras Derval, though not the town.

You could also look down, as it grew dark, on the lights in the cottage by the lake. His eyes were very good. He could see figures moving behind the drawn curtains. He watched them. After a while, he did begin to feel cold. It had all happened very fast.

He couldn't quite fit into this body or deal with the older mind he now had. He was still half in Dari's shape, in the blue winter coat and mittens. He still wanted to be carried down and be put to bed.

It was hard not to cry, looking at the lights, and harder when the lights went out. He was alone then with only moonlight and the snow and the voices again in the wind. He didn't cry, though, he moved back towards anger instead. *Why was he allowed to live?* Cernan had said. None of them wanted him, not even Finn, who had gone away.

It was cold and he was hungry. On the thought, he flashed red and made himself into an owl. He flew for an hour and found three night rodents near the wood. He flew back to the cave. It was warmer as a bird and he fell asleep in that shape.

When the wind shifted he woke, because with the coming of the south wind the voices had ceased. They had been clear and alluring but now they stopped.

He had become Darien again while he slept. Stepping from the cave, he looked all around him at the melting snow. Later, in the morning light, he watched his mother leave, riding off with the lios and the man.

He tried to make himself into a bird again but he couldn't. He wasn't strong enough to do it so soon. He walked down the slope to the cottage. He went inside. She had left Finn's clothes and his own. He looked at the small things he had worn; then he put on some of Finn's clothing and went away.

# CHAPTER 13

"And so, in the middle of the banquet that night, Kevin walked out. Liane saw him on the street and she says"—Dave fought for control—"she says he was very sure, and that he looked . . . he looked . . ."

Paul turned his back on them all and walked to the window. They were in the Temple in Paras Derval: Jennifer's rooms. He had come to tell her about Darien. She had listened, remote and regal, virtually untouched. It had moved him almost to anger. But then they had heard sounds outside and people at the door, and Dave Martyniuk and Jaelle herself had come in and told them what had happened to make the winter end.

It was twilight. Outside the snow was nearly gone. No flooding, no dangerous rising of rivers or lakes. If the Goddess could do this, she could do it harmlessly. And she could do this thing because of the sacrifice. Liadon, the beloved son, who was . . . who was Kevin, of course.

There was a great difficulty in his throat, and his eyes were stinging. He wouldn't look back at the others. To himself and to the twilight he said:

> *Love do you remember*
> *My name? I was lost*
> *In summer turned winter*
> *Made bitter by frost.*
> *And when June comes December*
> *The heart pays the cost.*

Kevin's own words from a year before. "Rachel's Song," he had called it. But now—now everything had been changed, the metaphor made achingly real. So completely so, he couldn't even grasp how such a thing could come to pass.

There was a great deal happening, much too fast, and Paul wasn't sure if he could move past it. He wasn't sure at all. His heart couldn't move so fast. *There will come a tomorrow when you weep for me,* Kevin had sung a year ago. He'd been singing of Rachel, for whom Paul had not yet cried. Singing of Rachel, not himself.

Even so.

It was very quiet behind him, and he wondered if they had gone. But then he heard Jaelle's voice. Cold, cold Priestess. But she wasn't now, it seemed. She said, "He could not have done this, not have been found worthy, had he not been travelling towards the Goddess all his life. I don't know if this is of aid to you, but I offer it as true."

He wiped his eyes and turned back. In time to see Jennifer, who had been composed to hear of Darien and tautly silent as Dave spoke, now rise at Jaelle's words, a white grief in her face, her mouth open, eyes blazing with naked pain, and Paul realized that if she was opening now to this, she was open to everything. He bitterly regretted his moment of anger. He took a step towards her, but even as he did, she made a choking sound and fled.

Dave stood to follow, awkward sorrow investing his square features. Someone in the hallway moved to block the way.

"Let her go," said Leila. "This was necessary."

"Oh, shut up!" Paul raged. An urge to strike this ever-present, ever-placid child rose fiercely within him.

"Leila," said Jaelle wearily, "close the door and go away."

The girl did so.

Paul sank into a chair, uncaring, for once, that Jaelle should see him as less than strong. What did such things matter now? *They shall not grow old, as we that are left. . . .*

"Where's Loren?" he asked abruptly.

"In town," Dave said. "So's Teyrnon. There's a meeting in the palace tomorrow. It seems . . . it seems Kim and the others did find out what was causing the winter."

"What was it?" Paul asked tiredly.

"Metran," Jaelle said. "From Cader Sedat. Loren wants to go after him, to the island where Amairgen died."

He sighed. So much happening. His heart wasn't going to be able to keep up. *At the going down of the sun and in the morning . . .*

"Is Kim in the palace? Is she okay?" It suddenly seemed strange to him that she hadn't come here to Jennifer.

He read it in their faces before either of them spoke.

"No!" he exclaimed. "Not her, too!"

"No, no, no," Dave rushed to say. "No, she's all right. She's just . . . not here." He turned helplessly to Jaelle.

Quietly, the High Priestess explained what Kimberly had said about the Giants, and then told him what the Seer had decided to do. He had to admire the control in Jaelle's voice, the cool lucidity. When she was done he said nothing. He couldn't think of anything to say. His mind didn't seem to be working very well.

Dave cleared his throat. "We should go," the big man said. Paul registered, for the first time, the bandage on his head. He should inquire, he knew, but he was so tired.

"Go ahead," Paul murmured. He wasn't quite sure if he could stand up, even if he wanted to. "I'll catch up."

Dave turned to leave but paused in the doorway. "I wish . . ." he began. He swallowed. "I wish a lot of things." He went out. Jaelle did not.

He didn't want to be alone with her. It was no time to have to cope with that. He would have to go, after all.

She said, "You asked me once if there could be a sharing of burdens between us and I said no." He looked up. "I am wiser now," she said, unsmiling, "and the burdens are heavier. I learned something a year ago from you, and from Kevin again two nights ago. Is it too late to say I was wrong?"

He wasn't ready for this, he hadn't been ready for any of what seemed to be happening. He was composed of grief and bitterness in equal measure. *As we that are left . . .*

"I'm so pleased we've been of use to you," he said. "You must try me on a better day." He saw her head snap back. He pushed himself up and left the room so she would not see him weep.

In the domed place, as he passed, the priestesses were wailing a lament. He hardly heard. The voice in his mind was Kevin Laine's from a year ago in a lament of his own:

*The breaking of waves on a long shore,*
*In the grey morning the slow fall of rain,*
*Oh, love, remember, remember me.*

He walked out into the fading light. His eyes were misted, and he could not see that all along the Temple slope the green grass had returned and there were flowers.

⊷═◑◖═⊷

Her dreams were myriad, and Kevin rode through all of them. Fair and witty, effortlessly clever, but not laughing. Not now. Kim saw his face as it must have been when he followed the dog to Dun Maura.

It seemed to her a heartbreaking thing that she could not remember the last words he had said to her. On the swift ride to Gwen Ystrat he had ridden up to tell her what Paul had done and of his own decision to let Brendel know about Darien. She had listened and approved; briefly smiled at his wry prediction of Paul's likely response.

She had been preoccupied, though, already moving in her mind towards the dark journey that lay ahead in Morvran. He must have sensed this, she realized later, for after a moment he'd touched her lightly on the arm, said something in a mild tone, and dropped back to rejoin Diarmuid's men.

It wouldn't have been anything consequential—a pleasantry, a gentle bit of teasing—but now he was gone and she hadn't heard the last thing he'd ever said to her.

She half woke from the hard dreams. She was in the King's House in Morvran. She couldn't possibly have stayed another night in the sanctuary. With Jaelle gone, with the armies returned to Paras Derval, the Temple was Audiart's again, and the triumph in the eyes of that woman was more than Kim could bear.

Of course they had won something. The snow was melting everywhere—in the morning it would be gone and she, too, would set forth, though not to Paras Derval. There had been a victory, a showing forth of Dana's power to balk the designs of the Dark. The power had been paid for, though, bought with blood, and more. There were red flowers growing everywhere. They were Kevin's, and he was gone.

Her window was open and the night breeze was fresh and mild with the promise of spring. A spring such as never before, burgeoning almost overnight. Not a gift, though. Bought and paid for, every flower, every blade of grass.

From the room next door she heard Gereint's breathing. It was slow and even, not ragged as before. He would be all right in the morning, which meant that Ivor, too, could depart. The Aven could ill afford to linger, for with the winter ending the Plain lay open again to the north.

Was everything the Goddess did double-edged? She knew the answer to that. Knew also that, this once, the question was unfair because they had so desperately needed this spring. She wasn't minded to be fair, though. Not yet. She turned over in bed and fell asleep, to dream again. But not of Kevin this time, though his flowers were there.

She was the Seer of Brennin, dreamer of the dream. For the second time in three nights she saw the vision that was sending her away from everyone she knew. It had come to her two nights ago, in Loren's bed, after a lovemaking they would each remember with gratitude. She had been inside this dream when Jaelle's voice, mourning the death of Liadon, had awakened them.

Now it came again, twisting, as such images always did along the timeloops of the Tapestry. There was smoke from burning fires and half-seen figures beyond. There were caves, but not like Dun Maura: these were deep and wide, and high up in the mountains. Then the image blurred, time slipped through the lattice of her vision. She saw herself—this was later—and there were fresh lacerations scoring her face and arms. No blood, though, for some reason, no blood. A fire. A chanting all around. And then the Baelrath flamed and, as in the dream of Stonehenge, she was almost shattered by the pain she knew it would bring. Worse, even, this was. Something monstrous and unforgivable. So immense a blazing to so vast a consequence that even after all that had come to pass her mind cried out in the dream the racking question she thought had been left behind: *Who was she that she should do this thing?*

To which there was no answer. Only sunlight streaming in through the window and innumerable birds singing in the light of spring.

She rose up, though not immediately. The aching of her heart cut hard against the flourish of that dawn, and she had to wait for it to ease. She walked outside. Her companion was waiting, with both horses saddled and ready. She had been planning to go alone, at first, but the mages and Jaelle—united for once—had joined Aileron in forbidding this. They had wanted her to have a company of men, but this, in turn, she had refused. What she was doing had to do with repaying a debt and not really with the war, she told them. She hadn't told them the other thing.

She'd accepted one companion because, in part, she wasn't sure of the way.

They'd had to be content with that. "I told you from the beginning," she'd said to Aileron. "I don't follow orders very well." No one had laughed or even smiled. Not surprisingly. She hadn't been smiling herself. Kevin was dead, and all the roads were parting. The Weaver alone knew if they would come together again.

And there was another parting now. Ivor's guard led out the blind shaman, Gereint, towards where the Aven waited with his wife and daughter. Liane, Kim saw, was red-eyed, still. So many smaller griefs there were within the larger ones.

Gereint, in his uncanny way, stopped right in front of her. She accepted the sightless touch of his mind. He was weak, she saw, but not finished yet.

"Not yet," he said aloud. "I'll be fine when I've had a haunch of eltor meat on the grass under the stars."

Impulsively, Kim stepped forward and kissed him on the cheek. "I wish I could join you," she said.

His bony hand gripped her shoulder. "I wish you could, too, dreamer. I am glad to have stood with you before I died."

"We may do so again," she said.

He made no reply to that. Only gripped her shoulder more tightly and, stepping nearer, whispered, so only she could hear, "I saw the Circlet of Lisen last night, but not who was wearing it." The last phrase was almost an apology.

She drew a breath and said, "That was Ysanne's to see, and so it is mine. Go easy, Gereint, back to your Plain. You will have tasks enough waiting there. You cannot be everything to all of us."

"Nor can you," he said. "You shall have my thoughts."

And because of who he was, she said, "No. You won't want to share what I think I'm about to do. Send them west, Gereint. The war is Loren's now, and Matt's, I think. In the place where Amairgen died."

She let him reach into her, to see the twin shadows of her dream. "Oh, child," he murmured and, taking her two hands between his own, raised them to his lips and kissed them both. Then he walked away as if weighted by more than years.

Kim turned around to where her companion waited patiently. The grass was green, the birds sang everywhere. The sun was well above the Carnevon Range. She looked up, shielding her eyes against the light.

"Are we ready?" she asked.

"We are," said Brock of Banir Tal.

She mounted up and fell into stride beside his horse for the long ride to Khath Meigol.

⤖〓◐〓⤗

*Travelling towards the Goddess all his life,* Jaelle had said of Kevin, and, alone of those in the room, Jennifer had truly understood. Not even the High Priestess could know how deeply true that was. Hearing the words, Jennifer felt suddenly as if every nerve within her had been stripped of its sheath and laid open.

All the nights, she saw now with terrible clarity. All the nights she had lain beside him after the arc of lovemaking was done, watching Kevin struggle to come back from so far. The one uncontrolled thing in him she had never understood, had feared. His was a descent, a downward spiral into passion, that her soul could not track. So many nights she'd lain awake, looking at the simplified beauty of his face as he slept.

She understood now, finally.

And so there was a last sleepless night for her shaped by Kevin Laine. She was awake when the birdsong began outside the Temple, and she had parted her curtains to watch the morning come. The breeze was fresh with the scents of spring, and there were leaves budding on all the trees. Colours, a great many colours in the world again, after the black branches and white snow of winter. There was green once more, so bright and alive it was stronger, at last, than the green unlight of Starkadh. As her eyes looked out on the spring, Jennifer's heart, which was Guinevere's, began to look out as well. Nor was this the least of Kevin's legacies.

There came a knocking at her door. She opened it to see Matt Sören with a walking stick in one hand and flowers in the other.

"It is spring," he said, "and these are the first flowers. Loren is meeting in the palace with a great many people. I thought you might come with me to Aideen's grave."

As they walked around the lower town and then struck a path to the west, she was remembering the story he had told her so long ago. Or not really as long as it seemed. The story of Nilsom, the mage who had turned evil, and of Aideen, his source, who had loved him: the only woman since Lisen to be source to a mage. It was Aideen who had saved Brennin, saved the Summer Tree, from Nilsom and the mad High King, Vailerth. She had refused to be source for her mage at the end. Had denied her strength to him and then killed herself.

Matt had told her the tale in the Great Hall at Paras Derval. Before she went riding and found the lios alfar. Before Galadan had, in turn, found her and given her to the swan.

Westward, they walked now, through the miracle of this spring, and everywhere Jennifer looked there was life returning to the land. She heard crickets, the drone of bees, saw a scarlet-winged bird take wing from an apple tree, and then a brown rabbit dart from a clump of shrubbery. She saw Matt drinking it in as well with his one eye, as if slaking a long thirst. In silence they walked amid the sounds of hope until, at the edge of the forest, Matt finally stopped.

Every year, he had told her, the Council of Mages would curse Nilsom at midwinter when they met. And every year, as well, they would curse Aideen—who had broken the profoundest law of their Order when she betrayed her mage—even though it had been to save Brennin from destruction, and the Tree that lay within this wood.

And every spring, Matt had said, he and Loren would bring the first flowers to this grave.

It was almost invisible. One had to know the place. A mound of earth, no stone, the trees at the edge of Mörnirwood for shade. Sorrow and peace together came over Jennifer as she saw Matt kneel and lay his flowers on the mound.

Sorrow and peace, and then she saw that the Dwarf was weeping, and her own tears came at last from the heart that spring had unlocked. For Aideen she wept, and bright Kevin gone; for Darien she cried, and the choice he had to make; for Laesha and Drance, slain when she was taken; for all the living, too, faced with the terror of the Dark, faced with war and the hatred of Maugrim, born into the time of his return.

And finally, finally by Aideen's grave in Kevin's spring, she wept for herself and for Arthur.

It lasted a long time. Matt did not rise, nor did he look up until, at length, she stopped.

"There is heart's ease in this place," he said.

"Ease?" she said. A weary little laugh. "With so many tears between the two of us?"

"The only way, sometimes," he replied. "Do you not feel it, though?"

After a moment she smiled as she had not done for a very long time. He rose from near the grave. He looked at her and said, "You will leave the Temple now?"

She did not reply. Slowly the smile faded. She said, "Is this why you brought me here?"

His dark eye never wavered from her face, but there was a certain diffidence in his voice. "I know only a few things," said Matt Sören, "but these I know truly. I know that I have seen stars shining in the depths of the Warrior's eyes. I know that he is cursed, and not allowed to die. I know, because you told me, what was done to you. And I know, because I see it now, that you are not allowing yourself to live. Jennifer, of the two fates, it seems to me the worse."

Gravely, she regarded him, her golden hair stirred by the wind. She lifted a hand to push it back from her face. "Do you know," she said, so quietly he had to strain to hear, "how much grief there was when I was Guinevere?"

"I think I do. There is always grief. It is joy that is the rarest thing," said the one-time King of Dwarves.

To this she made no reply. It was a Queen of Sorrows who stood with him by the Godwood, and for all the earnest certitude of his words, Matt knew a moment of doubt. Almost to himself, for reassurance, he murmured, "There can be no hope for anything in a living death."

She heard. Her gaze came back to him. "Oh, Matt," she said. "Oh, Matt, for what should I hope? He has been cursed to this. I am the agent of the Weaver's will. For what should I hope?"

Her voice went to his heart like a blade. But the Dwarf drew himself up to his fullest height and said the thing he had brought her there to say, and there was no doubt in him for this.

"Never believe it!" Matt Sören cried. "We are not slaves to the Loom. Nor are you only Guinevere—you are Jennifer now, as well. You bring your own history to this hour everything you have lived. You bring Kevin here within you and you bring Rakoth, whom you survived. You are here, and whole, and each thing you have endured has made you stronger. It need not be now as it has been before!"

She heard him. She nodded slowly. She turned and walked with him back to Paras Derval through the profligate bestowing of that morning. He was not wrong, for the Dwarves were wise in such things.

Nevertheless.

Nevertheless, even as they walked, her mind was turning back to another morning in another spring. Almost as bright as this, though not so long awaited.

There had been cherry trees in blossom all around when she had stood by Arthur's side to see Lancelot first ride into Camelot.

Hidden among the trees on the slopes north of them, a figure watched their return as he had watched them walking to the grave. He was lonely, and minded to go down to them, but he didn't know who they were and, since Cernan's words, he was deeply mistrustful of everyone. He stayed where he was.

Darien thought the woman was very beautiful, though.

⊹⊱══◉══⊰⊹

"He is still there," said Loren, "and he still has the Cauldron. It may take him time to put it to another use, but if we give him that time, he will. Aileron, unless you forbid me, I will leave to take ship from Taerlindel in the morning."

Tense sound rippled through the Council Chamber. Paul saw the High King's brow knitted with concern. Slowly, Aileron shook his head. "Loren," he said, "everything you say is true, and the gods know how dearly I want Metran dead. But how can I send you to Cader Sedat when we don't even know how to find it?"

"Let me sail," the mage said stonily. "I will find it."

"Loren, we don't even know if Amairgen did. All we know is that he died!"

"He was sourceless," Loren replied. "Lisen stayed behind. He had his knowledge but not his power. I am less wise, far, but Matt will be with me."

"Silvercloak, there were other mages on Amairgen's ship. Three of them, with their sources. None came back." It was Jaelle, Paul saw. She glittered that morning, more coldly formidable than ever before. If there was an ascendency that day, it was hers, for Dana had acted and the winter was over. They were not going to be allowed to forget it. Even so, he felt sorry for his last words yesterday evening. Hers had been a gesture unlikely to be repeated.

"It is true," Aileron was saying. "Loren, how can I let you go? Where will we be if you die? Lisen saw a death ship from her tower—what mariner could I ask to sail another?"

"This one." They all turned to the door in astonishment. Coll took two steps forward from his post beside Shain and said clearly, "The High King will know I am from Taerlindel. Before Prince Diarmuid took me from that place to serve in his company, I had spent all my life at sea. If Loren wants a mariner, I will be his man, and my mother's father has a ship I built with him. It will take us there with fifty men."

There was a silence. Into which there dropped, like a stone in a pool, the voice of Arthur Pendragon.

"Has your ship a name?" he asked.

Coll flushed suddenly, as if conscious for the first time of where he was. "None that will mean anything," he stammered. "It is a name in no language I know, but my mother's father said it was a ship's name in his family far back. We called it *Prydwen*, my lord."

Arthur's face went very still. Slowly the Warrior nodded, then he turned from Coll to Aileron. "My lord High King," he said, "I have kept my peace for fear of intruding myself between you and your First Mage. I can tell you, though, that if your concern is only for finding Cader Sedat—we called it Caer Sidi once, and Caer Rigor, but it is the same place I have been there and know where it is. This may be why I was brought to you."

"What is it, then?" asked Shalhassan of Cathal. "What is Cader Sedat?"

"A place of death," said Arthur. "But you knew that much already."

It was very quiet in the room.

"It will be guarded," Aileron said. "There will be death waiting at sea, as well."

*Thought, Memory.* Paul rose. "There will be," he said as they turned to look at him. "But I think I can deal with that."

It didn't take very long, after that. With a sense of grim purpose, the company followed Aileron and Shalhassan from the room when the council ended.

Paul waited by the doorway. Brendel walked past with a worried expression but did not stop. Dave, too, looked at him as he went out with Levon and Torc.

"We'll talk later," Paul said. Dave would be going north to the Dalrei, he knew. If there was war while *Prydwen* sailed, it would surely begin on the Plain.

Niavin of Seresh and Mabon of Rhoden went by, deep in talk, and then Jaelle walked out, head held very high, and would not meet his glance—all ice again, now that spring had returned. It wasn't for her that he was waiting, though. Eventually the room had emptied, save for one man.

He and Arthur looked at each other. "I have a question," said Paul. The Warrior lifted his head. "When you were there last, how many of you survived?"

"Seven," said Arthur softly. "Only seven."

Paul nodded. It was as if he remembered this. One of the ravens had spoken. Arthur came up to him.

"Between us?" he said, in the deep voice.

"Between us," said Paul. Together they walked from the Council Chamber and down the corridors. There were pages and soldiers running past them in all directions now—the palace was aflame with war fever. They were quiet, though, the two of them, as they walked in stride through the turmoil.

Outside Arthur's room they stopped. Paul said, very low so it would not be overheard, "You said this might be what you were summoned for. A while ago you said you never saw the end of things." He left it at that.

For a long moment Arthur was silent, then he nodded once. "It is a place of death," he said for the second time and, after a hesitation, added, "It would not displease me as events have gone."

Paul opened his mouth to say something, then thought better of it. He turned, instead, and walked down the corridor to where his own room was. His and Kevin's, until two days ago. Behind him, he heard Arthur opening his door.

***

Jennifer saw the door open, had time to draw a breath, and then he was in the room, bringing with him all the summer stars.

"Oh, my love," she said and her voice broke, after all. "I need you to forgive me for so much. I am afraid—"

She had space for nothing more. A deep sound came from within his chest, and in three strides Arthur was across the room and on his knees, his head buried in the folds of the dress she wore, and over and over again he was saying her name.

Her hands were cradling him to her, running through his hair, the grey amid the brown. She tried to speak, could not. Could scarcely breathe. She lifted his face that she might look at him and saw the tears of bitter longing pouring down. "Oh, my love," she gasped and, lowering her head, she tried to kiss them all away. She found his mouth with her own, blindly, as if they were both blind and lost without the other. She was trembling as with fever. She could hardly stand. He rose and gathered her to him and, after so long, her head was on his chest again, and she could feel his arms around her and could hear the strong beat of his heart, which had been her home.

"Oh, Guinevere," she heard him say after a space of time, "My need is great."

"And mine," she replied, feeling the last dark webs of Starkadh tear asunder so that she stood open to desire. "Oh, please," she said. "Oh, please, my love." And he took her to his bed, across which a slant of sunlight fell, and they rose above their doom for part of an afternoon.

After, he told her where it was he had to go and she felt all the griefs of the worlds return to rest in her. She was clear, though; she had spun free from Rakoth, and she was stronger for every single thing she had survived, as Matt had said. She rose up and stood in the sunlight of the room, clad only in her hair, and said, "You must come back to me. What I told you before is true: there is no Lancelot here. It has changed, Arthur. Only the two of us are here now, only us."

In the slant of sun she watched the stars sliding through his eyes. The summer stars, whence he had come. Slowly he shook his head, and she ached for his age and his weariness.

"It cannot be so," he said. "I killed the children, Guinevere."

She could find nothing at all to say. In the silence she could almost hear the patient, inexorable shuttling of the Loom.

Saddest story of all the long tales told.

# CHAPTER 14

In the morning came Arthur and Guinevere together out of Paras Derval to the great square before the palace gates. Two companies were gathered there, one to ride north, the other west to the sea, and there was not a heart among all those assembled that did not lift to see the two of them together.

Dave Martyniuk, waiting behind Levon for the signal to ride, looked past the five hundred men Aileron had given them to lead to the Plain, and he gazed at Jennifer with a memory flaring in his mind.

The very first evening: when Loren had told the five of them who he really was, and Dave, disbelieving and hostile, had stormed towards the door. To be stopped by Jennifer saying his name. And then, as he had turned, by a majesty he saw in her face. He could not have named it then, nor did he have words for it now, but he saw the same thing in her this morning and it was not transitory or ephemeral.

She left Arthur's side and walked, clad in a gown green as her eyes, green as the grass, to where he stood. Something of irresolution must have showed in his face, because as she came near he heard her laugh and say, "If you so much as start to bow or anything like that, Dave, I'll beat you up. I swear I will."

It was good to hear her laugh. He checked the bow he had, in fact, been about to offer and, instead, surprised them both by bending to kiss her cheek.

"Thank you," she said and took his hand in hers.

He smiled down on her and, for once, didn't feel awkward or uncouth.

Paul Schafer came up to join them, and with her other hand Jennifer claimed one of his. The three of them stood, linked so, for a moment.

"Well," said Dave.

Paul looked soberly at him. "You're going right into it, you know."

"I know," Dave replied. "But if I have a place in this, I think it's with the Dalrei. It . . . won't be any easier where you're heading." They were silent amid the bustle and clatter of the square. Then Dave turned to Jennifer. "I've been thinking about something," he said. "Way back, when Kim took you out of . . . that place, Kevin did something. You won't remember, you were unconscious then, but he swore vengeance for what had been done to you."

"I remember," said Paul

"Well," Dave went on, "he must have wondered how he would ever do it, but . . . I'm thinking that he found a way."

There was sunshine pouring down from a sky laced with scattered billows of clouds. Men in shirt sleeves walked all around them.

"He did more," said Jennifer, her eyes bright. "He got me all the way out. He finished what Kim started."

"Damn," said Paul gently. "I thought it was my charm." Remembered words, not his own.

Tears, laughter, and they parted.


Sharra watched the Aven's handsome son lead five hundred men away to the north. Standing with her father near the chariots, she saw Jennifer and Paul walk back to join the company that would soon be riding west. Shalhassan was going with them as far as Seresh. With the snow melted, there was urgent need now for his additional troops and he wanted to give his own orders in Cynan.

Aileron was already up on his black horse, and she saw Loren the mage mount up as well. Her heart was beating very fast.

Diarmuid had come to her again last night by way of her window. He had brought her a flower. She had not thrown water at him, this time, and had been at pains to point that out. He professed gratitude and later, in a different voice, a great deal more.

Then he had said, "I am going to a difficult place, my dear. To do a difficult thing. It may be wiser if I speak to your father if we. . . after we return. I would not have you bound to me while I am—"

She had covered his mouth with her hand and then, turning in bed as if to kiss him, moved the hand away and bit his lower lip instead.

"Coward!" she said. "I *knew* you were afraid. You promised me a formal wooing and I am holding you to it."

"Formal it is, then," he said. "You want an Intercedent, as well?"

"Of course!" she said. And then, because she was crying, and couldn't pretend any more, she said, "I was bound to you from Larai Rigal, Diar."

He kissed her, gently and then with passion, and then his mouth began to travel her and eventually she lost track of time and place.

"Formally," he'd said again, afterwards. In a certain tone.


And now, in the morning light, amid the busy square, a figure suddenly pushed through the gathered crowd and began a purposeful walk towards her father. Sharra felt herself going red. She closed her eyes for a moment, wishing desperately that she had bit him harder, much, much harder. And in a different place. Then, in spite of herself, she began to giggle.

Formally, he had promised. Even to the Intercedent who was to speak for him, after the old fashion. He had also warned her in Gwen Ystrat that he would never move to the measured gait, he would always have to play.

And so Tegid of Rhoden was his Intercedent.

The fat man—he was truly enormous—was blessedly sober. He had even trimmed his eccentric beard and donned a decent outfit in russet tones for his august mission. His round red face very serious, Tegid stopped directly in front of her father. His progress had been noted and marked by shouts and laughter. Now Tegid waited patiently for a modicum of silence. He absentmindedly scratched his behind, then remembered where he was and crossed his arms quickly on his chest.

Shalhassan regarded him with a mild, expressionless curiosity. Which became a wince a moment later as Tegid boomed out his title.

"Supreme Lord of Cathal," Tegid repeated, a little more softly, for his mighty lungs had shaped a silence all around with that first shout, "have I your attendant ear?"

"You have," her father said with grave courtesy.

"Then I am bid to tell you that I am sent here by a lord of infinite nobility, whose virtues I could number until the moon rose and set and rose again. I am sent to say to you, in this place and among the people here gathered in concourse, that the sun rises in your daughter's eyes."

There was a roar of astonishment.

"And who," asked Shalhassan, still courteously, "is the lord of infinite nobility?"

"A figure of speech, that," said Diarmuid, emerging from the crowd to their left. "And the moon business was his own idea. But he *is* my Intercedent and the heart of his message is true, and from my own heart. I would wed your daughter, Shalhassan."

The noise in the square was quite uncontrollable now. It was hard to hear anything. Sharra saw her father turn slowly to her, a question in his eyes, and something else that it took her a moment to recognize as tenderness.

She nodded once. And with her lips shaped a "Yes," for him to see.

The noise peaked and then slowly faded as Shalhassan waited beside his chariot, grave and unmoving. He looked at Diarmuid, whose own expression was sober now. He looked back at her.

He smiled. He *smiled.*

"Praise be to the Weaver and all the gods!" said Shalhassan of Cathal. "Finally she's done something adult!" And striding forward, he embraced Diarmuid as a son, in the manner of the ritual.

So it was amid laughter and joy that that company set forth to ride to Taerlindel, where a ship lay waiting to bear fifty men to a place of death.

Diarmuid's men, of course. It hadn't even been a subject of discussion. It had been assumed, automatic. If Coll was sailing the ship, then Diarmuid was commanding it and the men of South Keep were going to Cader Sedat.

Riding alone near the back of the party, Paul saw them, laughing and lighthearted, singing, even, at the promise of action. He looked at Coll and red Averren, the lieutenants; at Carde and greying Rothe and lean, agile Erron; at the other forty the

Prince had named. He wondered if they knew what they were going to; he wondered if he knew, himself.

Up at the front, Diarmuid glanced back to check on the company, and Paul met his blue gaze for a moment. He didn't move forward, though, and Diarmuid didn't drop back. Kevin's absence was a hollow place within his chest. He felt quite alone. Thinking of Kim, far away and riding east, made it even worse.

Shalhassan left them in the afternoon at Seresh. He would be ferried across to Cynan, almost immediately. The mild, beneficent sunshine was a constant reminder of the need for haste.

They turned north on the highway to Rhoden. A number of people were coming to see them off: Aileron, of course and Na-Brendel of Daniloth. Sharra was coming, as well; she would return to Paras Derval with Aileron and wait for her father there. Teyrnon and Barak, he saw, were deep in conversation with Loren and Matt. Only the latter two were sailing; the younger mage would stay with the King. They were spreading themselves very thin, Paul thought.

They didn't really have much choice.

Not far ahead he saw Tegid bouncing along in one of the Cathalian war chariots, and for a moment he smiled at the sight. Shalhassan had proved human, after all, and he had a sense of humour. Beyond the fat man rode Jaelle, also alone. He thought briefly of catching up to her. He didn't, though—he had too much to think about without trying to apologize to the Priestess. He could guess how she'd respond. A bit of a surprise, her coming, though: the provinces of Dana came to an end at the sea.

Which led him to thoughts of whose provinces began and of his statement to the Council the morning before. "I think I can deal with that," he'd said, in the quiet tones of the Twiceborn. Quiet, yes, but very, very rash. And they would be counting on him now.

Reflecting this, his features carefully unrevealing, Paul saw that they were turning west again, off the highway onto a smaller road. They had had the rich grainlands of the Seresh hinterland on their right until now, but, as they turned, the land began to drop slowly down in unfolding ridges. He saw sheep and goats and another grazing animal he couldn't recognize and then, before he saw it, he heard the sea.

They came to Taerlindel late in the day and the sun had led them there. It was out over the sea. The breeze was salt and fresh and the tide was in, the white-capped waves rolling up to the line of sandy beaches stretching away to the south towards Seresh and the Saeren mouth.

In front of them lay the harbour of Taerlindel, northward facing, sheltered by a promontory from the wind and surf. There were small fishing boats bobbing at anchor, a few larger ones, and one ship, painted gold and red, that would be *Prydwen*.

Once, Loren had told him, a fleet had anchored here. But the last war with Cathal had decimated the navies of both countries, and after the truce no ships had been built to replace them. And with Andarien a wasteland for a thousand years there was no longer any need, the mage had explained, to sail to Linden Bay.

A number of houses ringed the harbour and a few more ran back away from the sea into the sloping hills. The town was very beautiful in the late afternoon light. He only gave it a brief glance, though, before he stopped his horse to let the last of the party pass him by. On the road above Taerlindel his gaze went out, as far as it might, over the grey-green sea.

→⇒◯⇐←

They had let the light flare again from Atronel the past three nights, to celebrate and honor the spring returned. Now, towards evening of this fourth day, Leyse of the Swan Mark walked, in white for the white swan, Lauriel, beside the luminous figure of Ra-Tenniel, and they were alone by Celyn Lake gathering sylvain, red and silver.

Within the woven shadows of Daniloth, shadows that twisted time into channels unknown for all save the lios, it had never been winter. Lathen Mistweaver's mighty spell had been proof against the cold. For too long, though, had the lios gazed out from the shifting, blurred borders of the Shadowland to see snow sweeping across the Plain and the barren desolation of Andarien. A lonely, vulnerable island of muted colour had they been, in a world of white malevolence.

No longer. Ever bold, Ra-Tenniel took the long, slim hand of Leyse—and, for once, she let him do so—and led her past the muting of Lathen's shadows, out into the open spaces where the river ran into Celyn Lake.

In the sunset it was a place of enchantment and serenity. There were willows growing by the riverbank and aum trees in early leaf. In the young grass he spread his cloak, green as a vellin stone, and she sat down with him upon it, her arms full of sylvain Her eyes were a soft gold like the setting sun, her hair burnished bronze by its rays.

He looked from her to the sun, to the aum tree overhead, and the gentle flow of the river below them. Never far from sadness, in the way of the lios, he lifted his voice in a lament, amid the evening drone of bees and the liquescent splash of water over stone, for the ravaging of Andarien a thousand years ago.

Gravely she listened, laden with flowers, as he sang the long ballad of long-ago grief. The sun went down. In the twilight a light breeze stirred the leaves over their heads when, at length, he ended. In the west, above the place where the sun had set, gleamed a single star, the one named long ago for Lauriel, slain by black Avaia at the Bael Rangat. For a long time they watched it; then they turned to go, back into the Shadowland from where the stars were dim.

One glance Ra-Tenniel threw back over his shoulder at Andarien. And then he stopped and turned, and he looked again with the long sight of the lios alfar.

Ever, from the beginning, had the impatience of his hate marked Rakoth's designs. The winter now past had been a departure, terrifying in its implications of purposed, unhurried destruction.

But the winter was over now and, looking north with eyes whose colour shifted swiftly through to violet, Ra-Tenniel, Lord of the lios alfar, saw a dark horde moving through the ruin of Andarien. Not towards them, though. Even as Leyse turned to watch with him, the army of Rakoth swung eastward. Eastward, around Celyn, to come down through Gwynir.

And to the Plain.

Had he waited until dark, Rakoth might have sent them forth quite unseen for a full night's riding. He had not waited, and Ra-Tenniel offered a quick prayer. Swiftly he and Leyse returned to Atronel. They did not send their light on high that night, not with an army of the Dark abroad in the land. Instead they gathered together all the high ones of the Marks on the mound at Atronel. As the King had expected, it was fierce Galen who said at once that she would ride to Celidon. Again, as expected, Lydan, however cautious he might be, would not let his twin ride alone. They rose to go when Ra-Tenniel gave leave. He raised a hand to stop them, though.

"You will have to make speed," he said. "Very great speed. Take the raithen. It is time the golden and silver horses of Daniloth were seen again in Fionavar." Galen's eyes went blue, and a moment later so did those of her brother. Then they left to ride.

With the aid of those who remained, Ra-Tenniel made the summonglass come to urgent warning so that the glass in the High King's chambers in Paras Derval might leap to life as well.

It was not their fault that the High King was in Taerlindel that night and would not return to word of the summonglass afire until the afternoon of the following day.

⟡

He couldn't sleep. Very late at night Paul rose up and walked from Coll's mother's house down to the harbour. The moon, falling from full, was high. It laid a silver track along the sea. The tide was going out and the sand ran a long way towards the promontory. The wind had shifted around to the north. It was cool, he knew, but he still seemed to be immune to the cold, natural or unnatural. It was one of the few things that marked what he was. That, and the ravens, and the tacit, waiting presence in his pulse.

*Prydwen* rode easily at anchor. They had loaded her up in the last light of evening and Coll's grandfather had pronounced her ready to sail. In the moonlight the gold paint on her hull looked silver and the furled white sails gleamed.

It was very quiet. He walked back along the wooden dock and, other than the soft slap of the sea against the boats, his boots made the only sound. There were no lights shining in Taerlindel. Overhead the stars seemed very bright, even in the moonlight.

Leaving the harbour, he walked along the stone jetty until it ended. He passed the last house of the town. There was a track that curved up and east for a way, following the indentation of the bay. It was bright enough to follow and he did. After two hundred paces or so the track crested and then started down and north, and in a little while he came to sand again and a long beach open to the sea.

The surge and sigh of the waves was louder here. Almost, he heard something in them, but almost wouldn't be enough. He took off his boots and stockings and, leaving them on the sand, went forward. The sand was wet where the tide had washed back. The waves glowed a phosphorescent silver. He felt the ocean wash over his feet. It would be cold, he knew, but he didn't feel it. He went a little farther out and then stopped, ankle deep only, to be present but not to presume. He stood very still, trying, though not knowing how, even now, to marshal whatever he was. He listened. Heard nothing but the low sound of the sea.

And then, within himself, he felt a surging in his blood. He wet his lips. He waited; it came again. The third time he thought he had the rhythm, which was not that of the sea because it did not come from the sea. He looked up at the stars but not back at the land. *Mörnir*, he prayed.

"Liranan!" he cried as the fourth surge came and he heard the crash of thunder in his own voice.

With the fifth surge, he cried the name again, and a last time when the sixth pulse roared within him. At the seventh surging of his blood, though, Paul was silent and he waited.

Far out at sea he saw a white wave cresting higher than any of the others that were running in to meet the tide. When it met the long retreating surf, when it crashed, high and glittering, he heard a voice cry, "Catch me if you can!" and in his mind he dove after the god of the sea.

It was not dark or cold. Lights seemed everywhere, palely hued—it was as if he moved amid constellations of sunken stars.

Something flashed: a silver fish. He followed and it doubled back to lose him. He cut back as well, between the water stars. There was coral below, green and blue, pink, orange, shades of gold. The silver fish slipped under an arch of it, and when Paul came through, it was gone.

He waited. Felt another pulse.

"Liranan!" he called and felt thunder rock the deep. When the echoes rolled away he saw the fish again, larger now, with rainbow colours of the coral stippling its sides. It fled and he followed.

Down it went and he with it. They plunged past massive, lurking menaces in the lower depths where the sea stars were dim and colours lost.

Up it shot as if hurtling back to light. Past the sunken stars it went and broke water in a moonlit leap; from the beach, ankle deep in the tide, Paul saw it flash and fall.

And then it ran. No twisting now. On a straight course out to sea, the sea god fled the thunder voice. And was followed. They went so far beyond the memory of land that Paul thought he heard a thread of singing in the waves. He was afraid, for he guessed what he was hearing. He did not call again. He saw the silver fish ahead of him. He thought of all the dead and the living in their need, and he caught Liranan far out at sea and touched him with a finger of his mind.

"Caught you!" he said aloud, breathless on the beach where he had not moved at all. "Come," he gasped, "and let me speak with you, brother mine."

And then the god took his true form, and he rose up in the silvered sea and strode, shimmering with falling water, to the beach. As he came near, Paul saw that the falling water was as a robe to Liranan, to clothe his majesty, and the colours of the sea stars and the coral fell through it ceaselessly.

"You have named me as a brother," said the god in a voice that hissed like waves through and over rocks. His beard was long and white. His eyes were the same colour as the moon. He said, "How do you so presume? Name yourself!"

"You know my name," said Paul. The inner surge had died away. He spoke in his own voice. "You know my name, Sealord, else you would not have come to my call."

"Not so. I heard my father's voice. Now I do not. Who are you who can speak with the thunder of Mörnir?"

And Paul stepped forward with the retreating tide, and he looked full into the face of the sea god, and he said, "I am Pwyll Twiceborn, Lord of the Summer Tree," and Liranan made the sea waves to crash around them both.

"I had heard tell of this," the sea god said. "Now I understand." He was very tall. It was hard to discern if the sliding waters of his robe were falling into the sea about his feet, or rising from the sea, or the both at once. He was beautiful, and terrible, and stern. "What would you, then?" he said.

And Paul replied, "We sail for Cader Sedat in the morning."

A sound came from the god like a wave striking a high rock. Then he was silent, looking down at Paul in the bright moonlight. After a long time he said, "It is a guarded place, brother." There was a thread of sorrow in his voice. Paul had heard it in the sea before.

He said, "Can the guarding prevail over you?"

"I do not know," said Liranan. "But I am barred from acting on the Tapestry. All the gods are. Twiceborn, you must know that this is so."

"Not if you are summoned."

There was silence again, save for the endless murmur of the tide washing out and the waves.

"You are in Brennin now," said the god, "and near to the wood of your power. You will be far out at sea then, mortal brother. How will you compel me?"

Paul said, "We have no choice but to sail. The Cauldron of Khath Meigol is at Cader Sedat."

"You cannot bind a god in his own element, Twiceborn." The voice was proud but not cold. Almost sorrowful.

Paul moved his hands in a gesture Kevin Laine would have known. "I will have to try," he said.

A moment longer Liranan regarded him, then he said something very low. It mingled with the sigh of the waves and Paul could not hear what the god had said. Before he could ask, Liranan had raised an arm, the colours weaving in his water robe. He spread his fingers out over Paul's head and then was gone.

Paul felt a sprinkling of sea spray in his face and hair; then, looking down, he saw that he was barefoot on the sand, no longer in the sea. Time had passed. The moon was low now, over in the west. Along its silver track he saw a silver fish break water once and go down to swim between the sea stars and the colours of the coral.

When he turned to go back he stumbled, and only then did he realize how tired he was. The sand seemed to go on for a long way. Twice he almost fell. After the second time he stopped and stood breathing deeply for a time without moving. He felt light-headed, as if he had been breathing air too rich. He had a distant recollection of the song he had heard far out at sea.

He shook his head and walked back to where he'd left his boots. He knelt down to put them on but then sat on the sand, his arms resting on his knees, his head lowered between them. The song was slowly fading and he could feel his breathing gradually coming back to normal, though not his strength.

He saw a shadow fall alongside his own on the sand.

Without looking up, he said acidly, "You must enjoy seeing me like this. You seem to cultivate the opportunities."

"You are shivering," Jaelle said matter-of-factly. He felt her cloak settle over his shoulders. It bore the scent of her.

"I'm not cold," he said. But, looking at his hands, he saw that they were trembling.

She moved from beside him and he looked up at her. There was a circlet on her brow, holding her hair back in the wind. The moon touched her cheekbones, but the green eyes were shadowed. She said, "I saw the two of you in a light that did not come from the moon. Pwyll, whatever else you are, you are mortal, and that was not a shining wherein we can live."

He said nothing.

After a moment she went on. "You told me long ago, when I took you from the Tree, that we were human before we were anything else."

He roused himself and looked up again. "You said I was wrong."

"You were, then."

In the stillness the waves seemed very far away, but they did not cease. He said, "I was going to apologize to you on the way here. You seem to always catch me at a hard time."

"Oh, Pwyll. How could there be an easy time?" She sounded older, suddenly. He listened for mockery and heard none.

"I don't know," he admitted. And then, "Jaelle, if we don't come back from this voyage, you had better tell Aileron and Teyrnon about Darien. Jennifer won't want to, but I don't see that you'll have any choice. They'll have to be prepared for him."

She moved a little, and now he could see her eyes. She had given him her cloak and so was clad only in a long sleeping gown. The wind blew from off the sea. He rose and placed the cloak over her shoulders and did up the clasp at her throat.

Looking at her, at her fierce beauty rendered so grave by what she had seen, he remembered something and, aware that she had access to knowledge of her own, he asked, "Jaelle, when do the lios hear their song?"

"When they are ready to sail," she replied. "Usually it is weariness that leads them away."

Behind him he could still hear the slow withdrawing of the tide. "What do they do?"

"Build a ship in Daniloth and set sail west at night."

"Where? An island?"

She shook her head. "It is not in Fionavar. When one of the lios alfar sails far enough to the west, he crosses to another world. One shaped by the Weaver for them alone. For what purpose, I know not, nor, I believe, do they."

Paul was silent.

"Why do you ask?" she said.

He hesitated. The old mistrust, from the first time ever they spoke together, when she had taken him down from the Tree. After a moment, though, meeting her gaze, he said, "I heard a song just now, far out at sea where I chased the god."

She closed her eyes. Moonlight made a marble statue of her, pale and austere. She said, "Dana has no sway at sea. I know not what this might mean." She opened her eyes again.

"Nor I," he said.

"Pwyll," she asked, "can this be done? Can you get to Cader Sedat?"

"I'm not sure," he said truthfully. "Or even if we can do anything if we do get there. I know Loren is right, though. We have to try."

"You know I would come if I could—"

"I do know," Paul said. "You will have enough, and more, to deal with here. Pity the ones like Jennifer and Sharra, who can only wait and love, and hope that that counts for something beyond pain."

She opened her mouth as if to speak, but changed her mind and was silent. Unbidden, the words of a ballad came to him and, almost under his breath, he offered them to the night breeze and the sea:

*What is a woman that you forsake her,*
*And the hearth-fire and the home-acre,*
*To go with the old grey Widow-maker?*

"Weaver forfend," Jaelle said, and turned away.

He followed her along the narrow track to Taerlindel. On their right, as they went, the moon sank into the sea and they came back into a town lit only by the stars.

⤞═◉═⤝

When the sun rose, the company made ready to set sail in *Prydwen*. Aileron the High King went aboard and bade farewell to his First Mage, to Paul Schafer and Arthur Pendragon, to the men of South Keep who would man that ship, and to Coll of Taerlindel who would sail her.

Last of all he faced his brother. With grave eyes they looked at each other: Aileron's so brown they were almost black, Diarmuid's bluer than the sky overhead.

Watching from the dock, unmindful of her tears, Sharra saw Diarmuid speak and then nod his head. Then she saw him move forward and kiss his brother on the cheek. A moment later Aileron spun about and came down the ramp. There was no expression at all in his face. She hated him a little.

*Prydwen*'s sails were unfurled and they filled. The ramp was drawn up. The wind blew from the south and east: they could run with it.

Na-Brendel of Daniloth stood beside the High King and his guard. There were three women there as well, watching as the ship cast loose and began to slip away. One woman was a Princess, one a High Priestess; beside them, though, stood one who had been a Queen, and Brendel could not look away from her.

Jennifer's eyes were clear and bright as she gazed after the ship and at the man who stood in its stern gazing back at her. Strength and pride she was sending out to him, Brendel knew, and he watched her stand thus until *Prydwen* was a white dot only at the place where sea and sky came together.

Only then did she turn to the High King, only then did sorrow come back into her face. And something more than that.

"Can you spare a guard for me?" she said. "I would go to Lisen's Tower."

There was compassion in Aileron's eyes as if he, too, had heard what Brendel heard: the circles of time coming around again, a pattern shaping on the Loom.

"Oh, my dear," said Jaelle in a strange voice.

"The Anor Lisen has stood empty a thousand years," Aileron said gently. "Pendaran is not a place where we may safely go."

"They will not harm me there," Jennifer said with calm certitude. "Someone should watch for them from that place."

He had been meaning to go home to Daniloth. It had been too long since he had trod the mound of Atronel.

"I will take you there and stay with you," Brendel said, shouldering a different destiny.

# CHAPTER 15

Over and above everything else, Ivor thought, there were Tabor and Gereint.

The Aven was riding a wide circle about the gathered camps. He had returned from Gwen Ystrat the evening before. Two slow days' riding it had been, but Gereint had not been able to sustain a faster pace.

Today was his first chance to inspect the camps, and he was guardedly pleased with this one thing at least. Pending a report from Levon—expected back that night— as to the Council's decision in Paras Derval, Ivor's own plan was to leave the women and children with a guard in the sheltered curve of land east of the Latham. The eltor were already starting north, but enough would linger to ensure sufficient hunting.

The rest of the Dalrei he proposed to lead north very soon, to take up a position by the Adein River. When the High King and Shalhassan of Cathal joined them, the combined forces might venture farther north. The Dalrei alone could not. But neither could they wait here, for Maugrim might well come down very soon and Ivor had no intention of yielding Celidon while he lived. Unless there was a massive attack, he thought, they could hold the line of the Adein alone.

He reached the northernmost of the camps and waved a greeting to Tulger of the eighth tribe, his friend. He didn't slow to talk, though; he had things to think about.

Tabor and Gereint.

He had looked closely at his younger son yesterday on their return. Tabor had smiled and hugged him and said everything he ought to say. Even allowing for the long winter he was unnaturally pale, his skin so white it was almost translucent. The Aven had tried to tell himself that it was his usual oversensitivity to his children that was misleading him, but then, at night in bed, Leith had told him she was worried and Ivor's heart had skipped a beat.

His wife would have sooner bitten off her tongue than trouble him in such a way, without cause.

So this morning, early, he'd gone walking along the river with his younger son in the freshness of the spring, over the green grass of their Plain. The Latham ice had melted in a night. The river ran, sparkling and cold, out of the mountains; it was a bright blue in the sunlight. Ivor had felt his spirits lift, in spite of all his cares, just to see and be a part of this returning life.

"Father," Tabor had said before Ivor had even asked him anything, "I can't do anything about it."

Ivor's momentary pleasure had sluiced away. He'd turned to the boy. Fifteen, Tabor was. No more than that, and he was small-boned and so pale, now, he looked even younger.

Ivor said nothing. He waited.

Tabor said, "She carries me with her. When we fly, and especially this last time, when we killed. It is different in the sky, Father. I don't know how many times I can come back."

"You must try not to ride her, then," Ivor had said painfully. He was remembering the night at the edge of Pendaran Wood, when he watched Tabor and the winged creature of his dreaming wheel between the stars and the Plain.

"I know," Tabor had said by the river. "But we are at war, Father. How can I not ride?"

Gruffly, Ivor had said, "We are at war and I am Aven of the Dalrei. You are one of the Riders I command. You must let me decide how best to use such strength as we have."

"Yes, Father," Tabor had said.

*Double-edged*, Ivor thought now, looping back south along the western bank of the Latham towards where Cullion's fourth tribe was quartered. Every gift the Goddess gave was double-edged. He tried, not very successfully, not to feel bitter about it. The glorious winged creature with its shining silver horn was as mighty a weapon of war as anything they had, and the price of using it, he now saw, was going to be losing his youngest child.

Cullion, sharp-faced and soft-eyed, came riding out to intercept him, and Ivor was forced to stop and wait. Cullion was young to be Chieftain of a tribe but he was steady and alert, and Ivor trusted him more than most of them.

"Aven," Cullion said now without preamble, "when do we leave? Should I order a hunt or not?"

"Hold off for today," the Aven said. "Cechtar did well yesterday. Come down to us if you need a few eltor."

"I will. And what about—"

"An auberei should reach you soon. There's a Council tonight in our camp. I've left it until late because I'm hoping Levon will be back with news from Paras Derval."

"Good. Aven, I've been pushing my shaman since the snow started melting—"

"Don't push him," Ivor said automatically.

"—but he's offered nothing at all. What about Gereint?"

"Nothing," said Ivor and rode on.

\*\*\*

He had not been young when they blinded him. He had been next in line, waiting at Celidon for years, before word had come with the auberei that Colynas, shaman to Banor and the third tribe, was dead.

He was old now, and the blinding had been a long time ago, but he remembered it with utter clarity. Nor was that surprising: the torches and the stars and the circling men of Banor's tribe were the last things Gereint had ever seen.

It had been a rich life, he thought; more full than he could have dreamed. If it had ended before Rangat had gone up in fire, he would have said he'd lived and died a happy man.

From the time he'd been marked by the Oldest at Celidon, where the first tribe always stayed, Gereint's destiny had been different from that of all the other young men just called to their fast.

For one thing, he'd left Celidon. Only the marked ones of the first tribe did that. He'd learned to be a hunter, for the shaman had to know of the hunt and the eltor. He had travelled from tribe to tribe, spending a season with each, for the shaman had to know of the ways of all the tribes, never knowing which tribe he was to join, which Chieftain to serve. He had lain with women, too, in all the nine tribes, to sprinkle his marked seed across the Plain. He had no idea how many children he'd fathered in those waiting years; he did remember certain nights very well. He'd had years of it, seasons of travelling and seasons at Celidon with the parchments of the Law, and the other fragments that were not Law but which the shamans had to know.

He'd thought he'd had enough time, more than most of the shamans had, and he had begun it all by seeing a keia for his totem which had marked him inwardly, even among the marked.

He'd thought he was ready when the blinding came. Ready for the change, though not the pain. You were never ready for the pain: you came to your power through that agony, and there was no preparing for it.

He'd recognized what followed, though, and had welcomed the inner sight as one greets a lover long sought. He'd served Banor well for more than twenty years, though there had always been a distance between them.

Never with Ivor. No distance at all, and friendship, founded on respect, at first, and then something beyond. To fail the Chieftain of the third tribe, who was now Aven of all the Dalrei, would tear Gereint apart.

It was doing so now.

But he had, now that it had come down to war between the powers, no real choice. Two days ago, in Gwen Ystrat, the girl had told him not to track her where she went. Look west, she'd said, and opened her mind, to show him both what she was journeying to and what she'd seen of Loren's quest. The first had caused him pain such as he had not known since they blinded him. The second had revealed to him where his own burden lay, and his utterly unexpected inadequacy.

Long years he'd had, before he lost his eyes, to find a truer sight. Long years to travel up and down the Plain, to look at the things of the visible world and learn their nature. He had thought he'd done it well, and nothing until now had led him to change his mind. Nothing, until now. But now he knew wherein he had failed.

He had never seen the sea.

How could a Dalrei, however wise, ever dream that this one thing might undermine the deepest challenge of his days? It was Cernan of the Beasts whom the Dalrei knew, and Green Ceinwen. The god who left his place in Pendaran to run with the eltor on the Plain, and the hunting goddess who was sister to him. What did the Riders know of seaborn Liranan?

There would be a ship sailing west, the girl had shown him that. And seeing the image in her mind, Gereint had understood another thing, something beyond what even the Seer of Brennin knew. He had never seen the sea, but he had to find that ship wherever it might be among the waves.

And so he closed himself. He left the Aven bereft of any guidance he might have to offer. A bad time, the worst, but he truly had no choice. He told Ivor what he was going to do, but not where or why. He let the living force that kept his aged body still alive dwindle to a single inner spark. Then, sitting down cross-legged on the mat in the shaman's house of the camp beside the Latham, he sent that spark voyaging far, far from its home.

When the turmoil and frenzy overtook the camps later that night, he never knew of them. They moved his body the next day in the midst of chaos—he'd told Ivor he could be moved—but he was oblivious to that. By then, he had passed beyond Pendaran.

He had seen the Wood. He could place and focus himself by his memory of the forest and the contours of its emanations in his mind. He'd sensed the dark, unforgiving hostility of the Wood and then something else. He had been passing over the Anor Lisen, of which he knew. There was a light on in the Tower, but that, of course, he didn't realize. He did apprehend a presence there, and he had an instant to wonder.

Only an instant, because then he was past the end of land and out over the waves and he knew a helpless, spinning panic. He had no shape to give to this, no memory, scarcely a name to compass it. Impossibly, there seemed to be stars both above and below. Old and frail, blind in the night, Gereint bade his spirit leave the land he'd always known, for the incalculable vastness of the unseen, unimaginable, the dark and roiling sea.

⊹⇒◎⇐⊹

"You cannot," said Mabon of Rhoden, catching up to them, "drive five hundred men all day without rest."

His tone was mild. Aileron had made clear that Levon was leading this company, and Mabon hadn't demurred at all. Dave saw Levon grin sheepishly, though. "I know," he said to the Duke. "I've been meaning to stop. It's just that as we get closer . . ."

The Duke of Rhoden smiled. "I understand. I feel like that whenever I'm riding home." Mabon, Dave had decided, was all right. The Duke was past his best years and carried more weight than he needed to, but he hadn't had any trouble keeping up and had gone to sleep in his blanket on the grass the night before like an old campaigner.

Levon was shaking his head, upset with himself. When they reached an elevation in the rolling prairie he raised a hand for a halt. Dave heard heartfelt murmurs of relief running through the company behind him.

He was grateful for the rest himself. He hadn't been born to the saddle like Levon and Torc, or even these horsemen from the northern reaches of Brennin, and he'd been doing an awful lot of riding the past few days.

He swung down and stretched his legs. Did a few deep knee bends, touched his toes, swung his arms in circles. He caught a look from Torc and grinned. He didn't mind teasing from the dark Dalrei; Torc was a brother. He did a few pushups right beside the cloth that Torc was covering with food. He heard the other man snort with suppressed laughter.

Dave flopped over on his back, thought about sit-ups, and decided to eat instead. He took a dried strip of eltor meat and a roll of Brennin bread. He smeared them both with the mustardy sauce the Dalrei loved and lay back, chewing happily.

It was spring. Birds wheeled overhead and the breeze from the southeast was mild and cool. The grass tickled his nose and he sat up to grab a wedge of cheese. Torc was lying back as well, his eyes closed. He could fall asleep in twenty seconds. In fact, Dave realized, he just had.

It was almost impossible to believe that all of this had been covered with snow and exposed to an icy wind only five days ago. Thinking about that, Dave thought about Kevin and felt his restful mood slipping away like wind through his fingers. His mind began to turn from the open sky and the wide grasslands to darker places. Especially that one dark place where Kevin Laine had gone: the cave in Gwen Ystrat with the snow beginning to melt outside. He remembered the red flowers, the grey dog, and he would die remembering the wailing of the priestesses.

He sat up again. Torc stirred but did not wake. Overhead the sun was bright and warming. It was a good day to be alive, and Dave forced his mind away from its recollections. He knew, from bitter experience with his family, how unstable he became when he went too far with emotions like those that were stirring now.

He couldn't afford it. Maybe, just maybe, if there could come a space of time with leisure to work things through, he might sit down for a day or two and figure out why he had cried for Kevin Laine as he had not for anyone since he was a child.

Not now, though. That was perilous territory for him, Dave knew. He put Kevin, with some sorrow, in the same place he put his father—not forgotten, quite, but not to be addressed—and walked over to where Levon was sitting with the Duke of Rhoden.

"Restless?" Levon asked, looking up with a smile.

Dave hunkered down on his calves. "Torc isn't," he said with a backward jerk of his head.

Mabon chuckled. "I'm glad at least one of you is showing normal responses. I thought you were minded to ride straight through to the Latham."

Levon shook his head. "I would have needed a rest. Torc might have done it, though. He isn't tired, just smarter than we are."

"Do you know," said Mabon, "I think you are right." And he turned over on his back, spread a square of lace across his eyes, and was snoring within a minute.

Levon grinned and gestured with his head. He and Dave rose and walked a little away from the others.

"How much farther?" Dave asked. He turned through a full circle: in all directions he could see nothing but the Plain.

"We'll be there tonight," Levon replied. "We may see the outposts before dark. We lost a bit of time yesterday with Mabon's business in North Keep. I suppose that's why I was pushing."

The Duke had been forced to delay them in order to convey a series of instructions to the North Keep garrison from Aileron. He'd also had orders of his own to be carried down the road to Rhoden. Dave had been impressed with Mabon's unflappable efficiency—it was a quality, he'd been told, upon which men of Rhoden prided themselves. Those from Seresh, he gathered, were rather more excitable.

He said, "I slowed us up there, too. I'm sorry."

"I'd been meaning to ask. What was that about?"

"A favour for Paul. Aileron ordered it. Do you remember the boy who came when we summoned Owein?"

Levon nodded. "I am not likely to forget."

"Paul wanted his father posted back to Paras Derval, and there was a letter. I said I'd find him. It took a while." Dave remembered standing awkwardly by as Shahar wept for what had happened to his son. He'd tried to think of something to say and failed, naturally. There were, he supposed, some things he'd never be able to handle properly.

"Did he remind you of Tabor?" Levon asked suddenly. "That boy?"

"A little," Dave said, after thinking about it.

Levon shook his head. "More than a little, for me. I think I'd like to get moving."

They turned back. Torc, Dave saw, was on his feet. Levon gestured, and the dark Dalrei put fingers to his mouth and whistled piercingly. The company began preparing to ride. Dave reached his horse, mounted up, and jogged to the front where Levon and Mabon waited.

The men of Brennin were in place and mounted very fast. Aileron had sent them men who knew what they were doing. Torc came up and nodded. Levon gave him a smile and raised his hand to wave them forward.

"Mörnir!" the Duke of Rhoden exclaimed.

Dave saw a shadow. He smelled something rotting.

He heard an arrow sing. But by that time he was flying through the air, knocked cleanly from his horse by Mabon's leap. The Duke fell with him on the grass. *This*, thought Dave absurdly, *is what Kevin did to Coll.*

Then he saw what the black swan had done to his horse. Amid the stench of putrescence and the sickly sweet smell of blood, he fought to hold down his midday meal.

Avaia was already far above them, wheeling north. Dave's brown stallion had had its back broken with the shattering force of the swan's descent. Her claws had shredded it into strips of meat. The horse's head had been ripped almost completely off. Blood fountained from the neck.

Levon had been knocked from his mount as well by the buffeting of the giant wings. Amid the screams of terrified horses and the shouts of men, he hurried over. Torc was gazing after the swan, his bow held in white fingers. Dave saw that they were shaking: he'd never seen Torc like that before.

He found that his legs would work and he stood up. Mabon of Rhoden rose slowly, red-faced; he'd had the wind knocked out of his lungs.

No one said a word for a moment. Avaia was out of sight already. Flidais, Dave was thinking, as he tried to control his pulse. *Beware the boar, beware the swan.* . . .

"You saved my life," he said.

"I know," said Mabon quietly. No affectation. "I was looking to check the sun and I saw her diving."

"Did you hit her?" Levon asked Torc.

Torc shook his head. "Her wing, maybe. Maybe."

It had been so sudden, so terrifyingly brutal an attack. The sky was empty again, the wind blew gentle as before over the waving grasses. There was a dead horse beside them, though, its intestines oozing out, and a lingering odour of corruption that did not come from the horse.

"Why?" Dave asked. "Why me?"

Levon's brown eyes were moving from shock to a grave knowledge. "One thing, only, I can think of," he said. "She risked a great deal diving like that. She would have had to sense something and to have decided that there was a great deal to gain." He gestured.

Dave put his hand to his side and touched the curving shape of Owein's Horn.

Often, in his own world, it had come to pass that opposing players in a basketball game would single out Dave Martyniuk as the most dangerous player on his team. He would be treated to special attention: double coverage, verbal needling, frequently some less than legal intimidation. As he got older, and better at the game, it happened with increasing regularity.

It never ever worked.

"Let's bury this horse," Dave said now, in a voice so grim it startled even the two Dalrei. "Give me a saddle for one of the others and let's get moving, Levon!" He stepped forward and retrieved his axe from the ruins of his saddle. There was blood all over it. Painstakingly, he wiped it clean until the head shone when he held it to the light.

They buried the horse; they gave him a saddle and another mount.

They rode.

Ivor was in the shaman's house at sunset when they brought him word.

He had come at the end of the day to look in on his friend and had remained, helpless and appalled by what he read in Gereint's face. The shaman's body was placid and unmoving on his mat, but his mouth was twisted with a soundless terror and even the dark sockets of his eyes offered testimony of a terrible voyaging. Aching and afraid for the aged shaman, Ivor stayed, as if by bearing witness he could ease

Gereint's journey in some inchoate way. The old one was lost, Ivor realized, and with all his heart he longed to call him home.

Instead, he watched.

Then Cechtar came. "Levon is coming in," he said from the doorway. "He has brought the Duke of Rhoden and five hundred men. And there is something else, Aven."

Ivor turned.

The big Rider's face was working strangely. "Two others have come from the north. Aven . . . they are the lios alfar and—oh, come see what they ride!"

He had never seen the lios. Of all the Dalrei living, only Levon and Torc had done so. And Levon was back, too, with five hundred of the High King's men. With a quickening heart, Ivor rose. He cast one lingering glance at Gereint, then went out.

Levon was bringing his men in from the southwest; squinting, he could see them against the setting sun. In the open space before him, though, waiting quietly, were two of the lios alfar mounted up on raithen, and Ivor had never in his days thought to see either.

The lios were silver-haired, both, slim, with the elongated fingers and wide-set, changeable eyes of which he'd heard. Nothing he'd ever heard could prepare him, though, for their elusive, humbling beauty and, even motionless, their grace.

For all that, it was the raithen that claimed Ivor's speechless gaze. The Dalrei were horsemen and lived to ride. The raithen of Daniloth were to horses as the gods were to men, and there were two of them before him now.

They were golden as the setting sun all through their bodies, but the head and tail and the four feet of each of them were silver, like the not-yet-risen moon. Their eyes were fiercely blue and shining with intelligence, and Ivor loved them on the instant with all his soul. And knew that every Dalrei there did the same.

A wave of pure happiness went through him for a moment. And then was dashed to pieces when the lios spoke to tell of an army of the Dark sweeping even now across the northern Plain.

"We warned them at Celidon," the woman said. "Lydan and I will ride now towards Brennin. We alerted the High King with the summonglass last night. He should be on the Plain by now, heading for Daniloth. We will cut him off. Where do you want him to ride?"

Ivor found his voice amid the sudden babble of sound. "To Adein," he said crisply. "We will try to beat the Dark Ones to the river and hold them there for the High King. Can we make it?"

"If you go now and very fast you might," said the one called Lydan. "Galen and I will ride to Aileron."

"Wait!" Ivor cried. "You must rest. Surely the raithen must. If you have come all the way from Daniloth . . ."

The lios had to be brother and sister, so alike were they. They shook their heads. "They have had a thousand years to rest," said Galen. "Both of these were at the Bael Rangat. They have not run free since."

Ivor's mouth fell open. He closed it.

"How many do you have?" he heard Cechtar breathe.

"These two and three others. They do not breed since the war against Maugrim. Too many of them died. Something changed in them. When these five are gone, no raithen will ever outpace the wind again." Lydan's voice was a chord of loss.

Ivor gazed at the raithen with a bitter sorrow. "Go then," he said. "Unleash them. Bright be the moon for you, and know we will not forget."

As one, the lios raised open hands in salute. Then they turned the raithen, spoke to them, and the Dalrai saw two comets, golden and silver, take flight across the darkening Plain.

⟶⟞◯⟝⟵

In Paras Derval, Aileron the High King had just returned from Taerlindel. On the road back, he had been met with word of the summonglass alight. He was just then giving orders for an army to ride. They had too far to go, though. Much too far.

⟶⟞◯⟝⟵

On the Plain, Levon came up to his father. Mabon of Rhoden stood behind him.

Ivor said to the Duke, "You have been riding two days. I cannot ask your men to come. Will you guard our women and children?"

"You can ask anything you must ask," said Mabon quietly. "Can you do without five hundred men?"

Ivor hesitated.

"No," said a woman's voice. "No, we cannot. Take them all, Aven. We must not lose Celidon!"

Ivor looked at his wife and saw the resolution in her face. "We cannot lose our women, either," he said. "Our children."

"Five hundred will not save us." It was Liane, standing beside her mother. "If they defeat you, five hundred will mean nothing at all. Take everyone, Father."

She was not wrong, he knew. But how could he leave them so utterly exposed? A thought came to him. He quailed before it for a moment, but then the Aven said, "Tabor."

"Yes, Father," his youngest child replied, stepping forward.

"If I take everyone, can you guard the camps? The two of you?"

He heard Leith draw a breath. He grieved for her, for every one of them.

"Yes, Father," said Tabor, pale as moonlight. Ivor stepped close and looked into his son's eyes. So much distance already.

"Weaver hold you dear," he murmured. "Hold all of you." He turned back to the Duke of Rhoden. "We ride in an hour," he said. "We will not stop before the Adein, unless we meet an army. Go with Cechtar—your men will need fresh horses." He gave orders to Levon and others to the gathered auberei, who were already mounted up to carry word to the other tribes. The camp exploded all around him.

He found a moment to look at Leith and took infinite solace from the calm in her eyes. They did not speak. It had all been said, at one time or another, between the two of them.

It was, in fact, less than an hour before he laced his fingers in her hair and bent in the saddle to kiss her goodbye. Her eyes were dry, her face quiet and strong, and so, too, was his. He might weep too easily for joy or domestic sorrow, or love, but it was the Aven of the Dalrei, first since Revor was given the Plain, who now sat his horse in the darkness. There was death in his heart, and bitter hate, and fiercest, coldest resolution.

They would need torches until the moon rose. He sent the auberei forward with fire to lead the way. His older son was at his side and the Duke of Rhoden and the seven Chieftains, all but the Oldest one at Celidon, where they had to go. Behind them, mounted and waiting, were five hundred men of Brennin and every single Rider of the Plain save one. He forbade himself to think of the one. He saw Davor and Torc and recognized the glitter in the dark man's eyes.

He rose up in his saddle. "In the name of Light," he cried, "to Celidon!"

"To Celidon!" they roared with one voice.

Ivor turned his horse to the north. Ahead, the auberei were watching. He nodded once.

They rode.

Tabor deferred quietly to the gathered shamans, who in turn deferred to his mother. In the morning, following the Aven's instructions, they set about moving across the river to the last camp in the very corner of the Plain, where the land began to rise towards the mountains. The river would offer some slight defence, and the mountains a place to hide if it came to that.

It went quickly, with few tears, even from the very young ones. Tabor asked two of the older boys to help him with Gereint, but they were frightened by the shaman's face and he couldn't really blame them. He made the hammock himself, then got his sister to carry Gereint with him. They forded the river on foot at a shallow place. Gereint showed no awareness of them at all. Liane did well, and he told her so. She thanked him. After she had gone, he stayed a while with the shaman in the dark house where they had set him down. He thought about his praising Liane, and her thanking him, and of how much had changed.

Later, he went to check with his mother. There were no problems. By early afternoon they were all in the new camp. It was crowded, but with the men gone there was enough room in a camp built for four tribes. It was painfully quiet. The children weren't laughing, Tabor realized.

From the slopes of the mountain east of the camp a pair of keen eyes had been watching them all morning. And now, as the woman and children of the Dalrei uneasily settled in to their new camp, all their thoughts far away, in the north by Celidon, the watcher began to laugh. His laughter went on for a long time, quite unheard, save by the wild creatures of the mountains who did not understand or care. Soon enough—there was plenty of time—the watcher rose and started back east, carrying word. He was still laughing.

It was Kim's turn to lead. They had been switching after every rest period since they had left the horses behind and begun to climb. This was their fourth day, the third in the mountains. It wasn't too bad yet, here in the pass. Brock had said that the next day would be hardest, and then they would be close to Khath Meigol.

He hadn't asked anything about what would happen then.

In spite of herself, she was deeply grateful for his companionship and as deeply admiring of the stoic way in which he was leading her to a place more haunted than any other in Fionavar. He had believed her, though, had trusted her when she said that the ghosts of the Paraiko were not roaming with their bloodcurse in the mountain pass.

The Paraiko themselves were there. In their caves. Alive. And, in some way she still hadn't seen, being held.

She looked back. Brock was trudging sturdily along just behind, carrying most of their gear: one fight she'd lost. The Dwarves were even more stubborn than the Fords, it seemed.

"Break time," she called down. "Looks like a flat ledge where the trail bends up there." Brock grunted agreement.

She scrambled up; had to use her hands a couple of times, but it really wasn't too hard. She'd been right, there was a flat plateau there, even bigger than she'd guessed. A perfect place to stop and rest.

Unfortunately, it was occupied.

She was grabbed and muzzled before she could scream a warning. All unsuspecting, Brock followed her up and within seconds they were both disarmed, she of her dagger, he of his axe, and tied quite securely.

They were forced to sit in the middle of the plateau as the large level space gradually filled with their captors.

After a little while another figure leaped up from the trail along which they'd been climbing. He was a big man with a matted black beard. He was bald, and had a green tattooed design etched into his forehead and his cheeks. It showed beneath the beard as well. He took a moment to register their presence, then he laughed.

No one else had made a sound. There were perhaps fifty figures surrounding them. The bald, tattooed man walked commandingly into the centre and stood over Kim and Brock. For a moment he looked down at them. Then he drew back a booted foot and viciously kicked the Dwarf in the side of the head. Brock crumpled, blood pouring from his scalp.

Kim drew breath to scream, and he kicked her in the side. In agony, retching for air, she heard him laugh again.

"Do you know," the bald man asked his companions in a gutteral voice, "what the Dalrei have done down below?"

Kim closed her eyes. She wondered how many of her ribs were broken. If Brock was dead.

*Save us,* she heard within her mind. The slow chanting. *Oh, save us.*

❖❖=◉ ◉=❖❖

There had been a time when Dave hadn't regarded any of this as his concern at all. That had changed, long ago, and not because of any abstract awareness of the interwoven threads of all the worlds. It had been Ivor and Liane, his memories of them as he'd ridden south to Paras Derval a year ago. After the terror of the Mountain, it had been the presence of Levon and Torc beside him, and then it had been battle by Llewenmere, when men he knew had died—slain by loathsome creatures he could not help but hate. There had been brothers found in Pendaran Wood and, finally, there had been Jennifer and what had been done to her.

It was his war now, too.

He'd always been an athlete and had prided himself on that as much as surviving the rigors of law school. He'd never let himself get out of shape and, in the season after their return home when they waited to go back to Fionavar—for Loren to come for them, or Kim to have her long-sought dream—he had worked his body harder than ever before. He'd had an idea of what might lie ahead. Dave was in better physical condition than at any point in his life.

And he had never ached so much in every muscle and bone, or been more brutally exhausted. At any point in his life.

They had ridden through the night, by torchlight until the moon rose and then by its shining. He had been in the saddle from Paras Derval the two days before that, too, riding at speed. But that speed, for which Mabon had gently chided Levon, was as nothing compared to the headlong night ride of the Dalrei, north behind their Aven.

He'd wondered about the horses during the night and even more now as the sun rose on their right—wondered how long they could sustain this killing speed. They did, though, they kept it up, pounding over the grass without rest. They were not raithen, but every one of the horses had been bred and trained and loved by the Dalrei on this open prairie, and this was their finest hour in a thousand years. Dave stroked the streaming mane of the stallion he now rode and felt a great vein pulsing in its neck. It was a black horse—like Aileron's. Who, Dave prayed, silently, was riding his own black not far behind them now, alerted by the lios alfar.

It was Levon who made his father stop before the sun climbed overhead. Who ordered them all to stretch and eat. To walk their horses and let them drink of the waters of Rienna by Cynmere, where they had come. Men falling down with utter fatigue could not fight a battle. On the other hand, they had to win the race to Celidon and to Adein, if they could. Dave chewed some meat and bread, drank from the cold waters of the river, did his knee bends and flexes, and was back up in the saddle before the rest time was done. So, too, he saw, was every other man in the army.

They rode.

It would be the stuff of legend and of song if any generations came after them, to tell old stories and sing them. Sing the ride of Ivor, who rode to Celidon with the Dalrei behind him through a wild night and a day to meet the army of the Dark and to battle them on the Plain in the name of Light.

Dave let the black have its head as he had for the whole journey. He felt the churning power of its strides, unflagging even now, despite the weight it bore, and he drew grimmer resolution yet from the heart of the horse that carried him.

He was close behind the Aven and the Chieftains when they saw the lone auberei come streaking towards them. The sun was over to the west now, starting down. Ahead of them the single auberei stopped, then expertly turned his horse and began racing along with them in stride with Ivor's grey.

"Where are they?" the Aven screamed.

"Coming to the river, even now!"

Dave drew a breath. Rakoth's army had not reached Celidon.

"Will we beat them there?" he heard Ivor cry.

"I don't know!" the auberei replied despairingly.

Dave saw Ivor rise up in his saddle, then. *"In the name of Light!"* the Aven roared and urged his horse forward. Somehow, they all did. Somehow the horses increased their speed. Dave saw Ivor's grey hurtle past the auberei who were leading them and he threw the black after it, feeling the horse respond with a courage that humbled him. A blurred thunder on the Plain they were, akin to the great swifts of the eltor themselves.

He saw Celidon whip by on their right. Had an impression of standing stones much like Stonehenge, though not fallen, not fallen yet. He glimpsed, beyond the stones, the great camp at mid-Plain, this heart of the Dalrei's home for twelve hundred years. Then they were past, and flying, flying to the river in the waning of the afternoon and, seeing Torc, beside him, loosen his sword, Dave drew his axe at last from where it hung by his saddle. He caught Torc's eye; their glances held for a second. He looked ahead for Levon and saw him, sword drawn, looking back at them as he rode.

They cleared a rise in the land. He saw the Adein sparkle in the sun. He saw the svart alfar, hideous green creatures he knew, and larger dun-coloured ones, as well. They were beginning to wade across the river. Only beginning. Ivor had come in time. A thing to be sung forever, if there should be anyone to sing.

For there were very, very many foes coming to them. The Plain north of Adein was dark with the vastness of Rakoth's army. Their harsh cries rang in the air: alarm at the sight of the Dalrei and then high, mocking triumph at how few there were.

His axe held ready, Dave raced down behind Ivor. His heart lurched to see the ranks of the svart alfar part to make way for urgach mounted upon slaug, and there were hundred of them, hundreds upon hundreds, among thousands upon thousands of the svart alfar.

He thought about death. Then, briefly, of his parents and his brother, who might never know. He thought about Kevin and Jennifer, of the two brothers with him now, of the slaughter by Llewenmere a year ago. He saw the leader of the urgach, the largest of them all, saw that it was clad mockingly in white, and with his heart and soul he hated it.

"Revor!" he cried with all the Dalrei, and, "Ivor!" with all of them. Then he reached the Adein, weariness gone, blood frenzy rising like a flood, and there was war.

They did not cross the river; it was the only feature of the level grasslands that gave them any edge at all. The svart alfar were small, even the dun-coloured ones, and unmounted; they had to wade across Adein and up its banks into the swords of the Dalrei. Dave saw Torc sheath his blade and draw his bow, and soon the arrows of the Riders were flying over the river to wreak death on the other side. Only in passing did he grasp this, for he was in the midst of chaos and spurting blood, wheeling the black horse along the bank, hammering the axe down again and again, scything, chopping, once stabbing a svart with it when there was no room to swing. He felt the svart's breastbone crack under his thrust.

He tried to stay close to Levon and Ivor, but the ground was slippery with blood and river water, and then a cluster of the urgach came between on the terrifying, six-legged slaug, and he was suddenly fighting for sheer survival.

They were being forced back from the river; they could not stand and fight level with the urgach. The Adein was running red with blood now in the waning light, and there were so many svart alfar dead and dying in the stream that the living ones were crossing over the bodies of the dead behind the urgach and the slaug.

By Dave's side, Torc was fighting with a sword again. A tall warrior from North Keep was next to him, and desperately the three of them tried to hold close to the river, knowing how they would be overrun if they fell back too far. An urgach crashed up to Dave. He smelt the fetid breath of the horned slaug; the black horse wheeled sideways without command. The heavy sword of the urgach whistled past Dave's head, and, before it could come back, Dave leaned forward and with all his strength buried the axe in the ugly, hairy head. He jerked it free and lashed a backhand blow at the slaug even as the urgach slid like a tree to the bloodied ground.

A kill, but even as he drew breath, he saw another of the huge creatures angling for him, and he knew he could not keep this up, he could not hold this line. Torc, too, had killed and was desperately turning to face another slaug-mounted foe. The svarts were crossing the river now in numbers, and with a sickness in his heart, Dave saw how many were yet to come, and that they were using knives and short swords to cut open the Riders' horses from below.

Incoherently, he screamed, and as his battle rage rose up again, he kicked the black horse to meet the first oncoming slaug. He was in close too fast for the startled urgach to swing its sword. With his left hand Dave raked savagely at its eyes, and as it howled, he killed it with a short swing of the axe.

"Davor!" he heard. A warning too late. He felt pain lance through his left side and, looking down, saw that a svart had stabbed him from below. Torc killed it. Dave pulled the dagger free from his ribs, gasping. Blood followed. There was another urgach coming towards him, and two more beyond Torc. The North Keep man was down. They were almost alone near the river—the Dalrei were falling back; even the Aven was withdrawing. Dave looked at Torc, saw a deep gash on the other's face, and read bitterest despair in his eyes.

Then, from over the river, north where the Dark was, he heard the sound of singing, high and clear. Dave turned as the urgach hesitated and, looking, caught his breath in joy and wonder.

Over the Plain from the north and west the lios alfar were riding to war. Bright and glorious they were, behind their Lord, whose hair shone golden in the light, and they sang as they came out from the Shadowland at last.

Swift were their horses, passing swift their blades, fierce was the fire in the hearts of the Children of Light. Into the ranks of the svarts they rode, sharp and glittering, and the foot soldiers of the Dark screamed with hate and fear to see them come.

The urgach were all on the south bank now. The terrible giant in white roared a command, and a number of them turned back north, trampling scores of the svart alfar, living and dead, as they did.

Shouting with relief, ignoring the flowering pain in his side, Dave hastened to follow, to kill the urgach as they withdrew, to claim the riverbank again. Then, by the water he heard Torc say, "Oh, Cernan. No!" And looking up into the sky he felt joy turn to ashes in his mouth.

Overhead, like a moving cloud of death, Avaia descended, and with her, grey and black, darkening the sky, came at least three hundred of her brood. The swans of Maugrim came down from the unrelenting heavens and the lios alfar were blotted by darkness and began to die.

The urgach in white screamed again, this time in brutal triumph, and the slaug turned a second time, leaving the lios to the swans and the emboldened svarts, and the Dalrei were beleaguered again by overmastering numbers.

Hacking his way east towards where Ivor—still riding, still wielding his blade—had also regained the river, Dave saw Barth and Navon fighting side by side near the Aven. Then he saw the huge leader of the urgach come up to them and a warning shout tore from his raw throat. The babies in the wood, Torc's babies and his own, the ones they had guarded together. The sword of the giant urgach crashed in an arc that seemed to bruise the very air. It cut through Barth's neck as through a flower stem, and Dave saw the boy's head fly free and blood fountain before it fell into the trampled mud by Adein. The same sword stroke descending sliced heavily, brutally, into Navon's side, and he saw the boy slide from his horse even as he heard a terrifying sound.

He realized that he had made the sound. His own side was sticky with blood. He saw Torc, wild-eyed with hate, surge past him towards the urgach in white. He tried to keep up. Three svarts barred his way. He killed two with his axe and heard the other's head crack open under the hooves of his black horse.

He glanced north and saw the lios battling Avaia and the swans. There were not enough. There had never been enough. They had come out from Daniloth because they would not stand by and watch the Dalrei die. And now they were dying, too.

"Oh, Cernan," he heard someone say, in despair. Cechtar's voice. "This hour knows our name!"

Dave followed the big Rider's glance to the east. And saw. The wolves were coming. Both north and south of the river And leading them was a giant animal, black with a splash of silver between his ears, and he knew from what he had been told that this was Galadan of the andain, lieutenant to Maugrim. It was true. The hour knew their name.

He heard his name. From within.

Not the summoning of death as the Dalrei believed; not the call of the final hour. Absurdly, the inner voice he heard sounded like Kevin Laine's. *Dave,* he heard again. *You idiot. Do it now!*

And on the thought, he reached down and, bringing Owein's Horn to his lips, he sounded it then with all the strength that was left in him.

It was Light again, the sound, and the Dark could not hear it. Even so, they slowed in their advance. His head was tilted back as he blew. He saw Avaia watching him; saw her wheel suddenly aloft. He listened to the sound he made and it was not the same as before. Not moonlight on snow or water, nor sunrise, nor candles by a hearth. This was the noon sun flashing from a sword, it was the red light of a burning fire, it was the torches they had carried on the ride last night, it was the cold hard glitter of the stars.

And from between the stars, Owein came. And the Wild Hunt was with him, hurtling down from far above the swans, and every one of the shadowy kings had a drawn, upraised sword, and so too did the child who led them.

Into the phalanx of Avaia's brood they flew, smoke on flying horses, shadowy death in the darkening sky, and nothing in the air could withstand them, and they killed. Dave saw Avaia leave her sons and daughters to their doom and flash away north in flight. He heard the wild laughter of the kings he had unleashed, and he saw them circle one by one over him and raise swords in salute.

Then the swans were all dead or flying away and the Hunt descended on Fionavar for the first time in so many thousand years. Galadan's wolves were fleeing and the svart alfar and the urgach upon slaug, and Dave saw the shadowy kings wheel above them, killing at will, and there were tears pouring down his begrimed face.

Then he saw the Hunt split in two as four went with the child who had been Finn in wild, airborne pursuit of the army of the Dark. The other kings, and Owein was one of them, stayed by Adein, and in the evening light *they began to kill the lios and the Dalrei, one by one.*

Dave Martyniuk screamed. He leaped from his horse.

He began to run along the riverbank. "No!" he roared. "No, no, oh, no! Please!" He stumbled and fell in the mud. A body moved under him. He heard the unleashed laughter of the Hunt. He looked up. He saw Owein, grey like smoke on his black, shadowy horse, loom above Levon dan Ivor, who stood before his father, and he heard Owein laugh again for purest joy. He tried to rise; felt something give way in his side.

Heard a half-remembered voice above all the noise cry, "Sky King, sheath your sword! I put my will upon you!" Then he fell back, bleeding and brokenhearted in the filthy mud, and heard no more.

He woke to moonlight. He was clean and clothed. He rose. There was no pain. He felt his side and, through the shirt he wore, traced the line of a healed scar. Slowly, he looked around. He was on a mound in the Plain. Away to the north, half a mile perhaps, he saw the river glitter silver in the moonlight. He did not remember the mound, or passing this place. There were lights off to the east: Celidon. No sounds in the night, no movement by the river.

He put a hand to his hip.

"I have not taken it back," he heard her say. He turned to the west where she was, and when he had turned, he knelt, and bowed his head.

"Look at me," she said, and he did.

She was in green, as before, by the pool in Faelinn Grove. There was an illumination in her face, but muted, so he could look upon her. There were a bow and a quiver on her back, and in her hand she held out Owein's Horn.

He was afraid, and he said, "Goddess, how should I ever summon them again?"

Ceinwen smiled. She said, "Not ever, unless someone stronger than the Hunt is there to master them. I should not have done what I did, and I will pay for it. We are not to act on the Tapestry. But you had the horn from me, though for a lesser purpose, and I could not stand by and see Owein unchecked."

He swallowed. She was very beautiful, very tall above him, very bright. "How may a goddess be made to pay?" he asked.

She laughed. He remembered it. She said, "Red Nemain will find a way, and Macha will, if she does not. Never fear."

Memory was coming back. And, with it, a desperate pain.

"They were killing everyone," he stammered. "All of us."

"Of course they were," Green Ceinwen said, shining on the mound. "How should you expect the wildest magic to tamely serve your will?"

"So many dead," he said. His heart was sore with it.

"I have gathered them," Ceinwen said, not ungently. And Dave suddenly understood whence this mound had come, and what it was.

"Levon?" he asked, afraid. "The Aven?"

"Not all need die," she said. She had said that to him before. "I have put the living to sleep by the river. They sleep in Celidon, as well, although the lights burn. They will rise in the morning, though, carrying their wounds."

"I do not," he said, with difficulty.

"I know," she said. "I did not want you to."

He rose. He knew she wanted him to rise. They stood on the mound in the clear moonlight. She shone for him softly like the moon. She came forward and kissed him upon the lips. She motioned with a hand, and he was blinded, almost, by the sudden glory of her nakedness. She touched him. Trembling, he raised a hand towards her hair. She made a sound. Touched him again.

Then he lay down with a goddess, in the green, green of the grass.

# CHAPTER 16

At midafternoon on the second day, Paul caught a certain glance from Diarmuid and he rose. Together they went to the stern of the ship, where Arthur stood with his dog. Around them the men of South Keep manned *Prydwen* with easy efficiency, and Coll, at the helm, held their course hard on west. Due west, Arthur had instructed, and told Coll he would let him know when time came to turn, and where. It was to an island not on any map that they were sailing.

Nor were they sure what lay waiting there. Which was why the three of them, with Cavall padding lightly alongside on the dark planks of the deck, now walked together to the prow where two figures stood together as they had stood every waking hour since *Prydwen* had set sail.

"Loren," Diarmuid said quietly.

The mage slowly turned from staring at the sea. Matt looked around as well.

"Loren, we must talk," the Prince went on, quietly still, but not without authority.

The mage stared at them for a long moment; then he said, his voice rasping, "I know. You understand that I break our Law if I tell you?"

"I do," said Diarmuid. "But we must know what he is doing, Loren. And how. Your Council's Law must not serve the Dark."

Matt, his face impassive, turned back to look out at sea. Loren remained facing the three of them. He said, "Metran is using the Cauldron to revive the svart alfar on Cader Sedat when they die."

Arthur nodded. "But what is killing them?"

"He is," said Loren Silvercloak.

They waited. Matt's gaze was fixed out over the water, but Paul saw how his hands gripped the railing of the ship.

Loren said, "Know you, that in the Book of Nilsom—"

"Accursed be his name," Matt Sören said.

"—in that Book," Loren continued, "is written a monstrous way in which a mage can have the strength of more than his one source."

No one spoke. Paul felt the wind as the sun slipped behind a cloud.

"Metran is using Denbarra as a conduit," Loren said, controlling his voice. "A conduit for the energy of the svart alfar."

"Why are they dying?" Paul asked.

"Because he is draining them to death."

Diarmuid nodded. "And the dead ones are revived with the Cauldron? Over and over again. Is that how he made the winter? How he was strong enough?"

"Yes," said Loren simply.

There was a silence. *Prydwen* rode through a calm sea.

"He will have others with him to do this?" Arthur said.

"He will have to," the mage replied. "The ones used to source him will be incapable of moving."

"Denbarra," Paul said. "Is he so evil? Why is he doing this?"

Matt whipped around. "Because a source does not betray his mage!" They all heard the bitterness.

Loren laid a hand on the Dwarf's shoulder. "Easy," he said. "I don't think he can now, in any case. We shall see, if we get there."

*If we get there.* Diarmuid strolled thoughtfully away to talk with Coll at the helm. A moment later, Arthur and Cavall went back to their place at the stern.

"Can he make the winter again?" Paul asked Loren.

"I think so. He can do almost anything he wants with so much power."

The two of them turned to lean on the railing on either side of Matt. They gazed out at the empty sea.

"I took flowers to Aideen's grave," the Dwarf said, after a moment. "With Jennifer."

Loren looked at him. "I don't think Denbarra has her choice," he repeated after a moment.

"In the beginning he did," the Dwarf growled.

"Were I Metran, what would you have done?"

"Cut your heart out!" Matt Sören said.

Loren looked at his source, a smile beginning to play about his mouth. "Would you?" he asked

For a long time Matt glared back at him. Then he grimaced and shook his head. He turned once more to the sea. Paul felt something ease in his heart. Not to lightness, but towards acceptance and resignation. He wasn't sure why he found strength in the Dwarf's admission, but he did, and he knew he had need of that strength, with greater need yet to come.

He'd been sleeping badly since Kevin died, so Paul had volunteered to take one of the pre-dawn watches. It was a time to think and remember. The only sounds were the creaking of the ship and the slap of waves in the darkness below. Overhead, *Prydwen*'s three sails were full, and they were running easily with the wind. There were four other watchmen stationed around the deck, and red-haired Averren was at the helm.

With no one near him, it was a very private time, almost a peaceful one. He went with his memories. Kevin's death would never be less than a grief, nor would it ever be less than a thing of wonder, of glory, even. So many people died in war, so many had died already in this one, but none had dealt such a blow to the Dark as they passed over into Night. And none, he thought, ever would. *Rahod hedai Liadon*, the priestesses had moaned in the Temple at Paras Derval, while outside the green grass was coming back in a night. Already, through the net of sorrow that wrapped his heart, Paul could feel a light beginning to shine. Let Rakoth Maugrim fear, and everyone in Fionavar—even cold Jaelle— acknowledge what Kevin had wrought, what his soul had been equal to.

And yet, he thought, to be fair, Jaelle had acknowledged it to him twice. He shook his head. The High Priestess with her emerald eyes was more than he could deal with now. He thought of Rachel and remembered music. Her music, and then Kev's, in the tavern. They would share it now, forever, in him. A difficult realization, that.

"Am I intruding?"

Paul glanced back and, after a moment, shook his head.

"Night thoughts," he said.

"I couldn't sleep," Coll murmured, and moved up to the railing. "Thought I might be of some use up top, but it's a quiet night and Averren knows his business."

Paul smiled again. Listened to the easy sound of the ship and the sea. "It's a strange hour," he said. "I like it, actually. I've never been to sea before."

"I grew up on ships," Coll said quietly. "This feels like coming home."

"Why did you leave, then?"

"Diar asked me to," the big man said simply. Paul waited and, after a moment, Coll clasped his hands loosely over the rail and went on. "My mother worked in the tavern at Taerlindel. I never knew who my father was. All the mariners brought me up, it sometimes seemed. Taught me what they knew. My first memories are of being held up to steer a ship when I was too small to reach the tiller on my own."

His voice was deep and low. Paul remembered the one other time the two of them had talked alone at night. About the Summer Tree. How many years ago it seemed.

Coll said, "I was seventeen when Diarmuid and Aileron first came to spend a summer at Taerlindel. I was older than both of them and minded to despise the royal brats. But Aileron . . . did everything impossibly quickly and impossibly well, and Diar . . ." He paused. A remembering smile played over his face.

"And Diar did everything his own way, and equally well, and he beat me in a fight outside my mother's father's house. Then, to apologize, he disguised us both and took me to the tavern where my mother worked. I wasn't allowed in there, you see. Even my mother didn't know me that night—they thought I'd come from Paras Derval with one of the court women."

"Women?" Paul asked.

"Diar was the girl. He was young, remember." They laughed softly in the dark. "I was wondering about him, just a little; then he got two of the town girls to walk with us on the beach beyond the track."

"I know it," said Paul.

Coll glanced at him. "They came because they thought Diarmuid was a woman and I was a lord from Paras Derval. We spent three hours on the beach. I'd never laughed so hard in my life as I did when he took off his skirt to swim and I saw their faces."

They were both smiling. Paul was beginning to understand something, though not yet something else.

"Later, when his mother died, he was made Warden of the South Marches—I think they wanted him out of Paras Derval as much as anything else. He was even wilder in those days. Younger, and he'd loved the Queen, too. He came to Taerlindel and asked me to be his Second, and I went."

The moon was west, as if leading them on. Paul said, looking at it, "He's been lucky to have you. For ballast. And Sharra now, too. I think she's a match for him."

Coll nodded. "I think so. He loves her. He loves very strongly."

Paul absorbed that, and after a moment it began to clear up the one puzzle he hadn't quite understood.

He looked over at Coll. He could make out the square, honest face and the large many-times-broken nose. He said, "The one other night we talked alone, you said to me that had you any power you would curse Aileron. You weren't even supposed to name him, then. Do you remember?"

"Of course I do," said Coll calmly. Around them the quiet sounds of the ship seemed only to deepen the night stillness.

"Is it because he took all the father's love?"

Coll looked at him, still calm. "In part," he said. "You were good at guessing things from the start, I remember. But there is another thing, and you should be able to guess that, too."

Paul thought about it. "Well—" he began.

The sound of singing came to them over the water.

"Listen!" cried Averren, quite unnecessarily.

They all listened, the seven men awake on *Prydwen*. The singing was coming from ahead of them and off to starboard. Averren moved the tiller over that they might come nearer to it. Elusive and faint was that sound, thin and beautiful. Like a fragile web it spun out of the dark towards them, woven of sweet sadness and allure. There were a great many voices twined together in it.

Paul had heard that song before. "We're in trouble," he said.

Coll's head whipped around. "What?"

The monster's head broke water off the starboard bow. Up and up it went, towering over *Prydwen*'s masts. The moon lit its gigantic flat head: the lidless eyes, the gaping, carnivorous jaws, the mottled grey-green slimy skin. *Prydwen* grated on something. Averren grappled with the helm and Coll hurried to aid him. One of the watchmen screamed a warning.

Paul caught a glimpse in the uncertain moonlight of something white, like a horn, between the monster's terrible eyes. He still heard the singing, clear, heartachingly beautiful. A sick premonition swept over him. He turned instinctively. On the other side of *Prydwen* the monster's tail had curved and it was raised, blotting the southern sky, to smash down on them!

*Raven wings.* He knew.

"Soulmonger!" Paul screamed. "Loren, make a shield!"

He saw the huge tail reach its full height. Saw it coming down with the force of malignant death, to crush them out of life. Then saw it smash brutally into nothing but air. Prydwen bounced like a toy with the shock of it, but the mage's shield held. Loren came running up on deck, Diarmuid and Arthur supporting Matt Sören. Paul glimpsed the racking strain in the Dwarf's face and then deliberately cut himself off from all sensation. There was no time to waste. He reached within for the pulse of Mörnir.

And found it, desperately faint, thin as starlight beside the moon. Which is what, in a way, it was. He was too far. Liranan had spoken true. How could he compel the sea god in the sea?

He tried. Felt the third pulse beat in him and cried with the fourth, "Liranan!"

He sensed, rather than saw, the effortless eluding of the god. Despair threatened to drown him. He dove, within his mind, as he had done on the beach. He heard the singing everywhere and then, far down and far away, the voice of Liranan: "I am sorry, brother. Truly sorry."

He tried again. Put all his soul into the summoning. As if from undersea he saw the shadow of *Prydwen* above, and he apprehended the full magnitude of the monster that guarded Cader Sedat. Soulmonger, he thought again. Rage rose overwhelmingly in him, he channelled all its blind force into his call. He felt himself breaking with the desperate strain. It was not enough.

"I told you it would be so," he heard the sea god say. Far off he saw a silver fish eluding through dark water. There were no sea stars. Overhead, *Prydwen* bounced wildly again, and he knew Loren had somehow blocked a second crashing of the monster's tail. Not a third, he thought. He cannot block a third.

And in his mind a voice spoke: *Then there must not be a third. Twiceborn, this is Gereint. Summon now, through me. I am rooted in the land.*

Paul linked with the blind shaman he had never seen. Power surged within him, the godpulse of Mörnir beating fiercer than his own. Underwater in his mind, he stretched a hand downward through the ocean dark. He felt an explosion of his power, grounded on the Plain in Gereint. He felt it crest. Overhead, the vast tail was rising again. "Liranan!" Paul cried for the last time. On the deck of *Prydwen* they heard it like the voice of thunder.

And the sea god came.

Paul felt it as a rising of the sea. He heard the god cry out for joy at being allowed to act. He felt the bond with Gereint going, then; before he could speak again, or send any thought at all, the shaman's mind was gone from his. How far, Paul thought. How far he came. And how far back he has to go.

Then he was on the ship again and seeing with his own eyes, tenuously in the moonlight, how the Soulmonger of Maugrim battled Liranan, god of the sea. And all the while the singing never stopped.

Loren had dropped the protective shield. Matt was lying on the deck. Coll, at the helm, fought to steer *Prydwen* through the troughs and ridges shaped by the titans on their starboard bow. Paul saw a man fly overboard as the ship bucked like a horse in the foaming sea.

The god was fighting in his own form, in his shining water robe, and he could fly up like a wave flew, he could make a whirlpool of the sea below, and he did both those things.

By means of a power Paul could scarcely grasp, a hole suddenly formed in the sea. *Prydwen* bounced and rocked, her timbers screaming, on the very lip of it. He saw the vortex whirling faster and faster, and as its wildness grew he saw that even the vast bulk of the Soulmonger was no proof against the weight of the roused sea.

The monster was going down. The battle would be in the deep, and Paul knew this was for their sake. He watched the god, luminous and shimmering, hang suspended on a high wave overhead as he shaped the sucking whirlpool to draw the other undersea.

The Soulmonger's slimy scum-encrusted head came down. It was almost as large as the ship, Paul saw. He saw the huge lidless eyes up close, the man-sized teeth bared in fury.

He saw Diarmuid dan Ailell leap from *Prydwen*'s deck to land on the flat plane of the monster's head. He heard Coll cry out. The singing was all around them, even through the roaring of the sea. With disbelieving eyes, he saw the Prince slip, scramble for footing, then lurch over to stand between the eyes of Soulmonger and, with one mighty pull, tear free the white horn from its head.

The pull overbalanced him. Paul saw the monster going down, the seas closing over it. As he fell, Diarmuid turned and leaped, twisting, towards *Prydwen*.

To catch, one-handed, the rope Arthur Pendragon had sent flying out to him. They reeled him aboard against the pull of the closing sea. Paul turned just in time to see Liranan let fall the wave on which he'd hung and plummet down after the creature he was now allowed to fight because he had been summoned and compelled.

The singing stopped.

A thousand years, Paul thought, heartsick. Since first Rakoth had used Cader Sedat in the Bael Rangat. For a thousand years the Soulmonger had lurked in the ocean deeps, unable to be opposed. Invincibly vast.

Paul was on his knees, weeping for the captured souls. For the voices of all the bright lios alfar who had set sail to their song, to find a world shaped by the Weaver for them alone.

Not one of them would have gotten there, he now knew. For a thousand years the lios had set forth, singly and in pairs, over a moonless sea.

To meet the Soulmonger of Maugrim. And become its voice.

*Most hated by the Dark, for their name was Light.*

A long while he wept, whose dry eyes had brought so much pain once and then, later, had been rain. After a time he became aware that there was a kind of light shining and he looked up. He was very weak, but Coll was on one side of him and Diarmuid, limping a little, was on the other.

All the men of *Prydwen*—including Matt, he saw—were gathered at the starboard side. They made way for him in respectful silence. Passing to the rail, Paul saw Liranan standing on the surface of the sea, and the shining came from the moonlight caught and enhanced in the million droplets of his water robe.

He and the god looked at each other; then Liranan spoke aloud. "He is dead."

A murmur rose and fell along the length of the ship.

Paul thought of the singing and the bright lios in their small boats. A thousand years of setting sail to the high, sweet summons of their song. A thousand years, and none of them had known.

He said coldly, "Ceinwen gave a horn. You could have warned them."

The sea god shook his head. "I could not," he said. "We were enjoined when first the Unraveller came into Fionavar that we might not interfere of our own will. Green Ceinwen will have answer to make ere long, and for more than the gift of a horn, but I will not transgress against the Weaver's will. He paused. "Even so, it has been a bitter grief. He is dead, brother. I did not think you could summon me. Sea stars will shine here again because of you."

Paul said, "I had help."

After another moment, Liranan, as Cernan had done long ago, bowed to him. Then the god disappeared into the darkness of the sea.

Paul looked at Loren. He saw the tracks of tears on the mage's face. "You know?" he asked. Loren nodded jerkily.

"What?" said Diarmuid.

They had to be told. Paul said, over the grief, "The singing was the lios alfar. The ones who sailed. They never got farther west than here, since the Bael Rangat. Not one of them." *Brendel,* he was thinking. *How will I tell Brendel?*

He heard the men of South Keep. Their helpless rage. It was Diarmuid he watched.

"What did you go for?" he asked the Prince.

"Yes, what?" Loren repeated.

Diarmuid turned to the mage. "You didn't see?" He released Paul's arm and limped over to the steps leading up to the tiller. He came back with something that glittered white in the moonlight. He held it out to the mage.

"Oh," said Matt Sören.

Loren said nothing. It was in his face.

"My lord First Mage of Brennin," Diarmuid said, holding his emotion rigidly in check. "Will you accept as a gift from me a thing of greatest worth? This is the staff of Amairgen Whitebranch that Lisen made for him so long ago."

Paul clenched his hands. So many levels of sorrow. It seemed that someone else hadn't made it past this point either. Now they knew what had happened to the first and greatest of the mages.

Loren took the staff and held it sideways, cradled in both his hands. For all its years in the sea, the white wood was unworn and unsullied, and Paul knew there was a power in it.

"Wield it, Silvercloak!" he heard Diarmuid say. "Take revenge for him, for all the dead. Let his staff be used at Cader Sedat. For this did I bring it back."

Loren's fingers closed tightly around the wood.

"Be it so," was all he said, but the sound of doom was in his voice.

"Be it so now, then," said a deeper voice. They turned. "The wind has shifted," Arthur said.

"North," said Coll after a second.

Arthur looked only at Loren. "We reach Cader Sedat by sailing due north into a north wind. Can you do this, mage?"

Loren and Matt turned to each other as Paul had seen them do before. They exchanged an intensely private glance, unhurried, as if they had all the time in the world. Matt was desperately weary, he knew, and Loren had to be, as well, but he also knew it wasn't going to matter.

He saw the mage look up at Coll. He saw the bleakness of his smile. "Man your ship," he heard Loren say, "and point her to the north."

They hadn't noticed the dawn coming on. But as Coll and the men of South Keep sprang to obey, the sun leaped up behind them out of the sea.

Then it was on their right, as Coll of Taerlindel grappled his ship over straight into the strong north wind. Loren had gone below. When he reappeared he was clad in the cloak of shifting silver hues that gave him his name. Tall and stern, his hour begun at last, his and Matt's, he strode to *Prydwen*'s prow and he carried the staff of Amairgen Whitebranch. Beside him, equally stern, equally proud, walked Matt Sören, who had once been King under Banir Lök and had forsaken that destiny for the one that led him to this place.

*"Cenolan!"* Loren cried. He extended the staff straight out in front of him. *"Sed amairgen, sed remagan, den sedath iren!"* He hurled the words out over the waves, and power surged through them like a greater wave. Paul heard a roar of sound, a rushing of winds as if from all the corners of the sea. They flowed around *Prydwen* as Liranan's whirlpool had spun past her sides and, after a chaotic, swirling moment Paul saw that they were sailing on a hushed and windless sea, utterly calm, like glass, while on either side of them the wild winds raged.

And ahead, not very far at all, lit by the morning sun, lay an island with a castle high upon it, and the island was slowly revolving in the glassy sea. The windows of the castle were begrimed and smeared and so, too, were its walls.

"It shone once," Arthur said quietly.

From the very highest point of the castle a black plume of smoke was rising, straight as a rod, into the sky. The island was rocky and bare of vegetation.

"It was green once," Arthur said. "Cavall!"

The dog was growling and straining forward, his teeth bared. He quieted when Arthur spoke.

Loren never moved. He held the staff rigidly before him. There were no guards. Soulmonger had been guard enough. When they came close, the spinning of the island stopped. Paul guessed that they were spinning with it now, but he had no idea where they were. It was not Fionavar, though, that much he understood.

Coll ordered the anchors cast overboard.

Loren lowered his arm. He looked at Matt. The Dwarf nodded once, then found a place to sit. They rode at anchor in the windless sea just offshore from Cader Sedat.

"All right," said Loren Silvercloak. "Diarmuid, Arthur, I don't care how you do it, but this is what I need."

*It is a place of death,* Arthur had said to him. As they came near, Paul realized that it had been meant literally. There was a tomblike feel to the castle. The very doors—four of them, Arthur said—were set within the slopes of the grey mound from which Cader Sedat rose. The walls climbed high, but the entranceway went down into the earth.

They stood before one of these great iron doors, and for once Paul saw Diarmuid hesitate. Loren and Matt had gone another way to another door. There were no guards to be seen. The deep silence was unsettling. Nothing lived near that place, Paul saw, and was afraid.

"The door will open," said Arthur quietly. "Getting out again was the hard thing, last time."

Diarmuid smiled then. He seemed about to say something, but instead he went forward and pushed on the door of Cader Sedat. It opened soundlessly. He stepped aside and, with a gesture, motioned Arthur to lead them. The Warrior drew a sword and went in. Forty of them followed him out of the sunlight into the dark.

It was very cold; even Paul felt it. This chill went beyond the protection of Mörnir, and he was not proof against it. The dead, Paul thought, and then had another thought: this was the centre, where they were, everything spiralled around this island. Wherever it was. In whatever world.

The corridors were dusty. Spider webs tangled them as they walked. There were branching hallways everywhere, and most of them led down. It was very dark, and Paul could see nothing along those corridors. Their own path led upward, on a slowly rising slant, and after what seemed a long time they rounded a corner and, not far off, saw a glow of greenish light.

Very close to them, not five feet away, another corridor branched left, and up. From it, running, came a svart alfar.

The svart had time to see them. Time to open his mouth. No time to scream. Six arrows ripped into him. He threw up his arms and died.

Flat out, without thought, Paul dived. A guess, a glimpse. With one desperate hand outstretched he caught the flask the svart had carried before it could smash on the floor. He rolled as he landed, as silently as he could. They waited. A moment later Arthur nodded. No alarm had been raised.

Paul scrambled to his feet and walked back to the others. Wordlessly, Diarmuid handed back his sword.

"Sorry," Paul murmured. He had tossed it without warning when he leaped.

"I will bleed to death," Diarmuid whispered, holding up the scratched hand with which he'd made the catch. "What was he carrying?"

Paul handed over the flask. Diarmuid unstoppered it and sniffed at the neck. He lifted his head, mock astonishment visible even in the wan green light.

"By the river blood of Lisen," said the Prince softly. "South Keep wine!" And he raised the flask and took a long drink. "Anyone else?" he asked politely.

There were, predictably, no takers, but even Arthur allowed himself a smile.

Diarmuid's expression changed. "Well done, Pwyll," he said crisply. "Carde, get the body out of the hallway. My lord Arthur, shall we go look at a renegade mage?"

In the shadows Paul thought he saw starlight flash for a moment in the Warrior's eyes. He looked at Cavall, remembering something. In silence, he followed the two leaders down the last corridor. Near the end they dropped to their knees and crawled. Diarmuid made room for him, and Paul wriggled along on his belly and came up to the doorway beside the Prince. They lay there, the three of them, with the South Keep men behind, and looked out over a scene shaped to appall.

Five steps led down from the arched doorway where they were. There were a number of other entrances to the huge chamber below. The roof was so high it was lost in darkness. The floor was illuminated, though: there were torches set around the walls, burning with the eerie green light they had seen from the corridor. The doorway they had reached was about midway along the Great Hall of Cader Sedat. At the head of the chamber, on a dais, stood Metran, once First Mage of Brennin, and beside him was the Cauldron of Khath Meigol over a roaring fire.

It was huge. The Giants had made it, Paul remembered, and he would have been able to guess had he not known. It was black, as best as he could tell in the light, and there were words engraved on the outer rim of it, stained and coated with grime. At least fifteen svart alfar stood on a raised platform around it, and they were handling a net into which, one by one, others of their kind were laid and dropped, lifeless, into the boiling Cauldron.

It was hard to see in the green light, but Paul strained his eyes and watched as one of the ugly creatures was withdrawn from the water. Carefully, the others swung him away from the steaming mouth of the Cauldron and then they stood him up.

And Paul saw the one who had been dead a moment ago walk stumblingly, with others helping him, to stand behind another man.

Denbarra, source to Metran. And looking at the slackjawed, drooling figure of the source, Paul understood what Loren had meant when he said Denbarra would have no choice in the matter anymore.

There were well over a hundred svart alfar behind him mindlessly draining their lives to feed Metran's power, as Denbarra mindlessly served as a conduit for them. Even as they watched, Paul saw two of the svarts drop where they stood. He saw them collected instantly by others, not part of the power web, and carried towards the Cauldron, and he saw others still, being led back from it to stand behind Denbarra.

A loathing rose up in him. Fighting for control, he looked at last squarely on the mage who had made the winter Kevin had died to end.

A stumbling, senile, straggly bearded figure Metran had seemed when they first arrived. A sham, all of it, a seamless, undetected sham to mask pure treachery. The man before them now stood in complete control amid the green lights and black Cauldron smoke. Paul saw that he didn't look old anymore. He was slowly chanting words over the pages of a book.

He hadn't known he carried so much rage within himself.

Impotent rage, it seemed.

"We can't do it," he heard Diarmuid snarl as he grasped the same truth himself.

"This is what I need," Loren had said as *Prydwen* rode at anchor beside the island.

In a way it hadn't been much at all, and in another way it was everything. But then, Paul remembered thinking, they had not come here expecting to return.

Metran would be doing two things, Loren had explained with a terseness alien to him. He would be pouring the vast preponderance of his enhanced power into building another assault on Fionavar. But some of his strength he would be holding back to form a shield around himself and his sources and the Cauldron. They need not expect to find many guards at all, if indeed there were any, because Metran's shield—as Loren's own, that had blocked the Soulmonger—would be guard enough.

In order for Loren to have any hope of smashing the Cauldron, they had to get Metran to lower that shield. And there was only one thought that occurred to any of them—they would have to battle the svarts. Not those being used as sources, but the ones, and there would have to be a great many, who were there as support.

If they could create enough chaos and panic among the svarts, Metran might just be moved to turn his defensive shield into an attacking pulse levelled at the South Keep invaders.

"And when he does that," Loren said grimly, "if I time it right and he doesn't know I'm with you, Matt and I may have a chance at the Cauldron."

No one said anything about what would happen when Metran's might, augmented by the svart alfar and the inherent power of Cader Sedat, hit the South Keep men.

There was, really, nothing to say. This was what they had come to do.

And they couldn't do it. With the wily caution of years of secret scheming, Metran had forestalled even this desperate stratagem. There *were* no support svart alfar they could attack. They could see the shield, a shimmering as of summer heat rising from fallow fields. It covered the entire front of the Hall, *and all the svart alfar were behind it*. Only an occasional runner, like the winebearer they had killed, would make a darting foray out from the Hall. And they couldn't mount a threat against so few. They couldn't do anything. If they charged down onto the floor, the svarts would have a laughing time picking them off with arrows from behind the shield. Metran wouldn't even have to look up from his book.

Frantically, Paul scanned the Hall, saw Diarmuid doing the same. To have come so far, for Kevin to have died to let them come, for Gereint to have hurled his very soul to them—and for this, for nothing! There were no doors behind the screen, no windows over the dais whereon the Cauldron stood, and Metran, and all the svart alfar.

"The wall?" he murmured hopelessly. "In through the back wall?"

"Five feet thick," Diarmuid said. "And he'll have shielded it, anyway." Paul had never seen him look as now he did. He supposed he appeared the same way himself. He felt sick. He saw that he was shaking.

He heard from just behind them Cavall whimper once, very softly.

His sudden memory from the dark corridor came back. Quickly he looked past Diarmuid. Lying prone beyond the Prince, gazing back at Paul, was Arthur. Who said, a whisper of sound, "I think this *is* what Kim brought me for. I never see the end, in any case." There was something unbearable in his face. Paul heard Diarmuid draw a sharp breath and he watched Arthur move back from the entrance so he could rise without being seen. Paul and the Prince followed.

The Warrior crouched before his dog. Cavall had known, Paul realized. His own rage was gone. He hurt instead, as he had not since he'd seen the grey dog's eyes under the Summer Tree.

Arthur had his hands in the scarred fur of the dog's ruff. They looked at each other, man and dog; Paul found he could not watch. Looking away, he heard Arthur say, "Farewell, my gallant joy. You would come with me, I know, but it may not be. You will be needed yet, great heart. There . . . may yet come a day when we need not part."

Paul still could not look at them. There was something difficult in his throat. It was hard to breathe, around the ache of it. He heard Arthur rise. He saw him lay a broad hand on Diarmuid's shoulder.

"Weaver grant you rest," Diarmuid said. Nothing more. But he was crying. Arthur turned to Paul. The summer stars were in his eyes. Paul did not weep. He had been on the Tree, had been warned by Arthur himself that this might happen. He held out both his hands and felt them clasped.

"What shall I say?" he asked. "If I have the chance?"

Arthur looked at him. There was so much grey in the brown hair and beard. "Tell her . . ." He stopped, then slowly shook his head. "No. She knows already everything that ever could be told."

Paul nodded and was crying, after all. Despite everything. What preparation was adequate to this? He felt his hands released into the cold again. The stars turned away. He saw Arthur draw his sword in the corridor and then go down the five steps alone into the Hall.

The one prize that might draw the killing force of Metran's power.

He went quickly and was most of the way to the dais before he stopped. Scrambling back with Diarmuid to watch, Paul saw that Metran and the svarts were so absorbed they hadn't even seen him.

"Slave of the Dark, hear me!" cried Arthur Pendragon in the great voice that had been heard in so many of the worlds. It reverberated through Cedar Sedat. The svart alfar shouted in alarm. Paul saw Metran's head snap up, but he also saw that the mage was unafraid.

He gave Arthur an unhurried scrutiny from beneath his white eyebrows and bony forehead. And, Paul thought bitterly, from behind the safety of his shield.

"I intend to hear you," Metran said tranquilly. "Before you die you will tell me who you are and how you came here."

"Speak not lightly of dying in this place," Arthur said. "You are among the great of all the worlds here. And they can be awakened. As for my name: know that I am Arthur Pendragon, son of Uther, King of Britain. I am the Warrior Condemned, summoned here to battle you, *and I cannot die!*"

Only an arrow, Paul thought fearfully. An arrow could kill him now. But the svart alfar were gibbering in panic, and even Metran's gaze seemed less secure.

"Our books of lore," he said, "tell a different tale."

"Doubtless," Arthur replied. "But before you run to them, know this: I command you now to quit this place on the hour or I shall go down and wake the dead in their wrath to drive you into the sea!"

Metran's eyes wavered indecisively. He came slowly from behind the high table. He hesitated, then said, sharp and brittle in the huge room, "It is told you can be killed. Over and over, you have been killed. I will offer your head before the throne in Starkadh!"

He raised one arm high over his head. There came a low sound from Cavall. Arthur's head was lifted, waiting. This is it, Paul thought, and he prayed.

Then Metran lowered his hand slowly and began, brutally, to laugh.

It lasted a long time, corrosive, contemptuous. *He's an actor*, Paul remembered, wincing under the laceration of that mockery. *He fooled them all for so long.*

"Loren, Loren, Loren," Metran finally gasped, overcome by his own amusement. "Just because you are a fool must you take me for one? Come and tell me how you eluded the Soulmonger, then let me put you out of pain." His laughter ended. There was a bleak malevolence in his face.

From the far side of the Hall, Paul heard Loren's voice. "Metran, you had a father, but I will not trouble his rest by giving your full name. Know that the Council of the Mages has ordered your death, and so, too, has the High King of Brennin. You have been cursed in Council and are now to die. Know also that we did not elude the Soulmonger. We slew him."

"Hah!" Metran barked. "Will you bluster still, Silvercloak?"

"I never did," said Loren and, with Matt, he stepped into the green light of the Great Hall. "Behold the staff of Amairgen for proof!" And he held the Whitebranch high.

At that, Metran stepped back and Paul saw real dismay on his face. But for a moment only.

"Brightly woven, then!" said Metran sarcastically. "A feat to be sung! And for reward now, I will allow you to stand here and watch, Loren. Watch helplessly, you and whoever you coerced into this voyage, while I move a rain of death from Eridu, where it has been falling for three days now, over the mountains into the High Kingdom.

"In the name of the Weaver," Diarmuid said, horrified, as Metran deliberately turned his back on Loren and returned to his table by the Cauldron. Once more the svart alfar resumed their cycling of the living and dead. Through it all Denbarra stood, his eyes staring at nothing, his mouth open, slack and soundless.

"Look," Paul said.

Matt was talking urgently to Loren. They saw the mage stand irresolute a moment, looking at the Dwarf; then Matt said something more and Loren nodded once.

He turned back to the dais and, raising the staff of Amairgen, pointed it at the Cauldron. Metran glanced up at him and smiled. Loren spoke a word, then another. When he spoke the third, a bolt of silver light leaped from the staff, dazzling all of them.

The stones of Cader Sedat shook. Paul opened his eyes. He saw Metran struggling to his feet. He felt the castle trembling still. He saw the vast Cauldron of Khath Meigol sway and rock on its base above the fire.

Then he saw it settle back again as it had been.

The shield had held. He turned and watched Matt slowly rising from the ground. Even from a distance he could see the Dwarf trembling with what that power surge had taken from him. And, abruptly, he remembered that Matt had sourced a shield against the Soulmonger that same day, and then a steering of all the worlds' winds away from them as they sailed to the island. He couldn't begin to comprehend what the Dwarf was enduring. What words were there, what thoughts even, in the face of a thing like this? And how did you deal with the fact that it wasn't enough?

Shaken but unhurt, Metran stepped forward again. "You have bought the death you came for now," he said with no trace of idle play in him any more. "When you are dead, I can begin shaping the death rain again; it makes no matter in the end. I shall grind your bones to powder and lay your skull by my bed, Loren Silvercloak, servant of Ailell." And he closed the book on the table and began gesturing in a gathering motion with his arms.

He was bringing in his power, Paul realized. He was going to use it all on Loren and Matt. This was the end, then. And if that was so—

Paul leaped from the entranceway, down the stairs, and ran across the floor to Matt's side. He dropped to his knees there.

"A shoulder might help," he said. "Lean on me."

Without a word, Matt did so, and, from above, Paul felt Loren touch him once in a gesture of farewell. Then he saw the Whitebranch lifted again, to point squarely at Metran, who stood now between them and the Cauldron. He watched Metran level a long finger straight at the three of them.

Then both mages spoke together and the Great Hall shook to its foundations as two bolts of power exploded towards each other. One was silver, like the moon, like the cloak Loren wore, and the other was the baleful green of the lights in that place; they met midway between the mages, and where they met a fire leaped to flame in the air.

Paul heard Matt Sören fight to control his breathing. Above him, he glimpsed Loren's rigid arm holding the staff, straining to channel the power the Dwarf was feeding him. And on the dais he saw Metran, sourced by so very many of the svart alfar, bend the same power that had made winter in midsummer directly down on them. Easily, effortlessly.

He felt Matt begin to tremble. The Dwarf leaned more heavily on his arm. He had nothing to offer them. Only a shoulder. Only pity. Only love.

Crackling savagely, the two beams of power locked into each other as the castle continued to shake under their unleashed force. They held and held, the silver and the green, held each other flaming in the air while worlds hung in the balance. So long it went on, Paul had an illusion that time had stopped. He helped up the Dwarf—both arms around him now—and prayed with all his soul to what he knew of Light.

Then he saw that none of it was enough. Not courage, wisdom, prayer, necessity. Not one against so many. Slowly, with brutal clarity, the silver thrust of power was being pushed back towards them. Inch by bitter, fighting inch Paul saw Loren forced to give way. He heard the mage's breathing now, ragged and shallow. He looked up and saw sweat pouring in rivulets down Loren's face. Beside him, Matt was still on his feet, still fighting, though his whole body shook now as with a lethal fever.

A shoulder. Pity. Love. What else could he give them here at the end? And with whom else would he rather die than these two?

Matt Sören spoke. With an effort so total it almost shattered Paul's heart, the Dwarf forced sounds out of his chest. "Loren," he gasped, his face contorted with strain. "Loren . . . do now!"

The green surge of Metran's might leaped half a foot nearer to them. Paul could feel the fire now. Loren was silent. His breathing rasped horribly.

"Loren," Matt mumbled again. "I have lived for this. Do it now."

The Dwarf's one eye was closed. He trembled continuously. Paul closed his own eyes, and held Matt as tightly as he could.

"Matt," he heard the mage say. "Oh, Matt." The name, nothing more.

Then the Dwarf spoke to Paul and he said, "Thank you, my friend. You had better move back now." And grieving, grieving, Paul did so. Looking up, he saw Loren's face distort with wildest hate. He heard the mage cry out then, tapping into his uttermost power, sourced in Matt Sören the Dwarf, channelled through the Whitebranch of Amairgen, and the very heart and soul of Loren Silvercloak were in that cry and in the blast that followed it.

There came a flash of obliterating light. The very island rocked this time, and with that shaking of Cader Sedat a tremor rolled through every one of the Weaver's worlds.

Metran screamed, high and short, as if cut off. Stones shook loose from the walls over their heads. Paul saw Matt fall to the ground, saw Loren drop beside him. Then, looking up towards the dais, he saw the Cauldron of Khath Meigol crack asunder with a sound like a mountain shattering.

The shield was down. He knew Metran was dead. Knew someone else was, too. He saw the svart alfar, bred to kill, beginning to run with swords and knives towards them, and, crying aloud, he rose up and drew his own sword to guard those who had done what they had done.

The svarts never reached him. They were met by forty men of Brennin, led by

Diarmuid dan Ailell, and the soldiers of South Keep cut a swath of sheer fury through the ranks of the Dark. Paul charged into the battle, wielding a sword with love running high in his heart like a tide love, and the need to hammer through grief.

There were many svarts and they were a long time in the killing, but they killed them all. Eventually Paul found himself, bleeding from a number of minor wounds, standing with Diarmuid and Coll in one of the passageways leading back to the Great Hall. There was nowhere else to go, so they went back there.

In the entrance they paused and looked out over the carnage wrought in that place. They were near to the dais and walked up to it. Metran lay flung on his back, his face shattered, his body disfigured by hideous burns. Near him lay Denbarra. The source had been babbling through the fight, with the staring eyes of the hopelessly mad, until Diarmuid had put a sword through his heart and left him near his mage.

Not far from them, still smoldering, lay the thousand, thousand fragments of the Cauldron of Khath Meigol, shattered. Like a heart, thought Paul, and turned to walk the other way. He had to step over and around the dead svart alfar and the stones of the walls and ceiling dislodged in the final cataclysm. It was very quiet now. The green lights were gone. Diarmuid's men were lighting torches around the Hall. By their glow Paul saw, as he came near, a figure on his knees rocking slowly back and forth amid the devastation with a dark head cradled in his lap.

*I have lived for this*, Matt Sören had said; and had made his mage go into him for killing, uttermost power. And had died.

Looking down in silence, Paul saw then in the Dwarf's face, dead, a thing he had never seen in it, living: Matt Sören smiled amid the ruin of Cader Sedat, not the grimace they had learned to know but the true smile of one who has had what he most desired.

A thousand, thousand fragments, like a heart. Paul looked at Loren.

He touched the kneeling man, once, as the mage had touched him before; then he walked away. Looking back, he saw that Loren had cast his cloak over his face.

He saw Arthur with Diarmuid and went over to them. The torches were lit now, all around the Hall. Arthur said, "We have time, all the time we need to take. Let us leave him for a while."

Together the three of them walked with Cavall down the dark, mouldering corridors of Cader Sedat. It was damp and cold. A chill, sourceless wind seemed to be blowing among the crumbling stones.

"You spoke of the dead?" Paul murmured.

"I did," said Arthur. "Spiral Castle holds, below the level of the sea, the mightiest of the dead in all the worlds." They turned. Another darker corridor.

"You spoke of waking them," Paul said.

Arthur shook his head. "I cannot. I was trying to frighten him. They can only be wakened by name and, when last here, I was very young and I did not know—" He stopped, then, and stood utterly still.

*No!* Paul thought. *It is enough. It has been enough, surely.*

He opened his mouth to speak but found he could not. The Warrior took a slow breath, as if drawing it from his long past, from the core of his being. Then he nod-ded, once only, and with effort, as if moving his head against a weight of worlds.

"Come," was all he said. Paul looked at Diarmuid, and in the darkness he saw the same stiff apprehension in the Prince's face. They followed Arthur and the dog.

This time they went down. The corridor Arthur took sloped sharply, and they had to use the walls to keep their balance. The stones were clammy to the touch. There was light now, though, a faint phosphorescence of the corridor itself. Diarmuid's white tunic gleamed in it.

They became aware of a steady pounding noise beyond the walls.

"The sea," Arthur said quietly, and then stopped before a door Paul had not seen. The Warrior turned to the two of them. "You may prefer to wait out here," he said.

There was a silence.

Paul shook his head. "I have tasted death," he said.

Diarmuid smiled, a brief flash of his old smile. "One of us in there," he said, "had best be normal, don't you think?"

So they left the dog by the door and passed within, amid the incessant pounding of the sea on the walls.

There were fewer than Paul had thought there would be. It was not an overly large chamber. The floor was stone and without adornment. In the centre stood a single pillar, and upon it one candle burned with a white flame that did not waver. The walls gleamed palely. Set around the room in alcoves dimly lit by the candle and the phosphorescence of the walls were perhaps twenty bodies lying on beds of stone. Only that many, Paul thought, from all the dead in all the worlds. Almost he walked over to look upon them, to see the faces of the chosen great, but a diffidence overtook him, a sense of intruding upon their rest. Then he felt Diarmuid's hand on his arm, and he saw that Arthur was standing in front of one of the alcoves and that his hands were covering his face.

"It is enough!" Paul cried aloud and moved to Arthur's side.

In front of them, as if asleep, save that he did not breathe, lay a man of more than middle height. His hair was black, his cheeks shaven. His eyes were closed, but wide-set under a high forehead. His mouth and chin were firm, and his hands, Paul saw, clasped the hilt of a sword and were very beautiful. He looked to have been a lord among men, and if he was lying in this place, Paul knew, he had been.

He also knew who this was.

"My lord Arthur," said Diarmuid painfully, "you do not have to do this. It is nei-ther written nor compelled."

Arthur lowered his hands. His gaze never left the face of the man who lay on the stone.

"He will be needed," he said. "He cannot but be needed. I should have known it was too soon for me to die."

"You are willing your own grief," Paul whispered.

Arthur turned to him at that, and his eyes were compassionate. "It was willed long ago."

Looking on Arthur Pendragon's face in that moment, Paul saw a purer nobility than he had ever seen in his days. More, even, than in Liranan, or Cernan of the Beasts. Here was the quintessence, and everything in him cried out against the doom that lay behind this monstrous choice.

Diarmuid, he saw, had turned away.

*"Lancelot!"* said Arthur to the figure on the bed of stone.

His eyes were brown. He was taller than Paul had first thought. His voice was mild and low and unexpectedly gentle. The other surprising thing was the dog. Paul had thought Cavall's loyalty would make him hostile, but instead he'd come up to the dark-haired man with a quiet sound of joy. Lancelot had knelt to stroke the torn grey fur, and Paul could see him register the presence of the scars. Then he had walked in silence between Paul and Diarmuid back up to the living world.

He had only spoken at the very beginning. After he had first risen to the Warrior's command. Risen, as if, truly, he had only been asleep and not dead so very, very long.

Arthur had said, "Be welcome. We are at war against the Dark in Fionavar, which is the first world of all. I have been summoned, and so now are you."

And Lancelot had replied with courtesy and sorrow, "Why have you done this, my lord, to the three of us?"

Arthur had closed his eyes at that. Then opened them and said, "Because there are more at risk than the three of us. I will see if I can have us fight in different companies."

And Lancelot had answered mildly, "Arthur, you know I will not fight save under you and by your side."

At which point Arthur had turned on his heel to walk away, and Diarmuid and Paul had named themselves and, with Lancelot, had followed the Warrior back from the place of the dead amid the pounding of the sea.

Loren had risen. His cloak lay covering the body of Matt Sören. The mage, his face numb with weariness and shock, listened as Diarmuid and Arthur made plans for their departure. He hardly acknowledged Lancelot's presence, though the men of South Keep were whispering among each other with awe.

It was, Paul gathered, still daylight outside. Not long after noon, in fact. It seemed to him as if they had been on the island forever. In a way, he supposed, a part of him would always be on this island. Too much had happened here. They were going to be leaving almost immediately, it appeared. No one was minded to spend a night in this place.

Loren turned. Paul saw him walk over to one of the torches. He stood there with the pages of a book in his hand, feeding them one by one to the flame. Paul went over to him. Loren's face was streaked with the tracks of tears and sweat, running down through the soot and grime stirred up when the last bolt fell. Matt's last, Paul thought. And Loren's, too. His source was dead. He wasn't a mage anymore.

"The Book of Nilsom," said the man who had bade them cross with him so long ago. He gave Paul a number of pages. Together they stood, reaching up in turn to set each page alight.

It took a long time and they did it carefully. Somehow eased by the shared, simple task, Paul watched the last leaf burn; then he and Loren turned back to the others.

Who were staring, all of them, at one place in the Hall.

There were over forty men in that place but Paul couldn't hear any of them breathe. He walked towards Lancelot through the ring of men, saw the pure, unyielding will in his eyes, watched the colour begin to drain from his face, and he began to grasp the magnitude of this man who was trying to surmount, by sheerest resolution, the movement of the wheel of time and the shuttling of the Loom. They stood very close; he saw it all.

Beside him, Loren made a strangled sound and a gesture of denial. Paul heard the flap of wings. Even here. *Thought, Memory.*

"Loren, wait!" he said. "He did it once before. And this is Cader Sedat."

Slowly, the mage advanced, and Paul with him, to stand a little nearer yet. A little nearer to the place where Lancelot du Lac, newly wakened from his own death, knelt on the stone floor with the hands of Matt Sören between his own, and held up to his brow.

And because they were closer than the others, he and Loren were the first to see the Dwarf begin to breathe.

Paul could never remember what it was he shouted. He knew that the cry that went up from the men of Brennin dislodged yet more stones from the walls of Cader Sedat. Loren dropped to his knees, his face alight, on the other side of the Dwarf from Lancelot. The dark-haired man was white but composed, and they saw Matt's breathing become slowly steadier.

And then the Dwarf looked up at them.

He gazed at Loren for a long time, then turned to Lancelot. He glanced at his hands clasped in the other's, still, and Paul could see him grasp what had happened. Matt looked up at their hovering, torchlit faces. His mouth twitched in a remembered way.

"What happened to my other eye?" Matt Sören said to Lancelot, and they all laughed and wept for joy.

It was because of where they were, Lancelot explained, and because he was so newly wakened from death himself, and because Matt had suffered no killing wound, only a draining of his life force. And, he added in his courteous, diffident way, because he had done this once before at Camelot.

Matt nodded slowly. He was already on his feet. They clustered close to him, unwilling to leave him alone, to have any distance come between. Loren's tired face glowed. It eased the heart to look on him.

"Well," said Diarmuid, "now that we have our mage and source back, shall we sail?"

There was a chorus of agreement.

"We should," said Loren. "But you should know that Teyrnon is now the only mage in Fionavar."

"What?" It was the Dwarf.

Loren smiled sadly. "Reach for me, my friend."

Slowly they saw Matt's face drain of colour.

"Easy," Loren cautioned. "Be easy." He turned to the others. "Let no one grieve. When Matt died our link was broken and I ceased to be a mage. Bringing him back could not reforge what had been severed." There was a silence.

"Oh, Loren," Matt said faintly.

Loren wheeled on him and there was a fire in his eyes. "Hear me!" He spun again and looked at the company. "I was a man before I was a mage. I hated the Dark as a child and I do so now, and I can wield a sword!" He turned back to Matt and his voice deepened. "You left your destiny once to link it with my own and it led you far from home, my friend. Now, it seems, the circle is closing. Will you accept me? Am I a fit companion for the rightful King of Dwarves, who must go back now to Calor Diman to reclaim his Crown?"

And they were humbled and abashed at what blazed forth from Loren in that moment, as he knelt on the stones before Matt.

They had gathered what there was to gather, and had begun to leave the Hall. So much had happened. Every one of them was bone-weary and stumbling with it. So much. Paul thought he could sleep for days.

He and Arthur seemed to be the last ones. The others were walking up the corridor already. There would be light outside. He marvelled at that. Here there were only the torches, and the smouldering embers of the fire that had burned beneath the Cauldron of Khath Meigol.

He saw that Arthur had paused in the doorway for a last look back. Paul turned as well. And realized that they were not the last of the party, after all. Amid the wreckage of that shattered place a dark-haired figure stood, looking up at the two of them.

Or, not really the two of them. He saw Arthur and Lancelot gaze at each other and something so deep he could never have tried to name it passed between the two of them. Then Arthur spoke, and there was sorrow in his voice and there was love. "Oh, Lance, come," he said. "She will be waiting for you."

⊷⇒⦆⦅⇐⊷

*Here ends* THE WANDERING FIRE, *the second book of* THE FIONAVAR TAPESTRY

⊷⇒⦆⦅⇐⊷

# BOOK 3

# THE DARKEST ROAD

*At the end of this road*
*as at the beginning of all roads*
*are my parents*

*SYBIL AND SAM KAY.*

*This tapestry is theirs.*

# CONTENTS

# THE CHARACTERS

## The Five:

KIMBERLY FORD, Seer of Brennin
JENNIFER LOWELL, who is also GUINEVERE
DAVE MARTYNIUK ("Davor")
PAUL SCHAFER, Lord of the Summer Tree ("Pwyll Twiceborn")

KEVIN LAINE ("Liadon"), the sacrifice come freely on Midsummer's Eve

## FROM BRENNIN:

AILERON, High King of Brennin
DIARMUID, his brother

LOREN SILVERCLOAK, once First Mage of Brennin
MATT SÖREN, once his source, King of the Dwarves
TEYRNON, a mage
BARAK, his source

JAELLE, High Priestess of the Goddess
AUDIART, her second in command, in the province of Gwen Ystrat
LEILA, a young priestess, mind-linked to Finn dan Shahar
SHIEL, a priestess in Paras Derval

COLL of Taerlindel, lieutenant to Diarmuid, captain of the ship PRYDWEN
CARDE ⎫
ERRON ⎪
TEGID ⎬ the men of South Keep, members of
ROTHE ⎪ Diarmuid's band
AVERREN ⎭

GORLAES, Chancellor of Brennin
MABON, Duke of Rhoden
NIAVIN, Duke of Seresh

VAE, a craftswoman in Paras Derval
SHAHAR, her husband
FINN, their son, now riding with the Wild Hunt upon ISELEN
DARIEN, their foster child, son of Jennifer Lowell and Rakoth Maugrim

BRENDEL, a lord of the lios alfar, from Daniloth
BROCK, a Dwarf, from Banir Tal

# FROM CAThAL:

SHALHASSAN, Supreme Lord of Cathal
SHARRA, his daughter and heir ("the Dark Rose"); betrothed to Diarmuid

# FROM The PLAIN:

IVOR, Aven of the Plain, Chieftain of the third tribe of the Dalrei
LEITH, his wife
LEVON, his older son
CORDELIANE ("LIANE"), his daughter
TABOR, his younger son, rider of IMRAITH-NIMPHAIS

TORC, a Rider of the third tribe

GEREINT, shaman of the third tribe

# FROM DANILOTh:

RA-TENNIEL, Lord of the lios alfar
GALEN ⎫
LYDAN ⎭ twin brother and sister, of the Brein Mark
LEYSE of the Swan Mark

# IN The MOUNTAINS:

DALREIDAN, an exile from the Plain
FAEBUR of Larak, exiled from Eridu
CERIOG, leader of the mountain outlaws

RUANA of the Paraiko, in the caves of Khath Meigol

MIACH, First of the Dwarfmoot, in Banir Lök

# The DARK:

RAKOTH MAUGRIM the UNRAVELLER

GALADAN, Wolflord of the andain, his lieutenant
UATHACH, the urgach in white, commander of the army of Maugrim

FORDAETHA OF RÜK, Ice Queen of the Barrens
AVAIA, the Black Swan
BLÖD, a Dwarf, servant to Rakoth
KAEN, brother to Blöd, ruling the Dwarves in Banir Lök

# The POWERS:

THE WEAVER at the Loom

MÖRNIR of the Thunder
DANA, the Mother
CERNAN of the Beasts
CEINWEN of the Bow, the HUNTRESS
LIRANAN, god of the sea
MACHA
NEMAIN } godesses of war

OWEIN, Lord of the Wild Hunt, rider of CARGAIL
FLIDAIS ("Taliesin") of the andain, a power of Pendaran Wood
CURDARDH, the Oldest One, guardian of Pendaran's sacred grove

# FROM The PAST:

ARTHUR PENDRAGON, the Warrior, with CAVALL, his dog
LANCELOT du LAC, from the Chamber of the Dead in Cader Sedat

IORWETH FOUNDER, first High King of Brennin
CONARY, High King during the Bael Rangat
COLAN, his son, High King after him ("the Beloved")

AMAIRGEN WHITEBRANCH, first of the mages; slain by the Soulmonger
LISEN of the Wood, a deiena, source and wife to Amairgen

RA-TERMAINE, greatest of the Lords of the lios alfar; slain by Galadan in the
    Bael Rangat
RA-LATHEN ("Lathen Mistweaver"), his successor, who shaped the mists that
    made Daniloth into the Shadowland
LAURIEL, the White Swan, slain by Avaia in the Bael Rangat
REVOR, ancestral hero of the Dalrei; first Aven of the Plain
SEITHR, King of the Dwarves during the Bael Rangat
CONNLA, mightiest of the Paraiko, who bound the Wild Hunt and forged the
    Cauldron of Khath Meigol

# PART I

# THE LAST KANIOR

# CHAPTER 1

"Do you know the wish of your heart?"

Once, when Kim Ford was an undergraduate, young for university and young for her age, someone had asked her that question over cappuccino on a first date. She'd been very impressed. Later, rather less young, she'd often smiled at the memory of how close he'd come to getting her into bed on the strength of a good line and a way with waiters in a chic restaurant. The question, though, had stayed with her.

And now, not so much older but white-haired nonetheless, and as far away from home as she could imagine being, Kim had an answer to that question.

The wish of her heart was that the bearded man standing over her, with the green tattoos on his forehead and cheeks, should die an immediate and painful death.

Her side ached where he had kicked her, and every shallow breath was a lancing pain. Crumpled beside her, blood seeping from the side of his head, lay Brock of Banir Tal. From where Kim lay she couldn't tell if the Dwarf was alive or not, and if she could have killed in that moment, the tattooed man would be dead. Through a haze of pain she looked around. There were about fifty men surrounding them on the high plateau, and most of them bore the green tattoos of Eridu. Glancing down at her own hand she saw that the Baelrath lay quiescent, no more than a red stone set in a ring. No power for her to draw upon, no access to her desire.

It didn't really surprise her. The Warstone had never, from the first, brought anything but pain with its power, and how could it have been otherwise?

"Do you know," the bearded Eridun above her said, with harsh mockery, "what the Dalrei have done down below?"

"What? What have they done, Ceriog?" another man asked, moving forward a little from the circle of men. He was older than most of them, Kim saw. There was grey in his dark hair, and he bore no sign of the green tattoo markings.

"I *thought* you might be interested," the one named Ceriog said, and laughed. There was something wild in the sound, very near to pain. Kim tried not to hear it, but she was a Seer more than she was anything else, and a premonition came to her with that laughter. She looked at Brock again. He had not moved. Blood was still welling slowly from the wound at the side of his head.

"I am interested," the other man said mildly.

Ceriog's laughter ended. "They rode north last night," he said, "every man among them, except the blind ones. They have left the women and children undefended in the camp east of the Latham, just below us."

There was a murmur among the listening men. Kim closed her eyes. *What had happened?* What could have driven Ivor to do such a thing?

"What," the older man asked, still quietly, "does any of that have to do with us?"

Ceriog moved a step towards him. "You," he said, contemptuously, "are more than a fool. You are an outlaw even among outlaws. Why should any of us answer questions of yours when you won't even give us your name?"

The other man raised his voice very slightly. On the windless plateau it carried. "I have been in the foothills and the mountains," he said, "for more years than I care to remember. For all of those years, Dalreidan is what I have offered as my name. Rider's Son is what I choose to call myself, and until this day no man has seen fit to question it. Why should it matter to you, Ceriog, if I choose not to shame my father's grave by keeping his name as part of my own?"

Ceriog snorted derisively. "There is no one here who has not committed a crime, old man. Why should you be different?"

"Because," said Dalreidan, "I killed a mother and child."

Opening her eyes, Kim looked at him in the afternoon sunlight. There was a stillness on the plateau—broken by Ceriog's laughter. Again Kim heard the twisting note in it, halfway between madness and grief.

"Surely," Ceriog mocked, "that should have given you a taste for more!" He flung his arms wide. "Surely we should all have a taste for death by now! I had come back to tell you of women and boys for sport down below. I had not thought to see a Dwarf delivered into my hands so soon."

He did not laugh again. Instead, he turned to look down on the figure of Brock, sprawled unconscious on the sunbaked stone of the plateau.

A sick foreboding swept over Kimberly. A recollection, though not her own: Ysanne's, whose soul was a part of her now. A memory of a legend, a nightmare tale from childhood, of very great evil done, very long ago.

"What happened?" she cried, wincing with pain, desperate to know. "What did they do?"

Ceriog looked at her. They all did. For the first time she met his eyes and flinched away from the raw grief she read in them. His head jerked up and down convulsively. "Faebur!" he cried suddenly. A younger light-bearded Eridun stepped forward. "Play messenger again, Faebur. Tell the story one more time. See if it improves with age. She wants to know what the Dwarves have done. *Tell her!*"

She was a Seer. The threads of the Timeloom shuttled for her. Even as Faebur began his flat-voiced recitation, Kim cut straight past his words to the images behind them and found horror.

The background of the tale was known to her, though not less bitter for that: the story of Kaen and Blöd, the brothers who had led the Dwarves in search, forty years ago, of the lost Cauldron of Khath Meigol. When the Dwarfmoot had voted to aid them, Matt Sören, the young King, had thrown down his sceptre and removed the Diamond Crown and left the twin mountains to find another fate entirely, as source to Loren Silvercloak.

Then, a year ago, the Dwarf now lying beside her had come to Paras Derval with tidings of great evil done: Kaen and Blöd, unable to find the Cauldron on their own and driven near to madness by forty years of failure, had entered into an unholy alliance. With the aid of Metran, the treacherous mage, they had finally unearthed the Cauldron of the Giants—and had paid the price. It had been twofold: the Dwarves had broken the wardstone of Eridu, thus severing the warning link of the five stones, and then they had delivered the Cauldron itself into the hands of their new master, the one whose binding under Rangat was to have been ensured by the linked wardstones—Rakoth Maugrim, the Unraveller.

All this she had known. Had known, too, that Metran had used the Cauldron to lock in the killing winter that had ended five mornings ago, after the night Kevin Laine had sacrificed himself to bring it to a close. What she hadn't known was what had happened since. What she now read in Faebur's face and heard him tell, feeling the images like lashes in her soul.

The death rain of Eridu.

"When the snow began to melt," Faebur was saying, "we rejoiced. I heard the bells ring in walled Larak, though I could not return there. Exiled in the hills by my father, I, too, gave thanks for the end of the killing cold." So had she, Kim remembered. She had given thanks even as she mourned, hearing the wailing of the priestesses at dawn outside the dark cave of Dun Maura. *Oh, my darling man.*

"For three days," Faebur went on, in the same detached, numb tones, "the sun shone. The grass returned overnight, and the flowers. When the rain came, on the fourth day, that, too, seemed natural, and cause for joy.

"Until, looking down from the high hills west of Larak, I heard the screaming begin. The rain did not reach the hills, but I could see herdsmen not far away on the slopes below, with their goats and kere, and I heard them scream when the rain fell, and I saw huge black blisters form and break on animals and men as they died."

Seers could go—were forced by their gift to go—behind the words to the images suspended in the coils of time. Try as she might, Kim's second, inner sight would not let her look away from the vision caught in Faebur's words. And being what she was, twinned soul with two sets of memories, she knew more, even, than Faebur knew. For Ysanne's childhood memories were hers, and clearer now, and she knew the rain had been shaped once before in a distant time of dark, and that the dead were deadly to those who touched them, and so could not be buried.

Which meant plague. Even after the rain stopped.

"How long did it last?" she asked suddenly.

Ceriog's harsh laughter told her her mistake and opened a new, deeper vein of terror, even before he spoke. "How long?" he snapped, his voice swirling erratically. "White hair should bring more wisdom. Look east, foolish woman, up the valley of the Kharn. Look past Khath Meigol and tell me how long it lasted!"

She looked. The mountain air was thin and clear, the summer sun bright overhead. She could see a long way from that high plateau, almost to Eridu itself.

She could see the rain clouds piled high east of the mountains.

The rain hadn't ended. And she knew, as surely as she knew anything at all, that, if unchecked, it would be coming their way: Over the Carnevon Range, and the Skeledarak, to Brennin, Cathal, the wide Plain of the Dalrei, and then, of course, to the place where undying Rakoth's most undying hatred lay—to Daniloth, where dwelt the lios alfar.

Her thoughts, shrouded in dread, winged away west, far past the end of land, out over the sea, where a ship was sailing to a place of death. It was named *Prydwen*, she knew. She knew the names of many things, but not all knowledge was power. Not in the face of what was falling from that dark sky east of them.

Feeling helpless and afraid, Kim turned back to Ceriog. As she did, she saw that the Baelrath was flickering on her hand. That, too, she understood: the rain she had just been shown was an act of war, and the Warstone was responding. Unobtrusively she turned the ring inwards and closed her palm so it would not be seen.

"You wanted to know what the Dwarves had done, and now you know," Ceriog said, his voice low and menacing.

"Not all the Dwarves!" she said, struggling to a sitting position, gasping with the pain that caused. "Listen to me! I know more of this than you. I—"

"Doubtless, you know more, travelling with one of them. And you shall tell me, before we are done with you. But the Dwarf is first. I am very pleased," said Ceriog, "to see he is not dead."

Kim whipped her head around. A cry escaped her. Brock moaned, his hands moved slightly. Heedless of risk, she crawled over to help him. "I need clean cloths and hot water!" she shouted. "Quickly!"

No one moved. Ceriog laughed. "It seems," he said, "that you haven't understood me. I am pleased to see him alive, because I intend to kill him with great care."

She did understand and, understanding, could no longer hate—it seemed that clear, uncomplicated wishes of the heart were not allowed for her. Which wasn't all that surprising, given who she was and what she carried.

She could no longer hate, nor could she hold back her pity for one whose people were being so completely destroyed. But neither could she allow him to proceed. He had come nearer, had drawn a blade. She heard a soft, almost delicate rustle of anticipation among the watching outlaws, most of whom were from Eridu. No mercy to be expected there.

She twisted the ring back outwards on her finger and thrust her hand high in the air.

"Harm him not!" she cried, as sternly as she could. "I am the Seer of Brennin. I carry the Baelrath on my hand and a magegift vellin stone about my wrist!"

She was also hellishly weak, with a brutal pain in her side, and no idea whatsoever of how she could hold them off.

Ceriog seemed to have an intuition about that, or else was so goaded by the presence of the Dwarf that he was beyond deterrence. He smiled thinly, through his tattoos and his dark beard.

"I like that," he said, gazing at the Baelrath. "It will be a pretty toy to carry for the hours we have left before the rains come west and we all turn black and die. First, though," he murmured, "I am going to kill the Dwarf very slowly, while you watch."

She wasn't going to be able to stop him. She was a Seer, a summoner. A storm crow on the winds of war. She could wake power, and gather it, and sometimes to do so she could flame red and fly between places, between worlds. She had two souls within her, and she carried the burden of the Baelrath on her finger and in her heart. But she could not stop a man with a blade, let alone fifty of them, driven mad by grief and fury and awareness of coming death.

Brock moaned. Kim felt his life's blood soaking through her clothing as she held his head in her lap. She glared up at Ceriog. Tried one last time.

"Listen to me—" she began.

"While you watch," he repeated, ignoring her.

"*I think not*," said Dalreidan. "Leave them alone, Ceriog."

The Eridun wheeled. A twisted light of pleasure shone in his dark face. "You will stop me, old man?"

"I shouldn't have to," Dalreidan said calmly, "You are no fool. You heard what she said: the Seer of Brennin—with whom else and how else will we stop what is coming?"

The other man seemed scarcely to have heard, "For a Dwarf?" he snarled. "You would intercede, now, for a Dwarf?" His voice skirled upwards with growing incredulity. "Dalreidan, this has been coming between us for a long time."

"It need not come. Only hear reason. I seek no leadership, Ceriog. Only to—"

"Only to tell the leader what he may or may not do!" said Ceriog viciously. There was a frozen half second of stillness, then Ceriog's arm whipped forward and his dagger flew—over the shoulder of Dalreidan, who had dived and rolled and was up again in a move the Plain had seen rehearsed from horseback for past a thousand years. No one had seen his own blade drawn, nor had they seen it thrown.

They did see it, all of them, buried in Ceriog's heart. And an instant later, after the shock had passed, they saw also that the dead Eridun was smiling as might one who has found release from overmastering pain.

Kim was suddenly aware of the silence. Of the sun overhead, the finger of the breeze, the weight of Brock's head in her lap—details of time and place made unnaturally vivid by the explosion of violence.

Which had come and was gone, leaving this stillness of fifty people in a high place. Dalreidan walked over to retrieve his blade. His steps were loud on the rocks. No one spoke. Dalreidan knelt and, pulling the dagger free, cleaned it of blood on the dead man's sleeve. Slowly he rose again and looked around the ring of faces.

"First blade was his," he said.

There was a stir, a loosening of strain, as if every man there had been holding his breath.

"It was," said an Eridun quietly, a man older even than Dalreidan himself, with his green tattoos sunken deep in the wrinkles of his face. "Revenge lies not in such a cause, neither by the laws of the Lion nor the code of the mountains."

Slowly, Dalreidan nodded his head. "I know nothing of the former and too much of the latter," he said, "but I think you will know that I had no desire for Ceriog's death, and none at all to take his place. I will be gone from this place within the hour."

There was another stir at that. "Does it matter?" young Faebur asked. "You need not go, not with the rain coming so soon."

And that, Kim realized, brought things back round to her. She had recovered from the shock—Ceriog's was not the first violent death she'd seen in Fionavar—and she was ready when all their eyes swung to where she sat.

"It may not come," she said, looking at Faebur. The Baelrath was still alive, flickering, but not intensely so.

"You are truly the Seer of Brennin?" he asked.

She nodded. "On a journey for the High King with this Dwarf, Brock of Banir Tal. Who fled the twin mountains to bring us tidings of the treachery of others."

"A Dwarf in the service of Ailell?" Dalreidan asked.

She shook her head. "Of his son. Ailell died more than a year ago, the day the Mountain flamed. Aileron rules in Paras Derval."

Dalreidan's mouth crooked wryly. "News," he said, "is woven slowly in the mountains."

"Aileron?" Faebur interjected. "We heard a tale of him in Larak. He was an exile, wasn't he?"

Kim heard the hope in his voice, the unspoken thought. He was very young; the beard concealed it only partially. "He was," she said gently. "Sometimes they go back home."

"If," the older Eridun interposed, "there is a home to go back to. Seer, can you stop the rain?"

She hesitated, looking beyond him, east to where the clouds were piled high. She said, "I cannot, not directly. But the High King has others in his service, and by the Sight I have I know that some of them are sailing even now to the place where the death rain is being shaped, just as the winter was. And if we stopped the winter, then—"

"—then we can end the rain!" a deep voice rumbled, low and fierce. She looked down. His eyes were open.

"Oh, Brock!" she cried.

"Aboard that ship," the Dwarf went on, speaking slowly but with clarity, "will be Loren Silvercloak and my lord, Matt Sören, true King of the Dwarves. If any people alive can save us, it is the two of them." He stopped, breathing heavily.

Kim held him close, overwhelmed for an instant with relief. "Careful," she said. "Try not to talk."

He looked up at her. "Don't worry so much," he said. "Your forehead will set in a crease." She gave a little gasp of laughter. "It takes a great deal," he went on, "to kill a Dwarf. I need a bandage to keep the blood out of my eyes, and a good deal of water to drink. Then, if I can have an hour's rest in the shade, we can go on."

He was still bleeding. Kim found that she was crying and clutching his burly chest far too hard. She loosened her grip and opened her mouth to say the obvious thing.

"Where? Go where?" It was Faebur. "What journey takes you into the Carnevon Range, Seer of Brennin?" He was trying to sound stern, but the effect was otherwise.

She looked at him a long moment, then, buying time, asked, "Faebur, why are *you* here; why are you exiled?"

He flushed but, after a pause, answered, in a low voice. "My father unhoused me, as all fathers in Eridu have the right to do."

"Why?" she asked. "Why did he do that?"

"Seer—" Dalreidan began.

"No," said Faebur, gesturing at him. "You told us your reason a moment ago, Dalreidan. It hardly matters anymore. I will answer the question. There is no blood on the Loomweft with my name, only a betrayal of my city, which in Eridu is said to be red on the Loom, and so the same as blood. It is simply told. Competing at the Ta'Sirona, the Summer Games, at Teg Veirene a year ago, I saw and loved a girl from high-walled Akkaïze, in the north, and she . . . saw and loved me, as well. In Larak again, in the fall of the year, my father named to me his choice for my wife, and I . . . refused him and told him why."

Kim heard sympathetic sounds from the other Eriduns and realized they hadn't known why Faebur was in the mountains; nor Dalreidan, either, for that matter, until, just now, he'd told of his murders. The code of the mountains, she guessed: you didn't ask.

But she had, and Faebur was answering. "When I did that, my father put on his white robe and went into the Lion's Square of Larak, and he called the four heralds to witness and cursed me west to Carnevon and Skeledarak, unhoused from Eridu. Which means"—and there was bitterness now—"that my father saved my life. That is, if your mage and Dwarf King can stop Rakoth's rain. You cannot, Seer, you have told us so. Let me ask you again, where are you going in the mountains?"

He had answered her, and with his heart's truth. There were reasons not to reply, but none seemed compelling, where they were, with the knowledge of that rain falling east of them.

"To Khath Meigol," she said, and watched the mountain outlaws freeze into silence. Many of them made reflexive signs against evil.

Even Dalreidan seemed shaken. She could see that he had paled. He crouched down on his haunches in front of her and spent a moment gathering and dispersing pebbles on the rocks. At length, he said, "You will not be a fool, to be what you are, so I will say none of what first comes to me to say, but I do have a question."

He waited for her to nod permission, then went on.

"How are you to be of service in this war, to your High King or anyone else, if you are bloodcursed by the spirits of the Paraiko?"

Again, Kim saw them making the sign against evil all around her. Even Brock had to suppress a gesture. She shook her head. "It is a fair question—" she began.

"Hear me," Dalreidan interrupted, unable to wait for her answer. "The bloodcurse is no idle tale, I know it is not. Once, years ago, I was hunting a wild kere, east and north of here, and so intent on my quarry that I lost track of how far I had gone. Then the twilight came, and I realized I was on the borders of Khath Meigol. Seer of Brennin, I am no longer young nor am I a tale-spinning elder by a winter fire stretching truth like bad wool: I was there, and so I can tell you, there is a curse on all who go into that place, of ill fortune and death and souls lost to time. It is true, Seer, it is not a tale. I felt it myself, on the borders of Khath Meigol."

She closed her eyes.

*Save us*, she heard. Ruana. She opened her eyes and said, "I know it is not a tale. There is a curse. I do not think it is what it is believed to be."

"You do not think. Seer, do you know?"

Did she know? The truth was, she didn't. The Giants went back beyond Ysanne's learning or Loren's or that of the Priestesses of Dana. Beyond, even, the lore of the Dwarves, or the lios alfar. All she had was her own knowledge: from the time in Gwen Ystrat when she'd made that terrible voyage into the designs of the Unraveller, shielded by the powers of her friends.

And then the shields had fallen, she had gone too far, had lost them and was lost, burning, until another one had come, far down in the Dark, and had sheltered her. The other mind had named himself as Ruana of the Paraiko, in Khath Meigol, and had begged for aid. They were alive, not ghosts, not dead yet. And this was what she knew, and all she knew.

On the plateau she shook her head, meeting the troubled gaze of the man who called himself Dalreidan. "No," she said. "I know nothing with certainty, save one thing I may not tell you, and one thing I may."

He waited. She said, "I have a debt to pay."

"In Khath Meigol?" There was a real anguish in his voice. She nodded. "A personal debt?" he asked, straining to deal wlth this.

She thought about that: about the image of the Cauldron she had found with Ruana's aid, the image that had told Loren where the winter was coming from. And now the death rain.

"Not just me," she said.

He drew a breath. A tension seemed to ease from within him. "Very well," he said. "You speak as do the shamans on the Plain. I believe you are what you tell me you are. If we are to die in a few days or hours, I would rather do so in the service of Light than otherwise. I know you have a guide, but I have been in the mountains for ten years now and have stood on the borders of the place you seek. Will you accept an outlaw as companion for this last stage of your journey?"

It was the diffidence that moved her, as much as anything else. He had just saved their lives, at risk of his own.

"Do you know what you are getting into? Do you—" She stopped, aware of the irony. None of them knew what they were getting into, but his offer was freely made, and handsome. For once she had not summoned nor was she compelled by the power she bore. She blinked back tears.

"I would be honoured," she said. "We both would." She heard Brock murmur his agreement.

A shadow fell on the stone in front of her. The three of them looked up.

Faebur was there, his face white. But his voice was manfully controlled. "In the Ta'Sirona, the Games at Teg Veirene, before my father exiled me, I came . . . I placed third of everyone in the archery. Could you, would you allow—" He stopped. The knuckles of the hand holding his bow were as white as his face.

There was a lump in her throat and she could not speak. She let Brock answer this time.

"Yes," said the Dwarf gently. "If you want to come we will be grateful for it. A bowman is never a wasted thread."

And so, in the end, there were four of them.

⋅⊹⇒⊂⊹⋅

Later that day, a long way west, Jennifer Lowell, who was Guinevere, came to the Anor Lisen as twilight fell.

With Brendel of the lios alfar as her only companion, she had sailed from Taerlindel the morning before in a small boat, not long after *Prydwen* herself had dipped out of sight in the wide, curving sea.

She had bidden farewell to Aileron the High King, to Sharra of Cathal, and Jaelle, the Priestess. She had set out with the lios alfar that she might come to the Tower built so long ago for Lisen. And so that, coming there, she might climb the spiralling stone stairs to the one high room with its broad seaward balcony and, as Lisen had done, walk upon that balcony, gazing out to sea, waiting for her heart to come home.

Handling the boat easily in the mild seas of that first afternoon, sailing past Aeven Island where the eagles were, Brendel marvelled and sorrowed, both, at the expressionless beauty of his companion's face. She was as fair as were the lios, with fingers as long and slender, and her awakened memories, he knew, went back almost as far. Were she not so tall, her eyes not held to green, she might have been one of his people.

Which led him to a strange reflection, out among the slap of waves and the billow of the single sail. He had not made or found this boat, which would ultimately be required when his time came, but it was a trim craft made with pride, and not unlike what he would have wanted. And so it was easy to imagine that they had just departed, not from Taerlindel but from Daniloth itself. To be sailing west and beyond west, towards that place made by the Weaver for the Children of Light alone.

Strange thoughts, he knew, born of sun and sea. He was not ready for that final journey. He had sworn an oath of vengeance that bound him to this woman in the boat, and to Fionavar and the war against Maugrim. He had not heard his song.

He did not know—no one did—the bitter truth. *Prydwen* had just set sail. She was two nights and a dawn yet from the sound of singing in the sea, from the place where the sea stars of Liranan did not shine and had not shone since the Bael Rangat.

From the Soulmonger.

As darkness came on that first night, Brendel guided their small craft towards the sandy shore west of Aeven and the Llychlyn Marshes and beached it in the gentle evening as the first stars appeared. With the provisions the High King had given them, they made camp and took an evening meal. Later, he laid out a sleeping roll for each of them, and they lay down close to each other between the water and the woods.

He did not make a fire, being too wise to burn even fallen driftwood from Pendaran. They didn't need one, in any case. It was a beautiful night in the summer shaped by Kevin Laine. They spoke of him for a time as the night deepened and the stars grew more bright. They spoke, softly, of the morning's departures, and where the next evening would see them land. Looking at the night sky, glorying in it, he spoke to her of the beauty and the peace of Daniloth, and lamented that the dazzle of the stars was so muted there since Lathen Mistweaver, in defence of his people, had made their home into the Shadowland.

After that they fell silent. As the moon rose, a shared memory came to both of them of the last time they had lain beside each other under the sky.

*Are you immortal?* she had asked, before drifting to sleep.

*No, Lady*, he had answered. And had watched her for a time before falling asleep himself, beside his brothers and sisters. To wake amid wolves, and svart alfar, and red mortality in the presence of Galadan, Wolflord of the andain.

Dark thoughts, and too heavy a silence for the quicksilver leader of the Kestrel Mark. He lifted his voice again, to sing her to sleep as one might a cherished child. Of seafaring he sang, a very old song, then one of his own, about aum trees in leaf and sylvain flowering in spring. And then, as her breathing began to slow, his voice rode her to rest with the words of what was always the last song of a night: Ra-Termaine's Lament, for all those who had been lost.

When he finished, she was asleep. He remained awake, though, listening to the tide going out. Never again would he fall asleep while she was in his care, not ever again. He sat up all night watching, watching over her.

Others watched as well, from the dark edgings of Pendaran: eyes not welcoming, but not yet malevolent, for the two on the sands had not entered the forest nor burned wood of the Wood. They were very near, though, and so were closely observed, for Pendaran guarded itself and nurtured its long hate.

They were overheard as well, however low their voices, for the listening ears were not human and could discern speech at the very edge of unspoken thought. So their names became known. And then a drumming sound ran through that part of the Wood, for the two of them had named their destination, and that place had been built for the one who had been most loved and then most bitterly lost: Lisen, who would never have died had she not loved a mortal and been drawn into war outside the shelter of the Wood.

An urgent message went forth in the wordless rustle of leaves, the shadowed flicker of forms half seen, in a vibration, quick as a running pulse, of the forest floor.

And the message came, in very little time as such things are measured, to the ears of the only one of all the ancient powers of the Wood who wholly grasped what was at work, for he had moved through many of the Weaver's worlds and had played a part in this story when it first was spun.

He took thought, deliberate and unhurried—though there was a surge in his blood at the tidings, and a waking of old desire and sent word back through the forest, by leaf and quick brown messenger and by the pulse that threaded through the roots of the trees.

*Be easy*, he sent, calming the agitation of the Wood. *Lisen herself would have made this one welcome in the Tower, though with sorrow. She has earned her place by the parapet. The other is of the lios alfar and they built the Anor, forget it not.*

*We forget nothing.*

*Nothing,* rustled the leaves coldly.

*Nothing,* throbbed the ancient roots, twisted by long hate. *She is dead. She need never have died.*

In the end, though, he put his will upon them. He had not the power to compel them all, but he could persuade, sometimes, and this night, and for this one, he did.

Then he went out from the doors of his house and he travelled at speed by ways he knew and so came to the Anor just as the moon rose. And he set about making ready a place that had stood empty for all the years since Lisen had seen a ghost ship passing and had leaped from her high balcony into the darkness of the sea.

There was less to be done than might have been supposed, for that Tower had been raised with love and very great art, and magic had been bound into its stones that they should not fall.

He had never been there before; it was a place too sharp with pain. He hesitated on the threshold for a moment, remembering many things. Then the door swung open to his touch. By moonlight he looked at the rooms on the lower level, made for those who had stood guard. He left them as they were and passed upwards.

With the sound of the sea always in his ears, he climbed the unworn stone stairs, following their spiral up the single turret of the Tower, and so he came to the room that had been Lisen's. The furnishings were sparse but exquisite and strange, crafted in Daniloth. The room was wide and bright, for along the western curve of it there was no wall; instead, made with the artifice of Ginserat of Brennin, a window of glass stretched from floor to ceiling, showing the moonlit sea.

There was salt staining the outside of the glass. He walked forward and slid the window open. The two halves rolled easily apart along their tracks into recesses hidden in the curving wall. He stepped out on the balcony. The sea sound was loud; waves crashed at the foot of the Tower.

He remained there a long time, claimed by griefs too numerous to be isolated or addressed. He looked to his left and saw the river. It had run red past the Anor for a year from the day she had died, and it did so yet, every year, when the day came around again. It had had a name once, that river. Not anymore.

He shook his head and began to busy himself. He pulled the windows closed and, having more than power enough to deal with this, made them clean again. He slid them open a second time and left them so, that the night air might come into a room that had been closed a thousand years. He found candles in a drawer and then torches at the bottom of the stairs—wood of the Wood vouchsafed for burning in this place.

He lit the torches in the brackets set into the wall along the stairwell, and then placed the candles about the one high room, and lit them all.

By their light he saw that there was a layer of dust on the floor, though not, curiously, on the bed. And then he saw something else. Something that chilled even his wise, knowing blood.

There were footsteps in the dust, not his own, and they led over to that bed. And on the coverlet—woven, he knew, by masters of the art in Seresh—lay a mass of flowers: roses, sylvain, corandiel. But it was not the flowers that held his gaze.

The candles flickered in the salt breeze off the sea, but they were steady enough for him to clearly see his own small footprints in the dust and, beside them, those of the man who had walked into the room to lay those flowers on the coverlet.

*And those of the giant wolf that had walked away.*

His heart beating rapidly, fear shadowed by pity within him, he walked over to that bright profusion of flowers. There was no scent, he realized. He reached out a hand. As soon as he touched them they crumbled to dust on the coverlet. Very gently, he brushed the dust away.

He could have made the floor shine with a trace assertion of his power. He did not; he never did in his own rooms under the forest floor. Going down the stairs one more time, he found a sturdy broom in one of the lower chambers and then, with strong domestic motions, proof of long habit, Flidais swept out Lisen's chamber by candlelight and moonlight, to make it ready for Guinevere.

In time, for his was a spirit of play and laughter even in darkest times, he began to sing. It was a song of his own weaving, shaped of ancient riddles and the answers he had learned for them.

And he sang because he was filled with hope that night—hope of the one who was coming, that she might have the answer to his heart's desire.

He was a strong presence and a bright one, and there were torches and candles burning all through the Anor. The spirit of Gereint could not fail to sense him, singing, sweeping the dust with wide motions of the broom, as the shaman's soul went past overhead, leaving the known truths of the land to go spinning and tumbling out over the never-seen sea, in search of a single ship among all the waves.

As the sun went down on their left the following evening, Brendel guided the boat across the bay and past the river mouth towards the small dock at the foot of the Tower.

They had seen the upper lights come on as they swung into the bay. Now, drawing near, the lios alfar saw a portly, white-bearded, balding figure, smaller even than a Dwarf, waiting on the dock for them, and being of the lios alfar and more than six hundred years old himself he had an idea who this might be.

Gentling the small craft up to the dock, he threw a rope as they approached. The small figure caught it neatly and tied the end to a peg set in the stone dock. They rested there in silence a moment, bobbing with the waves. Jennifer, Brendel saw, was looking up at the Tower. Following her gaze, he saw the reflection of the sunset sparkle off the curved glass beyond the parapet.

"Be welcome," said the figure on the dock in a voice unexpectedly deep. "Bright be the thread of your days."

"And of yours, forest one," said the lios alfar. "I am Brendel of the Kestrel Mark. The woman with me—"

"I know who she is," the other said. And bowed very low.

"By what name shall we call you?" Brendel asked.

The other straightened. "I am pied for protection, dappled for deception," he said reflexively. Then, "Flidais will do. It has, for this long while."

Jennifer turned at that and fixed him with a curious scrutiny. "You're the one Dave met in the woods," she said.

He nodded. "The tall one, with the axe? Yes, I did meet him. Green Ceinwen gave him a horn, after."

"I know," she said. "Owein's Horn."

To the east just then, under a darkening sky, a battle was raging along the bloodied banks of the Adein, a battle that would end with the blowing of that horn.

On the dock, Flidais looked up at the tall woman with the green eyes that he alone in Fionavar had cause to remember from long ago. "Is that the only knowledge you have of me?" he asked softly. "As having saved your friend?"

In the boat Brendel kept silent. He watched the woman reach for a memory. She shook her head. "Should I know you?" she asked.

Flidais smiled. "Perhaps not in this form." His voice went even deeper, and suddenly he chanted, "I have been in many shapes. I have been the blade of a sword, a star, a lantern light, a harp and a harper, both." He paused, saw something spark in her eyes, ended diffidently, "I have fought, though small, in battle before the Ruler of Britain."

"*I remember!*" she said, laughing now. "Wise child, spoiled child. You liked riddles, didn't you? I remember you, Taliesin." She stood up. Brendel leaped to the dock and helped her alight.

"I have been in many shapes," Flidais said again, "but I was his harper once."

She nodded, very tall on the stone dock, looking down at him, memory playing in her eyes and about her mouth. Then there came a change. Both men saw it and were suddenly still.

"You sailed with him, didn't you?" said Guinevere. "You sailed in the first *Prydwen*."

Flidais's smile faded. "I did, Lady," he said. "I went with the Warrior to Caer Sidi, which is Cader Sedat here. I wrote of it, of that voyage. You will remember." He drew breath and recited:

> Thrice the fullness of Prydwen we went with Arthur,
> Except seven, none returned from—

He stopped abruptly, at her gesture. They stood so a moment. The sun sank into the sea. With the dark, a finger of wind arose. Brendel, watching, only half understanding, felt a nameless sorrow come over him as the light faded.

In the shadows, Jennifer's face seemed to grow colder, more austere. She said, "You were there. So you knew the way. Did you sail with Amairgen?"

Flidais flinched, as from an actual blow. He drew a shaken breath, and he, who was half a god and could induce the powers of Pendaran to accede to his will, said in a voice of humble supplication, "I have never been a coward, Lady, in any guise. I sailed to that accursed place once, in another form. But this is my truest shape, and this Wood my true home in this first world of all. How should a forest warden go to sea, Lady? What good would I have done? I told him, I told Amairgen what I knew—that he would have to sail north into a north wind—and he said he would know where to do so, and when. I did that, Lady, and the Weaver knows that the andain seldom do so much for men."

He fell silent. Her regard was unresponsive, remote. Then suddenly she said:

> *I will not allow praise to the men with trailing shields,*
> *They know not on what day the chief arose,*
> *When we went with Arthur of mournful memory—*

"*I wrote that!*" Flidais protested. "My lady Guinevere, I wrote that."

It was quite dark now on the path, but with the keen sight of the lios alfar Brendel saw the coldness leave her face. Voice gentle now, she said, "I know, Taliesin. Flidais. I know you did, and I know you were there with him. Forgive me. None of this makes for easy memory."

On the words she brushed past both of them and went up the pathway towards the Tower. Over the darkened sea the evening star now shone, the one named for Lauriel the White.

He had done it completely wrong, Flidais realized, watching her walk away. He had meant to turn the conversation to the name, the summoning name of the Warrior, the one riddle left in all the worlds for which he had no answer. He was clever enough, and to spare, to have led the talk anywhere he wanted, and the Weaver knew how deep his desire for that answer was.

The thing he had forgotten, though, was what happened in the presence of Guinevere. Even though the andain cared little for the troubles of mortal men, how could one be sly in the face of so ancient a sorrow?

The lios alfar and the andain, each with his own thoughts, gathered the gear from the boat and followed her into the Anor and up the winding stair.

⤙⟺◯⟺⤚

It was strange, thought Jaelle, to feel so uneasy in the place of her own power.

She was in her rooms in the Temple in Paras Derval, surrounded by the priestesses of the sanctuary and by the brown-robed acolytes. She could mind-link at a moment's need or desire with the Mormae in Gwen Ystrat. She even had a guest-friend in the Temple: Sharra of Cathal, escorted to the doors, but not beyond, by the amusing Tegid of Rhoden—who, it seemed, was taking his duties as Intercedent for Diarmuid with unwonted seriousness.

It was a time for seriousness, though, and for disquiet. None of the familiar things, not even the bells ringing to summon the grey ones to sunset invocation, were enough to ease the thoughts of the High Priestess.

Nothing was as clear as it once had been. She was here and she belonged here, would probably have scorned any request, let alone command, to be anywhere else. Hers was the duty and the power, both, to shape the spun webs of Dana's will, and to do so in this place.

Even so, nothing felt the same.

For one thing, hers also, as of yesterday, was half the governing of Brennin, since the High King had gone north.

The summonglass of Daniloth had blazed yestereve—two nights ago, in truth, but they had only learned of it on their return from Taerlindel. She had seen, with Aileron, the imperative coiling of light in the sceptre the lios alfar had given to Ailell.

The King had paused only long enough to snatch a meal as he gave terse commands. In the garrisons, the captains of the guard were mobilizing every man. It took very little time; Aileron had been preparing for this moment since the day she had crowned him.

He had done everything properly. Had appointed her with Gorlaes the Chancellor to govern the realm while he was away at war. He had even paused beside her in front of the palace gates and quickly, but not without dignity, besought her to guard their people as best her powers allowed.

Then he had been up on his black charger and galloping away with an army, first to North Keep to collect the garrison there, and then north, at night, over the Plain towards Daniloth and Dana alone knew what.

Leaving her in this most familiar of places, where nothing seemed familiar at all.

She had hated him once, she remembered. Hated them all: Aileron, and his father, and Diarmuid, his brother, the one she called the "princeling" in response to his mocking, corrosive tongue.

Faintly to her ears came the chanting from the domed chamber. It was not the usual twilight invocation. For eight more nights, until Midsummer's moon was gone, the evening chants would begin and end with the Lament for Liadon.

And so much power lay in this, so magnificent a triumph for the Goddess, and thereby for herself, as first High Priestess in uncounted, unknowable years to have heard the voice from Dun Maura cry out on Maidaladan, in mourning for the sacrifice come freely.

And with that, her thoughts circled back to the one who had become Liadon: Kevin Laine, brought from another world by Silvercloak to a destiny both dark and dazzlingly bright, one that not even the Seer could have foreknown.

For all Jaelle's knowledge, all her immersion in the nature of the Goddess, Kevin's had been an act so overwhelming, so consummately gallant, it had irrevocably blurred the clarity with which once she'd viewed the world. He was a man, and yet he had done this thing. It was, since Maidaladan, so much harder to summon the old anger and bitterness, the hate. Or, more truly, so much harder to summon them for anything and anyone but Rakoth.

The winter was over. The summonglass had blazed. There was war, somewhere north, in the dark.

And there was a ship sailing west.

That thought carried her back to a strand of beach north of Taerlindel, where she had watched the other stranger, Pwyll, summon and speak to the sea god by the water's edge in an inhuman light. Nothing was easy for any of them, Dana and the Weaver knew, but Pwll's seemed such a harsh, demanding power, taking so much out of him and not giving, so far as she could see, a great deal back.

Him, too, she remembered hating, with a cold, unforgiving fury, when she had taken him from the Summer Tree to this very room, this bed, knowing that the Goddess had spoken to him, not knowing what she had said. She had struck him, she remembered, drawing the blood all men should give, but hardly in the manner prescribed.

*"Rahod hedai Liadon,"* the priestesses sang under the dome, ending the lament on the last long, keening note. And after a moment she heard Shiel's clear voice begin the antiphonal verses of the evening invocation. There was some peace there, Jaelle thought, some comfort to be found in the rituals, even now, even in time of darkness.

Her chamber door burst open. Leila stood in the doorway.

"What are you doing?" Jaelle exclaimed. "Leila, you should be in the dome with—"

She stopped. The girl's eyes were wide, staring, focused on nothingness. Leila spoke, in a voice tranced and uninflected. "They have blown the horn," she said. "In the battle. He is in the sky now, above the river. Finn. And the kings. I see Owein in the sky. He is drawing a sword. Finn is drawing a sword. They are—they are—" Her face was chalk white, her fingers splayed at her sides. She made a thin sound.

"They are killing," she said. "They are killing the svarts and the urgach. Finn is covered in blood. So much blood. And now Owein is—he is—"

Jaelle saw the girl's eyes flare even wider then, and go wild with terror, and her heart lurched.

Leila screamed. *"Finn, no! Stop him! They are killing us!"*

She screamed again, wordlessly, and stumbling forward, falling, buried her head in Jaelle's lap, her arms clutching the Priestess, her body racked convulsively.

The chanting stopped under the dome. There were footsteps running along the corridors. Jaelle held the girl as tightly as she could; Leila was thrashing so hard, the High Priestess was genuinely afraid she would hurt herself.

"What is it? What has happened?"

She looked up and saw Sharra of Cathal in the doorway.

"The battle," she gasped, fighting to hold Leila, her own body rocking with the force of the girl's weeping. "The Hunt. Owein. She is tuned to—"

And then they heard the voice.

*"Sky King, sheath your sword! I put my will upon you!"*

It seemed to come from nowhere and from everywhere in the room, clear, cold, utterly imperative.

Leila's violent movements stopped. She lay still in Jaelle's arms. They were all still: the three in the room and those gathered in the corridor. They waited. Jaelle found it difficult to breathe. Her hands were blindly, reflexively stroking Leila's hair. The girl's robe was soaked through with perspiration.

"What is it?" whispered Sharra of Cathal. It sounded loud in the silence. "Who said that?"

Jaelle felt Leila draw a shuddering breath. The girl—fifteen, Jaelle thought, only that—lifted her head again. Her face was splotchy, her hair tangled hopelessly. She said, "It was Ceinwen. It was Ceinwen, High Priestess." There was wonder in her voice. A child's wonder.

"Herself? Directly?" Sharra again. Jaelle looked at the Princess, who despite her own youth had been trained in power and so evidently knew the constraints laid by the Weaver on the gods.

Leila turned to Sharra. Her eyes were normal again, and very young. She nodded. "It was her own voice."

Jaelle shook her head. There would be a price demanded for that, she knew, among the jealous pantheon of goddesses and gods. That, of course, was far beyond her. Something else, though, was not.

She said, "Leila, you are in danger from this. The Hunt is too wild, it is the wildest power of all. You must try to break this link with Finn, child. There is a death in it."

She had powers of her own, knew when her voice was more than merely hers. She was High Priestess and in the Temple of Dana.

Leila looked up at her, kneeling still on the floor. Automatically, Jaelle reached out to push a snarl of hair back from the girl's white face.

"I can't," Leila said quietly. Only Sharra, nearest to them, heard. "I can't break it. But it doesn't matter anymore. They will never call them again, they dare not—there will be no way to bind them if they do. Ceinwen will not intercede twice. He is gone, High Priestess, out among the stars, on the Longest Road."

Jaelle looked at her for a long time. Sharra came up and laid a hand on Leila's shoulder. The tangle of hair fell down again, and once more the Priestess pushed it back.

Someone had returned to the dome. The bells were ringing.

Jaelle stood up. "Let us go," she said. "The invocations are not finished. We will all do them. Come."

She led them along the curving corridors to the place of the axe. All through the evening chants, though, she was hearing a different voice in her mind.

*"There is death in it."* It was her own voice, and more than her own. Hers and the Goddess's.

Which meant, always, that what she said was true.

# CHAPTER 2

The next morning at the greyest hour, just before dawn, *Prydwen* met the Soulmonger far out at sea. At the same time, on the Plain, Dave Martyniuk woke alone on the mound of the dead near Celidon.

He was not, never had been, a subtle man, but one did not need deep reserves of subtlety to apprehend the significance of Ceinwen's presence beneath him and above him on the green grass tinted silver in the night just past. There had been awe at first, and a stunned humility, but only at first, and not for very long. In the blind, instinctive assertion of his own lovemaking Dave had sought and found an affirmation of life, of the living, after the terrible carnage by the river.

He remembered, vividly, a moonlit pool in Faelinn Grove a year ago. How the stag slain by Green Ceinwen's arrow had split itself in two, and had risen, and bowed its head to the Huntress, and walked away from its own death.

Now he had another memory. He sensed that the goddess had shared—had engendered, even—his own compelling desire last night to reaffirm the absolute presence of the living in a world so beleaguered by the Dark. And this, he suspected, was the reason for the gift she had given him. The third gift, in fact: his life, in Faelinn that first time, then Owein's Horn, and now this offering of herself to take away the pain.

He was not wrong in any of this, but there was a great deal more to what Ceinwen had done, though not even the most subtle of mortal minds could have apprehended it. Which was as it should be, as, indeed, it had always been. Macha knew, however, and Red Nemain, and Dana, the Mother, most surely of all. The gods might guess, and some of the andain, but the goddesses would know.

The sun rose. Dave stood up and looked around him under a brightening sky. No clouds. It was a beautiful morning. About a mile north of him the Adein sparkled, and there were men and horses stirring along its bank. East, somewhat farther off, he could make out the standing stones that surrounded and defined Celidon, the mid-Plain, home of the first tribe of the Dalrei and gathering place of all the tribes. There were signs of motion, of life, there as well.

Who, though, and how many?

*Not all need die*, Ceinwen had said to him a year ago, and again last night. Not all, perhaps, but the battle had been brutal, and very bad, and a great many *had* died.

He had been changed by the events of the evening and night before, but in most ways Dave was exactly what he had always been, and so there was a sick knot of fear in his stomach as he strode off the mound and began walking swiftly towards the activity by the riverbank.

Who? And how many? There had been such chaos, such muddy, blood-bespattered confusion: the wolves, the lios arriving, Avaia's brood in the darkening sky, and then, after he'd blown the horn, something else in the sky, something wild. Owein and the kings. And the child. Carrying death, manifesting it. He quickened his pace almost to a run. *Who?*

Then he had part of an answer, and he stopped abruptly, a little weak with relief. From the cluster of men by the Adein two horses, one dark grey, the other brown, almost golden, had suddenly wheeled free, racing towards him, and he recognized them both.

Their riders, too. The horses thundered up to him, the two riders leaping off, almost before stopping, with the unconscious, inbred ease of the Dalrei. And Dave stood facing the men who'd become his brothers on a night in Pendaran Wood.

There was joy, and relief, and all three showed it in their own ways, but they did not embrace.

"Ivor?" Dave asked. Only the name.

"He is all right," Levon said quietly. "Some wounds, none serious." Levon himself, Dave saw, had a short deep scar on his temple, running up into the line of his yellow hair.

"We found your axe," Levon explained. "By the river bank. But no one had seen you after . . . after you blew the horn, Davor."

"And this morning," Torc continued, "all the dead were gone, and we could not find you. . . ." He left the thought unfinished.

Dave drew a breath and let it out slowly. "Ceinwen?" he said. "Did you hear her voice?"

The two Dalrei nodded, without speaking.

"She stopped the Hunt," Dave said, "and then she . . . took me away. When I awoke she was with me, and she said that she had . . . gathered the dead." He said nothing more. The rest was his own, not for the telling.

He saw Levon, quick as ever, glance past him at the mound, and then Torc did the same. There was a long silence. Dave could feel the freshness of the morning breeze, could see it moving the tall grass of the Plain. Then, with a twist of his heart he saw that Torc, always so self-contained, was weeping soundlessly as he gazed at the mound of the dead.

"So many," Torc murmured. "They killed so many of us, of the lios. . . ."

"Mabon of Rhoden took a bad shoulder wound," Levon said. "One of the swans came down on him."

Mabon, Dave remembered, had saved his life only two days before, when Avaia

499

herself had descended in a blur of death from a clear sky. He swallowed and said, with difficulty, "Torc, I saw Barth and Navon, both of them. They were—"

Torc nodded stiffly. "I know. I saw it, too. Both of them."

The babies in the wood, Dave was thinking. Barth and Navon, barely fourteen when they died, had been the ones that he and Torc had guarded in Faelinn Grove on Dave's first night in Fionavar. Guarded and saved from an urgach, only to have them . . .

"It was the urgach in white," Dave said, bitterness like gall in his mouth. "The really big one. He killed them both. With the same stroke."

"Uathach." Levon almost spat the name. "I heard the others calling him. I tried to go after him, but I couldn't get—"

"No! Not that one, Levon," Torc interrupted, his voice fiercely intense. "Not alone. We will defeat them because we must, but promise me now that you will not go after him alone, ever. He is more than an urgach."

Levon was silent.

"*Promise me!*" Torc repeated, turning to stand squarely before the Aven's son, disregarded tears still bright in his eyes. "He is too big, Levon, and too quick, and something more than both of those. Promise me!"

Another moment passed before Levon spoke. "Only to the two of you would I say this. Understand that. But you have my word." His yellow hair was very bright in the sun. He tossed it back with a stiff twist of his head and spun sharply to return to the horses. Over his shoulder, not breaking stride, he snapped, "Come. There is a Council of the tribes in Celidon this morning." Without waiting for them, he mounted and rode.

Dave and Torc exchanged a glance, then mounted up themselves, double, on the grey, and set out after him. Halfway to the standing stones they caught up, because Levon had stopped and was waiting. They halted beside him.

"Forgive me," he said. "I am a fool and a fool and a fool."

"At least two of those," Torc agreed gravely.

Dave laughed. After a moment, so did Levon. Ivor's son held out his hand. Torc clasped it. They looked at Dave. Wordlessly, he placed his own right hand over both of theirs.

They rode the rest of the way together.

"Weaver be praised, and the bright threads of the Loom!" venerable Dhira, Chieftain of the first tribe, said for the third time.

He was beginning to get on Dave's nerves.

They were in a gathering hall at Celidon. Not the largest hall, for it was not a very large assembly: the Aven, looking alert and controlled despite a bandaged arm and a cut, much like Levon's, above one eye; the Chieftains of the other eight tribes with their advisers; Mabon, Duke of Rhoden, lying on a pallet, obviously in pain, as obviously determined to be present; and Ra-Tenniel, the Lord of the lios alfar, to whom all eyes continually returned, in wonder and awe.

There were people absent, Dave knew, people sorely missed. Two of the Chieftains,

Damach of the second tribe and Berlan of the fifth, were new to their titles, the son and brother, respectively, of men who had died by the river.

Ivor had, to Dave's surprise, left control of the gathering to Dhira. Torc whispered a terse explanation: the first tribe was the only one that never travelled the Plain; Celidon was their permanent home. They remained here at the mid-Plain, receiving and relaying messages through the auberei of all the tribes, preserving the records of the Dalrei, providing the tribes with their shamans, and always taking command of the gatherings here at Celidon. Always—even in the presence of an Aven. So it had been in Revor's time, and so it was now.

Checks and balances, Dave thought. It made some sense in the abstract but did little to reconcile him now, in the aftermath of battle, to Dhira's quavering voice and laggard pace.

He had made a rambling, discursive speech, half mournful, half in praise, before finally calling upon Ivor. Levon's father had then risen to tell, for the benefit of Ra-Tenniel, the story of their wild, improbable ride—a night and a day across half the length of the Plain—to just beat the forces of Maugrim to the river.

He had then deferred, with grace, to the Lord of Daniloth, who in turn told of how he had seen the army of the Dark crossing Andarien; how he had set his summonglass alight on Atronel, that it might flare a warning in Paras Derval, had sent two messengers on the magnificent raithen to alert the Dalrei, and, finally and most gallantly, had led his own army out of the protected Shadowland to battle by the Adein.

His voice carried music, but the notes were shaped by sorrow as he spoke. A very great many from Daniloth had died, and from the Plain and Brennin as well, for Mabon's five hundred men from Rhoden had fought their way to the thick of the battle.

A battle that had seemed lost, utterly, for all the courage on profligate display, until a horn had sounded. And so Dave, who was Davor here on the Plain, rose at Ivor's request and told his own story: of hearing a voice in his mind reminding him of what he carried (and in his memory it *still* sounded like Kevin Laine, chiding him for being so slow), and then blowing Owein's Horn with all the strength he had left in that hour.

They all knew what had happened. Had seen the shadowy figures in the sky, Owein and the kings, and the child on the palest horse. Had seen them descend from a great height, killing the black swans of Avaia's brood, the svart alfar, the urgach, the wolves of Galadan . . . and then, without pause or discrimination, without mercy or respite, turning on the lios alfar and the men of the Plain and Brennin.

Until a goddess had come, to cry, "Sky King, sheath your sword!" And after that only Davor, who had blown the horn, knew anything more until dawn. He told of waking on the mound, and learning what it was, and hearing Ceinwen warn him that she could not intercede another time if he blew Owein's Horn again.

That was all he told them. He sat down. He had, he realized, just made a speech. Once, he would have been paralyzed by the very thought. Not now, not here. There was too much at stake.

"Weaver be praised, and the bright threads of the Loom!" Dhira intoned once more, raising both his wrinkled hands before his face. "I proclaim now, before all of this company that it shall henceforth be the duty and the honour of the first tribe to tend that mound of the dead with fullest rites, that it remain forever green, and that—"

Dave had had more than enough of this. "Don't you think," he interrupted, "that if Ceinwen can raise the mound and gather the dead, she can keep it green if she wants?"

He winced, as Torc landed a punishing kick on his shin. There was a small, awkward silence. Dhira fixed Dave with a suddenly acute glance.

"I know not how these matters are dealt with in the world from which you come, Davor, and I would not presume to comment." Dhira paused, to let the point register. "In the same way," he went on, "it ill behooves you to advise us about one of our own goddesses."

Dave could feel himself flushing, and an angry retort rose to his lips. He bit it back, with an effort of will, and was rewarded by hearing the Aven's voice. "He has seen her, Dhira; he has spoken to Ceinwen twice, and received a gift of her. You have not, nor have I. He is entitled, and more than that, to speak."

Dhira considered it, then nodded. "It is so," he admitted quietly, to Dave's surprise. "I will unsay what last I said, Davor. But know this: if I speak of tending the mound, it is as a gesture of homage and thanksgiving. Not to cause the goddess to do anything, but to acknowledge what she has done. Is that inappropriate?"

Which left Dave feeling sorry in the extreme for having opened his mouth. "Forgive me, Chieftain," he managed to say. "Of course it is appropriate. I am anxious and impatient, and—"

"And with cause!" Mabon of Rhoden growled, raising himself on his cot. "We have decisions to make and had best get to them!"

Silvery laughter ran through the chamber. "I had heard," Ra-Tenniel said, amused, "of the urgency of mankind, but now I hear it for myself." The tenor of his voice shaded downwards; they all listened, entranced by his very presence among them. "All men are impatient. It is woven into the way time runs for you, into the shortness of your threads on the Loom. In Daniloth we say it is a curse and a blessing, both."

"Are there not times when urgency is demanded?" Mabon asked levelly.

"Surely," Dhira cut in, as Ra-Tenniel paused. "Surely, there are. But this must, before all else, be a time of mourning for the dead, or else their loss goes unremembered, ungrieved, and—"

"No," said Ivor.

One word only, but everyone present heard the long-suppressed note of command. The Aven rose to his feet.

"No, Dhira," he repeated softly. He had no need to raise his voice; the focus of the room was his. "Mabon is right, and Davor, and I do not think our friend from Daniloth will disagree. Not one man who died last night, not one of the brothers and sisters of the lios who have lost their song, will lie ungrieved beneath Ceinwen's mound. The danger," he said, and his voice grew stern, implacable, "is that they may yet have died to no purpose. This must not while we live, while we can ride and carry weapons, be suffered to come to pass. Dhira, we are at war and the Dark is all about us. There may be time for mourning, but only if we fight through to Light."

There was nothing even slightly prepossessing about Ivor, Dave was thinking. Not beside Ra-Tenniel's incandescence or Dhira's slow dignity, or even Levon's unconscious animal grace. There were far more imposing men in the room, with voices more compelling, eyes more commanding, but in Ivor dan Banor there was a fire, and it was matched with a will and a love of his people that, together, were more than any and all of these other things. Dave looked at the Aven and knew that he would follow this man wherever Ivor asked him to go.

Dhira had bowed his head, as if under the conjoined weight of the words and his long years.

"It is so, Aven," he said, and Dave was suddenly moved by the weariness in his voice. "Weaver grant we see our way through to that Light." He lifted his head and looked at Ivor. "Father of the Plain," he said, "this is no time for me to cling to pride of place. Will you allow me to yield to you, and to your warriors, and sit down?"

Ivor's mouth tightened; Dave knew that he was fighting the quick tears for which he took so much abuse from his family. "Dhira," the Aven said, "pride of place is always, always yours. You cannot relinquish it, to me or anyone else. But Dhira, you are Chieftain of the first tribe of the Children of Peace—the tribe of the shamans, the loremasters. My friend, how should such a one be asked to guide a Council of War?"

Incongruous sunshine streamed through the open windows. The Aven's pained question hung in the room, clear as the motes of dust where the slanting sunlight fell.

"It is so," said Dhira a second time. He stumbled towards an empty chair near Mabon's pallet. Obscurely moved, Dave began rising to offer his arm as aid, but then he saw that Ra-Tenniel, with a floating grace, was already at Dhira's side, guiding the aged chieftain to his seat.

When the Lord of the lios alfar straightened up, though, his gaze went out the western window of the room. He stood very still a moment, concentrating, then said, "Listen. They are coming!"

Dave felt a quick stab of fear, but the tone had not been one of warning, and a moment later he, too, heard sounds from the western edge of Celidon—and the sounds were cries of welcome.

Ra-Tenniel turned, smiling a little, to Ivor. "I doubt the raithen of Daniloth could ever come among your people without causing a stir."

Ivor's eyes were very bright. "I know they could not," he said. "Levon, will you have their riders brought here?"

They were on their way, in any case. Moments later Levon returned, and with him were two more—a man and a woman—of the lios alfar. The air in the room seemed brighter for their presence as they bowed to their Lord.

For all that, they were hardly noticed.

It was the third of the new arrivals who claimed the absolute attention of every person in the room, even in the company of the lios alfar. Dave was suddenly on his feet. They all were.

"Brightly woven, Aven," said Aileron dan Ailell.

His brown clothing was stained and dusty, his hair tousled, and his dark eyes lay sunken in deep pools of weariness. He held himself very straight, though, and his voice was level and clear. "They are making songs outside, even now. About the Ride of Ivor, who raced the army of the Dark to Celidon, and beat them there, and drove them back."

Ivor said, "We had aid, High King. The lios alfar came out from Daniloth. And then Owein came to the horn that Davor carries, and at the last Green Ceinwen was with us, or we would all have died."

"So I have just been told," said Aileron. He fixed Dave with a brief, keen glance, then turned to Ra-Tenniel. "Bright the hour of our meeting, my lord. If Loren Silvercloak, who taught me as a child, said true, no Lord of Daniloth has ventured so far from the Shadowland since Ra-Lathen wove the mist a thousand years ago."

Ra-Tenniel's expression was grave, his eyes a neutral grey. "He said true," he replied calmly.

There was a little silence; then Aileron's dark bearded face was lit by the brightness of his smile. "Welcome back, then, Lord of the lios alfar!"

Ra-Tenniel returned the smile, but not with his eyes, Dave saw. "We were welcomed back last night," he murmured. "By svart alfar and urgach, by wolves and Avaia's brood."

"I know it," said Aileron, swiftly changing mood. "And there is more of that welcome to come. I think we all know it."

Ra-Tenniel nodded without speaking.

"I came as soon as I saw the summonglass," Aileron went on after a pause. "There is an army behind me. They will be here tomorrow evening. I was in Taerlindel the night the message was sent to us."

"We know," Ivor said. "Levon explained. Has *Prydwen* sailed?"

Aileron nodded. "She has. For Cader Sedat. With my brother, and the Warrior, and Loren and Matt, and Pwyll also."

"And Na-Brendel, surely?" Ra-Tenniel asked quickly. "Or is he following with your army?"

"No," said Aileron, as the two lios alfar behind him stirred. "Something else has happened." He turned then, surprisingly, to Dave, and told of what Jennifer had said when *Prydwen* was out of sight, and what Brendel had said and done, and where the two of them had gone.

In the silence that followed they could hear the sounds of the camp through the windows; there were still cries of wonder and admiration from the Dalrei gathered about the raithen. The sounds seemed to be coming from far away. Dave's thoughts were with Jennifer, and with what—and who—she seemed to have become.

Ra-Tenniel's voice slid into the silence of the room. His eyes were violet now as he said, "It is well. Or as well as could be in such a time as this. Brendel's weaving was twined with hers since the night Galadan took her from him. We may have greater need of him in the Anor than anywhere else."

Only half understanding, Dave saw the diamond-bright lios alfar woman let slip a sigh of relief.

"Niavin of Seresh and Teyrnon the mage are bringing up the army," Aileron said, crisply coming back to solid facts. "I brought almost all of my forces, including the contingent from Cathal. Shalhassan is levying more men in his country even now. I have left word that those should remain in Brennin as a rear guard. I came here alone, riding through the night with Galen and Lydan, because I had to let the army have some rest; they had been riding for more than twenty-four hours."

"And you, High King?" Ivor asked. "Have you rested?"

Aileron shrugged. "There may be time after this meeting," he said, almost indifferently. "It doesn't matter." Dave, looking at him, thought otherwise, but he was impressed all the same.

"Whom did you ride behind?" Ra-Tenniel asked suddenly, an unexpected slyness in his voice.

"Do you think," Galen answered, before Aileron could speak, "that I would let a man so beautiful ride with anyone else?" She smiled.

Aileron flushed red beneath his beard as the Dalrei burst into sudden, tension-breaking laughter. Dave, laughing, too, met Ra-Tenniel's eyes—silver now—and caught a quick wink from the lios alfar. Kevin Laine, he thought, would have appreciated what Ra-Tenniel had just done. A sorrow, there. The deepest among many, he realized, with a twist of surprise.

There was no time to even try to deal with the complexities of that sort of thought. It was probably just as well, Dave knew. Emotions on that scale, running so deep, were dangerous for him. They had been all his life, and he had no room now for the paralysis they caused, or the pain that would follow. Ivor was speaking. Dave forced his thoughts sharply outwards again.

"I was about to initiate a Council of War, High King. Will it please you to take charge now?"

"Not in Celidon," Aileron said, with unexpected courtesy. He had recovered from his momentary embarrassment and was once again controlled and direct. Not entirely without tact, however.

Dave, out of the corner of his eye, saw Mabon of Rhoden nod quiet approval, and a look of gratitude suffused the features of old Dhira, sitting beside the Duke. Dhira, Dave decided, was all right after all. He wondered if he'd have a chance to apologize later, and if he'd be able to handle it.

"I have my own thoughts," the High King said, "but I would hear the counsel of the Dalrei and of Daniloth before I speak."

"Very well," said Ivor, with a crispness that matched Aileron's. "My counsel is this. The army of Brennin and Cathal is on the Plain. We have Daniloth here with us, and every fit Dalrei of fighting age. . . ."

*Except for one*, Dave thought involuntarily, but kept silence.

"We are missing the Warrior and Silvercloak and have no word from Eridu," Ivor continued. "We know that there will be no aid for us from the Dwarves. We do not know what has happened or will happen at sea. I do not think we can wait to find out. My counsel is to linger here only so long as it takes Niavin and Teyrnon to arrive, and then to ride north through Gwynir into Andarien and force Maugrim into battle there again."

There was a little silence. Then, "Ruined Andarien," murmured Lydan, Galen's brother. "Always and ever the battleground." There was a bittersweet sadness in his voice. Echoes of music. Memories.

Aileron said nothing, waiting. It was Mabon of Rhoden who spoke up, raising himself on his one good arm. "There is good sense in what you say, Aven. As much good sense as we are likely to find in any plan today, though I would dearly love to have Loren's counsel here, or Gereint's, or our own Seer's—"

"Where are they, Gereint and the Seer? Can we not bring them here now—with the raithen, perhaps?" It was Tulger of the eighth tribe.

Ivor looked at his old friend, worry deep in his eyes. "Gereint has left his body. He is soul-travelling. He did not say why. The Seer went into the mountains from Gwen Ystrat. Again, I know not why." He looked at Aileron.

The High King hesitated. "If I tell you, it must not leave this chamber. We have fear enough without summoning more." And into the stillness, he said, "She went to free the Paraiko in Khath Meigol."

There was a babble of sound. One man made the sign against evil, but only one. These were Chieftains and their hunt leaders, and this was a time of war.

"They live?" Ra-Tenniel whispered softly.

"She tells me so," Aileron replied.

"Weaver at the Loom!" Dhira murmured, from the heart. This time it didn't sound inappropriate. Dave, comprehending little, felt tension in the room like an enveloping presence.

"So we have no access to the Seer, either," Mabon continued grimly. "And we must accept, given what you have said, that we may never have her or Gereint or Loren again. We will have to decide this using what wisdom we have among ourselves, and so I have one question for you, Aven." He paused. "What assurance do we have that Maugrim will fight us in Andarien when we get there? Could his army not sweep around us among the evergreens of Gwynir and so run south to destroy what we have left behind: the mid-Plain here? The Dalrei women and children? Gwen Ystrat? All of Brennin and Cathal, open to him with our army so far away? Could he not do that?"

There was total silence in the room. After a moment, Mabon went on, almost whispering.

"Maugrim is outside of time, not spun on the Loom. He cannot be killed. And he has shown, with the long winter, that he is in no hurry this time to bring us to battle. Would he not glory and his lieutenants exult to watch our army waiting uselessly before impregnable Starkadh while the svarts and urgach and Galadan's wolves were ravaging all we loved?"

He stopped. Dave felt a weight like an anvil hanging from his heart. It was painful to draw breath. He looked at Torc for reassurance and saw anguish in his face, saw it mirrored deeply in Ivor's and, somehow most frighteningly, in the normally unreadable features of Aileron.

*"Fear not that,"* said Ra-Tenniel.

A voice so very clear. Blurring forever, Ivor dan Banor thought, the borders between sound and light, between music and spoken word. The Aven turned to the Lord of the lios alfar as might one desperate for water in a rainless land.

"Fear Maugrim," said Ra-Tenniel, "as must any who name themselves wise. Fear defeat and the dominion of the Dark. Fear, also, the annihilation that Galadan purposes and strives for, ever."

*Water,* Ivor was thinking, as the measured words flowed over him. Water, with sorrow like a stone at the bottom of the cup.

"Fear any and all of these things," Ra-Tenniel said. "The tearing of our threads from the Loom, the unsaying of our histories, the unravelling of the Weaver's design."

He paused. Water in time of drought. Music and light.

"But do not fear," said the Lord of the lios alfar, "that he will avoid a battle with us, should we march to Andarien. I am your surety for that. I and my people. The lios alfar are out from Daniloth for the first time in a thousand years. He can see us. He can reach us. We are no longer hidden in the Shadowland. *He will not pass us by.* It lies not in his nature to pass us by. Rakoth Maugrim will meet this army if the lios alfar go into Andarien."

It was true. Ivor knew that as soon as he heard the words, and he knew it as deeply as he had known any single thing in all his life. It reinforced his own counsel and offered complete answer to Mabon's terrifying question, an answer wrought from the very essence of the lios alfar, the Weaver's chosen ones, the Children of Light. What they were and had always been; and the terrible, bitter price they paid. The other side of the image. The stone in the cup.

Most hated by the Dark, for their name was Light.

Ivor wanted to bow, to kneel, to offer grief, pity, love, heart's gratitude. Somehow none of them, nor all of them together, seemed adequate in the face of what Ra-Tenniel had just said. Ivor felt heavy, clodlike. Looking at the three lios alfar he felt like a lump of earth.

And *yes,* he thought. Yes, he was exactly that. He was prosaic, unglamorous, he *was* of the earth, the grass. He was of the Plain, which endured, which would endure this, too, if they proved equal to the days ahead, but not otherwise.

Reaching back into his own history, as Ra-Tenniel had just done, the Aven cast aside all thoughts, all emotions save those that spoke of strength, of resistance. "A thousand years ago the first Aven of the Plain led every Dalrei hunter who could ride into the woven mists and the skewed time of Daniloth, and the Weaver laid a straight track for them. They came out onto a battlefield by Linden Bay that would otherwise have been lost. Revor rode from there beside Ra-Termaine across the River Celyn into Andarien. And so, Brightest Lord, will I ride beside you, should that be our decision when we leave this place."

He paused and turned to the other King in the room. "When Revor rode, and Ra-Termaine, it was in the army and at the command of Conary of Brennin, and then of Colan, his son. It was so then, and rightly so—for the High Kings of Brennin are the

Children of Mörnir—and it will be so again, and as rightly, should you accept this counsel, High King."

He was utterly unaware of the ringing cadences, the upwelling power of his own voice. He said, "You are heir to what Conary was, as we are the heirs of Revor and Ra-Termaine. Do you accede to this counsel? Yours is governance here, Aileron dan Ailell. Will you have us to ride with you?"

Bearded and dark, devoid of ornament, a soldier's sword in a plain sheath at his side, Aileron looked the very image of a war king. Not bright and glittering as Conary had been, or Colan, or even as his own brother was. He was stern and expressionless and grim, and one of the youngest men in the room.

"I accede," he said. "I would have you ride with me. When the army comes tomorrow, we set out for Andarien."

⊷⇒◉⇐⊶

In that moment, halfway and a little more to Gwynir, a lean and scarred figure, incongruously aristocratic atop one of the hideous slaug, slowed and then dragged his mount to a complete stop. Motionless on the wide Plain, he watched the dust of Rakoth's retreating army settle in front of him.

For most of the night he had run in his wolf form. In careful silence he had observed as Uathach, the giant urgach in white, had enforced an orderly withdrawal out of what had begun as blind flight. There had been a question of precedence there, to be resolved eventually, but not now. Galadan had other things to think about.

And he thought more clearly in his human shape. So a little before dawn he had taken his own form again and commandeered one of the slaug, even though he hated them. Gradually through the greyness of dawn he had let the army pass him by, making sure that Uathach did not notice.

He was far from afraid of the white-clad urgach, but he knew too little about him, and knowledge, for the Wolflord, had always been the key to power. It mattered almost not at all that he was reasonably certain he could kill Uathach; what was important was that he *understand* what had made him what he was. Six months ago Uathach had been summoned to Starkadh, an oversized urgach, as stupid as any of the others, a little more dangerous because of quickness and size.

He had come out again four nights ago, augmented, enhanced in some unsettling way. He was clever now, vicious and articulate, and clad by Rakoth in white—a touch that Galadan appreciated, remembering Lauriel, the swan the lios had loved. Uathach had been given command of the army that issued over the Valgrind Bridge. That, in the inception, Galadan had no quarrel with.

The Wolflord himself had been away, engaged in tasks of his own devising. It had been he, with the knowledge that came with being one of the andain, son of a god, and with the subtlety that was his own, who had conceived and led the attack on the Paraiko in Khath Meigol.

If attack it could be called. The Giants by their very nature had no access to anger or violence. No response to war, save the single inviolate fact that shedding their blood brought down any curse the injured Giant chose to invoke. *That* was the true, the literal concept of the bloodcurse; it had nothing to do with the superstitions about roaming, fanged ghosts haunting Khath Meigol.

Or so the Wolflord had continually reminded himself in the days he spent there while the Paraiko were penned like helpless sheep in their caves by the svarts and urgach, breathing the clever, killing smoke of the fires he'd ordered to be made.

He had only lasted a few days, but the true reason was his own secret. He had tried to convince himself of what he had told those he left behind—that his departure was dictated by the demands of war—but he had lived too long and too searchingly to really deceive himself.

The truth was that the Paraiko unsettled him deeply in some subconscious way his mind could not grasp. In some fashion they lay in his path, huge obstacles to his one unending desire—which was for annihilation, utter and absolute. How they could oppose him he knew not, for pacifism was woven into their very nature, but nonetheless they disturbed him and rendered him uneasy as did no one else in Fionavar or any other world, with the single exception of his father.

So, since he could not kill Cernan of the Beasts, he set about destroying the Paraiko in their mountain caves. When the fires were burning properly and the svarts and urgach made relentlessly aware of the need not to shed blood—as if they had to be reminded, for even the stupid svarts lived in abject terror of the bloodcurse—Galadan had withdrawn from the bitter cold of the mountains and the incessant chanting that came from the caves.

He had been in east Gwynir when the snow had, shockingly, melted. Immediately he had begun massing his wolves among the evergreens, waiting for the word of attack. He had just garnered tidings of his contingent slaughtered in Leinanwood by the High King when Avaia herself had swooped, glorious and malevolent, to hiss that an army had issued forth across the Valgrind Bridge, heading for Celidon.

At speed he had taken his wolves down the eastern edge of the Plain. He had crossed Adein near the Edryn Gap, unseen, unanticipated, and then, timing it flawlessly, had arrived at the battlefield to fall on the exposed right flank of the Dalrei. He hadn't expected the lios to be there, but that was only a source of joy, a deepening of delight: they were going to slaughter them all.

They would have, had the Wild Hunt not suddenly flashed in the heavens above. Alone among the army of the Dark he knew who Owein was. Alone, he grasped a hint of what had happened. And alone, he comprehended something of what lay beneath the cry that stopped the killing.

Alone in that army he knew whose voice it was.

He was, after all, her brother's son.

There had been a great deal to assimilate, and a very immediate danger, as well. And through all the pandemonium a thought, inchoate, little more than a straining towards, a possibility, was striving to take shape in his mind. Then, above and beyond all this, as if it had not been enough and more than enough, there came an intuition he had learned to trust, a vibration within the part of him that was a god, Cernan's son.

As the cold rage of battle passed, and then the chaos of flight, Galadan became increasingly aware that something was happening in the forest realm.

There was suddenly a very great deal to consider. He needed solitude. He always needed that—as being nearest to his long desire—but now his mind craved it as much as his soul. So he had detached himself from the army, unseen in the dawn shadows, and he was riding alone when the morning sunlight found him.

Shortly after sunrise he stopped, surveying the Plain. He found it deeply pleasing to his heart. Except for the cloud of dust, settling now, far to the north, there was no sign of life beyond the insentient grass he did not care about. It was almost as if the goal for which he had striven for past a thousand years had come.

Almost. He smiled thinly. Irony was nearly at the centre of his soul and would not let him dream for very long. The striving had been too lengthy, too deeply ingrained, for dreams to ever be remotely adequate.

He could remember the very instant his designs had taken shape, when he had first aligned himself with the Unraveller—the moment when Lisen of the Wood had sent word running through Pendaran that she had merged her fate and given her love to Amairgen Whitebranch, the mortal.

He had been in the Great Wood that morning, ready to celebrate with all the other powers of Pendaran her slaying of the man for his presumption in the sacred grove.

It had turned out otherwise. Everything had.

He had gone into Starkadh, once and once only, for in that place he, who was mightiest by far of the andain and arrogant with that strength, had been forced to humble himself before an obliterating magnitude of power. He had not even been able to mask his own mind from Maugrim, who had laughed.

He was made to realize that he was entirely understood and, notwithstanding that, had been accepted, with amusement, as lieutenant by the Dark. Even though Rakoth knew precisely what his own purposes were and how they differed from Maugrim's own, it hadn't seemed to matter.

Their designs marched together a very long way, Galadan had told himself, and though he was not—no one was—remotely an equal to the Unraveller, he might yet, ere the very end, find a way to obliterate the world Maugrim would rule.

He had served Rakoth well. Had commanded the army that cut Conary off by Sennett Strand so long ago. He had killed Conary himself, in his wolf shape, and he would have won that battle, and so the war, had Revor of the Plain not come, somehow, impossibly soon, through the mists of Daniloth to turn the tide of battle north to Starkadh itself, where it ended. He himself, badly wounded, had hardly escaped with his life from Colan's avenging sword.

They had thought he'd died, he knew. He almost had. In an icy cave north of the Ungarch River he had lain, bitterly cold, nursed only by his wolves. For a very long time he'd huddled there, damping his power, his aura, as low as he could, while the armies of the Light held parley before the Mountain and Ginserat made the wardstones and then shaped, with aid of the Dwarves, the chain that bound Rakoth beneath Rangat.

Through all the long waiting years he had continued to serve, having made his choice and set his own course. He it was who had found Avaia, half dead herself. The swan had been hiding in the frigid realm of Fordaetha, Queen of Rük, whose icy touch was instant death to a spirit less strong than one of the andain. With his own hands he had nursed the swan back to health in the court of that cold Queen. Fordaetha had wanted to couple with him. It had pleased him to refuse her.

His, too, had been the stratagem, subtle and infinitely slow, whereby the water spirit of Llewenmere, innocent and fair, had been lured into surrendering her most handsome swans. He had given her a reason that sufficed: his earnest desire, in the identity he had dissembled with, to bring swans north to Celyn Lake, on the borders of devastated Andarien. And she had released her guardianship and had, all unsuspecting, let him take them away.

He had only needed some of them: the males. North indeed, they had been carried, but far past Celyn into the glacier-riven mountains beyond Ungarch, where they had been bred to Avaia. Then, when they had died, she, who could not die unless slain, had coupled with her children, and had continued doing so, year after year, to bring forth the brood that had stained the skies on the evening just past.

The spirit of Llewenmere never knew for certain what she had done or who, indeed, he really was. She may have guessed, though, for in after years, the lake, once benign and inviting, had turned dark and weedy, and even in Pendaran, which knew a darkness of its own, it was said to be haunted.

It brought him no joy. Nothing had, since Lisen. A long, long life, and a slow, single purpose guiding it.

He it was who had freed Rakoth. Orchestrating, with infinite patience, the singling out and then the corruption of the Dwarf brothers, Kaen and Blöd; bringing into play the festering hatred of Metran of the Garantae, First Mage of Brennin; and, finally, cutting off, with his own sword, the hand of Maugrim when Ginserat's chain could not be made to break.

He had run then with Rakoth—a wolf beside a cloud of malice that dripped, and would forever drip, black blood—to the rubble of Starkadh. There he had watched as, inexorably, Rakoth Maugrim had showed forth his might—greater here than anywhere in any of the worlds, for here had he first set down his foot—and raised anew the ziggurat that was the first and the last seat of his power.

When it reared upwards again, complete, even to the green flickering of its lights, an obliterating presence among the ice, Galadan had stopped before the mighty doors, though they stood open for him. Once had been enough. Everywhere else his mind was his own. In one way, he knew, this resistance was meaningless, for Maugrim, in that one instant a thousand years ago, had learned everything of Galadan he would ever need to know. But in another way, the sanctity of his thoughts was the only thing that had any meaning left for the Wolflord.

So he had halted before the doors, and there had he received his reward, the offered image, never before seen, never known, of Maugrim's revenge against the lios alfar for being what they were: the Soulmonger at sea. Waiting for the lios as they sailed west in search of a promised world and destroying them, singly and in pairs, to claim their voices and their songs as a lure for those who followed. *All* of those who followed.

It was perfect. It was beyond perfection. A malevolence that used the very essence of the Children of Light to shape their doom. He could never have bound to his service a creature so awesome, Galadan knew. He could never even, for all his own guile, have thought of something so encompassing. The image was, among other things, a reminder to him of what Rakoth, now free again, was and could do.

But it was also a reward, and one that had nothing at all to do with the lios alfar.

The vision had been clear in his mind. Rakoth had made it clear. He had seen the Soulmonger vividly: its size and colour, the flat, ugly head. He could hear the singing. See the lidless eyes. And the staff, the white staff, embedded uselessly between those eyes.

The staff of Amairgen Whitebranch.

And so, for the very first time, he learned how that one had died. There was no joy. There could never again be joy, he had no access to such a thing. But that day, before the open doors of Starkadh, there had come an easing within him for a moment, a certain quiet, which was as much as he could ever have.

Alone now on the Plain he tried to summon up the image again, but he found it blurred and unsatisfying. He shook his head. There was too much happening. The implications of Owein's return with the Wild Hunt were enormous. He had to find a way to deal with them. First, though, he knew he would have to address the other thing, the intuition from the Wood that went deeper than anything else.

This was why he had stopped. To seek out the quiet that would allow the thing, whatever it was, to move from the edge of his awareness to the centre, to be seen.

For a while he thought it was his father, which would make a great deal of sense. He never ventured near Cernan, and his father had never, since a certain night not long before the Bael Rangat, tried to contact him. But this morning's sensation was intense enough, so laden with overtones and shadings of long-forgotten emotions, that he thought it had to be Cernan calling him. The forest was, somehow, part of this. It had—

And in that instant he knew what it was.

Not, after all, his father. But the intensity was suddenly explained, and more. With an expression on his face no one living had ever been allowed to see, Galadan leaped from the back of the slaug. He put his hand to his chest and made a gesture. Then, a moment later, in his wolf shape, covering ground faster than even the slaug might, he set out west, running as swiftly as he could, the battle forgotten, the war, almost.

West, to where lights were burning and someone stood in the Anor, in the room that had been Lisen's.

# CHAPTER 3

They had been climbing all morning, and the rough going was not made easier by the pain in Kim's side where Ceriog had kicked her. She was silent, though, and kept going, head down, watching the path and the long legs of Faebur climbing in front of her. Dalreidan was leading them; Brock, who had to be hurting far more than she was, brought up the rear. No one spoke. The trail was difficult enough without wasting breath on words, and there was, really, not a great deal to say.

She had dreamt again the night before, in the outlaw camp not far from the plateau where they had been captured. Ruana's deep chanting ran through her sleep. It was beautiful, but she found no comfort in that beauty—the pain was too great. It twisted through her and, what was worse, a part of it came from her. There was smoke in the dream again, and the caves. She saw herself with lacerations on her arms but, again, no blood was flowing. No blood in Khath Meigol. The smoke drifted in the starlit, firelit night. Then there was another light, as the Baelrath blazed into life. She felt it as a burning, as guilt and pain, and in the midst of that flaming she watched herself looking up into the sky above the mountains and she saw the red moon ride again and she heard a name.

In the morning, heavily wrapped in her thoughts, she had let Brock and Dalreidan make arrangements for their departure, and in silence all morning and into the afternoon she had climbed upwards and east towards the sun.

*Towards the sun.*

She stopped abruptly. Brock almost ran into her from behind. Shielding her eyes, Kim gazed beyond the mountains as far as she could, and then a cry of joy escaped her. Dalreidan turned, and Faebur. Wordlessly, she pointed. They spun back to look.

"Oh, my King!" cried Brock of Banir Tal. "I knew you would not fail!"

Over Eridu the rain clouds were gone. Sunlight streamed from a sky laced only with the thin, benevolent cirrus clouds of a summer's day.

Far to the west, in the spinning place of Cader Sedat, the Cauldron of Khath Meigol lay shattered in a thousand pieces and Metran of the Garantae was dead.

Kim felt the shadows of her dream dissolve as hope flared within her like the brilliant sun. She thought of Kevin in that moment. There was sorrow in the memory, there always would be, but now there was joy as well, and a burgeoning pride. The summer had been his gift—the green grass, the birdsong, the mild seas that had allowed *Prydwen* to sail and the men who sailed her to do this thing.

There was a keen brightness in Dalreidan's face as he turned back to look at her. "Forgive me," he said. "I doubted."

She shook her head. "So did I. I had terrible dreams of where they had to go. There is a miracle in this. I do not know how it was done."

Brock had come up to stand beside her on the narrow trail. He said nothing, but his eyes were shining beneath the bandage Kim had wrapped about his wound. Faebur, though, had his back to them, still gazing to the east. Looking at him, Kim sobered quickly.

At length he, too, turned to look at her, and she saw the tears in his eyes. "Tell me something, Seer," he said, sounding older, far, than his years. "If an exiled man's people are all dead, does his exile end or does it go on forever?"

She struggled to frame a reply and found none. It was Dalreidan who answered. "We cannot unsay the falling of that rain, or lengthen the cut threads of those who have died," he said gently. "It is in my heart, though, that in the face of what Maugrim has done no man is an exile anymore. Every living creature on this side of the mountains has received a gift of life this morning. We must use that gift, until the hour comes that knows our name, to deal such blows as we can against the Dark. There are arrows in your quiver, Faebur. Let them sing with the names of your loved ones as they fly. It may not seem like a true recompense, but it is all we can do."

"It is what we must do," said Brock softly.

"Easy for a Dwarf to say!" snarled Faebur, rounding on him.

Brock shook his head. "Harder by far than you could know. Every breath I draw is laden with the knowledge of what my people have done.The rain will not have fallen under the twin mountains, but it fell in my heart and it is raining there still. Faebur, will you let my axe sing with your arrows in mourning for the people of the Lion in Eridu?"

The tears had dried on Faebur's face. His chin was set in a hard, straight line. He had aged, Kim thought. In a day, in less than a day he seemed to have aged so much. For what seemed to her a very long time he stood motionless, and then slowly and deliberately he extended a hand to the Dwarf. Brock reached up and clasped it between both of his own.

She became aware that Dalreidan was looking at her.

"We go on?" he asked gravely.

"We go on," she said, and even as she spoke the dream came back, with the chanting and the smoke, and the name written in Dana's moon.

To the south and far below, the Kharn River flashed through its gorge in the evening light. They were so high that an eagle hovering over the river was below them, its wings shining in the sunlight that slanted down the gorge from the west. All around them lay the mountains of the Carnevon Range, the peaks white with snow even in midsummer. It was cold, this high up and with the day waning; Kim was grateful for the sweater they had given her in Gwen Ystrat. Lightweight and wonderfully warm, it was a testimonial to the value accorded all the cloth arts in this, the first of all the Weaver's worlds.

Even so, she shivered.

"Now?" Dalreidan asked, his voice carefully neutral. "Or would you like to camp here until morning?"

The three of them looked at her, waiting. It was her decision to make. They had guided her to this place, had helped her through the hardest parts of the climb, had rested when she had needed to rest, but now they had arrived, and all the decisions were hers.

She looked past her companions to the east. Fifty paces away the rocks looked exactly as they did where she was standing now. The light fell upon them the same way, with the same softening as evening came to the mountains. She had expected something different, some sort of change: a shimmering, shadows, a sharpening of intensity. She saw none of these, yet she knew, and the three men with her knew, that the rocks fifty paces to the east lay within Khath Meigol.

Now that she was here she longed with all her heart to be anywhere else. To be graced with the wings of the eagle below, that she might sweep away on the evening breeze. Not from Fionavar, not from the war, but far from the loneliness of this place and the dream that had led her here. Within herself she reached for, and found, the tacit presence that was Ysanne. She took comfort in that. She was never truly alone; there were two souls within her, now and always. Her companions had no such solace, though, had no dreams or visions to guide them. They were here because of her, and only because of her, and they were looking now for her to lead them. Even as she stood, hesitating, the shadows were slowly climbing the slopes of the ravine.

She drew a breath and slowly let it out. She was here to repay a debt, and one that was not hers alone. She was also here because she bore the Baelrath in a time of war, and there was no one else in any world who could make manifest the Seer's dream she'd had, however dark it was.

However dark. It had been night in the dream, with fires in front of the caves. She looked down and saw the stone flickering like a tongue of flame on her hand.

"Now," she said to the others. "It will be bad in the dark, I know, but it won't be that much better in the morning, and I don't think we should wait."

They were very brave, all three of them. Without a word spoken they made room for her to fall into line after Faebur, with Brock behind; and Dalreidan led them into Khath Meigol.

Even with the vellin shielding her she felt the impact of magic as they passed into the country of the Giants, and the form the magic took was fear. They are not ghosts, she told herself, over and over. They are alive. They saved my life. Even so, even with the vellin, she felt terror brushing her mind with the quick wings of night moths.

The two men and the Dwarf with her had no green vellin bracelets to guard them, no inner voices to reassure, yet none of them made a sound and none broke stride. Humbled by their courage, she felt her own heart flame with resolution, and as it did the Baelrath burned brighter on her hand.

She quickened her pace and moved past Dalreidan. She had brought them to this place, a place where no man should ever have had to come. It was her turn to lead them now, for the Warstone knew where to go.

For almost two hours they walked in the gathering darkness. It was full night under the summer stars when Kim saw smoke and the distant blaze of bonfires and heard the raucous laughter of svart alfar. And with the brutal mockery of that sound she found, suddenly, that her fears, which had walked with her until now, were gone. She had arrived, and the enemy ahead of her was known and hated and in the caves beyond those ridges of stone the Giants were imprisoned and were dying.

She turned and saw by starlight and the glow of her ring that her companions' faces were grim now, not with strain but with anticipation. Silently Brock unslung his axe, and Faebur notched an arrow to his bow. She turned to Dalreidan. He had not yet drawn a sword or unslung his own bow. "There will be time," he whispered, answering her unspoken question, scarcely a breath in the night air. "Shall I find us a place where we can look?"

She nodded. Calmly, silently, he moved past her again and began picking his way among the strewn boulders and loose rocks towards the fires and the laughter. Moments later the four of them lay prone above a plateau. Sheltered by upthrust teeth of rock, they looked down, sickened, on what the glow of the bonfires revealed.

There were two caves set into the mountainside, with high vaulted entrances and runic lettering carved over the arches. It was dark in the caves and they could not see within. From one of them, though, if they strained to hear past the laughter of the svart alfar, they could make out the sound of a single deep voice chanting slowly.

The light came from two huge fires on the plateau, set directly before each of the caves in such a fashion that the smoke of their burning was drawn inwards. There was another fire just over the ridge east of them, and Kim could make out the glow and the rising smoke of a fourth about a quarter of a mile away, to the northeast. There were no others to be seen. Four caves then, four sets of prisoners dying of starvation and smoke.

And four bands of svart alfar. Around each of the bonfires below them, about thirty of the svarts were gathered, and there were a handful of the nightmare urgach, as well. About a hundred and fifty of them, then, if the same numbers held true beyond the ridges. Not a very great force, in truth, but more than enough, she knew, to subdue and hold the Paraiko, whose pacifism was the very essence of their being. All that the svarts had to do, under the guidance of the urgach, was keep the fires burning and refrain from shedding blood. Then they could claim their reward.

Which they were doing now, even as she watched. On each of the pyres below lay the huge body, charred and blackened, of a Paraiko. Every few moments one of the svart alfar would dart close enough to the roaring flames to thrust in a sword and cut for himself a piece of roasted flesh.

Their reward. Kim's stomach heaved in revulsion and she had to close her eyes. It was an unholy scene, a desecration in the worst, the deepest sense. Beside her she could hear Brock cursing under his breath in a steady invocation, bitter and heartfelt.

Meaningless words, whatever scant easing they might afford. And the curses of the Paraiko themselves, which might have been unleashed had any one of them been killed directly, had been forestalled. Rakoth was too clever, too steeped in the shaping of evil, his servants too well trained, for the bloodcurse to have been set free.

Which meant that another sort of power would have to be invoked. And so here she was, drawn by a savesong chanted and the burden of a Seer's dream, and what, in the Weaver's name, was she to do? She had three men beside her, three men alone, however brave they might be. From the moment she and Brock had left Morvran, everything in her had been focused on getting to this plateau, knowing that she had to do so, with never a thought until now about what she could do when she arrived.

Dalreidan touched her elbow. "Look," he whispered.

She opened her eyes. He wasn't looking at the caves or the fires or the ridges beyond with their own smoke. Reluctantly, as always, she followed his gaze to the ring on her own hand and saw the Baelrath vividly aflame. With a real grief she saw that the fire at the heart of the Warstone was somehow twinned to the hue and shape of the hideous fires below.

It was deeply unsettling, but when had there been anything reassuring or easy about the ring she bore? In every single thing she had ever done with the Baelrath there was pain. In its depths she had seen Jennifer in Starkadh and carried her, screaming, into the crossing. She had awakened a dead King at Stonehenge against his will. She had summoned Arthur on the summit of Glastonbury Tor to war and bitterest grief again. She had released the Sleepers by Pendaran on the night Finn took the Longest Road. She was an invoker, a war cry in darkness, a storm crow, truly that, on the wings of a gathering storm. She was a gatherer indeed, a summoner. She was—

She was a summoner.

There was a scream, and then a raucous burst of laughter down below. An urgach, for sport, had hurled a svart alfar, one of the smaller green ones, onto the blazing fire. She saw, but hardly registered it. Her eyes went back to the stone, to the flame coiled in the depths of it, and there she read a name, the same name she had seen written across the face of the moon in her dream. Reading it, she remembered something: how the Baelrath had blazed in answering light on the night that Dana's red full moon had ridden through the sky over Paras Derval.

She was a summoner, and now she knew what she had to do. For with the name written in the ring had come knowledge that had not lain in the dream. She knew who this was and knew, also, what the price of her calling would be. But this was Khath Meigol in a time of war, and the Paraiko were dying in the caves. She could not harden her heart, there was too much pity there, but she could steel her will to do what had to be done and shoulder the grief as one more among many.

517

She closed her eyes again. It was easier in darkness, a way of hiding, almost. Almost, but not truly. She drew a breath and then within her mind, not aloud, she said, *Imraith-Nimphais.*

Then she led her companions back down and away from the fires to wait, knowing it would not be long.

Tabor's watch was not until the end of the night, and so he had been asleep. Not anymore. She was in the sky over the camp, and she had called his name, and for the first time ever he heard fear in the creature of his fast.

He was wide awake, instantly, and dressing as quickly as he could.

*Wait,* he sent. *I do not want to frighten them. I will meet you on the Plain.*

*No,* he heard. She was truly afraid. *Come now. There is no time!*

She was descending, even as he went outside. He was confused, and a little afraid himself, for he had not summoned her, but even with that, his heart lifted to see the beauty of her as she came down, her horn shining like a star, her wings folding gracefully as she landed.

She was trembling. He stepped forward and put his arms about her, laying his head against hers. *Easy, my love,* he sent, projecting all the reassurance he could. *I am here. What has happened?*

*I was called by name,* she sent, still trembling.

A shocked surge of anger ran through him, and a deeper fear of his own that he fought to master and conceal. He could conceal nothing from her, though, they were bonded too deeply. He drew a ragged breath. *Who?*

*I do not know her. A woman with white hair, but not old. A red ring on her hand. How does she know my name?*

His own hands moved ceaselessly, gentling her. Anger was still there, but he was Ivor's son and Levon's brother, both of whom had seen her, and so he knew who this was. *She is a friend,* he sent. *We must go to her. Where?*

The wrong question, though it had to be asked. She told him, and with the naming of that place fear was in both of them again. He fought it and helped her do the same. Then he mounted her, feeling the joy of doing so in the midst of everything else. She spread her wings, and he prepared to fly—

"Tabor!"

He turned. Liane was there, in a white shift brought back from Gwen Ystrat. She seemed eerily far away. Already. And he had not even taken flight. "I must go," he said, forming the words carefully. "The Seer has called us."

"Where is she?"

He hesitated. "In the mountains." His sister's hair, snarled in tangles of sleep, lay loose on her back. Her feet were bare on the grass; her eyes, wide with apprehension, never left his own.

"Be careful," she said. "Please." He nodded, jerkily. Beneath him, Imraith-Nimphais, restless to be gone, flexed her wings. "Oh, Tabor," whispered Liane, who was older than he but didn't sound it, "please come back."

He tried to answer that. It was important that he try; she was crying. But words would not come. He raised one hand, in a gesture that had to encompass far too much, and then they were in the sky and the stars blurred before their speed.

Kim saw a streak of light in the west. She raised her hand, with the ring glowing on her finger, and a moment later the power she had summoned descended. It was dark, and the clearing where they waited was rough and narrow, but nothing could mar the grace of the creature that landed beside her. She listened for alarms raised east of them but heard nothing: why should a falling star in the mountains be cause for concern?

But this was not a falling star.

It was a deep red through the body, the colour of Dana's moon, the colour of the ring she carried. The great wings folded now, it stood restlessly on the stones, seeming almost to dance above them. Kim looked at the single horn. It was shining and silver, and the Seer in her knew how deadly it was, how far beyond mere grace this gift of the Goddess was.

This double-edged gift. She turned her gaze to the rider. He looked very much like his father, only a little like Levon. She had known he was only fifteen, but seeing it came as a shock. He reminded her, she realized abruptly, of Finn.

Very little time had passed since the summoning. The waning moon had barely risen above the eastern reaches of the range. Its silver touched the silver of the horn. Beside Kim, Brock stood watchfully, and Faebur, his tattoos glowing faintly, was on her other side. Dalreidan had withdrawn a little way, though, back into the shadows. She was not surprised, though she sorrowed for that, too. This meeting would have to be a hard thing for the exiled Rider. She'd had no choice though. Just as she had none now, and there was deeper cause for sorrow written in the eyes of the boy.

He sat quietly, waiting for her to speak.

"I'm sorry," she said, and meant it with all her heart. "I have some idea of what this does to you."

He tossed his head impatiently, in a gesture like his brother's. "How did you know her name?" he asked, low, because of the laughter nearby, but challenging. She heard both the anger and the anxiety.

She shouldered her own power. "You ride a child of Pendaran's grove and the wandering moon," she said. "I am a Seer and I carry the Wandering Fire. I read her name in the Baelrath, Tabor." She had dreamt it, too, but she didn't tell him that.

"No one else is to know her name," he said. "No one at all."

"Not so," she replied. "Gereint does. The shamans always know the totem names."

"He's different," Tabor said, a little uncertainly.

"So am I," said Kim, as gently as she could. He was very young, and the creature was afraid. She understood how they felt. She had come crashing, she and her wild ring, into the midst of an utterly private communion the two of them shared. She understood, but the night of which she had dreamt was passing, and she didn't know if she had time to assuage them properly, or even what to say.

Tabor surprised her. He might be young, but he was the Aven's son, and he rode a gift of Dana. With calm simplicity he said, "Very well. What are we to do in Khath Meigol?"

Slay, of course. And take the consequences upon themselves. Was there an easy way to say it? She knew of none. She told them who was here, and what was taking place, and even as she spoke she saw the head of the winged creature lift and her horn begin to shine more brightly yet.

Then she was done. There was nothing more to tell. Tabor nodded to her, once; then he and the creature he rode seemed to change, to coalesce. She was near to them, and a Seer. She caught a fragment of their inner speech. Only a fragment, then she took her mind away. *Bright one*, she heard and, *We must kill*, and, just before she pulled away, . . . *only each other at the last.*

Then they were in the air again and Dana's creature's wings were spread and she turned, killingly bright, to flash down on the plateau and suddenly the servants of the Dark were not laughing anymore. Kim's three companions were already running for their vantage point again and she followed them as quickly as she could, stumbling over the rocks and loose stones.

Then she was there and watching how stunningly graceful death could be. Again and again Imraith-Nimphais descended and rose, the horn—with a cutting edge now—stabbing and slashing until the silver was so coated with blood it looked like the rest of her. One of the urgach rose before her, enormous, a two-handed sword upraised. With the preternatural skill of the Dalrei, Tabor veered his mount at full speed, up and to one side in the air, and the sharp edge of the horn sliced through the top of the urgach's head. It was all like that. They were elegant, blindingly swift, utterly lethal.

And it was destroying them both, Kim knew.

A myriad of griefs, and no time to deal with them: even as she watched, Imraith-Nimphais was soaring again, east to the next bonfire.

One of the svart alfar had been shamming death. Quickly it rose and began running west across the plateau.

"Mine," said Faebur quietly. Kim turned. She saw him draw an arrow and whisper something over its long shaft. She saw him notch it to his bow and draw, and she saw the moonlit arrow, loosed, flash into the throat of the running svart and drop it in its tracks.

"For Eridu," said Brock of Banir Tal. "For the people of the Lion. A beginning, Faebur."

"A beginning," Faebur echoed softly.

Nothing else moved on the plateau. The fires still roared; their crackling was the only sound. Over the ridge a distant screaming could be heard, but even as she picked her way down the loose slope towards the caves those sounds, too, abruptly ceased. Kim glanced over, instinctively, in time to see Imraith-Nimphais rise and flash north towards the last of the bonfires.

Making her way carefully amid the carnage and around the searing heat of the two fires she stopped before the larger of the caves.

She was here, and had done what she'd come to do, but she was weary and hurting, and it was not a time for joy. Not in the face of what had happened, in the presence of those two blackened bodies on the pyres. She looked down at the ring finger of her right hand: the Baelrath lay quiescent, mute. It was not finished, though. In her dream she had seen it burning on this plateau. There was more to come in the weaving of this night. What, she knew not, but the workings of power were not yet ended.

"Ruana," she cried, "this is the Seer of Brennin. I have come to the savesong chanted and you are free."

She waited, and the three men with her. The fires were the only sound. A flaw of wind blew a strand of hair into her eyes; she pushed it back. Then she realized that the wind was Imraith-Nimphais descending, as Tabor brought her down to stand behind the four of them. Kim glanced over and saw the dark blood on the horn. Then there was a sound from the cave and she turned back.

Out of the blackness of the archway and through the rising smoke the Paraiko came. Only two of them at first, one carrying the body of the other in his arms. The figure that moved out from the smoke to stand before them was twice the height of long-legged Faebur of Eridu. His hair was as white as Kimberly's, and so was his long beard. His robe, too, had been white once, but it was begrimed now with smoke and dust and the stains of illness. Even so, there was a gravity and a majesty to him that surmounted time and the unholy scene amid which they stood. In his eyes as he surveyed the plateau Kim read an ancient, ineffable pain. It made her own griefs seem shallow, transitory.

He turned to her. "We give thanks," he said. The voice was soft, incongruously so for one so enormous. "I am Ruana. When those of us who yet live are gathered we must do kanior for the dead. If you wish you may name one of your number to join us and seek absolution for all of you for this night's deeds of blood."

"Absolution?" growled Brock of Banir Tal. "We saved your lives."

"Even so," said Ruana. He stumbled a little as he spoke. Dalreidan and Faebur sprang forward to help him with his burden. "Hold!" Ruana cried. "Drop your weapons, you are in peril."

Nodding his understanding, Dalreidan let fall his arrows and his sword, and Faebur did the same. Then they went forward again and, straining with the effort, helped Ruana lower the other Giant gently to the ground.

There were more coming now. From Ruana's cave two women emerged supporting a man between them. Six, in all, came out from the other cave, sinking to the earth as soon as they were clear of the smoke. Looking east, Kim saw the first of the contingent from over the ridge coming to join them on the plateau. They moved very slowly, and many were supported and some were carried by others. None of them spoke.

"You need food," she said to Ruana. "How can we aid you?"

He shook his head. "After. The kanior must be first, it has been so long delayed. We will do the rites as soon as we are gathered." Others appeared now, from the northeast, from the fourth fire, moving with the same slow, strength-conserving care and in absolute silence. They were all clad in white, as Ruana was. He was neither the oldest nor the largest of them, but he was the only one who had spoken, and the others were gathering around the place where he stood.

"I am not leader," he said, as if reading Kim's thoughts. "There has been no leader among us since Connla transgressed in the making of the Cauldron. I will chant the kanior, though, and do the bloodless rites." His voice was infinitely mild. But this, Kim knew, was someone who had been strong enough to find her in the very heart of Rakoth's designs, and strong enough to shield her there.

He scanned the ranks of those who had come. "This is full numbering?" he asked. Kim looked around. It was hard to see amid the shadows and the smoke, but there were perhaps twenty-five of the Paraiko gathered on the plateau. No more than that.

"Full numbering," a woman said.

"Full."

"Full numbering, Ruana," a third voice echoed, plangent with sorrow. "There are no more of us. Do the kanior, too long delayed, lest our essence be altered and Khath Meigol shed its sanctity."

And it was in that moment that Kim had her first premonition, as the dark webs of her Seer's dream began to spin clear. She felt her heart clench like a fist and her mouth go dry.

"Very well," Ruana said. And then, to her again, with utmost courtesy, "Do you want to choose someone to join with us? For what you have done it will be allowed."

Kim said shakily, "If expiation is needed, it is mine to seek. I will do the bloodless rites with you."

Ruana looked down on her from his great height, then he glanced at each of the others in turn. She heard Imraith-Nimphais move nervously behind her under the weight of the Giant's gaze.

"Oh, Dana," Ruana said. Not an invocation. The words were addressed as to a co-eval. Words of reproach, of sorrow. He turned back to Kimberly. "You speak truly, Seer. I think it is your place. The winged one needs no dispensation for doing what Dana created her to do, though I must grieve for her birthing."

Again, Brock challenged him, looking up a long way. "You summoned us," the Dwarf said. "You chanted your song to the Seer, and we came in answer. Rakoth is free in Fionavar, Ruana of the Paraiko. Would you have us all lie down in caves and grant him dominion?" The passionate words rang in the mountain air.

There came a low sound from the assembled Paraiko.

"Did you summon them, Ruana?" It was the voice of the first woman who had spoken, the one from the cave over the ridge.

Still looking at Brock, Ruana said, "We cannot hate. Were Rakoth, whose voice I heard in my chanting, obliterated utterly from the tale of time, my heart would sing until I died. But we cannot make war. There is only passive resistance in us. It is part of our nature, the way killing and grace are woven into the creature that flew to save us. To change would be to end what we are and to lose the bloodcurse, which is the Weaver's gift to us in compensation and defence. Since Connla bound Owein and made the Cauldron we have not left Khath Meigol."

His voice was still low, but it was deeper now than when he had first walked from the cave; it was halfway to the chanting that Kim knew was coming. Something else was coming, too, and she was beginning to know what it would be.

Ruana said, "We have our own relationship with death, have had it since first we were spun on the Loom. You know it means death, and a curse, to shed our blood. There is more that you do not know. We lay down in the caves, because there was nothing else we could do, being what we are."

"Ruana," came the woman's voice again, "did you summon them?"

And now he turned to her, slowly, as if bearing a great burden.

"I did, Iera. I am sorry. I will chant it in the kanior and seek absolution with the rites. Failing which, I will leave Khath Meigol as Connla did, that the transgression might lie on my shoulders alone."

He raised his hands then, high over his head in the moonlight, and no more words were spoken, for the kanior began. It was a chant of mourning and a woven spell. It was unimaginably old, for the Paraiko had walked in Fionavar long before the Weaver had spun even the lios alfar or the Dwarves into the Tapestry, and the blood-curse had been a part of them from the beginning, and the kanior which preserved it.

It began with a low humming, almost below the threshold of hearing, from the Giants gathered around Ruana. Slowly, he lowered his hands and motioned Kim to come forward beside him. As she did so she saw that room had been made for Dalreidan, Faebur, and Brock in the circle surrounding them. Tabor and his winged creature remained outside the ring.

Ruana sank to his knees and motioned for Kim to do the same. He folded his hands in his lap and then, suddenly, he was in her mind.

*I will carry the dead,* she heard him say within. *Whom would you give to me?*

Her pulse was slowing, dragged by the low sounds coming from those around them. Her hands shook a little in her lap. She clasped them together, very tightly, and gave him Kevin and then Ysanne: who they were and what they had done.

Ruana's expression did not change, nor did he move, but his eyes widened a little as he absorbed what she sent to him, and then, within her mind, not speaking aloud, he said, *I have them, and they are worthy. Grieve with me.*

Then he lifted his voice in lament.

Kim never forgot that moment. Even with what followed after, the memory of the kanior stayed clear within her, the sorrow and the cleansing of sorrow.

*I will carry the dead,* Ruana had said, and now he proceeded to do so. With the textured richness of his voice he gathered them both, Kevin and then Ysanne, and drew them into the circle to be mourned. As the humming grew stronger, his own chanting twined through it and about it, a thread on a loom of sound, names offered to the mountain night, and into the ring began to come the images of the Paraiko who had died in the caves: Taieri, Ciroa, Hinewai, Caillea, and more, so many more. All of them approached to be gathered there, to stand in the place where Kim knelt to be reclaimed for this moment by the woven power of the song. Kim was weeping, but the tears of her heart fell soundlessly, that nothing might mar what Ruana shaped.

523

And in that moment he went even deeper; he claimed more. His voice growing stronger yet, he reached back through the tumbling ribbon of years and began to gather the Paraiko from the very beginning of days, all of them who had lived in their deep peacefulness, shedding no blood, and had, in the fullness of their time, died to be mourned.

And to be mourned now, again, as Ruana of Khath Meigol reached back for them, spreading the ambit of his mighty soul to encompass the loss of all the dead amid the carnage and the fires of that night. Kneeling so near, Kim watched him do it through her falling tears. Watched him try to shape a solace for sorrow, to rise above what had been done to them, with this majestic affirmation of what the Paraiko were. It was a kanior of kaniors, a lament for every single one of the dead.

And he was doing it. One after another they came, the ghosts of all the Paraiko in all the years, crowding into the wide circle of mourning for one last time on this night of deepest grief for deepest wrong done to their people. Kim understood, then, the source of the tales of ghosts in Khath Meigol, for there *were* ghosts in this place when the kanior rites were done. And on this night the pass in the mountains became a realm, truly, of the dead. Still they came, and still Ruana grew, forcing his spirit to grow great enough to reach for them, to carry them all with his song.

Then his voice went deeper yet, with a new note spun within it, and Kim saw that one had come into the circle who was taller than any Giant there, whose eyes, even from beyond the world, were brighter than any other's, and she knew from Ruana's song that this was Connla himself, who had transgressed in binding Owein, and again in making the Cauldron. Connla, who had gone forth from Khath Meigol alone in voluntary exile from his people to be reclaimed on this night when every one of them was being reclaimed and mourned anew.

Kim saw Kevin there, honoured among those gathered. And she saw Ysanne, insubstantial even among ghosts, for she had gone farther away than any of them, had gone so far, with her own sacrifice, that Kim scarcely grasped how Ruana had managed to bring even her shadow back to this place.

And at length there came a time when no new figures were drifting into the ring. Kim looked at Ruana as he swayed slowly back and forth, his eyes closed with the weight of all he was carrying. She saw his hands close tightly in his lap as his voice changed one last time, as it went deeper yet, found access to even purer sorrow.

And one by one, into the humbling amplitude of his soul, he summoned the dead svart alfar and the urgach who had imprisoned his people and slain them and devoured them when they were dead.

Kim had never known an act to match the grandeur of what Ruana did in that moment. It was an assertion, utter and irrefutable, of his people's identity. A clear sound in the wide dark of the night, proclaiming that the Paraiko were still without hate, that they were equal to and greater than the worst of what Rakoth Maugrim could do. That they could endure his evil, and absorb it, and rise above it in the end, continuing to be what they had always been, never less than such and never slaves of the Dark.

524

Kim felt purified in that moment, transfigured by what Ruana was shaping, and when she saw his eyes open and come to rest upon her, even as he sang, she knew what was to come and fearing nothing in his presence she watched him lift a finger and, using it like a blade, lay open the skin on his face and arms in long, deep cuts.

No blood flowed. None at all, though the skin curled back from the gashes he had made and she could see the nerves and arteries exposed within.

He looked at her. With no fear in her, none at all, in a spirit of mourning and expiation, Kim raised her own hands and drew her fingernails along her cheeks and then down the veins of her forearms, feeling the skin slice open to her touch. She was a doctor, and she knew that this could kill.

It did not. No blood welled from her wounds, either, though her tears were falling still. Tears of sorrow and now of gratitude as well, that Ruana had offered her this, had been strong enough to shape a magic so profound that even she, who was not one of the Paraiko, and who carried grief and guilt running so deep, might find absolution in the bloodless rites amid the presence of the dead.

Even as Ruana's voice lifted in the last notes of his kanior, Kim felt her gashes closing, and looking down on her arms she saw the skin knit whole and unscarred, and she gave thanks from the wellspring of her being for what he had given her.

Then she saw the Baelrath burning.

Nothing had ever been worse, not even the summoning of Arthur from his rest in Avalon among the summer stars. The Warrior had been doomed by the will of the Weaver to his long fate of summoning and grief, to restitution through all the years and worlds for having the children slain. She had shattered his rest with that terrible name cried out upon the Tor, and her own heart had almost shattered with the pain of it. But she had not shaped his doom; that had been done long ago. She and the Baelrath had created nothing, had changed nothing. She had only compelled him, in sorrow, to do what he was bound by his destiny to do.

This was different, and unimaginably worse, for with the flaming of the ring the image of her dream was made real, and Kim finally knew why she was here. To free the Paraiko, yes, but not only for that. How could it have been so, in time of war, and being who she was? She had come here drawn by the ring, and the Baelrath was a summoning power. It was wild, allowing no compunction or pity, knowing only the demands of war, the dictates of absolute need.

She was in Khath Meigol to draw the Giants forth. In the most transcendent moment of their long history, the hour of their most triumphant assertion of what they were, she had come to change them: to strip them of their nature and the defences that came with it; to corrupt them; to bring them out to war. Notwithstanding the peace woven into their essence. Notwithstanding the glory of what Ruana had just done, the balm he had offered her soul, the honour he had bestowed upon her two loved ones among the dead.

Notwithstanding everything. She was what she was, and the stone was wild, and it demanded that the Paraiko be undone so they might come to war against

Maugrim. What they could do, she knew not. Such healing clarity was not granted her. That would, she thought, with corrosive bitterness, have made things too easy, wouldn't it?

Nothing was to be made easy for her—or for any of them, she amended inwardly. She thought of Arthur. Of Paul on the Summer Tree. Of Ysanne. Of Kevin in the snow before Dun Maura. Of Finn, and Tabor behind her now. Then she thought of Jennifer in Starkadh, and Darien, and she spoke.

"Ruana, only the Weaver, and perhaps the gods, know whether I will ever be granted forgiveness for what I now must do." After the sonority of the kanior her voice sounded high and harsh. It seemed to bruise the silence. Ruana looked down on her, saying nothing, waiting. He was very weak; she could see the weariness etched into his features.

They would all be ravaged by weakness and hunger, she knew. Easy prey, the inward bitterness added. She shook her head, as if to drive those thoughts away. Her mouth was dry when she swallowed. She saw Ruana look at the Baelrath. It was alive, driving her.

She said, "You may yet wish you had never chanted the savesong to bring me here. But it might be that the Warstone would have drawn me to this place, even had you kept silent. I do not know. I do know that I have come not only to set you free, *but to bring you down, by the power I bear, to war against Rakoth Maugrim.*"

There was a sound from the Paraiko gathered around them, but watching only Ruana, she saw that his grave eyes did not change. He said, very softly, "We cannot go to war, Seer. We cannot fight, nor can we hate."

"Then I must teach you!" she cried, over the grief rising within her, as the Warstone blazed more brilliantly than it ever had before.

There was real pain. Looking at her hand she saw it as within a writhing nest of flame, brighter than the bonfires, too fierce, almost, to look upon. Almost. She had to look, and she did. The Baelrath was her power, wild and merciless, but hers was the will and the knowledge, the Seer's wisdom needed to turn the power to work. It might seem as if the stone were compelling her, but she knew that was not truly so. It was responding—to need, to war, to the half-glimpsed intuitions of her dreams—but it needed her will to unleash its power. So she shouldered the weight, accepted the price of power, and looking into the heart of the fire enveloping her hand she cast a mental image into it and watched as the Baelrath threw it back, incarnate, suspended in the air within the circle of the Paraiko. An image that would teach the Giants how to hate and so break them of their sanctity.

An image of Jennifer Lowell, whom they knew now to be Guinevere, naked and alone in Starkadh before Maugrim. They saw the Unraveller then, huge in his hooded cloak, faceless save for his eyes. They saw his maimed hand, they watched him hold it over her body so that the black dripping blood might burn her where it fell, and Kimberly's own burning seemed as nothing before what she saw. They heard Jennifer speak, so blazingly defiant in that unholy place that it could break the heart to hear, and they heard him laugh and fall upon her in his foulness. They watched him begin to change his shapes, and they heard what was said and understood that he was tearing her mind apart to find avenues for torture.

It went on for a very long time. Kim felt wave after wave of nausea rising within her, but she forced herself to watch. Jennifer had been there, had lived through this and survived it, and the Paraiko were being stripped of their collective soul through the horror of this image. They could not look away, the power of the Baelrath compelled them, and so she would watch it, too. A penance, in the most trivial sense she knew. Seeking expiation where none could possibly come. But she watched. She saw Blöd the Dwarf when he was drawn into the image, and she grieved for Brock, being forced to see this ultimate betrayal.

She saw it all, through to the end.

Afterwards, it was utterly silent in Khath Meigol. She could not hear anyone breathe. Her own numbed, battered soul longed for sound. For birdsong, water falling, the laughter of children. She needed light. Warmer, kinder light than the red glow of the fires, or the mountain stars, or the moon.

She was granted none of these. Instead she was made conscious of something else. From the moment they had entered Khath Meigol there had been fear: an awareness of the presence of the dead in all their inviolate sanctity, guarding this place with the bloodcurse that was woven into them.

Not anymore.

She did not weep. This went too far beyond sorrow. It touched the very fabric of the Tapestry on the Loom. She held her right hand close to her breast; it was blistered and painful to the touch. The Baelrath smouldered, embers seeming to glow far down in its depths.

"Who are you?" Ruana asked, and his voice broke on the words. "Who are you to have done this deed unto us? Better we had died in the caves."

It hurt so much. She opened her mouth, but no words came.

"Not so," a voice replied for her. It was Brock, loyal, steadfast Brock of Banir Tal. "Not so, people of the Paraiko." His voice was weak when he began, but grew in strength with every word. "You know who she is, and you know the nature of what she carries. We are at war, and the Warstone of Macha and Nemain summons at need. Would you value your peacefulness so highly that you granted Maugrim dominion? How long would you survive if we went away from here and were destroyed in war? Who would remember your sanctity when all of you and all of us were dead or slaves?"

"The Weaver would," Ruana replied gently

It stopped Brock, but only for a moment. "So, too, would Rakoth," he said. "And you have heard his laughter, Ruana. Had the Weaver shaped your destiny to be sacrosanct and inviolate, could you have been changed by the image we have seen tonight? Could you hate the Dark as now you do? Could you have been brought into the army of Light, as now you are? Surely this is your true destiny, people of Khath Meigol. A destiny that allows you to grow when the need is great, however bitter the pain. To come forth from hiding in these caves and make one with all of us, in all the Weaver's worlds afflicted by the Dark."

He ended ringingly. There was silence again. Then: "We are undone," came a voice from the circle of the Giants.

"We have lost the bloodcurse."

"And the kanior." A wailing rose up, heartrending in its grief and loss.

"Hold!" Another voice. Not Ruana. Not Brock. "People of the Paraiko," said Dalreidan, "forgive me this presumption, but I have a question to ask of you."

Slowly, the wailing died away. Ruana inclined his head towards the outlaw from the Plain. "In what you did tonight," Dalreidan asked, "in the very great thing you did tonight did you not sense a farewell? In the kanior that gathered and mourned every Paraiko that ever was, could you not find a sign from the Weaver who shaped you that an ending to something had come?"

Holding her breath, clutching her burned hand, Kim waited. And then Ruana spoke.

"I did," he said, as a sigh like a wind in trees swept over the bare plateau. "I did sense that when I saw Connla come, how bright he was. The only one of us who ever stepped forward to act in the world beyond this pass, when he bound the Hunt to their long sleep, which our people called a transgression, even though Owein had asked him to do so. And then he built the Cauldron to bring his daughter back from death, which was a wrong beyond remedy and led him to his exile. When I saw him tonight, how mighty he was among our dead, I knew that a change was come."

Kim gasped, a cry of relief torn from her pain.

Ruana turned to her. Carefully he rose, to tower over her in the midst of the ring. He said, "Forgive me my harshness. This will have been a grief for you, as much as for us."

She shook her head, still unable to speak.

"We will come down," he said. "It is time. We will leave this place and play a part in what is to come. But hear me," he added, "and know this for truth: *we will not kill*."

And with that, finally, words came to her. She, too, rose to her feet. "I do know it for truth," she replied, and it was the Seer of Breenin who spoke now. "I do not think you are meant to. You have changed, but not so much as that, and not all your gifts, I think, are lost."

"Not all," he echoed gravely. "Seer, where would you have us go? To Brennin? Andarien? To Eridu?"

"Eridu is no more." Faebur spoke for the first time. Ruana turned to him. "The death rain fell there for three days, until this morning. There will be no one left in any of the places of the Lion."

Watching Ruana, Kim saw something alter deep in his eyes. "I know of that rain," he said. "We all do. It is a part of our memories. It was a death rain that began the ruin of Andarien. It only fell for a few hours then. Maugrim was not so strong."

Fighting his weariness with a visible effort, he drew himself up very straight.

"Seer, this is the first role we will play. There will be plague with the rain, and no hope of return to Eridu until the dead are buried. But the plague will not harm the Paraiko. You were not wrong: we have not lost all of what the Weaver gave to us.

Only the bloodcurse and the kanior, which were shaped of the peace in our hearts. We have other magics, though, and most of them are ways of dealing with death, as Connla's Cauldron was. We will go east from this place in the morning, to cleanse the raindead of Eridu, that the land may live again."

Faebur looked up at him. "Thank you," he whispered. "If any of us live through the dark of these days, it will not be forgotten." He hesitated. "If, when you come to the largest house in the Merchant's Street of Akkaïze, you find lying there a lady, tall and slender, whose hair would once have gleamed the colour of wheat fields in sunlight . . . her name will have been Arrian. Will you gather her gently for my sake?"

"We will," said Ruana, with infinite compassion. "And if we meet again, I will tell you where she lies."

Kim turned and walked from the circle. They parted to make way for her, and she went to the edge of the plateau and stood, her back to everyone else, gazing at the dark mountains and the stars. Her hand was blistered and painful to the touch, and her side ached from yesterday. The ring was utterly spent; it seemed to be slumbering. She needed sleep herself, she knew. There were thoughts chasing each other around In her head, and something else, not clear enough yet to be a thought, was beginning to take shape. She was wise enough not to strain for the Sight that was coming, so she had walked towards darkness to wait.

She heard voices behind her. She did not turn, but they were not far away, and she could not help but hear.

"Forgive me," Dalreidan said, and coughed nervously. "But I heard a story yesterday that the women and children of the Dalrei had been left alone in the last camp by the Latham. Is this so?"

"It is," Tabor replied. His voice sounded remote and thin, but he answered the exile with courtesy. "Every Rider on the Plain went north to Celidon. An army of the Dark was seen sweeping across Andarien three nights ago. The Aven was trying to outrace them to the Adein."

Kim had known nothing of this. She closed her eyes, trying to calculate the distance and the time, but could not. She offered an inner prayer to the night. If the Dalrei were lost, everything the rest of them did might be quite meaningless.

"The Aven!" Dalreidan exclaimed softly. "We have an Aven? Who?"

"Ivor dan Banor," Tabor said, and Kim could hear the pride. "My father." Then, after a moment, as the other remained silent, "Do you know him?"

"I knew him," said Dalreidan. "If you are his son, you must be Levon."

"Tabor. Levon is my older brother. How do you know him? What tribe are you from?"

In the silence that followed, Kim could almost hear the older man struggle with himself. But, "I am tribeless," was all he said. His footsteps receded as he walked back towards the circle of Giants.

She was not alone, Kim thought, in carrying sorrows tonight. The conversation had disturbed her, stirring up yet another nagging thread at the corner of her awareness. She turned her thoughts inwards again, reaching for quiet.

"Are you all right?"

Imraith-Nimphais moved silently; Tabor's voice coming so near startled her. This time she did turn, grateful for the kindness in the question. She was painfully aware of what she had done to them. And the more so when she looked at Tabor. He was deathly pale, almost another ghost in Khath Meigol.

"I think so," she said. "And you?"

He shrugged, a boy's gesture. But he was so much more, had been forced to be so much more. She looked at the creature he rode and saw that the horn was clean again, shining softly in the night.

He followed her glance. "During the kanior," he said, wonder in his voice, "while Ruana chanted, the blood left her horn. I don't know how."

"He was absolving you," she said. "The kanior is a very great magic." She paused. "It was," she amended, as the truth hit home. She had ended it. She looked back towards the Paraiko. Those who could walk were bringing water from over the ridge—there had to be a stream or a well—to the others. Her companions were helping them. As she watched, she began, finally, to cry.

And suddenly, astonishingly, as she wept, Imraith-Nimphais lowered her beautiful head, careful of the horn, and nuzzled her gently. The gesture, so totally unexpected, opened the last floodgates of Kim's heart. She looked up at Tabor through her tears and saw him nod permission; then she threw her arms about the neck of the glorious creature she had summoned and ordered to kill, and laying her head against that of Imraith-Nimphais, she let herself weep.

No one disturbed them, no one came near. After some time, she didn't know how long, Kim stepped back. She looked up at Tabor. He smiled. "Do you know," he said, "that you cry as much as my father does?"

For the first time in days she laughed, and Ivor's son laughed with her. "I know," she gasped. "I know I do. Isn't it terrible?"

He shook his head. "Not if you can do what you did," he said quietly. As abruptly as it had surfaced, the boyishness was gone. It was Imraith-Nimphais's rider who said, "We must go. I am guarding the camps and have been too long away."

She had been stroking the silken mane. Now she stepped back, and as she did so, the Sight that had been eluding her, drifting at the edges of her mind, suddenly coalesced enough for her to see where she had to go. She looked at the Baelrath; it was dulled and powerless. She wasn't surprised. This awareness came from the Seer in her, the soul she shared with Ysanne.

She hesitated, looking up at Tabor. "I have one thing more to ask of you. Will she carry me? I have a long way to travel, and not enough time."

His glance was distanced already, but it was level and calm. "She will," he said. "You know her name. We will carry you, Seer, anywhere you must go."

It was time, then, to make her farewells. She looked over and saw that her three guides were standing together, not far away.

"Where shall we go?" Faebur asked.

"To Celidon," she answered. A number of things were coming clearer even as she stood here, and there was urgency in her. "There was a battle, and it is there that you will find the army, those who survived."

She looked at Dalreidan, who was hesitating, hanging back. "My friend," she said, in the hearing of all of them, "you said words to Faebur this morning that rang true: no one in Fionavar is an exile now. Go home, Dalreidan, and take your true name on the Plain. Tell them the Seer of Brennin sent you."

For a moment he remained frozen, resisting. Then he nodded slowly. "We will meet again?" he asked.

"I hope," she said, and stepped forward to embrace him, and then Faebur as well. She looked at Brock. "And you?" she asked.

"I will go with them," he answered. "Until my own King comes home I will serve the Aven and the High King as best I can. Will you be careful, Seer?" His voice was gruff.

She moved closer and out of habit checked the bandage she'd wrapped about his head. Then she bent and kissed him on the lips. "You, too," she whispered. "My dear."

At the very last she turned to Ruana, who had been waiting for her. They said nothing aloud.

Then in her mind she heard him murmur: *The Weaver hold your thread fast in his hand, Seer.*

It was what, more than anything else, she had needed to hear—this last forgiveness where she had no right to any. She looked up at his great, white-bearded patriarch's head, at the wise eyes that had seen so much. *And yours*, she replied, in silence. *Your thread, and that of your people.*

Then she walked slowly back to where Tabor waited, and she mounted behind him upon Imraith-Nimphais, and told him where it was she had to go, and they flew.

There were hours yet before dawn when he set her down. Not at a place of war but in the one place in Fionavar where she had known a moment's peace. A quiet place. A lake like a jewel, with moonlight glancing along it. A cottage by the lake.

He was in the air again, hovering, as soon as she dismounted. He wanted to be back, she knew. His father had given him a task and she had drawn him from it, twice now.

"Thank you," she said. There was nothing more she could think of to say. She raised a hand in farewell.

As he did the same she saw, grieving, that the moonlight and the stars were shining through him. Then Imraith-Nimphais spread her wings, and she and her rider were gone. Another star for a moment, and then nothing at all.

Kim went into the cottage.

# PART II

# LISEN'S TOWER

# CHAPTER 4

Leaning back against the railing of the afterdeck, Paul watched Lancelot duelling with his shadow. It had been going on for most of yesterday, from the time they sailed from Cader Sedat, and had continued for much of this second morning and into the afternoon. The sun was behind them now. Lancelot stood with his back to it and advanced and retreated along the deck, his feet sliding and turning intricately, his sword a blur of thrusts and parries, too fast to follow properly.

Almost every man on *Prydwen* had spent some time watching him, either covertly or, as Paul was, with open admiration. He had finally begun to pick out some of the disciplined patterns in what Lancelot was doing. And as he watched it go on and on, Paul understood something else.

This was more than merely training on the part of someone newly wakened from the Chamber of the Dead. In these relentless, driven repetitions Paul had finally begun to see that Lancelot was masking, as best he could, the emotions rising within himself.

He watched the dark-haired man go through his systematic drills without fuss or wasted motion of any kind. Now and always there was a quiet to Lancelot, a sense of a still pool wherein the ripples of turbulent life were effortlessly absorbed. On one level it was deeply reassuring and that reassurance had been present from the moment he had come among them, rising from his bed of stone to bring Matt Sören back from the dead, as well.

Paul Schafer was too wise, though, for that to be the only level on which he perceived what was happening. He was Pwyll Twiceborn, had spoken to gods and summoned them, had lived three nights on the Summer Tree, and the ravens of Mörnir were never far from him. *Prydwen* was sailing back to war, and Lancelot's training was apt and fit for the role he would play when they landed again.

They were also sailing back to something else, to someone else: to Guinevere.

In Lancelot's compulsive physical action, however disciplined it might be, Paul read that truth as clearly as in a book, and the themes of the book were absolute love and absolute betrayal, and a sadness that could bind the heart.

Arthur Pendragon, at the prow with Cavall, gazing east, was the only man on the ship who had not taken a moment to watch Lancelot duel his shadow's sword. The two men had not spoken since walking from the wreckage of Cader Sedat. There was no hatred between them, or even anger, or manifest rivalry that Paul could see. He saw, instead, a guarding, a shielding of the self, a tight rein kept on the heart.

Paul remembered—knew he would never forget—the few words they had spoken to each other on the island: Lancelot, newly wakened, asking with utmost courtesy, *Why have you done this, my lord, to the three of us?*

And Arthur, at the very end, the last doorway of that shattered, bloody hall: *Oh, Lance, come. She will be waiting for you.*

No hatred or rivalry there but something worse, more hurtful: love, and defences thrown up against it, in the sure foreknowledge of what was to come. Of the story to be played out again, as it had been so many times, when *Prydwen* came again to land.

Paul took his eyes from that fluid, mesmerizing form moving up and down the deck, repeating and repeating the same flawless rituals of the blade. He turned away, looking out to sea over the port railing. He would have to defend his own heart, he realized. He could not afford to lose himself in the woven sorrow of those three. He had his own burdens and his own destiny waiting, his own role to play, his own terrible unspoken anxiety. Which had a name, the name of a child who was no longer a child, of the boy who had taken himself, in the Godwood just a week ago, most of the way to his adulthood and most of the way to his power. Jennifer's son. And Rakoth Maugrim's.

Darien. He was not Dari anymore, not since that afternoon by the Summer Tree. He had walked into that place as a little boy who had just learned to skip pebbles across a lake and had gone forth as someone very different, someone older, wilder, wielding fire, changing shape, confused, alienated, unimaginably powerful. Son of the darkest god. The wild card in the deck of war.

Random, his mother had called him, knowing more, perhaps, than any of them. Not that there was reassurance in that. For if Darien was random, truly so, he could do anything. He could go either way. Never, Brendel of the lios alfar had said, never had there been any living creature in any of the worlds so poised between Light and Dark. Never anyone to compare with this boy on the brink of manhood, who was graceful and handsome, and whose eyes were blue except when they were red.

Dark thoughts. And there was no light, or approach to it, at the memory of Brendel, either: Brendel, to whom he was going to have to tell, or stand by while others told the story of the Soulmonger and the fate of all the lios alfar who had sailed west in answer to their song since the Bael Rangat. Paul sighed, looking out at the sea curling away from the motion of the ship. Liranan was down there, he knew, the elusive sea god moving through his element. Paul had a longing to summon him again, questions to ask, comfort, even, to seek, in the knowledge of sea stars shining again in the place where the Soulmonger had been slain. Wishful thinking, that. He was far too distant from the source of whatever power he had, and far too unsure of how to channel that power, even when it was ready to hand.

536

Really, when it came down to it, there was only one thing he knew for certain. There was a meeting in his future, a third meeting, and it drifted through his sleep and his daytime reveries. Along the very tracings of his blood, Paul knew that he would meet Galadan one more time, and not again. His fate and the Wolflord's were warp and weft to each other, and the Weaver alone knew whose thread was marked to be cut when they crossed.

Footsteps crossed the deck behind him, cutting against the rhythm of Lancelot's steady advance and retreat. Then a light, utterly distinctive voice spoke clearly.

"My lord Lancelot, if it would please you, I think I might test you somewhat better than your shadow," said Diarmuid dan Ailell.

Paul turned. Lancelot, perspiring slightly, regarded Diarmuid with grave courtesy in his face and bearing. "I should be grateful for it," he said, with a gentle smile. "It has been a long time since I faced someone with a sword. Have you wooden ones then, training swords aboard ship?"

It was Diarmuid's turn to smile, eyes dancing under the fair hair bleached even paler by the sun overhead. It was an expression most of the men aboard knew very well. "Unfortunately not," he murmured, "but I would hazard that we are both skilled enough to use our blades without doing harm." He paused. "Serious harm," he amended.

There was a little silence, broken by a third voice, from farther up the deck. "Diarmuid, this is hardly the time for games, let alone dangerous ones."

The tone of command in Loren Silvercloak's voice was, if anything, even stronger since the mage had ceased to be a mage. He looked and spoke with undiminished authority, with, it seemed, a clearer sense of purpose, ever since the moment Matt had been brought back from his death and Loren had vowed himself to the service of his old friend who had been King under Banir Lök before he was source to a mage in Paras Derval.

At the same time, the ambit of his authority—of anyone's, for that matter—seemed always to come to a sharp terminus at the point where Diarmuid's own wishes began. Especially this kind of wish. Against his will, Paul's mouth crooked upward as he gazed at the Prince. Out of the corner of his eye he saw Erron and Rothe handing slips of paper to Carde. Wagers. He shook his head bemusedly.

Diarmuid drew his sword. "We are at sea," he said to Loren with exaggerated reasonableness, "and at least a day's sailing, perhaps more, depending on the winds and our marginally competent captain"—a fleeting glance spared for Coll, shirtless at the helm—"from reaching land. There may never be a more felicitous occasion for play. My lord?"

The last question was directed at Lancelot, with a salute of the sword, angled in such a way that the sun glinted from it into Lancelot's eyes—who laughed unaffectedly, returned the salute, and moved neatly to the side, his own blade extended.

"For the sacred honour of the Black Boar!" Diarmuid said loudly, to whistles and cheers. He flourished his steel with a motion of wrist and shoulder.

"For my lady, the Queen," said Lancelot automatically.

It shaped an immediate stillness. Paul looked instinctively towards the prow. Arthur stood gazing outward towards where land would be, quite oblivious to all of them. After a moment, Paul turned back, for the blades had touched, ritually, and were dancing now.

He'd never seen Diarmuid with a sword. He'd heard the stories about both of Ailell's sons, but this was his initial encounter at first hand and, watching, he learned something else about why the men of South Keep followed their Prince with such unwavering loyalty. It was more than just the imagination and zest that could conjure moments like this out of a grim ship on a wide sea. It was the uncomplicated truth— in a decidedly complex man—that he was unnervingly good at everything he did. Including swordplay, Paul now saw, with no surprise at all.

The surprise, though thinking about it later Paul would wonder at his unpreparedness, was how urgently the Prince was struggling, from the first touch of blades, to hold his own.

For this was Lancelot du Lac, and no one, ever, had been as good.

With the same economic, almost abstract precision with which he had duelled his shadow, the man who had lain in a chamber undersea among the mightiest dead in all the worlds showed the men of *Prydwen* why.

They were using naked blades and moving very fast on a swaying ship. To Paul's untutored eye there was real danger in the thrusts and cuts they levelled at each other. Looking past the shouting men, he glanced at Loren and then at Coll and read the same concern in both of them.

He thought about interceding, knew they would stop for him, but even with the thought he became aware of his own racing pulse, of the degree to which Diarmuid had just lifted him—all of them—into a mood completely opposite to the hollow silence of fifteen minutes before. He stayed where he was. The Prince, he realized, knew exactly what he was doing.

In more ways than one. Diarmuid, retreating before Lancelot's blurred attack, managed to angle himself towards a coil of rope looped on the deck. Timing it perfectly, he quick-stepped backward, spun around the coil, and, bending low, scythed a cut at Lancelot's knees, a full, crippling cut.

It was blocked by a withdrawn blade, a very quickly withdrawn blade. Lancelot stood up, stepped back, and with a bright joy in his dark eyes cried, "Bravely done!"

Diarmuid, wiping sweat from his own eyes with a billowing sleeve, grinned ferociously. Then he leaped to attack, without warning. For a few quick paces Lancelot gave ground but then, again, his sword began to blur with the speed of its motion, and he was advancing, forcing Diarmuid back towards the hatchway leading belowdeck.

Engrossed, utterly forgetful of everything else, Paul watched the Prince give ground. He saw something else, as well: even as he retreated, parrying, Diarmuid's eyes were darting away from Lancelot to where Paul stood at the rail—or past him, actually—beyond his shoulder, out to sea. Just as Paul was turning to see what it was, he heard the Prince scream, *"Paul! Look out!"*

The whole company spun to look, including Lancelot. Which enabled Diarmuid effortlessly to thrust his blade forward, following up on his transparent deception—

—and have it knocked flying from his hand, as Lancelot extended his spin into a full pirouette, bringing him back to face Diarmuid but down on one knee, his sword sweeping with the power of that full, lightning-quick arc to crash into Diarmuid's and send it flying, almost off the deck.

It was over. There was a moment's stunned silence, then Diarmuid burst into full-throated laughter and, stepping forward, embraced Lancelot vigorously as the men of South Keep roared their approval.

"Unfair, Lance," came a deep voice, richly amused. "You've seen that move before. He didn't have a chance." Arthur Pendragon was standing halfway up the deck.

Paul hadn't seen him come. None of them had. With a lifting heart, he saw the smile on the Warrior's face and the answering gleam in Lancelot's eyes, and again he saluted Diarmuid inwardly.

The Prince was still laughing. "A chance?" he gasped breathlessly. "I would have had to tie him down to have a chance!"

Lancelot smiled, still composed, self-contained, but not repressively so. He looked at Arthur. "You remember?" he asked. "I'd almost forgotten. Gawain tried that once, didn't he?"

"He did," Arthur said, still amused.

"It almost worked."

"Almost," Arthur agreed. "But it didn't. Gawain could never beat you, Lance. He tried all his life."

And with those words, a cloud, though the sky was still as blue, the afternoon sun as bright as before. Arthur's brief smile faded, then Lancelot's. The two men looked at each other, their expressions suddenly unreadable, laden with a weight of history. Amid the sudden stillness of *Prydwen* Arthur turned again, Cavall to heel, and went back to the prow.

His heart aching, Paul looked at Diarmuid, who returned the gaze with an expression devoid of mirth. He would explain later, Paul decided. The Prince could not know: none of the others except, perhaps, Loren could know what Paul knew.

Knowledge not born of the ravens or the Tree but from the lore of his own world: the knowledge that Gawain of the Round Table had, indeed, tried all his life to defeat Lancelot in battle. They were friendly battles, all of them, until the very end—which had come for him at Lancelot's own hand in a combat that was part of a war. A war that Arthur was forced to fight after Lancelot had saved Guinevere from burning at the stake in Camelot.

Diarmuid had tried, Paul thought sadly. It was a gallant attempt. But the doom of these two men and the woman waiting for them was far too intricately shaped to be lifted, even briefly, by access to laughter or joy.

"Look sharp, you laggards!" Coll's prosaic, carrying voice broke into his reverie. "We've a ship to sail, and it may need some sailing yet. Wind's shifting, Diar!"

Paul looked back, south and west to where Coll's extended arm was pointing. The breeze was now very strong, he realized. It had come up during the swordplay.

As he looked back he could discern, straining, a line of darkness at the horizon.

And in that moment he felt the stillness within his blood that marked the presence of Mörnir.

✦⟾◉⟾✦

Younger brothers were not supposed to ride creatures of such unbridled power. Or to sound or look as had Tabor last night, before he took flight towards the mountains. True she'd overheard her parents talking about it many times (she managed to overhear a great deal), and she'd been present three nights ago when her father had entrusted the guarding of the women and children to Tabor alone.

But she'd never seen the creature of his fast until last night, and so it was only then that Liane had truly begun to understand what had happened to her younger brother. She was more like her mother than her father: she didn't cry often or easily. But she'd understood that it was dangerous for Tabor to fly, and then she'd heard the strangeness in his voice when he mounted up, and so she had wept when he flew away.

She had remained awake all night, sitting in the doorway of the house she shared with her mother and brother, until, a little before dawn, there had been a falling star in the sky just west of them, near the river.

A short time later Tabor had walked back into the camp, raising a hand to the astonished women on guard. He touched his sister lightly on the shoulder before he passed inside, unspeaking, and fell into bed.

It was more than weariness, she knew, but there was nothing she could do. So she had gone to bed herself, to a fitful sleep and dreams of Gwen Ystrat, and of the fair-haired man from another world who had become Liadon, and the spring.

She was up with the sunrise, before her mother even, which was unusual. She dressed and walked out, after checking to see that Tabor still slept. Aside from those on guard at the gates, the camp was quiet. She looked east to the foothills and the mountains, and then west to see the sparkle of the Latham, and the Plain unrolling beyond. As a little girl she'd thought the Plain went on forever; in some ways she still did.

It was a beautiful morning, and for all her cares and the shallow sleep she'd had, her heart lifted a little to hear the birds and smell the freshness of the morning air.

She went to check on Gereint.

Entering the shaman's house, she paused a moment to let her eyes adjust to the darkness. They had been checking on him several times a day, she and Tabor: a duty, and a labour of love. But the aged shaman had not moved at all from the moment they had carried him here, and his expression had spoken of such terrible anguish that Liane could hardly bear to look at him.

She did, though, every time, searching for clues, for ways of aiding him. How did one offer aid to someone whose soul was journeying so far away? She didn't know. She had her father's love of their people, her mother's calm stability, her own headstrong nature, and not a little courage. But where Gereint had gone, none of these seemed to matter. She came anyhow, and so did Tabor: just to be present, to share, in however small a way.

So she stood on his threshold again, waiting for the darkness to clear a little, and then she heard a voice she'd known all her life say, in a tone she'd also known all her life, "How long does an old man have to wait for breakfast these days?"

She screamed a little, a girlish habit she was still trying to outgrow. Then she seemed to have covered the distance into the room very fast, for she was on her knees beside Gereint, and hugging him, and crying just as her father would have and, for this, perhaps even her mother, too.

"I know," he said patiently, patting her back. "I know. You are deeply sorry. It will never happen again. I know all that. But Liane, a hug in the morning, however nice, is *not* breakfast."

She was laughing and crying at the same time, and trying to hold him as close as she could without hurting his brittle bones. "Oh Gereint," she whispered, "I'm so glad you're back. So much has happened."

"I'm sure," he said, in a different voice entirely. "Now be still a moment and let me read it in you. It will be quicker than the telling."

She did. It had happened so many times before that it no longer felt strange. This power was at the heart of what the shamans were; it came with their blinding. In a very little time Gereint sighed and leaned back a little, deep in thought.

After a moment, she asked, "Did you do what you went to do?"

He nodded.

"Was it very difficult?"

Another nod. Nothing more, but she had known him a long time, and she was her father's daughter. She had also seen his face as he journeyed. She felt an inner stirring of pride. Gereint was theirs, and whatever he had done, it was something very great.

There was another question in her, but this one she was afraid to ask. "I'll get you some food," she said, preparing to rise.

With Gereint, though, you seldom had to ask. "Liane," he murmured, "I can't tell you for certain, because I am not yet strong enough to reach as far as Celidon. But I think I would know already if something very bad had happened there. They are all right, child. We will have fuller tidings later, but you can tell your mother that they are all right."

Relief burst within her like another sunrise. She threw her arms around his neck and kissed him again.

Gruffly he said, "This is still not breakfast! And I should warn you that in my day any woman who did that had to be prepared to do a good deal more!"

She laughed breathlessly. "Oh, Gereint, I would lie down with you in gladness any time you asked."

For once, he seemed taken aback. "No one has said that particular thing to me for a very long time," he said after a moment. "Thank you, child. But see to breakfast, and bring your brother to me instead." She was who she was, and irrepressible.

"Gereint!" she exclaimed, in mock astonishment.

"I knew you would say that!" he growled. "Your father never did teach his children proper manners. That is not amusing, Liane dal Ivor. Now go get your brother. He has just awakened."

She left still giggling. "And breakfast!" he shouted after her.

Only when he was quite sure she was out of earshot did he allow himself to laugh. He laughed a long time, for he was deeply pleased. He was back on the Plain where he'd never thought to be again, once having ventured out over the waves. But he had, indeed, done what he'd set out to do, and his soul had survived. And whatever had happened at Celidon, it was not too bad, it could not be, or, even weakened as he was, he would have known from the moment of his return.

So he laughed for several moments and allowed himself—it wasn't hard—to look forward to his meal.

Everything changed when Tabor came. He entered the mind of the boy and saw what was happening to him, and then read the tale of what the Seer had done in Khath Meigol. After that his food was tasteless in his mouth, and there were ashes in his heart.

⤛⫘◖⫘⤜

She walked in the garden behind the domed Temple with the High Priestess—if, Sharra thought to herself, this tiny enclosure could properly be said to constitute a garden. For one raised in Larai Rigal and familiar with every pathway, waterfall, and spreading tree within its walls, the question almost answered itself.

Still, there were unexpected treasures here. She paused beside a bed of sylvain, silver and dusty rose. She hadn't known they grew so far south. There were none in Cathal; sylvain was said to flourish only on the banks of Celyn Lake, by Daniloth. They were the flower of the lios alfar. She said as much to Jaelle.

The Priestess glanced at the flowers with only mild attention. "They were a gift," she murmured. "A long time ago, when Ra-Lathen wove the mist over Daniloth and the lios began the long withdrawal. They sent us sylvain by which to remember them. They grow here, and in the palace gardens as well. Not many, the soil is wrong or some such thing—but there are always some of them, and these seem to have survived the winter and the drought."

Sharra looked at her. "It means nothing to you, does it?" she said. "Does anything, I wonder?"

"In flowers?" Jaelle raised her eyebrows. Then, after a pause, she said, "Actually, there *were* flowers that mattered: the ones outside Dun Maura when the snow began to melt."

Sharra remembered. They had been red, blood red for the sacrifice. Again she glanced at her companion. It was a warm morning, but in her white robe Jaelle looked icily cool, and there was a keen, cutting edge to her beauty. There was very little mildness or placidity about Sharra herself, and the man she was to wed would carry all his life the scar of a knife she'd thown at him, but with Jaelle it was different, and provoking.

"Of course," the Princess of Cathal murmured. "Those flowers would matter. Does anything else, though? Or does absolutely everything have to circle back to the Goddess in order to reach through to you?"

"Everything *does* circle back to her," Jaelle said automatically. But then, after a pause, she went on, impatiently. "Why does everyone ask me things like that? What, exactly, do you all expect from the High Priestess of Dana?" Her eyes, green as the grass in sunlight, held Sharra's and challenged her.

In the face of that challenge, Sharra began to regret having brought it up. She was still too impetuous; it often took her out beyond her depth. She was, after all, a guest in the Temple. "Well—" she began apologetically.

And got no further. "Really!" Jaelle exclaimed. "I have no idea what people want of me. I am High Priestess. I have power to channel, a Mormae to control—and Dana knows, with Audiart that takes doing. I have rituals to preserve, counsel to give. With the High King away I have a realm to govern with the Chancellor. How should I be other than I am? What do you all *want* from me?"

Astonishingly, she had to turn away towards the flowers, to hide her face. Sharra was bemused, and momentarily moved, but she was from a country where subtlety of mind was a necessity for survival, and she was the daughter and heir of the Supreme Lord of Cathal.

"It isn't really me you're talking to, is it?" she asked quietly. "Who were the others?"

After a moment Jaelle, who had, it seemed, courage to go with everything else, turned back to look at her. The green eyes were dry, but there was a question in their depths.

They heard a footstep on the path.

"Yes, Leila?" Jaelle said, almost before she turned. "What is it? And why do you continue to enter places where you should not be?" The words were stern, but not, surprisingly, the tone.

Sharra looked at the thin girl with the straight, fair hair who had screamed in real pain when the Wild Hunt flew. There was some diffidence in Leila's expression, but not a great deal.

"I am sorry," she said. "But I thought you would want to know. The Seer is in the cottage where Finn and his mother stayed with the little one."

Jaelle's expression changed swiftly. "Kim? Truly? You are tuned to the place itself, Leila?"

"I seem to be," the girl replied gravely, as if it were the most ordinary thing imaginable.

Jaelle looked at her for a long time, and Sharra, only half understanding, saw pity in the eyes of the High Priestess. "Tell me," Jaelle asked the girl gently, "do you see Finn now? Where he is riding?"

Leila shook her head. "Only when they were summoned I saw him then, though I could not speak to him. He was . . . too cold. And where they are now it is too cold for me to follow."

"Don't try, Leila," Jaelle said earnestly. "Don't even try."

"It has nothing to do with trying," the girl said simply, and something in the words, the calm acceptance, stirred pity in Sharra as well.

But it was to Jaelle that she spoke. "If Kim is nearby," she said, "can we go to her?"

Jaelle nodded. "I have things to discuss with her."

"Are there horses here? Let's go."

The High Priestess smiled thinly. "As easily as that? There is," she murmured with delicate precision, "a distinction between independence and irresponsibility, my dear. You are your father's heir, and betrothed—or did you forget?—to the heir of Brennin. And I am charged with half the governance of this realm. And—or did you forget that too?—we are at war. There were svart alfar slain on that path a year ago. We will have to arrange an escort for you if you intend to join me, Princess of Cathal. Excuse me, if you will, while I tend to the details."

And she brushed smoothly past Sharra on the pebbled walkway.

Revenge, the Princess thought ruefully. She had trespassed on very private terrain and had just paid the price. Nor, she knew, was Jaelle wrong. Which only made the rebuke more galling. Deep in thought, she turned and followed the High Priestess back into the Temple.

In the end, it took a fair bit of time to get the short expedition untracked and on the road to the lake, largely because the preposterous fat man, Tegid, whom Diarmuid had elected as his Intercedent in the matter of their marriage, refused to allow her to ride forth without him, even in the care of the Priestess and a guard from both Brennin and Cathal. And since there was only one horse in the capital large enough to survive martyrdom under Tegid's bulk, and that horse was quartered in the South Keep barracks on the other side of Paras Derval . . .

It was almost noon before they got under way, and as a consequence they were too late to do anything at all about what happened.

⋆⇒◉⇐⋆

In the small hours of that morning, Kimberly, asleep in the cottage by the lake, crossed a narrow bridge over a chasm filled with nameless, shapeless horrors, and when she stood on the other side a figure approached her in the dream, and terror rose in her like a mutant shape in that lonely, blighted place.

On her pallet in the cottage, never waking, she tossed violently from side to side, one hand raised unconsciously in rejection and denial. For the first and only time she fought her Seer's vision, struggling to change the image of the figure that stood there with her on the farther side. To alter—not merely foresee—the loops spun into time on the Loom. To no avail.

It was to dream this dream that Ysanne had made Kim a Seer, had relinquished her own soul to do so. She had said as much. There were no surprises here, only terror and renunciation, helpless in the face of this vast inevitability.

In the cottage the sleeping figure ceased her struggling; the uplifted, warding hand fell back. In the dream she stood quietly on the far side of the chasm, facing what had come. This meeting had been waiting for her from the beginning. It was as true as anything had ever been true. And so now, with the dreaming of it, with the crossing of that bridge, the ending had begun.

It was late in the morning when she finally woke. After the dream she had fallen back into the deeper, healing sleep her exhausted body so desperately needed. Now she lay in bed a little while, looking at the sunlight that streamed in through the open windows, deeply grateful for the small grace of rest in this place. There were birds singing outside, and the breeze carried the scent of flowers. She could hear the lake slapping against the rocks along the shore.

She rose and went out into the brightness of the day. Down the familiar path she walked, to the broad flat rock overhanging the lake where she had knelt when Ysanne threw a bannion into the moonlit waters and summoned Eilathen to spin for her.

He was down there now, she knew, deep in his halls of seaweed and stone, free of the binding flowerfire, uncaring of what happened above the surface of his lake. She knelt and washed her face in the cool, clean waters. She sat back on her heels and let the sunlight dry the drops of water glistening on her cheeks. It was very quiet. Far out over the lake a fishing bird swooped and then rose, caught by the light, flashing away south.

She had stood on this shore once, most of a lifetime ago, it seemed, throwing pebbles into the water, having fled from the words Ysanne had spoken in the cottage. Under the cottage.

Her hair had still been brown then. She had been an intern from Toronto, a stranger in another world. She was white-haired now, and the Seer of Brennin, and on the far side of a chasm in her dream she had seen a road stretching away, and someone had stood before her on that road. Sparkling brilliantly, a speckled fish leaped from the lake. The sun was high, too high; the Loom was shuttling even as she lingered by this shore.

Kimberly rose and went back into the cottage. She moved the table a little to one side. She laid her hand on the floor and spoke a word of power.

There were ten steps leading down. The walls were damp. There were no torches, but from below the well-remembered pearly light still shone. On her finger the Baelrath began to glow in answer. Then she reached the bottom and stood in the chamber again, with its woven carpet, single desk, bed, chair, ancient books.

And the glass-doored cabinet on the farther wall wherein lay the Circlet of Lisen, from which the shining came.

She walked over and opened the cabinet doors. For a long time she stood motionless, looking down at the gold of the Circlet band and the glowing stone set within: fairest creation of the lios alfar, crafted by the Children of Light in love and sorrow for the fairest child of all the Weaver's worlds.

*The Light against the Dark,* Ysanne had named it. It had changed, Kim remembered her saying: the colour of hope when it was made, since Lisen's death it shone more softly, and with loss. Thinking of Ysanne, Kim felt her as a palpable presence; she had the illusion that if she hugged herself, she'd be putting her arms about the frail body of the old Seer.

It was an illusion, nothing more, but she remembered something else that was more than illusory: words of Raederth, the mage Ysanne had loved and been loved by, the man who had found the Circlet again, notwithstanding all the long years it had lain lost.

*Who wears this next, after Lisen,* Raederth had said, *shall have the darkest road to walk of any child of earth or stars.*

The words she had heard in her dream. Kim reached out a hand and with infinite care lifted the Circlet from where it lay.

She heard a sound from the room above.

Terror burst inside her, sharper even than in the dream. For what had been only foreknowing then, and so removed a little, was present, now, and above her. And the time had come.

She turned to face the stairway. Keeping her voice as level as she could, knowing how dangerous it would be to show fear, she said, "You can come down if you like. I've been waiting for you."

Silence. Her heart was thunder, a drum. For a moment she saw the chasm again, the bridge, the road. Then there were footsteps on the stairs.

Then Darien.

She had never seen him. She endured a moment of terrible dislocation, over and above everything else. She knew nothing of what happened in the glade of the Summer Tree. He was supposed to be a child, even though a part of her had known he wasn't, and couldn't be. In the dream he had been only a shadowed presence, ill defined, and a name she'd learned in Toronto even before he was born. By the aura of the name she had known him, and by another thing, which had been the deepest source of her terror: his eyes had been red.

They were blue now and he seemed very young, though he should have been even younger. So much younger. But Jennifer's child, born less than a year ago, stood before her, his eyes uneasy, darting about the chamber, and he looked like any fifteen-year-old boy might look—if any boy could be as beautiful as this one was, and carry as much power within himself.

"How did you know I was here?" he said abruptly. His voice was awkward, underused.

She tried to will her heartbeat to slow; she needed to be calm, needed all her wits about her for this. "I heard you," she said.

"I thought I was being quiet."

She managed to smile. "You were, Darien. I have very good ears. Your mother used to wake me when she came in late at night, however quiet she was."

His eyes came to rest on hers for a moment. "You know my mother?"

"I know her very well. I love her dearly."

He moved a couple of paces into the room but stayed between her and the stairway. She wasn't sure if it was to keep an exit for himself or block it from her. He was looking around again.

"I never knew this room was here."

The muscles of her back were corded with tension. "It belonged to the woman who lived here before you," she said.

"Why?" he challenged. "Who was she? Why is it underground?" He was wearing a sweater and trousers and fawn-coloured boots. The sweater was brown, too warm for summer, and too large for him. It would have been Finn's, she realized. All the clothing was. Her mouth was dry. She wet her lips with her tongue.

"She was a very wise woman, and she had many things she loved in this room, so she kept it hidden to guard them." The Circlet lay in her hand; it was slender and delicate, almost no weight at all, yet she felt as if she carried the weight of worlds.

"What things?" said Darien.

And so the time, truly, was upon them.

"This," said Kim, holding it out to him. "And it is for you, Darien. It was meant for you. It is the Circlet of Lisen." Her voice trembled a little. She paused. He was silent, watching her, waiting. She said, "It is the Light against the Dark."

Her voice failed her. The high, heroic words went forth into the little chamber and fell away into silence.

"Do you know who I am?" asked Darien. His hands had closed at his side. He took another step towards her. "Do you know who my father is?"

So much terror. But she had dreamt this. It was his. She nodded. "I do," she whispered. And because she thought she had heard a diffidence in his voice, not a challenge, she said, "And I know your mother was stronger than him." She didn't, really, but that was the prayer, the hope, the gleam of light she held. "He wanted her to die, so you wouldn't be born."

He withdrew the one step he had advanced. Then he laughed a little, a lonely, terrible laugh. "I didn't know that," he said. "Cernan asked why I was allowed to live. I heard him. Everyone seems to agree." His hands were opening and closing spasmodically.

"Not everyone," she said. "Not everyone, Darien. Your mother wanted you to be born. Desperately." She had to be so careful. It mattered so much. "Paul—Pwyll, the one who stayed with you here—he risked his life guarding her and bringing her to Vae's house the night you were born."

Darien's expression changed, as if his face had slammed shut against her. "He slept in Finn's bed," he said flatly. Accusingly.

She said nothing. What could she say?

"Give it to me," he said.

What could she do? It all seemed so inevitable, now that the time had come. Who but this child should walk the Darkest Road? He was already on it. No other's loneliness would ever run so deep, no other's dangerousness be so absolute.

Wordlessly, for no words could be adequate to the moment, she stepped forward, the Circlet in her hands. Instinctively he retreated, a hand raised to strike her. But then he lowered his arm, and stood very still, and suffered her to place it about his brow.

He was not even as tall as she. She didn't have to reach up. It was easy to fit the golden band over his golden hair and close the delicate clasp. It was easy; it had been dreamt; it was done.

And the moment the clasp was fitted the light of the Circlet went out.

A sound escaped him; a torn, wordless cry. The room was suddenly dark, lit only by the red glow of the Baelrath, which yet burned, and the thin light that streamed down the stairs from the room above.

Then Darien made another sound, and this time it was laughter. Not the lost laugh of before, this was harsh, strident, uncontrolled. "Mine?" he cried. "The Light against the Dark? Oh, you fool! How should the son of Rakoth Maugrim carry such a light? How should it ever shine for me?"

Kim's hands were against her mouth. There was so much unbridled torment in his voice. Then he moved, and her fear exploded. It doubled, redoubled itself, outstripped any measure she'd ever had, for by the light of the Warstone she saw his eyes flash red. He gestured, nothing more than that, but she felt it as a blow that drove her to the ground. Thrusting past her, he strode to the cabinet against the wall.

In which lay the last object of power. The last thing Ysanne had seen in her life. And lying on the ground, helpless at his feet, Kim saw Rakoth's son take Lökdal, the dagger of the Dwarves, and claim it for his own.

"No!" she gasped. "Darien, the Circlet is yours, but not the dagger. It is not for you to take. You know not what it is."

He laughed again and drew the blade from its jewelled sheath. A sound like a plucked harpstring filled the room. He looked at the gleaming blue thieren running along the blade and said, "I do not need to know. My father will. How should I go to him without a gift, and what sort of gift would this dead stone of Lisen's make? If the very light turns away from me, at least I now know where I belong."

He was past her then, and by the stairs; he was climbing them and leaving, with the Circlet lifeless upon his brow and Colan's dagger in his hand.

"Darien!" Kim cried with the voice of her heart's pain. "He wanted you dead. It was your mother who fought to let you be born!"

No response. Footsteps across the floor above. A door opening, and closing. With the Circlet gone the Baelrath slowly grew dim, so it was quite dark in the chamber below the cottage, and in the darkness Kim wept for the loss of light.

When they came an hour later, she was by the lake again, very deep in thought. The sound of the horses startled her, and she rose quickly to her feet, but then she saw long red hair and midnight black, and she knew who had come and was glad.

She walked forward along the curve of the shore to meet them. Sharra, who was a friend and had been from the first day they'd met, dismounted the instant her horse came to a stop, and enfolded Kim in a fierce embrace.

"Are you all right?" she asked. "Did you do it?"

The events of the morning were so vivid that for a moment Kim didn't realize it was Khath Meigol that Sharra was talking about. The last time the Princess of Cathal had seen her, Kim had been preparing to leave for the mountains.

She managed a nod and a small smile, though it was difficult. "I did," she said. "I did what I went to do."

She left it at that for the moment. Jaelle had dismounted as well and stood a little way apart, waiting. She looked as she always did, cool and withdrawn, formidable. But Kim had shared a moment with her in the Temple in Gwen Ystrat on the eve of Maidaladan, so, walking over, she gave the Priestess a hug and a quick kiss on the cheek. Jaelle stood rigid for an instant; then, awkwardly, her arms went around Kim in a brief, transient gesture that nonetheless conveyed a great deal.

Kim stepped back. She knew her eyes were red from weeping, but there was no point in dissembling, not with Jaelle. She was going to need help, not least of all in deciding what to do.

"I'm glad you're here," she said quietly. "How did you know?"

"Leila," Jaelle said. "She's still tuned to this cottage, where Finn was. She told us you were here."

Kim nodded. "Anything else? Did she say anything else?"

"Not this morning. Did something happen?"

"Yes," Kim whispered. "Something happened. We've a lot to catch each other up on. Where's Jennifer?"

The other two women exchanged glances. It was Sharra who answered. "She went with Brendel to the Anor Lisen when the ship sailed."

Kim closed her eyes. So many dimensions to sorrow. Would there ever be an ending?

"Do you want to go into the cottage?" Jaelle asked.

She shook her head quickly. "No. Not inside. Let's stay out here." Jaelle gave her a searching look and then, without fuss, gathered her white robe and sat down on the stony beach. Kim and Sharra followed suit. A little distance away the men of Cathal and Brennin were watchfully arrayed. Tegid of Rhoden, prodigious in brown and gold, walked towards the three of them.

"My lady," he said, with a deep bow to Sharra, "how may I serve you on behalf of my Prince?"

"Food," she answered crisply. "A clean cloth, and a lunch to spread upon it."

"Instantly!" he exclaimed and bowed again, not entirely steady on the loose stones of the shoreline. He wheeled, and scrunched his way over the beach to find them provisions. Sharra looked sideways at Kim, who had an eyebrow raised in frank curiosity.

"A new conquest?" Kim asked with some of her old teasing, the tone she sometimes thought she'd lost forever.

Sharra, surprisingly, blushed. "Well, yes, I suppose. But not him. Um . . . Diarmuid proposed marriage to me before *Prydwen* sailed. Tegid is his Intercedent. He's looking after me, and so—"

She got no further, having been comprehensively enveloped in a second embrace. "Oh, Sharra!" Kim exclaimed "That's the nicest news I've heard in I don't know how long!"

"I suppose," Jaelle murmured dryly. "But I thought we had more pressing matters to discuss than matrimonial tidings. And we still don't have any news of the ship."

"Yes, we do," said Kim quickly. "We know they got there, and we know they won a battle."

"Oh, Dana be praised!" Jaelle said, suddenly sounding very young, all cynicism stripped away. Sharra was speechless. "Tell us," the High Priestess said. "How do you know?"

Kim began the story with her capture in the mountains: with Ceriog and Faebur and Dalreidan and the death rain over Eridu. Then she told them of seeing that dread rain come to an end the morning before, of seeing sunshine to the east and so knowing that Metran on Cader Sedat had been stopped.

She paused a moment, for Tegid had returned with two soldiers in his wake, carrying armloads of food and drink. It took a few minutes for things to be arranged in a fashion that, to his critical eye, was worthy of the Princess of Cathal. When the three men had withdrawn, Kim took a deep breath and spoke of Khath Meigol, of Tabor and Imraith-Nimphais, of the rescue of the Paraiko and the last kanior, and then, at the end, very softly, of what she and her ring had done to the Giants.

When she finished it was quiet on the shore again. Neither of the other women spoke. They were both familiar with power, Kim knew, in a great many of its shadings, but what she had just told them, what she had done, had to be alien and almost impossible to grasp.

She felt very alone. Paul, she thought, might have understood, for his, too, was a lonely path. Then, almost as if reading her thoughts, Sharra reached out and squeezed her hand. Kim squeezed back and said, "Tabor told me that the Aven and all the Dalrei rode to Celidon three nights ago to meet an army of the Dark. I have no idea what happened. Neither did Tabor."

"We do," Jaelle said.

And in her turn she told of what had happened two evenings before, when Leila had screamed in anguish at the summoning of the Wild Hunt, and through her link every priestess in the sanctuary had heard Green Ceinwen's voice as she mastered Owein and drew him from his kill.

It was Kim's turn to be silent, absorbing this. There was still one thing left to be told, though, and so at length she said, "I'm afraid something else has happened."

"Who was here this morning?" Jaelle asked with unnerving anticipation.

It was beautiful where they were sitting. The summer air was mild and clean, the sky and lake were a brilliant blue. There were birds and flowers, and a soft breeze off the water. There was a glass of cool wine in her hand.

"Darien," she said. "I gave him the Circlet of Lisen. Ysanne had it hidden here. The light went out when he put it on, and he stole Colan's dagger, Lökdal, which she'd also had in the cottage. Then he left. He said he was going to his father."

It was unfair of her, she knew, to put it so baldly. Jaelle's face had gone bone white with the impact of what she'd just said, but Kim knew that it wouldn't have mattered how she'd told it. How could she cushion the impact of the morning's terror? What shelter could there be?

The breeze was still blowing. There were flowers, green grass, the lake, the summer sun. And fear, densely woven, at the very root of everything, threatening to take it all away: across a chasm, along a shadowed road, north to the heart of evil.

"Who," asked Sharra of Cathal, "is Darien? And who is his father?"

Amazingly, Kim had forgotten. Paul and Dave knew about Jennifer's child, and Jaelle and the Mormae of Gwen Ystrat. Vae, of course, and Finn, though he, too, was gone now. Leila, probably, who seemed to know everything connected in any way to Finn. No one else knew: not Loren or Aileron, Arthur or Ivor, or even Gereint.

She looked at Jaelle and received a look back, equally doubtful, equally anxious. Then she nodded, and after a moment the High Priestess did as well. And so they told Sharra the whole story, sitting on the shore of Eilathen's lake.

And when it was done, when Kim had spoken of the rape and the premature birth, of Vae and Finn, when Jaelle had told them both Paul's story of what had happened in the glade of the Summer Tree, and Kim had ended the telling with the red flash of Darien's eyes that morning and the effortless power that had knocked her sprawling, Sharra of Cathal rose to her feet. She walked a few quick steps away and stood a moment, gazing out over the water. Then she wheeled to face Kim and Jaelle again. Looking down on the two of them, at the bleak apprehension in their faces, Sharra, whose dreams since she was a girl had been of herself as a falcon flying alone, cried aloud, "But this is terrible! That poor child! No one else in any world can be so lonely."

It carried. Kim saw the soldiers glance over at them from farther along the shore. Jaelle made a queer sound, between a gasp and a breathless laugh. "Really," she began. "Poor child? I don't think you've quite understood—"

"No," Kim interrupted, laying an urgent hand on Jaelle's arm. "No, wait. She isn't wrong." Even as she spoke, she was reliving the scene under the cottage, scanning it again, trying to see past her terrified awareness of who this child's father was. And as she looked back, straining to remember, she heard again the sound that had escaped him when Lisen's Light had gone out.

And this time, removed from it, with Sharra's words to guide her, Kim heard clearly what she'd missed before: the loneliness, the terrible sense of rejection in that bewildered cry wrung from the soul of this boy—only a boy, they *had* to remember that—who had no one and nothing, and nowhere to turn. And from whom the very light had turned away, as if in denial and abhorrence.

He'd actually said that, she remembered now. He'd said as much to her, but in her fear she'd registered only the terrible threat that followed: he was going to his father bearing gifts. Gifts of entreaty, she now realized, of supplication, of longing for a place, from the most solitary soul there was.

From Darien, on the Darkest Road.

Kim stood up. Sharra's words had crystallized things for her, finally, and she had thought of the one tiny thing she could do. A desperate hope it was, but it was all they had. For although it might still be proven true that it was the armies and a battlefield that would end things one way or the other, Kim knew that there were too many other powers arrayed for that to be a certainty.

And she was one of the powers, and another was the boy she'd seen that morning. She glanced over at the soldiers, concerned for a moment, but only for a moment; it was too late for absolute secrecy, the game was too far along, and too much was riding on what would follow. So she stepped forward a little, off the stony shoreline onto the grass running up to the front door of the cottage.

Then she lifted her voice and cried, "Darien, I know you can hear me! Before you go where you said you would go, let me tell you this: your mother is standing now in a tower west of Pendaran Wood." That was all. It was all she had left: a scrap of information given to the wind.

After the shouting, a very great silence, made deeper, not broken, by the waves on the shore. She felt a little ridiculous, knowing how it must appear to the soldiers. But dignity meant less than nothing now; only the reaching out mattered, the casting of her voice with her heart behind it, with the one thing that might get through to him.

But there was only silence. From the trees east of the cottage a white owl, roused from daytime slumber, rose briefly at her cry, then settled again deeper in the woods. Still, she was fairly certain, and she trusted her instincts by now, having had so little else to guide her for so long; Darien was still there. He was drawn to this place, and held by it, and if he was nearby he could hear her. And if he heard?

She didn't know what he would do. She only knew that if anyone, anywhere, could hold him from that journey to his father, it was Jennifer in her Tower. With her burdens and her griefs, and her insistence, from the start, that her child was to be random. But he *couldn't* be left so anymore, Kim told herself. Surely Jennifer would see that? He was on his way to Starkadh, comfortless and lonely. Surely his mother would forgive Kim this act of intervention?

Kim turned back to the others. Jaelle was on her feet, as well, standing very tall, composed, very much aware of what had just been done. She said, "Should we warn her? What will she do if he goes to her?"

Kim felt suddenly weary and fragile. She said, "I don't know. I don't know if he'll go there. He might. I think Sharra's right, though, he's looking for a place. As to warning her—I have no idea how. I'm sorry."

Jaelle drew a careful breath. "I can take us there."

"How?" said Sharra. "How can you do that?"

"With the avarlith and blood," the High Priestess of Dana replied in a quieter, different tone of voice. "A great deal of each."

Kim looked at her searchingly. "Should you, though? Shouldn't you stay in the Temple?"

Jaelle shook her head. "I've been uneasy there these past few days, which has never happened before. I think the Goddess has been preparing me for this."

Kim looked down at the Baelrath on her finger, at its quiescent, powerless flickering. No help there. Sometimes she hated the ring with a frightening intensity. She looked up at the other women.

"She's right," Sharra said calmly. "Jennifer will need warning, if he is going to her."

"Or comfort, afterwards, if nothing else," Jaelle said, surprisingly. "Seer, decide quickly! We will have to ride back to the Temple to do this, and time is the one thing we do not have."

"There are a lot of things we don't have," Kim amended, almost absently. But she was nodding her head, even as she spoke.

They had brought an extra horse for her. Later that afternoon, under the Dome of the Temple, before the altar with the axe, Jaelle spoke words of power and of invocation.

She drew blood from herself—a great deal in fact, as she had warned—then she linked to the Mormae in Gwen Ystrat, and in concert the inner circle of the priestesses of Dana reached down into the earthroot for power of the Mother great enough to send three women a long way off, to a stony shore by an ocean, not a lake.

It didn't take very long by any measure of such things, but even so, by the time they arrived the gathering storm was very nearly upon them all, and the wind and the waves were wild.

⊹⊱═⊙⊰═⊹

Even in the owl shape the Circlet fitted about his head. He had to hold the dagger in his mouth, though, and that was tiring. He let it drop into the grass at the base of his tree. Nothing would come to take it. All the other animals in the copse of trees were afraid of him by now. He could kill with his eyes.

He had learned that just two nights before, when a field mouse he was hunting had been on the verge of escaping under the rotted wood of the barn. He had been hungry and enraged. His eyes had flashed—he always knew when they did, even though he couldn't entirely control them—and the mouse had sizzled and died.

He'd done it three times more that night, even though he was no longer hungry. There was some pleasure in the power, and a certain compulsion, too. That part he didn't really understand. He supposed it came from his father.

Late the next night he'd been falling asleep in his own form, or the form he'd taken for himself a week ago, and as he drifted off a memory had come back, halfway to a dream. He recalled the winter that had passed, and the voices in the storm that had called him every night. He'd felt the same compulsion then, he remembered. A desire to go outside in the cold and play with the wild voices amid the blowing snow.

He didn't hear the voices anymore. They weren't calling him. He wondered—it was a difficult thought—if they had stopped calling because he had already come to them. As a boy, so little time ago, when the voices were calling he used to try to fight them. Finn had helped. He used to pad across the cold floor of the cottage and crawl into bed with Finn, and that had made everything right. There was no one to make anything right anymore. He could kill with his eyes, and Finn was gone.

He had fallen asleep on that thought, in the cave high up in the hills north of the cottage. And in the morning he'd seen the white-haired woman walk down the path to stand by the lake. Then, when she'd gone back in, he'd followed her, and she'd called him, and he'd gone down the stairs he'd never known were there.

She'd been afraid of him, too. Everyone was. He could kill with his eyes. But she'd spoken quietly to him and smiled, once. He hadn't had anyone smile at him for a long time. Not since he'd left the glade of the Summer Tree in this new, older shape he couldn't get used to.

And she knew his mother, his real mother. The one Finn had told him had been like a queen, and had loved him, even though she'd had to go away. She'd made him special, Finn had said, and he'd said something else . . . about having to be good, so

Darien would deserve the being special. Something like that. It was becoming harder to remember. He wondered, though, why she had made him able to kill so easily, and to want to kill sometimes.

He'd thought about asking the white-haired woman about that, but he was uncomfortable now in the enclosed spaces of the cottage, and he was afraid to tell her about the killing. He was afraid she would hate him and go.

Then she'd showed him the Light and she'd said it was meant for him. Hardly daring to believe it, because it was so very beautiful, he'd let her put it on his brow. The Light against the Dark, she called it, and as she spoke Darien remembered another thing Finn had told him, about having to hate the Dark and the voices in the storm that came from the Dark. And now, astonishingly, it seemed that even though he was the son of Rakoth Maugrim he was being given a jewel of Light.

And then it went out.

Only Finn's going away had ever hurt as much. He felt the same emptiness, the same hollow sense of loss. And then, in the midst of it, because of it, he'd felt his eyes readying themselves to go red, and then they did. He didn't kill her. He could have, easily, but he only knocked her down and went to take the other shining thing he'd seen in that room. He didn't know why he took it or what it was. He just took it.

Only when he was turning to go and she tried to stop him did it come to him how he could hurt her as much as she'd hurt him, and so, in that moment, he'd decided he was going to take the dagger to his father. His voice had sounded cold and strong to his own ears, and he'd seen her face go white just before he left the room and went outside and made himself into an owl again.

Later in the day other people had come, and he'd watched them from his tree in the woods east of the cottage. He'd seen the three women talking by the lake, though he couldn't hear what they said, and he was too afraid, in the owl shape, to go nearer.

But then one of them, the one with dark hair, had stood up and had cried, loudly enough for him to hear, "That poor child! No one else in any world can be so lonely!" and he knew that she was speaking of him. He wanted to go down then, but he was still afraid. He was afraid that his eyes would want to turn red, and he wouldn't know how to stop them. Or to stop what he did when they were that way.

So he waited, and a moment later the one with white hair walked forward a little, towards him, and she called out to him by name.

The part of him that was an owl was so startled that he flew a few wingbeats, out of sheer reflex, before he was able to control himself again. And then he heard her tell him where his mother was.

That was all. A moment later they went away. He was alone again. He stayed in the tree, in the owl form, trying to decide what to do.

She had been like a queen, Finn had said. She had loved him.

He flew down and took hold of the dagger again in his mouth, and then he started to fly. The part of him that was an owl didn't want to fly in the day, but he was more than an owl, much more. It was hard to carry the dagger, but he managed it.

He flew north, but only for a little way. West of Pendaran Wood, the white-haired one had said. He knew where that was, though he didn't know how he knew. Gradually he began to angle his flight northwest.

He went very fast. A storm was coming.

# CHAPTER 5

In the place where they were going—all of them, the Wolflord running in his wolf shape, Darien flying as an owl with a blade in his mouth, the three women sent from the Temple by the power of Dana—Jennifer stood on Lisen's balcony gazing out to sea, her hair blown back by the freshening wind.

So still was she that save for the eyes restlessly scanning the white-capped waves, she might have been the figurehead at the prow of a ship and not a living woman waiting at the edge of land for that ship to come home. They were a long way north from Taerlindel, she knew, and a part of her wondered about that. But it was here that Lisen had waited for a ship to return from Cader Sedat, and deep within herself Jennifer felt an awareness, a certainty, that this was where she should be. And embedded within that certainty, as a weed in a garden, was a growing sense of foreboding.

The wind was southwest, and ever since the morning had turned to afternoon it had been getting stronger. Never taking her eyes from the sea, she moved back from the low parapet and sat down in the chair they had brought out for her. She ran her fingers along the polished wood. It had been made, Brendel had said, by craftsmen of the Brein Mark in Daniloth, long before even the Anor was built.

Brendel was here with her, and Flidais as well, familiar spirits never far from her side, never speaking unless she spoke to them. The part of her that was still Jennifer Lowell, and had taken pleasure in riding horses and teasing her roommate, and had loved Kevin Laine for his wit as well as his tenderness, rebelled against this weighty solemnity. But she had been kidnapped after riding a horse a year ago, and Kim was white-haired now and a Seer with her own weight to carry, and Kevin was dead.

And she herself was Guinevere, and Arthur was here, drawn back again to war against the Dark, and he was everything he had ever been. He had broken through the walls she had raised about herself since Starkadh, and had set her free in the bright arc of an afternoon, and then had sailed away to a place of death.

She knew too much about his destiny and her own bitter role in that to ever truly be lighthearted again. She was the lady of the sorrows and the instrument of punishment, and there was little she could do, it seemed, about either of them. Her foreboding grew, and the silence began to oppress her. She turned to Flidais. As she did, her child was just then flying across the Wyth Llewen River in the heart of the Wood, coming to her.

"Will you tell me a story?" she asked. "While I watch?"

The one she'd known as Taliesin at Arthur's court, and who was now beside her in his truer, older shape, drew a curved pipe from his mouth, blew a circle of smoke along the wind, and smiled.

"What story?" he asked. "What would you hear, Lady?"

She shook her head. She didn't want to have to think. "Anything." She shrugged. Then, after a pause, "Tell me about the Hunt. Kim and Dave set them free, I know that much. How were they bound? Who were they, Flidais?"

Again he smiled, and there was more than a little pride in his voice, "I will tell you, all of what you ask. And I doubt there is a living creature in Fionavar, now that the Paraiko are dead and haunting Khath Meigol, who would know the story rightly."

She gave him an ironic, sidelong glance. "You did know all the stories, didn't you? All of them, vain child."

"I know the stories, and the answers to all the riddles in all the worlds save—" He broke off abruptly.

Brendel, watching with interest, saw the andain of the forest flush a deep, surprising red. When Flidais resumed it was in a different tone, and as he spoke Jennifer turned back to the waves, listening and watching, a figurehead again.

"I had this from Ceinwen and Cernan a very long time ago," Flidais said, his deep voice cutting through the sound of the wind. "Not even the andain were in Fionavar when this world was spun into time, first of the Weaver's worlds. The lios alfar were not yet on the Loom, nor the Dwarves, nor the tall men from oversea, nor those east of the mountains or in the sunburnt lands south of Cathal.

"The gods and the goddesses, given their names and powers by grace of the Weaver's hands, were here. There were animals in the woods, and the woods were vast then; there were fish in the lakes and rivers and the wide sea, and birds in the wider sky. And in the sky as well there flew the Wild Hunt, and in the forests and the valleys and across rivers and up the mountain slopes there walked the Paraiko in the young years of the world, naming what they saw.

"By day the Paraiko walked and the Hunt were at rest, but at night, when the moon rose, Owein and the seven kings and the child who rode Iselen, palest of the shadow horses, mounted up into the starry sky, and they hunted the beasts of woods and open spaces until dawn, filling the night with the wild terrible beauty of their cries and their hunting horns."

"Why?" Brendel could not forebear to ask. "Do you know why, forest one? Do you know why the Weaver spun their killing into the Tapestry?"

"Who shall know the design on the Loom?" Flidais said soberly. "But this much I had from Cernan of the Beasts: the Hunt was placed in the Tapestry to be wild in the truest sense, to lay down an uncontrolled thread for the freedom of the Children who came after. And so did the Weaver lay a constraint upon himself, that not even he, shuttling at the Loom of Worlds, may preordain and shape exactly what is to be. We who came after, the andain who are the children of gods, the lios alfar, the Dwarves, and all the races of men, we have such choices as we have, some freedom to shape our own destinies, because of that wild thread of Owein and the Hunt slipping across the Loom, warp and then weft, in turn and at times. They are there, Cernan told me one night long ago, precisely to be wild, to cut across the Weaver's measured will. To be random, and so enable us to be."

He stopped, because the green eyes of Guinevere had turned back to him from the sea, and there was that within them which stilled his tongue.

"Was that Cernan's word?" she asked. "Random?"

He thought back carefully, for the look on her face demanded care, and it had been a very long time ago. "It was," he said at length, understanding that it mattered, but not why. "He said it exactly so, Lady. The Weaver wove the Hunt and set them free on the Loom, that we, in our turn, might have a freedom of our own because of them. Good and evil, Light and Dark, they are in all the worlds of the Tapestry because Owein and the kings are here, following the child on Iselen, threading across the sky."

She had turned fully away from the sea to face him now. He could not read her eyes; he had never been able to read her eyes. She said, "And so, because of the Hunt, Rakoth was made possible."

It was not a question. She had seen through to the deepest, bitterest part of the story. He answered with what Cernan and Ceinwen had said to him, the only thing that could be said. "He is the price we pay."

After a pause, and a little more loudly because of the wind, he added, "He is not in the Tapestry. Because of the randomness of the Hunt, the Loom itself was no longer sacrosanct; it was no longer all. So Maugrim was able to come from outside of it, from outside of time and the walls of Night that bind all the rest of us, even the gods, and enter into Fionavar and so into all the worlds. He is here but he is not part of the Tapestry; he has never done anything that would bind him into it and so he cannot die, even if everything on the Loom should unravel and all our threads be lost."

This part Brendel had known, though never before how it had come to pass. Sick at heart, he looked at the woman sitting beside them, and as he gazed, he read a thought in her. He was not wiser than Flidais, nor had he even known her so long, but he had tuned his soul to her service since the night she'd been stolen from his care, and he said, "Jennifer, if all this is true, if the Weaver put a check on his own shaping of our destinies, it would follow—surely it would follow—that the Warrior's doom is not irrevocable."

It was her own burgeoning thought, a hint, a kernel of brightness in the darkness that surrounded her. She looked at him, not smiling, not venturing so much; but with a softening of the lines of her face and a catch in her voice that made him ache, she said, "I know. I have been thinking that. Oh, my friend, could it be? I felt a difference when I first saw him—I did! There was no one here who was Lancelot in the way that I was Guinevere, waiting to remember my story. I told him so. There are only the two of us this time."

He saw a brightness in her face, a hint of colour absent since *Prydwen* had set sail, and it seemed to bring her back, in all her beauty, from the realm of statues and icons to that of living women who could love, and dared hope.

Better, far better, the lios alfar would think bitterly, later that night, unsleeping by the Anor, that she had never allowed herself that unsheathing of her heart.

"Shall I go on?" Flidais said, with a hint of the asperity proper to an upstaged storyteller.

"Please," she murmured kindly, turning back to him. But then, as he began the tale again, she fixed her gaze once more out to sea. Sitting so, she listened to him tell of how the Hunt had lost the young one, Iselen's rider, on the night they moved the moon. She tried to pay attention as his deep cadences rode over the wind to recount how Connla, mightiest of the Paraiko, had agreed to shape the spells that would lay the Hunt to rest until another one was born who could take the Longest Road with them—the Road that ran between the worlds and the stars.

However hard she tried, though, she could not entirely school her thoughts, for the andain's earlier explanation had reached into her heart, and not just in the way Brendel had discerned. The question of randomness, of the Weaver's gift of choice to his Children, touched Arthur's woven doom with a possibility of expiation she'd never really allowed herself to dream about before. But there was something else in what Flidais had said. Something that went beyond their own long tragedy in all its returnings, and this the lios alfar had not seen, and Flidais knew nothing at all of it.

Jennifer did, though, and she held it close to her rapidly beating heart. *Random*, Cernan of the Beasts had said of the Wild Hunt and the choice they embodied. It was her own word. Her own instinctive word for her response to Maugrim. For her child, and his choice.

She looked out to sea, searching. The wind was very strong now, and there were storm clouds coming up fast. She forced herself to keep her features calm as she gazed, but inwardly she was as open, as exposed, as she had ever been.

And in that moment Darien landed near the river, at the edge of the trees, and took his human form again.

The sound of thunder was distant yet and the clouds were still far out at sea. But it was a southwest wind that was carrying the storm, and when the light began to change the weather-wise lios alfar grew uneasy. He took Jennifer's hand, and the three of them withdrew into the high chamber. Flidais rolled the curved glass windows shut along their tracks. They sealed tightly, and in the abrupt silence Brendel saw the andain suddenly tilt his head, as if hearing something.

He was. The howl of wind on the balcony had screened from him the alarms running through the Great Wood. There was an intruder. There were two: one was here, even now, and the other was coming and would arrive very soon.

The one who was coming he knew, and feared, for it was his own lord, lord of all the andain and mightiest of them, but the other one, the one standing below them at this moment, he knew not, nor did the powers of the Wood, and it frightened them. In their fear they grew enraged, and he could feel that rage now as a buffeting greater than the wind on the balcony.

*Be calm*, he sent inwardly, though he was anything but calm himself. *I will go down. I will deal with this.*

To the others, to the lios alfar and the woman he'd known as Guinevere, he said grimly, "Someone has come, and Galadan is on his way to this place even now."

He saw a look pass between the two of them, and he felt the tightening of tension in the room. He thought they were mirroring his own anxiety, knowing nothing of the memory they shared of the Wolflord in a wood east of Paras Derval a little more than a year ago.

"Are you expecting anyone?" he demanded. "Who would follow you here?"

"Who *could* follow us here?" Brendel replied quickly.

There was suddenly a new brightness to the lios, as if he had shed a cloak and his true nature was shining through. "No one has come by sea; we would have seen them—and how could anyone pass through the forest?"

"Someone stronger than the Wood," Flidais replied, vexed at the hint of apprehension that reached his voice.

Brendel was already by the stairwell. "Jennifer, wait here. We will go down and deal with this. Lock the door after us, and open only to one of our voices." He loosened his short sword in its scabbard as he spoke, then turned to Flidais, "How long before Galadan arrives?"

The andain sent the query out to the Wood and relayed the answer back, "Half an hour, perhaps less. He is running very fast, in his wolf shape."

"Will you help me?" Brendel asked him directly.

This was, of course, the question. The andain rarely cared for the affairs of mortals, and even more rarely intervened in them. But Flidais had a purpose here, his oldest, deepest purpose, and so he temporized. "I will go down with you. I told the forest I would see who this was."

Jennifer had gone very pale again, Brendel saw, but her hands were steady and her head very high, and once more he marvelled at her sheer, unwavering courage as she said, "I will come down. Whoever is here has come because of me; it may be a friend."

"It may not be," Brendel replied gravely.

"Then I should be no safer in this room," she answered calmly, and paused at the head of the curving stairs waiting for him to lead her down. One more moment he hesitated, then his eyes went green, exactly the colour of her own. He took her hand and brought it to his forehead and then his lips before turning to descend, sword drawn now, his tread quick and light on the stone stairs. She followed, and Flidais behind her, his mind racing with calculations, boiling over with considerations and possibilities and a frantically stifled excitement.

They saw Darien standing by the river as soon as they stepped out onto the beach.

The wind carried lashings of sea spray that stung when they struck, and the sky had grown darker even in the moments of their descent. It was purple now, shot through with streaks of red, and thunder was rolling out at sea beyond the rising waves.

But for Brendel of the lios alfar, who immediately recognized who had come, none of this even registered. Quickly he spun around, to fling some warning to Jennifer, to give her time to prepare herself. Then he saw from her expression that she didn't need his warning. She knew, already, who this boy standing before them was. He looked at her face, wet now with ocean spray, and stepped aside as she moved forward towards the river where Darien stood.

Flidais came up beside him, droplets of spray glittering on his bald head, an avid curiosity in his face. Brendel became aware of the sword he carried, and he sheathed it silently. Then he and the andain watched mother and child come together for the first time since the night Darien was born.

An overwhelming awareness filled Brendel's mind of how many things might lie in the balance here. He would never forget that afternoon by the Summer Tree, and the words of Cernan: *Why was he allowed to live?* He thought of that, he thought of Pwyll, far out at sea, and he was conscious every moment of Cernan's son, running towards them even now, as fast as the gathering storm and more dangerous.

He looked down at the andain beside him, not trusting the vivid, inquisitive brightness in Flidais's eyes. But what, after all, could he do? He could stand by, apprehensive and ready; he could die in Jennifer's defence, if it came to that; he could watch.

And, watching, he saw Darien step cautiously forward away from the riverbank. As the boy came nearer, Brendel saw some sort of circlet about his brow, with a dark gem enclosed within it, and deep in his mind a chime sounded, crystal on crystal, a warning from memories not his own. He reached back towards them, but even as he did he saw the boy hold out a sheathed dagger towards his mother, and as Darien spoke, Brendel's memories were wiped away by the urgent demands of the present.

"Will you . . . will you take a gift?" he heard. It seemed to him as if the boy were poised to take sudden flight at a breath, at the fall of a leaf. He held himself very still and, disbelieving, heard Jennifer's reply.

"Is it yours to give?" There was ice in her voice, and steel. Hard and cold and carrying, her tone knifed through the wind, sharp as the dagger her son was offering her.

Confused, unprepared, Darien stumbled back. The blade fell from his fingers. Aching for him, for both of them, Brendel kept silence though his whole being was crying out to Jennifer to be careful, to be gentle, to do whatever she had to do to hold the boy and claim him.

There was a sound from behind him. Quickly he glanced back, his hand gliding to his sword. The Seer of Brennin, her white hair whipping across her eyes, was standing at the edge of the forest east of the Anor. A moment later, his shocked eyes discerned the High Priestess, and then Sharra of Cathal's unmistakable beauty, and the mystery cleared and deepened, both. They must have come from the Temple, by using the earthroot and Jaelle's power. But why? What was happening?

Flidais, too, had heard them come, but not Jennifer or Darien, who were too intent on each other. Brendel turned back to them. He was behind Jennifer, could not see her face, but her back was straight and her head imperiously high as she faced her son.

Who said, small and seeming frail in the wild wind, "I thought it might . . . please you. I took it. I thought . . ."

Surely *now,* Brendel thought. Surely she would ease the path for him now?

"It does not," Jennifer replied. "Why should I welcome a blade that does not belong to you?"

Brendel clenched his hands. There seemed to be a fist squeezing his heart. *Oh, careful,* he thought. *Oh, please take care.*

"What," he heard Darien's mother say, "are you doing here?"

The boy's head jerked as if she'd struck him. "I—she told me. The one with white hair. She said you were . . ." His words failed him. Whatever else he said was lost in the tearing wind.

"She said I was here," his mother said coldly, very clearly. "Very well. She was right, of course. What of it? What do you want, Darien? You are no longer a baby— you arranged for that yourself. Would you have me treat you like one?"

Of course he would, Brendel wanted to say. Couldn't she see that? Was it so hard for her?

Darien straightened. His hands thrust forward, almost of themselves. He threw his head back, and Brendel thought he saw a flash. Then the boy cried, from the center of his heart, *"Don't you want me?"*

From his extended hands two bolts of power flew, to left and right of his mother. One hurtled into the bay, struck the small boat tied up to the dock, and blasted it into shards and fragments of wood. The other sizzled just past his mother's face and torched a tree at the edge of the Wood.

"Weaver at the Loom!" Brendel gasped. At his side, Flidais made a strangled sound and then ran, as fast as his short legs could carry him, to stand beneath the burning tree. The andain raised his arms towards the blaze, he spoke words too rapid and low to follow, and the fire went out.

A real fire this time, Brendel thought numbly. It had been only illusion the last time, by the Summer Tree. Weaver alone knew where this child's power ended or where it would go.

As if in answer to his thoughts, his unspoken fears, Darien spoke again, clearly this time, in a voice that mastered the wind and the thunder out at sea and the drumming, rising now from the forest floor.

"Shall I go to Starkadh?" he challenged his mother. "Shall I see if my father gives me a fairer welcome? I doubt Rakoth will scruple to take a stolen dagger! Do you leave me any choice—*Mother?*"

He's not a child, Brendel thought. It was not the words or the voice of a child.

Jennifer had not moved or flinched, even when the bolts of power flew by her. Only her fingers, spread-eagled at her sides, gave any hint of tension. And again, amid his doubt and fear and numbing imcomprehension, Brendel of the lios alfar was awed by what he saw in her.

She said, "Darien, I leave you the only choice there is. I will say this much and nothing more: you live, though your father wanted me dead so that you would never come into the Tapestry. I cannot hold you in my arms or seek shelter and love for you as I did in Vae's house when you were born. We are past the time for that. There is a choice for you to make, and everything I know tells me that you must make it freely and unconstrained, or it will never have been made at all. If I bind you to me now, or even try, I strip you of what you are."

"What if I don't want to make that choice?"

Struggling to understand, Brendel heard Darien's voice suspended, halfway, it seemed, between the explosion of his power and the supplication of his longing.

His mother laughed, but not harshly. "Oh, my child," she said. "None of us want to make it, and all of us must. Yours is only the hardest, and the one that matters most."

The wind died a little, a lull, a hesitation. Darien said, "Finn told me . . . before . . . that my mother loved me and that she had made me special."

And now, as if involuntarily, Jennifer's hands did move, up from her sides, to clutch her elbows tightly in front of her.

"*Acushla machree,*" she said—or so Brendel thought. She started to go on, then seemed to pull herself up short, as on a tight, harsh rein.

After a moment she added, in a different voice, "He was wrong . . . about making you special. You know that now. Your power comes from Rakoth when your eyes go red. What you have of me is only freedom and the right to choose, to make your own choice between Light and Dark. Nothing more than that."

"*No, Jen!*" the Seer of Brennin screamed, into the wind.

Too late. Darien's eyes changed again as the last words were spoken, and from the bitterness of his laughter Brendel knew they had lost him. The wind rose again, wilder than before; over it, over the deep drumming of Pendaran Wood, Darien cried, "Wrong, Mother! You have it all wrong. I am not here to choose *but to be chosen!*"

He gestured towards his forehead. "Do you not see what I wear on my brow? Do you not recognize it?" There was another peal of thunder, louder than any yet, and rain began to fall. Through it, over it, Darien's voice soared. "This is the Circlet of Lisen! The Light against the Dark—*and it went out when I put it on!*"

A sheet of lightning seared the sky west of them. Then thunder again. Then Darien: "Don't you see? The Light has turned away, and now you have as well. Choice? I have none! I am of the Dark that extinguishes the Light—and I know where to go!"

With those words he reclaimed the dagger from the strand before his feet; then he was running, heedless, contemptuous of the ominous drumming in the Wood, straight into Pendaran through the slashing, driving rain, leaving the six of them exposed on the shore to both the storm which had come and the rawness of their terror.

Jennifer turned. The rain was sheeting down; Brendel had no way to tell if there were tears or raindrops on her face.

"Come," he said, "we must go inside. It is dangerous out here in this!"

Jennifer ignored him. The other three women had come up. She turned to Kim, waiting, expecting something.

And it came. "What in the name of all that is holy have you done?" the Seer of

Brennin screamed into the gale. It was hard to stand upright; they were all drenched to the bone. "I sent him here as a last chance to keep him from Starkadh, and you drove him straight there! All he wanted was comfort, Jen!"

But it was Guinevere who answered, colder, sterner than the elements. "Comfort? Have I comfort to give, Kimberly? Have you? Or any of us, today, now? You had no right to send him here, and you know it! I meant him to be random, free to choose, and I will not back away from that! Jaelle, what did you think you were doing? You were there in the music room at Paras Derval when I told that to Paul. I meant everything I said! If we bind him, or try, he is lost to us!"

There was another thing inside her, at the very deepest place in her heart, but she did not say it. It was her own, too naked for the telling: *He is my Wild Hunt,* she whispered over and over in her soul. *My Owein, my shadow kings, my child on Iselen. All of them.* She was not blind to the resonances. She knew that they killed, with joy and without discrimination. She knew what they were. She also knew, since Flidais's tale on the balcony, what they meant.

She glared at Kimberly through the slashing rain, daring her to speak again. But the Seer was silent, and in her eyes Jennifer saw no more anger or fear, only sadness and wisdom and a love she remembered as never varying. There was a queer constriction in her throat.

"Excuse me." The women looked down at the one who had spoken. "Excuse me," Flidais repeated, fighting hard against the surging in his heart, straining to keep his voice calm. "I take it you are the Seer of Brennin?"

"I am," Kim said.

"I am Flidais," he said, unconscionably quick with even this casually chosen name. But he had no patience left; he was near now, so near. He was afraid he would go mad with excitement. "I should tell you that Galadan is very close to this place—minutes away, I think."

Jennifer brought her hands to her mouth. She had forgotten, in the total absorption of the last few minutes. But it all came back now: the night in the wood and the wolf who had taken her away for Maugrim and then had become a man who said, *She is still to go north. If it were not so, I might take her for myself.* Just before he gave her to the swan.

She shuddered. She could not help herself. She heard Flidais say, still for some reason addressing Kim, "I can be of aid, I believe. I think I could divert him from this place, if I go fast enough."

"Well then, go!" Kim exclaimed. "If he's only a few minutes—"

"Or," Flidais went on, unable now to keep the rising note from finally reaching his voice, "I could do nothing, as the andain usually do. Or, *if I choose, I could tell him exactly who just left the glade, and who is here.*"

"I would kill you first!" Brendel burst out, his eyes gleaming through the rain. A bolt of lightning knifed into the roiling sea. There came another peal of thunder.

"You could try," Flidais said, with equanimity. "You would fail. And then Galadan would come."

He paused, waiting, looking at Kim, who said, slowly, "All right. What is it you want?"

Amid the howling of the storm Flidais was conscious of a great, cresting illumination in his heart. Tenderly, with a delicate ineffable joy, he said, "Only one thing. A small thing. So small. Only a name. The summoning name of the Warrior." His soul was singing. He did a little dance on the wet strand; he couldn't help himself. It was here. It was in his hands.

"No," said Kimberly.

His jaw dropped into the soaked mat of his beard.

"No," she repeated. "I swore an oath when he came to me, and I will not break it."

"Seer—" Jaelle began.

"You must!" Flidais moaned. "You *must* tell me! It is the only riddle. The last one! I know all the other answers. I would never tell. Never! The Weaver and all the gods know I would never tell—but I must know it, Seer! It is the wish of my heart!"

Strange, fateful phrase crossing the worlds with her. Kim remembered those words from all the years that had gone by, remembered thinking of them again on the mountain plateau with Brock unconscious at her side. She looked down at the gnomelike andain, his hands writhing over and about each other in frantic, pleading desperation. She remembered Arthur, in the moment he had answered her summons on Glastonbury Tor, the bowed weight of his shoulders, the weariness, the stars falling and falling through his eyes. She looked at Jennifer, who was Guinevere.

And who said, softly, but near enough so as to be heard over the wind and rain, "Give it to him. Even so is the name handed down. It is part of the woven doom. Broken oaths and grief lie at the heart of it, Kim. I'm sorry, truly."

It was the apology at the end that reached through to her, as much as anything else. Wordlessly she turned and strode a little way apart. She looked back and nodded to the andain. Stumbling, almost falling in his eagerness and haste, he trotted to her side. She looked down on him, not bothering to mask her contempt. "You will go from here with this name, and I charge you with two things. To never repeat it to a soul in any world, and to deal with Galadan now, doing whatever must be done to keep him from this Tower, and to shield the knowledge of Darien from him. Will you do so?"

"By every power in Fionavar I swear it," he said. He could scarcely control his voice so as to speak. He rose up, on tiptoe so as to be nearer to her. Despite herself she was moved by the helpless longing, the yearning in his face.

*"Childslayer,"* she said, and broke her oath.

He closed his eyes. A radiant ecstasy suffused his face. "Ah!" he moaned, transfigured. "Ah!" He said no more, staying thus, eyes closed, head lifted to the falling rain as if to a benediction.

Then he opened his eyes and fixed her with a level gaze. With dignity she hadn't expected, so soon after his exaltation, he said, "You hate me now. And not without cause. But hear me, Seer: I shall do everything I swore to do, and more. You have freed me from desire. When the soul has what it needs it is without longing, and so it is with me now. From the darkness of what I have done to you there shall be light, or

I shall die trying to make it so." He reached up and took her hand between both of his own. "Do not enter the Tower; he will know if there are people there. Endure the rain and wait for me. I shall not fail you."

Then was gone, running on stubby, bowed legs, but fleet and blurred as soon as he entered the forest, a power of Pendaran, moving into his element.

She turned back to the others, waiting west of her, farther down the strand. They stood gathered together under this fury of the elements. Something, an instinct, made her glance down at her hand. Not at the Baelrath, which was utterly subdued, but at the vellin stone about her wrist. And she saw it twisting slowly back and forth.

There was power here. Magic in the storm. She should have known it from the first rising of the wind. But there had been no time to absorb or think about anything but Darien from the moment Jaelle had brought them here. Now there was. Now there was a moment, a still space amid the wild fury of the elements. She lifted her eyes past the three other women and the lios alfar and, looking out to sea, she saw the ship running helplessly before the wind into the bay.

# CHAPTER 6

For a long time Coll of Taerlindel at the helm of his ship had fought the wind. Tacking desperately and with a certain brilliance across the line of the southwesterly, he struggled through most of a darkening day to hold *Prydwen* to a course that would bring them back to the harbour from which they had set out. Bellowing commands, his voice riding over the gale, he kept the men of South Keep leaping from sail to sail, pulling them down, adjusting them, straining for every inch of eastward motion he could gain against the elements that were forcing him north.

It was an exercise in seamanship of the highest order, of calculations done by instinct and nerve on the deck of a wildly tossing ship, of raw strength and raw courage, as Coll fought with all the power of his corded arms to hold the tiller against the gale that was pulling the ship from his chosen path.

And this was only wind, only the first fine mist of rain. The true storm, massive and glowering to starboard and behind them, was yet to come. But it was coming, swallowing what was left of the sky. They heard thunder, saw sheets of lightning ignite in the west, felt the screaming wind grow wilder yet, were drenched by driving, blinding spray as they slid and slipped on the heaving deck, struggling to obey Coll's steadily shouted commands.

Calmly he called out his orders, angling his ship with consummate inbred artistry along the troughs and into the crests of the waves, gauging the seas on either side, casting a frequent eye above him to judge the filling of the sails and the speed of the oncoming storm. Calmly he did it all, though with fierce, passionate intensity and not a little pride. And calmly, when it was clear past doubt that he had no choice, Coll surrendered.

"Over to port!" he roared in the same voice he'd used throughout his pitched battle against the storm. "Northeast it is! I'm sorry, Diar, we'll have to run with it and take our chances at the other end!"

Diarmuid dan Ailell, heir to the High Kingdom of Brennin, was far too busy grappling with a sail roe in obedience to the command to do much in the way of dealing with the apology. Beside the Prince, soaked through and through, almost deafened by the scream of the gale, Paul struggled to be useful and to cope with what he knew.

With what he had known from the first rising of the wind two hours ago, and his first glimpse, far down on the southwest horizon of the black line that was a curtain now, an enveloping darkness blotting out the sky. From the pulsebeat of Mörnir within himself, the still place like a pool in his blood that marked the presence of the God, he knew that what was coming, what had come, was more than a storm.

He was Pwyll Twiceborn, marked on the Summer Tree for power, named to it, and he knew when power of this magnitude was present, manifesting itself. Mörnir had warned him but could do no more, Paul knew. This was not his storm despite the crashing thunder, nor was it Liranan's, the elusive god of the sea. It might have been Metran, with the Cauldron of Khath Meigol, but the renegade mage was dead and the Cauldron shattered into fragments. And this storm far out at sea was not Rakoth Maugrim's in Starkadh.

Which meant one thing and one thing only, and Coll of Taerlindel, for all his gallant skill, hadn't a chance. It was not a thing you tell a captain of a ship at sea, Paul was wise enough to know. You let him fight, and trusted him to know when he could not fight any longer. And after, if you survived, you could try to heal his pride with the knowledge of what had beaten him.

If you survived.

"By Lisen's blood!" Diarmuid cried. Paul looked up—in time to see the sky swallowed, quite utterly, and the dark green curling wave, twice the height of the ship, begin to fall.

"Hang on!" the Prince screamed again, and clutched Paul's hastily donned jacket with an iron grip. Paul threw one arm around Diarmuid and looped the other through a rope lashed to the mast, gripping with all the strength he had. Then he closed his eyes.

The wave fell upon them with the weight of the sea and of doom. Of destiny not to be delayed or denied. Diarmuid held him, and Paul gripped the Prince, and they both clung to their handholds like children, which they were.

The Weaver's children. The Weaver at the Loom, whose storm this was.

When he could see again, and breathe, Paul looked up at the tiller through the sluicing rain and spray. Coll had help there now, badly needed help, in the muscle-tearing task of holding the ship to its new course, running now with the full speed of the storm, dangerously, shockingly fast in the raging sea, at a speed where the slightest turning of the rudder could heel them over like a toy into the waves. But Arthur Pendragon was with Coll now, balancing him, pulling shoulder to shoulder beside the mariner, salt spray drenching his greying beard, and Paul knew—though he could not actually see them from where he crouched in the shadow of the mainmast—that there would be stars falling and falling in the Warrior's eyes as he was carried towards his foretold fate again, by the hand of the Weaver who had woven his doom.

*Childen*, Paul thought. Both the children they all were, helpless on this ship, and the children who had died when the Warrior was young, and so terribly afraid that his bright dream would be destroyed. The two images blurred in his mind, as the rain and the sea spray blurred together, driving them on.

Running before the wind, *Prydwen* tore through the seas at a speed no ship should have ever been asked to sustain, no sails to endure. But the timbers of that ship, screaming and creaking with strain, yet held, and the sails, woven with love and care and centuries of handed-down artistry in Taerlindel of the Mariners, caught that howling wind and filled with it and did not tear, though the black sky above might shred with lightning and the very sea rock with the thunder.

Riding the mad crest of that speed, the two men at the tiller fought to hold their course, their bodies taut with the brutal strain. And then, with no surprise at all, only a dulled, hurting sense of inevitability, Paul saw Lancelot du Lac grapple his way to their side. And so, at the last, it was the three of them: Coll conning his ship with Lancelot and Arthur at either side, their feet braced wide on the slippery deck, gripping the tiller together, in flawless, necessary harmony, guiding that small, gallant, much-enduring ship into the bay of the Anor Lisen.

And, helpless to do so much as veer a single point off the wind, onto the jagged teeth of the rocks that guarded the southern entrance to that bay.

Paul never knew, afterwards, whether they had been meant to survive. Arthur and Lancelot had to, he knew, else there would have been no point to the storm that carried them here. But the rest of them were expendable, however bitter the thought might be, in the unfolding of this tale.

He never knew, either, exactly what it was that warned him. They were moving so fast, through the darkness and the pelting, blinding sheets of rain, that none of them had even seen the shore, let alone the rocks. Reaching back, trying to relive the moment afterward, he thought it might have been his ravens that spoke, but chaos reigned on *Prydwen* in that moment, and he could never be sure.

What he knew was that in the fraction of splintered time before *Prydwen* splintered forever into fragments and spars, he had risen to his feet, unnaturally surefooted in the unnatural storm, and had cried out in a voice that encompassed the thunder and contained it, that was of it and within it—exactly as he had been of and within the Summer Tree on the night he thought he'd died—and in that voice, the voice of Mörnir who had sent him back, he cried, *"Liranan!"* just as they struck.

The masts cracked with the sound of broken trees; the sides cracked, and the deck; the bottom of the ship was gouged mercilessly, utterly, and the dark sea blasted in. Paul was catapulted, a leaf, a twig, a meaningless thing, from the deck of the suddenly grounded ship.They all hurtled over the sides, every man of what had been, a moment before, Coll's grandfather's beloved *Prydwen*.

And as Paul flew, a split second in the air, another fraction of scintillated time, tasting his second death, knowing the rocks were there and the boiling, enraged, annihilating sea, even in that instant he heard a voice in his mind, clear and remembered.

And Liranan spoke to him and said, *I will pay for this, and pay, and be made to pay again, before the weaving of time is done. But I owe you, brother—the sea stars are shining in a certain place again because you bound me to your aid. This is not binding; this is a gift. Remember me!*

And then Paul cartwheeled helplessly into the waters of the bay.

The calm, unruffled, blue-green waters of the bay. Away from the jagged, killing rocks. Out of the murderous wind, and under a mild rain that fell gently down, bereft of the gale that had given it its cutting edge.

Just beyond the curve of the bay the storm raged yet, the lightning still slashed from the purpled clouds. Where he was, where all of them were, rain fell softly from an overcast summer sky as they swam, singly, in pairs, in clusters, to the strand of beach under the shadow of Lisen's Tower.

Where Guinevere stood.

It was a miracle, Kim realized. But she also realized too much more for her tears to be shed only for relief and joy. Too dense this weaving, too laden with shadings and textures and a myriad of intermingled threads, both warp and weft, for any emotion to be truly unmixed.

They had seen the ship cannon towards the rocks. Then, even in that moment of realization and terror, they had heard a single imperative crash of sound, halfway between thunder and a voice, and on the instant—absolutely on the instant—the wind had cut out completely and the waters of the bay had gone glassily calm. The men who manned *Prydwen* were spilled over the disintegrating sides of the ship into a bay that would have destroyed them not two seconds before.

A miracle. There might be time enough later to search for the source of it and give thanks. But not yet. Not now, in this tangled sorrow-strewn unfolding of a long destiny.

For there were three of them, after all, and Kim could do nothing, nothing at all to stop the hurting in her heart. A man stepped from the sea who had not been on *Prydwen* when she sailed. A man who was very tall, his hair dark, and his eyes as well. There was a long sword at his side, and beside him came Cavall, the grey dog, and in his arms, held carefully out before him, the man carried the body of Arthur Pendragon, and all five people on the beach, waiting, knew who this man was.

Four of them stayed a little way behind, though Kim knew how every instinct in Sharra's soul was driving her to the sea where Diarmuid was even now emerging, helping one of his men out of the water. She fought that instinct, though, and Kim honoured her for it. Standing between Sharra and Jaelle, with Brendel a pace to the side and behind, she watched as Jennifer moved forward through the gentle rain to stand before the two men she had loved and been loved by through so many lives in so many worlds.

Guinevere was remembering a moment on the balcony of the Tower earlier that afternoon, when Flidais had spoken of randomness as the variable the Weaver had woven into his Tapestry for a limitation on himself. She was remembering, as if from a place infinitely far away, the explosion of hope in her mind, that this time might be different because of that. Because Lancelot was not here, no third angle of the triangle, and so the Weaver's design might yet be changed, because the Weaver himself had made a space in the Tapestry for change.

No one knew of that thought, and no one ever would. It was buried now, and smashed, and gone.

What was here, in its stead, was Lancelot du Lac, whose soul was the other half of her own. Whose eyes were as dark as they had been every single time before, as undemanding, as understanding, with the same pain buried in their depths that only she could comprehend, only she assuage. Whose hands . . . whose long, graceful fighter's hands were exactly as they had been the last time and the time before, every hurting time before, when she had loved them, and loved him as the mirror of herself.

Whose hands cradled now, gently, with infinite, unmistakable tenderness, the body of his liege lord, her husband. Whom she loved.

Whom she loved in the teeth of all the lies, all the crabbed, envious incomprehension, with a full and a shattering passion that had survived and would survive and would tear her asunder every time she woke again to who she had been and was fated to be. To the memory and the knowledge of betrayal like a stone at the centre of everything. The grief at the heart of a dream, the reason why she was here, and Lancelot. The price, the curse, the punishment laid by the Weaver on the Warrior in the name of the children who had died.

She and Lancelot faced each other in silence on the strand, in a space that seemed to the watchers to have somehow been cut out from the ebb and flow of time: an island in the Tapestry. She stood before the two men she loved, bareheaded in the falling rain, and she had memories of so many things.

Her eyes went back again to his hands, and she remembered when he had gone mad—truly so, for a time—for desire of her and the denial within himself of that desire. How he had gone forth from Camelot into the woods and wandered there through the turning of the seasons, naked even in the wintertime, alone and wild, stripped to the very bone by longing. And she remembered those hands when he was finally brought back: the scars, cuts, scabs, the calluses, and broken nails, the frostbite from scrabbling in the snow for berries underneath.

Arthur had wept, she remembered. She had not. Not then, not until later, when she was alone. It had hurt so much. She had thought that death would be better than that sight. And as much as any other single thing, it had been those hands, the palpable evidence of what love of her was doing to him, that had opened her own barricades and let him in to the hearthside of her heart and the welcome so long denied. How could it be a betrayal, of anyone or anything, to offer shelter to such a one? And to let the mirror be made whole, that its reflection of the fire might show both of them beside it?

Still she was silent in the rain, and he, and nothing of this showed in her face. Even so, he knew her thoughts, and she knew that he did. Motionless, wordlessly, they touched after so long and yet did not touch. His hands, clean now, unscarred, slender and beautiful, held Arthur in a clasp of love that spoke so deeply to her that she heard it as a chorus in her heart, high voices in a vaulted place singing of joy and pain.

And in that moment she recalled something else, and this he could not know, though his dark eyes might darken further, looking into hers. She suddenly remembered the last time she had seen his face: not in Camelot, or any of the other lives, the other worlds where they had been brought back to the working of Arthur's doom, but in Starkadh, a little more than a year ago. When Rakoth Maugrim, breaking her for the pleasure it afforded him, had ransacked the effortlessly opened chambers of her memories and come out with an image she had not recognized, an image of the man who stood before her now. And now she understood. She saw again the moment when the dark god had taken this shape in mockery, in a defiling, an attempt to stain and soil her knowledge of love, to besmirch the memory, sear it from her with the blood that fell from the black stump of his lost hand, burning her.

And standing here by the Anor as the clouds began to break up in the west with the passing of the storm, as the first rays of the setting sun sliced through, low down over the sea, she knew that Rakoth had failed.

Better he had not failed, a part of her was thinking, ironic, detached. Better he had scorched this love from her, made a kind of good from the abyss of his evil, freed her from Lancelot, that the endless betrayal might have an end.

But he had not. She had only loved two men in all her life, the two most shining men in any world. And she loved them yet.

She was aware of the changing light: amber, shades of gold. Sunset after storm. The rain had ended. A square of sky appeared overhead, blue, toning downwards towards the muted colour of dusk. She heard the surge of the surf, and the withdrawal of it along the sand and stones. She held herself straight as she could, quite still; she had a sense that to move, just then, would be to break, and she could not break.

"He is all right," Lancelot said.

*What is a voice?* she thought. What is a voice that it can do this to us? Firelight. A mirror made whole. A dream shown broken in that mirror. The texture of a soul in four words. Four words not about her, or himself, not of greeting or desire. Four quiet words about the man he carried, and so about the man he was himself.

If she moved, it would be to break.

She said, "I know."

The Weaver had not brought him to this place, to her, to have him die in a storm at sea; too easy, that, by far.

"He stayed at the tiller too long," Lancelot said. "He cracked his head when we hit. Cavall led me to him in the water." As quietly as that, he said it. No bravado, no hint of drama or achievement. And then, after a pause, "Even in that storm, he was trying to steer for a gap in the rocks."

*Over and over*, she was thinking. How many ways were there for a story to circle back upon itself?

"He was always looking for gaps in the rocks," she murmured. She said nothing else. It was difficult to speak. She looked into his eyes and waited.

There was light now, clouds breaking apart, clear sky. And, suddenly, the track of the sunset along the sea, and then the setting sun below the western clouds. She waited, knowing what he would say, what she would say in response.

He said, "Shall I go away?"

"Yes," she said.

She did not move. A bird sang behind her, in the trees at the edge of the strand. Then another bird sang. The surf came in and withdrew, and then it came in again.

He said, "Where shall I go?"

And now she had to hurt him very badly, because he loved her and had not been here to save her when it happened.

She said, "You will know of Rakoth Maugrim; they will have told you on the ship. He took me a year ago. To the place of his power. He . . . did things to me."

She stopped: not for herself, it was an old pain now, and Arthur had taken much of it away. But she had to stop because of what was in his face. Then after a moment she went on, carefully, because she could not break, not now. She said, "I was to die, after. I was saved, though, and in time I bore his child.

Again she was forced to pause. She closed her eyes, so as not to see his face. No one else, she knew, and nothing else, did this to him. But she did it every time. She heard him kneel, not trusting his hands any longer, and lay Arthur gently down on the sand.

She said, eyes still closed, "I wanted to have the child. There are reasons words will not reach. His name is Darien, and he was here not long ago, and went away because I made him go away. They do not understand why I did this, why I did not try to bind him." She paused again and took a breath.

"I think I understand," said Lancelot. Only that. Which was so much.

She opened her eyes. He was on his knees before her, Arthur lying between the two of them, the sun and its track along the sea behind both men, red and gold and very beautiful. She did not move. She said, "He went into this wood. It is a place of ancient power and of hate, and before he went he burnt a tree with his own power, which comes from his father. I would . . ." She faltered. He had only just now come, and was here before her, and she faltered at the words that would send him away.

There was silence, but not for very long. Lancelot said, "I understand. I will guard him, and not bind him, and leave him to choose his road."

She swallowed and fought back her tears. What was a voice? A doorway, with nuances of light, intimations of shade: a doorway to a soul.

"It is a dark road," she said, speaking more truth than she knew.

He smiled, so unexpectedly that it stopped her heart for a beat. He smiled up at her, and then rose, and so smiled down upon her, tenderly, gravely, with a sure strength whose only place of vulnerability was herself, and he said, "All the roads are dark, Guinevere. Only at the end is there a hope of light." The smile faded. "Fare gently, love."

He turned with the last words, his hand moving automatically, unconsciously, to check the hang of the sword at his side. Panic rose within her, a blind surge.

"Lancelot!" she said.

She had not spoken his name before that. He stopped and turned, two separate actions, slowed by a weight of pain. He looked at her. Slowly, sharing the weight, with very great care, she held out one hand to him. And as slowly, his eyes on hers and naming her name over and over in their depths, he walked back, and took her hand, and brought it to his lips.

Then in her turn, not speaking, not daring to speak or able, she took the hand in which he held her own and laid the back of it against her cheek so that one tear fell upon it. Then she kissed that tear away and watched him go, past all the silent people who parted to make way for him, as he walked from her into Pendaran Wood.

◦◦▭◑◖▭◦◦

Once, a long time ago, he had met Green Ceinwen by chance in a glade of the Wood by moonlight. Cautiously, for it always paid to be cautious with the Huntress, Flidais had entered the glade and saluted her. She had been sitting on the trunk of a fallen tree, her long legs outstretched, her bow laid down, a dead boar lying beside her with an arrow in its throat. There was a small pool in the glade, and from it the moonlight was reflected back into her face. The stories of her cruelty and capriciousness were legion, and he knew all of them and had started many of the tales himself, so it was with extreme diffidence that he approached, grateful that she had not been bathing in the pool, knowing he would very likely have died had he seen her so.

She had been in a mood of catlike languor that night, though, having just killed, and she greeted him with amusement, stretching her supple body, making room for him beside her on the fallen trunk.

They had spoken for a time, softly, as befitted the place and the moonlight, and it had pleasured her to tease him with stirred desire, though it was gently done, and not with malice that night.

Then, as the moon made ready to pass over into the trees west of them and so be lost to that glade, Green Ceinwen had said, lazily but with a different, more meaningful tone than hitherto, "Flidais, little forest one, do you not ever wonder what will happen to you if you ever do learn the name you seek?"

"How so, goddess?" he remembered asking, his nerves bared suddenly by this merest, most idle mention of his long desire.

"Will your soul not lie bereft and purposeless should that day come? What will you do, having gained the last and only thing you covet? With your thirst slaked will you not be stripped of all joy in life, all reason to live? Consider it, little one. Give it thought."

The moon had gone then. And the goddess, too, though not before stroking his face and body with her long fingers, leaving him rampant with desire by the dark pool.

She was capricious and cruel, elusive and very dangerous, but she was also a goddess and not the least wise of them. He sat in the grove a long time, thinking about what she said, and he had thought about it often in the years that followed.

And only now, now that it had happened, could he draw breath after breath that tasted of joy and realize that she had been wrong. It might have been otherwise, he knew: gaining his heart's desire might indeed have been a blight, not this transcendent brightness in his life. But it had fallen out differently; his dream had been made real, the gapped worlds made whole, and along with joy Flidais of the andain now finally knew peace.

It had come at the price of a broken oath, he knew. He had some fleeting, distant sense of regret that this had been demanded, but it scarcely even ruffled the deep waters of his contentment. And, in any case, he had balanced those scales with an oath of his own to the Seer, one that he would keep. She would see. However bitter her contempt for him now, she would have cause to change before the story spun to its close. For the first time, one of the andain would lend himself freely to the cause of the mortals and their war.

Starting now, he thought, with the one who was his lord.

*He is here*, the lone deiena in the tree above him whispered urgently, and Flidais barely had time to register the sudden easing of the rain and the passing of the thunder, and to fling the swift mental call he'd decided upon, before there came a sound of something crashing through the trees and the wolf had come.

And then, a moment later, Galadan was there instead. Flidais felt light; he had an illusion that he could fly if he wanted to, that he was only tied to the forest floor by the thinnest threads of constraint. But he had cause to know how dangerous the figure standing before him was, and he had a task to perform now, a deception to perpetrate on one who had been known for a long time as the subtlest mind in Fionavar. And who was also the lieutenant of Rakoth Maugrim.

So Flidais schooled his features as best he could, and he bowed, gravely and low, to the one who had only once been challenged in his claim of lordship over the elusive, estranged, arrogant family of the andain. Only once—and Flidais remembered, very well, how Liranan's son and Macha's daughter had both died, not far from here, by the Cliffs of Rhudh.

*What are you doing here?* said Galadan in his mind. Straightening, Flidais saw that the Wolflord looked lean and deadly, his features tight with anger and unease.

Flidais clasped his hands loosely together in front of his rounded belly. "I am always here," he said mildly, speaking aloud.

He winced, as a sudden knife of pain slashed into his mind. Before speaking again he put up his mental barricades, not displeased, for Galadan had just given him an excuse.

"Why did you do that?" he asked plaintively.

He felt the quick probe bounce away from his barriers. Galadan could kill him, with disturbing ease, but the Wolflord could not see into his mind unless Flidais chose to let him in, and that, at the moment, was what mattered.

*Do not be too clever, forest one. Not with me. Why are you speaking aloud, and who was in the Anor? Answer quickly. I have little time and less patience.* The mind voice was cold and arrogantly confident, but Flidais had knowledge of his own, and memories. He knew that the Wolflord was feeling the strain of being near to the Tower—which made him more, not less, of a danger, if it came to that.

Half an hour ago he would never have done it, never have dreamt of doing it, but everything had changed since he had learned the name, and so Flidais said, still carefully aloud, "How dare you probe me, Galadan? I care nothing for your war, but a great deal for my own secrets, and will certainly not open my mind to you when you come to me—in Pendaran, if you please—in this fashion, and with such a tone.

Will you kill me for my riddles, Wolflord? You *hurt* me just now!" He thought he had the tone right, grievance and pride in equal measure, but it was hard to tell, very hard, given the one with whom he was dealing.

Then he drew a quiet, satisfied breath, for when the Wolflord addressed him again it was aloud and with the courtly grace that had always been a part of him. "Forgive me," he murmured, and bowed in his turn with unconscious elegance. "I have been two days running to get here and am not myself." His scarred features relaxed into a smile. "Whoever that is. I sensed someone in the Anor, and . . . wanted to know who."

There was some hesitation at the end, and this, too, Flidais understood. In the cold, rational, utterly clinical soul that was Galadan's, the blinding passion that still assailed him in connection with Lisen was brutally anomalous. And the memory of his rejection in favor of Amairgen would be a wound scraped raw every time he neared this place. From the new harbour of peace where his soul was moored, Flidais looked at the other figure and pitied him. He kept that out of his eyes, though, having no pressing desire to be slain.

He also had an oath to keep. So he said, reaching for the right tone of casual appeasement, "I'm sorry, I should have known you would sense it. I would have tried to send word I was in the Anor myself, Galadan. I am just now leaving it."

"*You?* Why?"

Flidais shrugged expressively. "Symmetry. My own sense of time. Patterns on the Loom. You know they sailed from Taerlindel some days ago, for Cader Sedat. I thought someone should be in the Anor, in case they returned this way."

The rain had stopped, though the leaves overhead were still dripping. The trees grew too thickly to show much of the clearing sky. Flidais waited to see if his bait would be taken, and he guarded his mind.

"I did *not* know that," Galadan admitted, a furrow creasing his brow. "It is news and it matters. I think I will have to take it north. I thank you," he said, with much of the old calculation in his voice again. Careful, very careful, not to smile, Flidais nodded. "Who sailed?" the Wolflord asked.

Flidais made his expression as stern as he could. "You should not have hurt me," he said, "if you were going to ask questions."

Galadan laughed aloud. The sound rang through the Great Wood. "Ah, Flidais, is there anyone like you?" he queried rhetorically, still chuckling.

"There is no one with the headache I have!" Flidais replied, not smiling.

"I apologized," Galadan said, sobering quickly, his voice suddenly silken and low. "I will not do so twice." He let the silence hold for a moment, then repeated, "Who sailed, forest one?"

After a brief pause, to show a necessary flicker of independence, Flidais said, "The mage and the Dwarf. The Prince of Brennin. The one called Pwyll, from the Tree." An expression he could not read flashed briefly across Galadan's aristocratic face. "And the Warrior," he concluded.

Galadan was silent a moment, deep in thought. "Interesting," he said at length.

"I am suddenly glad I came, forest one. All of this matters. I wonder if they killed Metran? What," he asked swiftly, "do you think of the storm that just passed?"

Off balance, Flidais nonetheless managed to smile. "Exactly what you think," he murmured. "And if a storm has driven the Warrior to land somewhere, I, for one, am going to look for him."

Again Galadan laughed, more softly than before. "Of course," he said. "Of course. The name. Do you expect him to tell you himself?"

Flidais could feel a bright colour suffuse his face, which was all right; let the Wolflord think he was embarrassed. "Stranger things have happened," he said stoutly. "Have I your leave to go?"

"Not yet. What did you do in the Anor?"

A flicker of unease rippled through the forest andain. It was all very well to have successfully dissembled with Galadan so far, but one didn't want to push one's fortune by lingering too long. "I cleaned it," he said, with an edgy impatience he did not have to feign. "The glass and the floors. I rolled back the windows to let air in. And I watched for two days, to see if the ship would come. Then, with the storm, I knew it had been driven to land, and since it was not here . . ."

Galadan's eyes were cold and grey and fixed downwards on his own. "Were there not flowers?" he whispered, and menace was suddenly a vivid, rustling presence where they stood.

Feigning nothing at all, his heart racing, mouth suddenly dry, Flidais said, "There were, my lord. They . . . crumbled from age when I was dusting the room. I can get more for you. Would you desire me to—"

He got no further. Faster than eye could follow or most cunning mind anticipate, the figure in front of him melted away and in its stead a wolf was there, a wolf that leaped, even in the instant it appeared. With one swift, precisely calculated motion, a huge paw raked the forest andain's head.

Flidais never even moved. He was cunning and wise and surprisingly swift within his Wood, but Galadan was what he was. And so, an instant later, the little bearded andain lay, writhing in genuine agony on the sodden forest floor, holding both hands to the bloodied place where his right ear had been ripped away.

"Live a while longer, forest one," he heard, through the miasma of pain flowing over him. "And name me merciful in your innermost heart. You touched the flowers I laid in that place for her," the voice said, benign, reflective, elegant. "Could you really expect to have been allowed to live?"

Fighting to hold consciousness, Flidais heard, within his reeling mind, another voice then, that sounded near and very far away, at one and the same time. And the voice said, *Oh, my son, what have you become?*

Wiping away blood, Flidais managed to open his eyes. The forest rocked wildly in his vision, then righted itself, and through the curtain of blood and pain he saw the tall, naked, commanding figure and the great horns of Cernan of the Beasts. Whom he had called to this place just before Galadan came.

With a snarl of rage mingled with another thing, the Wolflord turned to his father.

A moment later, Galadan was in his human shape again, elegant as ever. "You lost the right to ask me that a long time ago," he said.

He spoke aloud to his father, a part of Flidais noted, even as he himself had spoken aloud to Galadan, to deny him access to his thoughts.

Majestic and terrible in his nakedness and power, the god of the forests came forward. Speaking aloud, his voice reverberating, Cernan said, "Because I would not kill the mage for you? I will not make answer to that again, my son. But will ask you once more, in this Wood where I fathered you, how have you so lost yourself that you can do this thing to your own brother?"

Flidais closed his eyes. He felt consciousness slipping away, ripple by ripple, like a withdrawing sea. But before he went out with the tide he heard Galadan laugh again, in mockery, and say to his father, to their father, "Why should it signify anything to me that this fat drudge of the forest is another byblow of your profligate seed? Sons and their fathers," he snarled, halfway to the wolf he could so easily become. "Why should any of that matter now?"

*Oh, but it does*, Flidais thought, with his last shred of consciousness. *Oh, but it matters so much. If only you knew, brother!* He sent it out to neither of the others, that thought. Closely to himself he clutched his memory of the torched tree, and Darien with the Circlet of Lisen on his brow. Then Flidais, having kept his oath, having found his heart's desire, was hit by another surge of pain and knew nothing more at all of what his father said to his brother in the Wood.

# CHAPTER 7

To the east, at Celidon, the sun was low in a sky unmarred by clouds or the hint of any storm as the army of Brennin came at last to the mid-Plain. Galloping beside Niavin, Duke of Seresh, at the front of the host, Teyrnon the mage, weary to the bone after three days of riding, nonetheless managed to pull his chunky body erect in the saddle at his first glimpse of the standing stones.

Beside him, his source chuckled softly and murmured, "I was about to suggest you do that."

Teyrnon glanced over, amused, at Barak, the tall, handsome boyhood friend who was the source of his power, and his good-natured face slipped easily into a self-deprecating grin. "I've lost more weight on this ride than I care to think about," the mage said, slapping his still-comfortable girth.

"Do you good," said Niavin of Seresh, on the other side.

"How," Teyrnon replied indignantly, over Barak's laughter, "can a complete scrambling of my bones possibly do me good? I'm afraid if I try to scratch my nose I'll end up rubbing my knee instead, if you know what I mean."

Niavin snorted, then gave way to laughter of his own. It was hard to stay grim and warlike in the company of the genial, unprepossessing mage. On the other hand, he had known Teyrnon and Barak since they were children in Seresh, in the early days of Ailell's reign, when Niavin's own father was the newly appointed Duke of Seresh, and he had little concern about their capabilities. They would be very serious indeed when the time called for it.

And the time, it seemed, was upon them now. Riding toward them from between the massive stones were three figures. Niavin raised a hand, unnecessarily, to point for the mage's benefit.

"I see them," said Teyrnon quietly. Niavin glanced over sharply, but the other man's face had lost its open ingenuousness and was unreadable.

It was probably just as well that Niavin could not discern the mage's thoughts. They would have worried him deeply, as deeply as Teyrnon himself was troubled, by self-doubts and diffidence and by one other thing.

Formally the two of them greeted Aileron the High King, and formally they returned to him the command of his army, in the presence of his two companions, Ra-Tenniel of the lios alfar, and the Aven of the Plain, who had ridden out to greet the host of Brennin. As formally, Aileron returned their salutations. Then, with the brusque efficiency of the war king he was, he asked Teyrnon, "Have you been contacted, mage?"

Slowly Teyrnon shook his round head. He had expected the question. "I have reached out, my lord High King. Nothing from Loren at all. There is something else, though." He hesitated, then went on. "A storm, Aileron. Out at sea. We found it while we were reaching. A southwest gale, bringing a storm."

"That should not happen," Ra-Tenniel said quickly.

Aileron nodded, not speaking, his bearded features grim.

"Southwest will not be Maugrim," Ivor murmured. "You have seen nothing of the ship?" he asked Teyrnon.

"I am not a Seer," the mage explained patiently. "I can sense, to some degree, an assertion of magic such as this storm, and I can reach out to another mage across a fair distance. If the ship had returned I would have found or been reached by Loren before now."

"And so," Aileron said heavily, "it has not returned, or else Silvercloak has not returned with it." His dark eyes met those of Teyrnon for a long moment, as a late-afternoon breeze stirred the grasses of the Plain all around them.

No one else spoke; they waited for the High King. Still looking at Teyrnon, Aileron said, "We cannot wait. We will push north towards Gwynir now, not in the morning as planned. We have at least three hours of light by which to ride."

Swiftly he explained to Niavin and the mage what had happened in the battle two nights before. "We have been handed an advantage," he said grimly, "one not of our own doing, but by virtue of Owein's sword and Ceinwen's intercession. We must turn that advantage to good effect, while the army of Maugrim is disorganized and fearful. Weaver knows what I would give to have Loren and the Seer with us now, but we cannot wait. Teyrnon of Seresh, will you act as my First Mage in the battles that lie before us?"

He had never been so ambitious, never aimed half so high. It had been derided as a flaw when he was younger, then gradually accepted and indulged as the years passed: Teyrnon was what he was, everyone said, and smiled as they said it. He was clever and reliable; very often he had useful insights into matters of concern. But the paunchy, easy-smiling mage had never been seen—or seen himself, for that matter—as being of real importance in any scheme of things, even in time of peace. Metran and Loren were the mages who mattered.

He'd been content to let that be the case. He'd had his books and his studies, which mattered a great deal. He'd had the comfort of the mages' quarters in the capital: servants, good food and drink, companionship. He'd enjoyed the privileges of rank, the satisfactions of his power, and, indeed, the prestige that went with both. Not a few ladies of Ailell's court had found their way to his bedroom or invited him to their own scented chambers, when they would have scorned to look twice at a chubby scholar from Seresh.

He'd taken his duties as a mage seriously, for all his genial good nature. He and Barak had performed their peacetime tasks quietly and without fuss and had served unobtrusively as buffers between the other two members of the Council of the Mages. He hadn't begrudged that, either. Had he been asked, in the last years of Ailell's rein, before the drought had come, he would have numbered his own thread on the Loom as one of those that shone most brightly with the glow of the Weaver's benevolence.

But the drought *had* come, and Rangat had flamed, and Metran, who'd had wisdom once, as well as cleverness, had proven himself a traitor. So now they found themselves at war against the unleashed power of Rakoth Maugrim, and suddenly he, Teyrnon, was acting First Mage to the High King of Brennin.

He was also, or so the nagging, unspoken premonition at the remotest turning of his mind had been telling him since yesterday morning, the only mage in Fionavar.

Since yesterday morning, when the Cauldron of Khath Meigol had been destroyed. He knew nothing specific about that, nothing about any of the consequences of that destruction, only this distant premonition, so vague and terrifying he refused to speak it or give it a tangible name in his mind.

What he felt, though, was lonely.

⤙⟫⟪⤚

The sun had gone down. The rain had stopped, and the clouds were scudding away to the north and east. The sky in the west still held to its last hues of sunset shading. But on the beach by the Anor Lisen it was growing dark, as Loren Silvercloak finished telling the truth that had to be told.

When he was done, when his quiet, sorrowful voice had come to an end, those gathered on the beach listened as Brendel of the lios alfar wept for the souls of his people slain as they sailed to their song. Sitting on the sand with Arthur's head cradled in her lap, Jennifer saw Diarmuid, his expressive features twisted with pain, turn away from the kneeling figure of the lios and enfold Sharra of Cathal in his arms, not with passion or desire but in an unexpectedly vulnerable seeking of comfort.

There were tears on her own cheeks; they kept falling, even as she wiped them away, grieving for her friend and his people. Then, looking down, she saw that Arthur was awake and was gazing back at her, and suddenly she saw herself reflected in his eyes. A single star, very bright, fell across her reflectlon as she watched.

Slowly he raised a hand and touched the cheek where Lancelot's hand had lain.

"Welcome home, my love," she said, listening to the brokenhearted grief of the lios alfar who had guided her to this place, hearing all the while, within her mind, the patient, inexorable shuttling of the Loom. "I have sent him away," she said, feeling the words as warp to the weft of the storm that had passed. The story playing itself out again. Crossings and recrossings.

Arthur closed his eyes. "Why?" he asked, only shaping the word, not quite a sound.

"For the same reason you brought him back," she answered. And then, as he looked up at her again, she hurt him, as she had hurt Lancelot: to do it and have it over and done, because he, too, had a right to know.

So Guinevere, who had been childless in Camelot, told Arthur about Darien, as the western sky gave up its light and the first stars came out overhead. When she was done, Brendel's quiet weeping came also to an end.

There was a star in the west, low down over the sea, brighter than all the others in the sky, and the company on the beach watched as the lios alfar rose to his feet and faced that star. For a long time he stood silent; then he raised both hands and spread them wide, before lifting his voice in the invocation of song.

Rough at first with the burden of his grief, but growing more crystalline with each word, each offering, Na-Brendel of the Kestrel Mark of Daniloth took the leaden weight of his sorrow and alchemized it into the achingly beautiful, timeless notes of Ra-Termaine's Lament for the Lost, sung as it had never been sung in a thousand years, not even by the one who had created it. And so on that strand at the edge of the sea, under all the shining stars, he made a silver shining thing of his own out of what evil had done to the Children of Light.

Alone of those on the beach below the Anor, Kimberly took no comfort, no easing of pain, from the clear distillation of the lament that Brendel sang. She heard the beauty of it, understood, and was humbled by the grandeur of what the lios alfar was doing, and she knew the power such music had to heal—she could see it working in the faces of those beside her. Even in Jennifer, in Arthur, in stern cold Jaelle, as they listened to Brendel's soul in his voice, lifted to the watching, wheeling stars, to the dark forest and the wide sea.

But she was too far gone in guilt and self-laceration for any of that easing to reach through to her. Was everything she touched, every single thing that came within the glowering ambit of the ring she bore, to be twisted and torn by her presence? She was a healer herself, in her own world! Was she to carry nothing at all but pain to those she loved? To those who needed her?

Nothing but sorrow. From the summoning of Tabor and the corruption of the Paraiko last night to her brutal mishandling of Darien, this morning and then again this evening—when she hadn't even arrived in time to warn Jennifer of what was coming. And then, most bitterly of all, the breaking of the oath she had sworn on Glastonbury Tor. Was the Warrior's portion of grief not great enough, she asked herself savagely, that she'd had to add to it by bandying about the terrible name he was cursed to answer to?

No matter, she swore, lashing herself, that Guinevere had said what she had said, giving dispensation. No matter how desperately they'd needed Flidais to aid them, to hold the secret of Darien. They would not have needed that aid, or anything at all from him, had she not presumed to send Darien to this place. She pushed her wet hair back from her eyes. She looked, she knew, like a half-drowned water rat. She could feel the single vertical crease in her forehead. It might, she thought derisively, fool someone into thinking she was wise and experienced: that, and her white hair. Well, she decided, trembling, if anyone was still fooled after tonight, it was their own lookout!

A last long wavering note rose up and then faded away as Brendel's song came to an end. He lowered his arms and stood silent on the strand. Kim looked over at Jennifer, sitting on the wet sand with Arthur's head cradled in her lap, and saw her friend, who was so much more than that, motion for her to come over.

She took an unsteady breath and walked across the sand to kneel beside them. "How is he?" she asked quietly.

"He is fine," Arthur replied himself, fixing her with that gaze that seemed to have no ending and to be filled, so much of the time, with stars. "I have just paid a fairly mild price for being a too-stubborn helmsman."

He smiled at her, and she had to smile back.

"Guinevere has told me what you had to do. She says she gave you leave, and explained why, but that you will still be hating yourself. Is this true?"

Kim shifted her glance and saw the ghost of a smile tracing the edges of Jennifer's mouth. She swallowed. "She knows me pretty well," she said ruefully.

"And me," he answered calmly. "She knows me very well, and the dispensation she gave you was also mine. The one you know as Flidais was Taliesin once—we both knew him a very long time ago. He is clearly part of the story, though I am not certain how. Seer, do not despair of brightness flowing from what you had to do."

There was so much comfort in his voice, in the calm, accepting eyes. In the face of this it would be hubris, mere vanity, to hold to her self-condemnation. She said, diffidently, "He said it was his heart's desire. The last riddle he did not know. He said . . . he said he would make light from the darkness of what he had done or die trying to do so."

There was a little silence, as the other two absorbed this. Kim listened to the surf coming in, so gentle now after the wildness of the storm. Then they sensed rather than heard someone approaching, and the three of them glanced up at Brendel.

He seemed more ethereal than ever in the starlight, less tied to the earth, to the pull of gravity. In the dark they could not see the colour of his eyes, but they were not shining. He said, in a voice like the whisper of the breeze, "My lady Guinevere, with your permission, I must leave you now for a time. It is . . . it is now my task, over and above all else I am afraid, to carry the tidings I have just heard to my King in Daniloth."

Jennifer opened her mouth to reply, but another voice made answer to the lios alfar.

"He is not there," said Jaelle, from behind them. Her hard voice, usually so imperious, was muted now, more mild than Kim had thought it could be. "There was a battle two nights ago by the banks of the Adein, near Celidon. The Dalrei and the men of Rhoden met an army of the Dark, and Ra-Tenniel led the lios alfar out of the Shadowland, Na-Brendel. He led them to war on the Plain."

"And?" It was Loren Silvercloak.

Kimberly listened as Jaelle, stripped of her usual arrogance, told the tale of how Leila had heard the blowing of Owein's Horn, and seen the battlefield through Finn's presence there, and then how all of them in the Temple had heard Ceinwen intercede. "The High King rode north in response to the summonglass the night *Prydwen* set sail," she concluded. "They will all be on the Plain by now, though what they will do I know not. Perhaps Loren can reach for Teyrnon and answer that for us."

It was the first time Kim could remember that High Priestess speaking so to the mage.

Then, a moment later, she learned that Loren wasn't a mage any longer. And even as the tale was being told the ring on her finger began to glow with returning life. She looked down upon it, fighting hard against the now-instinctive aversion she felt, and within her mind, as Loren and then Diarmuid spoke of Cader Sedat, an image began to coalesce.

It was an image she remembered, the first vision she'd ever had in Fionavar, on the path to Ysanne's Lake: a vision of another lake, high among mountains, with eagles flying over it.

Loren said quietly, "The circles, it seems, have been made complete. It is now my task to go with Matt to Banir Lök, to help him regain the Crown that he never truly lost, so that the Dwarves may be brought back from the edge of the Dark."

"We have a long way to go," Matt Sören said, "and not a great deal of time. We will have to set out tonight." He sounded exactly as he always had. Kim had a sense that nothing, absolutely nothing, would ever make him other than he was: the rock upon which all of them, it seemed, had rested at one time or another.

She looked at Jen and saw the same thought in her face. Then she looked down at the Baelrath again and said, *"You will not get there in time."*

Even now, even after so much had happened, it was with a deep humility that she registered the instant silence that descended over those gathered there when the Seer within her spoke. When she looked up, it was to meet the single eye of Matt Sören.

"I must try," he said simply.

"I know," she replied. "And Loren is right as well, I think. It does matter, somehow, that you try. But I can tell you you will not get there in time from this place."

"What are you saying?" It was Diarmuid who asked, his voice stripped of nuance as Jaelle's had been, pared clean to the simple question.

Kim held up her hand, so they could all see the flame. "I'm saying I'll have to go there, too. That the Baelrath will have to take us there. And I think all of us know by now that the Warstone is a mixed blessing, at the very best." She tried hard to keep the bitterness from her voice.

She almost succeeded, too. But in the stillness that followed, someone asked, "Kim, what happened in the mountains?"

She turned to Paul Schafer, who had asked the question, who always seemed to ask the questions that went below the surface. She looked at him, and then at Loren, beside Paul, gazing at her with the mix of gentleness and strength that she remembered from the beginning, and then, most vividly, from the night they'd shared in the Temple, before Kevin had died. Before she went to Khath Meigol.

So it was to the two of them, so different yet so much alike in some inexplicable way, that she told the story of the rescue of the Paraiko and what had followed. Everyone heard, everyone had to know, but it was to Loren and Paul that she spoke. And it was to Matt that she turned, at the end, to repeat, "And so you see what I mean: whatever blessing I carry will not be unmixed."

For a moment he looked at her, as if considering the point. Then his expression changed; she saw his mouth move in the grimace that she knew to be his smile and heard him say wryly, "No blade I have ever known to be worth anything at all has had only a single edge."

That was all, but she knew those quiet words were all the reassurance she had any right to seek.

Inclination matched training in the High Priestess of Dana. And so Jaelle, cold in the falling rain, chilled by what had happened with Darien and what was happening now, since the shipwreck, showed nothing at all of her apprehension to anyone on the strand.

She knew, being what she was, that it had been the voice of Mörnir that had thundered to still the waves, and so her gaze was on Pwyll first, of all of them, when he came ashore. She remembered him standing on another beach, far to the south, speaking with Liranan in a perilous light that came not from the moon. He was alive, though, and had come back. She supposed she was pleased about that.

They had all come back, it seemed, and there was someone new with them, and it was not hard to tell, from Jennifer's face, who this was.

She had made herself cold and hard, but she was not stone, however she might try to be. Pity and wonder had moved her equally to see Guinevere and Lancelot stand together in the rain, as the setting sun slanted through disappearing clouds low in the west.

She had not heard what they said to each other, but the language of gesture was plain, and, at the end, when the man walked away alone into the Wood, Jaelle found herself unexpectedly grieved. She watched him go, knowing the history, not finding it hard at all to guess what distancing quest Guinevere had now imposed upon her second love. What was hard was to preserve her own necessary image of detachment—in the presence of so many men, and in the turbulent wake of what had happened in the Temple before she had taken Kim and Sharra away, with blood and the earthroot tapped.

She had needed the Mormae in Gwen Ystrat to wield such a potent magic, and that meant dealing with Audiart, which was never pleasant. Most of the time she could manage it without real trouble, but that afternoon's exchange was different.

She had been on dubious ground, and she'd known it, and so had Audiart. It was beyond the irregular, bordering on a real transgression for the High Priestess to be leaving the Temple—and the Kingdom—even at a time like this. It was her sacred duty, Audiart reminded her, along the mindlink the Mormae shared, to remain in the sanctuary, ready and able to deal with the needs of the Mother. Furthermore, her second-in-command did not scruple to point out, had not the High King charged her to remain in Paras Derval and govern the country with the Chancellor? Was it not her further duty to exploit this unexpected opportunity as best she could in the service of their unwavering quest for Dana's return to primacy in the High Kingdom?

All of this, unfortunately, was true.

In response, all she could really do was pull rank, and not for the first time. Not actually dissembling, she had drawn upon the unease and restlessness she'd been feeling in the Temple and told the Mormae, without amplification, that it was her judgement, as High Priestess, that for her to leave at this time was according to the will of Dana—superseding any traditions or opportunities for gain.

There was also, she had sent along the mindlink, a very real urgency—which was true, as she had seen from Kim's white face and clenched hands as she waited tensely with Sharra under the dome, oblivious to the closed exchange of the priestesses.

She had made that sending white-hot with her anger, and she was, still, stronger than any of the others. *Very well*, Audiart had replied. *If you must do this, you must. I will leave for Paras Derval immediately to act as best I can in your absence.*

This was when the real clash had come, making what had gone before seem like a minor skirmish in a children's game.

*No*, she'd sent back, absolute firmness masking her inner anxiety. *It is my command, and so Dana's, that you stay where you are. It is only a week since the sacrifice of Liadon, and the rites of response are not complete.*

*Are you mad?* Audiart had replied, more nakedly rebellious than ever before. *Which of those chattering idiots, those insipid nonentities, do you propose to have act in your stead in a time of war?*

A mistake. Audiart always let her contempt and ambition show through too clearly. Sensing the response of the Mormae, Jaelle drew a breath of relief. She was going to get away with it. Every established pattern of precedent would have demanded that the Second of the Mother come to Paras Derval to take charge in her absence. Had Audiart said so quietly, with even the most cursorily assumed humility, Jaelle might have lost this battle. As it was, she sprang to the attack.

*Would you like to be cursed and cast out, Second of Dana?* she sent, with the silken clarity she alone could command over the mindlink. She felt the Mormae's collectively indrawn breath at the unveiled threat. *Dare you speak so to your High Priestess? Dare you so denigrate your sisters? Have a care, Audiart, lest you lose everything your scheming has won you thus far!*

Strong words, almost too strong, but she'd needed to throw them all off balance for what she had to say next.

*I have chosen my surrogate, and the Chancellor has been informed on behalf of the High King. I have this afternoon named the newest member of the Mormae, and she stands beside me, robed in red and opened new to the mindlink.*

*Greetings, sisters of the Mother,* Leila sent, on cue.

And even Jaelle, half prepared for it, had been stunned by the vividness of her words.

On the strand beneath the Anor Lisen, as the rain slowly came to an end and the sunset tinted the western sky, Jaelle was remembering that vividness. It offered a confirmation of sorts for her own instinctive actions and had served to still, quite effectively, whatever opposition to her peremptory behaviour might have been mounted in Gwen Ystrat. Even so, there was something profoundly unsettling about the mixture of child and woman in Leila, and her link to the Wild Hunt. Dana had not yet chosen to reveal to her High Priestess any indication of what all this might mean.

The voice of Loren Silvercloak, the mage she had hated and feared all her life, brought her fully back to the strand. She heard him reveal what had happened to him, and the triumph she might once have felt at such a revelation of weakness was quite lost in a wave of fear. They had need of Silvercloak's power, and they were not going to have it.

She'd hoped he might be able to send her home. So far from the Temple she had no magic of her own, no way to get back by herself—and, it now appeared, no one to help her. She saw the Baelrath come to life on the Seer's hand; then she heard where Kim was going with that power.

She listened to Pwyll's question—his first words spoken since *Prydwen* had run aground and they'd come ashore. She wondered about him, how one who could speak with the thundered voice of the God could be so quiet and self-contained and then surface, when his presence had almost been forgotten, with words that cut through to the heart of what was happening. She was, she realized, a little afraid of him, and her attempts to channel that fear into hatred or contempt were not really working.

Once more she forced her mind back to the beach. It was growing darker by the minute. In the shadows Diarmuid's fair hair was still bright, catching the last colour of the western sky. It was the Prince who spoke now.

"Very well," he said. "It seems that what we have been told is all we are going to learn. Let us be grateful to our charming Priestess for such information as we do have. Now, Loren can't reach Teyrnon anymore. Kim, I gather, has had a vision of Calor Diman but nothing of the armies. And Jaelle has exhausted her store of useful tidings." The gibe seemed reflexive, half-hearted; she didn't bother to respond. Diarmuid didn't wait. "Which leaves us dependent," he murmured, with what seemed to be a genuinely rueful shake of his head, "upon my own less than exhaustive store of knowledge about what my beloved brother is likely to do."

In some inexplicable way, the glib flow of words had a calming effect. Once more, Jaelle realized, the one she used to dismiss as the "princeling" knew exactly what he was doing. He had already decided, and now he was making the decision sound effortless and of little consequence. Jaelle looked at Sharra, standing beside the Prince. She wasn't sure whether or not to pity her, which was another change: once she would have had no trouble doing so.

"At a time like this," Diarmuid continued, "I can do no better than go back to my precocious childhood memories. Some of you may have known patient, supportive older brothers. I have been blighted sadly by the lack of such a one. Loren will remember. From the time I was able to take my first stumbling steps in my brother's wake, one thing was manifestly clear: *Aileron never, ever, waited for me.*"

He paused and glanced at Loren, as if seeking his confirmation, but then continued in a voice from which the flippancy was suddenly gone. "He will not wait now, nor could he, given where we went. If he is on the Plain with the army and the lios with him, Aileron will push for battle; I would stake my life on that. In fact, with your leave, I *will* stake my life on it, and all of yours. Aileron will take the fight to Starkadh as swiftly as he can, which to my mind means one thing only."

587

"Andarien," said Loren Silvercloak, who, Jaelle suddenly recalled, had taught both Diarmuid and his brother.

"Andarien," the Prince echoed quietly. "He will go through Gwynir to Andarien."

There was a silence. Jaelle was aware of the sea, and of the forest to the east, and, acutely now, of the dark shape of Lisen's Tower looming above them in the darkness.

"I suggest," Diarmuid went on, "that we skirt the western edge of Pendaran, going north from here, angle up through Sennett across the River Celyn to meet, if childhood memories have any merit at all, with the army of Brennin and Daniloth and the Dalrei on the borders of Andarien. If I am wrong," he concluded, with a generous smile at her, "then at least we will have Jaelle with us, to terrify whatever the fifty of us find there."

She favoured him with nothing more than a wintry glance. His smile grew broader, as if her expression had only confirmed his statement, but then, in one of his mercurial changes of mood, he turned and looked at Arthur, who had risen to stand.

"My lord," said the Prince, with no levity at all, "such is my counsel at this time. I will attend to any suggestion you might make, but I know the geography here, and I think I know my brother. Unless there is something you know or sense, Andarien is where I think we must go."

Slowly the Warrior shook his head. "I have never been in this world before," Arthur said in his deep, carrying voice, "and I never had a brother in any world. These are your men, Prince Diarmuid. Number me as one of them and lead us to war."

"We will have to take the women," Diarmuid murmured.

She was about to make a stinging retort, but in that moment something very bright caught her eye, and she turned to see the Baelrath on Kim's finger burst into even more imperative flame.

She looked at the Seer as if seeing her for the first time: the small slim figure with tangled hair, so improbably white, the sudden appearance of the vertical crease on her forehead. Again she had a sense that there seemed to be burdens here greater than her own.

She remembered the moment she had shared with Kim in Gwen Ystrat, and she wished, a little surprised at herself, that there were something she could do, some comfort she might offer that was more than merely words. But Jennifer had been right in what she'd said when Darien had gone: none of them had any real shelter to offer each other.

She watched as Kim walked over to Pwyll and put her arms around him, gripping him very hard; Jaelle saw her kiss him on the mouth. He stroked her hair.

"Till next," the Seer said, an echo, clearly, of the world the two of them had left behind. "Try hard to be careful, Paul."

"And you," was all he said.

The Priestess saw her walk over to Jennifer then, and saw the two women speak, though she could not hear what they said. Then the Seer turned. She seemed to Jaelle to grow more remote, even as she watched. Kim gestured Loren and Matt to either side of her. She bade them join hands, and she laid her own left hand over both of theirs. Then she lifted her other hand high in the darkness and closed her eyes. In that instant, as if a connection had been made, the Warstone blazed so brightly it could not be looked upon, and when the blinding light was gone, so were the three of them.

❖⟩━⟩◯⟨━❖

When he woke it was quite dark in the Wood. Putting a hand to his head, Flidais could feel that his wound had healed. The pain seemed to be gone. So, too, however, was his right ear. He sat up slowly and looked around. His father was there.

Cernan had crouched down on his haunches, not very far away, and was regarding him gravely, the horned head held motionless. Flidais met the gaze for a long moment in silence.

"Thank you," he said at length, speaking aloud.

The antlers dipped briefly in acknowledgment. Then Cernan said, also aloud, "He was not trying to kill you."

*Nothing has changed,* Flidais thought. *Nothing at all.* It was too old a pattern, laid down far too long ago, when both he and Galadan were young, for the anger or the hurt to be strong. He said mildly, "He wasn't trying not to, either."

Cernan said nothing. It was dark in the forest, the moon not yet high enough to lend silver to the place where they were. Both of them, though, could see very well in the dark, and Flidais, looking at his father, read sorrow and guilt both, in the eyes of the god. It was the latter that disarmed him; it always had.

He said, with a shrug, "It could have been worse, I suppose."

The antlers moved again. "I healed the wound," his father said defensively.

"I know." He felt the ragged edge of tissue where his ear had been. "Tell me," he asked, "am I very ugly?"

Cernan tilted his magnificent head in appraisal. "No more than before," he said judiciously.

Flidais laughed. And so, too, after a moment, did the god—a deep, rumbling, sensuous sound that reverberated through the Wood.

When the laughter subsided, it seemed very quiet among the trees, but only for those not tuned to Pendaran as were both of these, the forest god and his son. Even with only one ear, Flidais could hear the whispering of the Wood, the messages running back and forth like fire. It was why they were talking out loud: there was too much happening on the silent link. And there were other powers in Pendaran that night.

He was suddenly reminded of something. Of fire, to be precise. He said, "It really could have gone worse for me. I lied to him."

His father's eyes narrowed. "How so?"

"He wanted to know who had been in the Anor. He was aware that someone had. You know why. I said: only myself, which was not true." He paused, then said softly, "Guinevere was, as well."

Cernan of the Beasts rose to his feet with a swift animal-lithe motion. "That," he said, "explains something."

"What?"

In response, Flidais was offered an image. It was his father who was offering, and Cernan had never done him actual harm, although, until just now, little good, either. And so, in uncharacteristic trust, he opened his mind and received the image: a man walking swiftly through the forest with an utterly distinctive grace, not stumbling, even with the darkness and the entangling roots.

It was not the one he'd expected to see. But he knew, quite well, who this was, and so he knew what must have happened while he lay unconscious on the forest floor.

"Lancelot," he breathed, an unexpected note, most of the way to awe, in his voice. His mind raced. "He will have been in Cader Sedat. Of course. The Warrior will have awakened him. And she has sent him away again."

He had been in Camelot. Had seen those three in their first life, and seen them again, without their knowing him, in many of the returnings they had been forced to make. He knew the story. He was a part of it.

And now, he remembered with a flash of joy, like light in the darkness of the Wood, he knew the summoning name. That, however, brought back the memory of his oath. He said, "The child is in the Wood as well . . . Guinevere's child." And, urgently, "Where is my brother now?"

"He is running north," Cernan replied. For an instant he hesitated. "he passed by the child, not a hundred yards away . . . some time ago, while you slept. He did not see or sense him. You have friends in the Wood angry for your shed blood: he was offered no messages. No one is speaking to him.

Flidais closed his eyes and drew a ragged breath. So close. He had a vision of the wolf and the boy passing by each other in the blackness of the Wood in the hour before moonrise, passing by so near and not knowing, not ever to know. *Or did they?* he wondered. Was there a part of the soul that reached out, somehow, towards possibilities barely missed, futures that would never be, because of such a little distance in a forest at night? He felt a stir of air just then. Wind, with a hint—only imagined, perhaps—of something more.

He opened his eyes. He felt alert, sharpened, exalted still, by what had come to pass. There was no pain. He said, "I need you to do one thing for me. To help me keep an oath."

The dark eyes of Cernan flashed with anger. "You, too?" he said softly, like a hunting cat. "I have done what I will. I have healed the damage my son did. How many of the Weaver's bonds would you have me break?"

"I, too, am your son," Flidais said, greatly daring, for he could feel the wrath of the god.

"I have not forgotten. I have done what I will do."

Flidais stood up. "I cannot bind the forest in a matter such as this. I am not strong enough. But I do not want the child killed, even though he burned the tree. I swore an oath. You are god of the Wood as well as the Beasts. I need your help."

Slowly, Cernan's anger seemed to fade away. Flidais had to look up a long way to see his father's face. "You are wrong. You do not need my help in this," the god said, from the majesty of his great height. "You have forgotten something, wise child. For reasons I will never accept, Rakoth's son has been given the Circlet of Lisen. The powers and spirits of the Wood will not harm him directly, not while he wears it. They will do something else, and you should know what that is, littlest one."

He did know. "The grove," he whispered. "He is being guided to the sacred grove."

"And against what will meet him there," said Cernan, "what will meet him and kill him, I have no power at all. Nor would I desire such power. Even could I do so, I would not intervene. He should never have been allowed to live. It is time for him to die, before he reaches his father and all hope ends."

He was turning to go, having said all he intended to say, having done the one thing he felt bound to do, when his son replied, in a voice deep as tree roots, "Perhaps, but I think not. I think there is more to this weaving. You, too, have forgotten something."

Cernan looked back. There was a first hint of silver in the space where they stood. It touched and moulded his naked form. He had a place where he wanted to be when the moon rose, and the very thought of what would be waiting for him there stirred his desire. He stayed, though, for one more moment, waiting.

"*Lancelot,*" said Flidais.

And turned, himself, to run with that always unexpected speed towards the grove where Lisen had been born so long ago in the presence of all the goddesses and gods.

⟡

In his anger and confusion, the bitterness of rejection, Darien had run a long way into the forest before realizing that it was not the wisest thing to have done.

He hadn't intended to burn the tree, but events, the flow of what happened, never seemed to go the way he expected them to, they never seemed to go right. And when that happened, something else took place inside of him, and his power, the change in his eyes, came back and trees burned.

Even then, he'd only wanted the illusion—the same illusion of fire he'd shaped in the glade of the Summer Tree—but he'd been stronger this time, and uneasy in the presence of so many people, and his mother had been beautiful and cold and had sent him away. He hadn't been able to control what he did, and so the fire had been real.

And he'd run into the shadows of the Wood from what seemed to be the colder, more hurtful shadows on the beach.

It was quite dark by now, the moon had not yet risen, and gradually, as his rage receded, Darien became increasingly aware that he was in danger. He knew nothing of the history of the Great Wood, but he was of the andain himself and so could half understand the messages running through Pendaran, messages about him, and what he had done, and what he wore about his brow.

As the sense of danger increased, so, too, grew his awareness that he was being forced in a particular direction. He thought about taking his owl shape to fly over and out of the forest, but with the thought he became overwhelmingly conscious of weariness. He had flown a long way very fast in that form, and he didn't know if he could sustain it again. He was strong, but not infinitely so, and he usually needed a cresting tide of emotion to source his power: fear, hunger, longing, rage. Now he had none of them. He was aware of danger but couldn't summon any response to it.

Numbed, indifferent, alone, he stayed in his own shape, wearing the clothes Finn had worn, and followed, unresisting, the subtly shifting paths of Pendaran Wood, letting the powers of the forest guide him where they would, to whatever was waiting for him there. He heard their anger, and the anticipation of revenge, but he offered no response to it. He walked, not really caring about anything, thinking about his mother's imperious, cold face, her words: *What are you doing here? What do you want, Darien?*

What did he want? What could he be allowed to want, to hope for, dream of, desire? He had only been born less than a year ago. How could he know what he wanted? He knew only that his eyes could turn red like his father's, and when they did trees burned and everyone turned away from him. Even the Light turned away. It had been beautiful and serene and sorrowful, and the Seer had put it on his brow, and it had gone out as soon as it was clasped to him.

He walked, did not weep. His eyes were blue. The half-moon was rising; soon it would shine down through spaces in the trees. The Wood whispered triumphantly, malice in the leaves. He was guided, unresisting, the Circlet of Lisen on his brow, into the sacred grove of Pendaran Wood to be slain.

Numberless were the years that grove had lain steeped in its power. Nor was there any place in any world with roots so deeply woven into the Tapestry. Against the antiquity of this place even Mörnir's claiming of the Summer Tree in the Godwood of the High Kingdom had been but a blink of time ago—in the days when Iorweth had been summoned to Brennin from over the wide sea.

For thousands upon thousands of years before that day, Pendaran Wood had seen summers and winters in Fionavar, and through all the turnings and returnings of the seasons this grove and the glade within it had been the heart of the Wood. There was magic here. Ancient powers slumbered beneath the forest floor.

Here, more than a thousand years ago (a blink of time, no more), Lisen had been born in the rapt, silent presence of all the powers of the Wood and the shining company of the goddesses whose beauty had been hers from the beginning of her days. Here, too, had come Amairgen Whitebranch, first mortal, first child of the Weaver not born of the Wood, to dare a night in that grove, seeking a power for men that did not find its source in the blood magic of the priestesses. And here had he found that power, and more, as Lisen, wild and glorious, had returned to the violated glade of her birth to slay him in the morning and had fallen in love instead, and so left the Wood.

After that a great deal had changed. For the powers of the grove, for all of Pendaran, time ran up to the moment she had died, leaping from the balcony of the Anor, and then it moved forward more slowly, as if weighted down, from that day.

Since then, since those war-shattered days of the first coming of Rakoth Maugrim, only one other mortal had ever come into this place, and he, too, was a mage, a follower of Amairgen, and he was a thief. With guile and a cunning use of lore, Raederth the mage had known exactly when it might be safe to enter Pendaran in search of the thing he sought.

There was one day and one day only in every year when the Wood was vulnerable, when it grieved and could not guard itself. When the seasons came around to the day of Lisen's leap, the river running past the Anor ran red into the killing sea with the memory of her blood, and all the spirits of the forest that could do so gathered at the foot of the Tower to mourn, and all those that could not travel projected their awareness towards that place, to see the river and the Anor through the eyes of those assembled there.

And one year on the morning of that day Raederth came. Without his source, casting no aura of power, he had entered the sacred grove and knelt in the glade by the birthing place, and he had taken the Circlet of Lisen that lay shining on the grass.

By the time the sun went down and the river ran clear again into the sea, he had been running himself, for a whole day without pause, and was very near to the eastern fringes of the forest.

Pendaran had become aware of him then, and of what he had done, but all the mightiest powers of the Wood were gathered by the sea and there was agonizingly little they could do. They made the forest paths change for him, the trees shift and close menacingly about the fleeing man, but he was too near the Plain, he could see the tall grass in the light of the setting sun, and his will and courage were very strong, greater than those of any ordinary thief, and he made his way—though they hurt him, they hurt him badly—out of the forest and away south again with a shining thing held in his hands that only Lisen had ever worn.

So now it was with exultation, with a fierce collective joy, that Pendaran became aware that the Circlet had come home. Home and in pain, the spirits whispered to each other. It had to be in agony, with its light extinguished on the brow of one who had torched a tree. He would go mad and be flayed, mind and body both, before they released him to death. So they vowed, one to another: the deiena to the leaves of the sentient trees; the leaves to the silent powers and the singing ones; the dark, shapeless things of dread to the old, unmoving, deep-rooted forces that had once been trees and were now something more and intimately versed in hate.

For a moment the whispering stopped. In that instant they heard Cernan, their lord. They heard him say aloud that it was past time for this one to die, and they gloried in what he said. There would be no staying them, no god's voice to cry them off the kill.

The sacrifice was led to the grove: delicately he was guided, the forest paths made smooth and even for his tread; and as he walked his doom was decreed, and it was decided who would effect it. All the powers of the Wood were agreed: however bitter his sacrilege, however sharp the desire to kill lay upon them, they would not themselves act against one who wore Lisen's Circlet about his head.

There was another power, though, the mightiest of all. A power of earth, not of forest, not bound by the griefs and constraints of the Wood. Even as Darien was being guided, unresisting, to the sacred grove, the spirits of Pendaran sent down their summons to the guardian who slept below that place. They woke the Oldest One.

***

It was very dark in the forest, but even when he wasn't in his owl shape he could see very well at night. In some ways, in fact, the darkness was easier, which was another source of unease. It reminded him, this affinity, of the night voices calling from the winter of his boyhood and of how he had been drawn to them.

And *that* reminded him of Finn, who had held him back, and told him he had to hate the Dark, and then had left him alone. He remembered the day, he would always remember: the day of his first betrayal. He had made a flower in the snow and coloured it with the power of his eyes.

It was quiet in the grove. Now that he was here, the whisper of the leaves had died down to a gentle rustle in the night. There was a scent in the air he did not recognize. The grass of the glade was even and smooth and soft under his feet. He could not see the moon. Overhead, the stars shone down from the narrow circle of sky framed by the looming trees.

They hated him. Trees, leaves, the soft grass, the spirits present behind the trunks of trees, the deiena peeking through the leaves—all of them hated him, he knew. He should be terrified, a part of him acknowledged. He should be wielding his own power to break free of this place, to make them all pay in flame and smoke for their hate.

He couldn't seem to do it. He was tired and alone, and he hurt in ways he could never have expressed. He was ready for an ending.

Near the northern edge of the glade there was a mound, grass-covered, and upon it there were night flowers open in the darkness. He walked over. The flowers were very beautiful; the scent of the grove came from them. Carefully, so as to give no further injury or offence, Darien sat down on the grass of the mound between two clusters of dark flowers.

Immediately there came a surging, thrashing sound of fury from the Wood. He leaped to his feet, an involuntary cry of protest escaping his throat. He'd been careful! He'd harmed nothing! He'd only wanted to sit awhile in the starlit silence before he died. His arms went out, openhanded, in a hopeless gesture of appeasement.

Gradually the sound faded, though there remained, after it was gone, a kind of drumming, a rumbling, scarcely audible, beneath the grass of the grove. Darien drew a breath and looked around again.

Nothing moved, save the leaves rustling slightly in the breeze. On the lowest branch of one of the trees of the grove a small geiala perched, its soft furry tail held inquisitively high. It regarded him with a preternatural gravity. Had he been in his owl shape, Darien knew, the geiala would have fled frantically at first sight of him. But he appeared harmless now, he supposed. A curiosity. Only a boy at the mercy of the Wood—which was merciless.

It was all right, he decided, with a kind of desperate acceptance. It was even easier this way. Everyone, from the time of his first memories, had spoken to him of choice. Of Light and Dark, and choosing between the two. But they hadn't even been able to choose or decide about him among themselves: Pwyll, who'd taken him to the Summer Tree, had wanted Dari to be older, to come into this shape so he could come to greater knowledge. Cernan of the Beasts had wanted to know why he'd even been allowed to live. The white-haired Seer, fear in her eyes, had given him a shining object of Light and had watched with him as it went out. Then she'd sent him to his mother, who'd driven him away. Finn, even Finn, who'd told him to love the Light, had gone away without a farewell to find a kind of darkness of his own, in the wide spaces between the stars.

They spoke of choice, of his being balanced between his mother and his father. He was *too* finely balanced, he decided. It was too hard for all of them and, at the last, for him. It was easier this way, easier to surrender that need to decide, to give himself over to the Wood in this place of ancient power. To accept his dying, which would make things better for everyone. Dead, you couldn't be lonely, Darien thought. You couldn't be this hurt. They were all afraid of him, afraid of what he might do with the freedom to choose, of what he might become. They wouldn't have to be afraid anymore.

He remembered the face of the lios alfar that last cold morning of winter by the Summer Tree—how beautiful and shining he had been. And how afraid. He remembered the Seer with her white hair. She'd given him a gift, which no stranger had ever done, but he'd seen her eyes, the doubt and apprehension, even before the Light went out. It was true: they were all afraid of what he would choose.

*Except his mother.*

The thought found him totally unprepared. It hit with the force of revelation. *She* wasn't afraid of what he might do. She was the only one who hadn't tried to lure him, like the storm voices, or persuade him like the Seer. She had not tried to bind him to her, or even suggest a path to him. She had sent him away because the choice was his own, and she was the only one willing to allow that to be so. Maybe, he thought suddenly, maybe she trusted him.

In the grove, in the darkness, he saw the flowers on the mound where Lisen had been born, and he saw them clearly with the night vision of his father, thinking of his mother as he did.

For some reason, then, he remembered Vae and Shahar, the first mother and father he'd known. He thought about his two fathers: the one, a helpless minor soldier in the army of Brennin, obedient to the impersonal orders of the High King, unable to stay by his wife and sons in the winter cold, unable to keep them warm; the other, a god, and the strongest god, shaper of winter and war. Feared, as he, Darien, was feared for being his son.

He was supposed to choose between them.

Looked at one way, there was no choice at all to be made. His sight in the darkness, the fear he aroused, the dying of the Light on his brow, all spoke to that. It was as if the choice had already been made. On the other hand—

He never finished the thought.

*"It would please me if you pleaded for your life."*

If the rocks of the earth's crust could speak, they would have sounded like that. The words were a rumbling, a sliding, as of gigantic stones lurching into motion, a prelude to avalanche and earthquake.

Darien wheeled. There was a shape darker than darkness in the glade, and there was a huge hole in the ground, jagged and irregular, beside the creature that had spoken with the voice of the earth. Fear leaped in Darien, primeval, instinctive, despite all his resignation of the moments before. He felt his eyes explode to red; he lifted his hands, fingers spread, pointing—

And nothing happened.

There came a laugh, deep and low, like a shifting of boulders long at rest. "Not here," said the shape. "Not in this grove, and not untutored as you are. I have your name, and your father's. It is clear what you might become; enough, even, to test me somewhat had we met long after this. But tonight you are nothing in this place. You do not go nearly deep enough. It would please me," it said again, "to hear you plead."

Darien lowered his arms. He felt his eyes return to the blue he had from neither father nor mother, the blue that was his own; perhaps the only thing that was. He was silent, and in that silence he regarded what had come under the half-moon that rose at last above the eastern trees to shine palely down.

It held to no fixed shape or hue. Even as he watched, the creature oscillated ceaselessly through amorphous forms. It had four arms, then three, then none. Its head was a man's, then a hideous mutant shape covered with slugs and maggots, then a boulder, featureless, as the maggots fell back into the grass and the gaping hole beside it. It was grey, and mottled brown, and black; it was huge. In all the blurred shiftings of its shape it had two legs, always, and one of them, Darien saw, was deformed. In one hand it carried a hammer that was the grey-black colour of wet clay and was almost as large as Darien himself.

Again it spoke, amid the suddenly absolute, fearful silence of the forest, and again it said, "Will you not plead, Circlet-bearer? Give me a voice to carry back to my sleep under stone. They have asked me to leave you alive, tree-burner. They want your flesh and your mind to flay when the Circlet is gone from your brow. I will offer you an easier, quicker release, if you but ask for it. Ask, grove-defiler. Only ask; there is nothing else you can do."

The face was almost human now, but huge and grey, and there were worms crawling over it, in and out of the nose and mouth. The voice was the thickened voice of earth and stone. It said, "It is night in the sacred grove, son of Maugrim. You are nothing beside me, and less than that. You do not go nearly deep enough even to make me swing my hammer."

"*I do*," said another voice, and Lancelot du Lac entered the moonlit grove.

⋄⊨◉⊨⋄

They were sleeping on the beach just south of the Anor. Brendel had disobeyed Flidais's instructions to the extent of going inside alone and bringing out blankets and bedding from the lower rooms where Lisen's guards had slept. He did not go upstairs again, for fear of once more stirring Galadan's awareness of that place.

On a pallet beside Arthur, a little apart from the others, Jennifer lay in the motionless sleep of utter exhaustion. Her head was on his shoulder, one hand rested on his broad chest, and her golden hair was loose on the pillow they shared. Wide awake, the Warrior listened to her breathing and felt the beat of the heart he loved.

Then the heartbeat changed. She hurtled bolt upright, instantly awake, her gaze riveted on the high, watching moon. Her face was so white it made her hair look dark. He saw her draw a shuddering, afflicted breath. He felt it as a pain within himself.

He said, "He is in danger, Guinevere?"

She said nothing at all, her gaze never leaving the face of the moon. One hand was over her mouth. He took the other, as gently as he could. It trembled like an aspen leaf in an autumn wind. It was colder than it should ever have been in the mild mid-summer night.

He said, "What do you see? Is he in danger, Guinevere?"

"They both are," she whispered, eyes on the moon. "They both are, my love. And I sent them both away."

He was silent. He looked up at the moon, and he thought of Lancelot. He held one of Guinevere's hands clasped between both of his own broad, square ones, and he wished her peace and heart's ease with longing fiercer and more passionate than any he had ever felt for his own release from doom.

✦⟫═◑⟪═✦

"I go as deep as you," said the tall man quietly as he entered the glade. He had a drawn sword in his hand; it shimmered faintly, catching the silver of the moon. "I know who you are," he went on, speaking softly and without haste. "I know you, Curdardh, and whence you come. I am here as champion of this child. If you wish his death, you will have first to accomplish my own."

"Who are you?" the demon rumbled. The trees were loud again all around them, Darien realized. He looked at the man who had come and he wondered.

"I am Lancelot," he heard. A memory stirred at the back of his mind, a memory of games-playing with Finn in the winter snow. A game of the Warrior, with his King Spear and his friend, his *tanist*, Finn had said. First of the Warrior's company, whose name was Lancelot. Who had loved the Warrior's Queen, whose name, whose name . . .

The demon, Curdardh, shifted position, with a sound of granite dragging over grass. It hefted its hammer and said, "I had not thought to see you here, but I am not surprised." It laughed softly, gravel rolling down a slope. It shifted shape again. It had two heads now, and both were demon heads. It said, "I will claim no quarrel with you, Lancelot, and Pendaran knows that you lived a winter in a forest and did no evil there. You will come to no harm if you leave here now, but I must kill you if you stay."

With an absolutely focused inner quietude, Lancelot said, "You must try to kill me. It is not an easy task, Curdardh, even for you."

"I am deep as the earth's core, swordsman. My hammer was forged in a pit so deep the fire burns downwards." It was said as a fact, without bravado. "I have been here since Pendaran was here," said Curdardh, the Oldest One. "For all that time I held this grove sacrosanct, waking only when it was violated. You have a blade and unmatched skill with it. It will not be enough. I am not without mercy. *Leave!*"

With the last rumbled command, the trees at the edge of the grove shook and the earth rocked. Darien fought to keep his balance. Then, as the tremor came to an end, Lancelot said, with a courtesy strangely, eerily befitting to the place, "I have more than you think, though I thank you for the kindness of your praise. You should know, before we begin, for we are going to do battle here, Curdardh, that I have lain dead in Caer Sidi, which is Cader Sedat, which is the Corona Borealis of the Kings among the stars. You will know that that castle lies at the axle-tree of all the worlds, with the sea pounding at its walls and all the stars of heaven turning about it."

Darien's heart was racing, though he understood only a fragment of what he had heard. He had remembered something else: Finn, who in those days had seemed to know everything there was in the world to know, had told him that his mother had been a Queen. The knowledge made everything even more confusing than it had been already. He swallowed. He felt like a child.

"Even so," Curdardh was saying to Lancelot. "Even with where you have lain, you are mortal, swordsman. Would you die for the son of Rakoth Maugrim?"

"I am here," said Lancelot simply, and the battle began.

# CHAPTER 8

His secretary, Shalhassan of Cathal decided, at about the same moment, had not been born for the military life. Raziel on horseback was just a pale shadow—almost literally, in fact—of his usual efficient self. Already the Supreme Lord had been forced to pause twice in his dictation while Raziel rummaged frantically in his saddlebag to replace a broken stylus. Waiting, Shalhassan ran his fingers through his long pleated beard and scanned the moonlit road in front of his racing chariot.

They were in Brennin, on the road from Seresh to the capital, riding by moonlight and at speed because war demanded such things of men. It was a mild summer night, though the tail end of a major storm had whipped through Seresh late in the day, when he and his reinforcements from Cathal had crossed the river.

Raziel retrieved a stylus and promptly dropped it, as he attempted to shift his grip on the reins of his horse. Shalhassan betrayed not a flicker of response. With his feet firmly on the ground, Raziel was quite good at what he did; Shalhassan was willing, marginally, to allow him this deviation from absolute competence. With a wave of his hand he dismissed his secretary to fall back into the ranks. The dictation could wait until they reached Paras Derval.

They were not far away. Shalhassan had a sudden vivid recollection of the last time he'd taken this road eastward at the head of an army. It had been a winter's day, diamond-bright, and he'd been met in the road by a Prince in a white fur cloak and a white hat, with a red djena feather, brilliant against the snow, for ornament.

And now, not two weeks later, the snow was utterly gone and the glittering Prince was betrothed to Shalhassan's daughter. He was also away at sea; there had been no word in Seresh as to the fate of the ship that had sailed for Spiral Castle.

There *had* been word of the High King: he had ridden north at the head of the army of Brennin and those of Cathal who were already there, in response to a summonglass calling from Daniloth, the same night *Prydwen* had set sail. Shalhassan nodded tersely to his charioteer and gripped the front rail more firmly as they picked up speed. It was probably unnecessary, he knew. The odds were that he and this second contingent were too late to constitute anything but a rear guard at this stage, but he wanted to see Gorlaes, the Chancellor, to confirm that, and he also wanted to see his daughter.

They went very fast in the moonlight. A short time later he was in Paras Derval, and then he was being ushered, travel-stained, allowing himself no luxury of time to change his clothing, into the torchlit Great Hall of the palace where Gorlaes stood one dutiful step below the level of the empty throne. The Chancellor bowed to him, the triple obeisance, which was unexpected and gratifying. Beside Gorlaes, and a farther step below him, stood someone else who also bowed, as deferentially though rather less ornately, which was understandable, given who it was.

Then Tegid of Rhoden, Intercedent for Prince Diarmuid, told the Supreme Lord of Cathal that Sharra had gone away, and stood flinching in anticipation of the explosion that had to come.

Inwardly, it did. Fear and a towering rage exploded in Shalhassan's breast, but neither found expression in his face or bearing. There was ice in his voice, though, as he asked where and with whom.

It was Gorlaes who answered. "She went with the Seer and the High Priestess, my lord. They did not tell us where. If I may say so, there is wisdom in both . . . in all three of them. I do not think—"

He stopped short at a keen glance from Shalhassan, whose gaze had quelled more formidable speakers than this one. At the same time, Shalhassan was aware that his rage had already sluiced away, leaving only the fear. He himself had never been able to keep his daughter under control. How could he expect this fat man and the overextended Chancellor to do better?

He also remembered the Seer very well, and his respect for her went deep. For what she had done one night in the Temple at Gwen Ystrat—knifing her way alone into the darkness of Rakoth's designs to show them the source of winter—he would always honour her. If she had gone away it was to a purpose, and the same applied to the High Priestess, who was equally formidable in her own way.

However formidable they both were, though, he doubted they would have been able to stop his daughter from joining them, if she'd decided that was what she wanted to do. *Oh, Sharra*, he thought. For the ten-thousandth time he wondered if he had been wise not to remarry when his wife died. The girl had needed *some* sort of guidance, that much was more and more evident.

He looked up. Above and behind the Oak Throne of Brennin, set high in the walls of the Great Hall were the stained-glass windows of Delevan. The one behind the throne showed Conary and Colan riding north to war. The light of the half-moon, shining outside, silvered their yellow hair. Well, Shalhassan thought, it would be up to their successor, the young High King, Aileron, to wage whatever war the northlands would see now. The instructions were as he'd expected—as, indeed, they had to be. He would have done exactly the same thing. The men of the second contingent of Cathal, under the leadership of their Supreme Lord, were to remain in Brennin, distributed as Shalhassan and Gorlaes deemed wisest, to guard the High Kingdom and Cathal beyond, as best they could.

He drew his gaze slowly down from the glory of the window. Looking at Tegid—a contrast worthy of an aphorism—he said kindly, "Do not reproach yourself. The Chancellor is right—the three of them will know what they are doing. You may join me, if you like, in sympathizing with your Prince, who will have to deal with her from henceforth. If we survive."

He turned to the Chancellor. "I would appreciate food, my lord Gorlaes, and instruction to my captains for the quartering of my men. After that, if you are not weary, I wonder if we might share some wine and a game of ta'bael? That may be the closest we two get to war, it seems, and I find it soothes me to play at night."

The Chancellor smiled. "Ailell used to say the same thing, my lord. I will be glad to play with you, though I must warn that I am an indifferent player at best."

"Might I come watch?" the fat man asked diffidently.

Shalhassan scrutinized him. "Do you play ta'bael?" he asked dubiously.

"A little," said Tegid.

The Supreme Lord of Cathal pulled his sole remaining Rider backwards, interposing it in defense of his Queen. He favoured his opponent with a glance that had made more than one man contemplate a ritual suicide.

"I think," he said, more to himself than to either of the other two men, "that I have just been set up quite royally."

Gorlaes, watching, grunted in commiseration. Tegid of Rhoden picked off the intervening Rider with his Castle.

"Prince Diarmuid insists," he murmured, putting the captured piece beside the board, "that every member of his band know how to play ta'bael properly. None of us have ever beaten him, though." He smiled and leaned back in his chair, patting his unmatched girth complacently.

Studying the board intently, searching for a defence to the two-pronged attack that would be unleashed as soon as Tegid moved the Castle again, Shalhassan decided to divert some of his earlier sympathy to his daughter, who was going to have to live with this Prince.

"Tell me," he asked, "does Aileron also play?"

"Ailell taught both his sons when they were children," Gorlaes murmured, filling Shalhassan's wine flask from a beaker of South Keep vintage.

"And does the High King also play now at some rarified level of excellence?" Shalhassan noted the hint of exasperation in his voice. The two sons of Ailell seemed to elicit that in him.

"I have no idea," Gorlaes replied. "I've never seen him play as an adult. He was very good, when he was a boy. He used to play with his father all the time."

"He doesn't play ta'bael anymore," said Tegid. "Don't you know the story? Aileron hasn't touched a piece since the first time Diarmuid beat him when they were boys. He's like that, you know."

Absorbing this, considering it, Shalhassan moved his Mage threateningly along the diagonal. It was a trap, of course, the last one he had. To help it along, he distracted the fat man with a question. "I don't know. Like what?"

Pushing hard on the arms of his chair, Tegid levered himself forward to see the board more clearly. Ignoring the trap and the question, both, he slid his Castle laterally, exposing Shalhassan's Queen once more to attack and simultaneously threatening the Cathalian Lord's own King. It was quite decisive.

"He doesn't like to lose at anything," Tegid explained "He doesn't do things when he thinks he might lose."

"Doesn't that limit his activities somewhat?" Shalhassan said testily. He didn't much like losing, himself. Nor was he accustomed to it.

"Not really," said Tegid, a little reluctantly. "He's extremely good at almost everything. Both of them are," he added loyally.

With such grace as he could muster, Shalhassan tipped his King sideways in surrender and raised his glass to the victor.

"A good game," said Tegid genially. "Tell me," he added, turning to Gorlaes, "have you any decent ale here? Wine is all very well, but I'm grievously thirsty tonight, if you want to know the truth."

"A pitcher of ale, Vierre," the Chancellor advised the page standing silently in the doorway.

"Two!" Shalhassan said, surprising himself. "Set up the pieces for another game!"

He lost that one, too, but won the third decisively, with immense evening-redeeming satisfaction. Then both he and Tegid made cursory work of Gorlaes in two other games. It was all unexpectedly congenial. And then, quite late at night, he and the Chancellor further surprised themselves by accepting a highly unorthodox suggestion from the sole member of Prince Diarmuid's band remaining in Paras Derval.

What was even more surprising to Shalhassan, ultimately, was how entertaining he found the music and the ambience and the undeniably pert serving women in the huge downstairs room of the Black Boar tavern and in a smaller, darker room upstairs.

It was a late night.

⊹⟞⟝⊙⟞⟝⊹

If he did nothing further, Paul thought, nothing at all from now until whatever ending lay waiting for them, no one could tax him with not having done his share.

He was lying on the strand near the river, a little apart, as usual, from all the others. He had lain awake for hours, watching the wheeling stars, listening to the sea. The moon had climbed as high as it could go and was westering now. It was very late.

He lay by himself and thought about the night he had ended the drought and then about the predawn hour when he had seen the Soulmonger and summoned Liranan, with Gereint's aid, to battle Rakoth's monster in the sea. And then he let his mind come forward to the moment, earlier this evening, when he had spoken with the voice of Mörnir and the sea god had answered again and stilled the waves to let the mariners of *Prydwen* survive the Weaver's storm.

He had also, he knew, done something else almost a year ago: his had been the crossing between the worlds that had saved Jennifer from Galadan and allowed Darien to be born.

He wondered if those who came after would curse his name for that. He wondered if there would be anyone to come after.

He had done his part in this war. No one could question that. Furthermore, he knew, no one but himself would even think to raise the issue. The reproaches here, the sleeplessness, the striving, always, for something *more*—all of it was internal, a part of the pattern of his life.

The pattern that seemed woven into what he was, even in Fionavar. It lay at the heart of why Rachel had left him, it encompassed the solitariness Kevin Laine had tried so hard to break through—and had, in some way Paul still hadn't found time to assimilate.

But solitude appeared, truly, to be bound into the tangled roots of what he was. Alone on the Summer Tree he'd come into his power, and it seemed that even in the midst of a great many people, he still came into it alone. His gift seemed profoundly secret, even from himself. It was cryptic and self-contained, shaped of hidden lore, and solitary stubborn resistance to the Dark. He could speak with gods and hear them but never move among them, and every such exchange drew him farther away from everyone he knew, as if he'd needed something to do that. Not feeling the cold of the winter or the lash of the rain that had passed. Sent back by the God. He was the arrow of Mörnir, and arrows flew alone.

He was, he realized, hopelessly far from falling asleep. He looked at the half-moon, out over the sea. It seemed to be calling him.

He rose, with the sound of the surf loud in his ears. North, towards the Anor, he could see the shadows that were the sleeping men of South Keep. Behind him the river ran west towards the sea. He followed it. As he walked, the sand became pebbles and then boulders. He climbed up on one of them by the water's edge and saw, by moonlight, that he was not the only sleepless person on the beach that night.

He almost turned back. But something—a memory of another beach the night before *Prydwen* had sailed—made him hesitate, and then speak to the figure sitting on the dark rock nearest to the lapping waves.

"We seem to be reversing roles. Shall I give you a cloak?" It came out more sardonically than he'd intended. But it didn't seem to matter. Her icy self-possession was unsettlingly complete.

Without turning or startling, her gaze still on the water, Jaelle murmured, "I'm not cold. You were, that night. Does it bother you so much?"

Immediately he was sorry he'd spoken. This always seemed to happen when they met: this polarity of Dana and Mörnir. He half turned to climb back down and away but then stopped, held by stubbornness more than anything else.

He drew a breath and, carefully keeping any inflection from his voice, said, "It really doesn't, Jaelle. I spoke by way of greeting, nothing more. Not everything anyone says to you has to be taken as a challenge."

This time she did turn. Her hair was held back by the silver circlet, but the ends still lifted and blew in the sea breeze. He could not make out her eyes; the moonlight was behind her, shining on his own face. For a long moment they were both silent; then Jaelle said, "You have an unusual way of greeting people, Twiceborn."

He let out his breath. "I know," he conceded. "Especially you." He took a step, and a short jump down, and sat on the boulder nearest to hers. The water slapped below them; he could taste salt in the spray.

Not answering, Jaelle turned back to look out to sea. After a moment, Paul did the same. They sat like that for a long time; then something occurred to him. He said, "You're a long way from the Temple. How were you planning to return?"

She pushed a loop of hair back with an impatient hand. "Kimberly. The mage. I didn't really think about it. She needed to come here quickly, and I was the only way."

He smiled, then suppressed it, lest she think he was mocking her. "At the risk of being cursed or some such thing, may I say that that sounds uncharacteristically unselfish?"

She turned sharply, glaring at him. Her mouth opened and then closed, and even by moonlight he could see her flush.

"I didn't mean that to sting," he added quickly. "Truly, Jaelle. I have some idea of what it meant for you to do this."

Her colour slowly faded. Where the moon touched it her hair gleamed with a strange, unearthly shading of red. Her circlet shone. She said simply, "I don't think you do. Not even you, Pwyll."

"Then tell me," he said. "Tell someone something, Jaelle." He was surprised at the intensity in his voice.

"Are you one to talk?" she shot back reflexively. But then, as he kept silent, she added, more slowly and in a different voice, "I named someone to act in my stead, but I broke the patterns of succession when I did so."

"Do I know her?"

She smiled wryly. "Actually, you do. The one who spied on us last year."

He felt the edge of a shadow pass over him. He looked up quickly. No clouds across the moon; it was in his mind.

"Leila? Is it a presumption to ask why? Is she not very young?

"You know she is," Jaelle said sharply. Then, again as if fighting her own impulses, she went on. "As to why: I am not certain. An instinct, a premonition. As I told you all earlier this evening, she is still tuned to Finn, and so to the Wild Hunt. I am not easy with it, though. I don't know what it means. Do you always know why you do what you do, Pwyll?"

He laughed bitterly, touched on the raw nerve that had kept him awake. "I used to think I did. Not anymore. Since the Tree I'm afraid I don't know why I do *any* of what I do. I'm going by instinct, too, Jaelle, and I'm not used to it. I don't seem to have any control at all. Do you want to know the truth?" The words tumbled out of him, low and impassioned. "I almost envy you and Kim—you both seem so sure of your places in this war."

Her face grave, she considered that. Then she said, "Don't envy the Seer, Pwyll. Not her. And as for me . . ." She turned away towards the water again. "As for me, I have been feeling uneasy in my own sanctuary, which has never happened before. I don't think I need be an object of anyone's envy."

"I'm sorry," he said, risking it.

And seemed to fail, as her glance flashed swiftly back to him.

"That is presumption," she said coldly, "and unasked for." He held her gaze, refusing to yield to it but reaching, nonetheless, for something to say. Even as he did, her expression changed and she added, "In any case, such sorrow as you might feel would be balanced—overbalanced, in truth—by Audiart's pleasure, did she learn of this. She would sing for joy, and, Dana knows, she cannot sing."

Paul let his mouth drop open. "Jaelle," he whispered, "did you just make a joke?"

She gestured in exasperation. "What do you think we are in the Temple?" she snapped. "Do you think we stalk around intoning chants and curses day and night, and gathering blood for amusement?"

He left a little silence before answering, over the sound of the waves. "That sounds about right," he said gently. "You haven't been at pains to suggest otherwise."

"There are reasons for that," Jaelle shot back, quite unfazed. "You are sufficiently acquainted with power by now, surely, to be able to guess why. But the truth is that the Temples have been my only home for a long time now, and there was laughter there, and music, and quiet pleasures to be found, until the drought came, and then the war."

The problem with Jaelle, or one of the problems, he decided wryly, was that she was right too much of the time. He nodded. "Fair enough. But if I was wrong you must concede that it was because you wanted me to be wrong. You can't tax me with that misunderstanding now. That's one blade that shouldn't cut both ways."

"They all cut both ways," she said quietly. He had known she would say that. In many ways she was still very young, though it seldom showed.

"How old were you when you entered the Temple?" he asked.

"Fifteen," she answered, after a pause. "And seventeen when I was named to the Mormae."

He shook his head. "That is very—"

"Leila was fourteen. She is only fifteen now," she cut in, anticipating him. "And because of what I did this morning, she is of the Mormae now herself, and even more than that."

"What do you mean?"

She fixed him with a careful regard. "I have your silence on this?"

"You know you do."

Jaelle said, "Because I named her to act for me while I was away and in a time of war, it will follow, by the patterns of Dana, that if I do not return to Paras Derval, Leila is High Priestess. At fifteen."

Despite himself, he felt another chill, though the night was mild and the skies fair. "You knew this. You knew this when you named her, didn't you?" he managed to ask.

"Of course," she said, with more than a trace of her effortless scorn. "What do you think I am?"

"I don't really know," he said honestly. "Why did you do it then?"

The question was direct enough to give her pause. At length, she answered, "I told you a few moments ago: instinct, intuition. I have little more than those, much of the time, which is something for you to consider. You were lamenting your lack of control just now. Power such as ours is not so easy to manipulate, nor, in truth, should it be. I do not command Dana, I speak for her. And so, it seems to me, do you speak for the God, when he chooses to speak. You might give thought, Twiceborn of Mörnir, as to whether control matters too much to you."

And with the words, he was suddenly on a highway in the rain again, hearing the woman he loved tax him with the same cold flaw, hearing her announce that she was leaving because of it, unable to find a place in him where need of her found a true voice.

He seemed to be on his feet, standing above the Priestess by the sea. He wasn't sure how that had happened. He looked down and saw his hands clenched at his sides. And then he turned and was walking away, not from the truth, for that came with him under the stars, but from the icy green eyes and the voice that had spoken that truth here.

She watched him go, and suprised herself with regret. She had not meant to wound. Dana knew, she'd intended to hurt with so many things she'd said to him at one time or another, but not with that last. It had been kindly meant, as much so as lay within her nature, and instead she'd found a place where he was raw and vulnerable.

She should, she knew, keep that knowledge in readiness for encounters to come. But sitting on the rock, thinking back over what they each had said, it was hard to hold to such cold, controlling thoughts. She smiled a little to herself at the irony and turned back towards the sea—to see a ghost ship passing between herself and the setting moon.

"*Pwyll!*" She cried the name almost without thought. She was on her feet, her heart pounding with terror and awe.

She could not take her eyes from the ship. Slowly it moved from north to south across her line of sight, though the wind was from the west. Its sails were tattered and ragged, and the low moon shone through them easily. It lit the broken masts, the shattered figurehead, the smashed upheaval of the deck where the tiller was. Low down by the waterline she thought she could see a dark hole in the side of the ship where the sea must have rushed in.

There was no way that ship could remain afloat.

She heard Pwyll's quick, running footsteps, and then he was beside her again. She did not turn or speak. She registered the sharp intake of his breath and voiced an inward prayer of relief: he, too, saw the ship. It was not a phantom of her own mind, not a prelude to madness.

Suddenly he extended one hand, pointing in silence. She followed the line of his finger.

There was a man, a solitary mariner, standing near the front of the ship by the railing nearest to them, and the moon was shining through him as well.

He was lifting something in his hands, holding it out over the side of the ship towards the two of them, and Jaelle saw, with a second surge of awe, that it was a spear.

"I would be grateful for your prayers," said Pwyll.

She heard a beat of unseen wings. She looked up and then quickly back to him. She saw him step down off the rock where they stood.

*And begin to walk across the waves towards the ship.*

The provinces of Dana ended at the sea. Nevertheless, thought Jaelle, the High Priestess. Nevertheless. She closed her eyes for the first step, knowing she was going to sink, and set out after him.

She did not sink. The waves barely wet the sandals she wore. She opened her eyes, saw Pwyll striding purposefully in front of her, and quickened her pace to catch up.

She received a startled glance as she came abreast. "You may need more than prayers," she said shortly. "And invocations of Dana hold no sway at sea; I told you that once before."

"I remember," he said, stepping a little upwards to clear an advancing wave. "Which makes you either very brave or very foolish indeed. Shall we call it both?"

"If you like," she said, masking an unexpected rush of pleasure. "And accept that I am sorry if what I said before caused you pain. For once, I hadn't meant it."

"For once," he repeated dryly, but she was finally beginning to catch the shifting tones in his voice, and this was mild irony and nothing more. "I know you didn't mean it," he said, negotiating a trough between waves. "I did that one to myself. I'll try to explain someday, if you like."

She said nothing, concentrating on moving over the water. The sensation was uncanny. Jaelle felt perfectly, flawlessly balanced. She had to watch where they were going, and what the sea was doing in front of them, but having done so, it was no trouble to skim along the surface. The hem of her robe was wet; nothing more. If they hadn't been walking towards a ship that had been destroyed a thousand years ago, she might even have found it pleasurable.

As it was, though, the closer they came, the more eerily translucent loomed that hollow craft. As they came alongside, Jaelle could clearly see the gaping holes torn in it at the waterline, and in the exposed hold of Amairgen's ship, the sea sparkled with moonlight.

For such, of course, it was. There was nothing else it could be, not in the bay of the Anor Lisen. She had absolutely no idea what power kept it in the visible world, let alone afloat. But she did know, beyond doubt, who the one mariner high above them had to be. For a moment, when they stopped, standing upon the waves just below that tall, ghostly figure, Jaelle thought about the power of love, and she did pray then, briefly, for Lisen's peace at the Weaver's side.

Then Amairgen spoke, or what was left of him spoke, after so long a death, with the moonlight shining through. He said, in a voice like a deep-toned reed played by the wind, "Why have you come?"

Jaelle felt herself rocked, her balance slipped. She had expected—though she couldn't think why—a welcome. Not this cold, flat query. Suddenly the sea seemed terrifyingly dark and deep, the land a long way off. She felt an impersonal hand on her elbow steadying her. Pwyll waited until he saw her nod, before turning his attention back to the one who had spoken from the deck above their heads.

She saw him look up at the mage slain by the Soulmonger. Pale at the best of times, Pwyll was white and ghostly himself in the long moonlight. There was no flicker of doubt in his eyes, though, no hesitation in his voice as he made reply.

"We have come for the spear, unquiet one. And to bring you the tidings you have sought this many a year."

"Someone was in the Tower," the ghost cried. It seemed to Jaelle as if the wind lifted with the pain in the words, the long burden of loss. "Someone was in the Tower, and so I am come again, where I never came as living man, to the place where she died. Who stood in that room to draw me back?"

"Guinevere," said Pwyll, and waited.

Amairgen was silent. Jaelle was aware of the rocking of the sea beneath her. She glanced down a moment and then quickly back up: it had seemed to her, dizzyingly, that she'd seen stars below her feet.

Amairgen leaned forward over the railing. She was the High Priestess of Dana, and standing above her was the ghost of the one who had broken the power of Dana in Fionavar. She should curse him, a part of her was saying, curse him as the priestesses of the Goddess did at the turning of every month. She should let her blood fall in the sea below where she stood as she spoke the most bitter invocation of the Mother. It was, as much as anything had ever been, her duty. But she could not do it. Such hatred for his ancient deed was not within her tonight, nor would it ever be again, she somehow knew. There was too much pain, too pure a sorrow here. All the stories seemed to be merging into each other. She gazed up at him and at what he held and kept silent, watching.

He was foreshortened by the angle, but she could descry his chiseled, translucent features, the long pale locks of his hair, and the mighty gleaming spear he cradled in both his hands. He wore a ring on one finger; she thought she knew what it was.

"Is the Warrior here, then?" Amairgen asked, a breath on a moonlit reed.

"He is," said Pwyll. And added, after a moment, "So, too, is Lancelot."

*"What!"*

Even in darkness and from where she stood, Jaelle saw his eyes suddenly gleam like sapphires in the night. His hands shifted along the spear. Pwyll waited, unhurried, for the figure above them to absorb the implications of that.

Then, both of them standing on the tossing waves beside the ship heard Amairgen say, very formally now, "What tidings have you for me after so long?"

Jaelle, surprised, saw tears on Pwyll's face. He said, very gently, "Tidings of rest, unquiet one. You are avenged, your staff has been redeemed. The Soulmonger of Maugrim is dead. Go home, first of the mages, beloved of Lisen. Sail home between the stars to the Weaver's side and be granted peace after all these years. We have gone to Cader Sedat and destroyed the evil there with the power of your staff held by one who followed you: by Loren Silvercloak, First Mage of Brennin. What I tell you tonight is true. I am the Twiceborn of Mörnir, Lord of the Summer Tree."

There came a sound then that Jaelle never forgot for what was left of her days. It came not from Amairgen but, rather, seemed to rise from the ship itself, though no one at all was to be seen: a high keening sound, twinned somehow to the slanting moon in the west, balanced achingly between ecstasy and pain. She realized, suddenly, that there *were* other ghosts here, though they could not be seen. Others manned that doomed ship.

Then Amairgen spoke, over the sound of his mariners, and he said to Pwyll, "If this is so, if it has come to pass, then in the name of Mörnir I release the Spear into your trust. But there is one thing I will ask of you, one thing further that is needed before I can rest. There is one more death."

For the first time she saw Pwyll hesitate. She didn't know why, but she did know something else, and she said, "Galadan?"

She heard Pwyll draw a breath, even as she felt the sapphire eyes of the one who had found the skylore fix themselves on her own. She willed herself not to flinch.

She heard him say, "You are a long way from your Temples and your thirsty axe, Priestess. Do you not fear the killing sea?"

"I fear the Unraveller more," she said, pleased to hear her voice strong and unwavering. *The killing sea*, she registered, sorrowing: *Lisen*. "And I hate the Dark more than I ever hated you, or any of the mages who followed you. I am saving my curses for Maugrim, and"—she swallowed—"and I will pray, after tonight, to Dana, for your peace and Lisen's." She ended, ritually, as Pwyll had done, "What I tell you tonight is true. I am the High Priestess of the Goddess in Fionavar."

*What have I said?* she thought in bemused wonder. But she kept that, she hoped, from her eyes. Gravely, he looked down upon her from the ruined ship, and she could see, for the first time, something in him that went beyond power and pain. He had been loved, she remembered. And had loved so much that it had bound him in grief, beyond death through all the years, to this bay where Lisen had died.

Over the sounds that came from the torn hulk of his ship, Amairen said, "I will be grateful for your prayers."

Pwyll's words earlier, she thought, exactly his words. It seemed to her that this had become a night outside of time, where everything signified, in some way or another.

"Galadan," Amairgen repeated. The wailing from the dark ship was louder now. Joy and pain, she heard them both. She saw the moon shine through the sundered hulk. It was dissolving, even as she watched. "Galadan," Amairgen cried, one last time, looking down at the Twiceborn as he spoke.

"I have sworn it," said Pwyll, and Jaelle heard, for the first time, a doubt in his voice. She saw him draw a breath and lift his head higher. "I have sworn that he is mine," he said, and this time it carried.

"Be it so," said Amairgen's ghost. "May your thread never be lost." He was starting to fade; she could see a star shine through him. He raised the spear, preparing to drop it over the side to them.

The provinces of Dana ended at the sea; she had no power here. But she was still what she was, and a thought came to Jaelle then, as she stood on the dark waves.

"*Wait!*" she cried, sharp and clear in the starry night. "Amairgen, hold!"

She thought it was too late, he was already so translucent, the ship so ephemeral they could see the low moon through its timbers. The wailing of the invisible mariners seemed to be coming from very far away.

He came back, though. He did not let loose the spear, and slowly, as they watched, he took again a more substantial form. The ship had gone silent, bobbing on the gentle swells of the bay.

Beside her, Pwyll said nothing, waiting. There was nothing, she knew, he could say. He had done what he could: had recognized this ship for what it was, had known the spear and ventured forth out over the waves to claim it and set the mage free of his long, tormented sailing. He had brought tidings of revenge, and so of release.

The other thing, what might happen now, was hers, for he could not know what she knew.

The mage's cold, spectral gaze was fixed upon her. He said, "Speak, Priestess. Why should I hold for you?"

"Because I have a question to ask, speaking not only for Dana but in the name of Light." Suddenly she was afraid of her own thought, of what she wanted from him.

"Ask it then," Amairgen said, high above.

She had been High Priestess for too long to be so direct, even now. She said, "You were about to let go of the spear. Did you think thus to be so easily quit of your task in carrying it?"

"I did," he replied. "By giving it into your custody with the Warrior in Fionavar."

Summoning all her courage, Jaelle said coldly, "Not so, mage. Should I tell you why?"

There was ice in his eyes, they were colder than her own could go, and with her words there came a low, ominous sound from the ship again. Pwyll said nothing. He listened, balanced on the waves beside her.

"Tell me why," Amairgen said.

"Because you were to give the spear to the Warrior for use against the Dark, not to carry far off from the fields of war."

From the moonlit winter of his death, the mage's expression seemed acidly sardonic. "You argue like a Priestess," he murmured. "It is clear that nothing has changed in Gwen Ystrat, for all the years that have run by."

"*Not so,*" said Pwyll quietly, surprising both her and the mage. "She offered to pray for you, Amairgen. And if you are able to see us clearly, you will know that she was crying for you as she spoke. You will also know, better than I, what a change that marks."

She swallowed, wondering if she had really wanted him to see that. No time to think about it.

Instead, she lifted her voice again. "Hear me, Amairgen Whitebranch, long said to have hated Rakoth Maugrim and the legions of the Dark more than any man who ever lived. The High King of Brennin is riding from Celidon even now—so we believe. He is taking war to Maugrim in Andarien again, as the High King did in your own day. We have as far to go as the army does, and we are on foot. Neither the Warrior with his spear nor any of us here by the Anor will be there in time. We have three days' walking through Sennett, perhaps a fourth, before we cross Celyn into Andarien."

It was true. She had known it, and Diarmuid and Brendel, too. They'd had no other choices, though, once agreeing that Aileron would be riding north from the battle he'd missed by Celidon. They would simply have to walk, as fast and as far as they could. And pray.

Now they might have a choice. A terrible one, but the times were terrible and it seemed as if she might be charged with this part of their remedy.

"If what you tell me is true," the ghost said, "then, indeed, you have cause to fear. You had a question, though. I have stayed for it. Speak, for courtesy will not hold me any longer in this hour of our release."

And so she asked it: "Will your ship carry mortal men, Amairgen?"

Pwyll drew a sharp breath.

"Do you know what you are asking?" Amairgen said, very softly.

It was cold now among the waves, in the lee of that pale ship. She said, "I think I do."

"Do you know that we are released now? That tidings of the Soulmonger's death mark our release from bondage in the sea? And you would bind us longer yet?"

It had all become very hard. She said, "There is no binding I have, mage. I have no power here, no hold upon you. I have asked a question, nothing more." She realized that she was trembling.

For what seemed an interminable time, the ghost of Conary's mage was silent. Then, in a voice like a stir of wind, he said, "Would you sail with the dead?"

*The killing sea,* she thought for the second time. There was a marrow-deep fear within her, so far from the Temples she knew. She masked it, though, and then beat it back.

"*Can* we do so?" she asked. "There are some fifty of us and we must be at the mouth of the Celyn two mornings hence.

In front of them the timbers of the ship showed black and splintered. There were broken shards at the waterline and one vast, gaping hole where the sea was flowing in.

Amairgen looked down, his pale hair ruffled by the night breeze. He said, "We will do this thing. For a night and a day and a night we will carry you past the Cliffs of Rhudh into Sennett Strand and then down again to where Celyn finds the sea. I will earn the prayers you offered, High Priestess of Dana. And the salt of your tears."

It was hard to tell in the thin moonlight, and she was a long way below him, but it seemed to her there was some kindness in his smile.

"We can carry you," he said. "Though you will see none of the mariners, and myself only when the stars are overhead. There is a ladder aft of where you stand. You may both come aboard, and we will moor the ship by the jetty at the foot of the Anor for your companions."

"It is very shallow," said Pwyll. "Can you go so close?"

At that, Amairgen suddenly threw back his head and laughed, harsh and cold in the darkness above the sea.

"Twiceborn of Mörnir," he said, "be very clear what you are about to do. There are no seas too shallow for this ship. *We are not here.* Nor will you be, when once you stand upon this deck. I ask you again—would you sail with the dead?"

"I would," said Pwyll calmly, "if that is what we must do."

Together the two of them walked along the sea to where a rope ladder hung over the almost translucent side of the rotting ship. They looked at each other, saying nothing. Pwyll went first, entrusting his weight to the ladder. It held, and slowly he went up, to stand at length upon the deck. Jaelle followed. It seemed a long way to climb, upon nothing, to reach nothingness. She tried not to let herself think about it. Pwyll reached out a hand for her. She took it, and let him help her onto the deck. It held her weight, though looking down she could see right through the planks. There were waves washing through the hold below. Quickly she looked up again.

There seemed to be no wind suddenly, but the stars were brighter where they stood, and the moon also. Amairgen did not approach. He walked to the tiller and, with no one visible to aid him, began bringing the ship in towards the dock.

No one visible, but all around her Jaelle now heard footsteps, and then the creaking of the tattered sails as they suddenly flapped full, though still she could feel no breath of wind.

There were faint voices, a thread of what might have been laughter; then they were sailing toward the Anor. Looking to the land, she saw that all the others had awakened by now and were waiting there in silence. She wondered if they could see her and what she and Pwyll must look like, standing here; if they had become as ghosts themselves. And what they would be when they stepped down off this ship, if ever they did.

It did not seem that words were necessary. Diarmuid, unsettlingly quick as he always seemed to be, had already grasped what was happening. Amairgen gentled his ship to the foot of Lisen's Tower, a thing, Jaelle knew, that he had never done as living man. She looked over at him but could read nothing at all in his face. She wondered if she had imagined the smile she thought she'd seen from below.

There was no more time for wondering. The first of the men from the jetty were coming over the rail, wonder in their eyes and apprehension in various measures. She and Pwyll moved to help them. Last of all were Sharra, then Guinevere and Arthur; finally, Diarmuid dan Ailell came aboard.

He looked at Pwyll, and then his blue eyes swung to Jaelle to hold her with a long glance. "Not much of a ship," he murmured at length, "but I'll concede it was fairly short notice."

She was too strained to even try to think of a response. He didn't give her a chance, in any case. Bending swiftly, he kissed her cheek—which was not, by any measure, something to be permitted—and said, "Very brightly woven, First of Dana. Both of you." And he moved over and kissed Pwyll, as well.

"I didn't know," said Pwyll dryly, "that you found this sort of thing so stimulating."

And that, Jaelle decided gratefully, would do for her response as well.

They were all on board now, all silent among the tread of the invisible mariners, and the filling of sails that should have been too tattered to fill, in a wind that none of them felt.

Jaelle turned to see Amairgen walking slowly towards Arthur, the spear cradled in his hands. There was one more thing to be done, she realized.

"Be welcome," the dead mage said to the Warrior. "Insofar as the living can be welcome here."

"Insofar as I am living," Arthur replied quietly.

Amairgen looked at him a moment, then sank down on one knee. "I have had charge, in this world, of a thing that belongs to you, my lord. Will you accept the King Spear from my hands?"

They were moving out to sea, rounding the curve of the bay, swinging north under the stars.

They heard Arthur say, simply, in the deep voice that carried the shadings of centuries and of so many wars, "I will accept it."

Amairgen lifted the spear. Arthur took it, and as he did, the head of the King Spear blazed blue-white for a dazzling instant. And in that moment the moon set.

Guinevere wheeled abruptly as if she'd heard a sound. In silence she looked back at the strand, and at the forest beyond. Then, "Oh, my love," she whispered. "Oh, my dear love."

# CHAPTER 9

The battle had been going on for a long time when Flidais finally reached the sacred grove. He was the last to arrive, he realized. All the moving spirits of the Wood were here, ringing the circle of the glade, watching, and those who could not travel were present as well, having projected their awareness to this place, to see through the eyes of those assembled here.

They made way for him as he approached, though some more readily than others, and he registered that. He was the son of Cernan, though. They made room for him to pass.

And passing through that shadowy company he came to the very edge of the glade and, looking within, saw Lancelot battling desperately by starlight for his life, and Darien's.

Flidais had lived a very long time, but he had only seen the Oldest One once before, on the night the whole of Pendaran had gathered, as it had now, to watch Curdardh rise up from the riven earth in order to slay Amairgen of Brennin, who had dared to pass a night in the glade. Flidais had been young then, but he was always a wise, watchful child, and the memory was clear: the demon, disdaining its mighty hammer, had sought to smash and overwhelm the mind of the arrogant intruder who was mortal, and nothing more, and could never resist. And yet, Flidais remembered, Amairgen had resisted. With an iron will and courage that Cernan's younger son had never yet, in all the years that had spun between, seen surpassed, he had battled back against the Oldest One and prevailed.

But only because he had help.

Flidais would never forget the shocked thrill he'd felt (like the taste of forbidden wine in Macha's cloud palace, or his first and only glimpse of Ceinwen rising naked from her pool in Faelinn Grove) at his sudden realization that Mörnir was intervening in the battle. At the end, after Amairgen had driven back Curdardh, in the grey hour before dawn, the God—asserting after, with the daunting authority of his thunder voice, that he had been summoned and bound by Amairgen's victory—sent down a visitation of his own to the mortal, and so granted him the runes of the skylore.

Afterwards, Mörnir had had to deal with Dana—which had occasioned a chaos among the goddesses and gods that, Flidais thought, back in the glade again a thousand years later, had nothing and everything to do with what was happening now. But two clear truths manifested themselves to the diminutive andain as he watched the figures battling here under the stars.

The first was that, for whatever unknown reason—and Flidais was ignorant, as yet, of Lancelot's sojourn among the dead in Cader Sedat—the demon was using his hammer and his terrifying physical presence as well as the power of his mind in this battle. The second was that Lancelot was fighting alone, with nothing but his sword and his skill, without aid from any power at all.

Which meant, the watching andain realized, that he could not win, despite what he was and had always been: matchless among all mortals in any and all of the Weaver's worlds.

Flidais, remembering with brilliant clarity when he had been Taliesin in Camelot and had first seen this man fight, felt an ache in his throat, a tightness building in his broad chest, to see the hopeless, dazzling courage being wasted here. He surprised himself: the andain were not supposed to care what happened to mortals, even to this one, and beyond that he was a guardian of the Wood himself and the sacred grove was being violated by this man. His own duty and allegiance should have been as clear as the circle of sky above the glade.

A day ago, and with anyone else perhaps, they would have been. But not any more, and not with Lancelot. Flidais watched, keen-eyed by starlight, and betrayed his long trust by grieving for what he saw.

Curdardh was shifting shape constantly, his amorphous, fluid physicality finding new and deadly guises as he fought. He grew an extra limb, even as Flidais watched, and fashioned a stone sword at the end of it, a sword made from his own body. He challenged Lancelot, backed him up to the trees at the eastern side of the glade with that sword, and then, with effortless, primeval strength, brought his mighty hammer swinging across in an obliterating blow.

Which was eluded, desperately, by the man. Lancelot hurled himself down and to one side, in a roll that took him under the crushing hammer and *over* the simultaneously slashing sword, and then, even as he landed, he was somehow on his knees and lashing out backhanded with his own blade to completely sever Curdardh's newest arm at the shoulder. The stone sword fell harmlessly on the grass.

Flidais caught his breath in wonder and awe. Then, after a moment of wild, irrational hope, he exhaled again, a long sigh of sorrow. For the demon only laughed—unwearied, unhurt—and shaped another limb from its slate-grey torso. Another limb with another sword, exactly as before.

And it was attacking again, without slackening, without respite. Once more Lancelot dodged the deep-forged hammer, once more he parried a thrust of the stone sword, and this time, with a motion too swift to clearly follow, he knifed in, himself, and stabbed upwards at the earth demon's dark maggot-encrusted head.

That *had* to cause it pain, Flidais thought, astonished, still, to find how much he cared. And he seemed to be right for Curdardh hesitated, rumbling wordlessly, before sinuously beginning to change again: shaping this time into a living creature of featureless stone, invulnerable, impervious to blade, wherever forged, however wielded. And it began to track the man about the small ambit of the glade, to cut him off and crush the life out of him.

Flidais realized then that he had been right from the first. Every time Lancelot did damage, any kind of injury, the demon could withdraw into a shape that was impregnable. It could heal itself of any sword-delivered wound while still forcing the tiring man to elude its dangerous pursuit. Even with the crippled leg, Flidais saw—ritually maimed millennia ago to signify the tethering of the demon to guardianship of this place—Curdardh was agile and deadly, and the glade was small, and the trees of the grove around and the spirits watching there would not allow the man any escape, however momentary, from the sacrosanct place he had violated. And where he was to die.

He, and someone else. Tearing his eyes away from the grueling hurtful combat, Flidais looked over to his right. The boy, his face bone white, was watching with an expression absolutely unreadable. As he looked at Rakoth's son, Flidais felt the same instinctive withdrawal he had known on the beach by the Anor, and he was honest enough to name it fear. Then he thought about who the mother was, and he looked back again at Lancelot battling silently in darkness for this child's life, and he mastered his own doubts and walked over the grass at the edge of the glade to Darien.

"I am Flidais," he said, thereby breaking his own oldest rule for such things. What were rules, though, he was thinking, on a night such as this, talking to such a one as this child was?

Darien moved sideways a couple of steps, shying away from closer proximity. His eyes never left the two figures fighting in front of them.

"I am a friend to your mother," Flidais said, struggling uncharacteristically for the right words. "I ask you to believe that I mean you no malice."

For the first time the boy turned to him. "It doesn't really matter," he said, scarcely above a whisper. "You can't make any difference, can you? The choice is being taken away."

Chilled, Flidais seemed to see him clearly for the first time, suddenly aware in that moment of how young Darien was, and how fair, and, for his vision was keen in the darkness, of how blue the boy's eyes were.

He couldn't, though, however hard he tried, escape the image of their crimson flashing on the beach and the blaze of the burning tree.

There was a sudden loud rumble of sound from the glade and Flidais pressed quickly back against the trunk of one of the trees. Not six feet away, Lancelot was retreating toward them, pursued, with a sound like dragging scree, by the demon in its impervious rock shape.

As Lancelot drew near, Flidais saw that his whole body was laced with a network of cuts and purpling bruises. Blood flowed freely from his left shoulder and his right side. His clothing hung in tattered, bloodstained ribbons from his body, and his thick black hair lay plastered to his head. Rivulets of perspiration ran continuously down his face. Every few moments, it seemed, he had to lift his free hand, ignoring the wound, and claw sweat free from his eyes so he could see.

Insofar as he could see at all. For he was only mortal, and unaided, and even the half-moon had long since passed out of sight to the west, hidden by the towering trees that ringed the glade. Only a handful of stars looked down from above on this act of courage by the tormented, scintillant soul of Lancelot du Lac—the single most gallant, impossible act of courage ever woven into the Tapestry.

Bound by his own duty to the Wood and by the power of that place, Flidais watched helplessly as the two of them drew closer yet. He saw Lancelot, lithe and neat-footed, mastering pain and weariness, drop to one knee, just out of reach of the advancing demon and, lunging forward and down, level a scything blow of his sword at the demon's leg, the only part of the slate-grey rock shape that was not impervious to iron.

But nimbly, for all its grotesque, worm-infested ugliness, the demon of the grove spun away from the thrust. With terrifying speed, he shaped a new sword arm and, even as the weapon coalesced, launched a savage blow downwards against the sprawling man. Who rolled, in a racking, contorted movement, and thrust up his own bright blade to meet the overpowering descent of Curdardh's stone sword.

The blades met with a crash that shook the glade. Flidais clenched his fists, his heart hammering, and then he saw that even against this, even against the full brutal strength of the demon's arm, Lancelot had held firm. His blade did not break, nor his muscled arm give way. The swords met and it was the stone that shattered, as Lancelot rolled again, away from the edge of the glade, and scrambled, chest heaving convulsively, to his feet.

With, Flidais saw, another wound. A jagged fragment of the broken sword of the demon had cut him anew. His shirt shredded to confining strips, Lancelot tore it off and stood bare-chested in the middle of the glade, dark blood welling from a wound over his heart. He balanced on the balls of his feet, his unflinching eyes on his adversary, his sword held out once more, as he waited for Curdardh to come at him again.

And Curdardh, with the primeval, pitiless, unwearied power of earth, came. Once more shifting shape, away from the awkward though invulnerable guise of rock, once more it gave itself a head—almost human it was, though with only a single monstrous eye in the centre from which black grubs and beetles fell like tears—and once more, most terribly, it brought forth the colossal hammer from some place within itself. Taking hold of it with an arm so brawny it seemed as thick around as Lancelot was at the chest, the demon surged forward, seeming to cover the space of the glade with one huge stride, and, roaring like an avalanche, brought the hammer crashing down on the waiting man.

Who dodged yet again, though narrowly, for the demon was brutally swift. Flidais felt the ground shake again with the impact of the blow, and when Curdardh moved on, pursuing, always pursuing, the watching andain saw a smoking hole in the scorched grass of the glade where the hammer had fallen like doom.

On it went, on and on, till Flidais, driving his nails unconsciously into the palms of his hands, thought that his own heart would shatter from strain and weariness. Again and again Lancelot eluded the ruinous hammer and the slashing swords the demon shaped from its own body. Twice more the man succeeded in severing the arms that swung the stone blades, and twice more he was able to leap in, with a shining grace worthy of the watching stars, and wound Curdardh, once in the eye and then in the neck, forcing it each time into the protective, recuperative shape of rock.

This gave some respite to the man, but only a little, for even in that form the demon could attack, striving to corner Lancelot against the impervious wall of the trees ringing the glade and crush his life away against the dark, mottled mass of its body.

Once more an attack brought demon and man near to where Flidais stood beside Darien. And once more Lancelot managed to fling himself away. But this time his shoulder landed in one of the smoking holes the hammer had gouged, and Flidais heard him grunt involuntarily with pain, and saw him scramble, with an awkward desperation this time, away from the renewed assault. He was burnt now, the andain realized, horror and pity consuming his own soul.

He heard a strangled sound from beside him and realized that Darien, too, had registered what had happened. He looked over, briefly, at the boy, and his heart stopped, literally, for a moment. Over and over in his hands Darien was twisting a bright dagger blade, seeming almost oblivious to the fact that he was doing so. Flidais had glimpsed a telling flash of blue, and so he knew what that blade was.

"Be careful!" he whispered urgently. He coughed; his throat was dry. "What are you thinking of doing?"

For only the second time Darien looked directly at him. "I don't know," the boy said, painfully young. "I made my eyes red before you came . . . that is how I have my power." Flidais fought, successfully this time, to conceal his fear. He nodded. Darien went on, "But nothing happened. The rock thing said it was because I did not go deep enough to master it. That I had no power here. So I . . ." He paused and looked down at the knife. "I thought I might . . ."

Through the black night, and through the blackness of what was happening and the pity and horror he felt, Flidais of Pendaran seemed to see, within his mind, a faint, almost illusionary light gleaming in a far, far distance. A little light like the small cast glow of a candle in a cottage window at night, seen by a traveller in a storm far from home.

He said, in his rich, deep voice, "It is a good thought, Darien. It is worthy of you, and worthy of the one who is doing this for you. But do not do it now, and not with that blade."

"Why?" Darien asked, in a small voice.

"Once shall I tell you, and for your ears only, and once is enough for those who are wise," Flidais intoned, reverting, if briefly, to his cryptic elusiveness. He felt a familiar rush of pleasure, even here, even with what was happening, that he *knew* this. And that reminded him—past pleasure, reaching joy—of what else, now, he knew. And remembering that, he remembered also that he had sworn an oath earlier that night, to try to shape a light from the darkness all around. He looked at Darien, hesitating, then said, quite directly "What you are holding is named Lökdal. It is the enchanted dagger of the Dwarves, given to Colan dan Conary a long time ago."

He closed his eyes for a moment, to summon up the exact phrasing, given him by a wine-drowsy mage one spring night seven hundred years ago beside an evening fire on the edge of the Llychlyn Marsh. *"Who strikes with this blade without love in his heart,"* said Flidais, as the words came back, *"shall surely die."* And then he told the rest of it *"Who kills with love may make of his soul a gift to the one marked with the pattern on the dagger's haft."* Potent words, and a deep-delved, intricate magic.

Darien was looking down, gazing at the traced pattern on the hilt of the blade. He glanced up again and said, so quietly Flidais had to strain to hear him, "I wouldn't wish my soul on anything alive." And then, after a pause, the andain heard him say, "My gift was to be the dagger itself, before I was brought to this place."

"A gift to whom?" Flidais asked, though within himself he knew.

"To my father, of course," said Darien. "That I might find a welcome somewhere in the worlds."

There had to be something to say to that, Flidais was thinking. There *had* to be an adequate response, so much depended on it. But he couldn't think, for once. He couldn't find words, and then, suddenly, he didn't have time for them, either.

There came a rumbling crash from the glade, louder than any before, and this time there was a resonance of triumph within it. Flidais turned back just in time to see Lancelot hurtle through the air, clipped by the very end of a hammer swing he'd not quite dodged. It would have smashed the life from him had it hit more squarely. As it was, the merest glancing blow had knocked him flying halfway across the glade, to a bruising, crumpled landing beside Darien.

Curdardh, tireless, sensing an ending at last, was advancing towards him again. Dripping blood, desperately weary, his left arm now hanging uselessly at his side, Lancelot somehow, by an effort of will Flidais could not even comprehend, dragged himself to his feet.

In the instant before the demon was upon him he turned to Darien. Flidais saw their eyes lock and hold. Then he heard Lancelot say quickly, in a voice drained of all inflection, "One final cast, in memory of Gawain. I have nothing left. *Count ten for me, then scream. And then pray to whatever you like."*

He had time for no more. Sidestepping with a half-spin, he launched himself in another rolling dive away from the murderous hammer. It smote the ground where he had stood, and Flidais flinched back from the thunder of that stroke and the heat that roared up from the riven ground.

Curdardh wheeled. Lancelot was on his feet again, swaying a little. The demon made a loose, spilling sound and slowly advanced.

Flidais felt as if his heart was going to tear apart in his chest even as he stood there. The ticking seconds were the longest he had ever known in a long life. He was a guardian of the Wood, of this grove, as much as was Curdardh. These two had defiled the glade! *Three.* He couldn't look at Darien. The demon slashed with his sword. Lancelot parried, stumbling. *Five.* Again Curdardh thrust with the stone blade, the gigantic hammer held high, in readiness. Again the man defended himself. He almost fell. Flidais suddenly heard a rustling of anticipation in the leaves of the watching trees. *Seven.* Chained to silence, forced to bear witness, the andain tasted blood in his mouth: he had bitten his tongue. Curdardh, fluid, sinuous, utterly unwearied, moved forward, feinting with the sword. Flidais saw the hammer rise higher. He lifted his hands in a useless, pitiful gesture of denial.

And in that instant a sound such as Flidais had never heard in all his years exploded from Darien.

It was a scream of anguish and rage, of terror and blinding agony, torn whole and bleeding from a tortured soul. It was monstrous, insupportable, overwhelming. Flidais, battered to his knees by the pain of it, saw Curdardh quickly glance backwards.

And Lancelot made his move. With two quick strides and a straining upward leap he slashed his bright blade downward with stupefying strength and completely severed the arm that he'd never been able to reach until now.

The arm that held the monstrous hammer.

The demon roared with shock and pain, but even as it did, it was already causing itself to flow back over the amputated limb, growing it again. Flidais saw that out of the corner of one eye.

But he was watching Lancelot who had landed neatly from his unbelievable blow, who had hurled his sword away from him, towards Darien and Flidais, and who was bending now, breathing harshly, over the hammer of Curdardh.

His left arm was useless. He wrapped his right hand about the shaft and, groaning with the effort, fought to lift it. And failed. The hammer was vast, unimaginably heavy. It was the weapon of a demon, of the Oldest One. It had been forged in fires deeper than the chasms of Dana. And Lancelot du Lac was only a man.

Flidais saw the demon shape two new swords from its body. He saw it advance again, with a wet, gurgling sound of rage and pain. Lancelot glanced up. And Flidais, on his knees, unable to move, unable to so much as breathe, was given a new measure, in that moment, of the magnitude of mortal man. He saw Lancelot *will* himself—there was no other word—to raise the black hammer with one hand.

And it moved.

The handle came off the ground, and then, beyond comprehension, so did the monstrous head. The demon stopped, with a grinding sound, as Lancelot, his mouth wide open in a soundless scream of uttermost endeavouring, used the initial momentum of that lifting to wheel himself through a full circle, his arm extended flat out, the muscles ridged, corded, glistening, the hammer inexorably rising with the speed of his motion.

Then he let it fly. And that mighty hammer, forged in downward-burning fires, thrown with all the passion of an unmatched soul, smashed into the chest of Curdardh, the Oldest One, with a sound like the earth's crust cracking, and it shattered the demon of the grove into fragments and pieces and shards, killing it utterly.

Flidais felt the silence as a weight upon his life. He had never known Pendaran to be so still. Not a leaf rustled, not a spirit whispered; the powers of the Wood lay as if enchanted in an awed stupefaction. Flidais had a sense, absurdly, that even the stars above the glade had ceased to move, the Loom itself lying silent and still, the Weaver's hands at rest.

He looked down on his own trembling hands, and then, slowly, he stood up, feeling the motion like a returning into time from another world entirely. He walked over, amid the silence, to stand by the man in the centre of the grove.

Lancelot had pulled himself to a sitting position, his knees bent, his head lowered between them. His left arm hung uselessly at his side. There was dark blood on the grass, and it was welling still from half a dozen wounds. There was an ugly burn on his shoulder, raw and blistered, where he had rolled in the scorching pit of hammer blow. Then Flidais, coming nearer, saw the other burn, and his breath lodged painfully in his chest.

Where the man's hand—once so beautiful—had gripped the hammer of Curdardh, the skin of his palm was blackened and peeled away in thick strips of violated flesh.

"Oh, Lancelot," the andain murmured. It came out as a croak, almost inaudible.

Slowly the man lifted his head. His eyes, clouded with pain, met those of Flidais, and then, unbelievably, the thinnest trace of a smile lifted the corners of his mouth.

"Taliesin," he whispered. "I thought I saw you. I am sorry—" He gasped and looked down at the seared flesh of his palm. Then he looked away and continued. "I am sorry I could not greet you properly, before."

Flidais shook his head mutely. He opened his mouth, but no words came. He cleared his throat and tried again, formally. "It has been told for centuries that you were never matched in your day of earthly knight's hand. What you battled tonight was not mortal and should never have been defeated. I have never seen a thing to match it and I never will. What may I offer you, my lord Lancelot?"

The mortal eyes, holding his own, seemed to grow clearer. "Your silence, Taliesin. I need your silence about what happened here, lest all the worlds learn of my shame."

"*Shame?*" Flidais felt his voice crack.

Lancelot lifted his head to gaze at the high stars overhead. "This was single combat," he said quietly. "And I sought aid from the boy. It will be a mark against my name for so long as time shall run."

"In the name of the Loom!" Flidais snapped. "What idiocy is this? What about the trees, and the powers of the Wood that aided Curdardh and hemmed you in? What about this battleground where the demon's power was greater than anywhere else? What about the darkness, where it could see and you could not? What about—"

"Even so," murmured Lancelot, and the little andain's sharp voice was stilled. "Even so, I besought aid in single combat."

"Is that so terrible?" said a new voice.

Flidais turned. Darien had come forward from the edge of the glade. His expression was calm now, but Flidais could still see the shadow of its contorted anguish when the boy had screamed.

"We both would have died," Darien went on. "Why is it so terrible to have asked that one small thing?"

Lancelot swung to look at him. There was a moment's stillness; then he said, "Save in one thing only, a love for which I will make eternal redress, I have served the Light in everything I have ever done. In that service, a victory won with a tool of the Dark is no victory at all."

Darien took a step backwards. "Do you mean me?" he asked. "A tool of the—"

"No," Lancelot murmured quietly. Flidais felt his cold fear coming back, as he looked at the boy. "No. I mean the thing I did."

"You saved my life," Darien said. It sounded like an accusation. He did not step forward again.

"And you, mine." Quietly, still.

"Why?" Darien shouted suddenly. "Why did you do it"

The man closed his eyes for a moment, then opened them. "Because your mother asked me to," he said simply.

With the words Flidais heard a rustling in the leaves again. There was an ache in his heart.

Darien stood as if poised for flight, but he had not yet moved. "She knew I was going to my father," he said, less loudly. "Did she tell you? Do you know that you have saved me to do that?"

Lancelot shook his head. He lifted his voice, though clearly it took an effort. "I have saved you to follow your road."

Darien laughed. The sound knifed into Flidais. "And if it leads north?" the boy asked coldly, in a voice that sounded older suddenly. "Due north to the Dark? To Rakoth Maugrim?"

Lancelot's eyes were undisturbed, his voice utterly calm. "Then it leads there by your choice, Darien. Only thus are we not slaves: if we can choose where we would walk. Failing that, all is mockery."

There was a silence, broken, to Flidais's horror, by the sound of Darien laughing again, bitter, lonely, lost. "It is, though," said the boy. "It is all mockery. The light went out when I put it on. Don't you know that? And why, why should I choose to *walk* in any case?"

There was an instant of silence.

"No!" Flidais cried, reaching out to the child.

Too late. Perhaps it had always been too late: from birth, from conception amid the unlight of Starkadh, from the time the worlds first were spun, Flidais thought, heartsick.

The eyes blazed savagely red. There came a roaring sound from the powers of the Wood, a blurring of shapes in the grove, and suddenly Darien was not there anymore.

Instead, an owl, gleaming white in the darkness, darted swiftly down into the grass, seized a fallen dagger in its mouth, and was aloft and away, wheeling out of sight to the north.

To the north. Flidais gazed at the circle of night sky framed by the towering trees, and with all his soul he tried to will a shape to be there. The shape of a white owl returning, flying back to land beside them and turn into a child again, a fair child, with mild blue eyes, who had chosen the Light and been chosen by it to be a bright blade in the looming dark.

He swallowed. He looked away from the empty sky. He turned back to Lancelot—who was on his feet, bleeding, burnt, swaying with fatigue.

"What are you doing?" Flidais cried.

Lancelot looked down on him. "I am following," he said calmly, as if it were the most obvious thing imaginable. "Will you help me with my sword?" He held up his mangled palm; his left arm hung at his side. "Are you mad?" the andain spluttered.

Lancelot made a sound that managed to be a laugh. "I have been mad," he admitted. "A long time ago. But not now, little one. What would you have me do? Lie here and lick my wounds in a time of war?"

Flidais did a little dance of sheer exasperation. "What role can you play if you kill yourself?"

"I am aware that I'm not good for much, right now," Lancelot said gravely, "but I don't think these wounds are going to—"

"You're going to *follow*?" the andain interrupted, as the full import of Lancelot's words struck him. "Lancelot, he's an owl now, he's *flying*! By the time you even get out of Pendaran he will be—"

He stopped abruptly, in mid-sentence.

"What is it? What have you thought of, wise child?"

He hadn't been a child for a very long time. But he had, indeed, thought of something. He looked up at the man, saw the blood on his bare chest. "He was going to fly due north. That will take him over the western edge of Daniloth. "

"And?"

"And he may not get through. Time is very strange in the Shadowland."

"My sword," said Lancelot crisply. "Please."

Somehow Flidais found himself collecting the discarded blade and then the scabbard. He came back to Lancelot and, as gently as he could, buckled the sword about the man's waist.

"Will the spirits of the Wood let me pass?" Lancelot asked quietly.

Flidais paused to listen to the messages passing around them and beneath their feet.

"They will," he said at length, not a little surprised. "For Guinevere, and for your blood spilled tonight. They do you honour, Lancelot."

"More than I merit," the man said. He drew a deep breath, as if gathering reserves of endurance, from where, Flidais knew not.

He scowled upwards at Lancelot. "You will go easier with a guide. I will take you to the borders of Daniloth, but I have a condition."

"Which is?" Always, the mild courtesy.

"One of my homes lies on our way. You will have to let me dress your wounds when we come there."

"I will be grateful for it," said Lancelot.

The andain opened his mouth, a cutting retort readied. He never said it. Instead, he turned and stomped from the grove walking north. When he had gone a short way he stopped and looked back, to see a thing of wonder.

Lancelot was following, slowly, on the dark and narrow path. All about him and from high above, the mighty trees of Pendaran Wood were letting fall their green leaves, gently, on a night in the midst of summer, to honour the passage of the man.

# PART III

# CALOR DIMAN

# CHAPTER 10

She had flamed red to travel once before, in her own world, not this one: from Stone-henge to Glastonbury Tor. It was not like the crossings. Passing between the worlds was a coldness and a dark, a time without time, deeply unsettling. This was different. When the Baelrath blazed to let her travel, Kim felt as if she truly touched the im-mensity of its power. Of her own power. She could blink distance to nothingness. She was wilder than any other magic known, more akin to Macha and Red Nemain in those hurtling seconds than to any mortal woman ever born.

With one difference: an awareness harboured deep within her heart that they were goddesses, those two, profoundly in control of what they were. And she? She *was* a mortal woman, only that, and as much borne by the Baelrath as bearing it.

And thinking so, carrying her ring, carried by it, she found herself coming down with Loren and Matt—three mortals riding the currents of time and twilit space—onto a cleared threshold high up in sharp mountain air. Before them, two mighty bronze doors towered in majesty, worked with intricate designs in blue thieren and shining gold.

Kim turned to the south and saw the wild dark hills of Eridu rolling away into shadow. Land where the death rain had fallen. Above her, some night bird of the high places lifted a long lonely cry. She listened to its echoes fading, thinking of the Paraiko moving, even now, among those desolate tarns and the high-walled, plague-ravaged cities beyond, gathering the raindead, cleansing Eridu.

She turned north. A gleam of light from high above drew her eyes. She looked up, far up, beyond the grandeur of the twinned doors of the Kingdom of the Dwarves, to see the peaks of Banir Lök and Banir Tal as they caught the last light of the setting sun. The bird called again, one long, quavering, descending note. Far off, there was another gleam, as if in answer to the day's-end shining of the twin peaks overhead. To the north and west, higher by far than anything else, Rangat claimed the last of the light for its own.

None of them had spoken. Kim looked over at Matt Sören, and her hands closed in-voluntarily at her side. *Forty years*, she thought, gazing at her friend who had once been—who yet was—the true King of the realm beyond these doors. His arms were spread wide, hands open, in a gesture of propitiation and utmost vulnerability. In his face she read, clear as calligraphy, the marks of longing, of bitterness, and bitterest pain.

She turned away, to meet the eyes of Loren Silvercloak. In them she saw the burden of his own difficult, complex grief and guilt. She remembered—knew that Loren had never forgotten—Matt's telling them all in Paras Derval about the tide of Calor Diman in his heart, the tide he had fought ceaselessly for the forty years he'd served as source to the one-time mage.

She turned back to the doors. Even in the dusk she could make out the exquisite tracery of gold and thieren. It was very quiet. She heard the thin sound of a pebble, dislodged somewhere and falling. The twin peaks were dark now, overhead, and dark, too, she knew, would be Calor Diman, the Crystal Lake, high and hidden in its meadow bowl between the mountains.

The first stars appeared delicately in the clear sky. Kim looked down at her hand: the ring flickered quietly, its surge of power spent. She tried to think of something to say, of words to ease the sorrows of this threshold, but she feared there might be danger in sound. Beyond that, there was a texture, a woven weight to this silence that, she sensed, was not hers to shoulder or to shoulder aside. It encompassed the spun threads of the lives of the two men here with her, and more—the long, many-stranded destiny of an ancient people, of the Dwarves of Banir Lök and Banir Tal.

It went back too far beyond her, even with her own twinned soul. So she kept her peace, heard another pebble dislodged, another bird cry, farther away, and then listened as Matt Sören finally spoke, very softly, never looking around. "Loren, hear me. I regret nothing: not a breath, not a moment, not the shadow of a moment. This is truth, my friend, and I swear it to be such in the name of the crystal I fashioned long ago, the crystal I threw in the Lake on the night the full moon made me King. There is no weaving the Loom could have held to my name that I can imagine to be richer than the one I have known."

He lowered his hands slowly, still facing the awesome grandeur of the doors. When he spoke again, his voice was rougher and even lower than before. "I am . . . glad, though, that the threads of my days have brought me to this place again, before the end."

Loving him, loving them both, Kim wanted to weep. *Forty years*, she thought again. Something shone in the depths of Loren's eyes, shone as the twin peaks had with the last of the sun. She felt a swirl of mountain winds on the high threshold, heard a sound behind her of gravel sliding.

Was turning to see, when the blow fell on the base of her skull and knocked her sprawling to the ground.

She felt consciousness sliding away. Tried desperately to cling to it, as if it were a physical thing that could be held, that *had* to be held. But, despairing, she knew she was going to fail. It was going, sliding. Pain exploding in her head. Blackness coming down. There were sounds. She could not see. She was lying on the stony plateau before the doors, and the last thought she had was of brutal self-mockery. Akin to the goddesses of war, she had imagined herself, only moments ago. Yet, for all the arrogance of that, and for all the gifts of the Seers that Ysanne had lavished upon her, she'd not been able to sense a simple ambush.

That was her last thought. The very last thing she felt, with a helpless terror that went beyond thought, was someone taking the Baelrath from her hand. She tried to cry out, to resist, to flame, but then it seemed as if a slow wide river had come and it carried her away into the dark.

She opened her eyes. The room rocked and spun, both. The floor dropped sickeningly away, then rushed precipitously back towards her. She had a stupefying headache and, even without moving a hand to feel it, knew she had to have an egg-sized lump on the back of her head. Lying carefully motionless, she waited for things to settle. It took a while.

Eventually she sat up. She was in a windowless chamber by herself. There was a pearly light, mercifully gentle, in the room, though she couldn't see where it was coming from: the stone walls themselves, it seemed, and the ceiling. There was no door either, or none that she could see. A chair and a footstool stood in one corner. On a low table beside them rested a basin of water—which reminded her of how thirsty she was. The table seemed a long way off, though; she decided to wait a few moments before chancing that journey.

She was sitting—had been lying—on a small bed at least a foot too short for her. Which reminded her of where she was. She remembered something else and looked down.

The ring was gone. She had not imagined that last, terrible sensation. She thought she was going to be sick. She thought of Kaen, who was leader here, though not King. Kaen and his brother, Blöd, who had broken the wardstone of Eridu, who had found the Cauldron of Khath Meigol and given it to Maugrim. And now they had the Baelrath.

Kim felt naked without it, though she still wore the belted gown she'd been wearing all day, from the time she'd risen in the cottage and seen Darien. All day? She didn't even know what day it was. She had no idea of the time, but the diffused light emanating from the stone had the hue of dawn to it. She wondered about that, and about the absence of any door. The Dwarves, she knew, could do marvelous things with stone under their mountains.

They could also, under Kaen and Blöd, be servants of the Dark such as Maugrim had never had before. She thought about Lökdal and then, of course, about Darien: the constant fear at the bedrock of everything. Apprehension mastered sickness and pain, driving her to her feet. She had to get out! Too much was happening. Too much depended on her!

The surge of panic faded, leaving her with the sudden grim awareness that without the Baelrath not much, in fact, really did depend on her anymore. She tried to take heart from the simple fact that she was still alive. They had not killed her, and there was water here, and a clean towel. She tried to draw strength from the presence of such things: tried and failed. The ring was gone.

Eventually she did walk over to the low table. She drank deeply of the water—some property of the stone basin had kept it chilled—and washed herself, jolted breathlessly awake by the cold. She probed her wound: a bruise, large, very tender, but there was no laceration. For small favours she gave thanks.

*Things do happen,* she remembered her grandfather saying, in the days after her gran had died. *We got to soldier on,* he had said. She set her jaw. A certain resolution came back into her grey eyes. She sat down in the chair, put her feet up on the stool, and composed herself to wait, grim and ready, as the colour of the light all around gradually grew brighter, and then brighter still, through the hours of what had to be morning outside, echoed, by craft or magic or some fusion of both, in the glowing of the stones within the mountain.

A door opened. Or, rather, a door *appeared* in the wall opposite Kim and then swung soundlessly outwards. Kim was on her feet, her heart racing, and then she was suddenly very confused.

She could never have explained rationally why the presence of a Dwarf woman should surprise her so much, why she'd assumed, without ever giving it a moment's thought, that the females among the Dwarves should look like . . . oh, beardless, stocky equivalents of fighting men like Matt and Brock. After all, she herself didn't much resemble Coll of Taerlindel or Dave Martyniuk. At least on a good day she didn't!

Neither did the woman who had come for her. A couple of inches shorter than Matt Sören, she was slim and graceful with wide-set dark eyes and straight black hair hanging down her back. For all the delicate beauty of the woman, Kim nonetheless sensed in her the same resilience and fortitude she'd come to know in Brock and Matt. Formidable, deeply valued allies the Dwarves would be, and very dangerous enemies.

With everything she knew, with the pain in her head and the Baelrath gone, with the memory of what Blöd had done to Jennifer in Starkadh and the brutal awareness of the death rain unleashed by the Cauldron, it was still, somehow, hard to confront this woman as an avowed foe. A weakness? A mistake? Kim wondered, but nevertheless she managed a half smile.

"I was wondering when someone would come," she said. "I'm Kimberly."

"I know," the other woman said, not returning the smile "We have been told who you are, and what. I am sent to bring you to Seithr's Hall. The Dwarfmoot is gathering. The King has returned."

"I know," said Kim dryly, trying to keep the irony out of her tone, and the quick surge of hope. "What is happening?"

"A challenge before the Elders of the Moot. A word-striving, the first in forty years. Between Kaen and Matt Sören. No more questions; we have little time!"

Kim wasn't good with orders. "Wait!" she said. "Tell me, who . . . who do you support?"

The other woman looked up at her with eyes dark and unrevealing. "No more questions, I said." She turned and went out.

Pushing her hair back with one hand, Kim hastened to follow. They turned left out the door and made their way along a series of ascending, high-ceilinged corridors lit by the same diffused natural-seeming light that had brightened her room. There were beautifully sculpted torch brackets along the walls, but they were not in use. It was daytime, Kim concluded; the torches would be lit at night. There were no decorations on the walls, but at intervals—random, or regulated by some pattern she had no chance to discern— Kim saw a number of low plinths or pillars, and resting on top of each of them were crystalline works of art, exquisite and strange. Most were abstract shapes that caught and reflected the light of the corridors, but some were not: she saw a spear, embedded in a mountain of glass; a crystal eagle, with a wingspan fully five feet across; and, at a junction of many hallways, a dragon looked down from the highest pedestal of all.

She had no time to admire or even think about any of this or about the fact that the hallways of this kingdom under the two mountains were so empty. Despite the width of the corridors—clearly built to allow the passage of great numbers—she and the Dwarf woman passed only a few other people, men and women of the Dwarves, all of whom stopped in their tracks to gaze up at Kimberly with cold, repressive stares.

She began to be afraid again. The art and mastery of the crystal sculptures, the casual power inherent in the vanishing doorways and the corridor lighting, the very fact of a race of people dwelling for so very long under the mountains . . . Kim found herself feeling more alien here than she had anywhere else in Fionavar. And her own wild power was gone. It had been entrusted to her, dreamt by a Seer on her hand, and she had lost it. They had left her the vellin bracelet, though, her screen and protection from magic. She wondered why. Were vellin stones so commonplace here as to be not worth taking?

She had no time to think this through either, no time, just then, for anything but awe. For her guide turned a last corridor, and Kim, following her, did the same and stood within one of the vast, arched entranceways to the hall named for Seithr, King during the Bael Rangat.

Even the Paraiko, she thought, let alone mortal men or the lios alfar, would be made to feel small in this place. And thinking so, she came most of the way to an awareness of why the Dwarves had built their Moot Hall on this scale.

On the level she and her guide were on, there were eight other arched entrances to the circular chamber, each of them as lofty and imposing as the one wherein she stood. Looking up, dumbfounded, Kim saw that there were two other levels of access to the chamber, and on each of these, as well, nine arches allowed entry into the prodigious hall. Dwarves were filtering through all the arches, on all three levels. A cluster of Dwarf women walked past, just then, pausing to fix Kim with a collective regard, stern and unrevealing. Then they went in.

Seithr's Hall was laid out in the manner of an amphitheatre. The ceiling of the chamber was so high, and the light all around so convincingly natural, that it seemed to Kim as if they might, indeed, be outside, in the clear cold air of the mountains.

Caught in that illusion, still gazing upwards, she saw that there seemed to be birds of infinite variety wheeling and circling in the huge bright spaces high above the hall.

Light flashed, many-coloured, from their shapes, and she realized that these, too, were creations of the Dwarves, held aloft and in apparent freedom of flight by a craft or art beyond her comprehension.

A dazzle of light from the stage below drew her eye, and she looked down. After a moment she recognized what she was looking at, and as soon as she did, her gaze whipped back, incredulous, to the circling birds overhead, from which the reflection of colour and light was exactly the same as it was from the two objects below.

Which meant that the birds, even the spectacular eagles, were made not of crystal, as were the sculptures she had seen in the corridors as they approached, but of diamond.

For resting on deep red cushions on a stone table in the middle of the stage were the Diamond Crown and Sceptre of the Dwarves.

Kim felt a childish desire to rub her eyes in disbelief, to discover if, when she took her hands away, she would still see what she was seeing now. There were diamond eagles overhead!

How could the people who were able to place them there, who *wanted* them there, be allies of the Dark? And yet . . .

And yet from the real sky outside these mountain halls a death rain had fallen on Eridu for three full nights and days. And it had fallen because of what the Dwarves had done.

For the first time she became aware that her guide was watching her with a cool curiosity, to gauge her response to the splendour of the Hall, perhaps to glory in it. She was awed and humbled. She had never seen anything like it, not even in her Seer's dreams. And yet . . .

She put her hands in the pockets of her gown. "Very pretty," she said casually. "I like the eagles. How many of the real ones died in the rain?"

And was rewarded—if it really was a reward—to see the Dwarf woman go pale as the stone walls of Kim's room had been when she awoke at dawn. She felt a quick surge of pity but fiercely suppressed it, looking away. They had freed Rakoth. They had taken her ring. And this woman had been sufficiently trusted by Kaen to be sent to bring Kim to this place.

"Not all the birds died," her guide said, very low, so as not to be overheard, it seemed. "I went up by the Lake yesterday morning. There were some eagles there."

Kim clenched her fists. "Isn't that just wonderful," she said, as coldly as she could. "For how much longer, do you think, if Rakoth Maugrim defeats us?"

The Dwarf woman's glance fell away before the stony rage in Kim's eyes. "Kaen says there have been promises," she whispered. "He says—" She stopped. After a long moment she looked Kim squarely in the face again, with the hardihood of her race. "Do we really have any choice? Now?" she asked bitterly.

Looking at her, her anger sluicing away, Kim felt as if she finally understood what had happened, what was still happening within these halls. She opened her mouth to speak, but in the moment there came a loud murmur from within Seithr's Hall, and she quickly glanced over at the stage.

Loren Silvercloak, limping slightly, leaning on Amairgen's white staff, was making his way behind another Dwarf woman to a seat near the stage.

Kim felt an overwhelming relief: only momentarily, though—for as Loren came to his seat she saw armed guards move to take up positions on either side of him.

"Come," her own guide said, her cool detachment completely restored by the pause. "I am to lead you to that place as well."

And so, pushing back that one aggravating strand of hair yet again, walking as regally and as tall as she could, Kim followed her into the Moot Hall. Ignoring the renewed rustle of sound that greeted her appearance, she descended the long, wide aisle between the seats on either side, never turning her head, and, pausing before Loren, chanced and succeeded in the first curtsy of her life.

In the same grave spirit he bowed to her and, bringing one of her hands to his lips, kissed it. She thought of Diarmuid and Jen, the first night they had come to Fionavar. Most of a long lifetime ago, it seemed. She gave Loren's hand a squeeze and then, ignoring the guards, let her glance—imperious, she devoutly hoped—sweep over the assembled Dwarves

Doing so, she noticed something. She turned back to Loren and said, softly, "Almost all women. Why?"

"Women and older men. And the members of the Moot who will be coming out soon. Oh, Kim, my dear, why do you think?" His eyes—so kind, she remembered them being—seemed to hold a crushing weight of trouble within their depths.

"Silence!" one of the guards snapped. Not harshly, but his tone meant business.

It didn't matter. Loren's expression had told her what she had to know. She felt the weight of knowledge that he carried come into her as well.

Women, and the old, and the councillors of the Moot. The men in their prime, the warriors, away. *Away, of course, at war.*

She didn't need to be told which side they would be fighting on, if Kaen had sent them forth.

And in that moment Kaen himself came forth from the far wing of the stage, and so for the first time she saw the one who had unchained blackest evil in their time. Quietly, without any evident pride or arrogance, he strode to stand at one side of the stone table. His thick hair was raven black, his beard closely trimmed. He was slighter than Matt or Brock, not as powerful, except for one thing: his hands were those of a sculptor, large, capable, very strong. He rested one of them on the table, although, carefully, he did not touch the Crown. He was clad unpretentiously in simple brown, and his eyes betrayed no hint of madness or delusions. They were meditative, tranquil, almost sorrowful.

There was another footfall on the stage. Kim tore her eyes away from Kaen to watch Matt Sören step forward from the near wing. She expected a babble of noise, a murmur, some level of response. But the Dwarf she knew and loved—unchanged, she saw, always unchanged, no matter what might come to pass—moved to stand at the other side of the table from Kaen, and as he came there was not a single thread of sound in all the vastness of Seithr's Hall.

In the well of that silence Matt waited, scanning the Dwarves assembled there with his one dark eye. She heard the guards shift restively behind her. Then, without any fuss at all, Matt took the Diamond Crown and placed it upon his head.

It was as if a tree in a dry forest had been struck by lightning, so explosive was the response. Her heart leaping, Kim heard a shocked roar of sound ignite the hall. In the thunder of it she felt anger and confusion, strove to detect a hint of joy, and thought that she did. But her gaze had gone instinctively to Kaen, as soon as Matt claimed the Crown.

Kaen's mouth was crooked in a wry, caustic smile, unruffled, even amused. But his eyes had given him away, for in them Kim had seen, if only for an instant, a bleak, vicious malevolence. She read murder there, and it knifed into her heart.

Powerless, a prisoner, fear within her like a living, sharp-clawed creature, Kim turned back to Matt and felt her racing heartbeat slow. Even with a Crown of a thousand diamonds dazzling upon his head, the aura of him, the essence, was still a quiet, reassuring certitude, an everlasting calm.

He raised one hand and waited patiently for silence. When he had it, nearly, he said, "Calor Diman never surrenders her Kings."

Nothing more, and he did not say it loudly, but the acoustics of that chamber carried his words to the farthest corners of Seithr's Hall. When their resonance had died away, the silence once more was complete.

Into it, emerging from either wing of the stage, there came some fifteen or twenty Dwarves. They were all clad in black, and Kim saw that each of them wore, upon the third finger of his right hand, a diamond ring gleaming like white fire. None of them were young, but the one who came first was the eldest by far. White-bearded and leaning for support upon a staff, he paused to let the others file past him to stone seats placed on one side of the stage.

"The Dwarfmoot," Loren whispered softly. "They will judge between Kaen and Matt. The one with the staff is Miach, First of the Moot."

"Judge what?" Kim whispered back apprehensively.

"The word-striving," Loren murmured, not very helpfully. "Of the same kind as the one Matt lost forty years ago, when the Moot judged in favour of Kaen and voted to continue the search for the Cauldron—"

"Silence!" hissed the same guard as before. He emphasized the command by striking Loren on the arm with his hand, not gently.

Silvercloak turned swiftly and fixed the guard with a gaze that made the Dwarf stumble quickly backwards, blanching. "I am . . . I am ordered to keep you quiet," he stammered.

"I do not intend to say overmuch," Loren said. "But if you touch me again I will turn you into a geiala and roast you for lunch. Once warned is all you will be!"

He turned back to the stage, his face impassive. It was a bluff, nothing more, Kim knew, but she also realized that none of the Dwarves, not even Kaen, could know what had happened to the mage's powers in Cader Sedat.

Miach had moved forward, the click of his staff on the stone sounding loud in the silence. He took a position in front of Kaen and Matt, a little to one side. After bowing with equal gravity to each of them, he turned and addressed the assembled Dwarves.

"Daughters and sons of Calor Diman, you will have heard why we are summoned to Seithr's Hall. Matt, who was King once here under Banir Lök, has returned and has satisfied the Moot that he is who he claims to be. This is so, despite the passage of forty years. He carries a second name now— Sören—to mark the loss of an eye in a war far from our mountains. A war," Miach added quietly, "in which the Dwarves had no proper role to play."

Kim winced. Out of the corner of her eye she saw Loren bite his lower lip in consternation.

Miach continued in the same judicious tones. "Be that as it may, Matt Sören it is who is here again, and last night before the convened Moot he issued challenge to Kaen, who has ruled us these forty years—ruled, but only by the support and sufferance of the Dwarfmoot, not as a true King, for he has never shaped a crystal for the Lake nor spent a night beside her shores under the full moon."

There was a tiny ripple of sound at that. It was Kaen's turn to react. His expression of attentive deference did not change, but Kim, watching closely, saw his hand on the table close into a fist. A moment later, he seemed to become aware of this, and the fist opened again.

"Be that as it may," Miach said a second time, "you are summoned to hear and the Moot to judge a word-striving after the old kind, such as we have not seen in forty years—since last these two stood before us. I have lived long enough, by grace of the Weaver's hand upon my thread, to say that a pattern is unfolding here, with a symmetry that bears witness to interwoven destinies."

He paused. Then, looking directly at Kim, to her great surprise, he said, "There are two here not of our people. Tidings are slow to come across the mountains, and slower still to come within them, but the Dwarves know well of Loren Silvercloak the mage, whose source was once our King. And Matt Sören has named the woman here as Seer to the High King of Brennin. He has also undertaken to stand surety with his life that both of them will respect our laws here by the Crystal Lake, that they will not wield the magics we know they carry, and will accept whatever judgement the Dwarfmoot makes of this striving. Matt Sören has said this. I now ask that they acknowledge, by whatever oath they deem most binding, that this is true. In return, I offer the assurance of the Dwarfmoot, to which Kaen has acceded—indeed, it was his suggestion—that they will be conducted safely from our realm if such need be after the striving is judged."

*Lying snake,* Kim thought furiously, looking at Kaen's bland, earnest expression. She schooled her features, though, placed her ringless hand in the pocket of her gown, and listened as Loren rose from his seat to say, "In the name of Seithr, greatest of the Dwarf Kings, who died in the cause of Light, battling Rakoth Maugrim and the legions of the Dark, I swear that I will abide by the words you have spoken." He sat down.

Another rustle, quiet but unmistakable, went through the Hall. *Take that!* Kim thought as, in her turn, she rose. She felt Ysanne within her then, twin soul under the twin mountains, and when she spoke, it was with a Seer's voice that rang out sternly in the huge spaces.

"In the name of the Paraiko of Khath Meigol, gentlest of the Weaver's children, the Giants who are not ghosts, who live and even now are cleansing Eridu, gathering the innocent dead of the Cauldron's killing rain, I swear that I will abide by the words you have spoken."

More than a murmur now, an urgent cascade of sound. "That is a lie!" an old Dwarf shouted from high up in the Hall. His voice cracked. "The Cauldron we found brought life, not death!

Kim saw Matt looking at her. He shook his head, very slightly, and she kept quiet.

Miach gestured for silence again. "Truth or lies will be for the Dwarfmoot to decree," he said. "It is time for the challenge to begin. Those of you gathered here will know the laws of the word-striving. Kaen, who governs now, will speak first, as Matt did forty years ago, when governance was his. They will speak to you, not to the Moot. You who are gathered here are to be as a wall of stone off which their words will come to us. Silence is law for you, and from the weight of it, the shape, the woven texture, will the Dwarfmoot seek guidance for the judgement we are to make between these two."

He paused. "I have one thing, only, left to ask. Though no one else has known a full moon night by Calor Diman, at issue today is Matt Sören's continued right to wear the Diamond Crown. In fairness, then, I would ask him to remove it for the striving."

He turned, and Kim's eyes went, with those of everyone else in the Hall to Matt, to discover that, having made his initial point, he had already placed it again on the stone table between himself and Kaen. *Oh, clever,* Kim thought, fighting to suppress a grin. *Oh, clever, my dear friend.* Matt nodded gravely to Miach, who bowed in response.

Turning to Kaen, Miach said simply, "You may begin."

He shuffled over, leaning upon his staff, to take his seat among the others of the Dwarfmoot. Kaen's hand, Kim saw, had closed into a fist again, at Matt's smooth anticipation of Miach's request.

He's rattled, she thought. Matt has him way off balance. She felt a quick rush of hope and confidence.

Then Kaen, who had not said a single word until that moment, began the word-striving, and as he did, all Kim's hopes were blown away, as if they were wispy clouds torn by mountain winds.

She had thought that Gorlaes, the Chancellor of Brennin, was a deep-voiced, mellifluous speaker; she had even feared his persuasiveness in the early days. She had heard Diarmuid dan Ailell in the Great Hall of Paras Derval and remembered the power of his light, sardonic, riveting words. She had heard Na-Brendel of the lios alfar take speech to the edge of music and beyond. And within herself, engraved on her heart and mind, she held the close sound of Arthur Pendragon speaking to command or to reassure—with him, somehow, the two became as one.

But in Seithr's Hall within Banir Lök that day she learned how words could be claimed and mastered, brought to a scintillant, glorious apex—turned into diamonds, truly—and all in the service of evil, of the Dark.

Kaen spoke, and she heard his voice rise majestically with the passion of a denunciation; she heard it swoop downwards like a bird of prey to whisper an innuendo or offer a half-truth that sounded—even for a moment, to her—like a revelation from the warp and weft of the Loom itself; she heard it soar with confident assertions of the future and then shape itself into a cutting blade to slash to ribbons the honour of the Dwarf who stood beside him. Who had *dared* to return and strive a second time with Kaen.

Her mouth dry with apprehension, Kim saw Kaen's hands—his large, beautiful, artisan's hands—rise and fall gracefully as he spoke. She saw his arms spread suddenly wide in a gesture of entreaty, of transparent honesty. She saw a hand stab savagely upwards to punctuate a question and then fall away, open, as he spoke what he deemed to be—what he made them believe to be—the only possible response. She saw him point a long shaking finger of undisguised, overwhelming rage at the one who had returned, and it seemed to her, as to all the others in Seithr's Hall, that the denouncing hand was that of a god, and it became a source of wonder that Matt Sören had the temerity still to be standing upright before it, instead of crawling on his knees to beg for the merciful death he did not deserve.

From the weight of the silence, Miach had said, from the shape and texture of it, the Dwarfmoot would seek guidance. As Kaen spoke, the stillness in Seithr's Hall was a palpable thing. It *did* have a shape, and weight, and a discernible texture. Even Kim, utterly unversed in reading such a subtle message, could feel the silent Dwarves responding to Kaen, giving him back his words: thousands of voiceless auditors for chorus.

There was awe in that response, and guilt, that Kaen, who had laboured so long in the service of his people, should be forced yet again to defend himself and his actions. Beyond these two things—beyond awe and guilt—there was also a humbled, grateful acquiesence in the rightness and clarity of everything Kaen said.

He came one step forward from where he had been standing, seeming with that small motion to have come among them, to be one with all of them, to be speaking directly, intimately, to every single listener in the Hall. He said: "It may be thought that the Dwarf beside me now will see farther with his one eye than anyone else in this Hall. Let me remind you of something, something I *must* say before I end, for it cries out within me for utterance. Forty years ago Matt, the sister-son of March, King of the Dwarves, shaped a crystal for Calor Diman on a new moon night: an act of courage, for which I honoured him. On the next night of the full moon, he slept by the shore of the Lake, as all who would be King must do: an act of courage, for which I honoured him."

Kaen paused. "I honour him no more," he said into the silence. "I have not honoured him since another thing he did forty years ago—an act of cowardice that wiped away all memory of courage. Let me remind you, people of the twin mountains. Let me remind you of the day when he took the Sceptre lying here beside us and threw it down upon these stones. The Diamond Sceptre, treated like a stick of wood! Let me remind you of when he discarded the Crown he so arrogantly claimed just now—after forty years!—discarded it like a trinket that no longer gave him pleasure. And let me remind you"—the voice dipped down, laden with marrow-deep sorrow—"that after doing these things, Matt, King under Banir Lök, abandoned us."

Kaen let the grim stillness linger, let it gather full weight of condemnation. Said gently, "The word-striving forty years ago was his own choice. The submission of the matter of the Cauldron of Khath Meigol to the Dwarfmoot was his own decision. No one forced his hand, no one could. He was King under the mountains. He ruled not as I have striven to do, by consensus and counsel, but absolutely, wearing the Crown, wedded to the Crystal Lake. And in pique, in spite, in petulance, when the Dwarfmoot honoured me by agreeing that the Cauldron I sought was a worthy quest for the Dwarves, King Matt abandoned us."

There was grief in his voice, the pain of one bereft, in those long-ago days, of sorely needed guidance and support. "He left us to manage as best we could without him. Without the King's bond to the Lake that has always been the heartbeat of the Dwarves. For forty years I have been here, with Blöd, my brother, beside me, managing, with the Dwarfmoot's counsel, as best I could. For forty years Matt has been far away, seeking fame and his own desires in the wide world across the mountains. And now, now he would come back after so long. Now, because it suits him—his vanity, his pride—he would come back and reclaim the Sceptre and Crown he so contemptuously threw away."

One more step forward. From his mouth to the ear of their hearts. "Do not let him, Children of Calor Diman! Forty years ago you decided that the search for the Cauldron—the Cauldron of Life was worthy of us in our time. In your service, following the decision the Dwarfmoot made that day, I have laboured all these years here among you. Do not turn away from me now!"

Slowly, the extended arms came down and Kaen was done.

Overhead, high above the rigid, absolute silence, the birds fashioned from diamonds circled and shone.

Her chest tight with strain and apprehension, Kim's glance went, with that of everyone else in Seithr's Hall, to Matt Sören, to the friend whose words, ever since she'd met him, had been parcelled out in careful, plain measures. Whose strengths were fortitude and watchfulness and an unvoiced depth of caring. Words had never been Matt's tools: not now, not forty years ago when he had lost, bitterly, his last striving with Kaen, and, losing, had surrendered his Crown.

She had an image of how it must have been that day: the young proud King, newly wedded to the Crystal Lake, afire with its visions of Light, hating the Dark then as he did now. With her inner Seer's eye she could picture it: the rage, the anguished sense of rejection that Kaen's victory had created in him. She could see him hurling away the Crown. And she knew he had been wrong to do so.

In that moment she thought of Arthur Pendragon, another young king, new to his crown and his dreams, learning of the child—incestuous seed of his loins—who was destined to destroy everything Arthur shaped. And so, in a vain attempt to forstall that, he'd ordered so many infants slain.

For the sins of good men she grieved.

For the sins, and the way the shuttling of the Loom brought them back. Back, as Matt had come back again after so long to his mountains. To Seithr's Hall, to stand beside Kaen before the Dwarfmoot.

Praying for him, for all the living in search of Light, knowing how much lay in the balance here, Kim felt the cast spell of Kaen's last plea still lingering in the Hall, and she wondered where Matt would ever find anything to match what Kaen had done.

Then she learned. All of them did.

"We have heard nothing," said Matt Sören, "nothing at all of Rakoth Maugrim. Nothing of war. Of evil. Of friends betrayed into the Dark. We have heard nothing from Kaen of the broken wardstone of Eridu. Of the Cauldron surrendered to Maugrim. *Seithr would weep, and curse us through his tears!*"

Blunt words, sharp, prosaic, unadorned. Cold and stern, they slashed into the Hall like a wind, blowing away the mists of Kaen's eloquent imagery. Hands on his hips, his legs spread wide, seemingly anchored in the stone, Matt did not even try to lure or seduce his listeners. He challenged them. And they listened.

"Forty years ago I made a mistake I will not cease to regret for the rest of my days. Newly crowned, unproven, unknown, I sought approval for what I knew to be right in a striving before the Dwarfmoot in this Hall. I was wrong to do so. A King, when he sees his way clear, must act, that his people may follow. My way should have been clear, and it would have been, had I been strong enough. Kaen and Blöd who had defied my orders, should have been taken to Traitor's Crag upon Banir Tal and hurled to their deaths. I was wrong. I was not strong enough. I accept, as a King must accept, my share of the burden for the evils since done.

"The very great evils," he said, his voice uncompromising in its message. "Who among you, if not bewitched or terrified, can accept what we have done? How far the Dwarves have fallen! Who among you can accept the wardstone broken? Rakoth freed? The Cauldron of the Paraiko given over unto him? And now I must speak of the Cauldron."

The transition was clumsy, awkward; Matt seemed not to care. He said, "Before this striving began, the Seer of Brennin spoke of the Cauldron as a thing of death, and one of you—and I remember you, Edrig; you were wise already when I was King in these halls, and I never knew any evil to rest in your heart—Edrig named the Seer a liar and said that the Cauldron was a thing of life."

He crossed his arms on his broad chest. "It is not so. Once, maybe, when first forged in Khath Meigol, but not now, not in the hands of the Unraveller. He used the Cauldron the Dwarves gave him to shape the winter just now past, and then—grief to my tongue to tell—to cause the death rain to fall on Eridu."

"That is a lie," said Kaen flatly. There was a shocked whisper of sound. Kaen ignored it. "You are not to tell a pure untruth in word-striving. This you know. I claim this contest by virtue of a breaching of the rules. The Cauldron revives the dead. It does not kill. Every one of us here knows this to be true."

*"Do we so?"* Matt Sören snarled, wheeling on Kaen with such ferocity that the other recoiled. "Dare you speak to say I lie? Then hear me! Every one of you hear me! Did not a mage of Brennin come, with perverted wisdom and forbidden lore? Did Metran of the Garantae not enter these halls to give aid and counsel to Kaen and Blöd?"

Silence was his answer. The silence of the word-striving. Intense, rapt, shaping itself to surround his questions. "Know you that when the Cauldron was found and given over to Maugrim, it was placed in the care of that mage. And he bore it away to Cader Sedat, that island not found on any map, which Maugrim had made a place of unlife even in the days of the Bael Rangat. In that unholy place Metran used the Cauldron to shape the winter and then the rain. He drew his unnatural mage-strength to do these terrible things from a host of svart alfar. He killed them, draining their life force with the power he took, and then used the Cauldron to bring them back to life, over and over again. This is what he did. And this, Children of Calor Diman, descendants of Seithr, this, my beloved people, is what we did!"

"A lie!" said Kaen again, a little desperately. "How would you know this if he truly took it to that place? How would the rain have stopped if this were so?"

This time there was no murmuring, and this time Matt did not wheel in rage upon the other Dwarf. Very slowly he turned and looked at Kaen.

"You would like to know, wouldn't you?" he asked softly. The acoustics carried the question; all of them heard. "You would like to know what went wrong. We were there, Kaen. With Arthur Pendragon, and Diarmuid of Brennin, and Pwyll Twiceborn, Lord of the Summer Tree, we went to Cader Sedat and we killed Metran and we broke the Cauldron. Loren and I did it, Kaen. For the evil done by a mage and the evil done by the Dwarves we made what recompense we could in that place."

Kaen's mouth opened and then closed again.

"You do not believe me," Matt went on, inexorably, mercilessly. "You want not to believe, so your hopes and plans will not have gone so terribly awry. Do not believe me, then! Believe, instead, the witness of your eyes!"

And thrusting a hand into the pocket of the vest he wore, he drew from it a black shard that he threw down on the stone table between the Sceptre and the Crown. Kaen leaned forward to look, and an involuntary sound escaped him.

"Well may you wail!" Matt intoned, his voice like that of a final judgement. "Though even now you are grieving for yourself and not for your people to see a fragment of the broken Cauldron return to these mountains."

He turned back to face the high-vaulted Hall, under the ceaseless circling of the diamond birds.

Again the shift in his speech was awkward, rough. Again he seemed oblivious to that. "Dwarves," Matt cried, "I claim no blamelessness before you now. I have done wrong, but have made redress as best I might. And I will continue to do so, now and forward from this day until I die. I will bear the burdens of my own transgressions and take upon myself as many of your own burdens as I can. For so must a King do, and I am your King. I have returned to lead you back among the armies of the Light where the Dwarves belong. Where we have always belonged. Will you have me?"

Silence. Of course.

Scarcely breathing, Kim strove with all her untutored instincts to take its measure.

The shape of the silence was sharp; it was heavy with unnamed fears, inchoate apprehensions; it was densely, intricately threaded with numberless questions and doubts. There was more, she knew there was more, but she was not equal to discerning any of it clearly.

And then, in any case, the silence was broken.

"*Hold!*" Kaen cried, and even Kim knew how flagrant a transgression of the laws of the word-striving this had to be.

Kaen drew three quick sharp breaths to calm and control himself. Then, coming forward again, he said, "This is more than a striving now, and so I must deviate from the course of a true challenging. Matt Sören seeks not only to reclaim a Crown he tossed away, when he elected to be a servant in Brennin rather than to rule in Banir Lök, but now he also invites the Moot—commands it, if his tone be heard, and not only his words—to adopt a new course of action without a moment's thought!"

With every word he seemed to be growing in confidence again, weaving his own thick tapestry of persuasive sound. "I did not raise this matter when I spoke because I did not dream—in my own innocence that Matt would so presume. But he has done so, and so I must speak again, and beg your forgiveness for that mild transgression. Matt Sören comes here in the last days of war to order us to bring our army over to the King of Brennin. He uses other words, but that is what he means. He forgets one thing. He chooses to forget it, I think, but we who will pay the price of his omission must not be so careless."

Kaen paused and scanned the Hall for a long moment, to be sure he had them all with him.

Then, grimly, he said, "*The army of the Dwarves is not here!* My brother has led it from these halls and over the mountains to war. We promised aid to the Lord of Starkadh in exchange for the aid we asked of him in the search for the Cauldron—aid freely given, and accepted by us. I will not shame you or the memory of our fathers by speaking overmuch of the honour of the Dwarves. Of what it might mean to have asked assistance from him and to now refuse the help we promised in return. I will not speak of that. I will say only the clearest, most obvious thing—a thing Matt Sören has chosen not to see. The army is gone. We have chosen a course. I chose, and the Dwarfmoot chose with me. Honour and necessity, both, compel us to stay on the path we are set upon. We could not reach Blöd and the army in time to call them back, even if we wanted to!"

"*Yes we could!*" Kim Ford lied, shouting it.

She was on her feet. The nearest guard shifted forward but quailed at a paralyzing glare from Loren. "I brought your true King here from the edge of the sea last night, by the power I carry. I can take him to your army as easily, should the Dwarfmoot ask me to."

Lies, lies. The Baelrath was gone. She kept both hands in her pockets all the time she spoke. It was no more than a bluff, as Loren's words to the guard had been. So much was at stake, though, and she really wasn't good at this sort of thing, she knew she wasn't. Nonetheless she held her gaze fixed on Kaen's and did not flinch: if he wanted to expose her, to show the Baelrath that had been stolen from her, then let him! He would have to explain to the Dwarfmoot how he got it—and then where would his talk of honour be?

Kaen did not speak or move. But from the side of the stage there came suddenly three loud, echoing thumps of a staff on the stone floor.

Miach moved forward, slowly and carefully as before, but his anger was palpable, and when he spoke he had to struggle to master his voice.

"Bravely done!" he said with bitter sarcasm. "A striving to remember! Never have I seen the rules so flouted in a challenge. Matt Sören, not even forty years away can justify the ignorance involved in your bringing an *object* into a striving! You knew the rules governing such things before you had seen ten summers. And you, Kaen! A 'minor transgression'? How *dare* you speak a second time in a word-striving! What have we become that not even the oldest rules of our people are remembered and ob-served? Even to the extent"—he swung around to glare at Kimberly—"of having a *guest* speak in Seithr's Hall during a challenge."

This, she decided, was too much! Feeling her own pent-up fury rising, she began a stinging retort and felt Loren's punishing grip on her arm. She closed her mouth with-out saying a word, though her hands inside the pockets of her gown clenched into white fists.

Then she relaxed them, for Miach's rage seemed to have spent itself with that brief, impassioned flurry. He seemed to shrink back again, no longer an infuriated patriarch but only an old man in troubled times, faced now with a very great responsibility.

He said, in a quieter, almost an apologetic voice, "It may be that the rules that were clear and important enough for all our Kings, from before Seithr down to March himself, are no longer paramount. It may be that none of the Dwarves have had to live through times so cloudy and confused as these. That a longing for clarity is only an old man's wistfulness."

Kim saw Matt shaking his head in denial. Miach did not notice. He was looking up at the lofty half-filled Hall. "It may be," he repeated vaguely. "But even if it is, this striving is ended, and it is now for the Moot to judge. We will withdraw. You will all remain here"—the voice grew stronger again, with words of ritual—"until we have returned to declare the will of the Dwarfmoot. We give thanks for the counsel of your silence. It was heard and shall be given voice."

He turned, and the others of the black-garbed Moot rose, and together they all withdrew from the stage, leaving Matt and Kaen standing there on either side of a table which held a shining Crown, and a shining Sceptre, and a black sharp-edged fragment of the Cauldron of Khath Meigol.

Kim became aware that Loren's hand was still squeezing her arm, very hard. He seemed to realize it in the same moment.

"I'm sorry," he murmured, easing but not releasing his grasp.

She shook her head. "I was about to say something stupid."

This time the guards were careful not to test Loren's patience by intervening again. Indeed, all about the Hall there was a rising swell of sound as the Dwarves, released from the bond of silence that had held them during the striving, began animatedly to discuss what had taken place. Only Matt and Kaen, motionless on the stage, not looking at each other, remained silent.

"Not stupid at all," said Loren quietly. "You took a chance by speaking, but they needed to hear what you could do."

Kim looked over at him with sudden dismay. His eyes narrowed at the sight of her consternation.

"What is it?" he whispered, careful not to be overheard.

Kim said nothing. Only withdrew her right hand slowly from its pocket, so that he could see what, clearly, he hadn't seen before—the terrible absence of fire, the Baelrath gone.

He looked, and then he closed his eyes. She put her hand back in her pocket.

"When?" Loren asked, his voice thin and stretched.

"When we were ambushed. I felt it being taken. I woke this morning without it."

Loren opened his eyes and looked at the stage, at Kaen. "I wonder," he murmured. "I wonder how he knew."

Kim shrugged. It hardly seemed to matter at this point. What mattered was that, as things stood, Kaen had been quite accurate in what he'd told the Dwarves. If the army was west of the mountains, there was nothing they could do to stop them now from fighting among the legions of the Dark.

Loren seemed to read her thoughts, or else they were his own as well. He said, "It is not over yet. In part, because of what you did. That was brightly woven, Kimberly— you blunted a thrust of Kaen's, and you may have bought us time to do something." He paused. His expression changed, became diffident and strained.

"Actually," he amended, "you may have bought Matt time, and perhaps yourself. There isn't much of anything I can do anymore."

"That isn't true," Kim said, with all the conviction she could muster. "Wisdom carries its own strength."

He smiled faintly at the platitude and even nodded his head. "I know. I know it does. Only it is a hard thing, Kim, it is a very hard thing to have known power for forty years and to have none of it now, when it matters so much."

To this, Kim, who had carried her own power for only a little over a year and had fought it for much of that time, could find nothing to say.

There was no time for her to reply, in any case. The rustle of sound in the Hall rose swiftly higher and then, as swiftly, subsided into a stiff, tense silence.

In that silence the Dwarfmoot filed soberly back to their stone seats on the stage. For the third time Miach came forward to stand beside Kaen and Matt, facing the multitude in the seats above.

Kim glanced at Loren, rigid beside her. She followed the tall man's gaze to his friend of forty years. She saw Matt's mouth move silently. *Weaver at the Loom,* she thought, echoing the prayer she read on the Dwarf's lips.

Then, wasting no time, Miach spoke. "We have listened to the speech of the word-striving and to the silence of the Dwarves. Hear now the rendering of the Dwarfmoot of Banir Lök. Forty years ago in this Hall, Matt, now also called Sören, threw down the symbols of his Kingship. There was no equivocation in what he did, no mistaking his intention to relinquish the Crown."

Kim would have sold her soul, both her souls, for a glass of water. Her throat was so dry it hurt to swallow.

Miach went on, soberly, "At that same time did Kaen assume governance here under the mountains, nor was he challenged in this, nor has he been until this day. Even so, despite the urging of the Moot, Kaen chose not to make a crystal for the Lake or to pass a full moon night beside her shores. He never became our King.

"There is then, over and above all else, the Moot has decided, one question that must be answered in this striving. It has long been said in these mountain halls—so long it is now a catchphrase for us—that Calor Diman never surrenders her Kings. It was said today by Matt Sören, and the Moot heard him say it before we came forth for the judging. That, we have now decided, is not the question at issue here."

Kim, desperately struggling to understand, to anticipate, saw Kaen's eyes flash with a swiftly veiled triumph. Her heart was a drum, and fear beat the rhythm of it.

"The question at issue," said Miach softly, "is whether the King can surrender the Lake."

The silence was absolute. Into it, he said, "It has never happened before in all the long history of our people that a King in these halls should do what Matt did long ago, or seek to do what he strives for now. There are no precedents, and the Dwarfmoot has decreed that it would be presumption for us to decide. All other questions— the disposition of our armies, everything we shall do henceforth—are contained in this one issue: who, truly, is our leader now? The one who has governed us forty years with the Dwarfmoot at his side, or the one who slept by Calor Diman and then walked away?

"It is, the Dwarfmoot decrees, a matter for the powers of Calor Diman to decide. Here then is our judgement. There are now six hours left before sunset. Each of you, Matt and Kaen, will be guided to a chamber with all the tools of the crystal maker's craft. You will each shape whatsoever image you please, with such artistry as you may command. Tonight, when darkness falls, you shall ascend the nine and ninety steps to the meadow door that leads from Banir Tal to Calor Diman, and you shall cast your artifices into the Crystal Lake. I will be there, and Ingen, also, from the Moot. You may each name two to come with you to bear witness on your behalf. The moon is not full. This is not properly a night for the naming of a King, but neither has anything such as this ever confronted us before. We will leave it to the Lake."

*A place more fair than any in all the worlds,* Matt Sören had named Calor Diman long ago, before the first crossing. They had been still in the Park Plaza Hotel: five people from Toronto, en route to another world for two weeks of partying at a High King's celebrations.

*A place more fair . . .*

A place of judgement. Of what might be final judgement.

# CHAPTER 11

That same day, as the Dwarves of the twin mountains prepared for the judgement of their Lake, Gereint the shaman, cross-legged on the mat in his dark house, cast the net of his awareness out over Fionavar and vibrated like a harp with what he sensed.

It was coming to a head, all of it, and very soon.

From that remote elbow of land east of the Latham he reached out, an old brown spider at the centre of his web, and saw many things with the power of his blinding.

But not what he was looking for. He wanted the Seer. Feeling helplessly removed from what was happening, he sought the bright aura of Kimberly's presence, groping for a clue to what was shuttling on the loom of war. Tabor had told him the morning before that he had flown the Seer to a cottage by a lake near Paras Derval, and Gereint had known Ysanne for much of his life and so knew where this cottage was.

But when he reached to that place he found only the ancient green power that dwelt beneath the water, and no sign of Kim at all. He did not know—he had no way of knowing—that since Tabor had set her down beside that shore, she had already gone, by the tapped power of the avarlith, to Lisen's Tower, and from there that same night, with the red flaming of her own wild magic, over the mountains to Banir Lök.

And over the mountains he could not go, unless he sent his soul travelling, and he was too recently returned from journeying out over the waves to do that again so soon.

So she was lost to him. He felt the presence of other powers, though, lights on a map in the darkness of his mind. The other shamans were all around him, in their houses much like his own, here beside the Latham. Their auras were like the trace flickerings of lienae at night, erratic and insubstantial. There would be no aid or comfort there. He was preeminent among the shamans of the Plain, and had been since his blinding. If any of them were to have a role yet to play in what was to come, it would have to be him, for all his years.

There came a tapping on his door. He had already heard footsteps approaching from outside. He quelled a quick surge of anger at the intrusion, for he recognized both the tread and the rhythm of the knocking.

"Come in," he said. "What can I do for you, wife of the Aven?"

"Liane and I have brought you lunch," Leith replied in her brisk tone.

"Good," he said energetically, though for once he wasn't hungry. He was also discomfited: it seemed that his hearing was finally starting to go. He'd only heard one set of footsteps. Both women entered, and Liane, approaching, brushed his cheek with her lips.

"Is that the best you can do?" he mock-growled. She squeezed his hand, and he squeezed back. He would have ferociously denied it, if pressed, but in his heart Gereint had long acknowledged that Ivor's daughter was his favourite child of the tribe. Of the Plain. Of all the worlds, if it came to that.

It was to her mother that he turned, though, to where he heard her kneel in front of him, and a little to the side. "Strength of the Plain," he said respectfully, "may I touch your thoughts?"

She leaned forward, and he raised his hands to run them along the bones of her face. The touch let him into her mind, where he saw anxiety, a weight of cares, the burdens of sleeplessness, but—and he marvelled, even as he touched her face—not even a shadow of fear.

His touch became, briefly, a caress. "Ivor is lucky in you, bright soul. We all are. Luckier than we deserve."

He had known Leith since her birth, had watched her grow into womanhood, and had feasted at her wedding to Ivor dan Banor. In those far-off days he had first seen a certain kind of brightness shining within her. It had been there ever since, growing even stronger as her children were born, and Gereint knew it for what it was: a deep, luminous love that was rarely allowed to shine forth. She was a profoundly private person, Leith, never given to open demonstration, not trusting it in others. She had been called cold and unyielding all her life. Gereint knew better.

He drew his hands away reluctantly, and as he did he felt the reverberations of war sweep over him again.

Diffidently, Leith asked, "Have you seen anything, shaman? Is there something you can tell me?"

"I am looking now," he said quietly. "Sit, both of you, and I will tell you what I can."

He reached out again, seeking interstices of power along the webs of time and space. He was a long way off, though, no longer young and but recently returned from the worst journeying of his days. Nothing was clear, except for the reverberations: the sense of a climax coming. An end to war, or an ending to everything.

He did not tell them that; it would be needlessly cruel. Instead, he ate the lunch they had brought for him—it seemed he was hungry, after all—and listened to the dispositions Leith had made of resources within the crowded camp of women and children and the old. And eight blind, useless shamans.

All through that day and the next, as premonitions gathered more closely about him, Gereint sat on the mat in his dark house and strove, whenever his waning strength allowed, to see something clearly, to find a role to play.

Both days would pass, though, before he felt the touch of the god, of Cernan's offered gift of foreknowledge. And with that voice, that vision, there would come a fear such as he'd never known, not even out over the waves. This would be something new, something terrible. The more so because it was not directed at him, with all his years, with his long, full life behind him. It was not his price to pay, and there was not a single thing he could do about it. With sorrow in his heart, two mornings hence, Gereint would lift his voice in summons.

And call for Tabor to come to him.

⊹⊱══◉═⊰⊹

Over the Plain the army of Light was riding to war. North of Celidon, of the Adein, of the green mound Ceinwen had raised for the dead, they rode and the white magnificence of Rangat towered ahead of them, filling the blue, cloud-scattered summer sky.

Every one of them was on horseback save for a number of the Cathalians, racing in their scythe-wheeled war chariots at the outer rim of the army. When the summonglass had flamed in Brennin, Aileron had had too much need of speed to allow the presence of foot soldiers. By the same token, throughout the long, unnatural winter, he'd been laying his plans against such a time as this: the horses had been ready, and every man in the army of Brennin could ride. So, too, could the men and women of the lios alfar from Daniloth. And of the Dalrei there was not and never had been any question.

Under the benevolent, miraculous sun of summer returned they rode amid the smell of fresh grass and vibrant splashes of wildflowers. The Plain rolled away in every direction as far as the eye could follow. Twice they passed great swifts of eltor, and the heart of every one of them had lifted to see the beasts of the Plain, released from the killing bondage of snow, run free again over the tall grass.

For how long? Amid all the beauty that surrounded them, that remained the question. They were not a company of friends out for a gallop under summer skies. They were an army, advancing, very fast, to the door of the Dark, and they would be there soon.

They *were* going fast, Dave realized. It was not the headlong pace of the Dalrei's wild ride to Celidon, but Aileron was pushing them hard, and Dave was grateful for the brief rest period they were granted midway through the afternoon.

He swung down off his horse, muscles protesting, and he flexed and limbered them as best he could before stretching out on his back on the soft grass. As Torc dropped down beside him, a question occurred to Dave

"Why are we hurrying?" he asked. "I mean, we're missing Diarmuid and Arthur, and Kim and Paul . . . what advantage does Aileron see in pushing on?"

"We'll know when Levon gets back from the conference up front," Torc answered. "My guess is that it's geography as much as anything else. He wants to get close to Gwynir this evening, so we can go through the woods in the morning. If we do that, we should be able to be north of Celyn Lake in Andarien before dark tomorrow. That would make sense, especially if Maugrim's army is waiting for us there."

The calmness of Torc's voice was unsettling. *Maugrim's army:* svart alfar, urgach upon slaug, Galadan's wolves, the swans of Avaia's brood, and Weaver alone knew what else. Only Owein's Horn had saved them last time, and Dave knew he didn't dare blow it again.

The larger picture was too daunting. He focused on immediate goals. "Will we make the forest, then? Gwynir? Can we get there by dark?"

He saw Torc's eyes flick beyond him and then the dark man said, "If we were Dalrei alone, we could, of course. But I'm not sure, with all this excess weight of Brennin we're carrying."

Dave heard a loud snort of indignation and turned to see Mabon of Rhoden subside comfortably down beside him. "I didn't notice any of us falling behind on the way to Celidon," the Duke said. He took a pull of water from his flask and offered it to Dave, who drank as well. It was icy cool; he didn't know how.

Mabon's presence was a surprise of sorts, though a happy one. The wound he'd taken by the Adein had been healed last night by Teyrnon and Barak, after Aileron had finally let them make camp. Mabon had flatly refused to be left behind.

Since the journey from Paras Derval to the Latham where Ivor and the Dalrei had been waiting, the Duke seemed to favour the company of Levon and Torc and Dave. Dave wasn't displeased. Among other things, Mabon had saved his life, when Avaia had exploded out of a clear sky on that ride. Beyond that, the Duke, though no longer young, was an experienced campaigner, and good company, too. He had already established a relationship with Torc that had the otherwise grim Dalrei joking back and forth with him.

Now Mabon tipped Dave a surreptitious wink and continued. "In any case, this isn't a sprint, my young hero. This is a long haul, and for that you need Rhoden staying power. None of your Dalrei brashness that fades as the hours roll by."

Torc didn't bother to reply. Instead he tore up a handful of long grass and threw it at Mabon's recumbent figure. The wind was against him, though, and most of it landed on Dave.

"I wish I knew," said Levon, walking up, "why I continue to spend my time with such irresponsible people."

The tone was jocular, but his eyes were sober. All three of them sat up and looked at him gravely.

Levon crouched down on his heels and played idly with a handful of grass stems as he spoke. "Aileron does want to make Gwynir by tonight. I have never been this far north, but my father has, and he says we should be able to do it. There is a problem, though."

"Which is?" Mabon was grimly attentive.

"Teyrnon and Barak have been mind-scanning forward all day to see if they can sense the presence of evil. Gwynir would be an obvious place to ambush us. The horses, and especially the chariots, are going to be awkward, even if we keep to the edges of the forest."

"Have they seen anything?" Mabon was asking the questions; Dave and Torc listened and waited.

"After a fashion, which is the problem. Teyrnon says he finds only the tracest flicker of evil in Gwynir, but he has a feeling of danger nonetheless. He cannot understand it. He *does* sense the army of the Dark ahead of us, but far beyond Gwynir. They are in Andarien already, we think, gathering there. "

"So what is in the forest?" Mabon queried, his brow furrowed with thought.

"No one knows. Teyrnon's guess is that the evil he apprehends is the lingering trace of the army's passage, or else a handful of spies they have left behind. The danger may be inherent in the forest, he thinks. There were powers of darkness in Gwynir at the time of the Bael Rangat."

"So what do we do?" Dave asked. "Do we have a choice?"

"Not really," Levon replied. "They talked about going through Daniloth, but Ra-Tenniel said that even with the lios alfar to guide us, we are too many for the lios to guarantee that a great many of us would not be lost in the Shadowland. And Aileron will not ask him to let down the woven mist with the army of the Dark in Andarien. They would move south the moment that happened, and we would be fighting in Daniloth. The High King said he will not permit that."

"So we take our chances in the forest," Mabon summarized.

"So it seems," Levon agreed. "But Teyrnon keeps saying that he doesn't really see evil there, so I don't know how much of a chance we're taking. We're doing it, in any case. In the morning. No one is to enter the forest at night."

"Was that a direct order?" Torc asked quietly.

Levon turned to him. "Not actually. Why?"

Torc's voice was carefully neutral. "I was thinking that a group of people, a very small group, might be able to scout ahead tonight and see what there is to see."

There was a little silence.

"A group, say, of four people?" Mabon of Rhoden murmured, in a tone of purely academic interest.

"That would be a reasonable number, I would guess," Torc replied, after judicious reflection.

Looking at the other three, his heartbeat suddenly quickening, Dave saw a quiet resolution in each of them. Nothing more was said. The rest period was almost over. They rose, prepared to mount up again.

Something was happening, though. A commotion was stirring the southeastern fringes of the army. Dave turned with the others, in time to see three strange riders being escorted past them to where the High King was, and the Aven, and Ra-Tenniel of Daniloth.

The three were travel-stained, and each of them slumped in his saddle with weariness written deep into his features. One was a Dalrei, an older man, his face obscured by mud and grime. The second was a younger man, tall, fair-haired, with a pattern of green tattoo markings on his face.

The third was a Dwarf, and it was Brock of Banir Tal.

Brock. Whom Dave had last seen in Gwen Ystrat, preparing to ride east into the mountains with Kim.

"I think I want to see this," said Levon quickly. He started forward to follow the three newcomers, and Dave was right beside him, with Mabon and Torc in stride.

By virtue of Levon's rank, and the Duke's, they passed through into the presence of the Kings. Dave stood there, half a head taller than anyone else, and watched, standing just behind Torc, as the three newcomers knelt before the High King.

"Be welcome, Brock," Aileron said, with genuine warmth. "Bright the hour of your return. Will you name your companions to me and give me what tidings you can?"

Brock rose, and for all his fatigue his voice was clear.

"Greetings, High King," said the Dwarf. "I would wish you to extend your welcome to these two who have come with me, riding without stop through two nights and most of two days to serve in your ranks. Beside me is Faebur of Larak, in Eridu, and beyond him is one who styles himself Dalreidan, and I can tell you that he saved my life and that of the Seer of Brennin, when otherwise we would surely have died."

Dave blinked at the Dalrei's name. He caught a glance from Levon, who whispered, "Rider's Son? An exile. I wonder who it is."

"I bid you both welcome," Aileron said. And then, with a tightening in his voice, "What tidings beyond the mountains?"

"Grievous, my lord," Brock said. "One more grief to lay at the door of the Dwarves. A death rain fell for three days in Eridu. The Cauldron shaped it from Cader Sedat, and—bitter to my tongue the telling—I do not think there is a man or woman left alive in that land."

The stillness that followed was of devastation beyond the compassing of words. Faebur, Dave saw, stood straight as a spear, his face set in a mask of stone.

"Is it falling still?" Ra-Tenniel asked, very softly.

Brock shook his head. "I would have thought you knew. Are there no tidings from them? The rain stopped two days ago. The Seer told us that the Cauldron had been smashed in Cader Sedat."

After pain, after grief, hope beyond expectation. A murmur of sound suddenly rose, sweeping back through the ranks of the army.

"Weaver be praised!" Aileron exclaimed. And then: "What of the Seer, Brock?"

Brock said, "She was alive and well, though I know not where she is now. We were guided to Khath Meigol by the two men here with me. She freed the Paraiko there, with the aid of Tabor dan Ivor and his flying creature, and they bore her west two nights ago. Where, I know not."

Dave looked at Ivor.

The Aven said, "What was he doing there? I left him with orders to guard the camps."

"He was." The one called Dalreidan spoke for the first time. "He was guarding them, and was going back to do so again. He was summoned by the Seer, Ivor . . . Aven. She knew the name of his creature, and he had no choice. Nor did she—she could not have done what she had to do with only the three of us. Be not angry with him. I think he is suffering enough."

Levon's face had gone white. Ivor opened his mouth and then closed it again.

"What is it you fear, Aven of the Plain?" It was Ra-Tenniel.

Again, Ivor hesitated. Then, as if drawing the thought up from the wellspring of his heart, he said, "He goes farther away every time he flies. I am afraid he will soon be like . . . like Owein and the Wild Hunt. A thing of smoke and death, utterly cut off from the world of men."

Silence once more, a different kind, shaped of awe as much as fear. It was broken by Aileron in a deliberately crisp voice that brought them all back to the Plain and the day moving inexorably towards dusk.

"We've a long way to go," the High King said. "The three of you are welcome among us. Can you ride?"

Brock nodded.

"It is why I am here," said Faebur. A young voice, trying hard to be stern. "To ride with you, and do what I can when battle comes."

Aileron looked over at the older man who called himself Dalreidan. Dave saw that Ivor was looking at him, too, and that Dalreidan was gazing back, not at the High King but at the Aven.

"I can ride," Dalreidan said, very softly. "Have I leave?"

Abruptly, Dave realized that something else was happening here.

Ivor looked at Dalreidan for a long time without answering. Then: "No Chieftain can reclaim an exile within the Law. But nothing I know in the parchments at Celidon speaks to what the Aven may do in such a case. We are at war, and you have done service already in our cause. You have leave to return. As Aven I say so now."

He stopped. Then, in a different voice, Ivor said, "You have leave to return to the Plain and to your tribe, though not under the name you have taken now. Be welcome back under the name you bore before the accident that thrust you forth into the mountains. This is a brighter thread in darkness than I ever thought to see, a promise of return. I cannot say how glad I am to see you here again."

He smiled. "Turn now, for there is another here who will be as glad. Sorcha of the third tribe, turn and greet your son!"

In front of Dave, Torc went rigid, as Levon let out a whoop of delight. Sorcha turned. He looked at his son, and Dave, still standing behind Torc, saw the old Dalrei's begrimed face light up with an unlooked-for joy.

One moment the tableau held; then Torc stumbled forward with unwonted awkwardness, and he and his father met in an embrace so fierce it seemed as if they meant to squeeze away all the dark years that had lain between.

Dave, who had given Torc the push that sent him forward, was smiling through tears. He looked at Levon and then at Ivor. He thought of his own father, so far away—so far away, it seemed, all his life. He looked over and up at Rangat and remembered the hand of fire.

"Do you think," Mabon of Rhoden murmured, "that that small expedition we were planning might just as easily be done with seven?"

Dave wiped his eyes. He nodded. Then, still unable to speak, he nodded again.

Levon signalled them forward. Careful of the axe he carried, moving as silently as he could, Dave crawled up beside his friend. The others did the same. Lying prone on a hillock—scant shelter on the open Plain—the seven of them gazed north towards the darkness of Gwynir.

Overhead, clouds scudded eastward, now revealing, now obscuring the waning moon. Sighing through the tall grass, the breeze carried for the first time the scent of the evergreen forest. Far beyond the trees Rangat reared up, dominating the northern sky. When the moon was clear of the clouds the mountain glowed with a strange, spectral light. Dave looked away to the west and saw that the world ended there.

Or seemed to. They were on the very edge of Daniloth: the Shadowland, where time changed. Where men could wander lost in Ra-Lathen's mist until the end of all the worlds. Dave peered into the moonlit shadows, the drifting fog, and it seemed to him that he saw blurred figures moving there, some riding ghostly horses, others on foot, all silent in the mist.

They had left the camp at moonrise, with less difficulty than expected. Levon had led them to the guard post manned by Cechtar of the third tribe, who was not about to betray or impede the designs of the Aven's son. Indeed, his only objection had been in not being allowed to accompany them.

"You can't," Levon had murmured very calmly, in control. "If we aren't back before sunrise, we will be captured or dead, and someone will have to warn the High King. The someone is you, Cechtar. I'm sorry. A thankless task. If the gods love us, it is a message you'll not have to carry."

After that, there had been no more words for a long time. Only the whisper of the night breeze across the Plain, the hoot of a hunting owl, the soft tread of their own footsteps as they walked away from the fires of the camp into the dark. Then the rustling sound of grasses parting as they dropped down and crawled the last part of the way towards the low tummock Levon had pointed out, just east of Daniloth, just south of Gwynir.

Crawling along beside Mabon of Rhoden, behind Torc and Sorcha, who seemed unwilling to allow more than a few inches of space between them now, Dave found himself thinking about how much a part of his reality death had been since he came to Fionavar.

Since he had crashed through the space between worlds here on the Plain and Torc had almost killed him with a dagger. There *had* been a killing that first night: he and the dark Dalrei he called a brother now had slain an urgach together in Faelinn Grove, first death among so many. There had been a battle by Llewenmere, and then among the snows of the Latham. A wolf hunt in Gwen Ystrat, and then, only three nights ago, the carnage along the banks of the Adein.

He had been lucky, he realized, moving more cautiously forward as the moon came out from between two banks of cloud. He could have died a dozen times over. Died a long way from home. The moon slid back behind the clouds. The breeze was cool. Another owl hooted. There were scattered stars overhead, where the cloud cover broke.

He thought of his father for the second time that day. It wasn't hard, even for Dave, to figure out why. He looked at Sorcha, just ahead, moving effortlessly over the shadowed ground. Almost against his will, a trick of distance and shadows and of long sorrow, he pictured his father here with them, an eighth figure on the dark Plain. Josef Martyniuk had fought among the Ukrainian partisans for three years. More than forty years ago, but even so. Even so, a lifetime of physical labour had kept his big body hard, and Dave had grown up fearing the power of his father's brawny arm. Josef could have swung a killing axe, and his icy blue eyes might have glinted just a little—too much to ask?—to see how easily his son handled one, how honoured Dave was among people of rank and wisdom.

He could have kept up, too, Dave thought, going with the fantasy a little way. At least as well as Mabon, surely. And he wouldn't have had any doubts, any hesitations about the rightness of doing this, of going to war in this cause. There had been stories in Dave's childhood about his father's deeds in his own war.

None from Josef, though. Whatever fragments Dave had heard had come from friends of his parents, middle-aged men pouring a third glass of iced vodka for themselves, telling the awkward, oversized younger son stories about his father long ago. Or beginning the stories. Before Josef, overhearing, would silence them with a harsh storm of words in the old tongue.

Dave could still remember the first time he had beaten up his older brother. When Vincent, late one night in the room they shared, had let slip a casual reference to a railway bombing their father had organized.

"How do you know about that?" Dave, perhaps ten, had demanded. He could still remember the way his heart had lurched.

"Dad told me," Vincent had answered calmly. "He's told me lots of those stories."

Perhaps even now, fifteen years after, Vincent still didn't know why his younger brother had so ferociously attacked him. For the first time ever, and the only time. Leaping upon his smaller, frailer older brother and punching him about. Crying that Vincent was lying.

Vincent's own cries had brought Josef storming into the room, to block the light from the hallway with his size, to seize his younger son in one hand and hold him in the air as he cuffed him about with an open, meaty palm.

"He is smaller than you!" Josef had roared. "You are never to hit him!"

And Dave, crying, suspended helplessly in the air, unable to dodge the slaps raining down on him, had screamed, almost incoherently, "But I'm smaller than you!"

And Josef had stopped.

Had set his gangly, clumsy son down to weep on his bed. And had said, in a strained, unsettling voice, "This is true. This is correct."

And had gone out, closing the bedroom door on the light.

Dave hadn't understood any of it then, and, to be honest, he grasped only a part of what had happened that night, even now. He didn't have that kind of introspection. Perhaps by choice.

He did remember Vincent, the next night offering to tell his younger brother the story of the train bombing. And himself, inarticulate but defiant, telling Vince to just shut up.

He was sorry about that now. Sorry about a lot of things. Distance, he supposed, did that to you.

And thinking so, he crawled up beside Levon on the hillock and looked upon the darkness of Gwynir.

"This isn't," Levon murmured, "the most intelligent thing I've ever done." The words were rueful, but the tone was not.

Dave heard the barely suppressed excitement in the voice of Ivor's son and, within himself, rising over his fears, he felt an unexpected rush of joy. He was among friends, men he liked and deeply respected, and he was sharing danger with them in a cause worthy of that sharing. His nerves seemed sharp, honed; he felt intensely alive.

The moon slipped behind another thick bank of clouds. The outline of the forest became blurred and indistinct. Levon said, "Very well. I will lead. Follow in pairs behind me. I do not think they are watching for us—if, indeed, there is anything there beyond bears and hunting cats. I will make for the depression a little east of north. Follow quietly. If the moon comes out, hold where you are until it is gone again."

Levon slipped over the ridge and, working along on his belly, began sliding over the open space towards the forest. He moved so neatly the grasses scarcely seemed to move to mark his passage.

Dave waited a moment, then, with Mabon beside him, began propelling himself forward. It wasn't easy going with the axe, but he hadn't come here to share in something easy. He found a rhythm of elbows and knees, forced himself to breathe evenly and slowly, and kept his head low to the ground. Twice he glanced up, to make sure of his orientation, and once the thinning moon did slide out, briefly, pinning them down among the silvered grasses. When it disappeared again, they went on.

They found the downward slope, just where the trees began to thicken. Levon was waiting, crouched low, a finger to his lips. Dave rested on one knee, balancing his axe, breathing carefully. And listening.

Silence, save for night birds, wind in the trees, the quick scurrying of some small animal. Then a barely audible rustle of grass, and Torc and Sorcha were beside him, followed, a moment later, as silently, by Brock and Faebur. The young Eridun's face was set in a grim mask. With the dark tattoos he looked like some primitive, implacable god of war.

Levon motioned them close. In the faintest thread of a whisper he said, "If there is an ambush of any kind, it will not be far from here. They will expect us to skirt as close to Daniloth as we can. Any attack would pin us against the Shadowland, with the horses useless among these trees. I want to check due north from here and then loop back along a line farther east. If we find nothing, we can return to camp and play at dice with Cechtar. He's a bad gambler with a belt I like."

Levon's teeth flashed white in the blackness. Dave grinned back at him. Moments like this, he decided, were what you lived for.

Then the armed guard stepped into their hollow from the north.

Had he given the alarm, had he had time to do so, all of them would probably have died.

He did not. He had no time.

Of the seven men he stumbled upon, every one was terribly dangerous in his own fashion, and very quick. The guard saw them, opened his mouth to scream a warning—and died with the quickest blade of them all in his throat.

Two arrows struck him, and a second knife before he hit the ground, but all seven of them knew whose blade had killed, whose had been first.

They looked at Brock of Banir Tal, and then at the Dwarf he had slain, and they were silent.

Brock walked forward and stood looking down at his victim for a long time. Then he stooped and withdrew his knife, and Sorcha's as well, from the Dwarf's heart. He walked back to the six of them, and his eyes, even in the night shadows, bore witness to a great pain.

"I knew him," he whispered. "His name was Vojna. He was very young. I knew his parents, too. He never did an evil thing in all his days. *What has happened to us?*"

It was Mabon's deep voice that slipped quietly into the silence. "To some of you," he amended gently. "But I think we have an answer now to Teyrnon's riddle. There is danger here, but not true evil, only a thread of it. The Dwarves are sent to ambush us, but they are not truly of the Dark."

"Does it matter?" Brock whispered bitterly.

"I think so," Levon replied gravely. "I think it might. Enough words, though: there will be other guards. I want to find out how many of them there are, and exactly where. I also need two of you to carry word back to the camp, right now." He hesitated. "Torc. Sorcha."

"Levon, no!" Torc hissed. "You cannot—"

Levon's jaw tightened and his eyes blazed. Torc stopped abruptly. The dark Dalrei swallowed, nodded once, jerkily, and then, with his father beside him, turned and left the forest, heading back south. The night took them, as if they'd never been there.

Dave found Levon looking at him. He returned the gaze. "I couldn't," Levon whispered. "Not so soon after they'd found each other!"

Words were useless sometimes, they were stupid. Dave reached forward and squeezed Levon's shoulder. None of the others spoke, either. Levon turned and started ahead. With Mabon beside him again, and Brock and Faebur following, Dave set out after him, his axe held ready, into the blackness of the forest.

The guard had come from the northeast, and Levon led them the same way. His heart racing now, Dave walked, crouched low among the scented outlines of the evergreens, his eyes straining for shapes in the night. There was death here, and treachery, and for all his fear and anger, there was room within him to pity Brock and grieve for him—and he knew he would never have felt either a year and a half ago.

Levon stopped and held up one hand. Dave froze.

A moment later he heard it, too: the sounds of a great many men, too many to maintain an absolute silence.

Carefully he sank to one knee and, bending low, caught a glimpse of firelight in the space between two trees. He tapped Levon's leg, and the fair-haired Dalrei dropped down as well and his gaze followed Dave's pointing finger.

Levon looked for a long time; then he turned back, and his eyes met Brock's. He nodded, and the Dwarf silently moved past Levon to lead them towards the camp of his people. Levon fell back beside Faebur, who had drawn his bow. Dave looped his hand tightly through the thong at the end of his axe handle; he saw that Brock had done the same. Mabon drew his sword.

They went forward, crawling again, careful of their weapons, desperately careful of twigs and leaves on the forest floor. With excruciating slowness Brock guided them toward the glow of light Dave had seen.

Then suddenly he stopped.

Dave held himself rigidly still, save for his own warning hand raised for Levon and Faebur behind him. Holding motionless, hardly breathing, he heard the crunching footsteps of another guard approach on the right, and then he saw a Dwarf walk past, not five feet away, returning to the camp. Dave wiped perspiration from his brow and drew a long, quiet breath.

Brock was slipping forward again, even more slowly than before, and Dave, sharing a quick lance with Mabon, followed. He found himself thinking, absurdly, about Cechtar's belt, the one Levon had wanted to gamble for. It seemed farther away than anything had any right to be. He crawled, moving each hand and knee with infinite deliberation. He hardly dared lift his head to look up, so fearful was he of making a sound on the forest floor. It seemed to go on forever, this last stage of the journey. Then, out of the corner of his eye, Dave saw that Brock had stopped. Glancing up, he saw that they were within sight of the fires.

Dave looked, and his heart sank.

There was a huge clearing in Gwynir; it seemed unnatural, man-made. He wondered, briefly, how it had come to be there. But there were more pressing concerns than that. This was no raiding party waiting for them, no delaying contingent readying a skirmish. There were a great many watch fires in the clearing, the flames kept low to avoid discovery, and around them, mostly sleeping, was the entire army of the Dwarves of Banir Lök and Banir Tal.

Dave had a horrifying premonition of the kind of havoc these fighters could wreak among Aileron's horsemen. He pictured the horses screaming, hampered and dangerous in the congested woods. He saw the Dwarves, small, quick, deadly, far more courageous than the svart alfar, slashing horseflesh and men amid the encircling trees.

He looked over at Brock, and his heart ached for the transparent anguish he saw in the other's face. Then, even as he watched, Brock's expression changed, and a cold hatred invested the Dwarf's normally kind features. Brock touched Levon on the arm and pointed.

Dave followed his finger and saw a Dwarf beside the nearest of the fires, talking softly to three others, who then ran off to the east, obviously carrying orders. The one who had spoken remained, and Dave saw that he was bearded and dark, as were Brock and Matt, and that his eyes were deep-set and hidden under an overhanging brow. He was too far away, though, to make out anything else. Dave turned to Brock, his eyebrows raised in a question.

*Blöd*, Brock mouthed, not making a sound.

And then Dave knew. This was the one they'd spoken of before, the one who'd given the Cauldron to Maugrim and had been in Starkadh when Jennifer was taken there. He felt his own hatred rising, his own eyes going flinty and cold, as he looked back at the Dwarf by the fire. He tightened his grip on the axe.

But this was a reconnaissance, not a raid. Even as he stared at Blöd, hungering for his death, he heard Levon's soft whisper commanding them to turn back.

They never had a chance, though.

There came a sound to their right, a loud crashing at the edge of the clearing, and then sudden hoarse shouts of alarm very near them.

*"Someone's here!"* a Dwarf guard screamed. Another one echoed the alarm.

Dave Martyniuk thought of his father blowing up bridges in darkest night in a darkest time.

He saw Brock rise, and Levon, weapons out.

He rose, hefting his axe. Saw Faebur's strung bow, and Mabon's long sword glint in the red light of the fire. For a moment he looked up. The moon was hidden, but there were stars up there between the banks of clouds, high above the trees, the fires, high above everything.

He stepped forward into the open, to have room to swing the axe. Levon was beside him. He exchanged one glance with the man he called his brother; there was time for nothing more. Then Dave turned towards the roused army of the Dwarves and prepared to send as many of them as he could into night before he died.

⋄⟶◉⟵⋄

It was still dark when Sharra woke on the deck of Amairgen's ship. A heavy fog lay over the sea, shrouding the stars. The moon had long since set.

She pulled Diarmuid's cloak more tightly about herself; the wind was cold. She closed her eyes, not really wanting to be awake yet, to become fully aware of where she was. She knew, though. The creaking of the masts and the flap of the torn sails told her. And every few moments she would hear the sound of invisible footsteps passing: mariners dead a thousand years.

On either side of her Jaelle and Jennifer still slept. She wondered what time it was; the fog made it impossible to tell. She wished that Diarmuid were beside her, warming her with his nearness. She only had his cloak, though, damp with the mist. He'd been too scrupulous of her honour to lie anywhere near her, either on the ship or, before they'd boarded, on the beach below the Anor.

They had found a moment together, though, after Lancelot had gone into the woods alone, in the deceptively tranquil hour between twilight and full dark.

All tranquility was deceptive now, Sharra decided, huddling under the cloak and the blankets they'd given her. There were too many dimensions of danger and grief all around. And she'd learned new ones with the tale Diarmuid had unfolded as they walked along the northwest curving of the strand past the Anor, and saw—first time for both of them—the sheer Cliffs of Rhudh gleam blood-red in the last of the light.

He had told her of the voyage in a voice stripped of all its customary irony, of any inflections of mockery and irreverence. He spoke of the Soulmonger, and she held his hand in her own and seemed to hear, as backdrop to the musing fall of his voice, the sound of Brendel singing his lament again.

Then he told her of the moment in the Chamber of the Dead under Cader Sedat, the moment when, amid the ceaseless pounding of all the seas of all the worlds, Arthur Pendragon had wakened Lancelot from his death on the bed of stone.

Sharra lay on the boat, eyes closed, listening to wind and sea, remembering what he'd said. "Do you know," he'd murmured, watching the Cliffs shade to a darker red, "that if you loved someone else, as well as me, I do not think I could have done that, to bring him back to you. I really don't think I'm man enough to have done what Arthur did."

She was wise enough to know that it was a hard admission for him to make. She'd said, "He is something more than a mortal, now. The threads of their three names on the Loom go back so far, intertwined in so many ways. Do not reproach yourself, Diar. Or, if you must"—she smiled—"do so for thinking I could ever love another as I do you."

He had stopped at that, brow furrowed, and turned to make some serious reply. She wondered, now, what it was he'd been meaning to say. Because she hadn't let him speak. She had risen up, instead, on tiptoe and, putting her hands behind his head, had pulled his mouth down so she could reach it with her own. To stop him from talking. To finally, properly, begin to welcome him home from the sea.

After which, they *had* greeted each other properly, lying upon his cloak on that strand north of Lisen's Tower, slipping out of their clothes under the first of the stars. He'd made love to her with an aching tenderness, holding her, moving upon her with the gentle rhythm of the quiet sea. When she cried out, at length, it was softly—a sound, to her own ears, like the sighing of a wave, a deep surging on the sand.

And so it was all right, after a fashion, that he did not lie with her when they came back to the Anor. Brendel brought a pallet out from the Tower for her, and blankets woven in Daniloth for Lisen, and Diarmuid left her the cloak, so she might have at least that much of him next to her, as she fell asleep.

To awaken, not long after, along with every one else on the beach, to see a ghostly ship sailing towards them, with Jaelle aboard, and Pwyll, and a pale proud figure beside them both who was, they gave her to understand, the ghost of Amairgen White-branch, beloved of Lisen, dead these long, long years.

They had boarded that spectral ship by starlight, by the cast glimmer of the setting moon, and unseen sailors had brought it about, and they had begun moving north as a mist descended over the sea to hide the stars.

Footsteps passed again, though there was no one to be seen. It had to be close to morning now, but there was no real way to tell. Try as she might, Sharra could not sleep. Too many thoughts chased each other around and around in her mind. Amid fear and sorrow, perhaps because of them, she felt a new keenness to all of her memories and perceptions, as if the context of war had given an added intensity to everything, an intensity that Sharra recognized as the awareness of possible loss. She thought about Diar, and about herself—a solitary falcon no more and found herself yearning, more than she ever had before, for peace. For an end to the terrors of this time, that she might lie in his arms every night without fearing what the mists of morning might bring.

She rose, careful not to wake the others sleeping beside her, and wrapping the cloak about herself she walked to the leeward rail of the ship, peering out into the darkness and the fog. There were voices farther along the deck. Others, it seemed were awake as well. Then she recognized Diarmuid's light inflections and, a moment later, the cold clear tones of Amairgen.

"Nearly morning," the mage was saying. "I will be fading any moment. Only at night can I be seen in your time."

"And during the day?" Diarmuid asked. "Is there anything we must do?"

"Nothing," the ghost replied. "We will be here, though you will not know it. One thing: do not, for fear of your lives, leave the ship in daylight."

Sharra glanced over. Arthur Pendragon stood there as well, beside Diarmuid and Amairgen. In the greyness and the mist, all three of them looked like ghosts to her. She made a sudden gesture rooted in old, foolish superstitions, to unsay the thought. She saw Cavall then, a grey shadow upon shadow, and in the fog he, too, seemed to belong to some realm of the supernatural, terribly far from her own. From sunlight on the waterfalls and flowers of Larai Rigal.

The sea slapped against the hull with a cold, relentless sound, magnified in the fog. She looked over the rail but couldn't even see the waterline. It was probably just as well; one glimpse, on first boarding, of water foaming through the shattered timbers of the ship had been enough.

She looked back at the three men, then caught her breath and looked more closely yet. There were only two of them.

Arthur and Diar stood together, with the dog beside them, but the ghost of the mage was gone. And in that moment Sharra became aware that the eastern darkness was beginning to lift.

Peering through the grey, thinning mist, she could now make out a long, low, rolling tongue of land. This had to be Sennett Strand, of the legends. They had passed the Cliffs of Rhudh in the night, and if her geography master in Larai Rigal had told true, and she remembered rightly, before the day was out they would come to the mouth of Linden Bay and see the fjords of ice and the vast glaciers looming in the north.

*And Starkadh:* the seat of Rakoth Maugrim, set like a black claw in the heart of a world of whitest light. She honestly didn't know how she was going to deal with looking upon it. It had as much to do with the ice as with anything else, she realized, with how far north they were, in a world so alien to one raised amid the gentle seasons of Cathal and the shelter of its gardens.

Sternly she reminded herself that they were not sailing to Starkadh or anywhere near it. Their journey would take them back south down Linden Bay to the mouth of the Celyn River. There, Diarmuid had explained, Amairgen would set them down, if all went well, in the darkness before dawn tomorrow, bringing an end to this strangest of voyages. It would have to be in darkness, she now realized, given what Amairgen had just said: *Do not, for fear of your lives, leave the ship in daylight.*

The mist was still rising, quickly now. She saw a small patch of blue overhead, then another, and then, gloriously, the sun burst into the sky over Sennett and the lands beyond.

And in that moment Sharra, looking towards the morning, was the first to notice something about the strand.

"Diar!" she called, hoping she'd kept the fear out of her voice.

He was still speaking to Arthur, just along the rail, standing quite deliberately on a part of the deck where the timbers had been completely torn away. He seemed to be suspended in air. And she knew that below him, if she looked, she would see seawater rushing in to swirl through the dark hold of Amairgen's ship.

He broke off the conversation and came over, quickly. Arthur followed.

"What is it?"

She pointed. By now the mist was entirely gone from off the water and there was a great deal of light. Morning in summer, bright and fair. She heard a babble of sound along the deck. Others had seen as well. The men of South Keep were crowding to the rail, and other hands were pointing to the same thing she was.

They were sailing along a green and fertile coast. Sennett Strand had always been known (if she remembered her lessons rightly) for the richness of its soil, though the growing season was short this far north.

But Sennett had been ruined, as Andarien beyond the bay had been, in the time of the Bael Rangat, despoiled by a killing rain and then ravaged by Rakoth's armies in the late days of the war before Conary came north with the armies of Brennin and Cathal. Ruined and emptied, both of those once-fair lands.

How then could they be seeing what now they saw? A quilting of fields laid out under the blue summer sky, farmhouses of stone and wood scattered across the strand, the smoke of cooking fires rising from chimneys, crops flourishing in rich shades of brown and gold and in the reddish hues of tall solais growing in row upon row.

Nearer to the ship, at the water's edge, as they continued north and the light grew clearer yet, Sharra saw a harbour indenting the long coastline, and within that harbour were a score or more of many-coloured ships, some tall-masted with deep holds for grain and timber, others little more than fishing boats to chance the ocean waters west of the strand. With a catch in her heart, as the cries of wonder grew louder all about her, Sharra saw that the very tallest of the ships carried proudly upon its mainmast a green flag with a curved sword and a red leaf: the flag of Raith, westernmost of the provinces of Cathal.

Next to it she saw another tall ship, this one flying the crescent moon and oak flag of Brennin. And the mariners of both ships were waving to them! Clearly, from over the sparkling water, came the sound of their greetings and laughter.

Beyond the ships the quayside bustled with early-morning life. One ship was off-loading, and a number of others were taking on cargo. Dogs and little boys careened about, getting in everyone's way.

Beyond the docks the town stretched, along the bay in both directions and back up from the sea. She saw brightly painted houses under slanting shingled roofs. Wide laneways ran up from the waterside, and following the widest with her gaze Sharra saw a tall manor house to the north and east with a high stone wall around it.

She could see it all, as they sailed past the mouth of the harbour and she knew this town had to be Guiraut upon Iorweth's Bay.

But Iorweth's Bay had been reclaimed by the rising land hundreds and hundreds of years ago, and Guiraut Town had been burnt and utterly razed to the ground by Rakoth Maugrim in the Bael Rangat.

It was so full of life, so beautiful; she suddenly realized that if she wasn't careful she would weep.

"Diar, how has this happened?" she asked, turning to him. "Where are we?"

"A long way off," he said. "We're sailing through the seas this ship knew before she was destroyed. In the days after Rakoth had come to Fionavar, but before the Bael Rangat." His voice was husky.

She turned back to look at the harbour, trying very hard to deal with that.

Diarmuid touched her hand. "I don't think there is anything that endangers us directly," he said. "So long as we stay on the ship. We will return to our own seas, our own time, after the sun has set."

She nodded, never taking her eyes from the brilliant colours of the harbour. She said, wonderingly, "Do you see that ship from Raith? And the smaller one over there—with the flag of Cynan? Diar, my country doesn't even exist yet! Those are ships of the principalities. They only became a country after Angirad returned from the Bael Rangat."

"I know that," he said gently. "We're looking at a world that was destroyed."

From over the water now she recognized the sound of a t'rena, played high and sweet on the deck of the ship from Cynan. She knew that music; she had grown up with it.

A thought came to her, born of the ache lodged in her heart. "Can't we warn them? Can't we do something?"

Diarmuid shook his head. "They can't see us or hear us."

"What do you mean? Can't you hear the music? And look—they're waving to us!"

His hands were loosely clasped together as he leaned on the rail, but the strain in his voice gave the lie to that casualness. "Not to us, my dear. They aren't waving to us. What they see isn't this broken hulk. They see a beautiful ship passing, with a picked crew from Brennin. They see Amairgen's mariners, Sharra, and his ship as it was before it sailed for Cader Sedat. We're invisible, I'm afraid."

So, finally, she understood. They sailed north along the line of the coast, and Guiraut Town disappeared from sight soon to disappear forever from the world of men, its brightness remembered only in song. Soon, and yet long ago. Both. Loops in the weaving of time.

The sound of the t'rena followed them a long way, even after the town was lost behind the curve of the bay. They left it, because they had no choice, to the fires of its future and their past.

After that the mood of the ship turned grim, not with apprehension, but with a newer, sterner resolution, a deeper awareness of what evil was, and meant. There was a harder tone to the speech of the men on the deck, a crispness to the movements with which they cleaned and polished their weapons, that boded ill for those who would seek to oppose them in what was to come. And it was coming, Sharra knew that now, and she, too, was ready for it. Some of that same resolution had hardened in her own heart.

They sailed north up the seaward coast of Sennett Strand, and late in the afternoon, with the sun well out over the sea, they came to the northernmost tip of Sennett and rounded that cape, swinging east, and they saw the glaciers and the fjords, and the blackness of Starkadh beyond.

Sharra gazed upon it and did not flinch or close her eyes. She looked upon the heart of evil, and she willed herself not to look away.

She could not, of course, see herself in that moment, but others could, and there was a murmuring along the ship at how fierce and cold the beauty of the Dark Rose of Cathal had suddenly become. An Ice Queen from the Garden Country, a rival to the Queen of Rük herself, as stern and as unyielding.

And even here, on this doorstep of the Dark, there was a thing of beauty to be found. High above and far beyond Starkadh, Rangat reared up, snow-crowned, cloud-shouldered, mastering the northlands with its glory.

Sharra understood suddenly, for the first time, why the conflict of a thousand years ago had come to be called the Bael Rangat even though not one of the major battles had taken place by the mountain. The truth was that Rangat loomed so imperiously high, this far north, there was no place in these lands that could not be said to lie under the sovereignty of the mountain.

Unless and until Rakoth defeated them.

They sailed down the bay of a thousand years ago under the westering sun. To the east they could see the golden beaches of Andarien and, beyond them, a hint of a green fair land, rising in gentle slopes towards the north. It would be dotted with strands of tall trees, Sharra knew, and there would be deep blue lakes, sparkling in the sun, with fish leaping from them in curved homage to the light.

All gone, she knew, all gone to dust and barrenness, to bleak highlands where the north wind whistled down over nothingness. The forests were levelled, the lakes dry, the thin grasses scattered and brown. Ruined Andarien, where the war had been fought.

And would be again, if Diarmuid was right. If even now, Aileron the High King was leading his armies from the Plain towards Gwynir, to come on the morrow through the evergreens to Andarien. They, too, would be there, those on this ship, if Amairgen's promise held.

It did. They sailed southeast down Linden Bay, through the growing shadows of that afternoon and the long summer twilight, watching the golden sands where Andarien met the bay gradually grow dark. Looking back to the west, over Sennett Strand again, Sharra saw the evening star—Lauriel's—and then, a moment later, the sun set.

And Amairgen was among them again, shadowy and insubstantial, but growing clearer as the night deepened. There was a cold arrogance to him and she wondered for a moment that Lisen had loved this man. Then she thought about how long ago she had died, and how long he had wandered, a ghost, loveless and unrevenged, through lonely, endless seas. He would have been different, she guessed, when he was a living man, and young, and loved by the fairest child of all the Weaver's worlds.

A pity she could never have expressed rose in her as she looked upon the proud figure of the first mage. Later it grew too dark, and she could no longer see him clearly under the starlight. The moon, thinning towards new, rose very late.

Sharra slept for a time; most of them did, knowing how little rest might lie in the days ahead—or how much rest, an eternity of it. She woke long before dawn. The moon was over the Strand, west of them. They carried no lights on that ship. Andarien was a dark blur to the east.

She heard low voices speaking again—Amairgen, Diar and Arthur Pendragon. Then the voices were gradually stilled. Sharra rose, Diarmuid's cloak about her in the chill. Jaelle, the High Priestess, came to stand beside her, and the two of them watched as the Warrior walked to the prow of the ship. He stood there—Cavall beside him, as ever—and in the darkness of that night he suddenly thrust high his spear, and the head of the King Spear blazed, blue-white and dazzling.

And by that light Amairgen Whitebranch guided his ship to land by the mouth of the River Celyn where it ran into Linden Bay.

They disembarked in the shallows by that sweetest of rivers, which flowed from Celyn Lake along the enchanted borders of Daniloth. Last of all to leave the ship, Sharra saw, was the one they called Pwyll Twiceborn. He stood on the deck above the swaying ladder and said something to Amairgen, and the mage made reply. She couldn't hear what they said, but she felt a shiver raise the hairs of her neck to look upon the two of them.

Then Pwyll came down the rope ladder, and they were all gathered on land again. Amairgen stood above them, proud and austere in what was left of the moonlight.

He said, "High Priestess of Dana, I have done as you bade me. Have I still the prayers you promised?"

Gravely, Jaelle replied, "You would have had them even had you not carried us. Go to your rest, unquiet ghost. All of you. The Soulmonger is dead. You are released. May there be Light for you at the Weaver's side."

"And for you," Amairgen said. "And for all of you."

He turned to Pwyll again and seemed about to speak once more. He did not. Instead, he slowly lifted high both his hands, and then, amid the sudden enraptured crying of his unseen mariners, he faded from sight in the darkness. And his ship faded away with him, and the crying of the mariners fell slowly away on the breeze, leaving only the sound of the surf to carry its echo awhile from so far back in time.

In that place where the river met the bay they turned and, led by Brendel of the lios alfar, who knew every slope and shadow of this country so near his home, they began walking east, towards where the sun would rise.

# CHAPTER 12

"I will not go within," Flidais said, turning away from the mist. He looked up at the man standing beside him. "Not even the andain are proof against wandering lost in Ra-Lathen's woven shadows. Had I any words left that might prevail upon you, I would urge you again not to go there."

Lancelot listened with that always grave courtesy that was so much a part of him, the patience that seemed virtually inexhaustible. He made one ashamed, Flidais thought, to be importunate or demanding, to fall too far short of the mark set by that gentleness.

And yet he was not without humour. Even now there was a glint of amusement in his eyes as he looked down on the diminutive andain.

"I was wondering," he said mildly, "if it were actually possible that you might run out of words. I was beginning to doubt it, Taliesin."

Flidais felt himself beginning to flush, but there was no malice in Lancelot's teasing, only a laughter they could share. And a moment later they did.

"I am bereft neither of words nor yet of arguments of dappled, confusing inconsequentiality," Flidais protested. "Only of time am I now run short, given where we stand. I am not about to try to restrain you physically here on the borders of Daniloth. I am somewhat wiser than that, at least."

"At least," Lancelot agreed. Then, after a pause, "Would you really want to restrain me now, even if you could? Knowing what you know?"

An unfairly difficult question. But Flidais, who had been the wisest, most precocious child of all in his day, was a child no longer. Not without sorrow, he said, "I would not. Knowing the three of you, I would not constrain you from doing a thing she asked. I fear the child, though, Lancelot. I fear him deeply." And to this the man made no reply.

The first hint of grey appeared in the sky, overture to morning and all that the day might bring. To the west, Amairgen's ghostly ship was just then sailing north along Sennett Strand, its passengers looking out upon a town given to the fire long ago, long since turned to ashes and to shards of pottery.

A bird lifted its voice in song behind them from some hidden place among the trees of the dark forest. They stood between wood and mist and looked at each other for what, Flidais knew, might be the last time.

"I am grateful for your guidance to this place," said Lancelot. "And for the tending of my wounds."

Flidais snorted brusquely and turned away. "Couldn't have done the one without the other," he growled. "Couldn't have guided you anywhere, let alone through the whole of a night, unless I'd first done something about those wounds."

Lancelot smiled. "Should I unsay my thanks, then? Or is this some of your dappled inconsequentiality?"

He was, Flidais decided, altogether too clever, always had been. It was the key to his mastery in battle: Lancelot had always been more intelligent than anyone he fought. The andain found himself smiling back and nodding a reluctant agreement.

"How is your hand?" he asked. It had been by far the worst of the wounds: the palm savagely scored by the burning of Curdardh's hammer.

Lancelot didn't even spare it a glance. "It will do. I shall make it do, I suppose." He looked north towards the mists of Daniloth looming in front of them. Something changed in his eyes. It was almost as if he heard a horn, or a call of another kind. "I must go, I think, or there will have been no point in our having come so far. I hope we meet again, old friend, in a time of greater light."

Flidais found himself blinking rapidly. He managed a shrug. "It is in the Weaver's hands," he said. He hoped it sounded casual.

Lancelot said gravely, "Half a truth, little one. It is in our own hands, as well, however maimed they are. Our own choices matter, or I would not be here. She would not have asked me to follow the child. Fare kindly, Taliesin. Flidais. I hope you find what you want."

He touched the andain lightly on the shoulder, and then he turned and after a dozen strides was swallowed up by the mists of the Shadowland. *But I have,* Flidais was thinking. *I have found what I want!* The summoning name was singing in his head, reverberating in the chambers of his heart. He had sought it so long, and now it was his. He had what he wanted.

Which did not do anything to explain why he stood rooted to that spot for so long afterwards, gazing north into the dense, impenetrable shadows.

It was only afterwards, thinking about it, that she consciously understood that this was something of which she must have always been inwardly aware: the terrible danger that lay in wait for her if she ever fell in love.

How else explain why Leyse of the Swan Mark, fairest and most desired of all the women in Daniloth—long sought by Ra-Tenniel himself, in vain—had chosen to abjure each and every such overture, however sweetly sung, these long, long years?

How else indeed?

The Swan Mark, alone of the lios alfar, had not gone to war. Dedicated in memory of Lauriel, for whom they were named, to serenity and peace, they lingered, few in number, in the Shadowland, wandering alone and in pairs through the days and nights since Ra-Tenniel had led the brothers and sisters of the other two Marks to war on the Plain.

Leyse was one of those who wandered alone. She had come, early of this mild summer's dawning, to glimpse the muted light of sunrise—all light was muted here—through the waters of the upward-rushing waterfall of Fiathal, her favourite place within the Shadowland.

Though truly her favourite place of all lay beyond the borders, north, on the banks of Celyn Lake, where the sylvain could be gathered in spring by one who was careful not to be seen. That place was closed to her now. It was a time of war outside the protection of the mist and what it did to time.

So she had come south instead, to the waterfall, and she was waiting for the sunrise, sitting quietly, clad as ever in white, beside the rushing waters.

And so it was that she saw, just before the sun came up, a mortal man walk into Daniloth.

She had a momentary spasm of fear—this had not happened for a very long time—but then she relaxed, knowing the mists would take him, momentarily, and leave him lost to time, no threat to anyone.

She had an instant to look at him. The graceful, slightly stiff gait, the high carriage of his head, dark hair. His clothes were nondescript. There was blood on them. He carried a sword, buckled about his waist. He saw her, from across the green, green glade.

That did not matter. The mist would have him, long before he could cross to where she sat.

It did not. She raised a hand almost without thought. She spoke the words of warding to shield him, to leave him safe in time. And, speaking them, she shaped her own doom, the doom her inward self had tried to avoid, all these long years, and had instead prepared, as a feast upon the grass.

The sun came up. Light sparkled gently, mildly, in the splash of the upward-running falls. It was very beautiful. It always was.

She hardly saw. He walked towards her over the carpet of the grass, and she rose, so as to be standing, drops of water in her hair, on her face, when he came to where she was. Her eyes, she knew, had come to crystal. His were dark.

She thought, afterwards, that she might have known who he was before he even spoke his name. It was possible. The mind had as many loops as did time itself, even here in Daniloth. She forgot who had told her that.

The tall man came up to her. He stopped. He said, with deepest, gravest courtesy, "Good morning, my lady. I am come in peace and trespass only by reason of utmost need. I must ask of you your aid. My name is Lancelot."

She had already given her aid, she might have said, else he would not have walked this far, not be seeing her now. He would be locked in a soundless, sightless world of his own. Forever. Until the Loom was stilled.

She might have said that, were her eyes not crystal—past that, even—brighter, clearer than she had thought they could go. She might have, had her heart not already been given and lost even before she heard the name, before she knew who he was.

There were droplets of water in her hair. The grass was very green. The sun shone down gently through the shadows, as it always did. She looked into his eyes, knowing who he was, and already, even in that first moment, she sensed what her own destiny was now to be.

She heard it: the first high, distant, impossibly beautiful notes.

She said, "I am Leyse of the Swan Mark. Be welcome to Daniloth."

She could see him drinking in her beauty, the delicate music of her voice. She let her eyes slide into a shade of green and then return to crystal again. She offered a hand and let him take it and bring it to his lips.

Ra-Tenniel would have passed a sleepless night, walking through fields of flowers, shaping another song, had she done as much for him.

She looked into Lancelot's eyes. So dark. She saw kindness there, and admiration. Gratitude. But behind everything else, and above it all, shaping the worlds he knew and woven through them all, over and over, endlessly, she saw Guinevere. And the irrevocable finality, the fact of his absolute love.

What she was spared—a dimension of his kindness—was seeing in his calm gaze even a hint of how many, many times this meeting had come to pass. In how many forests, meadows, worlds; beside how many liquescent waterfalls, making sweet summer music for a maiden's heartbreak.

She was shielded by him, even as she shaped her own warding, from knowing how much a part of the long threefold doom this was. How easily and entirely her sudden transfigured blazing could be gathered within the telling, one more note of an oft-repeated theme, a thread of a colour already in the Tapestry.

Her beauty deserved more, the incandescent, crystalline flourishing of it. So, also, did the centuries-long simplicity of her waiting. That, too, by any measure, deserved more.

And he knew this, knew it as intimately as he knew his name, as deeply as he named his own transgression within his heart. He stood in that place of sheerest beauty within the Shadowland and he shouldered her sorrow, as he had done so many others, and took the guilt and the burden of it for his own.

And all this happened in the space of time it might take a man to cross a grassy sward and stand before a lady in the morning light.

It was by an act of will, of consummate nobility, that Leyse kept the shading of her eyes as bright as before. She held them to crystal—fragile, breakable crystal, she was thinking—and she said, with music in her voice, "How may I be of aid to thee?"

Only the last word betrayed her. He gave no hint that he had heard the caress in it, the longing she let slip into that one word. He said formally, "I am on a quest set me by my lady. There will have been another who came within the borders of your land last night, flying in the shape of an owl, though not truly so. He is on a journey of his own, a very dark road, and I fear he may have been caught within the shadows over Daniloth, unknowing in the night. It is my charge to keep him safe to take that road."

There was nothing she wanted more than to lie down again beside the rising, rushing waters of the falls of Fiathal with this man beside her until the sun had gone and the stars and the Loom had spun its course.

"Come, then," was all she said, and led him from that place of gentlest beauty and enchantment, in search of Darien.

Along the southern margins of Daniloth they walked side by side, a little distance between, but not a great deal, for he was deeply aware of what had happened to her. They did not speak. All around them the muted, serene spaces of grass and hillocks stretched. There were flowing rivers, and flowers in pale, delicate hues growing along their banks. Once he knelt, to drink from a stream, but she shook her head quickly, and he did not.

She had seen his palm, though, as he cupped it to drink, and when he stood she took it between both her own and looked upon his wound. He felt the pain of it then, seeing it in her eyes, more keenly than he had when he'd lifted the black hammer in the sacred grove.

She did not ask. Slowly she released his hand—did so as if surrendering it to everything in the world that was not her touch—and they went on. It was very quiet. They passed no one else walking as they went.

Once, only, they came upon a man clad in armour, carrying a sword, his face contorted with rage and fear. He seemed to Lancelot to be frozen in place, motionless, his foot thrust forward in a long stride he would never complete.

Lancelot looked at Leyse, clad in white beside him, but he said nothing.

Another time it seemed to him that he heard the sound of horses rushing towards them, very near. He spun, shielding her reflexively, but he saw no one at all riding past, whether friend or foe. He could tell, though, from the turning of her gaze, that she *did* see a company riding there, riding right through the two of them perhaps, lost, as well, in a different way, amid the mists of Daniloth.

He released his grip on her arm. He apologized. She shook her head, with a sadness that went into him like a blade.

She said, "This land was always dangerous to anyone other than our kind, even before Lathen Mistweaver's time, when these shadows came down. Those men were horsemen from before the Bael Rangat, and they are lost. There is nothing we can do for them. They are in no time we know, to be spoken to or saved. Had we space for the telling, I might spin you the tale of Revor, who risked that fate in the service of Light a thousand years ago."

"Had we space for the telling," he said, "I would take pleasure in that."

She seemed about to say something more, but then her eyes—they were a pale, quiet blue now, much like the last of the flowers they had passed—looked beyond his face, and he turned.

West of them lay a thicket of trees. The leaves of the trees were of many colours even in midsummer, and the woods were very beautiful, offering a promise of peace, of quiet shade, of a place where the sunlight might slant down through the leaves, with a brook murmuring not far away.

Above the southernmost of the trees of that small wood, at the very edge of Daniloth, an owl hung suspended, wings spread wide and motionless in the clear morning air.

Lancelot looked, and he saw the sheath of a dagger held in the owl's mouth glint with a streak of blue in the mild light. He turned back to the woman beside him. Her eyes had changed colour. They were dark, looking upon the owl that hung in the air before them.

"Not this one," she said, before he could speak. He heard the fear, the denial in her voice, "Oh, my lord, surely not this one?"

He said, "This is the child I have been sent to follow and to guard."

"Can you not see the evil within him?" Leyse cried. Her voice was loud in the quiet of that place. There was music in it still, but strained now, and overlaid by many things.

"I know it is there," he said. "I know also that there is a yearning after light. Both are part of his road."

"Then let the road end here," she said. It was a plea. She turned to him. "My lord, there is too much darkness in this one. I can feel it even from where we stand."

She was a Child of Light, and she stood in Daniloth. Her certainty planted a momentary doubt in his own heart. It never took root; he had his own certainties.

He said, "There is darkness everywhere now. We cannot avoid it; only break through, and not easily. In the danger of this might lie our hope of passage."

She looked at him for a long moment. "Who is he?" she asked finally.

He had been hoping she would not ask, for many reasons. But when the question came, he did not turn away. "Guinevere's child," he said levelly, though it cost him something. "And Rakoth Maugrim's. He took her by force in Starkadh. And therein lies the evil you see, and the hope of light beyond."

There was pain now, overlying the fear in her eyes. And under both of those things, at bedrock, was love. He had seen it before, too many times.

She said, "And you think she will prove stronger?" Music in her voice again, distant but very clear.

"It is a hope," he replied, gravely honest. "No more than that."

"And you would act and have me act upon that hope?" Music still.

"She has asked me to guard him," he said quietly. "To see him through to the choice he has to make. I can do no more than ask you. I have only the request."

She shook her head. "You have more than that," she said.

And with the words she turned away from him, leaving her heart. She looked at the motionless bird, child of Dark and Light. Then she gestured with her long graceful hands and sang a word of power to shape a space through which he could fly over the Shadowland. She made a corridor for Darien, a rift in the mists of time that coiled through Daniloth, and she watched with an inner, brilliant sight, as he flew north along that corridor, over the mound of Atronel and beyond, coming out at length above the River Celyn, where she lost him.

It took a long time. Lancelot waited beside her, silent all the while. He had seen Darien's flight begin, but when the owl had gone some distance north over the many-coloured leaves of the forest, it was lost to his mortal sight. He continued to wait, knowing, among many other things, that this was as far as he would be able to follow Guinevere's child, the last service he could offer. It was a sorrow.

He was conscious, as he stood beside Leyse and the pale sun climbed higher in the sky, of a great weariness and not a little pain. There was a fragrance in the meadow, and birdsong in the woods nearby. He could hear the sound of water. Without actually being aware of having done so, he found himself sitting upon the grass at the woman's feet. And then, in a trance half shaped by Daniloth and half by marrow-deep exhaustion, he lay down and fell asleep.

When the owl had passed beyond the northernmost borders of her land and she had lost him beyond the mist, Leyse let her mind come back to where she stood. It was early in the afternoon, and the light was as bright as it ever became. Even so, she, too, was very tired. What she had done was not an easy thing, made harder for one of the Swan Mark by the inescapable resonance of evil she had sensed.

She looked down upon the man, fast asleep beside her. There was a quiet now in her heart, an acceptance of what had come to her beside the waters of Fiathal. She knew he would not stay unless she bound him by magic to this place, and she would not do that.

One thing, only, she would allow herself. She looked at his sleeping face for a very long time, committing it to the memory of her soul. Then she lay down beside him on the soft, scented grass and slipped her hand into his wounded one. No more than that, for in her pride she would go no further. And linked in that fashion for a too-brief summer's afternoon, joined only by their interwoven fingers, she fell asleep for one time and the only time beside Lancelot, whom she loved.

Through the afternoon they slept, and in the quiet peace of Daniloth nothing came, not so much as a dream, to cause either of them to stir. Far to the east, across the looming barrier of the mountains, the Dwarves of Banir Lök and Banir Tal waited for sunset and the judgement of their Crystal Lake. Nearer, on the wide Plain, a Dwarf and an Eridun and an exile of the Dalrei reached the camp of the High King and were made welcome there, before the army set out for the last hours of the ride to Gwynir and the eastern borders of this Shadowland.

And north of them, as they slept, Darien was flying to his father.

They woke at the same time, as the sun went down. In the twilight Lancelot gazed at her, and he saw her hair and eyes gleam in the dusk beside him, beautiful and strange. He looked down at her long fingers, laced through his own. He closed his eyes for a moment and let the last of that deep peace wash over him like a tide. A withdrawing tide.

Very gently, then, he disengaged his hand. Neither of them spoke. He rose. There was a faint phosphorescence to the grass and to the leaves of the wood nearby, as if the growing things of Daniloth were reluctant to yield the light. It was the same gleaming he saw in her eyes and in the halo of her hair. There were echoes of many things in his mind, memories. He was careful not to let her see.

He helped her rise. Slowly the glow of light faded—from the leaves and the grass and then, last of all, from Leyse. She turned to the west and pointed. He followed the line of her arm and saw a star.

"Lauriel's," she said. "We have named the evening star for her." And then she sang. He listened, and partway through he wept, for many reasons.

When her song was done she turned and saw his tears. She said nothing more, nor did he speak. She led him north through Daniloth, sheltered from the mist and the loops of time by her presence. All the night they walked. She led him up the mound of Atronel, past the Crystal Throne, and then down the other side, and Lancelot du Lac was the first mortal man ever to ascend that place.

In time they came to the southern bay of Celyn Lake, the arm that dipped down into Daniloth, and they went along its banks to the north, not because it was quickest or easiest but because she loved this place and wanted him to see. There were night flowers in bloom along the shore, giving off their scent, and out over the water he saw strange, elusive figures dancing on the waves and he heard music all the while.

At length they came to the edge of a river, where it left the waters of the lake, and they turned to the west as the first hint of dawn touched the sky behind them. And a very little while later Leyse stopped, and turned to Lancelot.

"The river is quiet here," she said, "and there are stepping stones along which you may cross. I can go no farther. On the other side of Celyn you will be in Andarien."

He looked upon the beauty of her for a long time in silence. When he opened his mouth to speak he was stopped, for she placed her fingers over his lips.

"Say nothing," she whispered. "There is nothing you can say."

It was true. A moment longer he stood there; then very slowly she drew her hand away from his mouth, and he turned and crossed the river over the smooth round stones and so left Daniloth.

He didn't go far. Whether it was an instinct of war, or of love, or of the two bound into each other, he went only as far as a small copse of trees on the banks of the river near the lake. There were willows growing in the Celyn, and beautiful flowers, silver and red. He didn't know their name. He sat down in that place of beauty as the dawn broke—dazzling after the muted light of the Shadowland—and he gazed out upon the ruined desolation of Andarien. He looped his hands over his knees, placed his sword where he could reach it, and composed himself to wait, facing west towards the sea.

She waited as well, though she had told herself all through the long night's silent walking that she would not linger. She had not expected him to stay so near, though, and her resolution faltered as soon as he was not there.

She saw him walk towards the aum trees and then sit down amid the sylvain she loved in her most cherished place of any in this one world she knew. She knew he could not see her standing here, and it was not easy for her to see clearly, either, beyond the encircling billows of the mist

She waited, nonetheless, and towards the middle of the afternoon a company of some fifty people approached from the west, along the riverbank.

She saw him rise. She saw the company stop not far away from him. Leading them was Brendel of the Kestrel Mark, and she knew that if he looked to the south he would see her. He did not.

He remained with the others and watched with the others as a woman, fair-haired, very tall, walked towards Lancelot. It seemed to Leyse that the mists parted a little for her then—a blessing or a curse, she could not say—and she saw Lancelot's face clearly as Guinevere came up to him.

She saw him kneel, and take her hand in his good one, and bring it to his lips, the same as he had done with hers when he had first approached her over the grass by Fiathal.

Yet not the same. Not the same.

And it came to pass that in that moment Leyse of the Swan Mark heard her song.

She went away from that place, walking alone, hidden by the screening of the shadows, and within her a song was building all the time, a last song.

Along the riverbank farther west she found, amid the willows and corandiel, a small craft of aum wood with a single sail white as her own white robe. She had walked past this place a thousand times before and never seen that boat. It had not been there, she realized. The music of her song had called it forth. She'd always thought that she would have to build her boat, when the time came, and had wondered how she would.

Now she knew. The song was within her, rising all the while, shaping a sweeter and sweeter sadness and a promise of peace to come beyond the waves.

She stepped down into the boat and pushed off from the restraining shallows and the willows. As she drifted close to the northern bank of the Celyn she plucked one red flower of sylvain and one of silver to carry with her, as the music carried her and the river carried her to the sea.

She did not know, and it was a granting of grace that she was spared the knowing, how very much an echo this, too, was of the story she had been brought into, how deeply woven it was into that saddest story of all the long tales told. She drifted with the current with her flowers in her hand, and at length she reached the sea.

And that craft, shaped by magic, brought into being by a longing that was of the very essence of the lios alfar, did not founder among the waves of the wide sea. Westward it went, and farther westward still, and farther yet, until at length it had gone far enough and had reached the place where everything changed, including the world.

And in this fashion did Leyse of the Swan Mark sail past the waters where the Soulmonger had lain in wait, and so became the first of her people for past a thousand years to reach the world the Weaver had shaped for the Children of Light alone.

# CHAPTER 13

The sun had set and so the glow of the walls had faded. Torches flickered in the brackets now. They burned without smoke; Kim didn't know how. She stood with the others at the foot of the ninety-nine stairs that led to the Crystal Lake, and a feeling of dread was in her heart.

There were eight of them there. Kaen had brought two Dwarves she didn't know; she and Loren had come with Matt; and Miach and Ingen were present for the Dwarf-moot, to bear witness to the judgement of Calor Diman. Loren carried an object wrapped in a heavy cloth, and so did one of Kaen's companions. The crystals—fruits of an afternoon's crafting. Gifts for the Lake.

Kaen had donned a heavy black cloak clasped at the throat with a single brooch worked in gold, with a vein of blue thieren that flashed in the torchlight. Matt was dressed as he always was, in brown with a wide leather belt, and boots, and no adornment at all. Kim looked at his face. It was expressionless, but he seemed strangely vivid, flushed, almost as if he were glowing. No one spoke. At a gesture from Miach, they began to climb.

The stairs were very old, the stone crumbling in places, worn smooth and slippery in others, an inescapable contrast to the polished, highly worked architecture everywhere else. The walls were rough, unfinished, with sharp edges that might cut if not avoided. It was hard to see clearly. The torches cast shadows as much as light.

The primitive stairway seemed to Kim to be carrying her back in time more than anything else. She was profoundly aware of being within a mountain. There was a growing consciousness of raw power massed all about her, a power of rock and stone, of earth upthrust to challenge sky. An image came into her mind: titanic forces battling, with mountains for boulders to hurl at each other. She felt the absence of the Baelrath with an intensity that bordered on despair.

They came to the door at the top of the stairs.

It was not like the ones she had seen—entranceways of consummate artistry that could slide into and out of the surrounding walls, or high carved arches with their perfectly measured proportions. She had known, halfway up, that this door wouldn't be like any of the others.

It was of stone, not particularly large, with a heavy, blackened iron lock. They waited on the threshold as Miach walked up to it, leaning upon his staff. He drew an iron key from within his robe and turned it slowly, with some effort in the lock. Then he grasped the handle and pulled. The door swung open, revealing the dark night sky beyond, with a handful of stars framed in the opening.

They walked out in silence to the meadow of Calor Diman.

She had seen it before, in a vision on the road to Ysanne's lake. She'd thought that might have prepared her. It had not. There was no preparing for this place. The blue-green meadow lay in the bowl of the mountains like a hidden, fragile thing of infinite worth. And cradled within the meadow, as the meadow lay within the circle of the peaks, were the motionless waters of the Crystal Lake.

The water was dark, almost black. Kim had a swift apprehension of how deep and cold it would be. Here and there, though, along the silent surface of the water she could see a gleam of light, as the Lake gave back the light of the early stars. The thinning moon had not yet risen; she knew Calor Diman would shine when the moon came up over Banir Lök.

And she suddenly had a sense—only a sense, but that was a good deal more than enough—of how utterly alien, how terrifying this place would be when a full moon shone down on it, and Calor Diman shone back upon the sky, casting an inhuman light over the meadow and the mountainsides. This would be no place for mortals on such a night. Madness would lie in the sky and in the deep waters, in every gleaming blade of grass, in the ancient, watchful, shining crags.

Even now, by starlight, it was not easy to bear. She had never realized how sharp a danger lay in beauty. And there was something more, as well, something deeper and colder, as the Lake itself was deep and cold. Each passing second, while the night gathered and the stars grew brighter, made her more and more conscious of magic here, waiting to be unleashed. She was grateful beyond words for the green shielding of the vellin stone: Matt's gift, she remembered.

She looked at him, who *had* been here on a night of the full moon, and had survived and been made King by that. She looked, with a newer, deeper understanding, and saw that he was gazing back at her, his face still vivid with that strange, glowing intensity. He had come home, she realized. The tide of the Lake in his heart had drawn him back. There was no longer any need to fight its pull.

No need to fight. Only judgement to be endured. With so very much at risk here in this mountain bowl, most of the way, it seemed, to the stars. She thought of the army of the Dwarves across the dividing range of the mountains. She had no idea of what to do, none at all.

Matt came over to her. With a gesture of his head, not speaking, he motioned her to walk a little way apart. She went with him from the others. She put up the hood of her robe and plunged her hands in the pockets. It was very cold. She looked down at Matt and said nothing, waiting.

He said, very softly, "I asked you, a long time ago, to save some of your words of praise for Ysanne's lake against the time when you might see this place."

"It is past beauty," she replied. "Beyond any words I might offer. But I am very much afraid, Matt."

"I know. I am, as well. If I do not show it, it is because I have made my peace with whatever judgement is to come. What I did forty years ago I did in the name of Light. It may still have been an act of evil. Such things have happened before and will happen again. I will abide the judging."

She had never seen him like this. She felt humbled in his presence. Behind Matt, Miach was whispering something to Ingen, and then he motioned Loren to approach, and Kaen's companion, carrying their crystals wrapped in cloth.

Matt said, "It is time now, I think. And it may be an ending to my time. I have something for you, first."

He lowered his head and brought a hand up to the patch over his lost eye. She saw him lift the patch and, for the first time, she caught a glimpse of the ruined socket behind. Then something white fell out, and he caught it in the palm of his hand. It was a tiny square of soft cloth. Matt opened it—to show her the Baelrath gleaming softly in his hand.

Kim let out a wordless cry.

"I am sorry," Matt said. "I know you will have been tormented by fear of who had it, but I have had no chance to speak with you. I took it from your hand when we were first attacked by the doorway to Banir Lök. I thought it would be best if I . . . kept an eye on it until we knew what was happening. Forgive me."

She swallowed, took the Warstone, put it on. It flared on her finger, then subsided again. She said, reaching for the tone that used to come so easily to her, "I will forgive you anything and everything from now until the Loom's last thread is woven, except that wretched pun."

His mouth crooked sideways. She wanted to say more, but there really wasn't time. It seemed that there had never been enough time. Miach was calling to them. Kim sank to her knees in the deep, cold grass and Matt embraced her with infinite gentleness. Then he kissed her once, on the lips, and turned away.

She followed him back to where the others stood. There was power on her hand now, and she could feel it responding to the magic of this place. Slowly, gradually, but there was no mistaking it. And suddenly, now that it was hers again, she remembered some of the things the Baelrath had caused her to do. There was a price to power. She had been paying it all along, and others had been paying it with her: Arthur, Finn, Ruana and the Paraiko. Tabor.

Not a new grief but sterner, now, and sharper. She had no chance to think about it. She came up to stand beside Loren, in time to hear Miach speak, with a hushed gravity. "You will not need to be told that there is no history for this. We are living through days that have no patterns to draw upon. Even so, the Dwarfmoot has taken counsel, and this is what shall be done, with six of us to witness a judgement between two."

He paused to draw breath. There was no stir of wind in the mountain bowl. The cold night air was still, as if waiting, and still, too, were the starry waters of the Lake.

Miach said, "You will each unveil your crystal fashionings that we may take note of them and what they might mean, and then you will cast them together into the waters and we will wait for a sign from the Lake. If there is fault found with this, speak to it now." He looked at Kaen.

Who shook his head. "No fault," he said, in the resonant, beautiful voice. "Let he who turned away from his people and from Calor Diman seek to avoid this hour." He looked handsome and proud in his black cloak, with the golden and blue brooch holding it about him.

Miach looked to Matt.

"No fault," said Matt Sören.

Nothing more. When, Kim thought, a lump in her throat, had he ever wasted a word in all the time she'd known him? Legs spread wide, hands on his hips, he seemed to be as one with the rocks all around them, as enduring and as steadfast.

And yet he had left these mountains. She thought of Arthur in that moment, and the children slain. She grieved in her heart for the sins of good men, caught in a dark world, longing for light.

*The question at issue*, Miach had said in Seithr's Hall, *is whether the King can surrender the Lake.*

She didn't know. None of them did. They were here to find out.

Miach turned back to Kaen and nodded. Kaen walked over to his companion, who held up his hands, the covered crystal within them, and with a sweeping, graceful motion Kaen drew the cloth away.

Kim felt as if she'd been punched in the chest. Tears sprang to her eyes. Her breath was torn away and she had to fight for some time before it came back. And all the while she was inwardly cursing the terrible unfairness, the corruscating, ultimate irony of this—that someone so twisted with evil, with deeds so very black laid down at the door of his heart, should have so much beauty at his command.

He had shaped, out of crystal, in miniature, the Cauldron of Khath Meigol.

It was exactly as she had seen it, in her long, dark mind journey from the Temple in Gwen Ystrat. When she had ventured so far into the blackness of Rakoth's designs that she could never have come back without Ruana's chanting to shield her and give her a reason to return.

It was exactly the same, but with everything reversed, somehow. The black Cauldron she had seen, the source of the killing winter in midsummer and then the death rain that had unpeopled Eridu, was now a glittering, delicate, ineffable glorious thing of crystalline light, even to the runic lettering around the rim and the symmetrical design at the base. Kaen had taken the image of that dark, shattered Cauldron and made of it a thing that caught the starlight as brightly as did the Lake.

It was a thing to be longed for, to be heartachingly desired by every single one of the Weaver's mortal children in all the worlds of time. Both for itself, and for what it symbolized: the return from death, from beyond the walls of Night, the passionate yearning of all those fated to die that there might be a coming back or a going on. That the ending not be an ending.

Kim looked at the Dwarf who had done this, saw him gaze at his own creation, and understood in that moment how he could have come to release Maugrim and surrender the Cauldron into his hand. Kaen's, she realized, was the soul of an artist carried too far. The search, the yearning for knowledge and creation taken to the point where madness began.

Using the Cauldron would have meant nothing to such a one: it was the *finding* that mattered, the knowledge of where it was. It was all abstract, internalized, and so all-consuming that nothing could be allowed to stand between the searcher and his long desire. Not a thousand deaths or tens of thousands, not a world given over to the Dark or all the worlds given over.

He was a genius, and mad. He was self-absorbed to the point where that could no longer be separated from evil, and yet he held this beauty within himself, pitched to a level Kim had never thought to see or ever imagined could be seen

She didn't know how long they stood transfixed by that shining thing. At length Miach gave a small, almost an apologetic cough. He said, "Kaen's gift has been considered." His voice was husky, diffident. Kim couldn't even blame him. Had she been able to speak, that, too, would have been her tone, even with all she knew.

"Matt Sören?" Miach said.

Matt walked over to Loren. For a moment he paused before the man for whom he had forsaken these mountains and this Lake. A look passed between the two of them that made Kimberly turn away for a moment, it was so deeply private, speaking to so many things that no one else had a right to share. Then Matt quietly drew the cloth from his own fashioning.

Loren was holding a dragon in his hands.

It bore the same relationship to Kaen's dazzling artistry that the stone door at the top of the stairs did to the magnificent archways that led into Seithr's Hall. It was roughly worked, all planes and sharp angles, not polished. Where Kaen's cauldron glittered brilliantly in the starlight, Matt's crafted dragon seemed dull beside it. It had two great, gouged eyes, and its head was turned upwards at an awkward, straining angle.

And yet Kim couldn't take her eyes off it. Nor, she was aware, had any of the others there, not even Kaen, whose quick chuckle of derision had given way to silence.

Looking more closely, Kim saw that the roughness was entirely deliberate, a matter of decision, not inability or haste. The line of the dragon's shoulder, she saw, would have been a matter of moments to smooth down, and the same was true of the sharp edge of the averted neck. Matt had wanted it this way.

And slowly she began to understand. She shivered then, uncontrollably, for there was power in this beyond words, rising from the soul and the heart, from an awareness not sourced in the conscious mind. For whereas Kaen had sought—and found— a form to give expression to the beauty of this place, to catch and transmute the stars, Matt had reached for something else. He had shaped an approach—no more than that—to the ancient, primitive power Kim had sensed as they mounted the stairs and had been overwhelmingly conscious of from the moment they had come into the meadow.

Calor Diman was infinitely more than a place of glory, however much it was that. It was hearthstone, bedrock, root. It encompassed the roughness of rock and the age of earth and the cold depths of mountain waters. It was very dangerous. It was the heart of the Dwarves, and the power of them, and Matt Sören, who had been made King by a night in this high meadow, knew that better than anyone alive, and his crafting for the Lake bore witness to it.

None of them there could know it, and the one man who might have told them had died in Gwen Ystrat to end the winter, but there was a cracked stone bowl of enormous antiquity lying, even then, beside a chasm in Dana's cave at Dun Maura. And that bowl embodied the same unthinking awareness of the nature of ancient power that Matt Sören's dragon did.

"You did this before," said Miach quietly. "Forty years ago."

"You remember?" Matt asked.

"I do. It was not the same."

"I was young then. I thought I might strive to equal in crystal the truth of what I was shaping. I am older now, and some few things I have learned. I am glad of a chance to set matters right before the end." There was a grudging respect in Miach's eyes, and in Ingen's, as well, Kim saw. In Loren's face was something else: an expression that combined somehow a father's pride, and a brother's, and a son's.

"Very well," Miach said, straightening as much as his bent years would allow. "We have considered both of your craftings. Take them and cast them forth, and may the Queen of Waters grant her guidance to us now."

Matt Sören took his dragon then, and Kaen his shining crystal cauldron, and the two of them went, side by side, away from the six who would watch. And they came, in the silence of that night, under the stars but not yet the late-rising moon, to the shore of Calor Diman, and there they stopped.

There were stars mirrored in the Lake, and high overhead, and then a moment later there were two more shining things above the water, as both Dwarves who had come to be judged threw their crystal gifts in arcs out over the Lake. And they fell, both of them, with splashes that echoed in the brooding stillness, and disappeared in the depths of Calor Diman.

There were, Kim saw with a shiver, no ripples at all to ruffle the water and so mark the place where they fell.

Then came a time of waiting, a time outside of time, so charged with the resonances of that place it seemed to go on forever, to have been going on since first Fionavar was spun onto the Loom. Kimberly, for all her dreaming, all her Seer's gifts, had no hint of what they were waiting to see, what form the Lake's answer was to take. Never taking her eyes from the two Dwarves by the water, she reached within and found her own twin soul, searching for a reply to the question she could not answer. But neither, it seemed, could the part of her that was Ysanne. Not even the old Seer's dreams or her own vast store of knowledge were equal to this: the Dwarves had guarded their secret far too well. And then, even as Kim was thinking this, she saw that Calor Diman was moving. Whitecaps began to take shape in the centre of the Lake, and with them there suddenly came a sound, high and shrill, a wailing, haunted cry unlike anything she'd ever heard. Loren, beside her, murmured something that must have been a prayer. The whitecaps became waves and the wailing sound grew higher and higher, and then so, too, did the waves, and suddenly they were rushing hugely from the agitated heart of the dark water towards the shore, as if Calor Diman were emptying her centre.

*Or rising from it.*

And in that moment the Crystal Dragon came.

Understanding burst in Kimberly then, and with it a sense, after the fact, as so many times before, that it should have been obvious all along. She had seen the enormous sculpture of a dragon dominating the entrance to Seithr's Hall. She had seen Matt's crafting and heard what he and Miach had said to each other. She had known there was more than beauty in this place. She had been aware of magic, ancient and deep.

This was it. This crystalline, shimmering Dragon of the Lake was the power of Calor Diman. It was the heart of the Dwarves, their soul and their secret, which she and Loren had now been allowed to see. A fact, she was grimly aware, that made their deaths doubly certain if Kaen should prevail in what was coming.

She forced her mind from that thought. All around her everyone else, including Loren, had knelt. She did not. Not clearly understanding the impulse that kept her on her feet—pride, but more than that—she met the shining eyes of the Crystal Dragon as they fell upon her, and she met them with respect but as an equal.

It was hard, though. The Dragon was unimaginably beautiful. Creature of mountain meadow and the icy depths of mountain waters, it glittered, almost translucent in the starlight, rising from the agitated waves high above the kneeling figures of the two Dwarves on the banks of Calor Diman.

Then it spread its wings, and Kimberly cried aloud in wonder and awe, for the wings of the Dragon dazzled and shone with a myriad of colours like gems in infinite variety, a play of light in the meadow bowl of night. She almost did sink to her knees then, but again something kept her on her feet, watching, her heart aching.

The Dragon did not fly. It held itself suspended, half within the water, half rising from it. Then it opened its mouth, and flame burst forth, flame without smoke, like the torches on the walls within the mountain; blue-white flame, through which the stars could still be seen.

The fire died. The Dragon's wings were still. A silence cold and absolute, like the silence that might have lain at the very beginning of time, wrapped the meadow. Kim saw one of the Dragon's claws slowly emerge, glittering, from the water. There was something clutched in its grasp. Something the Crystal Dragon suddenly tossed, with what seemed to her to be contemptuous disdain, on the grass by the Lake.

She saw what it was.

"No," she breathed, the sound torn from her like flesh from a wound. Discarded on the grass, glinting, lay a miniature crafting of a crystal dragon.

"Wait!" Loren whispered sharply, rising to his feet. He touched her hand. "Look."

Even as she watched, she saw the Dragon of Calor Diman raise a second claw, holding a second object. And this was a cauldron, of shining, scintillant beauty, and this object, too, the Dragon threw away, to lie sparkling on the blue-green grass.

She didn't understand. She looked at Loren. There was a curious light in his eyes.

He said, "Look again, Kim. Look closely." She turned back. Saw Matt and Kaen kneeling by the Lake. Saw the Dragon shining above them. Saw stars, subsiding waves, dark mountain crags. Saw a crystal cauldron tumbled on the grass and a small crafted dragon lying beside it.

*Saw that the dragon discarded there was not the one Matt had just offered to the Lake.*

And in that moment, as hope blazed in her like the Dragon's blue-white fire, Kim saw something else come up from Calor Diman. A tiny creature exploded from the water, furiously beating wings holding it aloft. A creature that now shone more brilliantly than it ever had before, with eyes that dazzled in the night, no longer dark and lifeless.

It was the heart's crafting Matt had offered, given life by the Lake. Which had accepted his gift.

There was a flurry of motion. Kaen scrambled forward on his knees. He reclaimed his cauldron. Rose to his feet holding it outstretched beseechingly. "No!" he pleaded. "Wait!"

He had time for nothing more. Time ended for him. In that high place of beauty which was so much more than that, power suddenly made manifest its presence for a moment only, but a moment was enough. The Dragon of the Lake, the guardian of the Dwarves, opened its mouth, and flame roared forth a second time.

Not up into the mountain air, not for warning or display. The Dragonfire struck Kaen of Banir Lök where he stood, arms extended, offering his rejected gift again, and it incinerated him, consumed him utterly. For one horrifying instant Kim saw his body writhing within the translucent flame, and then he was gone. There was nothing left at all, not even the cauldron he had made. The blue-white fire died, and when it did Matt Sören was kneeling alone, in the stunned silence of aftermath, by the shore of the Lake.

She saw him reach out and pick up the sculpted dragon lying beside him, the one, Kim now realized—seeing what Loren had grasped from the first—that he had shaped forty years ago, when the Lake had made him King. Slowly Matt rose to stand facing the Dragon of Calor Diman. It seemed to Kim that there was a tinted brightness to the air. Then the Dragon spoke.

"You should not have gone away," it said with an ancient sorrow.

So deep a sadness after so wild a blaze of power. Matt lowered his head.

"I accepted your gift that night," the Dragon said, in a voice like a mountain wind, cold and clear and lonely. "I accepted it, because of the courage that lay beneath the pride of what you offered me. I made you King under Banir Lök. You should not have gone away."

Matt looked up, accepting the weight of the Dragon's crystal gaze. Still he said nothing. Beside her, Kim became aware that Loren was weeping quietly.

"Nevertheless," said the Dragon of the Lake, and there was a new timbre in its voice, "nevertheless, you have changed since you went from here, Matt Sören. You have lost an eye in wars not properly those of your people, but you have shown tonight, with this second gift, that with one eye only you still see more deeply into my waters than any of the Kings of the Dwarves have ever done before."

Kimberly bit her lip. She slipped her hand into Loren's. There was a brightness in her heart.

"You should not have gone away," she heard the Dragon say to Matt, "but from what you have done tonight, I will accept that a part of you never did. Be welcome back, Matt Sören, and hear me as I name you now truest of all Kings ever to reign under Banir Lök and Banir Tal."

There was light, there seemed to be so much light: a tinted, rosy hue of fiercest illumination.

*"Oh, Kim, no!"* Loren suddenly cried in a choked, desperate voice. *"Not this. Oh, surely not this!"*

Light burned to ash in the wake of knowledge, of bitter, bitterest, recurring understanding. *Of course* there was light in the meadow, of course there was. *She* was here.

With the Baelrath blazing in wildest summons on her hand. Matt had wheeled at Loren's cry. Kim saw him look at the ring he had only just returned to her, and she read the brutal anguish in his face as this moment of heart-deep triumph, the moment of his return, was transformed into something terrible beyond words.

She wanted desperately not to be here, not to understand what this imperative blazing meant. She *was* here, though, and she did know. And she had not knelt to the Dragon because, somehow, a part of her must have been aware of what was to come.

What had come now. She carried the Warstone again, the summons to war. And it was on fire to summon. To compel the Crystal Dragon from its mountain bowl. Kim had no illusions, none at all—and the sight of Matt's stricken face would have stripped them away from her, if she'd had any.

The Dragon could not leave the Lake, not if it was to be what it had always been: ancient guardian, key to the soul, heart-deep symbol of what the Dwarves were. What she was about to do would shatter the people of the twin mountains as much and more as she had smashed the Paraiko in Khath Meigol.

This crystal power of Calor Diman, which had endured the death rain of Maugrim, would not be able to resist the fire she carried. Nothing could.

Matt turned away. Loren released her hand.

*I don't have a choice!* she cried. Within her heart, not aloud. She knew why the stone was burning. There was tremendous power here in this creature of the Lake, and its very shining made it a part of the army of Light. They were at war with the Dark, with the unnumbered legions of Rakoth. She had carried the ring here for a reason, and this was it.

She stepped forward, towards the now-still waters of Calor Diman. She looked up and saw the clear eyes of the Dragon resting upon her, accepting and unafraid, though infinitely sorrowful. As deeply rooted in power as anything in Fionavar and knowing that Kim's was a force that would bind it and change it forever.

On her hand the Baelrath was pulsing now so wildly that the whole of the meadow and all the mountain crags were lit by its glow. Kim lifted her hand. She thought of Macha and Nemain, the goddesses of war. She thought of Ruana and the Paraiko, remembered the kanior: the last kanior. Because of her. She thought of Arthur, and of Matt Sören, who stood, not far away, not looking at her, lest his expression plead.

She thought upon the evil that good men had done in the name of Light, remembered Jennifer in Starkadh. War was upon them, it was all around them, threatening those living now, and all who might come after, with the terrible dominion of the Dark.

"No," said Kimberly Ford quietly, with absolute finality. "I have come this far and have done this much. I will go no farther on this path. There is a point beyond which the quest for Light becomes a serving of the Dark."

"Kim—" Matt began. His face was working strangely.

"Be silent!" she said, stern because she would break if she heard him speak. She knew him, and knew what he would say. "Come here beside me! Loren! And Miach, too, I'll need you!" Her mind was racing as fast as it ever had.

They moved towards her, drawn by the power in her voice her—Seer's voice—as much as by the burning on her hand. She knew exactly what she was doing and what it might mean, knew the implications as deeply as she had ever known anything at all. And she would shoulder them. If it made her name a curse from now to the end of time, then so be it. She would not destroy what she had seen tonight.

There was understanding in the Dragon's crystal eyes. Slowly it spread its wings, like a curtain of benison, many-coloured, glittering with light. Kim had no illusions about that, none at all.

The two Dwarves and the man were beside her now. The flame on her hand was still driving her to summon. It was *demanding* that she do so. There was war. There was need! She met the eyes of the Dragon for the very last time.

"No," she said again with all the conviction of her soul—both her souls.

And then she used the incandescent, overwhelming blazing of the ring, not to bind the Dragon of the Dwarves but to take herself away across the mountains, herself and three others with her, far from that hidden place of starlight and enchantment, though not so far as she had gone in coming there.

The Baelrath's power was rampant within her, flaming with the fire of war. She entered into it, saw where it was she had to go, gathered and channelled what she carried, and took them there.

They came down, in what seemed to all of them to be a corona of crimson light. They were in a clearing. A clearing in the forest of Gwynir, not far from Daniloth.

*"Someone's here!"* a voice screamed in strident warning. Another echoed it: voices of Dwarves from the army Blöd commanded. They had come in time!

Kim was driven to her knees by the impact of landing. She looked quickly around. And saw Dave Martyniuk standing not ten feet away from her with an axe in his hand. Behind him she recognized, with an incredulity that bordered on stupefaction, Faebur and Brock, swords drawn. There was no time to think.

"Miach!" she screamed. "Stop them!"

And the aged leader of the Dwarfmoot did not fail her. Moving more swiftly than she had ever thought he could, he stepped between Dave and the trio of Dwarves menacing him, and he cried, "*Hold arrows and blades, people of the mountains! Miach of the Moot commands you, in the name of the King of the Dwarves!*"

There was thunder in him for that one moment, a ringing peal of command. The Dwarves froze. Slowly Dave lowered his axe, Faebur his bow.

In the brittle silence of the forest clearing, Miach said, very clearly, "Hear me. There has been judgement tonight by the shores of Calor Diman. Matt Sören returned to our mountains yesterday, and it was the decision of the Moot, after a word-striving in Seithr's Hall between him and Kaen, that their dispute be left to the Lake. So did it come to pass tonight. I must tell you that Kaen is dead, destroyed by the fire of the Lake. The spirit of Calor Diman came forth tonight, and I saw it with my eyes and heard it name Matt Sören to be our King again, and more: I heard it name him as truest of all Kings ever to reign under the mountains."

"You are lying!" A harsh voice intruded. "None of this is true. Rinn, Nemed—*seize him!*" Blöd pointed a shaking finger at Miach.

No one moved.

"I am First of the Moot," Miach said calmly. "I cannot lie. You know this is true."

"I know you are an old fool," Blöd snarled in response. "Why should we let ourselves be deceived by that children's fable? You can lie as well as any of us, Miach! Better than any of—"

"Blöd," said the King of the Dwarves, "have done. It is over."

Matt stepped forward from the darkness of the trees. He said nothing more, and his voice had not been loud, but the tone of command was complete and not to be mistaken.

Blöd's face worked spasmodically, but he did not speak. Behind him a swelling murmur of sound rushed backwards through the army to the ends of the clearing and beyond, where Dwarves had been sleeping among the evergreens. They were sleeping no longer.

"Oh my King!" a voice cried. Brock of Banir Tal stumbled forward, throwing down his axe, to kneel at Matt's feet.

"Bright the hour of our meeting," Matt said to him formally. He laid a hand on Brock's shoulder. "But stand back now, old friend, there is a thing yet to be done."

There was something in his voice that evoked an abrupt image, for Kim, of the iron lock on the door to the meadow of Calor Diman.

Brock withdrew. Gradually the murmur and the cries of the army subsided. A watchful silence descended. Occasionally someone coughed or a twig crackled underfoot.

In that stillness, Matt Sören confronted the Dwarf who had served in Starkadh, who had done what he had done to Jennifer, who had been leading the Dwarves even now in the army of the Dark. Blöd's eyes darted back and forth, but he did not try to run or plead. Kim had thought he would be a coward, but she was wrong. None of the Dwarves lacked courage, it seemed, even those who had surrendered themselves to evil.

"Blöd of Banir Lök," Matt said, "your brother has died tonight, and your Dragon waits for you now as well in judgement, astride the wall of Night. In the presence of our people I will grant you what you do not deserve: a right to combat, and life in exile if you survive. As atonement for my own wrongs, which are many, I will fight you in this wood until one of us is dead."

"Matt, no!" Loren exclaimed.

Matt held up one hand. He did not turn around. "First, though," he said, "I would ask leave of those assembled here, to take this battle upon myself. There are a very great many here who have a claim upon your death."

He did turn, then, and of all of them it was to Faebur that he looked first. "I see one here whose face marks him as an Eridun. Have I leave to take this death for you and in the name of your people, stranger of Eridu?"

Kim saw the young man step forward a single pace. "I am Faebur, once of Larak," he said. "King of the Dwarves, you have leave to do this for me and for all the raindead of Eridu. And in the name of a girl called Arrian, whom I loved, and who is gone. The Weaver guide your hand." He withdrew, with a dignity that belied his years.

Again Matt turned. "Dave Martyniuk, you, too, have a claim to this, for the sufferings of a woman of your own world, and the death of a man. Will you surrender that claim to me?"

"I will surrender it," Dave said solemnly.

"Mabon of Rhoden?" Matt asked

And Mabon said gravely, "In the name of the High King of Brennin, I ask you to act for the army of Brennin and Cathal."

"Levon dan Ivor?"

"This hour knows his name," Levon said. "Strike for the Dalrei, Matt Sören, for the living and the dead."

"Miach?"

"Strike for the Dwarves, King of the Dwarves."

Only then did Matt draw forth his axe from where it hung by his side and turn again, his face grim as mountain stone, to Blöd, who was waiting contemptuously.

"Have I your word," Blöd asked now, in the sharp, edgy voice so unlike his brother's, "that I will walk safely from this place if I leave you dead?"

"You have," said Matt clearly, "and I declare this in the presence of the First of the Dwarfmoot and—"

Blöd had not waited. Even as Matt was speaking, the other Dwarf had thrown himself sideways into the shadows and hurled a cunning dagger straight at Matt's heart.

Matt did not even bother to dodge. With an unhurried movement, as if he had all the time in the world, he blocked the flung blade with the head of his axe. It fell harmlessly to the grass. Blöd swore and scrambled to his feet, reaching for his own weapon.

He never touched it.

Matt Sören's axe, thrown then with all the strength of his arm and all the passion of his heart, flew through the firelit clearing like an instrument of the watching gods, a power of ultimate justice never to be denied, and it smote Blöd between the eyes and buried itself in his brain, killing him where he stood.

There were no shouts, no cheering. A collective sigh seemed to rise and fall, within the clearing and beyond it, to where Dwarves stood watching among the trees. Kim had a sudden image in that moment of a spirit, bat-winged, malevolent, rising to fly away. There was a Dragon waiting for him, Matt had said. Let it be so, she thought. She looked at the body of the Dwarf who had savaged Jennifer, and it seemed to her that vengeance should mean more, somehow. It should be more of a reply, something beyond this bloodied, torchlit body in Gwynir.

*Oh, Jen,* she thought. *He's dead now. I'll be able to tell you that he's dead.* It didn't mean as much as she'd once thought it would. It was only a step, a stage in this terrible journey. There was too far yet to go.

She had no more time for thoughts, which was a blessing and not a small one. Brock came rushing up to her, and Faebur, and she was embracing them both with joy. Amid the steadily growing noise all around, there was time for a quick question and answer about Dalreidan, and for delighted wonder as she learned who he really was.

Then, finally, she was standing in front of Dave, who had, of course, been hanging back, letting the others approach her first. Pushing her hair from her eyes, she looked up at him. "Well—" she began.

And got no further.

She was gathered in an embrace that lifted her completely off the ground and threatened to squeeze every trace of air out of her lungs. "I have never," he said, holding her close, his mouth to her ear, "been so happy to see anyone in all my life!"

He let her go. She dropped to the ground and stumbled, gasping frantically for breath. She heard Mabon of Rhoden chuckle. She was grinning like an idiot, she knew.

"Me neither," she said, aware, abruptly, of how true that was. "Me neither!"

"Ahem!" said Levon dan Ivor, with the broadest stage cough she'd ever heard. They turned, to find him grinning as much as they were. "I hate to intrude with petty matters of concern," the Aven's son said, striving to sound sardonic, "but we do have a report to make to the High King on tonight's events, and if we're to get back before Torc and Sorcha raise a false alarm, we'd best get moving."

Aileron. She'd be seeing Aileron again, too. So much was happening so fast. She drew a breath and turned, to see that Matt had come over to her.

Her smile faded. In her mind, even as she stood among the evergreens of Gwynir, she was seeing a Crystal Lake and a Dragon rising from it, glittering wings spread wide. A place where she would never walk again, under stars or sun or moon. She was a Seer; she knew that this was so. She and Matt looked at each other for a long time.

At length, he said, "The ring is dark."

"It is," she said. She didn't even have to look. She knew. She knew something else, too, but that was her own burden, not his. She said nothing about it

"Seer," Matt began. He stopped. "Kim. You were supposed to bind it, weren't you? To bring it to war?" Only Loren and Miach, standing behind Matt, would know what he was talking about.

Picking her words carefully, she said, "We have a choice, Matt. We are not slaves, even to our gifts. I chose to use the ring another way." She said nothing more. She was thinking about Darien, even as she spoke about choices, remembering him running into Pendaran, past a burning tree.

Matt drew a breath, and then he nodded slowly. "May I thank you?" he asked. This was hard. Everything was hard, now.

"Not yet," she said. "Wait and see. You may not want to. I don't think we'll have long to wait."

And that last thing was said in her Seer's voice, and so she knew it was true.

"Very well," Matt said. He turned to Levon. "You say you must carry word to the High King. We will join you tomorrow. The Dwarves have gone through a time worse than any in all our days. We shall remain by ourselves in these woods tonight and try to deal with what has happened to us. Tell Aileron we will meet him here when he comes, and that Matt Sören, King of the Dwarves, will bring his people into the army of the Light at that time."

"I will tell him," said Levon simply. "Come, Davor. Mabon. Faebur." He glanced at Kim, and she nodded. With Loren and Dave on either side, she began to follow Levon south, out of the clearing.

"Wait!" Matt cried suddenly. To her astonishment, Kim heard real fear in his voice. "Loren, where are you going?"

Loren turned, an awkward expression investing his lined face. "You asked us to leave," he protested. "To leave the Dwarves alone for tonight."

Matt's grim face seemed to change in the firelight. "Not you," he whispered softly. "Never you, my friend. Surely you will not leave me now?"

The two of them looked at each other in that way they had of seeming to be alone in the midst of a great many people. And then, very slowly, Loren smiled.

As they followed Levon out of the clearing into the darkness of the evergreens, Kim and Dave paused for a moment to look back. They saw Matt Sören standing with Brock on one side and Loren Silvercloak on the other. Matt had placed his fingertips together in front of his chest, with his palms held a little way apart—as if to form a mountain peak with his hands. And one by one the Dwarves of the twin mountains were filing up to him, and kneeling, and placing their own hands between his, inside the sheltering mountain the Dwarf King formed.

# PART IV

# ANDARIEN

# CHAPTER 14

In one way, Leila thought, listening to the last notes of the morning's Lament for Li-adon, it had been easier than she'd had any right to expect. She stood alone behind the altar, looking out upon all the others, closest to the axe but careful not to touch it, for that the High Priestess alone could do.

She stood closest, though. She was fifteen years old, only newly clad in the grey of the priestesses, yet Jaelle had named her to act in her stead while the High Priest-ess was away from Paras Derval. Dun to grey to red. She was of the Mormae now. Jaelle had warned her that there might be difficulties here in the Temple.

The fact that there hadn't been, so far, had a great deal to do with fear.

They were all a little afraid of her, ever since the evening when, only four nights ago, she had seen Owein and the Wild Hunt arrive at the battle by Celidon and had served as a conduit for Ceinwen's voice to resound in the sanctuary, so far from the river where the goddess was. In the supercharged atmosphere of war, that manifesta-tion of her own unsettling powers was still reverberating in the Temple.

Unfortunately it didn't help much with Gwen Ystrat. Audiart was another matter entirely. Three separate times in the day and a half following Jaelle's departure, the Second of the Goddess had reached for Leila through the gathered Mormae in Morvran. And three times Audiart had graciously offered to make her way to Paras Derval to assist the poor beleaguered child, so unfairly taxed with such a heavy bur-den in such a terrible time.

It had taken all the clarity and firmness Leila could muster to hold her back. She knew the issues at stake as well as any of them: if Jaelle did not return, then Leila, named in a time of war to act as High Priestess, would *become* the High Priestess, notwithstanding all the normal peacetime rituals of succession. She also knew that Jaelle had been explicit about this one thing: Audiart was *not* to be allowed to come to the Temple.

During the last mindlink, the evening before, diplomacy hadn't worked at all. Jaelle had warned her it might not and had told her what to do, but that didn't make the doing any easier for a fifteen-year-old, confronting the most formidable figure of the Mormae.

Nonetheless, she had done it. Aided by the astonishing clarity—she even surprised herself with it—of her own mind voice during the linkings and speaking as acting High Priestess, invoking the Goddess by the nine names in sequence, she had formally ordered Audiart to remain precisely where she was, in Gwen Ystrat, and to initiate no further mindlinks. She, Leila, had far too much to do to tolerate any more of these avarlith-draining communications.

And then she had broken the link.

That had been last night. She hadn't slept very well afterwards, troubled by dreams. One was of Audiart, mounted on some terrible six-legged steed, thundering over the roads from Morvran to seize and bind her with cold curses from millennia ago.

There had been other dreams, having nothing to do with the Mormae. Leila didn't understand the way her own mind worked, where her swirling premonitions came from, but they had been with her all night long.

And most of them were about Finn, which, since she knew where he really was and with whom he rode, became the most unsettling thing of all.

⟡

Darien never even knew he'd been frozen in time over Daniloth. As far as he was concerned, he'd been flying north, the dagger in his mouth, all the while. It was evening and not morning when he left the Shadowland and came out over Andarien, but he didn't know the geography here, so that didn't concern him.

In any case, it was hard to think clearly in the owl shape, and he was very tired by now. He had flown from Brennin to the Anor Lisen, and then walked to the sacred grove, and flown again from there through an unsleeping night to Daniloth, and then through the whole of yet another day to where he now was, heading north to his father.

Through the growing darkness he flew, and his keen night sight registered the presence of an unimaginably vast army gathering beneath him on the barren desolation of this land. He knew who they were, but he didn't descend or slow to take a closer look. He had a long way to go.

Below him, a lean scarred figure lifted his head suddenly to cast a keen glance at the darkening sky. There was nothing there, only a single owl, its plumage still white despite the changed season. Galadan watched it flying north. There was an old superstition about owls: they were good luck or bad, depending on which way they curved overhead.

This one did not swerve, arrowing straight north over the massing army of the Dark. The Wolflord watched it, troubled by a nameless disquiet, until it disappeared. It was the colour, he decided, the strange whiteness at sunset over this barren desolation. He put it out of his mind. With the snow gone, white was a vulnerable colour, and more of the swans were due to be coming back down from the north tonight. The owl was unlikely to survive.

It almost didn't.

A few hours later Darien was even more tired than before, and fatigue made him careless. He became aware of danger only an instant before the unnatural claws of one of Avaia's brood reached his flesh. He screeched, almost dropping the dagger, and veered sharply downwards and to his left. Even so, one claw claimed a half dozen feathers from his side.

Another black swan swooped hugely toward him, wings lashing the air. Darien wheeled desperately back to his right and forced his tired wings into a steep climb-straight towards the last of the three black swans, which had been waiting patiently behind the other two for precisely this move. Owls, for all their vaunted intelligence, were fairly predictable in combat. With a carnivorous grin the third swan waited for the little white owl, keen to slake its continuous hunger for blood.

In Darien's breast fear beat back tiredness, and following upon terror came a red surge of rage. He did not even try to dodge this last pursuing swan. Straight at it he flew, and an instant before they collided—a collision that would surely have killed him—he let his eyes burn as red as they could go. With the same blast of fire he had used to torch the tree, he incinerated the swan.

It didn't even have time to scream. Darien wheeled again, fury pulsing within him, and he raked the other two swans with the same red fire and they died.

He watched them fall to the dark earth below. All around him the air was full of the smell of singed feathers and charred flesh. He felt dizzy, suddenly, and over-whelmingly weak. He let himself descend, in a slow, shallow glide, looking for a tree of any kind. There were none. This was Andarien, and nothing so tall as a tree grew here, not for a thousand years.

He came to rest, for want of a better place, on the slope of a low hill littered with boulders and sharp-edged stones. It was cold. The wind blew from the north and made a keening sound as it passed between the rocks. There were stars overhead; low in the east, the waning moon had just risen. It offered no comfort, casting only a chill, faint illumination over the stony landscape, the stunted grass.

Darien took his own shape again. He looked around. Nothing moved, as far as he could see in the wide night. He was completely alone. In a gesture that had become a reflex in the past two days, though he was unaware of that, he reached up to touch the stone set in the Circlet of Lisen. It was as cool and dark and distant as it had been from the moment he'd put it on. He remembered the way it had shone in the Seer's hands. The memory was like a blade, or the wound made by a blade. Either, or both.

He lowered his hand and looked around again. About him, in every direction, stretched the desolation of Andarien. He was so far to the north that Rangat was almost east of him. It towered over the whole of the northlands, dominant and magnificent. He didn't look at the Mountain for long.

Instead he turned his gaze due north. And because he was much more than mortal and his eyes were very good, he could discern, far off through the moonlit shadows, where the stony highlands reached the mountains and the ice, a cold greenish glow. And he knew that this was Starkadh, beyond the Valgrind Bridge, and that he could fly there by tomorrow.

He decided that he would not fly, though. Something about the owl shape felt wrong. He wanted to hold to his own form, he realized: to be Darien, whatever and whoever that might be, to regain the clarity of thought that came in his human shape, though at the price of loneliness. Even so, he would do it this way. He would not fly. He would go on foot over the stones and the barren soil, over the ruin of this wasteland. He would go, with an extinguished light upon his brow, bearing a blade in his hand as a gift for the Dark.

Not tonight, though. He was much too tired, and there was a pain in his side where the swan's claw had caught him. He was probably bleeding but was too weary to even check. He lay down on the south side of the largest of the boulders—for such scant shelter as it might offer from the wind—and in time he did fall asleep, despite his fears and cares. He was young yet, and had come a long distance to a lonely place, and his soul was as much overtaxed as his body was.

As he passed over into the far countries of sleep, his mother was sailing in a ghostly ship down Linden Bay, just beyond the moonlit western ridges of the land, towards the river mouth of the Celyn.

He dreamt of Finn all night, just as Leila did in the Temple, a long way south. His dream was of the last afternoon, when he had still been small, playing in the yard behind the cottage with his brother, and they had seen riders passing on the snow-clad slopes east of them. He had waved a mittened hand, because Finn had told him to. And then Finn had gone away after the riders, and then much farther than they had gone, farther than anyone else, even Darien, even in dream, could go.

He did not know, huddled in the shadow of a leaning boulder on the cold ground of Andarien, that he was crying in his sleep. Nor did he know that all night long his hand kept returning to the lifeless gem bound about his brow, reaching, reaching out for something, finding no response.

⟡⟡⟡

"Do you know," said Diarmuid, gazing east with an enigmatic expression, "this is almost enough to make one believe in fraternal instincts, after all."

Beside him on the banks of the River Celyn, Paul remained silent. Across the northwestern spur of the lake the army was coming. They were too far off yet for him to make out individual details, but that didn't matter. What mattered was that Diarmuid, for all the reflexive irony of his words, had indeed been right.

Aileron had not waited, for them or for anyone. He had carried this war to Maugrim. The army of the High King was in Andarien again, a thousand years after it had last swept through these wild, desolate highlands. And waiting for them in the late-afternoon light was his brother, with Arthur and Lancelot and Guinevere, with Sharra of Cathal, and Jaelle, the High Priestess, with the men of South Keep who had manned *Prydwen*, and with Pwyll Twiceborn, Lord of the Summer Tree.

For what, Paul thought, that last was worth. It didn't, at the moment, feel like much. He should be used to this by now, he knew: this sense of latency without control. Of holding power without harnessing it. He remembered Jaelle's words on the rocks, and he was acutely aware that she was right—aware of how much his difficulties were caused by his own overdeveloped need for controlling things. Particularly himself. All of this was true; it made sense; he even understood it. It didn't make him feel any better, though. Not now, not so near to whatever ending lay in wait, whatever future towards which they were toiling.

"He has the Dwarves with him!" keen-eyed Brendel suddenly cried. "Now that," said Diarmuid sharply, "is news!"

It was. "Matt succeeded, then!" Paul exclaimed. "Do you see him, Brendel?"

The silver-haired lios alfar scanned the distant army. "Not yet," he murmured, "but . . . yes. It has to be her! The Seer is with the High King. No one else has her white hair."

Paul looked quickly over at Jennifer. She returned his glance and smiled. It was strange, he thought, in some ways it was the strangest thing of all, how she could be at once so different, so remote, so much Guinevere of Camelot, Arthur's Queen, Lancelot's love, and then, a moment later, with the quickness of a smile, be Jennifer Lowell again, sharing his own flash of joy at Kimberly's return.

"Should we walk around the lake to meet them?" Arthur asked.

Diarmuid shook his head with exaggerated decisiveness. "They have horses," he said pointedly, "and we have been walking all day. If Brendel can see them, then the lios alfar in the army can see us. There are limits, I'm afraid, to how far I will stumble over those rocks in order to meet a brother who didn't bother to wait for me!"

Lancelot laughed. Glancing over at him, Paul was hit with a renewed sense of awe and, predictably, by another wave of his own frustrated impotence.

Lancelot had been waiting for them here, sitting patiently under the trees, as they had walked up along the river two hours ago. In the gentle restraint of his greeting of Guinevere, and then of Arthur, Paul had glimpsed again the depths of the grief that bound these three. It was not an easy thing to watch.

And then Lancelot had told, sparely, without inflection, the tale of his night battle with the demon in the sacred grove for the life of Darien. He made it sound prosaic, almost a negligible event. But every man and the three women there could see the wounds and burns of that battle, the price he had paid.

For what? Paul didn't know. None of them did, not even Jennifer. And there had been nothing at all to be read in her eyes as Lancelot told of freeing the owl in Daniloth and watching it fly north: the random thread in this weaving of war.

A war that seemed to be upon them now. The army had come closer; it was rounding the tip of Celyn Lake. Beneath Diarmuid's acerbic flippancy Paul could read a febrile tension building: the reunion with his brother, the nearness of battle. They could make out figures now. Paul saw Aileron under the banner of the High Kingdom, and then he realized that the banner had changed: the tree was still there, the Summer Tree for which he himself was named, but the moon above it was no longer the silver crescent of before.

Instead, the moon above the tree was the red full moon Dana had caused to shine on a new moon night—the Goddess's challenge to Maugrim and the challenge Aileron was carrying now, at the head of the army of Light.

And so that army rode up around the lake, and it came to pass that the sons of Ailell met again on the borders of Daniloth, north of the River Celyn among the broad-leafed aum trees and the silver and red flowers of sylvain on the riverbank.

Diarmuid, with Sharra holding him by the hand, walked a little forward from the others, and Aileron, too, stepped apart from the army he led. Paul saw Ivor watching, and a lios alfar who had to be Ra-Tenniel, and Matt was there, with Loren beside him. Kim was smiling at him, and next to her was Dave, a crooked, awkward grin on his face. They were all here, it seemed, here on the edge of Andarien for the beginning of the end. All of them. Or, not quite all. One was missing. One would always be missing.

Diarmuid was bowing formally to the High King. "What kept you so long?" he said brightly.

Aileron did not smile. "It took some doing to maneuver the chariots through the forest."

"I see," said Diarmuid, nodding gravely.

Aileron, his eyes unrevealing as ever, looked his brother carefully up and down, then said expressionlessly, "Your boots seem seriously in need of repair."

It was Kim who laughed, letting all of them know that they could. Amid the release of tension, Diarmuid swore impressively, his colour suddenly high.

Aileron finally smiled. "Loren and Matt have told us what you did, on the island and at sea. I have seen Amairgen's staff. You will know without my telling you how brightly woven a journey that was."

"You might tell me anyhow," Diarmuid murmured.

Aileron ignored that. "There is a man among you I would greet," he said. They watched as Lancelot stepped quietly forward, limping very slightly.

Dave Martyniuk was remembering something: a wolf hunt in Leinanwood, where the High King had slain the last seven wolves himself. And Arthur Pendragon had said, a strangeness in his voice, *Only one man I ever saw could do what you just did.*

Now the one man was here, and kneeling before Aileron. And the High King bade him rise and, gently, with care for the other's wounds, he clasped him about the shoulders as he had not clasped his brother. Who stood a little way behind, a slight smile on his face, holding the Princess of Cathal by the hand.

"My lord High King," said Mabon of Rhoden, stepping forward from the ranks of the army, "the daylight wanes, and it has been a long day's riding to this place. Would you make camp here? Shall I give the orders to do so?"

"I would not advise it," said Ra-Tenniel of Daniloth quickly, turning from conversation with Brendel.

Aileron was already shaking his head. "Not here," he said. "Not with the Shadowland so near. If the army of the Dark were to advance overnight we would have the worst possible ground for battle, with the river behind us, and no retreat beyond it into the mist. No, we will move on. It will not be dark for a few hours yet."

Mabon nodded agreement and withdrew to alert the captains of the army. Ivor, Paul noted, already had the Dalrei mounted up again, waiting for the signal to ride.

Diarmuid coughed loudly. "May I," he said plaintively, as his brother turned to him, "be so bold as to entreat the loan of horses for my company? Or did you want me to trundle along in your wake?"

"That," Aileron said, laughing for the first time, "has more appeal than you know." He turned to walk back to the army but over his shoulder, as if offhandedly, added, "We brought your own horse, Diar. I thought you would find a way to get back in time."

They mounted up. Behind them, as they left the river for Andarien's stony ground, a boat was drifting gently down the current of the Celyn. Within that craft Leyse of the Swan Mark was listening to the music of her song, even as she came out upon the waves, to follow the setting sun across the wideness of the sea.

Kim looked over at Dave for encouragement. She didn't really have a right to any support, but the big man gave her an unexpectedly shrewd glance, and when she began picking her way forward and to the left, to where Jennifer was riding, he detached himself from Ivor's side and followed her.

There was something she had to tell Jennifer, and she wasn't happy about it at all. Especially not when she thought about the disastrous results of her sending Darien to the Anor two days ago. Still, there was really no avoiding this, and she wasn't about to try.

"Hi," she said brightly to her closest friend. "Are you still speaking to me?"

Jennifer smiled wearily and leaned across in her saddle to kiss Kim on the cheek. "Don't be silly," she said.

"It's not that silly. You were pretty angry."

Jennifer lowered her gaze. "I know. I'm sorry." She paused. "I wish I could explain better why I'm doing what I'm doing."

"You wanted him to be left alone. It isn't that complicated."

Jennifer looked up again. "We *have* to leave him alone," she said quietly. "If I'd tried to bind him we'd never have known what he really was. He might have changed at any time. We'd never have been sure what he might do."

"We aren't very sure now," Kim said, rather more sharply than she'd intended.

"I know that," Jennifer replied. "But at least he'll do it freely, whatever he does. By his own choice. I think that's the whole point, Kim. I think it has to be."

"Would it have been so terrible," Kim asked, not wisely, but she couldn't hold the question back, "if you had just told him you loved him?"

Jennifer didn't flinch, nor did she flare into anger again. "I did," she said mildly, a hint of surprise in her voice. "I did let him know. Surely you can see that. I left him free to make his choice. I . . . trusted him."

"Fair enough," said Paul Schafer. They hadn't heard him ride up. "You were the only one of us who did," he added. "Everyone else has been busy trying to cajole him or make him into something. Including me, I suppose, when I took him to the Godwood."

"Do you know," Jennifer asked Paul suddenly, "why the Weaver made the Wild Hunt? Do you know what Owein *means?*"

Paul shook his head.

"Remind me to tell you, if we ever have the time," she said. "You, too," she added, turning to Kim. "I think it might help you understand."

Kim was silent. She really didn't know how to respond. It was too hard, this whole question of Darien, and since what she'd done, or refused to do, last night by Calor

Diman, she no longer trusted her own instincts about anything. Besides, this confrontation wasn't why she'd come over.

She sighed. "You may hate me after all," she said. "I interfered again, I'm afraid."

Jen's green eyes were calm, though. She said, "I can guess. You told Aileron and the others about Darien."

Kim blinked. She must have looked comical, because Dave grinned suddenly, and Jennifer leaned across again to pat her hand.

"I thought you might have," Jen explained. "And I can't say you were wrong. By now he has to know. Arthur told me that on the ship last night. I would have talked to him myself if you hadn't. It may affect his planning, though I can't see how." She paused and then, in a different voice, added, "Don't you see? The secret doesn't matter now, Kim. None of them can stop him from whatever he's going to do—Lancelot freed him from Daniloth yesterday morning. He's a long way north of us now."

Involuntarily, Kim's gaze went out over the land that stretched in front of them. She saw Dave Martyniuk do the same. Wild and empty in the late-afternoon light, Andarien rolled away, all stony hills and barren hollows, and she knew it was like this all the way to the Ungarch River. To the Valgrind Bridge across that river, to Starkadh on the other side.

As it happened, they did not have nearly so far to go, themselves.

They were very close to the front of the army, only a few paces behind Aileron and Ra-Tenniel, ascending a wide, lightly sloping ridge with yet another bleak depression beyond. The reddened sun was well over to the west and a breeze had come up, overture to twilight.

Then they saw the front-riding auberei suddenly reappear on the crest of the ridge. The High King reached the summit. He reined in his own black charger and froze, utterly still. They topped the rise themselves, the four of them riding together for the first and only time, and looked down onto a vast, stony plain and saw the army of the Dark.

The plain was huge, easily the largest expanse of level ground they'd yet reached in Andarien, and Paul knew this was no accident of chance. He also guessed, as he tried to control his accelerating heartbeat, that this would be the broadest such expanse in all the land between here and the Ice. It had to be. With subtleties of contour and land formation stripped away, less of Aileron's training in war, little of his life's studies, could be drawn into play. The ridge upon which they now were, looking down the gentle slope, was the only distinguishing feature in all the level land to east or west. This would be a battle of force on force, with nowhere to hide or seek advantage, where sheer numbers would tell the tale.

Between them and whatever lands lay beyond was an army so huge it numbed the mind. It could scarcely be registered. That was another reason why this plain had been chosen: nowhere else could such obliterating numbers have been assembled to move freely without hindering each other. Paul looked up and saw hundreds of swans, all black, circling ominously in the sky over Rakoth's army.

"Well done, Teyrnon," the High King said calmly. Paul realized with a shock that Aileron, as always, seemed to have been prepared, even for this. The mage had been using his powers to sense forward. Aileron had guessed the army was here; it was why he'd been so adamant about not camping overnight against the mist of the Shadowland.

Even as he looked down, heartsick, upon what lay waiting for them, Paul felt a quick pride in the young war king who was leading them. Completely unruffled, Aileron took the measure of the army he would have to somehow try to defeat. Without turning around, his eyes ceaselessly scanning the plain below, he began to issue a string of quiet instructions.

"They will not attack tonight," he said confidently. "They will not want to come at us up this ridge, and at night they'll lose the advantage of the swans' eyes. We will have battle with the sunrise, my friends. I wish we had some way of fighting them for control of the air, but it can't be helped. Teyrnon, you'll have to be my eyes, for as long as you and Barak can do so."

"We can do so for as long as you need us to," the last mage in Brennin replied.

Paul noticed that Kim had gone pale at Aileron's last words. He tried to catch her eye but she avoided his glance. He didn't have time to find out why.

"The lios can help with that," Ra-Tenniel murmured. There was music in his voice still, but there was nothing delicate about it anymore, nothing soothing. "I can post the most long-sighted among us up on this ridge to overlook the battle.

"Good," said Aileron crisply. "Do that. Place them tonight to keep watch. They will stay there tomorrow as well. Ivor, assign pairs of auberei to stay with each of the posted lios, to carry their messages back and forth."

"I will," said Ivor simply. "And my archers know what to do if the swans come too low."

"I know they do," said Aileron grimly. "For tonight, all of you bid your men divide into three watches and keep their weapons to hand when they rest. As for the morning—"

"Wait," said Diarmuid, from beside Paul. "Look. We seem to have a guest." His tone was as effortlessly light as it always was.

He was right, Paul saw. The red light of the sunset picked out a single huge white-clad figure that had detached itself from the heaving mass of the army on the plain. Riding one of the monstrous six-legged slaug, it picked its way over the stony ground to a position carefully out of bowshot from those watching on the ridge.

An unnatural stillness descended. Paul was acutely aware of the breeze, the angle of the sun, the clouds scudding overhead. He reached, a little desperately, for the place within himself that would mark the presence of Mörnir. It was there, but faint and hopelessly far. He shook his head.

"*Uathach!*" Dave Martyniuk said suddenly. It was a snarl.

"Who is he?" Aileron asked, very calm.

"He led them in the battle by the Adein," Ivor replied, his voice thick with loathing. "He is an urgach, but much more than that. Rakoth has done something to him."

Aileron nodded but said nothing more.

Instead, it was Uathach who spoke.

"Hear me!" he cried, his voice a viscous howl, so loud it seemed to bruise the air. "I bid you welcome, High King of Brennin, to Andarien. My friends behind me are hungry tonight, and I have promised them warrior meat tomorrow and more delicate fare after that, in Daniloth." He laughed, huge and fell on the plain, the red sun tinting the mocking white of his robe.

Aileron made no reply, nor did anyone else on the ridge. In grim, repressive silence, stony as the land over which they rode, they looked down upon the leader of Rakoth's army.

The slaug moved restlessly sideways. Uathach reined it viciously. Then he laughed a second time, and something in the sound chilled Paul.

Uathach said, "I have promised the svart alfar meat for tomorrow and offered them sport tonight. Tell me, warriors of Brennin, of Daniloth, of the Dalrei, treacherous Dwarves, tell me if there is one among you who will come down alone to me now. Or will you all hide as the frail lios do, in their shadows? *I offer challenge in the presence of these armies! Is there one who will accept, or are you all craven before my sword?"*

There was a stir along the ridge. Paul saw Dave, jaw clamped tight, turn quickly to look at the Aven's son. Levon, his hand trembling, had half drawn his sword.

"No!" said Ivor dan Banor, and not only to his son. "I have seen this one in battle. We cannot fight him, and we cannot afford to lose any man here!"

Before anyone else could speak, Uathach's coarse laughter spilled forth again, a slimy flood of sound. He had heard.

He said, "I thought as much! Then let me say one thing more to all the brave ones on that hill. I have a message from my lord." The voice changed; it became colder, less rough, more frightening. "A year ago and a little more, Rakoth took pleasure in a woman of your company. He would do so again. She offered rare, willing sport. Black Avaia is with me now, to bear her back to Starkadh at his bidding. Is there one among you who will contest against my blade Rakoth's claim to her naked flesh?"

A sickness rose within Paul, of revulsion and of premonition.

"My lord High King," said Arthur Pendragon, as Uathach's laughter, and the howls of the svart alfar behind him, rose and fell, "would you tell me the name of this place."

Paul saw Aileron turn to the Warrior.

But it was Loren Silvercloak who answered, a knowing sorrow in his voice. "This plain was green and fertile a thousand years ago," he said. "And in those days it was called Camlann."

"I thought it might be," Arthur replied very quietly. Without speaking again he began checking the fit of his sword belt and the tilt of the King Spear in his saddle rest.

Paul turned to Jennifer—to Guinevere. What he saw in her face then, as she looked at the Warrior's quiet preparations, went straight to his heart.

"My lord Arthur," said Aileron, "I must ask you to defer to me. The leader of their army should fight the leader of our own. This is my battle, and I lay claim to it."

Arthur didn't even look up from his preparations. "Not so," he said, "and you know it is not. You are needed on the morrow more than any other man here. I told you all a long time ago, on the eve of the voyage to Cader Sedat, that I am never allowed to see the end of things when I am summoned. And the name Loren spoke has made things clear: there has been a Camlann waiting for me in every world. This is what I was brought here for, High King."

Beside him, Cavall made a sound, more whimper than growl. The red sun was low, casting a strange light upon all their faces. Below them, the laughter had ended.

"Arthur, no!" said Kimberly, with passion. "You are here for more than this. You must not go down there. We need *all* of you too much. Can't you see what he is? None of you can fight him! Jennifer, tell them it is foolishness. You *must* tell them!"

But Jennifer, looking at the Warrior, said nothing at all.

Arthur had finished his preparations. He looked up then, straight at Kimberly, who had summoned him. Who had brought him to this place by the binding of his name. And to her he made reply, in words Paul knew he would never forget.

"How can we *not* fight him, Seer? How can we claim to carry our swords in the name of Light, if we are cowards when we stand before the Dark? This challenge goes further back than any of us. Further back, even, than I. What are we if we deny the dance?"

Aileron was nodding slowly, and Levon, and Ra-Tenniel's eyes were bright with his agreement. Within his own heart Paul felt some deep eons-old force behind the Warrior's words, and as he accepted them, grieving, he felt another thing: the pulse-beat of the God. It was true. It was a dance that was not to be denied. And it seemed that it was Arthur's, after all.

*"No,"* said Guinevere.

Every eye went to her. In the windswept silence of that desolate place her beauty seemed to burn like some evening star brought among men, almost too fierce to look upon.

Motionless astride her horse, her hands twisted in its mane, she said, "Arthur, I will not lose you again like this. I could not bear it. Single combat is not why you were summoned, my love, it cannot be why. Camlann or no, this must not be your battle."

His face, under the greying hair, had gone still. He said, "We are caught in a woven doom of no escape. You know I must go down to him."

There were tears welling in her eyes. She did not speak, but slowly she shook her head back and forth in denial

"Whose place is it, then, if not mine?" he asked, scarcely more than a whisper.

She lowered her head. Her hands moved in a little helpless, trapped gesture of despair.

And then, without looking up, she said, with sudden, terrible formality, "In this place and before these many people my name has been besmirched. I have need of one who will take this challenge upon himself and unmake it with his sword."

And now she lifted her head, and now she turned. To the one who had been sitting quietly upon his horse, not speaking, not moving, waiting patiently for what he seemed to have known was coming. And Guinevere said: "Wilt thou, who hast been my champion so many times before, be so yet again? Wilt thou take this challenge in my name, my lord Lancelot?"

"Lady, I will," he said.

"You can't!" Paul exclaimed, his voice crashing into the stillness, unable to stop himself. "Jennifer, he's wounded! Look at his palm—he can't even hold a sword!" Beside him someone made a curious, breathless sound.

The three figures in the centre of the circle ignored him. Completely. It was as if he hadn't even spoken. There was another silence, laden with unsaid things, with so many layers of time. A stir of wind blew Jennifer's hair back from her face.

Arthur said, "My lady, I have known too many things for too long to ever deny Lancelot's claim to be your champion. Or that, healthy, he is far more worthy than I to face this foe. Even so, I will not allow it now. Not this time, my love. You have asked him, sorely wounded, to take this upon himself, not for your sake, or his, but for mine. You have not asked him in love."

Guinevere's head snapped back. Her green eyes went wide and then they blazed with a naked, dazzling anger. She shook her head, so fiercely that the tears flew off her face, and in the voice of a Queen, a voice that froze and bound them into the power of the grief it carried, she cried aloud, *"Have I not, my lord? And shall you tell me so? Would you tear open my flesh that all men here might probe into my heart as Maugrim did?"*

Arthur flinched, as if stunned by a blow, but she was not done. With icy, relentless fury she said, "What man, even you, my lord, *dares* in my presence to say whether I have spoken in love or no?"

"Guinevere—" Lancelot began, but quailed in his turn as her burning glance swung to him.

"Not a word!" she snapped. "Not from you or anyone else!"

Arthur had slipped down from his horse. He knelt before her, pain raw as a wound in his face. He opened his mouth to speak.

And in that moment, precisely then, Paul became aware of an absence and he remembered the slight, breathless sound at his elbow a moment before, a sound he'd ignored.

But there was no one beside him anymore.

He turned, his heart lurching, and looked north, along the downward-sloping path to where Uathach waited on the stony plain.

He saw. And then he heard, they all heard, as a ringing cry rose up, echoing in the twilight air between the armies of Light and Dark:

*"For the Black Boar!"* he heard. They all heard. *"For the honour of the Black Boar!"*

And thus did Diarmuid dan Ailell take Uathach's challenge upon himself, riding forth alone on the horse his brother had brought for him, his sword uplifted high, his fair hair lit by the sunset, as he raced towards the dance his bright soul would not deny.

He was a master, Dave knew. Having fought beside Diarmuid at the winter skirmish by the Latham and then at the wolf hunt in Leinanwood, he had reason to know what Aileron's brother could do. And Dave's heart—halfway to his own battle fury— leaped to see Diarmuid's first swiftly angled engagement of the urgach.

And then, an instant later, battle frenzy gave way to chilled grief. Because he remembered Uathach, too, from the bloody banks of the Adein in the first battle of Kevin's spring. And in his mind, replayed more vividly than such a memory should ever have been, he saw Maugrim's whiteclad urgach swing his colossal sword in one scything blow from the slaug's saddle that had cleaved through Barth and Navon, both: the babies in the wood.

He remembered Uathach, and now he saw him again, and the memory, however grim, was less than the reality, far less. By the light of the setting sun, in that wasteland between armies, Diarmuid and his quick, clever horse, met, with a thunder of hooves and a grinding shock of blades, a foe that was too much more than mortal for a mortal man to face

The urgach was too large, too uncannily swift despite his massive bulk. And he was shrewder than any such creature could ever have been had it not been altered in some way within the confines of Starkadh. Beyond all this, the slaug was a deadly terror in and of itself. Constantly ripping with its curved horn, seeking the flesh of Diarmuid's horse, running on four legs and lashing out with the other two, it was too dangerous for Diarmuid to do much more than evade, for fear that his own mount would be gored or trampled, leaving him helpless on the barren ground. And because he couldn't work in close, his slim blade could scarcely reach Uathach—though Diarmuid was a perilously easy target for the urgach's huge black sword.

Beside Dave, Levon dan Ivor's face was white with affliction as he watched the drama below. Dave knew how desperately Levon had wanted the death of this creature, and how adamant Torc—who feared nothing else that Dave knew—had been in binding Levon by oath not to fight Uathach alone.

Not to do what Diarmuid was doing now.

And doing, despite the horror of what he faced, with a seemingly effortless grace that somehow had, woven within its movements, the unpredictable, scintillant wit of the man. So sudden were his stops and starts, his reversals of direction—the horse seeming an extension of his mind—that twice, within moments of each other, he managed to veer around the slaug's horn to launch brilliant slashing blows at Uathach.

Who parried with a brutal indifference that almost broke the heart to see. And each time, his pounding counterstroke sent Diarmuid reeling in the saddle with the jarring impact of parrying it. Dave knew about that: he remembered his own first urgach battle, in the dark of Faelinn Grove. He had barely been able to lift his arm for two days after blocking one of those blows. And the beast he'd faced had been to Uathach as sleep was to death.

But Diarmuid was still in the saddle, still probing for an opening with his sword, wheeling his gallant mount—so small beside the slaug—in arcs and half-circles, random and disorienting, calculated to the hairsbreadth edge of sword or destroying horn, seeking an angle, a way in, a gap to penetrate in the name of Light.

"Gods, he can ride!" Levon whispered, and Dave knew that there were no words of higher, more holy praise that a Dalrei could ever speak. And it was true, it was dazzlingly true; they were watching an exercise in glory as the sun sank into the west.

Then suddenly it became even more than that—for again Diarmuid scythed in on Uathach's right side, and again he stabbed upwards for the heart of the beast. Once more the urgach blocked the reaching thrust, and once more, exactly as before, his counterstroke descended like an iron tree falling.

Diarmuid absorbed it on his blade. He rocked in the saddle. But this time, letting the momentum work for him, he reared his horse upwards and to the right, and sent his shining sword slashing downwards to sever the slaug's nearest leg.

Dave began a startled, wordless cry of joy and then savagely bit it back. Uathach's mocking laughter seemed to fill the world, and behind him the army of the Dark let loose a raucous, deafening roar of predatory anticipation.

Too great a price, Dave thought, hurting for the man below. For though the slaug had lost a leg, and so was much less of a danger than before, Diarmuid's left shoulder had been torn through by a ripping thrust of the animal's horn. In the waning light they could see his blood flowering darkly from a deep, raking wound.

It was too much, Dave thought, truly too inhuman a foe for a man to face. Torc had been right. Dave turned his head away from the terrible ritual being acted out before them, and as he did, he saw Paul Schafer, farther along the ridge, looking back at him.

Paul registered Dave's glance, and the pain in the big man's expression, but his own mind was a long way off, along the twisting paths of memory.

A memory of Diarmuid on the first night they'd arrived. *A peach!* he'd said of Jennifer, as he bent to kiss her hand And then said it, and did it again, a few moments later, swinging lazily through a high window to confound Gorlaes sardonically.

Another image, another extravagant phrase—*I've plucked the fairest rose in Shalhassan's garden*—as he rejoined Kevin and Paul and the men of South Keep from within scented Larai Rigal. Extravagance always, the flamboyant gesture masking so many deeper truths. But the truths were there to be seen, if one only knew where to look. Hadn't he shielded Sharra afterwards, the day she'd tried to kill him in Paras Derval? And then on the eve of the voyage to Cader Sedat he had asked her to be his wife.

Using Tegid as his Intercedent.

Always the gesture, the deflecting glitter of style, hiding what he was, at root, behind the last locked doorway of his soul.

Paul remembered, hurting on that windy rise of land, unwilling to look down again, how Diarmuid had relinquished his claim to the throne. How in the moment when fate seemed to have come full circle, when Jaelle had been about to speak for the Goddess and proclaim a High King in Dana's name, Diarmuid had made the decision himself, flippantly speaking the words he knew to be right. Though Aileron had sworn he was prepared to kill him just moments before.

There was a grinding of metal on metal. Paul turned back. Diarmuid had somehow—the gods only knew what it must be costing him—managed to circle in again close to the monstrous urgach, and again he'd attacked, carrying the battle to his foe. To be beaten back once more with a bone-jarring force that Paul could feel, even up here.

He watched. It seemed necessary to watch: to bear witness and remember.

And one more set of memories came to him then, as Diarmuid's brave horse pirouetted yet again, just out of reach of slaug horn and urgach sword. Images from Cader Sedat, that place of death at sea. An island in all worlds and none, where the soul lay open, without hiding place. Where Diar's face, as he looked upon Metran, had shown the full unshielded passion of his hatred of the Dark. Where he had stood in the Chamber of the Dead beneath the sea, and where—yes, there *was* a truth in this, a kernel, a clue—he had said to the Warrior, as Arthur prepared to summon Lancelot and so bring the old, three-sided tragedy into the world again: *You do not have to do this. It is neither written nor compelled.*

And Paul glimpsed then, with a shiver of primal recognition, the thread that led from that moment to this. Because it was for Arthur and Lancelot, and for Guinevere, that Diarmuid, in all the wild anarchy of his nature, had claimed this dance as his own.

It was against the weaving of their long doom that he had defiantly rebelled, and had channelled that rebellion into an act of his own against the Dark. Taking Uathach unto himself, that Arthur and Lancelot, both, might go forward past this day.

The sun was almost gone. Only the last long rays slanted low and red across Andarien. In the twilight the battle seemed to have moved farther away, into a realm of shadows like the past. It was very quiet. Even the loosely spilling, triumphant cries of the svart alfar had ended. There were flecks of blood staining Uathach's snowy robe. Paul couldn't tell if they were Diarmuid's or the urgach's own. It didn't seem to matter much: Diar's horse, fiercely gallant but hopelessly overmatched, was visibly tiring even as they watched.

Diarmuid backed it off a few paces, to try to buy it a moment's rest, but this was not to be allowed. Not in this battle, with this foe. Uathach, not laughing now, grim death in his black sword, came on, and Diarmuid was forced to cruelly spur his mount to motion again. Amid the silence along the ridge, a single voice spoke.

"There is one chance, only, left for him," said Lancelot du Lac.

Only one man understood and made reply.

"If you call it a chance," Aileron said, in a tone not one of them had ever heard him use before.

To the west, out beyond Linden Bay, the sun went down. Paul turned instinctively and saw its last dying light touch the face of the Princess of Cathal. He saw that Kim and Jaelle had moved to either side of her. After a moment he turned back to the figures on the plain. In time to see it end.

It was, on the whole, just a little bit ridiculous. This ugly, hairy monster, oversized even for an urgach, was as quick as he was himself. And it was swinging a sword that Diarmuid doubted he could even have lifted, let alone swung in those pounding, ceaseless blows. It was cunning, too, unnaturally, viciously intelligent. By Lisen's river blood, urgach were supposed to be stupid! Where, the Prince thought, absorbing another blow like an avalanche on his sword, where was the sense of *proportion* in this thing?

He felt like asking the question aloud, but survival had become a matter of meticulous concentration these last few moments, and he had no breath to spare for even halfway witty remarks. A shame. He wondered, hilariously, what Uathach would say to a suggestion that this matter be settled with the gambling dice Diarmuid just happened to have in his—

*Gods!* Even with a leg gone, the slaug, twice the size of his own tiring horse, was death itself. With a movement of his sword as desperately swift as any he'd ever made, Diarmuid managed to block a thrust of the animal's ripping horn that would have disemboweled his own mount. Unfortunately that meant—

He resurfaced in the saddle, having passed clean under his horse on one side and up again on the other, with Uathach's annihilating slash a whistling sound in the darkening air where his own head had been an instant before. He wondered if Ivor of the Dalrei remembered teaching him how to do that so many years ago, when Diarmuid was a boy summering with his brother on the Plain. So many years, but for some reason it felt like yesterday, just now. Funny, how almost everything felt like yesterday.

The sweep of Uathach's last stroke had swung the urgach grunting, sideways in his saddle and carried the slaug a few paces away with the shift of weight. Fresh, Diarmuid might have tried to use that to renew some kind of attack, but his horse was sucking air with desperate, heaving motions of its lathered flanks, and his own left arm was gradually growing cold, a weakness spreading from the deep tear of the wound, reaching across his chest.

He used the brief respite the only way he could, to buy time for the horse. A handful of seconds, no more than that, and it wasn't enough. He thought of his mother then. And of the day his father had died. So much seemed to have happened yesterday. He thought of Aileron, and of all the things left unsaid in all the yesterdays.

And then, as Uathach turned the slaug again, Diarmuid dan Ailell whispered to his horse one last time and felt it steady bravely to the murmur of his voice. Within himself he let a calm take shape, and from within that calm he summoned up Sharra's face, through whose dark eyes—doorways to a falcon's soul—love had entered into him so unexpectedly, and had stayed.

To carry him to this moment, her image in his mind, and the certain, sustaining knowledge of her love. To carry him forward across the darkened ground of that plain in Andarien, towards the last thing he could do.

Straight at the slaug he rode, his horse gallantly reaching for a last flourish of speed, and at the final second he veered it sharply left and launched the sternest blow he could at Uathach's side.

It was blocked. He knew it would be; they all had been. And now there came the huge, descending counterstroke of the urgach's sword. The one, like all the others, that would drive him, shuddering, back, when he parried it. That would numb his arm, bringing the inevitable end that much nearer.

He didn't parry it.

He wheeled his horse, hard, to gain just a little space, so Uathach's blade would not sever his body entirely, and he took that terrible blow on his left side, just under the heart, knowing it was the end.

And then, as white pain exploded within him in the darkness, towering, indescribable, as his life's blood fountained to fall among the stones, Diarmuid dan Ailell, with the last strength of his soul, almost the very last of his self-control, with Sharra's face before him, not Uathach's, did the final deed of his days. He rose up above his agony, and with his left hand he clutched the hairy arm that held that black sword, and with his right, pulling himself forward, as towards a long-sought dream of overwhelming Light, he thrust his own bright blade into the urgach's face and out the back of its head, and he killed it in Andarien, just after the sun had set.

Sharra watched as though from very far away. At the descent of dark, through a blurring mist of tears, she saw him take his wound, saw him kill Uathach, saw the beautiful, rearing horse gored hideously from below by the ripping horn of the slaug. The urgach fell. She could hear screams of terror from the svart alfar, the scream of the dying horse. Saw Diar fall free as the horse rolled on the ground and thrashed in its death agony. Saw the enraged, blood-maddened slaug turn to rip the fallen man to shreds of flesh—

Saw a spear, its head gleaming blue-white, flash through the dark and plunge into the throat of the slaug, killing it instantly. Saw nothing after that but the man lying on the ground.

"Come, child," said Arthur Pendragon, who had thrown the King Spear in a cast almost beyond belief, in this light and from so far. He laid a gentle hand upon her arm. "Let me lead you down to him."

She let him lead her down, through the rainfall of her tears. She was aware, distantly, of utter confusion among the ranks of the Dark. Terror at the loss of their leader. She was conscious of people on horseback beside her, but not of who they were, save for Arthur, who was holding her arm.

She went down the slope and rode across the dark, stony ground and came to where he lay. There were torches, somehow, all around them. She drew a choking, desperate breath and wiped away her tears with the loose sleeve of the robe she wore.

Then she dismounted and walked over. His head was cradled in the lap of Coll of Taerlindel, blood pouring and pouring from the wound Uathach's sword had made, soaking into the barren soil.

He was not yet dead. He breathed with quick, shallow motions of his chest, but every breath sent forth another torrent of his blood. His eyes were closed. There were other people there, but it seemed to her that she and he were all alone in a wide night world without stars.

She knelt on the ground beside him, and something, the intuitive awareness of her presence, caused him to open his eyes. By torchlight she met his blue gaze for the last time with her own. He tried to smile, to speak. But at the last there was too much pain she saw, he would not even be allowed this much, and so she lowered her mouth to his, and kissed him, and said, "Good night, my love. I will not say goodbye. Wait for me by the Weaver's side. If the gods love us—"

She tried to go on, tried very hard, but the tears were blinding her and stopping her throat. His face was bloodless, bone white in the light of the torches. His eyes had closed again. She could feel his blood pouring from the wound, saturating the ground where she knelt. She knew he was leaving her. No power of magic, no voice of a god could bring him back from where this silent, terrible pain was taking him. It was too deep. It was final.

Then he opened his eyes, with a very great effort, for the last time, and she realized that words didn't matter. That she knew everything he would ever want to say. She read the message in his eyes and knew what he was asking her. It was as if, here at the very last, they had moved beyond all need for anything but looking.

She lifted her head and saw Aileron kneeling at Diarmuid's other side, his face laid open as if by a lash, distorted with grief. She understood something then, and could even find a place within herself to pity him. She swallowed and fought past the thickness in her throat to find words again: Diarmuid's words, for he could not speak, and so she would have to be his voice for this last time.

She whispered, "He wants you to set him free. To send him home. That it will not have been done by the urgach's sword."

"Oh, Diar, no!" Aileron said.

But Diarmuid turned his head, slowly, fighting the pain of movement, his breathing so shallow it was hardly there, and he looked at his older brother and he nodded, once.

Aileron was still for a very long time, as the two sons of Ailell looked at each other by the flickering torchlight. Then the High King stretched forth a hand and laid it gently against his brother's cheek. He held it there a moment, and then he looked at Sharra with a last question, asking dispensation with his own dark eyes.

And Sharra reached for all the courage that she had and granted it to him, saying, for herself and for Diar, "Let it be done with love."

Then Aileron dan Ailell, the High King, drew forth his dagger from a sheath that hung down at his side, and he laid its point over his brother's heart. And Diarmuid moved one hand, and found Sharra's, and Aileron waited as he brought it to his lips one last time. He was holding it there, and holding her eyes with his own, when his brother's knife, agent of love, set him free from his iron pain, and he died.

Aileron withdrew his blade and set it down. Then he buried his face in his hands. Sharra could hardly see, she was so blinded by her tears. It seemed to be raining everywhere, in that clear cool starry evening over Andarien.

"Come, my dear," said Jaelle, the High Priestess, helping her rise. She was weeping. The Seer came up on the other side, and Sharra went where they took her.

Diarmuid dan Ailell was borne back in his brother's arms from the place where he died, for the High King would suffer no man else to do so. Across the stony plain Aileron carried him, with torches buring on either side and all around. Up the long slope he went, the body cradled against his chest, and men turned away their heads so as not to have to look upon the face of the living brother as he bore away the dead.

They made a pyre that night in Andarien. They washed Diarmuid's body and clothed it in white and gold, hiding his terrible wounds, and they combed his golden hair. Then the High King took him up again for the last time and bore him to where they had gathered the wood of the pyre, and he laid his brother down upon it, and kissed him upon the lips, and withdrew.

Then Teyrnon, the last mage of Brennin, stepped forward with Barak, his source, and with Loren Silvercloak and Matt Sören, and all of them were weeping in the darkness there. But Teyrnon thrust forth his hand and spoke a word of power, and a single shaft of light flew forward from his fingers, blazing white and gold like the robes of the dead Prince, and the pyre roared suddenly to flame, consuming the body laid upon it.

So passed Diarmuid dan Ailell. So did his untamed brightness come in the end to flame, and then ash, and, at the very last, in the clear voices of the lios alfar, into song under the stars.

# CHAPTER 15

A long way north of that burning, Darien stood in the shadows below the Valgrind Bridge. It was very cold, here at the edge of the Ice with the sun gone and no other living thing to be seen or heard. He looked across the dark waters of the river spanned by that bridge, and on the other side he saw the massive ziggurat of Starkadh rising, with chill green lights shining wanly amid the blackness of his father's mighty home.

He was utterly alone; there were no guards posted anywhere. What need had Rakoth Maugrim for guards? Who would ever venture to this unholy place? An army perhaps, but they would be visible far off amid the treeless waste. Only an army might come, but Darien had seen, as he walked here, countless numbers of svart alfar and the huge urgach moving south. There were so many, they seemed to shrink the vastness of the barren lands. He didn't think any army would be coming: not past those hordes he'd seen issuing forth. He had been forced to hide several times, seeking shelter in the shadows of rocks, swinging gradually westward as he went, so the legions of the Dark would pass east of him.

He was not seen. No one was looking for him, not for a solitary child stumbling north through a morning and an afternoon, and then a cold evening and a colder night. With pale Rangat towering in the east and black Starkadh growing more oppressively dominant with every step he took, he had come at last to the bridge and crouched down under it, looking across the Ungarch at where he was to go.

Not tonight, he decided, shivering, his arms wrapped tightly about himself. Better the chill of another night outside than trying to pass into that place in the dark. He looked at the dagger he carried and drew it from its sheath The sound like a harpstring reverberated thinly in the cold night air. There was a vein of blue in the sheath, and a brighter one along the shaft of the blade. They gleamed a little under the frosty stars. He remembered what the little one, Flidais, had said to him. He rehearsed the words in his mind as he sheathed Lökdal again. Their magic was part of the gift he was bringing. He would have to have them right.

The metal of the bridge was cold when he leaned back beneath it, and so was the stony ground. Everything was cold this far north. He rubbed his hands on the sweater he wore. It wasn't even his sweater. His mother had made it for Finn—who was gone.

And not really his mother, either; Vae had made it. His mother was tall and very beautiful, and she had sent him away and then had sent the man, Lancelot, to battle the demon in the Wood for Darien's sake. He didn't understand. He wanted to, but there was no one to help him, and he was cold and tired and far away.

He had just closed his eyes, there at the edge of the darkly flowing river, half under the iron bridge, when he heard a tremendous reverberating sound as some mighty door clanged open far above. He scrambled to his feet and peered out from under the bridge. As he did, he was hit by a titanic buffet of wind that knocked him sprawling, almost into the river.

He rolled quickly over, his eyes straining up against the force of the sudden gale, and far overhead he saw a huge, featureless shadow sweeping swiftly away to the south, blotting out the stars where it passed.

Then he heard the sound of his father's laughter.

⋆⟊⟎⋆

Anger, for Dave Martyniuk, had always been a hot, exploding thing within himself. It was his father's rage, unsubtle, enormous, a lava flow in the mind and heart. Even here in Fionavar in the battles he'd fought, what had come upon him each time had been of the same order: a fiery, obliterating hatred that consumed all else within it.

This morning he was not like that. This morning he was ice. The coldness of his fury as the sun rose and they readied themselves for war was something alien to him. It was even a little frightening. He was calmer, more clearheaded than he could ever remember being in all his life, and yet filled with a more dangerous, more utterly implacable anger than he had ever known.

Overhead the black swans were circling, crying raucously in the early morning light. Below, the army of the Dark was gathered, so vast it seemed to blot out the whole of the plain. And at their head—Dave could see him now—was a new leader: Galadan, of course, the Wolflord. Not a blessing, Ivor had murmured, before riding off to receive Aileron's orders. More dangerous than even Uathach would have been, more subtle in his malice.

It didn't matter, Dave thought, sitting tall and stern in his saddle, oblivious to the diffident glances he was drawing from all who passed near to him. It didn't matter at all who led Rakoth's army, who they sent against him: wolves, or svart alfar, or urgach, or mutant swans. Or anything else, or however many. Let them come. He would drive them back or leave them dead before him.

He was not fire. The fire had been last night, when Diarmuid burned. He was ice now, absolutely in control of himself and ready for war. He would do what had to be done, whatever had to be done. For Diarmuid, and for Kevin Laine. For the babies he'd guarded in the wood. For Sharra's grief. For Guinevere and Arthur and Lancelot. For Ivor and Levon and Torc. For the dimensions of sorrow within himself. For all those who would die before this day was done.

For Josef Martyniuk.

***

"There is something I would ask," said Matt Sören. "Though I will understand if you choose to deny me."

Kim saw Aileron turn to him. There was winter in the High King's eyes. He waited and did not speak.

Matt said, "The Dwarves have a price to pay and atonement to make, insofar as we ever can. Will you give us leave to take the centre today, my lord, that we may bear the main shock of whatever may befall?"

There was a murmur from the captains gathered there. The pale sun had just risen in the east beyond Gwynir.

Aileron was silent a moment longer; then he said, very clearly, so it carried, "In every single record I have ever found of the Bael Rangat—and I have read all such writings there are, I think—one common thread prevails. Even in the company of Conary and Colan, of Ra-Termaine and fierce Angirad from what was not yet Cathal, of Revor of the Plain and those who rode with him . . . even in such glittering company, the records of those days all tell that no contingent of the army of Light was so deadly as were Seithr and the Dwarves. There is nothing you might think to ask of me that I could find it within me to deny, Matt, but I intended to request this of you in any case. Let your people follow their King and take pride of place in our ranks. Let them draw honour from his own bright honour and courage from their past."

"Let it be so," said Ivor quietly. "Where would you have the Dalrei, High King?"

"With the lios alfar, as you were by the Adein. Ra-Tenniel, can you and the Aven hold our right flank between the two of you?"

"If we two cannot," said the Lord of the lios alfar, with a thread of laughter in his silvery voice, "then I know not who can. We will ride with the Riders."

He was mounted on one of the glorious raithen, and so, too, behind him, were Brendel and Galen and Lydan, leaders of their marks. There was a fifth raithen, riderless, standing beside the others.

Ra-Tenniel gestured towards it. He turned to Arthur Pendragon, but he did not speak. It was Loren Silvercloak, no longer harnessing a mage's powers but still bearing a mage's knowledge, who broke the waiting silence.

"My lord Arthur," he said, "you have told us you never survive to see the last battle of your wars. Today, it seems, you shall. Although this place was once called Camlann, it carries that name no longer, nor has it for a thousand years, since laid waste by war. Shall we seek to find good in that evil? Hope in the cycle of years?"

And Arthur said, "Against all that I have been forced through pain to know, let us try." He stepped down from his horse and took the King Spear in his hand, and he walked over to the last of the gold and silver raithen of Daniloth. When he mounted up, the spear blazed for a moment with light.

"Come, my lord," Aileron said, "and my lord Lancelot, if you will. I bid you welcome into the numbers of Brennin and Cathal. We will take the left side of this fight. Let us seek to meet the Dalrei and the lios before the end of day, having curved our ranks inwards over the bodies of our foes."

Arthur nodded, and so, too, did Lancelot. They moved over to where Mabon of Rhoden was waiting, with Niavin, Duke of Seresh, and Coll of Taerlindel, stony-faced, now leader of the men of South Keep, Diarmuid's men. Kim grieved for him, but there would be griefs and to spare this day, she knew, and there might be final darkness for them.

It seemed that they had said what had to be said, but Aileron surprised her again.

"One thing more," the High King said, as his captains prepared to move off. "A thousand years ago there was another company in the army of Light. A people fell and wild, and courageous out of measure. A people destroyed now, and lost to us, save one."

Kim saw him turn, then, and heard him say, "Faebur of Larak, will you ride, in the name of the People of the Lion, at the forefront of our host? Will you join with the Dwarves today, at the side of their King, and will you take this horn I carry and sound the attack for us all?"

Faebur was pale, but not with fear, Kim saw. He moved his horse towards the black charger Aileron rode, and he took the horn. "In the name of the Lion," he said, "I will do so."

He rode forward and stopped at Matt's left hand. On the other side of Matt, Brock of Banir Tal was waiting. Kim's mouth was dry with apprehension. She looked up and saw the swans circling overhead, unchallenged, masters of the sky. She knew, without looking, how utterly lifeless the Baelrath was on her hand. Knew, as a Seer knew, that it would never blaze for her again, not after her refusal by Calor Diman. She felt helpless and a little sick.

Her place would be here on the ridge, with Loren and Jaelle and a number of others from all parts of the army. She still had her training, and they would have to deal with the wounded very soon.

Very soon indeed. Aileron and Arthur galloped quickly off to the left, and she saw Ivor cantering to the right beside Ra-Tenniel and the lios alfar, to join the Dalrei waiting there. Even at a distance she could make out the figure of Dave Martyniuk, taller by far than anyone around him. She saw him unsling an axe from where it hung by his saddle.

Loren came to stand beside her. She slipped her hand into his. Together they watched Matt Sören stride to the front of the host of the Dwarves, who had never fought on horseback and would not do so today. Faebur was with him. The young Eridun had dismounted to leave his own horse on the high ground.

The sun was higher now. From where Kim stood she could see the seething army of the Dark carpeting the whole of the plain below. To the left, Aileron raised his sword, and on the other side the Aven did the same, and Ra-Tenniel. She saw Matt turn to Faebur and speak to him. Then she heard the ringing note of the horn that Faebur sounded, and there was war.

Cechtar was the first man Dave saw die. The big Dalrei thundered, screaming at the top of his voice, towards the nearest of the urgach as the armies met with a crash that shook the earth. Cechtar's momentum and his whistling sword blow knocked the urgach sprawling sideways in his saddle. But before the Dalrei could follow up, his mount was viciously speared by the horn of the slaug the urgach rode, and as the grey horse stumbled, dying, Cechtar's side was exposed and a svart alfar leaped up, a long thin knife in its hand, and plunged it into his heart.

Dave didn't even have time to cry out, or grieve, or even think about it. There was death all around him, bloody and blurred. There were svart alfar shrieking amid the screams of dying men. A svart leaped for his horse. Dave dragged a foot free of his stirrups, kicked at it viciously, and felt the ugly creature's skull crack under the impact.

Fighting for room to swing his axe, he urged his horse forward. He went for the nearest urgach then, and every time thereafter, with a hatred and a bitterness (cold, though, icily, calculatingly cold) that drove him on and on, the head of his axe soon red and wet with blood, as it rose and fell, and rose and fell again.

He had no idea what was happening even twenty feet away. The lios alfar were somewhere to the right. He knew that Levon was beside him, always, through everything that happened, and Torc and Sorcha were on his other side. He saw Ivor's stocky figure just ahead, and in all that he did he fought to stay within reach of the Aven. Again, as in the fight by the banks of the Adein, he completely lost track of time. His was a narrowed maelstrom of a world: a universe of sweat and shattered bone, of lathered horses and slaug horns, and ground slippery with blood and with the trampled flesh of the dying and the dead. He fought with a silent savagery amid the screams of battle, and where his axe fell, where the hooves of his horse lashed out, they killed.

Time warped and twisted, spun away from him. He thrust the axe forward like a sword, smashing in the hairy face of the urgach in front of him. Almost in the same motion he drove the axehead down, to bite through the flesh of the slaug it rode. He rode on. Beside him, Levon's blade was a whirling thing of ceaseless, glinting motion, a counterpoint of lethal grace to Dave's own driven strength.

Time was gone from him, and the morning. He knew that they had been advancing for a time, and then later, now, with the sun somehow high in the sky, that they were no longer pressing forward, only holding their ground. Desperately, they strained to leave each other enough room to fight, yet not so much space that the quick svart alfar might slip between, to kill from below.

And gradually Dave began to acknowledge, however hard he tried to block the thought, something that a part of him had known the evening before, when first they'd topped the ridge and looked down. It was the numbers, the sheer brutal weight, that would beat them.

It isn't even worth thinking about, he told himself, hammering the axe right through the blocking sword of an urgach on his right, watching Torc's sword slash into the creature's brain at the same moment. He and the dark Dalrei—his brother—looked at each other for one grim instant.

There was time for no more than that. Time and strength had rapidly become the most precious things in all the worlds and were becoming more rare with each passing moment. The white sun swung up the sky and paused overhead, balanced for an instant, as were all the worlds that day, and then began sliding down through a bloody afternoon.

Dave's horse trampled a svart alfar, even as his axe severed the raking horn of a dark green slaug. He felt a pain in his thigh; ignored it; killed, with a mighty blow of his fist, the dagger-wielding svart that had slashed him. He heard Levon grunt with exertion, and he wheeled just in time to crash his mount into the side of the slaug menacing the Aven's son. Levon dispatched the unbalanced urgach with a sweep of his blade. There were two more behind it, and half a dozen of the svart alfar. Dave didn't even have room to stay with Levon. In front of him three more of the slaug pressed forward, over the body of the one whose horn he'd smashed. Dave fell back a couple of paces, sick at heart. Beside him, Levon was doing the same.

Then, disbelieving, Dave heard the ceaseless shrieking of the svart alfar rise to a higher pitch. The largest of the urgach advancing on him roared a sudden desperate command, and a moment later, Dave saw a space suddenly materialize on his left, beyond Levon, as the enemy fell back. And then, even as it appeared, the space was filled by Matt Sören, King of the Dwarves, fighting in grim, ferocious silence, his clothing shredded, saturated with blood, as he waded forward over the bodies of the dead to lead the Dwarves into the gap.

"Well met, King of Dwarves!" Ivor's voice rose high over the tumult of battle. With a glad cry Dave thrust forward, Levon just ahead of him, and they merged with Matt's forces and began to advance again.

Ra-Tenniel, dazzlingly swift on the raithen, was suddenly beside them as well. "How are they doing on the left?" he sang out.

"Aileron sent us this way. He says they will hold!" Matt shouted back. "I don't know for how long, though. Galadan's wolves are on that side. We have to break through together and then circle back west!"

"Come on, then!" Levon screamed, moving past them all, leading them northward as if he would storm the towers of Starkadh itself. Ivor was right beside his son.

Dave kicked his own mount ahead, hastening to follow. He had to stay close: to guard them if he could, to share in whatever happened to them.

He felt a wind suddenly. Saw a vast, onrushing shadow sweeping across Andarien.

"Dear gods!" Sorcha cried, by Dave's right hand. There came a tremendous roaring sound.

Dave looked up.

<hr />

At dawn Leila woke. She felt feverish and afraid after a terrible, restless night. When Shiel came to get her, she told the other priestess to lead the morning chants in her stead. Shiel took one look at Leila and went away without a word.

Pacing the narrow confines of her room, Leila struggled to hold the images that were flashing into her mind. They were too quick, though, too violently chaotic. She didn't know where they were coming from, how she was receiving them. She didn't know! She didn't want them! Her hands were damp and she felt perspiration on her face, though the underground rooms were as cool as they always were.

The chanting ended under the dome. In the sudden silence she became conscious of her own footsteps, the rapid beating of her heart, the pulsing in her mind—all seemed louder, more insistent. She was afraid now, more so than she had ever been.

There was a tapping at her door.

"Yes!" she snapped. She hadn't meant to say it that way. Timorously, Shiel opened the door and peeped in. She did not enter the room. Her eyes grew wide at the sight of Leila's face.

"What is it?" Leila said, fighting to control her voice.

"There are men here, Priestess. Waiting by the entranceway. Will you see them?"

It was a thing to do, an action to take. She brushed past Shiel, walking swiftly down the curving corridors towards the entrance to the Temple. There were three priestesses and a dun-robed acolyte waiting there. The doors were open, but the men waited patiently outside.

She came to the threshold and saw who was there. She knew all three of them: Gorlaes the Chancellor, Shalhassan of Cathal, and the fat man, Tegid, who had been so much in attendance while Sharra of Cathal had been here.

"What do you want?" she said. Again her voice was harsher than she meant it to be. She was having a hard time controlling it. It seemed to be a bright day outside. The sun hurt her eyes.

"Child," said Gorlaes, not hiding his surprise, "are you the one who is acting as High Priestess?"

"I am," she answered shortly, and waited.

Shalhassan's expression was different, more quietly appraising. He said, "I have been told about you. You are Leila dal Karsh?"

She nodded. Shifted a little sideways, to be in the shade.

Shalhassan said, "Priestess, we have come because we are afraid. We know nothing, can discover nothing. I thought it was possible that the priestesses might somehow have tidings of what is happening."

She closed her eyes. Somewhere, at some level, in the normal weaving of these things, this should be taken as a triumph—the leaders of Brennin and Cathal coming to the sanctuary thus humbly. She was aware of this but couldn't summon up the appropriate response. It seemed lifetimes removed from the brittle fevers of this day.

She opened her eyes again and said, "I, too, am afraid. I know very little. Only that . . . something is happening this morning. And there is blood. I think they are fighting."

The big man, Tegid, made a rumbling sound deep in his chest. She saw anguish and doubt in his face. For an instant longer she hesitated; then, drawing a deep breath, she said, "If you like, if you offer blood, you may enter within. I will share whatever I come to know."

All three of them bowed to her.

"We will be grateful," Shalhassan murmured, and she could hear that he meant it.

"Shiel," she said, snapping again, unable not to, "use the knife and the bowl, then bring them to the dome."

"I will," Shiel said, with a hardiness rare for her.

Leila didn't wait. Another inner vision sliced into her mind like a blade and was gone. She strode from the doorway, stumbled, almost fell. She saw the frightened eyes of the acolyte, as the young one backed away from her. *Young?* a part of her mind registered. The girl was older than she was.

Leila went on, towards the dome. Her face was bloodless now. She could feel it. And could feel a dark, cold fear rising within her, higher and higher all the time. It seemed to her that all around her as she went, the sanctuary walls were streaming with blood.

‹•◦═◉═◦•›

Paul tried. He wasn't a swordsman, nor did he have Dave's tremendous size or strength. But he had his own anger, and courage to spare, sourced in a driven nature, infinitely demanding of himself. He had grace and very fast reflexes. But swordsman-ship at this level was not a thing one mastered overnight, not matched against urgach and Galadan's wolves.

Through the whole of the morning, though, he stayed in the heart of the battle on the western flank, fighting with a passionate, coursing renunciation.

Ahead of him he saw Lancelot and Aileron dismount, side by side, the better to wade, swords blurred with intricate flashing speed, among the giant wolves. He knew that he was seeing something never to be forgotten, excellence on a scale almost unimaginable. Lancelot was fighting with a glove on his burned hand, that the hilt of his sword might not dig into the wound. The glove had been white when the morning began, but already the palm of it was soaked through with blood.

On either side of Paul, Carde and Erron were fighting savagely, slashing through the svart alfar, battling the wolves, holding back, as best they could, the terrible mounted urgach. And, Paul was painfully aware, doing their best to guard him all the time, even as they fought for their own lives.

He did the best he could. Bending on either side of his horse's neck to thrust and cut with the sword he carried. Seeing a svart fall under one blow, a wolf draw back, snarling, from another. But even as that happened, Erron had been forced to whirl, with his lithe speed, to skewer another svart that had been leaping for Paul's exposed side.

No time for gratitude to be expressed, no time for any words at all. And only chance scattered seconds amid chaos in which to reach within himself and vainly seek some clue, some pulsebeat from the God, that might show him how to be more than a liability here, more than a source of danger to the friends guarding his life.

"Gods!" Carde gasped, in one brief respite some time later. "Why are the wolves so much worse than they were in Leinanwood?"

Paul knew the answer to that. He could see the answer.

Ahead of them and to the right, lethally fluid in all his movements, a palpable aura of menace hovering about him, was Galadan. He was battling in his animal shape, providing the guiding spirit, malevolent and subtle, for the onslaught of his wolves. For the whole of Maugrim's army.

Galadan. Whom Paul had so arrogantly claimed for his own. It seemed a mockery here, an act of fatuous hubris on the part of someone who couldn't even defend himself from the svart alfar.

In that moment, as he looked across the surging crush of the battle, a space opened up in front of Galadan, and then, with a hurtful twist of his heart, Paul saw grey Cavall move to confront, for a second time, the wolf with the splash of silver between its eyes. Memory slashed through Paul like a different kind of wound: a memory of the battle in the Godwood that had served to foretell the war they were fighting now.

He saw the scarred grey dog and the proud Lord of the andain face each other for the second time. Both were still for a frozen moment, coiling themselves in readiness.

But there was to be no reprise of that primal clash in the glade of the Summer Tree. A phalanx of mounted urgach thundered into the space between wolf and dog, to be met with a ringing crash of blades by Coll of Taerlindel and redheaded Averren, at the head of a score of the men of South Keep: Diarmuid's band. Fighting with a bleak savagery that day, each of them driving back heart's grief with the fury of war. Glad of the chance to kill

On either side of Paul, Carde and Erron held their ground, covering his body as well as their own. The sight of the Prince's men struggling with the urgach just ahead decided him.

"Go join the others!" he shouted to the two of them. "I'm no help here! I'm going back up on the ridge—I can do more there!"

There was an instant to exchange a glance with each of them, an instant to know it might be the last. He touched Carde's shoulder briefly, felt Erron's hand grip his arm; then he wheeled his horse sharply and cut away, racing back to the high ground, bitterly cursing his uselessness.

To his left, as he rode, he saw another pair of figures break free of the press, galloping back towards the ridge as well. Angling his mount over, he intercepted Teyrnon and Barak.

"Where are you going?" he cried.

"Up above," Teyrnon shouted, sweat streaming down his face, his voice raw. "The fighting's too congested. If I try to throw a power bolt I'll hit as many of our own men as theirs. And Barak is hopelessly vulnerable when he has to source my magic."

Barak was weeping with frustration, Paul saw. They reached the slope and charged upwards. At the top, a line of lios alfar stood, scanning the stretch of the battle. Mounted auberei waited beside them, ready to race down with word for the High King and his captains.

"What's happening?" Paul gasped to the nearest of the lios, as he dismounted and spun to look.

But it was Loren Silvercloak, striding forward, who answered him. "Too finely balanced," he said, his lined features grim. "We're being held to a standstill, and time is on their side. Aileron has ordered the Dwarves to drive east, towards the Dalrei and the lios alfar. He's going to try to hold the western flank and half of the centre alone."

"Can he?" Teyrnon asked.

Loren shook his head. "For a time. Not forever. And see, the swans are telling Galadan everything we do."

Down below, Paul could see that the Wolflord had withdrawn to a cleared space towards the rear of the army of the Dark. He was in his mortal shape again, and every moment another of the hideous black swans would descend from the uncontested reaches of the air to give him tidings and carry away instructions.

Beside Paul, Barak began to curse, a stream of heartfelt, anguished invective. Below, to their left, a flash of light caught Paul's eye. It was Arthur, the King Spear gleaming in his hand, guiding his magnificent raithen all along the line of battle on the western flank, driving back the legions of Maugrim with the incandescent flame of his presence, shaping a respite for the beleaguered men of Brennin wherever he went. The Warrior in the last battle at Camlann. The battle he had not been meant to see. And would not have seen, had not Diarmuid intervened.

Behind Paul the embers of the pyre still glowed, and ashes drifted in the morning sun. Paul looked up: no longer morning, he realized. Beyond the circling swans the sun had reached its zenith and was starting down.

He jogged back towards the south. In a cleared space a handful of people, Kim and Jaelle among them, were doing the best they could for the wounded that the auberei were bringing up the ridge in frightening numbers.

Kim's face was streaked with blood and sweat. He knelt beside her. "I'm useless down there," he said quickly. "What can I do?"

"You too?" she answered, her grey eyes shadowed with pain. "Pass me those bandages. Behind you. Yes." She took the cloths and began wrapping the leg wound of one of the Dwarves.

"What do you mean?" Paul asked.

Kim cut the bandage with a blade and fastened it as tightly as she could. She stood up and moved on, without answering. Paul followed. A young Dalrei, no more than sixteen, lay in breathless agony, an axe wound in his side. Kim looked down on him with despair.

"Teyrnon!" Paul shouted.

The mage and his source hurried toward them. Teyrnon took one look at the wounded boy, glanced briefly at Barak, and then knelt beside the Dalrei. Barak closed his eyes and Teyrnon placed his hand over the jagged wound. He spoke under his breath, half a dozen words, and as he did the wound slowly closed itself

When he was done, though, Barak almost fell, fatigue etched into his features. Teyrnon stood up quickly and steadied his source.

"I can't do much more of this," the mage said grimly, looking closely at Barak.

"Yes, you can!" Barak snapped, glaring. "Who else, Seer? Who else needs us?"

"Go to Jaelle," Kim said tonelessly. "She'll show you the ones who are worst off. Do what you can, but try not to exhaust yourself. You two are all we have in the way of magic."

Teyrnon nodded tersely and strode off to where Paul could see the High Priestess, the sleeves of her white gown pushed back, kneeling beside the figure of a crumpled lios alfar.

Paul turned back to Kim. "Your own magic?" he said, pointing to the dulled Warstone. "What's happened?"

For a moment she hesitated; then she quickly told him the story of what had happened by Calor Diman. "I rejected it," she concluded flatly. "And now the swans have the sky to themselves, and the Baelrath is totally dead. I feel sick, Paul."

So did he. But he masked it and pulled her to him in a hard embrace. He felt her trembling against his body.

Paul said, "No one here or anywhere else has done as much as you. And we don't know if what you did was wrong—would you have gotten to the Dwarves in time if you'd used the ring to bind the creature in the Lake? It isn't over, Kim, it's a long way from over."

From not far off they heard a grunt of pain. Four of the auberei set down a stretcher they'd been carrying. On it, bleeding from half a dozen new wounds, lay Mabon of Rhoden. Loren Silvercloak and a white-faced Sharra of Cathal hurried to the side of the fallen Duke.

Paul didn't know where to look. All around them lay the dying and the dead. Below, on the plain of battle, the forces of the Dark seemed scarcely to have diminished. Within himself the pulsebeat of Mörnir seemed faint as ever, agonizingly far. A hint of something but not a promise; an awareness, but not power.

He cursed, as Barak had done, helplessly.

Kim looked at him, and after a moment she said, in a strange voice, "I just realized something. You're hating yourself for not being able to use your power in battle. You don't *have* a power of war, though, Paul. We should have realized that before. *I'm* that kind of power, or I was, until last night. You're something else."

He heard a truth, but the bitterness wouldn't leave him "Wonderful," he snapped. "Makes me awfully useful, doesn't it?"

"Maybe," was all she said. But there was a quiet speculation in her eyes that calmed him.

"Where's Jen?" he asked.

She pointed. He looked over and saw that Jennifer, too, was dealing with the wounded as best she could. At the moment she had just risen from someone's side to walk a step or two north, looking down over the battlefield. He could only see her in profile, but as he gazed at her Paul realized that he had never seen a woman look as she did then, as if taking the pain of all the worlds onto herself in the manner of a Queen.

He never, ever, knew what made him look up.

To see a black swan diving. Soundlessly, a terror against the sky, razored claws extended straight for Jennifer. Black Avaia, putrescent death in the air, returning to claim her victim for a second time.

Paul screamed a warning at the top of his voice and launched himself in a frantic sprint over the distance between. The swan was a black projectile hurtling down with annihilating speed. Jennifer turned at his cry and looked up. She saw, and did not flinch. She grappled bravely for the slim blade they'd given her. Paul ran as he'd never run before in all his life. A sob escaped him. Too far! He was too far away. He tried, reached for speed, for more, for *something*. A meaty stench filled the air. A shrieking sound of triumph. Jennifer lifted her blade. Twenty feet away, Paul stumbled, fell, heard himself screaming her name, glimpsed the raking teeth of the swan—

And saw Avaia, ten feet above Jennifer's head, smashed into a crumple of feathers by a red comet in the sky. A living comet that had somehow materialized, blindingly swift, to intersect her path. A horn like a blade exploded into Avaia's breast. A bright sword smote at her head. The black swan screamed, in pain and terror so strident they heard it on the plain below.

She fell, screaming still, at the feet of the woman. And Guinevere walked over then, not faltering, and looked down upon the creature that had delivered her unto Maugrim.

One moment she stood so; then her own slim blade thrust forward into Avaia's throat, and the screaming of the swan came to an end, as Lauriel the White was avenged after a thousand years.

The silence on the ridge was overwhelming. Even the tumult of war below seemed to have receded. Paul watched, they all watched in awe, as Gereint, the old blind shaman, climbed carefully down to the ground, to leave Tabor dan Ivor alone astride his winged creature. The two of them seemed eerily remote even in the midst of so many people, blood on his sword, blood on her deadly, shining horn.

The shaman stood very still, his head lifted a little, as if listening for something. He sniffed the air, which was foul with the corrupt odour of the swan.

"Pah!" exclaimed Gereint, and spat on the ground at his feet.

"It is dead, shaman," said Paul quietly. He waited.

Gereint's sightless eyes swung unerringly to where Paul stood. "Twiceborn?" the old man asked.

"Yes," said Paul. And stepping forward, he embraced, for the first time, the old blind gallant figure who had sent his soul so far to find Paul's on the dark wide sea.

Paul stepped back. Gereint turned, with that uncanny precision, to where Kim was standing, silent, inexplicable tears streaming down her face. Shaman and Seer faced each other, and no words at all were said. Kim closed her eyes, still weeping.

"I'm sorry," she said brokenly. "Oh, Tabor, I'm sorry." Paul didn't understand. He saw Loren Silvercloak lift his head sharply.

"Was this it, Gereint?" Tabor asked, in a strangely calm voice. "Was it the black swan that you saw?"

"Oh, child," the shaman whispered. "For the love I bear you and all your family, I only wish that it were so.

Loren had now turned completely away, staring north.

*"Weaver at the Loom!"* he cried.

Then the others, too, saw the onrushing of the shadow, they heard the huge, roaring sound, and felt the mighty buffet of the wind that had come.

Jaelle clutched at Paul's arm. He was aware of her touch, but it was at Kim that he looked as the shadow came over them. He finally understood her grief. It became his own. There was nothing he could do, though, nothing at all. He saw Tabor look up. The boy's eyes seemed to open very wide. He touched the glorious creature that he rode, she spread her wings, and they rose into the sky.

⊷⊰⊙⊱⊶

He had been ordered to stay by the women and children in the curve of land east of the Latham, to guard them if necessary. It was as much for his sake, Tabor knew, as it was for their own: his father's attempt to keep him from leaving the world of men, which was what seemed to happen whenever he rode Imraith-Nimphais.

Gereint had called for him, though. Only half awake in that grey predawn hour in front of the shaman's house, Tabor heard Gereint's words, and everything changed.

"Child," the shaman said, "I have been sent a vision from Cernan, as sharp as when he came to me and named you to your fast. I am afraid that you must fly. Son of Ivor, you have to be in Andarien before the sun is high!"

It seemed to Tabor as if there was an elusive music playing somewhere amid the ground mist and the greyness that lay all about before the rising of the sun. His mother and sister were beside him, awakened by the same boy Gereint had sent with his message. He turned to his mother, to try to explain, to ask forgiveness. . . .

And saw that it wasn't necessary. Not with Leith.

She had brought his sword from their house. How she had known to do so, he couldn't even guess. She held it out towards him, and he took it from her hands. Her eyes were dry. His father was always the one who cried.

His mother said, in her quiet, strong voice, "You will do what you must do, and your father will understand since the message comes from the god. Weave brightly for the Dalrei, my son, and bring them home."

*Bring them home.* Tabor found it hard to frame words of his own. All about him, and more clearly now, he could hear the strange music calling him away.

He turned to his sister. Liane *was* weeping, and he grieved for her. She had been hurt in Gwen Ystrat, he knew, on the night Liadon died. There was a new vulnerability to her these days. Or perhaps it had always been there and only now was he noticing it. It didn't really matter which, not anymore. In silence, for words were truly very difficult, he handed her his sword and raised his arms out from his side.

Kneeling, his sister buckled the sword belt upon him, after the fashion of the old days. She did not speak, either. When she was done, he kissed her, and then his mother Leith held him very tightly for a moment, and then she let him go. He stepped a little way apart from all of them.

The music had gone now. The sky was brighter in the east above the Carnevon Range, in whose looming shadows they lay. Tabor looked around at the silent, sleeping camp.

Then he closed his eyes and inside himself, not aloud, he said: *Beloved!*

And almost before the thought was fully formed, he heard the voice of his dreaming that was the voice of his soul respond, *I am here! Shall we fly?*

He opened his eyes. She was in the sky overhead, more glorious to see than even innermost knowledge remembered her to be. She seemed brighter, her horn more luminous, every time she came. His heart lifted to see her and to watch her land so lightly at his side.

*I think we must,* he answered her, walking over to stroke the glistening red mane. She lowered her head, so the shining horn rested on his shoulder for a moment. *I think this is the time for which we were brought together.*

*We shall have each other,* she said to him. *Come, I will take you up to the sunrise!*

He smiled a little at her eagerness, but then, an instant later, his indulgent smile faded, as he felt the same fierce exhilaration surge through him as well. He mounted up upon Imraith-Nimphais and even as he did, she spread her wings.

*Wait,* he said, with the last of his self-control.

He turned back. His mother and sister were watching them. Leith had never seen his winged creature before, and a far-off part of Tabor hurt a little to see awe in her face. A mother should not be awed by her son, he thought. But already such thoughts seemed to come from a long way away.

The sky was appreciably lighter now. The mist was lifting. He turned to Gereint, who had been waiting patiently saying nothing. Tabor said, "You know her name, shaman. You know the names of all our totem animals, even this one. She will bear you if you like. Would you fly with us?"

And Gereint, as unruffled as he always seemed to be, said quietly, "I would not have presumed to ask, but there may yet be a reason for me to be there. Yes, I will come. Help me mount."

Without being asked, Imraith-Nimphais moved nearer to the frail, wizened shaman. She stood very still as Tabor reached down a hand, and Liane moved forward and helped Gereint up behind Tabor.

Then it seemed that there was nothing else to be said, and no time to say it, even if he could have managed to. Within his mind, Tabor told the creature of his dream, *Let us fly, my love.* And with the thought they were in the sky, winging north just as the morning sun burst up on their right hand.

Behind him, Tabor knew without looking, his mother would be standing, straight-backed, dry-eyed, holding his sister in her arms, watching her youngest fly away from her.

This had been his very last thought, his last clear image from the world of men, as they had sped through the morning high over the rolling Plain, racing the rising sun to a field of war.

To which they had finally come, and in time, with the sun high, starting over into the west. They had come, and Tabor had seen a black thing of horror, a monstrous swan diving from the sky, and he had drawn his sword, and Imraith-Nimphais, glorious and deadly, had reached for even greater speed, and they had met the diving swan and struck her two mortal wounds with shining blade and horn.

When it was over Tabor had felt, just as he had before, each time they'd flown and killed, that the balance of his soul had shifted again, farther away than ever from the world through which the people all around them moved.

Gereint descended, unaided, and so Tabor and Imraith-Nimphais stood by themselves among men and women, some of whom they knew. He saw the blood dark on his creature's horn, and heard her say to him, in the moment before he formed the thought himself, *Only each other at the last.*

And then, an instant later, he heard Silvercloak cry aloud, and he wheeled about and looked to the north, above the tumult of the battlefield where his father and his brother were fighting.

He looked, saw the shadow, felt the wind, and realized what had come, here, now, at the last, and knew in that moment why he had dreamt his creature, and that the ending was upon them.

He did not hesitate or turn to bid farewell to anyone. He was already too far away for such things. He moved his hands a little, and Imraith-Nimphais leaped into the sky to meet the Dragon.

The Dragon of Rakoth Maugrim in the sky over Andarien.

A thousand years before it had been too young to fly, its wings too weak to bear the colossal weight of its body. Most secret, most terrible of all Maugrim's malevolent designs, it had been another casualty of the Unraveller's untimely haste at the Bael Rangat—his Dragon had been able to play no part in that war.

Instead, it had lurked in a vast underground chamber hollowed out beneath Starkadh, and when the end had come, when the army of Light had beaten its way northward, Rakoth had sent his Dragon away, flying with awkward, half-crippled motions, to seek refuge in the northern Ice where no man would ever go.

It had been seen from afar, by the lios alfar and the long-sighted among men, but they had been too distant, still, to discern it clearly or know what it was. There were tales told about it that became legends in time, motifs for tapestries, for nightmares of childhood.

It had survived, nurtured through the long, turning years of the Unraveller's imprisonment, by Fordaetha, the Queen of Rük, in her Ice Palace amid the Barrens. Gradually, as the years passed and then the centuries, its wings grew stronger. It began to fly on longer and longer journeys through that white and trackless waste at the roof of the world.

It learned to fly. And then it learned to harness and hurl forth the molten fire of its lungs, to send roaring tongues of flame exploding amid the white cold, far above the great ice floes that ceaselessly ground and crashed against each other.

Farther and farther it flew, its great wings beating the frigid air, the flame of its breath luridly lighting the night sky over the Ice where no one was there to see save only the Queen of Rük from her cold towers.

It flew so high it could see, at times, beyond the glacier walls, beyond the titanic prison of cloud-shouldered Rangat, to the green lands far away in the south. It was all Fordaetha could do, as the sweep of time pushed even the stars into newer patterns, to hold the Dragon back.

But hold it she did, having power of her own in the cold kingdom she ruled, and in time there came a messenger from Galadan, the Wolflord, and the message was that Rakoth Maugrim was free, and black Starkadh had risen anew.

Only then did she send it south. And the Dragon went, landing in a space prepared for it north of Starkadh, and Rakoth Maugrim was there. And the Unraveller laughed aloud to see the mightiest creature of his hate now full grown.

This time Rakoth had waited, savouring the malice of a thousand years, watching his own black blood fall burning from where his severed hand had been. He waited, and in the fullness of time he made the Mountain go up in flame, and he shaped the winter, and then the death rain over Eridu. And only when these were ended did he let his army issue forth in might, and only after that, saved for the very last, that its unforeseen coming might shatter the hearts of those who would oppose him, he sent out his Dragon to scorch and burn and destroy.

So did it come to pass that the sun was blotted out, and half the sky, over that battlefield in Andarien. That the armies of Light and Dark, both of them, were driven to their knees by the pounding force of the wind of the Dragon's wings. That fire blackened the dry ground of wasted Andarien for miles upon miles in a long, smouldering strip of twice-ravaged earth.

And so, also, did it come to pass that Tabor dan Ivor drew forth his sword, and the shining creature he rode lifted herself, wings beating in a blur of speed, even into the fury of that wind. They rose aloft, alone at the last, as both of them had known they would be from the very first, and they hovered in the darkened air, shining, gallant, pitifully small, directly in the path of the Dragon.

On the ground below, battered to his knees by the wind, Ivor dan Banor looked up for one instant only, and the image of his son in the sky imprinted itself forever onto the patterns of his brain. Then he turned away and covered his face with his bloodied sleeve, for he could not bear to watch.

High overhead, Tabor lifted his sword to draw the Dragon towards him. It was not necessary, though; the Dragon was already aware of them. He saw it accelerate and draw breath to send a river of flame towards them from the furnace of its lungs. He saw that it was vast and unspeakably hideous, with grey-black scales covering its hide and mottled grey-green skin below.

He knew that there was nothing, and no one, on the windswept ground below that could withstand this thing. He also knew, with an exquisite, quiet certainty—a last space of calm here in the teeth of the wind—that there was one thing and one thing only they could do.

And there was only a moment, this moment, in which to do it, before the Dragon's flame burst forth to turn them into ash.

He stroked her shining, glossy mane. In his mind, he said, *So here it is. Be not afraid, my love. Let us do what we were born to do.*

*I am not afraid,* she sent back in the mind voice whose every cadence he knew. *You have named me your beloved, since first we saw each other. Do you know that you have been mine?*

The Dragon was upon them, blackness filling the sky. There was a roaring, a deafening noise of wind pushed to its outermost limits. Still, Imraith-Nimphais held steady before it, her wings straining as fast they had ever gone, her horn a point of blinding light in the roaring chaos of the sky.

*Of course I know,* Tabor sent to her, his last such thought. *Now come, my darling, we must kill it as we die!*

And Imraith-Nimphais forced herself higher then, somehow, and forward, somehow, directly into the maelstrom of the Dragon wind, and Tabor clung to her mane with all his might, letting fall his useless sword. Above the Dragon's path they rose; he saw it lift its head, open its mouth.

But they were hurtling towards it, angling downwards like a shaft of killing light straight for the loathsome head. Making themselves, the two of them, having only each other at the last, into a living blade, that they might explode at this dazzling, incandescent speed, the sharp horn shining like a star, right into and *through* the skin and muscle, the cartilage and bone of the Dragon's brain, and so kill it as they died.

At the very edge of impact, the edge of the end of all things, Tabor saw the Dragon's lidless eyes narrow. He looked down and saw the first tongue of flame appear at the base of its gaping throat. Too late! He knew it was too late. They were going to hit in time. He closed his eyes—

And felt himself thrown free by Imraith-Nimphais in a tumbling, spiraling parabola! He screamed, his voice lost in the cataclysm. He spun in the air like a torn leaf. He fell.

In his mind he heard, clear and sweet, like a bell heard over summer fields, a mind voice say in the purest tones of love: *Remember me!*

Then she hit the Dragon at the apex of her speed.

Her horn sheared through its skull and her body followed it, truly a living blade, and just as Imraith-Nimphais had shone, living, like a star, so did she explode like a star in her dying. For the Dragon's gathered fire burst within itself, incinerating the two of them. They fell, burning, to the earth west of the battlefield and crashed there with a force of impact that shook the ground as far east as Gwynir, as far north as the walls of Starkadh.

And Tabor dan Ivor, thrown free by an act of love, plummeted after them from a killing height.

When the Dragon came, Kim was beaten to her knees, not only by the wind of its wings but by the brutal awareness of her own folly. *Now* she knew why the Baelrath had blazed for the Crystal Dragon of Calor Diman. Why Macha and Nemain, the goddesses of war whom the Warstone served, had known that the guardian spirit of the Dwarves would be needed, whatever the cost might be.

And she had refused. In her arrogance, her own imposed morality, she had refused to exact that price from the Dwarves, or to pay it herself. Had refused to accept, at the last test, the responsibility of the Baelrath. And so now Tabor dan Ivor, hopelessly overmatched, was rising into the sky, into the wind, to pay the price for her refusal.

If he even could. If they weren't *all* to pay that price. For the Dragon that was coming down upon them meant the end of everything. Kim knew it, and so did every person on the ridge or on the bloody plain below.

Stricken with a guilt that numbed her senses, Kim watched Imraith-Nimphais fight desperately to hold her place in the air against the annihilating whirlwind of the Dragon's approach.

There was a hand gripping her shoulder: Gereint's. She had no idea how the old shaman knew what she'd done, but nothing about Gereint could surprise her any more. It was clear that he did know and was seeking, even here at the end, to comfort her—as if she had any claim, or right, to comfort.

Blinking tears from her eyes, she saw the monstrous, jointed, grey-black wings of the Dragon pound the air. The sun was lost; a huge, rushing blackness lay over the land. The Dragon opened its mouth. Kim saw Tabor let fall his sword. And then, unbelieving, stupefied, she saw the glorious creature he rode, gift of the Goddess, shining, double-edged, begin to move forward into the maelstrom, straight towards the obliterating vastness of the Dragon of Maugrim.

Beside her, Gereint was still on his feet despite the force of the wind, stony-faced, waiting. Someone cried out in fear and awe. The horn of Imraith-Nimphais was a dazzling thing of glory at the edge of night.

And then it was a blur, moving almost too fast to be seen, as she found, from somewhere in her being, an even greater, more defiant dimension of speed. And Kim finally realized what was happening, and just how the price would be paid.

*"Teyrnon!"* Paul Schafer cried suddenly, at the top of his voice, screaming it over the wind. *"Quickly! Be ready!"*

The mage threw him a startled glance, but Barak, without questions asked, fought to his feet, closed his eyes, and braced himself.

And in that instant they saw Tabor thrown free.

Then Imraith-Nimphais met the Dragon and a fireball exploded in the sky, too bright to look upon.

*"Teyrnon!"* Paul screamed again.

"I see him!" the mage shouted back. Sweat was pouring down his face. His hands were outstretched to their fullest extent, reaching. Power surged from them in shimmering waves, as he struggled to break the fall of the boy tumbling helplessly earthwards from so high.

The Dragon crashed to the ground with a sound like a mountain falling. All around Kim, people tumbled like dominoes to the trembling earth. Somehow Gereint kept his balance, staying upright beside her, one hand still on her shoulder.

And so, too, did Teyrnon and Barak. But as Kim looked up, she saw that Tabor was still falling, if slowly, spinning like some discarded toy.

"He's too far!" Teyrnon cried in despair. "I can't stop him!" He tried, though. And Barak, shaking in every limb, fought to source the magic that could break that terrible fall.

"Look!" said Paul.

Out of the corner of her eye Kim saw a flashing movement on the plain. She turned. A raithen of Daniloth was streaking westward over the ground. Tabor fell headfirst, slowed by Teyrnon's magic but unconscious, unable to help himself. The raithen shot over the ground like a golden and silver brother of Imraith-Nimphais herself. On its back, Arthur Pendragon let fall the King Spear and rose to stand in the stirrups. The raithen gathered itself and leaped. And as it did, Arthur stretched forward and up towards the boy spinning down out of the sunlight, and with his strong hands he caught Tabor as he fell and cradled him against his chest as the raithen slowed and stopped.

Racing in his wake, Lancelot leaned sideways in his saddle and reclaimed the fallen spear. Then together the two of them sped southward up the rise of land, to halt on the ridge where Kim stood, and Gereint, and all the others watching there.

"He is all right, I think," the Warrior said tersely. Tabor was ash white but seemed otherwise unhurt. Kim could see him breathing.

She looked at Arthur. There was blood all over his body; one deep gash above his eye was bleeding freely, partially blinding him. Kim moved forward and waited until he had handed Tabor down to be taken by a great many hands; then she made Arthur dismount while she tended his wound as best she could. She could see the ruin of Lancelot's palm, even through the glove he wore, but there was nothing, really, that she or anyone else could do about that. Behind her, Jaelle and Sharra were dealing with Tabor, and Loren had knelt beside Barak, who had collapsed. They would recover, she knew. They both would, though Tabor would carry an inner wound that only time might salve. If time were granted them. If they were allowed to go forward from today.

Impatiently, Arthur endured her ministrations. He was speaking constantly as she worked on him, relaying crisp instructions to the auberei gathered around. One of them he sent to Ivor, with word of his youngest son. Down on the plain the army of Light was battling again, with a passion and hope that the afternoon had not yet seen. Glancing down, Kim saw Aileron carving a lethal swath through the urgach and wolves with Diarmuid's men beside him, moving forward and to the east, struggling to link with the Dwarves in the centre.

"We have a chance now," Teyrnon said, gasping with fatigue. Tabor has given us a chance."

"I know," said Arthur. He turned away from Kim, preparing to race back down.

Then she saw him stop. Beside him, Lancelot's face had gone ashen, as pale as Tabor's was. Kim followed their gaze and felt her heart thud with a pain beyond words.

"What is it?" Gereint asked urgently. "Tell me what you see !"

*Tell him what she saw.* She saw, at this moment, even as hope seemed to have been reborn out of fiery death, an end to hope.

"Reinforcements," she said. "A great many, Gereint. A very great many coming from the north to join their army. Too many, shaman. I think there are too many."

There was a silence on the ridge. Then: "There must not be," Gereint said calmly.

Arthur turned at the quiet words. There was a passion in his eyes beyond anything Kim had seen there before. He said, in echo, "You are right, shaman. There *must* not be." And the raithen leaped down the ridge, bearing the Warrior back to war.

For one second only, Lancelot lingered. Kim saw him look, as if against his will, to Guinevere, who was gazing back at him. Not a word was said between them but a farewell was in the air, and a love that even now was still denied the solace and release of being spoken.

Then he, too, drew his sword again and stormed back to the battle down below.

Beyond the battlefield, north of it, the plain of Andarien was lost to sight, dark with the roiling movements of the advancing second wave of Rakoth's army: a wave, Kim saw, almost as large as the first had been, and the first had been too large. The Dragon was dead, but that hardly seemed to matter. It had only bought them time, a little time, shaped in fire to be paid with blood, but leading to the same ending, which was the Dark

"Are we lost?" asked Jaelle, looking up from where she knelt by Tabor. Kim turned to her, but it was Paul who made reply, among all the people gathered there.

"Perhaps," he said, in a voice that suddenly carried more than his own cadences. "It is likely, I'm afraid. But there is one last random thread left for us, among all the weavings of this day, and I will not concede dominion to the Dark until that thread is lost."

Even as he spoke, Kim's own knowledge came sweeping over her, in an image like a dream. She looked at Jennifer for an instant, and then her gaze went north, beyond the battlefield, beyond the thunderous approach of Maugrim's reinforcements—they had been seen now, down below; there were cries of harsh, wild triumph rising everywhere—beyond the blackened line of fire-ravaged earth that marked where the Dragon had flown. Beyond all these, far, far beyond, Kim looked towards a place she'd only seen in a vision given her by Eilathen, rising from his lake so long ago.

To Starkadh.

# CHAPTER 16

The laughter had frightened him. Darien passed a cold, fitful night, shot through with dreams he could not remember when the morning came. With the sun came warmth; it was summer, even here in the northlands. He was still afraid, though, and irresolute, now that he had come to the end of his journey. When he went to wash his face in the river the water was oily and something bit his finger, drawing blood. He backed away.

For a long time he lingered there, hiding under the bridge, reluctant to move. Movement would be such a decisive, such a *final* thing. It was eerily silent. The Ungarch ran sluggishly, without sound. Aside from whatever had bit him, there was no sign of life anywhere. Not since the Dragon had passed away to the south, a black shape in blackness. Not since the laughter of his father.

No birds sang, even on a morning in midsummer. It was a place of waste, of desolation, and across the river stood his father's towers, challenging the sky, so black they seemed to swallow the light. It was worse, somehow, in daylight. There were no obscuring shadows to blunt the impact of Starkadh's oppressiveness. Fortress of a god, with its huge, brutal, piled stones, blank and featureless, save for a scattered handful of almost invisible windows set far up. Crouching under the bridge, Darien looked at the exposed path leading up to the iron doors, and fear was within him like a living thing.

He tried to master it. To seek strength from an image of Finn, a vision of his brother dealing with this terror. It didn't work; however hard he tried, he couldn't even picture Finn in this place. The same thing happened when he tried to draw courage from a memory of Lancelot in the sacred grove. That didn't help either, it couldn't be superimposed.

He stayed there, lonely and afraid, and all the while, unconsciously, his hand kept returning to stroke the lifeless gem upon his brow. The sun rose higher in the sky. To the east Rangat gleamed, its upper slopes dazzlingly white, awesome, inaccessible. Darien didn't know why, but it was after he looked at the Mountain that he found himself on his feet.

He walked out from his hiding place to stand in the open under the brilliant sun, and he set foot on the Valgrind Bridge. It seemed to him that the whole world for miles around reverberated to the ringing of his tread. He stopped, his heart pounding, then realized that it was not so. The sound was small and slight, as he was; its echoes were only magnified in the chambers of his mind.

He went on. He crossed the River Ungarch and stood at last before the doors of Starkadh. He was not seen, though he was utterly unshielded there in the bleak flatness of that landscape: a boy in an ill-fitting if beautifully knitted sweater with a dagger in his hand, his fair hair held back by some circlet about his brow. His eyes were very blue in the sunlight.

A moment later they were red, and then the boy had gone. An owl, white as the vanished snows, flapped swiftly upwards, to land on the narrow sill of a window slit, halfway up the black face of Starkadh. Had that been seen, there *would* have been an alarm.

It was not seen; there were no guards. What need had there ever been for guards about this place?

In his owl shape, Darien perched uneasily on the window ledge and looked within. There was no one there. He ruffled his feathers, fighting back a stifling apprehension, and then his eyes flared again and he was once more in his own form.

He slipped cautiously down from the window and so set foot at last in the fortress where he had been conceived. A long, long way below, his mother had lain in a chamber deep in the bowels of this place, and on a morning much like this one Rakoth Maugrim had come to her and had done what he had done.

Darien looked around. It was as if it was always night within these walls: the single window let in hardly any sunlight. The daylight seemed to die where it reached Starkadh. A green, fitful illumination was cast by lights set in the walls. There was an overpowering stench in the room, and as Darien's eyes adjusted to the baleful texture of the light he was able to make out the shapes of half-consumed carcasses on the floor. They were svart alfar, and their dead bodies stank. He understood, suddenly, where he was and why there was a window here: this was the place where the swans might return to feed. He remembered the smell of the ones he had killed. It was all around him now.

The foul putrescence made him gag. He stumbled towards the inner door. His foot squashed something soft and oozing as he went. He didn't look to see what it was. He opened the door and almost fell into the corridor, gasping, heedless if he was seen.

And he *was* seen. A single urgach, massive and sharp-clawed turned, five feet away from him. It grunted in disbelieving shock and opened its mouth to bellow an alarm—

And died. Darien straightened. His eyes receded back to blue. He lowered the arm he'd thrust forward at the urgach and took a deep breath. Power coursed through him, triumphant and exhilarating. He had never felt so strong. The urgach was gone; there was no sign it had ever even been there! He had obliterated it with one surge of his power.

He listened for the sound of footsteps. There were none. No alarm seemed to have been raised. *It wouldn't matter,* Darien thought.

His fear had vanished. In its place was a rushing sensation of might. He had never known how strong he was: he had never *been* this strong. He was in his father's fortress, the place of his own conception. The hearthstone, then, of his own red power.

He was a worthy son, an ally. Even an equal, perhaps. Bringing more than a Dwarvish dagger as a gift. He was bringing *himself.* In this place he could blast urgach to nothingness with a motion of his hand! How could his father not welcome him to his side in a time of war?

Darien closed his eyes, let his inner senses reach out, and found what he was looking for. Far above him there was a presence infinitely different from Darien's awareness of urgach and svart alfar all through the fortress, a presence unlike any other. The aura of a god.

He found the stairway and began to climb. There was no fear in him now. There was power and a kind of joy. The sheath of the knife gleamed blue in his hand. The Circlet was dull and dead. His hand no longer went up to touch it, not since he'd killed the urgach.

He killed two more as he went up, exactly the same way, with the same completely effortless flexing of his hand, feeling the power course outward from his mind. He sensed how much more lay in reserve. Had he known about this, he thought, had he known how to tap into this power, he could have blasted the demon of the sacred grove into fragments all by himself. He wouldn't have needed Lancelot or any other guardian his mother sent.

He didn't even break stride at the thought of her. She was a long way off and had sent him away. Had sent him here. And here he was more than he had ever imagined he could be. He went up, tireless, climbing stairway after twisting stairway. He wanted to run, but he forced himself to go slowly, that he might come with dignity, bearing his gift, offering all he was. Even the green lights along the walls no longer seemed so cold or alien.

He was Darien dan Rakoth, returning home.

He knew exactly where he was going. As he climbed, the aura of his father's power grew stronger with every stride. Then, at the turning of a stair, almost the last, Darien paused.

A rumbling tremor rolled northward along the earth, shaking the foundations of Starkadh. And a moment later there came a cry from above, a wordless snarl of balked desire, of soul-consuming rage. It was too great, too brutal a sound. It was worse than the laughter had been. Darien's surging hope quailed before the hatred in that cry.

He stood still, gasping, fighting back the horror that rolled over him in waves. His power was still with him; he knew what had happened. The Dragon was dead. The fall of nothing else in Fionavar could have so shaken the earth. The trembling of the fortress walls went on for a long time.

Then it passed, and there was silence again, with a different texture to it. Darien stood rooted to the spot where he was, and a thought born of lonely hope bloomed in his mind: *He will need me even more now! The Dragon is lost!*

He took one step upon the last stairway, and as he did he felt the hammer of a god fall upon his mind. And with the hammer there came a voice.

*Come!* Darien heard. The sound became his universe. It obliterated everything else. The whole of Starkadh resonated to it. *I am aware of you. I would see your face.*

He wanted to go there, he had been going there, but now his feet were independent of his will. He could not have resisted however hard he tried, regardless of his rising power. In his mind, with bitterest irony, he remembered his own arrogance of the moments before: an equal to Maugrim, he had thought himself.

There were no equals to Rakoth Maugrim.

And on that realization he ascended the final stair of Starkadh and came out into a vast chamber, ringed about entirely with glass, though it had seemed as black as all the other walls when viewed from outside. Darien's mind rocked and spun, dizzily, at the perspective of that window.

He was seeing the battle in Andarien.

Beyond those high windows of Starkadh, the battle plain far to the south lay beneath his feet. It was as if he were flying over it: and a moment later he realized that this was exactly so. The windows—by exercise of a power he couldn't even begin to fathom—were showing the vision of the swans circling over Andarien. And the swans were the eyes of Maugrim.

Who was here.

Who turned now, at last, huge, mighty beyond the telling in this seat of his power. Rakoth Maugrim the Unraveller, who had entered into the worlds from outside the walls of time, from beyond the Weaver's Halls, with no thread of the Tapestry marked with his name. Faceless, he turned from the window to the one who had come, who had dared come, and Darien trembled then in every limb and would have fallen had his body not been held upright by the red glance of Maugrim.

He saw the blood drip, black and smoking, from the stump of his father's hand. Then the hammer of before became as nothing, nothing at all, as he felt his mind battered by the probing of the Unraveller. He could not move or speak. Terror was a clawed thing in his throat. The will of Rakoth was all about him; it was everywhere, driving, pounding on the doors of his being. Demanding that he give way, hammering a single question over and over again until Darien thought he would go mad.

*Who are you?* his father screamed soundlessly, endlessly, beating about all the entrances to Darien's soul. There was nothing at all Darien could do.

Except keep him out.

And he did. Motionless, literally paralyzed, he stood in the presence of the darkest god in all the worlds and held Maugrim at bay. His own power was gone; he could do nothing, assert nothing. He *was* as nothing in this place, except for one single thing. He was strong enough, as none anywhere in any world had ever been, to hold to his mind in Starkadh: to keep his secret.

He could hear the question being screamed at him. It was the question he had come here to answer, to offer the knowledge as a gift. But because it was being demanded in this way, because Maugrim would strip it from him as a rag from a wound, leaving him raw and naked beneath, Darien said *no* within his soul.

Exactly as his mother had done within these halls. Though she had not been as strong. She was only mortal, if a Queen, and in the end she had been broken.

Or, not quite. *You will have nothing of me that you do not take,* she had said to Rakoth Maugrim. And he had laughed and set about taking everything from her. But he had not. She had been open to him, utterly. Maugrim had stripped and ravaged her soul, and when he was done he had left her, a broken reed, to be enjoyed and killed.

But she had not been broken. Somehow there had been a spar left in her soul to which the memory of love still could cling, and Kimberly had found her holding to that spar and had brought her out.

To bear the child who stood here now, refusing to surrender his mind or his soul.

Rakoth could kill him, Darien knew, as easily as he himself had killed the urgach or the swans. But there was something—he wasn't sure what, but there was *something* saved from the wreckage of his life in this resistance.

And then, as the Worldloom shuttled slowly about the axis of that chamber, with everything, all of time, suspended as in a balance, Maugrim stopped the whirlwind of his assault, and Darien found that he could move, if he wished to, and could speak.

Rakoth Maugrim said, aloud, "Not even Galadan, Lord of the andain, could hold his mind against my will in this place. There is nothing you can do to me. I can end your life in ten thousand different ways even as we stand here. Speak, before you die. Who are you? Why have you come?"

And so, Darien thought, dazed, there was still a way, still a chance. He thought he could hear respect, of a kind. He had proved himself.

He was very, very young, and he had no guidance here at all, and had not had any since Finn had gone away. He had been rejected by everyone and everything, even by the light he wore upon his brow. Cernan of the Beasts had asked why he'd been allowed to live.

Manning the walls of his mind, Darien whispered, "I have come to offer you a gift." He held out the sheathed dagger, hilt foremost.

And even as he did the hammer descended again, in an unspeakable, shocking assault upon his mind, as if Maugrim were a ravenous beast raging about fragile walls, bludgeoning away at Darien's soul, screaming in fury at being denied.

But denied he was, for a second time. And for a second time he stopped. He was holding the dagger, now, and had unsheathed it. He had come nearer to Darien. He was huge. He had no face. The talons of his one hand caressed the blue-veined blade. He said:

"I have no need of gifts. Whatever I want, from today to the end of time and beyond, I shall be able to take. Why should I want a bauble of the treacherous Dwarves? What is a blade to me? You have one thing only that I desire, and I shall have it before you die: *I want your name.*"

Darien had come to tell him. To offer all he was and might be so that someone, somewhere, might be glad of his presence. He could speak now. He could move, and see.

He looked beyond Rakoth, out the windows of that place, and he saw what the black swans saw far to the south. He saw the battlefield, with such clarity that he could make out individual faces fighting there. His father had no face. With a shock of recognition he saw Lancelot, battling with blood all over his hand, swinging his sword at the side of a grey-bearded man who wielded a spear that shone.

Behind them, a phalanx of men, some mounted, some on foot, were struggling to hold their ground against stupefying numbers of the Dark. Among them—and Darien had to blink to be sure that he saw true—a man he knew gripped a rusty spear he remembered: Shahar, his other father. Who had been so much away, but who had swung him in the air and held him when he'd come home. He was not a fighter, Darien could see that, but he laboured in the wake of his leaders with a desperate determination.

The vision shifted—the eyes of another swan—and he saw the lios alfar beleaguered in another part of the field. He recognized one of them from the morning beneath the Summer Tree. There was blood in the silver hair.

Yet another perspective: a ridge of land this time, south of the battlefield. And on the ridge stood his mother. Darien felt, suddenly, as if he could not breathe. He looked upon her, from so impossibly far away, and he read the sorrow in her eyes, the awareness of doom descending.

And he realized, a white fire igniting in his heart, that he did not want her to die.

He did not want any of them to die: not Lancelot, or Shahar, or the grey man with the spear, not the white-haired Seer standing behind his mother. He was sharing their grief he realized; it was his own pain, it was the fire running through him. It was his. He was *one* of them.

He saw the innumerable loathsome hordes descending upon the dwindling army of Light: the urgach, the svart alfar, the slaugs, all the instruments of the Unraveller. They were foul. And he hated them.

He stood there, looking down upon a world of war, and he thought of Finn. In the end, here at the very end, it came back to Finn. Who had said that Darien was to try to love everything except the Dark.

He did. He was one of that besieged army, the army of Light. Freely, uncoerced, he finally numbered himself among them. His eyes were shining, and he knew that they were blue.

And so there, in that moment, in the deepest stronghold of the Dark, Darien made his choice.

And Rakoth Maugrim laughed.

It was the laughter of a god, the laughter that had resounded when Rangat had sent up the hand of fire. Darien didn't know about that. He hadn't been born then. What he knew, terrified, was that he'd given himself away.

The window of the chamber still showed the high ridge of land above the battle. It showed his mother standing there. And Rakoth had been watching as Darien looked upon her.

The laughter stopped. Maugrim stepped very close. Darien couldn't move. Slowly his father raised the stump of his severed hand and held it over Darien's head. The black drops of blood fell and burned on Darien's face. He couldn't even scream.

Maugrim lowered his arm. He said, "You need not tell me anything now. I know everything there is to know. You thought to bring me a gift, a toy. You have done more. You have brought me back my immortality. *You* are my gift!"

It was to have been so, once. But not like this. And not now, not anymore! But Darien stood there, frozen in his place by the will of Rakoth Maugrim, and heard his father say, "You do not understand, do you? They were all fools, fools beyond belief! I needed her dead, that she might never bear a child. I *must* not have a child! Did none of them see? *A child of my seed binds me into time! It puts my name in the Tapestry, and I can die!*"

And then came the laughter again, brutal crescendos of triumph rolling over him in waves. When it ended, Maugrim stood only inches away from Darien, looking down upon him from his awesome height, from within the blackness of his hood.

He said, in a voice colder than death, older than the spinning worlds, "You are that son. I know you now. And I will do more than kill you. I will thrust your living soul out beyond the walls of time. I will make it so that you have never been! You are in Starkadh, and in this place I have the power to do that. Had you died outside these walls I might have been lost. Not now. *You* are lost. You have never lived. I will live forever, and all the worlds are mine today. All things in all the worlds."

There was nothing, nothing at all, that Darien could do. He couldn't even move, or speak. He could only listen and hear the Unraveller say again, "All things in all the worlds, starting with that toy of the lios that you wear. I know what it is. I would have it before I blast your soul out of the Tapestry."

He reached forth with his mind—Darien felt it touch him again—to claim the Circlet as he had claimed the dagger and take it unto himself.

And it came to pass in that moment that the spirit of Lisen of the Wood, for whom that shining thing of Light had been made so long ago, reached out from the far side of Night, from beyond death, and performed her own last act of absolute renunciation of the Dark.

In that stronghold of evil, the Circlet blazed. It flared with a light of sun and moon and stars, of hope and world-spanning love, a light so pure, so dazzlingly incandescent, a light so absolute that Rakoth Maugrim was blinded by the pain of it. He screamed in agony. His hold on Darien broke, only for an instant.

Which was enough.

For in that instant, Darien did the one thing, the only thing, that he could do to manifest the choice he'd made. He took one step forward, the Circlet a glorious radiance on his brow, rejecting him no longer. He took the last step on the Darkest Road, *and he impaled himself upon the dagger his father held.*

Upon Lökdal, Seithr's gift to Colan a thousand years ago. And Rakoth Maugrim, blinded by Lisen's Light, mortal because he'd fathered a son, killed that son with the Dagger of the Dwarves, and he killed without love in his heart.

Dying, Darien heard his father's last scream and knew it could be heard in every corner of Fionavar, in every world spun into time by the Weaver's hand: the sound that marked the passing of Rakoth Maugrim.

Darien was lying on the floor. There was a bright blade in his heart. With fading sight he looked out the high window and saw that the fighting had stopped on the plain so far away. It became harder to see. The window was trembling, and there was a blurring in front of his eyes. The Circlet was still shining, though. He reached up and touched it for the last time. The window began to shake even more violently, and the floor of the room. A stone crashed from above. Another. All around him Starkadh was beginning to crumble. It was falling away to nothingness in the ruin of Maugrim's fall.

He wondered if anyone would ever understand what had happened. He hoped so. So that someone might come, in time, to his mother and tell her of the choice he'd made. The choice of Light, and of love.

It was true, he realized. He was dying with love, killed by Lökdal. Flidais had told him what that part meant, as well, the gift he might have been allowed to give.

But he'd marked no one's forehead with the pattern on the haft, and in any case, he thought, he would not have wanted to burden any living creature with his soul.

It was almost his last thought. His very last was of his brother, tossing him among the soft banks of snow when he'd still been Dari, and Finn had still been there to love him and to teach him just enough of love to carry him home to the Light.

# CHAPTER 17

Dave heard the last scream of Rakoth Maugrim, and then he heard the screaming stop. There was a moment of silence, of waiting, and then a great rumbling avalanche of sound rolled down upon them from far in the north. He knew what that was. They all did. There were tears of joy in his eyes, they were pouring down his face, he couldn't stop them. He didn't want to stop them.

And suddenly it was easy. He felt as if a weight had been stripped away from him, a weight he hadn't even known he was bearing—a burden he seemed to have carried from the moment he'd been born into time. He, and everyone else, cast forth into worlds that lay under the shadow of the Dark.

But Rakoth Maugrim was dead. Dave didn't know how, but he knew it was true. He looked at Torc and saw a wide, helpless smile spreading across the other man's face. He had never seen Torc look like that. And suddenly Dave laughed aloud on the battlefield, for the sheer joy of being alive in that moment.

In front of them the svart alfar broke and ran. The urgach milled about in disorganized confusion. Slaug crashed into each other, grunting with fear. Then they, too, turned from the army of Light and began to flee to the north. Which was no haven anymore. They would be hunted and found, Dave knew. They would be destroyed. Already, the Dalrei and the lios alfar were racing after them. For the first time in that long terrible day, Dave heard the lios begin to sing, and his heart swelled as if it would burst to hear the glory of their song.

Only the wolves held firm for a time, on the western flank. But they were alone now, and outnumbered, and the warriors of Brennin led by Arthur Pendragon on his raithen, wielding the shining King Spear as if it were the Light itself, were cutting through them like sickles through a field of harvest grain.

Dave and Torc, laughing, crying, thundered after the urgach and the svart alfar. Sorcha was with them, riding beside his son. The slaug should have been faster than their horses, but they weren't. The six-legged monsters seemed to have become feeble and purposeless. They stumbled, careened in all directions, threw their riders, fell. It was easy now, it was glorious. The lios alfar were singing all around, and the setting sun shone down upon them from a cloudless summer sky.

"Where's Ivor?" Torc shouted suddenly. "And Levon?"

Dave felt a quick spasm of fear, but then it passed. He knew where they would be. He pulled up his horse, and the other two did the same. They rode back across the bloodied plain strewn with the bodies of the dying and the dead, back to the ridge of land south of the battlefield. From a long distance away they could see the Aven kneeling beside a body that would be his youngest son.

They dismounted and walked up the ridge in the late afternoon light. A serenity seemed to have gathered about that place.

Levon saw them. "He'll be all right," he said, walking over. Dave nodded, then he reached out and pulled Levon to him in a fierce embrace.

Ivor looked up. He released Tabor's hand and came over to where they stood. There was a brightness in his eyes, shining through his weariness. "He will be all right," he echoed. "Thanks to the mage and to Arthur he will be all right."

"And to Pwyll," said Teyrnon quietly. "He was the one who guessed. I would never have caught him, without that warning."

Dave looked for Paul and saw him standing a little way apart from everyone else, farther along the ridge. *Even now,* he thought. He considered walking over but was reluctant to intrude. There was something very self-contained, very private about Paul in that moment.

"What happened?" someone said. Dave looked down. It was Mabon of Rhoden, lying on a makeshift pallet not far away. The Duke smiled at him and winked. Then he repeated, "Does anyone know exactly what happened?"

Dave saw Jennifer coming towards them. There was a gentle radiance in her face, but it did not hide the deeper well of sorrow in her eyes. Before anyone spoke, Dave had an unexpected glimmer of understanding.

"It was Darien," said Kim, approaching as well. "But I don't know how. I wish I did."

"So do I," said Teyrnon. "But I could not see far enough to know what happened there."

*"I did,"* said a third voice, very gently, very clearly.

They all turned to Gereint. And it was the old blind shaman of the Plain who gave voice to Darien's dying wish.

In the soft light and the deeply woven peace that had come, he said, "I thought there might be a reason for me to fly with Tabor. This was it. I could not fight in battle, but I was far enough north, standing here, to send my awareness into Starkadh."

He paused, and asked gently, "Where is the Queen?"

Dave was confused for a second, but Jennifer said, "Here I am, shaman."

Gereint turned to the sound of her voice. He said, "He is dead, my lady. I am sorry to say that the child is dead. But through the gift of my blindness I saw what he did. He chose for the Light at the last. The Circlet of Lisen blazed on his brow, and he threw himself upon a blade and died in such a way that Maugrim died with him."

*"Lökdal!"* Kim exclaimed. "Of course. Rakoth killed without love, and so he

died! Oh, Jen. You were right after all. You were so terribly right." She was crying, and Dave saw that Jennifer Lowell, who was Guinevere, was weeping now as well, though silently.

In mourning for her child, who had taken the Darkest Road and had come at last to the end of it, alone, and so far away.

Dave saw Jaelle, the High Priestess, no longer so coldly arrogant—it showed even in the way she moved—walk over to comfort Jennifer, to gather her in her arms.

There were so many things warring for a place in his heart: joy and weariness, deep sorrow, pain, an infinite relief. He turned and walked down the slope of the ridge He picked his way along the southern edge of what had been, so little time ago, the battlefield whereon the Light was to have been lost, and would have been, were it not for Jennifer's child. Guinevere's child.

He was wounded in many places, and exhaustion was slowly catching up to him. He thought of his father, for the second time that day, standing there on the edge of the battle plain, looking out upon the dead.

But one of them was not dead.

Would the old estrangement never leave him? Paul was wondering. Even here? Even now, in the moment when the towers of Darkness fell? Would he always feel this way?

And the answer that came back to him within his mind was in the form of another question: *What right had he even to ask?*

He was alive by sufferance of Mörnir. He had gone to the Summer Tree to die, named surrogate by the old King, Ailell. Who had told him about the price of power during a chess game that seemed centuries ago.

He had gone to die but had been sent back. He was still alive: Twiceborn. He was Lord of the Summer Tree, and there *was* a price to power. He was marked, named to be apart. And in this moment, while all around him quiet joy and quiet sorrow melded with each other, Paul was vibrating with the presence of his power in a way he never had before.

There was another thing left to happen. Something was coming. Not the war; Kim had been right about that, as she had been right about so many things. His was *not* a power of war, it never had been. He had been trying hard to make it so, to find a way to use it, channel it into battle. But from the very beginning what he'd had was a strength of resistance, of opposition, denial of the Dark. He was a defence, not a weapon of attack. He was the symbol of the God, an affirmation of life in his very existence, his being alive.

He had not felt the cold of Maugrim's winter, walking coatless in a wild night. Later, his had been the warning of the Soulmonger at sea, the cry that had brought Liranan to their defense. And then again, a second time, to save their lives upon the rocks of the Anor's bay. He was the presence of life, the sap of the Summer Tree rising from the green earth to drink the rain of the sky and greet the sun.

And within him now, with the war over, Maugrim dead, the sap was beginning to run. There was a trembling in his hands, an awareness of growth, of something building, deep and very strong. The pulsebeat of the God, which was his own.

He looked down on the quiet plain. To the north and west, Aileron the High King was riding back, with Arthur on one side and Lancelot on the other. The setting sun was behind the three of them, and there were coronas of light in their hair.

*These* were the figures of battle, Paul thought: the warriors in the service of Macha and Nemain, the goddesses of war. Just as Kimberly had been, with the summoning Baelrath on her hand, as Tabor and his shining mount had been, his gift of Dana born of the red full moon. As even Dave Martyniuk was, with his towering passion in battle, with Ceinwen's gift at his side.

Ceinwen's gift.

Paul was quick. All his life he had had an intuitive ability to make connections that others would never even see. He was turning, even as the thought flared in his mind like a brand. He was turning, looking for Dave, a cry forming on his lips. He was almost, almost in time.

So, too, was Dave. When the half-buried feral figure leaped from the pile of bodies, Dave's reflexes overrode his weariness. He spun, his hands going up to defend himself. Had the figure been thrusting for his heart or throat, Dave would have turned him back.

But his assailant was not looking to take his life, not yet. A hand flashed out, precise, unerring, at this last supreme moment, a hand that reached for Dave's side, not for his heart or throat. That reached for and found the key to what it had so long sought.

There was a tearing sound as a cord ripped. Dave heard Paul Schafer cry out up on the ridge. He clawed for his axe, but it was too late. It was much too late.

Rising gracefully from a rolling fall ten feet away, Galadan stood under the westering sun on the bloodied ground of Andarien, and he held Owein's Horn in his hand.

And then the Wolflord of the andain, who had dreamt a dream for so many years, who had followed a never-ending quest—not for power, not for lordship over anyone or anything, but for pure annihilation, for the ending of all things—blew that mighty horn with all the power of his bitter soul and summoned Owein and the Wild Hunt to the ending of the world.

Kim heard Paul shout his warning, and then, in that same moment, all other sounds seemed to cease, and she heard the horn for the second time.

Its sound was Light, she remembered that. It could not be heard by the agents of the Dark. It had been moonlight on snow and frosty, distant stars the night Dave had sounded it before the cave to free the Hunt.

It was different now. Galadan was sounding it: Galadan, who had lived a thousand years in lonely, arrogant bitterness, after Lisen had rejected him and died. Tool of Maugrim, but seeking ever to further his own design, his one unvarying design.

The sound of the horn as he sent his soul into it was the light of grieving candles in a shadowed, hollow place; it was a half-moon riding through cold, windblown clouds; it was torches seen passing far off in a dark wood, passing but never coming near to warm with their glow; it was a bleak sunrise on a wintry beach; the pale, haunted light of glowworms in the mists of Llychlyn Marsh; it was all lights that did not warm or comfort, that only told a tale of shelter somewhere else, for someone else.

Then the sound ended, and the images faded.

Galadan lowered the horn. There was a dazed expression on his face. He said, incredulously, "I heard it. How did I hear Owein's Horn?"

No one answered him. No one spoke. They looked to the sky overhead. And in that moment Owein was there, and the shadowy kings of the Wild Hunt, and before them all, unsheathing a deadly sword with the rest of them, rode the child on pale Iselen. The child that had been Finn dan Shahar.

And who now was death.

They heard Owein cry in wild, chaotic ecstasy. They heard the moaning of the seven kings. They saw them weave like smoke across the light of the sun.

*"Owein, hold!"* cried Arthur Pendragon, with all the ringing command his voice could carry.

But Owein circled over his head and laughed. "You cannot bind me, Warrior! We are free, we have the child, it is time for the Hunt to ride!"

And already the kings were swooping down, wildly destructive, invulnerable, the random thread of chaos in the Tapestry. Already it seemed their swords were shining with blood. They would ride forever and kill until there was nothing left to kill.

But even in that moment, Kim saw them falter, rein in their plunging, smoky steeds. She heard them lift their ghostly voices in wailing confusion.

And she saw that the child was not with them in their descent. Finn seemed to be in pain, in distress, his pale horse plunging and rearing in the reddening light of the sunset. He was shouting something. Kim couldn't make it out. She didn't understand.

⊷⟝◉⊨⊷

In the Temple, Leila screamed. She heard the sound of the horn. It exploded in her brain. She could hardly form a thought. But then she understood. And she screamed again in anguish, as the connection was made once more.

Suddenly she could see the battle plain. She was in the sky over Andarien. Jaelle was on the ridge of land below, with the High King, Guinevere, all of them. But it was to the sky she looked, and she saw the Hunt appear: Owein, and the deadly kings, and the child, who was Finn, whom she loved.

She screamed a third time, aloud in the Temple, and at the summit of her mind voice in the sky far to the north:

*Finn, no! Come away! It is Leila. Do not kill them! Come away!*

She saw him hesitate and turn to her. There was white pain, a splintering all through her mind. She felt shredded into fragments. He looked at her, and she could read the distance in his eyes, how far away he was—how far beyond her reach.

*Too far.* He did not even reply. He turned away. She heard Owein mock the Warrior, saw the sky kings draw their burning swords. There was fire all around her; there was blood in the sky, on the Temple walls. Finn's shadowy white horse bared teeth at her and carried Finn away.

Leila tore desperately free of whoever was holding her. Shalhassan of Cathal staggered back. He saw her stride, stumble, almost fall. She righted herself, reached the altar, claimed the axe.

"In the name of the Goddess, no!" one of the priestesses cried in horror, a hand before her mouth.

Leila did not hear her. She was screaming, and far away. She lifted Dana's axe, which only the High Priestess could lift. She raised that thing of power high over her head and brought it crashing, thundering, echoing down upon the altar stone. And as she did she cried out again, building with the power of the axe, the power of Dana, climbing on top of them as upon a mighty wall to hurl the mind command:

*Finn, I command you. In the name of Dana, in the name of Light! Come away! Come to me now in Paras Derval!*

She dropped to her knees in the Temple, letting the axe fall. In the sky over Andarien she watched. She had nothing left; she was empty, a shell. If this was not enough it had all been waste, all bitterest waste.

Finn turned. He pulled his plunging horse, fought her around to face Leila's disembodied spirit again. The horse reared in enraged resistance. She was all smoke and fire. She wanted blood. Finn clutched the reins with both hands, battling her to a standstill in the air. He looked at Leila, and she saw that he knew her now, that he had come back far enough to know.

So she said, softly, over the mind link they had shared, with no power left in her, only sorrow, only love, *Oh, Finn, please come away. Please come back to me.*

She saw his smoky, shadowy eyes widen then, in a way that she remembered from before, from what he once had been. And then, just before she fainted, she thought she heard his voice in her mind saying one thing only, but the only thing that mattered: her name.

⊹⟹⟸⊹

There wasn't even the tracest flicker in her ring, and Kim knew that there wouldn't be. She was powerless, empty of all save pity and grief, which didn't count for anything. A part of her mind was savagely, despairingly aware that it was she who had released the Hunt to ride, on that night at the edge of Pendaran. How had she not seen what would come?

And yet, she also knew, without Owein's intercession by the Adein River, the lios and the Dalrei would all have died. She would never have had time to reach the Dwarves. Aileron and the men of Brennin, fighting alone, would have been torn apart. *Prydwen* would have returned from Cader Sedat to find the war lost and Rakoth Maugrim triumphant.

Owein had saved them then. To destroy them now, it seemed.

So went her thoughts in the moment Finn pulled his white horse away from the others in the sky and began to guide her south. Kim put her hands to her mouth; she heard Jaelle whisper something on a taken breath. She couldn't hear what it was.

She did hear Owein cry aloud, shouting after Finn. The sky kings wailed. Finn was fighting his horse, which had reacted to Owein's cry. The horse was thrashing and bucking in the high reaches of the air, lashing out with her hooves. But Finn held firm; rocking on the horse's back, he sawed at the reins, forcing her southward, away from the kings, from Owein, from the blood of the coming hunt. Again Jaelle murmured something, and there was heart's pain in the sound.

Finn kicked at his balking horse. She screamed with defiant rage. The wailing of the kings was like the howling of a winter storm. They were smoke and mist, they had fiery swords, they were death in the reddening sky.

Then the wailing changed. Everything changed. Kim cried aloud, in helpless horror and pity. For in the distance, west, towards the setting sun, Iselen threw her rider, as Imraith-Nimphais had thrown hers, but not out of love.

And Finn dan Shahar, flung free from a great height, shadow and smoke no longer, becoming a boy again, mortal, even as he fell, regaining his shape, recaptured by it, crashed headlong to the plain of Andarien and lay there, very still.

No one broke this fall. Kim watched him plummet to the earth and saw him lying there, crumpled, and she had a vivid, aching memory of the winter night by Pendaran Wood when the wandering fire she carried had woken the Wild Hunt.

*Do not frighten her. I am here,* Finn had said to Owein, who had been looming over Kim on his black horse. And Finn had come forward, and had mounted up upon pale white Iselen among the kings and had changed, had become smoke and shadow himself. The child at the head of the Hunt.

No more. He was no longer Iselen's rider in the sky, sweeping between the stars. He was mortal again, and fallen, and very probably dead.

But his fall meant something, or it *might* mean something. The Seer in Kim seized upon an image, and she stepped forward to give it voice.

Loren was before her, though, with the same awareness. Holding Amairgen's staff high in the air, he looked up at Owein and the seven kings. The kings were moaning aloud, the same words over and over, and the sound of their voices whistled like wind over Andarien.

*"Iselen's rider's lost!"* the Wild Hunt cried in fear and despair, and for all her sorrow, Kim felt a quickening of hope as Loren cast his own voice over the sound of the kings in the air.

"Owein!" he cried. "The child is lost again, you cannot ride. You cannot hunt along the reaches of the sky!"

Behind Owein and his black horse the kings of the Wild Hunt were wheeling and circling in frenzy. But Owein held black Cargail motionless over Loren's head, and when he spoke his voice was cold and pitiless. "It is not so," he said. "We are free. We have been summoned to power by power. There is none here who can master us! We will ride and slake our loss in blood!"

He lifted his sword, and its blade was red in the light, and he made wild Cargail to rear back high above them, black as night. The wailing of the kings changed from grief to rage. They ceased their frightened circling in the sky and drew their own grey horses into place behind Cargail.

*And so it was all meaningless,* Kim thought. She looked from the Hunt away to the twisted body of Finn, where it lay crumpled on the earth. It had not been enough. His fall, Darien's, Diarmuid's, Kevin's death, Rakoth's overthrow. None of it had been enough, and it was Galadan, here at the last, who would have his long desire. White Iselen, riderless, flashed in the sky behind the riders of the Hunt. Eight swords swung free, nine horses lashed out with their hooves, as the Hunt readied itself to ride through sunset into the dark.

*"Listen!"* cried Brendel of the lios alfar.

And even as he spoke, Kim heard the sound of singing coming over the stony ground from behind them. Even before she turned she knew who it had to be, for she knew that voice.

Over the ruined plain of Andaríen, covering ground with huge, giant strides, came Ruana of the Paraiko to bind the Wild Hunt as Connla had bound them long ago.

Owein slowly lowered his sword. Behind him the kings fell silent in the sky. And in that silence they all heard the words Ruana sang as he came near:

*The flame will wake from sleep,*
*The Kings the horn will call,*
*But though they answer from the deep*
*You may never hold in thrall*
*Those who ride from Owein's Keep*
*With a child before them all.*

Then he was among them, chanting still in the deep, timeless voice. He strode to the forefront of the ridge, past where Loren stood, and he stopped, looking up at Owein, and his chanting ceased.

Then, in the wide silence, Ruana cried, "Sky King, sheath your sword! I put my will upon you! And I am one whose will you must obey. I am heir to Connla, who bound you to your sleep by the words you have heard me chanting, even now."

Owein stirred. He said defiantly, "We have been summoned. We are free!"

"And I shall bind you back!" Ruana replied, deep and sure. "Connla is dead, but the power of his binding lives in me, for the Paraiko have never yet killed. And though we are changed now and forever changed, that much of what we were I still command. You were only released from your long sleep by the coming of the child. The child is lost, Owein. Lost as he was lost before, when Connla first laid you to rest. I say it again: sheath your swords! *By the power of Connla's spell, I put my will upon you!*"

For one moment, a moment as charged with power as any since the worlds were spun, Owein was motionless in the air above them. Then slowly, very slowly, his hand came down, and he laid his sword to rest in the scabbard at his side. With a cold, sighing sound, the seven kings did the same.

Owein looked down upon Ruana and he said, half demanding, half in plea, "It is not forever?"

And Ruana said quietly, "It cannot be forever, my lord Owein, neither by Connla's spell nor by your place in the Tapestry. The Hunt will always be a part of the

Weaver's worlds—all of them. You are the randomness that makes us free. But only in binding you to sleep can we live. To sleep only, Sky King. You will ride again, you and the seven kings of the Hunt, and there will be another child before the end of days. Where we will be, we children of the Weaver's hand, I know not, but I tell you now, and I tell you true, all the worlds will be yours again, as once they were, before the Tapestry is done."

His deep voice carried the cadences of prophecy, of truth that had mastered time. He said, "But for now, here in this place, you are subject to my will because the child is lost again."

"Only because of that," said Owein, with a bitterness that cut through the air as keenly as his unsheathed blade might have done.

"Only because of that," Ruana agreed gravely. And Kim knew then how narrow had been their escape. She looked to where Finn had fallen and saw that a man had gone over to that place and was kneeling beside the boy. She didn't know, at first, who it was, and then she guessed.

Owein spoke again, and now the bitterness was gone, replaced by a quiet resignation. He said, "Do we go to the cave again, Connla's heir?"

"Even so," Ruana replied from the ridge, looking up into the sky. "You are to go there and lay you down upon your stone beds again, you and the seven kings. And I will follow to that place, and weave Connla's spell a second time to bind you to your sleep."

Owein lifted his hand. For a moment he remained so, a grey shadow on a black horse, the red jewels in his crown gleaming in the sunset. Then he bowed to Ruana, bound to the Giant's will by what Finn had done, and lowered his hand.

And suddenly the Wild Hunt was flashing away, south towards a cave at the edge of Pendaran Wood, near to a tree forked by lightning thousands and thousands of years ago.

Last of them all, riderless, Iselen flew, her white tail streaming behind her like a comet, visible even after the horses of the kings were lost to sight.

Dazed by the intensity of what had just happened, Kim saw Jaelle going swiftly along the ridge to where Finn lay. Paul Schafer said something crisply to Aileron and then set out after the High Priestess.

Kim turned away from them and looked up, a long way up, at Ruana's face. His eyes were as she remembered: deeply, quietly compassionate. He gazed down upon her, waiting.

She said, "Ruana, how did you come in time? So narrowly in time?"

He shook his head slowly. "I have been here since the Dragon came. I have been watching from behind—I would not come nearer to war than that. But when Starkadh fell, when the war was over and the Wolflord blew the horn, I realized what had drawn me here."

"What, Ruana? What drew you here?"

"Seer, what you did in Khath Meigol changed us forever. As I watched my people set out for Eridu, it came to me that the Baelrath is a power of war, a summons to battle—and that we would not have been undone by it as we had been only to journey east, away from war, to the cleansing of the raindead, necessary as that might be. I did not think it was enough."

Kim said nothing. There was a tightness in her throat.

Ruana said, "And so I took it upon myself to come west instead of east. To journey to wherever the war might be and so to see if there was a truer part the Paraiko should play in what was to come. Something drove me from within. There was anger in me, Seer, and there was hatred of Maugrim, and neither of those had I ever felt before."

"I know that," Kim said. "I grieve for it, Ruana."

Again he shook his head. "Grieve not. The price of our sanctity would have been the Wild Hunt riding free, and the deaths of all living peoples gathered here. It was time, Seer of Brennin, past time, for the Paraiko to be truly numbered among the army of Light."

"I am forgiven, then?" she asked in a small voice.

"You were forgiven in the kanior."

She remembered: the ghostly images of Kevin and Ysanne moving among all the thronging dead of the Paraiko, honoured among them, reclaimed with them by the deep spell of Ruana's song.

She nodded. "I know," she said.

Around the two of them there was silence. Kim looked up at the grave, white-haired Giant. "You will have to go now? To follow them to the cave?"

"Soon," he replied. "But there is something yet to happen here, I think, and I will stay to see."

And with his words a dormant awareness came back to life within Kimberly as well. She looked past Ruana and saw Galadan on the plain, ringed about by a great many men, most of whom she knew. They had swords drawn, and arrows trained on the Wolflord's heart, but not one of them moved or spoke, nor did Galadan. Near to the circle, Arthur stood, with Guinevere and Lancelot.

Off to the west, Paul Schafer, for whom they were waiting, at the High King's command, knelt by the body of Finn dan Shahar.

When Leila lifted the axe, Jaelle knew it. How could the High Priestess not know? It was the deepest sacrilege there was. And somehow it didn't surprise her at all.

She heard—every priestess in Fionavar heard—when Leila slammed the axe down on the altar stone and ringingly commanded Finn to come to her, a command sourced in the blood power of Dana's axe. And Jaelle had seen the shadowy figure of the boy on his pale horse in the sky begin to ride away, and she saw him fall.

Then the lone Paraiko came among them, and he put the binding of Connla's spell upon the Hunt, and Jaelle saw them flash away to the south.

Only when they were gone did she let herself go west to where Finn lay. She walked at first, but then began to run, wanting, for Leila's sake, to be in time. She felt the circlet that held back her hair slip off; she didn't stop to pick it up. And as she ran, her hair blowing free, she was remembering the last time this link had been forged, when Leila in the Temple had heard Green Ceinwen turn back the Hunt by the bloodied banks of the Adein.

Jaelle remembered the words she herself had spoken then, spoken in the voice of the Goddess: *there is a death in it*, she had said, knowing it was true.

She came to the place where he lay. His father was there already. She remembered Shahar, from when he had been home from war in the months after Darien was born, while the priestesses of Dana, privy to the secret, had helped Vae care for her new child.

He was sitting on the ground with his son's head in his lap. Over and over, his calloused hands were stroking the boy's forehead. He looked up without speaking at Jaelle's approach. Finn lay motionless, his eyes closed. He was mortal again, she saw. He looked as he had back in the days of the children's game, the ta'kiena on the green at the end of Anvil Lane. When Leila, blindfolded, had called him to the Longest Road.

Someone else came. Jaelle looked over her shoulder and saw that it was Pwyll.

He handed her the silver circlet. Neither of them spoke. They looked down at father and son and then knelt on the stony ground beside the fallen boy.

He was dying. His breath was shallow and difficult, and there was blood at the corners of his mouth. Jaelle lifted an edge of her sleeve and wiped the blood away.

Finn opened his eyes at the touch. She saw that he knew her. She saw him ask a question without words.

Very carefully, speaking as clearly as she could, Jaelle said, "The Hunt has gone. One of the Paraiko came, and he bound them back to the cave by the spell that laid them there."

She saw him nod. It seemed that he understood. He *would* understand, Jaelle realized. He had been one with the Wild Hunt. But now he was only a boy again, with his head in his father's lap, and dying where he lay.

His eyes were still open, though. He said, so softly she had to bend close to hear, "What I did was all right, then?"

She heard Shahar make a small sound deep in his chest. Through her own tears, she said, "It was more than all right, Finn. You did everything right. Every single thing, from the very beginning."

She saw him smile. There was blood again, and once more she wiped it away with the sleeve of her robe. He coughed, and said, "She didn't mean to throw me, you know." It took Jaelle a moment to realize that he was talking about his horse. "She was afraid," Finn said. "She wasn't used to flying so far from the others. She was only afraid."

"Oh, child," Shahar said huskily. "Spare your strength."

Finn reached up for his father's hand. His eyes closed and his breathing slowed. Jaelle's tears followed one another down her cheeks. Then Finn opened his eyes again.

Looking directly at her, he whispered, "Will you tell Leila I heard her? That I was coming?"

Jaelle nodded, half blind. "I think she knows. But I will tell her, Finn."

He smiled at that. There was a great deal of pain in his brown eyes, but there was also a quiet peace. He was silent for a long time, having little strength left in him, but then he had one more question, and the High Priestess knew it was the last, because he meant it to be.

*"Dari?"* he asked.

She found that this time she couldn't even answer. Her throat had closed completely around this grief.

It was Pwyll who spoke. He said, with infinite compassion, "He, too, did everything right, Finn. Everything. He is gone, but he killed Rakoth Maugrim before he died."

Finn's eyes widened at that, for the last time. There was joy in them, and a grieving pain, but at the end there was peace again, without border or limitation, just before the dark.

"Oh, little one," he said. And then he died, holding his father's hand.

There was a legend that took shape in after days, a tale that grew, perhaps, because so many of those who lived through that time wanted it to be true. A tale of how Darien's soul, which had taken flight some time before his brother's, was allowed by intercession to pause in the timelessness between the stars and wait for Finn to catch up to him.

And then the story told of how the two of them passed together over the walls of Night that lie all about the living worlds, toward the brightness of the Weaver's Halls. And Darien's soul was in the shape he'd had when he was small, when he was Dari, and the eyes of his soul were blue and Finn's were brown as they went side by side towards the Light.

So the legend went, afterwards, born of sorrow and heart's desire. But Jaelle, the High Priestess, rose that day from Finn's side, and she saw that the westering sun had carried the afternoon well over towards twilight.

Then Pwyll also rose, and Jaelle looked upon his face and saw power written there so deeply and so clearly that she was afraid.

And it was as the Lord of the Summer Tree, the Twiceborn of Mörnir, that he spoke. "With all the griefs and joys of this day," Pwyll said, seeming almost to be looking through her, "there is one thing left to be done, and it is mine to do, I think."

He walked past her, slowly, and she turned and saw, by the light of the setting sun, that everyone was gathered on the plain about the figure of Galadan. They were motionless, like statues, or figures caught in time.

Leaving Shahar alone with his son she followed after Pwyll, carrying her silver circlet in her hand. Above her head as she walked down to the plain she heard the quick, invisible wings of his ravens, Thought and Memory. She didn't know what he was about to do, but in that moment she knew another thing, a truth in the depths of her own heart, as she saw the circle of men make way for Pwyll to pass within, facing the Wolflord of the andain.

Standing beside Loren, with Ruana at her other side, Kim watched Paul walk into the circle, and she had a sudden curious mental image—gone as soon as it came to her—of Kevin Laine, laughing carelessly in Convocation Hall before anything had happened. Anything at all.

It was very quiet in Andarien. In the red of the setting sun the faces of those assembled glowed with a strange light. The breeze was very soft, from the west. All around them lay the dead.

In the midst of the living, Paul Schafer faced Galadan and he said, "We meet for the third time, as I promised you we would. I told you in my own world that the third time would pay for all."

His voice was level and low, but it carried an infinite authority. To this hour, Kim saw, Paul had brought all of his own driven intensity, and added to that, now, was what he had become in Fionavar. Especially since the war was over. Because she had been right: his was *not* a power of battle. It was something else, and it had risen within him now.

He said, "Wolflord, I can see in any darkness you might shape and shatter any blade you could try to throw. I think you know that this is true."

Galadan stood quietly, attending to him carefully. His scarred, aristocratic head was high; the slash of silver in his black hair gleamed in the waning light. Owein's Horn lay at his feet like some discarded toy.

He said, "I have no blades left to throw. It might have been different had the dog not saved you on the Tree, but I have nothing left now, Twiceborn. The long cast is over."

Kim heard and tried not to be moved by the weariness of centuries that lay buried in his voice.

Galadan turned, and it was to Ruana that he spoke. "For more years than I can remember," he said gravely, "the Paraiko of Khath Meigol have troubled my dreams. In my sleep the shadows of the Giants always fell across the image of my desire. Now I know why. It was a deep spell Connla wove so long ago, that its binding could still hold the Hunt today."

He bowed, without any visible irony, to Ruana, who looked back at him unblinking, saying nothing. Waiting.

Once more Galadan turned to Paul, and a second time he repeated, "It is over. I have nothing left. If you had hopes of a confrontation, now that you have come into your power, I am sorry to disappoint you. I will be grateful for whatever end you make of me. As things have fallen out, it might as well have come a very long time ago. I might as well have also leaped from the Tower."

It was upon them, Kim knew. She bit her lip as Paul said, quietly, completely in control, "It need not be over Galadan. You heard Owein's Horn. Nothing truly evil can hear the horn. Will you not let that truth lead you back?"

There was a murmur of sound, quickly stilled. Galadan had suddenly gone white.

"I heard the horn," he admitted, as if against his will. "I know not why. How should I come back, Twiceborn? Where could I go?"

Paul did not speak. He only raised one hand and pointed to the southeast.

There, far off on the ridge, a god was standing, naked and magnificent. The rays of the setting sun slanted low across the land and his body glowed red and bronze in that light, and there was a shining brightness to the branching tines of the horns upon his head.

*The stag horns of Cernan.*

Only an act of will, Kim realized, kept Galadan steady on his feet when he saw that his father had come. There was no colour in his face at all.

Paul said, absolute master of the moment, voice of the God, "I can grant you the ending you seek, and I will, if you ask me again. But hear me first, Lord of the andain."

He paused a moment and then, not without gentleness, said, "Lisen has been dead this thousand years, but only today, when her Circlet blazed to the undoing of Maugrim, did her spirit pass to its rest. So, too, has Amairgen's soul now been released from wandering at sea. Two sides of the triangle, Galadan. They are gone, finally, truly gone. But you live yet, and for all that you have done in bitterness and pride, you still heard the sound of Light in Owein's Horn. Will you not surrender your pain, Lord of the andain? Give it over. Today has marked the very ending of that tale of sorrow. *Will you not let it end?* You heard the horn—there is a way back for you on this side of Night. Your father has come to be your guide. Will you not let him take you away and heal you and bring you back?"

In the stillness, the clear words seemed to fall like drops of the life-giving rain Paul had bought with his body on the Tree. One after another, gentle as rain, drop by shining drop.

Then he was silent, having forsworn the vengeance he had claimed so long ago—and claimed a second time in the presence of Cernan by the Summer Tree on Midsummer's Eve.

The sun was very low. It hung like a weight in a scale far in the west. Something moved in Galadan's face, a spasm of ancient, unspeakable, never-spoken pain. His hands came up, as if of their own will, from his sides, and he cried aloud, *"If only she had loved me! I might have shone so bright!"*

Then he covered his face with his fingers and wept for the first and only time in a thousand years of loss.

He wept for a long time. Paul did not move or speak. But then, from beside Kim, Ruana suddenly began, deep and low in his chest, a slow, sad chanting of lament. A moment later, with a shiver, Kim heard Ra-Tenniel, Lord of the lios alfar, lift his glorious voice in clear harmony, delicate as a chime in the evening wind.

And so the two of them made music in that place. For Lisen and Amairgen, for Finn and Darien, for Diarmuid dan Ailell, for all the dead gathered there and all the dead beyond, and for the first-fallen tears of the Lord of the andain who had served the Dark so long in his pride and bitter pain.

At length Galadan looked up. The singing stopped. His eyes were hollows, dark as Gereint's. He faced Paul for the last time, and he said, "You would truly do this? Let me go from here?"

"I would," said Paul, and not a person standing there spoke to gainsay his right to do so.

"Why?"

"Because you heard the horn." Paul hesitated, then: "And because of another thing. When you first came to kill me on the Summer Tree you said something. Do you remember?"

Galadan nodded slowly.

"You said I was almost one of you," Paul went on quietly, with compassion. "You were wrong, Wolflord. The truth is, you were almost one of us, but you didn't know it then. You had put it too far behind you. Now you know, you have remembered. There has been more than enough killing today. Go home, unquiet spirit, and find healing. Then come back among us with the blessing of what you always should have been."

Galadan's hands were quiet at his sides again. He listened absorbing every word. Then he nodded his head, once. Very gracefully, he bowed to Paul, as his father once had done, and moving slowly he walked from the ring of men.

They made way for him on either side. Kim watched him ascend the slope and then walk south and east along the higher ground until he came to where his father stood. The evening sun was upon them both. By its light she saw Cernan open wide his arms and gather his broken, wayward child to his breast.

One moment they stood thus; then there seemed to Kim to be a sudden flaw of light upon the ridge, and they were gone. She looked away, to the west, and saw that Shahar, only a silhouette now against the light, was still sitting on the stony ground with Finn's head cradled in his lap.

Her heart felt too large for her breast. There was so much glory and so much pain, all interwoven together and never to be untied, she feared. It was over, though. With this there had to have come an ending.

Then she turned back to Paul and realized that she was wrong, completely wrong. She looked at him, and she saw where his own gaze fell, and so she looked as well, at last, to where Arthur Pendragon had been standing quietly all this time.

Guinevere was beside him. Her beauty, the simplicity of it, was so great in that moment, that Kim found it hard to look upon her face. Next to her, but a little way apart and a little way behind, Lancelot du Lac leaned upon his sword, bleeding from more wounds than Kim could number. His mild eyes were clear, though, and grave, and he managed to smile when he saw her looking at him. A smile so gentle, from one unmatched of any man, living or dead or ever to come, that Kim thought it might break her heart.

She looked at the three of them standing together in the twilight, and half a hundred thoughts went through her mind. She turned back to Paul and saw that there was now a kind of shining to him in the dark. All thoughts went from her. Nothing had prepared her for this. She waited.

And heard him say, as quietly as before, "Arthur, the end of war has come, and you have not passed from us. This place was named Camlann, and you stand living in our presence still."

The Warrior said nothing. The heel of his spear rested on the ground, and both of his broad hands were wrapped about its shaft. The sun went down. In the west, the evening star named for Lauriel seemed to shine more brightly than it ever had before. There was a faint glow, yet, to the western sky, but soon it would be full dark. Some men had brought torches, but they had not lit them yet.

Paul said, "You told us the pattern, Warrior. How it has always been, each and every time you have been summoned. Arthur, it has changed. You thought you were to die at Cader Sedat and you did not. Then you thought to find your ending in battle with Uathach, and you did not."

"I think I was supposed to find it there," Arthur said. His first words.

"I think so, too," Paul replied. "But Diarmuid chose otherwise. He made it *become* otherwise. We are not slaves to the Loom, not bound forever to our fate. Not even you, my lord Arthur. Not even you, after so long."

He paused. It was utterly silent on the plain. It seemed to Kim that a wind arose then that appeared to come from all directions, or from none. She felt, in that moment, that they stood at the absolute centre of things, at the axletree of worlds. She had a sense of anticipation, of a culmination coming that went far beyond words. It was deeper than thought: a fever in the blood, another kind of pulse. She was aware of the tacit presence of Ysanne within herself. Then she was aware of something else.

A new light shining in the darkness.

"*Oh, Dana!*" Jaelle breathed, a prayer. No one else spoke.

In the east a full moon rose over Fionavar for the second time on a night that was not a full moon night.

This time she was not red, not a challenge or a summons to war. She was silver and glorious, as the full moon of the Goddess was meant to be, bright as a dream of hope, and she bathed Andarien in a mild and beneficent light.

Paul didn't even look up. Nor did the Warrior. Their eyes never left the other's face. And Arthur said, in that silver light, in that silence, his voice an instrument of bone-deep self-condemnation: "Twiceborn, how could it ever change? I had the children slain."

"And have paid full, fullest price," Paul replied without hesitation.

In his voice, now, they suddenly heard thunder. "Look up, Warrior!" he cried. "Look up and see the moon of the Goddess shining down upon you. Hear Mörnir speak through me. Feel the ground of Camlann beneath your feet. Arthur, look about you! Listen! Don't you see? It has come, after so long. You are summoned now to glory, not to pain. This is the hour of your release!"

Thunder was in his voice, a glow as of sheet lightning in his face. Kim felt herself trembling; she wrapped her arms about herself. The wind was all around them, growing and growing even as Paul spoke, even as the thunder rolled, and it seemed to Kim, looking up, that the wind was carrying stars and the dust of stars past her eyes.

And then Pwyll Twiceborn, who was Lord of the Summer Tree, turned away from all of them, and he strode a little way to the west, facing the distant sea, with the bright moon at his back, and they heard him cry in a mighty voice:

"Liranan, sea brother! I have called you three times now, once from the shore, and once from the sea, and once in the bay of the Anor Lisen. Now, in this hour, I summon you again, far from your waves. In the name of Mörnir and in the presence of Dana, whose moon is above us now, I bid you send your tides to me. Send them, Liranan! Send the sea, that joy may come at last at the end of a tale of sorrow so long told. I am sourced in the power of the land, brother, and mine is the voice of the God. I bid you come!"

As he spoke, Paul stretched forth his hands in a gesture of widest gathering, as if he would encompass all of time, all the Weaver's worlds within himself Then he fell silent. They waited. A moment passed, and another. Paul did not move. He kept his hands outstretched as the wind swirled all around him, strong and wild. Behind him the full moon shone, before him the evening star.

Kim heard the sound of waves.

And over the barren plain of Andarien, silver in the light of the moon, the waters of the sea began moving in. Higher and higher they rose, though gently, guided and controlled. Paul's head was high, his hands were stretched wide and welcoming as he drew the sea so far into the land from Linden Bay. Kim blinked; there were tears in her eyes, and her own hands were trembling again. She smelled salt on the evening air, saw waves sparkle under the moon.

Far, far off, she saw a figure shining upon the waves, with his hands outstretched wide, as Paul's were. She knew who this had to be. Wiping away her tears, she strained to see him clearly. He shimmered in the white moonlight, and it seemed to her that all the colours of the rainbow were dancing in the robe the sea god wore.

On the high ridge northwest of them, she saw that Shahar still cradled his son, but the two of them seemed to Kim to be alone on some promontory now, on an island rising from the waters of the sea.

An island such as Glastonbury Tor had once been, rising from the waters that had covered the Somerset Plain. Waters over which a barge once had floated, bearing three grieving queens and the body of Arthur Pendragon to Avalon.

And even as she shaped this thought, Kim saw a boat coming towards them over the waves. Long and beautiful was that craft, with a single white sail filling with the strange wind. And in the stern, steering it, was a figure she knew, a figure to whom she had granted, under duress, his heart's desire.

The waters had reached them now. The world had changed, all the laws of the world. Under a full moon that should never have been riding in the sky, the stony plain of Andarien lay undersea as far inland as the place where they stood, east of the battlefield. And the silvered waters of Liranan had covered over the dead.

Paul lowered his arms. He said nothing at all, standing quite motionless. The winds grew quiet. And borne by those quiet winds, Flidais of the andain, who had been Taliesin once in Camelot long ago, brought his craft up to them and lowered the sail.

It was very, very still. Then Flidais stood up in the stern of his boat and he looked directly at Kimberly and into that stillness he said, *"From the darkness of what I have done to you there shall be light.* Do you remember, Seer? Do you remember the promise I made you when you offered me the name?"

"I remember," Kim whispered.

It was very hard to speak. She was smiling, though, through her tears. It was coming, it had come.

Flidais turned to Arthur and, bowing low, he said humbly, with deference, "My lord, I have been sent to bring you home. Will you come aboard, that we may sail by the light of the Loom to the Weaver's Halls?"

All around her, Kim heard men and women weeping quietly for joy. Arthur stirred. There was a glory in his face, as understanding finally came to him.

And then, even in the very moment it appeared, the moment he was offered release from the cycle of his grief, Kim saw that shining fade. Her hands closed at her sides so hard the nails drew blood from her palms.

Arthur turned to Guinevere.

There might have been a thousand words spoken in the silence of their eyes under that moon. A tale told over so many times in the chambers of the heart that there were no words left for the telling. And especially not now. Not here, with what had come.

She moved forward with grace, with infinite care. She lifted up her mouth to his and kissed him full upon the lips in farewell; then she stepped back again.

She did not speak or weep, or ask for anything at all. In her green eyes was love, and only love. She had loved two men only in all her days, and each of them had loved her, and each the other. But divided as her love was, it had also been something else and was so, still: a passion sustaining and enduring, without end to the worlds' end.

Arthur turned away from her, so slowly it seemed the weight of time itself lay upon him. He looked to Flidais with an anguished question in his face. The andain wrung his hands together and then drew them helplessly apart.

"I am only allowed you, Warrior," he whispered. "We have so far to go, the waters are so wide."

Arthur closed his eyes. *Must there always be pain?* Kim thought. Could joy never, ever be pure? She saw that Lancelot was weeping.

And it was then, precisely then, that the dimensions of the miracle were made manifest. It was then that grace descended. For Paul Schafer spoke again, and he said, *"Not so. It is allowed. I am deep enough to let this come to pass."*

Arthur opened his eyes and looked, incredulous, at Paul. Who nodded, quietly sure. "It is allowed," he said again.

So there was joy, after all. The Warrior turned again to look upon his Queen, the light and sorrow of his days, and for the first time in so very long they saw him smile. And she, too, smiled, for the first time in so very long, and said, asking only now, now that it was vouchsafed them, "Will you take me with you where you go? Is there a place for me among the summer stars?"

Through her tears Kim saw Arthur Pendragon walk forward, then, and she saw him take the hand of Guinevere in his own, and she watched the two of them go aboard that craft, floating on the waters that had risen over Andarien. It was almost too much for her, too rich. She could scarcely breathe. She felt as if her soul were an arrow loosed to fly, silver in the moonlight, never falling back.

Then there was even more: the very last gift, the one that sealed and shaped the whole. Beneath the shining of Dana's moon she saw Arthur and Guinevere turn back to look at Lancelot.

And she heard Paul say again, with so deep a power woven into his voice, *"It is allowed if you will it so. All of the price has been paid."*

With a cry of joy wrung from his great heart, Arthur instantly stretched forth his hand. "Oh, Lance, come!" he cried. *"Oh, come!"*

For a moment Lancelot did not move. Then something long held back, so long denied, blazed in his eyes brighter than any star. He stepped forward. He took Arthur's hand, and then Guinevere's, and they drew him aboard. And so the three of them stood there together, the grief of the long tale healed and made whole at last.

Flidais laughed aloud for gladness and swiftly drew upon the line that lifted the white sail. There came a wind from the east. Then, just before the boat began to draw away, Kim saw Paul finally move. He knelt down beside a grey shape that had materialized at his side.

For one moment he buried his face deep in the torn fur of the dog that had saved him on the Tree—saved him, that the wheel of time might turn and find this moment waiting in Andarien.

"Farewell, great heart," Kim heard him say. "I will never forget. "

It was his own voice this time, no thunder in it, only a rich sadness and a very great depth of joy. Which were within her, too, exactly those two things, as Cavall leaped in one great bound to land at Arthur's feet even as the boat turned to the west.

And thus did it come to pass, what Arthur had said in Cader Sedat to the dog that had been his companion in so many wars: that there might come a day when they need not part.

It had come. Under the silver shining of the moon, that long slender craft caught the rising of the wind and it carried them away, Arthur and Lancelot and Guinevere. Past the promontory it sailed, and from that solitary height Shahar raised one hand in farewell, and all three of them saluted him. Then it seemed to those that watched from the plain that that ship began to rise into the night, not following the curving of the earth but tracking a different path.

Farther and farther it went, rising all the while upon waters of a sea that belonged to no world and to all of them. For as long as she possibly could, Kim strained her eyes to make out Guinevere's fair hair—Jennifer's hair—shining in the bright moonlight. Then that was lost in the far darkness, and the last thing they saw was the gleaming of Arthur's spear, like a new star in the sky.

# PART V

# FLOWERFIRE

# CHAPTER 18

No man living could remember a harvest like the one that came to the High Kingdom at the end of that summer. In Cathal, as well, the graneries were full, and the gardens of Larai Rigal grew more extravagantly beautiful—drenched in perfume, riotous with colour—each passing day. On the Plain the eltor swifts ran over the rich green grass, and the hunting was easy and joyous under the wide sky. But nowhere did the grass grow so deep as on Ceinwen's Mound by Celidon.

Even in Andarien the soil had grown rich again—literally overnight, with the receding of the waves that had come to bear the Warrior away. There was talk of settling there again and in Sennett Strand. In Taerlindel of the mariners and in Cynan and Seresh, they spoke of building ships to sail up and down the long coast, past the Anor Lisen and the Cliffs of Rhudh, to Sennett and Linden Bay. There was talk of many things as that summer came to an end, words woven of peace and a quiet joy.

Through the first weeks after the battle there had been little time to celebrate. The army of Cathal had ridden north under their Supreme Lord, and Shalhassan had taken charge, with Matt Sören—for the King of the Dwarves would not let his people rest until the last of the servants of Maugrim were slain—of cleaning out the remnants of the urgach and the svart alfar that had fled the Bael Andarien.

The Dalrei, badly ravaged by the wars, withdrew to Celidon to take council, and the lios alfar made their way back to Daniloth.

Daniloth, but no longer the Shadowland. Two months after the battle that ended the war, after the Dwarves and the men of Cathal had finished their task, men as far south as Paras Derval had seen, on a night glittering with stars, a glow rise up in the north, and they had cried aloud for wonder and joy to see the Land of Light regain its truest name.

And it came to pass that in that time, with the harvest gathered and stored, Aileron the High King sent his messengers riding forth all through his land, and to Daniloth and Larai Rigal and Celidon, and over the mountains to Banir Lök, to summon the free peoples of Fionavar to a week of celebration in Paras Derval: a celebration to be woven in the name of the peace won at last, and to honour the three who remained of Loren Silvercloak's five strangers, and to bid them a last farewell.

⊸⊷⇒◯⇐⊶⊷

Riding south with the Dalrei to what was to be his own party, Dave still had no clear idea of what he was going to do. He knew—beyond even his own capacity to feel insecure—that he was welcome and wanted here, even loved. He also knew how much he loved these people. But it wasn't as simple as that; nothing ever seemed to be, not even now.

With all that had happened to him, the ways he had changed and the things that had made him change, the images of his parents and his brother had been drifting through his dreams every night of late. He remembered, too, how thoughts of Josef Martyniuk had been with him all through the last battle in Andarien. There were things to be worked out there, Dave knew, and part of what he'd learned among the Dalrei was how important it was to resolve those things.

But the other thing he'd learned here was joy, a richness of belonging such as he'd never known. All of which meant that there was a decision to be made, and very soon—for it had been decided that after the celebration week was over, Jaelle and Teyrnon, sharing out the powers of Dana and Mörnir, would jointly act to send them home through the crossing. If they wanted to go.

It was beautiful here on the Plain, riding southwest over the wide grasslands, seeing the great swifts flash past in the distance under the high white clouds and the mild end-of-summer sun. It was too beautiful to be thinking, wrestling with the shadows and implications of his dilemma, and so he let it slip from him for a time.

He looked around. It seemed that the whole of the third tribe and a great many others of the Dalrei were coming south with him at the High King's invitation. Even Gereint was here, riding in one of the chariots that Shalhassan had left behind on his way south to Cathal. On either side of Dave, Torc and Levon rode easily, almost lazily, through the afternoon.

They smiled at him when he caught their eye, but neither had said much of anything on this journey: unwilling, he knew, to pressure him in any way. But such a realization took him right back to the decision he had to make, and he didn't want to deal with that. Instead, he let his mind return to images of the weeks gone by.

He remembered the feasting and the dancing under the stars and between the fires burning on the Plain. A dance of the ride of Ivor to the Adein, another of the courage of the Dalrei at Andarien. Other dances, still, intricately woven, of individual deeds of glory in the war. And more than once the women of the Dalrei shaped the deeds of Davor of the Axe in battle against the Dark. And more than once, afterwards, all through the mild nights of that summer, with Rangat an unmarred glory in the north, there had been women who came to Dave after the fires had died, for another sort of dance.

Not Liane, though. Ivor's daughter had danced for them all between the fires, but never with Dave in his room at night. Once he might have regretted that, found in it a source of longing or pain. But not now, not anymore, for a great many reasons. Even in this there had been a joy to be savoured, amid the healing time of that summer on the Plain.

He had been honoured and apprehensive, both, when Torc had come to him, a few weeks after the return to Celidon, to make his request. It had taken a long night of rehearsal, with Levon drilling him over and over and laughingly plying him with sachen in between sessions, before Dave had felt ready to go stand the next morning, with something of a hangover to complicate things, before the Aven of the Dalrei and say what was to be said.

He'd done it, though. He'd found Ivor walking amid a number of the Chieftains in the camp at Celidon. Levon had told him that the thing was to be done as publicly as possible. And so Dave had swallowed hard, and stepped in front of the Aven, and had said, "Ivor dan Banor, I am sent by a Rider of honour and worth with a message for you. Aven, Torc dan Sorcha has named me as his Intercedent and bids me tell you, in the presence of all those here, that the sun rises in your daughter's eyes."

There had been a number of marriages all over Fionavar that summer after the war, and a great many proposals were done after the old fashion, with an Intercedent—an act of homage, in a real sense, to Diarmuid dan Ailell, who had revived the tradition by proposing in this way to Sharra of Cathal.

A number of marriages. And one of them the third tribe celebrated not long after the morning Dave had spoken those words. For the Aven had given his consent with joy, and then Liane had smiled the secret smile they all knew so well and said, quite simply, "Yes, of course. Of course I will marry him. I always meant to."

Which was as maddeningly unfair, Levon commented afterwards, as anything his sister had ever said. Torc didn't seem to mind at all. He'd seemed dazed and incredulous all through the ceremony in which Cordeliane dal Ivor had become his wife. Ivor had cried, and Sorcha, too. Not Leith. But then, no one expected her to.

It had been a wonderful night and a wonderful summer, in almost every way. Dave had even ridden with the Riders on an eltor hunt. Again, Levon had tutored him, this time in the use of a blade from horseback. And one morning at sunrise Dave had ridden out with the hunters, and had picked an eltor buck from a racing swift, and had galloped alongside of it and leaped—not trusting himself to throw the blade from his horse to the back of the eltor, and had plunged the blade into its throat. He had rolled, and risen up from the grass, and saluted Levon. And hunt leader and all the others had returned his salute with shouted praise and blades uplifted high.

A glorious summer, among people he loved, on the rolling Plain that was theirs. And now he had a decision to make and he couldn't seem to make it.

A week later, he still hadn't made up his mind. In fairness to himself, there hadn't been much time for introspection. There had been banquets of staggering sumptuousness in the Great Hall of Paras Derval. There had been music again, and of a different sort this time, for the lios alfar were among them now, and one night Ra-Tenniel, their Lord, had lifted his own voice to sing the long tale of the war just past.

Woven into that song had been a great many things shaped equally of beauty and of pain. From the very beginning, when Loren Silvercloak had brought five strangers to Fionavar from another world.

Ra-Tenniel sang of Paul on the Summer Tree, of the battle of wolf and dog, the sacrifice of Ysanne. He sang the red moon of Dana, and the birth of Imraith-Nimphais. (Dave had looked along the table then, to see Tabor dan Ivor slowly lower his head.) Jennifer in Starkadh. Darien's birth. The coming of Arthur. Guinevere. The waking of the Wild Hunt, as Finn dan Shahar took the Longest Road.

He sang Maidaladan: Kevin in Dun Maura, red flowers at dawn in the melting snow. Ivor's ride to the Adein, battle there, the lios coming, and Owein in the sky. The Soulmonger at sea, and the shattering of the Cauldron at Cader Sedat. Lancelot in the Chamber of the Dead. The Paraiko in Khath Meigol, and the last kanior. (Across the room, Ruana sat by Kimberly and listened in an expressionless silence).

Ra-Tenniel went on. He encompassed all of it, brought it to life again under the stained glass windows of the Great Hall. He sang Jennifer and Brendel at the Anor Lisen, Kimberly with the Baelrath at Calor Diman, Lancelot battling in the sacred grove, and Amairgen's ghost ship passing Sennett Strand a thousand years ago.

And then, at the end, in shadings of sorrow and joy, Ra-Tenniel sang to them of the Bael Andarien itself: Diarmuid dan Ailell battling with Uathach, killing him at sunset, and dying. Tabor and his shining mount rising to meet the Dragon of Maugrim. Battle and death on a wasted plain. And then, far off in an evil place, alone and afraid (and it was all there, all in the golden voice), Darien choosing the Light and killing Rakoth Maugrim.

Dave wept. His heart ached for so much glory and so much pain, as Ra-Tenniel came to the end of his song: Galadan and Owein's Horn. Finn dan Shahar falling from the sky to let Ruana bind the Hunt. And at the very last, Arthur and Lancelot and Guinevere sailing away in gladness on a sea that seemed to rise until it reached the stars.

The tears of the living flowed freely in Paras Derval that night, as they remembered the dead and the deeds of the dead.

But it had been a week woven mostly of laughter and joy, of sachen and wine—white from South Keep, red from Gwen Ystrat—of clear, blue-sky days crammed with activity, and nights of feasting in the Great Hall, followed, for Dave, by quiet walks beyond the tents of the Dalrei outside the walls of the town, looking up at the brilliant stars, with his two brothers by his side.

But to settle the matter that was in his mind, Dave knew he needed to be alone, and so finally, on the very last day of the festival, he slipped away by himself on his favourite black horse. He looped Owein's Horn, on its new leather cord, about his neck and set out to ride, north and west, to do one thing and try to resolve another.

It was a route he had taken before, in the cold of the winter snows at evening, when Kim had woken the Hunt with the fire she carried, and he had summoned them with the horn. It was summer now, end of summer, shading towards fall. The morning was cool and clear. Birds sang overhead. Soon the colours of the leaves would begin to change to red and gold and brown.

He came to a curve in the path and saw the tiny jewel-like lake set in the valley below. He rode past on the high ridge of land, noting the empty cottage far below. He remembered the last time they had ridden by this place. Two boys had come out behind that cottage to look up at them. Two boys, and both of them were dead, and together they had acted to let all the peace of this morning come to be.

He shook his head, wondering, and continued riding northwest, angling across the recently harvested fields between Rhoden and North Keep. There were farmhouses scattered on either side. Some people saw him passing and waved to him. He waved back.

Then, around noon, he crossed the High Road and knew he was very near. A few minutes later he came to the edge of Pendaran Wood, and he saw the fork of the tree, and then the cave. There was an enormous stone in front of it again, exactly as there had been before, and Dave knew who lay asleep in the darkness there.

He dismounted, and he took the horn into his hand and walked a little way into the Wood. The light was dappled here, the leaves rustled above his head. He wasn't afraid, though, not this time. Not as he had been the night he'd met Flidais. The Great Wood had slaked its anger now, the lios alfar had told them. It had to do with Lancelot and Darien and with the final passing of Lisen, the blazing of her Circlet in Starkadh. Dave didn't really understand such things, but one thing he did understand, and it had brought him with the horn back to this place.

He waited, with a patience that was another new thing in him. He watched the shadows flicker and shift on the forest floor and in the leaves overhead. He listened to the sounds of the forest. He tried to think, to understand himself and his own desires. It was hard to concentrate, though, because he was waiting for someone.

And then he heard a different sound behind him. His heart racing, despite all his inward preparation, he turned kneeling as he did so, with his head lowered.

"You may rise," said Ceinwen. "Of all men, you should know that you may rise."

He looked up and saw her again: in green as she always was, with the bow in her hand. The bow with which she'd almost killed him by a pool in Faelinn Grove.

*Not all need die*, she had said that night. And so he'd lived, to be given a horn, to carry an axe in war, to summon the Wild Hunt. To return again to this place.

The goddess stood before him, radiant and glorious, though muting the shining of her face that he might look upon her without being stricken blind.

He rose, as she had bade him. He took a deep breath, to slow the beating of his heart. He said, "Goddess, I have come to return a gift." He held out the horn in a hand that, he was pleased to see, did not tremble. "It is a thing too powerful for me to hold. Too deeply powerful, I think, for any mortal man."

Ceinwen smiled, beautiful and terrible. "I thought you would come," she said. "I waited to see. Had you not, I would have come for you, before you went away. I gave you more than I meant to give with this horn." And then, in a gentler tone, "What you say is not wrong, Davor of the Axe. It must be hidden again, to wait for a truer finding many years from now. Many, many years."

"We would have died by Adein without it," Dave said quietly. "Does that not make it a true finding?"

She smiled again, inscrutable, capricious. She said, "You have grown clever since last we met. I may be sorry to see you go."

There was nothing he could say to that. He extended the horn a little towards her, and she took it from his hand. Her fingers touched his palm, and he did tremble then, with awe and memory.

She laughed, deep in her throat.

Dave could feel himself flushing. But there was something he had to ask, even if she laughed. After a moment, he said, "Would you be as sorry to see me stay? I have been trying for a long time now to decide. I think I'm ready to go home, but another part of me despairs at the thought of leaving." He spoke as carefully as he could, with more dignity than he'd thought he possessed.

She did not laugh. The goddess looked upon him, and there was a strangeness in her eyes, half cold, half sorrowing. She shook her head. "Dave Martyniuk," she said, "you have grown wiser since that night in Faelinn Grove. I had thought you knew the answer to that question without my telling it. You cannot stay, and you should have known you cannot."

Something jogged in Dave's mind: an image, another memory. Just before she spoke again, in the half second before she told him why, he understood.

"What did I say to you that night by the pool?" she asked, her voice cool and soft like woven silk.

He knew. It had been hidden somewhere in his mind all along, he supposed.

*No man of Fionavar may see Ceinwen hunt.*

That was what she'd said. He *had* seen her hunt, though. He had seen her kill a stag by the moonlit pool and had seen the stag rise from its own death and bow its head to the Huntress and move away into the trees.

*No man of Fionavar . . .* Dave knew the answer to his dilemma now: there was, had only ever been, one answer. He was going home. The goddess willed it so. Only by leaving Fionavar could he preserve his life, only by leaving could he allow her not to kill him for what he had seen.

Within his heart he felt one stern pang of grief, and then it passed away, leaving behind a sorrow he would always carry, but leaving also a deep certitude that this was how it was because it was the only way it could ever have been.

Had he not been from another world, Ceinwen could not have let him live; she could never have given him the horn. In her own way, Dave saw, in a flash of illumination, the goddess, too, was trapped by her nature, by what she had decreed.

And so he would go. There was nothing left to decide. It had been decided long ago, and that truth had been within him all the time. He drew another breath, deep and slow. It was very quiet in the woods. No birds were singing now.

He remembered something else then, and he said it. "I swore to you that night, that first time, that I would pay whatever price was necessary. If you will see it as such, then perhaps my leaving may be that price."

Again she smiled, and this time it was kind. "I will see it as such," the goddess said. "There will be no other price exacted. Remember me."

There was a shining in her face. He opened his mouth but found he could not speak. It had come home to him with his words and hers: he was leaving. It would all be put behind him now. It had to be. Memory would be all he had to carry back with him and forward through his days.

For the last time he knelt before Ceinwen of the Bow. She was motionless as a statue, looking down upon him. He rose up and turned to go from among the shadows and dappled light between the trees.

*"Hold!"* the goddess said.

He turned back, afraid, not knowing what, now, would be asked of him. She gazed at him in silence for a long time before she spoke.

"Tell me, Dave Martyniuk, Davor of the Axe, if you were allowed to name a son in Fionavar, a child of the andain, what name would your son carry into time?"

She was so bright. And now there were tears in his eyes, making her image shimmer and blur before him, and there was something shining, like the moon, in his heart.

He remembered: a night on a mound by Celidon, south of the Adein River. Under the stars of spring returned, he had lain down with a goddess on the new green grass.

He understood. And in that moment, just before he spoke, giving voice to the brightness within him, something flowered in his mind, more fiercely than the moon in his heart or even the shining of Ceinwen's face. He understood, and there, at the edge of Pendaran Wood, Dave finally came to terms with himself, with what he once had been, in all his bitterness, and with what he had now become.

"Goddess," he said, over the tightness in his throat, "if such a child were born and mine to name, I would call him Kevin. For my friend."

For the last time she smiled at him.

"It shall be so," Ceinwen said. There was a dazzle of light, and then he was alone. He turned and went back to his horse and mounted up for the ride back. Back to Paras Derval, and then a long, long way beyond, to home.

⋄⟜⟝◯⟞⟞⋄

Paul spent the days and nights of that last week saying his own goodbyes. Unlike Dave, or even Kim, he seemed to have formed no really deep attachments here in Fionavar. It was partly due to his own nature, to what had driven him to cross in the first place. But more profoundly it was inherent in what had happened to him on the Summer Tree, marking him as one apart, one who could speak with gods and have them bow to him. Even here at the end, after the war was over, his remained a solitary path.

On the other hand, there *were* people he cared about and would miss. He tried to make a point of spending a little time with each of them in those last days.

One morning he walked alone to a shop he knew at the end of Anvil Lane, near to a green where he could see that the children of Paras Derval were playing again, though not the ta'kiena. He remembered the shop doorway very well, though his images were of winter and night. The first time Jennifer had made him bring her here, the night Darien was born. And then another night, after Kim had sent them back to Fionavar from Stonehenge, he had walked, coatless but not cold in the winter winds, from the heat of the Black Boar, where a woman had died to save his life, and his steps had led him here to see the door swinging open and snow piling in the aisles of the shop.

And an empty cradle rocking in a cold room upstairs. He could still reach back to the terror he'd felt in that moment.

But now it was summer and the terror was gone: destroyed, in the end, by the child who'd been born in this house, who'd lain in that cradle. Paul entered the shop. It was very crowded, for this was a time of festival and Paras Derval was thronged with people. Vae recognized him right away, though, and then Shahar did, as well. They left two clerks to deal with the people buying their woolen goods and led Paul up the stairs.

There was very little, really, that he could say to them. The marks of grief, even with the months that had passed were still etched into both of them. Shahar was mourning for Finn, who had died in his arms. But Vae, Paul knew, was grieving for both her sons, for Dari, too, the blue-eyed child she'd raised and loved from the moment of his birth. He wondered how Jennifer had known so well whom to ask to raise her child and teach him love.

Aileron had offered Shahar a number of posts and honours within the palace, but the quiet artisan had chosen to return to his shop and his craft. Paul looked at the two of them and wondered if they were young enough to have another child. And if they could bear to do so, after what had happened. He hoped so.

He told them he was leaving, and that he'd come to say goodbye. They made some small conversation, ate some pastry Vae had made, but then one of the clerks called upstairs with a question about pricing a bale of cloth, and Shahar had to go down. Paul and Vae followed him. In the shop she gave him, awkwardly, a scarf for the coming fall. He realized, then, that he had no idea what season it was back home. He took the scarf and kissed her on the cheek, and then he left.

The next day he went riding, south and west, with the new Duke of Seresh. Niavin had died at the hands of a mounted urgach in Andarien. The new Duke riding with Paul looked exactly as he always had, big and capable, brown-haired, with the hook of his broken nose prominent in a guileless face. As much as anything else that had happened since the war, Paul was pleased by what Aileron had done in naming Coll to rank.

It was a quiet ride. Coll had always been taciturn by nature. It had been Erron and Carde or boisterous, blustering Tegid who had drawn out the laughter hidden in his nature. Those three, and Diarmuid, who had taken a fatherless boy from Taerlindel and made him his right-hand man.

For part of the way their road carried them past towns they had galloped furiously through so long ago with Diar, on a clandestine journey to cross Saeren into Cathal.

When the road forked towards South Keep they continued west instead, by unspoken agreement, and early in the afternoon they came to a vantage point from where they could look into the distance at walled Seresh and the sea beyond. They stopped there, looking down.

"Do you still hate him?" Paul asked, the first words spoken in a long time. He knew Coll would understand what he meant. *I would have him cursed in the name of all the gods and goddesses there are,* he had said to Paul very late one night, long ago, in a dark corridor of the palace. And had named Aileron, which was treason then.

Now the big man was slowly shaking his head. "I understand him better. And I can see how much he has suffered." He hesitated, then said very softly, "But I will miss his brother all the rest of my days."

Paul understood. He felt the same way about Kevin. Exactly the same way.

Neither of them said anything else. Paul looked off to the west, to where the sea sparkled in the bright sun. There were stars beneath the waves. He had seen them. In his heart he bade farewell to Liranan, the god who had called him brother. Coll glanced over at him. Paul nodded, and the two of them turned and rode back to Paras Derval.

The next evening, after the banquet in the Hall—Cathalian food that time, prepared by Shalhassan's own master of the kitchen—he found himself in the Black Boar, with Dave and Coll and all the men of South Keep, those who had sailed *Prydwen* to Cader Sedat.

They drank a great deal, and the owner of the tavern refused to let any of Diarmuid's men pay for their ale. Tegid of Rhoden, not one to let such largess slip past him, drained ten huge tankards to start the proceedings and then gathered speed as the night progressed. Paul got a little drunk himself, which was unusual, and perhaps as a result his memories refused to go away. All night long he kept hearing "Rachel's Song" in his mind amid the laughter and the embraces of farewell.

The next afternoon, the last but one, he spent in the mages' quarters in the town. Dave was with the Dalrei, but Kim had come with him this time, and the two of them spent a few hours with Loren and Matt and Teyrnon and Barak, sitting in the garden behind the house.

Loren Silvercloak, no longer a mage, now dwelt in Banir Lök as principal adviser to the King of Dwarves. Teyrnon and Barak were visibly pleased to have the other two staying with them, if only for a little while. Teyrnon bustled happily about in the sunshine, making sure everyone's glass was brimmmg.

"Tell me," said Barak, a little slyly, to Loren and Matt, "do you think the two of you might be able to handle a pupil for a few months next year? Or will you have forgotten everything you know?"

Matt glanced at him quickly. "Have you a disciple already? Good, very good. We need at least three or four more."

"We?" Teyrnon teased.

Matt scowled. "Habits die hard. Some, I hope, will never die."

"They need never die," Teyrnon said soberly. "You two will always be part of the Council of the Mages."

"Who is our new disciple?" Loren asked. "Do we know him?"

For reply, Teyrnon looked up at the second-floor window overlooking the garden.

"Boy!" he shouted, trying to sound severe. "I hope you are studying, and not listening to the gossip down here!"

A moment later a head of brown unruly hair appeared at the open window.

"Of course I'm studying," said Tabor, "but, honestly, none of this is very difficult!"

Matt grunted in mock disapproval. Loren, struggling to achieve a frown, growled fiercely. "Teyrnon, give him the Book of Abhar, and *then* we'll see whether or not he finds studying difficult!"

Paul grinned and heard Kim laugh with delight to see who was smiling down on them.

"Tabor!" she exclaimed. "When did this happen?"

"Two days ago," the boy replied. "My father gave his consent after Gereint asked me to come back and teach him some new things next year."

Paul exchanged a glance with Loren. There was a genuine easing in this, an access to joy. The boy was young; it seemed he would recover. More than that, Paul had an intuitive sense of the rightness, even the necessity of Tabor's new path: what horse on the Plain, however swift, could ever suffice, now, for one who had ridden a creature of Dana across the sky?

Later that afternoon, walking back to the palace with Kim, Paul learned that she, too, would be going home. They still didn't know about Dave.

On the next morning, the last, he went back to the Summer Tree.

It was the first time he'd been there alone since the three nights he had hung upon it as an offering to the God, seeking rain. He left his horse at the edge of Mörnirwood, not far (though this he didn't know) from the place of Aideen's grave, where Matt had taken Jennifer early one morning in Kevin's spring.

He walked the remembered path through the trees, seeing the morning sunlight begin to grow dim and increasingly aware, with every step he took, of something else.

Since the last battle in Andarien—when he had released Galadan from the vengeance he'd sworn and channelled his power for healing instead, to bring the rising waters that ended the cycle of Arthur's grief—since that evening Paul had not sought the presence of the God within himself. In a way, he'd been avoiding it.

But now it was there again. And as he came to the place where the trees of the Godwood formed their double corridor, leading him inexorably back into the glade of the Tree, Paul understood that Mörnir would always be within him. He would always be Pwyll Twiceborn, Lord of the Summer Tree, wherever he went. He had been sent back; the reality of that was a part of him, and would be until he died again.

And thinking so, he came into the glade and saw the Tree. There was light here, for the sky showed above the clearing, mild and blue with scattered billowy clouds. He remembered the white burning of the sun in a blank heaven.

He looked at the trunk and the branches. They were as old as this first world, he knew. And looking up within the thick green leaves, he saw, without surprise, that the ravens were there, staring back at him with bright yellow eyes. It was very still. No thunder. Only, deep within his pulse, that constant awareness of the God.

It was not a thing, Paul realized then, from which he could ever truly hide, even if he wanted to, which was what he'd been trying to do through the sweet days of this summer.

He could not unsay what he had become. It was not a thing that came and then went. He would have to accept that he was marked and set apart. In a way, he always had been. Self-contained and solitary, too much so: it was why Rachel had been leaving him, the night she died on the highway in the rain.

He was a power, brother to gods. It was so and would always be so. He thought of Cernan and Galadan, wondering where they were. Both of them had bowed to him.

No one did so now. Nor did Mörnir manifest himself any more strongly than through the beating of his pulse. The Tree seemed to be brooding, sunk deep into the earth, into the web of its years. The ravens watched him silently. He could make them speak; he knew how to do that now. He could even cause the leaves of the Summer Tree to rustle as in a storm wind, and in time, if he tried hard enough, he could draw the thunder of the God. He was Lord of this Tree; this was the place of his power.

He did none of these things. He had come for no such reason. Only to see the place for a last time, and to acknowledge, within himself, what had indeed been confirmed. In silence he stepped forward and laid one hand upon the trunk of the Summer Tree. He felt it as an extension of himself. He drew his hand away and turned and left the glade. Overhead, he heard the ravens flying. He knew they would be back.

And after that, there was only the last farewell. He'd been delaying it, in part because even now he did not expect it to be an easy exchange. On the other hand, the two of them, for all the brittleness, had shared a great deal since first she'd taken him down from the Tree and drawn blood from his face in the Temple with the nails of her hand.

So he returned to his horse and rode back to Paras Derval, and then east through the crowded town to the sanctuary, to say goodbye to Jaelle.

He tugged on the bell pull by the arched entranceway. Chimes rang within the Temple. A moment later the doors were opened and a grey-robed priestess looked out, blinking in the brightness. Then she recognized him, and smiled.

This was one of the new things in Brennin, as potent a symbol of regained harmony, in its own way, as would be the joint action of Jaelle and Teyrnon this evening, sending them home.

"Hello, Shiel," he said, remembering her from the night he'd come after Darien's birth to seek aid. They had barred his way then, demanding blood.

Not now. Shiel flushed at being recognized. She gestured for him to enter. "I know you have given blood," she said, almost apologetically.

"I'll do so again, if you like," he said mildly.

She shook her head vigorously and sent an acolyte scurrying down the curved corridors in search of the High Priestess. Waiting patiently, Paul looked beyond Shiel to his left. He could see the domed chamber and—strategically placed to be visible—the altar stone and the axe.

The acolyte came back, and with her was Jaelle. He had thought he might be kept waiting, or sent for, but she so seldom did what he expected.

"Pwyll," she said. "I wondered if you would come." Her voice was cool. "Will you take a glass of wine?"

He nodded and followed her back along the hallway to a room that he remembered. She dismissed the acolyte and closed the door. She went to a sideboard and poured wine for both of them, her motions brisk and impersonal.

She gave him a glass and sank down into a pile of cushions on the floor. He took the chair beside the door. He looked at her: an image of crimson and white. The fires of Dana and the whiteness of the full moon. There was a silver circlet holding back her hair; he remembered picking it up on the plain of Andarien. He remembered her running to where Finn lay.

"This evening, then?" she asked, sipping her wine.

"If you will," he said. "Is there a difficulty? Because if there—"

"No, no," she said quickly. "I was only asking. We will do it at moonrise."

There was a little silence. Broken by Paul's quiet laughter. "We really are terrible, aren't we?" he said, shaking his head ruefully. "We never could manage a civil exchange."

She considered that, not smiling, though his tone had invited it. "That night by the Anor," she said. "Until I said the wrong thing."

"You didn't," he murmured. "I was just sensitive about power and control. You found a nerve."

"We're trained to do that." She smiled. It wasn't a cold smile, though, and he realized she was mocking herself a little.

"I did my share of goading," Paul admitted. "One of the reasons I came was to tell you that a lot of it was reflex. My own defences. I wanted to say goodbye, and to tell you that I have . . . a great deal of respect for you." It was difficult choosing words.

She said nothing, looking back at him, her green eyes clear and bright. Well, he thought, he'd said it. What he'd come to say. He finished his wine and rose to his feet. She did the same.

"I should go," he said, wanting to be elsewhere before one of them said something that was wounding, and so spoiled even this goodbye. "I'll see you this evening, I guess." He turned to the door.

"Paul," she said. "Wait."

Not Pwyll. *Paul.* Something stirred like a wind within him.

He turned again. She had not moved. Her hands were crossed in front of her chest, as if she were suddenly cold in the midst of summer.

*"Are you really going to leave me?"* Jaelle asked, in a voice so strained he needed a second to be sure of what he'd heard.

And then he *was* sure, and in that instant the world rocked and shifted within him and around him and everything changed. Something burst in his chest like a dam breaking, a dam that had held back need for so long, that had denied the truth of his heart, even to this moment.

"Oh, my love," he said.

There seemed to be so much light in the room. He took one step, another; then she was within the circle of his arms and the impossible flame of her hair was about them both. He lowered his mouth and found her own turned up to his kiss.

And in that moment he was clear at last. It was all clear. He was in the clear and running like his running pulsebeat, the clear hammer of his heart. He was translucent. Not Lord of the Summer Tree then, but only a mortal man, long denied, long denying himself, touching and touched by love.

She was fire and water to his hands, she was everything he had ever desired. Her fingers were behind his head, laced through his hair, drawing him down to her lips, and she whispered his name over and over and over while she wept.

And so they came together then, at the last, the children of the Goddess and the God.

They subsided among the scattered cushions and she laid her head against his chest, and for a long time they were silent as he ran his fingers ceaselessly through the red fall of her hair and brushed her tears away.

At length she moved so that she lay with her head in his lap, looking up at him. She smiled, a different kind of smile from any he had seen before.

"You would really have gone," she said. Not a question.

He nodded, still half in a daze, still trembling and incredulous at what had happened to him. "I would have," he confessed. "I was too afraid."

She reached up and touched his cheek. "Afraid of this, after all you have done?"

He nodded again. "Of this, perhaps more than anything. When?" he asked. "When did you . . . ?"

Her eyes turned grave. "I fell in love with you on the beach by Taerlindel. When you stood in the waves, speaking to Liranan. But I fought it, of course, for many reasons. You will know them. It didn't come home to me until you were walking back from Finn to face Galadan."

He closed his eyes. Opened them. Felt sorrow come over to shadow joy. "Can you do this?" he said. "How may it be allowed? You are what you are."

She smiled again, and this smile he knew. It was the one he imagined on the face of Dana herself: inward and inscrutable.

She said, "I will die to have you, but I do not think it need happen that way."

Neatly she rose to her feet. He, too, stood up and saw her go to the door and open it. She murmured something to the acolyte in the corridor and then turned back to him, a light dancing in her eyes.

They waited, not for long. The door opened again, and Leila came in.

Clad in white.

She looked from one of them to the other and then laughed aloud. "Oh, good!" she said. "I thought this might happen."

Paul felt himself flushing; then he caught Jaelle's glance and both of them burst out laughing.

"Can you see why she'll be High Priestess now?" Jaelle asked, smiling. Then, more soberly, added, "From the moment she lifted the axe and survived, Leila was marked by the Goddess to the white of the High Priestess. Dana moves in ways no mortal can understand, nor even the others among the gods. I am High Priestess in name only now. After I sent you through the crossing I was to relinquish my place to Leila."

Paul nodded. He could see a pattern shaping here, only a glimmering of it, but it seemed to him that the warp and weft of this, followed back to their source, would reach Dun Maura and a sacrifice made on the eve of Maidaladan.

And thinking of that, he found that there were tears in his own eyes. He had to wipe them away, he who had never been able to weep.

He said, "Kim is going home or I would never say this, but I think I know a cottage by a lake, halfway between the Temple and the Tree, where I would like to live. If it pleases you."

"It pleases me," Jaelle said quietly. "More than I can tell you. Ysanne's cottage will bring my life full circle and lay a grief to rest."

"I guess I'm staying, then," he said, reaching for her hand. "I guess I'm staying after all."

⬦⭒⬦

She was learning something, Kim realized. Learning it the hardest way. Discovering that the only thing harder for her to deal with than power was its passing away.

The Baelrath was gone. She had surrendered it, but before that it had abandoned her. Not since Calor Diman and her refusal there had the Warstone so much as flickered on her hand. So, late last night, quietly, with no one else in the room, no one else to know, she had given it to Aileron.

And he, as quietly, had sent for Jaelle and entrusted the stone to the custody of the Priestesses of Dana. Which was right, Kim knew. She'd thought at first that he would give it to the mages. But the wild power of the Baelrath was closer, far, to Dana than it was to the skylore Amairgen had learned.

It was a measure of Aileron's deepening wisdom, one of the marks of the changing nature of things, that the High King would surrender a thing of so much power to the High Priestess and that she would agree to guard it in his name.

And thus had the Warstone passed from her, which left Kimberly, on this last afternoon, walking with her memories amid the strand of trees west of Ysanne's cottage, dealing with loss and sorrow.

It should not be so, she told herself sternly. She was going home, and she *wanted* to go home. She wanted her family very badly. More than that, even, she knew it was right for her to be crossing back. She had dreamt it, and so had Ysanne, in those first days.

*It is in my heart as well that there may be need of a Dreamer in your world, too,* the old Seer had said. And Kim knew it was still true. She had seen it herself.

So need and rightness had come together with her own desire to draw her back. This should have made things easy and clear, but it was not so. How, in truth, could it ever be, when she was leaving so much behind? And all her thoughts and feelings seemed to be complicated, made even more blurred and difficult, by the hollow of absence within her when she looked at the finger where the Warstone had been for so long.

She shook her head, trying to pull herself out of this mood. She had so many blessings to count, so many riches. The first, running deeper than anything else, was the fact of peace and the Unraveller's passing from the worlds, at the hands of the child whose name she had dreamt before he'd even been born.

She walked through the green woods in sunlight thinking of Darien, and then of his mother and Arthur and Lancelot, whose grief had come to an end. Another blessing, another place where joy might flower in the heart.

And for herself, she was still a Seer, and she still carried, and always would, a second soul within her as a gift beyond words or measurement. She still wore the vellin bracelet on her wrist—Matt had refused, absolutely, to take it back. It would serve no real purpose in her world, she knew, save for memory—which, in its own way, was as good a purpose as any.

Deep in the woods alone, reaching painfully towards an inner peace, Kim stopped and stood in silence for a time, listening to the birds overhead and the sighing of the breeze through the leaves. It was so quiet here, so beautiful, she wanted to hold this to herself forever.

Thinking so, she saw a flash of colour on the ground off to her right and realized, even before she moved, that she was being given a final gift.

She walked over, following, as it happened, the steps that Finn and Darien had taken on their last walk together in the depths of winter. Then she knelt, as they had knelt, beside the bannion growing there.

Blue-green flower with red at its centre like a drop of blood at the heart. They had left it, that day, gathering other flowers to take back to Vae but not this one. And so it had remained for Kim to take it for herself, tears welling at the richness of the memory it stirred: her first walk in this wood with Ysanne, looking for this flower; then a night by the lake under stars when Eilathen, summoned by flowerfire, had spun the Tapestry for her.

The bannion was beautiful, sea-coloured around the brilliant red. She plucked it carefully and placed it in her white hair. She thought of Eilathen, of the blue-green glitter of his naked power. He, too, was lost to her, even if she had wanted to summon him, if only to bid farewell. *Be free of flowerfire, now and evermore,* Ysanne had said, at the end, releasing him from guardianship of the red Warstone.

The bannion was beautiful but powerless. It seemed to be a symbol of what had passed from her, what she could no longer do. Magic had been given to her that starry night by this lake, and it had rested in her for a time and had gone. It would be better for her, in every way, to be in her own world, she thought, to be removed from the sharpness of these images.

She rose and started back, thinking of Loren, who had to be dealing with the same withdrawal. Just as, she realized suddenly, Matt had dealt with it for all the years he'd spent in Paras Derval, fighting the pull of Calor Diman. The two of them had come full circle together, she thought. There was a pattern in that, more beautiful and more terrible than any mortal weaving could ever be.

She came out from the trees and walked down to the lake. It was slightly choppy in the summer breeze. There was the hint of a chill; overture to the coming of fall.

Kim stepped out onto the flat surface of the rock that jutted out over the water, just as she had done before, with Ysanne, when the Seer had summoned the water spirit under the stars.

Eilathen was down there, she knew, far down among his twining corridors of seastone and seaweed, amid the deep silence of his home. Inaccessible. Lost to her. She sat on the stone and wrapped her arms about her drawn-up knees, trying to number blessings, to shape sadness into joy.

For a long time she sat there, looking out over the waters of the lake. It had to be late afternoon, she knew. She should be starting back. It was so hard to leave, though. Rising up and walking from this place would be an act as lonely and as final as any she'd ever done.

So she lingered, and in time there was a footfall on the rock behind her and then someone crouched down by her side.

"I saw your horse by the cottage," Dave said. "Am I intruding?"

She smiled up at him and shook her head. "I'm just saying my goodbyes before this evening."

"So was I," he said, gathering and dispersing pebbles.

"You're coming home, too?"

"I just decided," he said quietly. There was a calmness, an assurance in his voice she'd not heard before. Of all of them, Kim realized, Dave had changed the most here. She and Paul and Jennifer seemed to have really just gone further into what they'd already been before they came, and Kevin had remained exactly what he always was, with his laughter and his sadness and the sweetness of his soul. But this man crouching beside her, burned dark by the summer sun of the Plain, was a very far cry from the one she'd met that first evening in Convocation Hall, when she'd invited him to come sit with them and hear Lorenzo Marcus speak.

She managed another smile. "I'm glad you're coming back," she said.

He nodded, quietly self-possessed, looking at her in a calm silence for a moment. Then his eyes flickered with a certain amusement that was also new.

"Tell me," he said, "what are you doing on Friday night?"

A little breathless laugh escaped her. "Oh, Dave," Kim said, "I don't even know when Friday night *is*!"

He laughed, too. Then the laughter passed, leaving an easy smile. He stood up smoothly and held out a hand to help her up.

"Saturday, then?" he asked, his eyes holding hers. And bursting within her then like another kind of flowerfire Kim had a sudden feeling, a flashing certainty, that everything was going to be all right after all. It was going to be much more than all right.

She gave him both her hands and let him help her rise.

∗⊶⇒◯⇐⊷∗

*Here ends* THE DARKEST ROAD *and with it* THE FIONAVAR TAPESTRY

∗⊶⇒◯⇐⊷∗

# AFTERWORD

Looking back, more than two decades after the trilogy first appeared, there are many things that might be said. At the same time, I have to confess to a desire (a strong one) to say nothing at all, to let the work continue to speak for itself. Real as this feeling is, I'm aware that the idea of a book standing alone, unmediated, becomes an illusion after a certain amount of time has passed. There are, for *Fionavar*, reviews, scholarship, commentary, novels inspired by it. There is a remarkable variety of music, art, internet forums, blogs, even trivia contests and online casting couches.

So the notion of the *Tapestry* existing in some pure space of its own is long gone. As a result, it would feel unduly ascetic for me to decline my publisher's request to offer an afterword. For one thing, I'm deeply honoured by how the trilogy seems to be enduring. Every author dreams of writing something that might last, have an impact. It can't be more than a dream at the outset, though it is a necessary one. Lacking at least the ambition to do something that will survive, we're limiting our horizons. But there are so many books, and so few of them do endure.

By one measure, two or three decades are a blink, especially in the context of a novel that deals with motifs of myth and legend. By another, in a rapid-transit, disposable-object, high-turnover age, it is a very long time for something to remain in the culture. Who can ever assume or rely upon such a thing? What author can help but be grateful when it happens? And how then resist the invitation to look back?

⟿⟾

At times over the years, I have teased interviewers by saying that the style and structure of *Fionavar* were conceived with only one thing in mind: to create a work on a scale that would allow me, when Paul is on the Summer Tree, to write the sentence, "Rain, rain, rain, rain, rain." And to live to tell the tale. The line is flippant, an easy joke, but as is often the case with a throwaway, there's truth embedded in it. The principal reason the language of the trilogy differs from my later books is that this was my mythic endeavour. The others track a movement (not a consistent one) towards history. It seemed proper to me, back then, to pursue a way of telling the story that would fit that mythic dimension. I imagined the arc of the narrative in operatic terms, moving from set piece to set piece: Paul on the Tree, Galadan and Cavall, Tabor meeting Imraith-Nimphais in the wood, Jennifer in Starkadh, Kevin at Dun Maura,

Owein and the Hunt, Cader Sedat, Lancelot in the Grove … others, obviously, to the end, with Diarmuid and then Darien. Language was guided by that context: this is a book that involves gods imprisoned under mountains and a mythic wolf and dog battling at the root of a sacrificial tree.

I also remember wanting to spin out, as best I could, the implications of naming a particular world as the "first" one that others reflect (imperfectly). What flows from such an idea? Well, if one wishes to be wry, one could say an over-the-top panoply of legends from myriad cultures. Wry or not, that seemed right to me: the diverse folklore of our world shakily echoing the "true" versions. The sword in the stone of Arthurian legend is set here against the "real" idea of the king spear in the mountain in Fionavar. I wanted to bring in as much as I could: shamanistic tradition, Norse myth, Celtic legend, Maori motifs, the Arthurian triangle and the Welsh figures that come into it, including Taliesin, the Wild Hunt and a dog named Cavall. And, in the figure of Darien, a playing out of a fairly vivid Oedipal drama—which was another way of drawing upon myth, of course.

Joseph Campbell and Robert Graves were by my desk in this endeavour. Graves' maddening, absurd, quite wonderful White Goddess gave me a great deal, including Paul's defeat of Fordaetha with the naming of her name. (Read the Welsh Câd Goddeu, the "Battle of the Trees.") I think my fascination with the power of names, which came to fuller development in *Tigana*, likely began here.

I also set myself the task, quixotic or otherwise, of trying to shape a narrative large enough that the figures of the Arthurian triangle could come in without overwhelming it: that they might be a component of the story but not the story. I was driven to this, in part, by a deep dissatisfaction with most treatments in literature of the figure of Guinevere and also (I confess) by the creative force that came from the middle-of-one-night idea of Arthur as "Childslayer"… using his early transgression to invert the "once and future king" legend, making it a burden not a blessing.

I still like that. And I feel the same way about using the Wild Hunt to offer a mythic explanation for the philosophical "problem of evil" … how an omnipotent, benevolent deity allows so much suffering into his worlds. Linking Diarmuid's anarchic nature to the Hunt basically compelled his ending, much as I (and a great many readers, it seems, over the years) wished for a way to avoid it.

At a certain point, as many novelists have said, the shape of a story and the emerging nature of its characters begin to assert a hold on the author, not the other way around. This happened early and often with *Fionavar*. Sharra was not, in the inception, a major figure. She was conceived of as a way of playing against the romantic image of the wastrel prince. I wanted to show Diarmuid doing something indefensible in that night garden, undercutting the rose-tinted image of my Prince Hal (he has his Falstaff, too).

I learned a major lesson here—two of them, actually. One is that when you play with archetypes, you had best be aware of their power: very few readers have ever held that garden scene against Diarmuid to the degree I thought they would. Glamorous princes have more leeway than one might imagine. Stephen Sondheim and

James Lapine, in *Into the Woods*, have their feckless prince say, indignantly, "I was raised to be charming, not sincere!" A word to the wise.

But once the garden scene was written—from Sharra's point of view—there was no possible way that particular woman would allow an author not to bring her back to do what she so obviously was going to do in retaliation. It took next to no time for her to assert a claim to prominence, and the narrative adjusted to make room.

Oh. That elicits an admission. One of the most common laments from readers for over twenty years now has been their wish to know exactly what happens to Sharra at the end. Now, I don't believe in saying exactly what happens to characters after a novel closes—the ending of every book I've written makes this point. The future is open-ended, the end of the novel does not demand the tying down of all lives that passed through it; we don't always know what happens next, in life or fiction. But in the case of Sharra, I had a notebook entry to write a conversation between her and Kim towards the end, and I thought: *this is so unnecessary.* Everyone will know that she's going back to Cathal and will take up the duties of her position and carry on, as she must.

I didn't write that conversation. The scene idea felt static, flat—its only purpose to tie up a thread I didn't think was really loose. I still feel that way, but with so many readers asking after Sharra, I confess to some regret that I didn't do a variant of the scene.

Not too many other regrets. I think if there had been more, I'd have found it harder to stay faithful to the inner voice that told me the *Tapestry* was complete, and that to respond to requests that I write what I called "volume four of a trilogy" would be a mistake that would subvert and undermine the unity of a book that was conceived as three volumes, complete with a "solution" to the well-known middle-book problem. I did, as most people reading this will know, move on to other parts of the forest, never having done a formal sequel. There are grace notes in later novels, small nods back to *Fionavar*—a bit more than that in one book—but that is all they are, all they're meant to be.

The *Tapestry* felt done to me, offering whatever degree of pleasure and reward I was capable of giving readers in that vein and at that time. The pleasure for me today, and the reward, is that so many people seem to have looked upon it as something that matters in their lives.

Many years later, consider this a thank you.

Guy Gavriel Kay
August 2006
Toronto

**Guy Gavriel Kay** is the author of ten novels, including *Ysabel*, *The Lions of Al-Rassan*, *Sailing to Sarantium*, *Lord of Emperors* and *The Last Light of the Sun*, and of an acclaimed collection of poetry, *Beyond This Dark House*. He was retained by the estate of J.R.R. Tolkien to assist in the editorial construction of Tolkien's posthumously published, *The Silmarillion*. His work has been translated into 21 languages and has appeared on bestseller lists around the world. He is the recipient of the International Goliardos Prize for his contribution to the literature of the fantastic. Guy Gavriel Kay lives in Toronto. Kay's authorized website may be found at **www.brightweavings.com**.